Sturmtau

Book 2: April 19

Flight of The Shearwater

Alan Jones

Paperback Edition

ISBN 978-1-9997368-5-9

Copyright © Alan Jones 2021

Published by Ailsa Publishing.

For Michael, Fergus and Peter

CONTENTS

PREFACE

This is a work of fiction. Most of the characters are drawn from my imagination but some of the characters existed: world leaders, the higher echelons of the National Socialist Party, some senior SS and Gestapo officers, and prominent clergy and military figures. There are a few others, including Admiral Wilhelm Canaris, head of the Abwehr.

Many of the events in the book, or events like them, happened. Where they are fictitious, I have tried to write them with integrity, always having in mind that they could have taken place, and that none of them should distract from the truth of the terrible crimes committed across Europe during the darkest time in human history.

On a very few instances, I have changed a location or tweaked a timescale to suit the narrative, but it is rare, and I hope the historians will forgive me.

I made extensive use of maps and nautical charts from the 1930's and 40's during my research. It was the only way I could make sense of the global scale of the war, and the Holocaust. I have included a few maps and charts in the book but it would be impossible to show enough detail in them to be truly useful, but maps, charts, and diagrams are available in much larger format at www.alanjonesbooks.co.uk/maps_charts_plans_st.html, including an interactive chart which should help in following any sea voyages that might take place.

There is also a raft of other supporting material; photographs, documents, and links to other websites packed with information surrounding the events in the book, and a glossary. As a reader, I always find these resources useful, especially when reading books of the length and scope of the Sturmtaucher Trilogy. www.alanjonesbooks.co.uk/sturmtaucher_trilogy.html

The Schopenhauer Illustrated Dictionary

Ketch [ketʃ] noun: ketch.

A two-masted, fore-and-aft rigged sailing boat with a mizzenmast stepped forward of the rudder and smaller than its foremast.

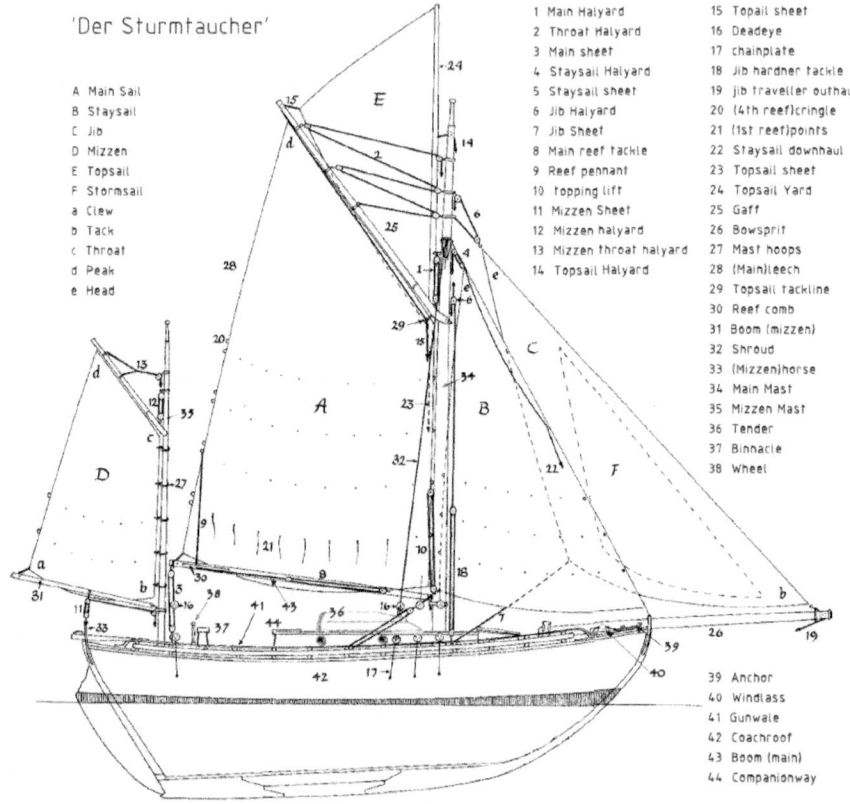

'Der Sturmtaucher'

A Main Sail
B Staysail
C Jib
D Mizzen
E Topsail
F Stormsail
a Clew
b Tack
c Throat
d Peak
e Head

1 Main Halyard
2 Throat Halyard
3 Main sheet
4 Staysail Halyard
5 Staysail sheet
6 Jib Halyard
7 Jib Sheet
8 Main reef tackle
9 Reef pennant
10 Topping lift
11 Mizzen Sheet
12 Mizzen halyard
13 Mizzen throat halyard
14 Topsail Halyard

15 Topail sheet
16 Deadeye
17 chainplate
18 Jib hardner tackle
19 jib traveller outhaul
20 (4th reef)cringle
21 (1st reef)points
22 Staysail downhaul
23 Topsail sheet
24 Topsail Yard
25 Gaff
26 Bowsprit
27 Mast hoops
28 (Main)leech
29 Topsail tackline
30 Reef comb
31 Boom (mizzen)
32 Shroud
33 (Mizzen)horse
34 Main Mast
35 Mizzen Mast
36 Tender
37 Binnacle
38 Wheel

39 Anchor
40 Windlass
41 Gunwale
42 Coachroof
43 Boom (main)
44 Companionway

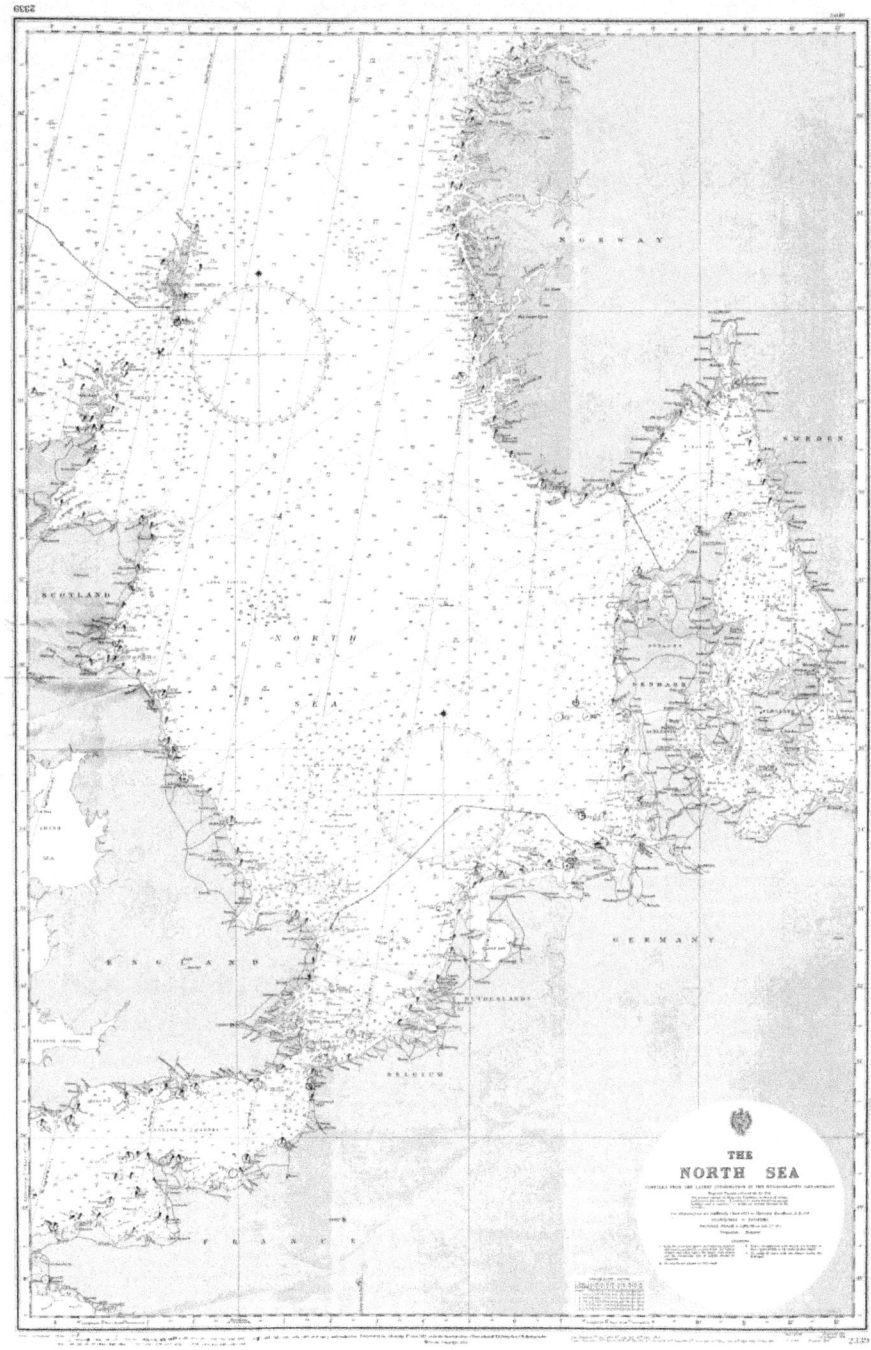

Plate 1. Chart of the North Sea

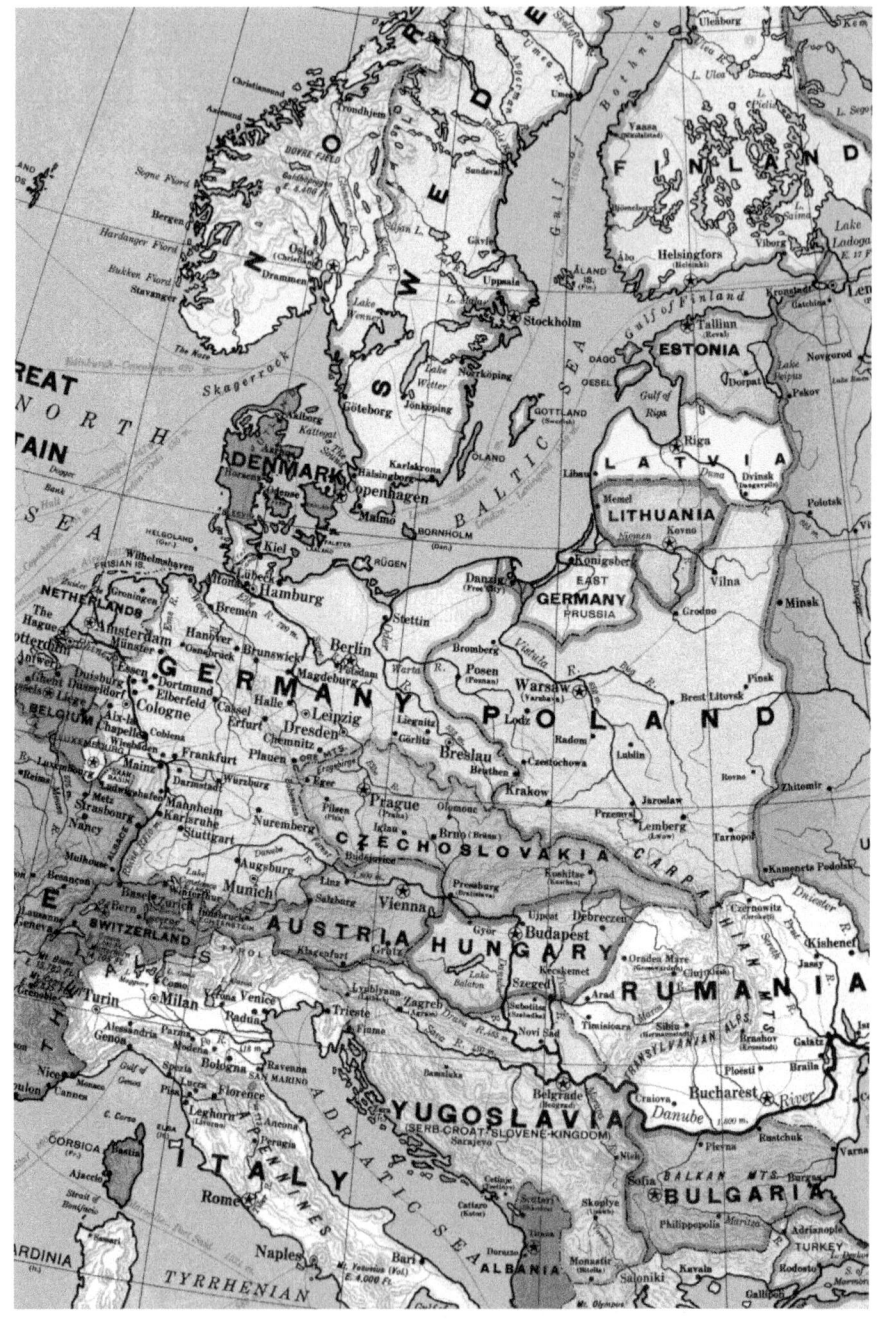

Plate 2. Map of central Europe

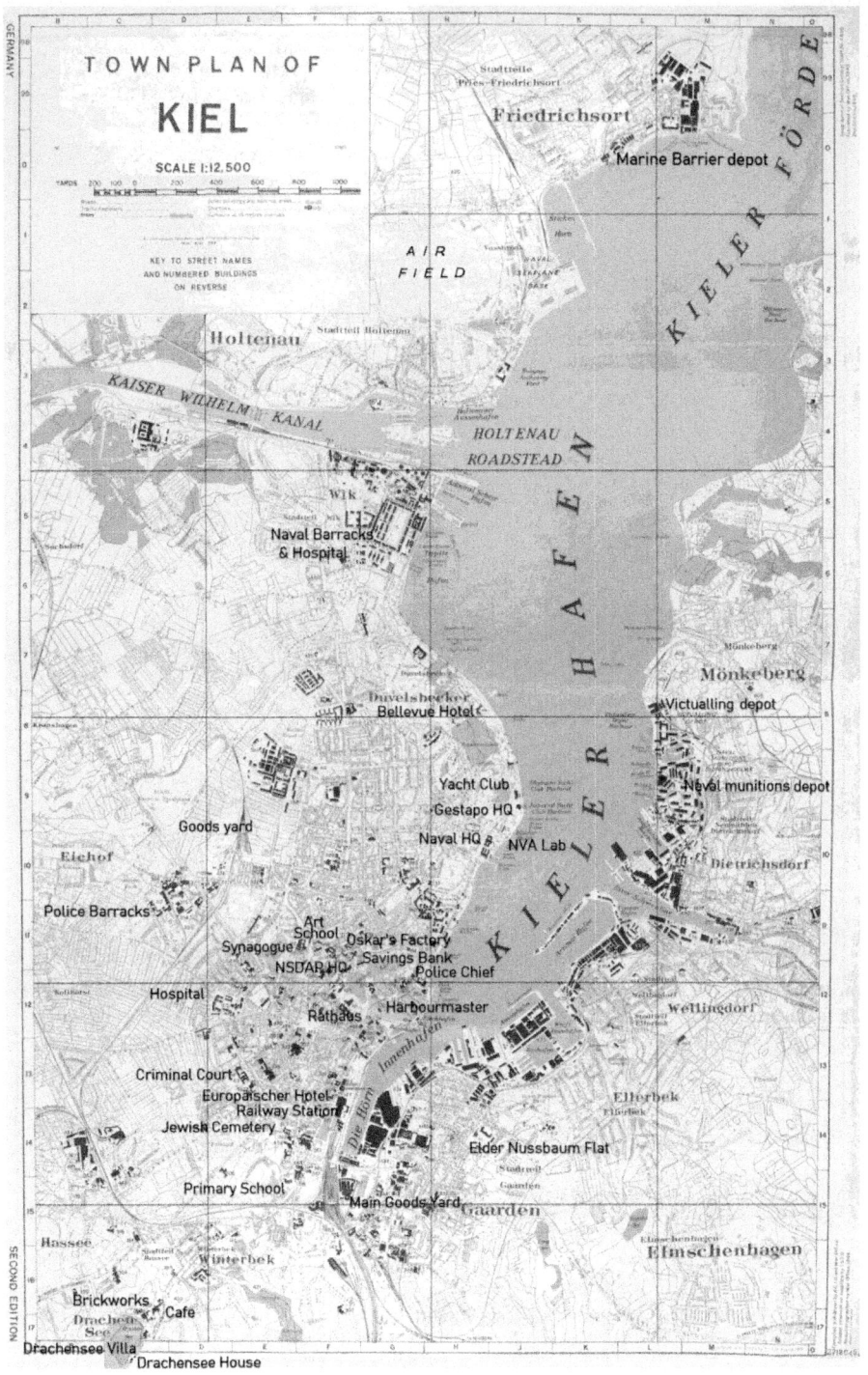

Plate 3. Street map of Kiel.

Plate 4. Map of Great Britain and Ireland.

For more detailed maps visit   https://www.alanjonesbooks.co.uk/maps_charts_plans_st.html

PROLOGUE

[15/07/2001 Sunday]

Maldon, England.

'The General wasn't to know,' Ruth said. *'It was just yet another misfortune to plague us. Our visas for Britain were only a month or two away from coming through when the war broke out, then the border with Denmark was closed the very day we left Kiel for Copenhagen.'*

The acute pain of disappointment showed in Ruth's face across the years, as if she were still standing at the border, gazing over at what she'd believed to be the first leg of her family's journey to freedom.

'We missed so many opportunities; if we'd tried to get out earlier to Britain, America or even, God forbid, Palestine, we'd have been separated from our families and our friends, but we would have been safe.'

A tear ran down Ruth's face and I looked down at my pad.

'Then there was Aunt Rosa. Within touching distance of America, they were turned away, with all the others. Even then, she should have stayed in Belgium, but what could she do? Her mother was ill. She didn't deserve to be put into Neuengamme, just for trying to get out of Germany, and failing.

Her words were clipped and angry, despite the passage of time.

'We should have known that it could only get worse; even Manny could see that, and he was a child. We'd lost any claim to be citizens in our own country and with it, every other right we'd once had. They'd taken our jobs and handed them to 'real' Germans, along with our businesses, our homes, and our land. And they were steadily robbing us of our money, and everything else we possessed.'

She closed her eyes, a frown furrowing her forehead. After a few moments, she spoke again.

'If that wasn't enough, they were going to rob us of our German homeland, the General told my parents, and send us to Poland. To ghettos, mostly, or to Konzentrationslager, with their barbed-wire fences, their unjust cruelty and their reek of death.'

I asked her if she wanted to stop for a rest, but she waved me away.

'Among us, there were thousands, especially the old, who refused to leave the country of their birth, my grandparents on both sides among them. They were the main reason we didn't try to leave earlier; that, and my father's unflinching loyalty to his employer, the General. If we'd known back then of the blackness that was to fall...'

She paused for a minute, breathing hard. I thought we might be finished for the day, but she put her hand on my arm.

'There we were,' she said, *'heading to the German border with Denmark, on the day the German Army massed a few kilometres away, waiting to invade.*

She sighed deeply.

'As I said, we didn't seem to catch the smallest break.'

CHAPTER 1

[08/04/1940 Monday]

Kiel, Germany.

By lunchtime, the General had almost managed to put the Nussbaums' journey to the back of his mind. He took himself off to one of the waterfront restaurants that lined Kieler Hafen but, when he sat back down at his desk on his return, he picked up the memo that was sitting on top of his in tray, in its familiar sealed envelope. He opened it and stared at its contents. His face blanched.

Memo: Geh.KdoS. ABW 08/04/40 CAC1021.1

For Attention Only: All senior executive officers, Abwehr.

From: Admiral Wilhelm Canaris, Chef der Abwehr.

Final preparations for Operation Weserübung, the invasion of Norway and Denmark, are in place. A combined naval and ground force operation will land Wehrmacht troops in Narvik, Trondheim, Bergen, Oslo, Egersund, Kristiansand and Arendal on the morning of the 9th of April.

Seven divisions of the 11th Army Corps, under General Nikolaus von Falkenhorst, including one mountain division and additional units from the 2nd Army, will be transported to Norway by two battleships, one heavy cruiser, two light cruisers, fourteen destroyers, and a variety of support vessels.

At the same time, two further battalions will cross the Danish border from Schleswig-Holstein into Denmark. This will be supported with simultaneous landings by the Kriegsmarine of troops at strategic positions in the Little Belt, the Great Belt, and in Copenhagen.

Air support for the naval forces and ground troops of both campaigns will be provided by the Luftwaffe.

This action has been sanctioned as a preventive manoeuvre against the proposed Franco-British occupation of Norway. The invasion of Denmark has been deemed necessary to provide bases for air support for the occupation of Norway and to secure the approaches to the Baltic through the Skagerrak and Kattegat. [END]

~~o~~

'Sir?'
The General raised his head, the captain's voice penetrating his daze.
'Yes, Captain, what is it?'
'I was just saying, sir, that you seem a little distracted today.'
The General grunted.
'Perhaps you should confine your comments to areas that concern you, Captain,' he snapped.
'I'm sorry, sir. I apologise for my rudeness.'
The General instantly regretted his loss of temper.
'I'm sorry, Captain. I shouldn't have barked at you. It's no excuse, but the Nussbaums left today, for Denmark.'

'I see, sir. I didn't know. Is that not what you wanted?'

'Yes, but unfortunately, this has put paid to their plans.'

He handed the memo to the captain.

As he read it, the captain's face slowly drained of colour.

'We're invading Norway, sir? And Denmark? Why?'

'Oh, there are a number of reasons,' the General replied, 'but the most important one is steel, or at least, the raw materials to make it.'

'I thought we imported most of our steel from Sweden, sir.'

'Yes, we do, Captain Bauer. Well, iron ore, the raw material for steel. Anyway, in summer, it's shipped direct from Sweden, straight across the Baltic sea but, during the winter, when the Baltic ports freeze, it's necessary to transport the ore by rail to the Atlantic port of Narvik, in the far north of Norway, then by ship to one of our North Sea ports.'

'Is that not a long way for it to travel, sir?'

'To a certain degree, but not as much as you'd imagine. The Swedish mines are in the northernmost part of the country, with a good rail link to Narvik. Although we will use the Baltic routes wherever possible, it's imperative that we retain the option to use Narvik in winter. Herr Hitler is worried that the British will try and influence Norway to block our ships.'

'I see, sir. Will the British not be forced to get involved once the invasion starts?'

'I would assume so. It's too close to their shores for them to ignore, and they'll know that Norway is vital for us to secure our supplies of iron and our capacity to rearm.'

The captain still looked shaken.

'What about the Nussbaums?' he said. 'They'll be caught up in the fighting.'

'That's what worries me. It's galling that I sent them there and, if the invasion succeeds, they will be back under German control, worse off than they were before.'

'You weren't to know, sir.'

'I know, but it doesn't make it any easier. We'll just have to wait and see how it pans out.'

'Are Franz and Johann involved, sir?'

The General sighed.

'I don't know, Captain. It says that units of the 2nd Army will be involved. They certainly didn't say anything to me before they returned to their garrison.'

'It's a worry, sir. On both fronts.'

'Thank you, Heinz,' he said, as the young officer headed for the door.

'Oh, and Captain,' he called across the room.

'Yes, sir. Is there something else?'

'I don't need to tell you, Captain, that you should keep all of this strictly to yourself.'

~~o~~

The General arrived home to be greeted at the front door by Yosef Nussbaum.

'Yosef!' he gasped. 'You're back.'

'Yes, sir. The border was closed, they told us. It was all very tense. They wouldn't let us through.'

'How did you get here?'

'The German border guards took a note of our names. They said we were Jewish rats trying to desert Germany in its hour of need. I thought they were going to arrest us but they put us on a train back to Kiel with the others, sir. We took a taxi from the station. We only arrived back a short while ago.'

'You were lucky not to be sent to a camp. You shouldn't be working. Are Miriam and the children not distraught?'

'Manny is upset. Ruth and Miriam are putting a brave face on it, but they're terribly disappointed.'

'You should be with them. They'll need you.'

'Miriam is preparing dinner, sir; Ruth is helping her. It keeps their minds occupied.'

The General's head was reeling. Shock had turned to relief that Yosef and Miriam had avoided finding themselves trapped in a war zone, but it took them no further forward in their attempts to get out of Germany.

'Listen,' he said. 'Don't say anything about this to Maria until I get a chance to talk to her.'

'I'll do that, sir. I'll tell Miriam and the children to do the same.'

'Danke. I'll speak to you both as soon as possible.'

He put his hand in his pocket and gave Yosef the note addressed to Antje.

'Give this back to Ruth,' he said.

~~o~~

'Hello, we're home.'

The General gave Maria a peck on the cheek.

'Hallo, darling. Did you have a nice trip? How is your mother?'

'My mother is very well, and she asks after you. Antje did nothing but stay in the garden and paint but, apart from that, it was most enjoyable. We went to the Opera. *La bohème*. It was wonderful, although your daughter sulked all the way through.'

'I thought Eva liked that sort of thing?'

She gave him a stare.

'You know I wasn't talking about Eva.'

The two girls appeared at the front door, lugging bags that appeared far too heavy for a weekend.

'Here, let me help,' he said, giving Eva a hug, and doing the same with Antje.

'Did we miss anything?' Maria asked.

'No, no,' he said. 'It was all very peaceful here without you. I had the most marvellous weekend,' he added, grinning.

'Papa,' Antje scolded. 'You know you missed us.'

'Of course I did, Schatzi, but I sat on the armchair in my socks, with my feet up on the table, and had long leisurely breakfasts with peace and quiet to read the whole paper without having to hide in my study.'

Maria and Eva shook their heads and smiled. Antje's face creased with amusement.

'I'm going to get changed, and go and see Ruth,' she said, dropping her bag behind her at the foot of the stairs.

The General waited a minute, until Maria and Eva had disappeared to unpack, and followed Antje up the stairs.

He knocked on her door.

'Come in,' he heard her say.

He stepped into her room.

'I need to tell you something before you go to see Ruth.'

A frown replaced her usual smile, and he quickly reassured her.

'Nothing's wrong,' he said. 'Well, at least, there…'

He fumbled for words.

'What I mean is, Ruth might say something to you, but don't tell your mother until I speak to her first.'

'You're not making much sense, Papa.'

'The Nussbaums left for Denmark, in the hope of getting to Britain.'

'Oh no. What happened?'

'They got turned back at the border,' the General said, closing his eyes and bowing his head.

'Ruth never said. I'm surprised she didn't at least say goodbye.'

'Yosef and Miriam didn't tell her until the day they were leaving. She left a note for you, but I gave it back to her when they returned.'

'Oh, I must go and see her.'

'On you go,' he said, smiling, 'but not a word to your mother. I want to speak to her first.'

~~o~~

He found his wife in their bedroom. She was wrapped in a towel; he heard the bath running in the adjoining room. He followed her through and drew a sharp breath when she dropped the towel and stepped into the steaming tub. He was always touched by the way the sight of her could still send shivers down his spine. She saw him looking and smiled.

'You can scrub my back for me, seeing you're here,' she said, sitting herself down into the bath with a long sigh.

She handed him the bath brush, and he obliged by washing her back while she leaned forward. He could feel her breath quicken as the soft brush raised a lather on the curve of her back, the tips of her vertebrae just showing through the suds.

'I can wash your front too,' he said, when he'd finished.

'That sounds wonderful,' she said with a hint of a smile, leaning back and handing him the sponge, and the soap.

He soaped up the sponge and began to wash her neck and shoulders. She tilted her head back against the rim of the bath.

'You didn't really lounge about all weekend, did you?' she said, her eyes closed.

'No, I didn't. Manny's Bar Mitzvah was on Saturday.'

He felt Maria stiffen under him.

'They tried to leave today,' he said.

She sat up in the bath and turned to look at him.

'Who?'

'The Nussbaums. They tried to leave for Denmark.'

'But what happened. Why are they still here?'

He told her the whole story, omitting the fact that he'd used her cousin's address on the travel permit.

'When were you going to tell me?'

She was sitting bolt upright now.

'I told nobody. It was safer that way.'

'What do you mean, safer? Don't you trust me?'

'Don't be silly. I just didn't want to put you or the girls in a difficult position or spoil your visit to your mother.'

'It's a bit hurtful, and smacks of you thinking I can't be discreet.'

'Maria, I'm sorry if that's the way you feel, but it wasn't intended that way.'

'Well, anyway, it's just a pity they were turned back. It would have been easier for everyone.'

The General stood up. All thoughts of intimacy had gone, and he felt foolish holding a handful of suds and a sponge.

'It would have been easier for us, you mean, not for the Nussbaums, although in the light of...'

He stopped himself. News of the invasion wouldn't be made public for another twenty-four hours, at least.

'There's no need for that tone,' she said. 'You know I care for them, but there's no denying that life would be much simpler without them here.'

'Perhaps it would be better if they were just deported to Poland,' he said, regretting the words as soon as they had left his lips.

She grabbed the towel and stood up, furious.

'That was cruel and uncalled for.'

She began to dry herself off, before pushing past him to the bedroom. He cursed himself for bringing the subject up, and for handling it so badly.

He was relieved that she'd missed his slip.

He followed her into the bedroom. She went behind the screen in the corner to dress, something she almost never did.

'Maria,' he said, 'I'm sorry. I shouldn't have said that. It was uncalled for. It has been an awful day, and it was so disappointing to find the Nussbaums here, when they should have been halfway to safety.'

'I sometimes wonder if you think more of them than you do of your own family.'

He shook his head, saying nothing. She stuck her head out from the screen and stared at him.

'Just out of interest,' she said, frowning, 'what did you mean when you said "especially

13

in the light of…" In the light of what?'

He sighed, cursing his gaffe. He took a deep breath.

'You say I don't trust you, but I'm going to tell you something now which cannot be repeated, to anyone. Do you understand?'

She stared at him. His voice had changed, and she knew it was his army voice, not raised, but it brooked no argument. He almost never used it with her.

'Of course I won't say anything,' she snapped, scowling at him.

'Tomorrow, we invade Denmark and Norway,' he said. 'They would have been caught up in it.'

For a moment, she stood still, her mouth open in disbelief.

'How do you…'

'How do I know? I get advance warning of almost every military action we take.'

Her face flushed with sudden fear.

'The boys. They're involved, aren't they?'

'I don't have full details, but it's possible. I won't know until later if they're part of it.'

'I wish you were as concerned about your own sons as you are about the Nussbaums.'

He didn't reply. With a deep sense of guilt, he realised that she was right. His first thought when he'd heard had been for the Nussbaums.

'You need to decide where your loyalties lie, Erich Kästner. I sometimes wonder.'

'I care about them all,' he said, his voice almost a whisper.

For a moment, her face softened, then she pushed passed him.

He stood for a minute, then made his way downstairs.

'Here,' Ruth said, handing Antje the note. 'You may as well read it.'

Antje opened it. It was short; Ruth had scribbled it at the last moment, while her father had spoken with the General, just before they left.

Dear Antje,

We have to leave immediately; Papa said not to say where, but your father might tell you if he thinks it is safe to do so.

I'm heartbroken to be leaving, but Mama says it's for the best. I know she is breaking her heart too, leaving Bubbe and Sabba Nussbaum and Bubbe and Sabba Sachs, and the rest of the family.

I'm saddest to be leaving without being able to say goodbye to you. You're the best friend I've ever had, and I will write to you every week, even if the letters don't get through.

I have the picture you gave me, and I will carry it with me always, to remind me of you, until we can meet again when this is all over.

Your best friend in the world,

Ruth Leonie Nussbaum

'I'm sorry you didn't make it,' Antje said, hugging Ruth. 'Papa says it would be better for you to leave, but part of me is glad you're here.'

'Me too, but we'll still have to go, Mama says.'

'I know, but let's make the most of it while you are here.'

CHAPTER 2

KIELER MORGENPOST

Tuesday 9th April 1940

LATE EDITION

NORWAY AND DENMARK INVADED

At 4am this morning, the forces of the Wehrmacht invaded Norway and Denmark, in a combined airborne, land-based and amphibious operation. A spokesman for the Reich Ministry of War said that this action on the part of the Third Reich had become unavoidable due to the openly discussed British and French plans to occupy Norway, with the intention of disrupting the import of Swedish iron ore to Germany.

"We cannot tolerate the imposition of an arbitrary blockade of legitimate trade between two free countries".

German warships landed units of the 11th Army at strategic objectives including Oslo, Bergen and Narvik. The battalion's mountain division and units from the 2nd Army also took part. Reports so far suggest that the invasion has been successful although there has been stiff resistance, especially at Narvik in the north of the country.

Sources from within Denmark report that the occupation there is almost complete, with limited resistance. German paratroopers took several objectives, including the airport at Aalborg, a key target, which will give the Luftwaffe enhanced access to Norwegian airspace in support of the campaign there.

~~o~~

Esther Weichmann tore the letter open, glancing at the Swedish postmark on the envelope. Unfolding the thin sheets of paper, she read Miriam's opening words and gasped.

Rosa. In a camp.

She read on, a tear falling onto the letter.

Mama and Papa Weichmann! Surely they are too old to be sent to Poland.

Normally greedy for news from home, she took little joy from the rest of Miriam's letter. Once she'd read it through once, she read it again, slower this time, trying to take it all in. She looked at the clock, knowing that Itsik would be home soon.

When he came through the door, he saw Esther's tear-stained face and rushed over to her.

'The baby. Is she all right? Nothing has happened to Moshe or Shoshana, has it?'

'No, no,' Esther sobbed, 'It's...'

She broke down.

'Mama and Papa. It's one of them, isn't it?'

'Itsik. It's not them. It's Rosa. She's in a camp.'

'Rosa? I thought the Liewermanns were in Belgium.'

'They were. She went back to Germany to see her mother. She was taken ill.'

'Who? Rosa?'

'No. Her mother, obviously.'

'So, what happened?'

'The Gestapo arrested her within a couple of days. She's been sent to a concentration camp near Hamburg. Neuengamme, it's called.'

'That's terrible. What about Emil and the children?'

'They stayed in Antwerp. Rosa's lawyer says she told him she doesn't want them to come home.'

'Did the lawyer give any hope?'

'I don't know.'

She bit her lip.

'Itsik,' she said. 'Can I ask you something?'

He reached out and touched her cheek.

'Of course. What is it?'

'Can we help Rosa?'

'How?' he said, a puzzled look on his face.

'The lawyer will cost a lot of money. Emil will be taking it out of their reserves. The Jewish community will try and help, but we could send a little, couldn't we.'

He hesitated, but he saw the pain and pleading in her eyes.

'Yes,' he said. 'We could spare a little. I'll send extra to Mama and Papa. Miriam can pick it up there.'

It had become impossible to send money to Germany, but Itsik had found a family of fellow immigrants in Haifa who still held reserves of money in Kiel, kept in safety by relatives. They were trying to get the money out of Germany.

In return for an envelope of Palestine pounds delivered to them every month, the equivalent amount of Reichsmarks were released to Itsik's parents from the cache in Germany. It would continue while the elder Weichmanns needed it, for as long as the hoard of money remained undiscovered.

It suited both families.

'Thank you,' she said, falling into his embrace.

'There,' he said, 'we'll try our best to sort it out.'

'I wish they'd came here when they'd had a chance. Miriam's family too.'

'They still could. I can talk to the people who are getting Mama and Papa out. It's risky though.'

'I know. I'm sure they would try if it weren't so dangerous.'

'There's also a waiting list. They can only smuggle a few people across the border at a time. Look at Mama and Papa. How long have we been waiting to hear?'

She sighed.

'Months. Have you contacted them again?'

'No. They told me to be patient; that they would get in touch with us.'

'The wait is terrible.'

'Yes, but it must be worse for them.'

~~o~~

[10/04/1940 Wednesday]

The General's face was creased with worry, but he smiled at Yosef and Miriam.

'I've pulled as many strings as I can,' he said. 'You should get travel papers in three to four weeks. You'll be going to Belgium first.'

'Thank you, sir. It's been a worry.'

'Once you get there, if the British embassy can't help you, I'd advise you to try and get into France, and make for Spain or Portugal. It might not be safe to stay in Belgium. I'll get you papers to travel.'

Miriam's eyes widened.

'They're going to invade Belgium?' she said, her voice trembling.

They.

The General flinched.

She doesn't think of herself as German, now.

'I can't say for sure,' he answered, 'but yes. Eventually. And France as well, I'd imagine.'

'What if we go, and we're caught in Belgium when the Wehrmacht invade?' Miriam asked.

'I can't see us taking on the French or the Belgians any time soon. Not while fighting still goes on in Norway.'

'I'm sorry, sir, I should have asked you about Franz and Johann. Are they involved?'

'Yes, I'm sure they are. They would have been in touch otherwise, and I know that sections of the 2nd Army have been deployed in both Norway and Denmark. I hear there is fierce fighting, especially in the north.'

'We pray for the boys, sir,' Miriam said. 'Every day.'

'Thank you,' he said, giving her a smile. 'We do too. They are both outstanding officers and being a good soldier is the best way to stay alive.'

'How is the campaign going, sir?' Yosef asked.

'It's going well, as far as I can tell, but war can be very confusing, as you know, Yosef. It will become clearer over the next few days.'

'I suppose it will, sir.' Yosef hesitated.

'Sir, how safe would Spain be?' he said. 'Are they not allied to Germany?'

'No, but it is a fascist state like Germany and Italy. Because Spain is a neutral country that still trades with Britain, you may be able to get a ship to England if we can resurrect your visas. There are very few options left otherwise.'

'I know, sir. We considered moving east, but Romania and Hungary both favour Germany, and have similar anti-Jewish laws. We thought about Greece, but we've been told the language is difficult and, with the invasion of Albania, it is under threat of Italian occupation.'

'No. You have to go west. Or to Palestine.'

'The consequences of failure if we try Palestine are unthinkable, sir. We should have gone earlier when we had a chance. We didn't realise…'

The General put his hand on Yosef's shoulder.

'I know, my friend. What's done is done. Let's just try and get you out, whatever way we can.'

CHAPTER 3

[09/05/1940 Thursday]

'Father, is that you? This line is Scheiße. I can hardly hear you.'

The General laughed and gave Frau Müller an apologetic shrug. She waited, notebook in hand, for the General to dictate a letter.

'Johann, I can just about make you out. Are you in Norway?'

'We were, but we've been withdrawn, after only a month. Colonel Schneider's division is being assigned back with the bulk of the 2nd Army. We're to join them near Koblenz. Something is going down. We've just disembarked in Kiel, but we're being loaded into trains on the dockside. Franz asked me to try and find a phone and let you know that we're both well.'

The General forced his face to remain neutral. He turned towards the window.

'I'll come and see you. It will only take five minutes.'

'No, I'm in the dockmaster's office. He let me use his phone; he says he knows you. I must go; the train is about to pull out. We'll try and phone once we get to our billets, but I wouldn't count on it. They're being incredibly tight on security.'

Johann's words were rushed. He could imagine him keeping one eye on the train, his friends gesticulating for him to hurry.

'Try and write to your mother.'

'We did, from Norway. Did she not get them?'

'No, but the post can be unreliable.'

'That's one of my men shouting. The train is moving. We'll see you soon.'

He heard the phone drop, and the beat of running footsteps. After a few crackles, a voice broke the silence.

'Herr General, how are you?'

'I'm fine. How are you?'

He half recognised the voice and managed to put a face to it – a large bushy moustache and broad, ruddy cheeks; a mountain of a man, if he remembered rightly. Christian Junge, the marshalling yard supervisor for the whole of Kiel, had introduced him on a visit to the dockside when a load of electrical parts for the Kriegsmarine had been delivered to the wrong quay.

'Oh, as well as could be expected,' the man said. 'We work from dawn until dusk. All these supplies and men, moving around the country, you know.'

'Yes, I suppose they are. Listen, thanks for letting my son use your phone. Did he make the train?'

The man laughed.

'Only just. His friends had the door open, and they hauled him up as he ran alongside. The whole train was laughing and cheering.'

The General smiled.

Typical Johann.

'I can't thank you enough.'

'Ach. You've always been kind to Wilhelm Aachen. Some of these fancy-pants officers wouldn't spit on you, far less pass the time of day.'

The General laughed.

'Nice speaking to you, Wilhelm, and thanks again. Auf Wiedersehen.'

He put the phone down and turned back to Frau Müller.

'My son,' he explained, with a shrug of his shoulders. 'He just about missed his train.'

He was sure she'd tried to listen to the other end of the conversation, but he'd held the earpiece tight to his ear, a trick he'd learned from Canaris.

'Let's get on with this letter, shall we?'

As he dictated, Johann's words simmered in his head.

Koblenz. Is it to be Belgium or the Netherlands? Or even France?

When she'd finished, he asked his secretary to send Captain Bauer in. The young naval

18

officer knocked on the door almost immediately and entered, standing to attention.

'Captain, see if there are any memos for me, would you?'

'Yes, sir.'

The young officer turned for the door.

'Just a minute, Heinz,' the General said, and Captain Bauer stopped.

'Yes, sir?'

'Were those two freight transport requisitions sent over to Herr Junge at the goods yard?'

'Yes, sir, they went this morning.'

'Good. Admiral Göpfert asked me personally to expedite them. It's new anti-aircraft guns for one of our destroyers. They're upgrading them.'

'We're doing quite a few of these requisitions now, sir.'

'Yes. It has made quite a difference to the Kriegmarine's efficiency. They seem to be quite pleased.'

'They are, sir. I overheard Admiral Göpfert talking with Admiral Schiffer last week. They were singing your praises.'

The General smiled.

'You shouldn't listen in to other people's conversations, Captain Bauer, and you should take flattery with a large grain of salt.'

'Yes, sir.'

'What do you think of Schiffer?'

Admiral Rolf Schiffer had taken over as Baltic Fleet commander from Admiral Raeder and had been in the job six months.

'He's good, sir, and the men like him, but they liked Raeder too.'

'That's what I'd heard. I was worried that when Schiffer came, we'd be getting one of Herr Hitler's Arschleckern in command.'

Heinz Bauer laughed.

'There are plenty of arse-lickers about, sir, but Schiffer doesn't appear to be one of them.'

'Good. Now go and check for these memos,' the General said.

While the captain was away at the communication centre, the General took out the old atlas that he always carried in his briefcase. Detailed military maps were better, but sometimes it was enough to see the overall lie of the land. He found Koblenz, about eighty kilometres south of Bonn.

It was within striking distance of the Belgian border.

The bulk of Southern Norway was under German control and only in the far north was there any resistance, where the British, French and Poles had strengthened the last of the Norwegian forces holding out against the Wehrmacht. The General was surprised that Colonel Schneider's battalion had been withdrawn.

The captain knocked on the door.

'Just two, sir.' He handed the General the small brown envelopes, each with the eagle crest and a swastika on the front.

He tore open the first one. It was a routine memorandum about recording payments for informants, and a brief thought about Dieter Mass passed through his mind, but he laid it aside and opened the second memo. He read it, then showed it to Captain Bauer. He watched the young man's face while he read.

Memo: Geh.KdoS. ABW 09/05/40 CAC1110.1

For Attention Only: All senior executive officers, Abwehr.

From: Admiral Wilhelm Canaris, Chef der Abwehr.

** HÖCHSTE GEHEIMHALTUNG **

135 divisions of the Heer have been positioned to invade Belgium, the Netherlands, Luxembourg, and France. The main attack, through the Forest of Ardennes, will start at 2100 tonight, the 9th of May, with further attacks in Northern

'The French are too strong for us. You said that yourself, sir.'

'I did, but that was for a conventional frontal attack; their army is bigger; it's more heavily motorised, with larger tanks, and France's fortifications along the Maginot Line on our border mean that they can concentrate their defence along the frontier with Belgium, but...'

He hesitated.

'If I hadn't watched the invasion of Poland,' he continued, 'I might still be saying the same thing.'

'Have we a chance of winning, sir?'

'Since the end of the last war, I've seen our army develop to fight in a different way. Damn, I helped to train them. It relies on a few central tenets, Captain. Speed, communication and adaptability.'

'But we're also much better equipped than the British and the French, and their allies, are we not?'

'That, my dear Heinz, is a fallacy promulgated by our leaders. Admittedly, we do have a few very well-equipped, modern divisions, but we also have a considerable number of old-fashioned infantry divisions who rely entirely on horses for transport.'

The captain stared at him.

'Are the French and the British the same?'

'No. Our intelligence tells us that they are both better mechanised than us, and their armour, especially the French, is heavier.'

'So, what chance do we have? We can't be faster if we rely so heavily on horses.'

'I read the reports of the Polish campaign. The one advantage we have is superior communications. Even back when I was regular army, we were beginning to train in the use of radios, almost as much as we practised firing weapons. It seems to work. We coordinate our forces better, and can react quicker, and take full advantage of our enemies' mistakes.'

'The navy is the same, sir, I believe. It's all radio now. We rarely use flags, or Aldis lamps these days.'

'Even between the services, Captain, communication is paramount. In the Polish campaign, our men on the ground could request air support that would arrive within an hour, or less. And don't forget, the one area where we are better equipped than France or Britain is in our power in the air. The Luftwaffe is bigger and more technologically advanced than the other two combined.'

'I see, sir. So, we could win?'

'It's possible and, ten years ago, I would have been behind them, cheering them on all the way. What soldier or patriot wouldn't? But now...?'

Heinz Bauer opened his mouth to say something, then stopped.

'It's true, Captain,' the General said, 'and it's not just those at the top. We're all to blame for what is happening in Germany's name.'

'But sir, we...'

The General shook his head. 'They couldn't do all this without the tacit support of the majority,' he said, 'although you could argue that it is understandable, that people are too frightened to speak out, that even the minority who see the wrong in it keep their silence, but it's no real excuse. And now it's too late. They have all the power.'

The young officer's face froze. He shook his head and stared at the General.

'We'll be tarnished forever by it,' Erich Kästner said.

~~o~~

That evening, Operation Fall Gelb was unleashed, and the tanks of the panzer divisions rolled into Luxembourg, Belgium and the Netherlands, the infantry behind them. The Luftwaffe dropped parachute divisions to take key bridges, forts, and airfields, in Belgium and in Holland.

A feint by several divisions of General Fedor von Bock's Army Group B drew a sizable portion of the French Army away from the main thrust of his divisions, who cut through the

Dutch, Belgian and French forces with devastating efficiency, taking large swathes of the low countries in the first few days.

The British Expeditionary Force, moving northwards from France, met the retreating Dutch, Belgian and French forces moving south.

Franz Kästner looked around. Their camp was strangely subdued, the forced idleness leaving his men with a restless lethargy.

A frustrated Colonel Schneider had been ordered to move his division to the border, then wait, the whole of the 2nd Army being held in reserve. They were close enough to hear the clamour of the guns fifteen kilometres ahead, and they watched as company after company thundered past, the men waving at them from the trucks.

'Look at that,' he said, pointing skywards. Countless waves of Luftwaffe planes droned above them, the lines of black crosses stark and menacing against the blue sky.

'I almost feel sorry for the poor bastards on the receiving end of that,' Franz said.

'Don't,' the colonel said. 'You'll thank them for every soldier killed and every gun or tank destroyed when we finally get to be part of it. Don't forget that I fought over these sorry fields and villages only twenty years ago, and we don't want to get bogged down in that sort of war again.'

'Sorry, sir. My father doesn't speak much about it, but from the little he does say, it sounds as if it was hell on earth.'

'It was sheer attrition. We killed a thousand of their men, they killed a thousand of ours. We advanced a few hundred metres, they won it back a few weeks later. In the end, the politicians sold us out. All these brave dead, for nothing.'

'The Führer won't sell us out, sir,' one of the junior officers said.

'No. I'm sure he won't,' the colonel said, nodding. 'What do you think, Franz?'

Franz knew the colonel was teasing him and refused to rise to the bait.

'You're right. He'll not sell us out, sir.'

'But you're not his greatest fan,' the junior officer said to Franz, trying to ingratiate himself with the colonel.

Franz closed his eyes for a second, then turned to the young lieutenant.

'I have issues with some of his policies,' he said.

The colonel interrupted, turning to the young man.

'I encourage my officers to have minds of their own, as long as I have no reason to doubt their loyalty to the Heer, and to Germany. Franz is one of my best officers and, from what I saw in Poland, I have no reason to worry. You, on the other hand, still have a lot to prove.'

The young officer blushed, and they all laughed at him.

'Like all armies, officers in the Heer are trained to obey orders but, as you know from your training, we teach ours to think on their feet, to be able to react to circumstances and take the initiative. You'd do worse than to watch Franz or Johann Kästner and learn from them. I should know. I learned from their father.'

CHAPTER 4

KIELER MORGENPOST

Friday 10th May 1940

LATE EDITION

DEUTSCHLAND UMFASST DIE NIEDERLANDE, BELGIEN, LUXEMBURG

In Berlin, at 9 O'clock this morning, Foreign Minister Joachim von Ribbentrop announced that Reich forces had launched military operations in the Netherlands, Belgium, and Luxembourg to protect the Low Countries' neutrality.

He stated that the action was in response to unimpeachable proof that Britain and France were planning an attack on the Ruhr, in a similar aggressive fashion to that which had taken place in the last war.

He further stated that collusion between the Dutch and British intelligence services to instigate a coup in Germany to oust its democratic leaders had been averted by the action taken by German forces.

140 army divisions, incorporating 3,000,000 soldiers 2,500 tanks and 7,500 field guns, are being deployed in the offensive, with critical support from the Luftwaffe's 2000 combat, 500 transport and 50 glider aircraft.

The Morgenpost has received early reports of significant advances in Southern Belgium and Luxembourg. An army spokesman said that the main thrust through the Forest of Ardennes had caught the French by surprise and if the armies of the Reich reached the Belgian coast, British, French, Belgian and Dutch forces would be completely cut off.

~~o~~

[18/05/1940 Saturday]

12th April 1940

Dear Miriam,

I was so glad to receive your letter. The talk is that mail isn't getting through at all now, so I think you are right – these will be our last letters to each other, for a while anyway. At least I have the chance to write this. Please thank the General for this opportunity.

I'm devastated about Rosa. What possessed her to come back to Germany, even though her mother was ill? Itsik and Abel have had to resist the urge to go back and see their parents as we know they would never get back out again.

We have arranged for a little extra money to be sent to Itsik's parents for you to give to whoever is dealing with Rosa's lawyer. It is the least we can do. I'm sorry it couldn't be more but most of our money is tied up in the house and the shops, and we need to have a little spare in case we get the go-ahead to bring Mama and Papa Weichmann over. We have had no news yet, but we've been told that it could be any time.

Please consider coming with the Haganah to Palestine if you can't get out any other way (we hear that Denmark has fallen now). I know it is dangerous, but people think the risk is being exaggerated by the British and the German authorities to try and stem the flow of Jews into Palestine.

Your little namesake is doing fine – she sleeps through the night now, so I'm less tired. Moshe and Shoshana dote on her although Moshe won't admit it.

The shops are doing better than we could have hoped, and the garden is coming along. I spend a lot of time in it, and I'm as brown as the other women now. I almost feel like a seasoned Palestinian, but I still miss both you and Rosa terribly. One day, we will all be together again, and I don't think I'll ever let you go!

It's not all roses here. Another Jewish settler was killed a few days ago, not far from us, and three Arabs. It is awfully sad, as we could all live together. The Arabs who work with us all say we've done miracles with the acres of land we have bought, but they are the friendly ones who appear happy for us to be here to provide work. They appear to be in the minority and many of the others are surly and rude, and we always wonder if they will turn on us one day. The British are a further concern. There are rumours that we might be interned, and we worry that if Germany defeats Britain, who will control Palestine?

I shouldn't be telling you my woes and putting you off coming, but I'd rather be honest and, despite all of it, we are much better off here than if we were still in Germany.

Please be safe, and all my prayers are for Rosa and you.

Esther.

~~o~~

Memo: Geh.KdoS. ABW 20/05/40 CAC01089.1

For Attention Only: General Erich Kästner, Abwehr, Kiel office, Abwehr.

From: Vice Admiral Wilhelm Canaris, Chef der Abwehr.

** HÖCHSTE GEHEIMHALTUNG **

SS authorities have opened the Auschwitz concentration camp close to the Polish town of Oświęcim, Upper Silesia. [END]

CHAPTER 5

[24/05/1940 Friday]

When the air-raid sirens went off for the first time, there was no panic; it was a practise, everyone knew. Kiel's children, excited and curious at first, laughed and squealed and shouted to each other, their eyes bright as they made their way towards their designated shelters.

But among their parents, holding tight to their children's hands as they entered the massive concrete mausoleums, the sense of unease was palpable. The persistent rising-and-falling wail of the sirens continued unabated as the lines of people were swallowed up, crowding together in the cold, harsh lights of the bunkers, finding neighbours to sit beside or, with awkward mumblings, introducing themselves to strangers.

General Kästner ushered Maria and his daughters in through the doors and into one of the cavernous rooms to the left, and motioned for the Nussbaums to follow him. He found a vacant section of wooden bench against the wall and indicated that the two women and the girls should sit down. Yosef, himself, and Manny stood in the narrow passage between the seats.

He knew, from his involvement in the coordination of Kiel's air defences, that not all the shelters were ready and that at some, people were simply gathering in a well-ordered group on the building sites earmarked as the location for their allocated bunkers.

As befitting the German character, they all attended, as directed by the announcement in the Morgenpost.

As the doors thudded shut and the locks slid home with a dull clunk, a collective intake of breath came from the citizen occupying the chambers. Those without benches sat on the floor. Wardens stepped carefully among the mass of people, chiding those who had forgotten their gas masks and showing others where the toilets were.

It didn't feel particularly stuffy; there was enough movement in the air from the large extractor fans humming noisily in the ventilator shafts, but the General was sure it would become uncomfortably stuffy if the power failed during a raid.

'That took over half an hour,' the General whispered to Yosef. 'They'll have to speed it up when it happens for real; there won't be that much warning in a proper air raid.'

'I'm sure people would speed up if there were bombs dropping.'

The General laughed.

'You may be right,' he said.

An hour passed before the faint sound of the all-clear signal filtered into the bunker through the ventilation shaft. As they waited patiently to join the river of bodies streaming through the door, the General heard a voice behind him.

'They've got a cheek, being in here. This shelter is for Germans.'

Standing next to him, he felt Yosef and Miriam stiffen and push towards the entrance. He craned his head backwards to try and catch sight of the speaker, but he couldn't tell who had spoken, so he scowled in the direction the words had come from.

A second person made a comment; a woman this time.

'It's terrible. I hope they're not taking up space intended for our own people.'

This time, the General caught a glimpse of the culprit, and stared at her. She looked away, and he pushed back towards her, against the throng, but he felt an arm tug the cloth of his coat.

'Sir, please leave it,' Yosef's voice whispered in his ear. 'We don't want a scene.'

The General was about to argue with him, but he saw the panic in Yosef's eyes and hesitated. He looked back towards the woman, but she was either keeping her head down, or had wormed her way to another part of the crowd.

He turned and saw Maria looking at him, her lips thin and set. She was close to the entrance and she and the others were slowly swept through the doors by the flow of people exiting. He followed, catching up with them as they made their way along the street.

'I'm sorry, sir,' Yosef said, walking with the General behind the ladies. 'I shouldn't have spoken like that, but you don't know how we live.'

'What do you mean?' the General said, bristling a little.

'As Jews, we try and make ourselves as invisible as we can. It's a triumph if we manage not to get noticed, sir. It's too dangerous to stick out from the crowd.'

A sense of horror struck the General. His indignant response to the barbs in the shelter would likely have caused nothing but trouble for the Nussbaums.

'I'm sorry, Yosef. I didn't think. These people rile me so much.'

'It's not just for us, sir. It's not safe for you to be seen taking that sort of stance either.'

The General glanced at Yosef.

'You do sometimes speak out when you shouldn't,' Yosef continued, with an apologetic shrug. 'Frau Kästner is correct. You should be more careful.'

'I only stand up for what I consider is right, Yosef.'

'I know, sir, and all of our people appreciate it, but I'm afraid the only reason you haven't been visited by the Gestapo is because of your position.'

~~o~~

THE LONDON EVENING TELEGRAPH

Sunday, May 26th, 1940

THOUSANDS OF TROOPS HOME SAFE.

Many more to follow.

An operation to evacuate nearly 400,000 men of the British Expeditionary Force from Dunkirk in France has begun. The BEF had become isolated from its French Allies when the German Army attacked unexpectedly in the southern part of Belgium. A controlled retreat to the harbour at Dunkirk and a staged evacuation to Dover and other English ports will hopefully prevent the capture of hundreds of thousands of soldiers and allow them to fight again another day.

Hundreds of small pleasure boats have made the hazardous trip across the channel to aid in the evacuation of the troops.

The importance of this vital evacuation cannot be understated with the threat to Britain of a Nazi Invasion.

~~o~~

Major Anthony Plenderleith frowned.

'It's impossible,' he said.

'What's impossible, dear?'

'They're trying to evacuate what's left of the British Army from France, in an armada of small boats.'

'Why don't they use big ships? It would be quicker.'

'They won't be able to get them close enough to the beaches, I suppose.'

'Well, if anyone can do it, Mr. Churchill can.'

CHAPTER 6

[27/05/1940 Monday]

Itsik recognised the man as soon as the shop door opened. He motioned for his assistant to mind the shop, and wordlessly ushered the new arrival to his office at the rear of the building.

'Have you any news?' he asked, before the man had a chance to speak.

'Yes. They move tomorrow. Do you have the money?'

'Yes. It's all here.'

Itsik turned and crouched in front of the safe, opening it with a key from his chain. He pulled out a brown envelope and handed it to the man.

Itsik watched him as he counted it. He was small, with tight curls of dark hair receding from his forehead. Although he was almost a head smaller than Itsik, and didn't seem particularly well-muscled, he had the hardened air of a fighter.

'It's all there,' Itsik said, his voice betraying his ragged nerves.

The man nodded as he counted the last note.

'You may think we're mercenary, asking for money,' he said.

'No, no,' Itsik protested. 'We understand.'

'It will help pay for others to come in, who have no money. Young people who will fight for our homeland.'

Itsik lifted his hand to bite a nail but dropped it again, like a nervous schoolboy.

'Yes. It is what we want too,' he said, meaning it, but he knew he would never have the hunger the young Haganah man had.

Moshe might, one day.

'You will know by this time next week,' the man said. 'It has been…'

For the first time, he sounded hesitant.

'… shall we say, difficult. There are no guarantees.'

'We know the risks, but if they stay, who knows what will happen.'

'Believe that, my friend. It will be a long seven days.'

~~o~~

[28/05/1940 Tuesday]

'Papa, this means we can never get out, doesn't it?'

Yosef looked at his daughter's face, then at the headline in the Morgenpost.

BELGIEN KAPITULIERT

Belgium surrenders.

'Not for certain, Ruth,' he said, unable to meet her gaze. 'There are other ways.'

He couldn't meet her eyes. First Holland, now Belgium. It was expected that France would fall next.

Was Britain even safe?

He heard her speak.

'Sorry, what did you say, Ruth?'

She sighed and shook her head, then repeated herself.

'The boys at school say the Haganah can help you get to Palestine, if you are young, and willing to fight.'

'Ha. That counts me out,' he said, a bitter laugh escaping his throat.

He saw her face cloud with hurt and bewilderment.

'I'm sorry,' he said. 'It is not the time for joking. What I mean is, it's young men they are looking for.'

'No. They want families too. But they won't take old people.'

'How do you know all of this?'

This time, it was her eyes that shifted from his.

'Chamudah?' he said.

'We were told not to say to anyone, even our parents.'

'Say what?' Yosef asked, trying not to sound angry.

'A man and a woman from the Haganah came to school, to talk to us about going to Palestine. During Herr Eliasowitz's lesson. It was just the older children, my age, and the students, who study next door to us.'

'I see. And what did they tell you?'

'That we must go to Palestine, even if it means leaving our parents behind, that there are places called Kibbutz, where we can live with other young people, and make a Jewish homeland.'

Yosef took her hand.

'Ruth, in a way they are right. These places do exist and, although it isn't without its risks, the Haganah can take you to Palestine.'

He paused, and looked at her young, serious face, and felt tears begin to prickle his eyes.

'But your mama and I want us all to get away from here together, as a family. I know you are growing up fast, into a clever and beautiful young lady, but you still need us and, without Manny and you, what else would there be for us?'

It crossed his mind that, perhaps, it was more about his and Miriam's needs than his children's but, deep down, he felt that they were still far too young to be without them.

'I wouldn't go, Papa. Not without you, Mama and Manny.'

'That's my girl. Try not to worry. We'll sort something out.'

But, in his heart, he wasn't sure he could.

~~o~~

[29/05/1940 Wednesday]

Itsik didn't have to wait a week. Two days after his meeting with the Haganah man, a woman knocked on the door of the house in Afula, just after the Weichmann family had eaten their evening meal.

Itsik got up from the table, and Esther heard the door opening, then a woman's voice. She heard Itsik invite her in and show her into the front room.

Through the closed door, she heard the murmur of voices, low and insistent. A few seconds later, she heard a cry.

'Stay here,' she told the children. 'Moshe, look after Miriam for me.'

She opened the door of the front room. The woman, in her twenties, *no more than a girl*, Esther thought, was standing next to Itsik, trying not to look at him.

Esther had never seen her husband in such distress. It was as if he was struggling to breathe, and she went to him.

'What's wrong, Itsik? What has happened?'

'It's Mama and Papa,' he gasped. 'They've been taken.'

He doubled over, almost retching.

'Herr and Frau Weichmann were arrested trying to leave Czechoslovakia,' the woman said, 'even though their papers appeared to be in order. We think they've been taken to one of the Auffangslager, but we don't know anything further. I'm sorry.'

A transit camp.

Esther could feel her eyes filling with tears, but she knew she had to stay strong for Itsik and the children.

She turned to the woman.

'Thank you for coming and telling us. It would be better if you left us now.'

The visitor nodded and let herself out.

'Mama, what is it?' a voice said.

Moshe was growing up so fast. Sometimes, she found herself beginning to think of him as a young man but, when she looked up and saw him standing, frightened in the doorway, he was her little boy again.

The baby struggled in his arms, desperate to get down on the floor to crawl around. Esther could see Shoshana's head peering round from behind Moshe, anxious to know what had upset her mama and papa.

'Go back through just now, please,' she said. 'I'll be there in a minute.'

Moshe hesitated, glancing at his father, but did as he was asked.

'I must go to Germany,' Itsik whispered hoarsely when the children had gone.

Esther bowed her head.

'You know you can't,' she told him, her voice soft. 'Look what happened to Rosa.'

'I can't just abandon them, and I can't send Abel.'

'Neither of you can go,' she said, harsher this time. 'Mama and Papa Weichmann wouldn't want you to go home and risk being sent to God knows what camp. They know that both of you are needed here.'

He looked at her, surprised by the hardness of her words.

'But...' he said, the words dying in his throat.

She put her hand on his.

'You can't go. I'll write to Miriam. Yosef and Jakob can try and find out more.'

Hope filled his face for a second, then died out again.

'What can they do?' he said.

'As much as you, if not more. They deal with this situation all the time.'

His head jerked up.

'I didn't realise...'

'I know, my love,' she said. 'The only reason I'm aware of these things is through Miriam's letters. She tells me everything.'

'I have to do something.'

'Send some money if you can.'

'It might be difficult. The last time, the Kreidls had real trouble getting in touch with their relatives.'

'Just try,' she said. 'Money helps more than anything. Now, I'm going to tell the children.'

'What will you say?'

'I'll tell Moshe the truth. He's old enough. I'll tell Shoshana that her Bubbe and her Sabba tried to come here but couldn't get out. She doesn't need to know about them being arrested.'

'Do you want me to...'

'No, I'll do it. You sit there, and I'll get you a cup of coffee.'

~~o~~

Esther made the coffee and, after telling Shoshana about her grandparents, sent her through to her father, the girl old enough to carry the tray holding the mug of coffee and a slice of fruitcake, balancing it with great concentration to avoid spilling it. When she heard Itsik and Shoshana talking, she closed the door and turned to Moshe.

'Thank you, Moshe. Your papa was in a terrible state, and I had to go to him.'

'It's Sabba and Bubbe, isn't it? Are they dead?'

'No, no,' Esther said, shaking her head, 'but they were caught trying to leave Germany. We don't know anything else. Your papa had arranged for the Haganah to bring them to Palestine, but something went wrong.'

'I knew they were coming. I overheard you, the other night. I prayed that they would make it here, Mama.'

She flinched at the distress on his face. The baby stretched a hand up and pulled his hair, but he didn't complain.

'Prayers are just requests for help,' Esther said. 'They're not always answered.'

'I know, but I so wanted them to be here. So did you, Mama, and Papa too.'

She ruffled his hair.

'I miss them terribly,' she said, closing her eyes. 'We all do. Bubbe and Sabba Weichmann mean more to me than my own parents ever did. Have I ever told you that?'

'No, Mama. Why?'

Her eyes blinked open, and she looked at him, her heart breaking.

'It's a long story. One day, I'll tell you, but your father always says I only married him because I wanted to be their daughter.'

A smile crept onto his face, and he rubbed his sleeve across his cheeks to wipe away the tears.

'Go and talk to your father,' she told him, giving him a hug, 'but don't say anything in front of Shoshana. I don't want her knowing about them being arrested.'

The baby wriggled, and she took her from him. She watched him go and marvelled at the tall, awkward youth who, only a blink before, had been her vulnerable little boy.

She sat down to write a note to Miriam.

When she'd finished, she sealed the envelope and glanced into the front room, nodding to Itsik before slipping out the front door. She knew that their neighbour, Herr Bacher, was leaving for China early the next morning, and would post it for her.

CHAPTER 7

'Have you anything you want to add to this message for Miriam?'

Itsik held up the piece of paper that he was about to wrap the bundle of Palestinian pound notes in and waited while Esther thought for a second.

'What have you written?' she asked.

'Just that Mama and Papa have been taken, and the money is for Jakob and Yosef to use to try and get them out, as they see fit.'

'How are you getting the message to Miriam?'

'The people I give this to will pass it on verbally. I believe they can contact them by telephone through a third party. Their relatives will write our message down and deliver a note with the money.'

'I've already written to Miriam, but in case it doesn't get through, tell them to add that she should get herself and her family out, that they should come here.'

'That's good. She'll get the message when she collects the money.'

'Why isn't it a verbal message, passed on when they give her the cash?'

'They won't take it to Drachensee. They say they can't risk it, but they'll leave the money and the note at Mama and Papa's flat. They were adamant.'

Esther chewed her lip.

'What if Miriam doesn't go to the flat?'

'She will,' Itsik said. 'You know what she's like. She'll feel duty-bound to keep an eye on it. And anyway, your letters still go to the flat.'

'I don't want her to go there anymore. Add that to the message. Tell her to stay away. You never know what these Gestapo people will do.'

Itsik put his hand on her arm and nodded.

'I'll do that.'

He added Esther's additions to the wrapper.

'I'll be back soon,' he said.

~~o~~

[30/05/1940 Thursday]

'That's it finished, sir.'

Yosef and the General stood back and looked at the summer house. It had taken much longer to build than either he or the General had anticipated. They'd found it harder to obtain materials than they'd expected, and the bitterly cold weather that had gripped Kiel in January had persevered into March.

'Wunderbar. Maria will love it. You've made a great job of it.'

Yosef shrugged.

'At least I know I've done something. I still feel bad about you paying me a salary and having to employ another driver.'

'Nonsense, Yosef. It gives you time to do all the jobs you'd never have managed. We should have taken someone else on years ago.'

Yosef looked around.

'The house and garden have never looked so good,' the General said, trying to make Yosef feel better, 'and the boathouse can get its roof redone, now that you've finished this…'

'Thank you, sir,' he said.

'Anyway, if it hadn't been for the invasion, you would have been gone, and Maria wouldn't have had a summer house. It was a great pity you didn't get out before it all kicked off. That's twice now you've been unlucky.'

'Or maybe lucky, sir. If we'd been in Belgium or Denmark when they fell, we could have been a lot worse off.'

'I suppose so. We still need to get you out though.'

The General still felt bad about being short-tempered with Yosef the day Belgium had fallen.

30

'You should have got out when it was possible, even if it had been to Palestine despite Miriam's reservations,' he'd snapped, his concern making him irritable.

'You're right, sir. I wish we had,' Yosef had replied, worry etched on his face.

The General winced, thinking about it.

'I'm sorry I lost the rag with you the other day, Yosef,' he said. 'I shouldn't have. Women, eh?'

'It wasn't just Miriam who dragged her heels, sir. It was me too. The place sounded so harsh and uncivilised. Now it sounds like heaven.'

'You could still go. I know it's dangerous, but people are getting in.'

'I know, sir. I'm meeting someone tomorrow. I'll let you know what they say.'

'That's excellent news. It would be a heavy weight off our shoulders,' the General said. 'although, needless to say, you'll be a big loss here.'

'Thank you, sir.'

'Now, let's show Maria the finished article.'

~~o~~

[31/05/1940 Friday]

Miriam rang the bell. Waiting was the time of danger for a Jew. She looked up, but the window didn't open and there was no familiar shout from Mama Weichmann.

After a minute, she pressed the bell push again. This time, when there was no response, she felt the familiar grip of fear take hold of her. The longer she stood, the more likely a neighbour would notice her, but she forced herself to try once again.

A curtain twitched across the street while she stood. She itched to leave, to scuttle around the corner and disappear homewards, but she swallowed her fear and stood for another few interminable minutes, before casually looking up for a final time, and turning towards home.

~~o~~

When Miriam reached the cottage, Ruth had just arrived home.

'Where's Manny?' Miriam asked.

'He's helping Papa in the garden. How were the Weichmanns?'

'It was very strange. They weren't in. I'm sure they would have said if they were going out.'

'Where would they be? Are they all right?'

'I do a bit of shopping for them but not all of it. They have no relatives left in Kiel, but I suppose they still have friends. I'll call back tomorrow. I hope nothing has happened to them.'

'I'll come with you, Mama, if you like. I have no violin lesson tomorrow.'

'Oh. Why?'

'Our music teacher has a family funeral in Lübeck. Herr Teubner says we shouldn't go in. Manny still has to go; one of the older students is going to teach the younger ones, but we could go and see the Weichmanns after we drop Manny off, if you like.'

'That would be nice. We could all have lunch in that little café on the way back.'

'Oh, Mama. That would be lovely. It's been ages since we've done that.'

It was the only café that would still serve Jews. For now.

~~o~~

Yosef lightly rapped and poked his head around the door of the General's study.

'Sir?' he said.

'Come in, Yosef. Any news?'

'It's not great, sir. The Haganah have been inundated and they say it will be months or even years before they can get us out.'

The General's face fell.

'That is bad luck. Is there anyone else doing it? I don't mind helping you out if you need money.'

'I don't think there is, sir. The Haganah are the only ones with the knowledge and the resources. I did ask if they would take the children earlier without us, but no, they'd prefer it if

31

we travelled as a family. It makes it easier once we get there, I suppose. I doubt Miriam would risk the children on the journey without us anyway.'

'No. I don't suppose she would. I'll ask around and see if there's any other way. If we defeat France, and it looks like we might, it may be possible to get you to Spain through the Pyrenees. I hear that the British have been driven into the sea at Calais and Dunkirk, and the French leadership, despite pockets of stern resistance from a few divisional commanders, appears to be caving in.'

'We'll take any way out, sir, whatever you suggest. If all else fails, we will have to wait for the Haganah.'

'I'll make enquiries,' the General said.

'Thank you, sir. Do you need anything?'

'No, Yosef. Carry on.'

CHAPTER 8

Somehow, having Ruth there made waiting in the street less conspicuous.

Miriam rang the bell and looked up at the Weichmanns' window but, like the day before, the window stayed resolutely shut.

'Press it again, Ruth,' Miriam said.

'Perhaps their doorbell isn't working,' Ruth said, pressing the bell push for the third time.

'I hadn't thought of that. If it were the first floor, we could throw a pebble at the window.'

'Ring one of the other bells,' Ruth said. 'Somebody will let us in.'

'We're Jews. We can't just do that. Someone might report us.'

A shadow passed over Ruth's face. Miriam hated having to destroy her daughter's youthful innocence, but it would be dangerous not to warn her.

They both jumped when the door opened, and a woman Miriam vaguely recognised appeared.

'Hello, are you here to visit the Weichmanns?'

Miriam realised that it was the neighbour, from the other flat on their landing.

'Yes. We have shopping for them.'

'I think they're away. I haven't seen them for a couple of days. Go up and try though. I'm off to the dentist. These wretched teeth.'

She let them past, and the door closed behind them. They climbed the stairs, relieved at not having to stand in the street any longer.

Reaching the top, Miriam rapped softly on the Weichmanns' door, not wanting to disturb the people in the flats on the landing below.

After a minute, she knocked again, a little louder.

'They really are away,' she said.

She checked the doorway for any sign of forced entry, but there was none.

'Did the Weichmanns leave a key out, like we do sometimes?'

'I don't know. They were always at home when I came. And there was never even any suggestion that I should have a key.'

Ruth lifted the mat, but there was nothing underneath, nor under the small plant pot beside the door, or inside it, hidden by foliage.

There was a small wooden tray, containing two pairs of shoes. Ruth checked underneath but there was nothing. She lifted the shoes out, but the box was empty.

'Try inside the shoes,' Miriam said.

Ruth turned them upside down, one after the other and, from the last shoe, a small key ring with two brass keys on it tumbled onto the stone of the landing, nearly falling through the cast-iron railings of the balustrade and down the stairwell to the ground below.

Miriam picked up the keys and tried the first one in the lock. It fitted, but it wouldn't turn.

She tried the second key; it turned, and she opened the door and stepped into the hallway.

'Frau Weichmann, Herr Weichmann,' she shouted, cautiously making her way through the flat. There was no answer and, when she glanced in the open bedroom door she passed, she saw a pile of clothes on the bed.

'Frau Weichmann,' she called again, worried they'd had a Gestapo house search. She reached the living room, but there was no one there and, when she looked in the kitchen, she found that it was empty too.

'There's no one in,' she shouted.

On the worktop, next to the sink, she saw a small, folded note, addressed to herself, propped up against a full jar of jam. She took her coat off, and her hat, and hung them up in the hallway. She returned to the living room and opened the note.

Dear Miriam,

If you are reading this, you have found the key and have let yourself in. We've left to go to Itsik and Esther. We are being picked up in ten minutes.

Thank you for everything you have done for us, from the bottom of our hearts. I exhort you to consider going to Palestine too. Itsik and Esther would not see you stuck if you could only get there.

Help yourself to anything in the flat. There's not much in the larder, or the cupboards, but take it for your family or give it to someone who needs it. The flat is mortgaged to a Jewish gentleman who will retain any money due to us for when we can come back, one day, Im Yirtzeh Hashem.

We will send a letter to the flat to let you know we've arrived safely, and Esther may continue to write to you here, but you have a key now, so it will be easy for you to check for mail.

God bless you, Miriam Nussbaum. You are an angel.

Else Weichmann.

~~o~~

There was no time or date on the note.

'What is it, Mama?' Ruth asked.

'I'm sorry, darling. I should have said something. It's good news. The Weichmanns are on their way to Palestine. Esther will be over the moon.'

Tears ran down Miriam's cheeks. Ruth ran to her.

'Why are you crying, Mama?' she said, tears welling in her own eyes.

'I'm happy for them,' she said, 'but part of me wishes it were us.'

'We could go, Mama,' Ruth said, her eyes bright.

'We'll see.'

~~o~~

[04/06/1940 Tuesday]

Wilhelm Canaris embraced Erich Kästner.

'To what do we owe this honour, Canaris,' the General said.

'That's a fine welcome, Kästner.'

'We thought you had better things to do than to visit us in Kiel. You know, consorting with the upper echelons of the party, visiting the troops in Norway, Belgium or France like some famous field marshal.'

Canaris laughed.

Captain Bauer entered with two steaming mugs of coffee. After he'd put them down, he stood to attention and saluted Admiral Canaris.

'Captain, it's nice to see someone maintaining military discipline around here,' the admiral said, returning his salute. 'At ease.'

'Good to see you, sir. Is there anything else, General?'

'No, Captain. That will be all. See that we're not disturbed, if you can.'

'Yes, sir,' the young officer replied and left, closing the door behind him.

'Well. What's new?'

Canaris smiled.

'I'm just back from Belgium, but they didn't see fit to invite me to Norway. There's the usual element of confusion, but the low countries are secure, as you know, and our advance across France is relentless. Our troops are fighting well.'

'Talking of which, have the 2nd Army been deployed yet?' the General asked, his voice level.

The admiral wasn't fooled by his friend's casual enquiry.

'They have. They've moved in behind the 12th and are supporting them now. I didn't get

34

a chance to see the boys, but I briefly spoke with Colonel Schneider at Advance Headquarters. He was itching to get involved.'

'He's a first-rate commander. He'll have had the sense to use their time in reserve to let his men recover. From what I hear, they had a tough time in Norway.'

'Yes. He said the further north they advanced, the stiffer the resistance. I believe the British, along with a few French and Polish units, are still fighting with the Norwegians at Narvik. The word is, though, that they're pulling out, and I can't imagine that the Norwegians will last too much longer on their own.'

'We appear to have got the tactics right, everywhere we've invaded.'

'Our communications and speed of deployment have been the biggest factors, and our training. And our boys can call in air strikes within minutes. The Stukas are dive-bombing a clear path for our troops, and completely demoralising the British and the French.'

'I told Captain Bauer that a few weeks ago. I understand the British Expeditionary Forces were annihilated.'

'Don't believe everything you hear. I have reasonably good intelligence that the British managed to evacuate at least eighty per cent of their troops from the beach. Kleist, von Kluge and Rundstedt halted the tanks of the 4th Army well short of Dunkirk. They were worried about a repeat of the Franco-British counter-attack at Arras the previous week when we overstretched ourselves. Anyway, the delay allowed the British to evacuate over 300,000 men, I'm told.'

'Why didn't we hear about it?'

'Any news that is in the remotest detrimental is suppressed. Orders from on high.'

'Can we take France?'

'I don't see why not, although I'm not sure we have the manpower to occupy the whole of France, but as long as we control the north, and Paris...'

'You've seen the plans, you old fox.'

'I attended a few of the strategy meetings when they finally decided that my input would be useful. Despite my warnings, they seem set on taking France, with a view to the eventual invasion of Britain.'

The admiral enjoyed the look of shock on his friend's face.

'It won't be right away, I would have thought,' he continued. 'We will need to regroup, but the British and the French will have left hundreds of thousands of tonnes of armour and machinery, and you know how quickly we can train soldiers these days.'

'Are they not starting to get suspicious about your over-pessimistic intelligence?'

'No, quite a few of my darker predictions were correct, and there were significant casualties and a few military setbacks; perhaps not on the scale I'd warned, but as I've said before, it's not an exact science. I'll say this for them, they do take note of the intelligence we give them and pass it on to our commanders. That's another factor in our domination of the British and the French. Both these countries have the resources to collect intelligence, but they don't disseminate it to those who need it.'

'How do you know all this?'

'I have a spider's web of spies at my disposal, all over the world. And I talk to high-up people in British politics and in the military. You surely must have guessed.'

The General shook his head.

'Who would have believed it? Do the party know about it?'

'Of course not. They know the Abwehr have intelligence contacts in Britain, France, and America. They'd be disappointed if we didn't, but they hopefully don't know that intelligence flows both ways.'

'What sort of information do you give them?'

'Similar to that I give to German High Command. Worst-case scenarios. I hope it will frighten them into taking action.'

The General whistled.

'It's a dangerous game you're playing. Why do you do it?'

'You know why. Take today, for example. Our bombers are destroying parts of Paris. Will history forgive us for that, or for Warsaw?'

'And there's the Jews,' the General said.

'Yes.' The Admiral sighed. 'There's the Jews.'

CHAPTER 9

'I'm looking forward to marching into Paris,' Fritz Aumeier said.

Johann grinned.

'They say Les Mademoiselles Parisiennes are the most beautiful and accomplished in all the world.'

'Knowing my luck, we'll be posted in some grim industrial city on the Belgian border,' Maxi groaned.

'You're such a pessimist, Maxi. Listen, why do you think they kept us in reserve?'

'I've no idea, Captain Kästner,' Maxi said, 'but I'm sure you're going to tell us.'

'Well, when we occupy Paris and the Führer holds a triumphant parade down the Champs-Élysées,' Johann explained, as if to a classful of sceptical children, 'he won't want a column of weary, dusty and battle-worn troops marching behind him. The crowds will be impressed beyond measure by smartly dressed, well-turned-out soldiers. And consider this; once Paris is occupied, nobody will welcome a bunch of ugly, boorish troops from the twelfth or the fourth divisions being billeted in the cultural capital of Europe; it stands to reason that they'll look for the sophisticated and charming German infantry officers from the 2nd Army to win the hearts and minds of the people of Paris.'

His friends doubled up laughing at Johann's ludicrous logic. Even Franz smiled. They were seated in the Café St. Martine, in the small French town of Château-Thierry, 100 kilometres short of Paris and eight kilometres behind the line of engagement with the French Army. They'd taken the town the previous day, and Colonel Schneider's battalion had been ordered to secure the town's three bridges across the Marne while the rest of the 2nd Army advanced.

Fuming again at being sidelined, the colonel had tasked Major Breit, Major Mandel and Major Dressel's companies to guard the bridges, while Franz and his men struck camp on the outskirts of the town and found billets for the colonel and his senior officers. Their job done, Franz's company had been given permission to have a few hours to themselves, providing it didn't get out of hand.

'There will be plenty fighting between now and Paris,' Franz said, 'for us all. But you might be right, Johann. Paris deserves a better class of officer. I presume you intend to visit the Louvre, Notre-Dame and the Sacré-Cœur?'

'If these are all bars, yes,' Johann whipped back at him, causing raucous laughter to spill across the street.

Franz smiled and shook his head, holding up his hands in defeat.

'I'll be visiting the Pigalle,' Maxi said, 'and Les Folies Bergère.'

'You shouldn't have to pay for it in Paris,' Heinrich said.

'It's all right for you lot,' Maxi retorted. 'You all have a smattering of French. I can't speak a word of their verdammte language.'

'We'll teach you,' Johann said, taking hold of Maxi's hand and kissing it. 'Quelle belle figure tu as, ma chérie.'

As the laughter resonated around La Place de l'Hôtel de Ville, Franz spotted Colonel Schneider walking across the square towards them.

Johann, his back to the square, was further educating Maxi in the art of seducing French girls as the colonel approached. The ribald laughter at his *Français pour les amoureux* began to stutter, then die. A puzzled expression came over his face and he faltered.

'Carry on, Captain Kästner,' the colonel said, clapping a hand on his shoulder. 'I heard the sounds of laughter from my billet and I wagered that you would have something to do with it. I believe you were giving French lessons…'

Johann bowed his head while his friends howled at his embarrassment.

He turned to see the colonel smiling.

'Perhaps the colonel would like to join us for a drink,' Franz said, 'and hear my brother's theories about the deployment of the Wehrmacht in Paris.'

'That would be very congenial, and truly educational,' the colonel said, smiling.

Johann glared at Franz. Franz shrugged.

'If you hand it out, you should be able to take it,' he mouthed.

~~o~~

Fritz Aumeier rose and gave Colonel Schneider his seat and fetched another chair from an adjacent table for himself. The garçon was summoned, and a further round of drinks was ordered.

The waiter returned, and the colonel sipped his brandy, enjoying his officers' sometimes biting exchanges, content that they were comfortable, but not complacent, in his presence. He'd watched every one of them during the Norway campaign, and when they'd taken Château-Thierry the day before. He knew that he'd moulded them into a formidable fighting unit and although they were all excellent soldiers, and good officers, three of them stood out.

Artur Schweitzer was unflappable and steady. He had rightly earned the rank of captain, making few mistakes, and he could be relied on to do as he was ordered.

Johann Kästner commanded an unparalleled loyalty from his men, had an instinctive awareness of battle tactics at a unit level, but he could be impulsive and didn't always grasp the overall strategy from a battalion or divisional perspective.

'Sir, you look a million miles away.'

'I'm waiting to hear Captain Kästner's latest military wisdom,' he said.

Through the ill-suppressed laughter of his friends, Johann outlined his reasons for believing that the 2nd Army would be stationed in Paris.

Colonel Schneider listened to him, his face a mask, ignoring the stifled laughs around him. As Johann reached the part about his and his fellow officers' social qualities, a twitch appeared at the corner of the colonel's mouth.

Johann finished and looked at the colonel.

'Well, Captain,' his commanding officer said, 'That was remarkable.'

The colonel turned away, making a fist with his hand, holding it between his teeth. Then, unable to hold it in, he let out a roar of laughter that had them all, even Johann, joining in.

'You're wasted as a captain,' he said, when he'd gained a modicum of control, 'with such an exceptional military mind.'

'I fully appreciate that it sounds presumptuous, and a little preposterous, sir, but wait and see. I'll let you all apologise to me when we're parading in the Place de la Concorde behind the Führer or drinking wine in the cafés of the Latin Quarter.'

The colonel shook his head and caught a glimpse of Franz doing the same.

Only Johann Kästner would have the balls to talk like that in front of his commanding officer.

His thoughts drifted back in time to himself at that age. Fighting under the then Colonel Kästner's command in the last war had been the making of him, and he knew that because Germany was now at war again, he would doubtless make General if he continued the work he'd already done and made no catastrophic errors. If he did, it would be because of Erich Kästner's guidance, twenty or so years before.

He saw Erich Kästner's oldest son very much like his father, maybe even better. Perhaps he'd inherited it from his father but, for whatever reason, Franz Kästner was by far the best soldier Walther Schneider had ever trained or nurtured. If he survived, the colonel was sure Franz would attain as high a rank as his father, or higher.

It wasn't just his maturity; it was his ability to process information and come up with a clear vision in his mind about what was happening on the field of battle, and what needed done. He found himself consulting Franz with increasing regularity and, as well as including him in most meetings with his senior staff, he seldom attended divisional briefings without him.

'Major Kästner,' he said. 'Perhaps it would be better if, the next time your brother has nothing better to do, you could enlighten him on one or two rather more pragmatic military theories. However, should he prove right, you may be in the unfortunate position of having a younger sibling promoted over your head.'

The whole table laughed again.

'And, just for the record,' the colonel added, 'We will be going to Paris. It is our main objective. Whether we are in the victory parade, which I'm confident will take place soon, or whether we'll be stationed in Paris, I can't tell you. For all I know, when this campaign is over, we might all be sent back to Norway.'

There were groans all around.

'Before then, enjoy the push for Paris, and the city itself. If we take Paris, you might just get a little leave before we move on, so let's make sure we get there in one piece.'

He saluted, and they all scrambled to their feet to return it.

He chortled to himself as he walked away.

~~o~~

'You bastards,' Johann hissed at them when the colonel was out of earshot. 'Especially you, *Major Kästner.*'

Franz grinned. 'You heard the man. One more drink. This one's on me. I'll happily pay, just to celebrate seeing you squirm for once, *Captain Kästner.*'

Johann smiled and held his hands up.

'You do realise, all bets are off now, don't you?'

'Yes, I do.' Franz sighed. 'But just remember, I am your superior officer.'

He smiled at Johann's scowl as the waiter brought their final drinks.

'Prost, gentlemen,' he said, raising his glass.

'Here's to Paris!' Artur toasted.

'Here's to the Fräuleins,' added Maxi. 'I mean Les Mademoiselles.'

'Here's to the colonel!' Heinrich said.

'And to the 2nd Army!'

'The Heer!'

'Deutschland!'

They drained their glasses.

As Franz walked across the bridge, at the back of the group of soldiers, he was struck by the fact that these men could have been soldiers from his father's war.

Army men, through and through, and not a toast to the Führer.

~~o~~

'I called round at the Weichmanns' flat today again,' Miriam said.

'Was there any further news?'

'No, but it's a bit too soon. I expect we'll not hear for a month. That's how long it takes for a letter to get here from Palestine.'

'Really?' Yosef said. 'I didn't realise. Why bother going round?'

'I don't mind. I'm due a letter from Esther anyway. I brought the last of the food back from the flat. We don't need it, with everything we get from the Kästners and what we can buy with our ration cards, but you must know somebody who is deserving of these.'

She showed him a selection of boxes, tins and packets. They'd handed out the perishables the week before.

'I'll take it to Jakob. I'm going over there on Thursday for a meeting of the committee. He'll find a use for it.'

CHAPTER 10

Yosef rushed home. By the time he opened the door, and burst into the kitchen, he was quite breathless.

'Emil Liewermann and the children are back,' he panted. 'Jakob told me.'

Miriam's hand went to her mouth and she gasped.

'The fool,' she cried. 'Rosa specifically told him to stay where he was.'

'It isn't his fault. They were deported from Belgium. They were lucky to be sent here, instead of Poland.'

'Where are they?'

'In one of the Kleiner Kuhberg houses. The one the authorities are using for displaced Jews. We're sure it's just a staging post before they send them onwards, I'm afraid.'

'Can't we bring them here? We have plenty room.'

'No, even if we could, it wouldn't be fair on the Kästners. Anyway, they are under curfew. Even during the day, they're restricted to the school building, the house with the synagogue in it, and the one they're living in. They can't even visit Rosa's mother.'

'That's terrible. Can I go to them?'

'Tomorrow. They'll be allowed over for the evening service.'

'Is there any news about Rosa?' She asked him this every week.

He shook his head. 'Nothing. The lawyer is doing his best; he was honest about her chances from the start.'

'If Emil and the children are deported to Poland, maybe there's a chance Rosa would be released, to join them.'

'I don't know, love. I doubt it. That would require the authorities to show a little compassion.'

~~o~~

KIELER MORGENPOST

Tuesday 11th June 1940

NORWAY CAPITULATES – SWEDISH STEEL SUPPLIES ASSURED

With the fall of Narvik, and the surrender of Norwegian forces, the Wehrmacht has ensured that supplies of iron ore from Sweden will be guaranteed summer and winter.

It is expected that significant numbers of ground forces and naval resources will be stationed in Norway to defend its western coastline from a British counter-invasion and to protect German and Norwegian merchant shipping from attack at sea.

The Führer praised each of the three branches of the Wehrmacht, saying that the fighting men of the Heer, the Kriegsmarine and the Luftwaffe had proved that no country in the world had armed forces to match those of the Third Reich.

In the war against the French and the British, sizable gains had been made in Northern France. A spokesman for the war ministry told the Morgenpost that advance forces of the

Wehrmacht were now within twenty kilometres of Paris, and that daily bombing of the city was taking place.

~~o~~

Frau Hueber watched from her window as the man turned the corner from Holtenauer into Jungmannstraße. Smartly dressed in a suit and a dark overcoat, he walked with purpose, as if he was heading home after a day's work in a bank, or an architect's office. As he came closer, she lost sight of him.

She heard the doorbell ring and she frowned. She opened the window and leaned out. The man was standing below, looking up at her.

'What do you want?' she shouted.

'I have a delivery for the Weichmanns in flat five, but they're not answering. Can you let me in?'

'Ja, ja. Come up.'

She went to the hallway and pressed the lock release. She stood in the doorway and listened to his footsteps echoing up the stairwell. When he reached the top, he nodded to her.

'Danke,' he said, removing a thick brown packet from his pocket. He waved it briefly at her, as if to prove his errand was genuine, then posted it through the Weichmanns' letterbox.

'They're away,' she told him. 'I haven't seen them for a week. The lady who helps the old couple was here though.'

'It's all right. I expect they'll get it when they return. Guten Abend.'

'Guten Abend,' she replied, watching him as he descended the stairs, until all she could see was his hand on the rail of the bannister, spiralling down into the gloom below.

~~o~~

[11/06/1940 Tuesday]

'Well, even if Italy had been a possible route of escape, it's out of the question now.'

The General put down the paper and took a sip of the coffee Yosef had just placed on his desk.

'We never considered it, sir. We would have had to travel through Austria, and we've heard that it's even worse there for Jews than it is here. And Italy, being fascist, and an ally of Germany, was never going to be much of a choice. Most Jews believe that Hitler will put pressure on the Italians to deal with their Jews in a similar fashion to here, like he did with Hungary and Romania.'

'I suppose you're right. It seems very opportunistic of Mussolini to declare war on France when we are attacking it in the north. The French won't be able to divert any troops southwards to counter the Italians. Where's it all going to end?'

'I don't know, sir. We've lost faith that anything will stop this madness. The British have scuttled back across the channel; they were our best hope, as the Americans seem hell-bent on staying out of it this time.'

'That might work in your favour if your visas come through. Has there been any news?'

'No, sir. I telephoned the consulate in Hamburg yesterday, but the lady I spoke to could tell me nothing. She said that the waiting time for visas had increased due to the heavy influx of applications. They couldn't give any idea of a timescale and she reminded me that only a small percentage of applications were successful, that we might not get visas at the end of the process.'

'Still, as long as the Americans remain neutral, there's still a chance that you will.'

'Yes, sir. She told me to phone back in six weeks.'

~~o~~

Sitting in the canteen, the General sipped his coffee. Lunch had been filling, if not particularly exciting, and he was just considering whether he could afford a ten-minute nap on his return to the office.

He smiled at the noise from the group of young officers sat at the next table. He caught snatches of their conversation, mostly about the vessels they were posted on, commanders they'd served under and the young women of the base, and of Kiel.

He was about to get up, when he heard one of them say the first line of a joke, so he waited, wanting to hear the punchline.

'Start again,' one of his friends said. 'I didn't catch the first bit.'

'Listen this time then.'

'All right, just get on with it.'

'Well,' the young lieutenant said, 'Hitler is told that Mussolini's Italy has joined the war. "We'll have to put up ten divisions to counter him!" says Göring. "No, he's on our side," says Hitler.'

The young lieutenant paused and looked around his friends for effect.

'"Oh, in that case we'll need twenty divisions",' he finished.

The General smiled to himself as the table erupted. He wondered if the young man would have got away with the joke in the army, or in a bar in town.

He got up. The young officers were all still laughing.

He still had a smile on his face when he reached his office.

CHAPTER 11

'Here's another pile for you, Kriminalassistentanwärter. Bigger than usual.'

The post-office driver dropped the small sack of mail on the desk of the duty sergeant. He shivered; the place always made him nervous, even though he dropped the mail at Gestapo Headquarters in Düppelstraße every day.

'I hope you sorted them for us this time.'

The man was only a sergeant, the same as the driver's brother-in-law, but he always felt uncomfortable talking to him. No one trusted the Gestapo. His sister's husband was regular police, the OrPo.

'Yes, Herr Kriminalassistentanwärter. Known Jewish addresses in one bundle, known Aryan addresses in another. Any we're not sure of are in the third pile. There are a few parcels as well.'

He could feel the dampness of cold sweat in his armpits.

'They're clearly marked,' he added.

'Good. Here are yesterday's letters.'

The desk sergeant handed him an identical sack. It contained the letters that had been checked and were deemed suitable for delivery.

'That will be all,' he added, 'unless you have anything you'd like to report?'

'Report? What do you mean?'

'Oh, you know. Neighbours or workmates acting suspiciously. Disparaging comments about the Third Reich, or the Führer. It's only being a good citizen to tell us.'

'No, no. I can safely say I've seen or heard nothing that you would be interested in.'

'Perhaps I should be the judge of that, eh? Well, be on your guard. Remember, if something you hear or see is brought to our attention, and you've not reported it, you'll be complicit in the act.'

'I'll keep that in mind, Kriminalassistentanwärter,' the man said, trying to keep the tremble from his voice. 'Heil Hitler,' he barked, saluting.

The Kriminalassistentanwärter returned his salute with the less formal Hitler greeting. The driver turned and left, his face pale, forcing himself not to hurry.

~~o~~

The Gestapo desk sergeant grinned. The post-office driver annoyed him somehow, and it pleased him to make the man squirm.

He picked up the sack and emptied the contents onto his desk. He glanced at the three bundles. Each contained between thirty and forty letters and packets. In addition, there were four loose parcels. These, he put back into the sack and strolled through the main office.

He dropped the Aryan bundle on the desk shared by six constables.

'Get these checked,' the desk sergeant said, saluting.

The junior Gestapo men acknowledged the older man's salute with one of their own.

'Yes, sir,' they chorused.

The Gestapo trusted nobody, even the post office. The constables checked each Aryan name and address against the electoral register and added it to the pile for delivery if it passed scrutiny. They selected one in ten letters to open as a random sample and, provided nothing unusual turned up, it was resealed with specially printed tape, and added to the others in the sack.

No one ever complained.

The desk sergeant handed the other two piles, and the sack containing the parcels, to Carl Meyer, a Kriminalassistentanwärter, or sergeant, like himself. They also held the SS rank of Sturmmann.

Storm trooper.

'Here's today's bundle of Juden mail,' he said.

'More work,' Carl Meyer said. 'The sooner we send them all to Poland, the better. There will be no one here for these people to write to.'

42

The desk sergeant laughed.

'No, I don't suppose they deliver post to the ghettos, do they?'

'They do, in fact, but there are strict rules, and soon it will be stopped altogether.'

'I heard that we're opening a new ghetto every week. My cousin says they sealed the ghetto at Łódź six weeks ago. Jews go in, but none come out.'

'Unless it's to a camp,' Carl Meyer said, laughing. 'He's an SS-Hauptsturmführer, your cousin, isn't he?'

'Yes. Though how the hell he made it to captain, I don't know. I inherited the brains in the family.'

Carl Meyer smiled.

'So, he's in Poland now?'

'Yes. He loves it. Lives like a king, he says, and the Fräuleins are grateful for anything warm inside, and that's not just the food.'

While they were still laughing, Kriminalassistent Heinrich Güllich walked in. An SS-Scharführer, he was the Gestapo counterpart of a detective inspector in the KriPo, the criminal investigation department, and Carl Meyer's immediate boss.

'What's so funny?' he asked, as the laughter died. The Kriminalassistent wasn't best known for his sense of humour or his tolerance.

'Nothing, sir. The desk sergeant was just telling me an amusing story about his cousin.'

'The Hauptsturmführer?'

'Yes, sir.'

'I can't imagine what you would find funny about him. From what the desk sergeant says, he sounds like a fine officer.'

'Yes, sir.'

The desk sergeant made a face behind Heinrich Güllich's back and returned to his post.

~~o~~

The Kriminalassistent picked up the pile of mail and leafed through it, grimacing. They'd only just started checking all the incoming and outgoing international post and without extra manpower, the department was under pressure, but it had already yielded fruit.

Around a quarter of the outgoing envelopes, packets and parcels had contained money; Reichsmarks, American dollars, French, and Belgian francs, even share certificates and, in one case, diamonds.

He'd been lucky enough to open that package. Addressed to a Herr Bruckner in Tel Aviv, he'd almost discarded the innocuous-looking beaded dress it had contained; it was too Jewish to be of any use as a present for his wife, but he wondered if it might make do as a sweetener for one of his Mischling informants.

He'd thrown it in the bottom drawer of his desk, where it had lain for a week until, with a clarity that took him by surprise, he'd realised that there was something bothering him about the garment. He'd retrieved it from the drawer and inspected it again.

The glass crystals that embellished the dress were not strung together by a thread running through each one; instead, each was suspended in fine silk macramé mounting, joined together in strings, glinting in the harsh light of the office. He'd peeled one of them out of its filigree pouch and examined it under a magnifying glass.

Looking around to check that no one had seen him, he'd placed the dress in a brown paper bag, and taken it home and secreted it in his loft. He put the small stone he'd removed into his wallet.

'It's a diamond,' the jeweller had said, peering at the stone through a loupe. 'And of superior quality.'

He'd returned the dress to the station, handing it to his superior, but not without carefully removing a couple of the decorative strings first.

'That's excellent policing,' Kamerad, his Kriminalsekretär had said. 'This will do your career no harm.'

He refused to feel guilty about the small *commission* he'd kept for himself. It might one day put his son, if he ever had one, through an expensive university, or help to buy that holiday lodge that would so please his wife. He was convinced that although most of the fines

43

and confiscations the Gestapo seized ended up in the coffers of the Reich Treasury, it was only after his superior officers had taken their own reasonable percentage.

A voice interrupted him and, for a brief second, the horrible thought that he'd been thinking out loud crossed his mind.

Carl Meyer, his Kriminalassistentanwärter, was speaking.

'What did you say?' Heinrich Güllich grunted, shaking the feeling loose.

'I was just saying that when we started, I wasn't convinced that checking mail would be worth the effort but look at this.'

The Kriminalassistentanwärter held up a small hardback book and smiled at the puzzled look on his boss's face.

'Look inside it,' he said.

Heinrich Güllich took if from him and opened it. Instead of pages, banknotes had been glued neatly in their place. The Kriminalassistent thumbed the edges of the notes, estimating that there were around 100, all of them the highest denomination

He whistled.

'10,000 marks. Not a bad haul.'

He looked at the cover and laughed.

'Die Prinzipien der Ökonomie,' he said. *The Principles of Economics*. 'How appropriate.'

The young Kriminalassistentanwärter forced a laugh. His sense of humour differed from that of his boss, but he knew when it was politic to react with amusement at his jokes.

'Sir, I can understand us opening the outgoing mail, but why bother with the post coming in from abroad?'

'An excellent question, Kriminalassistentanwärter. As you rightly say, opening the outgoing mail is probably of greater interest; it's the best way to stop these Judenschweine stealing our Reichsmarks and sending them overseas, and it will restrict the foul lies they spread about the Third Reich. That said, we can still learn a lot from reading letters coming in, however innocuous they may appear.'

'I suppose so, sir, but it seems a lot of work, for little return.'

'I would suggest you stop complaining and get on with it then.'

'Yes, sir,' the Kriminalassistentanwärter said. 'If you say so.'

'I do.' Heinrich Güllich sighed. He didn't have time to deal with sulky juniors, but Carl Meyer was a promising investigator for one so young.

'Opening the mail has additional benefits,' he said, trying to be patient. 'We know that Jews are filthy, devious little Schweine. They're forever finding ways to cheat or steal, or worse. There have been rumours of plots by Jews to assassinate high-ranking Reich officials, and that the resources to plan such attacks are coming from Jews abroad, where they poison the minds of foreigners and gain support for their dirty treachery. It's only by attention to detail that we can protect our leaders.'

He saw the younger man's back stiffen, and he turned away. He walked over to his office, one of four on the first floor. He handed his secretary his hastily scribbled list containing the next day's proposed house visits.

'Type these up for me, before you go home,' he said.

~~o~~

[12/06/1940 Wednesday]

When he arrived at work the next morning, his secretary handed him the day's duty sheet she'd typed up. He thanked her, and told her he needed a coffee as soon as possible.

He looked at the list and groaned. Carl Meyer was right. This mail business was generating a rash of leads that required to be followed up, and most of them ended up as nothing but the chance to turn over a Jew's home and rough them up a little. The contraband impounded from these house searches could be satisfactory, but he wanted to get his teeth into something more substantial.

Just as he was finishing his coffee, Heinrich Güllich heard a knock, and looked up to see Carl Meyer standing in the doorway.

'Yes? What is it?' he said, in his usual terse tone.

44

'Sir, I thought you might want to add this address to the list today.'

The Kriminalassistentanwärter handed him a note, and its envelope. He looked at the envelope first.

Weichmann
Flat 5, 34 Jungmannstraße
Kiel
Deutschland

He raised his eyebrows when he saw the postmark.

Shanghai. And no title. Strange.

He read the note.

M.

Sorry about the brevity. All well here. My in-laws are away. They were supposed to be with us but have been delayed. If you could look them up, that would be great. I have sent a small gift to you for them if it gets there.

You should pay us a visit sometime. A change of scenery is important to maintain your health.

All my love,

E.

'I see what you mean. It could be some sort of code.'

'I don't know, sir. It might be nothing, but I thought it was a bit cryptic. What stuck out for me was the use of initials instead of names. They certainly don't want to be identified.'

'What do we know about the people who live at the address?'

'Jews, obviously. Yosef and Else Weichmann. He owned Weichmann's hardware store, then his son took it over when he retired, until he emigrated in '37. The son's wife is called Esther.'

'That's two names beginning with 'E', but Else Weichmann would hardly likely be writing to her own address, would she?'

'No. I don't suppose she would. So, it could be the daughter-in-law. But who is M?'

'We're working on it, sir. What intrigued me is that a gift is mentioned, but none of the rest of it makes sense.'

'And you think we should pay them a visit?'

'Yes, sir. It will do no harm, though it might be a fool's errand. There's no rush.'

'I'll put it on the list. There's a visit just around the corner in Holtenauer. We'll do it after that. I'll take that one myself, and you can come with me today. Here's the other pairings. Give them their lists.'

He handed the young Gestapo man three sheets of paper.

'I'll meet you at the door in five minutes,' he added, pocketing the fourth sheet himself.

CHAPTER 12

'Yosef, I won't be long. I'm just going over to the Weichmanns. It's been a week.'

'Do you want me to come with you?'

'No. I'll be fine. Is there anything you need while I'm in town?'

He thought for a second.

'Yes, there is. A new catch for the cupboard in the hall. It will save me walking down later, and it's not far out of your way. If you give me a minute, I'll unscrew the old one, and you can show it to the shop assistant.'

'Is Itsik's shop the best to go to?'

'Yes, but it's Oskar's shop now,' he said, smiling.

Nearly everyone in Kiel still thought of it as *Weichmann's*.

By the time she'd put her coat and hat on, and retrieved her shopping basket from the pantry, he'd returned with the metal catch, wrapped in an old cloth.

She frowned. 'It's Wednesday,' she said. 'It's their half day. They'll not be open.'

'Damn,' he said. 'I forgot. I'll get it tomorrow.'

She smiled at him and opened the back door.

'Take care, love,' he said.

~~o~~

Miriam walked quickly across Martensdamm, glancing at the gently rippling waters of Kleiner Kiel on either side of the bridge. In former times, she would have stopped and taken in the view; the trees around the edge, the opera house reflected on the surface of the lake and the ducks paddling at the edges of the tree-lined bank, appealing to passers-by to feed them. It was what she'd loved about Kiel.

Leaving the open space behind, she joined Holtenauer Straße at its junction with Brunswicker. She followed the curve of the wide street with its elegant buildings as it climbed gently until she'd almost reached Jungmannstraße, when a tram stopped a few yards in front of her. She watched three people get off. As it pulled away, a black car passed it and drew into the side, 100 metres ahead.

Two men emerged and Miriam's flesh froze. They had the unmistakable look of Gestapo. She slipped round the corner into Jungmannstraße and walked as quickly as she could without breaking into a run.

She fumbled for the key that opened the door to the Weichmanns' building. Only once she was inside did she dare breath again.

She climbed the stairs and let herself into the flat. The door opposite was open a crack, and when she turned to close the Weichmanns' door behind her, she thought she caught a glimpse of a face, but she couldn't be sure.

She noticed that there was post, but it wasn't the letter that she'd expected. Picking up the package, she frowned. There was no name or address written anywhere on it, although the packaging had a slight tear where it had been squeezed through the letterbox. She straightened the torn paper and, sure enough, she could make out the letters M and N on the crumpled flap.

She tore it open. To her surprise, wrapped in a sheet of thick paper, there was a bundle of banknotes. As she flicked through them, she saw that they were large denomination notes, fifties and hundreds. She guessed there could be a few thousand Reichsmarks at least, perhaps more.

Why is Esther sending me money? Is it for Rosa?

She cracked open the door and glanced at the landing. It was empty. She stood still and listened for a second, but only her breathing broke the silence of the stairwell.

She closed the door over and locked it. Taking the money and the wrapper through to the living room where the light was better, she sat down. There was a handwritten note stuck to the inside of the wrapper. She carefully removed it and scrunched up the packing paper, tossing it into the fireplace. She began to read the note.

Mama and Papa have been arrested. They were caught crossing the border from Czechoslovakia to Romania. Our friends could do nothing. Please give this money to someone who can arrange a lawyer for them, to try and get them released. We can get you more if necessary.

Whatever you do, don't ever go back to the flat again. It is too dangerous – they are bound to search it. If you can, please try and get out and come to us, despite the risks.

By the time she'd finished, tears were running down her face.

Poor Esther. Poor Mama and Papa Weichmann.

She read the note again, with increasing disquiet. It wasn't Esther's handwriting, but she knew that they were her words. And her friend was right. With the Weichmanns' arrest, the flat would be searched in due course.

She picked up the money to put it into her handbag, but fumbled, and one of the bundles fell on the ground. As she stooped to pick it up, the doorbell rang.

She froze. She looked towards the door at the end of the hall, then cursed her stupidity, realising that it was the bell push on the street door that had sounded. She stuffed the money into her bag, crossed to the window and looked out. A black car was double-parked on the street below, directly opposite the door to the building.

It's the car from earlier.

One man was standing by it. Without opening the window and leaning out, she couldn't see the pavement directly beneath the flat, but she assumed it was his companion who had rung the bell.

She couldn't let them in; it would be a death warrant, more so because of the money but, sooner rather than later, someone would open the door for them. She thought about asking the woman across the landing if she could hide in her apartment, but she knew that, through fear, or a feeling of civic duty, the Weichmanns' neighbour might well give her up to the Gestapo.

She crept to the front door, lifted the snib, and gently opened it. She listened for any sounds from the stairwell, but it was silent. She stepped out, then stopped. She ran back to the living room and snatched the note from the table, slipping it into her coat pocket.

She made her way to the door again and, once out on the landing, she closed it softly behind her. She dropped the keys back into the shoes and started to run down the stairs but, fearing the clack of her shoes on the steps would be heard down below, she stopped and slipped them off, carrying them in one hand. She heard the ring of the doorbell again, sounding faintly behind her in the Weichmanns' flat.

She ran down the rest of the stairs, stopping at each landing to listen. As she reached the first floor, she heard a muffled voice from somewhere beneath, then another ring, from above her. It was followed by the sound of two further bells, on either side of her.

They're ringing all the doorbells.

She knew that one of the neighbours would let them in soon and doubted she had longer than ten or fifteen seconds. She hurried down the last flight of stairs, two at a time, and, reaching ground level, turned left, away from the front door, and down the back hallway of the building, towards the garden.

She'd been down here before, to hang out the Weichmanns' washing. She turned the handle of the door to the backyard. It was locked. She cursed.

The keys! She'd left them upstairs. She turned round. There was a small storeroom just inside the back door of the building where various pieces of garden equipment and bags of pegs were kept. She opened the door and slipped inside.

Her breaths were coming in deep rasps, and she fought to silence them. She'd no sooner pulled the door shut behind her when she heard the clack as the entrance door unlocked, echoing down the hallway.

In the darkness, she tried to control her rising panic, and the terror that was causing her whole body to shake. The blade of a garden spade dug into her side, but she didn't move for fear of making a noise. She heard footsteps coming towards her, then, to her relief, the clatter of leather soles on stone as they climbed the stairs. In guttural voices, she heard two men talking but could only make out snatches of their conversation, until it faded into echoed murmurs as they climbed.

Praying that there were only two of them, she opened the door of her hiding place and crept to the bottom of the stairs. Crouching, she peered around the corner and looked up. She saw two hands on the rail, sliding up almost in unison, close to the top.

She made herself wait a few seconds more, until she heard them knocking the Weichmanns' door. She straightened, intent on making her way to the front door but the clasp of her handbag chose that moment to strike the corner of the bannister with a loud clatter.

'Was ist das?' she heard clearly and, just as she pulled her head back, she saw a man lean over and look down. She froze again, hoping that the gloom of the stairwell would keep her hidden.

She waited for a step on the stairs but, after a few seconds, she heard a muffled voice, and the rap on a door again.

She inched past the bottom of the stairs, flattening herself as close to the wall as she could. When she reached the front door of the building, she reached down and slipped first one shoe, then the other, onto her feet.

She listened again. Another knock and the muffled tones of a man again, this time followed by a woman's voice. She presumed that the woman in the top flat must have opened her door to them.

Miriam wondered if the woman had seen her enter the flat, or leave.

If she did, will she tell the Gestapo?

The sound of the two men talking floated down to her and she closed her eyes and strained to listen. She heard the woman's voice again and the sound of a door opening.

She must have a spare key for the Weichmanns' flat. Or she told them about the one in the shoe.

She looked at the door in front of her. She knew the mechanism was noisy, but she saw no alternative. If the back door leading to the communal garden and the lane behind had been unlocked, she would have been away by now.

She pushed down the handle as gently as she could, but the release sprung open with a loud clunk that filled the hallway, and the stairwell. She slipped out, closing the door behind her, recoiling again at the loud thud of the lock as it latched.

Scheiße.

She turned right, instinctively heading in the opposite direction from the one she'd come, not knowing why. She imagined the scene in the Weichmanns' flat, hoping that as soon as they'd heard the click of the front-door lock, they would have leaned over the bannister on the top-floor landing, to see if anybody had entered. With any luck, when no one appeared at the bottom of the stairs, they would have assumed that it was someone leaving one of the other flats, and continued their search, or whatever it was they were doing.

She crossed the road and willed herself to keep a steady pace, as if she were an unconcerned Kiel housewife, heading out shopping or to visit a friend, but she felt almost naked, as if two pairs of Gestapo eyes were boring into her back from the flat halfway up the street.

She reached the corner and, before turning onto Knooper Weg, she risked a casual glance back. A figure stood at the window of the Weichmanns' flat, looking directly at her. Some instinct made her give a wave to an imagined person in one of the ground-floor flats below the Weichmanns', and she saw him look away.

Only when she was three blocks from Jungmannstraße did she begin to breathe easy again. She knew she could never go back to the flat.

I need to get rid of the money. I should find a litter bin.

She closed her eyes.

I can't. It's Esther's money. For Itsik's parents.

She hesitated for a second, then nodded to herself and walked briskly along the Knooper Weg until she reached Exerzierplatz. It was more crowded than the quieter side streets and she reasoned she would stick out less. Just as she turned down the side of the square, a black car coming towards her drew into the kerb a few metres away, and two men got out. With a sense of numb certainty, she continued to walk towards them, but they crossed the pavement and entered a tobacconist, laughing and joking.

There was no sense of relief; every shattered nerve ending cried for a rest from the

48

unremitting barrage of fear, but she continued to walk, the part of her mind that still functioned leading her on, like an automaton.

Reaching the end of Exerzierplatz, she continued onto Kleiner Kuhberg, counting down the house numbers on her right. 45, 43, 41… She risked a glance around her as she reached the Weber house at number 25 but forced herself to pass the soup kitchen and the temporary school, suppressing the urge to dive in to the first familiar refuge, knowing that the chance of assistance would be greater in number 15.

She reached it, and climbed the steps, pushing open the door and entering the relative sanctuary of the hallway. She ignored the doorway ahead, the entrance to the temporary synagogue, and took the wide staircase to the first floor, hoping that Jakob was in the committee office.

She knocked on the door and waited. When there was no answer, she knocked again, calling Jakob's name.

From behind her, she heard a voice and turned. Jakob was walking towards her. Seeing him, she felt her legs almost give way and she held out her hand to stop herself from falling.

He caught her elbow, his face a mask of concern.

'Miriam. What's wrong? Is Yosef all right? The children?'

'Yes,' she said, the tears not far away. 'They're all fine. I need your help.'

'You only have to ask,' he said.

He took her elbow and, opening the door next to the committee room, he guided her in. There was a cot in the corner, with a mattress and a folded blanket on it, a desk along one wall and a sink by the window. He showed her to one of the seats, and she sat down. He took the chair opposite.

'I sometimes don't get home,' he said, seeing her glance at the makeshift bed. 'If it's too late to walk the streets safely, I just stay here.'

She nodded, not surprised.

'What can I do for you?' he asked, leaning towards her, taking her hand.

'Oh, Jakob. I was so frightened. I thought they were going to catch me, that I'd never see Yosef or the children again.'

Tears rose to the surface, spilling out onto her cheeks.

Jakob took a clean handkerchief from his pocket and handed it to her.

'Here,' he said. 'Take your time and tell me everything. From the beginning.'

The story spilled out, releasing the fear and tension she'd dammed up inside her since the doorbell had rung in the flat. Jakob listened patiently, prompting her to repeat a word or two when he didn't quite catch her rushed, breathless account.

When she got to the bit about the money, she reached into her bag and pulled out the bundle and handed it to him.

He took it and let out a long, low whistle as he flicked his thumb across the edge, making a rough count in his head.

'It's a good job you didn't get caught with this,' he said. 'There could easily be 5,000 marks here. You did well. Very well. And you're brave; few people would have had the presence of mind that you had.'

'I didn't have time to think, to be honest.'

'That was maybe for the best.'

He got up and walked over to the desk. He put the bundle into the top drawer and returned to the chair opposite Miriam.

She handed him the note.

'It's not good,' he said. 'We can try but being arrested trying to flee the country will almost certainly get you sent to one of the concentration camps. I mean, look at Rosa Liewermann. She was leaving legally, and they still put her in a Konzentrationslager. I hear they are expanding the camp system in Poland, and that they're sending people there from the camps here.'

'Why?' she asked.

'Poland seems to be a dumping ground for those the government wants rid of. We believe their intention is to clear Germany of all its Jews and other undesirables and resettle them in the Generalgouvernement area. Out of sight, out of mind.'

'Can you get a lawyer for the Weichmanns?'

'I can try. It's getting harder and harder, and we have very few successes, but Itsik and his father were good friends of mine, so I'll give it my best efforts.'

'Thank you. There may be additional money available if you need it.'

'I saw that. It won't be easy for Itsik to get it to us. There's a bit of irony in that, eh? A Jew, trying to get money into Germany.'

'Yes. I suppose so. How did he get this in?'

Jakob explained how the money didn't need to be physically smuggled in.

'It's a useful exchange,' he said. 'For both parties.'

'Esther said not to go back to the flat,' she said.

'She's right. It wouldn't be safe.'

'How will they get in touch?'

'They know where you are. They'll find a way.'

She saw Jakob glancing at her. She looked in the small mirror stuck to the wall above the sink and dried her tears.

'Would you like me to walk you home, or send someone to get Yosef?' Jakob asked.

'No. I'm fine now,' she answered, getting up. 'I'm sure they didn't follow me, and, without the money, I feel better.'

He smiled.

'Yes. It must have been terrifying. It was probably just a routine check though. I'm sure they weren't looking for you, and it sounds as if you didn't arouse any suspicions. Did the Gestapo man get a good look at you?'

'Only from a distance. I couldn't really make him out, so I don't believe he'd have seen enough of me to be able to recognise me again.'

'That's good. It's a pity you looked back at all but it's understandable in the circumstances. Did you have your gloves on for the whole time?'

'Yes, I think so,' she said. 'I usually take them off if I'm cleaning, or putting the messages away, but I was only there to see if there was a letter from Esther.'

'That's good. You should have left no fingerprints. Leave this with me,' he said, 'and I'll see what we can do.'

She thanked Jakob for his help, and he promised to contact her as soon as he heard anything.

'Let me know if they get in touch again,' he said, showing her out. 'Are you sure you'll be all right?'

'Yes,' she said, composed again. She gave him a smile and waved as she walked away.

She felt strangely safe, walking down Kleiner Kuhberg, and along Sophienblatt, past the railway station. Even when a black car passed her on Hamburger Chaussee and pulled in ahead of her, she didn't flinch or feel the sense of dread she'd had earlier.

She'd almost reached home, when a sudden thought struck her, and her stomach lurched. *The packaging. I left it. It had my initials on it.*

CHAPTER 13

During their search of the flat, the Kriminalassistent had fished the crumpled piece of brown paper from the fireplace and turned it over slowly in his hand. The younger detective watched as he straightened it out and smoothed the torn section with his fingers, then walked to the front door and carefully inspected the letterbox. He picked a small scrap of brown paper from the hinge and matched it to the torn section. He peered closely at the packaging.

'M N,' he said. 'This must be the wrapper from the gift that they mentioned in the letter.'

Carefully flattening it out, he ran his fingers along the crease lines which marked the stiff paper where it had been folded.

'A book, sir?' the younger man suggested.

'I doubt it. The shape is all wrong.'

He removed his wallet from his inner coat pocket and extracted a twenty-mark note. He placed it on the paper, in the rectangle made by the four folds in the centre. It fitted almost perfectly.

The Kriminalassistentanwärter whistled.

'So, it was money,' he said.

The senior detective nodded. He looked closely at the paper again. He could see a second line of creases, about two centimetres from the others.

'That's the thickness of the pile, Kamerad Meyer,' he said. 'Let's see if you can work out how much money we missed out on.'

'But we don't know what kind of banknotes were in it,' the young detective said, looking confused.

'We have to assume that, if they went to all that effort, they would have made the package as small as possible. I suggest they would have used the largest denomination notes they could.'

'Thousand-mark notes, sir?'

'Probably not. That would be a huge sum. More likely hundred-mark notes, Meyer.'

'But how many would be in a pile that size, sir?'

'I don't know. You tell me. Here.'

The Kriminalassistent handed him the banknote.

'How will that help?' the younger man said.

'Fold it four times.'

Carl did as he was told.

'How thick is it?'

'About a millimetre, maybe a millimetre and a half.' The younger man's face lit up.

'It's like sixteen banknotes.'

'Yes,' the Kriminalassistent said. 'So, how many notes were there in total?'

He waited a minute while Carl Meyer counted in his head, using his fingers on a couple of occasions.

'Oh, for God's sake man, it's roughly ten notes to the millimetre and the bundle is twenty millimetres thick. That's 200 notes. That's about 20,000 marks.'

'That's a lot of money, sir, to be poking through a letterbox, assuming it was hundred-mark notes.'

'Even if it was only twenty-mark notes, it could still be 4,000 Reichsmarks. We need to look at these Weichmann people in a little more depth, I think. We'll start with her,' he said, nodding to the doorway, and the flat opposite.

~~o~~

'Frau Hueber.'

'Yes?'

'You said earlier that you hadn't seen anyone enter or exit the flat for a few days. Is that correct?'

'Yes. That's what I said.'

'I'd like you to remember that we are the Gestapo, and we don't take kindly to being lied to. Do you know what we do to people who aren't truthful with us?'

Heinrich Güllich was gratified to see a flicker of fear cross the woman's face.

'I am not lying, sir,' she said, a slight tremble in her voice.

Better.

'All right, let's suppose for the moment that you aren't.'

He paused and stared at her, until she dropped her eyes. He continued.

'You said the Weichmanns have been away for a while. Do you remember the last time you saw them?'

'I can't say for certain. Every day is the same to me. About a week or so. Maybe as much as a fortnight.'

'Were they carrying bags, or cases?'

'I didn't see them go. I would have remembered when it was if I'd seen them leave. I spoke to Els… I mean Frau Weichmann, when she was cleaning the landing one day, then nothing since.'

'And no one has been to the flat since?'

'I didn't say that. You asked me if anyone had entered or left the flat in the last few days.'

Carl Meyer saw a vein pulse in Heinrich Güllich's neck and wondered if the woman knew how much danger she was in.

'Do you know how serious this could be,' the Kriminalassistent said. 'We might be dealing with a murder here.'

It was on Frau Hueber's lips to say that the Gestapo would hardly bother if two old Jews had been killed but she saw the look on the detective's face and thought better of it.

'I'm sorry,' she said. 'The Weichmanns had few visitors. Just the lady who helps out. She called around a few days after they had gone.'

'Do you know her name?'

'No. I only saw her from time to time. I think she was there once a week.'

'What did she look like?'

'Difficult to say. About forty or fifty, but she was quite old-fashioned, so she could have been younger. Average height, mousy-brown hair, nondescript hairstyle. A nice face, but not striking. Arbeiter, I believe.'

'Of course she's a worker. She cleans houses.'

'I'm not sure. Her clothes were of a superior quality but not new, and she was better spoken than you'd expect for a cleaner. Her hands were those of a working woman though.'

'Was she on her own?'

She looked up, surprised.

'No. She had a girl with her that day. I supposed it was her daughter.'

'How old was the girl?'

'Maybe fifteen or sixteen. Sensible clothes, not like some of the young women nowadays, and no make-up. Very pretty though. Dark hair like her mother. Slim, and slightly taller. Striking eyes; very dark brown.'

'Were they Jews?'

'How would I know? I just said hello to them in passing at the front door. The Weichmanns are Jews, so I'd say they were too. I mean, who else would work for them nowadays?'

The young detective had been scribbling down everything she said. He looked up.

'Did the mother mention her daughter's name?' he asked.

'No.' She deliberated for a second. 'I don't think so.'

'So, Frau Hueber, now that you've been a little more forthcoming, did you see anyone else come to the flat.'

'Well, no one went into the flat, but a gentleman did deliver a parcel. He rang my bell and I let him in the main door. Just like I did for you.'

'Why didn't you tell us that, you old fool?'

Heinrich Güllich's voice rose, and the woman flinched.

'There's no need to be rude, young man,' she said. 'As I told you, he didn't enter or leave the flat, which was what you asked. He just delivered the parcel.'

Carl Meyer almost grinned.

~~o~~

For a moment, Frau Hueber thought she'd gone too far but the Kriminalassistent took a deep breath.

'And when was this?' he said.

'Two days ago.'

'Did you speak to him?'

'A few words. He thanked me, I told them the Weichmanns were away and he said they'd get it when they returned. He posted the packet through their letterbox and left.'

'What did he look like?'

'Like a lawyer or an accountant. Smartly dressed. About late forties, I would say. Clean-shaven.'

'Glasses? Hat?'

'No Glasses. Black fedora.'

'Accent?'

'Local, I'd say. Nothing remarkable.'

'And you saw nobody else?'

'No,' she said. It was the truth this time. She was sure she'd heard the door of the Weichmanns' flat softly close just before the two Gestapo men had arrived but, by the time she'd looked out, the person had already disappeared down the stairs.

If they hadn't been so loathsome and downright rude, she might have mentioned it to them, but it gave her a quiet satisfaction to withhold something from them, and they could never possibly know. Even so, a cold spasm of fear gripped her when they'd gone.

She'd got on well with her Jewish neighbours, without being terribly close, and she'd instinctively liked the woman who'd come to help them out. And she was sure that concern for the Weichmanns wasn't the Gestapo's motivation for their visit.

The irritated glare the men had given her before they'd left was reward enough for her small show of defiance.

~~o~~

Miriam entered the cottage, hanging up her coat and changing her shoes. She thought about putting the kettle on and settling herself with a cup of coffee but thought better of it.

I need to prepare the Kästners' evening meal.

She grabbed her pinafore and opened the door.

'Oh,' she gasped. Yosef stood in front of her, reaching for the handle to come in. She stepped back and let him enter.

'What's wrong?' he said, staring at her.

'I have to do the dinner,' she said, wondering how he knew.

'Five minutes won't make much of a difference. You're as white as a sheet. Tell me what's happened.'

'It's the Weichmanns,' she said. 'They've been arrested at the Romanian border. Itsik and Miriam sent me money to get them a lawyer. I only just escaped being caught in the flat by the Gestapo, with the money.'

'Do you have it now?' he gasped, shutting the door and glancing out of the window, as if expecting the cottage to be surrounded by Gestapo officers.

'No. I took it to Jakob.'

The look of relief on his face confirmed that she'd done the right thing.

'I need to go,' she said, resisting the urge to collapse into his arms. 'I'll speak to you later.'

She pushed past him, and he followed her over to the big house.

CHAPTER 14

Carl Meyer could see that the Kriminalassistent wasn't in the best of moods.

'Come in and sit down,' the senior Gestapo man snapped.

Moody swine.

Heinrich Güllich sipped his coffee while his Kriminalassistentanwärter pulled up a chair.

'Have we got anything else on the Weichmanns yet?'

'No sir. Just what we have already. And what the woman told us; that they've been away for a few days.'

'I think she's lying, the old hag.'

'Lying, sir?'

The older detective took out a cigarette and lit up. He glanced at his assistant and offered the packet to him.

'Cigarette?' he asked.

The younger man took one and lit up.

'I'm sure she saw someone there, that day. She had a shifty look about her and remember, she didn't offer us the key until we asked her.'

'Yes, sir.'

'And that door of hers. It was a little ajar. I bet you ten marks that it's always like that, so that she doesn't miss anything.'

'How can you be certain that somebody had been there?'

'I can't be a hundred per cent sure, but did you not smell it?'

'Smell what, sir?'

'It was faint, but I thought I could smell perfume.'

'Wouldn't it just be the old Weichmann woman's?'

'No, according to the woman, they've not been there for days. There's also the package wrapping.'

'That was clever, sir. I wouldn't have noticed it.'

'Well, you should have,' the Kriminalassistent growled. 'And I don't need to be told that I'm clever.'

Carl Meyer blanched. He'd forgotten that Güllich despised any attempts at flattery by his subordinates.

'What do you think, sir?' he said, changing the subject.

'There are a few possibilities. One – they've left Germany. Two – they're in hiding with family or friends, or three – they've been arrested. We need to establish if they have any relatives here and check the arrest lists for the last three weeks, although I don't believe they were detained during a house search; it's too tidy.'

'But their clothes were all emptied out on the bed, sir.'

'Yes, but they weren't strewn about the room, and nothing else had been pulled out. It looks as if they intended to leave for good but could only take a limited amount with them, and they were in a hurry. If they'd been coming back, they would have packed them all into drawers again.'

'Is there anything else you want me to do?'

'Yes. After you check the arrest lists, contact Berlin and ask for them to search central records in case they were arrested elsewhere in Germany.'

The Kriminalassistentanwärter got up and opened the door.

'One more thing, Kamerad Meyer.'

'Yes, sir?'

'Check the mortuary intakes.'

~~o~~

For the two hours of dinner service, Miriam buried herself in her work, tackling each task with greater zeal than normal. Even Maria noticed the change in her demeanour, remarking to the General that their housekeeper seemed tense and on edge.

'They have their worries, my dear,' he had said, drily.

~~o~~

Later, after Manny had gone to bed, and Ruth had retired to her room to study, Miriam told Yosef the whole story, gripping his hand tightly all the way through. She hadn't cried, but the shaking that took hold of her body came in waves until he wrapped her in his arms when she'd finished.

When she'd stopped trembling, he took her face in his hands.

'You're the bravest person I know, Miriam Nussbaum. And the most loyal. Did you consider getting rid of the money and just saying you were there to clean the flat?'

'No,' she said. 'I couldn't. It's the Weichmanns' only chance of getting out.'

'If you'd been caught, you would never have seen your children again.'

'I know, but I couldn't think like that. Anyway, where could I have put it?'

'Out of the window, up the chimney, at the bottom of the bin or you could have even burned it in the grate.'

'It didn't occur to me. If I'd done anything like that, and they'd found them, I'd have been in deeper trouble.'

'You're right, but it makes my blood freeze just thinking about it.'

'I only hope it's worth it.'

'Jakob will try his best.'

'I know.'

~~o~~

[13/06/1940 Thursday]

Carl Meyer knocked on the Kriminalassistent's office door and, hearing a grunted answer, he entered. He handed a telegram to Heinrich Güllich.

'I just got this from our office in Košice in Czechoslovakia. We have the Weichmanns in custody. They were caught crossing the border into Romania.'

'Ha,' he said, thumping the desk with his hand. 'They were trying to get to their son in Palestine. That's the route they take. Romania, Bulgaria, Turkey, Syria. The Haganah were almost certainly involved. If our orders weren't for us to catch these Judenschweine, I'd encourage them all to scuttle away like rats to that godforsaken hole in the desert. Let them wander around in their wilderness for another forty years.'

Carl Meyer joined in when the Kriminalassistent laughed but the joke eluded him. He knew nothing about the Jews save that they were the root of Germany's past troubles and, now that they were being dealt with, his beloved Fatherland would rise again.

'I've put a call through to one of their Kriminalassistenten,' he said. 'He'll phone back shortly.'

CHAPTER 15

SS-Obersturmbannführer Eicke sat on the couch. Lise handed him a cup of coffee.

'So nice of you to call in,' Lise said.

As usual, she was immaculate. Her hair and make-up were perfect, and she wore a figure-hugging floral print dress. The Obersturmbannführer's eyes drank it all in.

'I was passing through. I've been promoted and transferred out, so they gave me a five-day leave. My wife and I are staying at the Bellevue.'

'Where Rudolf and I got married,' Lise said.

'I know. I was honoured to be asked.'

'Rudolf talks very highly of you. He'll be disappointed that you're being transferred.'

'The SS value my talents so much that they've made me a lieutenant colonel, two steps up the ladder. And you needn't worry about Rudolf; I've recommended him for promotion, too, to take my place. He's more than capable. Did he tell you that, apart from us, only four of our original squad are still alive?'

'No,' she said, flinching. 'Those poor young men. How is he?' she asked, getting up from the chair and looking out of the window. 'I haven't seen him for three months.'

He raised an eyebrow.

'I'm surprised. They had a four-day furlough a few weeks ago. I thought he'd gone home. Perhaps he couldn't get transport. It can happen.'

She was silent. He looked at her, and she met his gaze. A look passed between them.

'That picture,' he said, pointing to the group photograph on the wall, of her with Rudolf's colleagues. 'You were wearing nothing underneath the dress.'

'Yes,' she said. 'I knew you'd noticed. I could feel your fingers asking questions through the cloth.'

'Why did you do that? On your wedding day?'

'It excited me. It excited Rudolf. You know we made love for the first time during the reception?' she said. 'I took him upstairs. No one noticed. I didn't even take the dress off.'

He laughed.

'I knew you were something special. I'm guessing our dear Rudolf isn't enough for you?'

'He was, for a while.'

'But now?'

'I think he sleeps around. I can't be sure.'

'He wouldn't be a soldier if he didn't.'

'But he's never going get anything like this, anywhere else,' she said, her voice close to a whisper.

He reached forward for her. She pulled away.

'Not here,' she said.

'Where?'

'Rent a room at the Europäischer Hof. I'll meet you there in an hour.'

'Where?'

'In the bar. I'll say hello as if I've just bumped into you. Leave a key when you go. I'll follow you up.'

'Do you do this often?' he asked.

'No,' she said. 'This is the first time.'

The Obersturmbannführer watched her go. Since he'd started bedding her mother, he'd vowed to have the daughter too, but even before that he'd coveted her, from the moment he'd seen her at the engagement party. At the wedding, when he'd felt her smooth uncovered contours under her dress, he'd thought of ways to put Rudolf at the heart of the fighting, hoping that he would die a hero's death. But he hadn't, and he loved the young man for it.

But Rudolf had made a mistake. He'd confided in his superior officer that he hadn't gone home to his wife, that they had problems.

Obersturmbannführer Eicke smiled.

It would be a pity to let a woman like that go to waste.

~~o~~

'I told you so, didn't I?'

'Keep your eyes forward and your mouth shut.'

Franz Kästner glanced at his brother as he spoke. The smug grin was there, as he'd expected. They were both immaculately turned out, as were the rest of the company Franz commanded, and the whole of Colonel Schneider's battalion.

They'd marched into Paris unopposed from the north-east, through the Aubervilliers Gate then on by Rue Saint-Denis to the Rue la Fayette. The citizens of Paris stood in sullen groups at every doorway, café, and street corner to watch the never-ending column of grey-green uniforms marching past. If they expected to view tired and battle-weary soldiers like their own troops who had just vacated the city, they were disappointed. Instead, they marvelled through gritted teeth and forced smiles at the well-nourished, well-drilled, and invincible troops of the Wehrmacht.

Luftwaffe fighters patrolled the sky above unmolested, protecting the advance of Franz and Johann's column, and the larger convoy from the north-west.

As they crossed the bridge over the Gare de l'Est, a series of commands had a machine-gun unit peeling off and setting up an emplacement in front of the Gare du Nord. Johann risked turning his head towards Franz again.

'They must love their city, these *Français*,' he said, in a low voice.

'What do you mean?' Franz asked, intrigued despite his previous warning for Johann to keep quiet.

'Well, to walk out without a fight, just to save Paris from further damage. I can't imagine the Wehrmacht doing that.'

'It's of no strategic importance in the defence of their country. They will fall back to positions further south that are easier to protect.'

'No. They just didn't want this reduced to rubble.'

He looked right and left, and Franz's eyes followed his gaze.

He saw the tall, elegant buildings, the shops, the cafés, the church spires, and the occasional tree-lined square, and understood why the Parisians did not want their city destroyed.

They reached the junction where the Rue la Fayette ended, and they crossed Boulevard Haussmann onto Rue Halévy.

'This time next week I'll be a major, like you,' Johann said, grinning.

'I don't think so. Not when you are reported by your senior officer for flouting marching orders like a tourist.'

Johann laughed.

'You heard Colonel Schneider. My prediction has proved correct. You only have to see the wonder and excitement on the faces of the young ladies lining the pavement to see why. The people of Paris are awestruck at the power and strength of the German Army and amazed how handsome their officers are.'

Franz stifled a laugh.

'Shut up and march,' he hissed.

Passing through the Place de l'Opéra, Franz thought that if there was a more beautiful city anywhere, he'd never seen it. They swung right and marched on until the boulevard opened out into the Place de la Madeleine. Johann's silence didn't last long.

'Impressive buildings, I'll give you that,' Johann said.

'That's Madeleine Church,' Franz said out of the corner of his mouth. 'Isn't it magnificent?'

Johann whistled under his breath, and Franz was surprised.

'I didn't think that was your sort of thing, brother. Maybe there's hope for you yet.'

Johann turned his head to Franz and nodded across the street.

'Church my Arsch. Look at them.'

Franz looked in the direction Johann was facing.

Three French women, in their early twenties, were standing under the trees in the small square opposite the church. They were wearing light summer dresses and had the effortless beauty that young French women wore with such ease.

Franz had to admit that they were a match for the splendour of the church opposite, but it annoyed him that Johann couldn't see beauty in anything other than female flesh.

He knew what the answer would be if he were to tackle Johann.

'I will concede that an elegantly designed yacht or a fast, sleek sports car might come close; maybe even one of our fighter planes, or a battleship at full speed, but nothing will get my blood racing like a pretty Fräulein,' he would say, grinning.

Turning into the Rue Royale, the crowds lining the street grew thicker, and a smattering of those watching the parade were applauding; a few even cheered and Johann asked Franz under his breath why they would do that.

'Those will be the anti-communists,' Franz said. 'They think we will solve all their problems.'

Johann leant closer to hear him as the thunder of marching men and idling machines echoed down the wide avenue towards them from the Place de la Concorde, increasing with every stride.

At the end of the street, the giant Egyptian obelisk towered above the square, its decorative hieroglyphics visible even from a distance, the gold cap at its peak glinting in the sun. Below, a sea of steel helmets of the rank and file of the Heer, and the caps of their officers, filled every corner of the largest square in Paris.

'Have you ever seen anything like this?' Johann said.

'One of the big rallies, I suppose, in Nuremberg or Berlin, maybe, but this is impressive.'

Surrounding the troops, all kinds of military vehicles stood parked in long lines at the edge of the square, the combined roar of their engines, even at tickover drowning out all but the loudest shouts, the air above the square thick with their exhaust fumes.

Only a fragment of the Wehrmacht forces taking Paris had been allocated to the parade. The remainder secured strategic positions all around the city, and even more were encamped outside, or were circumventing Paris to continue the advance southwards.

Colonel Schneider's battalion was one of the last to reach the square and, not long after they'd been directed to their allocated location, the engines of the tanks, half-tracks and lorries of the transport companies fell silent. The lone note of a bugle sounded and the voice of a Stabsfeldwebel cut across the Place de la Concorde. To a man, the assembled troops snapped to attention and saluted, their arms outstretched as one. Repeated waves of *Heil Hitlers* and *Sieg Heils* rolled across the Pont de la Concorde to the Assemblée Nationale on the opposite bank of the Seine.

As abruptly as it had started, the roar of the massed voices ceased, and the bugle sounded again. The Stabsfeldwebel barked the command to stand down and the troops began to file away in companies, to the posts they had been assigned outside the city, or to their respective billets in Paris.

Johann and Franz watched the square empty with typical German efficiency. They would be one of the last companies to leave and a few of their fellow officers took the opportunity to light cigarettes.

The colonel strode over to join them.

'Quite a show, eh?'

'Yes, sir,' they chorused.

'If this doesn't intimidate the French, nothing will,' he said.

'Sir, where are we going?'

'The battalion is being billeted in Caserne Monge; the French Republican Guard appear to have left it vacant.'

They laughed. The ceremonial regiment that provided Paris with pomp and circumstance when it was needed were spread over three or four barracks, dotted around the city, but they had retreated from the city with the regular French forces, leaving their accommodation vacant.

'I and my senior officers have been assigned a hotel just around the corner. Once you have the men settled, you will all join me for dinner, and I will detail the battalion's duties for the next couple of weeks.'

'Yes, sir.'

CHAPTER 16

'Scheiße.'

'Yes, sir.'

Heinrich Güllich glared at Carl Meyer. The junior detective flinched under his scrutiny.

'They shot them both?'

'Yes, sir. They were trying to escape.'

'Don't be so stupid, Meyer,' Heinrich Güllich hissed. 'It's a euphemism. They were executed. Not that I mind a couple of old Jews being shot but I needed to talk to this pair.'

'Perhaps they interviewed them first, sir.'

The Kriminalassistent rolled his eyes.

'And you imagine that a Dummkopf SS storm trooper at the back end of nowhere will have asked the questions we want answers to?'

'No, perhaps not, sir.'

'We'll find out when we get the full report, but I'd be amazed if we got anything useful.'

'I'll chase it up, sir. What else can we do?'

'We're going to go back and talk to that old fossil next door to them. I'm sure she's holding something back. There was someone in that flat that day, and I'd bet a month's salary that it was the cleaner, and she took the money. Thieving Jewish whore.'

He froze.

'Wait a minute, Meyer,' he said, getting up from his chair and walking over to the window.

'What's up, sir?'

'This housekeeper or cleaner woman. She's got to be Jewish, right?'

'Yes, sir. No one else would work for Jews.'

'And she has a teenage daughter.'

'Yes.' Carl Meyer's brow crinkled.

'Don't overwork your brain. We have records of all the Jews in Kiel. We can track her down. We need to get a better description from the old hag...'

He stopped, looking at his subordinate.

'What's the matter, Meyer? You look as if you swallowed a turd.'

'Sir, something just came to mind, when we searched the flat that first day.'

'Yes, what about it?'

'Well, sir, just as the woman let us in, do you remember hearing the door latch downstairs? You went to look over the bannister, to see if someone had entered the building.'

'Yes. There was no one there. The wind had blown it closed, I would imagine. We must have left it open.'

'No, sir. I'm sure I closed it, but when we came back in, I looked out of the front-room window. There was a woman walking along the street, on the other side.'

'So what? Did she come out of the Weichmanns' building?'

'I don't know, sir, but she turned around at the corner and looked back, straight at me.'

Heinrich Güllich stared at his assistant again.

'And you didn't think to tell me this?' he said.

'No, sir. I thought nothing of it, but she waved, sir.'

'At you?' The way the words were hissed reminded the young detective of the sound a poisonous snake would make, just before it struck.

'No, sir. She waved at somebody lower down, on the ground floor, maybe even further along the street. I just thought she'd turned to wave at whoever she'd been visiting.'

'If it was our woman, she made you look a fool, didn't she?'

Carl Meyer blushed, but bit back a retort. He didn't want to worsen his inspector's mood any further.

'Is there the remotest possibility that you would recognise this woman again, Kamerad Kriminalassistentanwärter?'

This time, the voice was dripping with sarcasm.

'I think so, sir. It was a distance away, but she definitely turned and looked straight at me.'

'Right, grab your coat. Let's go.'

'To the flat, sir?'

'Yes. We'll see if Frau Hueber can elaborate on her description of this woman, and if so, see if it does match your friend.'

'We'll still have a job finding her, sir.'

'Meyer, what do Jews do on a Friday?'

'I don't know, sir.'

'You have to know your enemy, Kamerad Meyer. You have a lot to learn. Jews go to the synagogue on Friday evening, and then on Saturday too.'

'Ah. I see, sir. We stake out the synagogue.'

A sudden worried look crossed his face.

'Sir, I thought the synagogue burned down in '38. I'm sure of it.'

'It did, you fool. They do their witchcraft in a house in Kleiner Kuhberg. For now, at least.'

He grinned.

~~o~~

'Canaris.'

'Kästner.'

'They're in Paris. All safe. I thought you'd like to know.'

'Thank you.'

The phone clicked dead.

He's in Paris too.

The General looked out of the window. A small part of him wondered what it would have been like if he and Canaris had reached Paris during their war.

He shook his head.

~~o~~

Carl Meyer drove. The visit to Frau Hueber had been interesting. When prompted, she'd agreed that the young detective's description of the woman was accurate.

And when Heinrich Güllich suspended her within a fraction of toppling over the balcony, she'd conceded that she might have heard the flat door close minutes before the two Gestapo men had climbed the stairs, but she would not be budged from her insistence that she hadn't seen anyone.

Heinrich Güllich had been disgusted when he stepped in the puddle of the old hag's urine and Carl Meyer had thought for a brief moment that his boss was going to let her drop the four storeys to the bottom of the stairwell, but the older detective had let her scurry back into her flat, whimpering, while he wiped his feet on the shawl he'd snatched from her.

'So,' he said, as the young Gestapo man swung the car right onto Lorentzendamm, heading for Exerzierplatz, 'we have this charwoman who is in the flat to do a weekly clean, she finds the money, hears the doorbell and panics. So, what does she do?'

'Hides in one of the other flats?'

'Possible, Kamerad. Possible. Could the old bag have hidden her?'

'No, she would have told us when…'

'Go on, say it. When she was hanging from the bannister?'

'Yes, sir.'

'I think you're right. We'll make a Gestapo investigator out of you yet.'

'Thank you, sir.'

'I was being ironic, Meyer. Let's see if you can work the rest of it out.'

'Someone she knew took her in, then she left once we went upstairs?'

'Do you really believe that anyone would hide a Jewish cleaner when there are two Gestapo men hammering at their door? Anyway, it would have taken her too long to persuade one of the neighbours to let her in. Did you observe that I checked out the back entrance of the building?'

'Yes, sir. I thought perhaps you were looking for something that had been tossed out of the window.'

'It had crossed my mind, Meyer, but the door was locked. I suspect it's always locked, but did you notice anything about the corridor that led to the backyard?'

'No, sir.'

'There was a door, just inside the back entrance. I had a look inside it; it was a small janitor's store. That's where she hid, I'm sure, and we passed within a few feet of her. Just imagine. Her little Jewish weasel face in the dark, sniffing for the chance to run. And then waving to you from the corner. They are sneaky, these little Judenschweine, aren't they?'

'Yes, sir. She didn't wave at me, sir.'

'She didn't, did she. But she might as well have done. Still, it should teach you a valuable lesson, shouldn't it?'

'Yes, sir.'

'Ah. Turn left here. Kleiner Kuhberg is straight ahead.'

'Which house is it, sir?'

Heinrich Güllich peered out of the window.

'That one,' he said. 'Number 15.' Park just short of it, on the other side of the road. It will give us a better view.'

Carl Meyer brought the car to a halt. The senior man looked at his watch.

'Now, Kriminalassistentanwärter, the filthy Jews will all be arriving soon. Keep your eyes sharp. It's all down to you now.'

'Yes, sir,' he said.

~~o~~

Ten minutes before the black car had drawn up opposite number 15, the Nussbaums had walked up the steps and entered the house. Jakob had met them at the front door and escorted them upstairs to the room he used as his private quarters.

He'd opened the door, and ushered them in. Emil Liewerman stood before them and Miriam couldn't quite hide her shock at his appearance.

'Emil, it's good to see you, but I wish you were anywhere else.'

She'd opened her arms and hugged him.

Yosef was also shocked. Emil had aged ten years in just over twelve months. His hair had greyed, and he appeared to have shrunk, or perhaps that was just a stoop he had gained during his time in Belgium.

'It's great to see you both,' Emil said, his voice quivering. 'I…'

He broke down, and Miriam patted his back. When he broke away, it was to give Yosef a handshake.

'I'm so sorry, Emil,' Yosef said, fighting the prick of tears in his eyes.

'Ach. It's happened. What can we do?'

'Listen,' Miriam said, holding his hand, 'Jakob is trying hard to get Rosa out. If they let her go, and you get your visas, you can still get to America. You have to believe that.'

'I try. I really do. But I'm lost without her.'

'I know,' Miriam said, 'but for the children, you must be strong.'

'I'll try.' Emil sniffed. 'I'm sorry I missed you last week, Yosef. They wouldn't let us leave the house. It's like a prison.'

'I know. Jakob told us. We're here now though. It was nice to get this extra time with you. Tell us all about the ship. I hear it was like living in luxury.'

Emil gave a wan smile.

'It was. The captain and the crew treated us like ordinary people. Even in Antwerp, we lived normal lives. It makes being brought back here even harder.'

For nearly an hour, the three of them talked until it was time to go down for the Shabbat service.

'Come on,' Miriam said, 'Everyone will be so pleased to see you, despite the circumstances. Jakob will maybe allow us a little extra time afterwards.'

'That would be good. I feel better having seen you both. And the children will be happy to be among all their friends again.'

CHAPTER 17

The Hotel Excelsior faced the barracks across the tree-lined gardens of Place Monge. The restaurant was on the ground floor and its tables spread outside onto the pavement, but Colonel Schneider had appropriated a table deep inside, in the alcove formed by the L-shaped bar.

'It's a little more discreet in here, as pleasant as it would be to eat outside,' he said to his assembled officers.

The colonel sat at the head of the table flanked by Franz Kästner and Major Briet. Of the ten captains in the battalion, five were present, the others deployed with their companies at strategic junctions in the sixth, thirteenth and fourteenth arrondissements, south of the river.

'First of all, don't tell your men yet, but I can confirm that we are being sent back to Norway.'

The announcement drew a collective groan from his staff.

The colonel held up his hand.

'It was always likely we'd return; our battalion was never part of the original plan for the invasion of France. The good news is that we will remain here for at least a week, and...'

He paused and looked at Johann and gave a concessionary nod, and a smile.

'... we are to be part of the honour guard when the Führer visits.'

The table erupted. Amid the laughter and cheers which filled the restaurant and spilled out into the street, the man next to Johann clapped him on the back.

The colonel held up his hand and waited for the table to fall silent.

'Although this was predicted by Captain Kästner,' he continued, 'before he gets carried away, there will be no immediate advancement in rank. Even I couldn't justify that to the promotion board.'

His officers laughed. Johann feigned disappointment, but there was a smile at the corner of his mouth.

'The whole battalion has performed as well as I could have hoped, although there is always room for improvement, and I will be addressing a few minor shortcomings once we return to Norway. In the meantime, our duties here in Paris are light, and I intend to treat this as the furlough that you and your men have rightly earned since the invasion of Poland.'

He looked around. There was a hint of a smile on a couple of their faces, but they were not boys anymore. He had turned them into fighting men, and they would take the well-deserved leave with the same stoic grins as they had during the periods of prolonged hardship they'd faced.

'So, make the most of Paris, and the delights it has to offer. Each day, one company will be on guard duty, another on fatigues. The remaining two companies will be off duty. This will run on a rolling basis so each of your companies will have two days off, two days on. This will exclude the day of the Führer's visit and the day before for preparation, for those units involved. Any questions?'

'No, sir,' they all chorused. 'Thank you, sir.'

'Now. Let us eat. This is Paris and the food is said to be the best in the world.'

~~o~~

If people leaving the synagogue noticed the two Gestapo men sitting in their car, they did their best not to show it, but the occasional glance at the black saloon betrayed their anxiety.

'It's been twenty minutes since the last person left, sir. I'd have noticed her going in, or out.'

'I know,' Heinrich Güllich snapped, lighting his third cigarette since they'd arrived. 'You needn't state the obvious. 'We'll come again tomorrow.'

'Yes, sir.' Carl Meyer hesitated. 'What if she took the money and ran, sir?'

'She'll either get away, and that's the last we'll hear of her, or she'll get caught crossing the border. And if she is, I want to get her back here, in the basement at Düppelstraße.'

The young man's eyes lit up.

'Do you think she would break, sir.'

'They all do, in the end. One way or another.'

~~o~~

[15/06/1940 Saturday]

Their vigil in Kleiner Kuhberg the following morning was no more successful.

When the stream of servicegoers had dwindled and died, and there was no sign of the mystery woman, the Kriminalassistent told him to drive back to the office, expressing his doubts about his assistant's observational abilities.

But Carl Meyer was sure that the woman he'd seen that day from the upper flat in Jungmannstraße hadn't entered or left number 15 while they'd been sitting outside.

'We'll pursue the matter further on Tuesday,' he said. I have to attend my nephew's christening tomorrow, in Frankfurt.'

He looked at his watch in disgust.

'The train is in an hour. My wife and I don't travel back until Monday.'

'Is there anything you want me to do in the meantime, sir?'

'Yes. Talk to the SD for me. Get me the records for all Jews in Kiel, if they have them.'

~~o~~

Memo: Geh.KdoS. ABW 16/06/40 CAC01172.1

For Attention Only: All senior executive officers, Abwehr.

From: Vice Admiral Wilhelm Canaris, Chef der Abwehr.

Marshal Pétain has been appointed the Prime Minister of France. An approach has been made via the Spanish ambassador requesting that Germany cease hostilities and make known its terms of peace. [END]

~~o~~

[16/06/1940 Sunday]

Oskar von Friedeburg leaned back in his chair.

'Do you know who I saw leaving the Europäischer Hof the other day. Saturday afternoon, to be exact?'

'No,' the General said. 'Is this some sort of game? Let me see… Goebbels, Heydrich, Himmler, or even the Führer himself?'

'No. But very droll,' Oskar said, with a polite laugh. 'You're on good form, today. Seriously, have a guess.'

'Oh, I don't know. Tell me before I burst with curiosity.'

'Lise Böhm.'

'Oh. Lise Mey, she is now. And why should that interest me?'

'I just wondered what she was doing there.'

'She was maybe asking the same question about you.'

'She didn't see me. I was sitting in the corner with a business associate.'

'A female business associate?'

'No, male. It was a business meeting. Of sorts. Anyway, that's irrelevant. Lise came down the stairs. Looking a little dishevelled, I'd say.'

'Then I'm glad Franz didn't marry her. I was dubious about her at the time, if you remember.'

'I just thought you'd like to know.'

'Thanks, Oskar. I must start reading your gossip column,' the General said, but a smile played on his lips, and Oskar knew that the information had pleased him.

CHAPTER 18

Ruth had been told not to open the door to anyone, but she was seventeen now and anyway, she had seen Jakob Teubner pass the kitchen window a moment before she heard the knock.

'Herr Teubner,' she said. 'Come in. What can I do for you?'

'Are your mama and papa in? I need to speak with them.'

'No. They are still over at the big house. They won't be long. Do you want me to tell them you're here?'

She noticed, with a start, that he was looking older. Lines of worry were etched deep on his face, and his eyes were rheumy, with a terrible depth of sadness in them.

'No, no,' he said, shaking his head. 'I'll wait.'

She made him a cup of coffee and sat him in the parlour. Manny had come down from his room and she made a face at him to stay with the old man.

She slipped out of the door and ran across to the Kästner house. Her mama was in the kitchen.

'Herr Teubner is here to see you and Papa. He said not to come and tell you, but I thought I should.'

Miriam glanced around, her eyes darting first to the clock, then to the doorway. She had almost cleared up, and the preparations for the evening meal were well in hand. She untied her apron.

'Your papa is down in the cellar fetching coal for the range. Go and tell him about Jakob.'

Ruth ran down the steps, meeting her father on the way, full scuttle in hand.

'I'll just put this in the drawing room,' he said. 'Tell Mama I'll be over in a minute.'

Ruth and Miriam hurried over to the cottage. As they reached the door, they turned at a shout behind them to see Yosef emerge from the Kästner house. They waited for him.

'What's going on?' he asked.

'It must be the Weichmanns,' Miriam said, opening the door, 'or news about Rosa.'

Jakob got up from the chair when the three Nussbaums entered the room. Miriam looked at his face and turned to Ruth.

'Take Manny next door,' she told her.

Reluctantly, Ruth did as she was told, glancing back at the three adults standing numbly in the centre of the room. She closed the door and, a second later, heard the low murmur of the older man's voice, then a gasp and a cry from her mother. She strained to hear, but she couldn't make out what they were saying.

'Go up to your room and play, Manny,' she said.

Her little brother was about to protest, but there was a quiet firmness in Ruth's voice, and he complied without argument. She poured two further cups of coffee and placed them on a tray. Knocking the door, she entered the parlour.

Her mother was in her father's arms. She was crying; racking sobs shook her body and Yosef looked over her shoulder at Jakob, shaking his head. They both turned when they saw Ruth.

'I just brought…'

'Put it down on the table,' Yosef said.

'What's up, Mama,' Ruth said, her face white.

Miriam turned her head. Ruth had never seen her mother cry like this. It was a shock to see tears streaming down her face, her eyes rimmed red. She felt her own tears welling up. Miriam broke away from Yosef and came to her.

'It's the Weichmanns,' she sobbed. 'They're dead. They've been killed.'

'Oh, Mama,' Ruth said, gasping. 'Why?'

'They were shot trying to escape,' Jakob said, glancing at Yosef, both men knowing the truth of it.

Yosef took his daughter's hand, his other arm around his wife.

'There can be no mistake?' Ruth asked Jakob.

'No,' the older man replied. 'We pay lawyers, Aryan lawyers, to make enquiries for us. They deal with the authorities all the time. They never give us the information until they're convinced it's reliable.'

'They were arrested trying to get to Palestine,' Yosef said. 'The lawyer told Jakob they were being brought back to Germany, but they tried to get away. The police shot them.'

'The police? Why would the police shoot people?'

'It was the Gestapo. I just didn't want you to…'

'Papa. I know about the Gestapo. I'm seventeen, not nine. Even Manny knows about the Gestapo.'

'I know, Bubbeleh. I just want to protect you. You shouldn't need to concern yourself with this… this evil.'

'We hear about them every day, Papa. At school, from friends. And I read the newspapers.'

'I'm sorry,' he said, stroking her hair. 'I still think of you as my little girl.'

He didn't tell her to leave the room. He turned to Jakob.

'What else can you tell us?'

'They almost made it to Romania. If they'd got as far as Bulgaria, the chances are they would have reached Palestine. Can you get a message to Itsik and Esther?'

'I don't know. We'll try.'

'The Haganah will already know. They have their own ways. They may have told Itsik by now.'

'It doesn't matter,' Miriam said. 'I'll write to Esther. There will be a way.'

She glanced at Yosef.

'I'm so sorry,' Jakob said. He hesitated, looking a little embarrassed.

'The money…' he said.

'Keep it. Use it to help someone else,' Miriam said. 'That's what Esther would want.'

'Thank you. I'll try and get their bodies back, for burial. I'll let you know.'

'Don't put yourself in danger by it, even though it would be a comfort to Itsik and Esther.'

'I won't.'

He shook Yosef's hand and kissed Miriam and Ruth, hugging them all in turn.

'Thanks for coming,' Yosef said, walking Jakob to the door. 'Shalom, my friend.'

'Aleichem Shalom.'

Jakob turned and walked up the drive.

~~o~~

Memo: Geh.KdoS. ABW 18/06/40 CAC01172.1

For Attention Only: All senior executive officers, Abwehr.

From: Vice Admiral Wilhelm Canaris, Chef der Abwehr.

The Führer and Benito Mussolini met in Munich today. Sources say Il Duce pushed for the Italian occupation of the Rhône valley, and that Corsica, Tunisia, and French Somaliland should be disarmed. The Führer refused his requests, stating that he would do nothing that would prompt a French government-in-exile to form in North Africa or London and that it was essential that the French fleet remained neutral. [END]

~~o~~

Obersturmbannführer Eicke kept the room at the Europäischer for the whole week he was home on leave. Lise visited every day. He was far more accomplished in bed than Rudolf, and better than Franz had been but, no matter how physically satisfied she felt each time she left to walk back to the flat in Lange Reihe, there was always something missing.

It's the sheer wonderment on Rudolf's face, every time he sees me, clothed or naked.

She'd seen the same light in Franz's eyes.

With the Obersturmbannführer, although his eyes drank her in as he watched her undress, it was possession of her that brought him to her bed. And while his hands and mouth knew expertly how to please her, she was sure he did it, at least in part, for the satisfaction of knowing he had the power over her to make her forget Rudolf, or any other man, when she was with him.

And he was always in control. With Rudolf and Franz, it was her who led them on and cooled them off, at her whim. When she was with Arnulf Eicke, he was the one in command, and she wasn't sure that she liked the way it made her feel.

On the third day, she'd deliberately stayed away, in an effort to regain control but, when she'd caved in to her desires by late afternoon, he'd opened the door without recrimination or disappointment and had taken her with an almost casual indifference.

When they'd finished, she lay back on his chest, her breasts still rising and falling sharply as the breath slowly returned to her.

'What do you tell your wife?' she asked him when she could speak, hoping to shake him.

'I tell her I have army business. I'm SS. My wife would never question it.'

The only godsend that made the whole sordid affair bearable was the knowledge that she wouldn't miss him when he'd gone.

It's his coldness.

It left her feeling used, to her surprise.

On the fifth day, he told her he couldn't meet with her.

'It's my wife, you know. I have to spend a little time with her.'

She laughed. Part of her was glad. Some time without him would give her back a modicum of normality.

She telephoned the villa at Drachensee and asked for her mother. A day at home was always a respite from the drudge of being a soldier's wife and now, from the restlessness that the Obersturmbannführer had let loose.

'I'm sorry,' the maid said, 'your mother is away meeting a friend. She left half an hour ago.'

'Oh,' Lise said, the disappointment in her own voice surprising her, 'tell her I'll see her on Sunday.' It was the Obersturmbannführer's last day in Kiel, but he'd be gone by late afternoon and she would stay over with her parents and make an evening of it.

'Who's she meeting?' she asked the maid. 'Not that horrible Hoffmann woman, I hope.'

She heard the maid laugh.

'No. She's having lunch with Frau Baumann, Fräulein Lise,' the maid said. 'In Elmschenhagen. She's usually back by six.'

She put the phone down and ran a bath, and lay soaking in it, imagining the Obersturmbannführer with his wife, doing the same. She had no real sense of jealousy; the man was too arrogant to want any lasting connection with her but, even now, she was looking forward to the thrill she knew she'd feel walking in through the entrance of the Europäischer the next day.

She felt no stab of guilt; her husband's failure to appear home on his last leave, and the memory of his violence on his previous visit, relieved her of that burden. And while the coldness of the Obersturmbannführer sometimes made her shiver, he'd taught her how to maximise her own pleasure, and his, in so many ways.

And she knew that, however good she'd been in bed before, she now had the power to drive almost any man to the brink of madness with desire, should she wish.

CHAPTER 19

[18/06/1940 Tuesday]

Heinrich Güllich wasn't in a good mood; that in itself, was nothing new, but there was a different, brooding element to his current malaise. Having to take a day's holiday for a family event hadn't improved his temper but he'd hardly set foot outside his office since his return and, when he did, it was to snap at one of his junior staff.

It hadn't helped that the SD were dragging their heels releasing the former synagogue records they held. He had muttered his suspicion to his assistant that they had mislaid them and were desperately trying to locate them again.

It's either that, or they don't want us to have them.

The truth of the matter was that the Jewish bitch, whoever she was, had slipped out from underneath Heinrich Güllich's nose, the money with her, and the Gestapo investigator was taking the failure hard.

The Kriminalassistent sat in his office torturing himself with the thought that a mere cleaner had outwitted them.

And the money she stole. Who was it intended for?

He froze. A brief frown furrowed his brow then his face lit up.

'She didn't steal it,' he shouted, thumping the desk.

Carl Meyer jumped at the Kriminalassistent's sudden exclamation. He got up and stood at the open door.

'You gave me a fright, sir. What did you say?'

'She didn't steal it. The money was meant for her all along. The flat was the drop-off, and she was there to pick it up. Frau 'M.N.' is the woman we're looking for!'

'But the Hueber hag said she came once a week to clean for the old Jews, sir. Why would anyone send money to her? At somebody else's home?'

'It must have been a cover. There's something more going on here than meets the eye. It explains everything.'

Carl Meyer's eyes widened.

'Some sort of agent, sir?'

'You've watched too many films, Kamerad,' he said, lighting a cigarette.

He paced up and down.

'No, not an agent,' he muttered, his excitement obvious, 'but she was the bag lady for one Jewish organisation or another. That has narrowed down the search. Finding her will be easy now.'

'It will take ages, sir, checking the records we retrieved from the synagogue, that's if the SD decide to give them to us. She may not even be from Kiel.'

'I have a better idea. Get your coat. We'll grab some Bratwurst on the way.'

~~o~~

Half an hour later, they drew up to the kerb outside number 15, Kleiner Kuhberg. Heinrich Güllich stepped out of the car.

'Sir, why are we back here?' Carl Meyer said, joining him on the pavement. 'She didn't turn up the other day.'

'This place also functions as an unofficial Jewish administration office. There's an old man, Teubner, who acts as their leader. The Judenrat is toothless so the authorities tolerate him and his friends; it helps them to keep an eye on the scum. If something is going on, he'll know about it.'

Carl Meyer followed him up the steps.

Heinrich Güllich thumped on the door. Thirty seconds later, a young man opened it. The Gestapo man flourished his badge and pushed past the youth.

'Get me Jakob Teubner,' he said.

'I'll f-fetch him for you,' he stammered.

They stood looking at the notices on the board.

Missing. Have you seen these men? My brother Solomon and his friend Jankel haven't been seen for two weeks. If you have any information, please contact David Levy via the Jewish Aid Committee office.

There was a picture of the two young men pinned below the text.

Heinrich Güllich laughed. He recognised them. The last time he'd seen them, they'd been lying on the floor of one of the rooms in the basement of the Gestapo building on Düppelstraße, blood oozing from their mouths and ears. It might have had something to do with having their heads stamped on by one of the thugs the Gestapo found useful as persuaders.

They'd been quite dead.

'Perhaps we should contact these Jewish Aid people. There may be a reward for information.'

Carl Meyer burst into laughter.

They were still laughing when Jakob Teubner came down the stairs.

'Can I help you?'

'I hope so, or I'll have a dozen angry SS men here in ten minutes to turn the place over for contraband.'

'There's no need for that. We always cooperate with the police.'

'Ah. But we're not the police, as you'll find out, if you aren't completely honest with us. You have lists of all the Jews in Kiel?'

'Not all of them. Only the ones that attend the synagogue here. Our records were lost at the time of the fire.'

'So, you only have lists of practising Jews. Not the ones who pretend they aren't Jews at all, who like to believe that they are real Germans?'

Jakob bit back a reply.

'What can I do for you?'

'There's a woman we'd like to trace. She is a witness in a case we are currently investigating. We are sure you can help us.'

'What kind of case? Why do you want her?'

'That's no concern of yours but, as you Jews are always whining, I'll tell you. We are investigating the disappearance of an elderly Jewish couple.'

'There seems to be a lot of Jewish people disappearing these days. Why are you interested in this couple?'

Heinrich Güllich stiffened. He was used to Jews cowering from him in his dealings with them, but this old bearded Jewmonger appeared to be unafraid; this in the same week that the Jewish bitch they were looking for was sitting somewhere, laughing at him.

The back of his hand connected with Jakob's cheek before the old man could react, and he staggered sideways, holding his jaw.

'Now that we have established the parameters of this interview,' the Gestapo man said, 'perhaps you would be kind enough to answer a few questions.'

~~o~~

Jakob Teubner rubbed his face, but he nodded, saying nothing.

'We are investigating the disappearance of a couple called Weichmann. Do you know them?'

'Yes,' Jakob said. 'They are members of our congregation.'

'There's a woman who cleans for them. In her forties, mousy brown hair, average height. Does it ring any bells with you?'

'I wouldn't have thought they would have had a cleaner. They were modest people, and self-sufficient.'

'Interesting you should say 'were'. Do you know anything about their disappearance?'

'I've heard rumours.'

'And what might these rumours be?'

'That they'd been arrested, and were in a camp, somewhere in Poland. That they'd been killed. I've been trying to retrieve their bodies for burial, if it's true.'

The Gestapo man grunted. Jakob couldn't tell if the Kriminalassistent believed him.

'I need to see your records.'

'All of them?'

'Yes, for completeness, but we are most interested in those whose surname begins with an 'N'.'

'That should narrow it down a bit. I'll go and get the ledger.'

Jakob tried to make himself breathe again.

How have they found out about Miriam and the money, and that her surname begins with the letter 'N'?

'My assistant will accompany you,' he heard the senior Gestapo officer say. 'We don't want you *losing* any pages now, do we?'

'By all means,' Jakob said, cursing himself. It ruled out the only action that he could think of that would prevent Miriam's name being found.

The younger Gestapo man didn't let him out of his sight while he collected the records from his office. They returned with the thin, hardbacked notebook that had taken the place of the heavy, leather-bound ledger that the Sicherheitsdienst had stolen.

The senior investigator almost snatched it from him, and Jakob watched as he opened it, and flicked to the 'N's.

Jakob listened as the Gestapo officer read out the names, his finger sliding down the list.

'Nachelski, Nachfalski, Nadelmann.'

He looked up.

'Nadelmann. Mascha Nadelmann. What do you know about her, old man?'

Jakob felt bad answering, but he couldn't see any way round it.

'About forty, married to Efraim. Two children.'

'Does she have a daughter?'

'No, they're both boys. Why?'

'I'll ask the questions,' he grunted, and returned to the ledger.

'Sir, can I have a word?'

Heinrich Güllich spun round to look at his assistant.

'What is it?' he said, scowling.

Carl Meyer swallowed but leaned over to the Kriminalassistent's ear and whispered something, cupping his hand to prevent Jakob hearing.

The senior Gestapo man nodded and turned back to Jakob.

'Does this woman have a niece?'

'I'm not sure. Not living in Kiel, but her family is from Lübeck.'

Heinrich Güllich pencilled a mark next to the woman's name and resumed his examination of the ledger.

Jakob caught only the odd name, muttered under his breath.

'Neubürger... Neuschüler... Niederländer... Nohlen.'

The Gestapo man looked up.

'Mendel Nohlen. What does his wife do?'

'She used to be a secretary in the Rathaus. She's a cleaner now.'

Jakob frowned. *Why just some of the names?*

'Does she have any daughters, or nieces?' he heard the Kriminalassistent ask.

'Yes. A daughter and two nieces. Twin girls.'

'What age are they?'

'Thirteen, fourteen, I suppose. They grow up so fast these days.'

The Kriminalassistent made another note in the ledger.

Jakob realised that one of the neighbours must have seen Miriam at the flat with Ruth. He knew that, somehow, he had to warn the Nussbaums.

'What about this woman,' the Gestapo man said, interrupting his thoughts. 'Maja Nowosilsky.'

'She's older. In her fifties. She has a grown-up daughter.'

'She's Polish, ja?'

'Her parents were from Poland.'

With sudden clarity, it dawned on Jakob.

Mascha. Maya. Even Mendel. They have Miriam's initials.

He had to buy time. It felt wrong to him, but the more people he could convince them to investigate, the longer it would take. It would allow him time to get in touch with Miriam or Yosef.

They must have been on something Miriam left behind. An item of jewellery perhaps.

He answered questions about another six or seven women and in all but one case, he was able to muddy the waters enough to keep them on the list.

Jakob felt his stomach tighten as the Gestapo man's finger reached Miriam's name.

'Miriam Nussbaum,' he heard the man say. 'I suppose she has a niece somewhere in Germany.'

'I don't know,' he replied, his voice remarkably even. 'She's originally from Altona. She does have a daughter though.'

He would have liked to have kept this information from him, but it was in the ledger, and he knew that it wouldn't be hard to find.

'What age is the daughter?'

'Seventeen or eighteen, perhaps.'

'Ah. This sounds promising. Was she employed as a cleaner?'

'I doubt it. She is the full-time cook and housekeeper for General Kästner and his family.'

The Gestapo man lit a cigarette.

'I'm surprised that a German Army officer would keep a Jewish housekeeper.'

'I'm told she is one of the best cooks in the city.'

'A Jewish cook though. This general is willing to risk his life, and the life of his family, being tended to by a treacherous Jew? Add her to the list; Jews are greedy. Perhaps she likes to make extra money on her days off.'

Jakob shrugged. Saying too much, in a bid to lead them away from Miriam, might make them suspicious.

He watched the man make a note on the page, and then count the number of names with a mark against them.

'I'll keep this,' the Gestapo man said, holding up the ledger.

'Do as you must, but may I have it back when you're finished with it? I'm sure your colleagues at the Rathaus wouldn't be pleased if we didn't keep proper records.'

'Old man, we'll do what we want with it; I'll burn it, if it so pleases me. And you may yet see the inside of a camp. In the meantime, don't contact any of these people. We'll be watching you.'

~~o~~

Jakob looked out of the second-floor window, careful to avoid being seen. The car the two Gestapo men had got into had driven away but another black Opel was parked further up Kleiner Kuhberg, on the opposite side of the street. Jakob couldn't make out if there was anyone in it, but he couldn't risk going to the Nussbaums' cottage to warn Miriam that they were watching him, and the phones to the Jewish properties in Kleiner Kuhberg had been disconnected a few months ago. He thought of sending someone else, but the young man who had answered the door was too nervous to brazen it out if he was challenged. He prayed that the Gestapo officer would go through the list in the same order as the ledger.

His only comfort was that it was now late afternoon and that the men wouldn't work into the evening on what was a routine case.

~~o~~

Jakob Teubner was wrong. By the time darkness fell, the two Gestapo officers had visited half of the women on the list, leaving terror and bewilderment in their wake, and no small measure of disarray and damage from their indiscriminate searches.

When Ruth arrived at school the next morning, Jakob was waiting for her, and drew her aside.

'Pretend you are sick and ask to be sent home,' he told her. 'Make sure you get a note from the teacher. I have an urgent message for your parents. Tell them…'

He hesitated.

'Tell them,' he continued, trusting her, 'that the Gestapo will be calling to ask about the Weichmanns and that I have told them nothing. They have information that you and your mother may have visited the flat. They believe she's their cleaner.'

Ruth paled, and her eyes widened with fright.

'Can you do that for me, Ruth?' Jakob said, laying a hand gently on her shoulder.

'Yes,' she said, in a voice fighting fear. 'Are we in trouble?'

'Not if your mama keeps a clear head. Tell her to admit to visiting the Weichmanns but not in the last week or so.'

He placed his hand on her head and smiled. 'Now go. God be with you all.'

Ruth turned and ran down the steps, but Jakob smiled when he saw her slow to a brisk walk, so as not to attract attention.

CHAPTER 20

'Sir, that's them, apart from this Nussbaum woman. None of them seem to fit, and she's the least likely of all.'

'She has a daughter the right age,' Heinrich Güllich said. 'We'll see what turns up. What's the address?'

'Hamburger Chaussee, 244.'

'An expensive part of town, Kriminalassistentanwärter. They're all plush houses out there.'

'Yes, sir. I did a quick check on this General Kästner. He's Abwehr. The woman and her husband are employed by the family.'

Heinrich Güllich grunted.

'He was regular army but retired in '33,' Carl Meyer continued, 'then joined the Abwehr as liaison officer with the Baltic Fleet Command. Asking around, he's highly respected by the Kriegsmarine and by local party officials. He's a little eccentric, especially in relation to his Jewish employees, but it's tolerated because of his standing. He's a close friend of Admiral Canaris, the head of the Abwehr.'

'I know who Canaris is,' the Kriminalassistent said, glowering at the junior man.

'Will we have to be careful, sir?'

Heinrich Güllich had been thinking along the same lines, but he baulked at his assistant's assumption that he would treat a suspect in a different manner just because they were in the pay of an unpatriotic general who didn't know that *all Jews were the same*, to be treated like vermin.

'No,' he snarled. 'We are investigators of the Secret State Police and we will not be influenced by status or position.'

The Kriminalassistent knew it was Scheiße. He'd been warned off looking into high-ranking party officials on more than one investigation, but this case was a splinter that had worked its way under his fingernail.

They passed the brickworks and could just see the waters of Drachensee beyond, through the trees.

'220, sir. We're almost there.'

The car drew up at the kerb just short of the Kästner house.

As they walked down the driveway, Heinrich Güllich took in the ivy-covered brickwork of the imposing house.

'It must pay well, being a general, eh?'

'It's a family home, sir. The general's father, Admiral Kästner, owned it before him.'

Despite himself, he was impressed with the young investigator's research.

'That will be the Jews' accommodation over there,' he said, pointing at the cottage. What he presumed to be the Kästners' car stood in front of the adjoining garage.

Their knock on the cottage door was unanswered, but Heinrich Güllich thought he caught a fleeting view of a face in the window next to the side door of the big house.

'Perhaps they're at work, sir,' he said, pointing to the Kästners' house.

'More than likely,' Heinrich Güllich said.

Carl Meyer began to walk towards the back door of the big house. His boss put his hand out and stopped him.

'We'll go round to the front. It looks better.'

And it will have these Jewish rats squirming.

They walked around to the front of the house and climbed the steps to the front door. A distant ringing sounded when Carl Meyer pressed the brass bell push.

A middle-aged man answered the door. The butler, the young Gestapo man assumed.

'Can I help you?'

'Yes,' Heinrich Güllich said, showing his identity card. 'Geheime Staatspolizei, Kriminalassistent Güllich. This is Kriminalassistentanwärter Meyer.'

The butler took the man's card and looked at it. He handed it back.

'Do you wish to speak to the General? He's currently at Naval Headquarters, and Frau Kästner is out.'

'No. We don't wish to bother him. We wish to speak to Miriam Nussbaum. I believe she works here.'

'That would be my wife. She's the housekeeper. I'm Yosef Nussbaum.'

Heinrich Güllich stared at Yosef. The man had flinched when his wife's name had been mentioned but had answered with calm reserve. He either felt very secure in his position, or they'd been warned.

He pushed past him and entered the hallway.

'Where is she?'

'I believe she's in the kitchen.'

'And where would that be, Jew?'

'Through here, sir,' he said.

Heinrich Güllich looked at him sharply, but the man's deference didn't appear to be loaded with sarcasm.

He's just well-trained.

He followed Yosef Nussbaum through to the kitchen. The Jew's wife was at the table, kneading bread dough, her hands covered in flour. She looked up when they entered.

She appears nervous, Heinrich Güllich thought, *but not overly so*. Almost everyone felt uneasy when the Gestapo called, more so if they were Jews.

Carl Meyer, at a nod from the Kriminalassistent, ushered Yosef back into the hall, telling him to wait.

~~o~~

Carl Meyer stepped back into the kitchen and closed the door behind him.

'Miriam Nussbaum?' he heard Heinrich Güllich ask the woman.

'Yes. I'm Miriam Nussbaum.'

'We'd like to ask you a few questions.'

'Do I have any choice?'

'Sit down,' he said, pointing to the chair.

She did as she was told.

He perched on the table close to her, half sitting, towering over her. He lit a cigarette.

'Do you know the Weichmanns, of...' – he looked at his notebook – '... 35 Jungmannstraße?'

Carl Meyer smiled. His superior knew the address, but all his little tricks, like the glance at the notebook, were part of his armoury designed to intimidate a witness.

'Yes,' she said. 'They are the parents of Itsik Weichmann. My friend Esther is married to Itsik.'

The young Gestapo man's pulse raced. He stared at the woman and, as if she sensed his gaze, she turned towards him.

He almost blurted it out but stopped himself.

It is her. The woman at the flat. It has to be.

'Have you ever visited them?'

The tone of Heinrich Güllich's voice remained remarkably neutral and Carl Meyer made a mental note of another lesson in the investigator's craft.

'Yes. Of course. Esther asked me to call in from time to time, when she left for Palestine a few years ago. I try and go once a week.'

'And recently? You've seen them?'

'Not since...' – she frowned – '... late May, I think.'

'But you've been to their flat since then?'

'I tried to visit, but they weren't there.'

'How many times did you go back?'

'Once. No, twice.'

'Always on your own?'

Miriam's eyes narrowed a little.

'My daughter went with me on one occasion.'

'When was that?'

'Let me see, it must have been two, no, three weeks ago. It was a Saturday because Ruth wasn't at school.'

'And you were never in the flat?'

'No. A neighbour let us into the building as she left, but when we knocked on the flat door, there was no one in.'

~~o~~

Miriam glanced at the younger Gestapo man. He was staring at her.

The man who was at the window. He recognises me. Why did I turn round at the end of the road?

'And you just left? You don't have a key?'

'No,' Miriam said. 'Why should I? I just visited them to keep an eye on them, for my friend.'

'And that was the last time you visited?'

Miriam weighed up her answer in the brief seconds before answering.

'Yes.'

'You were never in Jungmannstraße at any time after that?'

'No, well, yes, I may have walked along Jungmannstraße since then, but I didn't visit the flat.'

'Really? How convenient. And why were you walking along Jungmannstraße?'

'I was going into town that day, to pick up some haberdashery; buttons for a dress I was altering. My husband asked me to pick up something at the hardware store for him. Itsik's shop, well, it's not his shop now, but you know what I mean. It was closed; it's their half day but I thought that the one on Knooper Weg might be open.'

She knew that they both closed Wednesday afternoons; she'd heard people complain about the inconvenience.

~~o~~

Carl Meyer traced the route in his head. Itsik Weichmann's former shop was at the bottom of Brunswicker Straße. If she'd walked up Gerhard Straße, she could have taken Jungmannstraße to reach Knooper Weg. It was feasible.

'And did you see anyone you knew when you were in Jungmannstraße?'

'I don't think so,' Miriam said, her brow furrowing.

'So you didn't wave to anyone?'

'I suppose it's possible, but I can't say I remember.'

'And this something you were to purchase. What was it?'

'A catch. For a cupboard. He gave me the old one to take with me, to make sure I got the right size, but the other shop was closed too.'

'And where is this catch now?'

'I don't know. I gave it back to my husband. He must still have it.'

Heinrich Güllich nodded to Carl Meyer.

'Fetch the husband,' he said.

They waited in silence until the young Gestapo man returned with Yosef.

'Take her out,' the Kriminalassistent said.

Miriam rose, almost stumbling. Carl Meyer led her through to the hall and told her to wait.

'I have a couple of questions for you,' the Gestapo investigator said to Yosef. 'Did you send your wife to buy something for you recently? Last Wednesday perhaps?'

Yosef touched his chin for a few seconds, as if deep in thought.

'Yes,' he said. 'I asked her to pick up a catch for a cupboard. It was broken. I gave her the old one, so that she'd know what to buy.'

'Did she get it?'

'No, she didn't. She was too late getting to the hardware store. They're closed Wednesday afternoons. I got it myself a couple of days later.'

'And where is this catch now?'

'It's on the cupboard. I fixed it.'

'Show me.'

The Gestapo man followed Yosef through to the hall, past a puzzled Miriam. Yosef opened the small cupboard under the stairs and pointed to the shiny new catch.

'All right,' Heinrich Güllich said, rattled for the first time.

He turned to the Nussbaums.

'Come with us. We are going to search the cottage. You have the key?'

'It will be open,' Yosef said. 'We rarely lock it.'

'Ha. Such a genteel neighbourhood. I'm surprised they allow Jews like you to live here.'

The Nussbaums didn't respond. They followed the Gestapo man out of the back door. Carl Meyer walked behind them.

They left nothing undisturbed. In the kitchen, all the containers were overturned, and a mess of flour, sugar, split peas, and dried fruit littered the floor. In the front room, the coal scuttle was tipped onto the carpet and throughout the house, drawers and cupboards were emptied, their contents left strewn everywhere. The Nussbaums were made to look on in silence.

'Keys. Do you have any keys?'

Yosef handed Heinrich Güllich the bunch he always carried. They were nearly all for locks in the Kästner house. Miriam handed them her small collection of keys, tied on a loop of string. There were only four.

'What are these for,' the Gestapo man asked her.

'The front and back doors for here, and for the big house.'

'The fools trust you with the keys for their home? They're asking to be robbed.'

He took out a set of keys from his pocket, and held them up, comparing them with those on her key ring. None matched.

A sharp knock came at the door. Yosef glanced at the Gestapo man, who nodded. He walked over and opened it. The mistress stood on the doorstep.

~~o~~

Maria Kästner frowned.

'Yosef,' she said, 'why are you and Miriam not working? And why is Ruth sitting in my drawing room?'

Yosef closed his eyes for a second and, with a minimum of movement, shook his head. From behind him, he heard footsteps.

'Ah,' Heinrich Güllich said, easing Yosef to one side. 'You must be Frau Kästner.'

He held out his hand.

'I am Heinrich Güllich, Kriminalassistent, Geheime Staatspolizei. Did I hear you say the Nussbaums' daughter is in your house?'

Maria swallowed. She felt her stomach tighten.

'Yes,' she muttered, as if the Gestapo man wouldn't hear it.

'Perhaps you would be kind enough to ask her to come over here,' he said. 'My colleague will accompany you.'

Maria glanced through the doorway to the Nussbaums' kitchen. From the little she could see the normally tidy room was in complete disarray.

'Now, please,' the Gestapo man said.

She hurried across to the house and told Ruth to go the cottage. She watched as the younger Gestapo man led her roughly by the arm.

She'd arrived home to find the house empty apart from a pale Ruth, sitting alone, staring out of the window of the drawing room. She'd rushed through to the kitchen to ask Miriam what was going on, to find it empty. She'd noticed that the Nussbaums' back door was ajar and had stormed over to demand that they should provide an explanation for their behaviour. She wished now that she'd spoken to Ruth first, and had thought her actions through.

Erich will be furious with me.

~~o~~

Carl Meyer ushered Ruth into the cottage. When she saw Heinrich Güllich standing in the debris of the kitchen, she froze.

'What happened here…?'

'You don't need to concern yourself with that,' Heinrich Güllich said. 'When the Gestapo search a house, we do it thoroughly. Now, I must ask you a few questions. Your parents can stay but they will not say a word. And you will look at me, not them, when I am talking to you. Understood?'

'Yes,' she said, her voice barely audible.

'Speak up, girl,' Heinrich Güllich said.

'Yes,' she repeated, a little louder.

'That's more like it,' the Gestapo man said, smiling.

Carl Meyer thought it a masterful performance. Having the parents present and seeing their reaction to his questioning of their daughter was genius. Their facial expressions would provide as much information as her answers.

'Now, did you visit Herr and Frau Weichmann's flat with your mother, a few weeks ago,' Heinrich Güllich asked, smiling, the softness of his voice belying its menace.

Ruth tried to glance at her mother, but the Kriminalassistent leaned forward and gripped her jaw with one hand, his strong fingers keeping her facing him, and making her grimace with pain.

'Now, without help from your Jewish whore of a mother, answer the question.'

'Yes,' Ruth said, tears pooling in her eyes.

'Sorry, we didn't quite catch that.' He gripped harder.

Ruth whimpered. 'Yes,' she blurted out.

'And did you see the Weichmanns?'

'No. They weren't in.'

'Ah, but you went into the flat?'

'No. We couldn't get in. Mama didn't have a key.'

'But you got into the building, didn't you?'

'Y-yes,' Ruth said, stumbling on her words. 'A neighbour let us in. We thought the Weichmanns' bell might be broken, but there was no answer when we knocked the door.'

Carl Meyer had watched the Jew-bitch's parents while his boss questioned her. They flinched when the older investigator had gripped her face, his knuckles white. And they had bowed their heads when he'd asked her about her visit, almost freezing as she answered but, unless he'd imagined it, they'd let out long, slow breaths when she'd finished.

Heinrich Güllich opened his mouth to speak when the door burst open.

An older man in a Wehrmacht general's uniform stood at the door, his face red and his eyes blazing. Frau Kästner followed, white-faced.

'What the hell is going on here?'

Heinrich Güllich stepped forward and pulled his card from his pocket.

'Geheime Staatspolizei. Kriminalassistent Güllich.'

He held out his hand. The General ignored it and walked to the centre of the room.

'You'd better have a very good explanation for this desecration of *my* property.'

'Sir, we are conducting a criminal investigation. Your staff are witnesses, perhaps even suspects. We must not be impeded in our inquiry.'

'Do you know who I am?'

'Yes, sir. I know exactly who you are, which is why I find it strange that you should be trying to protect filthy criminals such as these…'

The Gestapo officer gestured towards the Nussbaums.

'I don't believe your accusations for one minute,' the General said, 'and I will not have my staff harassed in this way. I'm going to make a couple of phone calls. When I get back, it will not be in your best interest if you or your colleague are still on my property.'

'With respect, Herr General, you cannot interfere with a criminal investigation, no matter who you are.'

'We'll see what Herr Heydrich has to say about that,' the General said, and stormed out. His wife followed him.

Carl Meyer turned pale. He looked over at his boss. He'd never seen the Kriminalassistent look so unsure. Up until the mention of the Reich security chief, he'd watched with pride as Heinrich Güllich had stood up to the pompous general.

'Sir?' he said.

The older Gestapo man looked around.

'We're finished here anyway,' he said, spitting on the floor.

He turned to the Nussbaums, glaring at Miriam.

'We'll be back for you, soon, Jew-bitch. And your family.' He spat again. 'Your general can't protect his little Judenhund or her litter forever, you know, no matter how important he thinks he is. And when that happens, I'll make sure I deal with you myself.'

He motioned for his assistant to leave and followed him out, slamming the door behind him.

~~o~~

The Nussbaums stood frozen for a second, unable to move, then Yosef reached his arms around his wife and daughter, holding them tight as they sobbed.

They stood in the centre of their wrecked kitchen. A leg was broken on one of the chairs, and there were a couple of smashed jars on the floor, their contents splashed up the wall.

A soft knock at the door broke the silence.

Yosef released his wife and daughter and opened it. The General stood, a mixture of anger and sadness on his face.

'Yosef. Albert said they'd gone. Are you all right? How are Miriam and Ruth? Maria told me everything.'

'Come in, sir. We are all unharmed. Just a bit shaken. It's lucky Manny was at a friend's house.'

The General looked around.

'This is terrible,' he said. 'They'll pay for this.'

'Oh, don't worry, sir. We can have this cleared up in no time at all.'

'Is it just here?'

'No, sir. It's the whole house, but this is the worst, because of the flour and the eggs and the broken jars.'

'I'll give you a hand to clear up.'

'No, sir, that would never do. You've done more than enough, getting rid of them for us.' Yosef lowered his voice. 'I only worry that they'll come back.'

'They won't,' the General replied under his breath. 'I'll make sure of that. Admiral Canaris knows Heydrich well. I've asked him to have a word. With any luck, that Güllich fellow and his sidekick will be sweeping the streets tomorrow.'

'That would be wonderful, sir, though perhaps a little ambitious.'

The General looked at his employee and laughed. Yosef smiled. It was a release. Miriam and Ruth looked at them, bemused.

'Pour the General and I something to drink, Miriam,' he said, 'and pour one for yourself. And I think that Ruth should have a small one, too, for the shock.'

~~o~~

Miriam, in a daze, complied. She found four unbroken glasses in the cupboard and a bottle of brandy that had survived the search and poured four measures. She handed the larger two to her husband and the General, and the smallest one to Ruth.

They all drank. Ruth took a tentative sip from her glass, coughing with her first swallow. Miriam felt the warm glow reach her stomach and settle her racing heart. She watched Yosef and the General put their heads back and down their glasses in one and realised that their employer had been scared too.

'Sir, they will come back, won't they?'

'Not if I can help it, Miriam. I've had a word with someone high up who can sort it out.' He turned to Yosef.

'I must go. I need to placate Maria. It has been quite a shock for her. She is distraught that she mentioned Ruth being in the house.'

'She wasn't to know, sir. It couldn't be helped.'

'No, of course. But all the same. She feels bad about it.'

He slipped out of the door.

'He saved us again,' Miriam said. 'I don't know how long he can keep protecting us. Have the Haganah got back to you yet?'

'No, it will be months. And I haven't been able to get in touch with the Americans.'

'Can we not just make a run for it ourselves?' Ruth asked.

Miriam and Yosef turned to face their daughter, surprised at her question.

'Darling, it would be difficult, and almost suicidal if we failed.'

'It couldn't be much worse than this,' she said, looking around at the remains of the kitchen.

'You'll be surprised how soon we can tidy this up if we all help. We must try and get the worst of it cleared before Manny comes home. Papa will collect him when it's time.'

'I was so frightened, Mama, that I'd say the wrong thing.'

'You were the bravest girl. Coming home and warning us, and then answering all their questions perfectly.'

They'd had little time to get their stories straight. Ruth had arrived a few minutes before they heard the footsteps on the gravel and had seen the Gestapo men knock on the door of the cottage. She'd delivered her message and Yosef had told her to go to the drawing room, out of the way.

'Do what you were doing,' he'd told Miriam. 'I'll get the door if they come to the front.'

And, when they fetched her, Ruth had somehow known what to say. That was a miracle in itself, but Yosef also had the presence of mind to confirm Miriam's reason for being in Jungmannstraße, although he wasn't sure the two Gestapo men were convinced; they'd been lucky that it had been half-day Wednesday when Miriam had been at the Weichmanns' home.

As for the keys, Miriam knew it was fortunate that she'd returned them to the shoe outside the flat. If they'd found them in her possession…

They'd had further extraordinary luck, too, during the search of the house. The latest copy of the KJF was tucked inside an old magazine. *If they'd discovered that, it would have been harder for the General to intervene…*

Yosef rolled his sleeves up and sighed.

'There is no point in putting it off,' he said.

Miriam fetched a brush and bucket to pick up the broken shards of glass and stoneware, but he took it from her.

'Go and finish over at the big house,' he said, 'then come back as soon as you can. Ruth and I will make a start here.'

Numbly, Miriam left to complete the preparations for the Kästners' evening meal.

CHAPTER 21

'What made you tell the Gestapo about Ruth?' the General said.

'Frau Hoffmann's driver dropped me off,' Maria Kästner said. 'How was I to know the Nussbaums were being investigated?'

'Maria, they're not just employees, and they've just been subjected to the most horrendous ordeal of their lives.'

'As I have. I mean, Gestapo. In our house.'

'At least they left our kitchen intact,' the General snapped. 'And imagine what would have happened if Albert hadn't phoned me.'

As soon as he'd seen the Gestapo arrive, the Kästners' driver had slipped out, walked to the phone box, and made a call to Naval Headquarters. He told Captain Bauer that the General was needed urgently at home. Erich Kästner had left for Drachensee immediately.

Maria said nothing and looked away.

'No,' he said, staring at her in horror, 'You surely don't believe that it would have been better if I hadn't intervened, do you?'

'Of course not,' she said, exasperated, 'but we'll never hear the end of this, the way you spoke to them. You could have handled it with more diplomacy.'

'I could also have shot these criminals, breaking into my house like that, without a warrant.'

'Are you blind? They're part of the forces of law and order, and they don't need a warrant to arrest people like…' Her voice trailed off.

'You mean like the Nussbaums. Jews. You're right. But this is on my property, so they'll have to go through me first.'

'That's the problem. One day they will, if you keep fighting them. And where will that leave us?'

'I keep telling you, it won't come to that. And if all you're worried about is the neighbours and that countess of yours, I'm sorry, but they can think what they like.'

'It's easy for you to say that. You don't mix with anyone other than your Kriegsmarine people and the Nussbaums.'

'That's not true. I have close friends. Oskar, Doctor Speer, and Dieter Maas. And don't forget Canaris.'

'Hmmph,' she said. 'Doctor Speer and that Dieter Maas fellow are as bad as you, and as for Oskar von Friedeburg; he understands the importance of respect for the authorities, unlike the rest of you, but the women he associates with…'

The General laughed. He couldn't fault her assessment of his friends.

'I'm glad you find it funny. One day you'll wish you'd taken this all much more seriously.'

'Oh, I do,' he said. 'Make no mistake about that.'

He turned and left the room. He knew he'd left her infuriated with him, but he couldn't stomach her lack of empathy for the Nussbaums.

He thought of calling round to the cottage again but thought better of it.

'The office,' he told his driver, as the private held the staff car door open.

~~o~~

Heinrich Güllich brooded most of the way back until they reached the crossing of Holtenauer and Jungmannstraße. He told Carl Meyer to take a left and instructed him to park outside the Weichmanns' building. The door was opened for them by a resident on the second floor.

'The Jew-bitch is lying. And the Jew-bitch daughter. What I'd like to do to that young one to make her talk…'

Carl Meyer nodded, but he was worried; it was unusual for his boss to let matters get to him.

What madness will it lead to?

'Just because this General is flavour of the month with the intelligence services and the verdammte navy,' Heinrich Güllich ranted on, wheezing as he climbed the stairs, 'it doesn't mean his filthy Jew friends should get away with stealing from the Third Reich.'

'You're right, sir. I watched the parents while you were questioning the daughter. Their sense of relief when she confirmed her mother's story was palpable.'

'I'd hoped you'd have the wit to keep an eye on them. Perhaps I've underestimated you. We should give you a little interrogation of your own to do, sometime. Perhaps you should start with the Hueber woman. I'm sure she knows more.'

They'd reached the top landing but, this time, the door across the landing from the Weichmanns was firmly closed.

'Ha. She's learned her lesson,' the Kriminalassistent said.

Frau Hueber didn't answer when they rang the bell. Heinrich Güllich paced back and forward, fuming.

She's staying with relatives, most likely, until the investigation is over, Carl Meyer thought. He tried to hide his disappointment.

Heinrich Güllich unlocked the Weichmanns' door with the spare key he'd taken from Frau Hueber, then stopped.

'Have a look around,' he said. 'See if you can find another key to the Weichmanns' flat hidden somewhere. The Nussbaum woman must have got in somehow.'

Carl Meyer looked in all the places where a key could be secreted and, like Ruth Nussbaum, three weeks before, the last place he looked was in the shoe. This time, when the shoe was upended, the ring of keys bounced on the floor and eluded his desperate grasp, falling through the railings to the bottom of the stairwell.

~~o~~

'Fool,' Heinrich Güllich said, but he was smiling.

So, the woman could have had access. Everything else is a lie too.

He looked over the bannister and watched as his assistant rushed down the stairs.

'Be careful how you pick them up,' he shouted. 'We can get fingerprints from them.'

He heard Carl Meyer puffing his way back up the three flights again. He lit a cigarette while he waited. When the younger man reached the landing, his breath rasping, Heinrich Güllich held out his hand and took the keys from him, checking that one of them opened the lock.

He reached inside his coat and pulled a small brown envelope out. He dropped the keys into it, before returning it to his pocket.

'This is why we always wear gloves, Kriminalassistentanwärter,' he said. 'We'll see how clever the Jew-bitch is now. Have someone come over and check the rest of the place for prints and see if we can get any off the wrapping paper.'

'How will we know if any of them match the Nussbaum woman? We can't take prints from her now.'

Heinrich Güllich put his hand in his pocket and pulled out a hairbrush.

'I took this from the woman's dressing table, and another one from the daughter's bedroom. Have them dusted when we get back.'

Carl Meyer smiled and noted the Kriminalassistent's requests in his notebook. He followed the older man into the flat.

Heinrich Güllich took another look around, even though he knew there was nothing else to find. He opened a cupboard door and froze.

He looked in the remaining cupboards.

'Meyer,' he said. 'Have a look here.'

'Yes, sir. It's a cupboard.'

'Very perceptive, but what kind of cupboard?'

'Wood, sir?'

'Like what you have between your ears? No. It's almost empty. So are all the rest, but the Weichmanns left in a hurry, carrying next to nothing. So why is there nothing left?'

'Someone came in and emptied it, sir?'

'Yes. Somebody who knew they wouldn't be back.'

'The Weichmanns must have left her a note when they left, sir,' the young Gestapo man said, a hint of triumph in his voice.

'That's right, Meyer. That first time she came to the flat, with her daughter, she found it. She returned to the flat on several occasions, removing some of the foodstuffs and household goods on each visit, but she wouldn't take risks like that for the odd packet of sugar, when she works at the Kästner house, where there are no shortages.'

'She knew the money was coming, sir?'

'No, I doubt it, because we have the letter that told her about it. But it was addressed to the Weichmanns' flat, so I think she went there regularly to check for mail from the Weichmanns' daughter-in-law, because it was safer than having it sent to the cottage. If she'd received news that the Weichmanns had made it to Palestine, she would have never gone back there again.'

'So, when she turned up and found the money, it was a shock to her?'

'Correct, Kamerad. I'll wager there was a note in the package, confirming that the Weichmanns had been caught, and the money was to be used to try and get them released. Despite everything, she didn't panic, even when we showed up, and then the whole Jew-pig family stuck to their story. They might assume that they're safe now, but there may be a way to get them.'

'How, sir? If what that Jew-loving General Kästner says is true, we can't go near them.'

'The money, my young friend. The money. It must be somewhere.'

~~o~~

[20/06/1940 Thursday]

Lise cried when Obersturmbannführer Eicke left her in the hotel. He'd given her a perfunctory peck on the cheek and told her he would look her up when he was next on leave and closed the door behind him.

But they were tears of frustration, not sadness. She'd thought she'd done enough to make him want to stay, even if he couldn't, but he made it clear that she'd been nothing but a plaything that he could leave behind and pick up again whenever it suited him.

She hoped she'd have the strength to turn him away if there was a next time. It would redress the balance a little. She tidied herself up and left the hotel, hailing a taxi.

'Drachensee 242,' she said to the driver.

~~o~~

[21/06/1940 Friday]

'I've had a word with Heydrich. He says you should have no further problems. He didn't go quite as far as an apology, and he did hint that he couldn't hold off the hounds forever.'

'Thank you, Canaris,' the General said, slumping in relief. He'd been waiting for the admiral to call for two days since their conversation on the day of the Gestapo raid.

'It wasn't just me. Heydrich said he'd been ordered to the Reich Ministry. The head of the Baltic fleet had been on the phone to Himmler about it, and Himmler had lambasted Heydrich. You have friends.'

'As long as it works.'

'It's a one-time deal, Erich. Tell the Nussbaums to keep their heads down. This Güllich fellow has been warned that he'll end up in some Godless hole in Poland if the local Gestapo pull another stunt like that *unless* they are a hundred per cent sure of themselves.'

'I'll warn them. This all happened because the swine murdered Itsik's parents.'

'I know. I hear that heads will roll.'

'Oh, why?'

'Don't get carried away. It has nothing to do with your involvement. Those Gestapo officers in Czechoslovakia have killed off a goose that laid little golden eggs for the Third Reich.'

The General gave out a bitter laugh.

'Of course,' he said. 'Alive, their family would have continued to send money to try and have them released.'

'Exactly. But not now. And foreign currency is in short supply in Germany.'

'It will be of no comfort to Itsik's family, or to the Nussbaums.'

'No. I don't suppose it will.'

The admiral paused.

'Take care, my friend.'

'I will. And thank you again.'

~~o~~

Heinrich Güllich threw a mug across his office. It smashed against the wall, and a couple of shards landed on Carl Meyer's shoe.

'You knew it was coming, sir. It could have been worse.'

'Worse!' the older man shouted. 'Worse! We've been forced to drop the case. What could have been worse? Eh?'

'We could have been carpeted, sir. I've never seen the Kriminaldirektor so livid, sir.'

Heinrich Güllich glared at the younger man.

Carl Meyer flinched, but he could understand his boss's anger. For the Kriminaldirektor, the head of Gestapo in Kiel, to call the Kriminalassistent into his office was unusual; Heinrich Güllich rarely put a foot wrong.

'Even if takes me the whole of the thousand-year Reich,' the Kriminalassistent shouted, thumping his fist on the desk, 'I'll have those Jewish scum and their Jew-loving friends.'

'Surely we can't continue investigating them, sir? We'll be crucified if we get caught.'

'We'll keep our eyes and ears open. Watch them from a distance. They'll make a mistake, sooner or later. They'll try and use the money for something, wait and see. Remember, if we can get something watertight, we can go after them.'

'Yes, sir.' Carl Meyer wondered how easy it would be to get transferred. He wanted no part of an investigation that could go so horribly wrong. And he was sure that the Kriminalassistent was mistaken about the money. They hadn't found it when they searched the cottage.

'Don't worry, Kriminalassistentanwärter,' Heinrich Güllich said, giving him a withering glare. 'We'll be patient, and careful. Your career will not be at all affected.'

'I wasn't...' Carl Meyer blustered.

'Yes, you were. But don't worry about your prospects,' the Kriminalassistent said with a sneer, 'we can play the long game. We'll get them, even if we have to wait until they are the last Jews in Germany.'

'If you say so, sir. What can we do in the meantime?'

'Did you check if the results were back from the fingerprinting yet? Were there any on the keys?'

'Sorry, sir. Did you not see them? I put them on your desk.'

Heinrich Güllich glared at his assistant but said nothing. He sifted through the pile of papers in front of him and pulled out a large manila envelope. He opened it and extracted a single sheet of typewritten paper from it.

'Verdammt,' he said. 'Nothing.'

'Nothing, sir?'

'The only prints on the keys matched those that were found all over the flat. The Weichmanns, I presume. There were none on the paper.'

'All the prints in the flat were the Weichmanns', sir?'

'No, there were a few others; in the living room, and the kitchen. The Nussbaum woman's, and a few from the daughter, but they've admitted to being regular visitors to the Weichmanns. It does tell us one thing though.'

'What's that, sir?'

'The people who delivered the package were being incredibly careful. The man must have worn gloves, and even the person who packaged it must have done the same.'

'What about the Nussbaum woman. She unwrapped it.'

'She's either very clever, or just lucky. It will be interesting to find out if she makes a habit of wearing gloves; a lot of women do, including my wife. It's the fashion.'

'But we can't go near her, sir.'

'Not for now, but there are plenty other Jews in Kiel. Let's deal with them one at a time, and her turn will come round…'

Heinrich Güllich's eyes lit up.

'What, sir?'

'That Teubner Jew. I've only just realised. That's where she took the money.'

'Why would she do that?'

'He's the one who they go to when they need help. He finds the Jew-loving lawyers who are willing to act for them and he negotiates with the authorities. He's their spokesman.'

'If we go near him, they'll say we're still trying to get to the Nussbaums.'

'We don't target him directly. Anyway, we can think of a way for the OrPo, or KriPo, to put the squeeze on him. And we have all the time in the world.'

CHAPTER 22

KIELER MORGENPOST

Saturday 22nd June 1940

PEACE IN FRANCE. FRENCH GOVERNMENT AGREES TO CEASEFIRE

The Third Reich now occupies Northern France in addition to the Netherlands, Belgium, and Luxembourg. An agreement has been reached with Marshal Pétain that the French government, sitting in Vichy, will remain in control of Southern France, in the so-called "Zone Libre", or Free Zone.

~~o~~

'What a pleasant surprise, Erich. What brings you to this part of town?'

On presenting himself at Oskar's offices, the General had been shown into the businessman's inner sanctum. There had been no racing because of the war, and Kieler Woche had been cancelled that year. Although the General's boat was in the water, they'd only managed two short sails.

'Just passing, Oskar. I thought I'd call in. How's business?'

'Booming, my friend. The Third Reich have an insatiable appetite for everything I produce, from posters and pamphlets to cookware and tools.'

'You're looking well on it. How is Angelika?'

'Ah. It's sad, but the lovely Angelika has moved on. A mutual decision, I might add.'

Angelika had been the latest woman in Oskar's life.

'Really? I'm surprised that any woman would want to leave you, Oskar. I mean, you're charming, I'm sure you treat them well, you're not short of a Pfennig or two, and some might even say you're rather handsome, in your own way.'

Oskar laughed.

'Damned with faint praise. I'll be honest, Erich. Business is my bag. Don't get me wrong, I love the company of women, and if they happen to be beautiful…'

He held out his hands and shrugged.

'But I get bored after a while, and I find it stifling if they get too entrenched in my life. Angelika didn't try and do that, which is why I liked her so much, but we just drifted apart. I don't even know which one of us lost interest first.'

'It's your life, Oskar. As long as you're happy.'

'I am, my friend. Now, I suspect there is a reason for your visit?'

The General smiled.

'There is. I have a favour to ask. When are you next in Sweden?'

'I go next week. I'm there about once every six weeks or so.'

'I knew you had frequent business there. Can you post a letter for me?'

'For sure. I'm guessing it is to Palestine, yes?'

'Yes. To Itsik and Esther. His parents have been murdered by the Gestapo.'

Oskar bowed his head.

'I'm so sorry,' he said, his voice low.

'So am I. And angry, but what can I do? The Gestapo said they were shot trying to escape but I suspect that they were executed.'

'Itsik doesn't know yet? Is this the reason for the letter?'

'Yes.'

The General handed him Miriam's envelope.

'There's no direct post to Palestine now,' the General said. 'Even if it got out of

Germany, the British would never let it in.'

'I'll see that it's posted.'

'Watch yourself. They are searching people at the border. Hide it well.'

Oscar laughed.

'They won't stop me. I have friends in all the right places.'

'Well, take care anyway. If you hang out with dangerous animals, sooner or later you'll get mauled.'

'Very philosophical, my friend. When are we sailing next?'

'Soon, I hope. I'll have to check with the authorities. They're building a marine barrier across the Förde at Friedrichsort. I'm not sure if it's possible to get out of Kieler Hafen, but I'll keep in touch.'

They shook hands.

'I might call and say hello to Dieter if that's all right.'

'By all means.' He looked at the clock. 'He should be on a break soon.'

~~o~~

'Anything new?' the General asked Dieter when they were out of earshot of his fellow workers.

'Nothing much, other than the complete capitulation of any international opposition to the Third Reich.'

'There is that. We appear to be invincible. Unfortunately, I have a foot in both camps, and it is difficult not to be relieved that we've got this far with so few losses.'

'How are the boys?'

'They're in Paris, I'm told. I don't know when we'll see them. Perhaps after they've invaded Britain.'

Dieter Mass let out a brittle laugh.

'The English won't be as much of a walkover.'

'We said that about Poland, and France.'

'Yes. But they have the Channel.'

'That's true.' The General shivered.

'I hear that every third tank used in the invasion of France and the low countries was built in Czechoslovakia.'

The General raised an eyebrow. It often puzzled him where Dieter's information came from.

'That's no surprise,' he said, 'Adolf has been very clever; the spoils of each invasion pave the way for the next. We'll soon have the industries of France, Belgium and Holland to exploit for the Third Reich's war machine.'

'You knew Itsik Weichmann's parents were murdered?' Dieter said.

'You heard?'

The General shouldn't have been surprised. Dieter had always had contacts in the Jewish community although, day by day, these were getting less.

'Yes. Itsik was well known in Kiel.'

'Have you anything else for me?'

'There's a spate of court cases being brought by those who have been accused of being Mischling.'

'Mixed-race Jews? On what grounds?'

'So, the Aryan mother admits that her husband, a Jew, is not the father of the alleged Mischling, and that she had an affair with an Aryan man at the time of conception.'

'Surely the authorities wouldn't fall for that?'

'A surprising number of them succeed in being reclassified as Aryan.'

'Why?'

'Well, in a significant number of cases, the NSDAP are happy for the person to be reclassified, if they are useful to them, or are employed in a key position. Secondly, it's the state's responsibility to disprove these claims, and the main tenet of the prosecution is that the person must be found to have Jewish characteristics, such as an aquiline nose, swarthiness, tightly curled hair or even red hair.'

'But most Jews don't have any of these characteristics, far less all of them.'

'Exactly. That's why so many of them get reclassified. I hear that certain lawyers are making a fortune representing these people.'

They both laughed. Then the General frowned.

'And you? Are you all right?'

'I keep my head down and my ears open,' Dieter replied, 'and keep records.'

'Be careful, Dieter.'

'As always. When will we sail again?'

'I don't know. I'm working on it.'

'Take care.'

'You too.'

CHAPTER 23

[23/06/1940 Sunday]

'As much as I'm keen to meet the Führer again,' Johann grumbled, 'I'd rather be in sweet Celise's arms right now, a bottle of chilled wine on the bedside table.'

'I'm sure you would,' Franz said, not surprised that Johann spent nearly all his off-duty hours with the young Frenchwoman that he'd met on his second night in Paris.

'She's delicious,' Johann said, 'and I don't just mean metaphorically. She has a few friends, you know. I was going to ask her to bring them along tonight. The boys are desperate to meet them, but I'm sure you would get first pick.'

Franz laughed.

'Thanks for your thoughtfulness, but if I wanted a French girl, I'd have found one myself.'

This time it was Johann's turn to laugh.

'I don't think so, old boy. You're incapable of finding a girl anywhere in Europe, which seems such a waste. I mean, take Celise; she does the most amazing thing with her…'

The roar of a V8 engine drowned out the rest of his liturgy and the Führer's Mercedes-Benz swept onto the concourse in front of the Eiffel Tower and halted in front of Franz's unit.

'Stillgestanden!' Franz barked, calling his unit to attention. They were immaculate, he noted with pride.

One of the Führer's bodyguards, riding in the front, jumped out and opened the car door.

Adolf Hitler stepped out and saluted Franz as the leader of the honour guard. Franz and his men returned the salute.

'Heil Hitler,' they shouted in perfect unison.

Albert Speer, Hitler's architect, stepped out of the car and stood beside the chancellor. From the four cars behind, a gaggle of high-ranking army officers and government officials formed a loose cohort, trailing after the Führer as he walked towards the tower, looking up at its massive latticework of iron. Johann spotted Colonel Schneider amongst the attendant party and glanced at the honour guard. Franz's unit.

They're perfect.

A photographer shouted, and the group stopped to pose for a photograph in front of the iconic tower. It surprised Franz that Adolf Hitler hadn't wanted to view the captured city of Paris from the top, but within minutes, the group returned to the cars. The Führer walked up to Franz and saluted again.

Franz swallowed the bile in his throat.

'I've seen you before, Major,' he said, after Franz returned his salute.

'Jawohl, mein Führer. It was in Kiel. At a sailing regatta. I was fortunate enough to be presented with a trophy by you.'

'Ah. I remember,' Adolf Hitler said. 'And now you have taken Paris for me.'

'We only played a small part, mein Führer.'

Adolf Hitler leaned over and murmured in Franz's ear before walking away.

Franz watched as the cavalcade swept out of the square.

'Wegtreten,' Franz barked across the now silent concourse. *Dismissed.*

The men disbanded and talked in small groups, the excited chatter of soldiers who have just met their Führer. Johann stood with Franz and one of the other captains.

'I'd have thought he might have spoken to me,' he said. 'The charismatic one.'

Franz laughed. 'Rank will always prevail,' he said.

'It was the same in Kiel. He talks to the verdammte skipper, forgetting the crew that won the race for him. What did he say to you?'

'Oh, just that he was extremely impressed with Paris, that he'd heard a soldier could have a wonderful time here, and that we deserved a well-earned rest. "This is just the beginning",' he said.

'He said that? Do you think he means England?'

'Perhaps. I wouldn't read too much into it. He's not going to tell a junior officer his plans, is he?'

'I suppose not. Perhaps that's why we're going to Norway. Our battle group will attack from the north and the rest of the army will invade from France.'

'I'd be careful. You might get what you wished for.'

~~o~~

[29/06/1940 Saturday]

Erich Kästner hated society events but Admiral Canaris had made sure the invitation reached the Drachensee house. The Krupps were present, father and son, and almost all the senior navy staff were in attendance.

At least Maria is pleased, the General thought.

He didn't usually allow himself to be cajoled into going to these things and she'd been surprised when he'd told her they were going.

'Thank you, Wilhelm,' Maria said, putting her hand on the admiral's arm, 'for the invitation, and for persuading my anti-social husband to attend.'

'I'm delighted you both could come. Technically, the invitation isn't mine; it's Admiral Schiffer's affair but I'm sure Erich and you would have been on the list already. You usually are.'

He smiled at her, and at the General, receiving a scowl in return from his friend.

'I must introduce you to the admiral's wife,' Canaris said, taking the frowning Maria by the arm. 'If you haven't already met. She is completely charming.'

Canaris took Maria over to a handsome woman who stood in a group close to the string quartet. He returned to Erich Kästner alone.

'She knew most of the ladies,' he said, grinning, 'but I'm sure she has a new best friend. They seemed to hit it off. I wasn't lying when I said she was charming.'

'You enjoy dropping me in it, don't you?'

'My dear fellow, I'm not sure I like your tone.'

He laughed.

'It's not my fault that you don't accept invitations to any of these naval shindigs, and that your wife didn't know,' he added, 'and if I've inadvertently caused you any inconvenience, I apologise.'

'Oh, wipe that grin off your face. You knew fine well what you were doing.'

Canaris let out a soft laugh but didn't reply.

I'm here now,' the General said, shaking his head. 'You said that it would be advantageous for me to attend tonight, but I'm failing to see any benefit.'

'Hold still, my impatient friend. I have someone I'd like to introduce you to. I thought they might be able to help with your staff problem.'

'The Nussbaums,' the General said, lowering his voice. 'How?'

'Come with me.'

He took the General by the elbow and guided him across the large room and through into the conservatory.

In the centre of the glass-enclosed room, a cluster of people hung onto every word of Gustav Krupp, the shipyard owner. The group included Hinrich Lohse and Jürgen Hoffmann, and a few further high-ranking party officials. The General shook his head.

'Krupp hates Jews,' he whispered, 'and he hates me almost as much, after my stunt with the shipyard expansion.'

'Don't worry, it's not him.'

The admiral nudged the General in the direction of the corner, where a smaller group of men were standing. It included Krupp's son, Alfried.

'I don't suppose he'll have much time for me either,' he whispered again.

'Oh, don't concern yourself about Krupp Junior. He'll not hold grudges. Anyway, he's not the one I want you to meet either.'

As they approached the group, the men turned to look at them.

'Admiral Canaris.' Alfried Krupp held out his hand.

The two men greeted each other.

'And General Kästner. The Krupp nemesis.'

He laughed and gripped the General's hand. It was a firm handshake.

'Hardly,' the General said. 'More of a thorn in the pad.'

'My father was livid for days. His directors took the brunt, and my poor mother had to massage his bruised ego for a while, but do you know, I believe I've managed to convince him that you're simply a very astute and dedicated military man who was just doing his job.'

'I'm glad to hear it. I can't say I lost any sleep over your father's disapproval but it's never pleasant to have an atmosphere of rancour around the place.'

Alfried Krupp smiled.

'Quite,' he said. 'Have you managed any sailing this year?'

'Not much, I'm afraid. It has been a busy time for us here in Kiel, and the navy seem to be using more of the sea than they used to, or at least they claim they are.'

The group laughed. The General knew two of them; a vice admiral who had recently been stationed in Kiel, and a Korvettenkapitän who commanded one of the new light cruisers. Canaris introduced the first of the remaining two men as the naval attaché to the foreign office, stationed in Berlin.

The last of the group was a short, stout sort of man with round spectacles, and a rather elegant moustache.

'This is Alphonse Berac, the Swiss ambassador to Germany,' Admiral Canaris said to the General.

'So pleased to meet you,' the General said. 'I'm General Erich Kästner, army intelligence liaison to the navy.'

They shook hands, and Erich Kästner risked a glance at his friend, who gave an imperceptible nod.

'So, Ambassador, what brings you to Kiel?'

'Ah, I am a guest of the Krupp family. They have interests in Switzerland, and they thought I might like to see how they build the best ships in the world for the German Navy.'

'Well, you've come to the right place. Perhaps I could arrange a tour of the naval dockyards, and our headquarters, while you are here?'

'That would have been most interesting, Herr General, but alas, my time here is short, and Herr Krupp has already organised a very tight itinerary for me.'

'That's a shame. Another time perhaps.'

'Yes. I would look forward to that.'

He looked at the General and inclined his head.

'If I might ask,' he said, 'how did it happen that a General became such an integral part of the largest naval base in Germany?'

'It's a long story, I'm afraid.'

Erich Kästner noticed that Admiral Canaris was regaling the others with the account of his escape from Buenos Aires during the last war. He realised that he would have the Swiss ambassador on his own for just a few minutes.

He told an abridged version of his story, and asked after the ambassador's family for politeness, then took a deep breath.

'Perhaps you would permit me to pick your brains, Herr Ambassador.'

'I'd be surprised if I could help, but I'd be delighted to try.'

'It's a rather delicate matter, but I have a couple who work for me whose family have been part of our household staff for two generations. They are Jews, and I desperately need to get them out of the country. Is it realistic to try and get them into Switzerland?'

The ambassador's eyes clouded for a second, and a frown took the place of his previous smile.

'I'm afraid it would be almost impossible, Herr General.'

He lowered his voice.

'If I had a franc for every time I'd been asked that question, I would be a rich man. And that is exactly what you need to be to get into Switzerland now; richer than you or I could imagine. I don't suppose they have…'

'No. They have a little money, but I doubt it's on the scale you are alluding to.'

'It's a great pity. There are a couple of organisations who are taking orphans, I believe. Would they be willing to send the children?'

'No. I don't think so. They had the chance to send them to Britain a while ago, and they refused outright.'

'Then I'm sorry, my friend. I wish that I could have been of greater help, but my hands are tied.'

'I understand. I hope you didn't mind me broaching the subject, but I had to ask. I am very fond of this couple, and their children.'

'You aren't the first. I only wish I could do more.'

'Thank you for that. If I might ask one last favour?'

'Yes, go ahead.'

'If you could forget that I asked you about this, it would be much appreciated.'

The ambassador looked at him with the glimmer of a smile.

'Of course,' he said. 'It has already been erased from my mind.'

~~o~~

'Any luck?' Wilhelm Canaris said, as they made their way in for a light supper.

'No. Not unless, by some miracle, they can find a few hundred million Reichsmarks hidden away in a cupboard.'

'I'm sorry. I thought it was worth a try. He's reported to be sympathetic.'

'Thanks for the introduction. No stone left unturned, and all that.'

'What are you two scheming about now?' Maria asked, as she joined them.

'Nothing,' they chorused.

CHAPTER 24

[04/07/1940 Thursday]

'We're not going, sir.'

The General gripped Yosef's arm. The air above them was filled with the wail of air-raid sirens.

'You have to, Yosef. If this place gets hit, you'll be killed. The only safe place is the shelter. There were a number of casualties in the raid two days ago, and significant damage to property.'

'I know, sir. The NSDAP building on Gartenstraße was destroyed.'

The General smiled. The destruction of the National Socialists' Headquarters in the first British air raid on Kiel was a small, comforting irony to them both.

'All the more reason for you to take precautions.'

'They won't bomb here, sir, unless by accident, and we're far enough away from the dockyards to make it unlikely.'

'Why won't you go? These people can say what they like, but they won't dare stop you when you're with me.'

'Sir, they'll report us, if we haven't already been reported and, sooner or later, we'll receive another visit from the police, if we're lucky, or the Gestapo. You know we can't afford that.'

'Where can you take shelter? There must be somewhere.'

'I've cleared a space between the coal store and the laundry, in the basement. We'll be safe there, sir, from anything other than a direct hit.'

He looked at the General, who was shaking his head.

'None of our friends has been allocated a shelter either, sir,' Yosef added.

'That's awful. What do they do?'

'Mostly basements, sir. We've sandbagged the cellars of the houses in Kleiner Kuhberg. A lot of people go there.'

Yosef nodded towards the gate.

'You must go, sir.'

The General followed his gaze. Maria stood with the girls, trying to catch his attention. When she saw him glance at them, she shouted above the wail of the sirens, and waved for him to hurry.

'On you go, sir. We'll be fine.'

With a last reluctant look, the General strode up the drive and, gathering his family, hurried towards the bunker.

~~o~~

In the first week of bombing raids on Kiel, the Royal Air Force dropped over 150 tonnes of high explosive and around 20,000 incendiary bombs over the space of three nights. Most of the damage was limited to the area around the shipyards, and the industrial area to the south. A number of houses close to the yards were burned down but the fire service reacted with their usual efficiency and bravery, and by the time the sun fell each day, a sense of something approaching normality had returned to the city.

And then the sirens sounded again.

After the second night, Maria Kästner refused to return to the shelter.

'The smell is terrible,' she pleaded with the General, 'and the sense of being closed in is unbearable. It's like a tomb.'

'It's for your own safety, and that of the children, my dear,' the General said.

'I don't care. I'll take my chances. You can take Antje and Eva if you must.'

Maria turned to Yosef.

'Show me where you and Miriam go,' she said.

The General followed his wife and his handyman down the steps to the basement. He hadn't been down for years, but he knew that the coal store and the boiler room were at one end, and that they were filthy.

'This is the laundry; it's relatively clean but there's not much space in it. The next part is the store, and the boiler is over there,' he said, pointing to a closed door.

'The coal is bunkered next to it,' he explained. 'It's loaded in through the chute at the back. I fill the hopper on the boiler and the coal scuttles once a day, but I try to keep the mess here to a minimum.'

The General was surprised; he'd imagined black coal dust permeating everything, but he chided himself that he should have known better. Yosef was meticulous in everything he did.

'This would be better than that horrible shelter,' Maria said, looking around. Yosef had cleared an area about three metres square in the store, having moved the bulk of the heavy household supplies to one side.

'I could clear some additional space,' he said. 'I just made enough room for the four of us. I can put some of the stores in the laundry and the boiler room.'

Four old dining chairs sat in a circle. There was a small paraffin heater in the centre, and a couple of oil lamps hung on hooks from the roof. The General presumed they were for power cuts.

'I'll put out a few extra chairs if you'd like,' Yosef said. 'There's a pile of them in the corner.'

'That would be excellent, Yosef.'

The General looked at the heavy wooden shelfing bolted to the wall. It held everything from boxes of firelighters and neat stacks of bundled kindling to an array of cleaning and maintenance products that Miriam and Yosef used in their day-to-day work.

Strangely, for a cellar in a big house, it held no wine; the Kästners kept their modest wine collection in the ample larder that led off the kitchen.

'These shelves, Yosef, could pass for bunks if we could fashion mattresses for them.'

Yosef's face broke into a grin.

'You're right, sir. We all slept on rugs on the floor last night.'

'It's a bit narrow and cramped,' Maria Kästner said, wrinkling her nose.

'We can go to the public shelters, if you'd like,' the General said, ignoring the glare she gave him.

He examined the walls, and the ceiling.

'I'd thought about building a shelter in the garden, but I believe this will do, if we clear a larger space and reinforce parts of it.'

'What do you mean, sir?'

'Well, I don't think the ceiling would stand a direct hit on the house, but if we had a builder put a couple of metal beams in…'

'That would work, sir. And the door to the coal chute; we could pile sandbags on top of it when it's not being used.'

'I'll organise them today. We can also put a wall of sandbags at the entrance to the cellar. The rest of it is well protected by being underground.'

The General looked around.

Maria will rarely have to use public shelters again.

If the sirens sounded when Ruth and Manny were at school, they would be forced to use the Kleiner Kuhberg basement, and his own daughters would have to shelter in one of the university's bunkers while on campus.

The General, along with his Abwehr staff, had the bunker close to Naval Headquarters to make for when needed, or if he were visiting Tirpitzhafen, he would dash with the others to the Flandernbunker at the end of Hindenburgufer.

'This will do nicely, Yosef,' he said, satisfied.

CHAPTER 25

[06/07/1940 Saturday]

KIELER JÜDISCHES FREIHEITSNACHRICHTENBLATT

Volume 89

30th of Sivan, 5700

FURTHER RESTRICTIONS ON JEWS IN PUBLIC SPACES

The latest restriction on Jewish participation in everyday German life was announced at the Reichstag yesterday. From today, it is illegal for any Jew to be found in a park or other public place.

ŁÓDŹ GHETTO SEALED.

German authorities sealed the Jewish ghetto at Łódź, in Wartheland, just outside the Generalgouvernement zone in Poland. Although news of this has only just reached the KJF, our reports suggest that it happened in late April or early May. Our reports also state that no movement of people from the ghetto is permitted, other than escorted work parties to nearby factories.

This may be a pattern for future ghetto management by the National Socialists.

~~o~~

[23/07/1940 Saturday]

Yosef lifted the last sandbag into place.

'That should do the job, sir,' he said, wiping the sweat from his eyes with the back of his forearm.

'I hope it's never needed,' the General replied.

Both men stood in the sun, their vests soaked, their braces hanging loose from their trousers. Their shirts and jackets hung on a peg inside the cellar door.

Antje appeared, carrying a jug of Miriam's home-made lemonade, Ruth following with a tray of glasses. They handed out the drinks before exploring the new shelter, chattering with excitement.

'These will withstand almost anything,' the General told them, rubbing his hand along one of the iron H-beams. He took a long drink from the cold glass and let out a long breath of satisfaction.

'It's very cosy,' Ruth said. 'Will we all fit in there?'

'It will be a little cramped, especially if the boys are here, but it's more private than the public shelters, and we have everything here. Hurricane lamps, if the power fails; food, water, blankets.'

They'd even installed a small cast-iron stove, its flue jutting through the small bricked up and sandbagged window near the ceiling, at the back of the cellar.

'We should have cards,' Antje said, 'so that we can play games.'

'And you can bring your brushes down, and paint us all,' Ruth said, laughing.

The two girls ran to the new summer house and pulled out a couple of the deck chairs that Maria had ordered and placed a small table between them. In sunglasses and summer dresses the girls lay side by side, talking with earnest expressions that made their fathers laugh.

'They're getting very grown up, aren't they?' the General said.

'You sound disappointed, sir,' Yosef said, smiling.

'I suppose I am, in a way. You still have young Manny you can horse around with. Antje seems to have grown up in a matter of months. I wouldn't dream of throwing her over my shoulder now and threatening to dump her in the lake.'

Yosef laughed.

'I know what you mean. Look at them. They're young ladies.'

'I worry, though, about what's in front of them,' the General said. 'I see the Soviets are invading Lithuania, Latvia and Estonia.'

'Perhaps we should have considered them as an option,' Yosef said, bowing his head, 'but it's too late now. That's another door closed.'

'At least we've heard nothing else from our Gestapo friends,' the General said.

'No, thank God, but Jakob fears that the houses in Kleiner Kuhberg are being closely watched. He says that many of his contacts have told him that it's getting too dangerous for them to have any dealings with him and he was unable to get the Weichmanns' bodies released for burial, I'm afraid. We're not going to tell Itsik.'

'I'm sorry I can't be of any help. I can provide you and your family with a basic degree of protection, but that's as far as it goes, in the current climate.'

'I know, sir, and I appreciate your efforts.'

'How is Jakob?'

'Very downhearted, sir. We all are. Two million Frenchmen surrendered, Paris captured without a struggle and whole stretches of the Maginot Line failed to defend itself. Hundreds of thousands of Jews in France and the low countries will know what it is like to live under National Socialist rule. Hitler is now bombing London every night and the British are desperately trying to defend their skies with a rump of an air force, from what we're told.'

The General tilted his head and squinted at his employee.

'Where did you hear that?'

Yosef laughed. It had a cheerless ring to it.

'It only takes one Jew in Kiel to glean a little information, and we all know. In our position, we crave news of setbacks; anything that will weaken the National Socialists' power is welcome, but all we hear is success after success.'

'I'm afraid it's true. The British were completely unprepared for war. I'm relieved that the boys are safe for now, but I expect an invasion of England to happen any time.'

'That makes sense. There are fewer air raids on Kiel than there were at first. I suppose the British have enough to contend with fighting on their own shores.'

It wasn't strictly true. Sometimes weeks passed without a bomb dropping, then the sky would rain death for night after night. Only twice a bomb dropped close to Drachensee in the early days of the war; the first landed in a nearby garden but didn't detonate. The second fell in the lake and, apart from a few dead fish washed up on the shore, the large waterspout was witnessed only by old man Roetger, who refused to have anything to do with air-raid precautions.

In the unprotected cellar, the Kästners and the Nussbaums had felt the shock of the detonation. A cloud of dust and a trickle of sand from one of the bags were the only signs that it had happened, but they were all shaken.

But now the cellar was ready.

'I'm glad this is finished,' the General said. 'That one in the lake was a little too close for comfort.'

They lapsed into silence, sitting on the grass with their backs against the wall, savouring the slight breeze and the slaking cold of the lemonade.

'I phoned the American consulate again,' Yosef said, after a few minutes.

'Any progress?' the General said, daring to hope.

'It's slow, sir. Excruciatingly slow. They still say another ten months.'

The General exhaled through pursed lips.

'I'm not sure I can keep the wolves at bay that long. What about your Haganah people?'

'They've had a few setbacks, I'm told. There was a massacre of twenty Arabs in Haifa. They were killed when Jewish extremists mounted explosives on a donkey and detonated it in a marketplace in the Arab quarter of the city. The British have tightened up security, so the number of Jews making it into Palestine has dwindled to a trickle.'

'Haifa. That's close to where Itsik is, isn't it?'

'Itsik's brother lives in Haifa. He and Itsik have a shop there. He offered me a job, and accommodation, you know.'

'That was kind of him. If only we could get you there.'

'The timing of this attack is unfortunate; just when thousands of us are trying to get in.'

'Let's pray that the Americans come through, or the British relax their security measures in Palestine.'

CHAPTER 26

In Afula, Esther Weichmann grabbed the letter from the postman. It had a Swedish stamp, with a Malmö postmark.

She tore it open.

17th June

Dear Esther,

I don't know how to write this. Our hearts go out to you. Jakob found out that Itsik's mother and father have been killed. I'm so, so sorry to be telling you this, but I felt that you had to know, so that Itsik could say Kaddish for them.

Jakob said they had tried to escape and had been shot. It was the Gestapo, he said. He is trying to arrange for their bodies to be released so that we can give them a decent burial, here in Kiel.

They must have been so brave, and so desperate to see you all. Please remember that being with you and Itsik would have been in their hearts when they died, and it would have been quick; they wouldn't have suffered.

My only hope is that this letter gets to you, and that you know that we did everything we could.

You all have our deepest sympathies,

Miriam

The letter dropped from Esther's hand, and she gripped the hallstand to stop herself collapsing. A thin wail escaped her lips, unsettling the baby playing on the rug in the front room.

How can I tell Itsik?

~~o~~

[26/07/1940 Friday]

'We're home!'

Screams of joy from Antje and Eva drowned out Johann's next words as the girls and their mother smothered both men with hugs.

'Father will be home soon,' Antje squealed. 'You can tell us everything about France and Paris.'

She noticed her brothers staring at her.

'What is it?' she asked.

'You look so... grown up,' Franz said, looking her up and down.

'Quite the young lady,' Johann said, grinning and grabbing her and whirling her round.

'Stop it!' she squealed. 'Put me down.'

He stopped spinning but continued to hold her.

'And Eva,' Franz said, taking his sister into his arms in a rather gentler manner, 'how are you finding university?'

She smiled. 'It's amazing. I've learned so much, read so many books. And you get to meet such interesting people.'

'I'm glad you're enjoying it. How many languages do you speak now?'

'French, Italian and English. A smattering of Spanish too.'

He stepped back and looked at her.

'I can't believe my little sister is so accomplished.'

'The clever one in the family,' Johann said, laughing and taking Eva in his arms. 'It's great to see you.'

Maria Kästner looked on with pride, and a tear in her eye. They'd all turned out well, she thought, despite her husband's attempts to undermine the values she wanted them all to have.

'Mama,' Franz said. 'You look wonderful. How do you do it?'

'Oh stop,' she said, blushing. 'I feel old standing beside Eva and Antje. Aren't they both beautiful?'

'They are indeed. They take after you though.'

She laughed. 'Flattery will get you nowhere, but it's such a pleasant surprise that Antje has turned out to be a young lady after your father's best efforts to turn her into a surrogate son, even though she decided to go to art school.'

Franz and Johann laughed. Antje scowled at her mother but couldn't sustain it.

Franz spotted Yosef and Miriam, standing in the kitchen door, watching. Miriam, like Maria, had tears running down her face.

Franz walked over to them.

'Miriam, Yosef,' he said, 'It's lovely to see you both. How are you?'

'Very well, sir,' Yosef said, the form of address natural and seemly.

'We're delighted that you're both home, safe and well,' Miriam added. 'Ruth and Manny would love to see you when you have time to say hello, I'm sure.'

'Go fetch them,' Franz said, puzzled at the frown that crossed his mother's face.

'Oh, I'm sure they'll see you later. You'll want to spend time with your family first.'

But Franz insisted, and Yosef was dispatched to fetch the two younger Nussbaums.

'We should go into the drawing room,' Maria said. 'Miriam, can you bring in drinks for everyone, please?'

'At last. A drink. I'll have a cold beer if there is one.'

'I was talking about coffee, Johann,' Maria Kästner scolded. 'There will be plenty time after dinner if you wish to indulge.'

'Nonsense, Mama. We've had a long, hot journey and nothing would suit better than a bottle of cold beer. Wouldn't it, Franz?'

'Well…'

'There, Mama. Major Kästner approves, so it must be all right. And let's have it out in the garden. Why waste such a nice day.'

Maria's protests were stifled by the others, all talking at once.

She sighed and followed them.

Miriam brought a tray bearing coffee and iced lemonade. Ruth walked behind her mother, her own tray holding a bottle of beer each for the boys, and two glasses.

Manny ran in front of them. When he saw Johann, he made a beeline for him.

'Johann,' he shouted and tackled him, his arms around the younger Kästner brother's waist.

They fell to the ground, Johann pretending to be overpowered by the boy. After wrestling for a minute, Manny ended up astride the young officer, arms aloft in triumph.

'When you're quite finished, Johann,' Maria Kästner said.

Johann got to his feet, tousling Manny's hair.

'He's got so big. It was like being attacked by a bear.'

Manny grinned, his eyes gleaming with pride.

'Bring out the extra seats, boys,' Maria said. 'Make yourselves useful.'

Franz followed Manny into the summer house and picked up a chair. The boy had grown; Franz watched as he lifted a chair with ease and took it outside. As Franz placed his chair down beside the rest, he saw Ruth standing with their beers.

Johann had seen her too.

'Well, hello,' he said, his eyes wide. 'I'm sure we haven't been introduced. I'd have remembered such a beautiful woman.'

Ruth blushed but could do nothing but stand, holding the tray. Franz rushed forward, taking it from her and putting it on the table.

It was Antje who rescued her from Johann's scrutiny.

'Leave her alone, you great oaf.' She turned to Ruth. 'He says that to all the girls.'

They all laughed, except for Johann, who contrived to appear hurt.

'Mama,' Franz said, grinning, 'did Johann tell you about his latest girl?'

'No,' Maria said. 'He doesn't tell me anything.'

'Celise, isn't it, brother?' Franz asked Johann but didn't give him time to answer.

'She's French,' he continued. 'Johann is very much in love.'

Johann drew Franz a scathing look but turned to Maria.

'Elle est peut-être aussi belle que toi, Mama,' Johann said, his French accent making Antje and Ruth giggle.

'Elle est *presque* aussi belle que toi,' Eva said, correcting him.

'Yes, she is almost as beautiful as you, Mama. That's what I meant to say.'

'You'll not get away with trying to sound like a sophisticated Frenchman now, Johann,' Franz said.

He turned to the others. 'All the young officers think Johann is fluent in French, despite what I tell them.'

'La fortune favorise les courageux et gagne l'amour de la femme.'

They all turned to see who had spoken.

'Father,' Johann said, shaking the General's hand. 'At last, someone who understands me. Fortune indeed favours the brave and wins a lady's love. Somebody should tell that to Franz.'

Franz was on his feet. When he took his father's hand, the General's grip was strong and sustained, and he held his son's gaze for longer than usual.

'It's wonderful to have you both home. I presume you're heading back north?'

'Yes, it's Norway again for us,' Franz said. 'Johann was heartbroken to leave France. I only hope the Scandinavian fathers have locked up their daughters this time.'

Johann tried to protest, but the others laughed him down. Franz caught a glimpse of Ruth out of the corner of his eye. She looked a little hurt and confused.

Better that she knows what Johann is like.

Franz had vowed the last time they were home that he wouldn't allow his brother to play with Ruth's affections. The two families were too close to risk falling out over what would be a mere dalliance for Johann.

~~o~~

Much later, sitting in the drawing room when the ladies had gone to bed, and the General had disappeared to fetch a bottle of his favourite malt, Franz warned Johann about any misbehaviour with Ruth.

'She's worshipped you for years,' he said. 'Let her keep that idealised version of you intact until she finds someone who won't break her heart. Anyway, you didn't pay her that much attention until now.'

'But who knew she'd turn out like that?'

'I'll admit I got a shock when I saw her tonight, but she's no prettier than your own sisters, and she's just as off limits, do you understand?'

'Yes,' Johann conceded, his face heavy with disappointment.

Franz didn't know if his brother's sad expression was genuine, or if it was a blatant attempt to engender sympathy.

'If I thought for a moment that you would settle down...'

'You're right,' Johann said, shaking his head, 'but...'

'Do I hear correctly,' the General said, returning with the drinks. 'Johann, you surely aren't agreeing with your brother, are you?'

Franz saw Johann blush.

'I... I...' Johann stammered.

'Johann knows I'm right but finds it hard to concede. He'd suggested that the Wehrmacht could invade Britain from Norway.'

Johann shot Franz a grateful look.

'Ha,' said the General. 'I'm not sure that's so preposterous. I wouldn't discount anything where our wonderful leaders are concerned.'

'Father!' Johann said. 'You should be careful.'

'I'm among people I trust. You know how I feel about it. I'm careful with others.'

'Still, Johann is right,' Franz said. 'It is better to be prudent. There are ears everywhere.'

'Pah. Someone should be brave enough to speak out against these madmen. I only wish it were me.'

'Father, think of Mama and the girls,' Johann said. 'Anyhow, despite all his faults, what about the success that the Führer has brought. Germany is respected and feared the world over.'

The General raised an eyebrow.

'Feared, maybe,' he said, 'and respected by despots like Mussolini and Stalin, but not in many other places on earth.'

'Germany won't become great again without being tough and ruthless. It's impossible to argue against the glorious victories he has delivered. Czechoslovakia, Norway, Denmark, Holland, Belgium and now France. And we will take Britain too.'

'Johann, I know you see it in black and white but what will Europe be like with Hitler, Himmler, Goebbels and Göring in charge? What happens with people like Miriam and Yosef?'

'They'll be fine. They're with us.'

'What about Manny's grandparents, his friends at school? They're beginning to disappear.'

'They've been resettled.'

'You've seen what happens,' Franz interjected. 'You were there, in Poland.'

'They were isolated incidents,' Johann argued. 'It shouldn't happen but, sometimes in war, men behave out of character.'

Franz shook his head. 'It's not just Poland. You saw it in Austria, and in Czechoslovakia, and in Norway too. The Jewish population, and a few other minorities, are being persecuted, as they are here, in Germany.'

'You're exaggerating, blowing it all out of proportion.'

'He's not, Johann,' the General said, shaking his head. 'Last week, the Nussbaums' cottage was turned upside down by the Gestapo. If Albert hadn't phoned me to come home, they would have been arrested.'

'The Nussbaums? Arrested for what?'

'Nothing. Just looking after an old couple, Itsik Weichmann's parents. They tried to get to Palestine to join their sons, but they were caught. Miriam was seen at their flat. They believe she's some sort of accomplice.'

'They arrested the old couple? And now the Nussbaums are criminals too?'

'The Weichmanns were shot. "Trying to escape" was the phrase the Gestapo used, I believe.'

For the first time, Johann looked uncomfortable.

'What about the Nussbaums? Are they still under investigation?'

'No. I had the case quashed. But I don't know how long I can protect them.'

'It will all die down, wait and see.'

'No. The Nussbaums have to get out of Germany. We are trying our best to arrange it.'

'The Nussbaums leaving here? That's a tad dramatic.'

'You don't realise what life is like for them. They are constantly harassed; they have none of the rights that we take for granted. Yosef isn't permitted to drive now, and Ruth and Manny are banned from attending school. They can only travel to see Miriam's parents with a permit, which is almost impossible for them to obtain. The list is endless.'

'Once the war is won, these measures will be phased out.'

'Only if we lose, will there be any hope for Germany, or its Jews.'

Johann paled. He stared at his father.

'That's treason,' he said, his voice almost a whisper, glancing around.

'It's not treason to want to live in a country where the government don't torture and murder their own people every day.'

'I'll not listen to any more of this. We are fighting abroad, for the very survival of Germany, and you are talking like that!'

He spun round and stormed out of the door, slamming it behind him. Franz made to go after him.

'Leave him,' the General said, resting a hand on his elder son's arm. 'He just needs time. It's a lot to take in, when you find out that you're fighting for something that is rotten inside. He'll have a blowout, and tomorrow he'll have a raging hangover and lots of questions.'

He didn't. The hangover was there, and he acted as normal, teasing his mother and his sisters, and finding friends to drink with at night. One morning, he came home as the dawn broke with lipstick on his shirt and without a jacket.

But, aside from pleasantries and the odd piece of gossip, he didn't speak with Franz or his father. When they left to catch the train back to their barracks before shipping out, he shook hands with the General and hugged a tearful Maria, smiling as usual and as carefree as ever, without another mention of Germany, or the fate of its people.

'I'll keep an eye on him,' Franz murmured to his father as they made their goodbyes. 'We'll keep in touch as best we can.'

'Be careful,' the General said. 'Look after yourselves.'

~~o~~

On the train back, Johann said nothing. Franz thought over the conversation he'd had with his father and Yosef while Johann was drowning his sorrows.

'There are few safe places left, sirs,' Yosef had said. 'We're praying that the Americans come through with visas.'

'What about Sweden?' Franz had asked. 'You could get there through Denmark, surely?'

'Germany is the Swedish government's biggest customer for iron ore. Although they are neutral, they'll do nothing to upset the German authorities. They hand back any Jews that they catch entering illegally.'

'And Spain?'

'Again, neutral, but Franco is sympathetic to Hitler, and they'll not harbour any escaping Jews. The South of France is ostensibly free, and a lot of Paris's Jews have fled there, but the Vichy government will doubtless hand over their Jews in the end, if our government ask them to.'

'Switzerland? Greece?'

'Switzerland is closed unless you have a numbered account there,' the General said, bitterness discolouring his voice. 'Greece is under threat from the Italians.'

'Palestine is safe, for now,' Yosef said, 'but getting there is dangerous. Look at the Weichmanns.'

'That was terrible,' Franz said. 'What are we coming to when our government are killing innocent people in cold blood?'

'It's the tip of the iceberg, son. Yosef could tell you countless stories of his people being snatched, and sent to camps, or to the ghettos in Poland.'

'It's true, sir. Then there's house searches by the Gestapo, or the OrPo if you're lucky; evictions, repossessions. It happens every day.'

'And all the while we're helping take over Europe for them,' Franz said, shaking his head.

'I'll breathe better when Yosef and Miriam are away,' the General said.

'We all will,' Yosef replied. 'Here's to New York,' he said, raising his glass.

CHAPTER 27

Memo: Geh.KdoS. ABW 06/08/40 CAC01294.1

For Attention Only: All senior executive officers, Abwehr.

From: Vice Admiral Wilhelm Canaris, Chef der Abwehr.

The Soviet Union has completed the occupation and incorporation of the Baltic States of Latvia, Estonia, and Lithuania into the Union of Soviet Republics. [END]

~~o~~

[09/08/1940 Friday]

'Yosef, Miriam, may I have a word?'

Miriam put down her mixing bowl and looked up at Maria Kästner.

'Certainly, ma'am.'

Yosef gave the fork he was polishing a final rub and placed it next to the rest of the silver cutlery on the velvet cloth on the top of the dresser.

'What can we do for you, Frau Kästner?'

Maria drew in a deep breath.

'I don't know if you read today's paper but…'

She hesitated.

'… they've issued new regulations about the use of telephones.'

'Telephones, ma'am?' Miriam asked.

'Yes, you're not permitted to use a private telephone from today.'

'No one can use their telephone, ma'am?'

'No. Just you and Yosef. We can still use the telephone, naturally.'

'Ah, you mean Jewish people aren't authorised to use the telephone, ma'am,' Yosef said.

Maria Kästner blushed.

'That's right,' she said. 'You are still allowed to use public telephones,' she added with a fixed smile.

Yosef frowned.

'So, if the telephone rings,' he said, 'we shouldn't answer it, madam?'

'Well, if we're in, you can answer it and pass it over to one of us.'

'And if you're out, we've not to take a message for you, madam?'

'Well, yes…' Maria Kästner stopped. 'I don't know. Perhaps it's only that you can't make a call. We'll ask the General about that. It would be such an inconvenience if our staff couldn't take a message for us.'

'Indeed, madam. In the meantime, do you want us to answer the telephone or not?'

'Just answer the thing. But don't make any outgoing calls.'

'Yes, madam.'

Maria Kästner turned and left the room.

'When was the last time one of us made a call on the house telephone?'

'A personal call?'

'Yes.'

'Never, as far as I can remember.'

'Then why…' she said, nodding towards the door Maria Kästner had gone through.

He shrugged.

~~o~~

[11/08/1940 Sunday]

'Have you seen this, Major?'

Colonel Schneider handed Franz a piece of paper.

Memo: Geh.KdoS. HEER 11/08/40 OKW36523.1

For Attention Only: All senior officers, Heer.

From: Field Marshal Wilhelm Keitel

Any serving member of the Wehrmacht who is of mixed race is to be withdrawn from front-line duties as from today, in the interests of the security of the Reich. [END]

'Sir, do you want me to check? I know Sergeant Babst has a Jewish grandparent. There may be a number of others affected.'

'My adjutant has already completed the list. Here it is.'

The colonel handed Franz a typed sheet. It had twelve names on it. Franz stared hard at the list.

'One corporal,' he said, 'ten privates and Sergeant Babst. There are some excellent soldiers on there, sir.'

'I know, and the sergeant is one of the best we have, but my hands are tied.'

'I'll tell them all, sir, individually.'

'Thank you, Major.'

'Do you wish me to say anything to them, on your behalf, sir?'

The colonel grimaced and shook his head.

'Tell them that I thank them for their service,' he said, 'and that it's such a verdammte waste.'

~~o~~

'Arnulf.'

'Beate!'

The Obersturmbannführer gave Beate Böhm a chaste embrace and kissed both her cheeks.

'What are you doing here? I didn't know you were back.'

He stifled a smile at the accusatory tone in her voice.

'A flying visit, I'm afraid. Military matters. I'll telephone you next time, for sure,' he said.

'That would be lovely. Eberhard would be so pleased to see you again,' she said, glancing around. 'Unless you have time now for a coffee, or something to eat...'

'There's nothing I would like better but, unfortunately, I have a meeting to go to, and then I'm back with my Kompanie tonight.'

He smiled, taking cruel satisfaction from the disappointment that she didn't quite manage to hide.

'Next time,' he said, pecking her cheek again, his lips brushing hers in the passing.

They parted, each with smiles, and she walked briskly along Sophienblatt, into town.

He stopped and looked in a shop window and watched her out of the corner of his eye until she turned into Friedrichstraße, then strode in the opposite direction. Fifty metres further on, he stepped through the doors of the Europäischer Hof, and smiled.

It's a crying shame. They are so different, the mother and the daughter, but there just hasn't been time to fit them both in.

~~o~~

Beate Böhm stood for a minute at the corner of Sophienblatt and Friedrichstraße and frowned. She knew she'd been foolish to stop and look back; for all she knew, his meeting could be in the hotel, or perhaps he was staying there, and was hurrying to freshen up before being driven to the meeting. She walked on, slower now, chiding herself for caring.

CHAPTER 28

THE COLCHESTER ECHO

Sunday, August 25th, 1940

BOMBS FALL ON CENTRAL LONDON

Flames rose high above the capital last night from just before midnight as, for the first time since the Battle of Britain began, bombs fell on central London.

Extensive fires broke out in Hackney, Bethnal Green, Aldgate, Bloomsbury, Stepney, Shoreditch, Finsbury and West Ham, and hundreds of buildings throughout the East End have been destroyed, with many collapsing completely.

It is not yet known how many casualties have resulted from the bombing, but it is expected that at least a hundred civilians have been killed.

Winston Churchill, the prime minister, saw the devastation himself when he visited the area today.

Major Anthony Plenderleith put the paper down and lifted the letter that lay on the table beside it.

He knew the contents off by heart.

'Have you done nothing about that yet, darling?' his wife asked him as she came into the room.

'No. I can't believe that they would want to call me up at my age.'

'You're only forty-nine, dear.'

'I've been out of the army for ten years though. What would they want with me?'

'Experience, dear. You fought in the last war. They'll be looking for experience, to show these young whippersnappers. Look at the debacle in France.'

'I suppose so, but I'm getting a little long in the tooth to be sitting in a trench.' He shuddered.

'This war is not going to be about trenches,' she said.

'I didn't think you read the papers, dear,' he said, taken aback.

'I don't. Mildred mentioned it, and her Donald told her. It's this Blitzkrieg thing they do now. They move around in tanks these days.'

He'd never known her to take an interest in army matters, but he supposed that everyone in the country was talking about that damned man Hitler and his panzers now.

'I telephoned earlier,' he said, 'but I couldn't get through. I'll ring later, to see what it's all about,' he said.

KIELER MORGENPOST

Thursday 29th August 1940

BERLIN BOMBED

British bombers targeted civilian areas in the

first British air raid on Berlin last night, ignoring the convention that there should be minimal collateral damage to residential areas when attacking military targets.

A government spokesman said that Britain's cities would suffer retribution for this blatant act of aggression against innocent German men, women, and children.

Kiel continues to suffer sporadic heavy bombing raids, as it has done since the beginning of the war. They are confined mainly to industrial and naval areas in the immediate vicinity of Kieler Hafen, although several residential districts have been hit by stray bombs.

~~o~~

[29/08/1940 Thursday]

'Darling, what did they say?'

Marjorie Plenderleith took off her coat and put her shopping bag on the kitchen table.

'It's the damndest thing,' he said. 'They assure me that they want me to come back, but the good news is that it's not in a combat capacity.'

'Oh, that's a great relief, dear. I was a bit worried about you shooting at people at your age, or getting shot at.'

'Quite,' he said, filling his pipe. 'They want to release younger men for that sort of show, so I'll be based here in England, in some administrative role or another, or perhaps in a training camp. They are talking about a promotion though.'

'Oh, that would be marvellous. What would that make you?'

'I'd start as a lieutenant colonel, but there is the possibility that I could be made up to a full colonel, depending on my role.'

She could see that, despite himself, he was flattered and delighted with the offer of a return to the army, and she couldn't imagine him refusing it. She resigned herself to another move.

'It's a pity though,' he said, as if reading her mind. 'We were so settled here, and this new post will almost certainly mean we'll have to move.'

'That's all right, my dear. We've done it often enough. I'm sure it won't kill us, and it will only be for a short time, while this blasted war lasts.'

~~o~~

[07/09/1940 Saturday]

Memo: Geh.KdoS. ABW 07/09/40 CAC01348.1

For Attention Only: General Erich Kästner, Abwehr, Kiel office, Abwehr.

From: Vice Admiral Wilhelm Canaris, Chef der Abwehr.

** HÖCHSTE GEHEIMHALTUNG **

SS authorities have installed crematoria in the Auschwitz concentration camp. The area has been designated as Krema I. It is expected that the crematoria will be operational by the end of this month. [END]

CHAPTER 29

'Canaris.'

'Kästner.'

They shook hands and slapped each other's backs. The General studied his friend. Lines of care were appearing on Wilhelm Canaris's face, but he supposed his own would tell a similar story.

'It's been a while,' he said.

'I've been busy,' Admiral Canaris said with a sigh.

'A tour of France?'

'Among other places, yes. You guessed when I telephoned?'

'Yes. So, what have you learned?'

'That we are masters of all Western Europe, except for the British Isles.'

'But only half of France,' the General said, correcting him.

'The Vichy government are puppets. They control the rest of France for us, without the inconvenience of us having our troops deployed there.'

'So, it is Britain's turn next?'

'That will be a much tougher nut to crack.'

'I thought the British were ill-prepared and inadequately defended, that London is being pounded every night by our bombers and large parts of it have been levelled. The word is that surrender, or at least an armistice, is inevitable.'

'Don't believe everything our ministry for propaganda spits out. It is true that parts of London, and other cities, are being flattened, but we are losing vast numbers of planes in the process to British fighter aircraft. I was told by a senior member of the Luftwaffe command that the Royal Air Force always seem to be ready for us. They won't admit it, but they suspect that they have some kind of early warning system.'

'How? If they had operatives in northern Germany, or ships or submarines in the North Sea, we would intercept their radio traffic and eliminate them, surely.'

'It's nothing like that. It's a whole new technology. Our scientists are working on a beam that can identify incoming aircraft, and possibly ships. *Funkmessgerät*, it's called. We think they have it too.'

'How does it work?'

'Radio waves. I'm told they reflect off metal, and they can measure them when they bounce back. The British call it *radar*. We're currently trialling it on some Kriegsmarine ships, and at a few shore stations, but it's a defensive tool, first and foremost, and our military research has been geared to offensive technology for the last God knows how many years. A few of our boffins have been working on it, but it was given a low priority by those at the very top. We're at long last putting some resources into developing it, but we're playing catch-up.'

'The British have a more advanced system?'

'Yes. I'm sure of it, but the Luftwaffe are frightened to admit it. No one wants to be the one to tell the Führer that he and his advisors have made an error.'

'So, we can't see their bombers coming, but they can see ours, and plan accordingly.'

'We will get the technology, and it will be deployed on ships and along the coast, but it will take time. As a matter of fact…'

The admiral leaned forward.

'They're working on the latest naval version here in Kiel, at the NVA. Not a few hundred metres from your office.'

'The communications laboratory, next door?'

The *Nachrichtenmittel-Versuchsanstalt*, or NVA, was an unimpressive building adjacent to Naval Headquarters, overlooking the arsenal mole on the opposite side of the harbour. It was remarkable only for the plethora of unusual aerial masts protruding from its roof.

'Yes. Our top man there is Rudolf Kühnhold. Interesting fellow. You should meet him sometime.'

There was a knock at the door, and Frau Müller entered with two cups of coffee, and the bread, cheese, and cold ham that the General had asked her to send out for.

'Are you happy to have lunch here?' he asked the admiral when she'd gone.

'I've eaten in worse places.'

They helped themselves to the food, discussing the latest rumours of misbehaviour amongst the elite of the NSDAP while they ate.

It was the admiral who broached the subject of the Nussbaums.

'Your friends. Any progress?'

'No. They're just waiting for the Americans. I'm hoping they'll come through with visas, but they're still on the Haganah's list to go to Palestine.'

The admiral bowed his head.

'What?' the General asked.

'Our troops start moving into Romania today. Antonescu has, to all intents and purposes, invited the Wehrmacht in. It has been almost inevitable since King Carlos handed power over to the fascists.'

'That puts the border of the Reich 500 kilometres further south.'

'I'm afraid so. There's more.'

'Go on,' the General said in a resigned tone.

'The Tripartite Pact, signed at the end of September.'

'What about it? Us, the Italians, who were our allies anyway, and the Japanese. I didn't see much relevance.'

'Neither did I. Japan is on the other side of the world and, besides being a thorn in the British side, and perhaps sharing a few useful pieces of new technology, it doesn't seem of much significance.'

'But...' the General said.

The admiral nodded.

'There's a but. I've heard rumours that Hungary, Bulgaria and Yugoslavia are all in discussions with regards to joining the Tripartite Pact.'

'Do the Russians know?' the General said.

'I suspect they do. They've been asked to join, too, I've been told.'

'So, Adolf will, in effect, control the whole of Europe, and the Soviets will control what remains? An unholy alliance.'

'Yes. And we know what might happen to the Jews in these countries. Now you know why I wanted to talk to you.'

'What can be done?'

'Nothing. I am talking to the British, and the Americans. They're not listening, for different reasons.'

'How can they choose to ignore this?'

'Perhaps they think we're exaggerating. Roosevelt is sympathetic, but the American people don't want to get involved in another European war. The British are merely trying to survive.'

'So, Adolf Hitler can do as he wants?'

'Yes, and his ego won't let him stop. And that's when he will make a mistake.'

For a few moments, both men said nothing.

'Or his legacy will last a thousand years,' the General said.

'There is that,' the admiral agreed.

~~o~~

[11/10/1940 Friday]

'I'd forgotten how hospitable these Norwegians were,' Johann said, slurring his words.

'You're only saying that because Frieda there, is hanging onto you like you're something out of a chocolate soldier box,' Max said.

'You're jealous, Maximilian,' Johann said, laughing.' I'll ask her if she has a friend who's not as fussy as she is.'

He whispered something into the mass of blonde hair that covered the girl's ear. She turned her head towards Max.

'I will find girl for you, Max-a-million,' she said, almost as drunk as Johann. 'I promise.'

Max smiled and drained the last of his beer.

'What I find most annoying,' he said, slurring his words, 'is that the major, your brother, seems to attract girls with almost as much ease as you, but he does nothing with them. It's a criminal waste.'

'I agree,' Johann said. 'He likes to talk, he tells me. Well, I'm all right with that because it saves him lecturing me at every opportunity.'

It wasn't completely true. Franz had cornered Johann on a couple of occasions, trying to lure him into continuing the conversation they'd had in Kiel with their father, but Johann had always managed to change the subject, or had bailed out of the conversation on one pretext or another.

The girl, Frieda, whispered something in Johann's ear.

'Gentlemen,' he said. 'I'm going for a stroll with this young lady. If I'm not back at barracks by morning, send a search party in case she's a partisan.'

They all laughed. He looked around for Franz. He saw him by the bar, talking to two older women.

Johann slapped Franz's arm on the way past and received an indulgent smile and a shake of the head in return.

He hurried out into the cold, Frieda clutching onto him as they walked, one as unsteady as the other on the frozen, compacted snow, heading for her flat.

Damn Franz to hell. Better to get drunk and find a woman to hold than to fret about matters that don't concern us.

CHAPTER 30

[30/10/1940 Wednesday]

The next time the Nussbaums had a visit from the authorities, it wasn't the Gestapo.

A black car drew into the drive and two men in suits, each carrying a coat, walked round the side to the cottage, as the Gestapo had. When no one answered, they crossed to the back door of the Kästner house, seeing no need to walk all the way round to the front. Miriam answered.

'Miriam Nussbaum?' the shorter of the two men said.

'Yes. Can I help you?' she replied, glancing around to see if Yosef was behind her.

'Kriminalpolizei,' the man said, flashing a card at her. 'You applied recently for a travel permit to visit Hamburg?'

She'd attempted to visit her parents again, but she'd been refused a travel pass, and she hadn't persisted in reapplying, hoping that the General might offer her and Yosef a lift on his next trip to Hamburg.

'Yes. It was rejected.'

'Yes. We know that. We'd like to come in and ask you a few questions.'

'We can go to the cottage. Give me a second, please.'

They waited as she stepped into the kitchen and hung up her apron before closing the door behind her and leading them over to the cottage.

'My husband will be over shortly,' she said, as she showed them in.

The two men looked at each other, then the shorter detective narrowed his eyes at Miriam.

'We just want to ask a few routine questions.'

'I'd rather my husband was present,' she said.

'We can continue this at the police station, Frau Nussbaum, if you don't cooperate.'

'I'm perfectly happy to help. What do you wish to know?'

Before he could answer, the door opened, and Yosef entered, his face a mask of concern.

'This is your husband?' the shorter of the two policemen asked. He took out his notebook.

'Yes.'

'Your name,' the man asked.

Yosef gave his name and stood beside Miriam.

'Now, Frau Nussbaum, if we might continue,' the policeman said, his sarcastic tone not lost on Miriam.

'What was the purpose of your intended visit to Hamburg?'

'To visit my parents,' Miriam said.

'And for no other reason?'

'No.'

'Have you ever heard of a publication called the *Kieler Jüdisches Freiheitsnachrichtenblatt*?'

It was so unexpected that Miriam and Yosef couldn't stop themselves flinching.

'I've heard of it,' Miriam said. There was no point in lying. Every Jew in Kiel knew about it.

'Have you ever read it?'

Miriam and Yosef glanced at each other.

'No. That would be illegal,' Miriam said.

'Perhaps we should search the house,' the taller policeman said.

Miriam stared at him. *So, he can speak, after all.*

'By all means, help yourself,' Miriam said, relieved that they'd got rid of the copy of the KJF that had been so close to being unearthed during the Gestapo's house search.

The shorter policeman shook his head.

'Perhaps another time,' he said, and although the KriPo men lacked the menace of the Gestapo, Miriam shivered.

'You'll be hearing from us,' the taller man said.

~~o~~

When the General arrived home, his wife berated him that the Nussbaums were now bringing the police to their door. He made an unsuccessful attempt to placate her, then, before going across to the cottage, he telephoned his friend, Kiel police chief Uwe Müller.

'Erich,' Uwe had answered, in his usual booming voice. 'I always get nervous when you get in touch these days.'

The General didn't laugh.

'You know I wouldn't telephone you if it wasn't important.'

'I know,' the police chief said with a sigh. 'I can guess what you're phoning about.'

'You can?'

'The Jewish newspaper investigation. Have your Jews been interviewed?'

'Yes.'

'Well, don't worry. It's routine. Did they have any connection with the Judenhäuser in Kleiner Kuhberg?'

'Yosef helps out. He's a member of the committee, I'm sure, but it was his wife Miriam they wanted to talk to. She'd applied for a travel permit to Hamburg, to see her parents.'

'Ah. That's it then. Anyone who has travelled, or applies to travel, is being questioned. We suspect that they're printed here in Kiel, but they're turning up in Rendsburg, and Neumünster, and even in Hamburg, and the party are getting a little nervous that it will spread to further towns and cities.'

'Isn't it usually the Gestapo who investigate this sort of thing?'

'Yes, I was surprised that they gave it to the Kriminalpolizei, but the Gestapo complained that they are short-staffed and told us we were capable of handling it. I'm sure they'll take it over again when we find out where this rag is being printed.'

'And do you have any control over the KriPo?'

'Nominally, they and the Gestapo are under the umbrella of SiPo, the security police but in practice, the KriPo in Kiel work closely with us, and leave all the political stuff to the Gestapo. I have a little influence.'

'So, there's nothing to worry about?'

'Not unless they're involved.'

'No. They won't be,' the General said. 'Thank you.'

There was a short silence at the end of the line, then Uwe Müller spoke.

'You know, you won't be able to protect them forever.'

'I know, Uwe. I know.'

~~o~~

[01/11/1940 Friday]

'I'm glad we didn't go to Greece,' Ruth said. 'The Italians have invaded.'

Antje, lying on her bed, sketching a portrait of Ruth, looked up.

'I wish you didn't have to go anywhere, but I'd rather you were somewhere safe.'

'I don't want to go, but Mama and Papa are frightened now. First the Gestapo, and then the police. It has shaken all of us, except Manny. He's just angry.'

'It must be hard, not being able to fight back.'

'Mama is worried that he'll get into trouble. I didn't tell her, but a few friends of his got caught stealing paint. I'm sure he was involved, but they got away with just a warning. I think that they'd intended to daub a slogan on the wall of the local NSDAP building.'

Antje paled. 'He could have been arrested. That would have been terrible. I wish there were something I could do.'

'There's nothing you or I, or anyone can do. We'll just have to wait and pray. I'd prefer to go to America, but there is something exciting about Palestine.'

'Oooh, it would be. Imagine living in a desert.'

'I don't think it's all like that. I've seen pictures, and there are trees, and flowers. There are even swamps, in Galilee, we were told.'

'Still, it's like summer all year, they say. I'll come and visit you.'

They laughed. Antje showed Ruth her finished picture.

'It's lovely, Antje. It looks just like me.'

'I'm going to keep it. For when you go to America, or wherever you end up, so that I won't forget you.'

~~o~~

Erich Kästner changed trains at Hamburg, catching the Berlin train with five minutes to spare. He was normally driven to the monthly meeting in Berlin, at the Reich Ministry of War, but his army driver had twisted his ankle and was out of action for a few days.

He enjoyed travelling by train. In the relative comfort of first class, it was easier to catch up on paperwork or essential reading if he felt like it. And should he want to, the views of the Brandenburg countryside and the towns the railway passed through were better than those from the car. But it meant that he would have to stay in Berlin overnight.

The steward served him lunch as the train pulled out of Wittenberg with an hour and a half left of his journey. He considered these trips to be a waste of time, but Canaris liked to get his team together on a regular basis to foster a sense of cooperation.

When they pulled into Berlin's central station, he hailed a taxi to his hotel, a stone's throw from the Abwehr Headquarters on Tirpitzufer, part of the Bendlerblock complex that housed the offices of the OKW, or Oberkommando der Wehrmacht, the de facto Reich Ministry of War.

It was an indulgence, but he always stayed at the Grand Hotel Esplanade and as he ran a bath, and looked down Bellevuestraße towards the Tiergarten, he took a few moments to relax and soak before getting ready for the short walk to his meeting.

~~o~~

Kriminalassistent Werner Schmidt of the Kriminalpolizei thanked the two constables for their efforts and looked at the list of Jews he would have to visit that day, in the search for the criminals who published the *Kieler Jüdisches Freiheitsnachrichtenblatt*.

The detective sergeant was nothing if not thorough, and he'd asked to speak to the two younger detectives after reading their reports of the interviews they'd done a few days before. Now he was planning to revisit the ones that he thought might be withholding information.

Why the KriPo, the criminal police, had been given this task eluded him. If anything had Gestapo written all over it, this had, but he'd been assigned to the case by his harried Kriminalsekretär.

He called the two men back.

'One of you can come with me,' he said. The two constables looked at each other, then the short one stepped forward.

'I'll come,' he said.

'Oh, and there's one last thing, for future reference. You shouldn't have let the Nussbaum Jew stay when you were questioning his wife.'

'Yes, sir,' the shorter constable said. 'I'm sorry, sir.'

'You'll learn. Let's go.'

CHAPTER 31

The meeting was more fruitful than Erich Kästner had expected. Canaris had been called away on an urgent matter and it was left to his deputy to chair the meeting. In the admiral's absence, there was less jockeying for favour by the more obsequious heads of departments, and there had been genuine sharing of information across the table.

The General usually dined with Canaris afterwards, often accompanied by a couple of the latter's other acquaintances. On this occasion, he ate alone at the hotel and, after a brisk walk around central Berlin, he retired to his room for an early night, aided by a fine malt that was new to him, courtesy of the hotel bar.

He was woken by the insistent ringing of his bedside telephone. He scrambled to switch on the light and pick up the receiver. A glance at his watch told him it was only half past ten.

'I have a call for you, Herr General,' the switchboard operator said. 'It's from Kiel.'

The General's stomach lurched.

The boys. Something has happened to them.

'Erich.' He heard Maria's voice.

'What is it?' he asked, breathless.

'It's the Nussbaums. They've been arrested.'

The General's initial rush of relief was replaced by an immediate surge of guilt and worry.

'When did this happen?' he asked.

'After supper time. I have the children here. You need to come home.'

'I can't get transport tonight. The last train was hours ago.'

'Will the army not provide a car for you?'

'No. There would be too much red tape involved, and I would have to have a damned good reason.'

'I'll send Albert with the car.'

'No,' he said, raising his voice, then taking a deep breath. 'It wouldn't get me home much sooner, and you have to remember his age,' he said, his words measured now.

'What if they come back for the children?' Maria said.

'They won't,' he said, hoping it was true.

'This is just the end, Erich,' Maria said. He was shocked at the cold anger in her voice.

'I'll catch the first train in the morning. It leaves around six, so I'll be there by lunchtime. Have Albert meet me at the station, and I'll go straight to see Uwe.'

'You'll need to find a solution to all this, Erich. It's making me ill.'

He took a deep breath and tried to see it from her point of view.

'We'll discuss it when I get back. Now, try and get some sleep. Ruth will look after Manny. You could even take them to their grandparents first thing in the morning.'

He could sense that she was a little mollified at his suggestion.

'I'll be there as soon as I can,' he said, before replacing the receiver.

He sat slumped on the edge of the bed. He rang the reception and asked for a taxi to be ordered for five o'clock. He wasn't sure of the exact time of the first train, but he didn't want to miss it.

'And please ring me at four-thirty,' he said.

He lay back down and closed his eyes, but sleep eluded him.

~~o~~

'You are a colleague of Jakob Teubner, are you not?'

Yosef was tired. He didn't know the time, but it was late.

'Yes,' he answered. 'I am on the committee that runs the school for Jewish children in Kleiner Kuhberg.'

'And your wife. Is she involved?'

'Only as a parent.'

The detective pulled out a copy of the *Kieler Jüdisches Freiheitsnachrichtenblatt* from a folder and slid it across the table.

'You've read this rag here?'

'No, but I've seen a copy.'

'And you've never read it?'

'No.'

'I don't believe you. Was your wife going to make a delivery to Hamburg, for Teubner?'

'No. She wanted to see her family. It's almost impossible for them to talk on the telephone now.'

'You know who prints this,' the detective said, holding up the single-sheet newspaper. 'You must do, being part of the group that runs the Judenhaus school and the synagogue.'

'No. It has nothing to do with us. We wouldn't dare risk it, for the sake of the school.'

The hint of a smile appeared at the corner of the man's mouth.

Yosef watched the man put the KJF sheet back in the folder.

'Have it your own way,' the detective had said. 'A night or two in the cells might change your mind. And while you're sitting alone, worrying about your family, consider the possibility that we could have you sent to one of the camps.'

The detective watched Yosef for a few seconds while the threat sank in.

'Perhaps you'll be more talkative in the morning.'

In comparison with the Gestapo men, the policeman had been polite and reasonable, but it hadn't lessened Yosef's sense of dread.

The Kriminalassistent motioned for the younger man to take Yosef away. As he'd guided Yosef through the door, the detective spoke again.

'Your children. Is there anyone to look after them?'

'My daughter is old enough to see to my son.'

The detective had turned up at the door of the cottage not long after Miriam and he had returned after serving the Kästner ladies their evening meal. He'd introduced himself as Kriminalassistent Werner Schmidt of the Kriminalpolizei and he was accompanied by one of the young detectives who'd interviewed them.

He told them that they were being taken to the police station for questioning.

Miriam had barely been given time to throw on her coat and whisper to Ruth, listening in the hallway, to take Manny to the big house once the men had left, and to stay there.

'By the way,' the detective had said, as he led Miriam out, 'I'll be sending a couple of detectives over to search your house. Will they find anything?'

'No. We have nothing to hide.'

'We'll see.'

~~o~~

As Yosef was marched along the corridor, he looked up. Miriam was being brought in the opposite direction.

'Are you all right?' he gasped, and she looked up.

'Yes. I'm...'

'Nicht sprechen!' the man holding Yosef hissed, shoving Yosef past Miriam. Yosef looked over his shoulder, but Miriam was being pushed into the interview room he'd spent the last hour in.

The cell door clanged shut. Yosef sat on the bench that served as a bed, his head in his hands.

The General is away. No one can help us.

~~o~~

Maria Kästner watched from the kitchen window, her hands gripping the back of the chair as she stood in the dark. The two men had arrived within the hour and had already been in the cottage for forty minutes.

What if they come here? They might try and take the children. How could I stop them?

~~o~~

[02/11/1940 Saturday]

The maid answered the door. The General asked her if Chief Müller was at home and told her that it was imperative that he should speak to him.

She told him to wait, and returned a few seconds later and showed him in.

The General stood in the hallway, listening. From somewhere at the back of the house, he could hear the squeal of children's voices, interspersed with the laughter of adults.

The General sighed. *His grandchildren must be visiting.* He didn't know whether his intrusion would irritate Uwe, or if he would be glad of the excuse for a moment's respite.

'Erich,' Uwe Müller said, coming through the door from the kitchen in what the General would have called comfortable clothes.

'Uwe,' the General replied. 'I can't apologise enough, but there was no one else I could contact. The Nussbaums have been arrested. I'm not sure where they have been taken. We were told nothing. I'm worried they've been taken to one of these camps.'

'Sit down, Erich,' the police chief said, showing the General into the front room. 'Can I get you anything? Coffee, or something stronger?'

'No, no. Danke. I just need your help.'

'Right,' Uwe Müller said. 'First, when did this happen?'

'Late last night. I was in Berlin. My wife called, and I took the first train home this morning. I just got here.'

'They'll still be at Falckstraße. Yes, police district two is the most likely. Do you know who the arresting officer was?'

'I've not even been home. I came straight from the station.'

'So, they may have been released already.'

'No. My driver picked me up at the station. The Nussbaums haven't returned home.'

'All right. Wait there, and I'll make a phone call.'

He left the room. The General looked around. It was an austere room, the furniture heavy and ornate. He'd been once before, to a dinner party a few years back.

He was looking at the various photographs of the police chief's children and grandchildren when the man himself returned.

'Ah. The family. It has expanded somewhat, over the last few years, with all these grandchildren.'

'They must give you a lot of pleasure, Uwe.'

'Yes, but it's always nice when they go back home to their mamas and papas.' He laughed, then donned a serious look.

'They are still at Falckstraße. They are being questioned in connection with this investigation into the illegal Jewish newspaper. You've seen it, haven't you?'

'Yes. I've seen a copy. It's well written, I have to say.'

'Indeed,' the large man said, chuckling. 'It's perhaps the only newspaper that prints the truth, in all honesty, but the authorities can't be seen to ignore it. You understand?'

'Of course. But the Nussbaums aren't involved. I'm sure.'

'Are you? They could be using their privileged status to help their friends.'

'No. The Nussbaums have been with us for my whole life, two generations of them. They would never do anything that would jeopardise our family, or their positions.'

'It's a little naïve of you, I'd say. Although you may know them as well as anyone, these are desperate times, Erich, and it's surprising what people will do.'

'No. If you knew them, you would think the same. If they were involved, they'd have told me earlier in the week when the police first called.'

The police chief sighed.

'It may well be that the detectives are just fishing, in the hope that the Nussbaums will give them a name they've heard in connection with this rag. If so, they will release them when they discover that they know nothing, but it would be too risky to assume that. I'll find out who's in charge of the investigation and get back to you.'

'Should I not come with you?'

'No. Go home. I'll be in touch.'

CHAPTER 32

'When will Mama and Papa be home, sir?'

The General wished he could turn away and wipe his eyes, but he knew that not being able to meet Manny's gaze would destroy the boy's faith in him.

'We'll have them back in no time,' the General said, giving the boy an encouraging smile. 'In the meantime, would you rather stay here or go to your grandparents' house?'

He could feel Maria's eyes boring into the back of his neck.

'I'd rather stay here, sir, if that's all right with you and Frau Kästner.'

'Of course. You're always welcome here.'

Ruth interrupted.

'General, if you don't mind, Manny and I will go over to the cottage,' she said.

The General noticed Ruth's glance at Maria.

'I'm old enough to look after him,' she continued, 'and anyway, we need to see what sort of mess the police have left. I don't want Mama and Papa coming home to a house that is upside down.'

'I'll help,' Antje said, touching Ruth on the arm.

Ruth gave her a grateful smile.

'I'll help too,' the General said. 'It will give me something to do.'

He turned to his wife.

'Maria, would you mind staying here?' he said. 'If there's a phone call from Uwe, come and get me.'

She nodded.

~~o~~

By six o'clock, the Nussbaums' home had been restored to something approaching the way Miriam would have it. The KriPo men hadn't subjected the cottage to the same wilful vandalism of the Gestapo, but the search had been thorough, and it took a while to restore the spilled contents to the appropriate drawers and cupboards. The General had to smile when, despite the tension, Ruth followed them around, checking the work he and Manny had done, correcting them when their efforts weren't quite up to Miriam's standards.

They all had one ear cocked for the sound of an engine, or tyres on gravel. Hamburger Chaussee, once a busy road, saw scarcely a car on it now; since the bombing of Kiel had started, few ventured out at night, even on Saturday, not risking being stuck in one of the air-raid shelters in the city centre overnight.

Twice, the General had slipped over to the big house to ask Maria if there had been any calls, and to check that the telephone was working.

They'd finished clearing up when the clock struck six, and the General chased them over the yard where, he was pleased to see, Maria had set the table and cooked dinner of sorts.

The meat was overcooked, and the gravy had lumps in it, but they all devoured it as if it were one of Miriam's finest offerings, and the General flashed a smile of thanks at his wife.

'Hard work makes hungry mouths,' he said, beaming at Manny with a bonhomie that he didn't feel.

The boy gave him a thin smile.

'Perhaps we could play a game,' Maria suggested with a forced brightness, her nervous fingers playing with the sleeve of her dress.

Manny stared at the tablecloth. Ruth didn't answer. The General assumed that the girl's thoughts were a few kilometres away at a police station in central Kiel. Even Antje appeared subdued.

'Maybe another time…' Maria said.

An awkward silence fell on the table, broken only by the faint sound of Manny's leg swinging back and forth, hitting against his chair. Ruth glared at him and he stopped.

Five minutes passed then Manny looked up and turned his head towards the window. A moment later, they all heard the murmur of an approaching car.

The car slowed, and then sped up again as it passed, heading towards Hassee.

They all breathed out at once, and Manny looked at Ruth. She gave him a brief smile of reassurance.

'We'll go through to the drawing room,' the General said. 'It's more comfortable there.'

Ruth sometimes stayed over at the Kästners' house as a treat, sharing the bed in Antje's room, but this was different and, for the first time, she felt like a stranger.

Antje ran upstairs and returned with an old construction set that the boys had long since forgotten and gave it to Manny. It piqued his interest enough to keep him occupied, while the two girls and Maria cleared away the supper dishes.

'You should really stay here tonight,' the General said to Ruth, when they returned.

Ruth shook her head. 'No thank you, sir, it would be better for us to sleep at the cottage,' Ruth said. 'In case Mama and Papa come back. We'll be fine. We've imposed long enough.'

'Nonsense,' said the General. 'You'll stay here until your parents come home. I'll not have you on your own when we have all the room in the world. What would Yosef and Miriam think of us?'

'Thank you,' Ruth said, grateful for the General'skindness but wishing she and Manny could be at home, alone together.

When the doorbell rang, everyone, including the General, jumped. Ruth let out a gasp and her hand flew to her chest. Manny looked at his sister, his face tense and pale in the light from the table lamp.

'Stay here,' the General said, striding across the room. He closed the door behind him and walked down the hall.

When he opened the front door, Uwe Müller stood there, his hat in his hand.

'I have them,' he said. 'I've been told to release them into your custody, for now.'

'Where are they?'

'In the car.'

He stepped back and waved to his driver. The General watched as the man opened the back door of the car, and Miriam, then Yosef, climbed out.

The driver, a police constable, escorted them over to his chief. Yosef was pale and drawn, but he gave a nod and a half-smile of gratitude as he climbed the steps. The General clasped him on the shoulder and stepped to the side to let him through, followed by Miriam. She also gave him a tired smile.

They stood in the hall, Yosef's arm around his wife in support. The General turned back to Uwe.

'Thank you, my friend,' he said, his voice breaking.

'I can't help you the next time, Erich. I've told them to keep themselves to themselves for a while, even if that means staying away from Kleiner Kuhberg, for now, at least.'

He took a form from his pocket.

'I need you to sign this.'

The General took it and signed where the police chief indicated.

'Kriminalassistent Werner Schmidt may call on you. Be polite. He's just doing his job.'

'Why would he need to talk to me?'

'To make sure your Jews are behaving. You may also receive a visit from the Gestapo; they are involved in the investigation.'

He paused.

'Listen,' he continued, putting his hand on the General's shoulder. 'The only reason Kriminalassistent Schmidt let them go was because I told him who you are. You have a lot of friends in high places, and not just in Kiel, but that won't help you forever. Take my advice and get your Jews out.'

'It's not for the want of trying, Uwe. They've been unlucky.'

'For their sakes, and yours, sort it.'

The police chief shook the General's hand. He turned and walked down the steps.

'Remember,' he said, pausing as he got into the car. 'I don't want to hear from you again unless it's to go for a drink, or a meal with you and Oskar, and the Doc.'

The General waved as the car turned onto the main road.

'Now,' he said to Yosef and Miriam, 'Try and forget it for now. You have two young people who are desperate to see you.'

~~o~~

'What did they ask you?' Yosef said to Miriam when Manny had gone to bed, and Ruth had disappeared to her room.

'Oh, just if I'd read the KJF, and if I were involved in its distribution. Why do you think they are picking on us?'

'I'm not sure they are. I think this is completely by chance; if there had been a connection, the Gestapo would have been all over us last night.'

'Should we warn our friends?'

'We can't. We gave our word to the police chief that we wouldn't leave the grounds of the Drachensee house, and the General signed for our release.'

'We could ask the General.'

'No.'

'But Jakob, and the others…'

'They'll know about it. It wasn't only us.'

'Oh. I suppose that's true.'

She relaxed a little.

'Telephone again tomorrow,' she said. 'See what's happening with our visas. And we need to contact the Haganah.'

'How? We can't go near Kleiner Kuhberg.'

'Jakob will contact us when we don't appear.'

'If he's still there,' Yosef said, a tremor of fear in his voice.

~~o~~

[03/11/1940 Sunday]

Werner Schmidt sat at his desk. He lit a cigarette and lifted the release form. He stared at it. The police chief had handed it to him earlier that morning with a warning to leave the General's Jews alone.

The detective was a pragmatic man; although the police chief had no direct jurisdiction over him, the OrPo, the regular police, and the KriPo, the criminal investigation department, worked closely together.

In more serious investigations, when they needed the extra manpower, Uwe Müller always obliged KriPo by providing as many OrPo officers as they required, often cutting into his overtime budget to do so.

But this one was political. He was sure that the Nussbaums read the Jewish newspaper; all Jews did. He was also convinced that neither of them had anything to do with the newspaper's production, or its distribution.

Verdammt, I would have released them tomorrow anyway.

But it bothered him that the police chief had intervened; he'd never interfered with criminal investigations before. He'd understood just how much of a key military figure General Kästner was in Kiel when the chief had mentioned the names of the people who had been putting pressure on him to release the General's Jews. He cursed himself for not checking the Nussbaums' employer out before he'd arrested the pair.

But he hated double standards, and it pained him that he'd have to treat these two Juden differently from all the other Jews in Kiel. For all he knew, the Nussbaums could have been the ones who let a name slip that would have led to this investigation being wrapped up, and off his desk forever.

If only I'd been able to keep them in custody for another twenty-four hours.

He knew by experience that it was often the second night behind bars that reaped rewards from tired and fearful witnesses.

He sighed and slipped the release form into his desk drawer. There were still leads to follow, and he put the Nussbaums to the back of his mind.

~~o~~

Memo: Geh.KdoS. ABW 22/11/40 CAC01411.1

For Attention Only: General Erich Kästner, Abwehr, Kiel office,

Abwehr.

From: Vice Admiral Wilhelm Canaris, Chef der Abwehr.

Admiral Dönitz has officially adopted the "wolfpack" tactic for
the Unterseeboot fleet in the Atlantic.

The loss of over half of the ships in convoy HX 72 in
September, and the sinking of a quarter of the merchantmen in
convoy HX 79 without the loss of any U-boats, despite an escort
of two destroyers and four corvettes, has persuaded him that
the tactic he has developed of submarines hunting in groups,
with highly efficient communication, both with the pack and
with the onshore commanders, is the most effective way to
implement the blockade of Britain. [END]

CHAPTER 33

[22/11/1940 Friday]

'Your name has cropped up a couple of times in the wrong places.'

'Oh, I can't imagine why.'

Erich Kästner hadn't seen Gerhard Wendland since the young man had been a junior officer in his command, ten years or so ago. Now he was a Hauptsturmführer in the SD, seated in front of him. He put the contents of the memo aside and focussed his mind on his visitor.

Never, in his days in the army, would he ever have imagined that an officer of the *Sicherheitsdienst*, the security services, would be paying him a visit.

'Listen, Herr General. I'm here because you were a good officer to your men; you were kind to me when I was young and, shall we say, a trifle impetuous.'

The General gave his former lieutenant the smile he expected, and a chuckle to reinforce it.

'You were a handful at first,' he said, wondering why the Sicherheitsdienst, the SS's intelligence service, had sent this captain to see him.

'You straightened me out, General, and set me on the right path, and here we are now; me a Hauptsturmführer in the SD and you, a General in the Abwehr. Who would have thought it?'

The General shrugged. 'I saw potential in you once you knuckled down. I thought you could go far in the army. What made you leave?'

'Let's just say an opportunity came up. I was drafted into the military police and found I had a talent for detective work. I was approached two years ago by the Sicherheitsdienst and I liked the sound of it.'

'And your remit?' the General asked.

'Clever, Herr General,' the SD officer said, smiling. 'I almost forgot that you were in the intelligence game too. I'm with Section B, Inland-SD, if you must know.'

Canaris had once explained the inner workings of the Gestapo and the SD to him.

'Race and Ethnic Matters?' he asked.

'Bravo, Herr General. You've obviously done your homework. You know why I'm here, I would imagine.'

The General shrugged.

'Enlighten me.'

The SD man sighed.

'These pet Jews of yours are beginning to be an irritation.'

'My household staff? I'll admit to trying my best to keep hold of them. If you were to come and eat at my home, you would perhaps understand why. It would be almost impossible to find a cook half as good as Miriam Nussbaum.'

'Perhaps I'll take you up on that invitation sometime. If it were only that, it would be simple, but I'm not sure your motives are entirely of self-interest. I've been doing a little digging, my friend.'

When the General said nothing, Gerhard Wendland continued.

'Friedrich Schumm. Does that name ring any bells?'

'A close friend of my staff. I helped loosen a little red tape, to allow his parents to bury him.'

'The Jewish soup kitchen in Kleiner Kuhberg. I believe you were the chairman of the Rotary Club, when it just happened to make a significant donation.'

'Father Liebehenschel approached us. He is the priest at St. Augustine's. One of our members had suggested that we could help. He ran the soup kitchen for people who were destitute. If you remember, there was mass unemployment in the early part of the last decade.'

'Indeed there was, which the Führer has eliminated, but this soup kitchen was somewhat different, wasn't it?'

'It was?'

'Herr General. You know I shouldn't need to spell it out. Jews. They were all Jews.'

'The good father didn't break down his clientele by race for us.'

'And you never visited it?'

The General hesitated.

'I did once. It was my responsibility to make sure our funds were being used appropriately.'

'And you didn't notice that almost all of those clients of his were Jews?'

'No. One destitute person looks much like another. I saw only desperation.'

'You appear to have an answer for everything, Herr General.'

'Honesty, Hauptsturmführer. Mere honesty. I hoped you'd have remembered that from your service under my command.'

'Indeed, Herr General. Listen, my friend,' the SD man said, surprising the General with a softening of his tone. 'You might not believe this, but I am here to help you.'

The General's face must have revealed a little of his disbelief.

'General, you have thirty-five years of unblemished service. From everything I've learned over the last few days in Kiel, you are extremely well respected by the Kriegsmarine, the Heer and to my surprise, by senior local party officials. I heard a hundred times that you are a vital cog in the navy machine, that you're a man who makes things happen.'

The General shrugged again.

'I do my best and I'm good at my job.'

'Modest as ever, General. But that's only part of the reason I'm here. I wasn't lying when I said you were an inspiration to me; that you sorted me out and stopped me from destroying my career. You may or may not believe that I'm an honourable person. That's your prerogative.'

The General bit back a response. *How can a man in his position be considered honourable?*

'I'm here to warn you. As a friend. Your name has crossed my desk on several occasions and, if I've seen it, others have, too, and sooner or later, one of them will decide that you are a danger to the Third Reich.'

'And what I do for the Kriegsmarine, and the war effort. They would discard that?'

'Yes. Better men than you have been sacrificed. I don't want to see that happen to you.'

'If I believe what you say, this is a friendly warning?'

'Yes. I know that you have views diverse from my own. Don't let them destroy you.'

The SD man stood up.

'I'm sorry that you and I cannot be friends,' he said. 'I have a genuine respect for you, which is the only reason I'm here.'

'And all the information you have on me?'

'I'll keep it in a drawer. The Gestapo won't get anything on you from me. But if you are ever indicted for activities against the state, I'll have no hesitation in handing over what I have, for my own protection.'

'Even though you've sat on it?'

'Pah. I can present it any way I wish. Mere suspicion, the fear of accusing such a senior figure. There's a lot of that about.'

'I suppose I should thank you, Hauptsturmführer.'

'I'm not looking for thanks. I've paid my debt. It's your problem now.'

He held out his hand. The General took it.

'Thank you,' he said.

After the SD man had shown himself out, the General stared out of the window across Kieler Hafen.

There was a knock at the door. Heinz Bauer entered.

'Sir, is everything all right?'

'Yes, Captain. It's fine.'

'It's only…'

'I know. Even if one has done nothing, it's hard not to feel nervous with these people.'

'Is it trouble, sir?'

The General laughed.

'No. Not at all. The man served under me a few years ago. He was in Kiel, and thought he'd look me up.'

'Ah, sir. That's a relief.'

'He was a bit of a loose cannon. I like to think I sorted the fellow out. He's certainly done well for himself. A Hauptsturmführer, he was saying.'

'I wouldn't thank you for his job, sir. Everyone fears them.'

'I'm sure they do. But there can be a little good, even in a rotten barrel.'

'Just don't let them hear you say that, sir.'

CHAPTER 34

Memo: Geh.KdoS. ABW 23/11/40 CAC01414.1

For Attention Only: All senior executive officers, Abwehr.

From: Vice Admiral Wilhelm Canaris, Chef der Abwehr.

Today, Romania has signed the Tripartite Pact, following
Hungary's example. They join Germany, Italy, and Japan in the
alliance.

This move confirms the de facto agreement that already exists
between Romania and Germany, with thousands of Wehrmacht troops
already stationed in the country. [END]

~~o~~

[01/12/1940 Sunday]

'Jakob, come in.'

Yosef shepherded the older man into the cottage. He stuck his head out of the door and glanced around, then closed it.

By the time he'd followed Jakob into the kitchen, Miriam had taken his coat and seated him at the table. She filled the kettle and placed it on the range. Yosef hurried to shut the window blinds, then sat down opposite his guest.

'You shouldn't have come,' Miriam said, looking at the clock. 'It's dangerous. Especially at this hour.'

'Breathing is dangerous, these days,' Jakob replied, his laugh hollow.

'How are you, old friend?' Yosef asked, reaching out and putting his hand over Jakob's.

'Sick, Yosef. Sick and tired of all this. Where will it end?'

Yosef glanced at Miriam. He had never seen Jakob so low.

'Something will turn up,' he said. 'It has to.'

'I wish I could believe that. I'm at my wits' end. When I didn't see either of you for a few weeks, I was worried.'

'We were arrested by the police,' Yosef said, 'as part of the KJF investigation. The General got us out. He's a friend of the police chief.'

'We've been warned not to leave the Kästner property,' Miriam added. 'That's why we haven't been to Kleiner Kuhberg.'

'Ah. I'm relieved. I thought the Gestapo had taken you because of the Weichmanns. I felt so bad about sending them to you.'

'There was nothing you could do,' Miriam said, depositing three cups of coffee onto the table.

'All the same…'

'You said "too". Who else has been taken?'

'You didn't hear about Benno?'

'Benno Arndt? Used to work for the Morgenpost?'

'Yes. They killed him. The rumours are that he had a terrible death at the hands of the Gestapo.'

'Why? He was harmless.'

'He was the editor of the KJF.'

'Oh. I didn't know,' Miriam said, the colour draining from her face. 'The poor man.'

'Only a few key people knew it was Benno. He produced the paper on his own, with just one assistant, who got away, as far as we know. The story we're hearing is that Benno didn't give them his name, despite what they did to him.'

'That's what the police questioned us about; the KJF,' Yosef said. 'They thought Miriam was delivering copies to Hamburg.'

'Why?'

122

'She'd applied for a travel permit to visit her parents in Altona. They must have been checking all movements made by Jews.'

'They questioned half of the Jewish community. Somebody must have told them about Benno.'

Tears were running down Miriam's cheeks.

'I didn't know him well,' she said, 'but his bravery…'

'He knew that printing the newspaper would kill him. He told me that a while ago. But to be tortured. One day, I hope these animals will pay.'

Yosef snorted.

'Pay? Who's going to make them pay? The world doesn't care.'

'We care,' Miriam said, the firmness in her voice startling the two men.

'But what can we do?' Jakob asked. 'We're powerless.'

'We need to keep a record,' Miriam said, her eyes blazing. 'We need to write it all down. Rosa said that to me once, a while ago. She was right.'

'They'll find it, or they'll kill us. Whichever, it doesn't matter.'

'We hide it. We give it to Aryan friends. There are still one or two of them we can trust.'

Yosef saw her glance in the direction of the Kästner house.

Jakob looked up at her.

'You're right. Every Jew should chronicle their life in the Third Reich. They can't kill all of us or find every diary.'

Miriam rose from the table, and made a pot of coffee, then poured three cups.

'Why did you come so late?'

'The Gestapo watch us, but only during the day, because of the curfew.'

Since the outbreak of war, Jews were not allowed out of their homes during the hours of darkness. For those caught flouting the restriction, the penalties were severe.

'But if you get caught…'

I needed to get out. My home is gone; I moved my wife into Kleiner Kuhberg a fortnight ago. She's driving me crazy with her complaints about the accommodation.'

For a second, Yosef and Miriam stared at him, then they all burst out laughing.

The door to the hallway creaked open, and Ruth's head appeared around it, confused.

'Mama, why is Herr Teubner here at this time of night?'

'I went for a stroll, Ruth, and ended up here.'

Ruth gave a confused smile.

'It's all right, Chamudah,' Miriam said. 'Jakob was just checking we were all right, because we hadn't been to services and you hadn't been to school.'

'When can we go back?'

'Not yet, Ruth,' Yosef said. 'The General told us to stay close to home for a while, until all this fuss dies down.'

'I'll get some textbooks to you somehow,' Jakob said.

'Thank you,' Ruth said, her face brightening. 'I've been teaching Manny,' she added.

Jakob smiled at the hint of pride in her voice.

He turned to Yosef.

'Self-help,' he said. 'It's what we Jews do best.'

'She insists on keeping school hours,' Miriam said, managing a weary smile. 'Poor Manny thought he would have one long holiday.'

They all laughed, and Ruth blushed.

'Is Manny asleep?' Miriam asked.

'Yes. I was just reading when I heard voices.'

'Go back upstairs,' Miriam said, not unkindly. 'I'll be up in a while. Papa and Jakob need to talk.'

When Ruth had gone, Yosef turned to Miriam.

'We do?'

'I would imagine so, but I need to talk to Jakob first, then I'll go and leave you in peace.'

'What can I help you with, Miriam?' Jakob said.

'The Haganah. They haven't been in touch with us. Do you have contact with them?'

'From time to time, but it's difficult.'

'If you are talking to them, remind them that we are desperate to go, please.'

'I'll do that.'

'We hear rumours,' Miriam said. 'Is it true that they're sending more people to Poland?'

'They take more from the Judenhaus every day, but for every one of us they deport, the Gestapo bring in two. There are three families to every room now, and the sanitation is struggling to cope. And with rationing, it is difficult to feed them all.'

'Are Emil and the children still there?'

'For now, but I can't say for how long.'

'Can you use the Weichmanns' money to try and get Rosa out? I'm sure Esther and Itsik would have wanted that. If Emil and the children are deported, at least Rosa should be with them.'

'We're already trying. Emil asks me how we are getting on with it every day. But I will get our lawyer to try a bribe. It has its risks, but if we are lucky and find a greedy official, it could work.'

'Thank you. Shalom, Jakob.' She hugged him, tears in her eyes.

'Aleichem shalom,' the old man replied, releasing her.

She hurried out of the room, leaving the two men alone.

'Now, Yosef. I have a few pressing matters I was hoping you could help me with...'

CHAPTER 35

Kriminalassistent Werner Schmidt stirred three sugars into another cup of coffee. He shook his head.

No wonder I'm putting weight on.

He lit a cigarette and exhaled. It had been a difficult forty-eight hours, ever since he'd been invited to view the interrogation of Benno Arndt, the unfortunate publisher of the illegal *Kieler Jüdisches Freiheitsnachrichtenblatt*.

Involved as he was in the KJF investigation, he hadn't been able to find an excuse not to attend.

He'd slipped out after an hour, not having the stomach for it, but he'd seen the grin on Kriminalassistent Heinrich Güllich's face when the Gestapo man noticed him leave.

The phone rang.

It was Güllich. He listened, expecting to hear him gloat that the KriPo couldn't handle a bit of robust interrogation but, instead, the Gestapo man informed him that Arndt had died without giving them any names.

Both he and Güllich had been convinced that there was a second man involved in the printing process, and that there had to be others who distributed the KJF.

'He must have had a weak heart,' Güllich said. 'It is rare for us to fail.'

'At least we stopped it,' the policeman said, 'and the equipment has been destroyed.'

'We will get the others eventually, one way or the other,' the Gestapo man replied.

'No doubt, but from the Kriminalpolizei position, the case will now be closed, I would imagine.'

'Yes, my superiors have informed your department that we will take it from here.'

The Gestapo man paused.

'There's just one thing…'

'What is that, Kriminalassistent?' the KriPo man said.

'I was reading through your notes, and the constable's notes. I see that you interviewed a Miriam Nussbaum twice.'

'Yes. That's correct. She's a Jew, but she works for a General Kästner as a cook. He has some connection with the Kriegsmarine, as strange as that may sound.'

'Yes. We've had dealings with the Nussbaum woman, and this General Kästner.'

There was a pause.

'From your notes, I see that you had her in custody, but you were instructed to release her?'

'That's right. She and her husband. The chief of police himself asked me to let them go, if no charges were being brought against them.'

There was silence at the other end of the phone.

'There was no evidence they were involved,' Werner Schmidt added, his words running together. He cursed himself. 'They would have been released anyway, and we insisted on getting a signed declaration from this General Kästner with assurances that the Nussbaums would be restricted to the grounds of his residence, indefinitely.'

'I see. So, it was the police chief, Uwe Müller, who intervened personally?'

'Yes. He and General Kästner are good friends. There was also pressure from several of the admirals, and from the Rathaus too. General Kästner is very highly regarded by the city leaders and, as you know, they have a big say in how Kiel is run.'

The Gestapo man grunted.

'And you're sure these Jews weren't involved,' he said, 'even in a minor role?'

'I'm convinced that they read the wretched thing, like most of them, but beyond that, I'm almost certain they had nothing to do with it.'

He hesitated.

'Can I ask why you are interested in this woman, this couple?'

There was silence at the end of the phone, as if the man were weighing him up.

'I want these people. I've also been warned off investigating them. It came right from the top; Heydrich himself, maybe even Himmler. And I don't like justice being obstructed.'

Werner Schmidt smiled grimly. Justice wasn't a detail the Gestapo always concerned themselves with.

'The General is determined to keep them,' he said. 'He told me that Miriam Nussbaum is an irreplaceable cook and housekeeper, and the couple have worked for the General since he was first married.'

'That's the line he's taking,' Heinrich Güllich said, 'that they are indispensable to his well-being, and because he is so verdammte important, they can't be touched, but I suspect there's more to it than that. Yosef Nussbaum's parents worked for the General's father, the old admiral. It's just too cosy for my liking. I think our General is a Weisse Jude.'

A White Jew.

Werner Schmidt nodded.

He knew there were still a few Aryans around who insisted on associating with Jews, most of whom should have known better.

'Is he a Jew-lover in general, pardon the pun, or is it just his particular Jews?'

'That's for us to find out,' the Gestapo man said. 'I'm doing a little digging in the background. And let's see if we can turn up anything else about his Judenläuse.'

'Is there anything you want me to do?' the policeman said, out of politeness.

'No, just keep your eyes and ears open, please, and let me know if anything turns up.'

Heinrich Güllich hung up and Werner Schmidt sighed. They were both the same rank. Kriminalassistent. But the policeman got the distinct impression that the Gestapo man considered himself his superior.

Sitting in his office, in the fading late afternoon light from the weak sun outside, he thought about the Nussbaums, and the General, and that perhaps it would be a good idea to do a little rooting around on his own.

Why are the Gestapo investigating Miriam Nussbaum?

He picked up the phone and asked for central records.

CHAPTER 36

[21/12/1940 Saturday]

As the plane lifted off, its propellers biting into the sky, the General turned to Admiral Canaris, sitting next to him.

'I don't know how you talked me into this.'

'I need someone I can trust. You were available and, let's face it, they'll hardly miss you in Kiel.' He grinned.

'You'd be surprised. Maria will be heartbroken, and my staff will fret until I return.'

'I doubt it. Anyway, you're here now. And we'll be in Madrid sooner than you think.'

'If we get there,' the General said. 'Do you travel in these things often?'

Canaris laughed. He'd never seen Erich Kästner so miserable.

'I do prefer travelling by ship,' he said, 'but it takes far too long, so I fly when I need to, and the Reich ministry pays for it.'

'I'll be glad when we arrive, and in one piece,' the General said, looking uneasily out of the cabin window. 'Why are we going anyway? You're keeping it pretty close to your chest.'

'I'm being sent to try and persuade General Franco to join with us and fight, if and when a war starts between Germany and England.'

'Why did they send you?' the General said, raising his voice over the drone of the engines. 'I'm surprised they trust you enough.'

'They know my grasp of the language, my diplomatic skills, and my military brilliance are unmatched, and don't forget my experience in Spain and South America. Need I go on?'

'No, I understand. But there must be others who could do it. People who are more enthusiastic about this war.'

'They think I am a supporter, albeit a cautious one. I haven't done anything to persuade them otherwise.'

'What about the time you talked to Keitel about what went on in Poland?'

'He buried it. He told me that a few months back. Said that I'd had an uncharacteristic wobble but now I was back on track, that he'd covered for me.'

'That's terribly kind of him. So, you feel that you can do better by keeping in with them?'

'Yes. First, I'll know what's going on. Second, I might just get a chance to influence people and change minds.'

'I get that, but I still don't understand why they chose you.'

Admiral Canaris gave a knowing smile.

'I've met Franco before. He asked for me.'

'Ah. You said that you knew him. So, what do you want me to do?'

'Do you speak Spanish?'

'Only a smattering. You know that.'

'Just do as I say. I'll do most of the talking. I might ask you to speak to a few people, but those will all have reasonable German. Most of all, I just need someone who has my back, and who I can run things by if necessary.'

'I'm here to hold your hand and fetch coffee then?'

'Exactly. Now, sit back and enjoy the flight.'

~~o~~

Two days later, the two men walked into the foyer of their hotel. For Erich Kästner, it had been a long forty-eight hours, but fascinating.

'I'm not sure what happened today,' he said, as he and Canaris waited for the lift, 'but I'd like to find out. We flew in two days ago. You met with Franco three times with his entourage and once with him alone, then we all shake hands and go. That's it?'

'We're heading back tomorrow to tell Adolf Hitler that Spain will not go to war as an ally of the Third Reich unless Britain is defeated first.'

'Franco told you that?'

'Yes. And I'll tell you how it came about when we've had something to eat.'

~~o~~

They sat on the balcony of General Kästner's room. They could see into the adjacent balconies, which were empty, and Admiral Canaris had glanced over the balustrade to check that the ones below were also unoccupied. They were on the top floor, with a view over night-time Madrid, and the strains of a singer drifted up from the bar below. The hotel had unearthed a bottle of brandy of dubious provenance, but it was proving to be more palatable than it looked. Each man held a generous glass in his hand.

'So, how did you manage to persuade Franco not to fight with us? And why won't it go badly for you back at the Reichschancellery?'

'I didn't persuade him. I let him make his own decision, based on the facts, as he knew them.'

'But I heard you ask him, on Hitler's behalf, to ally himself to the Third Reich, in the event of a war in Europe.'

'I did, in the presence of Spain's minister of war, General Juan Vigón and our ambassador to Spain, Eberhard von Stohrer, and he was cautiously optimistic that he could help.'

'I know. He sounded quite positive. I was there, and there was an interpreter, so I heard it all. I was also present on the last day when Franco told you that, with regret, he was unable to support Germany, etc, etc, etc. It's what happened in between that I can't quite grasp.'

'I provided him with a few detailed pieces of intelligence about the forces available to all possible protagonists in a future European conflict and, in addition, the likelihood of further nations joining the conflict against Germany.'

The General thumped the table.

'You old sea dog.' He laughed out loud.

'It would have been remiss of me not to be completely open and honest with a potential ally. The Abwehr has access to a vast amount of intelligence data about all the major nations' political and military strengths, including our own.'

'You gave him information about the Wehrmacht?'

'And received information about his own military resources in return. You must remember that General Franco and I have built up a valuable friendship over the years. And, I might add, I shared our extensive knowledge of the strength of the British Armed Forces.'

The General's eyes narrowed.

'And some of the intelligence reports may have been played down, some exaggerated?'

'As you will know already, from your short time working within the sector, intelligence gathering is far from an exact science, and inaccuracies, while lamentable, cannot always be avoided, blah, blah, blah.'

The General looked at the straight face opposite him with astonishment. Not a twitch of a smile showed, even at the corners of his mouth.

Then, Erich Kästner threw his head back and roared with laughter, and his friend, the admiral, joined in.

~~o~~

The plane was almost empty. Of the twenty seats, only those in the front row were occupied, by the admiral's personal staff and two marines. Wilhelm Canaris and Erich Kästner sat together towards the rear.

About an hour before they landed at Tempelhof airport, the General, in a voice just loud enough to hear above the noise of the engines, spoke to Admiral Canaris.

'I didn't ask you why. It's been bothering me.'

'It's simple. I'm trying to avoid an invasion of Britain.'

'But surely, if we do attack Britain, it would be better to have Spain on our side?'

'If Spain is on our side, it will give our leaders the illusion that we can win. We can't win. At least, not yet. Maybe never.'

'So, you're just trying to get them to postpone it?'

'Yes, more or less. I'm trying to stop the bloodshed.'

'What about five years' time, when we are ready?'

'We'll worry about that in five years.' He turned to face the General.

'Erich, I mix with these people every day. I keep my ears open. Despite the victories in Poland, the low countries and in France, the army commanders know deep down that we're not ready. They're trying to stall for time as much as I am, but the reality of it is that Keitel, in overall command, is completely under Adolf's thrall, and if the Führer wants to cross the English Channel, he'll jump in a boat and paddle it there himself. Our leaders want to take over the whole of Europe and the High Command are too spineless to stand up to the likes of Göring, Goebbels and Himmler, and Adolf himself.'

'They'd risk everything to invade England? Just because no one is brave enough to stand up and say we'll lose?' the General said, incredulous. 'Why would they do that?'

'Because they're sleepwalking into it, like a flock of sheep led by a mad shepherd.'

'You were once a supporter,' the General said, softening his voice.

'I was. I am an advocate for our armed forces, and I still believe we need a strong nationalist leader who will stand up to communism and fight for Germany's rights as a nation...'

The head of the Abwehr hesitated.

'But we need to stop this despot, for the sake of a future Germany, and if that means putting a spanner in his plans, so be it.'

'You're taking quite a personal gamble here, you know, Canaris.'

'You're not averse to taking risks either, Kästner.'

The General laughed.

'What else can we do?'

'What we have been doing. Trying, where possible, to stall and moderate their excesses.'

He looked long and hard at his friend.

'Erich, why do you think I chose you to accompany me here?'

'I don't know, other than that you can trust me.'

'That's a big part of it, but not all. I know you have always had grave doubts about the direction Germany has taken. It has taken me longer to see the big picture like you have but, to my advantage, I come across like-minded people in my position.'

'Who are they? I see little evidence that anyone is standing up to the National Socialists.'

'These people have to be careful. They may only have one chance, and the timing has to be right.'

'You want me to help? To work with you; with them.'

'No. I want you to stay away from them. They will most likely fail, and I don't want them taking you down with them.'

'But you're involved.'

'Not directly, and I do enough to convince Hitler that he should have few doubts about my allegiance.'

'So why do you not want me to help?'

'I need you where you are. Someone I can trust, who isn't involved, and has the ear of the Naval Command.'

The General nodded.

'I work more closely with the Kriegsmarine than I do with the Heer,' he said.

'Yes, and I don't want you jeopardising that by trying to start a revolution. You will be betrayed.'

'They already know I'm not a big supporter of the National Socialists.'

'That's true, and many of them are the same, although they hide it better.' He smiled.

'And what about you?'

'I'll work away behind the scenes, sowing seeds here and there but keeping the Abwehr above reproach, and useful to the government. It's all about curbing their ambition and trying to avoid them getting Germany into a conflict that we can't win.'

'You think we'd lose again?'

'Yes. Even if we keep the Soviets out of it. But I wouldn't trust them either.'

'And if we don't invade Britain?'

'We will continue to organise. All the time, opposition to Hitler and his legions will get stronger, both militarily, and economically. He will continue to terrorise the people but, sooner or later, his power will wane when they realise all his promises are hollow.'

'And then?'

'We will have a new government.'

The General was silent for a few moments.

'It's a risky strategy, Canaris, like playing chicken in a snake pit. Be careful.'

'You never know. Friends of ours might one day be successful in removing Hitler and his followers. That's when you, and everyone like you, has to be ready.'

'But not before?'

'No.'

1941

"The enemy is at the gate. It is a question of life and death".

Andrei Zhdanov, leader of the Leningrad Party Committee.

CHAPTER 37

Lise unlocked the door.

'I'm home,' she shouted down the hallway. There was no answer.

I hope he hasn't found a bottle somewhere.

She'd hidden all the alcohol in the flat, except for the bottle of wine they'd shared the previous evening. They'd been out celebrating his promotion to Hauptsturmführer on his first night home on leave and, in the bedroom, she'd used all her new-found knowledge to make her husband's homecoming one to remember. She'd found his naked wonderment and happy subservience towards her a hundred times more captivating and satisfying when placed against the memory of the masterful Obersturmbannführer Eicke.

And she was sure in her heart that, despite his absence from her for nine months of his own choosing, and the violent interlude that framed his last visit in her mind, he loved her. In the sweating, rasping aftermath of their lovemaking he clung to her in silent tears, and she held her vulnerable and tender husband like a child, knowing that Frau Eicke would never command the same worship from the Obersturmbannführer that Rudolf had for her.

But again, his sleep had been interrupted by those rigid, sweating tremors and the fitful cries of nightmares, until he'd woken staring into space. She'd soothed him back to sleep, not knowing if he was conscious of her words, or the touch of her hands, or her lips on his face, but she sensed his rigid flesh melting under her fingertips.

And she vowed to never see the Obersturmbannführer again, even if he'd confirmed her doubts about Rudolf's fidelity during their brief affair. She knew they meant nothing other than a physical relief and, while distasteful, did not affect her husband's adoration of her.

Her sole irritation of the hours since his arrival the previous afternoon was his plaintive expression of regret at their inability to produce children for the Reich. She'd almost retorted that she could only have his child if he were there to impregnate her but had bitten her tongue and had retaliated by once again taking the necessary precautions to ensure that his seed never reached her womb.

She closed the door and shouted again, but there was still no answer. She'd slipped out to buy milk, leaving him in bed to sleep off the hangover from his overnight terrors; he would have had no time to dress and leave the flat, nor have reason for doing so.

She looked in the bedroom door and frowned, seeing the bed empty.

She walked into the tiny kitchen and placed the milk bottle into the larder. She ground enough coffee to fill the coffee pot and placed it on the stove to bubble away, assuming he was in the bathroom.

She took off her coat, hanging it up before entering the room that doubled as living and dining area. Rudolf was sitting at the table with his head in his hands.

She crossed to him and laid a soft hand on his neck.

'I have aspirin,' she said, 'if your head is sore.'

His fist caught her just below her ribs as he swung around. As she doubled over, winded, in pain and shock, she saw the tight, terrifying anger in his face. She stumbled, almost falling, and he grabbed her by the hair and drew her face close to the table.

Through eyes blurred by tears, she saw the white Bakelite box that housed her Dutch cap, sitting in the centre of the table.

How had he found it? She'd risen during the night and had taken it out, cleaning it as the nurse had told her to. If Rudolf had woken with the flame of passion in his eyes again, she would have made her excuses to empty her bladder and replaced it inside her, when it was needed.

For a horrible moment, she thought he was going to smash her head against the edge of the table. Instead, he lifted her face up to his, still gripping a handful of her hair, until his eyes, bloodshot and staring, were a few centimetres from hers.

'Was ist das?' he hissed.

She turned her eyes away from him and said nothing. He slapped her hard with his free hand across the side of her face.

'You lying, cheating whore,' he spat and hit her again. Her face burned where his hand had struck her, and her hair felt as if it was being pulled out from its roots.

'I was frightened,' she whimpered.

It startled him, and he froze, but his eyes narrowed again, and he hit her a third time.

'Frightened of what?' he said.

Tears were now running down her cheeks.

'Of carrying a child. Of giving birth.'

'Why? It is a woman's duty and privilege.' This time, he punched her stomach.

She retched and gasped for breath.

He swung her by the hair and threw her across the room. She struck one of the armchairs and fell over it, crumpling to a heap against the wall. He stood over her.

'My body. It's just for you. It would never be the same.'

He lifted the white box up and removed the rubber cap from it.

'This is an abomination. Not only is it against God, but it is against the Führer. He demands of the SS not just obedience and honour, but that we produce children for the Reich. How can I face my unit, knowing my wife disobeys me, humiliates me in this way?'

He lashed out with his foot and it caught her already bruised midriff.

She pleaded with him to stop.

'I'll have your children, Rudolf,' she cried. 'Please don't hurt me.'

'I know you will,' he hissed at her, undoing his belt.

~~o~~

She heard the door slam but lay for a while on the floor, unable to move. Her jaw throbbed, and a burning between her legs vied with the sharp pain of her ribs and stomach.

For an eternity she lay, fearful that he'd caused internal damage. Taking a deep breath, she turned on her side, then onto her stomach. She grimaced and drew her legs up, her forehead still pressed to the floor. She rested, catching her breath.

She looked at the clock, then, gathering her strength, she reached a hand up onto the armchair, and pulled herself to her knees.

She wiped her hands on her bloodied dress then, with a final effort, she stood, still stooped, and stumbled to the bathroom. On the floor, she saw the smashed box the Dutch cap had been in. The two halves of the diaphragm itself were in the toilet, along with the scissors he'd used to cut it with.

Chaotic thoughts echoed around her head.

Where will I get another one?

They were banned in Germany. She'd had to travel to Denmark to buy it, slipping across the border to Padborg on a trip to Flensburg with her mother and her ladies, no one commenting on her absence.

That won't be as easy now.

The wooden box on the windowsill that had held her personal toiletries, where she'd kept it hidden, was smashed, and the contents strewn next to it on the shelf, spilling onto the floor.

What made him look in the box?

She looked in the mirror. Her face was already turning blackish blue around her cheekbone and eye socket. She lifted her hand up and touched it with her fingers. It felt numb.

She glanced down at herself. Her dress was ripped, exposing one of her breasts and her bloody thighs.

How could he do so much damage, without hurting himself?

She ran a bath and, after making sure the front door of the flat was locked and bolted, she lowered herself in with great care, taking a sharp hiss of breath when the hot water reached her lacerations.

I have to get out of here, before he gets back.

There was nothing she wanted more than to have her mother with her, holding her, but she knew that she couldn't bring herself to call her, or drag herself to the villa in Drachensee, until she was whole again. She surrendered to the pain and vowed to survive.

I'll think of something.

~~o~~

Rudolf sat morosely in one bar, then another, then a third. By the time he was politely advised to go home, well after midnight, he'd been drinking all day, but it hadn't touched him, or dulled the pain.

He found a bench, in Exerzierplatz, and sat slumped on it. She'd betrayed him, and his mind got to working on how else she'd abused his trust. His anger began to build as he imagined a series of lovers. Perhaps it was his fault. He should have come home on his last two furloughs, but the shame of what he'd done to her the last time had kept him away. Now, he'd hit her again. He began to sob, then anger took over again, and the sob turned into an anguished shout.

He got up and stumbled towards the flat. He climbed the stairs not knowing if he would fall at her feet and beg forgiveness or confront her about her lovers. The door was locked, and the flat was in darkness. He fumbled for his key but, in his haste to leave, he'd forgotten it. He thumped on the door but there was no answer. He put his shoulder hard against it and it splintered and gave. He pushed the door open and stepped inside, calling Lise's name.

She'd gone. He stood in the middle of the living room and wept.

~~o~~

He stayed until the end of his leave, but she didn't come back. Twice he walked out to Drachensee and stood out of sight, down the road from the Böhm house, watching. He saw her parents come and go, and her brother, but there was no sign of Lise. As he boarded the train taking him back to his unit, he was already, in his mind, composing the letter he'd write to her apologising, and begging forgiveness.

And he hoped she was pregnant. A child would cure him, he knew. And her.

CHAPTER 38

[23/01/1941 Thursday]

In a small city like Kiel, it was perhaps inevitable that Franz and Lise would bump into each other.

He almost didn't recognise the woman in sunglasses and a headscarf who collided with him on Kaistraße.

'I'm so sorry,' she said, her head down, repositioning her glasses. 'I should be more careful.'

'Are you all right, Fräulein?' Franz said, more concerned for her than for himself.

'I'm fine, thank you,' she answered, turning to walk away.

'Lise?' Franz said.

For a moment, she said nothing. Then she gave him a weak smile.

'Franz? I'm sorry. I didn't recognise you. You look different.'

He laughed, surprising himself.

'A few years older, perhaps? How are you?' he asked, out of politeness.

'I'm well,' she said. 'Yourself?'

'Home on leave, but back to Norway again in a fortnight. We're being transferred to Bergen.'

'Is that good? I don't know much about Norway, I'm afraid.'

'Well, it is further south than we've been based for the last six months, so it shouldn't be quite as cold in winter. It is a beautiful country.'

'I'm happy for you,' Lise said, touching his arm. 'Now, I must go, I'm running late.'

'Are you sure you're all right? Are you hurt?'

He looked closer at her face.

'You're marked,' he said. 'That wasn't me, was it?'

She laughed, but to Franz it appeared rather forced.

'Oh, that,' she said. 'I walked into the kitchen door yesterday. I don't know where all this clumsiness is coming from.'

Franz reached out and removed her sunglasses.

'Lise!' he gasped. The left side of her face, almost hidden by the headscarf, was tinted blue and yellow. She'd attempted to apply enough make-up to hide it, but her efforts hadn't succeeded in covering all the bruises, and the deep scratch was still visible across her cheekbone.

She turned her face away, snatching her sunglasses back again and using her hand to screen herself from those passing by.

Franz moved to stand in front of her, shielding her from the crowd rushing up and down the street. He looked around, then guided her through the door of the café a few metres further down; she didn't resist.

He sat her down and ordered coffee for them both and looked out the large window to give Lise time to compose herself. In the yards on the far side of the Hafen, men were clambering over the tall, emerging superstructures of two large warships like insects, and he marvelled at their lack of fear.

He was glad Johann wasn't with him; he was sure his brother would have given Lise a hard time, despite her injuries. Franz had not long left his brother and his friends drinking in a sleazy bar on Wall, the road that curved round the front of Bootshafen and Fischhafen, where most of the city's strippers and working women plied their trade.

Why they enjoyed hanging around in low-life places watching disinterested women strip for them, Franz couldn't fathom, but he supposed they saw it as an integral part of being a soldier.

He'd left for home, his ears echoing to the sounds of their jeers as he stepped out into the street and had walked straight into his encounter with Lise.

He turned back to look at her. A little of the poise had been knocked out of the Lise he'd known, and whoever had done this to her had made a real job of it, but he was still wary. He couldn't forget the two years of hurt, and a further two of limbo, that she'd caused him.

'When I saw a woman in sunglasses in January in Kiel, I thought she'd watched too many American films.'

She gave a half-smile. 'It is a sunny day. Why not?'

'Who did that to you? Was it your husband?'

She shrugged.

'He lost his temper. He was drunk, and I goaded him.'

'Leave him then. Go back to your parents. Tell them you made a mistake. You don't have any children, do you?'

She laughed again.

'That's why he hit me,' she said. 'He wanted to know why I wasn't pregnant, that there must be something wrong with me.'

'He wanted a child that badly?'

'I don't know why I am telling you this. You're the last person I should be speaking to.' She paused for a second, then continued.

'He only wanted children for his ego. To show he was a man. To brag to his comrades.'

'But to hit you because you hadn't conceived? Why would he do that?'

'Because I told him I was using something.'

'Something? What...' Franz blushed. 'Oh,' he said, 'I see. But why?'

'I used a diaphragm because I didn't want to churn out little brats just to make him look good. I wanted to have fun, and would have been happy, even though he was just home for a week at a time. We would cram everything into that week...'

Franz blushed again at her forthrightness. 'But didn't you speak to him about it?' he said, asking himself how he'd got involved in such an intimate conversation.

'I knew he wanted me to have his children. I would have given in, in due course, but every time he came home, he would get drunk and ask me if I was "carrying a little soldier for the Reich yet".'

'You must have known that SS officers, if permitted to marry at all, are expected to produce children for the Fatherland. You were lucky to get permission.'

'Lucky? You think? There were two reasons for the wedding going ahead; maybe three.'

'I can guess the first,' Franz said.

'I suppose you can. When you look like this...' She gestured towards herself with her hands, and Franz had to agree that she still looked as good as she had back then, if not better.

'All they see is a breeding machine,' she continued, 'deserving of a suitable sire.'

She touched her face. 'This spoils it,' she said, 'at least for a while.'

'It will heal, although that scratch might leave a mark, if you're not careful.'

'It was his SS ring. He always likes to wear it. It comes in useful when he hits women.'

'You can't go back to him,' Franz said. 'Talk to your mother and father. They'll take you back when they see your face.'

She let out a bitter laugh.

'My father adores Rudolf. He thinks he's *quite a catch* for me. He spent a fortune on the wedding. He won't be as understanding as you imagine.'

'Your mother will talk him round, surely?'

'My mother cares more for appearances than anything else. How would it look if her daughter deserted a hero of the Third Reich?'

It wasn't strictly true. Her mother would see it from her daughter's side, she knew. In time.

'But if they saw your face...' Franz persisted.

'They'd tell me to be nicer to him, to stop making him angry. *Do you know how lucky you are? Most girls would die for a Schutzstaffel Obersturmführer. Give him a child.*'

'You can't live like this,' Franz said.

'He won't be home for another three, six or nine months, depending on when he sees fit. It might be better if my face does scar,' she said, touching her cheekbone. 'It will make him think twice about doing it again.'

She shuddered. For a while she stared out of the window, then she blushed, and laughed, but to Franz it sounded hollow.

'I shouldn't have told you. I'm sorry. Please never repeat any of this and, if you ever meet Rudolf, don't…'

She let the words hang.

'I'll say nothing. I'm not the type to break a confidence,' he said.

Lise flinched, but Franz didn't notice.

'I must go,' she said. 'A friend of mine is coming over tonight and I must get ready.'

'Will your friend not be shocked?' Franz asked, 'When she sees you?'

'She's an old friend from the BDM. She's witnessed this before and, anyway, she knows what SS men can be like.'

Franz shook his head.

'Be careful,' he said. He got up and pulled out her chair as she stood. She leaned forward and pecked him on the cheek.

'I made the wrong choice, Franz,' she whispered, and ran out of the café.

Franz stood for a minute, his mind in turmoil.

He paid the bill and left. A tram passed and he ran after it, jumping onto the rear platform as it slowed for the corner.

The conductor frowned at him but said nothing, his major's uniform enough to prevent the muttered disapproval that a civilian would have been subjected to.

He sat, staring at the seat opposite, thoughts of Lise whirling around in his head. When he finally looked up, he realised he was two stops beyond Drachensee, and jumped from the tram the next time it halted.

Walking back, he tried to put thoughts of Lise out of his mind.

CHAPTER 39

Knowing that Colonel Schneider, like the boys, was on leave, the General felt obliged to invite him for drinks one evening and, because he thought it might please Maria, he extended the invitation to include dinner.

'Katharina was distraught that she couldn't come,' the colonel said, standing in the Kästners' spacious entrance hall. 'She's chairing a committee of the *Lübeck women for the Reich* tonight and couldn't get out of it.'

'I fully understand, Herr Colonel,' Maria Kästner said, flashing a pleasant smile. 'I just wish Erich were as understanding about the importance of the charity work that I do,' she added, frowning at her husband.

Colonel Schneider laughed. 'Please call me Walther,' he said, taking her hand and kissing it. 'I'm sure Erich has great appreciation for what you do. Perhaps, like me, he is more apt to be effusive about it when talking to others.'

'The colonel is right, my dear,' the General said. 'I'm forever singing your praises to anyone who will listen.'

Yosef took the colonel's coat.

'We'll have drinks in the drawing room first,' Maria Kästner said. 'Johann and Franz are through there already.'

She turned to Yosef.

'Hang these up then sort everyone out for drinks, please.'

'Yes, ma'am,' Yosef said.

The General held his arm out in the direction of the drawing room, then followed Maria and Colonel Schneider through.

'Franz, my boy. Johann,' the colonel said.

'Herr Oberst,' Franz and Johann choroused, saluting. The General was a trifle disappointed to see that they used the Hitler greeting instead of a traditional army salute, but they were part of the colonel's battalion, and his way was law.

After shaking hands, Johann offered the colonel a drink.

'Have a malt whisky, Walther,' the General said. 'I have a couple here that might interest you.'

He turned to Yosef.

'Could you bring through the Macallan and the Glenfarclas, please, Yosef.'

'Are you enjoying Norway, Walther?' the General asked his guest, while he waited for Yosef to return.

'It's not Paris, but it has its own charm. The mountains and the fjords are stunning in their beauty.'

'I remember them well. Franz and I sailed *Snowgoose* there a few summers ago, with a couple of friends. The sailing was majestic, and I found the people to be exceptionally sociable.'

'Considering we have occupied their country, many of them still are. In fact, we are in negotiations to commission a Norwegian battalion in the Wehrmacht.'

'Really! That's extraordinary. I presume the officers will be German?'

'I know little detail, but one would assume so.'

'Will you manage any sailing while you are in Norway?' the General asked.

'I suppose I could talk my way into one of the local yachts. It wouldn't be the same as having my own boat there, but there are a few small sailing clubs in Bergen, I believe, and the waters around that area are very sheltered.'

The General laughed.

'Perhaps you could have *Der Sturmtaucher* shipped out to Bergen. You'll be there for the duration, by the looks of it.'

'It's possible, I suppose. There are ships plying back and forth all the time from Germany. It shouldn't be too much to ask for one of them to sit her on their deck, then drop her back in the water for me when they get to Bergen.'

'The season isn't long, but it is glorious. I'd look into it if I were you.'

'Excellent. I'll make a few enquiries tomorrow. Now, I see your man hovering with a bottle of that fancy whisky of yours…'

Towards the end of dinner, during which the colonel and the three Kästner men talked mostly about the war, and to what extent the British were on their knees, the colonel stated that he had some news for them.

The General saw Franz squirm slightly in his seat.

'Now we all know that Major Kästner here is not one to blow his own trumpet, but I have something to tell you, unless he has told you himself.'

He looked expectantly around the table but the blank faces that looked back at him confirmed his suspicions.

'Franz is following in his father's footsteps,' he said.

Johann groaned.

'Oh, don't tell me. He has been promoted to General.'

The colonel laughed.

'Not quite,' he said, pausing.

'Franz has been awarded an Iron Cross. He is to receive it when we return to Norway. General von Falkenhorst is going to present it to him in person.'

He beamed at their surprised faces.

Johann slapped his brother on the back.

'I told you they'd give you a medal,' he said.

'Two of my squad are to get Iron Crosses too,' Franz mumbled, his face reddening as they all crowded round him, everyone congratulating him at once.

'What was it for, Franz?' Antje said, her eyes wide with excitement.

'It was nothing much,' Franz said. 'We pulled a tank crew out of their damaged panzer.'

'Rubbish, Franz,' Johann said. 'It was a little more than that.'

'We all saw it,' the colonel interjected. 'We were following a panzer unit about twenty kilometres from Paris when the lead tank was hit by a shell from one of the few French tanks that were still making a fight of it. While the remaining panzers took on the French tank, we all watched in horror as the crippled tank began to burn.'

He turned to Franz.

'All except for Major Kästner. He shouted for two of his men to follow, racing across the open ground to the tank, even though there were machine guns and tank shells criss-crossing the clearing. When he reached the tank, he climbed up and managed to unjam the main hatch and help three of the crew to the ground, despite smoke billowing from the damaged section. With Corporal Hahnemann , he dragged the final crew member from the body of the tank and told the corp to carry the injured gunner to cover. I didn't see much more from where I was standing, as the smoke had completely occluded my view by then.'

He looked at Johann.

'We were on the opposite flank,' Johann said, continuing where the colonel had left off. 'The wind was blowing the smoke away from us. I saw Franz jump onto the turret and try opening the commander's hatch, but it was jammed. He jumped down and picked up a metal bar which had been ripped off by the shell, and climbed back up, using it to force the hatch open. At this point, flames were beginning to engulf the underside of the tank. We were all shouting to Franz to get clear, that it was no use, but he reached inside and pulled the unconscious commander out. We could see that he was gravely injured, but Franz wouldn't leave him. He jumped down and hoisted the man across his shoulder and ran towards us.'

He looked at Franz and shook his head.

'The whole platoon gave covering fire, and yelled for Franz to hurry, when the ammunition blew. Everyone threw themselves to the ground while chunks of metal flew over our heads. When we looked up, Franz and the injured man were nowhere to be seen.'

The colonel spoke again.

'When the smoke cleared, we crawled towards the still burning carcase of the tank, shouting Franz's name. We found him and the man he'd saved, both unconscious in a crater about halfway there. He must have thrown himself into it just as the tank exploded.'

The General looked at Franz, then Johann.

'And when were you going to tell us about this?' he said.

'Franz told me to say nothing,' Johann said. 'He thought it would just worry you both.'

'You were lucky you weren't killed, or severely injured,' Maria said, the vein in her temple throbbing. 'You both promised me you'd do nothing foolish.'

'Now you see why I didn't want to say anything,' Franz said.

'I must admit, when I first reached him, I thought he was dead,' Johann said. 'He wasn't moving, blood was pouring from the back of his head and I could smell burning flesh. We got Franz and the man he'd saved onto stretchers, but by the time we got a field ambulance, Franz was sitting up asking about the captain he'd hauled out.'

'What about your injuries?' Maria asked, still annoyed at what she thought was unnecessary recklessness.

'Several of his bruises were spectacular,' Johann said. 'He needed seventeen stitches for the wound on his scalp, and he had some minor burns to his hands. He was on light duties for a week until he insisted that he be returned to active service.'

'Did the tank commander survive?' Antje asked, surprising everyone.

'I don't know,' said Franz. 'He was in a pretty bad way. I asked around but no one could tell me.'

'He's making a slow recovery.'

They all turned at the colonel's words.

'They interviewed him for the citation,' he explained. 'He has serious burns to his arms, a fractured skull and two broken legs, and he might lose the sight in his left eye.'

'It's a relief to know that he'll live,' Franz said.

'It was a lieutenant, the tank's second in command, who cited Franz's squad for their medals,' Colonel Schneider said. He told them that none of them would have been here but for Franz and his men, and the captain wouldn't have made it if Franz hadn't gone back for him. That's why his Iron Cross is first class.'

He raised his drink.

'Major Franz Kästner.'

As Franz stood, his face colouring again, they rose and echoed the colonel's toast.

~~o~~

For once, Johann didn't disappear when the meal ended, and Franz joked that he was losing his touch with the ladies.

'Ach, there's nothing happening tonight. The boys have gone to Hamburg and by the time I got there, it wouldn't be worth my while.'

Maria smiled.

'That's wonderful,' she said. 'It's not often I have all four of you here at home these days.'

Miriam and Yosef entered to clear the dishes. The General told them of Franz's Iron Cross and insisted on Johann recounting Franz's heroics.

The Nussbaums congratulated Franz, then started to clear the table. Johann jumped up and offered to help, ignoring his mother's frown.

He lifted a stack of plates and, much to Yosef's embarrassment, walked through to the kitchen with them. Franz, listening to something the colonel was saying, noticed him out of the corner of his eye.

He heard his father tell the colonel that he had some rather nice Cuban cigars that he'd just received, and would the colonel like to retire from the ladies for a short while.

He turned and asked Franz to join them.

'Tell Johann to come too,' he added.

As the colonel and his father made their way through to the General's study, Franz looked around for Johann, but he hadn't returned.

Antje grabbed his arm.

'Were you frightened?' she asked, a worried look on her face.

'It happened too fast. I didn't have time to be afraid. Afterwards, I felt a shiver go down my spine when they told me how close it was.'

'Please be careful, Franz. I know you would always want to do the right thing but just imagine Mama and Papa, or Eva and I if anything happened to either of you.'

'I'll try, but we are soldiers. And it can be just as dangerous here for you. I heard that a bomb landed in the lake.'

'I stayed over with a friend from art school,' she said, 'but Mama told me there were dead fish all over the lawn. Anyway, we have the cellar now. Papa had it strengthened.'

'I know. He showed me. It certainly looks the part.'

He glanced around.

'Where has Johann disappeared to?'

'He'll be in the kitchen, chatting to Manny. You know what these two are like. Johann thinks of him as his little brother.' She laughed.

'I didn't realise Manny was here tonight.'

'Yes, he's doing his schoolwork in the kitchen, while Miriam and Yosef are working. Ruth is there, too, helping him. She does all his teaching now.'

Franz sighed.

'I wondered why he was being so helpful,' he said.

'Who? Manny?'

'No. Your idiot brother. He's finally noticed that Ruth is now an attractive young woman. I told him to keep away from her, but he'll be in there, talking to her, trying to worm his way into her affections.'

Antje giggled.

'I'm glad you find it amusing,' he muttered.

'I'm sorry, but don't worry yourself. Ruth is quite capable of fending off Johann if she wants to.'

'You don't know what he's like. He can charm any girl into…'

He stopped, blushing.

'Franz, I'm almost eighteen. I know what Johann's like with women. I've overheard Mama complaining about him to Papa.'

'And what does Papa say?' he whispered, wishing that she'd be as discreet.

'Oh, that Johann is just having fun, that he'll settle down when he's ready. Mama says he'll turn up one day with a ghastly trollop in tow, a little brat hanging on each arm.'

She giggled again.

'I'm going to get him,' he said, starting for the kitchen.

'I'll come with you' She said.

She followed him through, grinning.

~~o~~

'Thank you, Erich,' the colonel said, exhaling a cloud of rich cigar smoke into the air above him. 'The meal was exceptional. I can see why you do your best to hang on to your cook.'

Colonel Schneider didn't see the General's almost imperceptible stiffening.

'She's irreplaceable, and Yosef is too. I don't know what I'd do without them.'

'Yes, Franz always has a good word for them. It will be a sad day when you have to let them go.'

'I'll be damned if anyone is going to tell me who I can engage as my private staff, Walther.'

'In the end, you'll not have a choice, my friend. We've had the same problem in the battalion. We've lost a few excellent soldiers, but one has to make sacrifices for the good of the Reich.'

'Franz told me you'd had to let some of your best men go. We may live to regret that, one day.'

'I doubt it. We have a steady stream of young men coming in to replace them, desperate to fight for the Fatherland. Despite my initial disappointment, I can appreciate the dangers of leaving Jewish soldiers in place. Half of them have Bolshevik tendencies, I'm told.'

'Our erstwhile allies, the Soviets, are all Bolsheviks,' the General said, with a laugh.

'That's different. They've already had their revolution. We don't want one here.'

The General smiled and shrugged in defeat.

'So, the boys are doing well?'

141

'Exceptional young men, the pair of them, but I fear that I'm going to lose Franz in the near future.'

He looked at the General.

'I'm going to recommend him for an Oberstleutnant post. It may take him away from our battalion, but it will be a few months before it comes through. He deserves it, as much as I'd like to hold onto him.'

'That's very generous of you. Have you told him?'

'No, so if you'd keep it to yourself. He has done more than enough to merit it and, as you know, you rise faster through the ranks in time of war.'

He smiled at the General.

'Johann will make a capable replacement for him,' he said, 'given time. He's beginning to settle down now. They both have the Kästner blood in them.'

'I wouldn't know about that, but I am proud of them. I only hope our leader's ambition doesn't get them killed.'

'Oh, come now, Erich. We have taken Austria, Czechoslovakia, Poland, Holland, Belgium, Luxembourg, and France with less casualties than there was in one day on the Somme. The Führer has proved a master strategist, so far. We will take England when the time is right.'

'I'm not so sure they'll be as readily defeated, Walther. The channel is much easier to defend than any land border, and the British Navy is second only to that of the Americans, if that.'

'We invaded Norway by sea. Don't forget your sons were part of it. We were successful then, and we will be victorious again.'

'I wish I had your optimism, Walther.'

'Listen to me, Erich. You haven't seen the modern Wehrmacht in action, as I have. Ask your friend Canaris; he has been to the front. Even better, accompany him on one of his trips.'

'I might just do that. He has told me about the ruthlessness of our forces.'

'There's no room in war for weakness, Herr General.'

'That's true, Walther.' He hesitated, then spoke again.

'I've heard reports of atrocities by the SS, especially in Poland. If it's true, it must be stopped before Germany's name is tarnished forever.'

'The SS are a law unto themselves. I get nervous when we're involved in any operation that they're part of. They're bloodthirsty and undisciplined, but I'll say this for them; they don't lack courage, and they have a dying loyalty to the Führer.'

'My problem is their treatment of civilians, Jews in particular. *Massacre* is the word I'm hearing, over and over.'

'Erich, I'm sure there have been a few isolated incidents, but I don't believe it's widespread. And think about this. In each country we occupy, we need to control its people with a token number of soldiers and administrators. If the SS strike terror into the population, they will be much easier to control, no?'

'I suppose there is that, but when this war is over, one way or another, we will have to answer for our sins.'

'Not if we win, Erich.'

'With all due respect, Walther, we can't take over the whole world. And those nations who stay out of our grasp will be scrutinising what we are doing, make no mistake.'

The colonel stiffened but said nothing for a few seconds.

'Herr General, like you, I'm a little uncomfortable with a few of the Führer's policies but, in the light of what he's done for Germany in less than a decade, I'm willing to make allowances and, for the sake of your country, and your children, I would advise you to do the same, and pledge your loyalty to our leader. We are soldiers, after all.'

The General sighed.

'I know, and part of me celebrates our achievements over the last two years on the military front, but I keep asking myself, will it be worth it, or will we pay a price?'

'It's a price worth paying.'

Colonel Schneider's face softened.

'I hope I say this as a friend,' he continued. 'I believe that your views are coloured by your understandable concern and loyalty for your domestic staff, and I commend that. Get them out, if that's what it takes, but don't be pulled down by them.'

The General shook his head gently.

'Walther, I do consider you as a friend and, although I am anxious about my staff, who have been with us for my whole life, it runs deeper than that. I can see why, as a soldier, you'd need to concentrate on what you've been commanded to do. All I ask is that you keep your eyes open to what is going on around you.'

The colonel stubbed out his cigar and looked at his mentor.

'Of course, Erich. And you. Please take care. This is not the time or place to be out of step with the rest of Germany.'

The General smiled.

'You know me. Too much of a thinker.'

The colonel laughed.

'Now, where are those boys?' the General said, looking at the door. 'I thought they would be joining us.'

~~o~~

Manny was sitting, gazing up at Johann with the wonderment young boys have for their heroes. Ruth also sat, fascinated by what Johann was saying.

'Don't believe a word of it,' Franz said, smiling as he entered the kitchen, Antje behind him. 'He's prone to a little exaggeration.'

Johann laughed, and feigned a hurt look.

'I was just telling young Manny about our march into the centre of Paris.'

'Well, don't leave out the bit about all the young mademoiselles lining the streets, cheering.'

'He's right, Manny. They threw flowers at us. They'd never seen such handsome soldiers before.'

He winked at the young boy.

'Now you see what I mean by exaggeration,' Franz said, and they all laughed.

Franz turned to Johann.

'Father and the colonel are in the study. We've been asked to join them.'

'You go on ahead. I'm just catching up with this young man here. I haven't seen much of him since we got back.'

Johann smiled at Manny, who beamed back. Franz saw his brother's eyes flicker towards Ruth.

Franz looked back at Johann and nodded towards the doorway.

'You're expected,' he said.

Johann scowled, but he rose from the table, tousling Manny's hair.

'I'll see you later, my friend. I've been summoned by my boss...'

He nodded at Franz.

'... to go and see the colonel.'

Manny and Ruth laughed. Franz shook his head as he followed Johann out.

~~o~~

Antje touched Ruth on the arm.

'Come through,' she said. 'Mama won't mind.'

Ruth's eyes clouded a little.

'I'm not sure,' she said.

'You're my guest,' Antje replied. 'Mama told me to be sociable. Eva will talk about boys, fashion, and French literature to Mama, which are all boring, and I don't want to listen to army talk from Father and the boys, or their colonel. And Mama will be too busy fussing, so I need you to be there.'

She grinned.

'We'll just stay a short while, and then we can go up to my room,' Antje added, seeing Ruth's reluctance.

'All right, but I must tell Mama first.'

They joined Eva and Maria and Antje had been right; mother and daughter were discussing the latest young man the countess had introduced her to.

'Hugo has asked us up for the weekend,' Eva was saying.

'All of us?' Maria replied. 'I doubt very much that your father will come. He'll make his usual excuses.'

'I'll stay with Papa,' Antje said, a little too quickly.

'No, you won't,' Maria said, 'it will do you good to mix with Hugo's family, especially if Eva is going to marry the boy.'

'Mama!' Eva scolded. 'We've only just met.'

'Well, it could happen; it wouldn't be a bad thing.'

'It's not fair that I have to spend a whole weekend with *frightfully boring posh people*,' Antje said, mimicking the countess's diction.

~~o~~

Maria could see advantages in the General and Antje making their excuses; either of them could embarrass her, but if Eva were serious about Hugo, they'd all have to meet at some point.

She felt this was her oldest daughter's last chance. This time last year, she'd had high hopes when Eva began courting Frederick, one of the boys the countess had introduced, and it had lasted six months, but his mother had insisted he marry a minor princess from Prague who'd become available, to Maria's disgust, and a tearful Frederick had chosen privilege and position over Eva.

'We'll see,' she said.

Up until the month before, Maria had despaired of Eva ever liking another of the countess's young men, and her daughter had been showing what she considered an unhealthy interest in one of her fellow students at the university.

She'd wondered how long the countess would tolerate Eva's rejection of every potential suitor she found for her, but the old lady had made it her mission to find Eva a husband.

When she had almost run out of eligible young men, the countess asked her second cousin's third son to visit for the weekend, despite her misgivings about the boy. He was twenty but had a healthy disdain for the genteel society his parents so treasured.

The first time they'd met, his first word to Eva was 'wow.' Eva had blushed and the countess had frowned, giving her young relative a stern glare for daring to flout convention, but it was enough to break the ice and, to the elderly aristocrat's surprise, and Maria Kästner's delight, the two young people spent much of the evening in conversation, punctuated by a great deal of laughter.

And already, the boy had decided that Eva and her family should meet his parents.

~~o~~

'We should go through. Maria will want to hear all about the division, Walther. She complains that the boys tell her nothing.'

'Father, we don't tell her because we don't want to worry her,' Johann said, holding his hands up in defeat.

Since the boys had joined their father and the colonel, the conversation had been confined to the lighter side of army life, all four men shying away from anything too political or controversial.

The battalion's characters, and the serial miscreants who appeared in front of the officers after every weekend furlough, were described with amusement and, to be fair, not without fondness. The General reciprocated by telling of the most memorable men who'd served under him, and who he'd served under, including a general who insisted that his horse should be stabled in his quarters, feeding it three sugar lumps, night and morning, in its coffee.

The colonel reminded him of the Obergefreiter who'd got his head stuck in a bucket, which had to be cut off to release him, winning him demotion from corporal to private, and three Pfennigs being docked from his army pay for the bucket.

The General could see that both his boys had a genuine love and respect for Colonel Schneider, and that the colonel held Franz and Johann in the highest regard, leaving him in no doubt that his sons were in safe hands, and would follow their commanding officer anywhere.

They rejoined the ladies, and the colonel charmed and reassured Maria that her sons were professional soldiers of the highest order, and in the care of a commander who would do his best to look after his men.

'There's a new round of promotions coming up,' he told her, in an aside no one else could hear. 'I suspect both Franz and Johann will feature in it.'

'That would be wonderful,' she replied, her face beaming with pleasure and pride.

'But don't say a word, Frau Kästner. That can be our little secret.'

'My lips are sealed, colonel,' she said, her expression turning serious again.

~~o~~

'He's such a nice man,' Maria said, when the colonel had left and they were getting ready for bed. 'I do think the boys are in good hands. Thank you for inviting him.'

'I thought it might help if you met him,' the General said.

In bed, for the first time in months, Maria didn't turn away when the General kissed her goodnight.

CHAPTER 40

Franz couldn't fathom why he'd agreed to meet her. He sat in the bar, sipping a coffee, waiting for Lise to arrive.

The phone call had intrigued and worried him.

'A woman, looking to speak to you,' Miriam had said, as the Kästner family sat at the breakfast table.

Franz had got up and had taken the call in the hallway, Johann's loud speculations ringing in his ears.

'Hello?' he'd said, unable to hazard a guess as to who would be calling.

'Franz? It's Lise, I'm sorry to call you but I needed someone to talk to, would you meet me?'

Her words had tumbled out as if she'd rehearsed them and couldn't bear to be interrupted.

Franz's mind had been in a turmoil.

'Where?' he'd asked, cursing himself for not refusing.

'The bar at the Europäischer. Can you make twelve-thirty?'

'Yes, that should be fine. I'll see you there.'

When he'd returned to the dining room everyone was too polite to ask, apart from Johann.

'So, Brother,' he'd said. 'Who's the mystery woman?'

'The wife of a soldier. A problem has arisen and for some reason, she has turned to me.'

'One of our men?' Johann had asked.

'You know I can't say. She has asked me to keep it to myself.'

'Watch out, Franz, she may be after you,' Johann had joked.

'No. The poor woman was in a terrible state. I'll be quite safe.'

Johann had dropped his eyes, accepting the rebuke, but Franz knew it wouldn't burden his brother for long.

At midday, he'd slipped out and walked into town.

~~o~~

Franz drew a breath when she walked in; she had that effect on most men and he was no exception, despite the pain she'd caused him.

He ordered a coffee for her and sat down at a table near the back of the bar. The place was empty; guests at the Europäischer were businessmen, by and large, and party officials, so its restaurant and bar were only ever busy in the evenings.

The bruising had almost gone, and her make-up almost completely covered the line torn by her husband's ring.

'Lise,' Franz said, fumbling for his words a little, 'you look much better. Your face has healed remarkably well.'

'Thank you. You're very diplomatic. I'm skilled at covering it up now that the black has gone out of it.'

'Is it still sore?'

'Yes. The doctor said my cheekbone may have been fractured but there was nothing I could do but wait for it to heal.'

'You need to get out before he comes home again,' Franz said, his face a mask of concern.

'That's what I wanted to talk to you about. You don't realise what he's capable of doing if I leave him.'

'Tell your parents what the doctor said. Even they can't argue that you should go back to him if they hear what he's done to you.'

'My father wouldn't stand up to him; there would be no help there. My mother would, but I don't want to put either of them in that position. They'd never forgive me.'

'So, what can you do?'

'I need your help, Franz. I need someone to warn him off; somebody he'll think twice about crossing if he ever comes after me. I know I've done you a terrible wrong but you're the only person I can ask.'

Franz said nothing for a while. Lise watched him, her eyes wide and pleading. He'd never seen her look as vulnerable as she did at that moment.

'I'll speak with him the next time he's on leave. Send me word when he's back and I'll try and get leave myself. I can't promise anything, but I'll do my best, but on condition that you move back with your parents.'

'I will. Thank you, Franz.' She reached across the table and put her hand on his. 'I know I don't deserve this, but I'll make it up to you, I promise.'

Franz gave a hesitant smile. Something brushed his leg and he realised with a start that he could feel Lise's foot sliding up his calf, the unmistakeable sensation of nylon stocking against the twill of his army trousers.

For a brief second, he did nothing. His mind froze, but his body, to his horror, reacted in the old familiar way. The face that had so filled his thoughts teased him with a gentle smile, the tip of her tongue just visible between her lips.

Her foot travelled up past his knee onto his inner thigh.

'I have a room here,' she said, her voice low and husky, just as he remembered.

He reached down and pushed her foot away with more force than he'd intended and pulled his hand from hers.

'No,' he said. 'No. You're not thinking straight.'

'I am, Franz. I know I've been stupid but, if you forgive me, we could be together. I could get a divorce.'

'No. I don't think you realise what it did to me when you left. Besides, I've not changed, and you didn't find my views acceptable back then; why would it be any different now?'

'I can change, Franz. Please give me a chance. You know what I can give you,' she said, her tone soft again but with a hint of desperation.

He stood up.

'No, Lise,' he said. 'You broke my heart and I'll not risk it again.'

'If there's someone else, she'll never be as good for you as me. What we had was special.'

She rose from her chair and moved towards him.

'I know it was,' he said, taking a step back. 'I loved you; you were the most exciting and beautiful woman I'd ever met and, even now, part of me still craves to go up to that room with you, but I can't, and I won't. And it's not because there's anyone else; there's been no one since I was with you.'

'Come with me,' she said, grabbing hold of him, pushing herself against him. 'Make love to me, like you did before. Rudolf has never been a match for you, Franz.'

'No,' he said, pulling himself free, shoving her away. She almost fell against the chair but steadied herself.

'I'm going,' Franz said, a look of horror on his face. 'I truly hope you leave Rudolf and get yourself sorted out; I'll even have a word with him if I bump into him but please don't contact me again. My life has only just returned to normal and I won't have it shattered again.'

Her eyes clouded with anger.

'You're not a man,' she hissed. 'You're a eunuch or a faggot,' she added, taunting, looking around the bar. 'Ask any man here; they would kill for the chance to have me.'

He turned and walked away.

'Curse you, Franz Kästner, and your crazy, Jew-loving family,' she shouted, ignoring the barman's astonished look. He turned his head away in embarrassment.

'Give me a brandy,' she snarled, her voice shaking with anger.

Franz stumbled along Sophienblatt, bumping into people rushing for trains at the Bahnhof, apologising. A tram passed but he ignored it, needing to walk to clear his head.

He turned left onto Hummelwiese and stood on the bridge that crossed the railway tracks, looking into the mouth of the station, the platforms reaching out like fingers to catch the incoming trains.

For a while, he watched them arrive and disgorge their passengers from towns and cities all over Germany.

He didn't know how long he stood on the bridge, his head bowed, thoughts about his encounter with Lise rattling around in his mind. After a time, he gave himself a shake and turned and walked towards home, his footsteps heavy.

CHAPTER 41

Thoughts about Franz and the mystery woman flashed through Johann's mind while he sat listening to his friends' inane conversation.

He'd spoken briefly to his brother on his return, inviting him to join them for a few beers at the Ratskeller. He'd refused, heading up to his room, mumbling something about other people's problems.

It was so like Franz to become involved in that sort of affair, and he wasn't surprised that out of all the officers, Franz would be the one that they'd think of approaching.

But it still struck Johann as unusual that one of the soldiers' wives should contact an officer in their Kompanie, whatever the issue.

'Another beer?' Maxi Grabner asked, breaking into his thoughts.

'Yes. Why not. I'm going to empty my bladder first though.'

The third beer had done it, and now that he'd started, he knew he'd be pissing every half hour.

~~o~~

It was nothing more than an unfortunate coincidence that Lise Mey had also chosen the Ratskeller to have a drink.

She'd left the Europäischer with no clear intent, heading in the opposite direction to Franz, her cold fury at Franz's rejection blinding her to reason.

She loved the attention of men and the way they reacted to her. Now, when she'd fully expected to be in bed, naked, with Franz Kästner, showing him why they should put the past behind them, she realised that she craved the feel of a man's body next to hers, knowing that she could drive any red-blooded man wild, for her pleasure and for theirs.

It was such a fuss to find a new Dutch cap. It would be a shame for it to go to waste.

There were a few bars around where she could find an officer on leave, but she was sick of soldiers for now. In Kiel, there was a far greater chance of bumping into a midshipman than a major but even then, she wondered if she'd had her fill of military men, and that a businessman on his own, away from home, might be a better prospect.

But sitting in a sleazy bar, trying to pick up a stranger, was beneath her, and most of the hotels would be quiet, like the Europäischer, until the evening.

She decided that late-afternoon coffee would be a respectable way to keep an eye out for a suitable candidate to fuck, and that the Ratskeller would be open, busy, and respectable enough not to elicit comment or incite gossip.

She sat near the back, giving her a view of the whole room and, if anyone came in who she didn't wish to be seen by, it would be simple to avoid them and slip out once they were seated.

She'd been there twenty minutes when Johann and his friends arrived and, for one horrible moment, it occurred to her that Franz might be with them but, once they'd all filed in, she breathed a sigh of relief at his absence.

It made her task almost impossible; the last thing she wanted was for Franz to know what he'd driven her to do, but when Johann approached the back of the restaurant, heading for the toilet, it struck her that it would be a delicious revenge to bed her ex-fiancé's brother. It would be even sweeter if Franz were to somehow find out about it.

I'll make sure he does.

He spotted her. Because he was heading straight past her table, he had no way of ignoring her without appearing rude.

'Lise,' he said. She dropped her eyes to the table then looked up at him again.

'Johann,' she replied, sniffing. She used a handkerchief to blow her nose.

A tear ran down her cheek and he stopped, his face softening a little, banishing the disapproving frown that had been there a moment before.

'What's the matter?' he asked, his voice a mixture of concern and suspicion.

'Nothing. Just go, Johann.'

He fidgeted, his eyes darting from her face to the toilet door, and to his friends, laughing and joking at their table.

'Wait there,' he said. 'I'll be back in a second or two. A call of nature,' he added with an embarrassed smile.

Lise waited until he'd gone. Glancing towards his friends, she fished a tissue from her handbag and wiped some of her makeup off. She took out a small mirror and checked that she could see the remnants of the bruising, and the score that ran across her cheek.

By the time he came out again, she had composed herself, and dried her eyes.

'Look, Lise,' he said, 'tell me what the problem is. I may be able to help.'

She turned and showed him her face.

'Who did that to you?' he asked. She was pleased to see a mixture of shock and horror replace his guarded look.

'Rudolf, my husband. He gets drunk when he is home on leave, and he hits me.'

'The SS chap?'

'Yes. He's changed since he went to war.'

'Why don't you leave him?'

'I'm trying. I rented a room at the Europäischer Hof tonight, but I'm worried that he'll follow me.'

'We'll walk you there if you want. When are you going?'

She cursed to herself. It wouldn't do to have a group of drunken men turning up at the hotel.

'Oh, no,' she said, 'It wouldn't be right... a crowd of off-duty soldiers. I'd be the talk of Kiel.'

A burst of raucous laughter erupted from the table where Johann's friends sat.

'I see your point,' he said.

She gathered up her gloves. 'I'll be all right...'

He looked over as her voice trailed off. Maxi Grabner lurched to his feet and shouted for the barman to bring another round of beers.

He hesitated.

'Listen,' he said, frowning, 'I'll see you to your hotel, then catch up with my friends. They'll be heading down to Wall soon. Just give me a minute.'

He threaded his way back through the tables to his friends. She saw them give her curious glances while he spoke to them, and one of them laughed. She watched Johann shrug his shoulders and walk back to her.

'Come on then,' he said. 'Let's get you to this hotel of yours. How long will you stay there?'

'Two or three nights, I suppose.'

'What will you do then?' he asked. 'Why not move back with your parents?'

'Would you?' she asked.

'Lord, no,' he answered, and she was pleased to see the hint of a smile.

She put her coat on, and they left. She heard a wolf whistle as the door of the Ratskeller closed behind them.

'I apologise,' he said. 'They're philistines.'

'Don't be sorry,' she said. 'They seem nice fellows.'

'Yes. They're good friends. Most of them were originally friends of Franz...' He stopped and blushed.

'I'm sorry,' he said.

'Don't be. He's your brother. Truth be told, I made the biggest mistake of my life splitting up with him.'

~~o~~

Johann stared at her.

'It's true,' she said. 'We should have ironed out our differences. Now I'm married to a brute and I know Franz has found it difficult...'

'He has,' Johann said. He was surprised how contrite and regretful Lise was. And she was without doubt one of the most beautiful women he'd ever met.

When he'd gone over to tell his friends he was walking Lise home, he hadn't told them that it was Franz's ex-fiancée, just that it was an old friend who needed help. He was sure they'd never met her before, but he remembered Franz showing them a picture of a young Lise when they were first engaged.

Fortunately, they hadn't recognised her, but his announcement that he'd be back as soon as he'd walked her home prompted a series of nudges and winks and exaggerated looks of disbelief.

More than anything, he feared bumping into Franz, and the thought of having to explain Lise's presence, holding onto his arm as they walked towards the railway station, terrified him.

He noticed her looking from side to side every few paces and she gave an occasional nervous glance over her shoulder. He'd heard of the brutality of the Schutzstaffel troops and had seen it first-hand, so it didn't surprise him that they carried it over into their private lives, and that she was terrified.

When they reached the hotel, her eyes darted around the reception area, and she tightened her grip on his arm.

'Do you mind seeing me upstairs,' she asked, her voice still shaky. 'I'm embarrassed to be asking, but after this…'

'I don't mind, but you must telephone your parents and ask them to come and get you as soon as possible. You'd be much better off at home.'

'I will. I just need a little time to myself. You do understand, don't you?'

They took the lift and, getting out at her floor, he escorted her to the door of her room. She opened it and, feeling a little self-conscious, Johann turned on the light and looked around.

'It's all clear,' he said.

'Thank you so much,' Lise said, her voice starting to break. 'You've been so nice.'

What he took to be tears of relief overflowed and rolled down her cheek and, in contrast to her usual poise and elegance, she appeared terribly young and defenceless.

'I'm sorry,' she sobbed. 'I'm a mess.'

'Don't be silly,' he said, touching her arm. 'After what you've been through…'

She shivered and her legs gave way, almost stumbling. He caught her. She buried her head in his broad shoulder and sniffed.

Johann stood, not quite knowing where to put his hands but, not wanting to appear cold and heartless, patted her on the back.

'There,' he said. 'You're safe now.'

His eyes darted around the room, trying to find a way to escape without upsetting her further but the door had swung closed and, although her sobs had subsided, she was holding him tighter than ever.

He tried hard to ignore the effect it was having, but he couldn't help feeling her soft curves against him, and he forced his mind to think of training drills and the most troublesome men in his unit to avoid his body embarrassing him.

But, sweet Jesus, didn't she smell good!

To make matters worse, she moved her leg against his inner thigh, and her core pressed further into his.

Is she doing it on purpose?

Her head moved away from his chest and he breathed a sigh of relief until he looked down and saw that she was looking up at him, her lips slightly parted.

Christ. No wonder Franz lost himself in her.

Her face was near perfect, with a strange and mesmerising combination of innocence and knowing which he'd never seen in any other woman.

She reached up and pulled his head down, and kissed him on the lips, her fingers curling into the hair above his neck. His shocked mind responded without conscious thought, his tongue seeking hers, his body responding when she pushed against him. Her other hand slid down his back and pulled him to her, and his hands followed her cue, tracing the line of her body down to her hips without a wilful decision on his part.

She pushed her leg further between his, and he could feel her pubis hard against him, her legs gripping his thigh, her ankle wound around his calf. She gave a soft moan.

151

He gave in to his hunger, pulling her up onto him, pressing her warmness against his.

She gripped his hair tighter, causing him to flinch a little, not caring, then she brought her other hand around and slipped it between his legs. This time, it was Johann who groaned.

'No,' he whispered. 'No.'

He jerked away from her, his body screaming at him not to stop; that this would be the most exciting encounter with a woman he would ever have.

His love for his brother and his lust for this woman fought out a battle in his heart and in his mind. He knew, without doubt, that a night with Lise Mey would far and above surpass anything he'd ever experienced, but a mental picture of the anguish Franz would go through if he ever found out purged the thought of her lying on the bed, naked and desperate for him.

He pushed her away.

'I can't,' he panted. 'I can't do it to Franz.'

'He'll never know. It's just a fuck. You'll never forget a night with me. Your brother can't.'

He groaned and hung his head. His mind still wrestled with what she was offering, and what he was throwing away.

This is my thing. Women. Every millimetre of them.

He heard her speak and he looked up.

She'd dropped her coat to the floor. He watched as she unbuttoned her blouse, exposing the lace of her brassiere and the swell of her breasts, rising and falling in pace with her breathing.

She undid a button at the side of her skirt, and pulled the zip down, letting it slip over her waist and down to her ankles. She stepped out of it and stood in front of him.

'This is what you'd be giving up,' she said, reaching round behind her and unclipping herself. She let go, and the brassiere followed the skirt to the floor. She wiggled her underskirt over her hips, and it fell, too, joining the rest of her clothes. She wasn't wearing anything underneath.

'You'll never know what it would be like, the best night of your life, if you walk away now,' she said, her voice low and compelling.

She cupped a breast with one hand and with her other, traced a line across her belly and down through the triangle of hair between her legs, touching herself, watching his face, her eyes not leaving his.

'This could be you doing this,' she whispered, gently moving her fingers, toying with him.

'Stop,' he said. 'Stop, Lise.'

She laughed. 'Just like your brother. You're both cowards. You'll never know what it's like to have a real woman, just all those simpering girls you go with.'

She turned away from him and he swallowed, bowing his head. From the back, she looked just as desirable, maybe more so.

'I can't. I need to leave. I'm sorry.'

In a way, it was true. He was sorry. He knew he would always wonder about it, walking out instead of staying.

I'll regret it more if I stay.

He turned to the door and opened it.

'Don't go back to Rudolf,' he said.

She laughed.

'I haven't left him, you fool. I just wanted to fuck you. Just to say I'd done both Kästner brothers, and to spite your precious Franz. You very nearly did.'

His face paled.

'This was a set-up?'

She laughed again.

'Rejected by two Kästner brothers in the same day. What a pious, self-righteous twosome you are. You don't have a pair of testicles between you. At least Rudolf knows when a woman needs a good fuck.'

'But he hits you,' Johann gasped.

'And he rapes Jews, and Slavs and Gypsies, before he kills them, I'd imagine. But he still comes home to me, because I can give him something no other woman can.'

She began dressing, but in such a casual manner that Johann couldn't help watching. He imagined it was like watching a prostitute, after she'd been paid.

'And you're proud of that?'

'He loves the Führer. And the Third Reich. Not like the Kästner freaks.'

'I love my country as much as him, and I admire what the Führer has achieved beyond words.'

'But you don't love him, do you? Rudolf does, as much as he loves me.'

'So why does he hit you?'

'We get a little violent sometimes. You wouldn't have escaped without a few scratches yourself, if you'd had the balls to fuck me.'

He shook his head and opened the door.

He walked out without saying goodbye.

In the room, Lise picked up the lamp and threw it against the wall. Then she finished dressing.

~~o~~

Johann walked along Sophienblatt, mumbling to himself. In his chest, a deep sense of relief couldn't quite suppress the thought of Lise, naked, on top of him, her eyes wild, riding him like a feral, primitive savage.

Then a thought chased the image away.

The mystery woman. It was Lise who called Franz.

He began to walk faster, looking for his friends.

~~o~~

Lise tidied up the room, depositing the broken lamp in the bin, and took the lift down to the bar. She ordered a drink.

She glanced at the barman while he mixed her Martini. He was presentable,

mid to late thirties, maybe forty. *Not the over intelligent type,* she thought, but with an athletic build and a confident way about him, as if he were used to women finding him attractive.

She undid the top button on her blouse.

'Are you married?' she asked him, as he brought her drink over.

'Yes.' He sighed.

'What time do you finish here?' she said, leaning forward.

He looked at the clock.

'Another hour,' he said.

'Phone your wife. Make an excuse. You're about to have the best night of your life.'

CHAPTER 42

[09/02/1941 Sunday]

KIELER JÜDISCHES FREIHEITSNACHRICHTENBLATT

Volume 94

12th of Sh'vat, 5701

OBITUARY

BENNO ARNDT

Until Benno Arndt was murdered by the Gestapo in late November 1940, he was the editor and founder of this newspaper, the Kieler Jüdisches Freiheitsnachrichtenblatt, which he published almost single-handedly since he was sacked from the Kieler Morgenpost in April 1933.

It was his background as a subeditor at Kiel's most prestigious newspaper that prepared him for editing and publishing the only newspaper that reported the truth in Kiel, when the Morgenpost surrendered its integrity and honesty to the National Socialist Party.

Benno began working for the Morgenpost at sixteen, and unnamed members of the paper's staff say there is no doubt he would have become the paper's editor one day had the National Socialists not come to power.

Benno knew the risks he was taking by publishing the KJF but felt that it was important for the Jewish community in Kiel to have a voice and, of equal importance, to be informed.

The new editor of the KJF salutes Benno Arndt's bravery and urges readers to say Kaddish for him.

He leaves behind a wife and two children. He will be sadly missed.

~~o~~

On the top floor of Kleiner Kuhberg 15, Jakob Teubner lowered his copy of the *Kieler Jüdisches Freiheitsnachrichtenblatt*. He stared out of the attic window, across the rooftops of Kiel and sniffed twice, then once again.
 'You have a cold coming on, Jakob?' his wife asked him.

~~o~~

In the kitchen of their cottage, Miriam handed the KJF back to Yosef. Tears were running down her cheeks.
 'How could he have been so brave?' she said.

~~o~~

General Kästner swallowed as he read the article about Benno in his study. He closed his eyes, picturing the death the poor man had suffered, and the courage he'd shown in not betraying his friends.
 He put it down and opened the journal he'd been keeping. He wrote the date and a few lines about the KJF, its former editor, and its re-emergence. He slipped the book, and the copy of the Jewish news-sheet into the drawer and locked it.

154

He closed his eyes again and said a prayer for Benno Arndt.

~~o~~

Samuel Nussbaum, Yosef's father, laid down the KJF and picked up the mandolin he was working on. With gentle strokes, he dipped the cloth in the lacquer and applied it to the body of the instrument, then, with another cloth, polished the wood until it shone. As he worked, he chanted to himself the familiar verses of the Kaddish.

May His great name be blessed forever, and to all eternity,
Blessed be His name, whose glorious kingdom is forever.

~~o~~

[20/02/1941 Thursday]

Memo: Geh.KdoS. ABW 20/02/41 CAC01501.1

For Attention Only: General Erich Kästner, Abwehr, Kiel office, Abwehr.

From: Vice Admiral Wilhelm Canaris, Chef der Abwehr.

** HÖCHSTE GEHEIMHALTUNG **

Adolf Eichmann has agreed responsibility for the costs of transporting Jews within the incorporated Polish territories on behalf of the Reich Security Main Office. [END]

CHAPTER 43

'Kästner.'

'Canaris.'

The two only smiled; in the presence of a raft of Wilhelmshaven's top naval staff, their usual ebullient greeting would have been inappropriate.

'I'm glad you could come,' Admiral Canaris said. 'Our friends here in Wilhelmshaven would like to grill you about the work you do in Kiel, assisting the Baltic Command.'

A murmur of assent went around the table, heads nodding.

'I'd be delighted, but I'm not sure the reputation I have is quite justified.'

'Nonsense, Herr General,' one of the sitting admirals said. 'Our colleagues in Kiel speak very highly of the work you do assisting them with idiotic bureaucrats.' He smiled.

'It's just a matter of perseverance; a combination of the stick and the carrot and knowing which one to use, and when.'

'How so, Herr General?'

'I'll give you one example. Transport. Most of the railway staff are very patriotic, and are delighted to help the navy but, from time to time, if they drag their heels, the threat of an irate general having a chat with their superiors can often bring them into line. On the other hand, a guided tour of a destroyer for an official who has gone out of their way to help works wonders for their eagerness to please.'

'That's why we asked that you and Admiral Canaris come and speak to us. We wish to learn from your success because, frankly, we waste more time in Wilhelmshaven chasing orders and waiting for supplies than we do victualling and maintaining the Atlantic fleet.'

'We had similar problems, Herr Admiral. The secret is to find the right person to deal with. For instance, the head of the Reichsbahn for the Hamburg area is a very pleasant, hard-working fellow, but to all intents and purposes, it's his deputy managers who run the entire operation. I've made a point of cultivating relationships with lower-grade officials like him and, indeed, managers in key staging yards. I find we can cut through much of the red tape which clogs up the system and, often, just one or two phone calls will prioritise a delivery and save three or four days.'

'And your success in keeping the city councillors and regional politicians on the Kriegsmarine's side was accomplished in the same manner?'

'We try and cultivate similar relationships with civil servants, but in some instances, we are forced to work with politicians directly, and they require a different approach. It's perhaps unfair to generalise, but they are, as a rule, more self-serving, and one needs to find out what they want in return for their assistance. It can often be something intangible, perhaps a prominent position at the launch of a new ship, or a place on a committee which involves them sitting down with the admirals of Naval Command.'

'We have to talk to these people?'

'Yes, but it is just a formality and shouldn't be too onerous. Appoint a staff member you trust to do all the groundwork. With the right person in place, your own involvement will be minimal.'

'What sort of person are we looking for?'

'It has to be someone who can engage with civilians and who knows how to use tact and diplomacy, with a high enough rank to impress them and be forceful if necessary. And you must back them up at all times.'

'Perhaps we could be of help,' Admiral Canaris interjected. 'General Kästner could assist in the selection of an appropriate officer, having considerable expertise in assessing candidates' suitability.'

'That would be most generous,' the commander of the Wilhelmshaven base said, 'if you could spare the time.'

General Kästner smiled, and glanced at Admiral Canaris, who tried to hide a grin.

'I'd be delighted to be of assistance. I can extend my stay by a day if that would help.'

'Yosef, you can't go. What would the General say?'

Yosef sighed. He knew his wife was right, but he would be careful, and he wouldn't be away long.

'I have to go. The man deserves our love and respect. He knew what he was doing would get him killed but, for the sake of our people, he carried on.'

Benno Arndt's ashes had been returned to his family, and his funeral was being held that day. Jakob had sent word to Yosef, and it felt like a summons that he couldn't ignore.

It was Miriam's turn to sigh.

'If you must go, let me go with you.'

'No. One of us must stay with the children.'

'Ruth is old enough to look after Manny.'

'That's not what I mean. You know that.'

Miriam closed her eyes.

'Then why do you still go?' she said.

~~o~~

About fifty mourners stood in the large room that functioned as the synagogue. Most of the Jews who served on Jakob's unofficial committee were present; those missing had been deported or arrested over the last few months.

Jakob led the service, but it was one of Benno's close friends who gave the eulogy, a simple and fitting tribute to the newspaperman's life and bravery.

Yosef stood and listened. It had been too long since he'd stood in the house of God in Kleiner Kuhberg, and he closed his eyes, letting the feeling of belonging wash over him, cursing those who prevented his family from worshipping with their people.

He thought of the walk home, fraught with danger, but was glad that he'd come. It would be good to speak with Jakob and his other friends and colleagues after the service.

He didn't get the chance. A few minutes after the last Kaddish, the Gestapo forced their way through the front door and arrested every Jew who'd attended Benno Arndt's funeral.

~~o~~

By four o'clock, Miriam was becoming concerned, but she figured that Yosef might have had to wait for an opportune moment to leave the relative safety of the Jewish centre in Kleiner Kuhberg.

By six, she was almost out of her mind with worry, but she tried her best to hide it from Ruth, and above all, from Manny. Her daughter was not so easy to fool.

'Mama,' she said, when Manny was out of earshot, 'should Papa not have been home by now?'

Evening had fallen, and the curfew made it doubly dangerous for Yosef to be walking around the streets of Kiel after dark.

'He'll be home soon, Ruth. He must have a good reason for delaying the walk back. Perhaps the police were watching the place. They go home to their beds when the curfew starts; you heard Jakob the last time he was here.'

'You're right, Mama. We'll just have to wait.'

'You can help me serve the Kästners' dinner, seeing your father is shirking his duties,' Miriam said, trying to smile.

She shouted for Manny to come, and the three Nussbaums crossed the yard to the Kästner house.

~~o~~

Ruth had often helped her mother out, so waiting table for the Kästners had been part of growing up. She didn't see service as demeaning, but she hoped that it wouldn't be her lot in life, having her own aspirations for a career in teaching, law, or even medicine.

Maria smiled when she saw Ruth and thanked her when she placed her soup on the table, asking her how her day had been. Her bland reply was delivered with a smile and, as Frau Kästner turned her attention to her food, Ruth caught Antje's eye and was pleased to see her friend's almost imperceptible nod in return.

Five minutes later, Antje excused herself and met Ruth in the hallway.

'Mama is plating the next course, so I don't have much time,' Ruth said, her speech rushed.

'What's the matter?' Antje asked.

'Papa went to a funeral in Kleiner Kuhberg and hasn't returned. Mama and I are worried sick.'

'Oh,' Antje said, Ruth's worry reflected on her friend's face. 'He wasn't supposed to go anywhere.'

'I know. It was Benno Arndt's funeral. He felt he had to go.'

'The newspaper man you told me about?'

'Yes.'

'What do you want me to do?'

'Can you go and find out what has happened, after dinner?'

'I would have asked Papa, but he's away. Albert is still here. I'll ask Mama if he can drive me.'

'Won't she be suspicious?'

'No. I'll tell her I'm going to see a friend.'

'But Albert will tell your mother, won't he?'

'I'll just have to make it look convincing. Anyway, Albert is lovely. He won't say a word.'

Ruth smiled, despite herself.

'Thank you,' she said.

CHAPTER 44

'Kleiner Kuhberg, Albert,' Antje said.

The driver raised an eyebrow.

'Are you sure?' he said, his tone doubtful. 'You have a friend who lives there?'

'Yes. I have a message for her. It's about a boy,' she said, feigning a giggle.

'Whatever you say, Fräulein Antje.'

She cringed at the sceptical note in his voice.

The streets were empty of people, the biting cold February wind keeping them in the warmth of their homes. As the car sped into town, Albert kept glancing back at Antje.

She rummaged in her pocket for a bit of paper and scribbled on it.

'What number in Kleiner Kuhberg are you looking for, Fräulein?' he asked.

'I don't know,' Antje said, 'I'll recognise it when I see it. It's on the left-hand side, going up from the Hafen. It's somewhere near the middle.'

Ruth had told her the building she was looking for was number 15 and that the next three buildings were also used by Jews.

At the junction of Sophienblatt and Schevenbrücke, they swung left and continued for two blocks.

'Slow down, Albert,' Antje said. 'This is the start of Kleiner Kuhberg.'

The car slowed to a crawl, and Antje mouthed the house numbers to herself as she passed.

There it was. *Number 15.*

'Stop a minute, Albert.'

She stared. The front doors were lying open, one of them at an angle, hanging on one hinge. Glass littered the steps and a discarded hat lay on the pavement outside.

'They've been raided by the Gestapo, Fräulein, I imagine,' Albert said. 'I hope it's not your friend's house. Are they Jewish?'

'No,' she snapped, then softened her tone, cursing her slip. 'They live further up the street.'

She noticed Albert glancing at her again in the mirror and tried to look unconcerned.

'It's that one, I think,' she said, 'four or five buildings up from the one with the smashed doors.'

Albert pulled into the kerb and Antje jumped out. She ran up the steps and posted her note through the door. As she returned to the car, she looked up and waved. Albert, sitting in his seat, couldn't see above the ground floor.

'You have heard of the telephone, Fräulein?' he said.

Antje laughed.

'You are funny, Albert. I couldn't speak over the telephone. Her mother listens to her calls. It had to be a note.'

'How do you know she will get it?' he asked.

'I telephoned her first, to let her know I was coming,' she said.

He shook his head.

~~o~~

Ruth gasped when Antje told her what she'd seen.

'The police must have taken them all,' she said. 'Or the Gestapo. I must tell Mama.'

'I'm so sorry,' Antje said, putting her arm around her friend. 'Papa isn't back until the day after tomorrow, Mama says. He called earlier.'

Ruth put her head in her hands. 'Mama told him not to go,' she said, her voice breaking. 'Once Papa gets back, he'll sort it out.'

'I hope so. Thank you, Antje, for what you did.'

'I did nothing. A little trip in the car, that's all.'

'Still…'

~~o~~

It was Antje who told her father about Yosef. It was unfortunate that her mother was also present.

'This is intolerable,' Maria Kästner complained.

'It is, my dear. That they should dare to arrest Yosef after being warned to leave the Nussbaums alone. I'll have their hide for this.'

'You know that's not what I meant. Yosef was told not to leave here. Please don't cause a fuss, Erich. It's bad enough already.'

'I have to get him out, can't you see?'

'Please be polite about it. If you upset these people, they will harass us and the Nussbaums all the more.'

'These people don't understand the meaning of polite, but I can't do anything tonight. Anyway, they're not harassing us; it's the Nussbaums who're the victims here. I'll visit the police station first thing in the morning. In the meantime, I'm going to have a quick word with Miriam. She must be beside herself.'

'I'll come with you, Papa,' Antje said.

She didn't see her mother's frown, but it didn't escape the General's notice.

When Miriam answered the door, the General could see that she was trying to stay strong for Ruth and Manny but there was a tremor in her voice when she invited them in.

'I'm sorry,' she said. 'I tried to persuade him not to go.'

'That doesn't matter now,' the General said. 'What do you know?'

'I've heard nothing,' she told him when they were seated across the kitchen table. 'Nothing at all.'

'They want you to go to them, I imagine. Then they'll arrest you too. Leave it with me. I'll go and get him tomorrow.'

They kept their voices low. Antje and Ruth kept Manny busy in the other room, playing a card game with him.

'I have a bad feeling about this. It's as if they're taking revenge on us for the KJF surviving so long.'

'It was the Jewish community's one way to fight back, Miriam.'

'I know, sir. It has started up again, you know.'

'I know,' the General said, giving her a wry smile. 'I was given a copy.'

'It's only one sheet, and the printing's not as clear, but nobody complains. They say that Benno's former assistant is printing it now, and there are rumours that he's not a Jew.'

'A Gentile? I find that hard to believe. Why would...?'

'A friend of Benno's, I'm told. No one knows who he is. The latest edition just appeared.'

The General frowned.

'Would any of the people attending the funeral have had copies on them when the place was raided?' he asked, his brow creasing into a frown.

Miriam paled.

'I suppose they might have.'

'Reason enough to arrest them. Would Yosef have had a copy with him?'

'No. He wouldn't...'

She paused and chewed her lip.

'He might have,' she said. 'The last one was posted through the door. If there's a new edition, Yosef may have decided to bring it home for me.'

She covered her face with her hands.

'It's all right, Miriam,' he said, putting his hand on her shoulder. 'We'll get him back home, then talk about how we can get you out of the country.'

'It would be enough for us just to get Ruth and Manny out.'

The General froze.

'You can't mean that, Miriam.'

'We're desperate, sir. If it's the only way...'

Her voice trailed off. He could see that she was fighting back tears.

'What does Yosef think?' he asked.

'We haven't discussed it, but I'm sure he'd agree.'

'It might be easier. If we got the children out, you could risk the Haganah route; it would be safer with two adults travelling alone.'

'Just to know they were safe. That would be an enormous weight off our minds.'

'I'll make a few enquiries. I have a contact in Switzerland.'

CHAPTER 45

Franz watched on, knowing what his brother was going through.

Johann sat on his bunk, his head in his hands.

'You were right,' he said.

Franz sat down beside him. He put his arm around his shoulder.

'I felt like this the first time as well.'

'It's not the first time,' Johann said, his voice bitter. 'I just thought they were isolated incidents, the unfortunate consequences of war. That it was human nature for men to act out of character, now and then.'

He looked up at Franz, his eyes full of horror.

'This was premeditated,' he said, 'and part of some grand plan. I know that now.'

Johann's unit had been ordered to back up a combined SS and Norwegian action while they smoked out a group of alleged partisans from a village not far from Bergen.

'These were no partisans. Not a gun or other weapon between them unless you counted a fishing knife. And they were all Jews. I heard them praying, like Yosef and Miriam do. They shot them all, the women and children too.'

Franz gripped the back of his brother's shoulders, and gently shook him.

'It's not your fault. There was nothing you could have done.'

'Yes, there was, but we didn't lift a finger to stop it. Yes, a few of the lads brought up their breakfast afterwards; we were all disgusted, but we just stood there, watching, while they massacred whole families.'

'It happened in Poland. You didn't see the worst of it, but it was much the same. Admiral Canaris witnessed several massacres there, and to a lesser extent, it took place in France. And it's not just Jews. Do you know that when the French Army surrendered, our troops separated all the Moroccans and Algerians from the white soldiers, and shot them?'

'I didn't know that, but I'd heard stories about massacres. I just couldn't accept that our people could do that, and what was worse, that it was being condoned by our leaders.'

'I'm afraid there's more to it than that. They're not just turning a blind eye to it. It's official policy. I'm sure of it. So is father.'

Johann continued, as if he hadn't heard Franz speak.

'As for the Norwegians,' he said. 'Their soldiers took part. Against their own countrymen. There's a Norwegian brigade in the Wehrmacht, for God's sake!'

'Not all Norwegians are complicit, by any means,' Franz said. 'But there is a sizeable element here who approve of what the National Socialists are doing and want to be part of it. You don't have to look further than Vidkun Quisling and his puppet government. Although ultimate power resides with the Reichskommissariat, their cooperation makes it easier for our forces to control Norway.'

'I always thought that was a good thing; it kept the peace and allowed us to get on well with the Norwegian people.'

'You mean Norwegian girls,' Franz said, smiling.

Johann barely managed a grin.

'Now it's like Austria, and Czechoslovakia all over again. I should have believed you back then.'

It gave Franz no satisfaction that he was right; that his brother had been burying his head in the sand, denying what his eyes and ears were telling him. It had all happened in his periphery, allowing Johann to brush it aside. But this time, he'd been in command and, while it wasn't his unit who had wiped out the village, they'd stood by and let it happen.

'They don't want a Jew left alive in Europe,' Franz said.

'But why? What have the Jews done to deserve that?'

'Nothing. But they're getting blamed for everything from losing the last war to the depression, and for Germany's demise.'

'Yosef and Miriam must get out, with Ruth and Manny.'

'They've tried everything. They left it too late. Father has been making desperate attempts to get them to safety. It has become almost impossible.'

'What are we fighting for?' Johann asked, his voice cracking.

'I ask myself that every day,' Franz replied.

~~o~~

'General Kästner. It's good to hear from you. How is Kiel?'

'Oh, we have the odd bomb to dodge, Monsieur Ambassador, but otherwise, we are well.'

Alphonse Berac chuckled.

'I presume this phone call is not a social one, Herr General?'

'I wish it were, my friend. It concerns the matter we spoke about the last time we met.'

'Ah. The matter we didn't discuss?'

He chuckled again and the General laughed with him.

'Indeed,' the General said. 'You mentioned a couple of organisations who were taking in Jewish orphans.'

'Orphans, General Kästner. Of no particular race, I believe.'

There was a pause, then the General laughed again.

'I understand,' he said. 'I wonder if you could make discreet enquiries for me.'

'I'd be delighted to, Herr General. And please, call me Alphonse.'

'Thank you, Alphonse. And it's Erich.'

'How old are these children?'

'Seventeen and thirteen,' the General replied.

The Swiss ambassador sucked in his breath.

'Sixteen and thirteen, I believe you meant, Erich.'

'No, I…'

He stopped.

'Yes. Sorry. Sixteen and thirteen. Children. What about their papers?'

'I believe the organisations issue travel papers, with the correct details on them.'

'Ah,' the General said. 'I'd be most appreciative if you'd look into this for me.'

'It's the least I can do. I truly empathise with your position. I'll get back to you as soon as I can, but it may take a few days.'

'Thank you, sir. You are a gentleman.'

'Until then.'

The General put the telephone handpiece down. He breathed out a long sigh.

CHAPTER 46

[03/03/1941 Monday]

Erich Kästner sat in the back of his staff car and fumed. His visit to Uwe Müller, at the central police office, had been humiliating.

He'd sat and waited for forty minutes, only to be shown into the office of Uwe's deputy.

'Herr Müller has been called away on urgent police business,' the man had said. 'He asked me to have a word.'

'I can't impress how important it is that I speak with Chief Müller,' the General had said, in a voice that normally brooked no argument.

But it wasn't the army. The policeman had met Erich Kästner's stare with indifference.

'He asked me to tell you that, in light of your repeated requests for help,' he said, 'and in contradiction to your assurances that you would not contact him again on this matter, he is unable to offer any further assistance.'

'And that's it, is it? Do you realise who I am? I can be on the phone to Reinhard Heydrich if you'd rather I did that.'

'I know exactly who you are. Please feel free to call Herr Heydrich but, before you do, however, consider this. The man you are trying to have released from custody has been arrested with a number of others in an investigation involving the publication and the distribution of an illegal and subversive so-called newspaper, and I'm not sure that even the head of the entire German police force would wish to interfere in a matter as serious as this, just because you are a general in the Abwehr, with the ear of a few admirals, Herr Kästner.'

The General said nothing. He bowed his head.

'At least tell me which police station he's in.'

'Certainly. It's a matter of public knowledge. We don't hold them; the Gestapo do, and all those arrested, bar two, have been incarcerated in the camp at Neuengamme, for what I imagine will be an indefinite period.'

The General would have liked to wipe the smug grin from the policeman's face but, ignoring the cold barb of dread that almost paralysed him, he got up and gave the man a polite smile.

'Thank you,' he said.

~~o~~

On the way to Neuengamme, the General asked Captain Bauer for the custody forms.

'You've checked them twice already, sir, and I've been over them a couple of times myself.'

He hesitated.

'Are you sure we should be doing this, sir?'

'Just give me the bloody papers,' the General growled. 'I'll do whatever the hell I want.'

'Yes, sir,' Captain Bauer said, as he handed over the file. The General never held a grudge, and his bad humour would be forgotten by the end of the day.

The General checked the forms again. They were printed on official paper and requested the release into Abwehr custody of one Yosef Nussbaum, of the cottage, Drachensee house, Hamburger Chaussee, Kiel, and that the said prisoner was a key witness in an internal Abwehr investigation.

'They're fine,' the General said, after he'd read them through again.

'I know, sir.' Captain Bauer leaned forward to look out the front of the car.

'We're here, sir.'

'Keep your fingers crossed, Heinz,' he said, giving his assistant an apologetic nod.

'Yes, sir.'

~~o~~

It took four hours to have Yosef released.

'Against our better judgement, he is being discharged into your personal custody, sir,' the concentration-camp deputy Kommandant said.

'I understand. I will hold him in my own home if I have to,' the General said, qualifying his comment with a laugh.

The camp official smiled thinly.

'That won't be necessary, sir. Could you please sign here,' he said, pointing to a box on the release form, 'and here, here and here,' he added.

Once the General had completed the form, the man barked an order and, ten or so minutes later, a haggard and frightened Yosef was ushered into the room. He opened his mouth to say something, but the General's stare stopped him, and he stood in silence, his eyes straight ahead.

Captain Bauer stepped forward and, unable to look Yosef in the eye, asked him to hold out his arms and placed a set of handcuffs on him.

The General handed the deputy Kommandant the Abwehr custody papers, keeping a copy to accompany the prisoner, and motioned to the captain to lead Yosef out.

'I hope you find the prisoner is as useful to your investigation as you say he is,' the SS man said, the corner of his mouth turned down in a sneer.

'So do I, Herr Kommandant. I can't say much as you wouldn't have the necessary clearance, but I can tell you that this man is vital to my work with the Kriegsmarine.'

The concentration camp official grunted.

'I'm not the Kommandant, Herr General,' he said. 'I'm the Deputy Kommandant, SS-Oberscharführer Karl-Friedrich Höcker.'

He gave a Hitler salute.

Outside, under a dismal sky, the General looked around at the stark brutality of the camp on his way to the car.

On the site of an abandoned brickworks, he knew that it had been purchased by the SS to allow a new modern brick factory to be built and staffed by slave labour. Inside the high, sinister, barbed-wire fences, the construction of the new brickworks was well underway. The old factory was manufacturing bricks for its construction.

The General watched a large group of inmates on the opposite side of the site, excavating what looked to be a large ditch or lagoon.

'Was is das?' he asked the deputy Kommandant, who had accompanied him out to the car.

'Ah. It is to be a harbour, bringing in raw materials for the manufacture of bricks. We are building a short canal, to the Dove Elbe river, just over there.'

He pointed to the levees of the river, a kilometre to the north. The General was struck by how proud the man was of the construction.

"It joins the river Elbe at the docks in Hamburg," the man added.

The General saluted and got into the car. The large gates, three metres high, opened, and they turned onto the camp road, passing three guard towers on the short drive down to the main road. He looked through the fence across the mud and rain of the camp. Despite the biting wind, the inmates wore thin, striped work uniforms, their shaved heads making them look almost inhuman.

He looked away, his jaw set in anger.

'Are you all right, Yosef, my friend,' he murmured.

'I am now,' Yosef said, shivering. 'Thank you for getting me out of there. My only regret is that Jakob and the others aren't with me. God help them.'

The General, conscious of the last of the guard towers, laid his hand on top of Yosef's.

'I'm sorry it took so long. I was in Wilhelmshaven until late yesterday and the police were of no help.'

The car turned onto the main road, turning right in Neuengamme village for Bergedorf, and northwards to Kiel.

'Please stop,' Yosef said, gagging.

The General motioned for Captain Bauer to pull over. He helped Yosef out and looked the other way as his employee emptied the contents of his stomach on the verge at the side of the road.

Captain Bauer had wound down his window.

'Give me the keys,' the General said to him.

The General waited until Yosef had finished, then put his hand on his shoulder, giving him his handkerchief.

Yosef cleaned his mouth with difficulty, his hands still held in the handcuffs.

'Here. Let me get these,' the General said, unlocking one cuff, and then the other.

Yosef rubbed his wrists.

Back in the car, the three men remained silent for a kilometre or two.

'It's hell in there.'

Captain Bauer glanced in the mirror. The General put his arm around Yosef's shoulder.

'We saw that. It's inhumane, what they're doing to people.'

'You didn't see the half of it, sir.'

'What do you mean?'

Yosef said nothing, his head in his hands.

'You don't have to say, if you'd rather not,' the General said.

'No. I'm just so tired. But I want to tell you. To let you know what you had me released from.'

'Take your time, my friend.'

'I was there two days. Some poor souls have been in there for months, even years, perhaps, although I doubt anyone could survive that long.'

He paused, closing his eyes.

'They wake you up at six. You've been trying to sleep on a bunk of wooden slats, two of you to each one, three bunks stacked on top of the other. There are no covers, or mattresses. When you wake up, they line you up and make you call out your number. You're given a bowl of thin soup, with a couple of pieces of mouldy vegetables in it, if you're lucky, then they march you to work.'

He shivered. The General motioned for Captain Bauer to turn the heating up.

'They set us to digging the harbour. Others went to the brickworks; those were skilled men, I suppose. They sent us down into the pit, each armed with a spade. We dug all day, with only a short break around midday for another bowl of watery soup. The ground is heavy, with peat, then a thick band of clay. It's back-breaking work, especially on an empty stomach. Most of the men who have been there for a while are like skeletons.'

Yosef shut his eyes again. The General thought he had fallen asleep but, after a few seconds, he opened them and began to speak again.

'One of them, Arnold, he was called, fell to the ground; it was sheer exhaustion, I'm sure. The guards were on him in an instant, clubbing him and kicking him. They told two of the other inmates to drag him to the edge of the pit, and just left him there. He was still lying in the same spot when we left, just before it got dark. He was dead.'

A tear rolled down Yosef's cheek.

'My friends. They won't survive long in there. I don't suppose...'

'I'm so sorry, Yosef. I've overstretched my hand just getting you out. I'm afraid it will be impossible to help your friends.'

'That's not your fault, sir. I feel guilty to be out, though, leaving them in there.'

'Don't. You must be strong for Miriam and the children. We'll stop and get you cleaned up. I have fresh clothes in the back for you and we'll get you something to eat once we have you presentable. There's nothing we can do for the hair, I'm afraid.'

Yosef smiled.

'They shaved all of us the first day. For the lice, they said. They treated us with louse powder.'

The General steeled himself not to move away from Yosef, or to start scratching.

At the next village, Captain Bauer found a public lavatory. He parked next to it, and the General gave Yosef the bag of clothes, a cloth, a bar of soap, and a towel.

Five minutes later, Yosef emerged, a different man, though still looking drawn and tired.

The General handed him a cap.

'It will cover your hair until it grows again.'

In the same village, they found a small café, and ordered three large plates of Bratkartoffeln and a steaming beaker of coffee each.

'Take your time,' the General advised Yosef, watching him wolf into the fried potatoes, beef, and onions. 'We don't want you being sick again.'

Back in the car, the General marvelled at human resilience. Prisoner number 101357, with a plate of food inside him, looked almost like the Yosef of old, despite the stubbled head.

'How are they?' he asked.

'They're worried about you,' the General replied.

'I should have asked about them first. I wasn't thinking straight.'

'They'd understand. Let's get you home and see them. Then we'll have to have a long hard look as to what to do next.'

'I know. We're living on the edge of a cliff, sir.'

'You've fallen off that edge a couple of times, my friend. I'm not sure we can keep hauling you back up.'

Yosef tried to smile.

'The children. We need to get them out. Then worry about us.'

A sense of relief flooded the General. He'd been dreading confronting Yosef with the reality that the children should go first and had hoped that Miriam would be able to persuade him.

'I know. I spoke with Miriam yesterday. She feels the same.'

'Can anything be done?'

'I've already made enquiries. I'm just waiting for news. It shouldn't be too long.'

CHAPTER 47

[04/03/1941 Tuesday]

Deep down, the General had known that Admiral Wilhelm Canaris was his superior officer, but their relationship, even within the Abwehr, had been in essence an informal one. The General deferred to his friend when necessary, but there had never been a need for the admiral to pull rank on him.

When he was summoned to the Stadtheide barracks in Plön, without explanation, Erich Kästner knew that it was all going to change, and it wasn't hard to guess the reason for it.

But when Corporal Lubinus showed a tight-lipped Wilhelm Canaris into the General's office at the barracks, the General recalled what it was like being a junior officer, waiting for the axe to fall for one misdemeanour or another, back in the days.

'You fool,' the admiral said without preamble, his voice raised, if not quite a shout. 'Just what do you think you were playing at?'

The General flinched. He knew he deserved it, and he felt bad at letting down his closest friend.

'I mean, Erich, you've pulled a few stunts in your life but this...'

The General had never seen Wilhelm Canaris so angry. He glanced towards the door.

'Don't worry, I dismissed Corporal Lubinus. No one will hear what I have to say.'

He paused for breath.

'You're jeopardising everything we are striving for,' he continued. 'You'll have to learn to see the big picture.'

'But–'

'You needn't argue,' the admiral butted in. 'You'll draw the whole of the Gestapo, the SD and the police down on us, like a train.'

'What else could I do? He's my friend. I'd do the same for you.'

'I'm not a Jew, and I don't need your help.'

'I can't stand aside and watch them destroy Yosef and his family.'

'They have to go, Erich, however you do it. Get them away. If you can't get them out of the country, give them enough money and tell them to go into hiding. Plenty others are doing it.'

'They'll get caught, eventually. You know they will. If there's one thing we know about the machinery of the Reich, it's that it's damned efficient.'

'You can benefit the greater number by far if you keep yourself out of trouble,' the admiral said, his voice softening a little.

'I need you, Erich,' he added, holding up his hand to stop the General protesting. 'I need somebody I can trust, who I can talk freely with. But I need that person to be without blemish in the eyes of the security services. You are becoming a thorn in their sides.'

'I'll sort it. I have a contact who's trying to get the children out. After that, Miriam and Yosef are going to make a run for it with the Haganah, they say.'

'Good,' the admiral said, a little mollified, 'make it sooner rather than later.'

'I'm sorry, Canaris, for causing you trouble. How did you find out?'

'I'm in intelligence. I'm very good at it.'

'The paperwork. You saw the copy of the *transfer of custody form*.'

The admiral smiled.

'I keep an eye on you, like I do for all my heads of station, but with you, it's for a different reason.'

'Oh. What's that?'

'I need to keep you out of bother,' Canaris said.

'And who looks out for you?' the General asked.

~~o~~

[05/03/1941 Wednesday]

Maria Kästner moved out of the marital bed the day after Yosef came home. She told her children that the General's snoring had become impossible to sleep through and the General shrugged and smiled sheepishly, the lie confirming her story.

He thought it had fooled Eva, and the boys, but with Antje, he wasn't so sure. He caught her sometimes glancing at him with a look that said she knew that there was more to it.

And there was. The General's last attempt to keep Yosef out of prison had been the final straw.

'You continue to put this family at risk with your blind devotion to the Nussbaums, without caring what effect your behaviour has on the rest of us. From now on, you'll be sleeping on your own until you come to your senses. Don't you know that your own daughter is ashamed of you?'

The barb hurt him. He knew that Eva and Maria were close, and it was only natural that his oldest daughter should take her mother's part, but he'd always thought her sense of fairness and her intelligence would have been enough to see that there were two sides to every story.

'I'll have a word with her.'

'You can try, but it won't do any good. She's dreadfully upset with it all. She can hardly put her foot out of the door without a sense of humiliation.'

It crossed Erich Kästner's mind to say she was talking about herself, not Eva, but he thought it might be better to talk to his daughter first.

He didn't even consider that it could be Antje his wife had been talking about. His youngest daughter would fully back his stance on the Nussbaums, and on wider Jewish issues. He was sure of that.

And he wouldn't back down. Despite the pressure from Maria, and Admiral Canaris's warning, he knew that if the situation arose again, he'd do what he had to, just to keep them free, and alive.

He sighed and slipped out the back door. Albert was polishing the car.

'Do you need me, sir?' the driver asked.

'No. I'll walk. It's not a bad day.'

'Whatever you please, sir. They say a walk clears the head.'

The General laughed.

He didn't walk. As soon as he was out of the gateway, he jumped on a tram to Wellingdorf. He stayed on until Ellerbek, then got off at Franziusallee and crossed the road, looking around. He saw nothing amiss.

He boarded the next tram in the opposite direction, and sat near the back, getting off at Berlinerplatz.

He was sure he hadn't been followed. He'd recently taken the precaution of doing the same exercise once a week, just to dispel the hint of paranoia that Gerhard Wendland's visit, and the Gestapo's involvement, had induced.

He walked northwards.

The Admiralty had a small boatyard not far from the jetty, used to maintain the three navy launches that the admiral used to flit about the harbour. He'd been given permission to store *Snowgoose* there over the winter.

He opened the padlock with the key he'd been given, and closed it over behind him, leaving it unlocked. Ten minutes later, Dieter Maas slipped in through the gate and joined him.

The two men embraced and shook hands.

'Dieter, it's great to see you. Are you looking forward to a spot of sailing this summer, if they let us?'

'It would be good to get out on the water. It's surprising how quickly this sailing business gets under your skin.'

The General laughed.

'I was born with it in my blood, I fear,' he said. 'I've seen photographs of me as a babe in arms, in a sailing outfit, on my father's yacht.'

'There'll be no Kieler Woche this year again, will there?'

'I would doubt it. "Suspended for the duration of the war" is what I heard, however long that might be.'

'It won't be over quickly, I fear, if we keep invading other people's countries. Sooner or later, one of them is going to fight back.'

'The British are trying their best,' the General said, 'but it's mostly defensive for them at present. Still, there's no sign of Herr Hitler launching himself across the Channel, just yet.'

'There are rumours…'

'About us invading England?'

'No. Just the opposite.'

'The British invading us? That's preposterous. They don't have the resources. They're still licking their wounds over the disaster of their expeditionary force being hounded out of France and Belgium.'

'That's not what I meant. From what I've heard, our next move will be eastwards.'

'Another of the Balkan states? They're with us anyway. What would the point be?'

'I'll tell you what I've heard, and what I know, then you can make up your own mind. First, there's a general movement of troops and equipment to our eastern borders, when everyone is expecting an invasion of England.'

Dieter looked at the General but, seeing no reaction, he continued.

'Secondly, I hear that conscription is to be dramatically widened, both in age, and in the reduction of reserved occupation.'

'I'll interrupt you there, Dieter,' the General said. 'It's no real secret that there had been a gradual build-up of Soviet troops in the Baltic States and in Belarus. If Herr Hitler wants to strengthen our position in the east, as a precaution, but keep our options open for an invasion of Britain, he'd have no choice but to accelerate conscription.'

'That is what I argued to myself, Erich. And then we received orders to print these.'

He handed the General a one-page folded pamphlet.

'Is this in Russian?' the General said, looking at the script.

'Yes, it's Cyrillic, I think, but I haven't been able to get it translated yet.'

'How many copies have been ordered?'

'200,000.'

'200,000? That's a hell of a lot.'

'I know men on the shop floor of two of our competitors who also do work for the party. They have similar orders. That's only in Kiel.'

'Can I keep one?' the General asked.

'By all means. You'll get it translated?'

'Yes. The Abwehr has a Russian section. Can I ask you another favour?'

'Ask away. I can't promise I can help.'

'You've given me one of these,' the General said, picking up the pamphlet. 'Can you give me a copy of the next *Kieler Jüdisches Freiheitsnachrichtenblatt* before it is published?'

Dieter Maas paled.

'I… I…' he stammered.

The General put his hand on Dieter's arm.

'Don't worry. No one knows. Even I didn't, until now. It was just a wild guess. I'm sorry I shocked you like that.'

'How did you…'

'A couple of things. You mentioned a while ago that you'd been friends with Benno Arndt. He had an assistant, I'd heard, but that wasn't surprising; it would be difficult to produce a newspaper of that quality, even if it were only a one or two sheets, without help. But it wasn't until I heard a whisper that the new editor and publisher of the KJF might not be Jewish that I began to wonder.'

'Please mention it to no one, not even your most trusted colleagues.'

The blood drained from his face again and he stared at the General. 'You haven't spoken to anyone already, have you?'

'No. As I say, it was a wild guess. I wasn't expecting it to be true. And don't worry, I wouldn't dream of saying to anyone. However, it might be incompatible with our arrangement.'

'That would be sad. I've enjoyed our trading of information, knowing that someone else feels the same way I do. And it goes without saying that I'll miss the sailing.'

'It would look very suspicious if you were to suddenly stop sailing with me and, as for the trading of information, if something comes up in our conversation, who will know?'

Dieter smiled. 'I suppose you're right.'

'Our financial arrangement will have to end, I'm afraid,' the General said, 'if you wish to continue your publishing career.'

Dieter nodded.

'I didn't keep the money. It went to a deserving cause.'

'Oh. Which one?'

Dieter smiled at the General.

'Ah.' The General sighed.

'Benno and I financed the KJF between us. There was no one else involved. We thought it safer like that.'

The General laughed. 'So, the Third Reich financed the KJF, even if it was indirectly. Now, there's irony for you.'

'It doesn't cost much now. There are less Jews to read it, and it's only a single sheet these days, printed on an old Gestetner duplicator. There's another irony. It was manufactured in England.'

They sat for a while, soaking up the weak sun. The General produced a flask from his pocket. He took a sip and handed it to the newspaperman.

'Why do you do it?' the General asked.

'I was brought up to be a news editor. It matters to me that there's somebody who still prints the truth. When Benno started the KJF, he asked me to help. He figured a Jewish assistant would let something slip, and anyway, who would have suspected an Aryan of being his assistant? *A Weisse Jude.*'

The General smiled.

'And now?'

'I do it for Benno. And for the way he died. I like to picture the Gestapo's faces when they read it.'

'Take great care, my friend,' the General said. 'They'll not spare you Benno's fate just because you're not a Jew. It might even be worse for you. I'd try and find a way to scotch that Aryan rumour if I were you. Tell them your Bar-Mitzvah stories.'

Dieter smiled.

'And the sailing's still on?' he said.

'Of course.'

~~o~~

[07/03/1941 Friday]

'Canaris.'

'Kästner.'

'Are you still angry?'

'No. I've forgiven you. Are you behaving?'

'I'm trying my best. Did you get the items I sent?'

'Yes. They were of great interest. It is Russian, as you suspected. Instructions for local inhabitants under German occupation.'

'You knew?'

'Not exactly, but everything is beginning to stack up. The deployments, the new recruits. There was nothing concrete from my sources at the ministry, but your source has confirmed it for us. It was clever of the bastards to use provincial printers. There wasn't a whiff of it here in Berlin.'

'Our great leader hasn't confided in you?'

'Not yet. I don't believe it's imminent, so there is time.'

'But you think we're definitely moving east?'

'It looks like it.'

'It's a mistake.'

'I know. The biggest. Ask Napoleon Bonaparte.'

The General laughed.

When they hung up, Erich Kästner walked back to his office, and looked out a large-scale map of Eastern Europe, studying it with interest.

~~o~~

[10/03/1941 Monday]

'My husband's a fool. I'm livid with him. You would think these people were real family, the way he acts. Eva and I are being talked about because of him.'

She would never have spoken to the women in her usual circle of friends like this, but the countess was discreet, and surprisingly non-judgmental.

'They always said that the way to control a man is through his stomach. I always find, especially when you're young enough, and you still have your looks, like you have, that there are more reliable methods of keeping them on a short leash.'

Maria blushed. It was all very well withholding Erich's marital benefits. She wasn't sure she wanted to discuss it with the countess.

'I suppose you're right,' she said blandly, glancing out of the window at Eva and Hugo strolling together in the garden of the countess's beautiful home, deep in conversation, peppered with the occasional burst of laughter.

'They're getting along swimmingly, aren't they,' the countess said. 'You know, for a while, I was wondering if we'd ever find anyone suitable for either of them.'

Maria Kästner didn't know if she should be worried or flattered. She wasn't sure that she liked the sound of Eva ending up with a man no other respectable woman wanted.

'Why on earth would any girl not see Hugo as a catch, my dear Countess?'

The countess chuckled.

'It wasn't them. It was him. He just wasn't interested in any of them, until your Eva came along.'

Again, a doubt crept into Maria Kästner's mind. *Was Eva considered to be the last choice for Hugo?*

'I did wonder if he was going to be like his great uncle Ferdinand. Never married you know, and there were his boys…'

Maria Kästner blushed again, turning away to avoid the countess seeing her embarrassment.

'Still. All's well that ends well, my dear Maria.'

CHAPTER 48

'Erich.'

The General recognised the voice. His grip tightened on the telephone handset.

Alphonse Berac, the Swiss ambassador.

'Alphonse,' he replied. 'How are you?'

'Not good, my friend. I have a heavy heart.'

There was a short silence. 'Go on,' The General said

'The news is not great, I'm afraid,' the Swiss diplomat continued. 'The organisations we were talking about have been forced to suspend operations. "Difficulties with the German authorities", they say.'

The General slumped in his chair.

'I'm deeply sorry to hear that,' he said, his voice soft and flat.

'I'm sorry too. You must be devastated. I apologise for getting your hopes up.'

'Don't be ridiculous, Alphonse. It's not your fault. I don't suppose it is a temporary suspension?'

'I doubt it very much,' the ambassador said. 'The German border guards have made it almost impossible, I believe, and I can't see anything changing.'

'Thank you anyway, for what you have done. If you are ever in Kiel again, remember my promise to show you around.'

'I would enjoy that. I have a feeling that you and I would get on well, my friend.'

~~o~~

Five minutes after the Swiss ambassador had hung up, the telephone rang again. The General picked it up.

'I have Colonel Schneider for you,' Frau Müller said. 'He didn't give a reason for calling.'

The General's heart lurched.

My boys. Please God No.

'Colonel Schneider,' he said. 'It's good to hear from you. Are you home on leave?'

'Erich, how are you?' he said, his breeziness dispelling any concerns about Franz and Johann. 'I'm still in Norway, and it's still damned cold.'

The General laughed.

'The line is so clear. I assumed you were in Germany. Modern technology, eh?'

'Quite. We Germans are capable of anything we put our minds to.'

'What can I do for you, Walther?' the General asked, more than a little curious.

'Well, it's down to you, as it happens, or at least to a seed you planted in my mind the last time we spoke.'

'Me? I'm not sure I understand, but I'm intrigued. Go on.'

'Don't you remember? You suggested I should ship *The Shearwater* over here and get a little sailing in the fjords.'

'Ah. I'm not so sure I did but no matter. You wish me to help arrange transport?'

'No. I've already exhausted those avenues. There is no chance the navy, or even any of the merchantmen, will take a yacht on board. It would be seen as too wasteful of resources and not in the interests of the Reich. But I have a proposal, and I thought it only fair that I should run it past you first.'

'Certainly. I'm all ears, Walther.'

'I can arrange a couple of weeks' leave for Franz and Johann and they can sail her over here for me. Feel free to join them if you can get the time.'

'Why don't you do it?'

'Alas, I cannot be spared, as much as I'd enjoy the experience.'

'You're asking for my blessing?'

'Well, yes. I thought it only fair.'

'Hmmm. Franz and I have done it before. He's more than capable, I'd say, and he and Johann make a great crew. I'd be happy for them to do it. Have you spoken to them?'

'I've talked to Franz. He was happy to give it a go and said that Johann would jump at the chance.'

'When were you thinking of?'

'Early April, when the ice has melted, if we get the weather. The sooner the better; it will allow us to get a full season up here. If the war goes on much longer, I can keep her on the hard over the winter in Bergen, and she'll be here for next year.'

'Go for it, Walther. If there is anything I can do at this end, let me know.'

'There may be. *The Shearwater* has been in the Scheindorf boatyard in Kiel for a refit over the last month. They'll put it in the water for me and commission her, but if you could keep an eye on progress...'

'I'd be delighted, Walther. I can head over there tomorrow if you like. I know the Scheindorf brothers well.'

'That would be excellent. I'll keep in touch. Franz and Johann are catching a ride on a destroyer back to Kiel tomorrow, so they should be with you Monday. I will try and grab a few days home before they leave, to make any final arrangements.'

'That's fine, Walther. I look forward to hearing from you.'

The line went dead.

The General smiled. It crossed his mind to take up the colonel's offer and accompany the boys, but he discounted it almost immediately. He knew that if he went, Franz would defer to him, and he didn't want that.

This is their adventure.

For a few minutes, he allowed his mind to fill with pleasant visions of his sons' trip. Then his thoughts jerked back to the Swiss ambassador's call, wiping the smile from his face. He sat staring across Kieler Hafen, seeing nothing.

There has to be a way.

He walked to the window and looked to his left across to the Schwentine, the small inlet on the opposite side of the harbour between the enormous Deutsche Werke and Kriegsmarine yards, where the flow of the Schwentine river entered Kieler Hafen.

The colonel's boat, *Der Sturmtaucher*, was sitting on a cradle in one of the smaller boatbuilder's yards that lined the inlet. He would finish early and go and see how close she was to being back in the water.

He imagined the excitement his sons would feel as they headed for the mouth of Kieler Förde, at the start of a 600-mile voyage to Bergen in Norway.

He froze for a second, trying to grasp at a thought that was just out of reach.

That's it. *Der Sturmtaucher.*

The Shearwater.

His mind began work. He stood up and walked over to the framed chart of the North Sea and the Baltic on the wall of his office. He traced his finger from the mouth of Kieler Förde, along the narrow channel that separated Denmark from Sweden, up through the Kattegat and Skagerrak, where the Baltic became the North Sea, and around the west coast of Norway to Bergen. Then he let his hand drift to the west.

~~o~~

[17/03/1941 Monday]

'Sir, just before you leave, there was a note from the NVA for you. You'd shown an interest in a visit, sir.'

'The NVA. Who the devil are they? I hope this is important; the boys' ship is docking very soon.'

'I know, sir. Your car is ready. They've just passed the lightship at Stollergrund, so you have plenty time.'

'So, who are these NVA people?'

Captain Bauer read the note.

'Nachrichtenmittel-Versuchsanstalt,' he said.

The General remembered. *The Navy Transmissions Laboratory.*

'They have something to do with submarines, and early warning systems, I believe,' the young officer added.

'Oh, I remember now. One of the admirals asked me to get up to speed on it. They appear to be dragging their heels a bit.'

'When do you want me to schedule the visit? You're free on Wednesday morning.'

'That will do. Why don't you come as well; take notes for me. You have the necessary clearance, don't you?'

'Yes, sir.'

'Right. That's settled. Now, I'm off to meet my sons.'

CHAPTER 49

The General watched as destroyer Z4, the *Richard Beitzen*, docked expertly on the mole at the south end of Tirpitzhafen. A navy tug fussed around the ship, helping her berth with a nudge to her bow.

She'd made good time on her overnight passage from Bergen, having left at 0600 the day before, arriving in Kiel just over thirty-one hours later.

The General waved, seeing his sons leaning over the railing high above him, until they disappeared, making their way to the lower decks.

Ten minutes later, they were among the first to walk down the gangway onto the quay, shaking hands with the officer on watch.

The General could hear laughter as the boys walked towards them, the usual inter-service taunting between army and navy never letting up.

He walked towards them.

~~o~~

In the General's staff car, Johann talked excitedly about the upcoming voyage, naming all the possible ports of call on the way and asking his father about the readiness of *Der Sturmtaucher*.

'She's going in the water today,' the General replied. 'She appears to be in fine order. Final fitting out is tomorrow. I've taken the afternoon off to help, but they're expecting you two first thing in the morning.'

'I can't wait. Can we call round on the way home?' Johann asked.

'I don't see why not. It will give you a chance to inspect the hull, before she gets craned in.'

The General leaned forward.

'Private Zimmer, take us to the Scheindorf yard, please. Where we were the other day.'

'Yes, sir. Right away.'

The General turned to Franz.

'You're not saying much. Are you worried about the trip?'

Franz smiled, but the General noticed that it didn't reach his eyes.

'No. Not really. It would have been good to have you along, but I'm sure we'll manage.' He gave his father a half-smile.

'I can't get away for long enough to do a trip like that,' the General lied.

'I understand. The voyage should be straightforward, though, if we just watch the weather.'

The General frowned. There was no doubt that Franz wasn't himself.

I'll talk to him later when we're alone.

Franz took more interest at the yard, questioning the foreman carefully about the work they'd done. The yacht had been given a very thorough overhaul and all three of the Kästner men agreed that the boat was in great shape for the voyage ahead.

'I haven't told your mother yet,' the General said, as they sped past Krupp's shipyard, on the way home.

'I'll tell her,' Franz offered.

~~o~~

Maria Kästner took the news much better than the General had expected.

'They've sailed all their lives. Why should I start worrying now?' she said. 'Anyway, being part of this war is of much greater danger to them.'

They'd all smiled at that, knowing that she was right. Johann pulled out a chart from his father's study and laid it out on the table.

The General could see that his wife was only moderately interested, but because it was Johann, she was happy to let him describe the voyage in detail. Eva looked bored, but Antje followed the passage plan with eager fascination.

The General smiled. He knew it was only a matter of time before his youngest daughter asked him if she could leave her classes at art school for a fortnight and accompany her brothers, knowing that the answer would be no.

The General nodded to Franz, who followed him into his study.

He closed the door behind them.

'What's bothering you, son?' the General asked, his hand on Franz's arm.

He told the General about Johann witnessing the massacre of the Jewish families by the SS, and that the Norwegian Wehrmacht soldiers had taken part.

'In the light of what has gone on in Poland and elsewhere,' he finished, 'it's only a drop in the ocean but if it's happening in a place like Norway, nowhere is safe.'

'How did Johann take it?'

'Not well. I think he has realised what the National Socialists are all about, at long last.'

'Ah. This is the first time that he has seen acts like these at close quarters?'

'Yes. He was in command of the troops supporting the SS.'

'And you?'

'I wasn't there, but I could see on his face how bad it had been as soon as he came back to the billet. A ten-year-old boy was one of the victims, according to Johann. The SS maintained that they were all partisans.'

'I see reports like this every week. And the transports to Poland; they're increasing every day.'

'No sign of the Nussbaums' visas?'

'No. The last time Yosef contacted them, there were further delays. It could be another year, and I'm fearful that they won't have that time.'

The General told Franz about Neuengamme, and how he'd only just managed to arrange for Yosef's release.

'If it happens again, I'm not sure I can get any of them out. And if they're sent to Poland, I can do nothing.'

Franz stayed quiet, brooding.

'I need to ask you something,' the General said, 'but I'd fully understand if you refused.'

'I know what you're going to say. I've been turning the same question over in my mind.'

The General was momentarily flustered.

'You have?'

'Yes. I think so. You want us to take the Nussbaums to Sweden in the colonel's boat.'

The General stifled a smile.

'That's not exactly what I was going to suggest, but it does involve *Der Sturmtaucher*.'

It was Franz's turn to look flustered.

'What do you mean? Sweden is a neutral country. We can make landfall there on the way to Norway.'

'Sweden are handing any Jews that are caught entering the country back to the German authorities. Their economy relies too heavily on exports to Germany to risk upsetting us. And if they're handed back, they'll go straight to a camp, or to a ghetto in Poland.'

'But Denmark and Norway are both occupied. Where else could we…?'

He stopped.

'No,' he said, shaking his head. 'You can't mean… It's impossible. We'd be caught. As deserters, we'd be shot. As for carrying four Jews, trying to escape…'

'It wouldn't be four. You wouldn't have space to hide all of them on the yacht. It would just be Ruth and Manny. Yosef and Miriam will try and get out by other means, once the children are safe.'

Franz stared at his father, his mouth open.

'They'd never agree to it,' he said.

'Miriam asked me to find a way to get Ruth and Manny out when Yosef was arrested.'

'And Yosef went along with it?'

'Yes. He also suggested it, after he was released.'

'What about Ruth and Manny? Don't they get a say?'

'They'll do what their parents tell them to,' the General said, more harshly than he'd intended, 'but I'd imagine Miriam and Yosef would be able to persuade them that it's the right thing to do,' he added, his voice softening.

Franz stood in the centre of the room, his hand on his forehead, trying to take it all in. The General waited, giving his son time to consider his proposal.

'You *are* talking about us sailing across the North Sea to England?' Franz said, incredulity etched on his face.

'It's not as far as you'd imagine and, if you think about it, you only have to reach British waters to be safe, unless you are terribly unlucky.'

'But people will realise we've gone off course. They'll come after us. If they do, we'd be better off dead.'

'Not if you do it right and choose your weather. I'll show you how, once we get hold of the chart Johann is using.'

'You've put a lot of thought into this, haven't you?'

'Yes.' He hesitated. 'In principle, would you be willing to do it?'

'Yes, I think so. If Johann agrees.'

'Good. There's another reason for doing it. I didn't want to say until you'd decided so that it didn't influence your choice. If I tell you something, you must promise not to repeat it to anyone.'

'I'll not say a word. What is it you know?'

'Your Uncle Wilhelm and I both believe that our beloved Führer is going to order the Wehrmacht to invade Russia.'

Franz paled. He froze, his mouth open, for a second.

'That's madness,' he said. 'The Führer must know that.'

'He doesn't care, but it will be a war to end all wars. The Soviets might not have our technology or our tactical brilliance, but they have an almost unlimited supply of fighting men. I don't want you and Johann to be part of it.'

'I'm not scared of fighting, and I'd feel guilty that my friends will be sucked into it without me there to watch out for them, but I wouldn't want to be part of it, when I know it's wrong.'

'If you stay here, you will be part of it. Almost certainly. And if you think what we did in Poland was bad, can you imagine what they will do to people of the Soviet Union? And what will the Russians do to us if we're defeated, in retaliation? You'd be better off spending the rest of the war in a British POW camp.'

Franz shivered.

The General took hold of his son's shoulder.

'You did realise that you would be a prisoner of war,' he said, 'didn't you?'

'No. I suppose I didn't give it a thought. But it doesn't matter. I don't want to kill in the name of this so-called Reich anymore.'

'Then all we have to do is persuade Johann to be party to it,' the General said, walking towards the door.

'That won't be easy. He won't want to leave his friends to their fate. And we still need to put it to the Nussbaums,' Franz added, following him.

CHAPTER 50

'You can't be serious, either of you.'

Johann stared at his older brother, then at the chart still laid out on the drawing-room table. Albert had driven the ladies into town.

'We're deadly serious,' Franz said.

Johann turned to his father, his eyes wide in disbelief.

'I was lucky to get Yosef out this time,' the General said. 'If any of them are sent there again, I would be powerless to help, and being in one of these camps is almost certainly a death sentence. Even if they aren't sent to Neuengamme, or somewhere similar, they will be deported to Poland, and I've seen what the Third Reich plan to do there.'

'What?' Johann asked, his face grey.

'They plan to build death camps. Their aim is to eradicate Europe's Jews.'

Johann let out a brittle laugh.

'They can't,' he said. 'It's impossible.'

The General shook his head.

'The numbers are astounding, and if you'd asked me a few years ago, I would have scoffed at it like you, but not now. I believe that they will do as they say.'

'No,' Johann said, shaking his head. 'It can't be done.'

'The Nussbaums will not survive if they stay here in Germany, and I have exhausted every other way of getting them out.'

'If we didn't get caught on the way there, we'd sure as hell be caught on the way back, although at least we wouldn't have four Jews on board.'

The General and Franz glanced at each other, then looked back at Johann.

'It will only be Ruth and Manny,' the General said. 'There wouldn't be room to hide them all.'

He reached out and put his arm on Johann's shoulder.

'And you'll not be coming back,' he added.

'What do you mean? We can't just disappear. That's desertion.'

'This is a one-way trip,' Franz said. 'We'll be prisoners of war for however long this war goes on.'

'I'll not be a deserter,' Johann said, the vein on his forehead pulsing.

'We'll have no choice,' Franz said, finding it difficult to meet Johann's gaze. 'Even if we managed to elude the Royal Navy and land Ruth and Manny on English soil, I don't want to come back.'

'You'd condone this,' Johann said, looking at his father in disgust.

Erich Kästner flinched at the cold fury in his son's voice.

'Yes. There's something else you need to know.'

'You can't expect me to leave my friends in the lurch. I'd never forgive myself.'

'If you stay, you will be sent east. We are going to war with the Soviet Union.'

'That's madness. How do you...' He stopped.

'It will happen very soon. Later this year, in all probability. Perhaps sooner.'

'Then there's all the more reason for me to come back and serve. My friends need me. The army needs me, and it will need Franz too.'

'We cannot beat the Soviets,' the General said, 'and if we lose, no, when we lose, they will destroy us. Do you want to be part of that?'

'I signed up to fight for my country. I can't turn my back on it now.'

The General sighed.

'What you saw in Norway. The Jewish village. That will happen a thousand times in Russia, perhaps more. Do you want to be part of that?'

'I can't... I won't...'

He looked from his father to his brother, then back again.

'I need to think about it. There must be a way...'

The General put his arm around his youngest son's shoulder.

'Go away. Mull it over. But you mustn't tell a soul.'

'I'm not stupid,' Johann shouted, the anger spilling over.

He turned on his heel and left the room, slamming the door behind him. Franz made to follow.

'Leave him. He needs time.'

'But what if he confides in his friends?'

'He won't. He'll stay away from them.'

'How do you know?'

'I don't.' The General's voice softened. 'Not for sure, but I've dealt with men for nigh on forty years. You learn to read them. I'm sure you must do it too.'

'Sometimes. But I can't read Johann. He's too…'

'Volatile?'

'Yes.'

The General walked over to the window and looked down towards the lake. As Franz joined him, they saw Johann storm across the lawn towards the boathouse. A few minutes later, Johann hoisted the sails on one of the dinghies, and beat out against a stiff breeze to the middle of the lake, the small craft heeling over improbably close to the water, Johann's back only centimetres above the surface.

He tacked when he reached the other shore, and they saw him let the sails out, the boat almost flying across the Drachensee chop.

For an hour, he pushed the dinghy to its limits. His father and brother stood and watched, fascinated, until he pushed it too far, and capsized, dunking himself in the icy cold water.

Franz reached out to open the French windows, but the General stopped him.

They watched Johann pull himself up onto the hull then, leaning back and hauling on the halyard, he righted the small craft. Sorting the sails, he drifted in towards the shore, pulling it up on the small beach.

'Ask Yosef to run a hot bath for him,' the General said.

~~o~~

'I'll do it,' Johann said, but his eyes were clouded.

'I know what it means to you to leave your friends, the battalion, and the colonel,' the General said.

'No. I don't believe you do,' Johann said, almost in a whisper.

'Perhaps not, but you forget that I lived through the hell of the Great War, and I know what it will be like, warring in winter, in the mud and the cold.'

'I'm not frightened of fighting, or even dying,' Johann said, 'and, leaving my friends to face that without me, I might as well be dead, but if it will save Ruth and Manny, and it means that I don't have to take part in another act of evil like the one in Norway, I'll do it. Just don't expect me to feel good about it.'

'It will be worth it,' Franz said, 'if only to see them safe.'

'I know. Why can't we take Yosef and Miriam?'

'We may be searched,' Franz said, shaking his head. 'It won't be impossible to hide a girl and a child, but two adults…'

'I've spoken to Yosef and Miriam,' the General said. 'They asked me to try and get the children out if I could.'

'What about them?'

'There are other ways. We are trying to arrange it.'

'Why don't Ruth and Manny go with them?'

'We think this way is safer. Itsik Weichmann's parents were shot dead when they tried to get out.'

'Oh,' Johann said, the blood draining from his face. 'I remember.'

'Yosef and Miriam are prepared to take the risk, but it would make it much easier for them if they knew that Ruth and Manny were safe.'

Johann nodded.

'What do we have to do?' he said.

Franz rolled out the chart again.

~~o~~

Ruth had rarely seen her mother look so troubled. Her father, if anything, looked worse.

'We have something to say to you, and to Manny, but we want to speak with you first because we might need your help when we tell him.'

'Yes, Mama. What's the matter?'

'We can't wait for visas from the Americans. Sooner or later, we're all going to be arrested, or deported to Poland, and I don't have to tell you what that means.'

'Mama, you're frightening me.'

'I'm sorry, my love. It frightens me too.'

'What we're trying to say,' Yosef explained, 'is that we have to find other ways to get out. These days, it would be nearly impossible to travel as a family, but we have a chance of getting you and Manny to safety.'

'But Papa...' Ruth blurted, tears stinging her eyes.

'Shoosh,' he said. 'Listen to me. The General and I had a talk last night. He has found a way to get you to England, but it will be dangerous.'

'What about you and Mama?' Ruth said, sobbing.

'It will be much easier for us to travel without having to worry about you two,' Miriam said, trying her best to sound convincing. 'We'll have a go at getting into Palestine. The Haganah will find it much easier to smuggle two of us, rather than the whole family. We'll find a way to be together again once we're all safe.'

Ruth sniffed. 'Are you sure?' she said.

'Yes,' Yosef said. 'We're certain. It's the only way.'

Ruth looked at her parents and fought against her tears.

'How is the General going to get us to England?'

Miriam and Yosef glanced at each other.

'By boat,' Yosef said.

Ruth saw her mother's eyes close. Her father couldn't meet her gaze.

'A steamer? There haven't been any to England since the beginning of the war. And they wouldn't let us on one, anyway. We haven't got visas.'

'It would be on a yacht, Ruth,' Yosef said, trying to sound matter-of-fact. 'Franz and Johann have been asked to sail their commanding officer's yacht to Norway. They have offered to take you both with them and, instead of sailing to Bergen, they would make for England instead.'

'Across the North Sea? In a little sailing boat? They must be mad.'

Ruth's father tried to reassure her.

'The General and Franz have sailed in the North Sea countless times, and they've both been to Norway. Even Antje has sailed in the North Sea.'

'But Manny and I have hardly been on a yacht. I'd be terrified, and I don't know if I could live in a small boat for however long it would take to get there.'

'We know it won't be easy. I don't know how long it will take, but there's no one better than the Kästner boys to look after you. The General is convinced it will work and I'd trust him more than any man alive. Look at the number of times he's saved Mama and I already.'

'It's all too much to take in. I don't want to leave you.'

Ruth began to cry again. Yosef put his arms around her.

'It's only for a while,' he said. 'We'll find you, wherever you are, and we can be a family again. In the meantime, we need you to look out for Manny. Can you do that for us?'

'Yes,' Ruth said, so quietly that Yosef and Miriam had to strain to hear her.

'We must tell Manny, now,' Miriam said. 'Wash your face so that he can't see you've been crying.'

'Take a few minutes, Bubbeleh,' Yosef said.

Ruth looked up at him, and he turned away.

But not before she'd seen the tears gathering in his eyes.

~~o~~

Manny took it all in his stride. It required all of Yosef and Miriam's strength not to show their hurt when he enthusiastically embraced the idea without a qualm.

Only later, when the reality of being separated from his parents had hit home, did he sidle up to Miriam and have a quiet sob, burying his head in the folds of her dress.

'It's all right to have a little cry,' she told him, 'but I need you to be brave. I know Ruth is older than you, but you'll have to help her. She'll find it hard on the boat, and you'll be the only family she'll have.'

'But you'll come soon, won't you? You and Papa.'

'You can be sure we will, at the first chance we have, but it may take a little while to get to where you are. Travel is not easy these days, even outside of Germany.'

'I'll look after Ruth for you, Mama. I'll see that she's all right.'

'That's my little man. Now, I think we can let you off with your homework tonight. I've made your favourite; Matzah ball soup, and a lovely apple cake for afters.'

CHAPTER 51

[18/03/1941 Tuesday]

In the cellar, the Kästners and the Nussbaums listened to the crump of anti-aircraft fire, and the blasts of the thousands of bombs landing on Kiel.

'It's the biggest raid so far,' the General said, as the walls shook, and a little dust trickled onto the floor.

Yosef had been the last to enter.

'Sorry about that, sir,' he whispered in the General's ear while they stacked sandbags against the door. 'A friend called round, just as the sirens went off. I have some news.'

'What is it?'

'Jakob and a few of the others have been released,' Yosef said. 'They asked me to pass on their thanks.'

The General looked briefly away.

'I didn't have anything to do with it,' he said.

'They think you did, and so do I.'

'I spoke to one or two people, but I'm not sure it would have made any difference. Perhaps the Jewish community paid a bribe, not that it matters; it's a miracle that they were released. I only hope they are trying to get out of Germany now.'

Yosef shrugged.

'It's almost impossible, as you know. We'll not all get out.'

The General closed his eyes.

I'm powerless. How did we get to this?

It was three hours before the all-clear sounded.

~~o~~

[19/03/1941 Wednesday]

'Herr General, Welcome to the Nachrichtenmittel-Versuchsanstalt.'

The man held out his hand and Erich Kästner shook it warmly.

'I'm Rudolf Kühnhold, the lead scientist here,' the man continued. 'I'll show you around.'

'I'm delighted to meet you, Herr Kühnhold. I've heard a lot about you, and your facility.'

The General turned to the captain.

'This is Captain Heinz Bauer, my assistant. He's here to take notes. He has the necessary clearances.'

The tour of the NVA lasted about an hour. They saw experimental sonar systems that were being fitted to the new flush of submarines currently being built, allowing them to find targets while underwater.

'How does it work?' Heinz Bauer asked.

'We've had hydrophones for a while – they pick up the sound of the propellors, or screws as you navy types would have it, but we're working on active systems where we bounce sound pulses off a target to find its direction and bearing.'

'How accurate is it?' the General asked.

'The hydrophones are very good. They can even identify the size of a vessel by the sound its screws make – U-boat commanders can ignore small fishing boats, if they wish, and concentrate on more significant vessels. Active sound location systems are a little way off being of much practical use.'

Turning to technology above the surface, Rudolf Kühnhold enthused about the Kriegsmarine Seetakt radar, being fitted to the larger ships in the fleet.

'The navy feel that its priority is in range-finding, for the guns, but we're convinced that it will be increasingly used to detect approaching vessels and, just as importantly, approaching aircraft.'

'How accurate is radar technology?'

'We can easily detect a destroyer at 100 kilometres, in ideal conditions.'

'What about small objects? *Targets*, I believe you called them,' the General asked. 'A submarine conning tower, for example.'

'Not so good. We'd have to be quite close, and the operator would have to know how to tune the set well, and what to look for.'

The General affected a concerned frown.

'Don't worry. We're working on systems now that will roll out within the year that will detect objects that size.'

'And fishing boats? Will it help the Kriegsmarine avoid those unfortunate incidents that happen from time to time, when a trawler is sunk by one of our ships?'

'Again, the answer would have to be guarded. A wooden fishing vessel reflects radio waves poorly, although any significant steel in her superstructure might make a difference.'

'That's unfortunate. As well as the loss of brave German fishermen, the damage to our warships can be considerable.'

'As I've said, the advances we are making will offer considerable improvement in target identification and accuracy in the future, but it all takes time.'

'Time is something we don't have, Herr Kühnhold. I would urge you to spare no effort to get these new systems onto our ships. It could be the difference between success and failure.'

The scientist bridled a little.

'We progress as fast as we can, but the work is exacting and meticulous, and there are no shortcuts.'

'I wasn't suggesting otherwise. On the contrary, we have been most impressed with your work and will recommend that your budget should be increased, if funding can be found. Would I be correct in thinking that the British are perhaps a little more advanced than us?'

'We are playing catch-up in this area. The Luftwaffe, for instance, have an almost identical system to one the Kriegsmarine uses, but it's inferior to the British early warning array.'

'And do our aircraft have radar yet?'

'No. The aerials are becoming smaller, but the pulse generators are too heavy and power hungry at present.'

The General thanked the scientist profusely.

'Please keep me updated on progress,' he added as they left.

~~o~~

'I didn't realise you were so interested in technology, sir,' Captain Bauer said, on the short walk back to the office.

'I'm interested in everything, Captain. Always be curious, my father used to tell me. It's good advice.'

'I learned a lot today, sir. Science moves so fast. There was no radar on any of the ships I served on.'

The General thought he could detect a wistful note in the young man's voice.

Perhaps it's time to consider letting him go back to sea.

~~o~~

[20/03/1941 Thursday]

For over a week, Franz and Johann spent the large part of every day on *The Shearwater*. At first, they helped the yard workers, getting to know every millimetre of her, intimately.

Three days in, the elder Scheindorf brother took Franz aside.

'She's due her commissioning sail today,' he said. 'Now, normally, the owner would come and do that, with myself or my brother on board, and a yard hand to make notes of any snags, but I've had a letter from Colonel Schneider saying that he's happy for you to take his place.'

'Yes. He mentioned that we'd need to do that.'

'Norway,' he said. 'Quite a trip, young man, just for the two of you.'

'I've done it before, with my father, General Kästner.'

'Yes. The colonel said you were an experienced yachtsman, and we've done quite a bit of work for your father over the years.'

'He speaks highly of your yard.'

'That's kind of him. Well, there's no time like the present. Do you want to tell your brother? I'll meet you at the dock in ten minutes.'

For the next couple of hours, they put *The Shearwater* through her paces, in a steady brisk wind. Compared to their racing boat, she sailed like a bus; even their father's boat seemed like a sports car by comparison, but she had a solidity that neither of the other two boats had, and she virtually steered herself if the sails were properly set.

When they were satisfied with her, Franz expertly docked *The Shearwater*, the engine thudding away nicely.

'Everything's as it should be,' Franz said, shaking the yard owner's hand.

'I should hope so,' the man said.

He looked at Franz, the hint of a smile on his face.

'Do you know, I think you might be as good a sailor as your father, and your grandfather. It's not often I come across one as young as yourself who has the feel for a boat like you do, apart from a few of the fishermen's sons.'

Franz's face flushed red.

'It's nothing to be embarrassed about, lad. I'd be almost inclined to go on this trip to Norway with you, knowing I'd be safe.'

'Thank you, sir. I've learned most of it from my father. He has a little more experience than me though.'

'That's fair enough. Now, you can keep her here until tomorrow if you like. The colonel had arranged a berth at the base of one of the Kriegsmarine victualling jetties for you.'

For a brief second, Franz couldn't breathe. He swallowed a tide of panic and tried to steady his voice.

'The Kriegsmarine yard?' he said. 'Why? I thought we were leaving from here.'

'We have three boats coming in the day after tomorrow, and *The Shearwater* will get in the way. Didn't the colonel tell you?'

'No. He didn't. How will we get in and out of the naval yard?'

'I'm surprised he didn't mention it. He arranged for you to have these.'

The boatbuilder handed Franz two naval security passes.

'Keep them with you at all times. The Kriegsmarine people aren't very partial to non-navy personnel wandering about on their base unchecked.'

CHAPTER 52

[21/03/1941 Friday]

'How are we going to get Ruth and Manny on board?' Franz said.

The General looked up. He'd been thinking the same thing.

The three Kästner men sat in *The Shearwater*'s cockpit, a cup of steaming coffee in each of their hands. Behind them, the boatyard bustled with activity in preparation for the three vessels that would be the centre of the yard's attention for the next few weeks.

One of the new arrivals, a small fishing boat, was already at the dock, sitting astern of *The Shearwater*. The keel blocks and trestles were prepared, and the yard crane was being slowly moved into position.

'Just when you're ready, Shearwater,' the younger of the Scheindorf brothers shouted, grinning.

Franz waved and shook his head, smiling. Johann jumped up, gulping his coffee as he stood.

'Sit down and finish it. He's just pulling our legs. It will be an hour before they're ready for her.' Franz nodded to the fishing boat behind him. 'We'll be long gone.'

'We'll work something out,' the General said, 'about Ruth and Manny, I mean.'

'But security will be tight.'

'We could pick them up somewhere after we leave,' Johann suggested.

'We'd be seen, for sure,' Franz said. 'There will be no other yachts around and there may be a lot of curious eyes watching us.'

'Father could bring them to one of our stops along the way.'

'There's too much risk in that. He'd have to cross the Danish border with them, and even if they made it through, it would only take one person to see us. You know what the Third Reich is like; people are rewarded for reporting their neighbours and friends, or their own families, even in places like Denmark and Norway. Phoning the authorities about suspicious goings-on around a visiting yacht is becoming second nature to them.'

'Franz is right,' the General said. 'We must try and get them on while the boat is in the naval yard. We'll find a way.'

He threw the dregs of his coffee over the side. Franz and Johann did the same.

'Let's get her moved and see what the new berth looks like.'

Franz pressed the starter button and the engine roared into life. The General looked up and smiled, then let go the forward spring while Johann tended to the stern lines.

With only the stern spring left, Franz reversed the engine against it, and *The Shearwater*'s bow swung out into the Schwentine.

'Let go,' Franz shouted, kicking the engine into forward gear as the end of the rope slipped through the cleat.

The Shearwater edged out into the channel, the gentle flow of the river helping to turn her towards the wide expanse of Kieler Hafen.

It took them twenty minutes. Dwarfed by the ships in the Howaldtswerke Kriegsmarine yard, Franz guided her past the longer fuelling jetties, each one of them occupied by warships being loaded with enough ammunition, oil and supplies for weeks or even months at sea.

'It's one of the jetties within the victualling harbour we're looking for. It's mainly for smaller naval vessels. Our one will have two small harbour patrol boats tied up to it. We'll be berthed shoreside of them.'

'There it is,' Johann shouted, as they motored through the harbour entrance. Franz saw where he was pointing and steered *The Shearwater* towards it.

There were men everywhere, and dock cranes were loading supplies onto naval boats of all shapes and sizes but, as they approached their berth, a dockyard worker waved from the end of the pier and gestured that *The Shearwater* should go round to the far side, past the two patrol boats tied up together.

'Put out plenty fenders,' the man shouted as they passed.

They rounded the stern of the outer vessel and saw a Kriegsmarine officer and two naval ratings standing on the harbour wall, two metres above them, watching *The Shearwater* as Franz guided her in.

'What's the depth like?' he shouted up.

'You've plenty. Try and get the ladder to midships,' one of the ratings shouted back. 'And throw us your lines.'

When she was fast, the three Kästner men climbed up the ladder, helped the last foot or so by willing hands.

'Welcome to the navy, gentlemen,' the officer said, smiling.

'Captain Hössler,' the General said, 'How nice of you to meet us.'

'Not at all, General Kästner. It's not often that we get invaded by sea, by the army.'

They all laughed, even the two ratings.

'These are my sons,' the General said, 'Major Franz Kästner and Captain Johann Kästner.'

The captain gave an old-fashioned navy salute, the General was pleased to see, and the three Kästner men responded in kind.

'This is Captain Hössler,' the General said to his sons. 'He often looks after me when I visit. I presume he'll be doing the same for you while you're here.'

'Indeed, I will,' the captain said. 'If there's anything you need, just ask. Your father is a popular man around here. I doubt they would have given you this berth if your colonel fellow hadn't mentioned that it was General Kästner's sons who were sailing his boat to Norway.'

The General smiled.

'Kind words, Captain Hössler. How will it work, with Franz and Johann going back and forward to the boat, getting her ready?'

The captain turned to Franz. 'You were issued with passes, ja?'

Franz showed the captain the security passes the boatyard owner had given him.

'Keep these on you at all times when you are here. Show them at the gate when you wish to come in or out and please restrict yourself to this area only and go directly to and from the gate when you arrive or leave. There will always be someone about, if there's anything you need to ask but, do you see that telephone over there?' he said, pointing to a box on the wall with *Telefon* stencilled on it in black paint. 'That connects to the main gatehouse. If you need to, you can use it to contact me.'

'Is the gatehouse manned twenty-four hours a day?'

'Of course. This is the navy, not the army.'

They all laughed.

'General Kästner, you can use your normal pass. You can come and go as you please but, as with your usual visits to Kriegsmarine installations, you should be accompanied at all times. This will be waived, obviously, as long as you are within the confines of the small-craft harbour, or directly between here and the gatehouse.'

'Thank you, Captain Hössler. Now, my car should be here soon.'

'It's at the gate, sir. Would you like me to have it sent, or do you wish to walk? It's not far; I'm heading that way myself.'

The General turned to his sons.

'Are you ready? Will we walk up with the captain?'

'I just need a final check of the lines, then I'll be with you.'

Franz leaned over the edge of the quay and looked at *The Shearwater*. She sat snugly against the wall of the jetty and her lines ashore were seamanlike.

He caught up with the others, the ratings having disappeared to their next task.

'I was just saying, how excited you must be about your trip,' the Kriegsmarine captain was saying. 'It's the talk of our officer's mess.'

'I thought you'd be too busy to concern yourself about us.'

'It's busy, Major, but mostly routine, so the men like to gossip. They're all very intrigued by your little boat.'

'If any of them would like a look…'

'You might have a long queue if you make an offer like that, although I must admit, I would be the first to take you up on it.'

'You're welcome to come aboard. We'll even take you out for a sail if you have time.'

'Ha. That would be wonderful. Oh. there's one other thing I must tell you.'

He pointed to a large concrete structure ahead of them.

'If you're at the boat, and the air-raid siren sounds, get yourself into the shelter.'

'Have you had much damage?'

'We've had a few hits, but our fire-fighting teams deal with it, and we have the manpower to make repairs rapidly. We've been lucky. Most of the fuel tanks are underground beside the oiling jetties, where the ships refuel, and they haven't hit one of them yet.'

'Have you been based here long?'

'A year. I enjoy it but I'd prefer to be back afloat.'

He looked at them almost apologetically. 'The post came with a captain's epaulettes. I'd still be a lieutenant if I'd stayed where I was. I'll try for a command next year. They're generally fair-minded at rewarding people for taking a job like this.'

The General thought of his own Captain Bauer and reminded himself that the young man was ready for a seagoing command.

'You're doing a fine job, Captain,' he said, 'and it will make being back at sea the better for it.'

'I hope so, sir. Perhaps I could speak to you when the time comes. You do have a bit of clout with the admirals.'

The General laughed.

'I doubt it, but I'd be happy to put in a good word for you.'

The captain beamed. Franz looked at Johann. Neither had realised just how much sway their father had with the navy.

'Here you are, sir,' the captain said, as they turned the last corner. The General's car sat outside of the main gate, the driver leaning against the front wing, smoking a cigarette. He quickly dropped it and stubbed it out with his foot when he saw the General.

The captain shook their hands and saluted again.

'We'll be here most days, captain,' Franz said to him. 'It's been good to meet you.'

'And you, too, sir. I look forward to seeing the boat.'

The marine on the gate checked their passes, and the gates of the naval dockyard slid open. The three army men walked through.

The General glanced at his sons and wondered if their thoughts were the same as his.

How, in the name of God, are we going to get them through yard security?

CHAPTER 53

[27/03/1941 Thursday]

They waited while the marine officer in charge of the gatehouse issued Colonel Schneider with a one-time pass. As promised, he'd arrived in Kiel to make final arrangements for the voyage, although, in truth, there wasn't much for him to do, other than to pay all the outstanding accounts at the chandlers, the boatyard and the general stores.

The Kriegsmarine made no charge for berthing, or for the small amount of fuel Franz had been given to top up *The Shearwater*'s tank, and to fill the fuel cans they'd lashed in the stern locker. Instead, the colonel wrote a cheque the association for Kriegsmarine and Reichsmarine veterans, and handed it to Captain Hössler, thanking him for all his help.

'Anything for General Kästner,' the captain said.

The colonel looked out the guardhouse window and watched Erich Kästner and his sons talking easily to the marines, sharing a laugh with them. Despite the care the officer was taking with Walther Schneider's credentials, they'd hardly glanced at the Kästner men's passes, and their car had been given a cursory search.

The formalities over, they drove to the jetty where *The Shearwater* lay.

~~o~~

'So, tell me,' Walther Schneider said, sitting with the three Kästner men in *The Shearwater*'s cabin, 'how are the preparations going?'

'We're almost ready,' Franz said. 'The Kriegsmarine couldn't have been more helpful. We only have a few bits and pieces to put on the boat before we leave on Wednesday, weather permitting.'

'Wouldn't you rather leave earlier?' the colonel asked. 'It would give you a few extra days.'

'The navy say the last of the ice is just breaking up,' Franz said. 'It should all be cleared by next week. It's a good thing it didn't persist like last year.'

'No, quite. You would have needed to wait until May.'

'They also have radio reports from our weather station in Greenland. The barometer is dropping, and it's expected that an Atlantic storm will hit them tomorrow, meaning that we'd expect a bit of a blow in three or four days, on Sunday or Monday. It would be better to wait until that's passed.'

'Anyway,' Johann added, 'A fuel pipe ruptured on one of the injectors yesterday. One of the navy mechanics did a temporary repair, so it's usable, but we're waiting for a spare to come from Motoren-Werke Mannheim. It should be here by Tuesday.'

'Excellent,' he said, rubbing his hands and smiling. 'She's looking great. Let's take her for a sail and see how you two handle her.'

~~o~~

After the boat had docked, and while Franz and Johann squared everything away, the colonel poured a generous tot of rum for himself and the General.

Handing Erich Kästner the glass, he sighed.

'Franz sails *The Shearwater* better than I do,' he said, 'and I rate myself as a good yachtsman. How he's learned the subtleties of sailing a ketch, and working with the gaff rig, in such a short time, is beyond me.'

'He has a natural affinity for boats,' the General said. 'And don't forget, he has been around yachts since he was in his pram.'

'Even so, he trims her close to perfection. It's remarkable. It's taken me years to master that.'

'She sails well, Walther. She's a boat you could cross an ocean in if you wished.'

'I might do that one day. When I retire. She's strongly built, and sea friendly. I'm happy to sacrifice a bit of speed for that, and one man can handle her on his own, at a push.'

'She'll do well in Norway. I'd imagine you'd like to get her up as far as Spitsbergen.

She'd cope with the Arctic well, given a good summer.'

'Finding the time could be the problem, but perhaps I could use my leave, instead of going home, as long as my wife doesn't hear about it.'

He laughed. 'Maria might also be disappointed,' he added. 'Franz and Johann may decide to join me.'

'She will be, if they do. She misses them greatly when they're away. These last few weeks have been a godsend to her, having the boys home.'

'Me. A godsend,' Johann's voice interrupted, as he climbed down the companionway. 'I'm glad it's been recognised, and not before time.'

The two older men laughed, as Johann sat down beside him.

Franz followed his brother into the cabin. The colonel poured two extra glasses and refreshed his own and the General's.

He reached into the large bag he'd brought with him and pulled out a sheaf of sea charts. He turned to Franz.

'Now, show me your passage plans,' he said.

~~o~~

Franz sifted through the pile, and unfolded a large-scale chart of the North Sea, which included the sections of the Western Baltic they would need and, moving the other charts aside, he laid it out on the table.

'There's going to be a lot of naval and commercial traffic through the Great Belt,' he said. 'We don't particularly want to be evading a stream of Kriegsmarine ships and merchant vessels, especially if we are beating to windward at the time, so I propose that we go through the Lillebælt, to the West of Fyn. It's a little longer, but there will be less traffic, and it has better shelter, so if we do encounter bad weather, we wouldn't have to run for cover as early.'

'That's sound thinking,' the colonel said. 'It can be a little tricky; around Bågø, for instance, but it's nothing that you can't handle, especially as I imagine it will be all done in daytime.'

'I can't guarantee that. We haven't planned any night sailing, but most of our legs are around fifty miles long. Depending on how the wind holds up, we may not always be able to make it in daylight, and our longest leg, from Hjelm to Læsø will almost certainly finish after dark; it's around seventy miles.'

'The channels are all well marked with lights,' the General said, 'and Franz isn't inexperienced at night sailing.'

'I know,' the colonel said. 'I watched him take *The Shearwater* in to Wismarer Bucht in darkness. He did quite a job that night, with an inexperienced crew.'

Franz reddened and Johann grinned at him, deepening the colour in his face.

'It was well marked. We just followed the buoys and kept clear of the odd fishing boat, and one freighter.'

'The point is,' the colonel said, 'I have no qualms if you end up sailing at night. My only advice is to cross the Skagerrak in daylight. The stretch of water between Denmark and Norway can be treacherous.'

'I'll show you our route,' Franz said, his finger tracing a line starting at the mouth of Kieler Förde.

'We have a few options for stops in the Lillebælt, but I fancy the look of Bøjden Bro then, after we pass through the Middelfart narrows, there's a small harbour at Bogense, which we visited with father a few years ago.'

He turned to the General.

'Do you remember it?'

'Of course. We were all there. Johann, your mother, and the girls. It was a quaint little place, with a nice beach and a railway that ran right down to the harbour.'

'So where will you head from there?' the colonel said, interrupting the Kästner family memories.

'I thought we'd head for Hjelm. It's a little island just off the coast, north of Samsø.'

The colonel looked at the chart.

'Why there? Would Samsø not be better?'

'We'll see what the weather's like. Hjelm has shelter and good holding on three sides and, because it's fourteen miles further north than Samsø, it makes the long leg to Læsø the next day more achievable.'

'That makes sense,' the General said. 'If you only make Samsø, you could use Anholt as your next stop.'

Johann spoke for the first time.

'We could, but we wouldn't make Hirsthalls the following day; we'd need to stop at Skagen, which would add an extra day to the journey.'

'That wouldn't be a disaster,' Franz said, 'but it would be better if we make Hirtshals. We'd be ten miles shorter crossing to Norway the following day, and with a less westerly heading.'

The General nodded.

'The prevailing wind in the Skagerrak is from the west,' he said. 'From Skagen, you'd be crashing into the waves and wind the whole way, slowing you down and punishing both you and the boat.'

Now the Colonel was nodding.

'Franz's plan is good,' he said. 'It will have you sailing off the wind, if the weather holds to form, gaining extra speed, and giving you a more comfortable crossing.

'Once we're at Grimstad,' Johann said, 'we'd just be hopping up the coast thirty or forty miles at a time, depending on the wind.'

Franz, like the other two Kästner men, knew that this part of the journey was fantasy. From Hirtshals, if the weather played its part, they would strike out west, towards the east coast of Great Britain.

It was the other reason Franz had chosen Hirtshals; it was nearer the end of the Skagerrak, and further away from the main route large vessels would take from the Baltic to Norway. In peacetime, it would still have been busy with merchant ships plying their way to and from Britain, but since the war had begun, that traffic had ceased.

'We'll call in at three or four ports on the way to Bergen,' Franz said. 'Kristiansand or Mandal, Jøssingfjord or Rekefjord, Stavanger for sure, then cut inside Karmøy, if the weather is bad, to Lervik. From there, it's sheltered all the way to Bergen.'

'You could join us for several of the legs in Norway, sir,' Johann said.

The colonel laughed.

'I might just do that,' he said.

He looked at the chart again.

'It's a sound plan, Franz,' he said.

'And Johann, of course,' he added.

It's true, Franz thought. Both of us pored for endless hours over father's charts and through the sailing directions, deciding where we should stop each night, looking for quieter harbours and anchorages where Ruth and Manny would be less at risk of discovery, without making it look as if we are trying to hide something.

'I'm going home to Lübeck for the weekend to see the family,' the colonel said, 'and my transport back to Norway is in the early hours of Wednesday so I won't be able to see you off, but I'll try and call in again before I leave.'

'That would be great, sir. We should have that repair done by then. We aim to set off around seven on Wednesday.'

'Ha. I'll be halfway up the Great Belt by then,' the colonel said.

He looked around at them.

'I have a little further news for you. There has been a new round of promotions. I'll not be your colonel for much longer.'

Both brothers spoke, their words intermingling.

'I'm sorry to hear that,' Franz said, when he could make himself heard.

'Yes, sir,' added Johann. 'You'll be missed.'

The colonel laughed.

'I'm not going anywhere, but I'll be your Generalmajor now.' *Brigadier.*

'Congratulations, sir.'

'Yes,' said Erich Kästner, reaching over to shake the colonel's hand. 'You'll be a general before this war is over.'

The colonel laughed. 'One step at a time,' he said, 'but there were quite a few changes in the Kompanie. Majors Breit and Mandel have been promoted and have been transferred to a new battalion. They're being shipped out to eastern Poland, to beef up our border forces. Our allies, the Russians, have been strengthening the units they have posted on their side of the border, I'm told.'

'Do you think there's something in the wind?' the General asked. 'Are the Soviets mobilising?'

Franz glanced up, but his father's face was a mask of innocence.

The colonel laughed. 'No,' he said. 'They wouldn't dare and, anyway, Comrade Stalin still appears to be full of good intentions.'

He turned to Franz.

'You're being promoted to Oberstleutnant when you get back to Norway.' *Lieutenant colonel.*

Franz stared at the colonel.

'Why?' he asked.

'Because I recommended it and because the battalion is enlarging, and new men will need new leaders.'

He turned to Johann.

'You'll be one of our new majors,' he said.

'At last. My talents are recognised, but always one step behind my brother.'

They all laughed, the sound of it filling the cabin.

Franz looked around.

The world needs serious men, meticulous men like Father and I, and the colonel, but it also needs men like Johann, who can lighten a circumstance and bring a smile to men's faces.

The General reached for the bottle and refilled their glasses.

'As the only one here unlikely to gain further promotion, I congratulate all three of you, and I fully expect that you'll all end up in senior positions in the Wehrmacht.'

He raised his glass to them. Franz thought he saw a flash of pain in his father's eyes.

He knows Johann and I will never take up our new rank, whatever happens. And neither of us will see him again for years, if ever.

All four men touched their glasses together.

Colonel Schneider stood up and shook the Kästner men's hands.

'Until Monday,' he said. 'Sieg Heil.'

CHAPTER 54

Der Sturmtaucher, like most cruising yachts, carried an elementary toolbox; a set of spanners and wrenches for the engine, pliers, and screwdrivers for the rudimentary electrics, and even a small collection of woodworking tools to fix broken spars or boards.

Johann fished a bit from the leather roll that held the drills.

'Will this be big enough?' he asked.

Franz looked at it and nodded.

Johann fitted it into the jaws of the brace and, carefully positioning it on the cross marks Franz had made on the boards covering the bilge, he began turning the handle.

It took a while; he was careful not to split the wood and, when he was finished, he lifted the board out and rubbed it with a piece of fine sandpaper to smooth off any rough edges.

Franz took a brush and, using some old varnish tinted with some black ink, lifted the board from the floor and carefully coated the inside of the hole, to make it look as if it had been there a while.

'That should do,' he said.

Johann used a small scraper to scoop out the sawdust and shavings that had fallen into the bilges and emptied it into the old paint can they were using as a rubbish bin. With a rag, he cleaned out the remaining debris.

He shuddered.

'I'm not sure they'll be able to suffer it in there,' he said.

'They'll have to if anyone comes aboard.'

'But one little air hole?' he said, shaking his head. 'It could get very stuffy in there.'

'It's more likely to be cold, wet and dark, and damned uncomfortable,' Franz said.

He looked at the space at their feet. It was roughly coffin-sized, and not dissimilar in shape.

'Try it,' he said.

Johann lifted the second board and lowered himself in. It was barely long enough for him, and he had to bend his legs slightly to let Franz replace the boards on top of him. It was wide enough, though, for two people, at a push.

'How is it?' Franz asked, looking at the floor.

The boards were a very neat fit, and it was hard to tell that there was a space underneath them. The air hole that they'd just drilled was very discreet and, if anyone asked, it could easily be explained as a drainage hole, allowing any water that got into the cabin to seep down to the bilge, where it could be pumped out.

A pipe from the deepest part of the bilge led up to the back of the cockpit, where a hand-operated pump ejected the contents of the bilges through a fitting in the side of the hull.

'It's not very pleasant,' Johann said, his voice so muffled Franz could barely hear it.

Franz lifted the boards up, and his brother climbed out.

He looked at the open bilge and the corners of his mouth turned down.

'They'll need to have a mat of some description if they are going to be in here for any length of time.'

'Could you stand it for a few hours?' Franz said.

'You and I could cope, but we've been trained for situations like that. I'm not sure how Ruth and Manny will fare.'

'Don't underestimate them. They've had to deal with hardships you and I have no conception of.'

'What do you mean?' Johann said.

'Talk to Father. He can tell you everything that the Nussbaums have been through; what Jewish families have to endure.'

'I didn't know,' Johann said.

They replaced the bilge boards.

'You do realise what this trip means for us, don't you?' Franz said.

'What do you mean?'

'We'll not see Mother or Father, or Eva or Antje, for as long as this war goes on, perhaps never.'

'No. The war will end one way or another, and we will go back home.'

'If Adolf Hitler wins, and gets his thousand-year Reich, we will never see them again.' Johann shook his head.

'I don't understand.'

'If the British are defeated, we'll be handed back. If they find out we helped two Jews escape, and that we're deserters, we'll be shot.'

'They'll not find out. As far as they'll know, we were captured taking the colonel's boat to Norway.'

'The British will know. There will be records of our capture. We will never be safe.' Johann paled.

'I hadn't thought of that.'

'It shouldn't come to that. I don't think Hitler will win,' Franz said.

'He doesn't seem to be doing too badly at present. Who will stop him? The Russians don't have our training, or our equipment. We only need to get as far as Moscow.'

Franz reminded him of what their father had said about the Soviets, and their unlimited supply of men.

'The Red Army isn't a patch on the Wehrmacht. We'll annihilate them.'

Franz shook his head. 'It can't be ruled out, but Father and Uncle Wilhelm think that the Russian winter, the vastness of the country, and their almost unlimited resources, will make it difficult.'

'If the Führer takes Russia, he'll not stop. He'll come back for Britain.'

'I know. That's what frightens me. I just thought that you should go into this with your eyes open.'

'I refuse to believe we'll never see them again.'

'You must make your goodbyes, but Mother and the girls can't know. It would put them in danger. We must leave as if it's just another sailing trip.'

'I'll not say a word. Mama will imagine the worst anyway about us going to Norway, no matter what she says, so it will be quite natural to say our farewells.'

Franz smiled, but there was a sadness in his eyes.

'I guess that will have to do.'

The brothers sat for a while, both deep in their own thoughts.

'Do you think the colonel bought the story about the fuel pipe?' Franz asked, breaking the silence.

'Yes. Most definitely. He didn't suspect a thing.'

It had been Johann's idea to remove the fuel pipe and get a temporary one made. It gave them complete control of when they would leave, being able to produce the 'replacement' part when needed. They didn't want the colonel near the boat once Ruth and Manny had been smuggled on.

'We're finished here,' Franz said. 'Let's go home.'

~~o~~

[31/03/1941 Monday]

'Do we have to do this today?' Johann asked, untying the sail ties.

'Yes,' Franz snapped, regretting his crossness immediately. 'We need to be sure the guards at the gate are so acclimatised to us coming and going that we're part of the furniture. Look at today, for instance. They hardly looked at our papers and took no more than a cursory glance at the car.'

'I suppose you're right,' Johann said, ignoring Franz's unusual outburst. 'It was just that I wanted to go for a drink with the boys; Maxi and Fritz came over from Norway with the colonel and they asked if I could join them for a beer.'

'We would have done it yesterday, but the weather was foul.'

'I know. It's just…'

'Don't worry. We won't be out for long. You can join them later.'

Johann grunted.

In truth, Franz and the General had been delighted when battering rain and strong winds had hit Kiel late on Saturday, confirming the forecast from the weather station in Greenland.

'Where's Father?' Johann said. 'I thought he was coming.'

'He had to call at the office first. He'll be here shortly.'

Just as he finished speaking, the General's staff car rolled to a halt on the quayside.

'Catch this, boys,' he shouted, throwing down a hessian sack. 'More supplies.'

Johann deftly fielded the sack and stowed it in the cabin.

'Come on then, old man. You're holding us back.'

'He's just desperate to get finished, and join his friends for a drink,' Franz said, shaking his head.

'I thought you'd be coming too,' Johann replied, laughing.

'I'll leave you to it. Father and I will brief Ruth and Manny and talk to Miriam and Yosef.'

'Suit yourself. Remember you'll never see…'

'Sshh,' Franz hissed. 'You never know who might be listening.'

'Sorry,' Johann said, his tone a little sarcastic. 'There's no one within a hundred metres.'

'Even so, Franz is right. We have to be careful,' the General said.

Johann rolled his eyes and Franz could see him biting back a comment.

They were out for an hour. The brothers practised anchoring, watched over by their father, then the General surprised them by throwing a fender over, with a bight of rope attached to it, shouting 'man overboard' as he did so.

It took them less than four minutes to turn the boat and luff up to the fender, retrieving it with a boathook.

'Not bad, you two,' the General said. 'Out there, you wouldn't want to be in the water any longer than need be at this time of year.'

When they docked, Franz told Johann that he and the General would see to the boat.

'Take my car and park it in town. I'll collect it later. I'll go home with Father.'

'Thanks,' Johann said, flashing a grateful smile at Franz and his father. 'I'll telephone the house and let you know where I leave it. You might even change your mind and join us for one.'

'I might just,' Franz said. 'Don't say a word to them about our plans,' he added, as Johann hauled himself up the ladder, 'or Herr Hitler's plans.'

'I won't,' he said. 'I'm not stupid.'

'I know you're not, but it would be easy, with a few too many beers inside you, to confide in the boys.'

'My lips are sealed,' he said, with an exaggerated zipping motion across his mouth, before turning and running across the quay to Franz's little sports car.

'I'll check on him later,' Franz said to his father. 'He's closer to my friends than I am; they're as much his friends now. It will be a wrench for him, knowing that it might be years before he sees them again, and knowing what they might face.'

~~0~~

The marine stepped out and held his hand up. The General wound down his window and waited.

'General, how are you today? Not long until they leave now, sir.'

'No. if the spare part for the engine arrives, they'll be leaving in the early hours of Wednesday morning.'

The marine ducked his head in and looked in at Franz.

'Sorry, sir. I didn't know you were there. I thought you might have been in the car with Captain Kästner.'

Franz glanced at his father and wondered if he had the same thought.

They didn't check the car when Johann left.

'No. Johann wanted to leave early. A day out in the bars of Kiel with his friends.'

'Quite right, sir. I only wish I could join them.'

Franz and his father laughed. It all helped to foster the informal nature of their comings and goings.

'We'll not be bothering you too much longer,' Franz said.

'Oh, you've been no bother, sirs. We've enjoyed having you. It breaks up the monotony. Have you decided on your route yet?'

'More or less,' Franz replied.

'I'll bring a chart next time,' the General said, 'and show you. It makes more sense when you see it.'

'That would be great, sir. None of us can imagine doing a voyage like that in such a small boat.'

'It's quite a tough little boat,' Franz said, 'capable of going around the world, if you wanted.'

'Really, sir? If you don't mind, I think I'll stick to proper ships if I ever get back to sea.' Franz smiled.

'How long have you been based here?'

'Eighteen months, sir. I hope to get a move soon.'

'I'll have a word with the admiral,' the General said.

The marine's face brightened.

'Thank you, sir,' he said. 'I'd appreciate it. They say you are a man who gets things done around here.'

'I try my best. I'd be happy to help.'

The General wound up the window, then rolled it down again.

'Sergeant,' he called, as the marine walked to the gate.

'Yes, sir,' he said, turning. 'What can I do for you?'

'My daughter, and her young cousin would like to visit the boat, to see what Franz and Johann are sailing to Norway in. Is there any chance they would be allowed down to the yard tomorrow evening, after my daughter finishes school, and her supper?'

'Well, it's very irregular, sir, but I suppose this whole business has been out of the ordinary. I'll have to check with the captain, but he's usually very reasonable. I'd imagine it wouldn't be a problem. I'll let you know if there's an issue.'

He walked smartly to the gate and slid it open.

'Our cousin? Ulrich?' Franz asked, as they passed the saluting marine. 'That was clever.'

'Not really. He's almost the same age as Manny. There'll be no records; they'll never know.'

'But they'll question why two young people go in, and don't come back out.'

'I have a plan. It should work.'

~~o~~

Johann listened to the exchange with amusement, tinged with sadness.

'It's unfair,' he heard Maxi Grabner say. 'I mean, what is wrong with me?'

'Nothing, Maxi,' Fritz said. 'At least you've been promoted to a full lieutenant now.'

'At long last, but why are you all captains or majors now, and I'm still a junior officer?'

'Well, let me see,' Fritz said, rubbing his chin, a serious look pinned to his face. 'How many times did you fail your captain's exam?'

'I passed it. In the end.'

'How many times?' Fritz insisted.

'Seven or eight,' Maxi replied, counting the times on his fingers.

'Mmmm. More like ten,' Johann interjected.

'Well, whatever. I've passed now. You'd think they'd just make me straight up to captain. Now they'll have to wait another six months before they get the benefit of my experience.'

Like all of them, Johann loved Maximilian Grabner, but he was widely acknowledged to be the worst officer in the Kompanie. He was always assigned the least critical task and even the colonel did his best to keep him out of the line of danger. In all truth, he was more of a company mascot than a soldier.

'Your talents lie elsewhere,' Johann said. 'You keep everybody entertained and you're exceptional at finding good restaurants and bars, and great places to meet local women.'

'Hmmph,' he grunted. 'Not that I ever benefit from it. I rarely end up with a girl.'

'Maxi,' Johann explained, like a patient father to a child, 'we've told you before; you always set your sights too high and go for the most beautiful ones. You'd be better off accepting that you'll never be their first pick and go for the homelier girls, before they're all whisked off by desperate officers from other units, or, God forbid, the rank and file.'

The sad look of resignation that Maxi now sported, as he often did, occasionally engendered sympathy but, more often than not, provoked mirth among his friends, and through the rest of the battalion.

He'd played the sad clown for most of his life and was comfortable in the role.

'Well, now that Franz is going to be a lieutenant colonel, he'll not want to mix with the likes of us,' Maxi complained.

'Franz isn't like that. He's just never been as sociable as me,' Johann said. 'I'll still mix with the likes of you, Maxi, even though I'll be a major, and you a mere lieutenant.'

'Don't flatter yourself. Some of us find you just a bit too full of yourself.'

They both laughed, denying their exchange any possible malice, but Johann's grin faded first.

Fritz Aumeier glanced at him.

'This trip of yours,' he said, 'It sounds quite dangerous, does it not?'

'We've done this sort of thing before, and Franz sailed to Norway with my father once. It will all depend on the weather.'

'What about the British?' Maxi asked.

'We'd be very unlucky to encounter the Royal Navy. They don't venture into the Baltic, or even the Skagerrak; apart from the crossing to Norway, we'll be close to land for most of the route.'

'I suppose so,' Fritz said. 'You seem a little preoccupied. Are you worried about it?'

'I'm not, but it has its risks, I suppose.'

Fritz looked at his friend, the hint of a frown shading his face.

'Johann, can I ask you something?' Maxi interrupted, his tone now serious.

'Yes, of course. Fire away.'

'If, by any chance, the boat sinks, and you don't make it, can I have your knife?'

'Maxi!' Fritz hissed, giving his friend a dark look.

'What?' Maxi said, his arms spread wide in innocence.

Johann laughed. Maxi had always admired his whalebone-handled pocketknife, that the admiral, his grandfather, had given him.

'It's fine, Fritz. Maxi's right.' He turned to Maxi. 'You can have it, my friend, if anything happens to me. You can split the rest of my stuff between the others.'

'You two are far too morbid,' Fritz said, in disgust. 'We're supposed to be enjoying a quiet drink, and maybe pick up a few girls, and now we're discussing your demise.'

'I'm not going to drown, don't worry. But if something happens, tell the boys that it was a privilege to serve with them.'

Max and Fritz waited for the punchline, the twisted barb at the end, but it didn't come.

'You're being serious, aren't you?' Fritz said.

'I do have a deep side, you know,' Johann replied, 'but I keep it well hidden. Now, let's forget about it and find some Fräuleins to cheer us up.'

~~o~~

[31/03/1941 Monday]

The General sat opposite Miriam and Yosef, at the Nussbaums' table.

'Everything's in place. I just need to know if you are both a hundred per cent sure about it.'

The couple looked at each other.

'Yes,' Yosef said. His hair had grown in now, and he didn't look quite so much like a convict.

'If you're sure that Franz and Johann can do it,' Miriam said, receiving a glare from her husband.

'It is risky,' the General said. 'There's no getting away from it but, if anyone is capable of pulling it off, it's Franz and Johann.'

'When do they leave?'

Miriam's voice was close to cracking.

'Wednesday morning, but Ruth and Manny will need to get onto the boat on Tuesday evening.'

'Why?' Miriam asked.

'The yard will be too busy in the morning to smuggle them in. It should be quieter the evening before, and the blackout will help.'

'Will Franz and Johann be with them overnight?'

'No. It will only be for a few hours. The boys will be there early on the Wednesday.'

'They'll be ready,' Yosef said. 'We have to take this chance to get them out, and we trust Franz and Johann to do their best. We know they are risking everything too.'

'They believe it's the right thing to do,' the General said.

'So, what do we tell Ruth and Manny?'

'I need to talk to them. It would be better to do it now.'

'They're in the parlour. I'll call them through.'

Erich Kästner knocked on his daughter's bedroom door. He heard her call out to come in. He opened it.

Antje was sitting on her bed, reading a book.

'I need to speak with you,' he said, 'to ask you a very big favour.'

CHAPTER 55

[01/04/1941 Tuesday]

'The weather reports you asked for are on your desk, sir. They say they'll send them over every day, until you tell them otherwise.'

'Excellent. The boys will be delighted. I know they're not entirely accurate, but it will give them an idea of what the weather is going to do.'

'I believe they are better than they used to be, sir, although there is a worry that our weather station in Greenland is very vulnerable to British attack.'

'I suppose it is. Perhaps we should have a secondary base set up in the event of our main centre being shut down.'

'Do you want me to mention that to them, sir?'

'Yes. Good idea. Tell them it was your idea, Captain Bauer,' the General said.

He rummaged through the papers on his desk.

'Did the charts showing our minefields arrive?'

'They're in a large brown envelope, sir. I put it on your desk, sir.'

'Ah. I see it. Thank you.'

He'd requested the charts a week ago but had worried that they wouldn't arrive in time.

'Who sent them over?'

'It was Kommodore Boehm, sir.'

Rolf Boehm. He'd been based in Kiel for his whole career. As far as the General knew, the man had never had a seagoing commission. He remembered him as one of the navy contingent who'd been at his retiral party.

Was that really eight years ago?

'I know you only requested the minefields for the Ostsee and its approaches, but he's included the Nordsee ones as well.'

Good old thorough Rolf. Because the boys weren't supposed to be sailing in the North Sea, the General had been trying to come up with a way to get the information about the minefields there, in addition to charts for those in the Baltic and the Skagerrak.

'Send him a note of thanks… No, wait, get him on the line and I'll thank him personally.'

'Yes, sir.'

Within a couple of minutes, the phone rang.

'I have Kommodore Boehm on the line, sir,' the captain said.

'Rolf,' the General said. 'How are you. I just wanted to thank you for those minefield charts.'

'My pleasure, General Kästner. We've just finished updating them after the last minelaying operation. We're exceptionally well protected now. The British would be so slow picking their way through into the Baltic, we could knock them off like ducks at a fairground.'

'You did realise why I wanted them.'

The General heard a laugh at the end of the phone.

'Yes, your boys' trip is the talk of the base. I assumed that was what it was for.'

'Yes. It will be most helpful. How much technical stuff do you know about mines?'

'A fair bit. I've been coordinating minelaying operations for three years now. You have some questions?'

'Yes. It's regarding *The Shearwater*, Colonel Schneider's yacht; the one the boys are taking to Norway.'

'What about it?'

'If they do happen to stray into a minefield, how likely are they to set off a mine?'

'The vessel is wood, not steel?'

'Yes, but it has a lead keel.'

'What is her draught?'

'About two metres.'

'And what is her top speed?'

'About eight knots, but she'll mostly cruise at five or six.'

'Well, unless you're unlucky, and encounter a stray mine floating free, your boys should be safe enough. Mines are usually laid to float between three and five metres below the surface. Contact mines require a vessel to hit the mine and depress one of its 'horns' to explode it, so your boys should pass safely over.'

'What about magnetic mines?'

'Your boat's keel is made of lead, so it shouldn't set a magnetic mine off.'

'What about the keel bolts?'

'I doubt very much that there will be enough iron in them.'

'Thank you, Rolf. That has been most helpful.'

'My pleasure, General. Wish them good luck for me. The best way is to keep away from the minefields as much as possible, but to always keep a close eye out for mines that might have broken away, drifting on the surface.'

'I'll tell them that.'

He paused.

'Although we didn't need them, I was intrigued to see the charts for our mines in the North Sea.'

'Ach, I just put them in for completeness. I thought you might be interested.'

'I was. Our minelaying is more extensive than I thought.'

'Oh, we've put a lot of resources into it, Herr General.'

'I suppose the British have done the same?'

'We know they have. I can send you over a chart showing their minelaying strategy if you're interested. Obviously, we rely on intelligence reports, so they're not as accurate. I'll get them over to you within the next few days.'

'It would be fascinating to see them but, to save you the bother, Captain Bauer is up on your floor just after lunch. I'll tell him to call in and collect them.'

'Even better. I'll have them ready.'

When he put the phone down, the General sighed. That had been a lot easier than he'd feared.

Now, we just need the ship movements.

CHAPTER 56

Manny's fourteenth birthday was a muted affair. Yosef and Miriam tried their best to make it a celebration, but a pall hung over the Nussbaum house that no amount of food, drink, or attempts at cheerfulness could dispel.

The General attended, with Antje. Maria and Eva sent their apologies; Albert was driving them to the countess's country home for lunch, Maria furious with the General that he and Antje had refused to join them, citing Manny's birthday party as their excuse. Manny was delighted when Johann and Franz made an appearance.

Miriam had surpassed herself with the meal; the table groaned with the weight of food, but few attending had the appetite for it.

Yosef danced the Hora with Manny, the younger Nussbaum now surpassing his father, his youthful flexibility and strength outdoing the more experienced and skilful Yosef. They insisted that the General should give it a try and, for a short time at least, laughter filled the Nussbaums' kitchen at his enthusiastic but woeful efforts.

In the end, despite it being rarely danced by women or girls, Miriam, Ruth, and Antje joined in, allowing the traditional Hora circle to be formed.

~~o~~

After they'd eaten, Ruth took Antje by the hand, and led her upstairs.

Closing the door, they sat on Ruth's bed, facing each other.

'We'll not have a chance to say goodbye alone tonight. Thank you for helping,' Ruth said, a tear running down her cheek.

'I couldn't not help. I just hope it goes well. I couldn't bear to see you and Manny caught.'

'You would be in trouble too.'

They were both crying now.

'You've been the best friend anyone could have,' Ruth said.

'And you have too,' Antje replied, hugging her.

'I still have the picture you drew of the Sturmtaucher with me,' Ruth said. 'It's my lucky talisman, especially now that I know the name of the boat.'

'*Der Sturmtaucher*,' Antje said, smiling. 'I hope she skims over the waves, taking you all to safety.'

'I wish you were coming. I'm terrified.'

'I do too. You'll not get caught though. Franz and Johann will look after you.'

'It's not that I'm frightened of the most. It's the sea, and the wind and the waves. I hope I won't let them down.'

'You won't. You'll get used to it. It's the most marvellous feeling, flying along with just the wind pushing you.'

'We'll see,' Ruth said, and Antje could hear grave doubt in her voice.

They heard the General's voice float up the stairs.

'Antje. We should go now.'

'Just coming, Papa,' she shouted back. She turned to Ruth.

'I'll see you later, and we'll be together when it's all over,' she said.

They hugged again, clinging to each other, then Antje ran down the stairs, wiping her eyes.

~~o~~

The General gently touched her on the arm, and she followed him out of the door, closing it softly behind them.

'They need time to themselves,' the General said. 'There's no knowing when they'll be together again.'

'What time do we leave?'

'Around six. Have you got everything?'

'Yes. I checked with Ruth. We have the same clothes.'

'And a hat?'

'Yes. The same one exactly. Why do we need hats?'

'Ruth is going to cut her hair.'

'Oh my goodness! Why?'

'If she's seen on the boat from a distance, with a hat on, she might just pass as Franz or Johann.'

'Ah. I see. She'll be upset about that too. She loves her hair.'

'It might be the least of her problems. She's never sailed before and, for them to succeed, they're going to need to sail in some pretty rough conditions.'

'She told me she was worried about that. I could go and help her,' Antje said, looking hopefully at her father.

'I imagine you know the answer to that,' the General said, smiling.

~~o~~

In the General's study, the Kästner men pored over the weather charts the General had brought home. Franz and Johann listened as their father spoke.

'Our weather boffins don't claim that they are accurate all the time, but they're increasingly getting the trends right. As weather generally comes in from the west, data from our station in Greenland and information from our ships in the Atlantic give us a reasonable warning of approaching weather systems. In addition, our base in Spitzbergen and other Kriegsmarine installations on the coast of Norway send us reports, so if the weather closes in from the north, we should get a warning at least.'

'So, what are they saying?' Franz asked.

'It's looking fairly settled for the next few days.'

'What if we don't get the bad weather we need once we get to Skagerrak?' Johann said.

'Have another *engine problem*. You'll think of something. Wait for the weather to change.'

'What else have you got?' Franz said.

'Planned ship movements for the Baltic fleet, for a week in advance. It won't cover every naval vessel, but all the routine patrols and passages are included. I told them that you wanted to plan your route to avoid getting in the way of naval vessels. They were impressed by your consideration.'

Johann smiled, but the General could see that it was an effort.

'Try and find a telephone each night you are in port and call home,' he continued. 'It will seem quite natural for you to contact me for daily weather reports and navigational information. I should have the Baltic fleet movements for the following week by the time you reach Hirtshals, and I'm working on the same information for the Atlantic fleet at Wilhelmshaven.'

Both brothers nodded.

'I've asked around discreetly about the sea areas where you're least likely to be found. I've marked them on this chart here.'

He laid out a chart of the whole of the North Sea.

'Because of the British blockade, there's little merchant shipping. The Kriegsmarine patrols cover Norwegian coastal waters, the Skagerrak, the West coast of Denmark and the north coasts of Germany and Holland, Belgium, and France. You'll not be that far south.'

'What about Kriegsmarine ships on passage?' Johann asked.

'They nearly all go north, either to Norway or, giving the top of Scotland a wide berth, they head out into the Atlantic. On the whole, they stay in the eastern part of the Nordsee, but the occasional warship will head south, heading for ports in the north of France.'

He pointed out a large area in the middle of the North Sea.

'If you can get into this zone, your chances of making it increase dramatically.'

'What about submarines?' Franz said.

'You'd be unlucky to be spotted by one, according to the submariners I've talked to. They mostly stay submerged in the Nordsee and rely on surfacing occasionally to locate targets or using sonar if it's fitted. I'd use your engine as little as possible. They can listen out for the sound of a boat's propellor.'

A soft knock on the door startled them. Maria Kästner stuck her head into the study.

'We're home,' she said. She appeared to be in a good mood and the General breathed a sigh of relief.

'Did you have a nice day?' he asked.

'Yes. It was delightful. The countess is so charming, and her home...'

'I'm glad you enjoyed it. We won't be much longer here. We'll join you in the drawing room.'

'Dinner will be at eight. And don't any of you dare miss it,' she said, looking pointedly at Johann.

'Yes, Mama,' he said, smiling.

'We'll take a run down to the boat after dinner,' Franz said, 'just to check that everything is ready for tomorrow.'

'If you must,' she said. She shook her head and left, closing the door behind her.

The three men looked at each other.

'I still feel bad about not telling Mother or the girls.'

'It's for their own safety. And ours. Anyway, I'm afraid I've had to involve Antje.'

'But why?' Franz said. 'I thought...'

'I know I said that they shouldn't be part of it, but I had no option. It's the only way to get Ruth on board, without alerting the security detail.'

'You're going to use Antje as a decoy?' Johann said.

'Antje didn't hesitate. Ruth is her best friend. And she'll keep it to herself. She's a good girl.'

'I know,' Franz said. 'I just wish we could have kept her out of it.'

The General bowed his head.

'We'll just have to make sure it goes to plan.'

He opened his briefcase and pulled out an envelope.

'Now. We don't have much time. We need to discuss the minefields,' the General said, laying out the plans Rolf Boehm had given him.

~~o~~

If it hadn't been for Franz, Maria Kästner might have guessed there was more to their trip than they'd told her.

The General did his best to hide his worry, but Johann and Antje were both more subdued than usual.

'You're terribly quiet, Johann,' Maria said softly, her hand on his arm.

'He's missing his friends already,' Franz joked.

Johann didn't laugh. 'Just because you have no friends of your own...' he said, scowling.

'You're right,' Franz said, smiling. 'I don't have the energy to get up to all the nonsense you and Fritz and Maxi get up to. Perhaps I should tell Mama a few amusing stories about your exploits at officer training school?'

'There's no need. I'm sure she's heard them all before.'

'Oh, I don't think so. What about the one where you and Maxi smuggled a horse into the barracks?'

'A horse?'

Maria looked at her younger son, a quizzical smile on her lips.

'It was just for a laugh. We got a week on fatigues for our efforts. I vowed never to peel another potato again.'

Johann gave his account of the horse incident in detail. As the story went on Franz added to it every once in a while, with descriptions of their classmates' reactions, and the arrival of the college MPs, who Johann and Maxi hadn't seen at first, adding to its absurdity.

The General smiled, glad that Franz had lightened the mood, and made the family's last meal together a happy affair. Inside, his stomach turned with the thought of what lay in front of them in the days, weeks, and months ahead.

By the time coffee was served, even Eva had lost her usual reserve, and had joined in the raucous laughter at Johann and his friends' tales of misbehaviour.

'Were you never involved, Franz?' she asked.

Franz smiled.

'Once or twice, on the periphery, or as a curious observer.'

'Franz was usually there to extract us from situations like that, to save us from ourselves.'

'It was a good job I was there sometimes. You'd have never made it past second lieutenant if I hadn't saved your bacon, at least twice.'

'It's true; I can't deny it.'

Miriam entered to clear the table. She looked remarkably composed but the General could see signs of strain on her face. As she turned to the kitchen, he caught her eye. He nodded, almost imperceptibly and she lowered her gaze.

'Well, Johann. Let's go and check this boat,' Franz said.

'If we must,' Johann said.

When Maria turned away, Franz glared at him, but the General noticed the exchange.

'I'm surprised the colonel didn't phone,' he said, changing the subject. 'He must have changed his mind,' the General said.

'He may have already been down at the boat, but surely he would have telephoned us first? Oh well, we'll see him in Norway.'

The General smiled. It was a nice touch by Franz.

'You two go ahead,' he said. 'I'll be down shortly. I'll pack those charts for you.'

'Can I come and see the boat?' Antje said.

Maria Kästner frowned at her, surprised.

'Antje. Leave the boys in peace to do their infernal checks. They wouldn't want you getting in their way. And anyway, it's dark now.'

'It's all right, Mama,' Johann said. 'We should have taken her down before. She'll love it.'

He turned to Antje.

'You'll have to squeeze in the back.'

'That's fine,' Antje said, her face brightening up. I'll go and get my coat on.'

CHAPTER 57

Miriam hung her apron over the back of one of the kitchen chairs and hurried over to the cottage. Manny and Ruth were standing in the kitchen with Yosef. She saw that they were trying to fight back their tears, but when she entered, their resolve broke.

She hugged them both, Ruth first.

'Look after Manny,' she whispered hoarsely, squeezing her daughter tightly, 'until we're all together again. You have been the best daughter a mother could have asked for and I'm so proud of you both. I love you.'

'Yes, Mama. I love you too. You and Papa must get out as soon as possible.'

'We will,' she said, caressing Ruth's cropped hair with her fingers, her face crumpling.

She turned to Manny and wrapped him in her arms, squeezing him too tightly.

'Mama,' he wheezed, and she loosened her hold, enough for him to breathe.

'Sorry,' she said, not caring that her tears were flowing now. 'You are my little sunshine, and the best boy in the world, but I need you to be a young man now, and look after your sister.'

'I will, Mama,' he said, almost getting control of his voice. 'We'll be all right. I'm looking forward to it, really.'

Miriam tousled his hair.

'That's the spirit.'

She reached to include Ruth in her embrace, and Yosef wrapped his arms around them all. The family stood, four people together in the centre of the kitchen.

'I love you all more than life itself,' Yosef said.

He began chanting the traveller's prayer, *Tefilat HaDerech.*

'May it be your will, Lord, our God and the God of our ancestors, that you lead us toward peace, guide our footsteps toward peace, and make us reach our desired destination for life, gladness, and peace.'

They all intoned the words with him.

'May you rescue us from the hand of every foe and ambush, from robbers and wild beasts on the trip, and from all manner of punishments that assemble to come to earth. May you send blessing in our handiwork, and grant us grace, kindness, and mercy in your eyes and in the eyes of all who see us.'

There was a short pause.

'Blessed are you, Lord, who hears our prayer.'

When they finished, a silence fell on the warm familiar room, broken only by gentle sobbing.

~~o~~

No one was looking, but they didn't take any chances. Even before Antje and her brothers sauntered across the yard to the garage, Manny had crept out and hidden himself, crouching down in the cramped back seat of Franz's sports car, leaving just enough room for Ruth.

In the darkness of the garage, Antje passed Ruth, touching her hand lightly as she did so, and climbed into the open luggage compartment of her father's car, making herself comfortable, nestled on top of the sail bag that had been placed there earlier.

Johann shut the boot lid behind her, while Ruth, emerging from the shadows, got into the back seat of the sports car, only just managing to squeeze her legs in beside Manny. With the soft top up, there wasn't much headroom.

She wore an almost identical coat to Antje, and she had what was left of her hair tucked under the black beret worn tilted to one side. No one watching from the street, or from the big house, would have known it wasn't Antje in Franz's car.

Franz reversed the car and drove up the short drive to the road. In the mirror, he checked to see if Eva or Maria were watching, but the front of the house was in darkness.

The engine of the DKW Roadster growled as it accelerated down Hamburger Chaussee, but he kept his speed to a sensible level; it would be a disaster to be stopped by the police for speeding.

As they turned right, just before the Bahnhof, Johann told Manny to sit up.

'Remember, if they ask, you're our cousin, Ulrich.'

Johann gave Manny an encouraging smile.

Ruth mumbled quietly in the back.

'My name is Antje Kästner, I was born on the twenty-fifth of March, 1923. My name is…'

'You'll be fine, Ruth,' Johann said, still smiling. 'I doubt anyone will ask.'

The roads were quiet. An odd pedestrian walked along the pavement, coat collar folded up to protect them against the cold breeze. A tram passed, its solitary passenger looking wearily out of its window.

As Franz swung the car into the gateway of the naval yard, a marine stepped out from the gatehouse. He saluted as Franz drew to a halt.

He barely gave Ruth and Manny a glance.

'Ah, sir. Your sister and your cousin. The captain said we've just to let you through.'

'Thank you, Sergeant.'

'It's not a bad evening, sir.'

'No. A little cool, but dry. That's the main thing.'

The guard moved to the gate, then stepped back.

'There's just one thing, sir.'

'Yes,' Franz said, tensing.

'If I don't see you before you leave, good luck.'

He held his hand through the open window, and Franz shook it.

'Thank you, Sergeant. Your best wishes are very much appreciated.'

He hesitated.

'My father will be down shortly,' he said. 'He's calling round to Naval Headquarters to collect a chart we realised we were missing.'

'No problem, sir. Always happy to help the General. There's not many army men I'd say that about.'

'Oh, I don't know. You've been terribly kind to us.'

'I didn't mean…'

Franz laughed.

'It's all right, Sergeant, I know what you mean.'

The marine began to laugh and walked over to open the gate. He gave them a wave as they drove through, closing the gate behind them.

'We're in,' Franz said. He heard Ruth's sigh of relief from the back seat. 'Now it all depends on Father.'

~~o~~

Ten minutes later, the marine left his box again, this time to greet the General.

'Good evening, sir. It's a pleasant one. Your sons aren't far in front of you.'

'I had to fetch something for them.'

'Yes, a chart, they said. Just drive on through, sir. I'll open her up for you.'

'Thank you, Sergeant.'

The gate opened once again, and the General drove through, and down towards the quay.

'We're through,' he hissed. He hardly heard Antje's muffled reply.

Arriving at the quay, he parked as close as he could to Franz's car. As he got out, he looked around, whistling, scanning the quayside in each direction.

He walked to the edge of the jetty.

'Ahoy there,' he shouted, just loud enough for them to hear below.

'Father,' Johann replied, emerging from the lit cabin.

'It's all clear,' the General said.

He returned to the car, opened the boot, and pulled the sail bag out. Antje climbed from her hiding place keeping him shoreside of her. Hoisting the bag onto his shoulder, he walked in front of her towards the jetty and stood looking down, holding the bag, while she clambered down the ladder.

He gave another look around, as if checking the wind, then threw the bag onto the deck. He followed his daughter down the ladder.

In the cabin, he was greeted by relieved smiles from everyone, but he could almost smell the fear from the two Nussbaum youngsters, bubbling just underneath the surface.

'Well done, all of you. That was the hardest part.'

He turned to Franz.

'Have you shown them their hiding place?'

'Not yet,' Franz replied.

'Do it now,' the General said. 'They should know where to go. You can never tell if one of the base personnel will take it on himself to come down and come aboard.'

Franz looked at Ruth and Manny apologetically. Johann lifted the boards covering the bilge space and wiped away the little water that lay at the bottom of it with a cloth.

'Try it,' the General said.

Ruth looked at him, her face pale, then at her brother.

Manny clambered in, and Ruth followed. Johann replaced the boards.

For a half a minute, nobody said a word, then the General spoke.

'It's not pleasant, we know, but it could save your lives.'

He turned to Johann. 'Let them out,' he said.

Johann lifted the boards and Ruth and Manny climbed out. The General noticed Ruth shivering.

'Remember to take a blanket with you, maybe two. You can lie on top of one and use the other to cover you; it could get cold down there.'

'I have an old sailcloth sheet,' Franz said. 'Cover yourselves with that. If someone does lift the boards, there's always the chance that they'll think it's a pile of sails, and not look any further.'

He didn't sound convincing, even to himself.

'He's right,' the General said, keeping his doubts from his voice.

He turned to his sons.

'Now, I'm going to head home,' he said. 'Remember that I'm supposed to have Ulrich with me if they ask you at the gatehouse.'

'We'll remember,' Franz said.

'If I'm searched, I'll park just down the road, so that I can be seen from the gate, and flash my brake lights. You'll just have to come up with something.'

'Right. We'll see you back at the house. We'll give you ten minutes at least.'

CHAPTER 58

The marine sergeant saluted when the General's car came to a halt.

'That was a short visit, sir.'

'Yes. I just wanted to make sure they put that chart on board. We wouldn't want them going in circles, would we?'

The sergeant laughed.

'No, sir. You're right, sir.'

'Speaking of charts,' the General said, reaching over to the passenger seat, 'I have this for you.'

'For me, sir?'

'Yes. It's a chart showing the route the boys intend to sail.'

'Ah. You did say, sir. Thank you very much. The men have been asking about it.'

The marine took the chart.

'Thank you, Sir.'

He hesitated and held up the chart.

'You wouldn't mind showing me, sir?' he said.

'Certainly,' the General said, cursing under his breath, 'but we'll have to do it in the gatehouse, Sergeant. It's as black as coal out here.'

'Of course, sir. It's the infernal blackout. We're not authorised to switch all the lights on.'

Stepping out of the car, he couldn't help but glance at the back seat, where he'd laid an old coat on top of a couple of empty holdalls.

He followed the marine over to the gatehouse. Another marine sat at the window, drinking a mug of coffee.

When he saw the General, he jumped up, almost spilling its contents.

'At ease, Marine,' the General said, smiling. 'I'm just here to show your sergeant the route my sons will be following.'

'Yes, sir. Sorry, sir. We're all very taken with their trip, sir.'

'So I hear.'

The General flattened out the chart and pointed out the track he'd drawn on it.

'They may have to deviate a little from this plan, depending on the wind and the weather, but it shouldn't be too far off it. They're taking the Lillebælt route to keep out of the way of the Kriegsmarine ships. I can let you know how they are getting on if you like.'

'That would be great, sir. We've grown fond of *Der Sturmtaucher*, and it would be good to keep track of her progress. You can just send a note to the gatehouse here, or to the captain. We'll get it all right.'

'I'll do that. Well, thanks for everything.'

The General proffered his hand to the sergeant.

'I'll get the gate for you, sir.'

While the General got into the car, the sergeant opened the gate. As he drove past the saluting marine, he turned his head and spoke, as if there were someone in the car with him. The sergeant, caught unawares, glanced at the back seat as the car swept past, then waved. The General looked in his mirror and saw the gate slide closed behind him. He hoped that, despite the darkness, the Marine had glimpsed the bundle in the back.

He took a deep breath and closed his eyes for the briefest of seconds. When he opened them, he saw a car turn the corner 100 metres ahead and come towards him. As he watched it approach, he idly wondered if it was an officer from one of the ships in dock, or perhaps one of the new security detail coming on duty.

As the car passed, the General had a brief glimpse of the army driver, and his passenger, who sat with his face close to the window, looking out at the dockyard.

The General's grip tightened on the steering wheel, and his heart thudded in his chest.

The man in the back of the car was Colonel Schneider.

CHAPTER 59

'Now remember,' Franz said to Ruth. 'You can't use the lamps, I'm afraid, and you must keep deathly quiet. You can sleep up in the forepeak; it will be warm enough, with the two of you in there. If you hear anyone near the boat, though, hide in the bilges. It's better to err on the side of caution. You've got that?'

Ruth and Manny nodded.

'We'll be back here early, around five, and we'll set off as close to seven as we can. You'll both have to stay out of sight while we get ready to depart, which might mean hiding in the bilge again, but we'll try and keep that to a minimum.'

Ruth blushed.

'What do we do if we need to…' she said, her voice trailing off.

Franz blushed. Antje giggled.

'You can use the heads, but don't flush.'

He showed her the sea toilet.

'A patrolling guard might hear it if you pump it out. There are plenty blankets, so wrap up well; it could get quite cold.'

Ruth nodded. Manny clambered through into the forepeak and turned to face them, his eyes shining. Franz smiled.

It's all a big adventure to him.

He only hoped that the boy wouldn't find it too hard once the reality of being away from his parents hit him.

'We'd better go,' Franz said, turning towards Johann, but his brother had frozen, cocking his head to one side.

'What is it?' Franz said.

'Ssshh,' Johann hissed. 'I think I can hear a vehicle.'

'It's just a boat.'

'No, it's a car, I think, and it's coming this way.'

'It might be Father,' Franz said. 'Perhaps he's forgotten something, or he was searched at the gatehouse, and made an excuse to come back.'

Then they all heard it; the purring of an engine and the squeal of a car's brakes as it pulled to a halt on the quayside.

'I'll see what he wants,' Johann said, leaping up through the companionway.

Franz strained to catch the conversation.

'Colonel Schneider, sir,' he heard Johann say in a loud voice. 'Such a pleasure to see you. We thought you weren't coming.'

Without thinking, Franz lifted the boards on the floor and hissed at Ruth.

'Get Manny. You'll have to hide.'

Antje reacted first. She dashed forwards and grabbed Manny's arm, whispering in his ear that he needed to move fast.

Ruth lowered herself into the bilge, grabbing the sailcloth that Franz had shown her. Manny tripped and almost fell on top of her but caught himself just in time.

'Keep your fingers clear,' Franz hissed, dropping the boards into place with a clatter that caused him to wince.

One of the boards didn't quite sit properly but Antje nudged it with her toe and pushed it down with the ball of her foot.

Franz heard Johann's voice again.

'Colonel, you wouldn't mind catching this and leaving it by the car, seeing you're up there?'

Good thinking, Johann. Buy us a bit of time.

Franz stuck his head out of the companionway. He saw Colonel Schneider catch the sail bag that Johann had thrown up and carry it towards the sports car.

He looked back down into the cabin.

'Clear the extra mugs away,' he whispered to Antje.

She opened a locker and stowed Ruth and Manny's mugs, leaving the other three on the table.

The colonel saw Franz and waved.

'Permission to come aboard?' he shouted, smiling.

'Of course, sir. She's your boat.'

'Well, it might be, but for the next two weeks she's yours,' the colonel said, as he descended the ladder and stepped onto the side deck.

'A cup of coffee, sir?' Franz said.

'As long as it has a tot of rum in it.'

Franz ducked back into the cabin and lit the Primus stove. He checked that the kettle had enough water in it and put it on to boil.

~~o~~

Antje watched the colonel let himself down into the warm cabin. His face registered more than a little surprise when he saw her.

'A stowaway!' he joked.

'Our sister, Antje, sir,' Franz said. 'She wanted to come down and see the boat. Our young cousin was here as well, but he was tired, and left with my father.'

'I thought that was the General's car we passed on the way in,' the colonel said. 'I'm sorry I missed him, and I apologise for coming so late. Family stuff.'

'No need to apologise, sir,' Franz said.

'Antje would like to come with us on the trip, sir,' Johann said, 'but our mother put her foot down.'

The colonel laughed. He turned to Antje.

'I remember you from Wangerooge, my dear. You've changed a little,' he said with a smile. He looked at her fondly. 'Quite the swimmer if I recall. And I seem to remember that you were a bit of an artist too.'

'I'm studying at the Technische und Kunstgewerbliche Fachschule in Kiel.'

'Ah. So, the Kästners will have a real artist in the family one day.'

'I hope so,' Antje said, blushing.

'You've sailed in the North Sea before, so perhaps your mother should have let you go on the trip.'

'It was only that one time we visited Wangerooge and Helgoland,' Antje said, 'but I imagine that it will be a little more challenging so early in the year, and so far north.'

'You're quite right, I suppose. Your mother is only looking out for you, after all.'

Franz brewed a cup of coffee for the three men and added a tot of rum to each. Antje shook her head when he offered her a mug.

The cabin sole creaked as Franz sat and she glanced down at the boards concealing Ruth and Manny. She saw Franz give her a brief frown. She flushed a little but smiled and looked at the colonel.

'Do you not wish you were going, Herr Colonel?' she said.

She didn't listen to his reply. With a sudden certainty, if only in her imagination, she could hear Ruth and Manny's breathing, and she was terrified the colonel would hear it too.

~~o~~

In their hiding place, Ruth stared at Manny's face. In the faint light coming through the small air hole, she could see her own fear reflected in her brother's anxious stare. She was glad they'd taken positions facing each other. She tried to talk to him with her eyes, reassuring him. She was amazed to see him respond, his rigid features melting into a recognisable smile. He winked at her and, as she suppressed a giggle, a cold hand took grip of her heart.

I mustn't make a sound.

She listened as the three men talked, Antje saying little, and she tried to gauge the passage of time, but it was impossible. Every second dragged.

It wasn't long before she began to feel sore; at first, it was only her hip, where it pressed against the cold hardness of a keel bolt but soon, other parts of her body began to ache. She assumed that it was the same for Manny. She began shivering again and closed her eyes briefly.

She felt Manny's hand touch hers, then take hold of her fingers and squeeze. She opened her eyes and looked into his soft, smiling face. She forced her body to relax, taking strength from him.

A sense of shame washed over her. She was the eldest and she'd promised to take care of Manny. At the first real hurdle, it was he who was looking out for her. She steeled herself and nodded, then smiled.

It's bearable, she thought, surprised.

Then both she and Manny froze. They heard the colonel's voice, coming closer now.

'I've never noticed that before,' he said.

'What, sir?' they heard Franz say.

'The hole in the board, there. That's new.'

'Ah. We had it done, sir. My grandfather had one in his old boat. It's a drainage hole in case we get pooped, and water comes in the companionway.'

'What do you mean by pooped?' Ruth heard Antje ask, and she blessed her friend for trying to distract the colonel. Through the hole, she could just see part of his face. He appeared to be staring straight at her.

She heard him rise to Antje's bait.

'In a heavy following sea, my dear,' he said, 'if a wave catches up with you and breaks over the back of the boat, it can fill up the cockpit and even spill over into the companionway. If that happens a few times in succession, the boat could sink. Your brothers have shown a great deal of foresight, but I hope it will never be needed.'

'How so?' Antje asked, still pretending to be clueless.

'All boats let in water to some degree, which finds its way to the lowest part of the boat, the bilges. It's easy to pump it out from there, to keep the rest of the boat dry.'

'Oh, yes. The handle is in the cockpit. Papa made me pump it every so often. I think his boat had a bit of a leak.'

The colonel laughed.

'All boats let in a little water, but if there were to be a sudden large ingress, it would take a while to filter into the bilges, and slosh around in the cabin sole. By drilling the hole, your brothers have made sure the water drains freely, and it can be pumped out as fast as they can work the handle.'

The hole above Ruth darkened, and she held her breath as the colonel's eye appeared, centimetres away. She closed her eyes, gripping Manny's hand tightly, to warn him.

She heard the colonel speak again, his voice close now.

'Perhaps you should make another hole, Franz, in the other plank. It would look more...' He struggled to find the right word.

'Symmetrical?' Johann said.

'That's it. Symmetrical. What do you think?'

'We could do that when we get to Bøjden tomorrow, couldn't we, Franz?'

'Yes. It would give the varnish time to dry.'

'That would do,' the colonel said.

The boards creaked as he stood up. Ruth swallowed with relief and breathed out.

'I really must be going,' she heard him say.

'Will you be calling in to see father?' Antje asked.

'I hadn't thought of it. I'm due to report at my transport ship before midnight. I suppose my driver could drop me round to say hello to your father before heading up to Tirpitzhafen.'

'I'm sure he'd be delighted to see you, Herr Colonel,' Antje said. 'We're heading home shortly.'

Ruth heard the companionway hatch being slid open.

'No,' the colonel said, 'You should have some time with your parents. It might be a while before you get back home to see them. I'll just head straight for the base at Wik. Tell your father I was sorry I missed him and that I'll catch up with him the next time I'm home.'

'Very well, sir.'

'Have a safe voyage, gentlemen,' he said, 'and look after her. I'm very fond of the old tub.'

'We will, sir,' Franz said. 'As if she were our own.'

Ruth heard the companionway steps creak as the colonel, then Franz, climbed out into the cockpit. She began to shiver again.

~~o~~

When the colonel had gone, Antje removed the boards. Franz stayed on deck, keeping an eye open for any other unwanted visitors.

Ruth and Manny were cold, damp and shaken.

'You did extremely well,' Johann told them. 'We nearly died when he bent down to look at the hole we'd drilled. You must have been terrified.'

Ruth was still trembling. Antje put her arm around her shoulder.

'We have to go now,' she said. 'Will you be all right?'

'Yes,' Ruth said, gathering herself. 'We'll be fine. Won't we, Manny?'

'Yes.' He hesitated. When he spoke again, there was a tremor in his voice.

'Antje. Tell Mama and Papa... tell them not to worry.'

'I will,' Antje said, her eyes brimming with tears. She looked at Ruth again.

'Come here,' Ruth said, holding out her arms. They clasped each other, sobbing silently. Johann looked away and wiped his eyes.

For a minute, there was no sound but the lapping of the water on the hull, then Johann touched Antje's shoulder, and she pulled herself away, climbing up into the cockpit to join Franz. Johann extinguished the oil lamps and followed her up, putting the washboards in place and closing the hatch.

He turned the key in the padlock. It felt terrible shutting the two young Nussbaums inside.

They have the forehatch, in an emergency.

Franz helped Antje up the ladder, and they walked over to the car. He saw the sail bag sitting by the driver's door.

He told Antje to get in and he lifted the bag over to the edge of the quay.

'Johann, put this in one of the cockpit lockers. We can stow it away tomorrow.'

CHAPTER 60

Franz pulled the car up at the yard gate.

The marine sergeant, seeing them coming, was standing waiting for them.

'Is that you all shipshape, sirs?' he said.

'Yes. We're ready to go,' Franz said. 'We'll be back here about five in the morning. Will you be still on duty?'

'No. My watch ends at midnight, sir. The best of luck with the trip. We'll follow your progress with interest.'

'That's awfully kind. You've all been so good to us. Did my father show you our route?'

'Yes. He left us a chart, with all your stops marked on it and he said he'd keep us up to date on your progress.'

As he spoke, Franz saw him looking past him, into the back of the car. A trace of anxiety showed on his face.

'Your young cousin, sir. Is he not with you?'

'Did the General not say?' he asked, allowing a puzzled look to cross his face.

'No, sir. What do you mean?' the sergeant asked. Franz noticed that his body had tensed a little, and his smile had disappeared.

The second marine came to the door of the gatehouse and watched, his semi-automatic rifle at hand.

'I thought he'd have told you,' Franz said lightly. 'He took my cousin with him. The boy was tired and said he felt sick. Father said he could lie down in the back seat and he'd take him home.'

Both guards relaxed a little.

'Ah. I did see a bundle in the back seat,' the sergeant said. 'The General must have covered him up with his coat. He should really have told me. You gave me a start, sir.'

The second marine turned and went back inside.

The sergeant gave a brittle laugh.

'I thought he'd maybe stowed away on the boat,' he said. 'You might have discovered him halfway to Norway.'

'Not much chance of that; he was sick with the boat in dock. I don't suppose he'd cope with the crossing to Norway.'

The marine laughed again. Franz wasn't sure if it was because he was nervous. The man kept glancing at the boot, and Franz got the impression he would have liked to search the car.

After a silence that hung in the cool night air forever, the marine spoke.

'I'll get the gate for you, sir.'

'Thank you, sergeant. And all the best for the future.'

The gate slid open, and the roadster pulled away.

As they drove along in the darkness, the street lamps shrouded because of the blackout, Johann turned to Franz.

'I was nervous, even though we had nothing to hide this time,' he said, letting out a deep breath.

'Do you think he suspected something?' Antje said, frowning. 'They won't go and check the boat, will they?'

'No. I doubt it. He was just unsure of himself. He knew he'd made a mistake by not searching our vehicles each time, and it made him uneasy. He'll talk himself into thinking that there was a boy in the back seat of Father's car.'

'I hope so,' Antje said. 'For Ruth and Manny's sake.'

~~o~~

Despite the circumstances, the remainder of the evening in the Kästner house passed pleasantly. Maria insisted on a game of Poch, a card game played with the traditional thirty-two-card pack and a board, and the ensuing good-natured teasing that always accompanied such family fun disguised the unease that infected Antje and her brothers and, to a degree, their father.

~~o~~

In the Nussbaum house, the contrast couldn't have been greater. Miriam wept every time she thought of her children, unable to get them out of her mind.

'They're going to be safe,' Yosef told her, for the third time. 'I spoke with the General briefly when they returned. It all went like clockwork.'

'It might be the last time we'll ever see them,' Miriam cried.

'We will get out, somehow,' Yosef assured her. 'It will take a while, but we'll all be together, one day.'

But Miriam was inconsolable. She busied herself in the kitchen, baking braids of white Challah bread and preparing a brisket to cook overnight for supper the following evening.

Yosef sat in the parlour and tried to read the newspaper that the General had handed in earlier, such as it was, but his heart wasn't in it.

He got up and stood in the doorway, watching his wife's heart break.

He felt powerless to help.

~~o~~

Maria Kästner retired to bed around eleven, hugging both her sons before climbing the stairs to her bedroom.

'I'll not see you off in the morning,' she said. 'You're leaving at such an unearthly hour.'

Eva and Antje followed her up a short while later.

'We'll have a nightcap,' the General said, nodding to his study. Franz and Johann followed him through.

Franz and Johann each sat in one of the captain's chairs near the window.

The General crossed to the drinks cabinet.

'It's the last time we'll see Mama and Eva,' Johann said. 'We couldn't even say a proper goodbye.'

'You know we couldn't make a fuss,' Franz said, 'but it was difficult, I have to say.'

The General placed a bottle and glasses on the desk and poured three generous whiskies.

'What are we having tonight?' Franz said.

The General showed him the bottle.

'Glenfiddich,' he said. 'It arrived last week.'

'How the hell did you get that from Britain?'

'I didn't. It arrived by special delivery. Canaris found a couple of bottles in a little shop in Berlin. I sent one to your grandfather.'

Franz laughed, and tasted it.

'Very nice,' he said, savouring it.

'Yes. It's one of my favourites. It made up for that bottle of blended whisky your mother bought me last year, for my birthday. What was it?'

'Loch Scavaig.'

'That's the one. I don't know where she got it. She just liked that it was named after a sailing ship, with a picture of it on the label. The first time I opened it, Yosef and I had a nip, and your mother was watching. We had to smile politely and swallow it, until she left the room. I poured a little of it away every month, but not enough to make her think she should buy another bottle.'

They both laughed. Johann barely smiled. He got up and looked out of the window, into the dark night.

'Your friends,' his father said, joining him at the window. 'You're worried about them?'

'If I'm honest,' Johann said, 'it's breaking my heart. They'll say I'm a coward.'

'It takes more bravery to stand up to something that's not right than to go into battle, knowing the wrong of it.'

'My head tells me that, but my heart doesn't. It calls me a deserter, a traitor, and a man who leaves his friends to their fate.'

'Staying here would make no difference to them, but by going, you will be saving Ruth and Manny's life.'

'It's not that simple,' Johann said, his face pale now, his eyes defeated. 'I know that I should have listened to you both a long time ago, but it still doesn't make what we are doing entirely right, in my eyes.'

'Everyone has to make up their own mind. You know now what goes on in the name of the German people and, yes, there are dangers if we fail.'

'I'm not worried about getting caught, or what they would do to us. I'll take as many of them as I could with me and die doing it. I wouldn't want them to get Manny or Ruth, but if we could do this, and still find a way to come back to our unit, I'd consider it.'

'That can't happen,' the General said. 'You know that, and I can't say anything that will soften the pain you're feeling about your friends but consider the terrible acts you would be made to take part in if you stayed.'

He held out his hand. Johann hesitated, then shook it. Franz rose from the chair and did the same. The General put his arms around them both and held them tight against him, burying his head in their shoulders to hide his tears.

'I'm going to call it a night,' Johann said, breaking away. As he reached the door, he turned.

'I meant to ask,' he said. 'Why didn't we take Antje in the car with us, and Ruth hiding in your car, Father?'

'We could have done. In a way it would have been better; there was always the chance that marines might have noticed the difference between the girls, but I thought that Manny might be nervous on the way into the yard, and having Ruth there would settle him.'

Johann nodded. 'It makes sense. I just wondered. Well, goodnight.'

They watched him leave.

'He'll be all right, once you're on your way,' the General said as they listened to his heavy footfall on the stairs.

'I know. All he needs is to be doing something.'

The General poured another finger into their glasses.

They sat in silence for a while, savouring the whisky, and each other's company.

'Are you ready?' the General asked.

'Yes,' Franz said. 'As ready as one can be, for something like this.'

He hesitated.

'I worry about Ruth. I think Manny will cope. He's a tough young man.'

'Ruth will be tough, too, in a different way,' the General said.

'I'm going to keep her on watch with me.'

The General raised an eyebrow.

Franz stared at the carpet.

'Manny will come on leaps and bounds with Johann. My guess is that he'll be sailing the boat on his own within a week. I think Ruth will need to be looked after with a little more care.'

'And that's the only reason?'

Franz's head shot up. He stared at the General, then looked away.

'I don't want any complications. Johann has already commented that Ruth's short hair makes her look older and rather sophisticated, like the girls in Berlin.'

'Johann would never take advantage of her.'

'Not on purpose, but you know what he's like, even without trying. He oozes charm, and women can't seem to resist him. They'd be a long time together on watch.'

'And you won't swap around watches?'

'No. It will be much easier to get into a routine on the first part of the journey with set watches, four hours on, four hours off. We'll need that constancy once we head out into the North Sea.'

'I suppose you're right. Anyway, you're the skipper and it's your call.'

There was a comfortable silence, then Franz looked at his glass.

'You know we might never do this again?'

The General closed his eyes for a second.

'I do. But we could say that every time you step out of this house, with that uniform on.' Franz stared at him.

'It was the same for your mother when we were first married,' the General continued. 'Worse, perhaps. I was away fighting the war, and she had two, then three small children to look after, who she would have had to bring up on her own if I'd been killed.'

'You rarely speak of those times,' Franz said.

'I survived. I'll never forget the horror of it but it's hard to talk about. I lost too many friends; too many good men died, and I can't believe we're at war again. It's the other reason I believe you and Johann are doing the right thing. This is not a just war, and you're better out of it.'

'It will be a relief not to have to kill again in the name of this horror, but I understand Johann's pain. I also feel dreadful at leaving my friends to fight.'

'You'll be saving two innocent people. Always keep that at the front of your mind.'

'I'll try.'

CHAPTER 61

'What's that?' Manny hissed in Ruth's ear, his hand over her mouth to stop her crying out.

She looked around in the near darkness, only the light of the moon through the porthole casting a glimmer on Manny's face. She didn't know how long she'd been sleeping for.

'I can't hear anything,' she whispered.

'Listen.'

She strained to hear and, sure enough, a voice cut through the darkness, in the distance, then another. Then she heard the faint sound of boots on the paving of the quay, getting closer.

'We must hide,' Manny hissed.

'Move very slowly,' Ruth said, or they'll see the boat rock.'

Manny nodded and gave her a surprised look of respect.

Crouching down, and keeping to the centre of the boat, they crept to their hiding place, lifting the boards carefully, then lowering them once they were in.

The sounds were above them now.

'I'm not sure we should be doing this,' a man's voice said. 'What if somebody sees us?'

'We can just say we were checking their lines, that we saw that one was loose.'

'I still don't see why you want to check. You said yourself, there was a coat on the back seat, and that it could have been covering a child.'

'I know, but I just want to make sure.'

The boat rocked a little as someone stepped off the ladder, onto the gunwale. Ruth and Manny held their breath.

The padlock rattled.

'It's locked.'

Ruth closed her eyes.

The marines from the gatehouse.

'What did you expect, Sergeant?' she heard the marine say. 'And anyway, why would they leave a small boy on board?'

'I know it doesn't make sense, but I just had a feeling in my guts that something wasn't right. We should have checked both cars.'

Ruth heard the deck creaking, then footsteps on the coachroof above them.

The boat lurched suddenly to one side.

Ruth almost screamed, but she'd managed to stop herself. She lay still, not even daring to reach out her hand to Manny. The boat rolled a few times, side to side, then settled.

The man, the sergeant. He must have leaned out, holding onto the mast. That's why the boat rocked.

'Scheiße. What did you do that for, Sergeant?' she heard the marine on shore say. 'I thought you were going to fall in.'

'If a child was aboard, he would have cried out.'

The boat rocked again, but less this time. She heard the clank of boots on metal as the marine sergeant climbed the ladder. She breathed out.

'Are you satisfied now?' she heard the second marine say.

'Yes. And not one word of this to anyone, do you hear?'

'Not a word, Sergeant. You know me. My middle name is discretion.'

'I thought it was Theodore,' the sergeant said, laughing, as their footsteps receded along the jetty.

The two young Jews waited ten minutes before climbing out of their hiding place. Ruth glanced out of the porthole but the moon, which had bathed the jetty in pale light, had gone.

CHAPTER 62

[10/08/2001 Friday]

Maldon, England.

Ruth sighed. She took off her glasses and stared out of the window. When she spoke, I could see that she was back on board, the smell of the sea in her nostrils.

    '*Der Sturmtaucher.* The Shearwater. *It sounds better in English than it does in German. There were times I hated the sight of her. When the wind and the cold soaked into my bones or I leaned over the side, retching until my stomach ached, or I lay in that damp coffin of the bilge, I detested everything about her.*

    '*She wasn't a beautiful boat, like one of these elegant racing yachts; she was businesslike, but in the end, as much as I hated her, I grew to love her.*'

CHAPTER 63

Der Sturmtaucher

Log Entry

Wed 2nd April 1941

07:00 Depart KIEL, for BØJDEN BRO. Crew: Franz Kästner (Skip) Johann Kästner. Weather fair. Sea slight. Visibility Good. Wind 15 knots, westerly. Air pressure 1020mb. Full sail, 010°M, 4.5 Knots

~~o~~

'Good luck, you two. Fine morning for a sail.' The General forced himself to smile. 'Keep me posted of your progress, and I'll see you on your next leave.'

He worked to keep his voice casual, but not overly so. His sons were, after all, supposed to be heading out on a significant journey, and the sixty-mile leg across the Skagerrak, out of sight of land, would naturally cause any parent concern but, at the same time, most of the trip was in safe waters, the yacht was seaworthy, and the boys were very experienced sailors.

As they cast off, hauling in the sheets to fill the sails and edging the boat away from the jetty, he tried to put their real objective out of his mind and, knowing that the smattering of onlookers on the quay would not expect a general of the Third Reich to indulge himself in overt displays of emotion, he returned their wave for just a few seconds before turning his back on them and making briskly for his parked car.

The driver opened the door for him and, only when he was seated, and the car was moving across the wide quayside, did he allow the strain and worry to show on his face.

'Where to now, sir?' The driver's voice cut through his pain, and he shrugged off the feeling of dread, hoping the young soldier hadn't noticed anything amiss from his glance in the car's mirror.

'Turn left at the yard gates. Head for Heikendorf, then take the Laboe Road.'

The Opel purred as it weaved its way between the warehouses and workshops of the naval yard and the General marvelled as ever at the sheer might of the Wehrmacht machine that he was just a small part of. There was no doubt that the Führer and his party of thugs had galvanised Germany and transformed it from a nation on its knees to one that would dominate Europe for the foreseeable future.

As they reached the dockyard exit, they drew to a halt at the barrier. The sentry checked the papers the driver handed him, glanced at the General in the back, and waved them through. The General didn't recognise him.

A new posting. Perhaps the sergeant's wish to be shipped out has borne fruit.

The car swept through the gateway and turned onto the coast road that ran northwards, parallel to the shore of Kieler Förde.

'Don't you wish you were going with them, sir?' The driver had been with him for a considerable time, and the General saw no harm in allowing a little familiarity, provided the private remembered when it was appropriate.

He laughed, a bitter taste of bile rising from his stomach at the irony of the man's words.

'I'd love to make the trip with them, but time...'

... and the need to cover their backs and to protect the ones left behind, he thought to himself.

'Yes, sir, I could see that you were itching to go aboard,' the driver said, laughing.

The General scowled.

'Just drive on,' He snapped.

He saw the young soldier glance in his mirror, then fix his eyes firmly on the road, an injured look on his face.

The General cursed himself, knowing that he was lucky it was only his driver.

The truth was, he would have happily gone with them and left *Das Vaterland* behind forever.

~~o~~

When they'd left the jetty, Franz had looked back at his father crossing the stones of the quay, wondering if he would ever see him again, then he'd turned back to the boat, giving himself over to her, measuring the set of the sails and the wind, and urging her forward towards the mouth of Kieler Förde.

Ahead of them lay the marine barrier, a floating boom with a pair of anchored flat barges in the centre. A wire rope as thick as a man's arm stretched from each barge to the shore, threaded through a line of large cylindrical floats. Suspended from this, anti-submarine nets reached down to the seabed, where they were anchored at ten-yard intervals. A gap in the centre of the barrier was blocked by a forlorn-looking naval vessel, whose only task was to move 100 metres to one side or the other to let boats through. The two barges had bollards on their decks, where vessels could tie up, if boarding and inspection were necessary.

It took *Der Sturmtaucher* over half an hour to sail within hailing distance of the barrier, but Franz had flown code flag 'K', as required, telling the navy vessel that he wished to communicate with them, and as they got closer, he could see that flag 'C' was flying, as an affirmative.

On their approach, the vessel moved astern, and a gap opened up. As they drew closer, Franz feathered the sails, allowing them to luff, or flap, reducing boat speed. As they passed the bow of the dark-grey naval vessel, a bored sailor with a loudhailer told them to tie up to the barge nearest the Holtenau shore, and the ship began moving forwards again, closing the gap behind them. Franz let go of the sails and, as *The Shearwater* stalled, Johann used the last of their momentum to bring her alongside the barge.

After slipping their lines over the bollards, Franz ducked down below, and whispered to the hidden siblings that they were just tying up at the barrier. He heard a muffled sound from the bilge, and assumed it was an acknowledgement.

When he went back up on deck, he saw that there was another boat tied up on the barge on the opposite side of the barrier entrance, and he could see a naval officer, accompanied by two armed ratings, walking around on deck, lifting hatches, and talking to its harassed-looking master.

'Make a cup of coffee, Johann. We need to convince them that we're off on an unexpected but welcome chance of a sail to Norway.'

By the time the small freighter had been released to enter Kieler Hafen, the coffee was ready, and they watched as the inspection detail on the guard boat descended onto the barge *The Shearwater* was moored to.

The three men marched towards them, the officer leading the way, clipboard held in front of him.

Another inspection shouldn't have been necessary; *The Shearwater* had just left a naval dockyard, but Franz knew that the German military liked its interminable formalities and he told himself that any search of the yacht wasn't evidence of suspicion on their part. Even so, he had to fight a sense of panic as he looked out the sheaf of permits he'd collected the day before at the harbour office.

'It might take some time to pass through the barrier,' the harbour master had told him, 'especially if there were a few vessels waiting to exit or enter at the same time.'

For the sake of his nerves, Franz hoped it wouldn't take too long.

The senior officer looked down at his clipboard as he reached the yacht.

'May I see your papers, please?'

Franz handed them over.

'*Der Sturmtaucher*. Nice name. Is she yours?'

'No, we're just delivering her to Norway for our commanding officer, Oberst Schneider. It should be on the manifest.'

This didn't impress the man. He flipped a page over and glanced at the sheet. Franz got the feeling that, as a naval officer stuck on a small ship that travelled no further than fifty or sixty metres in either direction in a day, he was bored, and no doubt frustrated.

'You are Major Kästner,' he said.

'Yes, and my brother is Hauptmann Johann Kästner. We are stationed in Bergen. Herr Oberst is a keen sailor and wishes to make the most of his time in Norway.'

'It's a waste of the Wehrmacht's resources, if you ask me, but that's the *Heer* for you.'

Franz resisted the urge to defend the army's reputation and shrugged in agreement.

'We just follow orders. It's what good soldiers of the Reich do.'

Franz's implied disdain for his commanding officer's self-indulgence appeared to mollify the officer, who gave his name as Kapitänleutnant Meier.

'All the same, we must do an inspection of your vessel before you can leave.'

CHAPTER 64

Standing on the low rise just north of Heikendorf, General Kästner watched as the minutes ticked past. He had a good view across the Förde to Friedrichsort and the marine barrier that stretched towards him from the naval barracks just beyond the lighthouse and the fort.

It had taken him a quarter of the time to get to his vantage point, so he had been standing a while, watching *The Shearwater*'s slow but steady progress, admiring his sons' boat-handling as they deftly docked it at the barrier.

He'd also seen the other boat arriving at the barrier shortly before *The Shearwater* and had relaxed a little until it had been released to carry on towards Kiel.

He'd watched the tall, thin officer step onto the yacht, leaving the two marines standing guard on the flat deck of the barge, but he couldn't see much else. He didn't want to arouse suspicion in his driver by getting the binoculars from the car's glove compartment, so he waited, the minutes dragging by.

The driver said nothing, still smarting from being snapped at, and the General made a mental note to treat his subordinate to a breakfast in one of the beachfront cafés in Laboe as an apology.

He counted the seconds away, not daring to look at his pocket watch, allowing them the ten or so minutes that he had set aside in his head for the necessary clearances to be checked.

He knew that this was another moment of immense danger for them all, and if Ruth and Manny were discovered, he, his sons, and the whole family would be implicated.

The ship's officer disappeared down the yacht's companionway, and the General held his breath. Bile rose in his throat and sweat trickled down between his shoulder blades; as much as he wanted to turn away, he couldn't avert his eyes.

Please God, let them pass.

~~o~~

'I'd be delighted to show you around. There's not much to see on her. We are keen to make a start, however, as we intend to get to Bøjden tonight.'

'It won't take long,' Kapitänleutnant Meier said. 'We have been asked by Kriegsmarine Headquarters to expedite your progress. You must have friends in high places.'

'My father is General Kästner. He must have put in a good word for us.'

The man's eyes widened. 'General Kästner! I should have guessed. Everyone in the Kriegsmarine speaks highly of him, even if he is Heer.'

Franz judged it to be a suitable moment to start showing Captain Meier the yacht, so he invited him down below. He opened a few of the lockers for him, and showed him their supplies, but the man took little interest. One of the boards that covered the bilge spaces creaked, and the man looked down.

'We're just about to have a cup of coffee, such as it is. Would you like one?'

Franz was glad of Johann's interjection. This was yet another ordeal by confinement that Ruth and Manny were going through, and he wondered about their state of mind, having only just found out about the marines' midnight visit on arriving at the boat that morning.

He heard the petty official accept Johann's offer, and was relieved when he agreed that it was just the type of morning when it would be pleasant to sit out on deck to savour it.

For the next ten minutes, the man babbled on about the importance of keeping Kieler Hafen safe for the Reich's ships, and how critical his part in it was. He briefly asked about their journey, but it was obvious that his only interest in them was their high-ranking father.

At length, though, he rechecked the clipboard, handed Franz the mug, and told them they were free to continue.

After a brief handshake, the Kapitänleutnant stepped onto the barge. The three Kriegsmarine men stood to attention and saluted.

'Heil Hitler.' Franz returned the straight-arm salute and shouted to Johann to hoist the foresail. The wind caught it, and the bowline strained.

Franz asked the Kapitänleutnant to throw off the lines.

'Leave the stern spring until last, please.'

The man nodded curtly and motioned to the marines to release a line each. With only the stern spring holding the yacht, the bow swung around off the wind and, once the marine released it on Franz's command, *The Shearwater* eased away from the barge. Once she had enough way, or speed, on, Franz tightened her into the wind, and Johann hoisted the mainsail and the mizzen, settling into a steady reach.

With a steady fifteen knot wind on her beam, they hoisted the staysail and topsail, and *Der Sturmtaucher*, now fully canvassed, picked up her heels, driving them on towards the mouth of the Förde.

~~o~~

General Kästner watched them leave.

It had been the longest ten minutes of his life. When the officer had reappeared on deck, he'd breathed out slowly, but when the man sat down, brandishing his clipboard, a sense of foreboding had returned. *Is the officer remonstrating with Franz? Are the two marines more alert, more on edge?*

But, after an age, the man had stood up and, having shaken hands with Franz, had stepped onto the barge, and the General had watched his sons cast off, waving to the boarding party.

He murmured an almost silent prayer of thanks to whatever god was listening for *Der Sturmtaucher*'s release and followed the yacht's progress northwards towards the open sea.

The tension that had paralysed him dispersed with every nautical mile they put between themselves and Kiel, until they passed Bülk Lighthouse and the Kleverberg mark at the mouth of Kieler Förde and headed northwards.

He walked back to the car, smiled at the driver, and told him to make for Laboe.

Sitting on his own in the back, as the car wound its way down towards the resort's beachfront, he told himself that his sons and their two young Jewish wards had only crossed the first hurdle on their treacherous journey during which, at any point, they could be exposed by the authorities, with all the unthinkable consequences that went with being captured.

It's the last time I'll have to watch it unfold in front of me.

In a way, not knowing might be harder to live with, but he trusted his sons implicitly. He had two main worries. The first was keeping Ruth and Manny from being discovered during the first part of the journey. He didn't think the authorities would necessarily be looking for them but, in any random search, particularly a thorough one, they would almost certainly be found.

In his mind, the papers they carried, and the influence that the boat's owner and the General himself had in northern Germany and, to a lesser extent, Denmark, made an in-depth search less likely but not impossible.

If the stowaways remained undetected, his second concern, and perhaps his greatest worry, was what would happen when the yacht deviated from its agreed route, and they didn't turn up as expected. They would need help from the weather. They had chosen to go this early in the season for the best chance of a storm, with its wind, rain and reduced visibility, and the way it would empty the North Sea of some of the vessels that might otherwise spot them.

Most of all, they needed luck.

CHAPTER 65

08:30 KLEVERBERG LT. 090˚M and 5 fathom contour.

Wind 15 knots westerly, 025˚M, 5 knots

~~o~~

'You're safe to come out now but keep down below, in the cabin.'

Franz lifted the boards covering the bilge space, and helped Manny to crawl out first, then Ruth. They shivered and looked at each other with relief. Despite their efforts to dry it out, there was always a dribble of water in the bilges, and their clothes were damp and foul-smelling.

'Get yourselves cleaned up and put fresh clothes on, and I'll heat a pot of soup up for you.'

Ruth washed herself at the sink in the heads, then scrambled into the forecabin to change. Manny just stripped off where he stood, wiped himself with a flannel, and threw on his dry clothes.

Franz waited until Ruth was ready, then he sat them both down.

'We'll need to set a few ground rules, for everyone's safety. The most important point is that you two are never seen, so in sight of land or other ships, or especially in harbour, you must both stay down here, ready to get back in the bilge at a moment's notice. Do you understand?'

They nodded, but Franz saw a flicker of fear in Ruth's eyes.

'I know it's not pleasant, but it's the best place to hide, and you did incredibly well again today. I'm not sure I could have suffered it.'

Franz saw Ruth smile at the lie, but Manny's shoulders straightened at his efforts to lift the young man's spirits.

'When it's possible, one of you can be on deck with one of us, but you must wear our jackets and cap. If we're seen, from a distance at least, either of you could pass for one of us.' He turned to Ruth. 'That's why we asked you to cut your hair. Sorry.'

'I'm not. Whatever we need to do, we'll do. Even going in there.'

She pointed to the now covered bilge, and although she said it with determination, Franz saw her grimace.

'Because of the two-on-deck rule, and also to get into practice for when we have to sail overnight, we are going to start a watch system, so that there are always two people sailing the boat and keeping a lookout for other ships, buoys, lights, rocks and shoals.'

He paused to see if they were taking it in. They both nodded.

'So, Johann and I have had a chat, and we've decided that he and Manny will be on one watch, and Ruth and I will have the opposite one.'

He thought he saw a flash of disappointment in Ruth's eyes, and even though she hid it well, he knew he'd been right not to pair her with his brother. He suspected that she'd held a torch for Johann since childhood and doing it this way was as much to protect her and his brother, as it was to keep any trouble of the romantic kind off the boat.

Manny, on the other hand, was delighted, and unlike his sister, made no attempt to hide it. Franz smiled, knowing that he should be a little hurt to be second choice for both, but it was understandable that his younger brother, closest to Manny's age and always the most likely to tease the boy and play roughhouse with him, should be his favourite.

'We have a few further rules, and a few safety drills to teach you first, but we'll show you the rest of the stuff as you go along.'

He watched Manny's face. He knew that he had the lad's attention now.

On the way to the yard, that morning, he'd told Johann that he would be on watch with Manny, rather than with Ruth.

'Manny will learn quickly,' he'd told Johann. 'You'll have a capable deckhand in the first week, while the sailing is easy and it's all during daylight hours. Ruth, if she's anything like Antje, may pick it up just as quickly, but I suspect she won't be quite as keen as Manny to get stuck in, so she and I will take watches together. No offence, but I've done a lot more passage-making than you, and a fair bit of short-handed stuff, so I'm not too bothered about having to do most of it on my own.'

'You're just worried Ruth will fall hopelessly in love with me and I'll break her heart.' Johann had laughed, punching his arm. Franz couldn't admit to his brother that those were indeed his concerns.

'You're right all the same,' Johann continued, 'You have done far more sailing than me, outside of racing. I reckon I could take you one on one around the cans though.'

Franz had to concede that Johann would give him a run for his money in opposing racing boats but, truthfully, they worked better as a team; Johann often got the best out of the boat on the helm, Franz was a master of sail trim, and they shared a common knack for getting the tactics almost perfect, making them a formidable duo on the water, in whatever boat they raced.

Looking at Manny and Ruth now, he knew that he'd made the right decision. Although Ruth was four years older than her brother, she still looked pale and fragile from her ordeal in the damp and cold darkness of the bilge, while he wouldn't have guessed that Manny had been through the same nightmare.

'The next thing,' he told them, 'is the life preservers. There are four on board, and we'll tell you when to wear them. It may only be when we hit rough weather and big seas. There are also a few points to remember down here. Fire is a disaster on board, so it's imperative that we are careful with the paraffin for cooking and lighting, and the diesel oil when we're filling up the tank from the fuel cans.'

They nodded again.

'How much fuel do we carry?' Ruth asked.

'Not enough for the whole voyage, but we can fill up as we go along, so that we never arouse suspicion by taking on a whole lot in one go.' He looked at her. 'Is that all right?'

She nodded, and he went on.

'We'll get each of you to practise a man overboard drill on your first watch. It's one of the occasions when everyone on board is usually involved, no matter who's on watch, but on this voyage, depending where we are, there can be only one of us on deck so it's going to be a real challenge. We'll work something out, though it might take a bit of trial and error.'

He looked at their faces, serious now as they realised what he was saying.

'Don't worry, we don't throw one of you in to practise with; we use a fender and a length of coiled warp to mimic a body in the water.'

They all laughed at his lame attempt at humour, but it broke the tension.

'Now, we still have the minefields at the mouth of Kieler Förde to negotiate, so Johann and I will stay on deck until we're well clear, and because we'll be passing close to the lightship out by Stollergrund, it would be better if you both stayed hidden until it's out of sight. They may ask us to stop; my father said they have a couple of marines on board.'

~~o~~

09:30 KIEL LIGHTSHIP, STOLLERGRUND.

Wind 15 knots westerly, slight to moderate. 000°M, 5 knots

~~o~~

The passage through the minefield that protected Kieler Hafen should have been straightforward but weaving their way through a maze of high explosives designed to sink ships much larger than their own played tricks with their minds, and following the safe route, as shown on the chart supplied by the harbour master, stretched Franz and Johann's already frayed nerves and navigational abilities to the limit. For Ruth and Manny, Franz thought, hiding down below, it must have been worse.

The Kästner boys waved to the on-duty keepers and their protective marines on the light vessel as they passed, and received a ribald message from them, spelled out in signal flags, in return.

'They've heard about our trip and decided to give us a rude send-off,' Johann said.

'Send a message back,' Franz said, mindful of the necessity to act as if they were on nothing but an adventure.

They heard the receding laughter that greeted Johann's reply, and, within the hour, they were out of sight.

Franz lowered himself down the companionway. Ruth had washed out their wet clothes, drying them in front of the small charcoal stove on the bulkhead.

'Now, Manny, you're up for the first watch with Johann, so here's my jacket and my hat. Put them on and get up there and help him.'

He smiled as Manny almost flew up the steps. He sat back, listening to the boy's excited chatter and Johann's patient replies, the start of the teenager's maritime education.

He turned to Ruth. 'You're stuck with me, I'm afraid.'

She shrugged, and the tension in her face dissolved into a quiet smile.

'I have no preference. I hope you weren't too upset about Manny. He hasn't quite learned yet to be diplomatic. And he does know Johann very well…'

~~o~~

Ruth put the kettle on.

She listened as a laugh filtered through the hatch from the cockpit. She glanced at Franz.

'I sometimes envy Johann,' he said, as if he'd read her mind. 'He's still a teenager at heart in a lot of ways, and he doesn't take life too seriously. I used to watch him larking around with Manny and his friends and think that he wasn't just entertaining the children, but it wasn't just that; he was having as much fun himself.'

Ruth smiled. It was true. Franz had always been the sensible one and, at an early age, had seemed more comfortable in adult company.

'Don't get me wrong,' Franz said, 'Johann's an excellent soldier and an exceptionally good sailor; I trust him unreservedly with the boat, but he has this uncanny ability to switch off any sense of responsibility when it's not needed.'

Ruth looked at him, feeling a little sorry for him; he sometimes looked as if he had the weight of the world on his shoulders, and she wondered if he ever relaxed, and let off steam.

I don't think he does.

Despite her doubts, she sensed that he was happy in his own skin, and that he derived pleasure from life in different, quieter ways. And perhaps this slower, monotonous style of sailing was his thing.

If it is, it might just save our lives.

She watched him stand up, then slide into the seat at the chart table. He began making pencil marks on what looked like a map, although she knew it was a sea chart. He shouted up to Johann, and got an instant reply, neither of which she understood. She assumed that he was navigating the boat, and that Johann was driving it, if that was the right word.

She'd been out dinghy-sailing with the Kästner boys at Drachensee a few times each summer, and she'd sailed once or twice on the Kästner family's yacht on Kieler Förde, where she'd been given a line to hold, or shown how to turn a winch and, on the odd occasion, she'd even been permitted to steer.

But that was the depth of her sailing experience and she was honest enough to admit that she was terrified that she would be nothing but a hindrance on *The Shearwater*.

'I want to learn enough to be useful to you, so don't treat me any different from the way you would Manny,' she said.

He laughed. 'Sorry, I'm used to my sisters. Eva likes to sit back and sunbathe but Antje is useful to have on board when she's not immersed in her drawings.'

CHAPTER 66

13:15 Leave POLS-REV East buoy 2 cables to port. Full mizzen, main, jib and staysail. Wind 15 knots, westerly. 335°M, 4.5 knots.

~~o~~

'Franz, that's the mark. You asked me to shout when we passed it.'

Franz got up from the chart table. He looked across at the port bunk, where Ruth lay curled up, sleeping soundly.

She must have slept poorly last night.

He lit the stove and filled the kettle, then leaned over and gently shook her prone figure.

She stirred, then opened her eyes.

'You're on the boat,' Franz said, seeing her confused frown. 'It's our watch in fifteen minutes,' he said.

'Of course,' she said, with a little shake of her head. 'Give me a second.'

She went to the sink, in the small galley area, and ran the tap, pumping the pedal at floor level with her foot. She splashed water on her face and dried it with a towel.

Franz shouted to Manny, and the youngster descended the companionway, taking off the cap and jacket and handing it to Franz.

'The kettle's on,' Franz said. 'Make a mug of coffee for everyone if you don't mind.'

Manny scuttled to get the mugs from the locker. Franz turned to Ruth.

'I'll send Johann down. Don't forget to put on his oilskins.'

She nodded. Franz climbed up into the cockpit.

'We've made excellent progress since passing the lightship,' he said.

'Twenty-two miles in under four hours. She doesn't need much done with the wheel; she practically sails herself. We dropped the jib and the main, like you said, just a few minutes ago.'

'Thanks. I want to skirt the minefield, in close. Shortening sail, as we call it, will take a bit of speed off and just give me a little less to do if we have to tack in a hurry.'

Johann nodded.

'She's all yours,' he said. 'I'll send Ruth up.'

When Ruth appeared, Franz suppressed a frown. Despite the hat, and the jacket, she looked nothing like Johann, but he supposed, at a distance, she might just pass.

'What do you want me to do?' she said.

Franz held out a coiled line, with what looked like an iron weight tied to one end, like those on the scales that Miriam used in the Kästner kitchen when she measured out flour for cakes and bread.

'What is it?' she asked.

'It's a lead line. For finding the depth. I'll show you how to use it.'

He tied a rope around the wheel and lashed it loosely to the binnacle, the pedestal it was mounted on.

'There,' he said. 'She'll stay straight at that, for a while at least.'

He untied the small cord that held the coil together and dropped the line on the deck at his feet. He lifted the weight and turned it over. Ruth saw a recess in the bottom.

'If we want to know what type of seabed we are sailing over, we would fill the bottom up with tallow and it would pick up stones, gravel, sand or even mud from the bottom, which we could examine once we bring it up. It's useful to know that when we're anchoring.'

He looked up at her, and she nodded.

'This time, we just want to know the depth. Do you see these little knots?' he said, pointing to the line.

'Yes. Are they every metre?'

'No, but you're along the right track. They're every fathom, which is almost two metres. At sea, we use old-fashioned measurements like fathoms and nautical miles, unfortunately.'

'Oh,' she said. 'Why don't they use metres and kilometres?'

'Tradition, I suppose. Using nautical miles makes sense, because it is also one minute of latitude, but that's for another day. The point is that this lets us know the depth in fathoms. I'll show you.'

He lowered the line over the side and let it run through his fingers, counting out loud each time a knot passed through his fingers.

'Fourteen fathoms,' he said, when the line began to bounce and twitch. 'About twenty-five metres. Now you try.'

He pulled the line back up, dropping the spare coils on the deck, then handed it to her.

She lowered it over the side and counted the fathoms like he did.

'Twelve,' she said.

'That will be right. We want to get closer to the shore, into a depth of about two or three fathoms.'

'I wondered why we appear to be getting closer to land, when all that sea is out there.'

She pointed over the starboard gunwale to clear water between them and the island of Ærø, five miles to the east.

'We're just about to enter a minefield,' he said.

She gasped and looked around, the blood draining from her face.

'Don't worry. My father spoke with the man in charge of laying the minefields. He told him that it's highly unlikely that we would set off a mine. We don't have enough draught, or enough iron in our hull, but he advised us not to take chances. He said they don't lay mines in shallow waters near to land, at depths less than four or five fathoms. It's why we're skirting so close to the shore.'

'I see,' she said, a little relief showing on her face.

'So, I want you to measure depths for me, so that we can find the three-fathom contour, and sail along it.'

'But isn't that dangerous? What about rocks and sandbanks?'

'In certain places, you would be right, but I've checked the chart and this coast is clean all the way up; there are no rocks or shoals to catch us out, and the contours are relatively straight.'

He leaned over and reached down into the companionway, lifting the chart from the table. He laid it on the cockpit seat, and placed a couple of smooth stones on top, to stop it blowing away.

'I wondered what these were for,' she said, laughing.

'See, the seabed is quite uniform all the way. Once we reach here,' he said, pointing to a spot halfway between the small harbours of Mommark and Lystbådehavn, 'we're through, and we can head out into the middle again.'

'Lystbådehavn,' she said. 'Are we in Denmark already?'

'Yes. It didn't take us long to leave German waters.'

'It's still under German occupation though.'

'I know,' he said, bowing his head. 'Otherwise, you would all have been safe here.'

She stared at the land, then took another sounding.

'Nine fathoms,' she said, wincing as the line cut into her fingers.

Franz saw her grimace and reached into one of the cockpit lockers.

'Use these,' he said, handing her a pair of leather gloves, 'until your hands toughen up a little.'

The depths Ruth called out steadily decreased until they reached three fathoms. Franz straightened up *The Shearwater* and ran parallel to the shore, turning away from the land when the water shallowed, and towards it when it deepened.

They didn't see any mines.

~~o~~

As they approached Mommark, Franz warned Ruth not to look towards the harbour mouth.

'We're passing pretty close. From the back, you'd pass as Johann, but if somebody saw your face…'

She stared out across the Bælt, calling out the soundings. She noticed a distant puff of smoke in the distance, on the horizon.

She watched it, imagining an open fire in the grate of a little farmer's cottage, a mother mending clothes while her children played around her.

When she looked again, the smudge of grey against the pale-blue sky was bigger, with a flash of white at the bottom of it. She stared, then realised what she was looking at.

'There's a boat coming,' she shouted, and pointed. 'From over there.'

'It's all right. I've seen it, but well done for spotting it. It's of vital importance to keep a lookout.'

'But what if it sees us? What if it's a Kriegsmarine boat?'

'It's the ferry, from Faaborg to Als. I was expecting it. The timetables for all the ferries are down in the cabin. There's also a ferry from Ærø.'

'Do you want me to go down below, and get Johann up in case they see us?'

'The ferry docks at Mommark. By the time it gets there, we'll be far enough away to be safe.'

'So, what is Als? A region of Denmark?'

'Yes, but it's an island. Almost half of Denmark is made up of islands. Als, for instance, is separated from the mainland by Als Sund, a narrow channel sometimes only as wide as a few hundred metres. It looks more like a river than part of the sea.'

He showed her on the chart.

'The town of Sønderborg sits on both sides of the sound, with a bridge connecting the island to the mainland.'

Franz had been right. By the time the ferry reached Mommark, *The Shearwater* was almost a mile north of the harbour entrance.

'Why did the ferry go through the minefield?'

'When they laid the mines, they would have left a safe channel through it for the ferry. The captain will know the route exactly.'

'How can he tell? There are no markers. It all looks the same.'

'That's what navigation is all about. He'll use prominent features on land, and navigational marks in the water, to plot a route through it. He does it several times a day, so it will be second nature to him.'

'Still, if he makes a mistake…'

'He won't. There's too much at stake. Anyway, don't worry, we're past the minefield. We can head over towards Bøjden now.'

He checked the chart then turned the wheel, looking at the compass as he did so.

'Zero-one-zero,' he said, more to himself than to Ruth.

'What does that mean?' she asked.

He laughed.

'Habit. When there's somebody steering, and someone else navigating, we always call out course changes. If I were navigating, I would tell the helmsman the new course and he would confirm it, once before he turned, and then again once he was on the new course.'

'They do that on big ships,' she said. 'I saw it in a film; *S.O.S. Eisberg*, it was, with Gustav Diessl and Leni Riefenstahl. Antje and I went to see it a few years ago.'

'I think I remember it. I forgot you and Antje were never away from the cinema, until…' He stopped.

'Don't blame yourself, Franz. Your family weren't part of it.'

'There weren't enough of us though.'

'I know.'

A gust of wind heeled the boat a little and Franz instinctively veered away a couple of degrees until it passed.

'How do you do that?' Ruth asked.

'What?'

'You steer, without looking at the compass, or where we're going.'

'I do check our heading, and have a quick glance around every so often, but once you've done this for a while, you can feel when the boat is going the right way. My father does this trick with his eyes closed, steering courses by memory. It always spooks people who have never sailed before.'

'Is it not dangerous?'

'He only does it when there's somebody else who knows what they're doing to keep a lookout.'

His eyes swept the horizon.

'Have a go helming the boat,' he said. 'I'll hoist the foresail and the main again, now that the minefield is behind us.'

'I've never done much steering.'

'You'll be a natural. I can tell. Best to start now; this is the easiest point of sail to steer, when the wind is on the beam.'

'From the side, you mean?'

'Yes. The boat doesn't heel as much, and you don't have to fight the wind or waves to keep it on track. It almost steers itself.'

He took his hands off the wheel and held them up. For about a minute, *The Shearwater* sailed in a straight line then a small wave caught her and knocked her off a point. Franz lightly caught the wheel and made a small adjustment, then let go again. This time, the boat stayed in line for longer.

He moved aside and showed her where to put her hands.

'See? All you have to do when you're on course is find a point on the land, where you're heading, and aim to keep her pointing at it, but look around, every so often; be aware of other vessels, or of a wind change, which you can usually see on the surface of the water.'

She gently adjusted the wheel when another wave eased the boat a point to starboard, but she overcompensated, and had to turn it back.

'Don't oversteer. Let the boat have its way until you see that it's not going to come back itself.'

She stood, her feet planted slightly wider for balance. Franz watched her for a while and nodded.

'That's good,' he said.

When she glanced round a few minutes later, he'd closed his eyes, his face tilted back, the early-April breeze still cold enough to make the sun's heat welcome.

More nervous now, with Franz not supervising her, she gripped the wheel a little tighter. Her eyes flitted between the compass and the sea ahead, imagining hidden dangers if she strayed off route.

'Keep an eye out for stray mines,' he said, smiling when she turned to him in fright.

'Don't joke about things like that.'

'I'm not. With this sort of sea, you'll easily spot them a good distance away. In rough weather, we'll have to keep a sharper lookout.'

'I thought you were asleep.'

He smiled again. 'I just closed my eyes for a minute. You were doing fine.'

She gave him a scowl, but she couldn't keep the hint of a smile from it.

'Are there a lot of stray mines?' she asked.

'It's hard to say. I suppose the odd one might break loose and enemy submarines and planes sometimes drop random mines, but Rolf Boehm says there's been little of that in the Ostsee, so far.'

'He's the man in charge of the minefields?'

'Yes. You may have seen him at the house. At one of Mother and Father's parties.'

'They were always exciting. So many important people.'

'I suppose there were. I never really thought much of it.'

He closed his eyes again.

She smiled. They came from different worlds and here she was, and Manny, sailing, of all things, with two people from what she considered to be the privileged classes. And she knew it would never have happened if circumstances had been different, and Herr Hitler and his party hadn't turned her world upside down.

Her mind darkened, as it did whenever she dropped her guard. Her eyes misted, sick with worry about her parents, alone and scared for her and her brother, and in terrible danger themselves, at any point a hair's breadth away from being deported, or arrested.

She felt the boat lurch and looked up. The horizon was blurred by tears. She sniffed and wiped her eyes, trying to find her mark.

Franz felt the shift and opened his eyes. He looked at Ruth and saw her forearm rub her face. She sniffed again.

He stood up and took the wheel.

'Have a little break,' he said. 'Take a moment.'

'I'm sorry,' she said. 'I was thinking about Mama and Papa.'

His eyes dropped.

'It must be terrible,' he said, 'leaving them like that.'

'It's awful. It's the not knowing that's the worst. I only pray that they can get out too.'

'We'd have loved to have taken you all, but…'

'It would have been impossible, I know.'

'My father will do his best to help find a way out.'

'I know he will. He's a wonderful man.'

'He is. They're both wonderful men, your father and mine.'

She shook her head.

'Here I am, crying about not seeing our mama and papa, and not even giving you and Johann a thought, or your parents.'

'We will miss them, but they're not in danger, like Yosef and Miriam.'

'But it could be a long time before you see them. And Antje. And Eva.'

'I know, but we would have seen them only rarely if we'd stayed, and if they'd opened up an Eastern Front…'

She stared at him.

'What do you mean?'

'Nothing. It's just a rumour.'

'Russia?' she said, her eyes wide.

He gave a bitter laugh.

'I wasn't meant to say but who are you going to tell? My father believes that Hitler will have us attacking the Soviets soon.'

'Will that help us? My parents?'

'We don't know. But it may help you and Manny, in the short term.'

'How?'

'It makes it less likely we will attempt to invade England any time soon. The army would be too stretched. However, if the Wehrmacht defeat the Russians, it will give the Third Reich all the resources it needs. Once we get to Britain, you should perhaps try and move on elsewhere; Canada, Australia, New Zealand, or even America.'

'That's what Papa said. And your father. What will you and Johann do? You can't afford to stay in England any more than us.'

Franz stared at her.

She doesn't know.

'I'm not sure,' he lied. 'We'll just wait and see what happens.'

A sudden cry behind them, out to starboard, made Ruth jump.

'It's only a gannet,' Franz said, laughing. He pointed it out to her. The large, streamlined white bird with cream-coloured head and black, pointed wing tips soared past, a metre above the waves.

Hrak-hrak-hrak-hrak-hrak-hrak…

Ruth laughed this time; the loud, insistent call fading as the bird sped ahead of them.

'It's probably heading where we want to go,' Franz said, 'but it will get there a lot quicker.'

'They nest in Britain?' she said.

'Yes. Most of them. In enormous colonies, I've read.'

She looked at him, surprised.

He blushed.

'I take an interest in nature. When you sail, you're always close to it.'

They watched the elegant bird until it was a dot in the distance, and it disappeared. *The Shearwater* cut through the water cleanly, without effort, and Ruth found the movement soothing, sensing the tension melt from her body as she leaned back and watched the low-lying land ahead creep slowly closer.

A few other boats passed, but always in the distance; a couple of fishing boats, and a small freighter, but there were no other yachts.

'It's a little early in the season,' Franz said, 'and with the war, there may not be any…'

By four o'clock, they'd crossed the channel. Franz made an entry in the log.

'That's all Fyn,' he said, pointing to the land ahead of them. 'One of the larger islands in Denmark.'

A small boat appeared, rounding the low headland ahead of them, and crossed in front of them.

'You'd better change places with Johann,' Franz said. 'We'll be in Bøjden Bro soon.'

Ruth's eyes clouded.

'Will we have to hide in the bilges again?' she asked.

'Hopefully not. Bøjden is small fishing harbour. There will be few people about, and certainly no Germans. You'll be fine as long as you and Manny stay down below, out of sight.'

The lines of worry on Ruth's face softened.

'We'll not be in a harbour every night,' Franz added. 'When we spend nights at anchor, you'll not be as restricted.'

CHAPTER 67

17:02 Arr BØJDEN BRO.

Wind 10 knots, sou'westerly.

~~o~~

While Johann heated up a simple meal of tinned meat and boiled potatoes with fried onions, Franz called at the house nearest to the long single jetty that they berthed at.

He'd guessed right. It was the home of the fisherman who acted as the harbour master, for the little that the job entailed. A round, pleasant woman told him that her husband was still fishing, but he would certainly call and see Franz when he returned, if only out of curiosity. He asked if there was a telephone and was told that it was in the village, further up the street, next to the small store that sold a few basic supplies. When he got there, the shop, if you could call it that, was closed, but he found the phone kiosk next to it.

Franz made the call to the General, muttering thanks under his breath to his father for giving him a purseful of Danish kroner, notes and coins.

'Is everything well, son?' he heard the General say.

'Yes. We're both in fine form. It was a lovely sail; a reach most of the way. We made good time.'

'And the minefields?'

'We were anxious going through the one at the mouth of Kieler Förde, but we skirted the minefield at the south end of Als, keeping close to the shore as you suggested. It wasn't so bad. We're going to make for Bogense tomorrow if we can.'

'Excellent. I'll tell your mother, and your sisters.'

Franz replaced the handset. He'd wanted to say so much more to his father, but they'd discussed it before they left. The General was adamant that they should say nothing of the Nussbaums, that the Drachensee phone line could not be trusted to be secure; perhaps not even the one in his office.

They ate their food in near silence, and by nine o'clock, Ruth and Manny were snug in the forepeak, in their sleeping bags.

~~o~~

'How did you cope?' Ruth asked in a whisper.

'It was great,' Manny said. 'Johann showed me how to steer, and how to adjust the lines that control the sails. He says I'm a natural.'

She could hardly see his face, but she knew he was smiling. She smiled back. She'd known he would love being on the boat.

'It will take me a little longer than you to learn all that stuff, but I did try steering today for a while.'

He said nothing, and for a moment, she thought he'd fallen asleep, but then he spoke. There was a choke in his voice.

'Do you think about Mama and Papa?' he said.

'All the time. What about you?'

'I try to keep busy but then, without warning, they're there, in my head, and I want to cry.'

In the faint light from the porthole, Ruth could just see the shine in his eyes.

'Be brave,' she said, 'and I'll try too.'

They heard the tread of approaching footsteps, and a voice, in a language they didn't understand, called out.

~~o~~

'Mama, I'm going over to see Ruth,' Antje shouted, sticking her head in the drawing-room door.

'At this time of night? Whatever for?'

'I want to show her a new drawing I've done and tell her where the boys have got to. I'll not be long.'

'Erich, tell her,' Maria Kästner said, turning to her husband.

'Let her go. They're grown up now.'

'Don't wait up, Mama,' Antje said, and disappeared.

'I don't know why Antje doesn't have other friends. It's always Ruth this and Ruth that.'

'They've been close since they were toddlers. Leave them be.'

'That's easy for you to say, but if you ever manage to get the Nussbaums away, like you promised, she'll have no friends.'

'Nonsense. She has friends from art school. At least you have her home every night. She might have gone away to university in Berlin, or Frankfurt.'

'I don't know why she couldn't have gone to a finishing school, like I did.'

'And then get married?' he said, shaking his head. 'Let her follow her dreams first.'

She glared at him.

'Is that what you two were whispering about earlier?'

'We weren't whispering,' he said, sighing. 'We were just talking. About the boys, in fact. Antje was just asking what Bøjden was like.'

'You've been there?' Maria asked. 'I didn't know.'

'I was there a few years ago. It was the last time I went sailing with my father; it won't have changed much since then.'

'We haven't seen your parents in a while. Perhaps your father could talk sense into you and Antje.'

He shook his head again.

'She'll be fine. One day, there will be a place again for a friendship like Ruth's and Antje's.'

~~o~~

'Papa says they're safe,' Antje said. 'That they're over the first big hurdle and making good progress.'

Miriam and Yosef clung to her every word.

'He asked me to come over and tell you. I told Mama that I wanted to speak to Ruth, so that they think they are both still here.'

A tear rolled down her cheek. She looked at the Nussbaums.

'How can you carry on, as normal, with them gone?'

'We get by, minute by minute,' Miriam said. 'We try and act as if they are still here. Sometimes I convince myself they are.'

She reached out and took Antje's hand.

'We have to hold onto the belief that they're going to be safe, no matter how painful it is that they're gone.'

'Ask your father to pass on a message to Franz for them,' Yosef said. 'Tell them we love them, that we miss them terribly, but for every kilometre they're further away from here, we breathe easier.'

'I'll tell him. He would have come himself, but he felt that it would have raised a few eyebrows.'

'It was difficult, serving dinner, knowing that he'd taken a call from Franz or Johann,' Miriam said.

'He'll try and speak with you tomorrow. They're hoping to get to Bogense. It's on the other side of Fyn.'

Yosef pulled out a well-thumbed world atlas and turned to the double page showing Denmark on one side and, in inset boxes, Greenland and Iceland on the opposite page. He located Kiel, just showing near the bottom of the page, and traced his finger up until he found Bøjden. His finger moved across to the north of Fyn and found Bogense. He frowned with disappointment.

'Obviously, it's further by boat than it would be if one travelled across the island by land,' Antje said.

'It doesn't look very far,' Miriam said, leaning over her husband's shoulder.

'That's the thing about small boats,' Antje said. 'They don't sail terribly fast, but they get there, unnoticed.'

'I hope so,' Yosef said. 'I only hope so.'

Antje rested a hand on Yosef's arm.

'Every day away is one closer to safety,' she said.

Antje rose to leave, her heart breaking at the raw misery etched on their faces.

'Papa will speak to you tomorrow evening. Mama and Eva are going out, so we should be on our own at dinner.'

She said goodnight and left. As she walked the short distance she looked up at the stars. *I wish I were with them.*

~~o~~

The Bøjden fisherman and part-time harbour master didn't stay long, and he was civil enough. Franz gave him a five-kroner note as payment. He suspected that the man's role in charge of the small harbour had no stipend attached to it, and the occasional donation from visiting boats rewarded him for his efforts.

The man was more interested in what was happening in Germany than in where they were heading.

He accepted a glass of rum from them, but by ten he was gone and the Kästner brothers turned in for the night, relieved that the first day had gone well.

CHAPTER 68

08:15 Depart BØJDEN BRO, for BOGENSE HAVN. Weather fair. Sea slight. Visibility Good. Wind 12 knots, sou'westerly. Air Pressure 1023mb. Full sail, 270°M, 4.2 knots

~~o~~

They left Bøjden not long after eight, the slant of drifting smoke from the cottage chimneys confirming the wind direction in their favour.

Franz and Johann stayed on deck while they were in sight of the harbour and the village, with its fishermen and curious children around, and mothers lighting fires in their grates.

Half an hour later, when they'd cleared the small spit of land and its shoals that sheltered Bøjden Bro, they were alone again, and Ruth joined Franz in the cockpit.

'We have the first watch today,' Franz said.

'I know. Manny wasn't terribly impressed. He was itching to get out on deck.'

Franz laughed.

'He'll get his time up here. We're doing turn-about for who does the first watch.'

Ruth gripped the edge of the coaming, her face a little strained. The boat was tilting alarmingly, much more than it had the previous day, and she had to brace herself to avoid sliding off the seat.

'We'll be close to the wind for the first hour or so, until we clear the bottom of Helnæs,' Franz explained. 'When we're going into the wind the sails are much closer to the centre of the boat, and there's a greater sideways pressure on them. That's what causes her to heel over, but don't worry, the wind alone can never capsize her. If she goes too far over, the wind spills and she'll come up again.'

'So, it can't push us right over?'

He shook his head.

'Not wind alone, and anyway, before we ever got to that stage, we would reduce the amount of sail. That's called reefing.'

Ruth looked up. There was a lot of canvas above her head.

'The only way she can be rolled is if she gets beam-on, or side-on, to an exceptionally large wave, but that would only happen in the severest of storms, and away from shelter.'

'What about the Nordsee?' she asked.

'It's possible, in strong enough winds, but there are plenty of precautions we can take to prevent it, so don't worry. The main priority now is for you to learn how to steer into the wind, when the boat is heeling this far over.'

He motioned for her to take the wheel.

'The idea is to keep as near to the wind as possible, without being so close that the boat will stall.'

She gripped the wheel tightly, feeling it pull against her.

'Turn the wheel to port, into the wind,' he said, 'and see what happens.'

It was surprisingly easy to turn but it stiffened as the boat swung a degree or two to port.

'You want to feel like you're fighting it a little,' Franz said. 'Now, turn it further to port.'

She did as he asked and, almost immediately, the wheel slackened, the sails flapped, and the boat lurched upright. Ruth felt the speed fall off.

'The wind is now too far in front of you and it's not driving the sails, so we've stalled. We need to turn back to starboard to catch the wind again while we still have some momentum.'

He gestured for her to turn the wheel the opposite way. When she did, the boat seemed to pause for a second then, as it came round, and the wind filled the sail again, it heeled over and dug into the water and surged forward again.

'We want to sail at the point just before the sails start to flap, or luff, as we call it. After a while, you'll feel when it's just perfect, and you won't even have to think about it.'

Franz watched her as she fought to keep the boat close to the wind, stalling a few times then turning away to get her going again. It impressed him how quickly she got the hang of it, but the conditions were ideal for a beginner; he was glad she was getting the chance to learn in relatively light winds, and in sheltered waters.

'It's colder today, and windier,' she said.

'I'll take the wheel while you fetch an extra jumper,' he told her, 'Don't let yourself get chilled; it can be difficult to warm up again.'

She went below and put on an extra layer. When she returned, he handed her back the wheel.

'Anyway,' he said, 'it only feels colder today because we're sailing into the wind.'

She looked at him, her brow creased. He laughed.

'You don't believe me, but you know when you walk into town, and the wind is behind you?' he said. 'A pleasant breeze, not too cold?'

'Yes,' she said, still puzzled.

'You go into the shop, buy some groceries, and come back out. When you walk back home and the wind is in your face, it feels colder, and you have to fight against it.'

'Yes. It's because you're walking into the wind.'

'Well, it's the same with a boat. Yesterday, the wind was slightly behind us, and it was about fifteen knots. At the moment, it's in front of us and, although it's only around twelve knots, it feels much stronger than yesterday, and therefore colder.'

She thought about it.

'It's all about vectors,' she said, surprising him.

'Yes. It is.'

'We did them at school…'

Her face darkened, and Franz frowned.

'It must have been hard, being kept out of school,' he said.

'I kept my studies up, after I couldn't go,' she said. Her voice had a defiant tone, he thought.

'I loved school,' she continued. 'It was bad enough when we were forced to leave the Realschule, but the Jewish school was fine. I missed my friends, though, and then, when Mama and Papa were arrested, and we were told we couldn't go to Kleiner Kuhberg, I cried for days, though I tried not to let Mama see.'

'You've all been treated terribly. I can't believe how vile ordinary people could behave, and how cruel they could be.'

'We thought we were Germans, like everyone else,' she said, 'but now I'm not sure we can even call ourselves that.'

'You *are* German, the same as me,' Franz said.

'The law doesn't say so,' she murmured, her eyes glazed with a film of tears. She wiped them.

'It's the wind,' she said.

Franz said nothing. There was nothing to say.

~~o~~

09:19 HELNÆS LIGHT, 0.75 NM, 355°M

Wind 12 knots, sou'westerly. 4.7 kts, 325°M

~~o~~

'I see what you mean,' Ruth said. 'One moment my face smarted with the wind against it, the next it's a gentle breeze across the deck. Are you sure it hasn't dropped?'

'No. The wind is just the same. We've turned just forty-five degrees away from it, but it makes all the difference,' Franz said. 'Keep the compass at three-two-five.'

'It's hard,' she said. 'It keeps swinging around with the waves.'

He didn't tell her that it was only a chop, and that they might encounter waves later in the voyage that would dwarf the boat.

He reached down into the cabin and, from the small locker just inside the companionway hatch, he lifted out a small wooden box. Ruth watched him as he pulled out a brass dial and clamped it to a bracket near the stern of the boat. He connected a coil of line to the gauge, which ran to a shiny brass cylinder with a propeller on it.

'What's that?' she asked, curious. 'Are we going fishing?'

He laughed.

'It's a trailing log,' he said. 'It measures our distance. We should use it all the time but it's a bit of a fiddle and once you have been sailing as long as Johann and I, you get to know how fast you are going by the feel of the boat, and the sound of the water on the hull.'

He placed the brass rotator gently in the water and let the line out between his fingers until it was taut, and spinning. He looked at his watch.

A minute later, he read the dial, and wrote it down in the notebook he always carried in his inside pocket. He did a few quick calculations.

'Perfect,' he said. 'I'd estimated four and a half knots. We're doing four point seven.'

He retrieved the line and the brass propeller and dried them with a clean rag. He placed it all back in its box.

'How often will you do that?' Ruth asked.

'Once or twice a day, just to make sure it's working, and to keep our guesses honest. We don't really need it when we can see where we are, but it will come into its own when it's foggy, or when we're out of sight of land.'

He watched her standing, less rigid than before, as Helnæs receded behind them. Franz smiled. Yesterday, her gaze had been fixed dead ahead, her hands gripping the wheel hard enough to make her knuckles white. Now, she steered one-handed and looked around.

The sky was huge. Nearly all the land surrounding the Lillebælt, the smaller of the three channels that allowed passage from Kieler Bucht to the Kattegat and the mouth of the Baltic, was low-lying, and the horizon floated barely above the sandy shoreline.

Only the occasional stand of trees, granary tower, or church steeple broke the skyline.

After an hour, Franz took the wheel.

'You've done well. Have a rest for a while.'

~~o~~

Ruth sat back against the cockpit coaming and closed her eyes. The gentle rocking of the boat and the warming sun almost lulled her to sleep but, deprived of the concentration required to steer, her mind drifted to thoughts of home, and the pain returned.

She turned away, so as not to let Franz see her cry again. She wiped the tears from her cheek with her sleeve and tried to fill her head with pleasant memories of her parents, not the pale, drawn and anguished faces she remembered from their final farewells.

She saw Franz look up at the mainsail then lean over and adjust one of the lines, no more than a few centimetres.

'Tell me about setting the sails,' she said.

'Ah. That's a big subject. Where do we start?'

'Just the basics, to begin with. What if you all took ill, and I had to sail on my own?'

He laughed.

'Well, it would be tough, but not impossible; this boat does lend itself well to that situation. Because of its rig, and because it's a ketch, the sails are easier to hoist than in yachts like my father's.'

'Why is that?'

'Well, the sail area is split up into smaller, more manageable sections. We can use the main – the large one – or the mizzen – the small sail on the mast at the back of the cockpit – or both. Likewise, we can use the staysail – the smaller sail at the bow – or the jib – the one that flies from the bowsprit, or both.'

She looked up again.

'Why are the sails a different shape from the ones on your father's yacht?'

'Ah. This boat is what they call *gaff-rigged*. As well as the boom at the bottom of the mainsail, which all yachts have, *The Shearwater* has a pole at the top, called the gaff. When we hoist it, we pull the gaff up horizontally first with the throat halyard, then when it's where we want it, full or reefed, we haul on the peak halyard, which lifts the gaff towards the mast until it's tight, usually at about forty-five degrees from the vertical.'

He pointed to the top of the mainsail.

'That's what gives it its shape. The mizzen is just a smaller version,' he said.

'What are the rest of the ropes for?' she said.

He tied the wheel to the binnacle.

'Come with me,' he said, climbing over the coamings and up the side deck. He waited until Ruth had joined him at the main mast.

'Will she steer on her own?'

'For a while. I'll keep my eye on our heading, don't worry.'

She smiled, and he turned to the mast. He pointed to the ropes that ran down it, belayed to pins, or cleats, near to the base, and hung in coils on them.

'We have halyards to set the topsail, which fills the space between the gaff and the mast, the mainsail, and both foresails. Then, on the boom, at the bottom of the sail, we have the vang, or kicking strap, which holds the boom down and tensions the sail vertically, and the outhaul, which does the same, but along the bottom of the sail.'

As he explained, he took hold of each line or halyard, and showed her where they ran through their blocks and sheaves, letting her work out what each one did.

'Once the mainsail is set up, the mainsheet controls how much the boom can swing outward to port or starboard to allow for different points of sail. It's simple.'

'For you, maybe. I'm afraid it will take me a long while to grasp it.'

'It won't, really, I promise. Unfortunately, you and Manny have had to hide down below while we're hoisting the sails because there could be people about, but when we are at anchor, in a few days, you'll be able watch and help when we set off in the morning.'

They made their way back to the cockpit.

'But we'll still have only two on deck?' Ruth asked.

'Yes. Always. At least during daylight. Just in case anyone sees us, but once it's dark, if the weather is fair, we could all sit in the cockpit.'

She closed her eyes. It would be lovely not to be cooped up in the cabin during the long evenings, and to help hoist the sails the next morning.

She must have dozed off because she awoke with a start. Franz was steering with his left hand and writing in the boat's log with the other. She stood up and looked over his shoulder at what he'd written.

~~o~~

11:24 Leave TORØ REV BANK MARK 1ca to starboard, turn 045°M to TØMMEN PHM. Wind 12 knots, sou'westerly. Full sail, running. 025°M, 4.4 knots.

CHAPTER 69

Ruth looked behind her and, sure enough, there was a red buoy a few hundred metres astern.

I must have felt the boat turn. That's what woke me up.

'Ah. You're awake,' Franz said.

She blushed, ashamed of falling asleep on watch again.

'I'm sorry,' she said. 'I must have drifted off.'

He laughed.

'Don't worry. It's the sun, the fresh air, and the concentration you put into helming. It makes you sleepy. We only have another hour to go, then we're off watch.'

She pointed at the log book.

'PHM. Is that the buoy?'

'Yes. It stands for port hand mark. SHM would be a starboard hand mark.'

'Ah. I see. Do you want me to steer again?'

'Yes, that would be great. We're heading for that buoy straight ahead. Can you see it?'

'The red one?'

'Yes. Do you see the lighthouse on Bagø?'

He pointed to the left of where they were heading. She could see a stubby white tower at the left-hand edge of another low-lying island.

'Yes. I see it.'

'Once we reach the red buoy, turn and head for the lighthouse.'

'Why don't we just go straight for it?' she asked.

He unfolded the chart, which had been sitting under the polished stones.

'The same reason we didn't just head straight for the lighthouse when we rounded Helnæs.'

He pointed at the chart. She saw the darker shading of the shallow areas, with depths marked in fathoms dotted all over the seabed.

'There are sandbanks on both sides. Here, at Torø Rev and here, north of Arø, so we must pick our way through them, using the channel markers where we can, and using the transit from the Tømmen buoy to Bagø lighthouse as a guide through the channel between Arø and Bagø.'

'It looks straightforward on the chart, but when you look at the sea, it all appears the same.'

'That's why it's so important to read the chart properly and find the marks and any transits we can. Otherwise, we could end up aground.'

'Would we sink if we did that?'

'Most likely not, depending on what the seabed is made of, and there is usually a way to get off, but it could damage the boat if we hit it hard, or if it was rocky, and if there is a change of tide, or even wind, it could become altogether more serious. All in all, it's better not to touch the bottom.'

~~o~~

They'd reached the second red buoy, and Franz marked the chart with the time. Ruth turned the boat onto the new course, aiming for the white tower and, as they turned, Franz pulled in the mainsheet, then the jib sheets, and finally the mizzen sheet, so that the sails remained full.

He was happier with the wind on the beam. Running downwind was always a worry, with the risk of a gybe, and the boom hurtling across the deck, taking anything in its way with it, and he'd kept a hold of the mainsheet, ready to haul it in if the wind crossed behind them.

Now on a beam reach, they headed for Bagø. They would pass within two cables, or a fifth of a nautical mile, of the lighthouse.

'It's square,' Ruth said, her eyes lighting up. 'I thought lighthouses were round.'

Franz laughed.

'They come in all shapes, sizes and colours. You'll see quite a variety over the next few weeks.'

He stuck his head down into the cabin.

'Fifteen minutes until your watch,' he said.

'We're ready,' Johann said. 'We've just made a spot of lunch. Do you want it now, or when you come down?'

'What is it?'

'Bread, cheese and pickle.'

'We'll get it shortly. We'll be passing Bagø soon and, according to Father's charts, this area has been mined.'

'Have you seen anything?'

'No. The chart indicates that the channel is clear but there's a narrow 'gate' at either end next to the port hand markers. We're in a smaller channel for now, and it should be too shallow to mine, I hope.'

'How is Ruth coping?'

'I didn't tell her about this minefield. There was no point in making her nervous. She's helmed very well, even beating out of Bøjden.'

Johann turned to Manny.

'Do you hear that? You'll have to up your game.'

Franz laughed.

He stood up and took the wheel, telling Ruth to change places with Johann. Manny could come up in ten minutes.

It will give Ruth and Manny a little time alone.

~~o~~

12:30 2½ ca off SW corner BAGØ 0.5 knots tide in favour. Wind 10 knots, sou'westerly. 4.2 knots, 340°M. Full sail, broad reach.

~~o~~

'How's Manny doing?' Franz asked when Johann joined him.

'Good,' Johann said. 'Very good, considering. They talk at night when they go to bed, Manny told me. I think they have a bit of a cry to themselves.'

'I'm not surprised. They've never spent a day away from their parents before now. And to leave them like that, not knowing when they'll see them again…'

Johann shook his head.

'I don't know why it took me so long to see what was in front of my nose.'

'Don't be hard on yourself. The whole country sleepwalked into it.'

'I don't know,' Johann said. 'Some did, for sure, but for a lot of people, it was as if it were the opportunity they'd been waiting for.'

'I hate leaving Mother and Father and the girls in the thick of it.'

'We had no choice. I only wish we could have told Mother and Eva. I feel bad having lied to them.'

A head appeared at the companionway.

'That's twelve-thirty, I guess,' Franz said, handing the helm over to Johann.

He climbed down into the cabin and, before he'd had a chance to sit down, Manny was on deck. He heard Johann speak to him.

'Now, these two have been dawdling along all day. Let's see if we can get a little more speed out of this old tub.'

He smiled as Johann gave the youngster a series of sharp commands; a notch on a jib sheet here, a minor adjustment of the peak halyard, a sharp tug on the outhaul, then, when the footsteps across the deck had halted, he heard Johann tell Manny he had the helm.

He risked a glance out. The boy's face was glowing, a smile playing at the corner of his mouth.

I wish Yosef and Miriam could see him now.

CHAPTER 70

'Sir.'

The captain's insistent voice broke into the General's thoughts.

'Sorry, Captain. I was miles away.'

Heinz Bauer laughed.

'Sailing in the Lillebælt, sir?'

'That obvious, Captain Bauer?'

'It's understandable, sir. It's quite a trip.'

The General smiled. There were times he forgot that people who didn't sail thought the voyage to Norway was something exceptional, perhaps even foolhardy.

If only they knew.

'I'm afraid I have another pile of papers for you to read and sign, sir.'

He placed them on the desk in front of the General, who groaned.

The captain felt for him.

'Where are they now, sir?' he asked, giving the General the excuse he needed.

'They're heading through the straits at Middelfart for Bogense. It will be their second night on Fyn.'

He opened the doors of his cupboard and looked at the chart. Heinz Bauer saw the first day's track as far as Bøjden, marked in ink. Their proposed route for the next week or so was pencilled in, all the way to Bergen.

'We spent a week in the Lillebælt and the Kattegat on our training ship, the *Schlesien*. They were interesting waters to sail in.'

'A lot of shallows, Captain, and narrow channels. Was Admiral Canaris in command?'

'No, sir. He was second officer at the time. He took command of her a few years later.'

'Ah. What was he like to serve under?'

'Excellent, sir. He was a great teacher and had an easy way with us recruits. There were one or two lads who looked like they'd never make the grade, but he sorted them out. One of them even has his own command now.'

The General caught the wistfulness in the captain's voice and reminded himself to look at a seagoing commission for his assistant.

'How would you like a go at command, Captain?'

'A ship, sir?'

'Yes. I can pull strings. It might be one of the smaller vessels, to cut your teeth on.'

'Oh, sir, that would be wonderful…'

His voice trailed off.

'You don't sound entirely convinced, Captain Bauer,' the General said.

'It's not that, sir. I'd love to go back to sea, but this job has got under my skin, and I feel that I'm doing a lot of good here.'

'You'd be difficult to replace, certainly, but you always wanted a seagoing commission.'

'I feel as if there is still plenty to do here, and I'd hate to leave you in the lurch, sir.'

'I can postpone it for six months; we'll have another look at it then, if you want.'

'I think that would be best, sir. As much as the thought appeals to me, I know I'd miss being here at the centre of things.'

The General smiled. He'd been dreading getting someone new for the post and had considered promoting Chief Petty Officer Neuer, replacing him with a new NCO, but although he was reliable and trustworthy, he didn't yet have the grasp of the details that the young captain had developed.

'Well, that's settled for now. What's on the agenda today?'

Heinz Bauer smiled. 'You'll need to brief everyone. They're all asking how Franz and Johann are getting on. It's the talk of the navy.'

'Ah, well. If it keeps them all happy.'

'Yes, sir. I think it's a nice diversion from the bombing and stuff, sir.'

'I suppose it is, Captain, but I'll be glad when they get there. It's early in the year and the weather can be fickle. There are the minefields to worry about, and there's still the chance of ice. I'm glad they're not sailing at night.'

'I wouldn't worry, sir. The boys are excellent sailors, sir, and Franz won't take any chances.'

The General laughed.

'Johann might though. I'm glad Franz is there.'

'Do you need anything, sir?' the captain said.

'A cup of coffee would be great, before I tackle my in-box.'

He nodded at the pile of folders on his desk.

'I might just put a dram in it,' he added, 'if only to get through this mountain.'

Heinz Bauer laughed, and left to fetch the General's coffee.

He scribbled a short note and placed it in an envelope. It would keep the victualling yard captain and his marines up to date with *Der Sturmtaucher*'s progress. The internal navy post would pick it up and deliver it later that day.

The General always tried to keep a promise.

CHAPTER 71

13:20 Beacon on Eastern point of BRANDSØ 6 ca to west.
Following safe channel through Minefield. Mizzen and foresail
only. Wind 14 kts, sou'westerly. 3.3 kts, 355°M

~~o~~

'Why did you take the mainsail down and leave the staysail up, Johann?'

Manny stood at the helm, looking ahead for the next green lateral, mark four miles ahead.

They'd had to turn *The Shearwater* into the wind to take the mainsail down, and they'd dropped the jib, the larger and furthest forward of the two foresails, shortly after, leaving only the inner staysail and the mizzen sail at the back of the cockpit.

'We've had to reduce speed, to pick our way through this minefield. If the wind had been forward of the beam, I would have just lowered the foresails. Then, if we needed to stop, we would just sheet the mainsail in to depower it but, because the wind is coming from behind us today, there's no easy way to stop the boat, apart from turning it all the way round, which takes a lot of time and space in a tub like this.'

'So, by using only the foresail instead,' Manny said, 'if we let the sheets go, the sail will instantly collapse, and the boat will slow down?'

Johann nodded, impressed. 'You've got it. You catch on quick, but the boat will still take a little while to come to a halt.'

'What about the mizzen? Is it not like a miniature mainsail?'

'Yes, you're right, but it's much smaller, and we can take the wind out of it by scandalising it.'

'What do you mean? It sounds like something you read in the newspapers.'

Johann laughed.

'No, not in this case,' he said. 'We let go of the sheet and the kicking strap, and pull hard on the topping lift. The boom swings upwards and the sail collapses. That's scandalising. I'll show you once we're through this minefield.'

'Why don't we do that for the main?'

'We could, but it's got a much heavier boom, and it's hard to do quickly. You also need to go forward to the mast to do it. All the mizzen lines are right here, at the base of the mizzenmast, here in the cockpit.'

Manny looked up at the rigging. Johann could tell that he was trying to make sense of what he'd just been told. He was a quick learner, but it was a lot to take in.

By the time they'd reached the mark, a little tide was beginning to run with them, and Johann knew that it would get stronger in the winding channel that separated the island of Fyn from the mainland. At its narrowest it was around a third of a mile from bank to bank with three sweeping snake-like curves past the towns of Middelfart, on the south bank, then Fredericia, on the north side of the channel, on their port side.

As they rounded the first of the bends in the channel, Johann anxiously looked ahead. In the distance, passing under one of the central spans of the new Lille Bælt bridge, a small freighter was coming towards them.

'Steer over towards the south bank a little,' Johann told Manny. 'Let's keep out of her way.'

The heavily wooded land surrounding the channel was a little higher, and the light winds had turned flukey, blowing in three different directions in the space of a few minutes.

'Is steam not supposed to give way to sail?'

'Don't believe everything you read in books. Technically, if we were a large working sailing ship, they should give way to us, but in a narrow channel, his ability to manoeuvre is very restricted in comparison to ours, so we have to keep out of his way.'

The ship, a rusty vessel by the name of *Seepferdchen*, passed them with plenty of sea room and Johann and Manny returned the master's wave.

'Once we're clear of her, head back over to the middle of the channel. You wouldn't pass for Franz if someone were up close, and the town of Middelfart is coming up on the right, half a mile beyond the bridge.'

'What about people on the bridge itself?'

'If we see anyone, keep your head down.'

No pedestrians peered down on them from the walkway on the bridge, but they saw a few cars and lorries trundle across, and a train thundered overhead as they passed under it.

'Look,' Manny said, pointing towards the harbour at Middelfart.

Johann's stomach lurched. A small grey launch was heading their way, its substantial bow-wave an indication of how fast it was cutting through the water towards them.

'Get down below and send Franz up. Be ready to hide.'

Manny disappeared down the companionway and, a few seconds later, Franz appeared, in the same jacket and hat the boy had been wearing.

'It's a Kriegsmarine launch,' Johann said. 'Are Ruth and Manny hidden?'

'Not yet. I'll tell them.'

Franz stuck his head into the cabin and told Ruth and Manny to get into the bilge.

The boat was slightly larger than Johann had first thought; he saw that it was a converted pilot boat, painted battleship-grey, and that a machine gun had been mounted on her foredeck. It circled around behind them and a disembodied voice emanated from a speaker on the small bridge.

'Please stop. We wish to see your papers.'

Franz shouted over to the vessel.

'We'll heave-to if that's all right.'

'That will do. We'll come alongside.'

They turned the boat round the way they'd come, passing through the wind but, instead of releasing the foresails, to sail on the opposite tack, they left them backed, on the wrong side.

Johann let the main out a little, to spill a spot of wind, and Franz turned the wheel back fully to port and tied it off to the binnacle.

~~o~~

The boat lay stopped in the water. Franz, although he'd hove-to a hundred times before, always marvelled that a boat with full sails that could easily drive it along at five or six knots, could sit in the water, almost motionless.

He remembered the first time he'd seen his father do it, and the General's patient explanation of why it worked.

'It's all about balance,' his father had said. 'The rudder and the mainsail want to turn the boat to windward and drive her forward. The backed foresail pushes the nose of the boat off the wind. Both these forces work against each other, keeping the boat in equilibrium, about forty-five degrees off the wind.'

The General had looked up at the sails.

'It's a yachtsman's way of taking time out to make a cup of coffee, put a reef in, or check the chart,' he'd said. 'It's also a good way to survive a storm when the boat can't make way against wind and tide, and you don't want to turn back and run with the sea.'

The throb of an engine close by jerked Franz back from his memories. He looked up and saw that the launch was almost alongside.

The helmsman was skilled. The hulls barely touched as the launch glided to rest beside them. Two ratings caught the bow and stern lines from Franz and Johann and made them fast.

'Do you want springs on?' Franz asked.

A Kapitänleutnant, in command of the launch, stepped down from the bridge and leaned on the guardrail.

'That depends, my friend, on what we find. Permission to come aboard?'

'You're welcome,' Franz said. The man didn't need to ask, but it was good naval etiquette.

The Kapitänleutnant turned and spoke to the man on the helm.

'We'll drift a little with the tide but, as long as we have plenty room, don't try and hold position.'

He stepped over both rails onto *The Shearwater*.

He gave a Hitler salute.

'Heil Hitler,' he said.

'Heil Hitler.' Franz and Johann returned the salute.

'Now,' the Kapitänleutnant said. 'Your papers, please.'

Franz reached inside the companionway hatch and opened the small locker. He pulled out the folder containing their travel passes and port clearances and handed it to the naval officer.

He scrutinised the papers then handed them back to Franz. He held out his hand.

'We've been waiting for you to pass. We were told it would probably be today. It's good to meet the sons of General Kästner.'

The man's handshake was firm, and his face held a genuine warmth.

'You've met my father?'

'Once, but he won't remember it. It was when we picked the launch up from Kiel after her refit and he was touring the yard with one of the admirals. We were supervising her being craned in, and they came over to watch. They spoke with us for about ten minutes.'

Franz laughed.

'My father always likes to talk.'

'Ah, but he listens too. He asked us about our vessel, and about our patrols.'

'Yes. He has a curious mind.'

'Everyone in Kiel speaks highly of him.'

Franz sighed.

'So we keep hearing.'

The Kapitänleutnant laughed.

'Anyway. We won't keep you. Are you coming into Middelfart?'

'No, we're heading for Bogense.'

'That's a shame. We could have shared a Schnapps, or a beer.'

'Another time perhaps.'

He turned to go, then stopped.

'I don't suppose I could have a look around her. She looks a lovely yacht.'

Franz saw Johann stiffen. It was almost imperceptible, and he hoped none of the crew of the launch had noticed.

'I'd be delighted,' he said. 'She belongs to my commanding officer. We're delivering her to Norway for him.'

'We heard. That's quite a trip in a boat this size.'

'Not really. She's designed to take almost any sea in the world if she's sailed right.'

'I'll take your word for it. What's her accommodation like?'

'Come down and have a look,' Franz said, praying that Ruth and Manny had hidden themselves.

Johann climbed down into the cabin first. The Kapitänleutnant followed him.

'The cabin seats six at a push, but she is more comfortable for four. There are pilot berths on either side, for sleeping at sea, and a couple of berths in the forepeak. A further two could sleep on the saloon seating.'

The officer stuck his head through into the forepeak and saw the two sleeping bags.

'You sleep up there when you're in harbour?'

'Yes,' Franz said, glad that he and Johann had stowed their own sleeping bags in the locker under the saloon seating.

'A little galley as well, I see. She's well appointed.'

'She even has heads,' Johann said.

'Don't all yachts have toilet facilities?' the Kapitänleutnant asked.

'No. The smaller ones just use a bucket.'

The man laughed.

'As we do,' he said. He stepped back towards the companionway and the boards beneath his feet creaked loudly. He looked down.

'Squeaky floorboards,' he said. 'You should put a smear of linseed oil between them.'

Franz held his breath. The officer smiled at him.

246

'That's good advice,' Franz said, surprised that his voice remained steady. 'Just mind your head on the hatch as you go out.'

When the three of them were on deck again, the Kapitänleutnant shook Franz and Johann's hands and saluted again, this time an old-fashioned naval salute. The boys returned it.

'The best of luck with the rest of your voyage,' he said, stepping back onto the launch.

Franz and Johann watched as the larger craft edged away, then, at a safe distance, opened up her big diesel engine and sped back towards the harbour.

'Let's get going,' Franz said, untying the lashing from the wheel.

Johann let go of the foresail sheets and both sails flapped across the deck. He sheeted them in on the starboard side.

Franz steered away from the wind and the boat slowly picked up speed, still heading back the way they'd come.

'We'll gybe round,' he said, turning the boat away from the wind again.

Johann automatically reached for the mainsheet, to control the boom as the wind came round behind them.

'Gybe-ho,' Franz said.

They executed the manoeuvre with practised ease. Despite its dangers, the big advantage to gybing was that the boat didn't lose any speed in the turn, and they were soon heading for Fredericia, the town on the north side of the channel, just around the next bend.

Franz looked back at the harbour. The launch had tied up just inside the entrance, ready for its next task. He waited until they'd cleared Lyngodde, the point of land that hid Fredericia from Middelfart. He ducked down into the cabin below.

He lifted the boards on the cabin sole and helped Ruth and Manny out.

'You can go back up now, Manny,' he said, giving the boy his gear. Manny pulled the jacket on and donned Franz's cap and was up on deck within seconds, apparently unperturbed by his time in the bilge.

Ruth, on the other hand, was pale and Franz thought he could see a tremor in her hand when he passed her a cup of coffee five minutes later.

'You struggle with it, don't you?' he said.

'If it weren't for Manny, I don't think I could stay down there.'

'We will be in Bogense tonight, and you may have to hide again at some point. The following two nights, we hope to be at anchor and you'll not need to go down there at all.'

'That's a relief. I didn't know, but I suspect that I'm claustrophobic.'

He gave her a sympathetic look. 'Unfortunately, there's no other option,' he said.

'I know, and I can get through it. Having Manny with me helps.'

'He's coping remarkably well. Almost too well.'

'What do you mean?'

'It's not that... what I mean is...'

'You think he's not troubled enough, that he should be distraught at being wrenched away from his parents?' Her voice had risen a little, and her cheeks flushed.

He reddened.

'No, no. I just wonder if he's blocking it out, that he's burying it. It can't be good for him.'

'You don't hear him at night,' she said, her tone softening. 'I give him a hug each evening, before we go to sleep, and he smiles and tells me everything is all right. Then, when he thinks I'm asleep, he turns away from me and sobs, almost silently, so as not to wake me. He cries himself to sleep every night.'

Franz bowed his head and closed his eyes.

'I didn't know,' he said.

'How could you?' she said, the crossness in her voice now gone. 'I can't even let him see that I know. He wants to be strong for me.'

'He's a tough young man. How does he get through the day without breaking down?'

She gave a dry, brittle laugh.

'He's a German Jew. He's had plenty practice.'

Franz started at the bitterness in her voice.

'He's been through a lot,' she continued. 'At school, in the streets, being confined to the

247

house, Mama and Papa being arrested. And all the time, having to act as if it's of no consequence, just to be brave for them.'

'Should we talk to him?'

'No. Leave him be. We do speak about Mama and Papa, but we try and talk about the good times we had together. If he wants to unburden himself to me, or to you, or more likely Johann, he will.'

Franz stood up and glanced out through one of the small portholes in the coachroof.

'That's Fredericia over there' he said. 'We must have rounded the point at Strib. We'll have the watch soon.'

'It will be nice to get a little fresh air,' Ruth said.

'We'll be in Bogense in a couple of hours.'

'Is that a big place?'

'No, but it's busier than Bøjden.'

'And tomorrow?'

'We make for Hjelm. It's an island, off the coast. It's uninhabited, apart from the lighthouse keepers. We'll be safe there.'

The harbour at Bogense had a strange shape. Two fingers of land projected far out into the bay, creating a long, narrow harbour between them. The railway line ran halfway out the south pier.

'I'd forgotten the harbour was built with the railway in mind,' Johann said to Franz, as they negotiated the narrow entrance formed by two breakwaters extending from the piers, angled at forty-five degrees to afford protection from the sea for the boats berthed along its quaysides.

'Yes. It must have been quite a busy port in its day,' Franz replied, looking anxiously for a berth.

'We'll not go in too far,' he added. 'The closer we are to the entrance, the less likely we'll be disturbed.'

Johann nodded. Manny had told him that Ruth was struggling with the thought of hiding in the bilge again.

'She could hide in the locker below the berth in the forecabin, where the spare sails are,' he said.

'She could, but if the boat were searched, they'd be sure to look in there.'

'I suppose so. What if she refuses to hide in the bilge?'

'She won't,' Franz said.

Johann looked at him, an eyebrow raised.

'She won't,' Franz repeated. 'She knows what's at stake.'

Johann held up his hands in surrender.

'There's a space over there,' he said, pointing to a free length of harbour wall between two generations of fishing boats. One was a traditionally rigged fishing smack, built in the previous century, the other a modern trawler, a small mizzen its only sail.

The gap was more than enough for *The Shearwater* but when they cleared the shoulder of the fishing smack, Johann shouted to Franz that the berth was reserved; there were three trestles sitting on the edge of the quay with poles crossed between them.

One of the fishing smack's crew waved at them, indicating that there was a berth beyond the second fishing boat and, with the last of the wind in the foresail and mizzen, Franz steered *The Shearwater* into the much tighter space that the fisherman gestured towards and drifted *The Shearwater* just close enough for Johann to hand the bow line to the man ashore. He looped it over a bollard, and Johann pulled it tight. The gentle breeze nudged *The Shearwater* towards the harbour wall and the mizzen, sheeted in tight by Franz, blew the stern in a few metres in front of the trawler's bow.

The man took the stern line and nodded at Franz, who returned the nod.

'Tak skal du have,' he said. *Thank you.*

'Selv tak.' *You're welcome.*

The man smiled briefly and went back to his shipmates, mending nets on the sea wall.

'Great job, old boy,' Johann said.

'You can do it the next time,' Franz said. He knew that it was their teamwork that made berthing under sail possible. He hardly had to tell Johann when to ease or harden a sail to give him the speed required, and he fully believed that his brother would make as good a job of helming her in as he had.

They'd spent hours practising all sorts of manoeuvres under sail; anchoring, mooring, and berthing; starting with small dinghies and gradually moving up in size and complexity of vessel, with most of their big mistakes having been made in little boats, where the consequences of failure were often no worse than a dunking, or a coat of paint.

'I'll go and find the harbour master if you start making supper,' Franz said. He walked down the quay, looking with interest at the variety of boats moored on both sides of the harbour; a small freighter in the larger of the two basins, close to the entrance; fishing vessels of all shapes and sizes and a sailing cargo barque whose pale, sun faded rigging and bagged moulding sails told him it hadn't moved in a long while.

He reached the head of the railway siding. The tracks were rusted, and weeds grew up between the paving and the rails, but there were a couple of box wagons sitting on the track, opposite a small steam coaster. Two men were using a barrow to trundle wooden crates across the quay, handing them up to a man standing in the open doors of the wagon.

A pile of coal was heaped on the quay next to the boat.

Franz smiled to himself, inordinately pleased that small vessels like her still plied these waters.

The harbour master was a taciturn fellow; apart from churlishly checking Franz's custom clearances, collecting *The Shearwater*'s harbour dues, and telling him where he would find a telephone, he didn't engage Franz in conversation, despite Franz speaking to him in Danish.

Franz found the telephone kiosk in the market street, up from the church, and placed a call to the Drachensee house. Antje answered.

'Franz,' she squealed, and he smiled at the excitement in her voice.

'Antje. How is everybody?'

'We're all fine. Are you in Bogense?'

'Yes. We made it. Is Father in?'

'No. You'll have to make do with me. I'm the only one here.'

'Oh, that's fine. Tell him the minefield at Brandsø was a little tricky and that we were stopped by a Kriegsmarine launch in the Middelfart straits. They were very courteous though. Everyone in the Kriegsmarine seems to know about our trip, and they all believe that the sun shines out of his backside.'

She laughed.

'As long as you're all right.'

'We're fine. Give our love to the parents.'

'I will. Do you know that Manny Nussbaum is keeping a track of where you are, on an old atlas?'

Clever, Franz thought.

'That's great. You'll have to update the Nussbaums on our progress.'

'I'll do that. Mama and Papa left a message for you. I spoke to them last night. They said that they loved you very much and that with every kilometre you're closer to your destination, the happier they are.'

Franz instinctively knew that the message was for Ruth and Manny, from Yosef and Miriam.

Bright girl. Father must have told her not to trust the telephone line.

'I'll tell Johann,' he said. 'He'll have a smile at the thought of Manny keeping an eye on progress.'

He could almost hear the relief in her voice that he'd understood her message.

'And tell Mother and Father that we're thinking of them and let them know that we're doing well.'

'I will,' Antje said. 'Take care, Franz.'

He heard the catch in her voice and could feel his own eyes welling up. This unexpected conversation with his youngest sister could be their last.

'And look after Johann,' she added.

'I'll do my best,' he said.

He put the handset down.

When he'd recovered his composure, he picked up the telephone again and succeeded in persuading the operator to connect him to the garrison in Norway. He updated the colonel on their progress, and hung up, his commanding officer's good wishes ringing in his ear.

He strolled up the street, looking in the window of the chandlers; there was a selection of supplies for fishermen in the small window, but it looked as if the display hadn't changed in ten years.

He found the grocery store and bought bread, milk and cheese, and carrots and potatoes. He added a few turnips that sat forlornly in a wooden crate by the door.

He made his way back to *The Shearwater*. As he passed the cargo vessel he'd seen earlier, he saw that the men who'd been unloading the crates had finished and were now shovelling coal down the fuel chute on its side deck. A small shunting engine puffed behind him, making its slow way along the quayside to pick up the two loaded box vans, clouds of smoke and hissing steam surrounding it.

He gave a whistle as he reached *The Shearwater*, as they'd agreed, and stepped aboard; the yacht's gunwales were almost on a level with the quayside. An appetising smell wafted up to him from inside the cabin, and he wasted no time in removing the washboards and climbing down, replacing them once he was in.

He slid the hatch closed.

Johann stood in front of the cooker, giving his Rindereintopf, a hearty beef stew, a final stir. Behind him, on either side of the table, Ruth and Manny sat, talking quietly. Franz thought they looked a little on edge.

'It's a lot busier than Bøjden Bro,' Johann said. 'I put the washboards up so that no one could see in.'

'We were going to hide,' Manny said, the words rushing out, 'but Johann said it would be all right; that no one would come onto the boat without asking permission.'

'He's probably right,' Franz said. 'Just be ready to get in there quickly if you need to.'

'We will,' Ruth said, the relief softening her face.

'Let's eat,' Johann said.

CHAPTER 73

Half an hour later, Manny, standing in the cabin, almost stumbled as the boat suddenly rocked.

'Somebody's there,' he whispered, scrambling to lift the boards on the cabin floor.

'No. You're all right. That was the wash from a boat,' Franz said. 'We shouldn't have any visitors tonight. The harbour master might walk around and do a check later, but he's not the sociable type, and that fisherman, while helpful, didn't come across as the kind who'd pop in for a glass of rum.'

Johann laughed.

'I thought the Danes were a friendly bunch?'

Franz shook his head. 'It seems not, but it's not surprising when you think about it. We've invaded their country. What do you expect?'

Johann smiled.

'You're right, I suppose.'

'It's a good thing,' Franz said. 'We'll be left to our own devices, but there will be a German military presence here, and civilian administrators, so we must stay vigilant.'

Another wave rocked *The Shearwater*.

'It must be a fair-sized boat,' Johann said. 'I'm going to take a look.'

He slid the hatch back and climbed the first couple of steps of the companionway.

'Scheiße,' he hissed.

'What's the matter?' Franz said.

Johann stepped down and closed the hatch.

'There's a Kriegsmarine Vorpostenboot tied up on the berth that was reserved.'

Franz cursed under his breath. *A patrol vessel.*

'They may not bother us,' he said. 'And if they do, we have all the clearances.'

'I'd still rather not be sitting two boats along from the Kriegsmarine,' Johann said.

'We'll keep the hatch closed and pretend we're asleep.'

Johann looked at him sceptically.

'It's only half-past eight,' he said.

'We could have an early start, for all they know.'

'We'll just have to hope for the best.'

About fifteen minutes later, they heard German voices passing on the quayside. Johann caught snatches of the conversation from which he judged that a few of the men, and a couple of the officers, had been allowed ashore for a few drinks. There was a ribald comment about Danish women, then their voices receded down the quay.

They all breathed out at the same time.

'Where are we making for tomorrow?' Manny asked.

'A good point, Manny,' Franz said.

Johann pulled a chart out from under the chart table and placed it in front of them.

'We've just come through here,' he said, pointing to the Middelfart narrows, 'to Bogense, here.' He slid the tip of his finger across the chart. 'Tomorrow, we're heading north, passing the island of Endelave on its east side, through the gap between Tunø and Samsø, then on up to Hjelm, this tiny little island here.'

He pointed to a dot on the chart just off the coast, then pulled out a larger scale chart of the area.

'It's just over a kilometre long, and about half that wide.'

'We can anchor a reasonable distance off,' Franz interjected, 'on whichever side gives the best shelter, unless it's very blowy.'

'How far away is it?' Ruth said.

'We've less distance to cover than today, and it's much more straightforward; there are no minefields that we know of, and no tricky channels.'

She smiled. She helped gather the supper dishes, and she dried while Franz washed.

'Can we have a game of cards?' Manny asked.

The request caught the Kästner brothers by surprise.

'We used to play at home,' Ruth explained.

'Then we'll play cards,' Franz said.

Johann lifted the lid of the chart table and looked under the pile of folded sheets.

'Aha,' he said. 'I thought they were here.' He passed the box over to Manny. 'What do you want to play?'

'Skat,' Manny said. 'Mama never played. She didn't like cards. It was just Papa, Ruth and me.'

'I'll sit it out,' Franz said, knowing that Skat was a game for three players. 'I'll have a last check at the lines.'

When he returned, the game was well underway and he smiled, seeing the pleasure on Manny's face.

He fished out the sailing directions for the area they were passing through the next day. It listed all the lights, marks, and hazards that they would expect to find, and any other information that was relevant to navigation. He didn't have to worry about tides too much. The Ostsee, or Baltic, had no lunar tides. The only tidal currents that ran depended on wind direction, southwards during westerlies or northerlies and northwards when the wind was from the south or east.

Every so often, he looked over at the card players, immersed in their game. Although they had to keep their voices to a whisper, it added to their excitement, and the flickering light from the oil lamps increased their sense of adventure.

He looked at his watch. Ten o'clock. It would soon be time for them to turn in; they would have to be up at seven, to depart at eight, or shortly after.

He lit the stove and put the kettle on. He was just putting a couple of spoonfuls of ground coffee into the pot when he heard voices approaching. He held up his hand to the three card players and turned his head to listen.

'It's the sailors, coming back, I think.'

'Not much of a night out then,' Johann whispered, with a smile.

'I can hear the clinking of glass. Surely they're not taking bottles back to their boat?'

'Maybe the Kriegsmarine are quite lax. I mean, they drink rum as a matter of routine.'

'I'm not sure they still do that. Anyway…'

The boat rocked as someone stepped on the deck.

'Hello. Is anyone on board?' The voice was just outside the hatch.

'Ruth, Manny,' Franz hissed. 'Hide, quickly.'

The hatch cover began to slide back. Franz jumped up and gripped its underside, cursing under his breath when his fingers were caught between it and the frame.

'Hold on a second,' he shouted, turning with desperate eyes back to the cabin. He watched as Manny dived into the forward cabin and Ruth scrambled after him. Johann shoved her as she fell through onto the bunk and closed the door behind her and turned to face the companionway.

'Don't push,' Franz shouted, 'It's jammed.'

He heard the man outside talk to another sailor.

'It's jammed. He's just coming.'

'Tell him to hurry. I need a drink.'

Franz cursed again. The last thing they needed was the company of a couple of inebriated Kriegsmarine sailors.

He pushed the hatch closed a little, then removed his fingers, and began rubbing them with his other hand. He pulled the hatch open. Two grinning, ruddy faces filled the opening.

'Franz Kästner?' one of the men asked.

'Yes. That's me. What can I do for you?'

'Oberfähnrich zur See Bernd Vogel and Stabsoberfeldwebel Ehren Kruger at your service,' the man said, the fumes from his breath dispelling any notion that the two sailors hadn't made the most of local hospitality.

'We have a little nightcap here,' the midshipman continued. 'We thought you might join us.'

'We have an early start tomorrow,' Franz said, 'I…'

The warrant officer spoke up.

'Ach, come on. We want to toast your voyage, and your father.'

'Sweet Jesus,' Johann muttered. 'Will we ever be out of the old man's shadow?'

Franz smiled, despite himself, and hoped the two drunken officers hadn't heard Johann's comment.

'Let them in,' Johann whispered in Franz's ear. 'Otherwise, we'll have the whole harbour looking at us.'

'Come in for one drink, gentlemen,' Franz said, 'But we're leaving early, so we must get our sleep.'

The two officers clattered down the companionway steps.

Franz, his heart missing a beat, noticed the four mugs sitting on the table and nudged Johann, who grabbed two of them and slipped them into the starboard pilot berth, beneath Franz's sleeping bag.

A second later, the midshipman shrugged Franz drunkenly aside, and deposited a bottle of Schnapps on the table, and four glasses.

Franz and Johann glanced at each other.

'Where did you get the glasses?' Johann asked.

'The barman sold us the bottle. The glasses he threw in for free,' the warrant officer said in explanation.

'It was guilt,' the midshipman said, 'at the exor... exorbitant price he charged for the Schnapps.'

Johann laughed. The midshipman filled the four glasses with the clear spirit.

'Prost,' he said. 'Here's to a successful journey.'

'And here's to your father,' his companion said, raising his glass. 'What a man!'

They clinked their glasses together and downed them. The midshipman filled them up again.

'To the Kriegsmarine,' Johann toasted.

'And the Heer,' the midshipman said, 'despite their faults.'

Johann and Franz both laughed this time.

The two Kriegsmarine officers drank steadily. Franz and Johann nursed their drinks but couldn't prevent the midshipman from topping their glasses up from time to time. He told them that their patrol boat was heading to Norway too, but to Fredrikstad, where they would patrol the outer reaches of Oslofjorden and the eastern end of the Skagerrak. They insisted that Franz and Johann tell them all about *The Shearwater*'s proposed route.

'We'll not be as far east as that. We hope to cross from Hirsthals to Grimstad,' Johann said.

'A pity. We could have had a proper night out in Oslo. Those Norwegian girls!' He nudged his companion, who grinned.

The midshipman insisted on toasting the General a second time but, by now, the warrant officer was spilling more than he drank. His head gradually drooped, until his chin rested on his chest, his eyes closed.

Then, without warning, he lurched to his feet, catching the others by surprise.

'The heads!' he shouted.

'Go outside,' Franz yelled, but it was too late. The man burst through the door to the heads and closed it behind him. They heard him retching, and Franz hoped his aim was true.

'He can't hold his liquor,' the midshipman said.

'Do you need a hand to get him back on board?' Franz asked.

'Perhaps, to get him outside, but once he's on the quay, we should be fine. Have another drink,' he said, slurring his words.

'Thanks, but no, and if you two don't want to be on report, you'd be better off throwing that bottle in the harbour.'

'That would be a waste. I'll hide it in my bunk. They'll never find it.'

'It's up to you,' Franz said, shrugging his shoulders.

The door opened, and the warrant officer stepped out from the heads, catching the others unaware.

'Sit down for a minute,' Johann told him, comfortable with handling drunks when it wasn't him being the one carried back to barracks.

'Where do you sleep?' the man asked, slurring his words.

'In these,' he said, pointing to the two pilot berths, 'or sometimes in the forepeak.'

'In here?' he mumbled, pointing to the door into the forward cabin. 'I think I'll have a few moments' rest.'

Before Franz or Johann could stop him, he'd opened the door and fallen onto the forecabin berth. Franz and Johann held their breaths and waited for a scream from Ruth or a shout of surprise from the warrant officer, but after a few seconds, the only sound emanating from the forecabin was the loud snores of their visitor.

'He can't sleep there,' Franz said, looking at the drunken officer's prone body, horrified.

'Let him be. He'll wake up in a while. In the meantime, have another drink.'

The midshipman poured three more glasses.

'This is definitely the last,' Franz said, looking anxiously at the forecabin door jammed ajar, with the drunken seaman's legs protruding.

The midshipman waved him away.

'We'll see,' he said.

CHAPTER 74

In the forecabin, Ruth wrinkled her nose. The smell of the sailor's stale body, vomit, and alcohol almost made her gag, but she put her handkerchief to her nose, and the faint scent of lavender from the soapflakes her mother did the laundry with was enough to mask the worst of the man's odour.

She listened to the man's comedic snoring and saw Manny, despite the terrible danger they were in, make a face at her. She forced herself to stifle a giggle.

The sailor stirred and turned over to lie on his back. His arm flailed out to the side as he rolled, hitting Ruth on the shoulder. She flinched but resisted the urge to move. His hand rested on the berth a centimetre or two from her face. In the faint glow from the oil lamp in the main cabin, spilling through the open door, she could see a signet ring on the man's fingers and noticed that his nails were chewed down to the quick.

She wished they'd had time to hide under the forecabin berth; the locker contained a full set of older sails that were well worn but serviceable, just in case one of the working set was damaged, along with a number two jib and a balloon staysail for downwind sailing in light airs, but there would have been room to snuggle between the sail bags and stay out of sight.

But they hadn't and Ruth prayed fervently that the nightmare would end, and the man wouldn't grab her and raise the alarm.

Since the sailors had arrived on the boat, she and Manny had listened to the sounds in the forecabin with growing disquiet, glancing at each other in fear when they heard the man stumbling to the heads. When he burst headlong through the doorway onto the forecabin berth, Ruth only just managed to suppress a scream.

Now, lying listening to the loud snores of the drunken sailor, she prayed that his friend would finish drinking quickly and take his companion with him.

~~o~~

When the midshipman went out on deck to relieve himself, Franz took the opportunity to empty his own glass into the sink and fill it with water. He did the same for Johann's glass and tipped most of what was left in the bottle out too. As the sailor unsteadily climbed back down into the cabin, Franz poured the last of the bottle into the man's glass.

The midshipman held the bottle upside down and laughed.

'We polished that off in no time,' he said, lifting his glass.

'To the Fatherland,' he said, almost smashing the glass against Johann's, 'and the Führer.'

'The Fatherland. The Führer.' Franz and Johann gave a perfunctory Hitler greeting, and the junior officer followed suit, almost falling over.

Franz and Johann drained their glasses, screwing up their faces in pretence. The midshipman downed his in one.

'I need to go,' he said, his head beginning to loll.

'You have to take your friend here with you,' Franz said.

'He can stay here. He'll wander back when he wakes.'

'No,' Franz said, and the midshipman looked up, surprised at the firmness in his voice.

'All right, all right,' he said, huffing. He pulled half-heartedly at his friend's feet, but Johann told him to make way.

'Get out onto deck, and we'll pass him up to you,' he said.

While the man climbed the ladder, Johann and Franz somehow manhandled the unconscious warrant officer out of the forecabin onto the floor of the saloon then, using a bight of warp as a sling under the sailor's armpits, they hauled him up the companionway. The man hardly stirred.

From there, it was easier. They managed to hoist him onto the quayside first, then, with the midshipman following behind, the two brothers carried the man between them, his boots dragging along the ground, depositing him on the deck by the wheelhouse door of the patrol vessel.

'You can leave him here. I'll get help from the crew,' the midshipman said, disappearing down below. He returned a few seconds later with two ratings, who carried their warrant officer forward to his bunk.

He turned to Franz and Johann, his voice full of genuine emotion and filial love, the mark of the truly drunk.

'It has been a wonderful evening, gentlemen. Perhaps our paths may cross again.'

He shook their hands and turned round, almost falling over, before disappearing inside.

'I only hope it's not any time soon,' Johann said grimly as they made their way back to the boat.

~~o~~

'I'm sorry about that,' Franz said. 'There was nothing we could do.'

Ruth and Manny had stayed in the forward cabin until the two Kästner brothers returned.

'It's all right,' Ruth said. 'I thought he was going to see us.'

'Ha. He couldn't see his own thumbs,' Johann joked, but no one laughed.

'Do either of you want a cup of coffee?' Franz asked.

'No. But thank you. We'll just turn in, won't we, Manny?'

Manny nodded and began to lay out his sleeping bag.

Ruth closed over the forecabin door, but Franz put his hand out to stop her.

'I'm sorry,' he said. 'It slipped my mind earlier, with all the fuss with the men from the patrol boat. I spoke with Antje on the telephone. She asked me to pass a message on from your parents.'

Manny and Ruth looked at him, a mixture of pain and anticipation in their expressions.

'What did they say?' Ruth asked, her voice flat.

'That they love you very much and they miss you terribly, but the closer you get to safety, the more relieved they feel.'

'Can you get a message to Mama and Papa, the next time you phone home?'

'Of course,' Franz said softly. He saw Ruth take Manny's hand.

'Tell them,' she said, 'That we love them dearly, that we miss them terribly but that we're being brave, especially Manny.'

She smiled at her brother.

'Tell them that I'm learning to sail,' Manny said, wiping a tear from his cheek.

'I'll let them know.'

'I don't suppose…' Ruth said, then shook her head.

'What?' Franz asked her.

'No, it's all right. I just wondered if there was any way we could talk to Mama and Papa, but I know it's impossible.'

Franz bowed his head and shook it slowly, then looked up at Ruth again.

'I'm sorry. It's just too risky. Anyway, even if we could get you to a telephone, my father isn't sure that the line is safe. In all our calls, we can only talk about you and Manny indirectly. If the line is being monitored, you talking to your parents would give the game away, and we'd all be arrested.'

'I know. It was only…'

Franz touched her shoulder.

'We understand. If there was a way…'

He left the words hanging.

They all said goodnight, and Ruth closed the door. Johann lit the paraffin stove and filled the kettle. He and Franz sat silently, waiting for it to boil.

They could hear the low murmur of voices from the forecabin.

'Prayers,' Franz said, his voice low. 'And a little family time, I imagine.'

'It must be hard for them,' Johann said, nodding at the closed door.

'How's Manny been?' Franz asked. 'I've not seen much of him.'

'He's good. While we're sailing, he thinks of nothing else. I keep him busy; if he's not helming, I get him to trim sail or swing the lead. If there's nothing that needs doing, I make him practise his knots, or locate something on the chart.'

'Has he said anything to you about his parents?'

'Not really. I figured if he wanted to talk, he'd tell me.'

'I guess that's fair.'

'Has Ruth said much?'

'Bits and pieces. She's cried from time to time when she's talked about them, and what they've been through. We don't know the half of it.'

'One day, we'll come back, and there'll be a reckoning.'

'We have to get away first and someone has to stop Adolf Hitler.'

CHAPTER 75

Fri 4th April

08:15 Depart BOGENSE HAVN, for HJELM. Weather cloudy. Sea slight. Visibility Good. Wind 13 knots, westerly. Air Pressure 1012mb. Full sail, 035°M, 5.8 knots.

~~o~~

On a broad reach, it took only an hour to clear Æbelo light on the northern tip of the chain of islands that guarded the shallows east of Bogense.

'Why are we passing inside of the buoy?' Manny asked. 'Is the safe water not outside of it?'

'I'm impressed that you knew where the safe channel was.'

'I looked on the chart, like you showed me.'

'You're right, Manny, and if we were in a large ship drawing six or seven metres, we would stay to the other side of the red marker, but we only draw two metres and, between it and the lighthouse, there's plenty water as long as we don't go too close to the point. If you keep steering, I'll take soundings, just to be safe.'

Manny held the course and Johann smiled as he stayed closer to the buoy than the lighthouse.

He's not taking any chances.

As they approached the red marker, with its top light dormant in daytime, Johann asked Manny if he noticed anything about it.

'What do you mean?' he said, scrutinising it carefully as it came towards them.

'Well, what is the water doing around it?'

They were now passing the buoy, a boat-length to port.

'It looks as if it's moving through the water, like a boat.'

The buoy, larger now that it was up closer, was tilting away from them, and it looked like it had a small bow wave, as if it were propelling itself in the direction *The Shearwater* had just come from.

'That's the tide,' Johann said. 'It's flowing in the same direction as us, but the buoy is attached to the bottom. The whole sea is moving past it, creating that little wave.'

'I thought the Ostsee had no tide?'

'It doesn't have twice daily tides like they do in the Nordsee, and the Atlantic, but it does have currents caused by the wind, which act like tidal currents. Storms can also cause the sea level to rise and fall by as much as a metre or more but, on the whole, tides are weak and less significant than in other parts of the world.'

'So, it is helping us now?'

'Yes, but only a little. While the wind stays in the south-west, the tide will push us north and east, half a knot, perhaps.'

'How do you know that?'

'Just little details, like how much the current affects that buoy. Once we've travelled quite a distance, and know our boat speed, we can work out how much extra we've travelled. That will be tide.'

'We're going to use the log? Can I do it? I know how.'

'Yes,' Johann said, smiling. 'When you're navigating, you want as much information as possible. Franz will tell you that.'

'Is he really that good?'

'The best. Apart from my father, and even then…'

~~o~~

10:45 Pass through MØLLEHAGE CHANNEL west of ENDELAVE 3 cables
to port, in 2 fathoms of water. Wind 16 knots, West. Broad
reach. 035°M, 6.1 knots. 100 or so seals on MØLLEGRUND
sandbanks

~~o~~

'Look, Johann. Seals. They're everywhere.'

Johann smiled. Manny was steering but his eyes were on the seal colony on the barely visible sandbanks, just broaching the surface.

'Just wait,' Johann said. 'They'll come up to the boat, to see who we are. They're very curious.'

Sure enough, as *The Shearwater* approached, most of the seals slid into the water and, within seconds, heads were popping up all around the boat, the loud snorts of their exhaled breath causing Ruth to shout up from the cabin below, asking what the noise was.

'Seals, hundreds of them!' Manny shouted. He turned to Johann.

'Can Ruth come up and see them?'

Johann looked around. The island was deserted, as well as he could make out, and the sea around was empty as far as the eye could see, bar themselves and the seals.

'Just for a minute,' he said, 'but she'll need to keep her head as low as possible.'

Ruth climbed the steps and knelt in the cockpit, smiling gratefully at Johann, her head barely above the coaming. Flocks of gulls and terns wheeled overhead, calling loudly as if they, too, wanted to know what the commotion was.

Johann sheeted in the main, and the jib, until they luffed just enough to slow the boat down, but not stall her.

'What's Franz doing?' he asked.

'He's sound asleep,' Ruth said, smiling. 'I don't think he slept well last night.'

'No,' Johann said. 'He was restless. He finds it tough to relax.'

He gave Ruth a wide smile. She glanced away, blushing.

The seals close to the boat barked loudly, their mouths grinning wide, as if they found humans amusing. As more seals from the sandbar joined them, the noise became deafening, but neither Ruth nor Manny cared.

'I've never seen anything like it,' Ruth squealed, prompting another round of barking from their visitors.

Johann watched her with disquiet. He was glad Franz had put the two of them on separate watches. He fell in and out of love on a monthly basis, but he knew that he couldn't afford to indulge his growing feelings for Ruth, even though he'd caught her glancing at him out of the corner of her eye when she thought he wasn't looking. He asked himself how it had taken him so long to realise just how beautiful she was.

The seals followed the slow progress of the boat, breaking the surface every so often to inspect *The Shearwater* and her crew.

'It's a game to them,' Ruth said, still transfixed.

A loud blast of a ship's horn off their port side shattered her childlike wonder and Johann's complacency. It was followed by four other blasts. Ruth ducked her head down below the coamings.

'Stay down,' Johann hissed, looking around frantically. Less than a mile away, on their port side, he saw a vessel.

'It's that verdammte Vorpostenboot,' he said.

The glint from the sun on glass told him that someone on the bridge of the patrol vessel was watching them. He reached for his own binoculars and focussed on the patrol vessel. He then looked down at Ruth, crouching on the cockpit floor.

'I hope they didn't see you,' he said.

'It's too far away, surely,' she said.

'They're using a pair of these,' he said, tapping the binoculars. 'They might have spotted you.'

Johann lifted them up to his eyes again.

A figure on the bridge waved. He couldn't be sure, but it looked like the previous night's visitor, the now sober midshipman. The figure pointed to the masthead. Johann scanned upwards and saw what the man was pointing at.

'It's all right,' he said. 'I don't think they noticed you.'

He studied the signal flags and wrote down each one, then laughed.

'Sore head. Great night. Good luck,' he said.

He gave a wave and saw it returned. A moment later, they heard the muffled roar of the boat's diesel engines as its stern dug into the water and the boat accelerated away to the north.

~~o~~

On the bridge of the patrol vessel, the midshipman took another sip of black coffee. He had a puzzled expression on his face.

'What's wrong with you?' the first officer said. 'You look like you've swallowed a dung beetle.'

'Nothing that this won't cure,' he said, lifting his cup. 'It's strange though. I could have sworn I saw three people on the boat.'

'I thought you said it was only General Kästner's sons.'

'Yes. There were definitely only two of them last night.'

'Here, let me see.'

The first officer took the binoculars and trained them on *The Shearwater*.

'I only see two. There's a sail bag sitting in the cockpit that could look like a person, if your vision weren't quite clear for some reason or another.'

'Very funny, First. If you think I'm bad, wait until you see our Stabsoberfeldwebel. We had to carry him on board last night.'

'It's lucky for you that the old man didn't hear you. You'd have been confined to the boat for a couple of weeks.'

'Ach, he's not so bad. He knows it does a man good to let his hair down from time to time.'

'He's not the worst, I suppose.'

'Where is he?' the midshipman said, looking around.

'Talking to the engineer. There's an oil leak. We may have to stop in somewhere while it gets fixed.'

The first officer took a final look at *The Shearwater* through the binoculars.

'No, definitely only two. A nice boat, though, in an old-fashioned way.'

'It is, but Norway? Rather them than me if the weather turns.'

CHAPTER 76

'Frau Kästner,' the man said, smiling. He showed Maria his identification. She swallowed, but her mouth was dry, and she felt her heart thud in her chest.

'Geheime Staatspolizei,' she said.

'Gestapo is fine,' he said. 'Everyone calls us that, even ourselves.' He smiled, but Maria noticed that his eyes were cold and dark.

'What can I do for you?' she asked, her voice flat.

'Your staff. The Nussbaums. I need to see them. They're not in their cottage.'

'No. They're both working this morning. Miriam is in the kitchen. Yosef will be in the basement or in the garden. Do you want me to fetch him?'

'Yes, please. Is there somewhere I can talk with them?'

'Of course. Come in. Miriam is through here.'

She led the man into the kitchen. Miriam turned from the table, where she was kneading a ball of dough. She gave her employer a polite smile. Maria Kästner met her gaze for a brief second then looked away.

'This is Heinrich Güllich, Miriam, from the Gestapo,' she said. 'He wishes to speak with you and Yosef.'

The housekeeper's face paled as the Gestapo man stepped out from behind Maria but, when she spoke, she surprised her employer with the steel in her voice.

'I know who he is,' she said. 'He has interviewed us before.'

'Indeed, I have, Frau Kästner,' the Gestapo man said.

'I'll fetch Yosef,' Maria said, not able to look at Miriam, leaving her employee with the Gestapo man.

'So, Frau Nussbaum,' Heinrich Güllich said, smiling, 'You are a busy woman.'

'Yes. It's a large house to look after.'

'And I suppose the General and Frau Kästner entertain a lot?'

'Not so much as they used to but, yes, from time to time.'

'I'm told that you are indispensable to the Kästners. I mean, you seem to live a charmed existence, you and your husband.'

'Hardly charmed, Herr Güllich.'

Footsteps sounded in the hallway and Yosef entered.

'Ah. The equally indispensable Herr Nussbaum.'

Yosef came through the door, looked anxiously at the Gestapo man then walked over to Miriam. He put his arm around her shoulders.

'How touching,' the Gestapo man said.

'Why are you here?' Yosef asked. 'What have we done?'

The Kriminalassistent laughed.

'You misunderstand the nature of my call. I'm just here to confirm that you are both adhering to your conditions of release.'

'We go nowhere outside the confines of the Kästner property,' Miriam said.

'Excellent. It's all I came for. Call it a spot check if you like.'

He turned towards Maria Kästner, who stood at the doorway, neither in nor out.

'Frau Kästner, I'll get out of your hair now. The General will be home soon, I suppose, and you will want the dinner to be ready.'

'Yes. Miriam has it all in hand though. Can I offer you a cup of coffee?'

Heinrich Güllich gave her a polite smile.

'Thanks, but I must go. Criminals don't catch themselves, you know.'

'I'll show you out,' Maria said, relieved that her offer had been turned down.

She walked into the hallway and waited for him to pass. He followed her out.

~~o~~

As he passed through the kitchen doorway, he turned. Miriam saw a faint smile at the corner of his mouth.

A cruel smile.

'Herr Nussbaum, Frau Nussbaum,' he said, his tone almost casual. 'There's just one thing I'm a little curious about.'

'Yes, Herr Kriminalassistent?' Yosef said.

'Your children. I was over at the cottage, and no one answered the door. And I don't see them here. Are they also on the Kästner property?'

Miriam saw Yosef freeze. She willed him to say nothing. When she spoke, she marvelled at how level her voice was.

'Yes,' she said. 'They are in the cottage. They were told not to answer the door. One never knows what kind of person they'd find if they opened it.'

Miriam could feel Yosef stiffen with her lie.

'Ah. Very wise. These are dangerous times. You can never be sure that your children are safe.'

He turned again, leaving the kitchen. Maria Kästner followed him. Yosef and Miriam didn't move until they heard the front door close. Miriam looked through the window to the cottage, fearful that the Gestapo man would investigate the truth of her statement, but they heard a car crunch out of the driveway and accelerate towards Kiel.

Maria Kästner came back into the kitchen. She couldn't hide the anger on her face.

'This is really the limit, Yosef, Miriam. To have that man come into my house. If the General won't say it, I will. You and your family will have to find somewhere else to go.'

'I understand, Frau Kästner. We are trying every avenue to find a way out for us and the children.'

'Well, I'm going to have a word with the General when he comes home. If he won't do anything, I will.'

She turned and stormed out of the room.

'I'd never have thought…' Miriam said.

'There, Miriam. You must understand, it's difficult for her.'

Miriam said nothing. She dusted off her apron and placed the dough in the warming oven to prove.

CHAPTER 77

12:58 HOV HAVN 310°M, TUNØ beacon 035°M, SÆLVIG ferry pier
010°M. Wind 14kn west, sou'westerly. 035°M, 5.8 knots

~~o~~

Franz plotted the third bearing line on the chart.

'There,' he said. Ruth looked at the spot on the chart he was pointing at. The three lines almost intersected.

'They don't all meet at the same point,' she said. 'I thought the idea was to find out exactly where we were?'

'Yes, in an ideal world they would, but little errors always creep in, so you always end up with a triangle called a cocked hat. We're somewhere in that triangle.'

They'd been on watch for half an hour. The wheel was lashed amidships, and *The Shearwater* cut an almost straight line through the water. Every so often, Franz would make a small adjustment, keeping the compass sitting on zero-three-five degrees, heading straight for the beacon on Tunø.

Ruth had watched Franz take a bearing with the handheld compass to the red tower at the harbour entrance at Hov, then he'd let her take the second bearing to the end of the pier at Sælvig, made easier to locate by the fact that the ferry had docked there a few minutes earlier.

'That's two points of our fix. The third is the beacon on Tunø, directly ahead of us. We can read that one from the steering compass.'

She looked at the title of the chart.

'Why are some of our charts British, not German?'

'We have German charts too, but Britain ruled the earth's oceans for centuries, and charted much of the globe. All over the world, their charts are the best you can get and, for some regions, they are the only ones available. Father always held the British in the highest regard and used their charts when he considered them to be useful. We also use their sailing directions.'

'Oh. I never thought of it that way. I'm learning so much. It's like being in school.'

He laughed.

'It's only useful if you decide to take up sailing as a pastime.'

'Or become a sea captain.'

Franz laughed again.

'I did hear that a woman in Russia had become the first female captain of an ocean-going ship,' he said. 'The Soviets were immensely proud of her, but she's probably the only one in the world.'

'I could be the first German one,' she said, then, as she looked at Franz, her face paled.

Franz dropped his gaze.

'I-I mean…' Ruth stuttered.

Franz looked up.

'You're still German. You can go back when this is all over and be the first seagoing captain if that's what you want.'

'I'll have to wait and see what Mama and Papa want to do, but I don't know if I ever want to go back, knowing what our fellow Germans did to us.'

'Not all of them, Ruth,' Franz said softly.

'No. There are good people. They're just hard to find.'

She told him about their headmaster, when all the Jewish children were expelled.

'He was so sad. And he wished us all well. I'll never forget that.'

'It must have been terrible,' Franz said.

'It was.'

He listened as she spoke of how they'd stood in the cold and rain, and of the loathsome maths teacher who'd lambasted them with a stream of vile hatred.

'But the Jewish school was wonderful,' she said. 'The teachers tried their best to cover the syllabus and, besides, we had the chance to learn more about our Jewish heritage.'

'It's important to you, isn't it?'

'Yes, and even more so for Manny. But I sometimes wonder if it was our determination to retain our Jewishness that brought all this down on us.'

'Never think that,' Franz said, his voice hardening. 'You can still be German and Jewish, just as you can be Catholic, or Lutheran or a Buddhist, if you wished.'

'It might have been true once. But not now. Or we wouldn't be here.'

Franz bowed his head again.

'One day it will.'

~~o~~

As they slipped past the sandy spit off the western tip of Tunø, and skirted the shallows north of Samsø, two boats passed near to them; the first, the closest, was the small coaster that Franz had seen coaling up in Bogense, steaming northwards in the same channel as *The Shearwater*, between Lillegrund and Issehoved.

Franz steered to the starboard edge of the channel to allow the much larger vessel enough sea room. The master gave him a wave of thanks as the ship overtook them, and Franz was glad he'd sent Ruth below; two of the deckhands leaned over the side of the ship and eyed *The Shearwater* with curiosity.

The second was a small fishing boat which passed them in the opposite direction, a cloud of gulls following behind. Its crew of two were tailing prawns on their way home to Maarup on Samsø, or Tunø Havn. They barely gave the yacht a glance, and neither waved.

'It's safe to come up now,' Franz shouted down to Ruth, as the fishing boat receded southwards.

'How far is it now?' she asked, taking the wheel from Franz.

'About eight miles; an hour and a half, I reckon. That's it dead ahead.'

'That little hump?'

Franz unfolded the largest scale chart he had of Hjelm.

'Yes, Hjelm is Danish for helmet,' he said, pointing at the small island. 'Over half of it is low and flat, but there's a small hill in the middle. It's higher than all the other islands around here, so you can see it for miles. You can just about make out the lighthouse on top.'

'And we'll be anchoring there?'

'Yes. There should be no one near us. You can help me drop the anchor.'

Ruth looked at the chart again.

'I always wondered why you and your father bothered learning English. Now I can see why. None of the annotations are in German.'

'Yes. It is useful, but it's not just that. My father always said that if you had a good grasp of English you could get by in most parts of the world because of the British Empire, and the Americans, of course.'

'I'll need to improve my English,' Ruth said, 'if we're going to live there, or in the United States, or Canada even.'

'I would say it's a must if you want to get on.'

'You speak it well, don't you?'

'Ha, I'd never be taken for an Englishman, but I can follow a conversation and make myself understood, although some of the accents...'

'I've been attending classes but it's difficult, not being able to practise.'

'Didn't Antje help you? She learns it at school.'

'Yes, she did, and your father would encourage me to speak in English, but I was embarrassed.'

'Why?'

'His time was too important to be spending it teaching a teenager to speak English.'

'He wouldn't have thought of it like that.'

'I know. He is a wonderful man. He was so good to us all.'

For a few seconds they sat in silence, then Ruth took a deep breath.

'I don't like to ask, but could you teach me?'

Franz looked at her, and she turned away, blushing.

'Of course,' he said. 'We should have thought of it sooner.'

He glanced around in one of his periodic checks, but nothing moved between them and the horizon.

'We'll speak English as much as possible,' he said. 'The better your grasp of the language, the easier it will be for you and Manny in Britain.'

It set a pattern for the rest of the day, and the journey. Whenever they were on watch, they would switch from German to English, only returning to their native tongue when she didn't understand something, or she became too tired to concentrate.

And steadily, Ruth's English improved.

CHAPTER 78

15:52 Arr HJELM. Anchor off W of island in coarse sand. Wind backed to East. Light airs.

~~o~~

'Why didn't we just put the engine on?' Ruth asked.

'Because he's too stubborn.'

Franz grinned as Johann's voice floated up from the cabin below.

'It's a matter of principle,' Franz said. 'We had fair winds all the way until the last half mile or so, but there was still enough to sail, and we were in no rush. It's so much more satisfying to complete the passage under canvas.'

As the wind had backed from the south round to the east, it had slackened, and by the time they reached a point a cable and a half off the beach in seven metres of water, *The Shearwater* was barely making a knot and a half.

With Ruth at the helm, keeping the boat into the light wind as instructed, Franz went forward and dropped the anchor, letting it run out through the capstan before locking it off with forty metres of chain laid out on the seabed.

Now they sat at the centre of the wide bay, halfway up the west shore of the teardrop-shaped island. It's highest part, the helmet, heavily wooded with the lighthouse perched on top, took up most of the north-eastern half of the island, the rest low-lying and bereft of features, ending in a long grassy spit jutting to the south-west.

Not a soul stirred on the island, though Franz knew that the lighthouse was manned, and that at least one family lived in the keepers' houses close by.

Franz and Ruth dropped the sails, now luffing gently as the boat sat on the anchor, head into the wind.

Franz reefed the mizzen, but left it hoisted.

'Why are we leaving that one up?' Ruth asked.

'A couple of reasons. One, it keeps the boat nicely into the wind when it's lying at anchor and two, if the wind shifts and the anchor drags during the night, we can quickly hoist the staysail and, between them, we'll have enough steerage to keep us off the shore.'

'Oh. I thought that once the anchor was down, that was it for the night.'

'No, it's not like tying up in a harbour. You have to keep an eye on how the anchor's holding.'

'Does that mean we still have to do watches?'

'No. I'll probably check occasionally, but Johann or I would waken if something were to give. When you sail for a while, you get a feeling for that sort of thing.'

'But we can't still all go on deck together?'

'No. Johann told me about your little scare earlier. It could have been dangerous if you'd been seen. We can't risk it.'

'I know you're right, but sometimes, when I manage to forget all the bad things, I like to pretend that we're just on an ordinary sailing trip, with no constraints.'

Franz smiled.

'We can all take turns out in the cockpit; just not all of us at the same time.'

~~o~~

From the moment Erich Kästner walked in the front door, he knew that something was wrong.

Instead of Yosef welcoming him home and taking his coat, it was Maria who stood, holding the door open.

From the coldness in her eyes, he sensed that he was in trouble and when she said nothing, he followed her into the drawing room and closed the door.

'The Gestapo were here today,' she said. He'd never heard such cold fury in her voice.

'What did they want? Please tell me they haven't arrested Yosef and Miriam.'

'I've had a Kriminalassistent of the Geheime Staatspolizei interrogate me in my own

267

home and that's the first question you ask. Why does it not surprise me?'

'Why did he interrogate you? What did he ask you about?'

'Maybe you should be asking how I am,' she retorted.

'How are you? Did he treat you badly?' he asked.

She stared at him.

'I'm fine,' she said, reddening. 'That's not the point. He asked me if the Nussbaums were in the house. He was awfully aggressive.'

'That's how they work. They try and put the fear of God into people. Did he threaten you?'

She hesitated.

'No. I took him through to the kitchen, then went to fetch Yosef.'

'And did you hear what he said to them?'

'He said he was here to check that they were adhering to their terms of release.'

'And that's it?'

'He asked about Ruth and Manny, but they were over at the cottage.'

The General froze, then forced himself to breath. When he spoke, his voice was flat and steady.

'He didn't want to speak to them?'

'No,' she said, a puzzled look appearing on her face. 'Of course not. They're children.'

'That doesn't always stop them.'

'What is going on here?' she asked. 'It's gone past the stage where I can tolerate this. You'll have to tell them to go.'

'I can't. It would mean the end for them. I'll get them away, I promise.'

'You've been saying that for months. I don't believe you anymore. Anyway, it won't matter.'

There was a tap at the door, and Yosef entered. He asked if there was anything they needed before they retired.

The General shook his head. 'No, Yosef, and thank you,' he said.

~~o~~

Maria Kästner waited until Yosef had gone.

'You really must do something, Erich,' she said, determined to stand her ground.

'It's not as easy as you think,' the General said with a sigh.

He went to the drinks cabinet and poured a whisky for himself. 'Would you like a drink?' he asked.

'Yes. A small brandy.'

He poured her drink and walked towards her. He froze, staring at her.

'What?' she said, frowning.

'What did you mean, when you said it wouldn't matter?' he said.

For a second, Maria hesitated.

'I told them they'd have to go,' she said, annoyed at his condemnatory tone. 'They agreed that it was only right that they should do in the circumstances.'

She returned his stare, then looked away, frightened of the cold anger on his face.

'What have you done?' he said quietly, his face a mask of fury. 'I'll hold you personally responsible if they leave now, and something happens to them.'

She felt tears prick her eyes, but she was too angry to cry.

'You care more for the Nussbaums than you do for me, or your own children. I can't forgive you for that. Do you know that Eva is terrified of what will happen if people find out the Gestapo are investigating us?'

'Of what people will say, no doubt, if you have anything to do with it. And anyway, they're not investigating us, it's the Nussbaums they're after.'

'The poor Nussbaums. There you go again. Your own daughter is living in mortal fear and all you worry about is a family of Jews, who we owe nothing to. We've done all we can for them.'

'We'll see. I'm going to have a word with them and apologise for my wife's behaviour.'

'You *will* not apologise for me,' she shouted. 'I've done nothing wrong.'

His eyes, like hers, were blazing now, but his voice was low and coldly restrained. She couldn't hold his gaze.

'One day, you'll look back on today, Maria, and you'll wish you'd acted differently. Yosef, his family and his parents are at risk of being sent to a ghetto, or a concentration camp, or killed, and I'll never forgive myself, or my family, if that happens when we could have provided help.'

He turned and walked out of the room. Maria Kästner stood for a second, then lifted her head and followed him. As she reached the kitchen, she heard the back door slam shut.

~~o~~

'I'm sorry my friends,' the General said. 'She's just afraid.'

Miriam put the dish of Cholent into the oven. It would cook slowly overnight, and she wouldn't have to cook during Shabbat. It combined different meats, including goose and sausage, with barley or buckwheat and beans in plenty of goose fat. She knew that few other Jewish households had the luxury of those ingredients, having to make do with turnip and potatoes as a rule, with the odd piece of smoked fish to add flavour but, although she was grateful to the Kästners, it felt like a hollow privilege without her children here to enjoy it.

'It's all right, sir,' she said. 'We understand. We're putting your family at risk.'

'No, you're not,' the General said, allowing his irritation to show. 'There's no danger to us; merely inconvenience.'

'Still, it must be unpleasant for Frau Kästner to have people like that bursting into her house.'

'You and I both know that's not what happened. I presume he wasn't rude or threatening to Maria.'

'No, sir. He was very polite, even to us, but I'm sure that was because the mistress was present.'

'Maria told me that he mentioned the children.'

'Yes. I think it was just to threaten us, sir,' Miriam said. 'To put pressure on us.'

'Miriam told him they were in the cottage, sir,' Yosef added. 'I nearly died. It was fortunate that he didn't check.'

'You got away with it. That's all that matters, but we'll need to do something about it over the next few days.'

'What do you mean, sir?'

'If they come back, they'll not fall for that again. They'll demand to see Ruth and Manny.'

'So, what can we do?'

'We'll report them missing, to the police. We must make it look as if there's no connection between the boys leaving, and Ruth and Manny not being here. It's fortunate that Maria, Eva, and Albert think they're still around, but we have to come up with a plausible story.'

'We could have sent them to Miriam's parents.'

'They would check. And thoroughly investigate. Do you really want to bring that down on Miriam's family?'

Yosef shook his head, then brightened.

'I have a cousin who has a farm in Karstädt. We think they've been deported to Poland. As far as I know, the farm is empty.'

'That wouldn't work. Sending your children away is a criminal act. No. It needs to be simpler. We have to make it look like they went missing from here. One minute they were out in the garden, the next they were gone.'

'If you're sure, sir.'

'It's the only way.'

'So, what do I do, sir? Do I contact the police?'

'No. I will. On your behalf. If you go to the police station, they'll keep you there. And it's illegal for you to phone. We'll get the police to come here.'

'But Frau Kästner…'

'Let me worry about that,' the General said, his expression grim.

CHAPTER 79

Franz and Johann sat in the cockpit. It was around seven.

'They asked for an hour to themselves,' Franz said.

'That will be good for Manny. I think they need to talk about Yosef and Miriam.'

'No, you Dummkopf. It's preparation for their Shabbat. Manny takes his religious obligations very seriously, you know.'

'Oh. I forgot what day it was,' Johann said.

'Ruth wants to keep as much routine going as possible,' Franz said. 'It's why they didn't eat bread tonight. And they'll want a little time tomorrow to say prayers, around midday.'

'That will be our watch. I'll send Manny down.'

~~o~~

When the sun had set, and the moon disappeared behind a low bank of cloud, Franz reluctantly agreed that they could all sit in the cockpit for a while.

'No lamps, though, other than our anchor light.'

He told Ruth to bring a couple of cushions up. He placed them on the cockpit floor and sat down on one. Manny took the other. Neither of their heads was above the cockpit coamings.

'Look at the stars,' Manny said.

They all looked up. The oil lamp had been hoisted just as the sun had gone down, as was required of a vessel at anchor. Its paraffin would need replenished before they retired to their bunks but, with the wick barely showing, it would burn through until sunrise.

Above it, in the clear sky, a myriad of pinpricks of light lit up the blackness.

Johann, mainly for Manny's benefit, told them a ghost story. Franz smiled when he saw Ruth shivering. It wasn't cold.

'Here,' he said, as Johann finished, handing Ruth his jacket. She put it on and flashed him a grateful smile.

'I have a story,' Franz said. 'It's about this place, Hjelm. I'm told there are countless ballads about it.'

'Is it another ghost story?' Manny asked, his eyes wide with anticipation.

'No. It's a true story. In the middle of the thirteenth century, a nobleman, Marsk Stig, killed Eric, the king of Denmark, then fled to Norway. The Norwegian king, who hated the Danish royal family, gave him arms, and boats, and he set off back to Denmark. He landed here on Hjelm and built a fortress.'

He smiled as Manny, leaning forward, hung on his every word.

There's still a small remnant of childhood in him.

'For the next fifty years,' Franz continued, 'he pillaged and plundered the coasts around here, like a pirate, until he died in the year 1293. They say he was like the famous Englander, *Robin Hood,* and that poor and disadvantaged people flocked to him, to fight for him. He even minted his own coins. Legend has it that he's buried at the top of the island. A pirate king.'

Manny whooped with delight, then put his hand over his mouth.

'Sorry,' he said. 'It was such an exciting story. Pirates!'

He looked over towards the island. The only sign of life was the sweep of the lighthouse's beam which lit up the sky above them.

Franz glanced over at Ruth. She was talking quietly with Johann, smiling at something he was saying. He frowned and looked at his watch.

'Let's all get an early night. Hopefully, we'll not be interrupted by pirates, or drunken sailors. We have an early start in the morning.'

~~o~~

During the night, Ruth's monthly bleeding came. She'd expected it, but it made her acutely aware of the lack of privacy on the yacht. She whispered to Manny that she had to go to the toilet.

'The heads,' he said. 'It's the heads.'

'I know,' she said, a little exasperated.

'Are you all right?' he asked.

'I'll be fine. I just need to go and sort myself out. Girls' stuff.'

His eyes widened, and he mumbled an apology.

'Mama told me,' he said.

'I don't want Franz or Johann to know,' Ruth said, blushing, glad that Manny couldn't see her. She suspected he knew.

'I'll tell them in the morning that I had to go to the toilet,' he said, touching her arm.

'Danke,' she said.

Five minutes later, she was back in bed. Manny was either asleep or he was pretending to be. Neither Franz or Johann had said anything, nor had appeared to waken. She lay down, relieved.

~~o~~

In the darkness, Franz turned over, annoyed at not having given it a thought. He told himself he must find a way to give her a bit more privacy for the next few days, even if it meant Johann, Manny and him being up in the cockpit for a short while.

~~o~~

Sat 5th April

06:00 Dep HJELM for LÆSØ. Pressure dropping slowly.

Weather cloudy but dry. Sea slight. Visibility Good. Wind 14 knots, westerly. Air pressure 1009mb. Full sail plus topsail. 035°M, 6.0 knots.

~~o~~

By five, the wind had strengthened, and had veered back round to the west. Franz cooked a panful of scrambled egg.

'We'll need to keep an eye on the anchor,' he said, 'now we're on a lee shore.'

'What does that mean?' Manny asked.

'It means that the wind is blowing us towards the beach. It's not an ideal position for a sailing vessel because it's harder to sail upwind, away from danger.'

'Should we not leave now then?'

Franz shook his head. 'It's only a light breeze at present. We'll be fine to stay here until we finish breakfast and get squared away, unless the wind gets up quickly.'

'If we were anchored on the other side of the island, we'd be all right?'

'Yes. If we were staying here longer, we'd move round to the east of Hjelm.'

'I wish we were on watch first,' Manny said. 'It would be cool to leave in the dark.'

'It won't be dark for long. The sky will begin to lighten almost as soon as we leave, but it will be dark when we arrive at Læsø. Most likely you'll be on watch for that, if Johann has got out of bed by then. And you'll be on watch tomorrow morning when we leave.'

'Johann needs his sleep,' a muffled voice from the port pilot berth said.

'Manny, Johann's right. It only takes two to sail the boat, and you'll have two long watches today. You should jump in the other pilot berth and get some rest.'

'I'd rather be up and about. I can do the navigation for you, down here, if you like. You can check it, to make sure I'm doing it right.'

Franz looked at him. Underneath the surface of eager determination, he thought he saw a glimpse of desperation in the boy's eyes, of longing for his parents, and for the nightmare to end.

'Of course you can,' he said. 'It would be a great help. I looked out the relevant charts last night. Two-one-zero-eight covers the first part of today's passage, then two-one-zero-seven.'

~~o~~

Manny pulled out the two charts and put the one showing the southern Kattegat on top. He could see their track from the day before, with the final annotation at their current position.

'You'll want the large-scale chart of the whole of the Baltic as well, to plot the entire leg,' he heard Franz shout down. 'Two-five-nine, it is.'

Manny lifted the hinged lid of the chart table and leafed through the pile of charts. He found the one he was looking for and pulled it out. He could see that, while it would show the whole of the day's passage, there wasn't much detail. Still, it would allow him to plot the course to Læsø, then he could study the larger scale charts for any hazards. He set about his task, while Franz and Ruth donned their jackets.

~~o~~

In the moonless black of night, they hoisted the main and sheeted it in, along with the mizzen, which had never been dropped, and *The Shearwater* trembled as the wind luffed the sail. Ruth took the helm and Franz began to wind the windlass handle, the anchor chain rattling down the spurling pipe into the chain locker.

'Steer to starboard a little,' he called out.

The wind caught the sails, and nudged the boat forward, helping Franz by taking the weight off the anchor chain.

'Now to port.'

With each small turn, he brought in more chain until it was pointing vertically downwards.

'Anchor aweigh,' he shouted.

Ruth turned the wheel to starboard, falling off the wind, as she'd been told to do. With the anchor off the seabed, *The Shearwater* began to move slowly forward, parallel to the beach.

Franz quickly wound in the remainder of the chain and the anchor thumped up onto the bow roller. He lashed it onto the deck, so that it couldn't deploy accidentally, and hoisted the staysail. Back in the cockpit, he sheeted it in and told Ruth to come up closer to the wind, to draw them away from the beach. As *The Shearwater* came round, he sheeted the main and the mizzen in as tight as the staysail and, as the sails worked in concert, *The Shearwater* surged forward, and heeled.

'How do you know where we're going when it's so dark?' she said, looking anxiously in the gloom.

'First, if you look at the compass, you'll see we're heading north-west, away from the beach. Secondly, the beam of the lighthouse is directly behind us, which means we are going in the opposite direction from it, away from the island.'

She looked a little less worried.

'Then there's this,' he said.

He pulled out the lead line and called out depths.

'Three fathoms,' he said. 'Hold your course.'

He went forward and hoisted the jib. When he got back, he took another sounding.

'Four fathoms.'

He hauled in the jib sheet and adjusted the main. He swung the lead again.

'Five fathoms,' he said. Happy that they were far enough away from the island, he shouted down to Manny.

'We're four cables north-west of the lighthouse. Plot a fix and tell us our course.'

Thirty seconds later, Manny stuck his head through the hatch and told Ruth to change course to zero-three-five.

Squinting at the compass, lit by its tiny, internal, flickering red lamp, she turned the wheel until the numbers lined up.

'Zero-three-five,' she said.

Franz smiled. She was learning.

'We'll be on this course for three or four hours, Franz said, 'until we clear the point at Fornæs, on the mainland.'

Ruth frowned and leaned forward. 'Should you not check the course Manny gave me?' she said quietly to Franz.

He smiled. 'I have the courses in here,' he said, tapping the notebook in his pocket. 'I did them earlier, but he's not to know that.'

Ruth's face softened with a smile.

'He's turning out to be a fine sailor,' Franz added.

She was surprised that Manny had the confidence to set the course, without checking with Franz or Johann.

'Will we tie the wheel again?' she asked.

'Not while it's dark, if we can help it. We want to be able to act quickly if we see another boat. Once the sun comes up, it'll be quite safe to lash it off.'

'Do all boats have lights at night, like us?'

She'd watched him lower the anchor light and snuff it out, then light the three navigation lamps that warned other boats of their presence; a red light on the port side, a green on the starboard and a white light on the stern.

'Yes. Most yachts nowadays, including my father's, have electric lights, but the colonel didn't believe they would be appropriate on *The Shearwater*, which is a very traditional, old-fashioned sailing boat.'

He looked around the solid wooden boat.

'And, do you know, I think he's right,' he said.

'I like the oil lamps down below, the way they flicker,' Ruth said.

Despite the horror of their flight from Kiel, there was a small part of her that rather enjoyed being on the boat; in other circumstances, especially if Antje could have been on board, she might have relished it.

'You can't just flick a switch in the middle of the night though,' he said, 'when you need light.'

'No,' she said, laughing, 'and I'm trying to keep my torch for when I really need it.'

'Look,' Franz said. He pointed east. The faintest glimmer on the horizon signalled the beginning of sunrise.

She hadn't noticed, and she watched as the dim red glow spread upwards.

'It's beautiful,' she said, watching as the tip of the sun appeared, sending a spear of light across the surface towards them.

'It's not always a good sign, a red sky at dawn,' he said. 'It can foretell heavy weather.'

'Oh. When?'

'Often the next day, but not always.'

'I worry about that,' she said. 'When the wind and the sea get wild.'

'I'll not lie. It can be unpleasant. Sometimes it puts people off sailing for life.'

'But you're not worried?'

She saw him hesitate.

'I always respect the sea,' he said. 'It can bite you unexpectedly but, if you have a solid boat, and you do the right thing, you can get through most of what she throws at you.'

'And this boat. Is it sound enough? It seems terribly old.'

'She's not as old as she appears, but she's based on a Colin Archer design from the turn of the century, built along traditional lines as a rescue boat for the wild seas off Norway. She's heavy, with a long keel, and her gaff rig is more substantial than the likes of my father's boat, which is built for speed as much as it is for seaworthiness.'

'So, the General's boat is better?'

'It depends on what you're looking for. My father likes to cruise, mostly, but he also raced in his day, and was good at it, you know. *Snowgoose* is a compromise. She's not an out-and-out racing yacht like the one Johann and I race, but she can show a clean pair of heels if she's fully canvassed.'

'But it... she... wouldn't be so safe in heavy seas?'

'We've been caught out in a few storms, and we've never felt in real danger, but she won't ride it out like *The Shearwater* would. You couldn't be in a better boat than this to cross the North Sea, if it's stormy. She's built for heavy weather, like a working boat.'

'But they don't use sailing boats for cargo anymore, do they?'

'You'd be surprised how many are still working. There were a couple in Bogense, a fishing smack and a Baltic trader, although it hadn't moved in a while. They need a bit of a blow to get them moving.'

The wind must have heard him, she thought; it strengthened, and Ruth felt the wheel pull against her as *Der Sturmtaucher* surged forward, the rigging creaking as it tightened.

It was now light enough to see the low hills of Djursland on their port side. On their starboard, there was nothing but empty sea and an uninterrupted horizon that stretched from north to south.

'It looks wide,' Ruth said.

'The Kattegat is about fifty miles wide here, but once we're past the headland, it will get wider. We'll be out of sight of land for quite a while.'

'We're heading for another island, yes?'

'Yes. Why?'

'If we're out of sight of land, what if we miss it?'

'We keep plotting our progress on the chart. It's accurate enough for what we need. It's quite a big island and it's only ten miles away from the mainland.'

'But won't we be arriving at night?'

'Yes, but provided it isn't foggy, we'll be able to see the lightship at Læsø Rende, then make for whatever shelter we can find off Læsø. If it's very rough, we can go into Vesterø Havn, but I'd rather anchor. The less time we spend in harbour, the better for you and Manny.'

She smiled at him.

CHAPTER 80

'That's Havknude Flak buoy, Manny, about two cables to our port.'

'I've got it, Franz,' Manny shouted from the cabin. 'I'll put the fix in and make a log entry. There's a course change for you. Zero-zero-five degrees.'

Ruth turned the wheel and watched the compass needle swing round.

'Zero-zero-five,' she said.

The boat heeled a little more as the wind came round from the port quarter to the beam.

Franz did a sounding and shouted it down to Manny; it was just over ten fathoms, as expected. He fetched the brass log out of the locker and trailed it overboard.

'Six-point-five knots,' he said.

'What's the wind speed?' Manny asked.

'It has got up a bit. I reckon it's just under twenty-five knots. Force six, westerly. It's maybe time to put a reef in.'

Franz asked Ruth to steer close to the wind while he worked, and changed the jib first, for a smaller one, then reefed the mainsail. When he was finished, he told her to return to her original course.

'How does that feel?' he asked Ruth.

'Easier,' she said, 'and we're not heeling as much, but we've slowed down, haven't we?'

Franz took another log reading.

'Still six-point-five knots,' he said, smiling.

'How can that be?' she said, frowning. 'There's less sail up, and it feels slower.'

'It often happens when you reef. The boat works a little less efficiently when it's heeled over too far, and although it always feels as if you're going faster, it's not always the case.'

He went over to the hatch.

'Any chance of a cup of coffee, young man?' he said.

'Of course,' Manny said, looking up. 'I'll just put the kettle on.'

While he busied himself lighting the stove, swinging on its gimbals to keep it level, Franz took the chance to glance at the chart below. Manny had marked the fix in the right place and had drawn in their track from Hjelm. He checked the log entry.

```
08:23 Leave HAVKNUDE FLAK buoy to port. Weather overcast. Still
dry. Sea slight. Visibility Good. Wind 23 knots, westerly. 1
Reef Main, and Jib. 005°M, 6.5 knots. Unidentified small
Kriegsmarine vessel seen, about 5NM distance, 060°M
```

Franz nodded, smiling. The boy had meticulously mimicked Franz's neat script and, to anyone other than an expert, it would have appeared to be from the same hand. *Clever. I should have thought of that.*

Manny handed the two coffees up to Franz, then disappeared. Franz heard Johann's voice call from his bunk for a coffee, then Manny's excited chatter as he told Johann that he was navigating *The Shearwater*. Franz smiled again. Those two were forming a strong partnership.

As he did every few minutes, he scanned the horizon in all directions, then sat back and savoured the coffee. It was good; he mentally thanked his father for slipping a pack of his favourite coffee into the boat's provisions, instead of the ersatz rubbish which was all that was available these days.

'What do you think will happen to Mama and Papa?'

Ruth's question stunned Franz, coming from nowhere.

He looked at her face. Her eyes watered and he doubted it was from the wind. He glanced at the hatch, but he could still hear the murmur of Johann's and Manny's voices down below.

'The honest answer is that I don't know. I hope that they can get out quickly, either by themselves, through the Haganah, or with my father's help.'

'And if they don't?'

'He'll protect them as long as he can.'

'But not forever?'

'No. Not forever. There's only so much he can do, despite what he says. He's only one man.'

'I know.'

'He'll not give them up, Ruth, without a fight.'

'But he can't win. They'll be sent to a camp. Papa wouldn't talk about what it was like in Neuengamme.'

'Some of the camps are worse than others, from the little I've heard. Anyway, they might not be taken to a camp. Most of the…'

He swallowed and looked away.

I can't tell her. It's better she doesn't know.

'You can talk about it, Franz,' she said. 'I'm not stupid. Most of the Jewish people have been rehomed in Poland. And you're right. It would be far better than being in a camp. They may even be able to find my grandparents, and sit out the war until it is over, if Papa can find a job.'

'I hope it doesn't come to that. The General will get them away, I'm sure.'

He told himself to come up with a way to ask his father if he'd made any progress when he spoke to him next.

CHAPTER 81

The General looked at the clock on the wall of his office.

Nine-thirty. Time to make the call.

He wondered where *Der Sturmtaucher* was. Halfway to Læsø, he hoped.

It took a while for his call to be put through to Uwe Müller's office. The police chief answered curtly.

'Erich,' he said. 'What can I do for you?'

'Uwe, how are you?'

'I was fine. Now I'm worried. Your calls always mean trouble.'

'I'm sorry. I should call you when nothing is wrong.'

'You do on the odd occasion, I must admit but, this time, you have a problem. With your Jews again, I guess.'

'Well, yes and no. It's not Miriam and Yosef this time. It's–'

Uwe Müller interrupted.

'Please don't tell me it's on behalf of friends of theirs. That would be stretching my patience, even for you.'

'No, It's not their friends. It's their children. They've gone missing.'

'Missing? When?'

'Yesterday. They were out in the garden. Miriam went to call them for dinner, and they'd gone.'

'How old are they?'

'Well, Manny is fourteen, Ruth is almost eighteen.'

'The girl is hardly a child, Erich.'

'That's not the point. They're missing, and we've searched everywhere.'

There was silence at the end of the phone, then Uwe Müller sighed.

'And what do you expect me to do about it? Organise a city-wide search for them? Do you know how short-staffed we are currently, what with losing so many men to the Wehrmacht?'

The General hoped the police chief would do nothing, as long the Nussbaum children were reported as missing.

When the police chief spoke, there was a hint of weariness in his voice.

'Erich, my advice to you is to let this go. Have a look for them yourself. Enlist the help of your minions. If I record this as an incident, your Jews will be investigated again.'

The General knew that what his former friend said was true, but he believed it was more dangerous not to report it.

'I'll do as you say, but I'd still like it recorded in case they turn up somewhere.'

The police chief sighed again.

'All right. If you insist, but don't blame me if you receive a visit from one of my men.'

'Thanks, Uwe. I appreciate it.'

'I told you the last time. I didn't want to hear from you again.'

'I know. But you have children, Uwe. So do I. You know I couldn't leave it.'

~~o~~

'1000 hours. Change of watch,' Franz said. 'You go down first. Send Manny up.'

Ruth stood aside as Franz took the wheel.

She looked around. To port, the land had receded rapidly to the west since they'd passed Fornæs point. Now it was gone. In front of them, there was nothing but sea, in all directions. As they'd left the lee of the land, the waves had grown, and the boat lifted and rolled a little more as each crest reached them.

Ruth glanced back for a last look at the headland they'd passed half an hour before, for reassurance, but it had disappeared. She shivered, the feeling of disorientation unnerving without land in sight as a reference.

She climbed down the companionway.

Manny took her jacket and cap, and he dived up past her, eager to be on deck.

Johann was sitting on the edge of the bench seat, tying up his boots.

'How's it looking out there?'

'Frightening,' she said.

'Oh. Is the wind getting up?'

'No. It's not that, although it's a bit rougher than it was. It's just that the land is disappearing. We'll soon be out of sight of it, I think.'

'Ah. We're in Aalborg Bugt now. Once we cross that, we'll be back close to land again. Here, I'll show you.'

He nodded to the chart and she stood beside him while he pointed to the large bay cutting nearly twenty miles into the land.

'It's about forty miles across. It will take us six or seven hours, but we should see land long before that.'

'Still, it's strange, feeling that you might be in the middle of the ocean.'

'Just wait until we're in the Nordsee. Then we'll be out of sight of land for days.'

Ruth shivered, and Johann gave her an encouraging smile.

~~o~~

'Don't worry,' he said. 'You'll get used to it and remember, if we're out of sight of land, it's less likely we'll be seen.'

'I suppose you are right,' she said. 'We just seem so... so small out here.'

The Shearwater lurched as a larger wave caught the hull, and she almost fell. He caught her, his arm around her shoulders. She smiled gratefully at him.

'It's all yours, Johann.'

He quickly dropped his arm when he heard Franz's voice. He looked up to see his brother's face in the companionway, frowning.

He blushed, and moved away from Ruth, lifting his sweater and pulling it over his head.

Franz climbed down the steps and handed his foul-weather gear to Johann.

'It's a little cooler now, with the spray and the wind. You'll need this. Hold our course for another couple of hours and we'll keep well clear of the shoals.'

There was enough water for the boat to safely pass over the cluster of sandbanks that guarded the bay; the depth never got less than three or four fathoms, but they could kick up the sea, forming larger, sharper waves which would make the boat less comfortable for its crew. It was better to avoid them.

Johann nodded. Ruth smiled at him.

'Thanks,' she said.

He returned her smile then, seeing Franz glare at him again, scowled and climbed the companionway steps.

~~o~~

Ruth frowned, noticing the exchange of looks between the two brothers but, as the boat lurched again, her stomach turned, and she sat down, feeling a little light-headed and nauseous.

'Are you all right?' Franz said. 'You look a little pale.'

'I feel a bit strange,' she said.

'Do you feel sick?'

'A little. It feels stuffy all of a sudden,' she said. She wiped her brow with the back of her hand. It was damp with sweat.

'I don't know if it was because the land disappeared or if it was the movement of the boat, or just being down below,' she said, 'but I do feel unwell.'

'If it's seasickness, it could be all three,' Franz said.

He reached into one of the lockers above the galley and pulled out a biscuit tin. He opened it, and loosened the paper covering the contents.

'Here,' he said, handing her a biscuit. 'Eat one of these.'

She took it from him, unconvinced.

'It's ginger,' she said, taking a small bite.

'Yes. Ginger is good for seasickness, but it's easier to take it before you get sick.'

She took another bite of the biscuit. When she'd finished that one, Franz gave her another.

'After you've eaten that, take a small drink, and lie down in Johann's bunk. I'll get your sleeping bag.'

'I don't know if I could. Anyway, I could lie in my own bunk.'

'No, you'd get thrown around too much. Johann's bunk is on the lee side of the boat. It's lower down because the boat is heeling, so it has less movement. You'll also not be at risk of falling out.'

She gave a weak laugh but did as he said.

~~o~~

Ten minutes later, she was sound asleep.

Franz smiled. *The best thing for her.*

He checked the chart. Manny had put a fix in when they were abreast of Fornæs Light. He followed the course marked on the chart. It was correct.

He's really coming along.

He stood up and slid the hatch back.

'You're perfect on that course, Manny,' he said. 'Your chartwork was right on the mark.'

~~o~~

Johann looked around. There was nothing but sea. He thought of Ruth, and the fear he'd seen in her eyes.

No wonder she's terrified.

Then he thought of the smile she'd given him.

It's simpler this way.

Part of him wished that it was him, not Franz, who was on watch with Ruth, but he knew that the look he'd had from him had been a warning. He couldn't blame his brother.

He'd caught a glimpse of her figure as she stretched herself to scatter the tingling numbness in her arms and legs, and he'd had to turn away, worried that she or Manny or Franz might have caught him looking.

His track record with women wasn't something to boast about, even if it impressed his friends.

He shut his eyes.

Women always complicate things.

CHAPTER 82

Werner Schmidt was not in the best of moods. When he had a Sunday off, he liked to finish early on the Saturday to make the most of the weekend, so he'd arranged only one visit, to interview a witness who had been away all week on business. The man had returned late the night before, and the detective had arranged to call at his house around ten o'clock to take a statement.

He'd almost made it out the door when his Kriminalsekretär shouted to him.

'You've dealt with these people before. Go and find out what the problem is after you're finished,' he'd said, handing him a piece of paper with General Kästner's name on it, and the Nussbaums' below it.

There had been no point in protesting, even though his superior knew he worked his arse off during the week to allow him to finish early on the Saturday, the one day when he could relax with his sons without worrying about going to church or visiting his wife's family.

He knew it wouldn't be a case of conducting a quick interview and shelving it until Monday; this one had politics written all over it; as well as having his own boss looking over his shoulder, he would have the chief of police breathing down his neck and, if Heinrich Güllich got wind of it, he could kiss the whole weekend goodbye.

By the time he'd finished his first call, it was nearly eleven. The witness hadn't furnished as much information as he'd hoped, which didn't improve his temper, and, as he drove out to Drachensee, he snapped when the young detective he'd brought with him had the temerity to ask if the Kriminalassistent would normally be sent to investigate missing Jewish children.

'Only if their parents work for someone high up in the Kriegsmarine, with friends in the right places.'

'I still don't get it, sir. This man is a general, yet he works with the Kriegsmarine?'

'He's Abwehr. Army intelligence but works closely with the navy. He has the ear of all the top admirals, and most of the OKW too. The Gestapo were warned off him by Heydrich himself when they tried to investigate his Jews.'

The young KriPo man whistled.

'So, you see,' the Kriminalassistent continued, 'we need to tread carefully with this one.'

~~o~~

General Kästner opened the door himself.

'Kriminalassistent Schmidt, sir, Kriminalpolizei.' The detective showed the General his card.

'This is my colleague, Kriminalassistentanwärter Reiter.'

'Come in. The Nussbaums are through in the drawing room. I thought it would be quieter in there.'

The two policemen followed the General through. Yosef and Miriam sat nervously on the small couch set at right angles to the General's desk. The General invited the KriPo men each to take a seat in the other two chairs, then walked around and sat at his desk.

Werner Schmidt cleared his throat.

'I believe two children have gone missing,' he said.

'Yes,' the General said. 'Since yesterday.'

'And you only reported this today?'

'I only discovered that they were missing today. Understandably, considering their recent experiences with the Gestapo, the Nussbaums didn't want to make a fuss last night, hoping that Ruth and Manny had decided to go for a walk and had got stranded somewhere because of the curfew. Even when they didn't turn up this morning, they were still reluctant that I should phone the police, but I managed to persuade them that it was the right course of action to take.'

'I see,' the Kriminalassistent said.

The General glanced at the Nussbaums. They did look extremely uncomfortable about the involvement of the KriPo.

'Perhaps we could hear from the Nussbaums,' he said to the General, turning to Yosef and Miriam.

'Tell me exactly when you last saw your son and daughter.'

'We left them in the cottage while we served the Kästners their evening meal,' Miriam said. 'We often do that. Ruth has been looking after Manny for several years while we do our duties in the big house.'

'And did they indicate to you that they were going to *go for a walk* at any time?'

'No,' Yosef said. 'They were told always to stay in the confines of the cottage, the Kästners' house, or the gardens.'

'Ruth would often take Manny out to let him play in the garden, or down by the lake,' Miriam said. 'She would read a book while he played.'

'Ah. The lake,' Werner Schmidt said, raising his eyebrows. 'I don't suppose they could have gone swimming, could they?'

The General got the impression that two drowned Jewish children would be a welcome outcome for the detective, saving further effort on his part.

'No,' the General interjected. 'We've already looked. Their clothes aren't lying around. Anyway, it's a bit early in the year and they were both good swimmers.'

'What about a boat?'

'None of the dinghies are out of the boathouse.'

'We don't have the manpower to search the lake for missing…'

He was going to say Jews but thought better of it, given the General's cold stare.

'… persons,' he said, 'but I'd strongly advise you to have a thorough search yourselves. It would be a shame if the resources of the police were being wasted when all the time, the missing children were close to home.'

'We'll drag the lake this afternoon,' the General said, his voice cold but remarkably polite. He hoped that the Nussbaums' fear and loathing of the policemen translated as concern for their children and anger at his apparent disinterest.

'I'll need photographs. And descriptions. The constable will take them while I have a look around. I'll need full access to the house, and the Nussbaums' cottage, and the gardens.'

'Be my guest, Herr Schmidt.'

Erich Kästner was glad that Maria was at a charity event but the Kriminalassistent's next words dashed his hopes that Maria's involvement could be avoided.

'I'll have to interview all of you individually, including your family, Herr General, and any other staff you have.'

'My wife is currently out at a charity fundraiser, but she will be back just after lunchtime. My eldest daughter is with her, and our driver. My youngest daughter was concerned about Ruth and Manny and felt that her time would be better served by going out and looking for them. I suspect she'll be back home shortly.'

'Good. I'll speak to your wife and daughters before I leave. I'll also have a word with your neighbours, Herr General. They may have seen something.'

'As you must, Herr Kriminalassistent but I'd appreciate it if you could do it unobtrusively. The local residents are, shall we say, not accustomed to answering their doors to the police.'

'I understand. We will be very discreet.'

The General was impressed with the man's restraint. The man's voice remained polite, like his own, but he could see the suppressed anger in his eyes.

Good. He thinks I'm arrogant.

He hoped his goading of the man fitted in with the detective's expectations and would convince him that he and the Nussbaums were telling the truth.

CHAPTER 83

He was thorough. The General gave him that.

He made a careful round of the gardens and stood staring out at the lake for a while.

He went into every room in the big house. The General accompanied him. He opened the occasional drawer or cupboard, but it was by no means an exhaustive search. The General concluded that he just wanted to have a look around, to see how he and his family lived.

'It's a large house,' he said. 'I presume that is why you need your domestic staff.'

'The house was my father's. The staff are essential to me. Without being conceited, I have a key role in the Wehrmacht. I work long hours, sometimes at home, and I need no interruptions or inconveniencies. You may see that as frivolous but, I can assure you, the Kriegsmarine don't.'

'Yes. You have substantial backing. There's no other way your Jews would still be here.'

He paused and lit a cigarette, offering one to the General, who shook his head.

'You know, it's ironic,' the detective said. 'You and your Jewish staff have always been very uncooperative with us, but now you want our help.'

'We've always been happy to assist the police. Can you honestly say you ever had any real suspicions about the Nussbaums?'

'By association, yes, but nothing concrete. It's the only reason they were released, you must understand.'

'Then why did they send you today? I would have expected someone from the OrPo.'

The KriPo man said nothing. He shrugged.

After he'd finished with the big house, the detective searched the Nussbaums' cottage. It was more thorough than his look round the Kästner house, but he didn't pull the place apart, like previous searches.

When Maria and Eva returned, with Albert, he interviewed each of them in the General's study.

The General and Albert took one of the dinghies out of the boathouse, and using a grappling hook and two long poles, began searching the part of the lake closest to the house.

When the Kriminalassistent returned from questioning the Kästners' neighbours, he walked to the lakeside and spoke with the General.

'The Böhms don't have a very high opinion of your family,' he said.

'No. My son, Franz, and their daughter, Lise, broke off their engagement a few years ago. It was very acrimonious and, unfortunately, our families have not been on speaking terms since.'

'They say it was over your family's 'Jew-loving' inclinations; their words, not mine,' he said, suppressing a smile.

'As I say, they were bitter. They also accused my son of being a coward. He has an Iron Cross, first class.'

'Are you a Jew-lover?'

'I treat everyone as I find them, no matter who they are. If some of my friends happen to be Jews, I'm not going to change my opinion of them.'

'Friends, you say. I thought they were employees?'

'They are, and excellent ones at that, but you must remember that Yosef and I grew up together. His father held the same position in my father's household that he holds now in mine.'

'Can I give you a word of advice, Herr General?'

'If you must, Herr Schmidt.'

'You would be stupid to put your reputation, and your family's welfare at risk for a couple of Jews. In the end, you will not be able to hold onto them, and in the meantime, you'll be antagonising people much more ruthless than me.'

The General stared at him.

'Is that a threat, Herr Kriminalassistent?'

'No, General Kästner. Just an observation.'

For a moment, they stared at each other.

'Did the neighbours see anything?' the General asked.

'No. Nothing. No stranger, hanging around. No car speeding off. It's all a little unusual. I mean, without papers, they wouldn't get far on their own.'

'That's why I telephoned the police chief. You can surely see that it wasn't a decision that was taken lightly.'

'When did you last see them, Herr General?'

'I'm almost certain it was Friday morning. Ruth would sometimes help her mother do breakfast, and Manny usually tagged along. I could be wrong. It may have been the day before.'

'Thank you, Herr General. I'll do my best to find them, but I can't promise anything.'

They both knew he was lying. Werner Schmidt had done what was necessary to satisfy the police chief, who didn't want the General hounding him, and his own boss, who didn't want the police chief on his back.

Erich Kästner hoped they'd done enough to convince the detective that the children had gone missing the day before. It had been a dangerous game, deliberately involving the police, but he knew that sooner or later Heinrich Güllich would be back, and he wanted control of the narrative of the children's disappearance.

He coughed.

'I don't quite know how to say this, but…'

He hesitated, as if unsure.

'Go on, Herr General. I assure you, any information you can provide will be most useful.'

'I… I worry that the Gestapo might have something to do with their disappearance.'

The policeman gave him a thin smile.

'That's quite an accusation. Even for a high-ranking member of the armed forces.'

'It's not an accusation, Herr Kriminalassistent. It's merely a suggestion that it's possible.'

'Even if it were true, preposterous as it is, it's not an area I would care to investigate.'

'Then I will ask Herr Güllich myself the next time he makes a social call.'

~~o~~

The Kriminalassistent collected his constable, who'd taken descriptions of the children from Yosef, and he pocketed the photographs that Miriam reluctantly handed over.

He shook the General's hand.

'We'll be in touch,' he said.

The General stood at the window and watched them drive away. Yosef came into the room and asked the General if he needed anything.

'No. Not at present, Yosef.'

'How do you think that went, sir,' Yosef asked.

'Good,' he replied. 'Very good. I'm sure they believe us.'

'He was very meticulous, sir.'

'It was all for appearance's sake,' the General said. 'The Kriminalassistent isn't the worst. At times he sounded almost human.'

'Both of them thought it was a waste of their time trying to find two Jewish children.'

'I know, and despite my distaste, that's not a bad thing.'

'It may be for nothing, if they're caught, sir.'

'Another few days and they'll be crossing the North Sea. Until then, we need to be careful.'

'I know, sir, and Miriam does too.'

CHAPTER 84

'How are you feeling now?'

'Better,' Ruth said, leaning up on one elbow, her short hair dishevelled, her eyes trying to focus.

'I've just brewed a pot of coffee. I'll pour you one.'

'Thank you. How long did I sleep?'

'A couple of hours. Maybe a little more.'

It was nearly one o'clock, but he'd left her sleeping, thinking it would do her the world of good. He'd even dozed off himself on a couple of occasions, waking from time to time only to check the boat and plot their estimated position when they cleared the bottom end of the shallows, calling the course change up to the helmsman.

'I don't feel sick now,' she said. 'The ginger must be working.'

A little colour had returned to Ruth's cheeks, and she'd stopped staring at the sea in morbid fascination.

'Your mama baked these before we left,' he said, 'just in case.'

She looked at him, then turned away, her eyes clouded with tears. He thought that it would have pleased her.

How could I have been so stupid?

She wiped her eyes and turned back to him.

'I'm sorry,' she said.

'Don't be. I shouldn't have said anything.'

'No. It's nice that Mama made them. If it weren't the biscuits, something else would have brought her to mind, or Papa.'

'We're on deck again soon. Are you feeling up for it? Manny wouldn't complain if I asked him to do an extra watch.'

'No. As much as he'd enjoy it, the only way I can get through this is to do my bit.'

'That's the spirit. There's still an hour to go; we'll have lunch and make some for the boys. We'll be on from two until six so hopefully they'll return the favour for dinner.'

~~o~~

'We have a different use for the bilges tonight,' Franz said, adjusting the jib sheet when it luffed a little.

'Really?' Ruth said, checking the compass.

'We're going to dye the second set of sails grey,' Franz said.

'Why on earth would we do that?'

'They'll not show up against the sky and the waves when we strike out across the North Sea.'

'Oh. I suppose that makes sense. What if we have to hide in the bilge tonight?'

'You and Manny will be dyed grey too,' Franz said, smiling.

Ruth laughed.

'It will only take a couple of hours, then we'll leave them out to dry, and stow them away again before we leave Læsø.'

~~o~~

'Is the lightship bearing two-three-five yet?' Johann heard Franz shout.

They'd changed watch again at six, and Manny was helming. Johann lifted the sighting compass to his eye.

'Two-three-zero,' he said, opening the hatch.

'Another half a mile,' Franz said, looking up from the chart table. 'Five minutes, then take another bearing. We're looking for two-three-five. Are our navigation lights on?'

'Yes, I lit them ten minutes ago. The wind has backed to the south, but it has dropped a little.'

Johann scanned the horizon. The sky was darkening fast as the sun touched the land to the west, then fell below it. The beam from the lightship that marked Læsø Rende, the deep-water channel between the island and the sandbanks, had been lit for half an hour, shining brighter as the night closed in.

'Why do you want the bearing of the lightship to be so accurate?' Manny asked.

'We're going to use the lightship to give us a course over the shoals of Nordvest Rev,' Johann said. 'When the hand compass reads two-three-five to the lightship, we turn so that it is right behind us. If we keep the lightship bearing constant, we will clear all the hazards.'

'I always thought lighthouses and lightships were just to warn ships away from dangers. They're so much more useful than that.'

'They are, and there's another neat trick I'll show you sometime, but enough for one day. Now, let's see what this bearing is.'

He lifted the sighting compass.

'Two-three-five,' he shouted.

Franz echoed the bearing, then shouted the new course. 'Steer zero-five-five degrees.'

Manny grinned at Johann and began turning the wheel.

'Wait,' said Johann.

'What's wrong?' Manny said, turning the wheel back to midships.

'Nothing,' Johann said, 'but the wind is almost behind us now, just off our starboard quarter, and our sails are out to port. When we turn, the wind will pass behind the boat to the other side. It's called a gybe.'

He was sure Franz had already told the boy, but he quickly explained the dangers of the heavy boom whipping across the deck.

'How do you stop it?'

'Before we turn, we pull in the mainsheet until the boom is at the centre of the boat. That way, it can go nowhere while we are turning. As the wind crosses to the other side, we let the mainsheet gradually out, but in a controlled manner. Do you understand?'

~~o~~

In the cabin, Franz heard them start the gybe and felt the boat begin to turn. He told Ruth to expect a slight lurch as the boat turned across the wind.

He felt *The Shearwater* swing upright as it turned, then, with a soft thump, it began heeling a little the opposite way. The flapping of the foresails lasted only seconds before he sensed the boat surge forward again.

'That was a smooth gybe,' Franz said. 'It can be a fearful thing if someone gets it wrong.'

Ruth looked at the chart.

'It only shows half a fathom of water over the reef,' she said, pointing to where the shoals were marked.

'With the strong westerlies today, and the low air pressure, there should be enough water to get us over. In very strong winds, the water levels can rise as much as a fathom. It will save us going round, but we'll check the depths carefully once we get close.'

Franz wasn't sure she was convinced.

He told Johann to take another sighting.

'Læsø Rende two-three-five.'

'Get me a log reading.'

He stuck his head through the hatch and watched Johann trailing the log behind the boat.

'Six knots,' he said as he stowed the log.

Franz nodded and sat down at the chart table again. Unless the wind changed, they wouldn't need another log reading.

An hour later, Franz poked his head through the hatch again.

'Start swinging the lead, please, and luff the mainsail. Let's lose some speed. We're getting close to the reef.'

Johann hauled in the mainsheet and the sail fluttered in the breeze, and their speed dropped by two knots. He lowered the lead line over the side. In the darkness, Franz heard him count the knots on the cord with his fingers.

'Ten fathoms,' he shouted.

'Nine fathoms.'

Johann immediately lifted the line and lowered it again.

'Eight and a half.'

The line flew through his hands.

'Eight.'

'Seven.'

'Luff the jib.'

Johann released the sheet. The jib flapped and half-wrapped itself around the forestay. A little more way came off the boat.

'Brace yourself in case she grounds,' Franz said to Manny.

Johann swung the lead again.

'Four.'

~~o~~

Manny glanced at Johann. Despite the speed dropping, the seabed was still coming up fast. The wheel almost slipped through his sweating palms.

What if they've got it wrong?

He braced himself for the sudden wrenching stop if their keel dug into the sandbank.

'Three,' Johann shouted. Manny couldn't believe how calm his voice sounded.

'Two.'

Manny held his breath and looked ahead, as if something in the darkness was looming towards them.

'Two.'

The Shearwater surged forward, cutting through the water as if she had a thousand fathoms under her keel.

'Three,' Johann shouted.

'Four.'

'Five.'

'Seven.'

'We're over,' he said to Manny, who breathed out again.

'That was scary,' he said.

'Not really, although the sandbanks can shift.'

'Is that why you call the depths so often?'

'No. We do that so that we can tell when we cross the sandbank. Because we know our bearing from the lighthouse, and where the sandbank is on the chart, we know exactly where we are, within a hundred metres. There's also a lighthouse ahead of us; it should be off our port bow.'

'I thought the island was on our starboard?'

'It is, but there's another shoal that runs out from Læsø, about three miles offshore, with a little islet at the end of it that barely sticks its head above sea level. It's called Nordre Rønner; there's a lighthouse on that and there's also a light at the entrance to Vesterø Havn, but that one may be difficult to see against the lights of the town.'

'Do we have to cross that shoal too?'

'Yes, I would think. If you don't mind giving up the helm, you could go down below to check. Franz will show you.'

Reluctantly, Manny left the wheel to Johann, and disappeared below. Within a few minutes, he was back.

'Franz showed me. He said that when the lighthouse is due north, we should be on top of the shoal. Once we're over it, we need to sail south-west for two miles. We can anchor close inshore in about five fathoms.'

'You can take her in, and I'll swing the lead.'

Johann talked Manny through the anchoring drill and made him repeat it.

When they reached the shallow ridge that separated Vesterø Havn from the bay beyond, Johann called the soundings again. This time, as the depth decreased, the youngster felt less anxious than he'd been before, trusting the Kästner brothers and the chart that Franz had shown him. It took the best part of half an hour to reach a suitable place to anchor; like the previous evening, the wind died with the sun.

As the chain rattled down, *The Shearwater* drifted backwards in the wind. The anchor dug in with a sharp tug, and she shuddered to a halt.

'It's holding,' Johann yelled. He waited until the boat settled.

'Come and help me drop these sails,' Johann said.

In the darkness, he and Manny worked quietly and efficiently, dropping the staysail first, tying it down before lowering the main and lashing the gaff to the boom.

A reef in the mizzen completed their work, apart from putting a match to the wick on the anchor light and hoisting it up the mast. It cast a faint glow which barely illuminated the deck.

~~o~~

They stood looking out towards where land should be. In the blackness, only a solitary light from an isolated farmhouse flickered on Læsø.

'You did well today,' Johann said. 'You've come a long way in a few days, but it will get much harder from here on in, as soon as we round Skagen.'

'I'll be all right. Nothing the sea can do could be worse than what they've done to us.'

Johann froze, shocked by the boy's venom.

'We'll get you to a place where you won't have to worry about that again.'

'I'm not concerned for myself. Only for Ruth, and what is happening to Mama and Papa.'

Johann didn't quite know what to say. He thought that Franz would have had the right words, but the boy had opened up to him, not to his brother.

'My father will do his very best to get them out,' he said. 'Whatever it takes.'

'And if that's not enough?'

'Then pray for them. Pray for us all.'

Manny stared at Johann.

'I didn't think you held much with religion,' he said.

'I don't, but I know you do, and your parents do. If you believe it will help, do it.'

'Ruth and I pray before we go to sleep. We talk about Mama and Papa. And all the others. It keeps them alive in our hearts.'

Johann looked away. The young man had suffered so much in his short life while he, Johann, had led a charmed and privileged existence, caring only of soldiering and women, and not always in that order. And of his friends, of course, whose hedonistic bents matched his own.

'I can't imagine what you've been through,' he said, 'or how you cope with the fear of what is happening to your family.'

He paused.

'I'm the last person who should give you advice,' he said, his hand on Manny's shoulder, 'but all I can tell you is try and get through each day and hope that, when this is all over, you'll be back with them.'

'They'll pay, one day, those who've done this,' Manny said, the coldness in his voice catching Johann unawares.

'Yes. They should,' he mumbled.

The two young Germans, poles apart, stood together in the dark, the minutes passing in silence.

Then, from the companionway, they heard Franz call them.

'There's coffee ready once you're squared away.'

Johann put his hand on Manny's shoulder and nodded to him.

'Keep hoping,' he said.

CHAPTER 85

06:00 Dep LÆSØ for HIRTSHALS. Cooler. Barometer dropping 1003mb. Wind 18 knots, nor'westerly. Sea state slight to moderate. Full sail 355°M, 5.5 knots.

~~o~~

They'd arrived after dark and they left before dawn. Manny saw nothing of Læsø, save the flash of the Nordre Rønner light as they passed it, a few cables off.

With the wind ahead of the beam on a close haul, the boat heeled significantly more than it had, and the waves crashed into the bow, sending the odd burst of spray back to Johann and Manny in the cockpit.

'It's much colder,' Manny said, glad of the extra layers Johann had told him to wear, and the heavy oilskins that kept out most of the dampness.

Even so, his eyes stung every time a wave caught the boat and showered them with spray.

'It is cooler. The thermometer is back a couple of degrees, but it always feels colder still when you're sailing into the wind, even on a fine day.'

'You can't see the spray coming in the darkness. The first thing you know is when it hits you in the face.'

'The Nordsee will be worse. It's much saltier, and your eyes will sting with every driven drop.'

'Bring it on,' the boy said, grinning. It felt good to fight nature. *To fight anything.*

He stood, one foot on the edge of the cockpit seat, the other on the sloping deck, wrestling the wheel, the rudder, the wind, and the sea, keeping the boat on the course as close to the wind as the elements would allow.

An hour later, he watched with envy as Johann huddled in the lee of the coachroof against the biting rain, the collar of his oilskin jacket fastened up to his nose, leaving only his eyes showing.

It had started at first light and it fell, not continuously, but in a series of sharp squalls whose gusts threatened to broach the boat. *The Shearwater* felt over-canvassed when the wind strengthened but Johann, rather than put a reef or two in, let the sheets off to spill a bit of wind, taking the pressure off the helm, until the gusts subsided.

'It's difficult to maintain a course,' Manny said. 'I keep getting pushed eastwards.'

'You can only do what the wind will let you and, don't forget, we have as much as a knot of tide against us now, with some north in the wind. We either tack soon, and get further westwards now, at the expense of making ground northwards, or we carry on as best we can, and hope that there's a wind change.'

'What did Franz say?'

'He's leaving it up to us. I say we carry on. If the wind shifts to the west, we can make for close round the Skaw. If it shifts to the north, we'll put a series of tacks in.'

'And if it stays in the north-west?'

'We punch out into the Skagerrak far enough to close-haul her all the way down to Hirtshals.'

'Is there a problem with that?'

'Yes, we might end up halfway to Sweden.'

~~o~~

Werner Schmidt looked at his watch.

How had the bastard found out so quickly?

He thought he'd have at least a day's grace and be able to enjoy his Sunday, then write up his report on Monday morning; true, he'd have to attend church with his family, and visit his brother-in-law, Willi, for lunch, but the afternoon would be his, to spend time with his sons, playing ball, or flying kites, making up for losing most of Saturday to the damned missing Jew children.

Now, with Heinrich Güllich's voice grating in the telephone's earpiece, he realised that he would have to go into the office, write up the case, and deliver it to Gestapo Headquarters, no doubt to be grilled about it by the Gestapo investigator.

'I want to interview them this afternoon,' he heard the Gestapo man say. 'When can you have your report on my desk?'

Werner Schmidt sighed. It wouldn't do to let the security police think he wasn't as fanatical as they were.

'I can be at your office around about twelve, but I must be away by one. A family occasion, you understand.'

'For me, my work always comes first, but you must do as you see fit,' the Gestapo man said.

'I'll be there at twelve,' Werner Schmidt said. He put the phone down.

He looked at his watch again. Ten o'clock. On a Sunday morning.

He returned to the bedroom and began washing himself at the sink his wife had insisted they had installed.

'You're going to work,' she said, her tone accusing him.

'I have to. It's the Gestapo. You can't refuse them.'

'Why not? They're just police, like you, but more…'

She searched for a word.

'Dangerous?' he said.

'No. Zealous,' she said.

'Perhaps you'd rather they came here to discuss the case.'

Her face blanched and he felt terrible.

'There's no need for that. They're just men like the rest of you. They have wives too.'

'Güllich does, but his love for the Führer comes first.'

'Werner,' she hissed, as if the Gestapo man were in the hallway, 'don't say things like that.'

'You see, that's why I comply with their requests; why everyone does.'

She relented.

'Just try and be at Willi's,' she said.

'I'll do my best. I've told Herr Güllich that I must be away by one. I'll meet you there.'

He finished dressing and left the house.

~~o~~

By the time he'd typed up his report and deposited the carbon copy for one of the secretaries to file, his ashtray was full, and a fog of smoke shrouded his corner of the office.

The case annoyed him.

It crossed Werner Schmidt's mind that these people were fundamentally different from the likes of him; a private lake, a boathouse, and the arrogance to suppose that because of who they are, the police would jump at their command.

But they'd all pretty much told the same story.

Most of them couldn't say specifically when they'd last seen Ruth and Manny, but they were sure that, if it wasn't yesterday, then it must have been the day before.

Antje had been more definite. She told the detective that she and Ruth had talked every day, the last time being late in the afternoon of the day they'd gone missing.

'Was there anything different about her?' he'd asked her.

'No,' Antje had replied. 'She was just her usual self. And Manny was full of fun, as he normally was.'

She'd been believable. They'd all been believable.

He had enough time to stop for a coffee in one of Holtenauer Straße's cafés before driving the short distance to Gestapo Headquarters on the corner of Düppelstraße and Moltkestraße.

He was shown in by the junior Gestapo officer he'd met before but whose name eluded him.

Güllich took the report from him and indicated that he should take a seat while he read it.

'So,' he said, looking up at Werner Schmidt, 'you think they're telling the truth?'

'I believe so. Apart from the parents and the Kästner girl, the younger one, they're all very vague about when they last saw the children. If they'd made it up, they would have had their stories better rehearsed.'

'I wouldn't trust these Judenläuse not to pull the wool over their employer's eyes. And in this case, I wouldn't trust that General fellow either. He's already intervened once too often on behalf of these Jews of his.'

'He does seem determined to retain them, but he maintains that it's because they are indispensable to him. I've been told by others, particularly one of the neighbours, who hates the family, incidentally, that she is an excellent cook. "One of the best in Kiel", she said.'

'I've heard that too, but it's no excuse to harbour criminals,' Heinrich Güllich said. He paused.

'I don't just want those Jewish scum,' he said.

'What do you mean, Herr Kriminalassistent?'

'I want him too. The General. I don't like him. There's no excuse for his liberal attitudes.'

'For Christ's sake, Herr Güllich,' Werner Schmidt said, 'you can't be serious. He's an Abwehr general, with a prominent role in the Kriegsmarine in Kiel, a navy town. And he has the ear of Heydrich and the mayor and the police chief. Do you want to end up in some backwater in Poland?'

'This is not about Heinrich Güllich. It is about justice, and the Third Reich. I have a feeling about Herr Kästner, and his family, and I'm willing to risk my career on finding out what it is about them that bothers me.'

Werner Schmidt took out a pack of cigarettes. He offered one to Heinrich Güllich and lit it for him.

What have I become involved in?

He took a long draw of smoke into his lungs and tried to think of a way to drop the investigation. He cursed to himself.

While the children are missing, it is still technically a police matter.

'What else did the General say? Are you sure that's all you spoke about?'

'I wrote everything down, Herr Güllich. It's all in my report.'

It wasn't. He hadn't mentioned the General's comment about the Gestapo. Was this his way out of the case?

He weighed it up, then gambled.

'He did say something that I was loathe to put in my report.'

'Yes. What was it?'

'He asked, hypothetically, he said, if the Gestapo could have anything to do with the children's disappearance.'

The Gestapo man laughed. It surprised Werner Schmidt, as much for the coldness of it as for the fact that the man had a sense of humour.

'And what did you say?'

'I said the Gestapo would never take children like that, illegally.'

'You're wrong, Herr Kriminalassistent. I would happily take their children if I thought it would bring them to heel. But no, it wasn't us. Do you know what I think?'

'No, Herr Güllich.'

The detective felt as if he was sitting in front of his Kriminaldirektor, receiving a dressing-down. It annoyed him.

We're equal in rank.

'I think they have spirited these children away,' Heinrich Güllich said, 'and they are trying to cover for it because they know we are monitoring them.'

For a moment he froze, then his face clouded, and he thumped the table with his fist.

'Verdammt!' he shouted.

'What is it?' the KriPo man said.

'The children. When I visited the other day. They said they were in the cottage, that they'd been told not to answer the door. I should have checked.'

'I don't know what you're talking about, Herr Güllich.'

'I visited the Nussbaums. A routine check, to make sure they were adhering to their conditions of release. I spoke with them, and also to the Kästners, at the big house, after getting no answer at the Nussbaums' cottage. When I asked about the children, they told me that they were at home, but wouldn't answer the door; that it was too dangerous these days. I took them at their word. Fool!'

Werner Schmidt wasn't going to agree with the Gestapo man and irk him even more, but he was glad that Güllich had screwed up. It would be ammunition, should he ever need it.

'Perhaps it was the truth, Herr Kriminalassistent?'

'You're as bad as them. Can you not see they're a nest of vermin, the lot of them?'

'I don't know, Herr Güllich. The General has an Iron Cross and one of his sons does too. Both his sons are making rapid progress through the ranks and they say the General saves the Kriegsmarine millions of marks and thousands of hours of time every year.'

'Nepotism, favouritism. The elite looking after the elite. Well, this is a new Reich, and that sort of way of thinking is on the way out. Our Führer was an ordinary man. A corporal. Those that surround him have come from humble beginnings. One day, all these privileged hangers-on will be ousted, and Germany will be run by people like you and me. And there won't be a Jew in sight.'

A speck of phlegm dribbled from the corner of the Gestapo man's mouth.

Werner Schmidt said nothing. Where it impinged on his job, or his family, he took notice of politics and public opinion, but as for the rest of it, he wasn't interested.

Out of the corner of his eye, he saw the young Gestapo sergeant approach, perhaps curious at the reason for his boss's outburst.

Meyer. That's it! The young Gestapo officer's name is Carl Meyer.

He smiled. He prided himself on his good memory.

'Meyer,' Heinrich Güllich said, 'get ready to go. We're going to pay General Kästner and his Jews another visit.'

'Yes, sir,' the young man said, scurrying away to collect his coat.

'Are you sure there's nothing else, Kriminalassistent Schmidt?' the Gestapo man said.

'No. That's everything. Let me know how you get on.'

'You're welcome to accompany us. To see how our methods compare with yours, and our results.'

He smirked.

'I would normally accept, but I have a family affair I must attend.'

'It's your loss, Kriminalassistent. And thank you for your work so far. It sometimes does no harm to have… what do the Americans call it in their movies… a *good cop, bad cop*, is that it?'

'I believe so.'

He was happy to be the good cop. There were times when he had to rough up a suspect as part of his job, but he didn't tackle it with the relish that Heinrich Güllich applied to his work.

'I'll show myself out,' he said, shaking the hands of the Gestapo men.

CHAPTER 86

By the time *The Shearwater*'s watch changed for the second time, just after lunch, they'd reached the point where the Kattegat, the sheltered stretch of water that ran northwards from the Danish islands between Sweden and Denmark, met the Skagerrak, the exposed straits that separated Denmark from the southernmost parts of Norway, running westwards, and open to the wildness of the North Sea. Before they reached it, with the wind strengthening, Franz had put a reef in the main, and dropped the jib. They'd only seen one other vessel, a destroyer heading south, almost certainly to Kiel.

The Skaw, the world's largest sandspit, jutted thirty kilometres out into the sea, separating the two stretches of water, like a giant talon, piercing the expanse of water that flowed from the Baltic to the North Sea. A mile beyond it, the Skagen Rev lightship marked the end of the shallow reef that extended from its tip.

Franz and Ruth, who'd done their stint between nine and one, sat in the cabin, eating bread and cheese, and drinking coffee.

Ruth shivered, despite the many layers she had on, but the hot coffee, and escaping the cold and wet of the cockpit, began to warm her.

'How are you?' Franz asked her, a concerned frown creasing his face.

'Better for this,' she said, holding up the mug.

'You didn't feel sick, even when the wind got up. That's promising.'

'Yes. It was a good idea to eat a few of Mama's ginger biscuits though. I'm sure it helped.'

'You did well. It's not easy to learn to sail close to the wind, trying to point the boat as far up as possible without losing way. Most people take years to master it, so don't worry about the odd mistake.'

'I'd imagine that Manny is much better than me.'

Franz shrugged. 'Johann says Manny is a natural. He's taken to it like a duck to water, and he's thrown himself into it as if nothing else matters. Johann wonders if it helps him forget everything else.'

'Maybe. He hasn't spoken so much about home in the last few days,' she said. 'I hope he's not bottling it all up.'

'Manny has talked to Johann a little; about Drachensee, and your parents, and about what he's been through.'

'That's good,' she said, but to Franz, she sounded a little hurt. 'It will do him no harm to get it off his chest,' she added.

'If you feel the need to talk, I'm a good listener.'

'I know. It's all a bit raw for now. I don't know what to think.'

'We'll get news tonight. I'll phone Father. Your mama and papa will be desperate for news too.'

'Is that why we're going into harbour tonight?'

'One of the reasons. We need a few supplies; milk, bread, butter, cheese and some fresh vegetables and, anyway, there's no other shelter.'

'I thought we would have had enough provisions for the journey. We have tins of milk, and vegetables. We have flour and eggs.'

'But not enough. Remember there are four of us on board. We couldn't take enough food for us all. It would have raised suspicions with the colonel when he was on board, so we had to buy a few extra supplies in Bogense, and we'll need to do the same in Hirtshals.'

'I see,' she said. 'Won't they get suspicious if you buy too much? After all, we're supposed to be in Norway by the following night.'

'That's not a problem. We can say we intend to anchor for a few nights, but beyond that...'

He glanced at her, wondering how much he should say.

'It may take us a week to cross the Nordsee,' he said, 'depending on the wind direction. You realise that, don't you?'

'I didn't know how long it might take,' she said, blushing. 'I suppose I imagined two or three days.'

'It's nearly 400 miles, in a straight line. If we had the right winds, we can average six knots, which would allow us to do almost 150 miles a day, so, you're not far off. But we may have to deviate from our route if we see Kriegsmarine ships, then there's the weather, and the direction of the wind to consider.'

'Oh. I didn't realise. Could we run out of food?'

'It's unlikely, although it might get less appetising as time goes on. Water might be more of an issue. We'll fill our tank at Hirtshals, along with a few extra Einheitskanisters we have stowed in the stern locker. It should be enough.'

'There's a lot to take into account, isn't there? It hadn't really occurred to me.'

'We do it all the time in the army, planning ahead. Food supplies, fuel, ammunition. It's not just about fighting.'

'I suppose so. Don't they say an army marches on its stomach?'

He laughed.

The boat lurched and she grabbed the table to stop herself falling forward.

'It's a bit rougher here, isn't it?'

'Yes. There's a lot less shelter in the Skagerrak, now that we've lost the protection of land.'

'I think I'll take another ginger biscuit,' she said.

'It might be better if you can chew a little piece of raw ginger. That would be even more effective.'

He rummaged in the locker above the galley and pulled out a little bag. He extracted a dried ginger root and cut off a small sliver with his pocketknife and handed it to her.

She grimaced, but put one end in her mouth and chewed, tentatively.

'It's not so bad,' she said, a slow smile spreading across her face. 'It looked foul.'

He smiled.

'You know where it is if you need it. Another trick that can help is to look at the horizon. I know you can't go out on deck when we're not on watch, but you can still look out through one of the portholes in the coachroof, or through the hatch, as long as you keep your head down.'

'I will, if you think it will help.'

'And keep as warm as you can. Being cold is a sure way to get seasick.'

'I'll try. It was a little cold today. I'll wear extra clothes for the next watch, even if it makes me look like the Michelin Man.'

Franz laughed out loud. Johann stuck his head through the hatch.

'What did you say?' he asked Ruth. 'I haven't heard my brother laugh like that in a long while.'

She blushed.

She explained about the extra clothes being unflattering.

'You still look pretty,' Johann said, before disappearing.

She blushed again and looked at the chart to hide it.

Franz frowned. He made a mental note to have another word with his brother.

'What is this?' she asked. Franz looked at the chart. She was pointing to an area shaded in pencil with cross-hatching that ran from the point of the Skaw to the Swedish mainland, forty miles away.

Franz looked away for a second.

When he turned back to her, he couldn't quite hold her gaze.

'It's another minefield,' he said.

'That whole area?'

'Yes.'

'Aren't we in it now?'

'Possibly. I don't know for sure.'

'Isn't that dangerous?'

'I don't think so, unless we come across a stray mine, which could happen anywhere, to be honest. As I told you before, most of the mines are suspended well below our keel.'

'Why didn't you tell us we were in a minefield?'

'Johann knows. We've been keeping an eye out. I didn't want to worry you, and there was nothing you could do about it anyway.'

'So, we could be sitting here, a couple of feet from however many kilograms of high explosive, primed to go off.'

'Yes, but...'

'But what?'

'We wouldn't know much about it,' he said, his eyes lowered.

She shrugged.

'I suppose you're right. It still makes me nervous though.'

'Me too, I'll be glad when we're through it.'

He looked at the chart again, then at his watch.

'I'll see if we can turn yet. We don't want to end up in Norway. Or Sweden.'

He stood up and looked out of the hatch.

'Can you give me a bearing to the Skagen light?' he asked.

'Yes, but it's not easy see,' Johann said.

Franz poked his head out. He could just make out the lighthouse, its unpainted stone blending in with the grey of the sky.

He watched Johann lift the hand compass and sight it on the tip of the lighthouse.

'Two-three-zero degrees,' Johann said.

'How much of it do you reckon you can see? Half of it?'

'No, but it's hard to say. The top third perhaps?'

Franz did a quick calculation.

'I reckon that matches up with where our estimated position is; about ten to twelve miles away, which means we have all that ground to make up.'

'Yes,' Johann said, 'but we've gone a little further north than I'd thought. We might not be just so close to the wind on this tack.'

A few points off the wind would increase their speed and it would make for a more comfortable sail.

'You can tack, but keep close to the wind for now,' Franz said. 'We can always fall off it later. I'd rather keep upwind of Hirtshals while we can in case it backs to the west later.'

'Fair enough,' Johann said with a groan.

'Ready about,' he shouted.

'Ready,' Manny said.

'We're going about,' Franz said to Ruth. 'Hang on.'

She clung to the handrails in the cabin as Manny, on the helm, turned ninety degrees to port. The boat, leaning hard over to starboard, righted herself, then heeled the opposite way as Manny straightened her onto her course.

Johann tacked the staysail, and for the first time, they headed westwards, crashing through the waves again, this time on the starboard bow.

Franz marked their estimated position on the chart, and, as always, marked the time against it. He filled in the boat's log.

~~o~~

13:50 Skagerrak. SKAGEN Lt 230°M approx.11NM.

Wind 25 knots, nor'westerly. Tack to 260°M. 4.5 knots Passing through minefield at entrance to Kattegat.

CHAPTER 87

Miriam cleared the lunch dishes from the table in the dining room while the Kästners retired to the drawing room for coffee.

Maria and the two girls had returned from church around twelve-thirty and the General had joined them for lunch not long after.

The General heard the doorbell ring and, as Yosef and Miriam were both busy, he asked Antje to see who their caller was.

She returned a few moments later.

'It's Herr Güllich, again. From the Gestapo,' she said, ashen-faced, ushering the Kriminalassistent in, Carl Meyer in tow.

The General got to his feet. He returned the Gestapo officer's Hitler greeting and echoed his barked *Heil Hitler.*

'Ah, Herr Güllich,' he said. 'I suspected you'd pay us a visit. I just didn't expect it so soon.'

'The Gestapo don't sleep, Herr General. Nor do we rest at weekends. Why should we when the Führer doesn't?'

'Indeed. When I was young, like you, I was the same. Alas, I'm now at the age when I need a day's rest.'

He turned to his family.

'You've met my wife, Frau Kästner, of course, and these are my daughters, Eva and Antje.'

'Yes, I met your wife on my last visit, and I've read your daughters' statements.'

The General didn't blink. He saw Maria and the girls stiffen.

'Yes,' the General said, keeping is voice affable. 'Kriminalassistent Schmidt was very thorough when he was here. Most helpful indeed. Has he made any progress?'

'No. But I wonder if his premise is perhaps mistaken.'

'I'm sorry, Herr Güllich?' the General said, frowning.

'He's still convinced that the children are missing, that they've been snatched, or have wandered off.'

Maria Kästner, despite the undercurrent of unease the man provoked, interrupted.

'Herr Kriminalassistent, whatever do you mean? Obviously, the children are missing. Why would we lie about something like that?'

The Gestapo man said snorted. 'I can think of a number of reasons,' he said.

Maria stared at him for a second, then looked away as Yosef came through the doorway, carrying a tray.

'Should I serve the coffee, sir?' he asked.

'Please do, Yosef,' the General said. He turned to Heinrich Güllich. 'Perhaps our guests would like to join us?'

'No thank you, Herr General,' the Kriminalassistent said. 'We will only take a little of your time. Perhaps if I might be permitted to ask a few questions of each of you, somewhere more private.'

'By all means. You can use my study. I'll show you myself. Who do you wish to speak to first?'

'We'll have the mother through to begin with,' the Kriminalassistent said curtly, pointing at Miriam.

The General smiled kindly at Miriam, and she walked slowly to the door. He turned to Yosef.

'There's no reason not to pour the coffees, we'll be back in a moment.'

He motioned for Miriam to go in front of them, then led the two Gestapo men through to his study.

He showed them in.

He told Miriam to sit down. He rounded his desk, to take his own seat.

'We wish to question the woman alone, Herr General,' Heinrich Güllich said. 'We will speak with you later.'

'Oh. I see,' the General said, his voice apologetic and unconcerned, for Miriam's benefit. 'I'll leave you to it.'

~~o~~

When the General had left, Heinrich Güllich nodded at one of the chairs in front of the desk, and Carl Meyer grabbed Miriam's arm, moving her to it.

He had puzzled as to why his superior had shown his hand earlier, asking questions in front of the whole family. He had expected him to interview everyone separately, trying to drive wedges between the cracks in their stories until they fell apart.

But when the Nussbaums had entered carrying trays of coffee and Pralinen, the young Gestapo man wondered if Heinrich Güllich might have been right after all.

Out of the corner of his eye, he'd seen both Nussbaums glance at the General, for reassurance, he presumed, but only briefly. Almost immediately, they'd recovered their composure.

Once Miriam Nussbaum was seated, the Kriminalassistent took the General's chair and regarded her across the desk with unconcealed disgust.

'Your employer is under the illusion that we are here to help you find your children,' the Kriminalassistent said.

He gave a cold smile.

'In a way, he's right.'

Carl Meyer watched for signs of fear, but Miriam Nussbaum didn't flinch, staring instead at a spot on the wall behind the Kriminalassistent.

~~o~~

The General was the last to be questioned. He smiled at the conceit of the man sitting at his desk, in his chair.

'I must say,' the Gestapo man said to the General, 'Your Jewish *friend*s appear to have their stories well rehearsed.'

'That's not a surprise,' the General countered. 'They're telling the truth.'

'Let's not pretend I'm wrong, General. I'll tell you what I think.'

The Kriminalassistent paused, and took out a cigarette from a black case, inscribed with a silver swastika. He offered one to the General, who shook his head, and gave one to his assistant.

'You don't mind?' he said to the General, lighting the cigarette.

'Not at all,' the General said, indicating the ashtray that was on the desk. 'I indulge in the occasional cigar.'

'Now, where was I?' the Gestapo man said. 'Ah, yes. The truth, as I see it. The Nussbaums have reported their children missing, presumably on your advice, something that no other Jews would do in the circumstances. Admittedly, you consider them to be special, privileged Jews, above the law because they provide services to you that are indispensable.'

'I can't argue with that. They are a key part of my household and, as my position allows, they live and work here under my protection, and that of the Abwehr, for whom my work is considered critical.'

Erich Kästner watched, fascinated, as a vein on the Kriminalassistent's neck began to pulse.

'That may be, but it is illegal for Jews to travel in Germany without a permit and it is a serious criminal act for a Jew to leave the country without permission, or for anyone to be complicit in such an act.'

The anger in Heinrich Güllich's voice was barely disguised and, despite appearances, the General felt drops of cold sweat trickling down his spine.

'The Nussbaums, with or without your involvement, have arranged for their brats to be spirited out of the country, or into hiding. I intend to get to the truth of the matter. If they are still in Germany, as I suspect, we will find them and take them into custody, along with their parents. No amount of *protection* from you or the Abwehr could stop me in the face of such a flagrant criminal act.'

'As I say, I have no worries on that score. I have complete faith that the Nussbaums are telling the truth.'

'Then you are either a fool, which I doubt, or are so embroiled in their disappearance that your own position will be put into question.'

The General laughed.

'You overreach yourself, Herr Kriminalassistent, and your fervent imagination is going to get you into trouble. I pray that Kriminalassistent Schmidt will find the Nussbaums' children and that, when the truth is known, you and your assistant here will find yourselves with a great deal of explaining to do.'

'You do realise, Herr General,' Heinrich Güllich said, his eyes almost bulging, 'that when you are disgraced, your sons, who I believe are doing well in the Wehrmacht, will find their careers in the doldrums, if they're lucky; and your daughters, well, they will be pariahs of the genteel society that they are so much part of.'

The General smiled.

'Herr Güllich,' he said, still in the most reasonable voice, 'we are both working for the good of the Reich, but in different ways. The government considers my work to be of enough importance to indulge me in the matter of retaining my Jewish employees, but I can assure you there is no wrongdoing here.'

Heinrich Güllich stood up and leaned across the desk. The General noticed a fleck of spittle at the corner of his lips and subconsciously wiped his own mouth.

'You forget the number of senior military men who have made the mistake of overestimating their importance. I could give you a list but I'm sure you know them all well.'

The Gestapo man walked to the door. He turned.

'As for your importance,' he said, 'you and your kind are dinosaurs. When history looks back on the Third Reich, it is the SS and the Gestapo's part in it that will be remembered.'

'You may be right, Herr Güllich. I just hope for Germany's sake that you're not.'

~~o~~

'Order a tap on the General's phone.'

'Is that wise, sir?'

Heinrich Güllich closed his eyes. Half an hour before, he would have torn a strip off the young officer, but the Kriminalassistent had regained his self-control again since returning from Drachensee and climbing the stairs to his first floor office.

'Yes. It is,' he said, calmly lighting a cigarette. 'Sooner or later, they will communicate with someone about these children, and I want to hear about it.'

'But, sir, we were told to stay away from the General and his Jews.'

'No, you fool. We were told to stop investigating his staff. We are now helping the police with their enquiries into two missing children.'

'Is there any chance they could be telling the truth, sir?'

Heinrich Güllich gave Carl Meyer a withering stare.

'No. The children are either out of the country already, they are in hiding, or they are in transit. If it is either of the latter, we will catch them and, through them, we will prove that the parents and their Jew-loving employer are criminals of the lowest order.'

'And if they're already out of the country?'

'If we can confirm that, we can still use the evidence to deal with the Jews. I doubt if we could pursue the General.'

Carl Meyer opened his mouth to speak, then stopped.

'What is it, Meyer?' Heinrich Güllich said.

'I… I… How do you know they are lying, sir? I mean, all their stories were consistent.'

'I just know, Kriminalassistentanwärter. They were well rehearsed; I'll give them that. And they kept it simple. No over-elaboration, and only a few of them are involved.'

'Sir?'

'They're not all part of it. The Jews are, obviously. The General, nearly certainly. Frau Kästner, most certainly not; she was angry, but at the Nussbaums, and her husband, not at us. I doubt the driver is part of it, or the daughters, although…'

'You think there's a possibility the girls could be involved?'

'Not the older one. She was almost as indignant as the mother. But the younger daughter.

What was her name?'

'Antje, sir.'

'That's right. She admitted she was friendly with the Nussbaum girl. Was she a close enough friend that the Jewish brat would confide in her?'

'She gave no indication of it, sir, but she did look over to her father a couple of times.'

'I think she's her father's daughter. It would make sense if she were a Jew-lover too.'

'The mother didn't seem so keen on their Jewish staff.'

'No. She appears to be a good German. I wonder how she ended up marrying someone so pro-Jewish?'

'Perhaps he wasn't always like that, sir?'

The Kriminalassistent shook his head.

'No. He was always a Jew-lover,' he said. 'He told Werner Schmidt that he and his manservant grew up together as childhood friends. And I've checked. The Jew's father and mother did work for the General's father.'

'We should visit the children's grandparents, sir. Perhaps they're hiding them'

Heinrich Güllich stubbed out his cigarette and glared with a sneer at Carl Meyer.

'I've already looked into it,' he said 'A couple of OrPo constables did a round of the houses in their street. A routine check for unexploded ordnance, they were told. Our colleagues in Hamburg are checking the woman's parents.'

He laughed. 'Why would they send the children there anyway?' he continued. 'They'll all be deported sooner or later.'

'Will the Nussbaum children be deported when we find them?' Carl Meyer asked.

'No, you fool. They'll be sent to a camp if they're not shot immediately. Why should they get a second chance to live like real people?'

'What else can we do, sir?'

'I've requisitioned a car for you, and another Kriminalassistentanwärter. The pair of you can keep an eye on them.'

'You mean, follow them, sir?'

'Just the General. The Nussbaums won't dare set foot outside the property. Just don't let him see you doing it.'

'Yes, sir.'

When Carl Meyer left, Heinrich lit another cigarette and stared across the room, unseeing.

Should I tell the Kriminaldirektor?

He stood, picked up his jacket, and made for the stairs. He stood for a second, his hand on the banister leading up to the Gestapo chief's office, then turned and took the stairs down, two at a time.

CHAPTER 88

After the two Gestapo men had left, the General excused the Nussbaums from service for the rest of the day, ignoring his wife's frown. The supper only needed heating up and he thought that he and Maria were quite capable of doing that themselves.

Since then, no one had spoken to him. Albert the driver, had left, and Maria and Eva had avoided him, strolling outside in the garden. He could see them talking earnestly and looking back at the house. He didn't need to be a lip-reader to know what they were talking about.

His wife's accusing look, after the men had gone, had been more eloquent than any tirade she might have flown into. He didn't think she suspected he was part of a plan to spirit the two younger Nussbaums away, but she detested his attempts to protect them. He still felt terrible about keeping her in the dark, but her innocent indignance had sown enough doubt on the Kriminalassistent's suspicions, he thought, that made upsetting her worthwhile. The same applied to Eva, and Albert too, to a lesser extent.

The Nussbaums had been strong and had stuck to the simple story that they'd agreed on. Antje too, had been convincing, he was sure, although he'd caught Heinrich Güllich looking at her and at himself a couple of times for signs of collusion.

He got up from his chair and looked out. Eva and Maria were sitting at the summer house.

He walked through to the hall and glanced into the empty kitchen, then climbed the stairs, two at a time.

At the top landing, he paused for breath, telling himself that he wasn't as young as he used to be, then crossed to Antje's bedroom. He knocked gently on the door and, hearing a soft voice, let himself in.

He could see that she'd been crying.

He crossed the room and took her in his arms.

'I'm sorry you had to go through that,' he said.

'It wasn't them,' she said. 'I'm just terrified for Ruth; for all the Nussbaums. And I can't talk to anyone about it, but I have to be strong for Miriam and Yosef.'

He felt guilty; he should have realised.

'You can talk to me.' He held her at arm's length and looked at her.

'I'm tremendously proud of you,' he said. 'You did well today. I almost believed you myself.'

She smiled.

'If it's any consolation, I feel the same as you,' he continued. 'The boys, Ruth and Manny, Miriam and Yosef. I'll not rest until they're all safe.'

'I know, Papa. Is there anything else we can do?'

He thought for a second.

'Yosef has been in contact with the Haganah. They're a–'

She interrupted him.

'I know who they are. Ruth told me about them.'

'They haven't got back to him. We need to get a message to them, but I think the Gestapo will be watching me.'

'Do you want me to try?'

'I don't know. They may be watching you too.'

'I'll be careful. How do I get in touch with them?'

'I don't know. I'll have to ask Yosef.'

'Let me know. I'd feel better if I were doing something to help.'

'I'll speak to Yosef. In the meantime, try and act as normal, for your mama. She's not happy about all the goings-on.'

'I know. Are you and Mama all right, Papa?'

He shrugged.

'It's difficult. She's just very worried about everything, and I'm not helping. I'm very bull-headed about the Nussbaums, and Mama just wants it all to go away. She'll come round once we get the Nussbaums to safety.'

'She's wrong, Papa. We must do everything we can for them. We owe them that.'

'I know,' he said, squeezing her hand. He looked around.

On her easel, there was a drawing of Ruth. He stood up and walked over to it. He felt the hotness of tears fill his eyes.

'That's wonderful,' he said, his voice breaking.

'It's almost finished. I started it a while ago, in case I forgot what she looked like.'

He smiled over at her.

'Did Ruth see it?'

'Yes, when it was partly done. She sat for it.'

'Keep it in a safe place. Best not to let Mama see it.'

He closed the door softly behind him. He had to see the Nussbaums.

CHAPTER 89

16:24 SKAGEN LT directly abeam. 3NM (running fix).

Wind 15 knots, nor'westerly. 235°M. 6.0 knots. Close reach.

~~o~~

'That's more like it,' Manny yelled, as *The Shearwater* picked up her heels and flew.

Johann grinned.

'I knew you'd be pleased,' Franz shouted up.

He'd waited until they had a bit of sea room, then called up the course change Johann and Manny had been waiting for.

It was only a twenty-five-degree change, but it made all the difference. Instead of *The Shearwater* sailing tight to the wind, hard-heeled and crashing into every wave, full sail had been hoisted and the sheets had been eased, and they were riding the waves at a shallower angle. The cant of the deck up top and down below, was also less, and more comfortable for her crew.

Manny's job on the helm was easier too. The boat didn't fight him as much and he savoured the chance to look around.

Three miles off the port beam, according to the running fix Johann had done, Skagen lighthouse and the large keeper's house adjoining it were the only objects on land that rose higher than a few metres above the level of the sea.

The long sandy spit and the trailing line of surf that extended a mile or so from the lightship to the lighthouse told of the dangers to ships that they guarded against.

'As far as you can see, that's the Skaw,' Johann said. 'It's the largest natural sandspit in the world and it has grown over thousands and thousands of years, by sand being washed by the sea up the Jutland coast and deposited here. They say it is the equivalent to 80,000 lorryloads of sand every year!'

Manny whistled. He tried to imagine a line of lorries driving along the beach, dumping sand beyond the lighthouse, and hurrying to fetch another load.

'That's over 200 lorryloads a day,' Manny said.

'That's if they work Sundays,' Johann said, laughing.

'The whole of the North Sea coast of Denmark is sand dunes, often with large tidal lagoons in behind them. It's the same with the north German coast, and Holland, with the Frisian Islands.'

'I learned about them at school, in geography.'

Manny's face darkened.

'Didn't you like school?' he asked.

'Yes. Sometimes. I liked to learn, and some of the teachers were great, but most were cruel. And the other children; I had a few friends, but many of them hated us and wouldn't miss a chance to hit us or put us down.'

Neither of them said anything for a minute.

'It was worse when we had to stop going to our Hebrew school,' Manny said, breaking the silence.

'Why? Was it better than your other school?'

'Yes. No. I mean yes,' he said, flustered, then continued.

'What I mean is, it was different. I missed football and a few of the boys who stuck by me, but when I was at Hebrew school, for the first time in a long while, I felt that I belonged.'

Johann shook his head sadly.

'I didn't know,' he said. 'No one should ever have to feel like that.'

'I missed the lessons we got in our old school. We didn't do so much science, or learn about technology at Kleiner Kuhberg, but we studied the Torah and read about our own history, instead of the Kaiser and the Führer.'

'What do you mean?'

'I learned about our spiritual home in Canaan, or Israel, and how Jews from all over the world, especially Germany, are returning. It's called the Diaspora, you know.'

'To Palestine?'

'Yes. My friend Moshe moved there a few years ago, with his family. He used to write to me, but the Gestapo steal all his letters now.'

'It's a pity you didn't go,' Johann said, almost to himself.

'I told them I wanted to, but Mama and Papa said I had to stay with them.'

He paused. A tear trickled down his cheek and he brushed it away quickly, lest Johann see it.

'I wouldn't really have wanted to go without them anyway.'

'Your mama and papa will get there. My father will see to it. Then, after the war, you can be all together again.'

'How long do you think it will last?'

Johann thought for a minute.

'I don't know for sure; I'm just a soldier, but I worry that it will go on for a long time. A year, maybe? It won't be as protracted as our fathers' war; this is a different kind of conflict. It's faster moving, and we have planes that can travel thousands of kilometres to bomb the enemy. No one appears to have the ability or the technology to resist us.'

'If Germany wins, will the whole world be Nazi?'

'Nazi?' Johann said, frowning. 'Is that not what the British call us?'

Manny blushed.

'It's short for Nationalsozialisten. Me and my friends use it. Mama and Papa too.'

'I didn't realise it was used in Germany,' Johann said. 'Anyway, I don't think Germany can invade America. If we can get you there, you'd be safe. Is that why you asked?'

'Yes. Papa tried his hardest to get us there. I suppose there's still a chance that he and Mama will get visas.'

'I'm sure he and the General are trying their hardest. We just need to worry about you.'

'Will Franz be phoning the General tonight?'

'Yes. Once we get to Hirtshals.'

'Can you ask him to pass on a message again?'

'I'll try my best. What do you want him to say?'

'Tell Mama and Papa I know how to sail a boat now.'

Johann laughed. He stared at Manny for a second.

'Do you know,' he said, 'I really think you do. Perhaps we should make you the skipper,' he teased.

'Oh, no. I didn't mean that. I just want them to know that they don't need to worry.'

'I know,' Johann said. He almost ruffled the boy's hair but held back, not wanting to patronise him.

'I'll say to Franz. We shouldn't be long getting to Hirtshals at this speed.'

He looked at his watch.

'Ten minutes to change of watch.'

Manny's face fell.

'Can we not just carry on? They might not notice.'

'No. We have to keep the routine going. It will be important later. Anyway, you and I have done the tough bit, around Skagen. Few young men of your age have done that.'

Another tear fell down Manny's cheek.

If Papa could see me now, he would be so proud.

CHAPTER 90

'Sir, do you think he knows?' Yosef asked.

The General shook his head.

'He suspects that Ruth and Manny are in hiding, or have been sent away, but he has no idea about the boat.'

'How did he know?' Miriam asked. 'We didn't give anything away, did we?'

'No. It's nothing like that. He's just a suspicious bas…'

He stopped.

'Sorry, Miriam.'

'You were right, sir. He is a bastard.'

The General smiled.

'He is indeed, but a clever one. I'm not sure his assistant is convinced, and the policeman certainly had no idea.'

'So, it's just a shot in the dark, sir?' Yosef said.

'I think so. But he'll be watching us closely now, and he'll have put out a bulletin to all Gestapo offices with Ruth and Manny's pictures.'

'Even in Denmark, sir?'

'Yes. And Norway too. Anywhere the Gestapo have a presence.'

Etched lines of worry showed on both the Nussbaums' faces.

'They only have one further stop, before they strike out across the North Sea and they know to remain hidden, so it makes no difference if the Gestapo sends out all the photographs in the world.'

'Unless they get caught, sir.'

The General flinched at Yosef's words.

He's right. If they are caught, there had been a slim chance that Franz and Johann could have talked their way out of it, but not now.

'They won't get caught, but we must do our part. Herr Güllich and his sidekick will probably return, most likely when I'm not here. Just remember to stick to your story and, for God's sake, don't try and embellish it. Keep it simple. It will only be for another few days, or perhaps a week, then they're safe.'

'How will we know, sir?'

'We won't. At least for a while. But they'll get word through to us, somehow.'

He hesitated.

'Now, we have to do something about you two. I'm going to telephone the American consulate today, to try and get them moving on your visas. In the meantime, we need to get in touch with the Haganah. How do I contact them?'

Yosef and Miriam glanced at one another.

'Look,' the General said. 'You'll have to trust me.'

'I'm sorry, sir. It's just that we've been told never to give out the information to anyone who isn't Jewish. I don't know how they'll react if you try and get in touch with them.'

'Well, you can't. Anyway, it won't be me. Antje will do it.'

'Sir. You can't risk her doing this.'

'She wants to. She's breaking her heart about Ruth. She wants to help.'

Yosef turned to Miriam.

'They might be more willing to trust Antje.'

Miriam shook her head, but Yosef gripped her hand.

'It may be our only hope,' he said.

'Yosef's right,' the General added. 'Anyway, I'll have someone keep an eye on her. From a distance.'

He racked his brain to think of who would be best. Captain Bauer didn't have the guile. Oskar would be ideal, but his face was too well known and, anyway, he didn't want to test Oskar's loyalty.

Dieter. He would do it.

The General froze.

'What's wrong, sir?' Yosef said, his face a mask of concern.

'Dummkopf!' he hissed. 'How could I be so stupid?'

'What, sir?'

'We don't have to use Antje. I have another way.'

'How, sir?'

It was the General's turn to be secretive.

'Don't worry, my friends. You don't need to know. Give me your contact anyway in case it doesn't work.'

Yosef wrote the name on a piece of paper, along with an address.

'Sir, will Franz be calling you today?'

'I hope so. They should get to Hirtshals tonight. I'll let you know.'

'Be sure and pass on our love, sir.'

'Of course I will.' He lowered his eyes, unable to face the depth of their sadness.

'This will be their last contact, won't it, sir?'

'Yes. I hope so.'

'Will you also tell Franz and Johann that we can never repay them for what they've done for us. We know what it means for them.'

'I will. Is there anything else?' The General struggled to keep his voice from breaking.

'Yes,' Miriam said firmly. 'Ask him to tell Manny to say his prayers and be respectful.'

The General laughed and it broke the spell of gloom.

'They'll be all right,' he said, almost believing it.

~~o~~

The telephone rang on Heinrich Güllich's desk. He picked up the handset.

'Kriminalassistent Güllich.'

'Elmar Dürer, Deutsche Reichspost.'

'Ah. Guten tag.'

'It's about your call-monitoring request.'

'Yes,' he said, the cold chill of doubt sending a trickle of sweat running down his back; in the past, he'd always gone through his superiors when setting up a wiretap.

'It's in place, although it is a little irregular.'

'Irregular? Why?' Heinrich Güllich fumbled for a cigarette. He lit it at the third attempt.

'The phone number is for a General Kästner, sir.'

'That's correct. Just because the man is a general, it doesn't mean he shouldn't be investigated. Anyway, this is mainly to eliminate him from our enquiries,' he lied.

'Oh, it's not that, sir. More than a few of our requests are for the telephone lines of high-ranking officials. It's not even that this man is a member of the Abwehr.'

'Then what's the problem?'

'There's no problem, Herr Kriminalassistent. It's just that the General's phone is already being monitored.'

Heinrich Güllich sat back in his seat, his face drained of colour.

'Who authorised it?' he croaked, his voice half an octave higher. He took a long, slow draw on his cigarette.

'I'm sorry, sir. I can't divulge that information,' he heard the man say.

'I understand. Will the other party be informed of our request?'

'I can't tell you that either, sir. Do you wish to proceed with the monitoring request?'

For a second, he hesitated. He was getting himself involved in something outside his jurisdiction. It could be opening a giant can of worms.

'Yes. Carry on. The usual process?' he said brusquely, as if he did this every day.

'Yes, sir. We will send you daily transcripts of all calls. Recordings are available. Do you have any key words, Herr Güllich?'

'Key words?' he said, still speculating on who else could be listening to the General's calls.

'Yes, sir.'

'Of course,' Heinrich Güllich said, cursing his stupidity. If the Reichspost operator heard any words that had been flagged up, he or she would contact the Gestapo immediately.

He thought for a second.

'Any of these,' he said. 'Jew. Haganah.'

'Could you spell that please, sir'

'H-A-G-A-N-A-H.'

'Thank you. Anything else?'

'Nussbaum. Immanuel. Ruth. Miriam. Yosef. And Jakob Teubner.'

'Is that all, Herr Kriminalassistent?'

Heinrich Güllich wondered if he could detect a hint of sarcasm in the man's voice, but he let it go.

'Yes. Thank you.'

He put the phone down and stubbed out his cigarette.

The office door opened, and Carl Meyer walked in.

'What are you doing here?'

'Sir. I left Kriminalassistentanwärter Seidel at the General's house, with the car. I hailed a taxi. The General has settled in for the night. I said I'd come and see you. We were wondering if we should do shifts.'

Heinrich Güllich cursed himself. He should have told them. He was getting too immersed in the case.

'You should have stayed,' he said harshly. 'I was just about to come and tell you to do shifts.'

The Kriminalassistentanwärter paled.

'I'm sorry, sir. It was just…'

'Try not to tax your brain too much, Meyer. It isn't built for it.'

'When will I relieve Kriminalassistentanwärter Seidel, sir?'

'Do four hours each.' He looked at his watch. '6pm. I'll run by Drachensee and tell Seidel.'

'I can go home, sir?'

'What do you think this is, Meyer? A holiday camp? We are in the middle of a critical investigation.'

Carl Meyer paled again.

'Send out for food and get a cup of coffee down you,' Güllich said, 'and don't move from that phone. If there's a call from the Reichspost about the General, let me know.'

'Where will you be, sir?'

'I'll telephone. Just take a note.'

CHAPTER 91

Manny cursed, and tried to peer out the starboard porthole.

He'd only just come off watch, around ten minutes before, when he heard Franz shout.

'Whales. Off the starboard bows. Two of them.'

He heard Ruth's squeal of delight and looked, pleading, at Johann.

'What kind are they?' Johann shouted.

'Orcas,' Franz replied.

'I didn't think they'd come this far into the Skagerrak,' Johann said.

'Look, they're awfully close,' Ruth shouted.

Manny still couldn't see them.

'Come up, Manny,' Franz said. 'I'll swap with you for a minute.'

Manny waited until Franz had descended the companionway steps, then shot up into the cockpit. Johann and Franz watched through the companionway as brother and sister stared at the two killer whales, looks of wonderment on their faces.

'Remember to keep an eye out for other boats, and mines,' Franz shouted up, smiling. 'You two are in charge now.'

Ruth looked around nervously. It was the first time neither of the Kästner brothers had been on deck, telling them what to do, but Manny laughed.

After a while, he stuck his head down into the cabin.

'Do you want to see them, Johann? They're fantastic.'

'Ach, no. You enjoy them,' Johann replied.

'You've got to see them, Johann,' Ruth shouted, so he nodded and gestured for Manny to come down.

~~o~~

Once Johann was on deck, he was glad of it. The two graceful sea mammals effortlessly kept pace with the yacht, and they were wonderful to watch.

He looked up at the sails. Franz had put a reef in to make the steering lighter for Ruth, and he'd dropped the larger of the two foresails.

'I reckon we're doing six and a half knots and they're not even trying,' he said to Ruth. 'Let's see if they speed up when we do.'

He went forward and shook out the reef on the main and hoisted the jib. *The Shearwater* surged forwards, spray flying as the waves caught her beam and lifted her over the crests.

He thought about the topsail but decided against it in case the wind backed and left them over-canvassed, in a sea that wouldn't make reducing sail easy.

Ruth was infected by his boyish excitement, fighting the wheel to ride the waves and extract every ounce of speed from the heavy boat.

Johann watched her. Even with all her layers on, and a woollen hat covering her short hair, he thought she looked wonderful. She was too wrapped up watching the sea, and the whales, to notice his brazen scrutiny. If she had, she would have blushed.

'She sails well when you get enough canvas flying,' he shouted, over the gusting of the wind.

'Franz says it's better not to have so much sail up that you have to fight it.'

'He's an old man,' Johann said. He laughed. 'Too much excitement isn't good for his heart.'

'Now you're being cruel,' she said, giggling. 'I thought Franz loved racing.'

'He does, but deep down he prefers cruising. My father is the same. A great racing sailor but happiest on a quiet anchorage, listening to nature.'

'And you?'

'I need speed, and excitement, like this. I mean, look at these whales. We're probably doing over seven knots now, with every halyard and stay straining, but these animals are keeping up with us without even trying.'

'We're not racing them,' she said, laughing.

'If we had our competition boat, I reckon we could give them a run for their money.'

'How fast does that go?'

'Eleven, twelve knots on a reach, with full sail in sheltered waters.'

'That's nearly twice as fast as us. What does it feel like?'

'Like you're flying. And you want to beat the other boat so badly.'

He smiled at her. A wave knocked the bow off and she fought to bring it back round. He reached over and gripped the wheel, helping her.

She gave him a grateful smile.

'So, you're better than Franz at racing then? Why is he always the skipper?'

'Ah,' he said, laughing. 'There's a question.'

He paused and took a deep breath.

'If Franz and I were sailing dinghies on our own, against each other, and in decent winds, I might just edge it, because I'll push it just that little bit harder. In light winds, or in very strong winds, Franz would win. He's a better tactical sailor when the wind drops and has this uncanny knack of knowing when to reduce sail in a blow.'

'What about big yachts, like your army one?'

'If Franz isn't there, I'll skipper her, and do it well, but when it comes to someone choosing a skipper for a boat, they'll pick Franz nine times out of ten.'

'Why, if you're just as good?'

'On the water, I can compete, but Franz can train a crew and manage them much better than me, and he looks after the boat like a mother with a child. And he's shrewd.'

'What do you mean?'

'I love nothing better than screaming past another boat or flying round inside them at a mark, leaving them trailing in our wake. Franz beats other boats by out-thinking them. It's not always as exciting, but it wins more races.'

'So why don't you do all the stuff Franz does?'

He shrugged and smiled.

'I get bored,' he said. 'Anyway, the thing is that it turns out that together, we make a great team. There are times during a race when he'll let me push the boat as hard as I can, burying the gunwales under water with two men on the wheel just to hold our course. On other occasions, when I think we should be going all out for it, he'll take a different tack to the other boats. Before you know it, we're at the head of the fleet.'

'You don't resent him for it?'

'Hell, no. I'll be sitting in the bar celebrating with the crew and Franz will still be going over the boat with a fine-tooth comb, making sure there's not a screw loose or a frayed rope anywhere and that the covers are properly on, and that all the warps are correct.'

'And on this trip. You're happy to leave it to Franz?'

'Even here, we work as a team. We did all the passage planning together and we both navigate but Franz does all the victualling, and a host of things behind the scenes that make everything go smoothly. If something happened to him, I'd step in and do his job but, while he's here, I'm more than happy he's the man in charge. Don't worry, there'll be no mutiny.'

She laughed this time.

'Look,' she said, pointing at the sea, 'they're even closer now.'

Sure enough, the two whales were almost within touching distance. It was as if they were playing with the boat, daring her to go faster.

'The other thing,' Johann said, looking back at Ruth, 'is that if something terrible happens, like we're knocked down, or get holed, or someone falls overboard, there's no one else I'd rather have in command, except perhaps my father.'

~~o~~

Ruth shivered. It was as if he'd flicked a switch, and the day had lost its warmth. His face, so carefree a moment ago, had mislaid its perpetual grin, and had a bleakness on it that she would not have believed possible.

She looked ahead, and could see nothing but grey sky, dark sea and white crests and wondered if he was thinking the same. Very soon, they would turn the boat westwards, and head out into that emptiness.

For a minute, neither of them said anything, then the sun broke through the clouds and lit up *The Shearwater*, and the sea around them.

The greys and blacks turned blue again, and a smile lit up Johann's face.

'I'd better go. Let the old man up,' he said, laughing.

'It's been good talking to you,' she said softly.

He slipped down below.

When Franz came up, she smiled at him.

'They're still here,' she said, seeing his frown.

He smiled, but it barely reached his eyes.

He's worried about tonight. Going into harbour. About Manny and I.

~~o~~

Franz was worried about their visit to Hirtshals. It was their last stop, he hoped, in German-held territory, and it was a busy harbour, but that wasn't what was at the forefront of his mind. Neither was the threat of Ruth falling for Johann's charms although he could have done without the distraction.

The weather concerned him the most.

We need a storm to hide us.

He knew that they could delay a day, or maybe two, waiting for the weather to close in, but every hour spent in the harbour risked exposure, and the catastrophe that would accompany it for both the Nussbaums and the Kästners.

He wasn't an intensely religious man, but he muttered a short prayer under his breath, then stared out across the Skagerrak westwards, willing a storm to come.

He didn't know how long he'd sat until he heard Ruth's voice.

'When will we get to Hirtshals?' she asked.

'A couple of hours at most,' he said, giving himself a shake.

'We'll have to hide again, won't we?'

'I'm afraid so. And it may have to be in the bilges. They might want to do a quick search of the boat, seeing as we're leaving Denmark.'

'Don't worry,' she said. 'It won't be for long. We can suffer it.'

He looked up at her.

Was she falling under Johann's spell?

He'd heard their laughter and had seen the excitement on Ruth's face when he had come back out. He wouldn't have minded if she and Johann became more than friends, if Johann had been the type to be serious and considerate, but he wouldn't see her used and discarded like most of his brother's women.

He made a mental note to get Johann off the boat with him tonight.

We need to talk.

He wondered if he should warn Ruth but, if he did, he might ruin the easy closeness of the crew and introduce undercurrents that would put them in danger, when conditions became critical.

He cursed Johann for giving him an extra worry, when it was the last thing he needed.

Then he relented.

There wasn't a bad bone in Johann's body. He was sure he didn't deliberately set out to break girls' hearts and, in all probability, Johann had been let down often enough by girls to know what it felt like.

On the positive side, the opportunities for Johann and Ruth to be together would disappear once they struck out across the North Sea; they couldn't afford to deviate from the schedule of watches, and anything between them would be snuffed out before it started.

He looked out at the two orcas, then at Ruth. This time his smile was genuine.

Enjoy these simple pleasures while you can.

For another ten minutes, they watched as the whales kept station with *The Shearwater*, sometimes a hundred metres away, often closer.

Then, with an imperious flick of their flukes, first one was gone, and then the other. Franz looked up at the sails and smiled. He thought about putting a reef back in; he could see Ruth fighting the helm at times, but she appeared to be enjoying the battle, and *The*

Shearwater was singing. He eyed the bar-tight stays and their tackles but put them out of his mind. On a boat like this, everything was over-engineered and could take almost anything the sea could throw at it, if the crew did the right thing.

CHAPTER 92

Two miles out from Hirsthals, with a fishing boat in sight, Franz sent Ruth below. Johann joined him on deck and began preparing the boat for entering the port.

'Are we going in under sail?' he asked, half a mile from the harbour mouth.

'We'll see how busy it is with fishing boats. If it's too tight, we'll motor in.'

'I'll drop the main first, and the jib, until we see what's happening.'

'No. You take the helm. I'll work the deck.'

Johann grinned.

'I'll try not to wreck anything,' he said.

Franz frowned and shook his head. He knew Johann was joking and was as capable as he was of berthing *The Shearwater*.

Once they'd stowed the main on the boom, they approached the harbour mouth and heaved-to on the mizzen and foresail, slowly drifting past the entrance to get a look inside.

'There are a lot of boats,' Franz shouted, standing at the bow, 'but there's plenty room to swing round. We can tie up to one of the fishermen. They'll soon move us if they need to.'

He walked back to Johann.

'Go on the inside of the Tværmolen,' he said. 'That's the pier that runs across the way. There's only one boat abreast at the end.'

'I'll be coming in starboard-side-to. Are you happy with that?'

'Yes. As long as you're into the wind. Go for it.'

Franz let out the staysail sheet as the boat turned slowly and Johann steered it through the entrance.

'Watch your speed,' Franz said, luffing the mizzen to the centre line to depower it. He could see fishermen on the boats clustered around the harbour, and others on the harbour wall, stopping what they were doing and lifting their heads to watch.

Johann twisted the wheel from side to side in successive quick turns which barely deflected *The Shearwater*, but the rudder acted like a brake, slowing her down.

They swung wide and approached the pier almost upwind, using the last of the way on the boat to sidle up to a large fishing vessel. A couple of hands caught their ropes and sullenly slipped them over the bollards on the trawler's stern quarter and shoulder.

'Another surly bunch,' Johann whispered under his breath.

'What do you expect? It's the same as in Bogense. Why should they be friendly to us when we've invaded their country?'

'Were they always like that?'

'No. When father and I sailed to Norway in '34 we found the Danes and the Norwegians to be more than friendly.'

'Ah well, at least this way we shouldn't get visitors and, with any luck, there'll be no Kriegsmarine vessels berthed here.'

They led their spring lines fore and aft and ran a bow line and a stern line loosely to the shore. If the fishing boat wanted to leave before them, it could slip *The Shearwater*'s stern line, and pass it round behind them. It would then be up to Franz and Johann to tighten it up, and pull themselves against the jetty when it left, and rig new spring lines.

'God aften,' Franz said, in passable Danish. *Good evening.*

'God aften,' one of the fishermen replied, a flicker of surprise on his face.

'Havnenmesteren. Vil han stadig være her?' Franz said.

The harbour master. Will he still be here?

'Ja. Han kommer snart ned. Han så dig komme ind.'

Franz smiled and nodded. The harbour master had seen them come in. He told Johann that they could expect a visit shortly.

'Jig lavir noget koffe,' Johann said, going below, trying out his own Danish on the fisherman.

Franz relaxed a little, knowing he would tell Ruth and Manny to hide.

'Your Danish is excellent,' the man said, speaking slowly so that Franz could understand. 'Your friend is not so good.'

Franz laughed. 'He's my brother. I have Danish enough to get by.'

The man grunted.

'It's better than that. You are German, I see,' he said, pointing to the flag. 'You are sailing around Denmark during a war?'

'No,' Franz said, smiling. 'We are heading for Norway, tomorrow.'

Franz explained that they were delivering their commanding officer's boat to Bergen.

'Good luck,' he said. 'The weather is to turn, they say.'

'We hope to get to Bergen by the end of the week.'

The man's eyebrows rose.

'That's a trip,' he said.

'We'll aim for Grimstad tomorrow, then, when we get the weather, hop up the coast over three or four days to Bergen.'

'It's feasible. In fair weather. But I wouldn't risk it if a storm is coming.'

'We're tight for time. If we can get across the Kattegat, we can leave it at any port, and return to our Kompanie. We can collect it later when the weather improves.'

The man turned. A short stocky man in a dark uniform was approaching.

'Our harbour master. I will leave you to it.'

'One thing,' Franz said. 'When are you leaving in the morning?'

'Around five. We will slip out behind you and tie you up, don't worry.'

'Thank you. I'll get up to redo our lines. Just give me a shout.'

The man shrugged and shook Franz's hand. He turned to the harbour master and spoke rapidly, too quick for Franz to understand it all, but he caught enough to realise that the fisherman was recounting Franz's story to him.

The harbour master stepped aboard *The Shearwater* and spoke gruffly to Franz, in rusty German.

'You stay overnight? Norway tomorrow?'

'Yes. We hope to buy a few provisions at the shop. When does it open in the morning?'

'Around seven-thirty. My wife runs it. You want her open early?'

'No. Seven-thirty is fine. We hope to leave at eight. How much do we owe for the berth?'

'Ach. I not require payment. If feeling generous, place kroner in collection box for seamens' mission. Is in my wife's shop.'

'We'll do that. Would you like a coffee? It's freshly made.'

The man's eyes lit up.

'Perhaps something in coffee?' he said, grinning.

'Ah,' said Franz. 'A man after my own heart.'

Franz showed the harbour master down the companionway and followed him below.

The man greeted Johann in German and Franz smiled at his brother's relieved grin. Johann offered him a mug of coffee and Franz found the rum bottle and added a tot to each mug.

For the next half hour, Franz and Johann were treated to a potted history of Hirtshals Havn, learning that it was only completed ten years before, and that it had been a key fishing harbour and ferry port, with daily sailings to Kristiansand in Norway.

'The ferry has been suspended since beginning of the war,' the harbour master said. 'Now only get German troop transports from Norway.'

'What about the fishing boats?' Franz asked, trying to make it sound like idle curiosity.

'There are less boats, and they make us paint them black, and remove our radios. The fuel is heavily rationed, and our fishermen given strict areas to fish by German authority, but our boys constantly flout the rules to find catch. The Germans sometimes make example of one or two. Quite a few boats still fish over near England.'

'Don't they ever get captured?' Johann asked.

'By British? One or two, yes.' He weighed up Franz and Johann for a few seconds.

'Sometimes think they do on purpose, to go Britain.'

'Does the Kriegsmarine not patrol those areas?' Franz asked.

'Not so much. They have bigger fish to cook.' He laughed.

~~o~~

In the bilges, Ruth shut her eyes and groaned silently as the man accepted yet another drink and rabbited on about his harbour. An age dragged past before she heard him get to his feet and tell them that his wife would have his evening meal ready. She breathed out and looked across in the dimness to Manny.

He was asleep. She couldn't decide whether to laugh or cry.

She heard the man climbing the companionway steps, followed by Franz. The boat rocked slightly as they stepped off onto the quay.

She winced. Despite the blanket she was lying on, the bilge was cold, hard, and uncomfortable. Five long minutes later, Johann lifted the boards and Manny woke up, blinking in the light coming in the hatch.

'We shouldn't have any more visitors tonight,' Johann said. 'Franz is away with the harbour master, who has offered to let him use the telephone in his office. I'll make the dinner.'

'I'll help,' Ruth said, and she was rewarded with one of Johann's smiles. She blushed. For a moment, she forgot where she was and who they both were.

She understood why women were so attracted to him.

Franz would be just as handsome if he weren't so serious.

She watched Johann make a face at Manny, and her brother's face crack into a grin.

Sometimes, he doesn't appear to have a care in the world.

She shook her head, remembering her promise to her nine-year-old self that she would marry him one day, then reached into the locker behind the stove, lifting out a handful of potatoes from the sack, putting the memory out of her mind.

She began preparing the potatoes while Johann chopped the cabbage and set it to boil in water and vinegar.

By the time Franz returned, the food was cooked. Johann drained the water from the potatoes and added a wedge of lard. He put it back on the stove and threw in the salted beef he'd chopped up, and a few small onions.

As it sizzled, Ruth laid out the bowls and the cutlery, and drained the cabbage.

The kettle was set to boil and, when Franz returned, they sat down to eat.

They were all ravenously hungry. It had been a long time since their lunch of bread and cheese, and the cold wind had sapped their energy.

'Did you get through?' Johann asked, between mouthfuls.

'Yes.' He turned to Ruth and Manny. 'My father couldn't say much, but he told me that everyone at Drachensee is missing us terribly and they all hope that the rest of the voyage is just as successful. I'm guessing that message was for all of us, but especially you two.'

Manny and Ruth fought to keep the disappointment from their faces.

'Oh, and we've to remember and say our prayers,' Franz added, laughing.

'That's Mama,' Ruth said, smiling now. 'It's for you, Manny.'

Manny blushed, and turned away, worried that the Kästner brothers would see the wetness in his eyes.

'Did you tell them what I asked you to?' he asked, anxiously.

'I couldn't mention you or Ruth as such, but I told them that the youngster was learning fast and enjoying his first trip this far north. My father will know I wasn't talking about Johann.'

It appeared to satisfy Manny.

Ruth poured mugs of coffee for everyone. As they sat eating the last of the scones that Miriam had baked, dunking them in their coffee to take away the staleness, Ruth yawned.

She immediately apologised.

'Don't be sorry. It's been a long day, and hard too,' Johann said. 'You both did a great job today.' He gave her a broad smile, making her blush.

'Manny somehow managed to fall asleep in the bilges,' she said. 'I wish I could.'

'That's because he has nerves of steel,' Johann said, patting Manny on the back. The teenager grinned at him.

'I think we'll head to bed, as soon as we've cleared up here,' Ruth said.

'That's not a bad idea,' Franz said. 'Get as much sleep as you can because from tomorrow, it will be harder to come by.'

'I might have a nightcap,' Franz said to Johann. 'Care to join me?'

Because the wind had dropped, they sat out in the cockpit, hanging an oil lamp on the boom to see by. They each had a measure of rum, seeing the bottle had been cracked open.

'Ruth knew that there was more to that phone call,' Johann said.

Franz cocked his head.

'You think so?'

'Yes. I could tell you were holding back, and I'm sure she could too. That's why she went to bed so early and took Manny with her.'

Franz nodded.

'Well, you're both right. There have been developments.'

'With the authorities? Already?'

'Yes. Father made a point of informing me that Ruth and Manny had gone missing the day before yesterday and said that he'd reported it to the police.'

'He'd only do that if he had to. Something must have happened.'

'I don't know. He couldn't say. But there's worse. The Gestapo are now involved. They suspect that the Nussbaums, perhaps with his help, are trying to get Ruth and Manny out of Germany.'

'They haven't guessed that they're with us, have they?'

'No, I doubt it. When he asked about our trip, he sounded very casual and unconcerned.'

'What else did he say?'

'That everyone; he, Mother, Albert, Eva and Antje all had seen them the day they went missing, or the day before.'

'How did he manage to get them to do that? He must have told them.'

'I don't think he would. He'd keep it between the Nussbaums, Antje and himself, I'm sure.'

'Anything else?'

'It appears that we're going to get our storm. The weather station in Greenland is reporting cyclonic winds, associated with an area of low pressure to the south of Greenland, travelling rapidly east, and so far, the forecasts have been reliable.'

'Good. It's our chance,' Johann said, rubbing his hands.

'We'll have to make for Grimstad to start with; Father says there's a small Kriegsmarine squadron just leaving Kiel, heading for Stavanger. They're going to keep an eye out for us.'

Johann groaned. 'That's all we need.'

'It's not a bad thing. They'll be passing us by about midday. It will corroborate our passage plan if they see us, and they'll not look for us further west when we go missing.'

'True. What about fishing boats?'

'The harbour master says they'll head round into the Kattegat if the barometer's dropping fast. The fishing is poorer, but it's sheltered, and they can run for Skagen Havn if they need to.'

'So, this is it. We're going.'

'It looks like it. If we can get 100 miles out before the storm passes, we should be outside any shipping lanes, not that there is much merchant shipping out there, but the Kriegsmarine use the same routes, even on patrol.'

'We're keeping the same watches?' Johann asked.

'Yes. It's working fine. No point in changing it.'

Johann sighed.

'It's maybe for the best. I think I'm falling in love.'

'I know. I suspect Ruth has a soft spot for you too.'

Johann shook his head. 'It doesn't matter now, does it?'

Franz put his hand on Johann's shoulder.

'No. It wouldn't work,' he said. 'If we make it to Britain, we will be in separate camps from them. If Ruth and Manny are released, Ruth is going to try and arrange for them to travel to America.'

'I know, but it will be a painful week.'

Franz grinned. 'Once you see those English roses, you'll forget all about Ruth.'

Johann laughed, but it had a hollow ring to it.

'I don't think we'll see an English rose, or any other woman, for a long time.'

Franz was relieved. He'd wondered how he would bring the subject of Ruth up, and how he would warn his brother off without being cruel about it.

'Another?' Johann said, pulling the cork from the bottle.

'I think I'll pass. I want to be sharp for tomorrow.'

'What time do we leave?' Johann said, replacing the cork with a wistful look.

'Around eight, but we need to pick up some supplies first. You can come with me; it will take two of us to carry them back.'

Johann lifted the two glasses and took them down below. Franz sat, looking at the lights of the small town.

He thought about Ruth, and his brother. He could be wrong; perhaps Johann was serious about Ruth. She certainly liked him, immensely. He knew he had a duty to protect her, but an uneasy question kept swimming around in his mind.

Is it jealousy? Aren't you a little in love with her yourself?

CHAPTER 93

'Dummkopf. Scheißkerl.'

Heinrich Güllich stood over a cowering Carl Meyer, his face red, the veins in his neck standing out. The young Kriminalassistentanwärter's hands came up in self-defence.

'I'm not going to hit you, fool,' the Kriminalassistent spat, 'but it is tempting.'

'But, sir, there was nothing suspicious in the telephone calls.'

'That may yet prove to be the case, but it is I who'll be the judge of that. Never, I repeat, never, make that mistake again.'

Carl Meyer shrank from the venom in his superior's voice.

'I'm sorry, sir.'

'You should have told me the moment I got back.'

'I apologise, Herr Kriminalassistent. I forgot in all the excitement.'

Heinrich Güllich had returned just as two suspected communists had been brought in. One had been living underground for over a year and had been organising whatever opposition there was in Kiel from his bolthole.

Even the Kriminalassistent had got caught up in the uproar that had greeted him when he stepped into the office. It wasn't until an hour later, when he'd left the crowd of spectators watching the initial stages of the traitors' interrogations, that Carl Meyer had remembered the call, and had told him.

'That's no excuse,' he said, still shouting.

Carl Meyer glanced around, glad that the office was deserted. A muffled scream rose from the interrogation room, in the basement.

'Have you had a look at it, sir?'

'Briefly. You're lucky it's not more critical or I'd have your testicles for Christmas decorations.'

Carl Meyer flinched. He wasn't even sure that the Kriminalassistent was joking.

'There were a few other calls, sir,' he said, trying to distract his boss. 'The Reichspost man only mentioned them because he telephoned about this one.'

'And you've written everything down?'

'Yes, sir. And they're sending over a transcript in the morning, first thing.'

'I should make you walk over to the exchange and get it now.'

He picked up Carl Meyer's notes and studied them again, then threw them at the Kriminalassistentanwärter.

'As I said, it's lucky for you.'

Relief flooded into the young Gestapo man's face. There were times he wished he'd stayed with the KriPo.

'I would have said, sir, if I'd thought…'

'I've told you, don't think the next time. Just do as you're told.'

Carl Meyer fumed. He couldn't win. First, the Kriminalassistent tells him to use his brain; the next, to act like a drone.

His face showed only contrition.

'The Nussbaums' name triggered the call from the Reichspost,' Heinrich Güllich said. 'Either the General wasn't involved, or he suspects he has a wiretap. I wonder how long they've been listening to him.'

'Who are they, sir?'

'It has to be the SD.' *Sicherheitsdienst.* The security services' intelligence unit. Like the Gestapo, it was part of the SS.

'But why are they listening to General Kästner?'

'Because the state security service doesn't trust military intelligence. For all we know, they're all listening to each other. The one thing we do know is that it must have been sanctioned at the highest level. The Reichspost man had no intention of telling us anything.'

'You mean Heydrich, sir?'

'It could be, but it may even have come from Himmler. Herr Kästner seems to move in those sorts of circles.'

'Are you sure we should be meddling, sir?'

'We're not meddling. We're doing our jobs. Anyway, they'll either ignore us, watch what we're doing to see if we stir anything up, or pay us a visit to warn us off.'

Heinrich Güllich reached out and picked up the sheet closest to him.

'Give me the others,' he said.

His assistant picked up the rest of the sheets and handed them to his superior.

The Kriminalassistent read them again, scrutinising each word with care.

'What a waste of a time,' he said, his face screwed up in disgust. 'Don't they realise there's a war on? Sailing indeed.'

'Everyone in Kiel is talking about it. At least, those with any connections with the Kriegsmarine.'

'Why? Because two privileged army toffs decide to sail to Norway? It's a waste of Wehrmacht resources, in my opinion. It verges on the criminal. Their commanding officer should know better, but he's from the same privileged background as the General.'

'Yes, sir,' Carl Meyer said, wishing he'd kept his mouth shut.

'I'll tell you what it does confirm. The whole family, well, most of them, are Jew-lovers. The way they talk about *their* Jews is sickening, as if they're part of the family. I mean, what good German would care if two Jewish brats were missing?'

'You think that's what happened, sir?' Carl Meyer said, a hint of hope in his voice.

'No,' Heinrich Güllich growled. 'I'm sure they're on their way to the border somewhere, and while I can't rule out the possibility that the General isn't involved, my gut instinct tells me that he is.'

'What about the other calls, sir?'

'The call to Colonel Schneider was just to update the supercilious fool about his precious boat. If it were up to me, I'd tell them all to forget about sailing and get on with fighting for the Fatherland. As for the General's calls to his friends, who do they think they are?'

The Kriminalassistent looked down at the list of phone calls made from the Drachensee house.

'I've heard of Oscar von Friedeburg,' he said. 'He's a rich businessman with close ties to the party, and Speer is a bit of a self-righteous loudmouth; he's an excellent doctor, I'm told, but we suspect him of treating Jews illegally.'

He looked at the list again.

'I'm not sure who this Dieter Maas is,' he said.

'He works for von Friedeburg,' Carl Meyer said. 'He used to be the editor at the Morgenpost. They all raced together in the General's boat at the last Kieler Woche before the war.'

Carl Meyer was relieved to be useful for once, but Heinrich Güllich gave him a look of disbelief.

'How in hell's name do you know that?'

'My father, sir. He used to crew on one of the boats, a few years ago. It was his job. He still follows the Kiel racing calendar. We often go and watch together. It can be quite exciting.'

'Exciting? I'd rather watch my wife paint her nails.'

Carl Meyer couldn't do the mental gymnastics required to imagine Heinrich Güllich interacting in any way with his wife. He said nothing.

'Have a nap if you must but don't move from that phone,' the Kriminalassistent added with a sneer. 'I'll go out and relieve our friend on Hamburger Chaussee. You can take over for me when I come back.'

'Will you take a car, sir?'

'No. I'll drag one of the Kriminalassistentanwärteren away from their show. He can drop me off.'

'How long will you be out there, sir?'

'I'll see how it goes. Three or four hours at least. Maybe more.'

When Heinrich Güllich had left, Carl Meyer folded his jacket and sat it on the desk as a pillow. Within five minutes, he was asleep.

CHAPTER 94

The wind awoke Franz at six. It whistled through *The Shearwater*'s rigging, punctuated by the rubbing of old tyres used by the fishermen as fenders, and wet hemp ropes creaking on a hundred restless fishing boats, like an orchestra warming up before a symphony.

Men moved about on the fishing vessel *The Shearwater* lay against and he nodded a good morning to the man he'd spoken with the previous evening.

'Still intending to go?' the fisherman asked.

'Yes. We need to stock up with supplies, then we'll be off. Yourselves?'

'Yes. We're going within the hour. I'll give you a shout and you can tend your lines.'

Half an hour later, the fishing boat slipped out past them, waves crashing over the bow as soon as it had cleared the pier ends.

Franz went down below and began preparing breakfast.

~~o~~

It wasn't the wind that roused Heinrich Güllich. He woke to the sound of tapping on the car window. A policeman leaned down, looking at him through the glass.

He wound the window down.

'Officer,' he said.

'Morning. A late night, sir? One too many?'

Heinrich Güllich fished his Gestapo warrant card from his pocket and flashed it at the policeman.

'Sorry, sir,' the constable said, the smile evaporating from his face.

Heinrich Güllich checked his watch and glanced over at the General's house. Seven o'clock, and there was no sign of life. He lit up a cigarette and drew the welcome smoke into his lungs, hoping that the General was still at home. He didn't relish explaining to his two juniors how he'd missed him leaving.

The policeman still hovered.

'Is there anything else, Constable?'

'No, sir. I'll be off.'

He walked away, glancing back once.

The Gestapo man rubbed the back of his neck, sore from the cramped position he'd fallen asleep in. He'd checked his watch at five-thirty but could remember nothing after that.

He looked over at the Kästner house again and saw Yosef Nussbaum leave the cottage and walk over to the big house. A few minutes later he saw the man's Jew-bitch wife follow him over.

It bothered him that they could carry on with their lives with impunity, immune from the laws that governed the rest of their kind.

He rubbed his forehead. There was something niggling him, but he couldn't quite get hold of it.

He looked up as an army car approached and was relieved to see it turn into the General's driveway.

Ten minutes later, the car emerged again and, before ducking down, Heinrich Güllich glimpsed the General in the back seat. He waited until the car had reached the brick factory, then followed, staying as far behind them as he could without risking losing them.

He watched the car head north through Kiel and as expected, it took the road down to the foreshore. When it reached Naval Headquarters, it stopped at the kerbside. The Gestapo man watched from a distance as the General got out and walked through the front doors of the building.

He drove past, and turned left onto Karolinenweg. The Gestapo building was only a couple of blocks away. When he reached it, he parked the car and ran up the stairs to the office. He found Carl Meyer still at his desk.

When he saw the Kriminalassistent, the younger man stood up.

'I thought you'd call sooner, sir, to be relieved.'

317

'I waited until the General had gone to work. He's there now so I took the opportunity to come back here. Send someone over there to keep an eye on him.'

'Yes, sir. There have been no more calls made to or from the Kästner house, but the Reichspost have sent over the transcripts of last night's calls.'

He handed Heinrich Güllich the sheets, watching the older man as he read them, frowning now and again.

'When did the Kästner boys leave Kiel on this voyage of theirs?' Heinrich Güllich asked.

'I don't know, sir, but I can phone my father. He's been following their progress.'

'Has everyone gone mad? What is it about these time-wasters that interests Kiel's mindless masses?'

~~o~~

Carl Meyer ignored the slur on his father's character.

'They're mostly people connected with the Kriegsmarine, or with sailing, sir. I suppose it's a distraction from the bombing, and the shortages. And my father has a lot of experience at sea.'

Heinrich Güllich grunted. The young Kriminalassistentanwärter picked up the telephone and dialled. When his father answered, he asked him about the Kästner boys' itinerary.

He listened to his father, nodding at intervals and making occasional notes.

'Well?' Heinrich Güllich asked when Carl Meyer ended the call.

'They left last Wednesday, sir. The second of April.'

'Verdammt. When did the Nussbaum brats go missing?'

'It was Friday, sir. Could there be a connection, sir?'

'I'm not sure, but I find it all too coincidental that the Jewish brats go missing at the same time as the General's sons make a boat journey to another country.'

'But, sir, how could they be on the boat if it left two days before they disappeared?'

'We only have the Kästners' and the Nussbaums' word for that and, anyway, they could have joined the boat after it left. I presume they called in at a few ports on the way?'

Carl Meyer smiled to himself; the Kriminalassistent was quite happy to use his father's information when it suited him.

'Yes. They did. But my father said they were all in Denmark, sir. Bøjden and Bogense, the first two nights, then probably Hjelm and Læsø, before Hirtshals.'

'I've never heard of any of these places,' Heinrich Güllich said.

'I'll get a map, sir. We have them for all the occupied territories.'

He walked across the room to the bookcase and ran his finger along the spines of books and maps until he found what he was looking for.

'Who would have driven the children to Denmark to pick up the boat?' he said, returning with a map of Denmark.

'The General, or his driver, or even the General's wife,' Heinrich Güllich said, then shook his head.

'No. I don't believe she would,' he said. 'She wasn't as enthusiastic about the Nussbaums as her husband.'

'There will be records of border crossings, sir. Do you want me to request them?'

'Please do, and I think I'd like to interview the Nussbaums and the Kästners again. It's more than possible that the children have been away longer.'

Carl Meyer hid his scepticism but supposed that it was possible that the Kriminalassistent was right.

He spread the map out on the table and pointed out each port in turn.

'They're all difficult to get to, by road, sir. If the children are on the yacht, they must have boarded here in Kiel.'

'Suppose they did. Could they have paid a visit to Sweden, to drop them off there?'

'If they'd wanted to go to Sweden, they'd have gone through the channels further east. And Hirtshals would be a hell of a detour if Sweden was their intended destination.'

'Perhaps they dropped them off at one of their stops in Denmark?'

'If they have, sir, they could be difficult to find.'

'You'd be surprised. We can send photographs to the local police in each of the places they visited. Offer a small reward to the public. In rural places like that, they'll be turned in sooner or later. They'll stick out like whores in a convent.'

The Kriminalassistent looked at the map again.

'When are they due at Hirtshals?'

'My father said they should have arrived yesterday, sir.'

'How long would it take us to get to Hirtshals?'

'It's about 500 kilometres, sir. It would take most of the day, but it's probable they've left by now.'

'Damn. Even so, contact the local police and find out if they have left. Get them to hold onto them if they haven't.'

He looked up at the younger man.

'Get me a map of Norway,' he said. 'Let's see where this Grimstad place they're making for is located.'

It took Carl Meyer a little longer this time. When he returned, he unfolded a map of Norway and Sweden, including the northernmost tip of Denmark. He laid it out on top of the first map.

'Here, sir,' he said, pointing to a small town almost directly across the Kattegat from Hirtshals.

'Where is our nearest Gestapo office?'

Carl Meyer opened his desk drawer and pulled out the directory of Gestapo offices. He flicked through until he found the page listing Norway.

'Kristiansand, sir. It's our headquarters for southern Norway.'

He looked at the map and did a rough calculation.

'It's about seventy kilometres. Just over an hour.'

'Contact them. Get them to send a car to Grimstad when the yacht is expected to arrive. How long would it take them if they left this morning?'

'That would depend on the wind, sir. If they made good time it could be around ten hours. That would get them in about 6 or 7pm.'

He paused.

'That's assuming they go there. They could choose any port along that coast.'

Heinrich Güllich raised his eyebrows and looked at his assistant.

'I had the same thought myself, but let's see if you're reasoning is the same as mine.'

Carl Meyer hesitated, feeling a little less sure of his ground.

'Well, sir,' he said. 'If your assumption is correct, and the Jews are on board, they haven't given a single clue away in their conversation, which means that they know, or suspect, that someone is listening in. So, if they wanted to drop them off in a quiet harbour somewhere, they'd try and throw the listeners off the scent.'

'Well done, Kamerad. I may have underestimated you.'

Carl Meyer beamed. He'd never addressed him as Kamerad before. And to get actual praise from the man!

'Thank you, sir,' he said. 'I'm just doing my job.'

'So, what do we do next?'

'You're asking me, sir?'

'Yes. Let's see how far you can take this.'

'Well, sir, I'd ask all ports within thirty kilometres of Grimstad, east and west, for their vessel movement records. Although it will take a while to get that information to us, it will give us a good idea of where they are. We can find them and track them from there and apprehend them as soon as they dock at their next port of call.'

'Excellent, Meyer, but there's something else we can try, that will get the job done even quicker.'

'What's that, sir?'

'Have a read at the transcripts again.' He handed the Kriminalassistentanwärter the three sheets of paper.

The younger man still had a puzzled expression on his face when he'd finished.

'Sir?'

'Do we have anyone within the Kriegsmarine command?'

'I don't think so, sir, but SD do, I'm sure. Don't you have contacts in the SD?'

319

'I know a few people. And while you were away getting the map of Norway, I telephoned one of them. He's going to get back to me.'

'I still don't get…'

He stopped.

'The flotilla, or whatever you call it, sir. The squadron. It's going to be in that area.'

Heinrich Güllich smiled.

'But, sir, the Kriegsmarine hold these Kästner boys in high regard. How will you convince them to stop their boat and arrest them?'

'We don't. If we can get someone inside the Kriegsmarine to put a request in that requires all small boats crossing the Kattegat to be searched, they'll think nothing of stopping the Kästners' boat. I'll go further. They'll be very apologetic about it until they find our hidden Jews.'

'Are you sure, sir? General Kästner's name carries a lot of weight in the Kriegsmarine.'

'You forget one thing, Herr Kriminalassistentanwärter. The unflinching resolve of the German soldier or sailor to follow orders.'

Heinrich Güllich laughed.

'And if the Jews aren't on the boat?'

'Then there's no harm done, is there? We start looking in Denmark, and back in Kiel.'

'Sir!' Carl Meyer said, jumping to his feet.

'What now, man?'

'The General. If the Kriegsmarine put an order through to search all vessels, he'll know we're onto them.'

'So what? He'll not be able to warn his sons.'

'But sir, I don't think you realise the power he has. He could easily get the order rescinded, or perhaps he's clever enough to get it changed to just, let's say, fishing boats.'

'I'd be more worried if the General were going to be at headquarters.'

'But that's where he is, sir. You said so yourself.'

The phone rang.

Heinrich Güllich picked it up and said a few words, then cupped his hand over the mouthpiece.

'I'm going to take this in my office. Put this down once you hear me on the line.'

Carl Meyer took the handpiece from the older man and listened. When he heard the click of the phone being picked up, and the Kriminalassistent's voice, he replaced the handpiece on the telephone and sat down.

Five minutes later, Heinrich Güllich came out of his office, a smug grin on his face.

'Get your coat,' he said. 'We have half an hour.'

'To do what, sir?'

'What's the surest way to get the General out of that building?'

Carl Meyer's eyes widened, and then he laughed.

'We're going back out to the Kästner house!'

Heinrich Güllich clapped him on the back.

'We'll make a Gestapo man out of you yet.'

CHAPTER 95

Mon 7th April

07:45 Dep HIRTSHALS for GRIMSTAD. Dull. Cooler. Barometer dropping. 998mb. Wind 25 knots, westerly.

Sea state moderate. 1 reef main, staysail, No.2 jib, 1 reef mizzen. 315°M, 5.0 knots.

~~o~~

They raised sail in the inner harbour. A fair bit of swell was entering between the outer arms of the east and west piers, but it was calm in comparison to the sea outside the entrance, and neither Franz nor Johann relished the thought of being thrown about on the foredeck, trying to hank on the foresails while waves crashed over the bow, threatening to wash the feet from under them.

The harbour master had called down at the boat at seven, telling them that his wife had opened the shop early for them. By seven-thirty, they were back at the quayside with two large bags of supplies, enough to keep them for three or four days at a push, but not so much as would arouse suspicion. Added to the food already on the boat, they expected it to last until they were picked up by the Royal Navy, or in the unlikely event that they eluded British coastal defences, they could survive a little hunger until they made one of the ports on the east coast of England.

Their fuel tanks were still full; they'd hardly used the engine, and the harbour master had shown them where the tap was, to fill up their water tanks.

He'd been there when they left; he shook hands with Franz and Johann, then stepped off the boat.

'Sikker rejse,' he called down from the quay. *Safe journey.*

'Tak min ven,' Franz replied. *Thank you, my friend.*

The harbour master switched back to bad German.

'If all Germans like you would welcome in our Denmark,' he said, casting off *The Shearwater*'s lines.

'If all Germans were like us, Denmark would still be yours,' Franz shouted back, as the wind blew them off the wall.

The boat slowly began to make way in reverse, the thud of the big diesel reassuring as the rudder slowly bit into the water, trying to find steerage.

Once the sails had been hoisted, Johann made for one pier first, then the other, in a series of short tacks using the engine and the sails to power them towards the entrance.

'Did you warn them?' Johann said, as they neared the narrowest point, where the waves piled up into peaks between the two pier ends.

'Yes. They know it's going to be rough for a stretch, until we're clear. And to hang onto something.'

'Here we go,' yelled Johann, grinning through gritted teeth as a wave crashed over the boat, the spray strafing the cockpit.

For a couple of minutes, *The Shearwater* laboured, caught in a maelstrom, the wheel having a mind of its own and the boat barely making way against the sea. But slowly, as if dragged forwards by the will of the two men wrestling with her, the gap between them and the foam-covered piers began to stretch.

A cable northward, the confused sea of the harbour entrance settled down into the sharp heavy chop typical of the shallower southern part of the Skagerrak.

Laying a course for Grimstad, they found themselves on a close reach and, although *The Shearwater* rose and fell with each successive wave on her shoulder, she shrugged them off and settled into her stride.

~~o~~

It turned out to be a bad morning for Maria Kästner.

Around eight, just as Johann went below to allow Ruth to come on deck for the first watch, Heinrich Güllich knocked once more on the front door of the Kästner house.

Yosef paled when he saw who was outside, but he steeled himself, and opened the door.

'Herr Güllich,' he said. 'You're back. I'll tell the mistress you're here.'

'Are you not going to invite us in, Jew?' Carl Meyer said, standing slightly behind and to the left of his boss.

'Carl. Please,' Heinrich Güllich said. 'We mustn't be rude.'

'I'm sorry, Herr Güllich,' Yosef said, 'I'm not sure if the mistress is dressed yet and it would be inappropriate for me to invite strangers into the house without informing her.'

'That's entirely understandable. Please give Frau Kästner our regards and ask her if it would be possible for us to have a few words at her convenience.' He looked at his watch.

'Yes, sir. I'll go and ask. I don't imagine it will be longer than a minute or two.'

Yosef shut the door.

'He deserves to be shot, sir. The impertinence of the man beggars belief.'

'Oh, don't worry,' Heinrich Güllich said, lighting a cigarette. 'His turn will come. In the meantime, he, or someone else, is doing exactly what we want. It will be most illuminating to read the transcript of the telephone call that is currently being placed to the General.'

Carl Meyer smiled.

'That's clever, sir,' he said.

The Kriminalassistent gave him a withering look but said nothing.

Less than two minutes later, the Jewish manservant opened the door again and ushered them in. Maria Kästner stood in the hall and greeted them formally.

'What can we do for you, Herr Kriminalassistent,' she said.

'Oh, we just have a few follow-up questions to ask. We have one or two leads on the missing children, and there are a few details we need to clear up. Is the General at home?'

'No, he's not, but I believe he is due home shortly.'

'Excellent. That's most fortuitous. I wonder if it would be possible to interview yourself and your daughters first, so as not to waste time.'

Maria Kästner felt her stomach turn. She couldn't imagine what it must feel like if she'd had something to hide.

'Of course,' she said. 'Would you like to talk to us in the study?'

'No. We will speak to you all here, in the hallway, individually. If everyone else could kindly assemble in one of the other rooms, we will call each person out when we are ready for them.'

Maria sent Yosef to the kitchen to collect Miriam, and she herself went upstairs to call the girls. Part of her wanted the General here, as soon as possible, but a voice inside her head warned her to expect a confrontation that could easily lead to disaster for her family.

She headed towards the drawing room, her daughters behind her.

'We'll talk to you first, Frau Kästner,' Heinrich Güllich said.

~~o~~

'When do we turn west?' Ruth asked, huddled in the lee of the coachroof.

'There's a squadron of Kriegsmarine ships passing through the Kattegat about midday,' Franz told her. 'They'll expect to see us heading to Norway. After they've passed, we can bear out to the west.'

She looked out at the waves.

'It will be hard, won't it?'

'I'll not lie to you. It'll be tougher than anything we've seen yet, and it will get worse. The barometer has dropped two points since first light.'

'Is that bad?'

'The faster it falls, the stronger the wind will get.'

She shivered.

'I'm frightened.'

'I'll let you in to a secret. I'm frightened too, but fear keeps us alive, as long as we control it, and don't let it make us panic.'

'How do you do that?'

'I trust myself, and Johann. And above that, I trust *The Shearwater*. She'll not let us down if we treat her right.'

'You talk about the boat as if it's a woman.'

He laughed. 'All sailors, all seamen do. It's the way of the sea. Men are simple creatures. They remember the safety of their mother's arms as a child and when they're at sea, it makes them feel safe.'

'Is it always their mothers?'

He laughed again.

'No. I suppose for some, it might be their wives, or their girlfriends.'

'And what about women at sea?'

'There aren't many. And they have mothers too.'

It was Ruth's turn to laugh.

CHAPTER 96

By the time the General arrived at Drachensee, Maria had already been questioned and Eva had just been called through. Carl Meyer opened the door and asked him to wait in the drawing room along with his family and the other members of his household.

'I wish to speak with my wife first,' the General said, in such a reasonable tone that Carl Meyer wondered why he had felt as if he'd been torn off a strip.

Heinrich Güllich stepped forward.

'That will not be possible, Herr General. We are reinterviewing everyone involved individually and would rather the people who've spoken to us already do not converse with those who have yet to be questioned. Do you have a problem with that? It's fairly standard procedure in a case like this.'

'Firstly, I thought this was a police matter and secondly, unless you've arrested all of us, you can't insist on such a ludicrous arrangement in our own home and, thirdly, have you advised anyone of their rights to a lawyer?'

'Very good questions, Herr General, and I will try and address them. This is a police matter; we are simply assisting the police because of the delicate nature of the investigation and indeed, we can't insist on your compliance, but we would ask politely that you would indulge us on this occasion. We don't want to be forced down the road of making arrests at this time. Imagine how embarrassing that would be for someone like Frau Kästner, or your daughters. Lastly, no one has been charged or cautioned, so we have no requirement to inform you of your rights. Incidentally, because of the state of war we are currently in, we have been given the power to waive the rights of citizens in exceptional circumstances.'

'And in what way are the circumstances of this case exceptional, Herr Güllich?'

'That's for us to decide, Herr General. Now, if you don't mind. We'd like to ask your daughter a few questions.'

The General opened his mouth to argue but when he glanced at his daughter, he saw pleading in her eyes.

'It's all right, Eva. Just tell the truth. We've done nothing wrong. Tell your mother that I'll talk to her afterwards.'

He saw Eva close her eyes in relief. Carl Meyer led the General to the drawing-room door and gestured for him to go through, then closed the door.

The General crossed towards the windows, where Antje stood with the Nussbaums. Albert, the driver, sat in one of the chairs.

'How are we all?' he said, giving them a confident smile.

'Nervous, sir,' Yosef said.

'Don't be. The only thing we should be worrying about is finding Manny and Ruth.'

'I don't understand all this, sir,' Albert said. 'It's an effrontery, to treat us all like this. I've never been subjected to anything like this in my whole life.'

'I'm sorry you're involved, Albert. Just remember to speak honestly with them.'

'I will, sir.'

The door opened, and Carl Meyer called Albert's name. The General gave him an encouraging smile and touched his shoulder.

'Remember. You have nothing to hide,' he said quietly.

The door closed behind him. Antje began to say something, but the General put his finger to his lips.

'Later,' he mouthed and gave his daughter a hug, then, in as normal a voice he could muster, he told her that they were going sailing that evening, and that she was invited.

She smiled, and he watched a little of the tension seep away.

'Who's all going?' she asked.

'Myself, Oskar, Doc Speer and Dieter, and you, if you feel up to it.'

'Of course I'll come. I'll not let these people spoil my day.'

He flashed her a grateful smile and looked at Yosef and Miriam. They'd aged ten years in a week.

'I'll speak to you tonight,' he murmured in Yosef's ear, squeezing his shoulder and patting Miriam on the arm.

He picked the newspaper up from the table, sat down in one of the chairs, and began to read.

~~o~~

Yosef Nussbaum smiled. He'd forgotten how good it was to have Erich Kästner as a friend at times like this.

He recalled the man sitting opposite them as a young colonel in the last war, leading his men with a calmness that every one of them believed had pulled them through with the least casualties of all the front-line battalions.

He squeezed his wife's hand and gave an almost imperceptible nod towards their employer, calmly reading. She looked over and the hint of a smile appeared at the corner of her mouth. He saw Antje doing the same and caught her eye. She gave him a faint shake of her head and rolled her eyes. Yosef returned her smile.

She's been the best of friends to Ruth, whatever happens.

He frowned.

If Ruth and Manny were caught and returned to Germany, the girls' friendship would cost the Kästner family dear.

He closed his eyes.

Where are they now?

~~o~~

09:30 HIRTSHALS LT 150°M. 11NM (dead reckoning)

Wind 20 knots, nor'westerly. 345°M. 5.0kts. Close-hauled.

~~o~~

'We're not making Grimstad now,' Franz said, pointing in the direction they wanted to go. 'The wind has veered to the north, so we're getting pushed further east than we'd like.'

'Can't we just turn west?' Ruth asked. 'The shift in wind suits us, doesn't it?

'It does, but we can't turn westwards until the Kriegsmarine flotilla has passed us. This course is still the one they'd expect us to take for Grimstad, so we have to hold it.'

'The wind has died a little. Even though we're heading into it, the gusts aren't as strong as they were earlier.'

'It has, but it's the lull before the storm, I think. The barometer's still dropping. Nine-nine-six the last time I looked.'

'I don't like the look of these clouds coming,' Ruth said.

Franz looked to the west and nodded. A thick band of dark cloud filled the horizon. He closed the hatch, and secured it, and told Ruth to fasten up her oilskins and hold on tight.

Within a couple of minutes, the squall had struck. For quarter of an hour, Franz fought to keep *The Shearwater* on track but every so often a large wave, or a vicious gust, would knock her nose round and she'd wallow, losing way.

But almost as quickly as it had started, the darkness of the squall lifted, and they could see further than a few hundred metres again.

'That's a taster of what's to come,' Franz said, trying to prepare her for the days ahead.

CHAPTER 97

The General was the last to be interviewed. The questions were as before, but Güllich was more insistent in tying down the time that Ruth and Manny were last seen, and the General's movements on that day, and for the week before.

Then they were finished.

Heinrich Güllich stood up and thanked the General for his patience, and for the understanding of his family.

'Is there any news on the children's whereabouts?' the General asked. 'I'm sure the Nussbaums would have liked to ask but would be far too reticent.'

'We're following a few interesting leads, with a wide geographical spread, so these things take time, but I suspect we will have more concrete information in the very near future.'

'Well, thank you,' the General said, walking them slowly to the door.

The younger Gestapo man stopped in front of a photograph of the General with Franz and Johann, all in uniform.

'Your sons,' he said. 'You must be immensely proud.'

'Yes. They've done well. Franz in particular.'

The man smiled.

'My father is extremely interested in their trip to Norway. He used to be around yachts, you know. It's a remarkable undertaking at any time, but this early in the year, and with the war...'

'I know. We do worry about them, but they've been through the campaigns in Poland, Norway and France, so they know all about danger, and they've both done their bit in the war.'

Colour flushed to Carl Meyer's face.

'Very honourable, I'm sure,' he said, through tight lips.

Heinrich Güllich interrupted.

'They called at quite a few places on the way, didn't they?'

'Yes. Mostly in Denmark but they're crossing over to Norway today. That's their biggest challenge, I'd say.'

'You didn't think about meeting up with them at one of their stops?'

'No. There was no point.' The General frowned. 'Why do you ask?'

'Just a thought.'

'Did they stop at Hjelm and Læsø,' the younger Gestapo man said, knowing the answer. 'My father wasn't sure.'

'Yes. They did.'

'We should visit all these places,' Heinrich Güllich said. 'They sound charming.'

The General forced himself to smile.

'They are. I've had the pleasure to sail these waters myself. Perhaps your father has too,' he said, turning to Carl Meyer.

'Yes. We've heard all the stories. He was part of the professional crew on a yacht owned by the Krupps.'

'Ah. The Krupps always had beautiful boats, and they loved their sailing.'

'Well, we must go,' Heinrich Güllich said. 'We'll be keeping a close eye on *Der Sturmtaucher* and your famous sons. I hear that one or two of their Kriegsmarine friends might bump into them today. And who knows, we may have news soon about your missing Jews.'

His face broke into a smile but the General saw nothing but malice in his eyes. He returned the smile, shook his hand and that of Carl Meyer's, and showed the two men out.

When he closed the door, he breathed out and closed his eyes.

They know.

There was nothing he could do about it and it didn't matter if they'd arranged a reception committee in Grimstad. One way or another, *Der Sturmtaucher* would never arrive in Norway.

He went to the kitchen. They were sitting around the table, apart from Maria. They all started talking at once, but he held up his hand.

'They're just trying to put pressure on us; that's what they do. It's just to hide their own failings.'

He turned to Eva.

'Where's Mama?'

'She's upstairs. She has a headache.'

'Go to her. I'll be up shortly.'

Eva left, and the General turned to Albert.

'Albert,' he said. 'Get the car ready. I dismissed my driver, and I need to get back to the office.'

When the old man had left, the General asked the three of them how it had gone.

'The same questions, sir,' Miriam said, 'and several new ones about what happened the previous week. We don't think we made any mistakes.'

'What about you, Antje?'

'They wanted to know details of my friendship with Ruth. I didn't try to hide it. They asked what I was doing when the boys left. I had to tell them I'd visited the boat the night before.'

'That's unfortunate, but necessary. Several people saw you.'

'They said that they believed that Ruth and Manny were attempting to leave the country and if anyone in the house has any information, they should consider the consequences if they don't divulge it. They said that to all of us, apart from Yosef and Miriam.'

He didn't tell them about the Gestapo's questions to him about the boys, and *The Shearwater*. There was no point in adding to their worries.

'I'm going up to see your mother,' he said to Antje, 'then I'm going back to work.'

He turned to Miriam and Yosef.

'Remember, your children are missing so none of the others expect you to carry on as normal but be careful. Don't let anything slip. I'll try and speak to you later.'

~~o~~

The conversation with Maria had been a difficult one. Eva was trying to comfort her mother but left when the General arrived.

She'd been lying in bed, looking pale and drawn, and her make-up had run where she'd been crying. His heart had gone out to her, but she'd given him a cold stare and spoken in a flat voice that he hardly recognised.

'This is the end, Erich. You and your *friends* have brought disaster to this house. If the Nussbaums are not away by the end of the week, I'm going to stay at my mother's house for a while. I simply can't put up with all this aggravation.'

'What about Eva and Antje?'

'Eva is coming with me. I haven't spoken to Antje yet, but I suspect she will stay with her precious father.'

The last words were spoken with venom, and the General flinched.

'I'm sorry, Maria, that you feel like that. You knew when you married me that the Nussbaums were part of this family.'

'But I didn't know that all this would happen.'

'All the more reason for us to protect them.'

'No. Your own family should be your priority. And it's not.'

He wondered how she'd react if she knew that he'd involved her two sons, and her youngest daughter, in a high-risk attempt to smuggle Ruth and Manny out of Germany.

'I can't change who I am. And I know that having the Gestapo stamping all over our house is terrible but just imagine how Miriam Nussbaum is feeling at present.'

'See? That's what I mean. You always have to bring it back to the Nussbaums.'

'I thought Miriam was your friend, once. She was there when you needed her, with Eva.'

Maria's third pregnancy had been her most difficult, and Miriam had been such a godsend to her during her confinement that they'd become good friends.

'That was a long time ago.'

'I've never forgotten it, and I don't suppose Miriam has.'

He looked at his wife. She couldn't meet his gaze.

'That's not fair,' she said.

'I'm going back to work. We'll be sailing this evening, but we can speak tomorrow night.'

She said nothing, but she turned her back to him.

He took one last look at her and left, closing the door behind him. Eva was downstairs.

'Eva. I'm sorry for everything you're having to go through. Trust me when I say I didn't mean for any of this to happen, but I couldn't stand by and do nothing.'

'I'm sorry too, Father, but Mama's right. You've forgotten all of us in this.'

He didn't know what to say. He realised that he'd lost Eva, and it was his own fault.

'Miriam helped bring you up. When I wasn't there, the Nussbaums looked after you all.'

'They were paid to do it. They're servants. And I know it's not their fault but they're breaking up this family.'

'I'm sorry you think like that, Eva, but they're our friends, and I can't turn my back on them.'

'You'd rather turn your back on Mama and I.'

'It's not as simple as that, Eva.'

'For Mama and I, it is. I'm going to see her now,' she said, climbing the stairs without looking back.

CHAPTER 98

Albert dropped the General at Naval Headquarters. In his office, he stood in front of the chart of the Skagerrak. Hirtshals was the last point marked on it.

He traced his finger to where he thought they would be by now, almost a third of the way across the open tract of water that separated Denmark from Norway.

As long as they get away, it will all be worth it.

Captain Bauer entered, with a sheaf of papers.

'Is everything all right, General?' he asked. 'Frau Müller said you'd been called home.'

'Nothing to worry about, Captain. The police called at the house, wanting further information about the Nussbaums' children.'

'A terrible thing, sir, but you hear so much of it, these days.'

'Quite. Now what do you have for me?'

'The weather forecast, sir. There's going to be a blow. It's a good job *The Shearwater* will be in Grimstad tonight.'

The General took the report and scanned it. Fighting the urge to cheer, he made his face sombre and spoke with a slight tremor.

'I hope they get in safely. Weather has a habit of coming in early when you least need it.'

He turned back to the captain.

'You have some papers for me?'

'Yes, sir. Could you check these and sign the relevant copies, please.'

The General was glad of the distraction, spending an hour signing forms and going over requisition requests with the captain.

'Here are today's command orders, sir,' the captain said, when they'd finished. 'I know you like to glance at them.' He smiled.

'Is something amusing, Captain?' the General asked.

'Sorry, sir. I thought you would find this one comical.' He leafed through the orders sheets and pulled one out, handing it to the General.

```
KRIEGSMARINE OSTSEE COMMAND

ORDER K/OSC/1297867

April 7th, 1941

Time: 08:45

TO: ALL KRIEGSMARINE SHIPS IN KATTEGAT BETWEEN LINE FROM
SKAGENS REV LIGHTSHIP [57°46'60N, 10°44'00E] TO PATER NOSTER LT
[57°54'10N, 11°24'50E] AND LINE BETWEEN HANSTHOLM LT
[57°06'78N, 8°36'08E] TO LINDESNES LT [57°58'90N, 7°3'33E]

ALL VESSELS UNDER 50 METRES IDENTIFIED IN THE AREA DEFINED
ABOVE ARE TO BE STOPPED AND SEARCHED FOR ILLEGAL PERSONS ON
BOARD DURING THE PERIOD 08:45 TODAY AND 08:45 TOMORROW.

END
```

A chill hand gripped the General's stomach and he had to concentrate hard to stop his hand trembling.

It's over.

He looked at his watch. Eleven-thirty.

He knew now the true purpose of the Gestapo's visit. He was too late to try and rescind the order, or even amend it. He heard the captain speaking to him.

He forced himself to smile.

'Sorry,' he said. 'I was a million miles away. What did you say?'

'I asked you if you were all right, sir.'

'I'm fine. I find myself a little preoccupied. I suppose it is the thought of the Skagerrak in bad weather.'

'They'll be sensible, sir. They'll hole up in a small harbour somewhere until it clears. There's plenty shelter, in any of a hundred places.'

'Just as long as they reach Norway.'

'Yes, sir. Franz and Johann are very experienced. They'll be fine.'

~~o~~

The captain retrieved the forms that the General had signed and made for the door. He looked back just before he closed it behind him. The General was still standing, staring at the chart on the wall, his face strained and pale.

He closed the door softly, leaving the General to his thoughts.

He walked to the records office, a frown on his face, and spoke to one of the clerks, giving him the sheaf of forms. He found it difficult to get the image of the General's face out of his mind, so, instead of going straight back, he called in at the command centre, and struck up conversation with a young lieutenant.

'General Kästner is a bit worried about his sons. Have there been any sightings yet?'

'I don't think so, but I can ask for you. It should definitely come through; all small vessels in the area are to be boarded.'

The lieutenant smiled.

'It's comical,' he said. 'Imagine the Kästners' boat being stopped and searched. Perhaps they'll find a beautiful English lady spy on board.'

Captain Bauer laughed.

'From what the General says of Johann, I wouldn't put it past him,' he said.

'I doubt they'll bother searching them. I mean, everyone in the Kriegsmarine has been following their progress. They'll hardly want to hold them up.'

'Still, let me know the minute they've made contact. It will perhaps relieve the General's anxiety.'

'I'll do that, sir. Anything for General Kästner.'

CHAPTER 99

'There's a ship off our starboard side, Franz.'

Franz followed Ruth's outstretched hand.

A smudge of smoke rose barely above the horizon

'You have good eyesight,' he said. 'Hopefully, that might be the Kriegsmarine. You'd better get down below and send Johann up.'

Ruth relinquished the wheel to Franz and disappeared down the companionway. By the time Johann replaced her in the cockpit, Franz could make out the dark grey bow of a naval ship.

'It's coming up fast,' Johann said. 'It's not big enough to be a destroyer; probably a torpedo boat.'

'It's making for us anyway. Father did say they would make contact if they saw us.'

The ship was increasing in size with every minute. It was now less than a mile away.

'They're signalling,' Franz shouted. 'With an Aldis lamp. Get a pencil.'

Johann reached down to the chart table and grabbed a pencil, and a dog-eared notebook they often used on deck. He muttered the letters as he wrote.

'-U-R-M-T-A-U-C-H-E-R- -S-O-F-O-R-T- -A-N-H-A-L-T-E-N.'

'They want us to stop,' Franz said, frowning. 'That's strange. I thought they'd just steam alongside and hail us.'

'I'll send a reply.'

Johann hoisted the 'C' flag to signal their affirmative and Franz steered the boat through the wind, then tied off the wheel hard to starboard. *The Shearwater* sat still in the water, rising and falling as the waves passed under her, comfortably hove-to.

The torpedo boat circled behind them and took position a cable upwind of them, creating a calm patch of sea in their lee. Even with that, *The Shearwater* rocked in the unpleasant swell.

Franz saw the large letters on the torpedo boat's bow as it slid into view.

T4

An officer on the bridge waved at them, then picked up a loudhailer.

'Ahoy. *Shearwater.*'

Franz reached into one of the cockpit lockers and pulled out a similar, but smaller, device.

'Ahoy, *T4*. How are you?'

'We're good. How is the trip so far?'

'Excellent. All to plan.'

'We're in for rough weather, I think.'

'Yes. We might have to hole up in Grimstad for a few days.'

Johann nudged Franz, who turned around.

'It's Rainer Schulze,' Johann said. '*Helga-II*. He beat us in the '38 Kieler Woche, and we took him the following year.'

'I remember him. A decent fellow, and a good sailor.'

The loudhailer boomed again from the torpedo boat's bridge.

'Hold your position. We're coming aboard.'

He disappeared from sight.

'Scheiße,' Johann said.

He poked his head down the companionway and hissed a warning to Ruth and Manny to hide in the bilge as quickly as possible.

Franz watched as four sailors prepared the torpedo boat's tender to be lowered. The davits had been swung out, and two seamen had already climbed into it. A young officer stood by, waiting to board it.

A figure emerged onto the ship's deck just below the bridge and walked quickly back to the tender. Even from a distance, Franz could see that it was Rainer Schulze.

The ratings helped both officers climb aboard, and the chief petty officer pulled the lever to lower the tender into the sea.

As soon as the lifting gear had been released, the seamen pushed off from the side of the torpedo boat and the junior officer steered it towards *The Shearwater*. Franz and Johann set fenders out on the starboard side and the tender approached her, bow to bow.

Lines were thrown and slipped over cleats; stern, bow and springs. Even in the calmer waters in the torpedo boat's lee, the boats rose and fell together in the swell, and Rainer Schulz had to be careful when stepping across to *The Shearwater*. One of the able seamen accompanied him.

'Kapitänleutnant, welcome on board. This is an unexpected pleasure.'

'I'm honoured to be on board,' Rainer Schulze said. 'We've all been following your trip with interest.'

'We're a little surprised that it's created such a stir. We're sure it's only on account of our father.'

'Ah. We're very fond of the Kriegsmarine's only general. I think I told you before how highly thought of he is, which makes the next part a little difficult for us.'

'What do you mean?' Franz asked.

'An order came through to search all boats in the Skagerrak of less than fifty metres in length.'

'What for?' Johann laughed. 'Are the Norwegians or Danes running arms and ammunition?'

'No. *Illegal persons* was the reason given.'

'But surely it doesn't apply to German vessels?' Franz said, smiling.

Inside, his stomach turned, and he had to swallow to get rid of the bile at the back of his throat.

'I'm sorry. We've been given the task to do, without exception.'

'By all means, Rainer, go ahead,' Franz said. 'Orders are orders.'

'Thank you for being so understanding. We'll get it over and done with and let you get on your way as quickly as we can. You do realise there's a storm coming?'

'Yes, I spoke to father last night. Naval Command had given him a forecast. We hoped to get to Grimstad tonight, then hole up for a few days, while the storm passes.'

'I'm not sure you'll make Grimstad. The wind is coming round to the north, or slightly west of north. You'd be better running further east along the Norwegian coast, to Kragerø, Langesund or Larvik, or even turn back to Denmark.'

'We can't go back, but we'll take your advice into consideration. It will be disappointing if we can't make Grimstad.'

Rainer Schulze looked around.

'We'll do a quick search of the topsides first, then go down below.'

As their former sailing rival moved around the deck, opening lockers, and peering in, Franz prayed that Ruth and Manny were in their hiding place in the bilge.

'It all seems to be in order,' he said, smiling at them. 'She's a fine boat, if a little… um… clumsy.'

The Kästners laughed.

'She's no racing boat,' Franz said, 'but she holds a sea well. I wouldn't be quite so complacent about crossing to Norway in *Brünhilde* or *Helga-II* with a storm coming.'

Those were the army and the navy eight-metre racing yachts.

'Or even *Snowgoose*,' Johann added.

'*Snowgoose*?' Rainer Schulze asked, a slight frown on his face.

'My father's yacht.'

'Ah. The General's boat. I've seen her race, but I'd imagine she was built more with fast cruising in mind.'

'Yes, she handles well enough in a blow, but nothing like *Der Sturmtaucher*, I would think.'

'No. This has the look of one of these old boats from when sail was still to the fore, designed to survive anything the elements could throw at them.'

'She's very comfortable to sail when it's rough. It's a pity you couldn't join us.'

'Ha. My commanding officer wouldn't be quite as indulgent as yours, gentlemen. Shall we go below?'

'Be our guest,' Franz said, trying hard to keep concern from his voice.

Franz showed him the way, and Johann followed behind the Kriegsmarine man.

'Impressive accommodation,' Rainer Schulze said, looking around.

'Yes, she's well finished. The colonel had her refitted this winter.'

Franz glanced at the floor and froze. From between the boards that covered Ruth and Manny's hiding place in the bilges, a small piece of white cloth protruded, standing out conspicuously against the dark wood of the floor. Franz stepped across and covered it with his foot, standing awkwardly in the centre of the cabin.

He glanced at Johann. From the dazed look on his face, he assumed that he had seen it and had observed Franz's attempt to hide it. With a sideways glance of his eyes, he signalled to Johann to show Rainer Schulze around.

Johann began opening the lockers next to the companionway, and around the galley, but Rainer Schulze stopped him.

'I'm not doing a full search of *The Shearwater*. I just have to satisfy myself that you are not carrying any English spies on board,' the Korvettenkapitän joked. 'If I can just have a look forward, that should do us,' he added.

'Certainly,' Johann said.

Franz stood rooted to the spot for a second, then moved back to let the navy man pass, as he knew he'd have to. He saw Johann look down at the piece of cloth, and that Rainer Schulze had seen his glance.

'You are worried about your bilges. That is not a good sign,' he said, then frowned as he saw the protruding cloth.

He looked at Johann, then Franz, a puzzled look on his face.

'Lift the boards for me,' he said, his voice now clipped and cold.

Franz looked desperately at Johann then knelt on the cabin floor. Behind Rainer Shultz, he saw Johann lift a belaying pin, and gave him the barest shake of his head.

Johann put it down. Dozens of thoughts ran through Franz's mind, but he tried to focus on a way out of their predicament.

Would Rainer Schulze be sympathetic, and would he listen to reason?

He lifted the board, closing his eyes in despair, expecting Ruth or Manny to scream. Instead, he heard a soft gasp from Johann, and he opened his eyes.

The bilges were empty, save for the old blanket and a couple of cotton sheets that Ruth and Manny made themselves more comfortable with when they were hiding in the cramped space. He tried to make sense of what his eyes were telling him, but it took a few seconds for it to sink in.

He lifted out the blanket, and the sheets. They were sodden with the residual dampness that inhabited nearly all boats' bilges.

'You keep bedlinen in your bilge?' Rainer Schulze said, his voice sceptical.

'We'd stored our excess canned food in the bilge when we left Kiel,' Johann said, interrupting. 'The blankets were to stop them rattling about.'

Franz could have hugged Johann for his quick thinking, but he knew that Rainer Schulze was not convinced.

'We'll have a look at the rest of the boat.'

He made Franz lift the cabin seats and show him the lockers underneath, then opened the door of the heads and stuck his head in, looking behind the door for good measure.

'What's in the forecabin?' he asked.

'We sometimes use it when we're in port,' Franz said, still in a daze, 'but it's mostly just sails.'

Rainer Schulze unlatched the door and crawled through, onto the padded mats that functioned as a double bunk.

'Give me a light. I need to see what I'm doing in here.'

Johann passed him a lighter, and the Kriegsmarine man lit one of the oil lamps on the bulkhead and looked around. He shifted a couple of the sail bags that lay against the boards of the hull making sure that no one was hiding behind them.

'What's below this?' he asked.

'There's another locker,' Franz said, at the doorway.

Rainer Schulze reversed back out of the forecabin and lifted one of the padded mats, and the plywood cover supporting it.

Franz peered over his shoulder, glimpsing the large sailcloth bags that he'd expect to be there. The navy man moved the top bag to one side and prodded the two beneath it.

He replaced the wooden cover, and the mat, and scrambled to his feet again.

He nodded to Franz and Johann and climbed up the companionway. They followed close behind him. He looked about on deck and walked across to the dinghy, lashed upside down on top of the coachroof.

'Please untie it,' he said.

'As you wish,' Franz said. He began to loosen the knots on one side, and Johann did the same on the other. When they had finished, Rainer Schulze asked them to lift it from one side. He looked under it and nodded curtly.

'You can tie it back down again,' he said.

'Are you quite satisfied?' Franz asked, his voice surprisingly free of rancour.

'Yes. I'm sorry, but I had my orders,' the Korvettenkapitän said. 'I hope the next time we meet it is in less trying circumstances.'

'I do, too,' Franz said, still finding it hard to believe that the Nussbaums had completely disappeared from *The Shearwater*. 'We fully understand.'

A sudden thought sent a shaft of fear through his heart.

Christ Jesus, I hope they're not in the water.

The possibility that Ruth and Manny had lowered themselves over the side of the boat while the search was being conducted or, worse still, had slipped into the water and drifted away so as not to incriminate himself and Johann, made his chest tighten and he struggled to take a breath.

He heard Rainer Schulze talking but he didn't catch what the navy man said.

'We'll look forward to it,' Johann said, covering Franz's lapse.

'Take care, and make for the best shelter you can,' the Kriegsmarine man said.

Franz glanced up and saw the radar dish that his father had told him about.

'That's our radar,' Rainer Schulze said, seeing Franz's look. 'It allows us to see ships miles away, even at night.'

'Is that how you found us?' Franz asked.

'Not really. It was just chance that we came across you. We saw your masts long before you showed up on our radar. You're wooden, you see. The fishing boats are the same, but steel ships show up from over twenty miles away, on a good day.'

Franz feigned a disappointed look.

'I thought you might be able to keep an eye on us; make sure we got to shelter safely.'

Rainer Schulze laughed.

'For one, we're going in the opposite direction, and we won't be hanging around. We want to get in before the worst of the storm hits and, anyway, you'll not show up on our radar for more than a few miles at best. But good luck, my friends.'

Rainer Schulze shook hands with Johann first, then Franz. The three men saluted, and the Korvettenkapitän stepped back onto the torpedo boat's tender, followed by the able seaman. Franz and Johann let go of their lines and watched as the launch curved round to the side of the torpedo boat where the lifting lines had been lowered, ready for it.

CHAPTER 100

'Where are they?' Franz said as the tender was winched up into the davits, then swung onto the deck of the torpedo boat.

He spoke in a whisper, knowing that it was irrational, as if their voices would carry to the ears of those on the torpedo boat.

'I don't know,' Johann replied, his eyes frantic with worry.

'Please God, I hope they're not in the water,' Franz said, and turned to see Johann's face blanch.

'They can't be. They wouldn't survive.'

'Unless they sacrificed themselves for us; so that we wouldn't be caught with them on board.'

'No. They wouldn't. Never.'

'Then where are they?'

'I don't know,' Johann snapped.

'I'm sorry,' he said, after a pause.

The deep sound of the torpedo boat's engines interrupted the silence, then its horn sounded twice.

'We'd better get moving and let them see the direction we're heading,' Franz said. 'Look over the port side first,' he added.

Johann walked up the port side of the boat, crouching as if fixing one of the sheets. He peered over, then returned to the cockpit.

'I don't see them.'

'If they're out there, they're lost,' Franz said.

Johann nodded, and released the foresail sheets. Franz unlashed the wheel, and *The Shearwater* began to turn, sluggishly at first, then with more purpose.

'Zero-one-zero,' Franz said, automatically. 'Course set for Langesund.'

The torpedo boat, as if satisfied they were moving, began to make way, drawing apart from them, turning to port to avoid the wash swamping *The Shearwater*. From the bridge, Rainer Schulze waved, and they waved back.

'Take the wheel,' Franz told Johann. 'I'm going below in case they're down there, though God knows where. Keep spilling wind in case we need to come back and search for them.'

Rainer Schulze might still be watching.

Johann nodded. He slackened all the sheets, depowering them without them luffing too much.

Down below, Franz looked around frantically. He lifted the pads on the pilot berths and checked the lockers below, knowing in his heart that they weren't large enough for Manny to hide in, far less Ruth.

He moved forward, checking the wet locker. Their oilskins all hung in a row but when he moved them aside, only the planking of the hull looked back at him.

He opened the door to the forecabin and looked in. Ruth and Manny hadn't miraculously appeared from God knows where, and the chain locker wasn't large enough for one, let alone two people to hide in.

The only thing for it, he thought, was to wait until the torpedo boat was out of sight then retrace their route, hoping against hope that they would find them. If they didn't, they would have to carry on to Norway and phone the General with the terrible news that they'd failed, and that the two young Nussbaums had drowned.

His head dropped, and he covered his face with his hands.

'Ruth. Manny,' he said, the names like a lament.

'Franz.' A muffled voice pierced his despair.

He looked behind him, wondering what Johann wanted.

'Franz,' the voice repeated, but he realised it came from in front of him.

It can't be.

He grabbed hold of the padding and threw it to the side then did the same with the plywood cover, but he realised he must have been hearing things; the only contents in the locker were the three sail bags. Perhaps Johann was above him, on deck, although he couldn't think why.

There was a hatch above his head, which they used to pass sails up and down from the forepeak to the deck. He reached up to undo the clamp that held it shut, then he heard a voice below him.

'Franz. Is it safe yet?'

He looked down at the sail bags and saw one of them move.

'Ruth,' he said, relief melting the cold slab of fear and desolation that had pressed down on him.

He moved the top sail bag aside and stared at the one below. The bag moved. Either Ruth or Manny was inside it.

'You can come out now,' he said. 'They're away. We thought you'd gone overboard.' It sounded ridiculous now that he'd found them.

'I can't get out. I tied the knot and pulled it tight, and I can't get it open now.'

He stifled a smile, despite himself.

He undid the knot and slackened off the drawstrings. He pulled the neck of the bag open and Ruth stuck her head out, gulping for air. Her hair was plastered to her scalp and sweat ran in rivulets down her face. He saw that she'd slipped herself in between the folds of the sail; it was the only reason Rainer Schultze hadn't discovered her.

It must have been hellish in there.

He opened the hatch above them, to give her some air.

'Let Manny out,' she gasped. There was no movement from the third bag.

Franz undid the drawstring. It wasn't tied as tight as Ruth's, but a sudden fear that Manny had been smothered washed over him. He hesitated, then peered into the bag.

He burst out laughing, shaking his head. Manny Nussbaum was fast asleep.

He woke with a start, the fresh breeze from the hatch and Franz's laugh rousing him. He blinked and saw Franz looking at him.

'We're safe?' he asked.

'Yes. For now.'

Franz turned to Ruth. Covered in sweat, and sticking to the sails surrounding her, she struggled to get out of the bag. Franz tried to help her, but it was difficult in the confined space of the forecabin until Manny, clambering out of his own sail bag, lent a hand.

'Johann!' Franz said, glancing sternwards. 'I must tell Johann.'

He ducked out into the saloon and scrambled up the steps. Johann was still at the wheel, staring ahead, unseeing.

'They're safe,' Franz shouted from the companionway. 'They were hiding in the sail bags in the forepeak locker.'

Johann's head slumped for a second, then he looked across the cockpit to Franz. There were tears running down his face and he raised one hand to the sky, his fist clenched.

Franz reached him and they embraced, leaving the wheel untended.

The Shearwater, as ever, ploughed on her course regardless.

CHAPTER 101

'We can turn now,' Franz said.

They'd watched the torpedo boat recede to the north-west until she was just a dot on the horizon, the plume of smoke from her funnel disappearing ten minutes later.

'How far do you think they're away, Manny?' The boy was peering out of the companionway.

'Ten, fifteen, twenty miles?'

'About ten, I think,' Franz said, showing Manny how to work out distances from when any object disappeared over the horizon. 'All you need to know is the height of the object and your height above sea level.'

'Rainer said their radar would be lucky to pick us up at two or three miles,' Johann added. 'That gives us a good margin for error, and they're going away from us all the time anyway.'

Johann turned the wheel hard to port, and *The Shearwater*'s bow came through the wind. Franz tacked the foresails and they set a course south-south-west, on a beam reach.

Franz untied one of the life rings from the back of the boat and threw it overboard, along with a spare life preserver and a name board that hung in the saloon. They were all marked with the yacht's name. He also collected a few of his and Johann's personal items that would float and discarded them over the side along with the others.

'The wind and current will take them eastwards,' he said.

He and Johann had stayed on deck, just in case another Kriegsmarine vessel came up on them, but he'd allowed Manny and Ruth to stand on the lower companionway steps, their heads under the hatch but able to breathe the fresh air of the cockpit and watch the boat's wake snake over the now mounting waves running eastwards behind them.

'Would you have really hit Rainer?' Franz asked.

'I don't know. I wasn't thinking clearly,' Johann said, blushing.

'I wonder what he would have done if he'd found Ruth and Manny.'

'He might have listened to reason.'

'I don't know. I'd like to think so, but I doubt it.'

Both men fell silent, deep in their own thoughts.

When an hour had passed, and there were no sightings of other vessels, Franz relented and went below, sending Manny up to take his place. He made a pot of coffee and handed two mugs up into the cockpit and sat down at the saloon table opposite Ruth.

'So, tell me what happened, and why you disregarded everything we talked about,' Franz said, a hint of a smile at the corner of his mouth.

She blushed and lowered her eyes.

'We put the blankets into the bilge,' she said, in a quiet voice, 'then I just knew that I couldn't get in. Just being in the cabin was making me feel unwell and I realised that if I started retching in the bilges, I'd be bound to be heard. I told Manny that we would have to hide in the forepeak.'

She looked at him apologetically.

'Manny tried to talk me out of it, but I insisted. In the end, he got into one of the sail bags, as I told him, and I fastened it loosely. Then I climbed into the other one and pulled the drawstring almost closed and tied a slip knot in it. Unfortunately, when I tightened it, I must have pulled too hard, and it almost closed the bag completely.

'I nearly panicked,' she said, and he could see from her eyes that she'd been terrified. 'I thought I was going to suffocate but I managed to push my hand into the gap and open up a small airway. It was hot and stuffy, and when the man came to search, I nearly died.'

'At least you weren't sick.'

'I was too worried about getting enough air, I didn't have time to feel sick, and anyway, it didn't smell as bad as the bilge.'

'We were lucky. He got very suspicious at one point.'

'You knew him, didn't you?'

'Yes. We've sailed against him. You might have even met him yourself, at Kieler

337

Woche. I can't remember if you were there that year.'

They sat, saying nothing for a minute.

'You thought we'd jumped overboard?' Ruth said.

'Well, when you didn't show up, we wondered if you'd slipped over the side to hide. That would have been extremely dangerous. You would nearly certainly have died.'

'How could we have done it? Someone would have seen us.'

'The sails were still up. You could easily have slipped out of the front hatch, or through the companionway when we were waiting for the launch to arrive.'

'I suppose so.'

'They were the worst moments of my life,' Franz said. 'The thought of you, in the water, drowning.'

'Me?'

Franz blushed. 'You and Manny. I thought of what I'd have to say to my father, and that he'd have to tell your parents.'

'Oh,' she said, and tears welled up in her eyes. 'I didn't think of that.'

'It doesn't matter now. You're both here, and *The Shearwater* is heading west.'

'Can I ask a question, Franz?'

'Yes.'

'Why are we heading so far south?'

'You noticed?' he said, smiling again.

'I saw you mark it on the chart.'

'There are a few reasons. We need to get as much distance as possible between us and where they expect us to be. If we punched straight into twenty-five-knot winds and waves like this, we would make terribly slow progress. Going this way, our direction is now the exact opposite of the one we were on. If there's a search later, they won't look for us this far south.'

'Oh. I see.'

He lifted a chart down and laid it out on the table. She looked at the title.

Chart 2181. Texel to Bergen.

'There's also a need to get out of the main shipping lanes the Kriegsmarine use,' Franz said, pointing out several areas on the chart, 'but, as well as that, we have no way of knowing for sure where we are now, with all that's gone on in the last few hours. This way, we should be able to see Hanstholm lighthouse in the distance, which will give us a last true fix before we head across the North Sea and, apart from the danger of the odd vessel passing close to Hanstholm, we should be well clear of any shipping after that.'

'I'm sorry. You've thought this all through, you and Johann, haven't you?'

He smiled.

'Yes,' he said, 'but you're right though. It may seem for a while that we're going back to Denmark but it's the best way, I promise.'

'Thank you,' she said, laying her hand on top of his.

He blushed again and quickly lifted the chart, putting it back on the chart table.

'Another coffee?' he asked, in the awkward silence.

'No thanks,' she said. 'I think I might lie down. Unlike Manny, I could never have gone to sleep in that sail bag.'

Franz laughed.

'He's quite a young man,' he said. 'Hardly a nerve in his body.'

She smiled, and Franz saw pride at her little brother shine in her eyes.

When she lay down on the pilot bunk, he sat back and closed his eyes. Before long, he drifted off to sleep.

In his dream, he saw Ruth far out to sea, calling his name but, no matter how hard he tried, he couldn't make *The Shearwater* fight the wind and get to her.

CHAPTER 102

'Sir, that was the police station at Hirtshals. The Kästner brothers left early this morning.'
'Verdammt. We missed them. Still, the Kriegsmarine won't.'
They both laughed.
'Here's the transcript of Frau Kästner's call to her husband, sir.'
Heinrich Güllich took the sheet of paper from his assistant, sat down at his desk, and read it.

DEUTSCHE REICHSPOST

TRANSCRIPT. 7TH April 1941 07:59

From Kiel 3457. Drachensee House. Kästner.

To Kiel 1358 Naval HQ, Kiel.

BEGIN CALL

Female 1: Guten Morgen. Kriegsmarine Headquarters. How can I help you?
Female 2: General Kästner's office, please.
Female 1: Who's calling?
Female 2: Frau Kästner.
Female 1: I'll put you through.
-
Female 3: Guten Morgen, General Kästner's office. Can I ask who is speaking?
Female 2: It's Frau Kästner, Frau Müller. I need to speak to my husband.
Female 3: Certainly, Frau Kästner. I'll see if he's available.
Female 2: It's urgent, Frau Müller.
Female 3: I'll get the General on the line.
-
Male 1 : Maria. What's the matter?
Female 2: Erich, that man is here again. Herr Güllich. From the Gestapo.
Male 1 : What does he want?
Female 2: I don't know. Yosef stalled him at the door so that I could call you.
Male 1 : Don't panic. They're just trying to frighten us.
Female 2: But what do I do?
Male 1 : Just answer truthfully. We've done nothing wrong. For all we know, they may have news about Ruth and Manny.
Female 2: Oh. I didn't think of that. What if it's not, and they arrest the Nussbaums. You won't cause a scene, will you?
Male 1 : Just calm down, and let them in. Do what they say, and I'll be home presently.
Female 2: Hurry, Erich.

END CALL

Heinrich Güllich smiled grimly.
'I'll say this for the old bastard. He's a cool customer for a Judenknecht.'
A servant of the Jews.
Carl Meyer nodded.

'He is good, if he knows something about it, sir.'

'He knows. I'm sure. But she doesn't. She's scared because she's innocent.'

'Why is that, sir, about people?'

Heinrich Güllich smiled.

'It's the same with the police, to a lesser extent. Everyone thinks they are guilty of something. Even the innocent.'

'What do we do now, sir?'

'We just wait. These Jewish brats will turn up somewhere. When they do, we'll have them.'

'They all stuck to the same story, sir. Frau Kästner and her oldest daughter aren't convinced about when they last saw the children, but the younger daughter is adamant that she saw them the day they went missing. And the driver now seems sure he saw Ruth the same day too.'

'The power of collective suggestion, my young friend. He wants to be the same as the others and, as the General and his youngest daughter are the most convincing, he's aligned himself with them, without even knowing why.'

'What about the Nussbaums? They were more nervous today.'

'I thought the Nussbaums might crack, but they're proving harder than I thought. We need to get them away from the General's protection.'

'How do we do that, sir?'

'Let's widen the net. Talk to those the General and his family come in contact with. And to who's left of the Nussbaums' circle of friends.'

CHAPTER 103

Just after four, Ruth awoke. The wind had increased and the noise of the waves crashing against the side of the hull was louder than before.

Franz, sitting at the chart table, looked up and smiled at her.

'Good sleep?' he asked, smiling.

'It took me a while to doze off but after that, I heard nothing, until now. You went to sleep almost instantly. Did you sleep for long?'

'Around an hour,' he said.

'You must have been dreaming,' she said. 'You were crying out in your sleep.'

He reddened. 'What was I saying?'

'I couldn't make it out. You sounded so distressed that I nearly woke you up.'

'I can't remember any of it.'

She sat up.

'Did you put the blanket over me?'

'Yes. There was a chill in the cabin. I thought you might be more comfortable.'

She thanked him, and stood up, a little unsteadily.

'We're on watch at quarter past four,' he said, looking at the brass clock on the bulkhead. 'It gives us ten minutes to grab a slice of bread and cheese.'

'I'm not sure I'm hungry,' Ruth said.

'You should try and eat something if you can,' he said gently. 'You'll need to keep your energy levels up. It's going to be cold and wet out there.'

He watched her force food down and, when Johann shouted down the watch change, he told her to take a piece of ginger with her, to chew on if she felt sick.

'Just in case,' he said.

~~o~~

During Franz and Ruth's watch, the wind backed steadily to the west, and continued to increase in strength. By now, to hold a course to Hantsholm, at the north-western tip of Denmark, *The Shearwater* was close-hauled, sailing as near to the wind as she could. Helming was tough; the waves were much steeper now and whoever was on the wheel had to judge the right time to come off the wind to climb each wave, then turn back into the wind to slide down the back of it.

Franz patiently showed Ruth how to master it and watched as she did her best, but she could only manage short spells, leaving him to do more than his share of the steering. And it was cold. The constant spray from the sea breaking over the bow permeated through their outer layers, and the wind bit into their soaked clothing, chilling them to the core.

~~o~~

'I'm just taking a walk along to the command centre, Frau Müller,' the General said.

'It's five o'clock, sir. I'll be away by the time you return.'

He nodded and grunted a goodbye, then strode off down the corridor.

A young captain gave him a smart salute and grin when he entered.

'General Kästner, what can I do for you, sir?'

'I was hoping you had news about those sons of mine.'

'Ha, sir. Everybody keeps asking. There's nothing yet, sir, but there's a radio blackout, other than for critical communications. We'll hear more when the routine reports come in by telephone.'

'Thank you. I wonder if you could let me know when you hear anything, although Franz and Johann may have phoned from Norway by then.'

'They may be quite late getting in, sir. The weather has deteriorated quite a bit up in the Skagerrak. I'd imagine they would have to run before the wind, to one of the fjords further east.'

'They told me they were expecting a storm. Perhaps it has come a little earlier than expected.'

'I'm sure they'll be all right, sir. There are plenty of places with good shelter up there, and I'm sure the Kriegsmarine will be keeping an eye out for them.'

'You're right, Captain. I'll just have to be patient.'

'The city took a terrible pounding last night, sir. Everyone is talking about it.'

Shortly before midnight, the heaviest air raid of the war on a German city had begun. It lasted five long hours. Targeting the shipyards, the indiscriminate nature of high-altitude bombing left whole swathes of the city alight.

'It's terribly sad,' the General said, shaking his head. 'Over 200 dead, and at least 8000 poor souls have lost their homes, they say.'

'The yards are still working, though, sir.'

'Yes. People are incredibly resilient. I saw that in the last war.'

'Hopefully, this one doesn't last as long, sir.'

'Amen to that, Captain.'

The General returned the captain's salute and left. As he exited the command centre, he glanced along the corridor and ducked back into the doorway. Heinrich Güllich was talking to one of the marines who provided the security for the Naval Headquarters.

Immediately, he knew the Gestapo officer was here to arrest him, and that meant that the boys must have been caught. Frau Müller must have told him that her boss had gone to the command centre. If it weren't for the marine checking his credentials, Heinrich Güllich would have already had him in custody.

The General looked around. On the opposite side of the wide corridor, there was a doorway, but the Gestapo man would see him crossing to it. Just then, a group of young naval officers rounded the corner and walked past him, laughing and joking. As they walked towards the Gestapo officer and the marine, the General took his chance and strode across the corridor and slipped in through the doorway, closing it behind him, not quite latching it.

His hiding place was a janitor's store cupboard, shelved along one wall, the other side lined with stepladders and an assortment of brushes and mops, all propped up against a rack to hold them in place. He went to switch on the light then changed his mind.

With the door open a crack, he could see a little of the corridor and had a view across to the doorway of the command centre, and into the small reception area where reports were dropped off and visitors were received.

A minute passed, then he heard footsteps coming along the corridor. Through the gap, he saw the marine, then Heinrich Güllich, come into view.

'Here we are, sir,' he heard the marine say, pointing to the command centre doorway.

'Thank you, Corporal. Heil Hitler,' the Gestapo man said, giving him a Hitler salute.

Heinrich Güllich waited a few seconds until the same captain the General had been speaking to a few moments before came to the desk and asked if he could help.

'Yes,' the Gestapo man said, showing his Geheime Staatspolizei identification card. 'I'm looking for any results from the stop-and-search order that went out yesterday for all small vessels in the region of the Skagerrak.'

'Oh. That was a Gestapo investigation? We wondered where the order had come from.'

'It's not your place to speculate about such matters, Captain. This is an extremely sensitive investigation. Now, can you give me the reports from the searches that have been conducted?'

'I'm sorry, sir. We don't have that information yet. There is a radio blackout for all but the most important communications. We won't hear anything until the vessels concerned reach harbour, and report to their shore station. Our staff there will then forward the details on to us by telephone.'

The General watched as Heinrich Güllich fought to keep his temper under control.

'This is of the utmost importance. I insist that any of your ships that has intercepted a vessel with illegal persons on board should contact the Kriegsmarine Headquarters at once and that I should hear about it immediately.'

He took a card from his pocket and gave it to the captain.

'You can get me at this number. If I'm not there, leave a message for me to contact you.'

He paused and leaned over the desk towards the young naval officer.

'You do not want me investigating your personal circumstances,' he said, his voice cold and matter of fact.

Even from his hiding place, the General could see the sudden pallor in the young captain's face.

'Yes, sir,' he said. 'We'll let you know as soon as we hear. I'll talk to the head of communications and get a message sent out immediately.'

Heinrich Güllich turned and walked back the way he'd come.

The General allowed himself a grin and punched his palm with his fist in relief.

They haven't been caught. He isn't in the building to make an arrest.

He knew the way the Kriegsmarine worked and, if his sons had been intercepted and the Nussbaums had been found, the repercussions would have been considered important enough for a message to be sent over R\T communications, if for no other reason than to warn him before his world collapsed in on him.

He could only assume that Heinrich Güllich was getting impatient.

He waited a few minutes and scanned the corridor again. It was empty. He slipped out of the store cupboard and glanced around, but no one had seen him.

He returned to his office and sat at his desk, staring into space. He telephoned home and instructed Albert to drive Antje to the dock for seven. He checked the clock. An hour to go before he was due to meet his crew, and hardly worth going home. He would grab something before the shoreside cafés closed for the evening and sit at the boat.

He got up and looked at the chart on the wall and tried to imagine what it would be like out there in the steadily worsening conditions of the Nordsee.

Over the next few days, the worst part would be not knowing, and it might be years before he heard from Franz and Johann again. If ever.

~~o~~

Franz sent Ruth down below after a couple of hours to fetch coffee for them, but she knew it was an excuse for her to warm up and dress in dry clothes. It gave her a chance to have a quick wash and feel almost human again.

While she was down, she looked at their course, speed, and time for the last few log entries, and even she could see a steady decline in the amount of way they were making. The six knots they had been managing just after they turned around now appeared ridiculously fast and, with every second wave almost bringing them to a standstill, they were lucky to be travelling through the water at three and a half knots.

To add to their misery, the rain was now falling in earnest. At first, it came in isolated showers but, by six, those downpours had coalesced into a dismal constant deluge.

'You thrive on this, don't you?' Ruth said, when she climbed up from the cabin, into the rain, bearing two steaming cups of coffee.

'Normally, yes. But, this time, there's too much riding on it to be enjoyable. And sadly, we don't have the option of running for shelter.'

She looked ahead at the waves breaking over the bows.

They're hell-bent on destroying us.

She glanced at Franz for reassurance. She shivered; for the first time, she saw real worry etched on his face.

CHAPTER 104

They arrived in dribs and drabs. Oskar was the first to walk down the jetty and hail the General in a cheerful voice, five minutes before Doc Speer and Dieter arrived from different directions, with Antje close behind them.

'Let's sail,' the General said.

There was a stiff breeze, the forerunner of the storm that the crew of *The Shearwater* were grappling with; the same one that would hit Kiel early the following day. The boat, and the crew, performed well and the General was delighted that his friends had absorbed Antje into their group, the Doc in particular taking her under his wing and teaching her the finer points of setting sail and staying safe in the hustle and bustle of a racing yacht.

'This is great,' she said, halfway through, her eyes shining, 'although I do love cruising too. I think I'd get bored with this quicker.'

The General laughed.

'It's much the same with me, but we have a good laugh, and there aren't so many races that it gets tedious,' he said.

Back at the dock, once the boat was squared away, the General whispered to Antje that there were a few bottles of beer in the bilge and that, if she didn't mind, could she pass them around.

'Have one yourself, if you like,' the General said, or there's a bottle of white wine if you'd rather.'

'No. Beer is fine, Papa.'

It was cold now, so Doc Speer and Oskar followed Antje down the companionway.

'Aren't you two coming down?' Oskar shouted up.

'In a minute,' the General replied, accepting the two bottles that were handed up.

The General stood up and went forward. He leaned against the mast. Dieter sat on the tender.

'How goes it?' the General asked, in a low voice.

'Much the same. Work. Eat. Sleep. Watch our country become the most hated in the world.'

The General laughed, but even to himself, it sounded hollow.

'And your work?'

'Ach, Oskar keeps me busy. And the Third Reich provides him with all the work we need.'

'That's not what I meant.'

'I know. I prefer to pretend I have two lives, but my audience is shrinking; soon there will be no one to read it.'

'What will you do then?'

'I'll still write it. And maybe post copies to prominent Nazis in Kiel.'

The General laughed, then frowned.

'I was joking,' Dieter said, smiling.

'I need a favour,' the General said.

'Yes. Anything, as long as I can help.'

The General lowered his voice still further.

'I need to make contact with the Haganah,' he said. 'Do you know how to get in touch with them?'

Dieter looked around sharply.

'It's dangerous for them, and for you. It would be best done through a third party.'

'You?'

'No. Not me. I couldn't afford to risk the KJF.'

'Who then?'

'You don't need to know. They'll contact you.'

'When?'

'Tomorrow. Next week. Next month. Who knows when they'll feel it's safe? I hope you have plenty cash at your disposal.'

'Why?' the General said, frowning again. 'Are they trying to profit from the movement of refugees?'

Dieter Maas shook his head and gave the General a disappointed look.

'They're having to pay higher bribes to German officials, and those of our Axis allies. It will cost you at least 5000 marks.'

'I'm sorry,' the General said. 'I shouldn't have said that. Tell them I'll pay anything.'

'It's not your fault. Everyone's on the take these days.'

'Even Oskar?' the General said, nodding in the direction of the companionway.

'No. Oskar, he's usually the one who has to pay. Sizeable sums. But for him, it's an acceptable business expense. He reaps the rewards.'

'Perhaps I shouldn't be mixing with him? It would be a shame. I like Oskar.'

'I wouldn't be too hasty. He's a useful man to know, and he does a lot of good. The few Jews, or Mischlinge, who still have jobs in Kiel work for Oskar.'

The General turned to Dieter, surprised.

'Their paperwork has somehow been overlooked,' the newspaperman said. 'The best way to survive as a Jew these days is to work for someone with influence, or someone high up in the party. You should know that.'

He stared straight at the General.

The General closed his eyes and bowed his head.

'The Nussbaums. I try my best.'

'You've done remarkably well to keep them safe, but I hear the children are missing?'

'Yes. Yosef and Miriam are distraught.'

Dieter looked at the General, his eyes narrowing. The corner of his mouth twitched in a smile.

'Let's hope they stay missing,' he said.

The General's head came up sharply.

'What do you mean by…'

Dieter Maas held up his hand.

'You ask me about the Haganah,' he said, 'a week after their children go missing. This is a newspaper editor you're talking to.'

The General had the grace to look sheepish.

'It's safe with me,' Dieter said, 'and I'll try my best to help.'

'Thank you.'

'How are the boys doing, by the way? I imagine they'll have reached Norway by now?'

The General glanced at his friend. Dieter had an ironic smile on his face.

'I haven't heard yet,' the General said. 'I'm expecting news soon.'

Dieter put his hand on the General's arm.

'I feel for you, my friend. It will hurt to have to keep such a heavy burden to yourself.'

'Thank you. You know I can't speak about it, don't you?'

'It's easier for me. The less I know, the better. If I'm ever taken, I'll try my best not to mention you, if I'm asked, but I can't promise anything.'

The General closed his eyes again and shook his head slowly from side to side.

'These are the worst of times,' he said.

'Ah. Good old Dickens. I admire the English a lot, you know.'

'They're the only ones who can save us,' the General said. 'Them, and the Americans.'

Dieter Maas sighed, and nodded.

~~o~~

A short distance away, in the Gestapo Headquarters at Düppelstraße 23, Kriminalassistent Heinrich Güllich slammed the phone down.

'No news, sir?' Carl Meyer asked.

'Nothing. We know that they left Hirtshals. The local police confirmed with the harbour master. I'd hoped that our colleagues in Norway would have located them, if they've somehow managed to elude our wonderful Kriegsmarine friends.'

He thumped the desk with his fist.

'How the hell can they not find a yacht in a stretch of water that size, with all their ships?'

'The Skagerrak is bigger than you'd think, sir, and if the weather's bad…' His voice trailed off.

'It's more likely that they're just not trying very hard, because they're all besotted by General Kästner and his wonderful sons.'

'They'll show up, sir. They must. If not in Grimstad, then in one of the other ports in southern Norway. And our men will get them.'

'I hope so. Because it's not just two Judenschweine we're searching for here. In the Third Reich, there's no place for criminals like General Kästner and those in the Kriegsmarine and the Heer who protect him and his criminal family.'

'Yes, sir,' Carl Meyer said.

CHAPTER 105

When the General got home, Maria had already gone to bed. He slipped out the back door and knocked on the door of the Nussbaums' cottage.

Yosef let him in.

'How are you holding up?' the General asked.

'It's difficult, sir, but we have to carry on the best we can.'

'I can't stay long. I just wanted to give you an update. As far as I know, they left Hirtshals this morning, but I've heard nothing since.'

He hesitated.

'The Gestapo are extremely suspicious. This Heinrich Güllich is a dangerous fellow and is not going to let it go, so be prepared; he'll be back again, no doubt.'

The General decided not to tell Yosef about the Kriegsmarine's orders to intercept and search *The Shearwater*. It would serve no purpose other than to worry the Nussbaums unnecessarily.

'I've talked to someone who can get in touch with the Haganah, but it might take a while.'

'They know about us, sir, but it won't do any harm to remind them that we're still willing to give it a go.'

'Excellent. Now, we just sit tight and wait. For Ruth and Manny, every day there's no news is good for them, and us. If all goes to plan, we should hear something in the course of time, but it might take months.'

'Thank you, sir.'

'I'll see you both in the morning.'

~~o~~

Just before dark, at the end of Ruth and Franz's watch, Johann and Franz turned *Der Sturmtaucher* into the wind and changed the sails. It took them half an hour, and twice Johann was almost washed overboard, working on the foredeck with waves crashing over him, the boat pitching heavily in the steep seas.

But the difference was remarkable. Gone was the off-white of the tanned flax canvas, replaced with a grubby mottled grey from their uneven attempts to dye the second set of sails, melting *Der Sturmtaucher* into the dark clouds and the sheets of rain which filled the blackening sky.

Then night was upon them.

~~o~~

Antje was still up when her father returned from the Nussbaums.

'How are they?' she asked.

'Miriam was in bed, but they're just about holding it together, I think.'

'It must be awful for them. It's the not knowing that's so hard.'

'I know, and it will get worse, but the longer we know nothing, the better for them.'

'Do you think that horrible Gestapo man will come back?'

'Yes. I have no doubt. He is taking all this as a personal affront, and he'll not let it go. I'm afraid we'll have to put up with him for a while yet.'

He gave her a hug.

'You're a remarkable girl,' he said.

~~o~~

As midnight approached, Ruth lay in the port berth, trying to snatch what little sleep she could. *The Shearwater*, hard on the wind, tilted at an alarming angle. It seemed that Franz, held in by a lee cloth in the berth on the opposite side of the cabin, lay almost directly above her and, each time a wave slammed against the bow, the whole boat juddered.

She wondered how much of this punishment it would take before something gave.

~~o~~

Up on deck, Manny, tied by a lifeline to a steel eye on the side of the cockpit, fought with the wheel as each wave threatened to bury them in black mountains of water and white foam.

Twice, Johann reduced sail; he dropped the jib, then put another reef in the mainsail. He took to holding the mainsheet in his hand. When the wind began to overpower *The Shearwater*, he would release it, spilling just enough wind to give Manny a chance to hold her on course.

'What speed is the wind now?' Manny asked.

'Around thirty knots,' Johann said, shouting to make himself heard above the noise. 'That's a force seven, a near-gale.'

'If that's a near-gale, I can't imagine what a gale would be like.'

'You won't have to. We'll have a force eight or even a force nine before the night is out; the barometer is still dropping.'

For a second, Johann thought he saw a flash of fear in the boy's eyes, but then Manny laughed.

And Johann smiled.

~~o~~

Tue 8th April

01:13 Estimated position 36NM NNE HANSTHOLM.

Barometer still dropping. 993mb. Wind 30 knots, westerly. Sea state rough. 2 reefs main, staysail, 1 reef mizzen. 220°M, 3.5 knots.

~~o~~

Johann dried himself off and marked up the boat's log, then plotted their position on the chart. It was only a guess, extrapolated from their speed, measured by the brass log they trailed from time to time, and their direction, which they'd tried to keep as constant as possible.

Manny watched over his shoulder, tired from just coming off watch.

'We've been making 220 degrees on the steering compass,' he said, 'but you've marked a course on the chart that barely makes Hanstholm, which has a bearing of 205 degrees from us. Are the wind and the waves pushing us that far off?'

'No. It's only partly that; there's variation, the difference between the magnetic course and the true course on the chart, and there's leeway, that's the wind. Because we have a long keel, it's maybe only about five degrees, with variation slightly less. But the rest is tide. We think it's pushing us eastward by one knot at least.'

He pointed to part of the chart where Franz had drawn three lines, forming a triangle.

'This one is our course and speed through the water,' he said, tapping his finger on a line heading almost south-east, 'and this one is the tide.'

The second line ran from the end of the first one, in an easterly direction. He pointed to the line Franz had joined that made up the third side of the triangle.

'This is our course over the ground.'

'I see. He's made an allowance for the tide.'

'Yes, and normally, if the tide was changing constantly, as it does in many places, we would plot each hour, with its own tide, to find out where we are.'

'Why aren't we doing that now?' Manny asked.

'The Skagerrak and the Kattegat don't have much true, or lunar tide. All the tidal flow is caused by the wind and, if it blows in the same direction, the tide is more or less constant. Once we get to Hanstholm, we'll begin to see lunar tides, but in the North Sea, they will be less strong than the ones we're experiencing now.'

'So, we'll be able to travel faster?'

'That depends on what the weather does. And remember, the tide in the North Sea will push us one way, then the other, so, over a few days, it will cancel itself out.'

'If the wind stays like this, we can't just head west anyway, can we?'

'No. We'll have to continue south-west for a while, then tack north-west, and so on, unless the wind goes more to the north or to the south and allows us to head west.'

'I hope it does. We would get to England quicker.'

'We would, but most of all, we need the storm to continue, so that we won't be seen.'

'And if the storm dies, what do we do then?'

'We hope that it doesn't but, if it dies, we pray for fog. It's another good reason to head south.'

Manny looked at the chart again, his brow furrowed like an old man. Johann waited for more questions, but they didn't come. He saw Manny stifle a yawn.

'Let's try and get a few hours' sleep,' he said, putting his hand on Manny's shoulder. 'We'll be on watch again just after four. Do you want the high bunk or the low bunk?'

'What's the difference?'

'Well, it doesn't hurt as much if you fall out of the low bunk.'

'I'll take that one then.'

CHAPTER 106

By sunrise, the weather had worsened, and Ruth had succumbed to seasickness.

It had begun shortly after they came off watch at four; Franz knew that it was a combination of tiredness, the cold, and the boat's motion in the confines of the cabin.

She barely made the heads. Franz hovered outside the door, listening to the constant retching that went on forever, knowing there was little he could do.

When she emerged, she was pale and haggard and, with the boat being thrown about mercilessly, she struggled to stand. He helped her into the port bunk and tied a bucket nearby; it was likely that she'd be sick again.

'I know it's the last thing you want to hear,' he said, 'but try to keep nibbling the ginger, and take small sips of water. It will help immensely.'

He smiled and was rewarded with a faint smile in return.

She slept fitfully, waking twice to be sick again and by eight, Franz was resigned to being on watch on his own and let her sleep on.

But as he was putting on his oilskins, Ruth stirred, insisted on getting ready and following him up. As Johann and Manny fell into the berths they'd just vacated, Ruth propped herself up in the corner of the cockpit, getting a little shelter from the bulkhead and watching the sea with horror.

Before he went below, Johann remained at the helm while Franz put a second reef in the main, and another in the mizzen. It appeared to steady *The Shearwater*, and she shook herself off like a wet dog and bounded forward again.

Franz found an old sail bag and made Ruth sit in it, like a sleeping bag, and made sure her lifeline was tied on. The sail bag did the job, repelling most of the spray that crashed over the coach house with every second wave.

'Look at the horizon,' he told her.

'I'll try,' she said.

In truth, the horizon hardly existed. The sun barely penetrated the thick cloud and the wind, rain and spindrift that blew off the crests of the breaking waves made visibility less than a few hundred metres. Only the blurred junction between the dark sky and the black sea, and the crests of the waves gave them any idea of where the horizon might be.

The Shearwater would claw her way up the steep front of each wave and crash through it when it was impossible to climb any higher, then steady herself down the back of the wave, into the deep trough, and the next wall of water ahead.

'This is a gale,' Franz said, trying to keep her alert. 'Force eight, and the barometer's still going down.'

'Can the boat take any more of this?' she asked, a tremor of fear in her voice.

'Yes. She's as good a boat as you'd want in these conditions. She's heavy, with a big lead keel, and her spars are stouter than anything on a modern yacht. Provided we keep reducing sail and don't let her get side-on to a big wave, we should be fine.'

He looked at the worry on her face.

'It won't be pleasant though,' he said.

She leaned over the side to be sick again and he was powerless to help, other than to keep an eye on her.

She sat down again and wiped her mouth with the back of her hand.

'I must look terrible,' she said.

'Don't worry. No one can see you,' he said.

'Just you. And Johann. And Manny.'

'By the time the storm's passed, we could all be like you. None of us are immune to seasickness.'

'Have you ever had it?'

'Well, no, as a matter of fact, but it could happen.'

~~o~~

Ruth watched him.

She doubted he'd ever succumb to the nightmare of seasickness. He looked so at home, bracing himself with ease and, although he barely moved the wheel, the boat seemed to respond to his touch, finding the kindest path through the chaotic sea.

She closed her eyes for a second and tried to remember what it felt like to be on dry land. When she opened them again, Franz was staring past her, at something out to sea.

It must be a boat. Please let it not be a Kriegsmarine ship.

'Look,' he said, pointing.

She turned around, but could see nothing but waves, rolling away from them.

'What is it?' she asked, her tone a little irksome.

'Ein Sturmtaucher,' he said.

A Shearwater.

She looked again, then she saw it, the white of its underside flashing against the darkness of the sea as it turned, skimming along the trough beneath two waves, centimetres above the surface, disappearing when it turned away from them, the muddy brown of its back blending in with the sea behind.

~~o~~

'It looks so easy,' she said. 'It just glides, as if there's no storm.'

'It's sheltered from the wind, down in the trough,' Franz said.

He looked at her face and saw what he thought were tears running down it. He wondered if he was mistaken; that it was just the rain, or the spray until he saw her shoulders jerk in a sob.

'What's wrong?' he said, in a lull between gusts.

'Oh, nothing,' she said. 'Just me being silly.'

She turned to face him.

'Antje gave me a picture of a Shearwater that she'd painted,' she said. 'I brought it with me, to remind me of her. I'll show you sometime.'

Franz looked away. The mention of his sister had caught him by surprise. He recalled the day she'd drawn the birds on their trip to Wangerooge and Helgoland.

He looked back at her.

'She wanted to come, you know. She pleaded with my father.'

Ruth smiled.

'I know. She told me. She was the best friend anyone could have had.'

'We'll see her again, I promise.'

'I wish I could believe that,' Ruth said.

~~o~~

'The weather has deteriorated, sir. There's no chance of them moving anywhere today, wherever they've holed up.'

'I know, Captain, and no matter how good the shelter, unless they are in a harbour, they'll not be able to get ashore to contact anyone.'

'That's true, sir,' Captain Bauer said.

'Have you spoken with the command centre today, sir? Do you want me to go along and find out if there's any news?'

'No, Captain, but thanks. I've already spoken to them.'

'Ah. I'll leave you to it then, sir.'

The captain closed the door behind him. Frau Müller glared at him.

'Well?'

'No news, I'm afraid,' the captain said.

'I pray they're safe,' she said.

Despite her disapproval of most of General Kästner's ways, Captain Bauer was surprised to read genuine sympathy for him in her eyes. He sensed that the General's unaccustomed agitation, out of character for him, had unsettled everyone in the small unit.

'If anyone phones, let me know straight away,' he told her.

351

CHAPTER 107

'It is, you know. We did it.'

Johann pointed.

Through the gloom, perhaps a mile away, a white smear appeared atop the dark strip of land they had been following for almost two miles.

'That's Hanstholm light,' he said. 'We were only two miles out.'

'How can you be sure?' Manny said, as the rain and foam obscured the tower again.

'We'll go a little closer, just to make certain, but we've been running parallel to the land since we spotted it half an hour ago, heading west. There's no other lighthouses nearby and, anyway, if it is Hanstholm, the land will fall away to the south-west once we pass it.'

Johann had been taking soundings every quarter-hour since the start of their watch at midday and comparing them to the depth contours on the chart, so it hadn't been a shock when Manny shouted out that he could see the rough shades of land ahead. The rain had eased, and the wind had moderated a little to a force seven again, improving the visibility as a result.

They'd crept along a mile or so off the shore, never too close to make him fear they'd be spotted from the land in the grey mirk they sailed in, until the lighthouse emerged from the gloom, half a mile to the west.

'Look,' Manny said. 'What's that?'

Johann squinted. To the east of the lighthouse, three long fingers, barely visible against the dark clouds, reached up and pierced the skyline, pointing inwards towards each other.

'They're cranes,' Johann said. He could see their latticed arms now and could just make out the hooks suspended from the steel wires. 'It must be a construction site of some kind. I'll ask Franz.'

He slid back the hatch and peered into the cabin below. Franz was making lunch of bread and cheese, but he looked up when the hatch opened.

'We think we can see the Hanstholm light. We'll know for sure when the land drops away to the south, but there's a large construction site east of the lighthouse which is a little puzzling.'

'Father mentioned it. They're building a massive naval battery. Hanstholm fortress. He says the range of the guns that are being installed will cover halfway to Norway, and they're going to build another one in Kristiansand, to guard the Skagerrak and control access to the Baltic.'

Johann laughed.

'That's what it must be. A good job it isn't ready yet or we might have been blown out of the water.'

'I would imagine that they're more concerned about the British and their Royal Navy.'

~~o~~

Five minutes later, Franz heard Manny say something to Johann.

'Are you sure?' he heard Johann ask then the hatch slid open again. Johann's head appeared.

'That's the land dropping away now. It's Hanstholm light, all right.'

He disappeared again and returned a half a minute later.

'The bearing to the lighthouse is one-seven-zero degrees and the depth is eleven fathoms.'

Franz drew a line on the chart at a bearing of one-six-five, to allow for variation, then made a mark just past the point where it crossed the ten-fathom contour. It was a fix that he knew was accurate to within a cable or so, and he was more than satisfied by how accurate their navigation had been.

But he worried that the storm was subsiding. This close to land, it was imperative that they were not seen, and that other boats should think twice before venturing out.

'Aren't there minefields around here?' Johann called down.

'We've been skirting the edge of one for the last hour or two but we're almost out of it, if father's information is accurate.'

'I'm relieved to hear it, although I don't know if we would spot a mine with this sea running.'

'No, I suppose not. How's it looking out there?'

'We're in a lull at the present time. The wind has dropped a shade, and the rain is almost off. The trouble is, I can see the shore a little too well now. I hope we're not spotted.'

'They might be able to see us but, in this sea, and with the dull background, I doubt it.'

'It was a good idea to dye the sails grey. The light sails would have stood out like a wart on a tart's nose.'

'Johann!' Franz said.

'Ach, don't be so uptight. I'm teaching Manny how to curse properly.'

'It's not just Manny,' Franz hissed. 'We have a girl on board.'

'From what I know, girls aren't as easily shocked as you might think. You should hear what some of them call my–'

Franz slid the hatch shut, cutting off Johann's words.

He turned, embarrassed, but Ruth was dozing, curled up in her berth. He would wake her up soon; she needed to take a little nourishment and now was an ideal opportunity, while conditions were less unsettled.

Johann slid the hatch back open.

'I meant to say. It looks very dark out to the west. There's more heavy weather heading our way.'

CHAPTER 108

'Herr Kriminalassistent, we have the reports from our operations in the Skagerrak you were looking for. We can send them over later if you like.'

Heinrich Güllich looked at his watch and smiled grimly.

Five past two and a day late. With a little luck, the Kästners will get the rewards they deserve.

'No,' he said, not wanting to wait. 'I'll send someone over to collect them.'

He looked around for Carl Meyer, but he'd sent him to follow up a lead on another of their cases.

I'll go myself.

He left the office and walked the short distance down to Naval Headquarters, despite the strong wind, and the threat of rain.

The same captain he'd spoken to the day before was waiting for him at the command centre.

'Herr Kriminalassistent, how are you?'

'I'm fine. Where are my reports?'

The young captain flinched.

'I have them here, sir. I'm not sure there's much in them of interest.'

He turned away, but Heinrich Güllich didn't miss the grin he gave the lieutenant sitting at a desk nearby.

'You've read them?' the Kriminalassistent asked, scowling.

'Yes, sir. These are just copies. The reports will be made available to the whole Kriegsmarine.'

'And you, as a mere captain, decided that it would be beneficial to the Third Reich for you to study these documents? Documents that were requested by the Geheime Staatspolizei?'

'The decision was not mine, Herr Güllich. My commanding officer instructed me to go through the reports and summarise them for our department. It's routine. Would you like to see the summary, sir?'

'No thank you, Captain. I'd rather trust my own judgement. Heil Hitler.'

He clicked his heels and stretched his arm out in salute.

'Heil Hitler,' the captain intoned, giving a weary Hitler greeting in reply.

~~o~~

The lieutenant stifled a grin.

'You really got up his nose, Captain. Are you sure that was wise?'

The satisfaction that he'd felt in goading the Gestapo officer had staled a little, and the young captain began to wonder if the lieutenant was perhaps right, but it was done now.

He shrugged, but his nonchalance was unconvincing.

'What did the report say?' the younger officer asked.

'The Kriegsmarine intercepted and searched fifty-two vessels under fifty metres yesterday. Forty-one of them were fishing boats and most of the others were commercial vessels of one type or the other. Only one wasn't.'

'What vessel was that, sir?'

A smile appeared at the corner of the captain's mouth.

'*Der Sturmtaucher*, the yacht that General Kästner's sons are delivering to Norway for their commanding officer.'

The lieutenant laughed.

'Did they find anyone illegal? A couple of Danish girls on the Kästner yacht?'

'That's what I thought, but no girls. However, the search did turn up two illegals. One was a Polish man who worked on a Norwegian fishing boat. He had no visa. The other was a fourteen-year-old boy who had lied about his age to go to sea on a lobster boat, working out of Skagen in Denmark.'

Both the men laughed.

'Has there been any news of the Kästners' arrival in Norway?' the lieutenant asked.

'No,' the captain said, his face now serious. 'They haven't been seen by anyone since torpedo boat *T4* left them, and they haven't made contact with General Kästner or their commanding officer either. I telephoned the General a short while ago to tell him that they'd last been seen heading for Langesund. He appears rather worried, although he's hiding it well. He's sure that they'll have taken refuge somewhere, without access to communications.'

'What do you think?'

'He's probably right. They had time enough to reach safety before the storm struck.'

'They say it's a bad one. The worst in years.'

'It seems to be. God rest their souls if they are caught out in it.'

~~o~~

Carl Meyer blanched. He'd seen the Kriminalassistent's anger on quite a few occasions over the last week, but he'd never seen him in such a cold fury.

'The sycophantic, Jew-loving, treasonous bastards,' he said. 'One day, Germany will be rid of them all, and we will have loyal National Socialists in their place.'

'What happened, sir?'

'The Kriegsmarine fools stopped the Kästner boat and found nothing.'

'Perhaps the Nussbaums have been dropped off in Denmark, as you suggested.'

'They were on board. I'm sure of it now, in my gut. The navy have either lied and turned a blind eye when they found them, or they didn't bother searching with any real diligence. It's the usual *old boys' network* of patronage and nepotism at its worst.'

Carl Meyer had glanced at the report on the search of *Der Sturmtaucher*. As far as he could tell, it had been conducted thoroughly.

'It might be worthwhile interviewing this Kapitänleutnant Schulze, sir, even if just for completeness.'

'Why bother? He'll be just like the rest, protecting his own kind. Never mind, one day, they'll all pay for it.'

Carl Meyer waited a minute before speaking again.

'What about Norway, sir? Has there been nothing at all?'

'Do you think I would be sitting here talking to you if they'd been spotted? I sometimes wonder if there's an investigator in you at all.'

'Sorry, sir,' said Carl Meyer, seething inside.

The man can sometimes be a complete Arschloch.

For a time, Heinrich Güllich sat at his desk, fuming, then stood up, pacing across the room, back and forward. He lit another cigarette, the fourth in as many minutes.

'They have to turn up somewhere, unless they've sunk,' he said.

'Perhaps it's what they deserve, sir?'

'No,' Heinrich Güllich shouted. 'I don't want them at the bottom of the sea, with a quick death. I want them here, in front of me, in our interrogation rooms downstairs, to see how superior they would feel then. And to make their father watch…'

Carl Meyer thought the Kriminalassistent was losing it but there was something very compelling to him about the thought of Heinrich Güllich interrogating the members of the Kästner family when they'd lost the protection that was now afforded them.

CHAPTER 109

When the second part of the storm hit, it did so with a wrath that shocked the Kästner brothers.

'Stick your head up and look at this,' Johann said, sliding open the hatch.

Franz climbed the steps and glanced past the stern. He could just about make out Hanstholm light in the murk as the land receded. He turned and looked towards the bow, where Johann was pointing.

'Let's drop the main, get the storm jib up, and put a reef in the mizzen,' he said abruptly.

He looked again. As far as his eyes could see, a black wall of cloud and rain stretched left and right, and the angry white line at its base told Franz that it was whipping up the sea as it rushed towards them. In front of it, the waves had increased in size in the short time he'd last looked, a sure sign that a severe blow was on the way.

He turned and spoke to Manny.

'When Johann has finished reefing, make sure you're both tied on and hand the wheel to him. You take charge of the jib sheet but take a turn on the cleat, and watch your hands if it starts to run through.'

'Why? What is that?' he said, pointing at the approaching blackness.

'That, Manny, is going to make what we've been through earlier feel like a sail round Kieler Hafen on a summer's day. I'm going down to make sure everything is secure, including your sister. And I'm going to tie this hatch shut. Just knock if you need anything.'

He gave a last glance at the looming bank of black cloud advancing towards them. It was much closer now, and he shouted to Johann to hurry back to the cockpit. If he were caught on the foredeck, he could be washed overboard by the first wave.

He closed the hatch. He woke Ruth and told her what to expect. Then he waited.

The first gust rocked *The Shearwater* and, despite having next to no canvas set, she heeled over to an alarming angle. Ruth, safe in her bunk, screamed as the side of the hull almost became the floor.

Franz knew she'd come back up; it hadn't been a wave that had flattened them. A second later, sails, close to horizontal, spilled the wind and she began to right herself, but Franz knew the danger hadn't passed. A broach, while righting herself, could put her side-on to the sea, and if a wave were large enough, it could roll them.

He waited, holding his breath, but out on deck, Johann must have been alert to the danger because, even as she threatened to stall, she swung hard to starboard and met the next wave on the shoulder.

Franz heard the storm jib fill with a crack and pull *The Shearwater* round, and she bit into the wall of water, burying her bow in the crest of the wave to emerge on the other side.

A tonne of water crashed into the cockpit, filling it almost instantly. Franz saw a stream pour down the steps of the companionway through the small gap between the hatch cover and the washboards and knew he'd have to fashion something from spare canvas to proof it against further ingress of water, or the cabin, their refuge from the cold and the wet, would become damp and miserable.

~~o~~

In the cockpit, the weight of water almost swept Manny over the side but his lifeline held, and he grabbed onto the guardrails and clung on, while the water emptied through the cockpit drains. Johann saw him gasp as the water penetrated his clothing.

Johann had been knocked over but managed somehow to regain his feet, and steered off the wind a little, just to keep *The Shearwater* from burying herself again.

The waves were mountainous now and he knew that they were in trouble. He took the next wave just forward of the beam and she tilted alarmingly again, but she climbed up the side of it and broke through the crest without burying herself and he swung her to port, trying to make way westwards, away from land.

The cockpit had emptied of water. He thanked God, the boatbuilder, and Colonel Schneider for fitting large cockpit drains that allowed the water to run away quickly. The extra weight of a full cockpit would have done nothing for *Der Sturmtaucher*'s stability.

He managed another four waves without burying her, but he mistimed the fifth one, and they were engulfed again.

This time, both he and Manny were ready for it. As the water ran away, they looked at each other and grinned.

He looked at the compass. They were getting pushed further and further northwards and he knew that they'd have to do something about it, but he didn't know how safely he could tack *The Shearwater* through a wind and a sea like this.

'Take the wheel, Manny. Try and do what I was doing; take the front of the wave at this angle.'

He showed Manny as *The Shearwater* climbed up the next wave.

'And just as you come to the top,' he said, turning the wheel, 'put her to port, and keep her that way until you meet the next wave.'

'I'll try,' Manny said, taking the wheel and gripping it with whitened knuckles.

Johann tied him on and moved his own lifeline to the forward eye at the companionway entrance. He knocked a couple of times on the hatch.

He looked forward. The boat was climbing the next wave as it should and, as it reached the top, he felt the turn to port and *The Shearwater* steadied herself on the back of the wave.

The hatch slid open a crack.

'We need to talk,' he said to Franz. 'But we can't afford to keep this hatch open.'

'I'll come up,' Franz said. 'No one will see us in this.'

Johann closed the hatch again and waited. He watched Manny work the waves, impressed by how quickly the boy had caught onto what he had to do, but he knew he'd need to be ready if a wave came that the youth couldn't cope with.

I'll worry about that when it happens.

~~o~~

The hatch slid open and Franz climbed out, fastening it quickly behind him. He fitted the piece of canvas he'd cut and roughly stitched to seal the companionway. To be extra safe, he tied a cord around the handles to avoid any chance of it springing open if worst came to worst, and they were knocked down.

'Use this from now on,' he told Johann. 'It will keep the water out from below.'

He glanced up at the sails, took a long look at the sea and watched Manny steer.

'He's a natural,' he said to Johann.

'He had a good teacher,' Johann said, smiling.

'That might be so, but we're being pushed back north again,' Franz said.

'Yes. That's why I wanted you up. We need to turn and run south.'

'We'll be on a lee shore,' Franz said.

'I know, but we need to find shelter. This appears to be getting worse, and it's up to force ten already, maybe even an eleven. If we make one mistake, we could roll her.'

Franz closed his eyes for a second, not wanting to visualise the boat being upside down but unable to prevent the picture from entering his head.

'I think she'd come up again,' he said.

'Those on deck would be lucky to survive, and she would likely lose a spar or two.'

Franz knew he was right.

'We'll have to run down the coast, find somewhere to tuck in to ride this out.'

'It would need to be somewhere we wouldn't be seen.'

'That's going to be difficult. There aren't many places like that close by.'

'How far is it to Thyborøn?'

'About thirty miles. But the entrance will be guarded.'

'If we get there at night, we might be able to slip through unnoticed.'

'I'm not sure we will. There's plenty room inside to hide but getting back through the entrance unseen once the storm blows over would be nigh on impossible.'

The Thyborøn Kanal, a short, narrow channel between two long sandspits, opened out into Nissum Bredning, a large, shallow inland sea running into a series of fjords which connected the west coast of Denmark with the Kattegat in the east.

They could anchor behind the north spit, where there were large mudflats and a number of small cuts where they could hide, but the German fortifications at the entrance would have to be negotiated on the way in, and on the way out, and smaller Kriegsmarine vessels might still patrol the sheltered waters, Franz was sure.

'You've sailed this coast before. Where else is there?'

'There's no shelter at Thorsminde, and little at Hvide Sande. It has the same problem as Thyborøn, but worse; we'd have to go through a lock to get into Ringkøbing Fjord, so that's not an option.'

The yacht lurched and they heard Manny's warning shout just as *The Shearwater* buried herself in a wave. As she lurched to starboard Johann scrambled along the cockpit and took hold of the wheel, helping Manny wrench it round, but it was too late to stop them being swamped again.

'Come over, you bitch!' Johann screamed, and *The Shearwater*, as if she'd heard his cry, met the next wave halfway round. Another wall of water crashed into the cockpit again, but she'd broken the crest of the wave and the sails were driving her forward, pointing better for the next one.

She settled again on her course, but Johann stood by the wheel, ready to help if needed.

'There is a place, another thirty miles on from Hvide Sande,' Franz said. 'The ferries used to leave there for England before the war.'

'I know it. Esbjerg. It's a busy port, though, so we'd have the same problem of being seen.'

'From what I remember, the entrance between the outlying islands is quite a distance from the port itself, and there's a lot of quiet shelter in the lee of Fanø, or in Ho Bucht, a quiet inland sea to the north. We once anchored there, behind a large sandspit, amongst the marshes. I can't remember its name, but it was very isolated.'

'That's a hundred miles from here,' Johann said, shaking his head. 'In this weather, it could take us two days.'

'The only other option is to heave-to here and try and ride out the storm.'

'We'll be too close to the shipping lane, once the storm blows over. We need to get a substantial distance between us and where they think we'll be.'

Franz thought for a minute.

'We must go south,' he said, his mind made up. 'We have no option, really. If the weather improves, we can strike out west for England at any point.'

'There's another problem,' Johann said.

'What's that?' Franz asked.

'The storm jib is working fine but the mizzen isn't doing enough, and if we let out its reef, there would be too much sail, too far aft.'

'Even one reef in the main would be too much,' Franz said, 'but we do have the trisail.'

'What's a trisail?' Manny asked and both the Kästners turned, not realising that he was listening to them.

'It's a small triangular sail that takes the place of the mainsail,' Johann said, 'for storms.'

'It doesn't attach to the boom; we lash it to one of the stern cleats, so we can keep the boom tied down, out of the way,' Franz explained. 'It takes away the danger that it will fly across the boat, if we accidentally gybe, or if the mainsheet comes loose.'

'Unfortunately, we have to rig it,' Johann said, 'and we'd be better doing it while we can still see.'

Franz looked at his watch.

Six o'clock. An hour's daylight at most in these conditions.

'It means someone has to go up to the mast,' he said.

'That would be me,' Johann said.

'Or me,' Franz said.

'No. I'll go. You take the wheel and Manny can help with the lines.'

Franz didn't argue with him. On helm, in these seas, he could probably keep the boat steadier than Johann.

He opened the hatch and looked down into the cabin. Ruth wasn't in her bunk, then he saw the door to the heads swinging.

Scheiße, she's being sick again and no one's looking out for her.

He put her out of his mind as he took the wheel, knowing he had no choice.

'We'll get the trisail rigged, ready to go up, then drop the mizzen and hoist the trisail at the same time,' he said to Johann.

They explained to Manny his part in the process, and Johann retrieved the trisail from its locker at the back of the cockpit.

Franz waited until they were through the next wave then pointed her higher into the wind.

~~o~~

Johann clambered from the cockpit, dragging the sail behind him. He unscrewed the shackle on the main halyard and transferred it to the head of the trisail, then tied the tack down to the gooseneck, which held the boom onto the mast.

'Look out,' he heard Franz shout, and he wrapped his lifeline around one of the cleats on the mast and clung on, just as the wave broke over the bow, burying him chest deep in water. The wave pulled the canvas from his hands and he gasped as the cold water penetrated his oilskins, soaking his inner clothing again, but he held on and, when the wave had passed, he gathered the sail back in and got hold of the line tied to the clew. He looked back and signalled to Franz that he was ready to hoist.

'Hauuuulll away,!' Franz screamed above the roar of the storm.

Johann pulled hard on the halyard and the trisail shot up the mast in a few seconds. He tightened it as much as he could, then used the purchase, a simple system of pulleys, to remove any residual slackness.

Again, he heard the warning shout and, this time, he tucked in behind the mast, sparing himself the worst of a drenching.

Untying his lifeline, he made his way back to the cockpit, noticing with satisfaction that Manny had dropped the mizzen and was tying it down to its boom, with the gaff lying neatly on top of it.

He tied off the trisail to one of the stern cleats and helped Manny do up the last few sail ties on the mizzen.

The Shearwater steadied up, and bit through the next wave more easily.

~~o~~

'She feels better,' Franz shouted. 'Let's get her round.'

She tacked much better than Franz thought she would, or maybe they just got lucky with a series of smaller waves but, once the wind was on her starboard side, he found that he could just about sail parallel to the coast, and perhaps even edge her seawards, to gain a little room.

He sent Johann down to dry off and change clothes and asked him to check on Ruth. To his surprise, no sooner had Johann disappeared than Ruth emerged from the hatch, fully geared up in her oilskins.

'You should have stayed below,' he said.

'I needed fresh air,' she answered. 'And anyway, I'm not going to act like a weakling just because of a little seasickness.'

She took out a piece of ginger and put it in her mouth, chewing slowly.

Franz saw her fighting the urge to gag.

He nodded to Manny.

'Go and get a fresh set of clothes, and a cup of coffee. We'll move the watches back a little to make up for you and Johann doing overtime.' He smiled.

'It's all right,' Manny said. 'I'd rather just stick to our usual watch if you're fine with that.'

Franz wasn't surprised. He watched Manny climb down the companionway and close the hatch behind him. The boy was proving to be tougher than they could have dreamed of, and Franz knew he'd do anything to help his sister.

He found himself quickly in touch with the waves and the wind, steering across the steep fronts of the breakers and down their long backs, only once in a while burying the yacht's nose in a wave or being knocked sideways. Ruth wasn't sick again but the fear he'd seen in her eyes, when she first came up and caught sight of the size of the waves, never left her.

When he wasn't looking, Ruth watched Franz. He looked so easy on the helm, despite the conditions, and it was this alone that kept her fear under control. She liked Johann, but she didn't know quite how she felt about Franz. She was coming to trust him more by the day, and her liking for him grew every hour they were thrown together.

Don't fall for him, she told herself, knowing that their backgrounds were too far apart for anything ever to come of it. He was also older than her and, besides, the way she looked now, more like a boy, and a sick one at that, she was sure he wouldn't give her a second glance.

'We're heading south, aren't we?' she said, watching the compass.

'Not quite,' he said. 'There's a bit of west in our course, but the coast runs south and west, so we're just keeping our distance from it.'

'It's not getting us any closer to Britain, is it?'

'Not at present, but the storm's too severe to try and fight it, and with the barometer still not bottoming out, it could get worse yet. We're trying to find somewhere to shelter, until the wind changes direction.'

'Do you know where to find somewhere like that?' she asked.

'Yes, but it will take us a while to get there.'

'How long?'

'We hope to get there by late tomorrow.'

She gasped.

'Do you think the storm will last that long?'

He shrugged.

'No one can tell. All I know is that there's no sign of it passing.'

He glanced at her, and she saw the look of concern in his eyes.

What must I look like? Pale. Terrified. Ill. Pathetic.

'You were about to tell me about your Bat Mitzvah,' he said, 'the last time we were on watch.'

Ruth stared at him.

How can he even think of having a normal conversation when it's like this?

She tasted bile in her throat as the boat lurched again, but she'd been brought up not to be rude. And she appreciated his attempts to take her mind away from the horrors surrounding her.

She swallowed and forced herself to speak.

'It doesn't have the significance of a Bar Mitzvah,' she said, 'but it was important to me.'

'My father said it's a recent thing. When Yosef had his Bar Mitzvah, girls didn't take part.'

'No, the rabbi introduced it, but the Orthodox Jews, the Ostjuden, didn't approve, and wouldn't let their daughters take part.'

'There's a lot of ceremony, being a Jew, isn't there? We only have Christmas and Easter, really.'

'We love our holy days. We have Pesach, that's Passover, which will be next week. We'll be in England by then, won't we?'

'I hope we will,' Franz lied, glancing at the steep seas surrounding them. 'Is it terribly important that you attend synagogue that day?'

'Yes, but there's also the whole cleaning thing, and the meal. I hope we can find a Jewish family to celebrate it with but, if not, Manny and I will just have to observe by ourselves.'

'How would I wish you a happy Passover?'

'You'd say *chag Pesach samech,*' Ruth told him, 'but happy Passover would do.'

'Isn't there a holiday around Christmastime? I've seen the candles in your window.'

'That's Hanukkah, in early December, the Festival of Lights. We light the Menorah to symbolise the light that burned in the temple for eight days, even though there was only enough oil for one day, but it's not as important as Pesach, Rosh Hashanah, or Yom Kippur.'

'What are they?' he asked.

She briefly wondered how much of it was genuine interest, or if it was just to keep her mind off the sea.

'Rosh Hashanah is the Jewish New Year,' she said. 'It also marks the creation of man, in the Garden of Eden. It's in the autumn.'

'Would I say Happy New Year to you?'

'If you want to impress a Jewish person, you should say *Shanah Tovah Umetukah.*'

'Shanah Toveh Umtekah,' Franz said.

'Close,' Ruth said, smiling, 'but it's *Shanah Tovah Umetukah.*'

She spoke slowly, enunciating each syllable and when he repeated it, it was much better.

'Watch out,' Franz said, pulling Ruth towards him as a wave, larger than the rest, spilled into the cockpit.

'That's cold,' Ruth gasped. She began to shiver.

'Go down and dry yourself off. I'll be fine for a while. Make a cup of coffee while you're down.'

Gratefully, she slid the hatch back and removed the washboards. She disappeared down the companionway, closing them over behind her.

~~o~~

'Shanah Tovah Umetukah,' Franz said, then repeated it.

He smiled as the next wave descended on him.

I must remember that.

CHAPTER 110

'Is there any news of the boys yet?'

Erich Kästner turned towards the kitchen door with a start. Maria had hardly spoken to him in a week, and she hadn't been in when he returned late from work so he'd eaten his meal in the kitchen, served up by Miriam. He hadn't heard his wife coming in the front door.

He gave her what he hoped was a reassuring smile.

'There's nothing yet, but the reports from Norway say that the storm is still raging.'

'What if they were caught in it?'

Although they were estranged, he still loved his wife and it pained him to have to lie to her.

'I'm sure they had enough time to reach safety,' he said. 'They're tucked away in some fjord, miles away from civilisation. We'll not hear from them until the storm passes.'

'You're worried, aren't you?'

'I worry about a lot of things but, yes, I'd be a fool not to be concerned.'

She bit her lip.

'I don't know what I'd do if anything happened to them. I know it sounds silly, with them both being soldiers, but this is different.'

'I know what you mean but they've been lucky so far. The Wehrmacht has swept all before it with minimal resistance, and remarkably few casualties. It won't always be like that.'

'Have you heard something?' she said sharply.

'Nothing concrete,' the General answered. 'Just rumours.'

'Are we going to invade Britain? Will the boys be part of it?'

The General almost laughed.

If their luck held, at least two German soldiers would be in England by the end of the week.

'It's not Britain,' he said. 'And yes, the boys' Kompanie could be involved.'

She frowned for a moment then a knowing look crossed her face.

'It must be Turkey or Arabia,' she said. 'We need oil, don't we, for our ships and our tanks.'

He didn't disabuse her of her error. If rumours did start about the proposed Eastern Front with the Soviets, he didn't want them traced back to his wife.

~~o~~

It appeared to Manny that when the daylight faded, the storm fed on the darkness and redoubled its ferocity. Since coming back on watch at eight, with the daylight gone, every second wave engulfed *Der Sturmtaucher*, dropping tonnes of water on her decks and in her cockpit. It made helming nigh on impossible at times, save to mitigate the worst of what the sea was doing to her.

They took short spells on the wheel; any longer than half an hour stretched tired muscles beyond fatigue and strained their levels of concentration to breaking point. Johann, the stronger of the two, both physically and mentally, lasted longer than Manny, but not by much.

Halfway through the watch, Manny glimpsed the flash of a red light less than a mile off their beam. He slid the hatch open a few centimetres. Franz was studying the chart and looked up.

'That's the Vorupør light,' he said. 'A little less than a mile. 'Just forward of the beam.'

He watched as Franz checked the bulkhead compass and made a log entry.

22:35 VORUPØR LT 120°M, 8 Ca. Wind 45 knots, westerly. Massive seas. Barometer still dropping. 988mb. 4.0kts 215°M. Storm jib and trisail.

He slid the hatch shut and followed the beam from the lighthouse, illuminating the sea and the low cloud surrounding them in blood-red flashes like a scene from a watery hell, until it faded and disappeared behind them.

~~o~~

For a further two hours, Johann and Manny fought the storm without speaking to one another; little could be heard above the roar of the wind and the crash of the sea as it slammed *The Shearwater*. Twice, the boat almost broached, and Johann was thrown across the cockpit by the wheel spinning but both times, she found her own way back just as it looked certain she'd roll. As midnight came and went, they counted down the minutes until they could escape the onslaught for the relative sanctuary of the cabin.

'I'm sorry you've had to go through this,' Johann shouted, during a brief lull.

'It's better than being back in Kiel,' Manny said. 'At least I can fight back here.'

Johann looked at Manny.

He's not a boy anymore.

He wondered if Manny had lost his childhood forever.

'What was the worst for you?' he asked.

'School,' Manny said, without hesitation. 'I loved school, until the National Socialists destroyed it for us. They turned the teachers and our school friends against us.'

He wiped the rain and the spray from his eyes with his sleeve.

'I remember once,' he continued, 'three Hitlerjugend boys grabbed Fischel Liewermann and dunked his head down the toilet. They'd pissed in it first. Another two boys held me, so I could do nothing.'

'The teachers; they did nothing to stop this?'

Manny laughed.

'Stop it? Fischel went into class, all wet, and smelling of urine. The teacher asked him why, and he told him. The teacher took us all out to the toilets and asked which toilet they'd dunked him in. Fischel showed him and the teacher took hold of him and asked him if this was the way they did it and dunked him again. All the HJ boys were rolling around, laughing.'

'That's terrible,' Johann said, bowing his head. 'I was in the Hitler Youth. We never did anything like that.'

'How many Jewish boys were at your school?'

'Just one. Everyone treated him all right. Then one day, in our last year, he was gone.'

Manny gave a brittle laugh.

'The funny thing is,' he said, 'when I first saw you and Franz in the Hitlerjugend uniform, I wanted nothing more than to join.'

~~o~~

Just before Tuesday became Wednesday, Manny was sick for the first time. As he leaned over the coaming, bringing up the little he had eaten, Johann realised that he, too, was feeling queasy and wouldn't be far behind him.

He was sick a few moments later, for the first time ever at sea, but he made no effort to lean overboard, concentrating instead on keeping the boat on course; close to every wave which scoured the cockpit, so the contents of his stomach were washed away almost as soon as they landed on the deck.

~~o~~

Antje padded downstairs in her dressing gown and slippers. She'd lain in bed for the last hour, unable to sleep through the noise of the wind and the rain battering the window, worrying about *The Shearwater* and the worst storm of the year.

In the kitchen, she made herself a mug of hot chocolate, a cure she'd often found effective for insomnia, and put it on a tray. Coming out into the hallway, she saw a light under the door of the study and paused before crossing to it.

She gently knocked on the door and entered.

Her father sat in the shadows, barely visible behind the pool of light that illuminated a nautical chart spread out on the top of his desk.

'Antje!' he said. 'What are you doing up?'

'The same as you, I'd imagine. Worried about the boys, and Ruth and Manny.'

'I can't tell you not to worry. When we prayed for a storm to cover their escape, we didn't envisage one quite this extreme.'

'You think they're in a lot of danger?' she asked him.

She looked at him across the desk. His face mirrored her own deep concern, and she knew it was unfair to ask him.

'I'd be lying to you if I said they'll be safe, but they couldn't be in a better boat for the conditions they'll be fighting. If it were *Snowgoose* they were in, I'd say they would have far less chance of surviving it, but *The Shearwater* has a longer, heavier keel, her spars and rigging are stronger, and she's stouter built and more stable than any other yacht I've sailed on.'

'It's the not knowing that's so difficult.'

'I know,' he said softly, 'But it's double-edged, like the storm. If we hear from them, they've failed, and not knowing is the best we can hope for, at least for a while.'

A tear ran down her cheek and he came around the desk and put his arms around her.

'Be strong,' he said. 'And remember, in the next few days, when they are reported as lost, use the grief and worry you feel now, and show it, but always keep belief in your heart.'

'I'll try,' she said.

CHAPTER 111

Just after midnight, the hatch slid back and Franz emerged, closing it behind him and securing it firmly. His eyes took in the mountainous seas, the hard-pressed sails and the exhaustion engraved on Johann's and Manny's faces.

He scaled his way across the tilted, heaving deck and put his mouth close to Johann's ear.

'The wind has come round to the north a little,' he said.

'Yes,' Johann shouted back, Franz reading his lips as much as hearing him. 'Only in the last fifteen minutes.'

'We have a bit more sea room now. I think we should set the boat to fore-reach and stay below for a while. If she gets knocked down, someone will get hurt, or washed overboard.'

Johann nodded.

Fore-reaching was a technique Franz had used on a few occasions. It involved centring the foresail just in front of the mast, hauling the main or the trisail fully in and lashing the rudder amidships. Set up like this, the boat made its own way about sixty degrees off the wind and would still travel forwards at a knot or two, holding her course and critically, meeting the waves shoulder-on.

They sent Manny down, then checked that everything was secure on deck, and followed him, securing and sealing the hatch behind them.

'Make sure everything down here is stowed,' Franz said, 'and the lockers are all firmly closed.'

A few minutes later they huddled together in the main cabin, listening to the fury of the noise outside. Johann checked and tied the lee cloth across the starboard pilot berth holding Manny and Ruth, huddled together for warmth, to prevent them falling out, then did the same for the port berth, after climbing into it.

Franz lay on the cabin floor, wedging himself in with a couple of sail bags.

Every so often, he got up and checked the compass. Most of the time, it swung between one-nine-five degrees and two-one-five, close enough to keep them three or four miles offshore.

Twice, she broached, but found her nose again and battled on. Franz closed his eyes and thanked God that the colonel had chosen the heavy, stable, sea-friendly *Sturmtaucher* and not a modern, Bermuda-rigged greyhound like his father's boat.

He lay his head down and tried to sleep.

~~o~~

Franz awoke with a jerk, two hours later, thrown against the table leg with a painful crash. Disorientated, he tried to work out which way was up but what his eyes and his brain were telling him didn't make sense.

Then Ruth screamed, and the lee cloth stretched, taking the weight of her and Manny as the boat tipped further over, threatening to throw them out of the pilot berth.

'She's going over,' he shouted, hanging onto the table to prevent himself landing on top of Johann, directly below him.

The roar of the wave that had flattened them drowned out any other sound, and Franz crouched, unable to move as the crippled yacht continued its roll.

A spray of water erupted from a corner of the hatch as the sea flooded in from the cockpit, and the port side of the coachroof became submerged. Franz heard a loud crack and the sharp snap of a rigging line breaking.

For an eternity, *The Shearwater* lay on her side and Franz waited for the next wave to roll her all the way over. An inversion might not sink them, but he doubted the spars and the rigging would survive it.

Then, though hard to discern at first, the weight of *The Shearwater*'s lead keel began to right her and, as Franz watched, the gimballed lamp, swinging free, began to turn, and he felt the cabin sole slowly become the floor again.

Another wave hit them and threatened to push them back over, but *The Shearwater* shook herself and fought back, her bow biting into the water, slewing her round to crash through the wave, righting herself as she did until, with a final shudder, they were upright again.

'Stay where you are,' Franz shouted to Ruth and Manny.

Johann had already untied his lee cloth and was scrambling out of his berth.

'She must have got broadside on to a wave. You check everything down here, I'll go up top,' Franz said, throwing on his oilskins and his life preserver.

He undid the cord holding the companionway hatch in place and slid it back, expecting to see a scene of devastation. He heard the sails flap a little, then fill.

The mast is still intact, and the sails are still there.

He climbed out and looked around. The cloud had thinned and there was just enough moonlight filtering through for him to see. He cursed. The cover of the stern locker had been forced open and it was full of water.

The rigging looked to be intact, by and large. The topmast had broken, and it hung, swinging loosely by its halyard.

We'll have to get it down.

One of the jib sheets had come loose and was snaking around the forestay.

He tied his lifeline onto the hemp jackstay that ran the entire length of the boat and crawled along the deck, retrieving the jib sheet and cleating it off, hanging on with grim determination as each wave threatened to throw him into the frothing sea.

Returning aft, he grabbed the bailing bucket from the forward cockpit locker and began to empty the seawater from the stern locker. He realised with dismay that they'd lost much of its contents; a couple of fenders wouldn't be missed, where they were going, but most of the bulkier stores had been kept in that locker, including a sack of potatoes and another containing their supplies of fruit and vegetables.

Both had vanished.

The can of diesel was still there, lashed firmly to an eye on one side of the locker, but the top had sprung off, and Franz recognised the smell of diesel in the water he was bailing. He poured the remainder of its tainted contents out, muttering apologies to the gods of the sea as the slick of diesel oil momentarily settled the turbulent surface.

He lashed the empty container back on and clipped shut the cap.

The two spare metal containers of drinking water were there, their lids intact.

We still have an almost full tank of water anyway.

He lashed the stern-locker lid down and checked the remaining lockers. They'd lost a whisker pole from the deck, but they could fashion another from a spare spar, should they need it.

He untied the line on the wheel and, waiting for the right wave, he tacked her through the wind, and lashed the wheel again.

There's one more job to do.

He fetched the two longest mooring lines from the forward cockpit locker. And lashed their ends securely to cleats on the stern, port and starboard, then threw the coils overboard.

He looked around one last time then climbed back down into the cabin, securing the hatch behind him.

Ruth handed him a cup of coffee after he'd got out of his oilskins, then took a sip from her own mug.

She gagged and almost spat it out.

'Yeuch,' she said. 'It tastes awful. Did you put salt into it instead of sugar?'

'No, I did not,' protested Johann, tasting his, with the same result.

He fished the jar of sugar from the locker and opened it. Sticking a wet finger in, he licked it.

'It's sweet,' he said.

Franz lifted the kettle and half-filled a fresh cup. He took a sip and shook his head.

'It tastes salty,' he said, grimacing. He pressed the water-pump pedal below the sink with his foot and rinsed the cup out, then filled it and took a mouthful.

He spat it into the sink.

'The water's contaminated,' he said. 'We must have siphoned seawater into the tank when we were on our side.'

'Do we still have the spare cans?'

'Yes. Luckily, we filled them up in Hirtshals, and they were lashed down. We'll just have to be careful with our water.'

'We can cook with seawater,' Johann said, although any thoughts of heating up anything more involved than a can of beans while the storm raged were largely redundant.

'We'll survive,' Franz said. 'If worst comes to worst, we can harvest rainwater. There's plenty of it.'

Johann grinned, then the smile disappeared from his face.

He checked the cool locker. Two of the four bottles of milk had smashed along with half the eggs and two jars of pickles.

'Leave it just now, Johann,' Franz said. 'We'll sort it when the weather settles a bit.'

'Should we go back to having a watch on deck?' Johann asked.

'No. If one or more of us had been up on deck, we'd have been overboard, even with lifelines. I set some trailing warps. We should have done it before now.'

'What's a trailing warp?' Manny asked and Franz smiled at him, amazed that, despite the desperate plight they were in, the boy was still curious, and eager to learn.

'We tie a couple of long ropes to the back of the boat in a large bight, or loop, and trail them in the water,' Johann said. 'It slows us down, and it keeps our stern steady and less likely that we'll be knocked sideways by a wave.'

'There's so much to learn, isn't there?'

'Manny, we're all learning,' Franz said. 'Johann and I have never sailed in anything as bad as this.'

Ruth stared at him.

'It's true. The wind speed out there could be gusting to sixty knots; that's force eleven.'

She looked at Manny, then back at Franz. He wondered if he could see accusation in her eyes, but she blinked, and a tear rolled down her cheek.

'It won't last forever,' he said. 'We just need to survive the next few hours.'

The storm would last another six days.

CHAPTER 112

By sunrise, the wind had dropped a little. Prior to the previous twenty-four hours, Johann and Franz would have considered forty knots of wind to be at the top edge of their capabilities and, in certain sea conditions, downright dangerous.

Now gale force eight felt like a reprieve.

'I think we should try and get a little more distance off Thyborøn,' Franz said, looking at the chart.

'Why? It would be good to see the entrance and know exactly where we are.'

'The leading lights will be lit until an hour after sun-up and we should be able to see them up to seven miles out, according to the chart.'

'In this visibility?' Johann said, his expression doubtful.

'If you look out, you'll see it has cleared a little. I don't want us to go close enough to be seen. We should be passing any time soon.'

'If we want to beat out to the west, we'll have to helm her.'

'I know. Do you and Manny want to do a spell?'

'Yes,' Johann said, jumping up. 'Definitely. It would be better than sitting down here waiting for God knows what.'

Manny's face echoed Johann's enthusiasm.

Within five minutes, they were on deck, and Franz felt the boat heel and surge forward as Johann trimmed the sails and Manny steered *The Shearwater* into the wind.

A short while later, Johann opened the hatch and shouted down.

'I can just see the leading lights at Thyborøn; they're almost in line, but it's going to close in again; there's more rain coming.'

'What's the depth?' he called before Johann had closed the hatch.

After a minute, it slid open again.

'Fourteen fathoms.'

Franz found the leading line on the chart and traced his finger along it to where it crossed the ten- and twenty-fathom contour lines. He made a mark on the line, equidistant between the two. It was a decent fix.

He marked up the log.

Wed 9th April

07:00 4NM off THYBORØN CANAL 087°M. Leading lights just visible. Wind 40 knots westerly. Close-hauled. Storm jib and trisail. 988mb. Tide 0.2 knots 000°T.

It gave him some sense of relief. Now that he knew exactly where they were, the decreasing visibility suited them, and the enduring storm was enough to keep fishing vessels and other commercial ships in harbour.

Most small Kriegsmarine vessels wouldn't venture out in a storm as bad as this one, so the only risk of discovery came from sizeable navy ships, and it would be unlikely anything bigger than a patrol vessel that would be so close inshore.

He slipped in to the heads and took a chance to for a quick wash, and a change of clothes. Feeling better, he closed the door behind him and looked around the main cabin.

Ruth had been sick again, and she lay pale and exhausted in her berth. Franz encouraged her to take small sips of water and he watched over her until she fell into a fitful sleep, only rousing a little when a particularly large wave crashed with a roar over the coachroof.

Once she'd settled, he arranged himself in the corner of the cabin and closed his eyes, trying to catch a little sleep himself before the next watch.

~~o~~

'That's Colonel Schneider on the telephone, sir.'

The General picked up the handset.

'Walther, how are you?'

'Apart from taking an age to get through on this damned line, I'm very well, thanks. And you?'

'Oh, holding up.'

'Have you heard from your sons yet? The last time we spoke, they'd called you from Hirtshals.'

'No. The Kriegsmarine phoned me a short while ago. One of their vessels bumped into them halfway across the Skagerrak. They were last seen heading a tad further east than they intended, towards Langesund, but it could have been anywhere along that coast. They'll be stormbound in some remote anchorage, with no access to a telephone, I imagine.'

'You're not worried then?'

'No. Why should I be?'

'I've been told that one of the biggest storms of the year has hit southern Norway and northern Denmark. It's hellish here, and we've not had the worst of it, they say.'

'I know, but there was plenty time for them to find shelter before the storm set in.'

Colonel Schneider grunted.

'I suppose you're right,' he said.

'Once the storm passes, they'll be back on the move and will contact you as soon as they reach civilisation.'

'I'll look forward to it. I don't want them away any longer than they need to be,' the colonel said gruffly.

'They could always leave the boat somewhere and return to the Kompanie, and you could sail it up the coast of Norway yourself, at a time convenient to you. It would be a sail I'd thoroughly recommend.'

The colonel's voice brightened.

'I might do that. I talked about joining them further up the coast for a day or two anyway.'

'Well, keep it in mind, Walther,' the General said, bidding him goodbye.

When he'd put the phone down, he took a long breath. In his whole life, he'd never told so many lies as he had in the last few days.

~~o~~

11:10 BOVBJERG LT 110°M 2NM Poor visibility. Wind 40 knots westerly. 988mb. Storm jib and trisail. Close-hauled. 3 knots, 195°M.

CHAPTER 113

Around lunchtime, Kriminalassistent Heinrich Güllich phoned the Gestapo office in Kristiansand.

'Have you checked *everywhere*?' he demanded.

He was told that Gestapo personnel were currently visiting every sizeable port in southern Norway and that port movement records for them, and all the smaller harbours, were on their way, but that their delivery would be delayed a day or two because of the storm.

'Keep looking,' he said, angry now. 'If their boat does turn up, I want it torn apart, plank by plank, until we find these two Judenscheiße, or at least some evidence that they've been on board.'

He put the phone down and rang the Kriegsmarine command centre.

'There's no further news, Herr Kriminalassistent,' the familiar smug voice of the captain said. 'None of our vessels have reported any further contact with the Kästner yacht.'

'Can't one of your ships have a look for them?'

'Herr Kriminalassistent, northern Europe is in the grip of the worst storm of the decade and the Kästner boat will be sheltering in a secluded anchorage on the Norwegian coast. We couldn't risk one of our ships and their crew for something so…'

He struggled to find the right word.

'Trivial! Inconsequential! Are these the sort of words you're looking for? What kind of navy are you?' the Gestapo man snarled.

'A very capable one, sir, but we do not risk lives and ships unnecessarily.' The captain paused. 'Can you tell me why the Gestapo are so interested, anyway, sir?'

'It's none of your b…' He stopped. He didn't want any hard-to-answer questions being asked by the Kriegsmarine command at Gestapo Headquarters. He took a deep breath and spoke in his most reasonable voice.

'Johann Kästner is an essential witness in an ongoing Geheime Staatspolizei investigation.'

'Ah. That's good to know. We couldn't work out how it was possible that the Kästner brothers were under investigation themselves.'

'That does not surprise me,' the Kriminalassistent said drily. 'Anyway, I trust you will inform me if there is any news of this boat of theirs?'

'By all means, sir. We hope to have something soon.'

'Are you sure?' the Gestapo man said, sarcastically.

'Oh yes, sir. All our vessels have been asked to report by radio as soon as they make contact.'

Heinrich Güllich smiled. At least the bastards had learned to jump at the Gestapo's requests.

'I'm sure they'll contact us as soon as they hear something,' the captain continued. 'They all know General Kästner is anxious for any news.'

The smile disappeared from the Kriminalassistent's face. He slammed the phone down.

Carl Meyer turned away to hide a smile.

'The old Jew,' Heinrich Güllich asked. 'What is his name?'

'Teubner, sir. Jakob Teubner. You wish to interview him?'

'Yes. Him and a few others. We need to widen the net, just in case this whole trip is a red herring.'

~~o~~

By mid-afternoon, the wind had risen again, and the seas, which had died down a little, were once more mountainous. Franz checked the barometer; it remained stubbornly at nine-eight-eight, where it had been for the last twelve hours.

He put on his oilskins and looked at Ruth. In between bouts of sickness, she was managing to sleep, but he knew she wouldn't be fit enough to go on watch in a few hours' time.

It didn't bother him to do a watch on his own, but it was easier with two, and he knew it would annoy her if she thought she wasn't pulling her weight.

The boat thudded against another wave, then another.

He slid back the hatch and climbed up, closing it behind him.

Looking around, he realised it had once more become almost untenable to have people on deck again; Johann and Manny were barely clinging on and it took two of them to steer the boat.

If that wasn't enough, they both had the grey, haggard faces of those suffering from seasickness and as he watched, Manny turned downwind and vomited, so as not to catch Johann with a faceful of wind-strewn bile.

He shouted to them to heave-to and come down below, but they couldn't hear him, so he fought his way to the wheel and, putting his mouth close to Johann's ear, repeated his command.

Johann nodded and began turning *The Shearwater* through the wind. Once the storm jib was fully backed, he turned the wheel hard to starboard and Franz lashed it to the binnacle.

They waited to see how she would settle but, as Franz expected, she lay with her bow just off the wind and her shoulder taking the worst of the waves.

Franz followed Johann and Manny down below and made sure they all chewed a piece of root ginger and took a drink of water before sending them to their bunks. He made a note of their estimated position in the log and noted down that they were hove-to.

He wedged himself into the chart-table seat and closed his eyes. He dozed for short periods but got up and looked out of the brass-rimmed portholes at regular intervals and, once or twice, he slid back the hatch and checked the sails.

He'd give them all a few hours' respite, then, if the wind and waves allowed, they'd start moving south again.

CHAPTER 114

'Open up,' Carl Meyer said, banging on the glass of the door to Kleiner Kuhberg 15. 'We know you're in there.'

Jakob Teubner shuffled down the stairs. Since his stay in Neuengamme, he'd had problems with his digestion and had never regained the weight, and the strength, that he'd lost during his incarceration.

'Ach, have patience,' he muttered to himself, putting his glasses on to see who could be calling on him.

There weren't many visitors these days. The bulk of the city's Jews had moved away or had been deported to Poland, and most of those that remained lived as virtual prisoners in the Judenhaus at Kleiner Kuhberg 21, and 25, a few doors along, a holding pen for imminent deportation.

Of those who remained free, few would risk attending services or sending their children to school; the curfew and the random stop-and-search policy of the Third Reich had seen to that.

He was allowed access to the Judenhaus, as much to assist the authorities as to provide succour to his former friends and neighbours.

As he reached the door, he recognised the two Gestapo men and stiffened his back defiantly. They would do what they wished with him, but he wasn't going to be intimidated by a pair of nasty Gestapo puppies.

'Hurry up, old man,' Carl Meyer snarled through the glass. 'Don't you know who we are?'

'I know very well who you are, Kriminalassistentanwärter,' Jakob said, unlocking the door and opening it to allow the men to enter. 'Have you come to take me away, again?'

'We might well do, if you aren't of any help to us, you old fool.'

'So, what do you want?'

'You don't have much of a congregation these days, do you?'

'I'm not a rabbi. I was just the man they turned to for help.'

'Including your friends, the Nussbaums?' Heinrich Güllich said, speaking for the first time.

'Ah. Yosef and Miriam were more likely to offer help than look for it.'

'When was the last time you saw them?'

'I was with Yosef in Neuengamme, but he was released before me. Let me see, that would be a month ago, perhaps. Miriam, I've not seen for many months.'

'So, you say you have no contact with them?'

'No. None. In case you haven't noticed, we Jews are not allowed to wander about in Kiel, visiting each other.'

The Kriminalassistent punched Jakob in the stomach, and he doubled over, collapsing to the floor, his breath coming out in a long, slow wheeze.

'Lift him up,' Heinrich Güllich said, and Carl Meyer jumped to comply. He lifted the old man up by the hair, forcing him to scramble to his feet.

'Now, that was just a soft, friendly warning,' Heinrich Güllich hissed. 'The next one will hurt. Answer the question.'

'I've had no contact with either of them,' Jakob gasped, still fighting for breath.

Heinrich Güllich slapped Jakob across the cheek.

'You'd think he'd have learned from the last time we interviewed him,' he said, turning to his assistant. 'Wouldn't you?'

'Yes, Kriminalassistent.'

'Now, old Jew, if I were a Judenhund and I wished to escape, how would I do it?'

'By paying vast sums of money to corrupt Reich officials.'

This time, the blow was with the back of Heinrich Güllich's hand, and it knocked Jakob Teubner to the floor again. The Gestapo man's ring also left a deep gouge in the old man's cheek, which dripped blood onto the rug in the entrance hall.

'Now, Jew. I asked you a question,' Heinrich Güllich said.

Jakob rose to his knees and tried to get to his feet.

'Stay there,' Heinrich Güllich barked, gripping the old man's ear and twisting it to reinforce his order.

'All I know is what I've heard. Jews with wealthy relatives abroad have been able to buy themselves visas.'

He flinched, waiting for another blow, but it didn't come.

'And wealthy Jews here in Germany?' Heinrich Güllich asked.

'Those in power know they'll get their money in the end, so it's not as likely to be so persuasive, but it depends on how scrupulous a local official is.'

'What about organisations trying to smuggle Jews out. How would a person contact them?'

'I wouldn't know, Herr Kriminalassistent.'

Heinrich Güllich took hold of Jakob Teubner's ear again and twisted it, harder this time.

'I don't believe you, Jew.'

'It's true,' Jakob grunted, through the pain.

'You must have heard of these Haganah people,' the Gestapo man said.

'I've heard of them, of course, but they won't deal with anyone who has any contact with the authorities, and, against my own wishes, I seem to have been appointed as an intermediary between the government representatives and the Jewish community, at least until my usefulness runs out.'

'So, you didn't arrange for the Nussbaum brats to escape?'

Jakob Teubner gasped and lifted his head sharply.

'No. Have they gone?'

Heinrich Güllich let out a sneering laugh.

'Gone,' he said, snapping his fingers in front of Jakob's face. 'Just like that. Their Jew-loving General reported them missing. Would you believe that? I mean, missing Jews? He expects the security forces to look for them, when all the time, he has them secreted away somewhere, whisking them out of the country.'

Jakob looked down at the ground, not daring to let the Gestapo men see the glint of satisfaction in his eyes at the thought of at least two Jews evading the grip of the National Socialist machine.

'And you say you know nothing about it,' Heinrich Güllich growled.

'No, sir,' Jakob said, contrite now, the joy hidden deep within him.

'They'll be in custody soon, along with their parents. As for the General…'

He lashed out a foot and caught Jakob on the side of the head. Jakob's world went black.

~~o~~

'Check him,' Heinrich Güllich said.

Carl Meyer put his finger on the old man's neck.

'He's alive, sir. His pulse is strong.'

'What do you think?' he said. 'Did he know?'

Carl Meyer had watched the old Jew closely. The old man hadn't known about the Nussbaum children, he was sure. He could see from the Kriminalassistent's face that he thought the same.

'I don't think so, sir,' he said.

'Teach him a lesson, but don't kill him,' the Kriminalassistent said.

CHAPTER 115

In the Kästner house, a visitor could have been forgiven for thinking that everything was as normal.

The General had left early and would return late, just before dinner, as was his habit. Antje had cycled to art school and returned in the afternoon to paint in the garden.

Albert was on hand to drive Maria Kästner to lunch first, then to an art exhibition sponsored by the Kiel district branch of the NSDAP, heavily promoted by Mayor Hoffmann and his wife. It displayed works by Arno Breker, Adolf Wissel and Adolf Ziegler, all favourites of the Führer. Maria Kästner made all the right noises as she walked around with Irmgard Hoffman but told Eva later that the pictures were hideous. Albert was there again to collect her and take her back home.

Eva attended three classes critical to her degree at Kiel University and spent the remainder of the day in the library, studying hard for her final exams. When she arrived home, she sought out her mother.

'Mama,' she said, her face flushed with excitement, 'I've been offered a job.'

'Already? You haven't even graduated. What is it?'

All the way through her course, she'd watched the growth of the National Socialist regime with interest. She'd been approached a few weeks previously, as one of the top students in her year. She'd been told about the job only that morning.

'The government, Mama. They want me to work for them as a translator.'

'That's wonderful, Eva, but will you need a job if you marry Hugo?'

'We'll not get married right away. I can work in the meantime. Anyway, Hugo might be quite happy for me to work. He's not as stuffy as the rest of his family.'

'If you think so. I wouldn't want you to jeopardise your prospects.'

'I won't, Mama. Hugo is quite modern in some ways.'

She couldn't tell her mother that the job offer had come from one of the government's less public departments; one that the general population heard little about. Or that Hugo was more relaxed in other ways, too.

She felt the familiar tingling of arousal that appeared every time she thought of him.

~~o~~

Miriam Nussbaum knocked softly on the drawing-room door and entered.

'Ma'am, here's the order for the grocer,' she said.

Maria Kästner took the list from Miriam and glanced at it.

'I'll telephone them shortly. Thank you.'

She gave Miriam an awkward glance.

The Nussbaums had cleaned, cooked, and served up the family's meals as usual, with a subdued efficiency that Maria Kästner was forced to concede as above and beyond what could be expected of parents whose children had gone missing.

But since their disappearance, she'd found herself looking for excuses to leave the house as often as possible and, when she was at home, keeping away from the kitchen.

It wasn't that Miriam or Yosef appeared judgemental about her lukewarm support; the Nussbaums had accepted her need to put her own family first a long time before but it made conversation difficult.

How does one find the right thing to say?

She'd tried, but she knew that her attempts to comfort them sounded insincere.

When dinner was served, it was a stilted affair that even Eva's talk of her new career couldn't lift from near silence. The boys were only mentioned briefly, as if not talking about them created the illusion that nothing was amiss.

~~o~~

As soon as the dessert was cleared and coffee had been served and consumed, the General disappeared to his study, and Maria complained of a pounding headache and retired to bed.

Eva and Antje looked at each other. They had never been truly close as children; Ruth was more like a sister to Antje, and the two Kästner girls had grown further apart as their values and priorities diverged but, that evening, they found themselves with a shared concern for their brothers.

'They'll be fine,' Eva said, desperately trying to dispel the disquiet that had pervaded the house since reports of the storm had reached Drachensee. 'They've been around yachts since they could walk, and they've been away with Father every year since Mama stopped going, and Franz has been to Norway before with him.'

Antje sighed. 'I know, but it's still a worry. Part of me would have loved to have gone with them, but the storm sounds terrible,' she added.

'Yeuch,' Eva said. 'It would be damp, cramped, uncomfortable, cold, and miserable. Need I go on?'

'Nonsense. We've had some lovely summer sails and, anyway, I don't mind when it's wet and windy; they're the most exciting bits.'

'I'll stick to dry land, and now I wish they had too. It's a real worry. Even Papa looks anxious at times.'

'He gets all the weather reports, and he knows what it can be like up there; it's not like the Ostsee, with plenty of shelter.'

'But the ship they encountered; the captain said they were halfway across, and that they were heading for safety.'

Antje saw the moistness in her sister's eyes and her heart went out to her, knowing what the week ahead would bring.

'They'll be fine, one way or the other,' she said.

It was lame, but it was all she could offer. It pained her to lie to her sister and her mother, but her biggest fear was that she would let slip that her brothers and her closest friend were in the middle of the Nordsee, in a storm that even hardened seamen were saying would cost lives.

'Let's wait and see,' she added.

~~o~~

Johann opened the hatch and let himself down into the cabin. He saw Franz sitting at the chart table, slumped over in an uncomfortable sleep. He checked the log. The last entry was thirty-five minutes before; an estimated position that put them a mile or two short of Thorsminde. He touched his brother on the arm.

Franz shook himself awake.

'What's the matter?' he asked.

'Nothing,' Johann said. 'It's still blowing out there but we're coping. The only thing is that the wind has backed to the south-west, and we're going to be a bit close to Thorsminde. I'm going to start the engine, and motorsail for a while.'

Franz nodded.

For the couple of hours they'd been hove-to, they'd drifted a little close to the shore, and if Johann and Manny hadn't managed to make much ground to seaward, it made sense to put the engine on.

With the storm jib dropped, to stop it flailing, they could sail much closer to the wind, and claw their way westwards, away from the coast. The trisail, while adding little forward propulsion, would keep the boat stable and less inclined to roll.

Johann reached in behind the companionway and turned the battery key, then climbed out into the cockpit again.

Franz heard the click of the heater, then, twenty seconds later, the big diesel engine thudded into life.

Ruth woke, hearing the noise, and looked enquiringly at Franz.

'We're putting the engine on for a while, just to give us extra sea room to pass Thorsminde without being seen.'

'Oh,' Ruth said. 'Why don't we just tack out for a while?'

Franz laughed. 'You're thinking like a yachtswoman now,' he said, 'but it would probably mean losing ground, and we must arrive at the entrance to Esbjerg during the night,

375

and at the right state of the tide, so we can't afford to be forced too far north.'

'You've calculated all that already?'

'We've allowed a safety margin; it's better to arrive a little early than too late. We worked it out as soon as we turned to run south,' he said.

'I'm glad you're here,' she said. 'I feel safe, despite how horrible it is at times.'

Franz blushed, and pretended to check the chart.

She flinched as *The Shearwater*, now heading almost directly into the sea, slammed down with each wave, causing her timbers to shudder alarmingly.

Franz gave Ruth a reassuring smile.

'If I weren't here, Johann would do it,' Franz said.

'He told me that, but he said he wouldn't do it as well as you, and that he'd rather have you around if it all went terribly wrong.'

'He said that? When?'

'When we were watching the whales the other day. It's the only chance I've had to speak with him. It was nice, and he's always great fun.'

'I suppose he is,' Franz said morosely. 'Just watch him though,' he continued, his face reddening again. 'He has a way with girls, well…'

'Don't worry, Franz,' she said, smiling. 'I'm not fifteen. I can handle Johann.'

Franz turned away in embarrassment and crouched in front of the companionway steps. He unclipped the catches at both sides, and the entire step assembly swung upwards, allowing access to the engine. Franz watched it for a while and took a clean rag and ran it across the injectors and around the oil filters. He reached under the engine and wiped the sump.

He looked at the rag. There was no diesel on it, and just a smear of oil.

He replaced the companionway steps and fastened the catches.

'No leaks,' he said, 'and running like a dream.'

He grinned sheepishly.

'We check the oil levels and fuel filters once a day, but I like to take a look at her while she's running.'

She smiled at him and he blushed again.

'How are you feeling?' he asked.

'Not too bad at the moment. I've not been sick for a while now.'

'You're looking better.'

'I had a wash, and changed, though it's not easy when the boat is being thrown around.'

'It's going to be rough while we motorsail out,' Franz said.

She took a piece of ginger from the small pouch she'd started carrying around her neck and chewed it, grimacing.

'I know it's not pleasant,' Franz said, 'but it might just make a difference.'

He closed the engine compartment and marked up the chart with their new course and got into his bunk.

'I'd advise you to do the same,' he said. 'Another couple of hours and we'll be on watch again.'

CHAPTER 116

Thur 10th April

04:55 NØRRE LYNGVIG LT, [Fl(W)5s] 3NM off 090°M Moderate visibility. Wind 35 knots west, sou'westerly. 988mb. Storm jib and trisail. 4 knots 190°M. Approx. 4NM to pass HVIDE SANDE.

~~o~~

There had been two watch changes since Thorsminde; Franz and Ruth had gone on deck at midnight and were relieved by Johann and Manny just after four, having observed the flash of Nørre Lyngvig lighthouse ten minutes before. Since then, the weather had closed in again.

'Bear one-nine-zero for an hour,' Franz told Johann. 'That should take us well clear of Hvide Sande, on our beam. Your course from there will be one-eight-zero.'

Every time Franz checked the compass, it read one-nine zero. After an hour, he marked the new estimated position and popped his head through the hatch to confirm that once they could see the lights of Hvide Sande, their new course would be directly south.

'We can see nothing, Franz,' Manny said, huddled close to the hatch.

Franz looked around. The weather had worsened again. The wind had increased further in strength, and the rain was battering *The Shearwater*'s deck in solid sheets. He reckoned that visibility was down to less than a mile.

'I'll have to redo the course. We need to find the shore before we reach Horns Rev.'

He climbed down and closed the hatch, drying his hair with a towel to avoid dripping on the chart.

He removed the large-scale chart they'd been using covering the western coast of Denmark and replaced it with chart number 3678, *Esbjerg Approaches*. It covered the coast twenty or so miles north and south of Esbjerg, including Blåvand, just beyond Horns Rev.

He stared at it. Horns Rev was a sandy reef that extended thirty-five miles out into the North Sea from Blåvand point. To reach Esbjerg, they would have to either go through the Slugen channel halfway along the reef, a detour of almost fifteen miles, or take a risk with one of the narrower channels that crossed the reef closer inshore.

Franz was loathe to beat all the way out to Slugen just to come back in and, anyway, it put them in the main channel for vessels heading to Esbjerg from the north and, although it was unlikely that a great many boats would be at sea, there was always the chance of being spotted.

He studied the chart. The channel closer inshore, Ringkøbing Dyb, was for the most part, wider and deeper, but its northern end was unmarked, and it narrowed to less than half a cable at its southern end.

Søren Bovbjergs Dyb, a couple of miles further out, was marked with a lit buoy at both ends and, although narrower along the whole of its two-mile length, its width never dropped below a cable and a half.

Still, he knew it would be tricky at night, especially with a storm raging, and if he got it wrong, they would be wrecked on a desolate lee shore, with minimal chances of survival and little hope of evading capture if they somehow made it to dry land.

He took a deep breath and plotted a route through Søren Bovbjergs Dyb, then on to Graa Dyb, the entrance channel for Esbjerg and Ho Bucht.

He made a drawing of the route on a piece of paper and sandwiched it between two sheets of Perspex. He clamped the aluminium frame holding them together and grabbed a chinagraph wax pencil from the cubbyhole below the chart table.

He handed it up to Johann.

'Your course is one-five-five until you reach the ten-fathom contour. Then follow it. I want you to identify the Kærgård beacon, then the Ringebjerg beacon.'

'All right. Have you marked what lights are on the beacons?'

Franz shook his head.

'They're both unlit so we'll have to creep along, just keeping the shore in view so that we're not seen. I've made small drawings of what the beacons should look like. Beyond them, we should see the Blåvands Huk lighthouse, but it's directly inshore of Horns Rev. I don't want us to be too close to it.'

Johann nodded.

'I'll let you know when we catch sight of the shore.'

Franz ducked his head back in and sat at the chart table. He marked an entry in the log and plotted their estimated position on the chart.

```
05:45 Off HVIDE SANDE (EP). 4NM. 130°M Poor visibility. Wind 40
knots, sou'westerly. 988mb. Tide 0.5kt 010°T. Storm jib and
trisail. 4 knots 155°M.
```

~~o~~

Ruth and Franz both slept. When they woke at seven-thirty, there was a semblance of light outside but, when Franz looked out the porthole, the morning was dismal and grey, and the rain was still driving horizontally across the deck.

On a close reach, and with the boat less heeled, Franz cooked eggs for everyone and toasted the last of their bread, reckoning that hot food, washed down with a mug of scalding coffee, would be a good morale booster.

For the first time in days, Ruth devoured her breakfast and Franz smiled as he ate his with a little less haste. Once they'd finished, they dressed in their oilskins and called up to the boys on deck.

Manny came down first and, seeing the hot meal, sat down at the table and attacked it with the same enthusiasm as his sister.

'Stay here until I have a word with Johann,' Franz told Ruth. 'Come up when he comes down.'

He disappeared through the hatch and Ruth smiled at her brother.

'How is it?' she asked.

'It's wonderful. I think I might go to sea when I'm older.'

She smiled. In a way, she was glad that the danger of the voyage was a distraction, saving him from dwelling on the pain and the worry about their parents and grandparents that was sure to hit him when it was over. She wished that she could do the same but, every so often, the thought of them all still in Germany crept into her mind, bringing tears to her eyes.

She ruffled his hair.

'You've seen what the sea can throw at you. Perhaps you will make a seaman one day.'

'From what Johann said, the worst might yet be to come.'

Ruth shivered.

CHAPTER 117

Once on deck, Franz looked around. The sea looked horrendous, but *Der Sturmtaucher* felt at home in it, Franz thought.

Perhaps I'm beginning to trust her.

'We reached the ten-fathom contour,' Johann said. 'I changed course so that we're coming in at a shallower angle, so that we don't beach her. I've been taking soundings every five minutes, but we've not sighted the shore yet.'

'Stay up on deck for a while, until we see land, just to be on the safe side. I don't want to put Ruth under any pressure, and it will give her and Manny a chance to talk.'

Franz dropped the lead line over the side and counted the fathoms.

'Eight fathoms,' he said, hauling the line back in. 'It's going to be tough going through Horns Rev tonight.'

'I know. Would we not be better beating out and coming in the Slugen channel?'

'It's too risky. We'd be in the main shipping channel for twice as long, maybe more.'

'There'll be nothing out in weather like this.'

'We can't be sure of that.'

Neither man said anything for a while.

'Six fathoms,' Franz intoned, his head cocked to one side. 'I can hear surf, I think.'

Johann peered out to port, forward of the beam.

'I still can't see anything,' he said, 'but you're right, I can hear it now.'

'Come round five degrees to starboard,' Franz said.

'Five degrees to starboard,' Johann acknowledged, turning the wheel.

'Five fathoms,' Franz said.

'I can see it,' Johann shouted. 'Sand dunes. They're high.'

'Yes, they're up to twenty metres in places, according to the chart. Steer two-one-zero. That should take us parallel to the shore.'

'Two-one-zero,' Johann replied.

'Now we look out for the beacons. Kærgård has a dome shape, Ringebjerg is a diamond. Both are on tripod legs.'

'How far apart are they?'

'What? The legs?'

'No, you fool. The beacons.'

Johann glanced at Franz, who grinned. Johann shook his head.

'They're five miles apart,' Franz said. 'If we've missed Kærgård, it will be a while before we see Ringebjerg.'

'We've not missed it,' Johann said, pointing.

Franz followed his outstretched arm and saw it, for all the world like a giant insect standing sentinel on the land, looking out to sea. Then it was gone, fading into the rain and the mist.

'Take a break,' Franz said. 'Send Ruth up for the rest of the watch. You'll need to be rested.'

'What about you?'

'I managed an hour or two earlier. I'll sleep when we get in.'

~~~o~~~

On the shore, in a valley between the dunes, a tall figure saw the mast rolling from side to side in the distance, almost buried under the waves.

He crossed himself and turned away.

'God rest their souls,' he said.

CHAPTER 118

'Here are the port reports, Herr Kriminalassistent.'

Carl Meyer handed his boss a manila envelope, which he opened, and spilled the contents onto his desk.

The Kriminalassistent flicked through them.

'There's nothing in these,' he said, throwing them on the desk.

'I didn't think there would be, sir. I'm sure our colleagues in Norway would have checked them.'

'They have to be hiding somewhere.'

'How long do we search for, sir?'

'Until we have reason not to. If they're in Norway, the Nussbaums will be far away from any port by now. I want you to send their photographs to the Kristiansand office and ask them to disseminate them around the whole of southern Norway.'

'What if they've reached Sweden? Or if they've left Germany by another route?'

'Then we've lost them, and they win.'

Carl Meyer was astounded that the Kriminalassistent could be so phlegmatic about it, after his extraordinary efforts to catch them.

'However, I don't believe they are in Sweden, or that we've lost them yet. Even if we have, we still have the parents in our jurisdiction, don't we?'

'But, sir, what about our instructions not to harass them?'

'We tread carefully. There are always ways around problems like this. Anyway, one day, they'll make a mistake, these Jews and their guardian angel.'

The sneer in the Kriminalassistent's voice was tempered by the tightness of his jaw.

'And in the meantime, sir?'

'We keep the pressure on them. Phone Werner Schmidt. Get him to contact the Nussbaums and order them to appear at the police station on Monday.'

'What reason does he give?'

'Use your imagination. Tell them it's something to do with the children.'

'Why Monday, sir?'

'Let them stew over the weekend. A few jangling nerves might soften them up.'

~~o~~

Beate Böhm sat on the edge of the bed and looked at Obersturmbannführer Eicke while he dressed, with a strange uneasy thrill.

When he'd phoned that morning, he'd caught her by surprise. Eberhard had just left for work, and she'd hurried to wash and dress, and tell the maid the now accustomed lie of a meeting with her friend in Elmschenhagen.

As soon as she'd arrived at the door of the familiar room in *their* hotel, she'd known it would be different.

He'd pulled her inside and almost ripped the clothes from her in his haste, but she'd responded, feeling the rush of excitement of something new, and almost frightening. He hadn't hurt her, but there had been an undercurrent of violence which she matched with her own, rolling fiercely on the bed, like two cats rutting.

Afterwards, she'd accepted a cigarette from him, and they'd smoked, glancing at one another, as if deciding which one of them would make the next move.

'Why the rush?' she said, trying to sound careless.

'I have a meeting at Plön this afternoon. At the Stadtheide barracks, between ourselves and a group of regular army commanders. It's a routine thing, and a waste of time, in my opinion. I arrived this morning, early, with a few hours to spare, and thought of you.'

'How long have we got?' Beate asked.

'I have to be away by twelve-thirty, at the latest,' he said.

'Then let's not waste time,' she said, her eyes narrowing as she straddled him, wondering why she'd lived so long in dullness with Eberhard, without a man like the

Obersturmbannführer every once in a while, to make her feel alive again.

~~o~~

Arnulf Eicke hadn't been entirely truthful. He'd telephoned Lise first, but she'd made an excuse, real or otherwise, and he'd shrugged and called Beate, thanking his foresight for having an older version of Lise Mey in reserve.

But he'd been angry at Lise, sure that she was punishing him in some way, and it had given his meeting with her mother a hard edge. In fairness, the woman had responded, giving as good as she'd got.

The daughter would suffer in a different way. It would be a few visits before he would call her again, until she regretted not being available when he felt the need for her.

~~o~~

Franz watched Ruth as she sat huddled in the cockpit.

She'd found her sea legs at last, or so he hoped. She still seemed weak from not having been able to eat or drink for a few days, but the constant nausea and the retching had ceased, at least for the moment. Knowing that the cold wind would cut through the extra layers of clothing she had on, he made her take a break now and then, sending her down below to make coffee and take the chance to warm up.

But, refreshed, she managed to helm for short spells as they crept southwards, beating out to sea, then back in again until they glimpsed the high dunes, before turning seawards once more.

The wind had dropped, and was now in the high thirties, but the waves kicked up by the shallows still broke over the boat every few minutes and the rain was unremitting.

'Why are we going so slow?' Ruth asked.

'There are several reasons,' Franz said. 'We need to keep land just in sight to know exactly where we are, to find our way to the entrance of the channel through Horns Rev. Finding the Ringebjerg beacon is critical to doing that, and we must do it in daylight, but we can't sail too close to shore in case we're spotted, so we have to juggle our distance from the dunes.'

He stopped talking while they tacked back out, until the dunes once again disappeared behind them.

'We've arrived here in plenty time,' he continued. 'Almost too early, in fact, so we have to wait until darkness falls to begin our passage through Horns Rev.'

'Why, if there are no boats out here?'

'Once we pass over Horns Rev through Søren Bovbjergs Dyb, we will be joining the main Slugen channel. There is always the chance that a Kriegsmarine boat, or a merchant freighter, will be entering or leaving Esbjerg, so we can't pass through during daylight.'

He paused, wondering how much she could take in at once.

'We don't want to enter Hobo Dyb, the place where we're hoping to hide, on a falling tide because, if we get stuck, we will have no chance of getting free.'

Ruth nodded and moved the wheel without thinking, as the staysail luffed. Franz smiled.

'And you know exactly what time low water is going to be?' Ruth asked.

'Yes, it's just after midnight, from the tide tables in the almanac.'

'You had all this planned from the time we passed Hanstholm?'

'More or less, but with a little slack built in.'

Franz checked his watch.

'Ready about,' he said, and she swung the wheel hard to port, onto the shoreward tack.

As *The Shearwater* turned through the wind, a blast of spray from the bow caught her full in the face.

Franz gripped the wheel to stop it spinning away from her as she bent double, blinded and in pain, but a few seconds later, she opened her eyes.

Franz looked at her, concerned. As her vision cleared, she blushed and apologised for being so pathetic.

'Don't be silly,' he said. 'That was a sore one. You'll learn to see these coming and close your eyes or turn away.'

He looked ahead.

'Now, we must find this beacon.'

CHAPTER 119

Maria Kästner frowned as she put down the phone.

'Has something happened, ma'am?' Miriam asked.

Maria stared at her for a second, then frowned.

'You've to attend the police station at some point; yourself and Yosef. You'll be notified when in the next couple of days.'

'Was it the Gestapo, ma'am?' Miriam said.

How can she be so calm? Maria Kästner thought.

'No,' she snapped. 'It was Kriminalassistent Werner Schmidt. He wishes to question you further concerning the whereabouts of Ruth and Manny.'

She stared again at Miriam.

'Is there something I should know?' she asked.

'No, ma'am. They just don't believe that we, as Jews, would report our children missing.'

'Oh. I see,' Maria said, flustered. 'Perhaps they have new information?'

'Then why wouldn't they come and tell us, ma'am?'

'Yes. I suppose that's true.'

'Did he say anything else?'

'No, not really. Well, it was rather curious. He asked after Franz and Johann. I didn't know he was acquainted with them.'

Not knowing what else to say, Maria turned and went into the drawing room.

When would the nightmare end?

~~o~~

Captain Bauer watched the General out of the corner of his eye. He'd been staring at the same piece of paper for over ten minutes.

Heinz Bauer was worried about his commanding officer. He was always so efficient in getting his daily mountain of paperwork squared away by eleven, allowing him to meet with those he had to and telephone those he didn't.

Most days, it cleared the way for an afternoon of visits to installations, vessels, factories or even a civil servant or a politician, in the interest of the Kriegsmarine and the Abwehr.

But for seventy-two hours, the General had been distracted and had left many of his documents unread or unsigned, disinterested in attending all but the most urgent appointments.

'Any news yet?' the captain said, cursing himself as he said it. Someone had once told him never to ask a question when you knew the answer was going to be one you didn't want to hear.

'Nothing at all, Heinz,' the General said with a sigh. 'Nothing at all.'

'Have you spoken to Naval Command today, sir?'

'No. They said they'd contact me when they heard anything.'

'I'm going there now,' the young officer said, picking up the papers on the General's desk. He would sign them himself; his ability to replicate his commanding officer's signature was proving useful.

'I'll come along with you, Captain,' the General said.

The two men walked together to the command centre. The young officer on duty greeted them with his usual smile.

'Any news, Lieutenant?' the General asked.

'Nothing, Herr General, I'm afraid, but the storm rages on, I'm told. It's almost unheard of, a storm of this duration and ferocity. Even the lulls have thirty-five knot winds.'

'Any sign of better weather coming in?' Heinz Bauer asked.

'The weathermen reckon it should tail off in two or three days. I'm told that three anti-cyclones have travelled across the Atlantic in quick succession, each catching up with the other. A very unusual pattern, they say.'

'There you go, sir,' Captain Bauer said. 'In a couple of days, we'll find out where

383

they've been sheltering.'

'There have been a couple of our ships patrolling the Kattegat since yesterday, sir, but I don't expect that your sons would have dared to venture out; the storm has abated a little, but it's still raging. At least we've heard nothing untoward, yet.'

Captain Bauer frowned at the young lieutenant, but the General just nodded and thanked the young officer.

'I'm going to see Admiral Schiffer, Captain. I should be back in the office in an hour.'

'Yes, sir. Could you ask him if the appropriations committee have met yet? There's that matter of the access road to the munitions depot that you promised to sort out.'

'Yes, I will. Thank you for reminding me. I'll ask him.'

'And don't forget, sir. You have the meeting in Plön this afternoon.'

'It had slipped my mind, Captain. You might as well come too. It will be an education. The Waffen-SS are sending a few of their people.'

'I'll order the car for twelve-thirty, sir. That should give us enough time.'

He hesitated.

'Sir,' he said, 'the lieutenant meant nothing. I'm sure the boys will be safe and well.'

The General gave him a tired smile, and the captain saluted and walked away.

~~o~~

Erich Kästner sighed. It went against every principle he had, deceiving all these decent people, but he had no option but to continue. Only if the people surrounding him were convinced could he ever hope that the Gestapo would lose interest.

And only then could he start to hope that Yosef and Miriam might also be on their way.

~~o~~

As they sped through the outskirts of Kiel on their way to Plön, Captain Bauer attempted to make conversation, but the General answered in monosyllables, then rudely ignored him. At the corner of Werftstraße and Gablenzstraße, a tram and a lorry had collided, and the General barked at the army driver to find a way round the jammed traffic.

By the time they'd got through, they were running ten minutes late, but they made good progress as far as Elmschenhagen. Where Preetzer Chaussee crossed Wiener Allee, there was another hold-up, and the General fumed at the delay.

'We have plenty time, sir,' the Captain said.

The General grunted and looked away.

It made for an uncomfortable journey.

It pained Erich Kästner to treat the two young men with such indifference, but he needed to convince them that he was a worried man, and that the source of his concern was that the boys hadn't been in touch. His ill-tempered silence also gave him time to think, without having to make idle conversation with them.

When the traffic at last began to move, he suddenly stiffened and stared out of the window.

'Pull over,' he barked, leaning forward.

A surprised Private Zimmer found a space to stop and looked at the captain in the mirror. The General saw the puzzled look that passed between them but ignored them, continuing his scrutiny of the street.

After a minute or so, the General nodded to Private Zimmer to carry on with their journey, which they did in uneasy silence.

Returning to his solitary slouch, the General mulled over what he'd just witnessed.

While stuck in traffic, he'd seen Beate Böhm get out of a car parked on the other side of the street. As he'd watched, she'd leaned in and spoken with the driver for a minute, and then walked past them in the opposite direction, looking around her, as if wary of being seen.

When they drove on, the General had caught a good view of the driver, an SS officer, a handsome brute of a fellow, from what the General had seen, with the typical arrogant sneer of the Schutzstaffel.

Very strange, he thought.

CHAPTER 120

By the time they changed watch again, just after midday, the crew of *Der Sturmtaucher* still hadn't seen the Ringebjerg beacon. They'd skirted the shore until it had shallowed at its southern end and Franz had turned the boat round and retraced her track northwards, barely making way.

But around one, Johann opened the hatch and told Franz that he'd caught sight of it, but that they'd had to go in much closer than he'd expected.

'It's not quite as prominent as Kærgård,' he added.

'No. It may be somewhat smaller.'

'And the visibility has closed in, significantly. Less than half a mile, I'd say. We could hardly see the shore most of the time.'

'Is it still as rough?'

'Yes. We're taking a hammering, Franz. Let's hope she's as sound as she feels.'

'I'm sure she is. Have you seen Blåvands light, yet?'

'No. I doubt we went far enough south. We'd be almost on top of Horns Rev before we were close enough to see it.'

'It will be lit by six, tonight. We'll see it then.'

'I hope it is. Father did say that a number of lighthouses aren't, so as not to give directions to enemy shipping.'

'They've all been lit, so far,' Franz said. 'We'll heave-to for a few hours. Keep the watches going. Use sightings of the beacon and depth soundings to hold station.'

~~o~~

'General Kästner, this is Obersturmbannführer Eicke.'

'I'm delighted to meet you, Herr General. I've heard a great deal about you.'

'Ha. Almost none of it is true, Obersturmbannführer.'

'On the contrary, if just half of it is fact, the Kriegsmarine have managed to steal one of the most capable generals in the Wehrmacht but, aside from that, I believe one of my former officers is married to your neighbour's daughter.'

'Ah. The young SS officer who married Lise Böhm. Rudolf, I believe. I'm afraid his surname or rank escapes me.'

'Well remembered, Herr General. It's Hauptsturmführer Mey now. He has my old command. I believe he met you once, briefly.'

'I remember him. A decent young man.'

'And he certainly has one of the most beautiful wives in Germany,' the Obersturmbannführer said, chuckling. 'I believe he is the envy of the Kompanie.'

'You know the family well then?' the General said.

'Yes. I was at their wedding, and indeed, the engagement party. The parents are such lovely people, most welcoming.'

'Indeed. It's such a coincidence. I saw Beate Böhm on my way here, in Elmschenhagen.' The SS man smiled.

'Such a pity. If I'd known Frau Böhm was so close, I would have arranged to meet her. Such a charming woman, and Lise is such a credit to her and her father.'

He turned as a warrant officer appeared in the doorway.

'Ah,' the Obersturmbannführer said. 'Our meeting is about to start. It's been good talking to you. Perhaps our paths will cross again.'

The two men shook hands. As he walked away, the General watched him. He'd recognised the man immediately. It was the same SS officer whose car he'd seen Beate Böhm getting out of.

He took his seat in the meeting, deep in thought.

~~o~~

Waiting for darkness was the hardest part.

Ruth was sick again. *The Shearwater* sat hove-to remarkably well, but the motion, the confinement to the cabin and the mind-numbing struggle without making progress took its toll. By the time she was due to go on watch again, she was almost back to square one again.

Franz tried to sleep between her retching, but he couldn't switch off the thought running over and over in his mind.

Am I putting them all in far too much danger?

He shook his head. They desperately needed shelter, and rest. And supplies were getting low. The bread and milk had gone, water was running short and they'd used twenty litres of diesel during the long hours the engine had battled to keep them offshore. And there were a few repairs needed to *The Shearwater*.

This was their only chance to replenish the boat's stores, and their own bodies.

He ran through the plan again but could find no better option.

Then it was their turn on watch.

Johann and Manny had borne the brunt of the waiting, sitting in the cockpit, sounding the depths, keeping track of where the beacon should be and, every half hour, counteracting *The Shearwater*'s slow drift by sailing her back to her starting point. It was monotonous, and it required immense concentration.

When Franz slid back the hatch and climbed into the cockpit, he could see the exhaustion in their haggard faces, and he watched as they stumbled down the companionway and fell into their bunks.

Ruth joined him, and the fresh air and the occasional sight of land revived her a little.

'Not long to go now,' Franz said, still worried about her. The rain dripped constantly from the brim of her sou'wester and she shivered from time to time. He sat beside her, sandwiching her between him and the bulkhead to provide a bit of shelter. She rewarded him with a tired smile.

Twice they couldn't find the beacon and had to return to their trawl along the shore to locate it and, once, a large breaking wave threatened to knock her down again, but Franz managed to turn her into the sea before she rolled.

Despite the conditions, they talked, as they had done through almost every watch they'd shared. Having lived a stone's throw apart for all their childhood years, it had shocked them both how little they truly knew of each other's lives. Often in English, the substance of their conversations ranged from Ruth's Jewish faith to Franz's military career, and what he'd seen in Poland, and Norway, and France.

They even talked about sailing.

He told her of the ragged grandeur of the Norwegian fjords and of the stark beauty of the Frisian Islands, with their mudflats and reed beds, teeming with nature, and Ruth drank in his every word, asking questions and repeating the unfamiliar English phrases until they lay imprinted in her mind, every one a building block in her drive to speak the language of her new and wished-for homeland.

But when they talked of their parents, their families, and their friends, they found themselves speaking in German.

~~o~~

Darkness fell early in the gloom, and the welcome beam from Blåvands Huk lighthouse pierced the dark skies long before the sun had set. It made the last hour of their wait easier, having a constant point to navigate from; only depth soundings were required to fix their position.

'I wonder if the keepers know how comforting their light is?' Ruth asked.

'I'd never thought about it,' Franz said. 'I guess I always took it for granted.'

After that, they sat in easy silence until Franz told Ruth to get everyone up on deck.

'Now,' he said, when they'd all sat, huddled together, 'while we're passing through Horns Rev, and going in the main channel, I want no one down below. It's just too easy to be trapped down there if we do founder; at least this way we have a slim chance of making it ashore.'

He looked around at them. His words had scared Ruth and Manny. He took two knives, each with a cord lanyard attached, and handed them to the Nussbaums.

'Hang these around your necks. You'll be tied on, but if I tell you to, or if the boat goes over and you're trapped, use them to cut your lifeline and do what you must to get to shore. Make sure your life preservers are fastened correctly, and if you do make it, try for the nearest farmhouse. It's your best chance of getting help. If you do, don't try and find Johann and I. We can take care of ourselves.'

He paused.

'Have you got that?' he asked, more harshly than he'd intended.

'Yes,' Ruth and Manny answered, unable to look at him.

'When we're in the main channel, keep out of sight as best you can unless we tell you otherwise. It's unlikely we'll meet any other boats, but it would be stupid to be careless at this point.'

'Good luck, everyone,' Johann said, and Manny returned his grin with a broader one of his own, but Franz could see real fear behind their bravado.

'You take her,' he said to Johann, handing the wheel over and picking up the Perspex-covered passage plan, and the chinagraph pencil.

'Manny, you can swing the lead. Ruth, keep a lookout to port. I'll watch to starboard.'

He turned to Johann.

'Two-six-zero.'

'Two-six-zero.'

Johann turned the wheel, and *The Shearwater*'s storm jib fluttered, then filled.

'I can't make two-six-zero,' Johann said.

'Get as close to the wind as you can get. We might have to tack out to the first mark. It's a white light. Everyone keep an eye out for it.'

CHAPTER 121

It took them half an hour to beat out the short distance to the buoy that marked the northern edge of Horns Rev.

'What does *Rev* mean?' Ruth asked.

'It's a reef,' Johann told her. 'Horns Rev is a sandy reef that runs for miles out into the North Sea. A lot of ships have foundered on her over the years.'

'Two-two-five,' Franz called, frowning at Johann as they passed the mark.

'The next mark has a red light,' he said, hoping Ruth hadn't picked up on Johann's comment. 'Two flashes every ten seconds. It's at the start of Søren Bovbjergs Dyb, the channel we're looking for. We leave it to starboard. We should be able to see the following mark on the same heading. Red again, one flash every ten seconds.'

Johann leaned forward.

'The waves are breaking on the reef, Franz,' he said. 'It's going to be hard to keep her on course.'

'She has a good grip of the water. Trust her and keep her as straight as you can.'

As they approached the reef, the crash of pounding waves made talking difficult and, all around, ribbons of white froth streaked the air. Franz could feel *The Shearwater* shuddering as each crest fell on her, shifting her sidelong towards the shore one minute, and sucking her back to seaward the next.

Johann fought to keep the boat heading for the faint, flashing red light that flickered through the crashing surf and driving rain.

Manny called out the depths and Franz was pleased to see him hold his fingers up as a visual indicator, knowing that his voice might not carry over the roar of the sea.

Franz peered ahead, hoping for a patch of darkness on the surface of the swirling water that might indicate the channel, but there was none. The sea in front of them was an endless churning sheet of white and he began to fear that he'd been reckless, gambling with all their lives.

Then, almost at the mark, he noticed that the tumbling wall of water on its seaward side flattened out ahead, and a few degrees to port, in the distance, there was a glimpse of a single flash of red from the buoy at the far end of the channel.

'Five points to port,' he shouted, and he heard Johann acknowledge the course change.

The boat, on a reach now, with the wind on the beam, surged forward. Franz didn't worry much about speed; because the trisail was fixed amidships, its drive would reduce when the wind was anywhere but in front of the beam, and the tiny storm jib was doing most of the work. If he needed more sail in a hurry, he could hoist the mizzen in seconds; it still had a reef in it.

'Four fathoms,' Manny called out, his four fingers in the air.

'Watch out!' Franz shouted as a wave, much bigger than the rest, broke over the side, swamping the cockpit with a solid wall of water that almost washed Manny over the side. Franz grabbed his arm and held on, not entirely trusting the boy's lifeline.

Manny shot him a grateful look as *The Shearwater*'s stern slewed to port, and Johann fought to keep the yacht from heading straight into the confused wall of white water on the seaward side of the channel. Franz jumped up and helped Johann force the wheel round, feeling the rudder biting into the swirling sea and clawing *The Shearwater* back from the brink.

Once she'd started to recover, the bow, caught by the next wave, came round too far and Johann cursed and turned the wheel to starboard.

Again, her response was sluggish but, this time, he brought her out of the turn early, and she straightened up. The red light ahead had disappeared in a cloud of spindrift, but Johann helmed to Franz's tersely delivered course changes and, a minute later, the blink of the channel mark appeared again, straight ahead.

'You beautiful girl!' Johann screamed. Even above the thunder of the sea, they all heard him.

Franz reckoned they were halfway through when Ruth shouted something, and pointed ahead, and to port of them.

Franz followed her gaze and saw a white light, higher up than the channel markers, then another, moving left to right.

'A ship,' he shouted. 'In the Slugen channel. Heading out from Esbjerg.'

Johann had seen it too and stared at Franz in horror.

Franz sprang up, undid the catches of the starboard cockpit locker, and threw open the cover. He drew out an open-ended canvas cone, with two lines attached, one at each end. He leaned over to the stern Samson post and threw a couple of turns of the thicker of the two ropes onto it.

'What's that?' Manny yelled in Johann's ear.

'The drogue,' Johann shouted. 'It's like putting on the brakes.'

Franz threw the drogue over the stern and waited. He braced himself against being thrown forward and Manny saw him and put out his arm to steady his sister.

The rope tightened with a crack as the cone opened out and bit into the water and halved *The Shearwater*'s speed, almost throwing Johann over the binnacle.

The lights of the ship were now dead ahead. He counted them, three or four white lights, and one green one. Then another white.

It's a sizeable vessel.

Even with the drogue deployed, reducing *The Shearwater*'s speed, she was still closing on the passing vessel and, in the faint moonlight, Franz could make out the unmistakable grey steel of a Kriegsmarine ship.

As they approached the end of the channel, the gap between them and the warship shrinking, the crew of *The Shearwater* had to crane their heads back to see the ship's lights, high above them on her superstructure, and by the time the stern light passed them, it towered above their bow.

Franz prayed that there was no one on the warship's stern deck, but grimaced; even if there was though, the chance of them looking down, or seeing *The Shearwater* appear beside them out of the gloom, was remote. All the same, it had been a close call, and if they hadn't deployed the drogue…

He shuddered. Another wave caught *The Shearwater*'s bow and Johann steered into it. They were now almost on top of the red light marking the end of Søren Bovbjergs Dyb.

'We're almost in the Slugen channel,' he shouted.

'I know,' Franz said, his voice almost lost in the howl of the wind and the crash of the sea. 'I can hear the whistle.'

Many of the channel markers had sound signals in addition to lights; often it was a bell but the one marking the edge of the Slugen channel, and the end of Søren Bovbjergs Dyb, had a whistle.

Franz pulled on the drogue's tripping line and felt it collapse, it's power to slow down the boat disrupted, and he hauled both lines in, lifting the canvas cone back on board.

The Shearwater shot forward into the deeper waters of Slugen Dyb.

'One-one-five degrees,' Franz shouted.

'One-one-five.'

'Ease the jib sheet,' Franz said to Ruth, pointing at the cleat it was tied off to.

Ruth let out a few turns and looked up at the foresail. It had filled, bellying out as the wind caught it.

'I'm going to drop the trisail,' Franz shouted in Johann's ear. 'It's doing nothing and it's going to flog, with the wind behind the beam.'

'All right. Be careful.'

Franz looped his lifeline around the jackstay and scrambled, low to the deck, towards the mast. He loosened off the main halyard and hauled the sail down, securing it on top of the boom with a couple of sail ties. Within seconds he was back in the cockpit.

He grabbed the sighting compass from the locker and took a bearing from the Blåvands light. He used the chinagraph pencil to make a note of it on his passage plan.

He leaned into Ruth and Manny and showed them the drawing. They could just make out the thick black lines in what little moonlight filtered through the clouds. With the wind behind them, the noise had dropped a little.

'We're through the reef now,' he told them. 'It runs out from Blåvands Huk, or point, and the land beyond that turns almost ninety degrees eastwards.'

He pointed out to port.

'We'll run downwind from here along Blåvand foreshore, then along the length of Skallingen. It's about ten miles, and we aim to judge it to be there just before midnight, when the tide is turning.'

'Is that low water or high?' Manny asked.

'Low water.'

'Why are we going in at low tide?'

'A good question, Manny. It has its drawbacks; the shallower water will kick up the sea more, and there's always the danger with big waves that, if we're in a trough, the keel could sink low enough to touch bottom.'

'So why not go in on high water, or at least until the tide comes in a bit?'

'The tidal range here is only a metre and a half at present, so we'd have to wait a long time for it to make much of a difference, and we must get in long before sunrise. But there's another reason.'

He pointed to his drawing again.

'Once we're through the main channel, we're looking to turn sharply to port, into a smaller one called Hobo Dyb. Although it sounds counter to what you'd expect, it's much easier to see the channel when the tide is out because the sandbanks around it will be showing. There should just be enough moonlight for us to see them, with a bit of luck. If we wait, the tide will cover them, and finding it will require much more guesswork.'

'What is Skallingen?' Ruth asked.

Franz turned to her.

'It's a narrow spit of high sand dunes with sea marsh behind them, about six kilometres long. It's where we'll be hiding behind; between that and an island called Langli.'

He showed her the board with his drawn plan on it, then gave it to Manny, and told him to hang onto it for him, for a while.

Ruth smiled as Manny pored over it, examining every detail.

Franz moved back to the binnacle and tapped Johann on the shoulder.

'I'll take her in,' he said.

Johann nodded and moved aside.

Franz had no concerns that Johann would resent him taking over the helm. Making a passage through a narrow channel, over a bar in storm-force winds with a following sea was a recipe for disaster and he doubted any of them would survive if the boat struck one of the many hazards they faced, and foundered. As skipper, it was his place to take the helm and the responsibility, and the consequences if he failed.

He put his hand on Johann's arm.

'On the approach to the main channel, we'll deploy the drogue again,' he said, 'but I want you to hang on the tripping line so that we can slow down or speed up as needed, and to prevent us being broached when a wave overtakes us. Whatever happens, we must be going slow enough when we pass the lighthouse, so that I can make the turn.'

'Are you going to use the engine?'

'I'd rather stick with the foresail; this boat was built to sail, and she works better under canvas, but we'll keep the engine ticking over in neutral, for emergencies, and I can always stick her into reverse if we need to slow her down a little, although I suspect it will have little effect.'

Johann nodded again.

'Anything else?' he said.

'Once we're past the lighthouse, go up forward and look out for the channel. It won't be marked but it should be obvious between the sandbanks. When you see it, point it out. I'll be keeping one eye on you for a signal. Once we're in Hobo Dyb, I want you to call out the depths and look for withy sticks.'

In smaller channels which did not warrant marker buoys being laid, long, thin poles, or *withy sticks*, were stuck into the mud to mark the edges of the channel, port and starboard, sometimes with their own distinctive mark. They were often put there by local fishermen for their own use and were moved whenever the channels shifted, as they were prone to do.

'You want to go as far up Hobo Dyb as we can?'

'Yes. We'll try and find a deep enough cut that branches to seaward and hide among the marshlands.'

Johann nodded again. He put his hand on his brother's shoulder.

'Good luck,' he said. 'I wouldn't trust anyone else with this.'

Franz laid his hand on top of his brother's and squeezed.

'Thank you.'

CHAPTER 122

Ruth sat, wedged into the corner of the cockpit, gripping the handrail until her knuckles shone white.

The weak moonlight barely penetrated the low, heavy clouds, and solid banks of driven rain still swept across *The Shearwater*'s decks. The roar of the waves pounding the shore terrified her, and the fact that she couldn't see the land when it was so close didn't help.

Without appearing obvious, she watched Franz.

He helmed without effort, and his eyes took in everything – the sea, the boat, the sails, and the crew. He was welded to the wheel, and stood easy, without effort, despite the heaving of the deck.

She'd been astounded at his patience, taking the time to answer her and Manny's questions in the middle of a storm, while trying to navigate a boat through a maze of sandbanks.

It was ironic, perhaps, that he sometimes had the look of one of the men on the posters for the National Socialist Party, yet that she was still able to like him as much.

She heard another whistle ahead of them and saw the flashing red light of the next mark. As they passed it, they saw the sea boil and churn behind it.

'That's the end of the inshore channel, Ringkøbing Dyb,' Johann said. 'It looks terrible, where it narrows. We made the right choice.'

'Manny, what's the next mark?' Franz asked.

Manny checked Franz's diagram.

'Two red flashes, five seconds. And a whistle.'

'I'm going to keep shoreside of it by half a cable, to stay out of the main channel; we were lucky to avoid that last vessel.'

'We'll be in the main channel going in Graa Dyb,' Johann said.

Ruth glanced at the Perspex-covered passage plan Manny held. Franz had written Graa Dyb in large letters adjacent to the straight, narrow channel that ran between the tip of Skallingen, and Langli Sand behind it on one side, and the island of Fanø and Søren Jessens Sand on the other. There didn't look to be much room to pass another ship and there were shallows at the entrance. She presumed that was the bar Franz was talking about.

'It can't be helped,' Franz said. 'There's no other way in, and we'll only be in it until we turn into Hobo Dyb, just past the lighthouse.'

'It's still over halfway,' Johann said, and Franz frowned at him.

'Most vessels won't use the channel at low water,' Franz said.

'The Kriegsmarine vessel must have passed through well under half-tide,' Johann said.

Franz shrugged.

'It can't be helped. We need shelter.'

'How long will we be in the channel for?' Ruth asked.

'Half an hour to three quarters, but we can stick to the side of the channel at first. Without lights, we'd still have a fair chance of remaining unseen.'

'How far are we away from the entrance?' Ruth asked, her face white in the gloom.

Franz looked at his watch. 'Another hour. We'll see Skallingen light soon.'

The weather had closed in again, and the beam from Blåvand light had disappeared, and the light from the smaller Skallingen lighthouse had not penetrated the murk yet. On a night with good visibility, they would have seen both lights at the same time, offering a certain way to fix their position.

'Franz,' Ruth shouted, pointing behind him. He turned just as a wave twice the height of the others lifted the starboard quarter and threw *The Shearwater*'s stern to the side and heeled her over.

Franz, instead of trying to correct the turn, swung the wheel to starboard, using the yacht's momentum to bury the bow into the crest of the wave, swinging her into the wind. The jib collapsed and Johann hauled on its sheet to stop it flailing.

The Shearwater swung violently from side to side, threatening to throw the four of them overboard, then settled. Franz wrenched the wheel to port and *The Shearwater* spun again, filling the sail and, before the next wave, the turn had brought her back onto her original course.

'Well done,' Johann said, thumping Franz on the arm.

'That's what you call a broach,' he said, turning to Ruth and Manny.

'I just saw the big wave coming,' Ruth said, still breathless. 'The next thing I knew we were going sideways.'

'If we'd stayed that way, the wave might have rolled us,' Johann said, 'but old Franz here managed to get her bow into the wave and keep us upright.'

Ruth saw Franz shake his head.

'It's not a bad thing that it happened here,' he said, 'where we had a bit of room to manoeuvre, and the waves and the wind weren't directly behind us. In the main channel, the waves will be much bigger, and right on the stern; the wind will be coming from behind too. If we broach in the narrows, it will be hard to stop her going over, or being pushed onto the shoals lining the channel.'

'If it does happen,' Johann said, 'and she's beached, the same applies as before. Cut your lifelines and make for safety.'

'We'll use the drogue again,' Franz added, 'which should stop us broaching, and we'll try and time our run to come in on the back of a wave, if we can.'

'But if you want to say a little prayer, now's the time to do it,' Johann joked.

~~o~~

23:10 Graa Dyb, No.2 channel marker 3 ca ahead, R, occ. Whistle, poor to moderate visibility. Wind increasing 40-45 knots, west-nor'westerly. 988mb. Storm jib. 4 knots 115°M.

~~o~~

Even before they rounded the outer mark, Franz grimaced as the weather took one last swipe at them.

The wind, which had dropped to a steady thirty-five knots between Horns Rev and Graa Dyb, howled harder again, kicking up the swell by another metre.

And the rain, almost off at one point, began to fill in, making it impossible to see more than half a mile ahead.

Only the beam from Skallingen light penetrated the sheets of heavy rain that passed over them in waves, and Franz headed straight for it. He prayed that he'd know when to veer to starboard just at the right time to round the point the lighthouse sat on, and not crash straight into the tip of the Skallingen bank.

He was having to work hard just to keep *The Shearwater* on course. Every wave that overtook them kicked the stern out; first to port and then to starboard but he managed to hold her steady until, halfway in, a larger wave flung her sideways like a piece of driftwood.

Ruth screamed and clung onto Manny.

'Pull on the drogue line,' Franz shouted. 'It's collapsed. But mind your fingers.'

Johann hauled on the now slack line until it seized taut again, as the drogue's cone filled. With the rudder hard over to port, the drogue's pull straightened *The Shearwater*, and the headsail filled again.

'It must have been too close to the surface, and the wave tripped it,' Franz said. 'Let it out another twenty metres; it will sit a little deeper in the water.'

Johann let the line out a few metres at a time, not wanting it to collapse again.

Franz looked at his watch and calculated the distance in his mind and held steady on his course.

They could all hear the thunderous crashing of waves breaking on the shore ahead, and on the sandbanks on either side of them.

'We're getting pretty close to the lighthouse, Franz,' Johann shouted, the edge in his voice barely audible above the roar of the sea and the wind.

Franz peered forward. The rain had eased to almost nothing. The air had cleared, and he imagined he could see the dunes of Skallingen in the pale moonlight that filtered through the clouds. He checked his watch again.

'Another minute,' he yelled, holding firm.

The sweeping beam of the lighthouse was above their heads now, and Franz knew they were close. He squinted ahead and saw the massive line of white surf, directly in front of them.

He turned the wheel to run across the surf and scanned ahead but couldn't see a break in the line of tumbling froth. He began to worry that he'd gone too far in towards the shore when he saw the gap. It was little more than a thinning of the surf line, perhaps twenty metres ahead, but it was all he had, so he turned the wheel and committed *The Shearwater* to it.

'Hang on tight,' he yelled, as the wind came across the deck and heeled *The Shearwater*. It was what he'd counted on. The boat was less likely to broach when the wind wasn't straight behind them.

As the line of white surf grew closer, it enlarged and intensified into a tumbling mass of troubled foam. Flumes of it filled the wind, which whistled in fury through the rigging. Franz prayed that no ship was coming out because he knew that there was nothing he could do but share the channel with it, praying they'd slip by unseen.

As they entered the surf and crossed the bar, he wrenched the wheel to port, then starboard, to counteract the ferocious swirling eddies that threatened to deflect *The Shearwater* onto dark, menacing shadows on either side that would claim her, and drown them.

Completely in tune with the boat, he felt the wave behind them lift the stern a second before Ruth saw it and screamed a warning. He looked back and saw a huge wall of water building behind them, falling towards them.

'Trip the drogue,' he shouted to Johann, pointing to the line in case his voice was lost in the wailing of the storm.

Johann grabbed the thinner of the two lines and hauled on it, collapsing the canvas cone.

The Shearwater surged forward, surfing the front of the wave. Franz, at the binnacle, saw the deck sloping down away from him and hoped beyond hope that the nose wouldn't dig in and pitchpole the boat, end over end, killing them all.

The stern rose higher as the crest of the wave gained on them, at an angle that Franz thought was impossible for a thirty-ton boat and he knew for sure that the wave was going to catch them, and toss them aside, onto the shore.

~~o~~

Ruth watched in horror as the stern of the boat rose almost directly above her, the crest of the wave looming over the lone figure of Franz, still fighting to keep *The Shearwater* from broaching.

'Let go of the tripping line!' Franz screamed, turning to Johann.

Johann released it and the drogue line snapped tight with a loud bang.

Ruth saw it stretch to breaking point, the Samson post it was lashed to bending backwards, but it held. The stern of the boat, checked hard by the drogue, buried itself in the crest of the wave as it swept over it, dumping tonnes of water into the cockpit.

Franz, crushed against the wheel, fought to stay upright.

Johann was flung from one end of the cockpit to the other, barely missing Manny, coming to a sudden painful stop against the cockpit bulkhead.

Ruth had seen the wave coming and turned away, burying her head in her arms, in the corner of the cockpit. She caught the brunt of the crushing force of the water but, with her mouth closed, and holding her breath, she avoided breathing in lungfuls of ocean.

The drogue held for a few seconds, then the line parted, whipping through the cockpit, passing close to Franz's head with a velocity that would have been fatal had it struck.

But it had done its job. *The Shearwater*, her stern now behind the wave's crest, balanced for a second in mid-air then fell backwards, levelling off as she fell onto the back of the wave. Released from the hold of the drogue, she surged forwards again.

The beam from the lighthouse was now almost abreast of them.

'The channel,' Franz shouted to Johann, still waist deep in cockpit water. 'Go forward.'

Ruth saw Johann jump up, staggered by how quickly he'd recovered while she sat numbed.

She watched as he undid his lifeline, tying it onto the jackstay then clambering over the

394

deck to the mast, his eyes searching ahead for any signs of the channel.

Ruth sucked in deep breaths, shocked by the weight of the water, and the numbing coldness of it. She looked back at Johann, then back at Franz, both searching the blackness ahead in desperation for any sign of the narrow entrance to Hobo Dyb. She peered into the darkness ahead.

There's nothing there.

~~o~~

The lighthouse was now on their beam. Franz faintly made out its round body and its metal legs as they passed it. There was still no shout from Johann so, gambling, he turned a few degrees to port, knowing that the channel they were searching for swung almost immediately round to the north, behind Skallingen.

'Nothing?' he yelled, but his voice didn't carry. Still in the main channel, the roar of the waves crashing behind them on the bar and the howl of the wind above them drowned out his voice.

With the lighthouse off the port quarter, Franz again took a risk, turning another few points to port. He groped for the image of the chart in his head and tried to place *The Shearwater* on it, working out angles and distances by instinct, as if he were flying above her, watching her curve round the back of Skallingen, threading her way into the narrow passage between the dunes and Langli Sand. He knew that a mistake now could leave them foundering within touching distance of safety.

'Thirty metres ahead.'

Franz couldn't be sure he heard it, but then he saw Johann point forwards and hold up his hands, flashing his fingers three times in quick succession.

Franz looked, but could see nothing. He glanced towards Skallingen, but there was no break in the shadowy sands on that side. He hesitated for a second, then putting his trust in his brother, turned the wheel hard to port.

For a second or two, *The Shearwater*'s momentum and the rush of the sea through Graa Dyb continued to throw her forward, and he thought he'd left it too late, but the rudder bit into the current and she began to turn, slowly at first, but gathering pace. The foresail billowed with a crack as the wind filled it, and she heeled in the turn, throwing Ruth and Manny across the cockpit, and forcing Johann to cling to the mast to keep him from sliding down the sloping deck.

Franz, unbalanced, had the presence of mind to centre the wheel, not wanting to be pushed round too far by the force of the wind on the sail and by the waves on *The Shearwater*'s stern.

She continued her turn, but it slowed, and she steadied herself and pitched forward into the darkness.

'Ease the sheet,' Franz shouted and Manny, picking himself up, took a turn off the cleat and let a length out.

The Shearwater lost a little of her heel but was still hurtling forward too fast.

'A bit more,' Franz shouted, and Manny obliged, easing the sheet until it started to luff.

The yacht's speed slackened, and Franz worked the wheel from side to side to slow her still further.

'There's a withy stick dead ahead,' Johann shouted. In the lee of Skallingen, the noise of the surf and the scream of the wind had decreased, and Franz could hear him now. He turned to starboard.

'Ruth, look out on your side. You're looking for withy sticks.'

'How do we know if they're port marks or starboard marks?' Manny asked.

'We don't, but they're most often port marks. We'll creep in as slowly as we can, to give us time to work it out.'

Incredibly, the foresail flapped on the foredeck; the wind had dropped in the sheltered waters of Hobo Dyb, behind the dunes, but enough of a breeze remained, blowing across the boat.

'Johann, can you take soundings forward?'

Manny grabbed the lead line from the cockpit locker and hurried forward to Johann.

'Two fathoms,' Johann shouted, a few seconds later, as Manny dived back into the cockpit.

'Haul in the sheet,' Franz called to him, conscious that *The Shearwater* had almost stalled.

'Work the sail until it just fills, and no more. We want her creeping forward with just enough way on to steer.'

Manny pulled on the sheet until the sail filled, with a soft slap, and the yacht's speed began to pick up again.

~~o~~

There was a short chop in the shallow channel, but there were no real waves to speak of. A gentle swell pushed in behind them from Graa Dyb, gently rocking them as it passed under the hull. Ruth found it difficult to reconcile the difference a few minutes could make, and a couple of hundred metres.

Above them, the wind still howled but the rain was no more than a greasy smir.

Through a thinning in the cloud, enough moonlight filtered through, and Ruth, seeing something ahead, shouted and pointed it out to Franz.

'Yes. That's a withy stick. Well done.' He steered to starboard, away from it, leaving it twenty metres to port.

'The channel curves away to the right,' he said, 'for about half a mile, then it runs straight for about the same distance to the tip of Langli. After that, it curves round to port, between the island and the marshes behind Skallingen. That's where we're aiming for.'

'You've been here before?' Ruth asked.

'A long while ago. With my father,' he said, the hint of a smile reaching his exhausted face, 'but it was during the day and in fine weather.'

She returned his smile, one of immense relief, she conceded.

They could see the withy sticks with ease now, and Johann gave directions from the bow, still checking the depths every minute or so.

In the moonlight, as they curved round to port, she could make out the low-lying dunes and grassland of Langli to the east and the higher dunes and extensive marshland of Skallingen to the west.

As the depths decreased, and they drew level with the middle of Langli, Franz turned to port and steered the boat towards a cut in the marshy hillocks of Skallingen, and *Der Sturmtaucher* bumped to a halt in the mud.

'Let's get this anchor out,' he said, joining Johann at the bow. The two brothers embraced, and Johann turned away, unlashing the anchor to hide his tears.

In the cockpit, Ruth stared at the two men. During the terrifying passages through Horns Rev and Graa Dyb, she'd hardly taken her eyes off Franz. He'd saved all their lives; she had no doubt about that, and she knew, even before she could see it in daylight, that he'd found a place where they might just escape discovery.

She'd come to believe, no matter how irrational it was, that during the worst of the night, he was almost immortal. She'd taken strength from her belief, but had feared that to look away would somehow jeopardise their chances of making it to safety.

But that wasn't the only reason.

She knew, deep down, that she was falling in love with him.

CHAPTER 123

[10/08/2001 Friday]

Maldon, England.

'Hobo Dyb. A wretched place in many ways, but it was heaven on earth. The wind howled above us for three days, but Der Sturmtaucher barely moved, tucked in behind the sand dunes and salt marshes of Skallingen. I slept through the storm for ten hours that first night, hearing nothing; I didn't even dream. We stayed for five days and, before we left, my life had changed forever.'

Ruth stared past me, out of the window, the occasional whitecap hardly troubling the bay's surface, and I knew she had slipped back across the cables of time to their refuge from the raging North Sea gale.

CHAPTER 124

Hobo Dyb, Denmark.

The anchor had no sooner settled into the mud of Hobo Dyb than Ruth and Manny crawled into the forepeak, their exhausted bodies and minds surrendering to unconsciousness almost instantly. In *The Shearwater*'s saloon, Franz and Johann, both numb with relief and close to collapse themselves, sipped the rum Franz had poured into their mugs, letting their minds and bodies slowly uncoil, knowing they'd won the battle to reach landfall.

Johann looked at his older brother's pallid face, the lines of worry ageing him beyond his twenty-four years. He presumed that his own appearance would be just as haggard if he were to look in the small shaving mirror that hung inside the door of the heads.

Franz gave a weary smile.

'We forgot to start the engine,' he said.

Johann laughed, and shook his head.

'It would have made no difference. Like you said, she was born to sail.'

'Yes. She's a wonderful girl,' Franz said, leaning his head back against the bulkhead.

'I'll do the first watch,' Johann said, 'You've been awake for the best part of thirty-six hours.'

'No, we'll not need a watch tonight; there'll be no boats anywhere near us while this is blowing, and even if there are any vessels passing through the main channel to Esbjerg, they'll never see us. Let's get a few hours' sleep and we'll rise at first light and lower the masts.'

Johann raised an eyebrow. 'Do you think that's necessary?'

'Yes. With the masts down, there's little or no chance we'd be seen from the main channel or Skallingen, but if we left them up…'

'It won't be easy.'

'It shouldn't be too bad getting them down. Hauling them back up will be difficult, but at least the masts are deck-stepped; it would have been impossible if they'd been keel-stepped.'

Johann nodded. The base of *Der Sturmtaucher*'s main mast was at deck level and could be lowered with care by undoing the rigging. The mizzen was the same.

A keel-stepped mast penetrated the deck all the way down through the cabin. It would have taken a crane to lift it out.

'I'm surprised they are deck-stepped,' he said.

'The colonel insisted on that design. To get to *Der Sturmtaucher*'s winter berths in Lübeck, she has to pass under the Wipperbrücke. The bridge only clears three metres, hence the need for the masts to be lowered without a crane.'

'That makes sense. Even so, I hope we can raise them again when the time comes.'

'We'll manage, somehow,' Franz said.

CHAPTER 125

Heinrich Güllich put the phone down. Yet again, there was nothing from Norway, but he hadn't given up hope; by all accounts the storm that had raged for almost a week was still blowing, even if its ferocity had reduced to something approaching a gale.

He decided to put the Nussbaums aside for a day; he was almost certain he was getting a stomach ulcer, and that his frustration with the Jews and their General was largely to blame.

He looked around for his assistant; he was nowhere to be seen, then he remembered. Carl Meyer was going to call in with his father and pick up one or two old sea charts of the Kattegat and Skagerrak to try and give his boss a better understanding of the voyage the Kästner traitors had made.

He called to one of the Kriminalassistentanwärteren and asked for a coffee and returned to his office. That was the good thing about the Geheime Staatspolizei. If you did your work well and produced results, they would let you get on with it, with minimal interference; going off on a tangent wasn't frowned upon, provided it furthered the aims of the Gestapo.

The Kriminalassistentanwärter, a recent recruit, brought the coffee just as Carl Meyer came through the door, carrying an oversized leather folio case the size of a small kitchen table. He took it straight into Heinrich Güllich's office.

The Kriminalassistent frowned.

'Sorry, sir,' he said. 'My father wouldn't let me fold the charts and it was either this or rolling them up.'

'It doesn't matter. Let's see what all the fuss is about.'

They cleared the Kriminalassistent's desk and Carl Meyer opened the case and laid out the nautical charts on top of it.

'Your father keeps all these charts in his home?'

'Yes, sir. He was in the Reichsmarine during the Great War, then he worked for the Krupps. It's a bit of nostalgia for him, I suppose. They gave him an out-of-date set when he retired; they're old, but he still keeps them corrected, so they'll be just as useful now as they were ten years ago.'

Heinrich Güllich grunted and lit a cigarette.

'My father has plotted what he thinks is *Der Sturmtaucher*'s course on the charts, for your information.'

'Ah. That was most kind of him. You must thank him for me.'

'I will, sir,' Carl Meyer said, a look of surprise on his face at the Kriminalassistent's expansive mood.

They pored over the charts. Carl Meyer explained the symbols and how distances were measured and answered as many of his boss's questions as he could.

Heinrich Güllich pointed at the chart.

'I can see the difficulties that Bødjen and Bogense would have presented for delivering the Nussbaum brats to the boat, but there are places in Schleswig-Holstein where they could have picked them up.'

He tapped several points on the chart.

'The Schwansen peninsula, the Angeln peninsula and the Schlei estuary, all in Schleswig-Holstein. Then there's Als in Denmark, or even Aarøsund or Middelfart.'

'Sir, the Schlei estuary has a narrow entrance, and it's well guarded. And there's nowhere easy to berth, or even anchor, on the rest of the Schleswig-Holstein coast, unless they made a big detour into Eckernförder Bucht or Geltinger Bucht, but they didn't have time.'

'What about the Danish mainland?'

'It's possible, but it's the same as Bogense and Bødjen; how would they have crossed the border?'

'He's a general. With unlimited powers, it seems.'

Carl Meyer looked sceptical.

Heinrich Güllich examined the chart again.

'All right, Meyer, I'll concede that if they're on the boat, they must have boarded at Kieler Hafen. The next problem is where they landed them. I'd guess somewhere in Sweden.'

'I've checked the distances, sir. If they'd wanted to do that, they'd have gone through the Great Belt, or more likely Øresund, between Copenhagen and Malmö. The only opportunity they had on the route they took was between Læsø and Hirtshals, and I don't believe they had time, sir. It would have added almost fifty miles to their journey. It's just not possible.'

'So, you think the rats are still on the boat?'

Carl Meyer shrugged.

'There are a number of permutations, sir, but it still comes down to the three most likely ones.'

Heinrich Güllich gave a cold smile. On the rare occasion his assistant crossed the line into arrogance, he needed slapped down, but he was interested to see if the young officer had reached the same conclusions as him.

'What are they?'

'One. They're in Norway, on the boat or already off it. The Kästner brothers are based there. They could have arranged a safe hiding place for them.'

'Two?'

'They've been dropped off in Demark. We should check out if the Kästners or the Nussbaums have relatives there.'

Heinrich Güllich nodded, impressed.

'And three?'

'This whole voyage thing is a red herring, intentional or not, and they've been spirited away by another route.'

'You've discounted the possibility that the Judenläuse are genuinely missing.'

'Yes, sir. Sorry, but you were right. They're trying to get them out of Germany. The Nussbaums and the General are doubtless involved, and maybe the girl too.'

'I'm glad you've come round to my way of thinking. I like your idea about checking for Danish relatives, but I also want you to get me the names and telephone numbers of the harbour administrators of all the places they've been to, and of any others where it's conceivable that they might have called in.'

'Yes, sir.'

The Kriminalassistent looked at the chart of the Skagerrak.

'So, they're somewhere on this chart?'

'Yes, sir. In southern Norway. Almost certainly.'

'Or Sweden, perhaps?'

'It's possible, but it would have taken them an extra five or six hours. They'd have been caught out in the storm. Do you want me to check? The Swedes are helpful for the most part.'

'No. It would flag up at the NSDAP office for foreign affairs.'

The Kriminalassistent stared at the chart for a long time.

'There is another possibility, my young friend,' he said. 'Do you have a larger chart of the area?'

'You mean one with more detail?'

'No, I want one that covers a wider area. Including the whole of the Nordsee.'

Carl Meyer gave a puzzled frown.

He reached to the bottom of the pile and pulled out a small-scale map that covered the entire North Sea, including much of Norway, Denmark, north-west Germany, Holland, Belgium, northern France, and the east coast of Britain.

Heinrich Güllich studied it for a while.

'How long would it take for them to sail to England?'

Carl Meyer burst out laughing, but Heinrich Güllich glared at him, and it died in his throat.

'Perhaps three or four days, sir, if the winds were favourable, but in this case, they weren't. The wind was from the west and as strong as it gets, sir. They'd never have survived a storm of that magnitude in the North Sea.'

Heinrich Güllich let the disappointment show on his face.

'What if they holed up, and made a break for it later?'

'Our ships would spot them, sir.'

Carl Meyer swept his hand across the mouth of the Skagerrak and from the northern tip of Norway, down the eastern half of the North Sea to the Frisian coasts of Germany and

Holland.

'Our ships criss-cross this area all the time. I believe a few have been back out in the last twenty-four hours, since the wind dropped.'

He made a circle with his finger in the north-east corner of the Skagerrak.

'The Kästners must be somewhere in here.'

'And you're sure they wouldn't have tried to sail west, under cover of the storm.'

'No, sir. It would have been suicide.'

CHAPTER 126

By the time Ruth cautiously removed the washboards and poked her head out from the companionway, Franz and Johann had lowered both masts.

'You should have called us to help,' she said.

'You needed your rest. The mizzenmast was easy; it's smaller and lighter. The main mast was tougher, but we managed it.'

She was surprised at how denuded the yacht looked without its masts, which were lashed along the port side of the deck, on cradles the brothers had fashioned from the spare planks they stowed aboard for repairs, and she was curious.

'Why are the masts down? Were they damaged?'

'Partly, but it's not the only reason; it will allow us to repair the topmast but above all else, we wanted to have less chance of being discovered.'

Franz handed her his cap.

'Tuck your hair in, and put this on if you are on deck, and remember, only two of us can be topside at any one time, the same as before.'

'I thought no one could see us here?'

'It's pretty well hidden from anywhere on land, but there are cattle grazing on drier parts of the salt marsh, so there's always a risk that the farmer will come to feed them. The road to the lighthouse is nearly a mile away from us, so that's not as much of a problem and Langli is uninhabited, as far as I'm aware, though animals graze there too, I think.'

She looked across the salt marshes through the sheets of rain that still blew in from the west. The flat spongy bog by the water's edge gave way at the head of the creek to large soft hummocks covered with coarse grass, coalescing into the solid strip of land that made up Skallingen. Plumes of sand blew into the air from the dunes on the seaward side which protected the anchorage from the worst of the storm.

She peered through the murk, the rain stinging her face and blurring her vision. 'I can't see a road, or any cows.'

'They're there all right. I heard them lowing during the night when there was a lull in the wind. And if you look closely, you can see the telegraph poles by the roadside. It's more of a track than a road, really, and the farmer feeds his cattle close to it, so I doubt he'll be in sight of us, but there could be a small fishing boat or two out in Ho Bucht and Hobo Dyb, once the storm dies down a bit.'

He pointed out the creel markers, and the poles that held fishing nets.

'Oh,' she said. 'I didn't notice them. It looks so wild here.'

~~o~~

Franz watched her look around, her interest piqued. Although frail and still tired, despite her long sleep, she had recovered a little of her usual self.

'How are you feeling now?' he asked. 'I was worried about you.' He blushed. 'About both of you,' he added, hoping she hadn't noticed.

She smiled, and something inside him broke a little.

'We'll be fine,' she said. 'Manny's still sleeping. I'll waken him before long or he'll never sleep tonight. Where's Johann?'

'He's gone back to his bunk for an hour or two, to try and catch up on his sleep.'

'Oh, I didn't notice him, but I know how he feels; I'm still tired despite being out cold since we arrived. What time is it?'

'It's half past ten,' Franz said, looking at his watch.

'Goodness,' she said. 'I didn't realise I'd slept so late.'

'I wouldn't worry. You'll sleep ten or twelve hours a night for the next few days to recover from what you've been through. If it's any consolation, you both did remarkably well. We've got thousands and thousands of nautical miles under our belts, but that's by far the worst conditions Johann or I have ever sailed in, so for both of you, it must have been horrific.'

'I was worse than useless. I was sick much of the time, and nowhere as good as Manny with the boat.'

'You managed a good deal more helming than I could ever have hoped for, and you kept me awake on watches, talking to me in English, keeping my mind alert when I was exhausted.' He smiled at her, knowing that she'd shown greater bravery than anyone he'd ever met.

She'd hauled herself up on deck for every single watch she'd been expected to do and, although she'd spent much of the last part of the journey huddled in the corner of the cockpit, retching, and clinging in desperation to whatever she could find on the heavily pitching yacht, she hadn't complained once.

In contrast, Manny had only been sick for a day or so, and although he hadn't shared any watches with the youngster, he knew that, despite being sometimes fearful when the sea was at its worst, the boy had relished the challenge.

'How long will we stay here do you think?' Ruth asked.

'It's hard to tell. It depends how long the storm lasts. And we could do with heavy fog for the next bit of the journey.'

'Why? Surely fog is dangerous?'

'Yes, it is. We wouldn't ordinarily choose to sail in it if we could avoid it, but this end of the North Sea is much busier with traffic, and we can't risk being seen. The good news is that fog is commonplace around here at this time of year, when warm air from the westerly breezes comes in contact with the cold waters off western Denmark. We'll hide here until the visibility becomes poor enough, at least to get part of the way.'

'Isn't it easy to get lost in fog? You were always on the lookout for lights at night, or buoys or landmarks during the day, so that you knew where we were.'

'You're right, but during the storm, visibility was never more than a couple of miles, and there were very few, if any, boats about. And we were close to land, looking for shelter, so we needed to know where we were with some precision. Now, we're heading out to open sea, and although we'll still try our best to keep a track of where we are, there's little risk of us not finding England. Come down below, and I'll show you how we find our way in the fog.'

He climbed down the companionway and she followed.

~~o~~

Ruth looked across the cabin. She spotted Johann's blond hair; he had indeed taken a nap, crawling into his sleeping bag in one of the narrow pilot berths on the port side of the cabin. They'd been glad of these coffin-like bunks during the storm when the yacht was heeled over, but she hadn't thought he'd use one when they were at anchor.

Johann didn't rouse, and they talked in low voices so as not to disturb him.

Franz fished out a North Sea chart.

'So, we start here,' he said, pointing to Graa Dyb, the main channel into Ho Bucht and Esbjerg. On the small-scale chart, the island of Langli was not much more than a squiggle inside the long spit of land that protected them from the storm. He made room for Ruth to sit beside him on the navigator's bench, sandwiched between the chart table and the bulkhead at the rear of the main cabin.

'We place a fix here.' He pointed. 'And write the time beside it. Then we plot the course we would like to sail, and adjust it for tide, if there is any.'

After drawing a small cross with a circle around it on the chart, to mark the starting position, he added a line going westwards away from the land, just over forty miles in length, which he labelled with a single arrow. He looked up the tide table, checked the tidal diamond on the chart, and calculated the tidal flow that was running. He then drew a short line on the chart, starting once more at the circular mark, and added three arrows to indicate that the line he'd just drawn represented the tide.

'With tide, we always work in intervals of an hour. This allows for reasonable accuracy as the tide changes constantly. There are two high tides and two low tides in just over twenty-four hours, about fifty minutes later each day.'

She watched, fascinated, as he added individual tidal flows for the next five hours, conscious of his proximity and the warmth within her that being close to him stirred.

We've got to know more about each other's lives in a couple of weeks than we did in the previous eighteen years we've lived on each other's doorsteps.

From an early age, she'd worshipped Franz and Johann; they were the older brothers she didn't have, but she always saw Franz as closer in nature to her father and the General, and it was easy to have a greater affinity with the fun-loving Johann.

She blushed, remembering her childish daydreams of marrying him when she grew up.

She'd outgrown that as she journeyed through her tough teenage years, which made her grow up all too fast. Changing from a girl into a young woman, she'd realised Johann's take on life, especially where women were concerned, was not what she wanted in a man, despite his obvious charms, but thoughts of Franz in any romantic sense had never entered her mind, until now.

She was well read and wasn't completely naïve about what her body and mind were telling her, but she also knew the realities of life; that she and Franz lived in different worlds and any affection she had for him could never be reciprocated, nor could she ever speak about her feelings to anyone.

His voice broke into her thoughts.

'You were miles away there. And here I am, trying to teach you the intricacies of navigation.'

'Sorry,' she said, but she could see that he was laughing so she gave him a nudge in his side with her elbow. 'Carry on. I'll ty and concentrate.'

He returned to the chart in front of them.

'We've added six hours of tide, so now we have to work out the approximate distance the boat would travel during that time.'

He picked up the dividers and gave them to her.

'They're just like a drawing compass but with two metal points instead of one, and no pencil.'

He pointed to the latitude scale up the side of the chart.

'It just so happens that each degree of latitude is sixty nautical miles. We want to measure thirty miles, because the boat will travel around five miles each hour.'

Ruth measured the distance required. She found it awkward to adjust the dividers, so he helped her to open them out, then gently squeezed her fingers to close them to the correct distance.

He told her to place one arm of the dividers on the end of the tidal stream vectors and make an arc with the other arm until it crossed the line he had already drawn.

'Make a little mark with the pencil on our route where the dividers cross it,' he told her, and once she had done as he had asked, he gave her the parallel rulers, and made her draw a line from the end of the tidal flows to the mark she'd made on their route line.

'Now for the clever bit,' he said.

He showed her how to use the parallel rulers to read off their course from the compass rose, printed on the chart.

'It's marked off in degrees,' he said. '360, just like geometry at school.'

She laughed. 'I'm not stupid. We did geography at school, so I know how a compass works.' She nudged him again.

'Don't be cheeky to your elders.' He grinned. 'I'm just trying to make it easy so that I don't confuse your simple mind.'

That earned him another nudge, from her elbow this time.

He made a painful grimace, and for an instant, she was fooled.

She saw a smile at the corner of his mouth, and she laughed.

'Get on with it,' she told him.

He showed her how take the reading from the compass rose, and wrote the number next to the line, and added two arrows.

'The arrows show the direction we need to steer on top of the water to travel along our desired ground track, as we call it.'

'So, we point in a completely different direction from the one we want to go?'

'Well, with exceptional tides, that could be the case, but with the sort of tides we have here, the differences aren't much more than a few degrees overall, but we still have to take several other things into account as well. Leeway, magnetic variation, and compass deviation all affect the course we steer, but we've done enough for one day. We'll have lesson two tomorrow.'

~~o~~

Franz stood up and looked out of the hatch.

'There's nothing stirring,' he said.

'I'm going to have a coffee,' Ruth said. 'Would you like a cup?'

'I'd love one. Although we're getting low on water. As for food…'

'I thought there was a cupboard full of tinned goods?'

'There are some, but not enough. We used more than I'd expected. Plus, we could do with some fresh bread, vegetables, milk, and cheese. We lost most of it when we were knocked down. And we'll need to get more fuel. We'll put it on the colonel's bill.'

She laughed again.

'I nearly died when he came aboard the night before we left,' she said. 'Do you still think he didn't suspect anything?'

'I'm sure he didn't, or he'd have done something about it. He was just anxious about his yacht.' He furrowed his brow. 'He'll be more worried now. I'd almost feel sorry for him, but…' His voice trailed off.

'What?'

'You don't want to know. It would only distress you.'

'I'm leaving my parents behind in a country that hates all Jews, and you're worrying about something upsetting me? You've got to start treating me like an adult, Franz,' she said. 'I'm sorry, I don't mean to be rude, but I'm not a child anymore.'

'I know that,' he said, rubbing his forehead with his hand. 'It's just… you have enough to cope with.'

'Don't worry about me. I'm stronger than you think. It's Manny I worry for. He's only fourteen and having to leave Mama and Papa, on top of what he's already been through.'

Despite her show of courage, Franz could see she was struggling, and he wanted nothing more than to put an arm around her to comfort her.

But it would have felt wrong. He took a deep breath.

'He told me that it would do Johann and I good to distance ourselves from our father.'

'Why would he do that?'

'Because of his attitude to the National Socialists.'

'That's absurd, there are plenty people who don't like what they stand for.'

'There aren't so many now, and those that don't choose to keep quiet about it.' He hesitated, then continued.

'He also said that my father should stop being a Jew-lover.'

CHAPTER 127

They sat in silence for a while. He was sorry he'd said anything, but he supposed she'd suffered those sorts of barbs every day since the National Socialists came to power.

The yacht creaked and lurched to one side. Ruth jumped, and let out a small cry. Franz put a reassuring hand on her arm.

'It's getting towards low water now. We're touching the bottom. When the tide is at its lowest, we'll be fully aground. Don't panic, it's thick, soft mud here and *The Shearwater* will just sink into it and list a little. It could be as much as twenty degrees.'

He used his arm to demonstrate how far the hull would lean over. For a second, he paled, wondering if she realised how like a Hitler salute it looked.

'She'll make her own hollow in the mud,' he said, covering his lapse, 'as she'll always sit in the same spot, because of the kedge anchor.'

He pointed to the rope tied to the back of the boat which disappeared under the water in the direction of Langli.

'We moved *Der Sturmtaucher* a little further up the creek and reset the main anchor, then laid out the kedge anchor at the back to stop her swinging round when the tide comes in.'

'Oh. I suppose that makes sense.'

'Lying like this also keeps the cockpit sheltered from the worst of the wind and the rain, and it means that from Skallingen or Langli, only the bow or the stern can be seen, making us much harder to spot.'

'You did an awful lot when I was sleeping. I feel quite bad about that.'

'Don't. You were completely done in. We didn't do it when we came in. We got up at high water, at about half past six, took the masts down, and moved the boat further up this little inlet, to be better hidden. It only took a few minutes to row the kedge anchor out and drop it fifty metres from the stern. We were surprised you didn't wake, but you were both out cold.'

She smiled, blushing.

'We'll rig an awning today,' he continued. 'The rain has passed now, but it looks as if further squalls are on their way; it will save the four of us being cooped up down below all the time.'

'Will we still always have to keep watch?' she asked.

'Only during the day. At night, we would normally show an anchor light so that other boats could see us, but that would m̲a̲k̲e̲ us stick out like a sore thumb. Anyway, Hobo Dyb is a blind, shallow channel going now̲ ̲ ̲ ̲ ̲ ̲ ̲ ̲ ̲ ̲ ̲ ̲ ̲ ̲ ̲ ̲-̲h̲o̲red in a small cut to the side of it. Apart from a small fishing boat or two, no vessels will ever use this channel. With any luck, we'll just look like a yacht that has been moored up and left for a while.'

'Won't a fisherman come on board, to check it out?'

'I doubt it. There's a kind of unwritten rule that moored boats are sacrosanct; a bit like you wouldn't walk into someone else's house.'

'So, will I still be on watch with you?'

He looked up at her, but her face gave nothing away and he blushed.

'We won't need to set watches; as long as someone on deck is keeping an eye out during daylight hours, it'll be enough.'

She looked disappointed, he thought.

Johann stirred in his bunk and grunted.

'I know you two think you're talking quietly,' he said, 'but there's no chance of me sleeping with all this idle chatter.' He grinned, half-shutting his eyes as they adjusted to the weak sunlight shining down the hatch through a break in the clouds.

'You couldn't have been sleeping very soundly if our talking woke you up,' Franz countered. 'We barely spoke above a whisper.'

'I woke before you came down from the cockpit,' Johann admitted. 'I enjoyed listening to the navigation lesson though. I learned a lot.'

Franz picked up a towel and threw it at him.

'We need to talk. Get dressed and I'll pour you a coffee.'

Johann glanced at Ruth.

'I'll go outside for some fresh air,' she said, reddening again.

Johann grinned again, and her blush deepened.

She climbed up the steps and closed the washboards behind her. Johann sniffed at his shirt and decided that it would do another day. Glancing at the door, he poured a shallow basin of water and washed himself before throwing his clothes on.

'That's me decent,' he said, opening the hatch again and poking his head out.

'I'll sit here for a while,' she said, not looking at him.

He lowered himself back down into the cabin, laughing.

'I think I've upset Ruth, Franz,' he said.

'Leave her alone, Dummkopf. Let's concentrate on the job in hand.'

Johann gave Franz his trademark apologetic smile.

Franz spoke in a low murmur and gestured that Johann should do the same.

'One of us is going to have to go and get water, and fuel, and some food, if we want to eat properly. This storm could blow for another few days yet, eating into the little supplies we have. And we don't know how long the next part of the voyage will take.'

'I know,' Johann said. 'It was the first thing that went through my mind this morning.'

He took a deep breath.

'I should go,' he said. 'If something happens to me, you've a greater chance of getting away. You're a better sailor than me.'

Franz started to protest, but he knew that Johann was right. While there wasn't much between them, Franz had the greater cruising experience of the pair, and he had the edge over his younger brother in terms of navigation and seamanship.

'All right, so you go. Take the tender towards the top end of Hobo Dyb but avoid the road that goes over to Langli at low water; there's always the chance that a farmer will go over to the island and see either you or the dinghy. Find a place you can beach it at one of the small creeks that cut into the fen. There's a small village called Ho, about a kilometre and a half along the road. We visited it the last time we were here, but we weren't trying to hide then...'

Johann hesitated. 'I could take young Manny. He'd be useful as a lookout, and he could come back and tell you if I get into trouble.'

'No, definitely not. Ruth would never allow it, and anyway, he's too young.'

'Hear me out. I've watched him over the last two weeks. He's tough for a boy his age, and he doesn't get flustered. He'll get sick to death of being cooped up on the boat for another week or so. When you hear the Scheiße he's had to put up with over the last few years, you'll realise he's as tough as either of us, if not tougher. Anyway, we will be able to carry twice the supplies with us both there.'

'But what happens if you get caught? Ruth won't leave without him.'

'We won't get caught; I'll make sure that he keeps out of sight, and if I get caught, he can make his way back here. I can either bluster it out or get myself sent back home in disgrace.'

Franz looked unconvinced, but he shrugged his shoulders. 'I'll have to ask Ruth.'

'That goes without saying, if she hasn't heard us talking.' He smiled.

Franz slid back the hatch and peered over the washboards. The yacht now had an alarming tilt, but Ruth was sitting on the low side of the cockpit, leaning on the coaming, staring at something in the water. Not wanting to disturb her, he didn't speak, but climbed up the steps and slid himself onto the seating beside her.

He could see now what had caught her eye. A heron was fishing the water's edge not more than ten metres from the boat. Ruth turned towards him, motioning him to be quiet. The tall, elegant bird was oblivious to them, intent only on studying the surface of the water. Every few minutes, it would lift one of its legs with exaggerated care, take a long step, and place it back in the water, leaving barely a ripple. As they watched, its patience was rewarded when it stabbed at the water, coming up with a fish gripped across its beak, which it flipped and swallowed, its long slender neck bulging as the fish slid down its gullet.

Ruth let out a stifled squeal of delight, and the heron, startled, took off with laboured beats of its large wings, less elegant now, but still magnificent, as it flew across the mudflats, settling out of sight to continue its search for food in solitude.

Franz watched Ruth's face. Amidst the horror that her life had become, she still managed to find innocent wonder in a gift from nature. Reluctant to spoil the moment, he waited until she'd stopped staring, long after the bird had disappeared. He wondered if she'd slipped back into her childhood, before the National Socialists had ripped her youth away from her.

He gently touched her elbow.

'I'm sorry. We need to ask you something.'

'Oh, I was miles away. It's so peaceful here.'

'I know. It's a pity we're here for all the wrong reasons. You'd have loved sailing around this place. It's so different from anything we have in the Ostsee.'

'It's the wildness,' she said. 'Despite everything, there were parts of the journey I liked, mostly before we got into the North Sea; the Lillebælt was beautiful, and I enjoyed the islands we sailed past, but I find this place much more fascinating.'

'Perhaps it's just because we're so relieved to have survived this far, but I know what you mean. I love places that are shaped by storms and tides. It makes them difficult to get to, and magical. And it means there are no people here. I mean, look at it now, at low tide. We could be in a different world.'

He looked around. The marsh grasses were now above head height and steep mudbanks hemmed them in, with only a shallow ribbon of water between them.

She must find it hard to believe that much of this will be covered in another six hours.

'It smells a little,' Ruth said with a smile, wrinkling her nose.

He laughed, then nodded towards the companionway.

'Johann is going to try and get water, and a few other basic supplies. He wants to take Manny with him.'

'Oh,' she said, 'why?'

'Well, he thinks Manny would be a big help as a lookout, but,' he added, 'he'll keep him out of trouble.'

'I don't see how he can do that. Manny is rather good at getting himself into scrapes,' she joked, to Franz's surprise.

'You're comfortable with this?'

'Yes, I think so. I'm sorry, I shouldn't have joked about something so important.'

Franz shrugged.

'No. It's good to smile, even in these terrible times.'

Ruth hesitated, then sighed.

'Manny has been through a really tough time,' she said. 'He was in a wretched place before my parents told him we had to get out of Germany and, although it broke his heart to leave them behind, he's pitched himself into everything this journey has thrown at him. How can I stop him helping Johann, who has restored his faith in people?'

'I'd never have guessed you'd see it like that. I've not spent much time with Manny, but it's no surprise how close he and Johann have become.'

'When we weren't on watch, you were always planning the next stage of the voyage, or fixing something, or looking after us and the boat. I was watching Manny when I could; how Johann was teaching him, and giving him responsibility. Manny would do anything for you two.'

'He'll keep him safe. I promise. And I wouldn't consider letting him go if it weren't important, but Johann is right. He needs Manny with him.'

'I know. Don't worry about Manny. He's already safer because he's here. And if they need to do this to help us escape, then you have my blessing.'

He gave her a grateful smile.

'We need an hour again, tonight, Manny and I,' she said, looking down at her hands.

'Ah. Shabbat.'

'Yes. And again tomorrow, before they go.'

'That's no problem. Johann and I will keep out of the way.'

'Thank you. It means a lot to Manny. And I think we should thank God, for getting us here.'

Franz smiled. 'You're right.'

She stared out across Hobo Dyb to Langli.

'And, Franz,' she said.

'Yes?'

'Nothing.'
He blushed again.

~~o~~

Yosef placed the pot of coffee on the General's desk, and poured it for him.
'Nothing, sir?' he said.
'Nothing, Yosef. We can only hope it stays that way.'
'It's harder than we ever imagined it would be, sir.'
'I know,' the General said softly.
He waited until Yosef had gone out of the room and took a rolled-up chart of the North Sea from the bookshelf and laid it on the desk.
He stared at it for a long while.

CHAPTER 128

'Here's the last one, sir.'

Carl Meyer handed his boss a sheet of paper.

'Hirtshals,' Heinrich Güllich said. 'This is the place they left for Norway?'

'Yes, sir. The harbour master is expecting your call.'

Heinrich Güllich nodded. Carl Meyer was proving to be more of an asset with every passing day. For every call placed by the Kriminalassistent, Carl had rung ahead and made sure that the people he needed to talk to were waiting by the telephone, ready to speak to him.

He dialled the number.

'Herr Harbour Master, Sprechen sie Deutsch?'

The call followed the same pattern as that of the five or six previous calls.

Had *Der Sturmtaucher been in the harbour?

When did it arrive, and when did it depart?

Did you, or anyone else, speak with either of the Kästners?

Was their paperwork correct?

Did anyone see any other persons on board?

Were there any suspicious comings and goings?

The answers from Hirtshals were almost identical to those in Bøjden and Bogense. Each harbour master had paid a visit to the boat or had at least spoken with one of the brothers; they'd berthed for one night in each place and had kept themselves to themselves.

When pushed, the Hirtshals harbour master said that Franz and his brother had spoken briefly with his wife when he picked up their supplies, and had also talked with one of the fishermen.

And the harbour master at Bogense had told Heinrich Güllich that Franz and Johann had shared a drink with a couple of sailors from a Kriegsmarine Vorpostenboot that berthed next to them; he'd heard them talking and laughing when he did his last inspection of the harbour before bed, as was his habit.

'They'd had quite a few by the sounds of merriment that was coming from the Kästners' boat,' he'd said.

Heinrich Güllich had taken a note of the patrol vessel's name, and the name of the fisherman in Hirtshals.

When he put the telephone down, he turned to Carl Meyer.

'At least four people have been inside the Kästner boat on this trip of theirs. We need to pay them all a visit. I feel that our presence might loosen their tongues.'

Carl Meyer blanched.

'We're going to Hirtshals?' he said. 'How will we explain that to the Kriminaldirektor?'

'Don't worry, Meyer,' he said, glad for a chance to put his assistant in his place. 'You leave the thinking to me and telephone the Kriegsmarine and find out where we can find that patrol vessel, and the torpedo boat that intercepted the yacht.'

CHAPTER 129

[12/04/1941 Saturday]

'Good luck.'

Johann untied the dinghy's painter from the toe rail of the yacht, coiled it, and pushed off. It was still dark; the full moon hadn't yet risen, so Franz had lit the starboard navigation lamp, shrouded all around with a piece of canvas apart from a narrow slit facing the shore at the east end of Hobo Dyb.

On land, only someone looking out from a small stretch of shorefront would see the light, and the chances of that, he reckoned, were slim. All that Johann and Manny had to do was to keep the green light directly on their stern, and they would reach the end of Hobo Dyb, without rowing in circles in the darkness.

They left at quarter to nine, just after sunset, to make sure the tide would be high enough to avoid them having to wade through the acres of mud that would be exposed when the water receded. They carried the two empty water canisters, a fuel container for diesel, and an oilskin bag with dry clothes and boots. In their haversacks, they each had a jute sack, empty apart from a couple of metal canisters wrapped in sailcloth to muffle any noise.

Johann rowed, and because his back was to the direction he was travelling in, he had no difficulty in keeping Franz's green guiding light in line with the middle of the transom at the stern of the dinghy. He told Manny to kneel in the bow, testing the depth of the water with an eight-foot willow withy stick that he dipped in, feeling for the bottom. As the moon rose, Johann could just make out the cast of the land in the distance, the tops of the trees making a jagged dark outline against the almost black-grey of the sky.

When Manny offered to take a spell on the oars, Johann hesitated, worried about the time, but he nodded and swapped positions with the boy, figuring that they'd built in a good margin of error when they'd planned the foraging expedition, and he reasoned that he could always take the oars back if they weren't making suitable progress.

They didn't speak; Franz had impressed upon them how far sound travelled over water. Johann kept an eye on the green light behind them, but he needn't have worried. Although he was having to put more effort in to achieve it, Manny maintained almost as much speed as he had, and was managing to keep their course close to perfect, no mean accomplishment when there was a strong breeze blowing them towards Langli and the mainland beyond.

Johann, who was already impressed with the young Jewish boy's tenacity and strength of will, revised his high opinion of him even further.

'You're doing great,' he whispered, 'I suspect we're almost there. Slow down a bit, and the oars will make less noise.'

No one will hear in this wind anyway, but best not to take chances.

Manny did as Johann had asked, and the oars, instead of splashing on each stroke, slid into the water with hardly a sound. Johann continued to probe with the withy stick, and the depth decreased with each stroke of the oars. A couple of times he whispered to Manny that it was getting shallow and, at one point, the boat grounded on the mud before releasing itself and progressing once more towards the shore.

'That's us,' Johann said. 'Turn up this creek a little, and we'll find a spot to leave the boat.'

With a surprising assurance, Manny turned the small boat into the narrow inlet. When rowing became impossible, he gave an oar to Johann, and they paddled the tender like an Indian canoe towards the dunes of Skallingen. When the creek shallowed and they bottomed out, Johann removed his boots and socks, rolled up his trousers, and stepped out from the bow of the boat.

He'd guessed the depth of the water correctly, but he'd underestimated how much he would sink into the mud. The water came almost up to his waist, soaking his trousers and causing him to curse.

He heard Manny stifle a laugh.

He grinned, himself, despite the cold, but he knew that he'd chill within minutes in wet clothes, and he was glad they'd each packed a dry set, along with spare boots and socks.

He pulled the boat along by its painter, and Manny steered it with one of the oars to keep it from snagging in the clumps of reeds that lined the narrow channel. After a few attempts, they found a shelved beach of sandy shingle among the mudbanks and pulled the boat up as far as they could. Once they'd reached the high waterline, they stopped to take a breath.

There was just enough light now from the freshly risen moon, flickering behind the clouds, for them to make out a stand of firmer ground across the marshes, stretching towards the treeline in the distance.

'Let's turn her over; she won't fill up with rainwater if it pours, and it will be easier to hide.'

They removed the fuel and water cannisters from the tender, along with the rest of their belongings, and piled them on the driest patch they could find. Between them, they manhandled the small wooden dinghy over, and covered the upturned hull with weed from the creek. Johann broke off a bit of the withy stick and drove it into the ground with a stone from the beach, then tied the painter to it.

'Why did you do that?' Manny asked.

'In case we've got the tide wrong, and she floats away.'

'Oh, I didn't realise that it would float upside down.'

Johann nodded. 'It would, being full of air, but not very well, and it could flip and sink anywhere, leaving us stranded. At least this way, if it does sink, we'll know where to start looking.'

'There, you can barely see it now,' he said, satisfied at their handiwork.

'How will we find it when we come back?'

'This is the clever bit,' Johann said, grinning.

Telling Manny to wait by the boat, Johann grabbed the remainder of the withy stick, now slightly shorter, and made his way towards the trees. Keeping the green light from the yacht in line with Manny, who gave an occasional low whistle, he paced out 100 metres as best as he could in the circumstances; he had to wade through a couple of boggy areas, and another small creek, but when he was satisfied, he drove the withy stick into the peat.

From his pocket, he took out a small piece of silver foil that he'd brought and wrapped it around the top of the pole. He stood back to admire his handiwork and removed the small flashlight from the waterproof pouch that hung from his neck, inside his shirt, and briefly shone it on the silver mark, quivering in the strong wind.

Satisfied that it would reflect light, he pocketed the torch and returned the way he had come, counting his steps again until he'd reached Manny.

'A hundred paces, direct in line with *The Shearwater*. As long as we can locate the marker, we can find the tender. I have a small compass if we can't see the light.'

'That's all very clever. I'd never have thought of that.'

'Neither did I,' Johann admitted. 'Franz came up with the idea of the silver foil and the withy stick.'

He looked around and turned to Manny.

'Now, let's find somewhere to fill these water containers.'

He lifted the two green water containers and waded off up the little creek they'd rowed up. Manny grabbed the fuel can and followed him.

The creek narrowed gradually, but it wasn't long before they came to a spot where it widened out into a small pool, and a stream bubbled into it at the far end. Johann cupped his hands and tasted the water in the pool.

'It's still too brackish to drink,' he whispered. 'We'll have to go on a bit.'

'It might always be brackish.'

Johann shook his head. 'There has been heavy rain for almost a week now. The marshes will be sodden. We just need to get above the high tidemark.'

They followed the little stream up twenty metres and found a place where the water burbled over a small waterfall, barely six or seven centimetres high. Above it, the little pool was deep enough to immerse one of the water containers on its side. They both tasted the water this time and, satisfied that there was no saltiness to it, they filled both cannisters.

'That's one job done,' Johann said.

It took longer than expected. The wind still whistled across the marsh, cutting through their saturated clothes. Shivering, they wasted no time in screwing the caps on the containers and wading back down the creek to the beach, where they stashed the water cans beneath the upended dinghy.

They packed their boots and socks, bags of spare clothes, the sacks with the metal flasks and a couple of spare flashlights into the haversacks that they had brought with them, and Johann added the fuel can to his load. It was red in colour and, in the pallid moonlight, Manny could see that it was marked in white paint with the word DIESEL, in large letters.

Johann saw Manny staring at it, and he grinned.

'Franz was taking no chances. He must think we're a couple of idiots.'

Manny laughed, breaking the tension that had gripped them both since they'd left the yacht.

'Let's go,' Johann said, as he retraced his steps to their marker pole, Manny in tow.

He stopped when he got to it, fished out the flashlight and pointed it towards Franz and Ruth in the yacht. He flashed out the letter 'C' in Morse code, repeated three times, and watched as the green light flashed a reply, before being extinguished.

'They'll switch it back on tomorrow night, for us coming back, and they insisted that they'll keep a watch now until first light in case we have to return sooner. We're not going to, though, but if it makes them feel better…'

Manny said nothing, so Johann turned and headed towards the line of trees, wading at first through boggy marsh, small muddy channels, and thick reeds, but the ground under their feet firmed up with each step until, a stone's throw from the treeline, their feet stopped sinking in with every pace.

When they reached the trees, Johann halted again. He pulled his folding knife from his pocket and gave it to Manny.

'Make a couple of marks on one of the trees; about waist height.'

Manny walked over and chose one that stood out a little from the rest, with a limb emerging just above the ground.

Johann nodded. It would be easy to pick out when they returned, even without the mark Manny was carving into its trunk.

'Why waist height?' the boy asked. 'Would it not be better at eye level.'

'It would be easier for us to see, but if someone else passes, it would be very noticeable. Down there, it could easily have been made by deer, or by cattle.'

Manny nodded. He folded the knife and handed it back to Johann.

'No, you keep it. I'll get it back from you if I need it.'

Manny turned the knife in his hand, and smiled, before pocketing it.

The strong wind had chilled them both to the core. Johann wasted no time in getting changed into dry clothes, and they both put their boots back on. Finding a suitable bush a few paces into the wood from the tree they'd marked, they stashed the oilskin bag with its spare clothes next to Johann's wet bundle under its lower branches.

Shouldering their backpacks, they skirted the edge of the wood, stumbling over the odd root that protruded from the ground, until they came to the road that led out to Skallingen, and to the lighthouse at the end of it.

They turned along the road in the opposite direction, towards the village, and the dim moonlight disappeared in the dark tunnel between the trees, but it was sheltered from the wind, and their exertions soon warmed them up. They managed to maintain a reasonable pace, feeling their way on the metalled road, now and again stumbling onto the verge, mumbling curses. By the time the first of the daylight began to paint the sky with dirty grey, they had reached the perimeter of a small farm on the roadside, and the trees gave way to fields.

Beyond the farm, they could make out the spire of a small church, and a few chimneys above the hedges and trees of the leafy village.

'We'll find somewhere to hide and watch a while. This place will have everything we need. It's just a matter of getting it without being seen.'

They scouted around and found a small wooden shed between the wood and the farm, open towards the east, with a pitched roof above, enclosed at the sides with rough-laid larch.

In the dim light, they climbed up a ladder attached to the back wall and through a large open hatchway, finding themselves in a small loft stacked with hay. Set into the tiles above, there were vents on both sides of the sloping roof, and one on the back wall. Johann clambered up on the piled hay and looked out each of the vents in turn.

'We can see pretty much in every direction from here – we might have to stick our heads down below the hatch to look out the front, but this is as safe a place as any.'

'I'll keep an eye open first, if you want,' Manny said. 'You haven't had as much sleep as I have since we came through the storm.'

Johann thought about it for a moment but, in truth, he was exhausted. He knew that he could trust Manny, so he relented.

'I think we should make ourselves a bolthole at the back of the pile of hay in case the farmer comes up here to throw hay down to his cattle.'

He hollowed out a hiding place up against the wooden wall and left a loose pile of hay ready to cover himself if he needed to. He made Manny prepare a refuge for himself, before settling down for a well-earned rest.

'Wake me if there's anything at all,' he murmured, before he slipped into unconsciousness.

CHAPTER 130

After the boys had rowed off into the night, Franz kept a close eye on the wick in the green lamp, knowing it was the only guide that Johann and Manny had. He could see nothing of them; within a few metres, they'd faded into the blackness of Hobo Dyb, the soft slap of their oars in the water receding to nothing in the wind, still whistling above their heads.

It had been a strange day of recuperation and rest, punctuated only by Ruth and Manny's meal together, in the cabin of *Der Sturmtaucher*, observing Pesach, and the rituals that had been repeated over thousands of years since the Israelites' exodus from Egypt.

The Kästner brothers had retreated to the cockpit, giving them space, and using the time to prepare for Johann and Manny's expedition.

It wasn't wasted time; they'd set up an awning using one of the grey sails, to protect the cockpit from the elements, leaving one side open, facing towards Ho Bucht, and a loose corner on the port side, as a viewing flap towards Graa Dyb.

When it was finished, they emptied the contaminated water tank and flushed it through with rainwater, already collecting on the awning.

Now Johann and Manny were gone.

There was no significant movement in the boat while the sea to the west still threw itself with savage ferocity on the Skallingen shore, less than a mile away.

'It's remarkable,' Ruth said. 'How can it feel so safe here when the wind is still howling, and I can hear the waves pounding on Skallingen shore?'

'We're tucked in here, with shelter on all four sides. We're lucky to be here.'

'I know. And it's good to know the boys are safe.'

About an hour after they'd left, Franz had seen the prearranged flashes from Johann's torch out of the corner of his eye, and he'd passed a hand in front of the lamp to return the signal, before extinguishing it.

'They're on shore,' he'd told Ruth. 'They'll hole up somewhere once they get to the village. I suspect it will be tomorrow evening before they'll be able to get hold of what we need, but it's possible a chance might present itself earlier.'

'There's nothing we can do now but wait. It's going to be a long night.'

'One of us will have to check for any signals every couple of hours. In a real emergency outside of those times, they have a whistle to catch our attention but, being honest, if they're being pursued, it would be unlikely that we'd manage to get out of here and away, without being seen. And if they see us, we'll be too slow to outrun them.'

'Let's not talk about that. The boys will be back tomorrow night with everything we need. I know they will.'

Franz wished he could be so confident, but he couldn't say anything to dent her mood of optimism.

'So, we're on our own.' Her statement startled him from his black thoughts, and he smiled at her. The full moon had now risen, and although it was mostly obscured by the clouds scurrying across the night sky, enough of it filtered through to cast a dim light on the darkness.

'I know. It feels strange, even though we did all these watches together.' He looked at her. It was less than a day since they'd made the shelter of Hobo Dyb, but already she'd regained her composure and the healthy glow of youth.

'It made it easier to bear,' he added. 'Even the bad bits.'

'I struggled with the storm,' she said, 'but besides that, there's nowhere I'd rather have been.'

'We'll have plenty time on watch in the coming week or more.'

'I know,' she said, 'but, after that...'

They'd avoided speaking about it, but neither of them was under any illusion of what would happen if they reached the safety of England.

She shivered. He didn't know if it was because of the cold, or that she'd seen what their future held. He reached out and touched her shoulder.

'You're cold?'

'No, not really. Just thinking.' She reached up and met his hand with her fingers. The contact was electric; more so, he thought, than the accidental brushings or nudges of earlier, because of its deliberate nature.

And it signalled that they both now acknowledged a truth that, at home, would have been an impossibility.

'Are you sure about this?' he asked her.

She turned towards him and moved her hand up to the side of his face.

'I've never been surer about anything.'

Wrapping his arms around her, he drew her towards him, and with great tenderness, they kissed for the first time. He closed his eyes, but when he opened them, he saw that her eyes, a striking dark brown with fine olive tracks, were wide open too.

He drew back a little, to look at her. She was, to his mind, perfect. He'd noticed, of course, that she'd changed from a pretty girl to an attractive young woman over the space of one summer, but he'd been in a dark place for most of that time and it had been largely academic to him. Even if he had been interested, he felt she was far too young for him and she would surely have wanted someone with more sense of fun.

And because of religion and class, and the need to consider others around them, affection from either of them could never have been reciprocated.

The war, and the desperate attempt to save Ruth and Manny's lives, had changed all that.

They kissed again, and this time she surprised him with the ferocity of her desire, turning her body towards him and entwining her fingers in his hair. For a moment, he responded, letting the fear that had stifled his heart dissolve.

He hesitated.

Am I taking advantage because she's vulnerable?

~~o~~

Ruth leaned against him, conscious of the deep and conflicting feelings of contentment, terror, excitement, and longing coursing through her body, but his arms around her banished almost every darker thought.

My parents. Manny. It's Pesach.

She gave them a moment's thought then shut them away.

This can't be wrong.

She gave into her need for him but sensed a reluctance and pulled away. Her face fell with disappointment, and confusion.

'Don't you want this?' she asked him.

'More than anything but, it's just that...'

'Just what? You do know that I love you, don't you?'

'I didn't. I mean, I do, but it's all happened so fast, and I don't want you to jump into something that you'll regret. You're still terribly young compared to me.'

'Franz, you're only seven years older than me, not twenty. During the last fortnight we've had a wonderful chance to get to know one another, good and bad. In an ideal world we could take our time over this, but we don't even know if we'll be alive next week, and if we are, we won't be together. I don't want to waste this chance.'

She watched his face as her words dissolved his fears.

'You're right,' he said. 'And yes, I love you too. I just don't want to see you get hurt.'

'You couldn't hurt me. I'm sure of that because I've known you since I was born, and from what I've seen, you're the best man I know.'

He laughed. 'I doubt it. What about your father?'

'That's not fair.' She smiled. 'But, truth be told, yes. You're as decent as he is.'

'I don't believe that, and I don't want you to be disappointed if I don't come up to your expectations.'

She laughed out loud this time and teased him with a smile.

'I'm sure you'll surpass them, Franz Kästner. I'll be surprised if you don't.'

The blood flushed to his face. She smiled again.

He's like an awkward teenager sometimes.

'I only want you to be sure that this is what you want.'

'Listen to me carefully. It's you I want to be with, and I don't want to wait until life is back to whatever normal will be. That day might never dawn.'

She hesitated, then continued. 'And just so you know, there are no boundaries. We don't have time for that. I'm not as naïve as you might think I am. I have read books, and not always the ones that were prescribed by my teachers.'

He stared at her. Ruth watched his face.

I've shocked him, she thought, but she saw his eyes soften. He blinked.

'You're right,' he said. 'It's just…'

'Franz, we have one day. We can't stop worrying about Johann and Manny, but we can try and pretend, just for a while, that there are only the two of us, and that no one else exists in the world. Will you do that for me?'

He nodded, took her hand, and let her lead him down into the cabin below.

~~o~~

In the cottage at Drachensee, Yosef and Miriam sat on opposite sides of the kitchen table. A tear fell from Miriam's cheek as she intoned the words from the Haggadah that should have been Manny's.

'Why is this night different…?'

CHAPTER 131

[13/04/1941 Sunday]

Low water had passed an hour after midnight, and Ruth had succumbed to a fit of giggles when Franz had fallen out of the steeply sloping starboard berth as the boat settled into the mud at a twenty-degree angle. They'd drifted off to sleep in each other's arms, Franz lying on the outside of their narrow, makeshift bed, waking up with a start on the floor.

'We should have put a lee cloth on,' he said, rubbing his hip.

'I doubt you were in any frame of mind earlier to think about details like that,' she said, smiling. 'Anyway, it's time for your two-hourly check.'

She lit the stove and put the kettle on in the dim light of the oil lamp while he threw on his clothes and climbed aloft to check for any signal from the boys. There was none.

'They must have found the way towards the village,' he said.

While Ruth was waiting for the water to boil, her mind drifted to the events of the previous few hours.

Undressing had been a clumsy but beautiful tangle of bodies and clothing, kissing all the while and finding a blanket to lie on, and another to cover them; the main cabin was still cool, and although they lit the small charcoal burner that functioned as the only form of heating on the boat, it took a while to warm up.

Ignoring the damp chill for as long as they could bear it, they'd drank their fill of each other's nakedness, until the cold drove them under the covers.

During clandestine and deliciously guilty conversations with her girlfriends in their mid-teens, the terrifying descriptions of what the first time with a man would be like had filled them all with dread; stories of pain, blood and regret dominated their understanding, but nothing, for her, could have been further from the truth. Franz had been gentle, almost shy with her but, as their excitement had grown, they'd both given in to their overwhelming need and abandoned any pretext of restraint.

She had memories of him touching her everywhere, and she'd not held back in her own exploration of his body. As waves of pleasure swept over her, she'd clung onto him and whispered his name, over and over. She wasn't sure, but she thought he had tears in his eyes when he held her, his arms wrapped tight around her, lying together in their own warmth.

Afterwards, when their breathing had quietened, they'd managed a few soft words before both falling into a contented and dreamless sleep, fortunate to be woken by the tide's rude and painful alarm call.

Once Franz had made sure that Johann and Manny had made no attempt to contact them, he climbed back down through the companionway, and sat close beside her, as she filled the coffee pot on the gimballed stove and waited for it to brew.

Neither one wanted to break the spell, so they drank in silence, perched at an uncomfortable angle but happy just to be breathing in each other's air, their bodies charged with meaning where their skin touched.

It was the gentle final incline of the boat, as the ebb tide reached its lowest point, that brought them out of their trance.

He looked at his watch. 'I'll set the alarm clock for half past four. We should try and get a few hours' sleep.'

'I'm not feeling tired right now,' she said, reaching for him, smiling.

'You're a bad girl,' he said, laughing with her, 'but I suppose we'll have plenty time to sleep later.'

'You might never want to sleep again,' she teased. 'Come on,' she said, taking the mug from his hand, 'show me again how much you love me, but we'll use the forecabin this time. I don't want you to get any more bruises.'

~~o~~

Kriminalassistent Heinrich Güllich threw his overnight bag into the trunk of the car and got into the passenger seat.

'Did you bring the photographs?'

'Yes, sir. They're on the back seat.'

'Excellent. Let's get moving. We have a long journey ahead of us.'

He settled back into his seat. Meyer could do most of the driving, giving him time to think.

But first, a nap would be good.

He'd had a fitful night and hoped that the journey would give him a chance to catch up on some sleep.

As soon as they reached the outskirts of Kiel, on the Eckernförde road, he closed his eyes.

'Sir, did you get hold of the Kriegsmarine this morning?'

He gave his assistant the kind of stare he used on his suspects, but Carl Meyer's eyes were fixed on the road.

'Yes, we're in luck,' he said, hoping that the younger man would hear the irritation in his voice. 'The patrol vessel docks at Skagen later today, around six. We'll go to Hirtshals first.'

'We should be there by one, sir.'

'Good. It's not far from Hirtshals to Skagen, then we'll head back south to this Bogense place. We may have to stop overnight somewhere, but I'd like it to be back in Kiel tonight, if it's possible.'

'We should definitely make Bogense, sir, but I suspect that's as far as we'll get today.'

Heinrich Güllich grunted. 'I want to call in at Aarhus on the way up, at our headquarters there. We pass through anyway.'

'Yes, sir. Might I ask why?'

The Kriminalassistent sighed.

'Because, you fool, people are always more inclined to be helpful if you make the effort to meet them in person, and it's so much easier to explain the delicacies of a situation face to face.'

'I see, sir. I suppose you're right.'

'I am right, Meyer.'

'We can give them photographs too, sir,' Carl Meyer said, his eyes lighting up.

'Indeed, Meyer. You should consider becoming a detective.'

He closed his eyes again.

'What about the Nussbaums, sir? Aren't they getting questioned again tomorrow?'

Heinrich Güllich opened his eyes once more.

When is this Dummkopf going to give me some peace?

'They can wait until Tuesday. They're not going to run away.'

'Does Kriminalassistent Schmidt know, sir?'

'No, but you can phone him from Aarhus or Hirtshals,' Heinrich Güllich snapped.

He glanced at his underling.

He's taken umbrage. Good.

He tilted his head back and closed his eyes.

~~o~~

As Heinrich Güllich slept, the car sped northwards through Eckernförde, then Schleswig, reaching the border just beyond Flensburg around ten.

He woke up, with Carl Meyer touching his arm. He blinked and looked out. They were approaching the checkpoint.

'We're almost in Denmark, sir.'

CHAPTER 132

'Wake up, Johann.'

At first, he didn't know where he was, and it took a few seconds to realise that it wasn't Franz trying to rouse him.

'Manny, what's up?'

'There's movement. Someone is leaving the house. I presume they are going to church.'

'Merde. What time is it?' Johann's stint in Paris with Celise, the young woman he'd met while stationed in the French capital, had left him with the occasional habit of cursing in French, considering it sophisticated, much to Franz's amusement.

'It's about ten-thirty. I didn't want to wake you up earlier because you needed your sleep.'

They'd each taken a watch during the night, but Johann had last handed over to Manny at about half past four.

'Let me take a look.'

Manny had found a gap between the boards in the gable facing the farmhouse, and Johann put his eye to it. A man and a woman were walking together down the short dirt track that led from the house to the road, a continuation of the one that Manny and Johann had walked along a few hours before. From the back of the farmhouse, they could hear a dog barking, trying to attract its master's attention, not pleased with the one morning in the week when it wasn't out in the fields with him, checking the livestock.

The couple were dressed well, the man in a dark suit, his wife in a frock and a heavy black coat with a dark beret, which she held on her head with one hand, lest it blow away in the strong wind. They somehow still managed to look like farmers; they both had on footwear suitable for the conditions; boots rather than shoes, and their clothes would have been unfashionable in any large town or city.

'Will there be anyone else in the house?' Manny asked.

'If they had children, they would have gone with them, surely?'

'I suppose so. This village looks like the sort of place where everyone goes to church.'

Johann glanced at Manny. The boy was sharp for his age.

'Franz said this little place is called Ho, and it has around twenty houses in it, quite a few of them small farms. He reckoned one of them, like this one, would be our best bet.'

'If they're at church, we only have an hour.'

'Maybe a little longer, by the time they walk there, chat with their neighbours after the service is finished, then walk back.'

The couple had reached the road and had turned right towards the village. Within a few minutes, they had disappeared behind the leafy copse that obscured most of the village from their vantage point.

Johann turned to Manny.

'You stay here. If anything happens to me, go back to the boat and tell Franz.'

'I want to come with you. I'd be more help.'

'No. Ruth and Franz only agreed to you coming if you stayed out of sight.'

'I know. But think about it; you'll need several trips without me, and it will take twice as long. There'll be more risk of you getting caught. If I come, we'd be in and out in half the time.'

Johann glanced at the farmhouse, then back at Manny.

'I don't know…'

'It's deserted. It will be safer if we both go.'

Johann looked across at the barn, and the house. Nothing was stirring.

'All right,' he said, shaking his head, 'but so much as a mouse squeaks, get back here as quickly as you can, without being seen.'

Manny nodded, grinning.

Johann shook his head again, but there was the hint of a smile in his eyes.

'Right, let's go for it,' he said. 'We'll check the barn first, and we must find fuel.'

They sprinted for the barn, the nearest building to them, using the stone walls and hedges as cover, and made it without hearing a shout, or seeing anyone. Pulling back the wooden bar that locked the door, they slipped inside.

'Look, there's the diesel tank. Fill up the fuel can while I look around.'

~~o~~

Manny unscrewed the lid and, once he'd found the stop valve on the tank, he squeezed the handle on the nozzle and filled the container, careful not to spill any. He left the full can by the door and went in search of Johann.

A smaller door in the far corner of the barn was open, and he could hear the soft lowing and gentle movement of cows tied in stalls; he presumed Johann had gone through, so he followed.

Perched on a stool, much to Manny's surprise, was Johann, attempting to milk one of the cows into the metal flask that he'd taken out of his bag, but the bulk of the warm milk squirting from the teat was missing the narrow neck.

Manny looked around. The warm smell of the hay, the cows and their manure was strangely comforting. In the small dairy at the end of the cowshed, he found a clean galvanised bucket. He returned and gave it to Johann.

'Here, you'll find this easier.'

Johann took the bucket, giving Manny a sheepish look. Manny watched him; most of the milk squirted into the bucket instead of half of it ending up on the cowshed floor. In a short time, to their relief, they had enough milk to fill up both their containers, which they sealed by tying pieces of leather over the lids and securing them in place with rough sisal string.

'You grab the milk, and I'll get the fuel. We'll hide them at the edge of the woods and come back and see if we can find food.'

Johann grabbed the diesel can, and Manny followed him, retracing their steps back the way they had come until they reached the cover of the trees. They hid their haul as best they could, and checking that all was still quiet, they returned to the barn, making sure they closed the doors, and edged their way around the yard to the house.

This set off the dog barking again, but neither of them took notice; it appeared to bark at the slightest noise and the neighbours, a distance away, would surely be inured to its clamour.

The back door opened when they turned the handle, as they'd expected. Nobody in these parts would feel the need to lock their house, trusting their neighbours and knowing that strangers were few and far between. They entered a large warm kitchen and sucked in deep breaths of freshly baked bread.

'It smells wonderful,' Manny whispered.

~~o~~

Johann grinned, but not wasting time, they helped themselves to three of the five loaves and, in a pantry, they found several large cheeses, of which they took one, and added a cured beef joint, potatoes and a selection of vegetables to their sacks: kale, carrots and cauliflower. They took one of the strings of onions that were hanging under a shelf, a side of smoked fish, and two greaseproof-paper-wrapped lumps of butter.

Satisfied, Johann removed the oilskin pouch from his neck, and extracted six five kroner notes that they'd retained from the money they'd been given to purchase supplies on their journey up the east coast of Denmark. He found a jar containing dried bay leaves and placed the notes inside it, hoping the farmer's wife would find it when they were long gone from Hobo Dyb and realise that the goods had been paid for.

'Franz said we shouldn't leave money, but I didn't think it was right,' he whispered to Manny, who was watching him, frowning.

They shouldered their now substantial sacks, closed the pantry door, and turned towards the door leading out to the yard.

'Stop. Rør jer ikke.'

They both turned towards the voice, flinching at the barked command. Johann understood enough Danish to freeze.

Stop. Do not move.

A young man stood facing them, framed in the kitchen's third doorway, the one that led to the rest of the house. He held a shotgun. It was pointed at them.

CHAPTER 133

Carl Meyer was pleased that the Kriminalassistent's mood had improved.

They hadn't stayed long in Aarhus, but Güllich had seemed satisfied with the meeting they'd had with one of the area's Kriminalassistenten. The man had a mindset like his, and the man had been impressed with the Kiel Gestapo officer's doggedness in trying to locate the two Jewish runaways.

'You're a credit to the Gestapo, Kamerad,' he'd said. 'If we allow even one Judenschwein to get away with it, the rest will think that we are a soft touch.'

He'd promised to circulate the children's photographs to the Danish police stations on the east coast, as Heinrich Güllich had requested, but added that it would be advisable to include the whole country, on the assumption that the Nussbaum children could have been moved.

Wishing them good luck and promising to provide any help should they require it, he'd shaken their hands and saluted.

'The Kriminalassistent was a great help, Herr Güllich,' Carl Meyer said, driving again.

'Yes. A man after my own heart. He understood the case perfectly, the more so when I mentioned our Jew-loving general.'

The man had been incensed when Heinrich Güllich had told him the lengths the General had gone to, just to keep his Jewish cook and her family.

'I can't understand someone like that, with such a prominent position in the Reich, who would risk his reputation for Untermenschen,' he'd said.

Subhumans.

Carl Meyer smiled. The man had a nice turn of phrase.

They passed through Hobro.

'It's good to see German flags flying from the town hall.'

'Yes, sir. And it's only the beginning.'

'How far is it now?'

'About 120 kilometres, sir,' Carl Meyer said. 'I phoned Werner Schmidt from Aarhus, sir. He wasn't happy being telephoned on a Sunday again.'

'The man is just a policeman. He doesn't live for the KriPo the way we do for the Schutzstaffel, and the Geheime Staatspolizei. For him, it's just a job.'

'He says he will speak with you when you return but is unhappy about stirring up more trouble with his chief.'

'He'll do as we tell him when we show him what we have found.'

Carl Meyer wasn't so sure. He had to concede that Heinrich Güllich's theories were, in many ways, beginning to look plausible, but they were, he believed, still largely unsubstantiated.

'What about our friends in Norway?' he asked.

'I telephoned them this morning. They say they don't have the staff to do a search of the coastline. As if it were too much to ask.'

'It is a difficult coast to police, sir. There are numerous fjords, and islands, and much of the area is uninhabited.'

'Nonsense. From what I hear, they have the Norwegian police in their pockets. They should use them and get out there looking, instead of sitting with their hands in their pockets, relying on useless port reports.'

'Yes, sir,' Carl Meyer said, hoping the Kriminalassistent wasn't about to go off on a rant.

'We'll be in Aalborg soon,' he said, changing the subject.

'We'll stop for something to eat. We want to be fresh for our interviews this afternoon.'

CHAPTER 134

Johann did exactly as he was told, not knowing if the shotgun the youth was pointing at them was loaded or not. He sensed Manny doing the same.

Scheiße. I should have checked the rest of the house first. Johann cursed his stupidity.

'Sorry. Not understanding much Danish,' He said, hoping the little he'd learned over the years was enough to talk themselves out of the situation.

'Sæt dem ned nu.'

Even without being able to understand the words, the motion of the young man's free hand left no doubt that they should place their sacks on the floor.

With great care, Johann laid his load down, and told Manny to do the same. When they'd straightened up, the stranger spoke again, and motioned for them to sit down at the table, with their hands showing.

He must have been satisfied that he had them completely under control, because his shoulders relaxed, and he pointed the gun towards the floor, but Johann was under no illusions that this would make it easy to overpower the youth; the gun could be raised and aimed at them long before they could cover the distance between them.

The long silence was broken only by a clock ticking in a distant part of the house, and by the occasional bark of the dog.

'Parlez-vous Français?' Johann asked, praying that their captor wasn't a fluent French speaker, and that his own French was good enough to convince him that he was a native of France. He willed Manny to stay quiet.

The barrel of the gun rose a few centimetres, and the youth made a gesture with his finger across his throat, indicating that Johann would be better served by remaining silent. Johann supposed the words he spoke had the same meaning.

The young man sat on the edge of the table opposite them, still pointing the gun in their general direction. How long they stayed like that, Johann or Manny couldn't tell; only the ticking clock behind them marked the passage of time, and he didn't dare turn around.

Just as the silence became almost intolerable, they heard footsteps outside. The back door opened, and an older man of about forty, the one they'd seen earlier with the woman, entered the room. Behind him, two men stood at the doorway, looking around the yard, making sure there was no one else nearby.

The new arrival said a few words to the younger man who, nodding to his sitting captives, spoke in rapid Danish, only interrupted by an occasional question from the older man. Johann could just catch a few words, but it wasn't difficult to guess what they were talking about.

Tyve. *Thieves.* Brød. *Bread.* Hus. *House.*

Johann judged that the older man was the owner of the farm, and that the younger man was his son.

When they'd finished, the farmer turned to the door and beckoned for his two companions to come in. After satisfying themselves that all was clear outside, they entered the kitchen and stood just inside the door. They all carried weapons.

The first of the new arrivals was older than the farmer, in his sixties, Johann guessed, and he shouldered a well-worn rifle. The second was younger. Like the farmer's son, he held a shotgun. They were both dressed in working clothes, in contrast to their host.

At a nod from the farmer, the son prodded Johann and Manny, and motioned for them to stand up. He roughly shoved them to the middle of the kitchen.

The farmer took a tobacco pouch from his pocket, removed a pipe from it, and filled it, taking care to tamp it down before striking a match. The flame dipped into the tobacco with each draw, and the man took a few puffs before settling his eyes on Johann and Manny.

'Wo kommen Sie her?' *Where are you from?* The man's German was good but that, in itself, didn't surprise Johann. Many Danes spoke German fluently; after all, much of Denmark's trade was with Germany, but he was a little puzzled that a farmer living in such a remote part of the country had such an excellent grasp of the language.

They must be German sympathisers.

'Ich habe nicht viel Deutsch,' he replied. *I don't have much German.* 'Parlez-vous Français?' he added, committing himself to the path he'd taken earlier.

The man continued in fluent German. 'You are not French. You are German. A soldier, almost certainly.'

Johann thought about trying to bluster again, but looking into the man's eyes, he could not hold his stare, and he lowered his gaze.

'The boots give you away,' he told Johann, and took another long draw at his pipe. 'German Army issue.'

Johann cursed under his breath. *Another mistake.*

'So, we know you are a German soldier, not in uniform, and you have a friend who is quite clearly not in the Wehrmacht, unless they are now recruiting boys.'

Johann found his voice. 'He is my younger brother, Franz.'

The farmer nodded at Johann's tacit admission in German that the Dane had been right.

'Why are you here? Are you a deserter? Why is your brother here?'

Fighting the panic deep within his chest, Johann forced himself to take a breath. Being turned over to the German authorities as a deserter would be terrible but having Manny with him would make it worse for him, and a catastrophe for the boy.

'We have trekked from Rendsburg. Franz is older than he appears. He's due to be called up, and our mother asked me to get him to friends of hers in Denmark. I am going to return once I have delivered him.'

The farmer turned to his companions.

'There will be a good reward for turning in a German deserter. Even more for two, no?'

His three fellow Danes laughed. A cold shaft of fear tore through Johann's chest. He chanced a quick glance at Manny and was surprised to see how calm he looked, then he remembered Manny telling him that he'd got used to not showing fear. It let the bastards know they hadn't won.

Johann took a little comfort from Manny's stoic resistance, but as soon as he'd got his breathing under control, he heard the farmer speaking again, and his blood turned to ice.

'Young Franz here doesn't look much like a brother of yours, nah?'

He stepped towards Manny, and when Johann moved to block him, the three guns were raised, pointing straight at his chest. He froze.

'That's what a brother would do, I have to say, but this one here has dark hair, and yours is blond.' He stood between the young Germans and rubbed a lock of hair on each of their heads between a finger and thumb, first Johann's, and then Manny's.

'And your eyes are a kind of greyish-green...' He stared at Johann, his face a few centimetres from him before turning to Manny and gripping the young Jew's chin.

'His are a dark brown. Do you not find that a little strange?'

Johann made to speak, but a shake of the head made him bite back his reply.

'As for your noses, well, yours is quite narrow and, if I might say so, one of your best features. Noble, almost, while your young friend's beak,' he said, 'is a little more like mine, is it not?'

'Brothers don't always look the same,' Johann said, his face flushed.

'No, I agree, but there are almost no similarities between you. I'd say that you must have different fathers, at least. Are you trying to say your mother was a whore?'

Johann tensed, but the farmer was ready for him, and laid a restraining hand on his chest. He motioned for the older man with the rifle to stand behind Johann.

'If he has to shoot you, he will, but he'll make sure it's not fatal, and you'll still be worth something.' He turned towards Manny. He gestured towards the young man by the table, and the youth handed him his gun. He pointed it at Manny.

'Drop your trousers,' he told him.

For the first time, Manny reacted, with a slight stiffening of his stance. Johann could picture him gripping the knife in his pocket, and he prayed that Manny wouldn't do anything reckless. He slowly exhaled when the boy's shoulders slumped, and he made no attempt to pull the knife out.

'I mean it. You're worth almost nothing, so it doesn't matter if I have to shoot you.'

Manny's face tightened. Johann watched as he fought to keep his eyes from filling with tears. Despite the shame and disgust he must have felt, he did as the man asked, loosening his belt and buttons, letting his trousers fall to his feet. Johann flinched when the knife spilled from Manny's pocket, clattering onto the floor.

The man picked it up. He unfolded the blade and ran his finger along the edge.

'Now your underpants.'

This time, Manny couldn't stop himself, and Johann saw a tear roll down his cheek. Reaching down, the teenager pulled his pants down with as much dignity as he could muster, and straightened, his eyes boring into the farmer's face.

'Aha, friends, what have we here?' The others looked at Manny's circumcised penis.

Johann's head slumped on his shoulders. A deserter sheltering a Jew could only expect one punishment, and that was bad enough, but knowing he'd failed Manny, the boy's family, Franz, and his own family, was worse. He'd been too sure of himself, failing to check that the house was unoccupied, and in doing so, he'd sentenced them both to death.

I should have listened to Franz, and left Manny in the woods.

To salvage anything from the hell he was in now, he had to make sure that Franz and Ruth were not pulled down with them. Close to desperation, he groped in his fatigued mind for an explanation that would lead their captors away from the suspicion that there were others involved.

'Pull your trousers back up.'

Johann's head jerked up, and Manny scrambled to obey, still staring with hatred at his tormentor.

'Sit down at the table, both of you, and tell me who else is on the boat.'

Johann and Manny looked at each other, and the dark knowledge that they'd utterly failed passed between them.

'How long have you known?' Johann asked, in a quiet voice. He had nothing left to fight them with.

'Since the morning after you arrived, during the worst of the storm. It must have taken astonishing seamanship to sail her in. At what time of night did you come over the bar?'

'Around midnight.' They knew everything. There was no point in lying. Perhaps Franz could persuade them to let them go. A thought flashed into his head.

Father. Could money be the answer? It won't be impossible to contact him.

Before he could formulate a way of offering a bribe without calling it one, the farmer spoke again.

'At low water, eh? Brave, but probably best. At least you could see the sandbanks. Good job it was a full moon.'

He gestured towards his companions.

'We are all farmers. But we are all fishermen too. We need to do both, to scratch a living here. We watch the sea, and we tend our cattle. Jens here saw your mast from Skallingen, just before you took it down.'

He nodded at the younger of the two men who'd followed him in.

'And one of our neighbours told us that there was a report of a boat that had been glimpsed off the Kærgård beacon on Thursday. They said you must have perished.'

'That was us. I've never been in anything like that before. At least, not without shelter to run to.'

The man shook his head. 'Crazy, but brave.'

Johann allowed himself a brief smile, proud that he and Franz had got them to safety, and proud of the Nussbaums for their part in it. A little of the worry slipped from his face.

'Now, we can understand why you would want to lie to us,' the farmer said, 'but we needed to be sure that you were not sent by the German authorities, and we had to be certain of your reasons for being here. We have seen betrayal before.'

The men had lowered their weapons and stacked them in the corner of the room. Apart from the farmer, the others sat down at the table, opposite Manny and Johann.

CHAPTER 135

'What we need now is for you to be entirely truthful with us.' He turned to Manny.

'I'm sorry about having to do that to you. It was necessary. No German would have faulted us for our behaviour, no matter who you'd been; on the contrary, we may have been praised as collaborators by our new masters.' He opened the back door and spat out into the yard.

'So, you're not going to turn us in?' Johann said, his relief almost palpable.

'That depends very much on what you tell us next. But it needs to be the truth this time.'

Johann didn't take long to consider their options. If they knew about the boat, Franz and Ruth were already as good as captured, so there was no reason not to level with these people. It was their sole chance of survival.

'My brother Franz is on the boat with–'

The man interrupted. 'Oh, you have two brothers called Franz. That's unusual.'

The farmer and his companions all laughed and, despite himself, Johann laughed too. When he glanced at Manny, he was also smiling.

'This young man is called Manny. His sister, Ruth, is on the boat with my brother.'

The men laughed again.

'So, there are two German... soldiers, I presume, but out of uniform... on a boat with two Jewish children. Now that is even more unusual.'

'Ruth isn't a child. She's older than me.' Manny spoke for the first time.

'Ah, she must be incredibly old then. Perhaps twenty or thirty?' he said.

Manny frowned, but there was the trace of a smile in his eyes.

He knows he's being teased, Johann thought, but after what he's just been through, he must almost welcome it.

Manny said nothing, but Johann spoke for him.

'Ruth is eighteen, so she's not a child. Manny and Ruth's parents worked for my father and mother since before I was born. They are part of our family,' he said, defiance in his voice.

'Don't worry, we feel the same about our Jewish neighbours too.'

He looked out of the window.

'None of our Danish Jews have been taken,' he continued. 'They are Danes, just like us, and the Germans know that if they want Denmark to remain peaceful, they can't touch them.'

He bowed his head for a second.

'Yes, a few Danes handed back fleeing German Jews to the German authorities at the beginning,' he said, pausing, '*but not on my watch.*'

He looked straight at Manny.

'And there are thousands like me.'

Manny's eyes filled with tears. Johann could understand why.

The thought of all these thousands of ordinary people risking the worst of sanctions to protect him, and others like him, must be hard to accept, after years of abuse and hatred.

The farmer's words seemed to release a dam inside the boy and, although Johann could see him trying to fight it, he gave in and allowed silent tears to run down his face.

There will be relief in those tears, too, that they weren't being handed over.

Johann put his arm round Manny's shoulders, and the others turned away, giving him a little dignity.

They allowed him a few minutes, but when the farmer could see that Manny had regained his composure, he took a seat at the head of the table.

'I don't know how many Danes feel as we do, but I can assure you that, while you are here, you will be safe in our village.'

He looked at Manny, now recovered. He put his hand on the young Jew's shoulder.

'Once again, I apologise for putting you through that. It was rough on you, especially for one so young, but it was necessary. These are dangerous times.'

He grimaced, and Johann could see that it must have been difficult for the older man to have been so cruel, in such a deliberate fashion.

'We understand. You have nothing to fear from us.'

'So, who are you? And, while I understand why you run, is it not crazy to try and escape in a small boat like that?'

Johann smiled. 'My name is Johann Kästner, and yes, it might be madness, but when every single option had been taken from them, and the chance presented itself to get Manny and his sister away, we felt we had to take it. They'll be looking for us now, but we hope that it's on the south coast of Norway, and they have no reason to suspect that we are trying to cross the North Sea.'

He told them the full story. How they'd struck out west from the Skagerrak during the storm, but the winds and the waves had forced them southwards down the coast of Denmark until they'd found shelter and safety in Hobo Dyb.

'You certainly have that here. The Germans are in this area in small numbers, and they have limited resources, but it's enough.'

He opened the door and spat again.

'They sometimes send a patrol out to Skallingen, and they seem to be planning some form of defensive structure out there, but their purpose is to watch out over the Nordsee, not keep an eye on Hobo Dyb or Ho Bucht for runaway Jews.'

His eyes hardened, and a slight tremor edged his voice.

'Our armed forces saw the might of the Third Reich and capitulated within six hours. Maybe if we'd known how thin on the ground they were going to be, we would have put up more of a fight. Still, perhaps it's for the best, as we had few casualties and no damage to our towns or roads. Sooner or later, we'll be ready to resist, if we get the chance.'

Johann wondered if this band of men were, in all but name, the local resistance to the occupying forces, but he said nothing.

Instead, he asked them what their names were.

The farmer, who Johann assumed to be the leader, and the one with the best command of German, turned and gestured at the younger man who had caught them in the house.

'This is Peder, my son.'

Peder stretched out his hand, and Manny and Johann shook it.

'You already know Jens. Jens Simonsen.'

The man shook Johann's hand first, then Manny's, and nodded.

'And this old bugger is Morten. Morten Østergaard.'

When they'd shaken the older man's hand, the farmer introduced himself.

'Last but not least,' he said with a smile, 'I'm Børge Lund. My farm is called Skallmosegard. My boat is the *Arktisk Måne*. Morten's is the *Havfrue*.'

Johann smiled.

The *Arctic Moon and *The Mermaid. Both good names for fishing boats.

The man who called himself Børge continued. 'Jens works on the *Havfrue* with Morten. What is the name of your boat?'

'*Der Sturmtaucher*. She's a wonderful boat. She carried us through the storm.'

The men murmured in agreement. They all knew what the conditions would have been like, exposed to all that the North Sea could throw at them. And they'd seen the storm.

'So, you have a few decisions to make, don't you?'

'I hadn't considered us having too many choices.'

The farmer laughed.

'Well, your Jewish friend here, and his sister, could stay in Denmark. We should be able to find a place for them, if they could learn to speak Danish quickly.'

Johann sensed Manny stiffening.

'I presume the story about your mother's friend in Denmark was a fabrication?' Børge added.

Johann blushed. 'Yes. I'm not so good at lying, am I? My mother does have a distant relative somewhere in Denmark, but I wouldn't know where.'

He looked at Manny, then back to Børge. 'We would have to talk it over, with Manny and Ruth, and Franz too.'

'I'd rather take my chances with you, Johann.'

They all looked at Manny. His voice was controlled and steady, and the steel had returned and Johann could see from their faces that every one of the Danes admired the boy for his courage.

Børge shrugged, his hands held up. 'It is only a suggestion. I cannot guarantee that our Jews will remain safe, or that Manny and his sister will remain well hidden here, but I know my people would do their best.'

'It's a fair offer, and while Manny has a big say in it, we'll need to talk it over with the others.'

Johann placed his hand on Manny's shoulder to reassure him.

'You can let us know, and we will make the necessary arrangements,' the older man said, turning to Manny.

'I don't need to tell you how hard and perilous your journey will be if you decide not to stay,' he said. 'You've already been through hell out there, but also bear in mind that Johann and his brother will be burning their bridges. As it stands, if you and your sister stayed here with us, they could call at the local German garrison and tell them that they were safe, that they could continue their voyage to Norway, or even abandon it. Think about that.'

Manny opened his mouth to speak, but Johann interrupted him. 'Please don't concern yourself with my brother and me. The only question we need to take heed of is what is best for Manny and Ruth. We promised our father, and their parents too, that we would get them to safety. That is what we will do.'

'Of course, it is a decision to be made by all of you. But the offer stands until such time as you leave.'

Johann thanked him. 'About the stuff we took.' He looked at them, and blushed, but there were no accusatory stares. 'We took a few litres of diesel too, and a container of milk. It's over in the woods by the cattle shed. We left some money, though. It's in a jar in the pantry.'

'Ah. Kroner, I hope.'

Johann nodded in reply, and the farmer continued. 'The authorities would be suspicious of how Reichsmarks had come into our possession out here.' He paused. 'If there is anything else you need, let us know. It would be better if you would stay here until evening and return to your boat after dark. There is no point in risking being seen by someone for a matter of hours.'

'That's very fair, though it's a shame to impinge on your hospitality when we set out to steal from you.'

'As you said, you paid for the goods you took, which was stupid, by the way. If we hadn't been keeping an eye on you, and stuff had gone missing, it would have been very suspicious. Thieves would never leave payment for their plunder.'

'That's why we left it in a jar. To give us time before you discovered it.'

'Still, there should be no room for sentiment while you're on the run. Remember that. In the meantime, you both look tired and hungry. My wife, Tove, will have finished teaching the kinder in Søndagsskole, and will be home soon to make food for everyone.'

Johann smiled at the mixture of German and Danish.

He realised why the man had returned from church without his wife, leaving her with her Sunday school children, while he and his friends dealt with a situation that could easily have had a much uglier conclusion.

He wondered if, should they not have turned out to be runaways on the wrong side of German law, they would have ended up dead, dumped in an isolated bog, or weighted down at the bottom of Ho Bucht.

'In the meantime,' Børge Lund said, 'have a rest for a few hours.'

He showed them next door to a small room with a couple of upholstered benches, and shelves containing farm and fishing equipment. 'I sometimes have a quick sleep here if I'm in and out at the barn, watching a cow at the calving, or checking the sheep at lambing time. It's comfortable enough. Here's something to cover yourselves up with.' He handed them each a rough blanket and left them to it, closing the door behind him.

CHAPTER 136

Captain Bauer held his hand over the telephone mouthpiece.

'There's a phone call for you, sir. It's Colonel Schneider again. He sounds annoyed.'

'I'll take it in my office,' the General said. 'Can you let the admiral know I'll be a few minutes late?'

He slipped back into the office, sat down at his desk, and picked up the phone.

'Walther,' he said.

'Any news yet, Erich?'

'None, I'm afraid. They must be still holed up. The storm has been terrible, hasn't it?'

'Yes. From what I hear, the worst for years.'

'I'd hoped they'd contacted you. It might be easier, in provincial Norway.'

'I suppose they may not have been able to get ashore yet.'

'There are quite a few Kriegsmarine ships out now. They're going to keep an eye out for them.'

'That's good to hear. It's been a worry. I'm beginning to regret having instigated the whole enterprise.'

'You weren't to know the storm would last this long, Walther.'

'There will be repercussions if anything has happened to them.'

The General froze.

'Walther, you surprise me,' he said, his voice still genial. 'Are Army Command giving you a hard time about it?'

'I've had one or two comments, yes. Frivolous use of Wehrmacht personnel, and the like.'

'Nonsense. You've always used sailing as a tool for officer development. Tell them this is just an extension of that.'

'If there had been a full crew, that might have passed muster, but with only two of them...?'

'Ach, don't worry, Walther. It will all blow over. You're one of the best commanders in the Wehrmacht, and they know it. That's why they're promoting you. You get the best out of your men.'

'You're probably right,' the colonel said.

'I am right. In a few days it will all be forgotten.'

He paused.

'Walther, I have to go. I have a meeting with Admiral Schiffer which I can't be late for. I'll speak to you soon.'

The two men said their goodbyes. The General put the phone down and sat for a second or two, looking out across the waves whipping the length of Kieler Hafen.

He wished that the next few days and weeks could be different for Walther Schneider but there was nothing he could do about it.

*With any luck, he'll get *Der Sturmtaucher back one day. When the war is over.*

He got up, already thinking about his meeting with the admiral.

~~o~~

The smell of pork and gravy woke Johann. After a dearth of cooked meals during the storm, and the restricted fresh ingredients over the last few days of the voyage, his stomach craved something warm and appetising. He left Manny sleeping and slipped out the door of their makeshift bedroom.

In the kitchen, he could hear a woman humming, and the clatter of pans on the range. The wonderful smells made him ache for the large, warm kitchen at home; his mother throwing around commands, while Miriam, without apparent effort, sliced, poached, baked, pickled, and roasted, unnoticed in the background.

He poked his head around the open kitchen door and watched the cook. She was a compact, middle-aged woman with hair pulled back in a tight bun, the way farmers' and fishermens' wives dealt with the hard practicalities of life.

'Hej. Dig hedder Johann.' His Danish was limited, but he thought it only fair to try and greet her in her own language and tell her his name.

'Hej,' she replied, turning to him. She switched to German.

'Hello. I'm surprised to see you risen,' she said. 'Børge tells me that you both looked most tired.'

She did remind him of Miriam Nussbaum, although she was smaller in stature.

'You speak excellent German,' he said.

'I'm not as much good as Børge,' she told him, 'but I can have myself understood.'

'I have almost no Danish. I used it all up in one sentence.'

She laughed. 'I must tell you; I think you meant to say "Jeg hedder Johann", *I am Johann*, but instead you stated "Dig hedder Johann", *you are Johann*. It is most easy mistake to make. Only very small difference.'

He blushed but smiled when he saw the amusement it had given her.

'I'm Tove, Børge's wife and mother of Peder. Welcome to my home.'

'I can't thank you enough for what you are doing, it must be dangerous for you all.'

'Pah,' she said, in an echo of her husband, 'the Germans are too few to check everyone, and if we have chance to help, we must give.'

'Still, Manny and I are most grateful.'

'Does your young friend still sleep?'

'Yes, I'll leave him to rest as long as possible. He stayed awake last night while I slept; for part of the night at least.'

'Yes, I scold men for not making you come inside during cold night, and for giving you such frights today.'

'That's all right. We understand why they did what they did. It's hard to know who to trust these days.'

'The men will be back soon, then we all eat. You must be hungered.'

'I'm very hungered,' he said, smiling. 'I could eat the side of a cow with no trouble.'

She laughed again, and when she did, she looked younger, and less severe.

'We need cow for milk, so we can't spare side, but I have a potful of Frikadeller. It's old Danish meatball dish. With gravy, boiled potatoes, red cabbage, beets, and pickles too, and I've made many more rye bread.'

He could feel his salivary glands constrict, and he swallowed before he embarrassed himself by drooling, the smells were so intoxicating.

'If you call your friend now, he will have woken enough to enjoy the food. I hear the men coming in the yard, so they will be arrived shortly.'

Later, Johann couldn't remember a meal that he'd enjoyed more. Encouraged by Tove, he'd eaten two heaped and steaming plates of the pork meatballs and gravy, with their accompanying side dishes, and big chunks of bread.

It was only when the farmer had said grace that the significance of the horrified look on Manny's face hit home to Johann, when the young Jew discovered that pork was on the menu. He tried to kick Manny's leg, his eyes exhorting him to eat the non-kosher food just this once, but he knew that Manny's reawakened passion for his Jewishness, tempered by his treatment at the hands of the German state, wouldn't allow him to deviate from his beliefs. He was about to explain Manny's predicament, when Tove, with an insight that surprised him, made an interjection unnecessary.

'Manny, I have fried chicken made for you. I know you can't eat pork.' She handed him a plate that had been sitting on the range. 'I have Jewish friend I meet from time to time; she is married to Danish man, but still she must eat your kosher food.'

She was rewarded by a grateful look of relief in the boy's eyes, and the room wasn't long in filling up with talk and laughter, then more talk and less laughter as darker matters were discussed. The awful events happening in Germany troubled the Danes almost as much as their own country's capitulation to the Wehrmacht.

CHAPTER 137

Johann cleaned his plate with the last of the bread and Tove served steaming mugs of coffee and a rich fruit loaf, which they spread with a thick layer of home-churned butter. Manny told the much-amused group of Johann's attempts at milking a cow. As he came to the end of the story, Peder held up the hand holding his knife and hissed for them to be quiet.

'What is it?' Børge said, his voice low.

'A truck. Maybe two.'

'Jens, see where they are. Peder, take Manny and Johann out to the barn. Keep them out of sight.'

He switched to Danish, and Johann only caught a couple of words, but his meaning was clear.

Peder wasted no time in leading the two young Germans over the yard to the barn in a crouching run behind the cover of a stone wall.

Inside, Peder climbed up the large wooden silo wall at the back of the cow stalls, using a series of wooden pegs hammered into the planks, a ladder of sorts. He motioned for them to follow him. When they got to the top, he opened one of two small doors, and gestured for Johann and Manny to enter.

'If you hear anyone coming up, dig down into the barley, and cover yourselves. Cup your hand in front of your nose and enough air will trickle down to let you breathe. Keep your eyes shut tight, or you'll suffer.'

Johann jumped into the silo, followed by Manny, and berated himself for staying at the house for a meal when they could have been back hiding in the woods, in relative safety.

The door closed above them, and they heard the bolt sliding across.

Børge waited in the yard, looking in the direction of the village, until Jens appeared around the corner, running into the yard.

The deep rumble of engines increased, and there was another sound too.

'Two trucks, I think. One of them is a half-track, or possibly a tank. It doesn't sound heavy enough though. They're coming through Ho now, heading this way. They'll be here in a couple of minutes.'

'All right, Jens, you and Morten head off back home, I'll start the milking.' He opened the back door and stuck his head inside.

'Tove, get the extra dishes washed and stacked away. Leave three sets out on the table; makes sure you're clearing them up if they stop here.'

There was a shout of reply from inside.

'It's done already. Do you take me for a dumb farmer?'

Børge chuckled to himself and strolled over to the barn. As he entered the cowshed, Peder jumped down the last few steps from the silo.

'Let's get these cows milked. They're not going to do it themselves.'

Listening out for the trucks, or sounds of soldiers shouting, the two set about their usual routine like they had, twice a day, for all their lives.

Johann and Manny sat in the dark silo, also listening. The sounds of the trucks had ceased and for a few moments, there was silence, broken only by the gentle lowing of the cows.

Then, in the distance, they heard voices.

Manny turned to Johann. 'Definitely German, but I can't make them out.'

'They'll have stopped at the village. Random searches. That's what they do on patrol. Keeps the local population nervous, and under control. They don't know who's next.'

'Is that the sort of stuff you do in the army?'

'Yes, sometimes, but our battalion is more of an active unit which goes where the fighting is. It's often the reservists that move in and take over after we've captured a town, or village. Older men, from the last war, in the main, or young recruits.'

'Were you in Denmark?'

'No, Poland, then Norway, then France. Then Norway again. Our stiffest opposition was in the north of Norway, and in Warsaw, but elsewhere, resistance was light, and once our tanks and aircraft showed up, it often evaporated.'

'No one was ready for this, were they?'

'The French thought they were, with their Maginot Line. We just skirted around it. The English thought they were, too, but they were ill-prepared and poorly trained to fight against our armoured divisions, and their air cover was virtually non-existent. We drove them into the sea at Dunquerque. They say few survived. That's half the British Army gone in one go.'

'So, the Nazis can do what they like?'

'I'm sorry, Manny, but I can't see anything stopping us taking over the whole of Europe. With the Russians on our side, carving up Poland and the Baltic States from the east, we had little opposition. Even...'

He stopped.

'What is it?'

'I shouldn't really say but...' He looked at Manny.

'Oh, what the hell,' he said, shrugging. 'My father says there are plans to invade Britain next year when we defeat Russia – we are already bombing their cities to oblivion.'

'Then why are we going there?'

'There's nowhere else to go and at least when you are in England, you and Ruth could try and get to America or Canada.'

Manny froze. 'They're starting up again,' he said.

Johann listened and, sure enough, he could hear one of the trucks moving. After a minute, the heavier-engined truck appeared to be on the move as well. *Don't stop here, he thought.*

~~o~~

Down below, father and son listened too, waiting for the Germans to pass.

The cow Peder was milking gave an irritable kick.

'Don't grip the teats so tightly,' his father told him. 'Relax. If the Germans do stop, so what? They've been here before. It's just routine. Think of something nice. We'll have a beer after they're gone.'

One of the trucks passed by, but they heard the second vehicle's tracks grind to a halt in the gravel at the entrance to the lane.

In the silo, the cowshed, and in the kitchen, they listened as soldiers shouted to each other above the rumble of the idling engine. They expected to hear the thump of boots marching down the lane, but they were either being cautious, approaching the farmhouse in single file, or they were so sure of themselves that they were strolling in as if they were visiting old acquaintances.

~~o~~

Tove saw them enter the yard and turn towards the kitchen door. She busied herself tidying up the kitchen, dropping the dirty plates and cups into the sink just as they knocked on the door. Cloth in hand, she opened the door and said hello in Danish, and asked them how she could help.

There were four of them. Two stood, guns ready, covering the rest of the farmyard. The others faced Tove, but for part of an occupying army, they weren't at all threatening.

They're just boys.

'Do you speak German?' the taller one asked.

'A little.' She didn't want to lie in case they ever heard her speak their language.

'We are doing a routine check. How many people are here?' He removed a clipboard from under his arm and ran his finger down the paper.

'There are three of us here. My husband and son are milking the cows. Do you want me to fetch them?'

'No, madam. Are they over in the barn?'

'No, but the cowshed is attached to the barn. You'll hear the cows.'

He turned and motioned to his men.

'You two, go and check out the barn. Wenzel, you come with me.'

He turned back to Tove. 'I presume that you are Frau Tove Lund?'

'Yes, that is my name.'

'We will need to take a look around. Please show us the way.'

He pushed in past her, and she followed. The remaining soldier closed the door after him, and Tove led them through the house, pointing out each room in turn. They opened all the cupboards and checked behind every piece of furniture. When they found the blankets in the small room that Manny and Johann had slept in, the Obergefreiter, a taller man, raised an eyebrow and asked her why there were two beds made up downstairs.

'My husband and son use them when they are in and out at night, tending cows having calves, or looking after sick animals.'

He nodded, as if he'd known that already.

As they toured the rest of the house, she realised that although he was the officer in command of the group, the tall soldier was barely out of his teens. She wondered how this army had conquered their nation with such ease. She was sure that her husband, or son, could have dealt with these soldiers without having to think twice about it, but she knew that it was the state machinery behind these *boys* that gave them their absolute authority.

CHAPTER 138

'What a godforsaken place.'

Carl Meyer nodded in agreement.

His boss stood beside the car, at the top of the small incline that ran down to Hirtshals harbour. The Kriminalassistent held onto his hat in one hand and the lapels of his coat with his other, to stop them flapping, leaning into the wind to save himself from being blown backwards.

The sea beyond the harbour was a dark grey, mottled with the foam of countless wind-whipped waves, and Carl Meyer shivered at the thought of being out there in any sort of vessel.

Large rollers crashed over the harbour walls, sending plumes of spray ten metres into the air, blowing onto the boats sheltered inside.

'If they're out there in a yacht, I don't give much for their chances,' Carl Meyer said.

'They're too cunning for that,' the Kriminalassistent said. 'They'll be hiding in a little hole somewhere like the rats they are.'

'I presume that's the harbour master's office over there,' the younger man said, pointing.

'Let's go. I've no intention of staying in this place for any longer than we have to.'

They got back in the car and drove to the building on the quayside. The notice beside the door confirmed that it was indeed the office of the Hirtshals harbour master but there was a note pinned on the door.

Back in an hour. On vessel Lille Bjørn.

'Verdammt!'

Heinrich Güllich walked to the end of the offices and looked out at the harbour. He didn't take account of the shelter that the building gave and, stepping round the corner, the wind caught his hat and blew it towards the eastern basin.

Carl Meyer sprinted after it and, a metre before it slithered and rolled off the edge, caught it. He returned it to the Kriminalassistent.

'Thank you,' Heinrich Güllich said, with gruff embarrassment.

'Let's try and find this *Lille Bjørn*,' he added, his hat now clasped tight in his hand.

They walked further along the quay, looking at the names of the vessels berthed alongside. Heinrich Güllich struck a match, but it blew out before he could light his cigarette. He cursed.

'This will take forever, sir. There's someone on that boat over there,' Carl Meyer said, nodding towards a tired-looking freighter, where a swarthy-looking seaman stood leaning on the rail in the lee of the wheelhouse, smoking.

The young Gestapo officer walked over to the rusty ship and stopped a short distance from the edge. His leather coat flapped in the gusting wind, and he gripped his fedora tightly to stop it flying away.

The man on the boat looked up. He leaned over the rail and spat into the dark, slopping water between the hull and the harbour wall.

Carl Meyer stiffened.

'Sprechen Sie Deutsch?' he said, trying to sound menacing.

The man looked at him, then spat again.

'Kun Dansk,' the seaman replied. *Only Danish.*

Carl Meyer didn't fully understand the words, but he caught enough to know the man didn't speak German. He stared at the sailor.

'*Lille Bjørn*,' he said, and turned, sweeping his arm at the other boats.

The man took a draw of his cigarette and blew the smoke towards him.

'Den anden kaj,' he said. *The other quay.*

Carl Meyer looked at him, a blank expression on his face.

The man pointed at the far side of the basin.

Carl Meyer gave him a stare and nodded.

'It's round there,' he said to Heinrich Güllich, nodding to the pier on the opposite side of the harbour.

The two Gestapo men walked back along the end of the basin, then up the furthest quay, checking the boats as they went. Closer to the west harbour wall, the occasional fleck of spray reached them from the waves still crashing against it. When they reached the end of the pier, they turned and began walking back down the other side, pulling their collars up against the wind, stronger now away from the shelter afforded by the storehouses in the centre of the quay.

There were fewer boats on the windward side, and they reached the end closest to the shore again, puzzled at having missed it.

'Someone's going into the harbour master's office,' Heinrich Güllich said, striding off in the direction of the low building close to where they'd parked the car.

When he arrived, with Carl Meyer scuttling behind him, he knocked, and pushed the door open.

'Ah. Kriminalassistent Güllich,' the man said, still in the process of hanging up his coat. 'You make good time. I hope you see note.'

'Yes. We tried to find the *Lille Bjørn*, but we couldn't see it. One of the seamen told us it was on the other quay.'

'The other quay? Not possible. *Lille Bjørn* is there.'

He went to the window and pointed. The two Gestapo men peered through the glass. The *Lille Bjørn* was the next-but-one boat in front of the rusty freighter.

'The Schweinhund. I'll have him for that.'

Carl Meyer made for the door but Heinrich Güllich put a restraining hand on his arm.

'We'll deal with him later.'

He turned to the harbour master.

'We have a couple more questions to ask you, and we'd like to talk with your wife, if you don't mind, and to the fisherman who spoke with the Kästner boys.'

'My wife is in shop. I will give directions to you. The fisherman speaking with Franz Kästner is now at sea. I believe he is returned late this evening. You are staying Hirtshals tonight?'

'We hadn't intended to, Herr Harbour Master,' Heinrich Güllich said, his disappointment evident on his face.

'We could go to Skagen and come back later,' Carl Meyer said. 'Is there a hotel or guest house here?'

He doubted a place like this, at the end of the earth, would have a decent hotel but presumed that a room or two would be available in one of the houses.

'We have hotel. Two, in fact. For ferry passengers, most of all. Sadly, the war has stopped ferry, but some of Wehrmacht men use.'

'Fine. You said on the phone that you met both Kästner boys?'

'Yes. I visited boat. We drink together, one or two. They nice boys, for Ge...' He stopped.

'For who?' Carl Meyer asked.

'General's sons,' the harbour master said, quick to cover his lapse.

Carl Meyer wondered if everyone in Hirtshals thought it was acceptable to disrespect the Gestapo.

'And you didn't see any evidence of anyone else on board?' Heinrich Güllich asked.

'No,' the harbour master said, frowning. They'd asked the same questions on the telephone. 'Only two on board. For sure.'

'And they left first thing the next day?'

'Around eight. They went shop of my wife to fetch supplies.'

'Did they buy many supplies?'

'You should ask wife. But I doubt; they made only one time back to boat.'

'And did you see them go?'

'I waved. They were fine guests in harbour.'

'What direction did they go in?'

The harbour master laughed.

'Up and down, a lot, at first. Harbour entrance, it was rough. Very rough.'

He looked at the sour expression on the Gestapo men's faces.

'Ach. They went north, as far as I watch. Grimstad.'

'And none of your boats have seen them since.'

This time, the laugh was louder.

'You see weather today? This very good compare with last week. You believe much boats out?'

'We were told the storm was bad.'

'Was terrible. Worst for maybe five, ten year. If out in sea…'

He made a cutting gesture across his throat.

Carl Meyer shivered again. There was something about these men of the sea that troubled him.

The harbour master told them how to get to his wife's shop.

Outside, Carl Meyer walked over to the freighter and called out, but no one answered. He eased his way across the gangway spanning the gap between the deck and the quay, its lack of guardrails unsettling.

He walked around the wheelhouse, trying to open the two doors, one at the back and one on the port side.

He crossed to the quay again.

'There's no one there, sir.'

'You can come back down when we return from Skagen. If you find him, you have my permission to throw him overboard.'

Carl Meyer wasn't sure if the Kriminalassistent was being serious, but it was tempting to believe that he was.

~~o~~

They got back in the car and drove the few hundred metres to the general store run by the harbour master's wife.

A bell rang as they opened the door.

A woman behind the counter was serving an old man and they waited until he went out, staring at them on his way to the door.

'Can I help you?' the woman said. Her German, unlike her husband's, was almost flawless.

'Yes,' Heinrich Güllich said. 'Your husband sent us up. We believe you sold a few supplies to the young German sailors that were here a week or so ago?'

'Yes. They were charming young men.'

The Kriminalassistent was sick and tired of the affection the Kästner men spawned everywhere they went.

'How much did they buy from you?'

'Oh, quite a bit,' she said.

'What exactly did they buy?'

'I can tell you if you like. I keep a ledger of everything I sell. It helps me with the ordering, and with my bookkeeping.'

She reached under the counter and pulled out a bound notebook and flicked back through a week's worth of pages.

'Here we are,' she said. 'A sack of potatoes, two litres of milk, cheese and bread. A half-kilo of butter.'

She listed half a dozen other items.

'Quite a lot for a trip to Norway?' Carl Meyer said.

'Not really,' she said. 'They were going to Bergen, which could take up to a week, and they said that they might not be able to provision again before they got there.'

'And they didn't purchase any items that would be particular to females?'

The woman bristled.

'I'm not sure what you mean.'

'Do you sell sanitary napkins here?' Heinrich Güllich said with a sigh.

'Few women here can afford them, but we do stock a few for those that do. But why would two men buy them?'

'There is a possibility that there was a woman on board. A young woman.'

The harbour master's wife's eyes were wide now.

'I'd find that hard to believe. My husband visited the boat and I think he might have noticed.'

'They would have been trying to conceal her, madam. We have deep suspicions they were attempting to smuggle a girl and a young boy out of Germany.'

Heinrich Güllich cursed himself. He had been drawn into giving away more than he'd meant to.

'Well, did they buy any?' he said, his face flushed angry now.

'No. I would have spotted that. And it would be on the list.'

'Unless they took you into their confidence,' Carl Meyer said, surprising himself, and he wondered if the Kriminalassistent would be annoyed. He glanced at his boss, but his face betrayed no irritation.

'Certainly not. I am not a person who tells lies,' the woman said, bristling again.

Heinrich Güllich was inclined to believe her. Her indignation appeared genuine.

He thanked her and they left.

'Right,' he said. 'To Skagen.'

CHAPTER 139

'You are Peder Lund, ja?' The two privates must have been primed with villagers' names.

Peder looked up from his seating position and nodded.

'I need you to answer me,' the soldier said, pointing his machine pistol at the young Dane.

'Yes, I'm Peder Lund.'

The man turned to Børge, who didn't wait to be asked.

'I'm Børge Lund,' he said, looking him in the eye.

The soldier stared back at the farmer but said nothing. It was the German who looked away first.

'As you see, we are in the middle of milking,' Børge said. 'Feel free to look around. Are you searching for anything in particular?'

Peder was impressed by how matter of fact his father sounded.

'Just routine,' one of the soldiers told him, saying nothing more after a cold frown from his colleague.

'Help yourself. Give us a shout if you need anything. Watch out when you are walking behind the cows. They tend to pish and shit when they sense a stranger in the cowshed. And number twenty-eight kicks, so watch her.'

The two soldiers glanced at the cows then back at Børge Lund but, not wanting to ask which animal was the kicker, they scurried past them to the far end of the cowshed, fearful of flying hooves and excrement.

When they'd finished checking the dairy, the soldiers ran the gauntlet of cows again. One of the beasts unleashed a kick in their direction, and although she missed, it set off a chain reaction in the others. Three of them made attempts to kick the soldiers, one landing a glancing blow on the taller of the two Germans, and the remaining cows released a volley of urine and faeces which landed in the gutter, splashing up onto the soldiers' uniforms and boots.

Cursing the cows, the soldiers stood in front of Børge again. The taller one nursed his bruised thigh.

Splattered and reeking of bovine waste, they glared at the farmer, daring him to laugh at their predicament, but both father and son kept their heads down and suppressed their mirth.

'Where does that go?' the frowning soldier asked, pointing to the line of pegs leading up to the roof.

'That's to allow us access to the silos, when we load them up with grain at harvest time.'

The pegs disappeared into the dim loft space. A rope hung on a block and tackle, to allow sacks of barley to be hoisted to the top.

The soldier looked up and, hanging his weapon over his back, made to start climbing.

'I'd dry your feet off first. These pegs are lethal if they get wet.'

Having disregarded the farmer's warning before, and suffered as a result, he picked up a handful of loose straw and dried his boots off, before starting the ascent.

'Watch out for the rats at the top. The cats are struggling to keep on top of their numbers.'

Peder watched the soldier's face blanch but allowed him some grudging respect when the man, younger than himself, shrugged and continued to climb.

The two farmers returned to their task, and the rhythmic squirt of milk into the buckets fell in time to the soldier's upward steps.

~~o~~

In the silo, Manny and Johann had heard the commotion below. Johann tapped Manny on the arm and motioned for him to cover his face with his handkerchief and burrow his way into the grain. By the time they registered the soldier's boots climbing the pegs on the outside of the wooden silo wall, they were well covered.

Trying to control their breathing and supressing their rising fear, they heard the man reach the top and the muffled sound of the first silo door opening. There was a long silence. Johann presumed that the soldier was having a good look inside. There followed a thump as the door closed and the bolt slid home.

Three short steps shook the wooden floor, and the bolt on the door above their heads shot back. The door creaked open, and the click of the torch being switched on echoed in the chamber above the surface of the barley. The silence grew as seconds turned to minutes.

What was the bastard doing?

A muffled voice reached them. Buried under a layer of grain, Johann couldn't make out his words clearly, but he did catch snatches of it. Something to do with dust.

Scheiße. The dust.

The air in the first silo would have been clear, Johann realised, the dust long settled. Because they had been scrabbling about, burying themselves, the air above their hiding place would be thick with dust and, when the soldier shone the torch in it, the beam would highlight every single particle.

An audible click told him the worst. He hoped they'd buried themselves deep enough, at least the length of a bayonet, but their faces were closer to the surface to allow enough air to filter through the barley. Johann steeled himself for the penetrating steel in his flesh. He doubted that the soldier considered the possibility of people hiding in the grain but that wouldn't matter.

More likely they're searching for weapons or ammunition, or illicit stocks of fuel.

A couple of times, he felt the grains around his body shift as the blade came close, and he was once again awestruck that Manny had the composure to lie still and not succumb to panic; it would have been easy for the boy to jump up and surrender, or even launch a suicidal attack on the soldier. Either action would have been fatal for them, and the farmers.

Thinking about it later, he knew that laziness saved them. If the soldier had jumped down onto the surface of the grain, he would either have sunk down onto them or, without having to reach down at arm's length, the thrusts from his bayonet would have been deeper, finding flesh or bone, ending any hope of escape.

The last stab was so close to Johann's face, he could almost smell the gun oil on the blade, but after a pause of a few seconds, another muffled series of shouts followed, and the door banged shut. The clang of the bolt sliding home was the sweetest sound that Johann had ever heard.

They lay, not moving a millimetre for a further ten minutes. Even when they heard the rumble of a heavy engine being gunned, and the rhythmic slap of the metal tracks on the tarmac, they remained still, not daring to move until one of the Danes told them it was safe.

For a few terrifying minutes before the bolt was unlatched, and the door flung open, Johann feared that one of the bayonet's thrusts had penetrated something vital in Manny and that the young boy had bled out, unwilling to make a sound even in death, or that he'd been unable to stop the grain from entering his mouth and nose, and had suffocated.

As soon as he heard Peder's voice, he jumped up and clawed at the grain, digging in desperation, expecting the worst. Tears blinded him but, just as he touched something cold and hard, a hand emerged a metre in front of him, and Manny pulled himself out from the grain, his face blackened with dust and sweat, only his teeth and the whites of his eyes showing through. Realising he must look the same, Johann looked towards Peder and the three young men, united in the relief at their closeness to disaster, burst into uncontrollable laughter.

Manny and Johann's mirth dissolved into coughing fits, exacerbated by the dust they'd inhaled during their ordeal. By the time they had climbed down, and washed themselves clean at the water trough, Børge had returned from the house with a wooden crate of beer, brewed on the farm.

He hesitated when handing Manny his bottle, but only for a second.

'If you're man enough to hold your nerve like that, you're entitled to a beer.'

The dark liquid slaked the dust from the two young German's throats, and Børge decided that Johann should learn to milk a cow properly, just in case he ever felt the need to steal a jug of milk again.

Tove arrived, and to Johann's surprise, she took the beer that Børge offered her and watched Johann's clumsy, but steadily improving technique with much amusement. She took over his agricultural education, and by the time the others had finished milking, she had him proficient enough to be useful, if still a little slow.

'The other truck checked the Jorgensen place,' Johann heard Tove say, 'then they both headed out to Skallingen.'

Børge grunted and glanced at Johann. 'They'll be all right out there. The Germans won't see them.'

Peder opened another beer for Manny and himself and, as the two of them talked, laughing together, Børge took Johann aside.

'It would be too dangerous to go back tonight. That patrol will return along the Skallingen road at some point, and you don't want to run into them. And anyway, the rain is torrential now; you'd be frozen by the time you got back to the boat. Wait until tomorrow night; you can stay here in the meantime. The weather will be better.'

'We can't. Franz and Ruth will be worried. They're expecting us back tonight.'

'That's true, but you surely discussed the possibility that you might need longer than twenty-four hours to get back.'

'Well, yes,' Johann admitted, 'we agreed that they would keep a two-hourly watch tonight, and if we didn't appear by daybreak, they'd do the same again the following night, for as many nights as it took. It won't stop them thinking the worst, though, especially with those army trucks running about.'

'If it's any help, we'll get word to them first thing in the morning. We check the nets in Hobo Dyb every couple of days anyway, so we'll not rouse any suspicion.'

Johann had to concede that the farmer was right; any sign of lights or movement out on Hobo Dyb when the Wehrmacht were in the area could attract unwanted attention and put them all in danger.

'All right, we'll stay. But leave it to me to tell Manny. He'll not want Ruth worried sick about him.'

The trucks returned from Skallingen just after dark.

They passed the farm without stopping, speeding through Ho and Bredmose on their way back to Esbjerg.

CHAPTER 140

By the time they returned from Skagen, Heinrich Güllich knew that he'd been right all along, and that Carl Meyer was almost as convinced as he was.

The hour-long journey to yet another harbour in the middle of nowhere had been made in silence. Heinrich Güllich had seen that his assistant was brooding about having been made a fool of by the insolent seaman, but he left him to drive in silence, using the time to mull over everything they'd learned so far.

Part of him couldn't help thinking that they were no further forward.

It hadn't taken them long to find the patrol vessel. It stood out from the fishing boats and working craft in the harbour. They were welcomed aboard by the first mate, and shown to the officers' mess, a rather grand name for a room with a table and a few chairs in it, with two portholes that let little natural light in. The two junior officers who'd drank with Franz and Johann were shown in.

The Kriegsmarine men had repeated their stories, recounting the evening as they remembered it. For the warrant officer, much of it was hazy, but the midshipman remembered almost everything, including the warrant officer being sick, his impromptu sleep in the forecabin, and the Kästner boys helping him back to his own vessel.

'So, there was nowhere on the boat anyone else could have been hiding?'

'No, the warrant officer was in the heads, and the only other compartment was up front. And he was snoring in there for a good half hour. Why do you ask?'

'We have reason to believe that *Der Sturmtaucher* was being used to smuggle two people out of Germany to Sweden or Norway.'

'Well, they weren't on the boat when we were on it,' the warrant officer said.

The midshipman rubbed his chin.

'It is funny you should mention it though,' he said.

'Why is that?' Heinrich Güllich said, leaning forward.

'Well, we passed them the next day, close to Endelave. I could have sworn there were three people on board, but the first lieutenant had a look and told me that my previous night's drinking had blurred my vision.'

'How close were you?'

'About a mile, maybe.'

'So how could you see?'

'I was looking at them through binoculars. They didn't see us at first, until we sounded the horn.'

'Could it have been a girl, or a young boy?'

'It was too far to tell, even with binoculars. It's possible though.'

'And no one else saw three people?'

'There were only two of us on deck. The warrant officer was sleeping it off.'

'What are you doing here in Skagen? We were told you were based in Norway.'

'We followed a suspicious fishing boat into the Kattegat yesterday. It was our first day out. We just passed Skagen when the oil seal blew again. We're in here until it's repaired.'

They two Gestapo men thanked the Kriegsmarine officers and left. In the car back, Heinrich Güllich thumped the dashboard, then lit a cigarette.

'I told you, Meyer, didn't I?'

'Yes, sir,' the junior man conceded. 'You were right.'

'Now all we have to do is find them. If they were still in the boat after Bogense, they must have got off in Hirtshals, or they're still on *The Shearwater*.'

'So, what's next, sir?'

'We ask around in Hirtshals; stir it up a little. And we call on the local police. Then tomorrow, we go to Bogense. Perhaps someone else saw them.'

~~o~~

If they hadn't been nervous about watchkeeping, Franz and Ruth wouldn't have moved from the cabin all that day, but despite the wonder they found in each other's bodies, and with the knowledge hanging over them that the afternoon and evening might be their only time alone together in any of the futures they could imagine, neither of them could ignore the need for frequent checks for other boats. In the end, they found it more relaxing and less disruptive to wrap up well and sit close together in the cockpit, content just to be alone, talking or sitting, comfortable in their shared silence.

'Franz, the rings, are they the ones you exchanged with Lise?'

Franz's hand shot up to his neck. Usually, only the coarse fisherman's twine was visible in the open collar of his shirt, but every time he'd been naked with her, the two rings had been visible, jangling gold against his fair skin.

'Yes,' he said, unable to lie. 'I've worn them every day since she threw her ring back at me. To remind me...'

He laughed.

'... it was my way of inoculating myself against women.'

'What do you mean?'

'Well, if ever I felt the need to get close to someone, it was always there as a warning.'

'I've seen the string before; you sometimes run it through your fingers when you're deep in thought, but I've never seen the rings.'

'I'm sorry,' he said. 'I should have taken them off.'

'No. Don't. They seem... part of you.'

He blushed.

She leaned forward, trailing her hand around the back of his neck, touching the soft frayed string. She kissed him.

'So, you don't wish to be involved with women,' she said, her eyes boring into his.

'Well...'

~~o~~

Later that day, they had good reason to be watchful.

Just after they'd eaten, they heard heavy diesel engines in the distance, getting louder, coming from the south. They stared in the direction of the sound as it got closer but, just when Ruth imagined she could see a boat through the murk, coming straight for them, the note of the engine changed as the ship passed the mouth of Hobo Dyb, and headed away from them, out to sea, the throb of its screws receding to the west.

Franz told her that it might be a fishing boat or a small commercial vessel leaving Esbjerg through the main channel but, when she asked him, he conceded that it could just have easily been a Kriegsmarine patrol boat.

An hour later, the roar of a diesel engine again pierced the silence, this time from the direction of Ho and Bredmose. The weather had cleared enough by then for them to see the telegraph poles that marked the road out to Skallingen lighthouse and, although they only glimpsed the top of the truck for a few brief seconds, they were able to follow its progress towards them by the pillar of dirty smoke rising from its exhaust. It slowed down as it approached, and the chilling thought that Johann and Manny had been caught, and that their captors were now coming for Ruth and him, filled Franz's mind.

There was no real way of running. Ruth flinched as his hand, holding hers, gripped too tightly. Powerless to act, Franz could only watch, paralysed, as the truck paused, then sped up again, its exhaust marking the vehicle's retreat towards the end of the strip of dunes and marsh that separated Hobo Dyb from the North Sea.

No sooner had relief flooded over them than the growl of a second engine began to build from the same direction as the first. Once again, the truck that came into sight slowed down at the same point, before speeding up like the first vehicle.

'That was a half-track, this time. They both must have slowed down for a bend in the road. I thought for a second they were stopping for us,' he said, when they could breathe again.

Ruth rubbed the hand that Franz had been holding. He noticed and muttered his apologies, horrified that he'd hurt her.

When the trucks returned along the road in the gloom of the evening a couple of hours later, the watching eyes from the yacht were less troubled when they slowed down again. Even if the vehicles' occupants had been looking towards them, they would have seen nothing; the yacht was well hidden behind the grassy hillocks of Skallingen and its marshy reedbeds.

Knowing it would be dark soon and realising that keeping a watchout for the boys could be a long and cold vigil, they went below while they could, shutting the hatch and pulling the washboards into place. With the curtains pulled, and the oil lamp burning, they grabbed the last chance to be alone. Lying naked under the blanket, they made love again for the last time before Johann and Manny's return would make it impossible. Their confidence with one another had grown every time they were together, and any residual shyness had completely evaporated, replaced by an increasing willingness to please the other without inhibition.

But long before midnight, when the boys were expected, they had dressed and cleared away the blankets, leaving no sign that they were anything more than friends.

'I'm not embarrassed about us,' Ruth said, 'and I don't feel guilty, it's just…'

'It's the same for me,' Franz told her, holding both her hands, 'but it will be simpler this way, and we have the hardest of times ahead of us; we can't afford for there to be any discord on *Der Sturmtaucher*.'

'We'll still be together for the rest of the voyage. We just won't be alone…'

The sad smile she gave him almost broke his heart.

'You'll still be stuck with me all these long watches,' he said, 'and, don't forget, when we get to England, we won't be separated forever.'

They'd kissed and clung to each other for one last time before going up on deck.

For the rest of the night, they kept watch for a flashing torch, and not only during the prearranged ten minutes at the top of every hour; they took turns at scanning the shore in the direction of Ho, talking softly to one another every so often to avert tired and careless eyes.

The hours dragged, and still nothing broke the blackness of night.

CHAPTER 141

By first light, they knew, deep down, that they weren't coming back.

'I feel terrible,' Ruth said, tears filling her eyes. 'Something bad has happened to them. We're being punished.'

'No,' Franz said, gripping her hand, 'There was always a possibility that they would take longer to find supplies and, anyway, they were maybe afraid of moving about in the dark with the Wehrmacht all over Skallingen.'

He did his best to keep his voice reassuring, despite his own deep misgivings.

'But what if the patrol was for them?' Ruth said. 'Perhaps they were spotted, and they've been picked up.'

'I don't think so. Why would the Germans have driven out to Skallingen with them? I'm sure Johann just didn't want to risk getting seen last night or leading the Wehrmacht to us.'

She appeared to believe him, and they managed a short sleep just as daylight broke. An hour later, Ruth, who had been dozing curled up against Franz, awoke with a start.

'What is it?' Franz asked, startled by her sudden movement.

'I hear something.'

'It's only the wind, or the boat creaking, or perhaps the water slapping against the hull.'

'No, I'm sure I heard something else, like a humming sound. Listen, there it is again.'

He turned his head towards the spot she was gazing at but heard nothing above the wind and the sea.

'It's an engine,' she said. 'Maybe an aeroplane passing over.'

They waited in silence. Then ever so faint, from the north-east, Franz heard it.

'It's a small boat, and it's coming from Ho Bucht,' he said, 'so it may just be a fisherman. Get below and be ready to hide in the bilge.'

She grimaced but did as he had asked. He crouched down in the cockpit and peered over the coamings. He could see nothing yet; the wall of swirling rain obliterated everything. Then the engine stopped.

Or has it? he thought. He imagined he could still hear its faint beat, as if the engine were ticking over. *Picking up pots, or laying nets,* he hoped.

Five minutes passed, then he heard the boat moving again, its engine getting louder.

'They're coming closer,' he hissed.

He heard the clatter of the bilge boards being lifted, and he felt for her, steeling herself to lower her body into that dank, suffocating hole in the bowels of the boat.

Through the driving rain, he began to make out a dark shape. It was a small cuddy boat; low, open, with a tiny wheelhouse up front, just large enough to hold a man, or two at a push. It continued towards them but, as it approached, it veered off and slowed, circling them at a distance. There were two men on board, standing on the open deck, one behind the wheelhouse, steering, and one further back at the transom. They were staring at the yacht, but in the gloom, and with his limited view of them, Franz couldn't make out their faces, or what they were wearing.

He kept his head down, hoping that they were indeed fishermen, that they would have a cursory look to satisfy their curiosity, then carry on to their next pot or net but, to his dismay, he heard the boat engine cut to idle and the rippling sound of the bow nosing the water as it drifted in towards them.

'Ahoy, *Sturmtaucher*.' The words, in German, shocked Franz, and his heart sank. He had hoped it would be local fishermen. *Why would the German authorities use a small boat like this?*

He remained out of sight and didn't respond. The fact that the men had hailed the yacht by name wasn't an issue; it was there in clear lettering on the hull. There was still a slim chance that whoever they were, they would move on, perhaps just noting the boat's details in a routine report.

'Ahoy, *Sturmtaucher*,' the cry came again. 'We know you're aboard.'

Franz cursed under his breath but, although his stomach bunched into a tight knot and his head pounded, he realised that, despite having hailed him in German, there was something that didn't quite fit with his concern that this was a German patrol, sent to investigate a sighting of an unfamiliar vessel in the area. There was a slight accent to the man's voice, and his enunciation was that of someone having to consider the words they were using. No matter though; their persistence wasn't welcome or helpful, whatever the man's nationality.

'Franz, I have a message for you from Johann.'

He heard Ruth's gasp from the cabin, and his heart thumped in his chest. He heard himself exhale slowly.

They must have caught Johann and Manny.

He wondered if this was going to be a shakedown; bartering with a Danish ethnic German or a well-educated local fisherman for their lives was better than the German military having found them, but only just, and could these people be trusted to let them go even if what they could give them was deemed sufficient?

But he had no choice. They were finished either way, so he stood up and waved for the boat to come alongside.

He caught the midship line that the man steering the boat handed to him and tied it to the cleat just in front of *The Shearwater*'s cockpit. The younger man looped a line over one of the yacht's stern cleats and pulled the boats together as the skipper gave it a touch of reverse to help him. Up close, it was clear that the pair were fishermen, and the various bits and pieces of equipment lying about on the deck confirmed this.

The older man, the one at the wheel, held out his hand, and Franz hesitated, then shook it, frowning.

'What have you done with Johann and Manny?'

The man smiled. 'They're fine. Sleeping it off in a warm bed after a rough time the night before last.' He paused, looking Franz up and down. 'He's like you, young Johann.'

Franz relaxed just a little, but still he didn't trust the strangers.

'Why didn't you bring them back?'

'We couldn't. Not in daylight. There's too much risk that they would be seen. The less people that know about this, the better it is for you, and for us.'

Still rather reluctantly, Franz beckoned for the men to come aboard.

'I'm Børge Lund. This is my son Peder. He caught your brother and his young friend breaking into our home, trying to steal food. They were lucky it was our house they broke into.'

Franz's heart sank again. He was sure now that there were going to be a series of difficult negotiations to get the boys back.

'I'm sorry about that. I'm sure that they intended to pay for it. They had money with them.'

'Don't worry, my friend, they did.' He smiled. 'Apart from getting caught, they've not let you down. We saw you the first morning after you arrived. A couple of friends watched Johann and Manny come ashore and hide in one of our farm sheds. When we went to church, we left Peder in the house. They didn't check it was empty.'

Franz didn't know what to say.

'Tell Ruth she can come out of hiding. I have a message for her from her brother.'

Franz slid back the washboards and told Ruth to come out.

A few moments later, a pale and worried-looking Ruth climbed into the cockpit.

'Are you sure he's fine?' she asked, as the man made a short bow to her, a soft grin on his face.

'He's great. He told me to say "Chazak v'ematz", if I've pronounced it correctly.'

'Yes. That's almost perfect. It means *be strong and of good courage*. Your German is excellent too.'

He shrugged. 'People assume that we're ignorant peasants living out here. Many of us speak a little German, I more than most; I spent a few years working on a German trawler while my father was still alive.'

'So, you're not going to turn us in?' Franz asked, a nagging doubt still troubling him.

'Ha. That was what Johann asked too. You Germans must be very untrusting people.'

His face creased into a smile as he said it, taking away any offence from his words.

'No, we know your circumstances,' he said, after a moment, 'and we'll do anything to keep you out of the hands of those Nazi bastards.' He turned his head to the side and spat.

'Sorry,' he said, turning back to Ruth, but she didn't know if he was apologising for the language or for the expectoration.

'That's all right,' Franz said, now laughing. 'She's learned a few words she shouldn't have heard during our trip.'

'Why would you help us?' Ruth asked.

The fisherman took out his pipe and lit it before answering.

'There are a few reasons,' he said, 'We are good people, like you, and we don't like what your country is doing to itself, or to her neighbours. One day, we will rise up and beat them, but not today. In the meantime, any small victory we can steal, and stick it up their...' He stopped and looked at Ruth. They both laughed.

'You know what I mean.'

~~o~~

Franz offered them coffee, and while he was making it, the two fishermen talked with Ruth, telling her about Manny. She was shocked when they told her what they'd done to him to make sure he and Johann were genuine fugitives, and her heart went out to her brother for the humiliation he must have endured, even if she understood the necessity for it.

'How is Manny now?' she asked. 'He could be a bit touchy about that sort of thing. He has gone through so much, which has made him feel persecuted on the one hand, but more determined to be Jewish on the other.'

'He was very brave. It felt wrong, treating him like that, but I had to be sure. I think he has almost forgiven us, although he had a knife gripped in his fist at one point. I'm not sure if he would have tried to use it.' He smiled.

'He can be deep. He hasn't even said much to me about leaving our parents behind, but that must be hard for him. He's only fourteen.'

'Scheiße. I thought he was older, maybe fifteen or sixteen. That makes it worse.'

'He's had to grow up fast. He should be playing football, collecting bird's eggs, or teasing girls instead of having to worry about life and death every waking minute.'

Her eyes filled up as the hopelessness of their circumstances washed over her.

Børge Lund placed a hand on her arm. 'These are the hardest of times, Fräulein. We'll do our best to get you all to safety, but even if you leave here, there'll be danger all the way, of one sort or another. The sea can be cruel, and there's the German Navy to worry about too.'

'We all know that. We should have got out long ago, but none of us thought it would get as bad as it has. They'll not be happy until they get rid of us all. My parents were heartbroken at us going, but they made us leave. They told me that even England might not be safe, that we should try and get to America if we survive the journey to Britain without drowning or being captured.'

The fisherman took a heavy draw on his pipe and blew the smoke out across the water.

'That's one of the reasons we came out. There's something that you should consider. I've already spoken to Manny and Johann about it.'

Franz handed up the four steaming mugs and listened as Børge outlined their options.

'... so you either trust that the Danish people can keep Ruth and Manny safe, and you and your brother can go back to Germany, or carry on to Norway as you were meant to, or you take the risk of all four of you trying for England,' he finished.

'And what did Manny say?' Ruth asked.

'I'd hoped to hear your thoughts before I tell you, but if you'd rather know first...?' He left the question hanging in the air.

'No, I suppose that's fair.' She thought for a few moments. 'It's terribly kind of you to offer...' She hesitated.

'But?' he said.

'Yes, there's a *but*. Even if you could guarantee our safety, which I know would be impossible, my parents made me promise to get Manny to England. I'd feel that I was betraying them if we did anything else. I'm sorry.'

'Don't apologise.' He shrugged. 'It will be easier for us if you leave, but we had to give you the chance. What do you think, Franz?'

'I'll go along with whatever Ruth wishes. I'm sure she's right; I've seen what the so-called Third Reich can do, and I believe that this war will last a long time. Like Ruth, I gave my word to her father, and mine, that I would get them both to safety, and I'll succeed in doing that or die trying.'

A tear slid down Ruth's cheek, but Franz ploughed on.

'There's another factor which makes my decision easier. I don't want to be part of the horror that is infecting Germany, not because I'm afraid of fighting for my country, or for what we are doing to other nations' armies, but for what we are doing to our own people, and to innocent civilians abroad.'

'You know if you are caught, they shoot deserters?' Børge said.

'Yes, I'm willing to take that risk. So is Johann. We've spoken about it.'

'And you also know that if you are caught attempting to aid in the escape of two Jews over and above this, you will be crying out for a bullet, in the end?'

Ruth gave a small cry, but Franz didn't flinch.

'Yes. We know.'

The fisherman, grave now, turned to Ruth.

'And you and Manny will be separated, and you will both go to work camps. I hear that most die there, but they are sure to rape you first. And not just once.'

Ruth spoke in such a hushed tone, the others had to lean in to hear her voice above the whistle of the wind outside.

'Yes. I understand,' she said.

CHAPTER 142

Father and son handed Johann and Manny's sacks to Franz and passed over the fuel can, before they left, along with four cans of water. Franz filled *The Shearwater*'s tanks and passed the empty containers back to the Lunds.

'The storm has almost passed but the wind will blow for one more day,' Børge had said. 'Maybe two.'

Franz knew from the past that it was never prudent to ignore what men who worked the sea had to say about the weather.

'And when will the fog come?' he asked.

'Ah, yes, you'll need the fog. I can't say for certain, but if it comes, it will be when the wind dies. You should get your light winds then. If you are lucky, there'll be a bit of north in them, but more likely from the west.'

'I'll take that. I'll let you know one day if you were wrong.'

'Oh, I'm often wrong. But I'm right plenty too.' He laughed.

He'd turned and motioned to his son, who'd lifted a bundle from one corner of the deck.

'Here, drape these over the stern, it will make you less conspicuous, from a distance at least. Hang them on one of the stick markers when you leave.'

Børge and Peder grappled to pass over an old fishing net, festooned with cork floats and tied with a manila rope.

Franz grabbed the end, dragged it to the back of the cockpit and, ducking out from under the awning, hauled it up onto the stern rail, securing it with a couple of turns of line around the dropped mizzenmast, impressed at the fisherman's shrewdness.

'The *Arctic Moon*,' Franz said. 'It's quite a name for a boat.'

Børge laughed. 'You mean for a boat that never leaves sheltered waters?'

'No,' Franz said, blushing. 'I didn't mean that.'

'I was in the Arctic, on a trawler, when I was younger. I never saw a moon like it. When I bought this boat, that's what I called her.'

'I like it,' said Franz. 'She's a nice boat.'

Børge nodded.

'Johann and Manny will bring your own water containers,' he said. 'They left them on the shore by the tender. They should be with you by midnight at the latest. My wife packed a few extras in with the rest of your stuff. Just a few items that might make your voyage a bit less unpleasant.'

'Tell her we can't thank her enough, and we'll never forget the kindness you've shown us.' Franz had gripped the older man's hand and held onto it for a few seconds.

'Pah. We do this sort of thing every week.' The fisherman smiled. He gave Ruth a hug and whispered something in her ear that Franz didn't catch.

Blushing, she hugged Peder. 'Stay safe,' she told him, but he just grinned. While his father started the engine, he picked half a dozen fish from one of the wooden crates stacked on deck, tied the tails together with a piece of twine, and handed them to her, before unlooping the line from the yacht's stern cleat and pushing off with a gentle shove. When she looked up again, he was readying the gear at the back of the boat for their next haul.

Franz and Ruth watched as the *Arktisk Måne* puttered across towards Langli. They stood under their makeshift awning until the boat disappeared into the band of mist and rain that shrouded Hobo Dyb.

~~o~~

The telephone on the General's desk rang. He picked it up.

'Sir,' Frau Müller said, 'There's a call from Denmark for you. I couldn't quite make out his name.'

The General paled.

'Can I help you?' he said, when he heard the click of the connection being put through.

'Yes. I wish talk with General Kästner.'

'The General speaking. Who's calling?'

'I'm harbour master in Hirtshals. I speak with your sons, week ago.'

'Herr Harbour Master. Delighted to talk to you. Your German is very good, vi kan tale Dansk hvis du vil.' *We can speak Danish if you like.*

The man laughed.

'Danish or German, it doesn't matter to me. Perhaps you should speak Danish and I should speak German.'

It was the General's turn to laugh.

'My friend, what is your number? Can I call you back in a few minutes?'

'Of course.'

Erich Kästner scribbled the number on a scrap of paper. He replaced the handset and grabbed his coat, telling Frau Müller he would be out for a short while.

A few minutes later, in the first telephone kiosk he could find, he picked up the handset and dialled.

'I'm sorry about that,' he said to the Hirtshals harbour master when the man answered.

'That's not a problem,' the man said. 'You must be a busy man, with all these countries you're invading.'

The General laughed. He knew the man was taking a risk, but he either had no fear or was covering over his nerves with a flash of dark humour.

'The reason I called, Herr General,' the man continued, 'was let you know that two Gestapo mens have been nosing about up here, asking all strange sorts of questions.'

'Like what?' the General replied, glad that he'd had the foresight to call from a public telephone.

'Listen, Herr General. I took shine to your sons. They are decent Germans, and there are very few of them, these days. It doesn't matter to me what these Nazis do, but I thought you might like knowing. From what they say I think you are good man too.'

'Carry on, my friend,' the General said.

'They ask people if they'd seen anyone else on boat, or if they'd seen anyone leaving yacht, or if they meet with any fishing boat after leave. They even asked my wife if they buy feminine hygiene goods.'

The General laughed.

'My housekeeper's children went missing a few days *after* the boys left. Was it this Güllich fellow who visited you?'

'Yes. Vile small man. With equal bad friend.'

'He has a bee in his bonnet that my sons are somehow trying to smuggle these children out of Germany. It's preposterous.'

'I'm sure you say truth, Herr General. I thought you need know.'

'I do appreciate it, Herr Harbour Master, but there's no need to concern yourself, although we're still waiting for news of their safe arrival in Norway.'

'Your boys are being safe. They strike me as fine seaman. Fishermen here still talking about way they come in to Hirtshals Havn under sail.'

He paused.

'There's one last thing, General.'

'Yes, my friend?'

'We all wish them best luck.'

The General heard the phone click. He put the phone down and looked around.

This Güllich chap is more dangerous than I thought. And much brighter than I gave him credit for.

~~o~~

He wasn't back in the office more than a few minutes when the telephone rang again. It was the General's now daily call from Colonel Schneider. The General was still thinking about the harbour master's call and was only half-listening.

'I visited Konteradmiral Otto Schenk, in Kristiansand yesterday,' he heard Walther Schneider say. 'It appears that you two know each other.'

The General forced himself to concentrate.

'Yes. He used to be based in Kiel. He's Admiral der Norwegischen Südküste now.'

Norway was split up into four naval regions. The southern region's base, like the Gestapo's, was in Kristiansand. Otto Schenk was its commander.

'He's sending out two ships to scour the coast.'

'That's good news, Walther, although the boys will be embarrassed to have caused such a fuss.'

'He said they were heading to sea today anyway, and that they may as well patrol the coast as anywhere. I assure you that he didn't make a big deal of it, but…'

'Go on, Walther.'

'I may have dropped your name to get in to see the man.'

The General laughed.

'I have no problem with that. I've already spoken to Admiral Schiffer who assures me that all Kriegsmarine vessels in the Skagerrak are keeping an eye open for *Der Sturmtaucher*, but it does no harm to have a couple of ships doing a more thorough search.'

'Excellent. We should find them by the end of the day, or at least by tomorrow, I imagine, if they don't show up of their own accord before that.'

'I'll speak to you tomorrow, Walther.'

CHAPTER 143

On *The Shearwater*, when the gentle thud of the boat's engine faded to nothing, Franz turned, and seeing Ruth's face crumple, took the fish from her and laid it at the back of the cockpit.

'They're safe,' she mumbled.

He wrapped his arms around her and held her until her sobbing ceased.

'Sorry,' she said, giving him a smile, 'it was such a relief.'

He sat her down and lifted one of the sacks of supplies onto the cockpit seat.

'We'll eat well for a while,' he told her, opening first one and peering inside. 'Let's get this all stowed away first, then work out what to do with this fish.'

'Thank you,' she said. 'They were so kind. I couldn't help it. They were telling the truth, weren't they?'

'As far as I can judge a character, these were two of the finest people you'll come across. I'm sure Johann and Manny will say the same when they come back tonight.'

'That was so clever with the net. Do we really look like a fishing boat?'

'From a mile or more away, yes, and nobody should get any closer than that, unless we're very unlucky.'

Helping Franz stow the contents of the sacks in the lockers below deck seemed to distract her, cheering her up a little, and they were pleasantly surprised at just how much extra food Peder's mother had added to their list of essentials. It included vinegar, and a note from Tove.

Pickle some of the fish. It will last for the rest of your journey.

Franz looked out a couple of the jars that had been emptied on the voyage from Kiel and took them up on deck. Watched closely by Ruth, he gutted, filleted and salted the fish and, laying aside enough for their evening meal, he had her stack the rest into the jars and fill them to the brim with vinegar.

'There, that will last us a while. If we run out, we might even try and catch a few fish ourselves. We have handlines on board. I'm sure I've seen them somewhere.'

'Oh, that would be fun.' She looked at him and frowned. 'When you were talking about the weather, I was trying to listen. Does it mean we might be leaving tomorrow?'

'It will be the next day again at the earliest. Why?'

'I just want to get as far away from Germany as we can, and as soon as possible; the longer we stay here, the more likely we are to get caught. I mean, you never intended for us to come this far south, did you?'

'No, that was unfortunate, but we were always going to be at the mercy of the wind. Don't worry, we are better off tucked in here while there's no fog; it's an almost perfect spot. We'll just have to wait.'

'But what if it doesn't come? What do we do then?'

'It will. Fog is commonplace in this part of the North Sea at this time of year.'

~~o~~

Because Franz didn't sound too concerned, Ruth relaxed a little. She cut a few slices from one of the fresh loaves and they ate it in the cockpit with some cheese, and some salted beef, watching a pair of curlews as they probed along the mudflats with their long and slender curved beaks. She delighted in trying to mimic their call, *rrrrrrheww – rrrrrrheww – rrrrrrheww*, trying to entice them closer, but they took no notice.

Nestled up against Franz, sheltering from the wind that found the gaps in the canvas cover, she fell asleep. When she awoke, she was alone on deck, but she could hear him whistling in the cabin below. She peered over the washboards and watched him, trying not to make a sound.

He was working at the chart table, a jumble of equipment and navigational paraphernalia surrounding him. Everything he did was exact and methodical. She could have sat watching him all day, but he must have sensed being scrutinised and he looked up to see her leaning on the lip of the hatch, looking down at him.

'You're awake.'

'I have been for a while. I've been watching you work.'

'That would have been dull. Why don't you come inside?'

'It wasn't dull. I love watching you. You are quite handsome, you know, though you may be developing a bald spot.'

He laughed. 'You've seen my father. His bald spot is substantial. I'll end up the same.'

'I was only joking. You've just got a high forehead, and maybe a tiny little patch at the back with a few hairs missing.'

He reached up and grabbed her, and she toppled, screaming, into the cabin. He caught her easily, and lay her on the berth, tickling her sides until her laughs and squeals were loud enough to worry him.

He stopped teasing her and smothered her with kisses.

'We can't have you attracting attention,' he said.

~~o~~

All day, Johann and Manny stayed out of sight on the farm. Børge gave them jobs to do, to keep them from becoming nervous, or bored, as much as the need for help on his part.

He told them of Ruth's decision, that she'd made the same choice as Manny, and that Franz had agreed. He'd added that it was a decision which he respected.

'Do you want a rest before you leave?' he said. 'Tove says go into the house and get a few hours' sleep before tonight.'

'Tell her thanks, but we'd rather hole up in the loft we used the other day. It's close to the woods, and if the trucks come again, we can slip away into the trees.'

'That might be wise. When you do leave, better to go to the east side of the wood, facing Ho Bucht, rather than use the Skallingen road. Just in case.'

Børge showed Johann and Manny the map. It was old, but not much had changed in his part of the world since it was printed forty years or so before.

'Once it's dark, make your way down this edge of the wood then along between the wood and the shore of Ho Bucht. Keep following the treeline round and you'll reach the point where you came ashore yesterday, from the opposite direction. You'll find your mark on the tree, no bother.' He smiled when Johann looked at him, surprised.

'No one else would have seen it, don't worry. We just knew where to look.'

Johann shrugged. 'We'll leave just after sunset and try and get as far as we can with what light is left. Once it's too dark, we'll hole up in the woods until the moon comes up. That should be about half past ten.'

'Sounds about right. Good luck. And pass my best to Franz and Ruth. They make a nice couple.'

Johann wasn't sure if he'd heard right.

'I suppose they would,' he said, unsure.

Børge put his pipe in his mouth but didn't light it.

'Listen, I maybe shouldn't say this but try and cut them a little slack out there. Take care of Manny too.'

Johann nodded, confused, but he didn't want to appear stupid, or disagree with this man, whom he'd grown immensely fond of.

'We'll keep away from Hobo Dyb until you leave. If you need help, move the net to the bow of the boat, and someone will come to you.'

'Thank you.'

'There's something you should know. Tove was in Esbjerg today. She saw a notice on the wall of the police station. It had a picture of Ruth and Manny on it. Now, even more, you can't afford to get caught.'

'It makes no difference. If we're caught, we're dead.'

Børge flinched.

He held out his arms and embraced Johann. 'You'll get there. I can feel it in my bones.'

'Thank you. I don't have the words to say how much your help has meant. I'm not stupid either.'

He hesitated.

453

'When we were burying ourselves in the grain, in the silo...'

Børge's face hardened.

'Go on.'

'My hand touched something that wasn't meant to be there. Something hard and metallic.'

'Ah, that would be my old shovel. I wondered where it had gone.'

'Yes, an old shovel, indeed.' Johann smiled. 'Or possibly something else.'

'Sometimes it's useful to keep a shovel hidden somewhere just in case you need it.'

'Well, please take care; you don't want to get caught hiding something like that. And don't underestimate the German state's power, its efficiency, or its ability to be cruel and heartless.'

Børge smiled and put his hand on Johann's shoulder.

'These are dangerous days, for the likes of you and I. We must do what is right, but don't worry, we will take care.'

Børge walked over to Manny.

'Look after your sister and these two boys. I'm relying on you. And don't ever forget something that Børge Lund once told you. You are a unique young man, perhaps the bravest person I have ever met, and for someone your age...' He gave the boy a huge hug.

'Chazak v'ematz, Manny.'

He turned away and walked across the yard before any of them could see the tears in his eyes.

~~o~~

Out on Hobo Dyb, the remains of Franz and Ruth's second day alone had been strange. Almost like a holiday, *or a honeymoon*, Franz thought, but full of underlying tensions; neither of them could rid their minds of thoughts of their siblings, holed up, apprehensive, waiting for night to fall.

The raw physical need to consume each other, for the present, had gone, and just being together, talking about the past and avoiding the future, was enough. The remnants of the storm still whipped up plumes of sand from the dunes protecting them, but with nowhere near the intensity as before, and in their sheltered haven, they passed the rest of the day cleaning and airing the boat, making minor repairs to the masts and mending a couple of small rips in the sails.

As evening approached, they both caught the other taking covert glances at the shore, despite knowing that Johann and Manny would not show themselves before darkness fell.

Eating their evening meal, of fresh fish and bread, gave them less pleasure than it should have, and even though the clock was running down on their time alone together, they felt no need to return to the forecabin and make love one last time.

Instead, they sat close together, each with their own thoughts, but never uncomfortable.

Ruth got up and reached in to the forecabin and drew out her small leather bag, one of the few things she'd brought with her; it held a few personal items and, Franz suspected, a little money and perhaps a few pieces of jewellery, enough to give her and Manny something to start with when they reached England.

'Here,' she said, pulling out a piece of paper and handing it to him. 'I promised you I'd show you this.'

He unfolded it, and he felt his eyes fill with tears.

'Antje's drawing. Ein Sturmtaucher. I was there when she drew it. She gave it to you?'

'Yes. For me to remember her by. Not that I'd ever forget. She is a true friend.'

'She's the one I'll miss most of all, besides my father.'

'I'll miss them all. Every one of them,' Ruth said.

They sat together for an hour until it was time to go up on deck, talking about those they had left behind. Both their parents, Antje and Eva, and their grandparents.

As the light faded, and their second night of vigil began, the wind, which had died down a little during the day, began to build and veer to the north, stinging their faces as they peered into the darkness.

CHAPTER 144

Carl Meyer was tired and not a little annoyed. Not once had Heinrich Güllich offered to drive.

They'd arrived back in Kiel around six and, hoping to get home for a bath, and a fill of his father's Rindereintopf, the hearty beef stew that they had every Monday evening, he'd brought the car to a halt outside Gestapo Headquarters and got his bag from the trunk.

'Goodnight, Herr Kriminalassistent,' he said, giving a quick salute, and walking away.

'And where do you think you're going, Kriminalassistentanwärter?'

Carl Meyer stopped, frowning.

'Home, sir?' he said.

'No, no, no,' Heinrich Güllich said, wagging his finger. 'We aren't finished yet.'

It had been a frustrating twenty-four hours since they'd left Skagen with the information that, if not conclusive, had set their own minds at rest that the Nussbaum siblings had been on *The Shearwater.*

On their return to Hirtshals, they went back to the port, asking about the Kästners and *The Shearwater*, and looking for the sailor who'd sent them on a wild goose chase, but the freighter had left and wouldn't be back for a week, at least. The harbour master didn't recognise the man they described but said he would be happy to call them when the ship returned, if they wished to visit again.

Nobody they questioned had noticed anything strange about *The Shearwater*, or the Kästner brothers' behaviour. The fisherman who'd spoken to Franz had not arrived in Hirtshals until midnight and, after spending an hour grilling him with little return, it had been one-thirty by the time Heinrich Güllich and Carl Meyer had fallen into their beds in the worst room in Hirtshals, next door to the hotel kitchen.

Four short hours later, they woke, still tired, as the room echoed to the sounds of clattering pans and shouting cooks, preparing breakfast for the early risers.

At Bogense, the harbour master reiterated what he'd said on the telephone, adding little else, and the people of Bogense had scant knowledge that *The Shearwater* had even docked there. Only a couple of fishermen and a dockworker remembered anything about the yacht, and their comments were limited to the fact that she was a good-looking, solid boat, of the kind that's rarely seen nowadays.

It had been a long journey back to Kiel, and Carl Meyer was exhausted.

'But I-I...' he stuttered, when Güllich vetoed his plans for a restful evening with his father.

'But nothing,' the Kriminalassistent said, striding towards the headquarters' entrance. 'We have work to do.'

Carl Meyer followed his boss, the anger bubbling up within him.

It's all right for you. You slept for much of the journey.

'We need to phone Werner Schmidt. Tell him to leave the Nussbaums until later in the week; we should have found *The Shearwater* by then. And tell him that we'll come and talk to him first, to show him what we've got.'

'Yes, sir. Would it be easier if he came here?'

'Yes. Good thinking, Meyer. It will unsettle him a little, perhaps. Even policemen get nervous in Gestapo Headquarters.'

He laughed for a few seconds then stopped, as if every joke he made was allotted a specified measure of amusement.

'While you're doing that,' he said, 'phone our friendly Kriminalassistent in Aarhus; get him to visit Hirtshals next week. I'm sure he would be delighted to have a word with our clever friend from the freighter when he hears how obstructive the man was in our investigation.'

Carl Meyer laughed, but he would rather have been there himself to deliver a message in person to the man who had made a fool of them in so casual a manner.

'And the woman. The harbour master's wife, with the shop. I believe the local tax inspector should make a thorough examination of her affairs, and her husband's.'

'They'll both be as clean as a newborn's Arschloch,' Carl Meyer said. 'They seemed like very upright citizens.'

'It doesn't matter. Any investigation will cause them endless worry and, despite what you say, everyone has something to hide.'

CHAPTER 145

Johann and Manny watched from the loft while the family worked long into the evening, completing the daily tasks that filled most of their waking hours. As night fell, and they readied themselves for the journey back to the boat, Johann wondered if Ruth and Manny had made the right decision.

They set out as soon as the light had faded enough for them to slip unseen into the wood, and crept along the edge, a few metres inside the outermost trees. The farm was all quiet now, and only a lamp in the kitchen gave a clue that someone was still awake.

At first, they made good progress, but as the light failed, it became difficult to avoid bumping into trees, stumbling over roots, or being whipped across the face by low branches.

'We'll stop here,' Johann told Manny. 'It's too dark to see my hand in front of my face.'

He heard Manny breathe a sigh of relief and found a low bush that they could crawl under.

'It'll be easier when the moon's up. When is that?'

'About half past ten. Try and get some rest before then.'

They settled down for the wait. By the time the moonlight began to filter through the branches, they were anxious to get moving. In places, there was a sort of path; they couldn't tell if it had been made by human or animal but at times it disappeared, and they would find themselves scrabbling through thick undergrowth, not quite knowing where they were putting their feet.

They had hoped to find the tree that marked their way before midnight, but it was well after one by the time they reached it and changed back into the muddy clothes and boots they'd hidden.

Shining their torch out into the marsh, Johann hoped that their reflective beacon would still be visible, despite the strong wind.

Nothing. When Manny spoke, there was an edge to his voice.

'What do we do if it's not there?'

'They'll see our torch flashing on *The Shearwater* when they next check. That'll be at two o'clock. I only hope we're not too far away for them to see us. Worst comes to worst, we can wait till first light, but that would be risky.'

Manny took a turn with the torch, and this time Johann stood ten paces to his left.

'Stop there.'

Manny froze, keeping the beam steady.

'Go back a little, nice and slowly.'

'There.' Both Manny and Johann spotted the faint glimmer in the distance. It flickered, but it was there all the same.

'I'll walk towards it. You keep shining the torch on it.'

Johann made to set off

'What if someone sees the light?'

'I wouldn't worry, Manny, it's pointing out across Hobo Dyb. Apart from Franz and Ruth, there should be no one else out there. The beam's not strong enough to be seen in the main channel.'

Johann stumbled forward in the dark, trying to keep sight of the small point of reflected light, and when he got halfway, he hissed to Manny that he should follow him. Looking at the moon, he gauged the direction they were heading in case they couldn't find the silver mark again.

Manny switched the torch off. Johann gave a few low whistles to guide him, and after one or two minor detours, Manny stood beside him.

'Why didn't you use the torch?' Johann asked.

'To save its batteries,' Manny replied, 'but I was also worried that a moving torch would be a giveaway if there was anyone around.'

'Good thinking, Manny. Now, Let's get to the tender before we freeze.'

This time, being closer, it was easy to pick up the silver marker, trembling in the wind, and they reached it without mishap.

Johann checked his watch. *One-fifty.* 'Flash the torch towards *The Shearwater*, over there.' He looked at the position of the moon and pointed where he thought the yacht should be. 'Long-short-long-short.'

Manny pointed the torch and tapped out the rhythm on the switch.

'That's Morse 'C', isn't it?' he said to Johann.

'Yes, how the hell do you know that?'

'We did it at school. I remembered it.'

'I'm impressed.' Johann nodded out to Hobo Dyb. 'Flash once more. If they don't reply, we'll wait until two o'clock, then try again.'

Manny flicked the switch twice and, in the distance, ten degrees to the left of where they'd been looking, a double green flash answered them.

'They've seen us,' they both said, turning and hugging each other.

'You'd better answer,' Johann said, and Manny flashed back again. The green light flickered twice then went out but, a few seconds later, it lit again, and this time it stayed on.

'Now, all we need to do is find this tender. You stay here. Shine the torch if I ask.'

Johann walked towards *The Shearwater*'s light, stumbling at times where the grassy loam gave way to marsh or small creeks, but it didn't take him as long as he expected, counting out the paces.

The dinghy was where it was meant to be, and he breathed out a sigh of relief. He whistled to Manny, who uprooted the withy stick, and made his way towards Johann, guided by the green light out on Hobo Dyb.

'You brought the marker. Good thinking,' Johann said, clapping Manny on the back.

Wasting no time, they turned the tender onto its keel, and loaded up the water containers and their spare clothes. Johann tied a second painter onto the bow of the boat and, grabbing one line each, they began pulling it towards the light.

'This will be a bit of a wade. It's nearly low water, and it could be a long time before we're afloat. We were meant to be here a couple of hours ago.'

'I don't care. I just want to get back.'

Johann looked at him in the darkness.

He's desperate to see Ruth. It's easy to forget he's still a child, deep down.

At first, the going was easy, because they could walk on the solid ground, one on each side of the narrow channel, but when they reached the end of the small creek, a vast expanse of mud stretched out before them.

Placing one foot in front of the other, they had sunk in above their knees at first, and every half metre was an effort. They discovered that it was easier to take three or four steps, letting the rope run through their fingers, then pull the boat towards them across the mud, taking up the slack.

Once or twice, especially as the mud grew deeper, Manny became stuck fast, struggling to free either of his feet from the sucking mud.

'Pull the tender as close to you as possible and use it to lift yourself up.'

It worked, and twice more Manny had to release himself again.

It took them an hour of slogging before they reached the water's edge and, even then, it was only a couple of centimetres deep. The boat slid a little better, but the mud became deeper, now above Manny's waist, and movement became so much of an effort for him, that progress almost stopped.

It's not his fault. He's exhausted, but he is slowing us up.

Johann told him to climb in. At first, Manny tried to argue, but Johann insisted, so he hauled himself up over the gunwale of the small dinghy. It took all his strength, and Johann's help, pushing from below, before he flopped into the bottom of the boat, gasping for air.

Johann gave him a minute to recover.

'Use the paddle in the mud to help me,' he said.

Although Manny's weight made the tender sink a little deeper into the mud, Johann found it easier to pull with Manny's assistance.

Progress was slow. It took all Johann's strength and resilience just to move one step and, with each metre, the mud deepened. As he sank in further, what little water there was crept up to the top of his chest. The boat was afloat, but he knew that with his weight in it, the keel would sink back into the mud and they would be stuck, so he battled on for another five minutes. When a small wave caught him unawares and splashed his face, causing him to choke on a mouthful of brackish water, he felt the cold fear of panic rise, and he began to struggle.

Sensing himself sinking further into the mud with every movement, he forced himself to stay calm, and hauling on the painter, tried to pull himself up. The mud's grip tightened on his legs, and another wave washed over his face. He couldn't remember the exact time the tide turned, but a vision of being stuck in the ooze on the rising flood flashed into his thoughts. His heart hammered loudly in his chest, and he began to shake.

From above, he felt a hand grip the scruff of his shirt and heave, and he made a determined effort to free himself, pulling on the rope as hard as he could.

He wriggled his toes and felt his right foot slide from his boot. The left foot refused to let go but with a final effort, he managed to straighten it out and, with less resistance, the boot slowly released itself from the mud, bubbles of putrid gas bursting at the surface as his foot slowly slid upwards. As he grabbed at the gunwale of the boat with his left hand, his own weight and Manny's on the same side of the boat threatened to capsize it.

'Let go, Manny,' Johann warned.

As Manny did as he was told, Johann slipped back a little, and the boat righted itself, throwing Manny onto his back.

'Pass me down the other rope and sit on the far side of the boat to pull me up. It will act as a counterbalance.'

Manny nodded, and after giving Johann the spare painter, he leaned back, bracing his feet against the inside of the hull. Johann tied the rope under his arms and around his chest and told Manny to pull. With his help, Johann hauled himself up and grabbed the gunwale, first with one hand, then the other. He hung there for a second to catch his breath then, summoning up the last of his reserves, he pulled himself up until his chest was resting on the edge. Ignoring the pain, he clung on while Manny tied the rope he was holding to the rowlock, grabbed hold of him under his arms, and hauled him into the tender.

Gasping, Johann tried to thank him, but he hardly had the strength, and his violent shivering rendered what words he managed to utter unintelligible.

Manny took off his coat and wrapped it around him. Johann, drenched and mud-caked, had lost one of his boots, and his chest heaved from his efforts to haul himself up.

Manny grabbed an oar, and kneeling in the bow, tried to pull them along, first on one side, and then the other. The small dinghy swung from side to side, making almost no headway. Behind him, he heard movement, and to his surprise, he felt Johann push in beside him with the second oar and together, they began to move forward, a centimetre or two at a time.

With each metre the boat edged through the mud, it began to slide forward a little easier until, with a sudden lurch, it released itself from the mud, afloat at last.

'Do you want me to row?' Manny said. 'You look terrible.'

'No,' Johann said, talking through chattering teeth. 'I need to keep warm, and sculling will help.'

They worked together, one kneeling on each side, keeping the green light straight ahead of them. The north wind worked in their favour, coming from behind them, and although it had an extra bite of chill to it, it pushed them towards the yacht in half the time. As they approached, Johann sat back and let Manny steer the dinghy with his oar, slowing down and curving into *The Shearwater*'s hull as if he'd done it all his life. A hand reached out from behind the light and grabbed the painter that Manny held out and lashed it to one of the cleats.

~~o~~

'Are you all right?' Franz said, grabbing the tender's gunwale to steady it. 'We thought you'd got lost.'

'We were late getting there, and the tide had gone out. We had to wade through half a mile of mud. Johann is just about freezing to death, and we're covered in sludge.'

'Get him aboard as quick as we can.' Franz turned to Ruth, standing beside him, desperate to see that her brother was all right.

'Fetch a few blankets and light the charcoal burner in the cabin.'

He handed Manny a bucket, and a soft brush.

'I know it sounds cruel but help Johann to get his clothes off and wash him down before he gets on board. We'll get him warmed up quicker that way.'

From what he could see of Johann, Franz knew that if he didn't get him into the cabin and warmed up quickly, he could collapse.

'Put the kettle on too,' he shouted to Ruth. 'He'll need something warm inside him.'

Manny had already removed Johann's one remaining boot, and his trousers. With what little help Johann could give, he pulled his jumper and shirt over his head. Most of the mud was on his clothes, so it only took one bucketful of seawater to clean the rest from his legs and arms. Stripped to his underpants, he staggered to his feet and clambered up onto the yacht with Manny's help. Franz caught him as he fell into the cockpit, wrapping a blanket round him with a big bear hug.

'I'm fine, I'm fine,' Johann whispered, barely audible. 'Help Manny.'

'Let's get you below first. Ruth will get you warmed up,' Franz said.

He helped Johann descend the companionway steps, and Ruth gently sat him down. Even in the moonlight, Franz saw the shock on her face at Johann's appearance. He touched her arm in thanks.

'He'll be all right. Get him another blanket. And fill a hot water bottle.'

'Of course,' she said, shaken into action.

Franz turned his attention to Manny. Not only had the boy already stripped off and washed himself, but he'd also put all the filthy clothes in the empty bucket and had lifted it over the gunwale into the cockpit.

Franz helped him aboard and handed him a blanket, which he wrapped around himself. He was shivering a little, but managed a smile when Franz embraced him too.

'Well done, Manny, you did a great job. Thanks for that.'

The teenager blushed, but the smile on his face grew wider.

An arm around him, Franz ushered him over to the companionway, and once they were both in the warm cabin, he slid the washboards in, and closed the hatch, leaving just a sliver of a gap for ventilation.

With the hatch closed, Ruth lit the oil lamp, and looked at the two half-naked men wrapped in their blankets. Tears flowed down her cheeks as she busied herself making coffee for them all. Franz rummaged about in Johann's sea bag and produced a dry pair of underpants. Holding Johann's towel to shield him, he helped Johann change his last piece of wet clothing.

'It's good to have you both back,' Franz said.

~~o~~

Manny, because his things were up front, disappeared into the forecabin and emerged a minute later, dressed in fresh clothes.

'You've recovered quickly,' Ruth said.

'I wasn't in the mud for as long, or in so deep. Johann was up to his neck by the end. I never want to see another mudflat again.'

Franz and Ruth laughed. They were all clasping steaming cups of coffee, and the heat in the cabin had brought a tinge of colour and life back into Johann's face, but he still shivered, in bouts that shook the whole table. He took a long sip of coffee and sighed as the warm glow in his stomach spread.

'I'll have nightmares about it. I thought I was done for. If it hadn't been for Manny...'

The boy blushed, delighting in the praise, first from Franz, and now from Johann, knowing deep down that he'd earned it. The truth was, despite the pain of leaving his parents behind, he felt more alive and worthwhile than he ever had.

Growing up under the National Socialists as a young Jewish boy had robbed him of a large part of his childhood, and his self-respect, despite his family and the Kästners doing everything possible to shield him from the worst of it.

Now, he was on a remarkable adventure and, even with the dangers and discomforts, he, of the four of them, relished it the most.

'Let's all get some sleep, and we'll talk about it in the morning,' Franz said. 'We're exhausted. I'll do two-hourly checks, but everyone else stays in their bunks. Tomorrow, we'll make our preparations. It looks like we'll be leaving the following day.'

CHAPTER 146

Yosef watched as General Kästner's army car pulled into the driveway. The driver jumped out and climbed the steps to the front door.

Yosef opened it.

'The General will be with you shortly,' he said. 'He's taking a telephone call at present.'

Yosef closed the door again. He turned and looked down the hall. The General was quietly remonstrating with someone, and Yosef couldn't help but overhear.

'Walther,' the General said, 'I understand that you're upset, but it's ridiculous to suggest that Franz and Johann would have been careless, or reckless.'

The General's face darkened as he listened, and Yosef turned away, embarrassed.

'I agree. It is a matter of grave concern that the two Kriegsmarine boats have seen nothing and, yes, I would have expected the boys to be on the move by now, as the wind has reduced considerably.'

Yosef stood still, not knowing quite where to look.

'Walther, I'm afraid I cannot leave that unanswered. You and I both agreed that the boat couldn't have been in better hands and...'

The General turned and rolled his eyes at Yosef, before speaking again, a hint of anger in his voice for the first time.

'Don't forget that a boat is replaceable, Walther. People aren't. If, as you're implying, *The Shearwater* has sunk, I'd be sorry for your loss, but it would be *nothing* compared to ours.'

The General listened for a minute.

'It's all right, Walther. I know that you didn't mean it like that, and that you always have your men's welfare at heart. I'll speak with the Kriegsmarine command and get them to redouble their efforts, and telephone you tomorrow, if not later today.'

He listened again.

'Uh-huh,' he said. 'That's fine. Auf wiedersehen.'

The General put the handpiece down.

He looked around and gave Yosef a long-suffering look.

'I take it that Colonel Schneider is suspicious,' Yosef said.

'No, Yosef. Just worried, and angry.'

He sighed.

'This is just the start of it. I'll have to call them in as missing now; I only hope they're far enough away to stay undetected. Don't say anything to Frau Kästner just yet.'

'I won't, sir.' He handed the General his briefcase.

~~o~~

At eleven-thirty, the General reported *The Shearwater* and her crew missing. He spoke with a few of the senior commanders first, and they all agreed it was the right thing to do; by officially listing the boys as missing, crews on board Kriegsmarine ships in the area would be more vigilant in looking for them.

'But remember we're at war,' Admiral Schiffer told him, in the Baltic commander's office, 'so we can't launch a full-scale search per se.'

'I fully understand. Please do what you can.'

'We will, Erich. The best I can do is to increase patrols for forty-eight hours. We can claim we've had intelligence about enemy ship movements.'

'Thank you.'

'I believe Wilhelmshaven have offered support as well.'

'I appreciate that, but I'd hate to see the whole of the Kriegsmarine mobilised just because of who I am, so please tell them that it won't be necessary.'

'That's very commendable of you, Erich, especially as you must be worried sick.'

The General slumped.

'I fully expected them to appear from one of the many sheltered anchorages, Rolf, but perhaps I was kidding myself.'

'From all accounts, they should have been able to make it to safety but, as you know, the sea can be a harsh mistress. Don't lose hope yet; even if the yacht has foundered, they could still have made it ashore, somewhere.'

'If I'm honest, it's becoming difficult to stay hopeful. And I haven't even told Maria yet.'

'Go home. Be with your family. I promise we'll let you know the moment we have any news.'

The General thanked him and left. It saddened him to have to be untruthful to so many good people, but it had been the only way to buy *Der Sturmtaucher*'s crew time. If, as he hoped, it would get the younger Nussbaums to safety, it would be worth it.

And, he admitted to himself, it might allow his sons to survive the war, and not be tainted by the madness that had engulfed their country.

~~o~~

'I've reported *Der Sturmtaucher* as missing, Walther,' the General said, his voice flat and resigned.

'I believe that's the right thing to do, Erich.'

There was none of the former belligerence in the colonel's manner now.

'I know there's still hope for them, but I'm afraid *Der Sturmtaucher* has gone.'

'No matter. I just pray that Franz and Johann will be found safe. That's all that matters now.'

'Thank you for your understanding, Walther. I'll do everything from this end to find them, and I know you'll do the same.'

The General hung up.

'This will be the most difficult time of all,' he said to Antje, who was standing in the door of the drawing room. She'd been listening.

'I know. It's keeping up the lies that's so hard, but I suppose that every day we can keep it going gives them a fighting chance to get away.'

'I keep telling myself that,' he said, sighing.

He looked her in the eye.

'I'll be straight with you, Antje. We may not be lying; the storm may have claimed them already and, the worst of it is, we might never know.'

A tear rolled down Antje's cheek. The General took her in his arms and held her. They waited for Maria and Eva to return.

~~o~~

Maria took the news that both her sons were missing with a cold anger that shocked the General. He'd expected tears, and maybe blame but she spoke in a chilled even tone without shedding a tear.

'You and your friend, the colonel, should have known,' she said. 'And Franz. He should have known too.'

'None of us could have predicted that storm, Maria. There hasn't been one like it in a decade.'

'That's not an excuse. You encouraged them. Admit it.'

He bowed his head.

'It was my suggestion in the first place for the colonel to take the boat to Norway, but it was the boys themselves who jumped at the chance. Part of me wishes I'd gone with them, but Franz is as capable as I am, and Johann isn't far behind. It would have made little difference.'

'They would always have chosen to do something like that if it were offered to them. And you and the colonel did just that. And now they're gone, drowned at sea.'

Eva let out a cry.

'There's still hope,' the General said, a desperate note in his voice. 'The Kriegsmarine are doing their best.'

'I'm not willing to listen to your platitudes, Erich. You know as well as I do that they're not coming home. If I'd lost them to the war, it would have been terrible, but like this...'

She turned to walk out of the room.

'I'll be upstairs,' she said. 'I don't wish to be disturbed.'

When she'd gone, Eva looked at her father, her eyes red, with tears running down her cheeks. She glanced at the door, confused as to whether to go after Maria, or if her mother's desire to be away from everyone included her.

His voice softened. 'Give her a little time, Eva, then go to her,' he said.

'I can't believe anything has happened to them, and I wish I'd said goodbye properly to them when they went away.'

'We all do,' the General said, his voice cracking. It broke his heart to lie to his own daughter, but he knew it was for her own protection. If they were ever caught, and it all came out, her genuine protestations that she wasn't a part of it might just save her life.

~~o~~

When Antje passed her mother's door an hour later, she heard crying and presumed that Eva was in the room with her, but when she heard the toilet flush, and her sister appeared from the bathroom and headed straight to her own room without noticing her, she realised it was her mother who was in tears.

She gripped the door handle, but hesitated. Blurting out the truth to save her mother from her grief would help no one, and she couldn't trust herself not to tell her.

She crept along the landing to her own bedroom. She looked at the collection of framed photographs on her dresser; one of the whole family, another of the boys as junior officers, in their uniforms, and one of her and Eva, by the lake in summer, a few years before.

She didn't want to think they would never be together again.

CHAPTER 147

At an hour past midnight, torpedo boat *T4* docked in Kiel. Korvettenkapitän Werner von Loringhoven turned to Rainer Schulze.

'You have the ship, Kapitänleutnant.'

The lines were all fast and the vessel's engines had been shut down, the generators taking over the task of providing power to run the ship on her berth.

'Have a good trip home, sir,' Rainer Schulze said. He turned to the third officer, who would help run the skeleton crew taking care of *T4* while she was in harbour.

'Take a signal to command HQ, third. Torpedo boat *T4* on berth.'

'Yes, sir.' The man turned and made for the gangplank, and the telephone on the mole.

'I'll be back in forty-eight hours, Kapitänleutnant. See to it that the repairs are completed before then,' the captain said.

'Yes, sir.'

~~o~~

'It's the talk of Kiel, sir,' Carl Meyer said.

'I find it hard to believe. Missing? I mean, really?'

'Yes, sir. They're looking at an area from where the Kästner brothers were last seen right across to Oslo fjord.'

Heinrich Güllich thumped his fist onto the table, then sat down, rubbing his temples.

'They're lying. They've fooled everyone. I can't believe they're running a search for a missing yacht in the middle of a war.'

'The Kriegsmarine deny that it's a search,' Carl Meyer said. 'They say they are merely doing extra patrols due to an escalation in the risk of enemy shipping in the area and that all Kriegsmarine vessels have been instructed to look out for signs of *Der Sturmtaucher* and the Kästner brothers while on patrol.'

'Bullshit. Where did you get this from?'

'I took the liberty of visiting the command centre as soon as I heard. I couldn't get hold of you.'

'I was out. Another case.'

'I thought you would want all the information I could get, sir.'

'You did well, Meyer,' the Kriminalassistent said. 'Part of me hopes they all drowned; all four of them. But I want their bodies recovered, so that I can see them lying on the slab and watch General Kästner's face when he has to identify them.'

'They may not find them, sir, or it may be months before they turn up on shore somewhere.'

Heinrich Güllich grunted. He lit a cigarette.

'Tell the Kriegsmarine to keep us posted. And we need to keep looking in Denmark for the Nussbaum brats, and maybe even Norway. The Kästners could have landed them, then tried to move up the coast, away from the drop-off area.'

'How long do we search for, sir?'

'Until we know they are dead, or we've exhausted every lead.'

'And the General?'

'We're going to pay him a visit.'

~~o~~

'Kapitänleutnant.'

'General.'

Grim-faced, Rainer Schulze and General Kästner shook hands.

'I hope you don't mind me coming aboard. I came as soon as I heard you'd docked.'

'Not at all, General. It's a shame that we meet again in such distressing circumstances.'

'I had to speak to you. You were the last person to see my sons. Thank you for allowing me on board.'

'For you, General, anything.'

'Thank you, Kapitänleutnant. I need to know what happened when you met them.'

Rainer Schulze took a deep breath.

'We'd received a command by radio to intercept and search any small vessel we found in the Skagerrak. We assumed we were looking for fishing boats transporting partisans from Denmark to Norway, or vice versa, or even Jews from Denmark to Sweden.'

'That makes sense,' the General said.

'We knew *The Shearwater* was on her way to Norway and I joked with Captain von Loringhoven that we might come across her. When we saw their sails a few miles in front of us, we were surprised, and delighted.'

'What was the weather like, at that point?'

'It was lumpy. There was a decent wind blowing but nothing that they couldn't cope with. We stopped and hailed them, kept them in our lee.'

'And you boarded them, I'm told.'

Rainer Schulze reddened.

'We discussed whether we should or not, but the captain decided that it would be unfair and unprofessional to make any exceptions to our orders. I said that I'd like to go, since I knew your sons, and it tickled me to meet with them like this, in the middle of the Skagerrak.'

'So, you went on board.'

'Yes. It was good to see them, and I was a tad jealous, I'll admit. I'd have loved to have done the trip with them. I'm sure we would have got on well. Anyway, I apologised to them for having to conduct a search, but they were very understanding, and showed me through every locker and cubbyhole on the boat.'

'You found nothing, I'd imagine, unless Johann had somehow hooked up with a Danish girl.'

'Nothing,' Rainer Schulze said, laughing, 'not even a girl, though I got the feeling that they were rather nervous. They kept glancing at each other. I presume that they just wanted to get on; I'd told them that there was some serious weather on the way.'

'And you said in your report that you advised them to divert to Langesund, or somewhere further east?'

'Yes. There was no way they were going to make Grimstad. They had already been forced off course, and we'd been told that all vessels should make harbour by nightfall.'

'And when you left them, they were heading in the direction of Langesund?'

'Yes. We tracked them on our radar for a few miles until we lost them. They were heading north-east. They should have made it to shelter by early evening, before the worst of the storm hit. I was surprised to learn that they hadn't shown up, but the storm was terrible, sir. Even in harbour we had an uncomfortable time of it, forever having to adjust warps and fenders.'

'I assumed they'd taken shelter somewhere isolated, where they were out of contact,' the General said, bowing his head.

'That's what we thought, General. Part of me still expects them to sail into Kristiansand and wonder what all the fuss has been about.'

'I keep hoping that myself, Kapitänleutnant.'

He held out his hand.

'Thank you.'

CHAPTER 148

'Heavvvvvve.'

The main mast moved upwards two or three centimetres in the darkness, and Ruth slid the batten forward, supporting the thick round spar in its new position. Standing at the bow, Johann let the strain off the rope, and took a breather. Towards the stern, where the top of the mast had lain on the deck, Franz and Manny rubbed their hands, sore from pulling on the rope running through the block lashed to the top of the bare mizzenmast, lifting the main mast like a crane.

'The first bit is the hardest, as we're lifting the whole weight of the mast,' Franz said.

They had hoisted the mizzenmast first, with relative ease.

Raising the masts was the last big task they had to complete before their departure the following day and they'd left it until dark, so as not to attract unwanted attention.

'Heavvvvvve.'

This time, the mast rose half a metre, and again Ruth moved the support forward, taking the strain off the rope.

'Well done everyone. Keep it going like this and we'll have it done in no time.'

Inwardly, Franz was worried. It was a heavy mast, and once it was nearly upright, it would be difficult to hold steady. If it fell, it could kill someone, or damage itself, or the boat.

'Heavvvvvve.'

It rose another half metre.

Franz made sure the shrouds, the part of the rigging that stopped the mast from falling sideways, were running through their blocks. As the mast lifted, he would cleat them off with just enough slack for the next hoist. The running backstays were loose and would stay like that until the mast was vertical, when they would act to stop the mast toppling forward. He'd calculated the final length they should be and had tied them off on a cleat. He could tighten each rope and make fine adjustments to all the rigging once the mast was fully raised.

He checked the tabernacle, the large, hollowed block of wood at the bottom of the mast which acted like a hinge.

Once the main mast was almost at the top of the mizzen, and Ruth had securely wedged it with a thicker batten, Franz and Manny moved to the bow of the boat with Johann, and they all pulled on the forestay, which now had enough angle to swing the mast forwards.

Franz adjusted the shrouds; he didn't want too much strain on the tabernacle at the mast's base and, although the thick metal pin and the bearings it sat in had a little give in them, too much sideways movement could have grave consequences.

In their favour, the wind had dropped during the day, and the surface of the water was smooth. The fog they were waiting for had arrived at sunset, the day after the boys had returned to the boat. There wasn't a breath of wind, but Franz hoped that Børge was right about it filling in again; they needed a breeze to move the yacht without having to resort to using the engine.

Twenty minutes later, with a final lurch, the mast reached the vertical. Franz secured the forestay to the deck and adjusted it at the block on the mast, before cleating it off. He did the same with the backstay and the shrouds and let out a long, slow, breath. It would still need adjusting, but at least the danger of it falling had gone.

Over the next two hours, working almost blind in the blackness, they added the gaff, the large wooden pole that held the top edge of the mainsail up, and the boom, which held the sail down, to the mast. The sails were next, and they hoisted them to check that all the lines were running, with no snags. The canvas hung limply in the damp stillness, and Johann looked at his brother, wondering, like Franz, if Børge's light westerlies would materialise.

~~o~~

[16/04/1941 Wednesday]

As soon as Franz woke the next morning, he knew that their wind had arrived. He felt the faint tremble through the boat's rigging and heard the soft slap of ripples on her hull. He pulled back the curtains, worried that the wind had blown the fog away, but he exhaled in relief when he could see nothing beyond fifty metres, except for the mist swirling over the water in the light westerly breeze.

He worked in silence, stowing all loose gear, readying the yacht for departure. He was in no rush; although he'd risen early, unable to sleep beyond sunrise, he had no intentions of leaving until after eight, an hour and a half before high tide, when there should be enough water in the small channel he aimed to pass through.

He was soon joined by the others; no matter how quiet he'd tried to be, the compact nature of the boat and the wooden construction of the decks meant that every little sound was amplified.

During breakfast, he ran through the plan to get out of Hobo Dyb unseen.

'Even with the fog, we can't use the main channel, because vessels could come in or out at any time, and although we may be able to keep to the edges, even if we didn't get washed ashore or swept under, I'm sure we would be seen.'

He pulled out a chart and pointed to Graa Dyb. 'The main channel runs straight out for about four miles, but it would be deep enough on either side at high water for us to veer off after half that distance, but that two miles will take us at least twenty minutes, longer if we don't put the engine on.'

'Can't we just chance it? Hardly anything's moved in or out since we've been here.' Johann was always more of a risk-taker than Franz.

'There were one or two when you and Manny were onshore, but anyway, now that the storm is over, I would imagine Kriegsmarine ships and the odd fishing vessel will start heading out today.'

As if to prove his point, a distant horn sounded, and Franz couldn't resist opening out his hands in a told-you-so gesture.

Johann punched his arm, and Franz grinned. His smugness had perhaps warranted the punishment.

'There's a narrow cut almost directly across the main channel from the entrance to Hobo Dyb,' Franz continued, his face becoming serious again. 'It's very shallow, but it runs between Fanø island and Søren Jessens Sand, and it takes us well south of any boats going in and out of Esbjerg.'

Johann looked at the chart. 'We'd be in the main channel for a short time, and if the wind is still in the west, on the beam, we won't have to use the engine.' He pointed the route out to Manny, who was peering at the chart.

The boy nodded.

'In the main channel,' Franz said, 'we'd either have to tack, which would be difficult, and would take forever, or we'd have to use the engine.'

Manny nodded; his understanding of the workings of the yacht, and how it sailed, were growing every day. Ruth lagged a little behind, not having quite as intense a hunger to learn, or as strong a desire to impress.

'Those depths on the chart, some are as low as a quarter of a fathom; is it going to be deep enough?' he asked.

'That's why we're leaving soon. High tide is at twenty to ten, so we should have almost a fathom of water on top of these depths, allowing us to scrape out.'

Franz sounded more confident than he felt, and he could see by Johann's glance that his brother knew it was going to be tight.

'We'll be fine. What else needs done, before we leave?' he asked.

'Nothing. We're good to go. We just need to weigh anchor.' He looked around the boat, giving it a final check.

Everything had been stowed and all the charts needed for the next part of the journey had been looked out.

'Wait, there is something,' Franz said. 'Can you and Manny row out and hang Børge's nets over one of the poles?'

They could have waited until the tide was higher and dropped them off as they were leaving, but Franz preferred having one less job to do once they were under way.

With the nets draped over the pole, Johann and Manny rowed back and recovered the kedge anchor; with the wind in the west, the nose of the yacht was holding position on the main anchor alone. Its work done, the tender was hoisted on board and lashed to the top of the coachroof. While Franz went below, and fetched the notepad with all his bearings, depths, and distances, the others removed the covers from the mainsail, hanked on the foresails and made all the halyards ready to haul.

CHAPTER 149

At quarter to nine, Franz gave Ruth the wheel and, with Johann's help, raised the mainsail. Pointing into the wind, it flapped and flailed but as soon as Franz stepped back to the cockpit and hauled on its sheet, it filled. The yacht took a bite into the water of Hobo Dyb and eased forward with a slight tremble.

'Weigh anchor.' Franz's voice didn't have to be loud to carry to the foredeck, and Manny heard it and began cranking the windlass, pulling in the slack on the anchor chain as the boat crept forward.

'Steer a point or two to starboard to keep the sail from collapsing.'

Ruth turned the wheel, and the boat paused, then swung around. As she veered away, creeping forward, more and more chain clattered down the hawsepipe into the locker, and Manny, sweating, watched the angle of the anchor rode steepen.

'Tack to port now,' Franz said. As the bow inched round again, Manny wound the windlass a last few furious turns until it rose almost vertically from the surface of the water and, with a slight shudder, freed itself from the mud.

'Hard to starboard.'

Ruth turned the wheel hard over and the bow came round, slowly at first.

'Let's get the foresail up,' he said to Johann, who hauled hand over hand on the jib's halyard. The sail shot up the stay, catching Manny by surprise as he worked at the bow, dipping the anchor in and out of the water to clean the black oozing mud from its flukes, before stowing it on deck.

As the top of the sail reached the block, and the leech tightened, Franz pulled in on the sheet until the sail billowed, turning the boat faster. As she wheeled away from the wind, he eased out both the mainsheet and the jib sheet, allowing the gentle breeze to fill the sails and drive her round.

As *The Shearwater* continued to turn, the wind swung round towards her stern.

'Ready to gybe,' he said, loud enough for everyone on board to hear.

Manny stepped back across the foredeck to the mast to join Johann, and Franz pulled in the sheet just as the mainsail began to flap, the wind now on its starboard side. As it caught the sail, the boom swung across, but he'd taken in almost all the slack, and it came to rest midships with a soft jerk. Johann jumped down into the cockpit and released the foresail sheet. The sail, now free, blew over to the port side of the bow, and Johann pulled in on the port sheet until the sail stopped flapping. Franz eased out the mainsail again until it filled, then checked the compass.

'Start to straighten up now,' Franz told Ruth. 'Course one-six-zero magnetic.'

As the boat's turn decreased, he trimmed the main again until the tell-tails on the sail flew free. The wind was now over his right shoulder, and he could feel it ruffling the hair behind his ear.

Satisfied that the sails were set, Franz watched as one of the sticks that marked the channel appeared out of the mist ahead of them and, as it passed the bow, he counted the seconds it took to clear the stern. He did a quick calculation in his head, knowing the boat length, and worked out that they were doing about three knots. He looked at his watch and marked the time in his notebook.

Johann lifted the lead line and made his way to the bow. Manny grabbed a withy stick that was lashed to the side of the coachroof, the one with the depth markings nicked into the bark. He followed Johann forward.

A few seconds later Franz heard the shout.

'Two fathoms.'

In the fog, Johann's voice easily carried to Franz.

'Use the withy stick once it gets shallower,' Franz shouted and was rewarded with a thumbs up from Manny.

Franz peered into the gloom, hoping he didn't miss one of the thin poles that marked the edge of the safe channel.

He checked the time and calculated that they'd reached the first bend in the channel. He told Ruth to turn thirty-five degrees to port. They held that course for another few minutes before following the poles marking the sweeping bend to starboard. He strained his ear for the sounds of other vessels.

'Listen out,' he hissed at the others, 'and keep a close watch too.'

They redoubled their concentration as the channel swung round again, this time to the left.

Franz counted out the distance in his head; he knew that they were approaching the edge of Graa Dyb, the main deep-water channel. He heard Ruth give a start when, ahead of them on the starboard side, the grey wall of mist lit up for a second.

'It's Skallingen light,' Franz said. 'It's still lit. We're close to Graa Dyb.'

He waited thirty seconds and told Ruth to steer one-two-five degrees, trusting that his calculations were correct. He'd judged that, in the last half hour of the incoming tide, there would be little or no current running in the main channel. He counted out the long minutes that he'd allowed to see them across.

Johann continued to shout out the depths, increasing while they transited the dredged channel that allowed large vessels to enter and leave Esbjerg.

'Five fathoms… seven fathoms… nine fathoms.' Franz tried to judge if the boat was being pushed one way or the other by the tide, but in the swirling mist, there was nothing to gauge it against. Just when he reckoned they were halfway across, his straining ears registered the faint sound he'd been dreading and, above the unmistakable throb of an engine, a blast from a ship's horn sounded somewhere towards the direction of Esbjerg.

'Vessel to port,' came the shout from the bow, and Franz acknowledged it.

'Coming out the channel,' he said. 'Hopefully, it's not too close, and it won't have too much speed on in this fog.' It was a guess at best, and in any other circumstance, he would have sounded his own horn to warn the other boat of his presence, but it was the one action he couldn't risk taking.

'Keep her steady, Ruth.' He looked at his watch. 'A few more minutes.'

He thought about running the engine, but it might give them away if one of the deckhands on the ship had a good ear.

Every time he looked at his watch, he was convinced the hands were barely moving. The thump of the big diesels grew in volume far faster than he'd anticipated, and he feared that he'd condemned them all to a horrible drowning, crushed by the bows of a ship that might not even notice their demise.

I should have started the engine.

He glanced to port.

It's too late now.

The urgency in Johann's voice alerted Franz as much as the rapidly decreasing fathoms being shouted at him.

We've reached the edge of the channel.

The instant relief he felt was replaced by a new worry.

'Can you see the cut?' he shouted to Johann.

'No. Will it be marked?'

'I doubt it.'

Franz looked at Ruth. She stood rigid, gripping the wheel, knuckles white.

'I'm going forward. Be ready to turn when I shout.'

Glancing at Ruth with some misgiving, he stepped onto the side deck and made to make his way forward. He stopped at the sound of Johann's voice from the bow.

'There's an eddy ahead on the port side. Ten metres. I think it's the channel.'

Franz hesitated, but only for a second, trusting his brother's judgement. He stopped and turned to Ruth.

'Hard over to port. Quick.'

He raced to assist her as she turned the wheel as fast as she could. Slipping in behind her, he grabbed the wheel, helping her to throw the boat round, sails flapping, but retaining enough momentum to keep the hull cutting through the water. Almost as soon as they'd wrestled the boat parallel to the side of the main channel, Johann shouted.

'Turn to starboard. The cut is abreast.'

This time, Franz didn't hesitate.

Almost shoving Ruth aside, Franz turned the wheel as fast as he could, hand over hand, in a full circle.

The yacht leaned heavily in the turn, then further still as the sails caught the wind again and accelerated her forward. Franz could see nothing but mist, and he waited for Johann's directions.

'Two fathoms. Ten degrees port.'

Franz made the adjustment. The ship's horn sounded, almost behind them now and, over and above the thudding of the engine, he could hear the rush of its bow wash, and readied himself for the significant wave that would hit their stern as soon as the boat passed.

'One and a half fathoms.'

He quickly looked at his pad. From the small sketch he'd made, he saw that the cut he hoped they were in, between the sandbank and the shore, ran almost directly north to south, so he turned again, until his course read one-eight-zero degrees on the compass.

'One and a quarter fathoms.'

We need to slow down in case we ground.

'Ruth, release the jib sheet.'

She grabbed the rope and released it from its cleat.

'Watch out for the foresail, boys,' he shouted.

The jib sheet ran loose, and the foresail flapped around Johann and Manny's heads on the foredeck.

'Thanks for that, Franz,' Johann murmured, but Manny could see he was grinning.

'Start reading the depths with your stick,' Johann told him, 'it's going to get shallower soon.'

'Do I tell you, or shout to Franz?'

'Just shout, no point in wasting time by having me pass it on.'

Franz felt the boat slow, the drive from the foresail lost, and he pencilled a line on his pad, marking the point on the course where he estimated *Der Sturmtaucher* was. He checked his watch and noted the time.

The bow of the ship had now passed behind them, and he could feel the small dip in the water level that warned him the wave was just about to hit.

'Watch out forward. We're about to get the wash from the ship.'

Everyone grabbed something to hold onto, and Franz gripped the wheel, bracing his legs as wide as he could.

'One fathom.' Manny this time.

The stern rose, and swung sharply to port as the ship's bow wave hit them, amplified by the shallowness of the cut they were in. Franz swung the wheel hard to starboard, to counteract the yacht's violent lurch before it drove them straight onto the shore but he oversteered and had to adjust again to compensate. As the wave passed under them, they dropped down into the trough that followed, and they all felt the thump, and the sudden deceleration, as the keel touched the sand. Johann looked back towards Franz, expecting the boat to twist on its keel but, within seconds, the sea had picked her up and she was moving forward again.

The heavy sound of the ship's engines passed behind them, and they could hear the screws churning up the water as she headed out to sea.

'Careful. There will be another few waves to follow.' Franz pictured a small freighter, making its way in the fog, the captain unaware of just how close he'd been to sinking them.

'Just over a fathom,' Johann shouted again.

'Shout it in feet,' Franz said. He turned to Ruth.

'There's six to a fathom,' he said.

He glanced back at their wake.

'Slacken the mainsheet a little,' he told Ruth, 'We'll take a little more speed off her while it's this shallow.'

He knew that the depth of their keel was just over a fathom but, because you couldn't rely on the accuracy of the soundings, it was natural for the person shouting them out to err on the side of safety and underestimate the depth.

Even so, they were running with barely enough water to clear the bottom, and he suspected that the shallowest part was still to come at the end of the sandbank before it dropped away again into deeper water.

'Where's the bloody sandbank?' he yelled, more to himself than anyone else. It showed on the chart as being visible at high water, but only just.

'Seven feet,' Manny shouted.

He glanced at his sketch. The Søren Jessens bank should have been twenty metres off the starboard beam.

It was Ruth who spotted it.

'There,' she said, pointing. 'Some white crests, and I can hear the waves breaking on it.'

He followed the line of her arm and saw the disturbed water, and maybe a glimpse of the sandbar itself. It was almost exactly where it should be.

Perhaps a bit too close, he thought.

He steered a couple of points to port, and continued to check his watch, counting down the minutes. The channel, if you could call it that, was about a mile long and at their current speed, it would take about twenty minutes until they were out of it.

The stern dipped again, and he repeated his warning about the wash, but this one was less forceful, and they didn't bottom out.

CHAPTER 150

The fog hid everything, and Franz made use of all his senses to know where they were.

The smell of the sea, the taste of the salt in the air. The feel of his hand on the wheel, the sounds of the breeze in the sails, the ripple of their wake and the touch of the wind on his face.

Johann and Manny, at the bow, were nothing but shadows shrouded in mist. Blind to anything more than a few metres in front of him, he glanced down at the crude diagram he'd drawn of Fanø, the Søren Jessens bank, and the temporary channel between them that would be nothing but a puddle in a few hours' time, and he pictured the boat in the centre of it, halfway along.

Manny continued his monotonous seven-feet chant, with the odd eight thrown in, creeping through the otherwise silent grey. Had anyone been walking on shore, they may have thought they'd just seen a ghost ship, gliding past where no sailing boat should ever be.

Five minutes passed, then seven, then ten.

'That's us halfway to the turn,' Franz told them.

'Scheiße, I thought we were nearly through,' Johann muttered to Manny.

Manny laughed, breaking the tension that had been building, and continued to shout out his soundings.

Another five nervous minutes passed, feeling more like ten, and still the depths stayed constant. Once or twice, Franz thought he felt the boat graze the bottom; there was no thump or apparent decrease in speed, just a sense of catching on the seabed for the briefest of seconds.

As his watch told him the twenty minutes would soon be up, he called out to the others to look out, and hang tight.

'Nineteen minutes,' he told them. 'It might get shallower at the end of the channel.'

'Eight feet,' Manny intoned.

The time dragged on.

'Twenty.' Another minute.

He itched to turn to seaward, but he didn't want to catch the tail of the sandbank.

'Twenty-one. Twenty points to starboard.'

He turned. Towards deep water.

'Eight feet.'

They all let out a breath.

The luff of the mainsail flailed as the wind came round to the bow. Franz turned to Ruth.

'Pull in on the main.'

She grabbed the mainsheet and hauled it in, until the flapping stopped.

'Let's get the foresail working. Pull in the port sheet.'

Ruth bent down to pick it up.

The yacht's keel bit into the sand with a grating thump, and she stopped dead, slewing around almost ninety degrees. Ruth was thrown forward, hitting the top of the coachroof, and landed, sprawling, on the tender.

On the foredeck, Johann had been standing, holding the lead line ready. The sudden stop hurled him forwards, and as his legs hit the guardrails, he toppled over towards the sea. Manny, on his knees, ready to take his next sounding, grabbed the corner of his sea coat as he disappeared over the side. The wire of the handrail bit into Johann's forearm as he grabbed it, forcing a yell from him, but he held on and hung there for a few seconds. Swinging his leg upward, he managed to hook his foot over the bowsprit and cling on.

Manny threw the withy stick onto the deck behind him and managed to reach Johann's right arm. Johann clasped his hand onto Manny's sleeve and, between them, they got Johann turned to face the boat. Somehow, Johann still had a hold of the lead line, and he flung it onto the foredeck; with this hand now free, he grabbed the lower guard rail and began hauling himself up.

Franz, when they grounded, felt the thump of the keel on the sandbank at the same time as the wheel was snatched from his hands, almost breaking his fingers. He lurched to one side, but managed to grab onto the binnacle, and stay upright.

The yacht had listed a little but was in no immediate danger and, noticing that Ruth lay in a heap across the top of the tender, he released all the sheets and dived forward to check if she was hurt.

Stunned and in pain, she didn't move for a few seconds but, just as Franz reached her, she tried to push herself up.

'Careful. Take your time.' Franz's arms were around her, helping her sit up, feeling for anything broken, his face pale with concern.

'I'm all right,' she said, gripping his arm and wincing, 'but it's going to hurt a little.'

She stood up, and hobbled, wincing and rubbing the front of her thighs where they'd hit the coachroof, but everything appeared to be working.

'Go and see to the boat. I'll be fine,' she told him.

Reluctant to leave her, but knowing that she was right, he told her to tend the helm, and that he'd be back once he'd spoken to Johann.

He rushed forward, just as his brother scrambled back over the guard rails, flopping onto the deck. Johann nursed his arm, where the wire rail had dug in.

'Are you two all right?'

Johann, his breath coming in short, harsh gasps, shook his head.

'Give me a minute,' he managed to rasp, crouching on one knee, head bowed. Manny stood up, holding the slackened foresail to prevent it slapping Johann around the head.

'What do we do now? I thought we'd made it through, then bang.'

'It's either the very end of the Søren Jessens bank or it's just an isolated lump of sand. We'll need to get off it soon, as the tide will be ebbing shortly.' Franz said, then turned to Johann.

'Are you good to help?'

Johann stood up, still breathing heavily, and ran his hands over his chest and his legs.

'Everything's still there. I guess I'll survive. We'd better get her off this bitch of a sandbar or we're done for.'

'I know. I'm not hurt, so I'll go out on the boom.'

He turned to Manny.

'There's a preventer attached to the end of the boom.'

He paused, realising Manny didn't know what he was talking about. 'It's a rope which we sometimes use to prevent the boom gybing. It goes from the tip of the boom and we rig it to the bow. Its free end is coiled on a cleat on the mast. Go and take it forward.'

Manny unhooked the coil of line and did as he'd been asked. Meanwhile, Franz tied a small bight of rope around his waist and passed the free end behind him and back through between his legs as a makeshift harness. He pulled the mainsheet tight, then climbing onto the binnacle, reached for the end of the boom. Tying himself to it, he hugged the boom beneath the foot of the mainsail, and clung on, swinging his legs up and hooking them around the thick spar, tucking them under the loose foot of the mainsail. He nodded to Johann.

'Manny, pull your end of the rope as hard as you can while I let the boom out,' Johann shouted, releasing the mainsheet. Manny hauled on the preventer, swinging the boom forward and out over the water, taking Franz with it.

'Keep pulling. As quick as you like.'

As the boom moved further out, Franz's weight on its far end began to heel the boat over to that side. By the time the boom was out as far as it could go, the mast was tilting twenty degrees, and Franz's backside was dipping into the water.

Of more importance, under the waterline, the keel tilted at the same angle on the opposite side and, because of that, it swung upwards by almost a foot, easing it off the sand. As it floated, the wind threatened to blow the hull towards the shore, but as soon as Johann felt it lift, he pulled in the foresail sheet as hard as he could and told Ruth to straighten up the rudder. He felt the yacht begin to move forwards as the sail filled, and because they were now closer to the wind, the air pressure on the sail made the boat heel even harder, dunking Franz's body under the water.

'Give me a bit of slack, Manny, I need to pull Franz in a bit. Nice and steady though.'

Manny released the preventer a couple of metres, allowing Johann to shorten the mainsheet, pulling in the boom just enough to lift Franz clear. The mast should have swung back to the vertical as Franz's weight moved towards the centre of the boat but the wind filling the mainsail fought against it, keeping the boat heeled. He told Ruth to keep the yacht's nose close the wind. It allowed him to get the end of the boom inboard of the guard rails while keeping enough angle of heel to avoid grounding again.

Franz released himself from the boom, dripping wet, and took charge of the jib sheet, pulling it in hard and allowing Johann to concentrate on the main.

Ruth looked pale and apprehensive; he didn't know if it was from watching him getting dumped in the sea, or from her earlier fright, or her injuries. He gave her a reassuring smile.

'One and a half fathoms.'

Johann and Franz looked at one another, and grinned, impressed that young Manny had taken it on himself to resume his soundings again, without having to be asked.

They touched once more before they reached charted deep water. This time, although the boat slewed a little and almost stopped, she had enough momentum to release herself and pick up again, sliding off the sand into deeper water.

Before long, Manny had dispensed with the withy stick, and was calling the soundings using the lead line.

'Two fathoms… three fathoms… five fathoms… six fathoms…'

Franz checked that the boat was sailing as close to the wind as she could manage without stalling, took a note of the compass reading, and descended into the cabin. After a quick change into dry clothes, he sat himself at the chart table. He marked their position, estimated at three miles south-south-west of Skallingen light, and drew a line on the chart from the fix, running south-westwards. In front of them lay the whole of the North Sea, 300 miles clear to the west, and over 100 miles to the north and south, all of it with enough depth for their draft, and more.

CHAPTER 151

The fog remained as dense, maybe even more so, as it had been when they left, and Johann hoped it wasn't just a narrow strip of haar along the coast.

He glanced out of the companionway at Ruth, helming, and Franz standing beside her.

He'd watched them since he'd returned to the boat, not quite believing Børge's claim that she and his brother were a couple.

But, a day later, he'd come to the conclusion that the Danish fisherman was right. Not only that, but he realised with a shock that they had slept together.

He was almost certain, from Lise's venomous words and the few remarks his brother had let slip over the years, that Franz had been sexually intimate with Lise before they'd broken up, and that he may have had a brief fling or two before he met her, but he was almost certain that his brother had not slept with a woman since, despite Johann's best efforts to encourage it.

And he was a hundred per cent sure that Ruth had been a virgin when she first boarded the yacht.

But he'd known enough women, and had slept with too many of them, perhaps, not to miss the signs that Ruth Nussbaum and his brother were lovers.

He knew that, prior to the start of the voyage, they were no more than friends and, with the age gap between them, their relationship had been more akin to that of an older brother and a much younger sister.

And there had been no opportunities on the first part of the voyage, between Kiel and Hobo Dyb, for them to sleep together, but now he wondered about the long watches Ruth and Franz had seen out, and he knew that they would have had interminable hours to talk, and for their friendship to turn into something more intimate.

It all fits.

Unlike Johann, Franz wouldn't jump into a woman's bed without some sort of prolonged courtship; it wasn't in his nature.

And for his brother to overcome the sense of betrayal of Ruth's parents and the General, for breaking the trust that they had put in Franz and Johann to keep Ruth and Manny safe, they must both have fallen so deeply in love that nothing else mattered.

For the second time in his life, Johann was jealous of his brother.

~~o~~

Heinrich Güllich looked around.

'A fine office you have here, Herr General,' he said, smirking.

'It does the job. I share it with my captain,' Erich Kästner said, nodding towards the second desk on the far side of the room.

'And a view of Kieler Hafen to boot,' Heinrich Güllich added, looking out of the window, across the harbour to the shipyards. 'They say you've made a significant impact on our production of warships.'

'I do my job.'

'As we all do, Herr General. It would be a pity if your reputation were ruined, and all this crumbled around you, wouldn't it?'

'As I say, I do what needs to be done. I let others worry about my reputation.'

'How very humble of you,' Heinrich Güllich said. He paused, clasping his hands together.

'I must say,' he continued, 'I'm surprised that you are here today. I thought that you might be at home, consoling your lovely wife.'

'There's a war on. We must put personal grief aside. Enough of my fellow citizens are suffering the same torment as I am.'

'Yes. I must pass on the Gestapo's sincere commiserations. It must be a worrying time although, for most people who have sons reported as missing, it isn't because of a sailing trip that, in all truthfulness, should never have been undertaken.'

'That is a matter of opinion. They were on leave. What they did with it is entirely up to

477

them.'

'And the wasted time the Kriegsmarine is spending looking for them? Is that helping the war effort?'

'If you'd taken the trouble to ask the Kriegsmarine, they would have told you that I rejected the offer of additional help. Admittedly, those ships that are in the area are looking out for any sign of *The Shearwater* or my sons, but only as part of their standard, routine patrols.'

Heinrich Güllich gave an ironic smile.

'If you say so, General Kästner.'

'Was there anything in particular you wished to see me about?'

'Your wife. She has relatives in Denmark?'

The General smiled.

'Yes,' he said. 'I believe the only one still alive is in a home for the elderly.'

The General was pleased to see a flash of irritation pass over the Gestapo man's face.

'But there is a house, I believe?'

'As far as I know, yes.'

If Güllich wanted to go on a wild goose chase all over Denmark, the General was happy to let him.

'You don't seem as distraught as you should, Herr General, having just had the news that your sons are missing, presumed drowned.'

'I reported them missing. They've not yet been presumed drowned. I still hope they will be found, alive and well.'

'Oh. So do I, General. So do I. And I fully expect them to. Somewhere in Denmark, or Norway, or trying to cross the border into Sweden.'

'What do you mean?' the General blustered, smiling inside.

'I know,' Heinrich Güllich hissed, spittle marking the corner of his thin, cruel mouth.

He stared at the General, his face centimetres away.

'Your sons,' he said, when the General didn't reply, 'have landed their sorry commander's boat somewhere and are, as we speak, hiding with their Jewish rats, imagining that they can lie low until we give up looking for them.'

'That's preposterous,' the General said. 'You dare to come in here and make unfounded accusations about my sons. I'll have your rank for this.'

'I don't think so, Herr General. The tide is turning. There's less and less support for your misguided efforts to protect your filthy Jews. You'll be on your own soon, and that's when we'll be ready for you.'

Heinrich Güllich's eyes almost bulged out of his head, and the veins in his forehead protruded, almost pulsing in time with his words.

The General laughed.

'We'll see. You've gone too far this time. My staff can hear you through that door.'

But it was as if Heinrich Güllich hadn't heard him.

'You, and your sons forget. We rule Norway and Denmark. The Gestapo are there in force and we're already looking for four rats, scurrying away, trying to find a hole to slink into. If we find the boat, we've got them. We know they are out there, and we have all the time we need.'

'I wish you good luck in your search,' the General said, opening the door to the outer office with a pleasant smile.

For the briefest second, he thought the Gestapo officer was going to whip out his pistol and shoot him, but he saw Heinrich Güllich relax, and force a smile to his face.

He stood in front of Erich Kästner, his eyes sweeping the room.

'Look around you, General Kästner. One day, you'll exchange all this for a prison cell. And I'll be the one locking the door.'

He smiled and walked out.

In his office, the General stood for a second, then walked over to the window.

Captain Bauer tapped his knuckle on the open door, hesitated, then entered the office.

'Are you all right, sir,' he said.

'Yes. I'm fine,' the General replied, not looking round.

'That man,' the captain blustered, 'he's…'

'Don't worry, Captain. He's just a small angry man with an enormous chip on his shoulder. I'll deal with him later.'

'Yes, sir,' the captain said, a doubtful look on his face. 'Do you need anything?'

'A cup of coffee would be nice,' the General said, turning round and giving the captain a strained smile.

'Yes, sir. Right away.'

He left, closing the door behind him. The General looked out at Kieler Hafen again and allowed himself a broad smile.

CHAPTER 152

The fog soaked everything. It permeated their clothes, and every surface was coated in its creeping dampness. Droplets of water gathered on the ends of Ruth's eyelashes, causing Franz to smile.

They'd taken the first watch to let Johann rest. His ribs and his arm were more painful than Ruth's injuries and Franz, despite Johann's protestations, had insisted that his brother should lie down and take a couple of aspirin.

He'd also changed the watches to six hours, having talked it over with Johann the day before they left.

'It'll give us a better sleep off-watch, and the navigation is less intense,' Franz had said.

The westerly wind steadied around the ten- to twelve-knot mark, and *The Shearwater* made slow but steady progress to the south-west.

'Try and keep the compass steady at two-three-zero,' Franz said to Ruth who was on the helm. 'For us to know where we are, our course must be consistent, and we need accurate speed measurements. He lowered the brass log into the water and fed the line out.

'Four and a half knots,' he said, and wrote it down in his notebook. 'A plot every hour will be sufficient unless the wind changes direction.'

'It feels strange, not being able to see more than a few metres,' she said.

'You have to rely on your ears. All ships should sound their horns at regular intervals in fog, but you have to listen out for their engines too, and if you're down below, you'll feel the throb of their screws through the hull.'

As he finished speaking, the mournful sound of a ship's horn split the silence.

'It's impossible to tell which direction that came from,' Ruth said, looking around as if she expected the vessel to appear any second.

'It's easier if you hear the engine; because it's a constant sound, you can turn your head to work out where it's coming from but, even then, the fog can play tricks on you.'

She sat, her head cocked to one side, listening.

The sound came again, and she swivelled her head one way, and then the other, then frowned.

'See what I mean?' Franz said.

They strained to hear an engine and she told Franz she could hear a faint thrum in the distance.

'It's quite far away,' she said. 'The sound of the horn travels further than the engine.'

They heard the horn a few times more, then it melted into the distance, but they got into the way of talking in short bursts, then listening for a minute or two. For the rest of the day, there was nothing to interrupt them but the burble of the sea slipping past the hull and the occasional straining of the rigging as the yacht beat gently to windward.

'How easy do you think it will be for us to get to America, or Canada?' Ruth asked.

Franz glanced at her, then looked away.

'Ruth, I…'

'What?'

Franz took a deep breath.

'You will be refugees, at best. More than likely, you'll be interned, at least for a while.'

'But why? They can't.'

'You're German. The British are at war with us. That's all that will matter.'

A tear spilled over Ruth's cheek.

'I thought…'

'I know.'

'And you and Johann will be prisoners until the war is over?'

'Yes. It won't matter how we got there, or why.'

For a while they sat, saying nothing.

'How long will it last?' Ruth said, breaking the silence.

'It's impossible to say. Years, for all we know.'

They sat in quietness until, with a start, Franz realised it was the end of the fourth hour of their watch, and his stomach told him it was lunchtime.

Franz took a log reading and, leaving Ruth on the helm, he crept down the companionway and put the kettle on, trying his best not to wake the other two. While it was boiling, he sat down at the chart tables plotting the tide and their progress through the water, estimating their position as best as he could.

Absorbed in his task, he failed to hear the kettle bubble as it heated until its loud whistle alerted him to the fact that it had boiled.

He cursed his carelessness as Johann and Manny both roused from their sleep.

'Is it our watch?' Johann said, stretching.

'No. I'm sorry. I didn't mean to wake you. I was just getting us a bite to eat, and a cup of coffee.'

'Make me one too, if you don't mind.' He turned to Manny, who was lying with his head up, supported on one arm. 'Do you want a cup, Manny?'

Manny nodded. Franz cut enough bread and cheese for four.

'How are you feeling?' he asked Johann.

'Still sore, but better than I was. I'll be fine.'

'Here,' he said, handing them a plate of food each, and a steaming cup of coffee. 'I'll take Ruth's up. We'll give you a shout in a couple of hours.'

He disappeared back up to the cockpit and closed the hatch behind him.

Johann stared at the hatch for a while, wrestling with what he had to say, then turned to Manny.

'We need to have a talk,' he said.

'About Ruth and Franz?' Manny replied.

Johann stared at him for a second. 'You know about them?' he said. 'Did Ruth tell you?'

'No. She didn't, but she talks about him a lot.'

'I didn't see it, until Børge said to me. I can't believe I missed it.'

He hesitated.

'What do you think about it?'

Manny frowned.

'It's difficult. I'm sure if I asked Herr Eliasowitz, our Cheder teacher, he would say it was wrong of them being together, Franz not being Jewish you see, but…'

Johann got up and looked out of the hatch, then sat down again.

'I think there's more to it…' he said, faltering for words, a first for him. 'What I mean to say is, well…'

'You're trying to tell me that they've slept together.'

Johann stared at Manny again. He laughed to hide his embarrassment, then stopped when he saw Manny's face.

'I'm sorry,' he said. 'You're making me nervous now.'

'It's all right. I'm not a child. I know what goes on.'

'I suppose you do,' Johann said. 'I just didn't know how you'd feel about it.'

Manny bowed his head, then lifted it.

'My teacher, and the men at the synagogue, would condemn them, and Mama and Papa might too…'

He stopped and stared out of one of the portholes.

'Neither Franz nor Ruth would do this without a good reason,' Johann said. 'They must have fallen deeply in love for them to… you know.'

'It doesn't stop me being angry at Franz, and at Ruth. I'd rather it hadn't happened, but…' Manny said, his voice trailing off, his frown deepening.

'These aren't normal times,' Johann said. 'We don't know if we are going to be alive tomorrow, or next week, and they won't know when they will see each other again, even if we make it to England.'

Manny stood up and thumped the side of his fist against the forward bulkhead.

'That's the difficult bit. I know it's wrong but there's part of me that just wants Ruth to be happy. She deserves a break from all the misery she's had to face.'

'Listen, I'm no saint, you must know that, and I can find no wrong in it, but I know what your religion means to you, and that you and your family's values are different to mine but think hard before you say anything to Ruth that you might regret or, at least sit on it for a couple of days before you speak to her. If you're still uncomfortable with it, talk to her, but be kind. Consider what you'd be taking away from her.'

'It's easy for you to say. What if it were Antje, or Eva?'

'It would depend on the man,' Johann said, after a moment.

Manny stared at him, then looked away.

'Do you think Franz could ever be bad to Ruth,' Johann said softly.

'No.' Manny scowled. 'Of course not. It still doesn't make it right.'

'No.' Johann sighed. 'I suppose it doesn't. Still, think about what I've said, and watch them. I've never had what they have, and part of me envies them.'

For a minute, Manny said nothing.

'I don't need any time,' he said, sighing. 'I'll say nothing. I can't spoil her happiness just because I'm not comfortable with it.'

Johann put his hand on Manny's shoulder.

'That's what makes a big man, my friend. You'll not regret it.'

'I hope so. I only hope my parents see it the same way.'

'They will, Manny. They will.'

They sat, one a hardened soldier, the other barely a man, a boy still in age only.

Johann closed his eyes. He had been dreading telling Manny about Ruth and Franz, and he'd been turning ways to word it over in his mind, for hours on end.

'I'd like to give them a bit of slack,' he said, standing up, 'but only if you're all right with it.'

'How?'

'Leave it with me. It mustn't appear deliberate; they'd be mortified if they thought we knew.'

Manny nodded.

CHAPTER 153

During their afternoon watch, Johann began to teach Manny how to sail a boat blind. Unlike Ruth, who had been introduced to it earlier in the day and still seemed nervous about the whole concept, Manny embraced it.

It was the appliance of maths and physics that sold it to him, he'd told Johann, both subjects he adored at school, and he'd pushed Johann's knowledge of the science of sailing to the limit with the myriad of questions he asked.

'You'll have to ask Franz about that,' Johann said, when Manny asked him why a yacht could travel faster with the wind from the side than from behind.

'We did the right thing,' Manny said. 'Did you see their faces?'

Johann smiled. He could still picture Franz and Ruth, framed in the companionway, trying to hide their pleasure when he'd suggested offhand that, whoever the off-watch pair was, they should sleep in the forecabin.

'It will give the other two access to the main cabin to do chartwork, and make coffee, without waking them,' he'd argued, 'like you did with us today.'

'It's not necessary,' Franz had said. 'I know I disturbed you both, but it won't happen again.'

'It's not just that,' Johann had insisted, leaning back in the cockpit. 'The pair on watch will be able to prepare meals, or use the cabin to warm up. It can get pretty cold out there and, as long as it's not too rough, the forecabin is fine to sleep in.'

'He's right, Franz,' Ruth had said. 'I don't mind sharing a cabin if you're all right with it. We each have our own sleeping bags.'

Franz had slowly been persuaded. Johann couldn't bring himself to look at Manny, and he'd turned away to hide his smile at his brother's reluctance.

'It suits me,' Manny had said, his face betraying nothing. 'I find it easier to sleep up forward.'

At that moment, Johann loved Manny for his humanity, knowing how difficult it must have been for the young Jewish boy.

Now, sitting watching Manny make minor adjustments to the sail trim while keeping the yacht true to its course, he did so with quiet satisfaction.

Checking his watch, he took a log reading and filled in the figure in Franz's notebook.

'Pretty constant,' he said. 'Four and a half. That's over 100 miles in a day.'

'But is it in the right direction?' Manny asked.

'Not quite. Twenty degrees further west would be better, but we can tack later and, besides, the fog will persist for longer the further south we are, so I think Franz is quite happy with us heading that way.'

~~o~~

17:00 EP: 55°3'92'N, 7°49'50'E. Watch change FK.

Sea slight. Dense fog. Wind 10 knots, westerly. Air pressure 1010mb. Full sail & topsail. 230°M, 4.5 knots. Tide 0.5 knots, 340°.

~~o~~

'I can't rid myself of the feeling that we'll still get caught, despite the fog,' Ruth said, standing close to Franz at the wheel, leaning her head on his arm.

'We haven't seen another boat all day, or even heard an engine since a few miles out of Esbjerg. We'll cross the shipping lane from Hamburg and Wilhelmshaven to Norway and the Skagerrak during the night if we stay on this course but, since the start of the war, very few merchant ships risk being targeted by the British Navy, and there are less fishing boats in these parts because of the risk of mines.'

'We're in another minefield? Doesn't that worry you?'

'My father was told that the British have mined large parts of the Helgoland Bight to disrupt our shipping, but our own protective minefields are further west. In a way, they could be our saviour, keeping Kriegsmarine ships away from much of the area we'll be sailing in.'

'So, how can our shipping lanes pass through the British minefield?'

'They clear safe channels with minesweepers on a regular basis, so our naval vessels all stick to the same route.'

'But surely, the longer we're out there, the greater the chance they'll catch us?'

'Not necessarily. The closer we get to British waters, the more likely it is that we'll be intercepted by a Royal Navy vessel, not a German one.'

'Until then, we need the fog?'

'I doubt we'll get it for that long, but if it gets us into an area where there isn't a lot of naval traffic, it'll be a start.'

'What about aeroplanes, once we're out of the fog?'

'Bombers fly mostly at night, or at high altitudes. I doubt they'll take much notice of us. The biggest danger is a reconnaissance flight. We'll fly a Swedish flag once we're in view. It might just be enough to fool them.'

As the light faded and the smothering fog grew colder, she put her arms around his waist and hugged him.

~~o~~

22:00 EP: 54°39'52'N, 7°14'84'E.

Sea slight. Visibility very poor (fog). Wind 10 knots, westerly. Air Pressure 1012mb. Full sail & topsail. 230°M, 4.5 knots. Tide 0.5 knots, 340°.

~~o~~

Franz looked at the log entry he'd just made and compared it to the previous few entries. He smiled. Apart from a small amount of tide running across them in the opposite direction, and the new latitude and longitude, they were identical.

He knew that sailing a constant course for hours, even days or weeks at a time, would bore most of his fellow sailors but it gave him a quiet satisfaction and he resolved, if he survived the war, to try and cross one of the world's oceans one day.

He looked at the clock on the bulkhead. In another hour, it would be Johann and Manny's watch.

CHAPTER 154

The General was climbing the stairs, heading for bed, when he heard the telephone ring.

As had been the case since the boys had left, his heart raced every time it rang, the terror of there being news of *The Shearwater*'s capture or sinking always at the front of his mind.

He ran down the stairs to answer it.

'Erich,' the familiar voice said.

'Walther. You're phoning late.'

'I'm sorry,' Colonel Schneider said, his voice betraying his dismay. 'I just had a phone call. A fishing boat docked last night in Engalsvik, near Fredrikstad, close to the Swedish border. They reported finding one of *Der Sturmtaucher*'s life rings two days ago, fishing off the Koster Islands, in Swedish waters. The Kriegsmarine are going to do a search of the area tomorrow and the Swedish coastal authorities have been informed.'

For a few seconds, there was silence, then Erich Kästner spoke.

'Thanks for letting me know. If I'm honest, I was expecting it. They must have foundered on the Norwegian coast. Wind and tide will have taken the flotsam across to the Swedish side.'

'They might still have made it ashore. I'm trying to get in touch with the Swedish coastguard.'

'It was a lee shore, Walther. In a force eleven. There's very little chance.'

The colonel didn't reply.

'Listen,' the General said, 'No matter what has happened, the boys made the decision to go, rightly or wrongly. I don't reproach you for anything.'

'No. But I reproach myself.'

'Don't.'

The General paused.

'I must go and tell Maria, Walther,' he said, after a few moments. 'I'll be in touch.'

He put the phone down and walked back upstairs to tell his wife the biggest lie of his life, if he could bring himself to do it, or to tell her the truth.

~~o~~

'Franz. I can see stars.'

Franz looked up. Sure enough, bright pinpricks of light shone in a black sky. There was just enough starlight to reveal a long wall of fog, like a cliff face of cloud, stretching as far as the eye could see to the south, with a little west in it.

'We'll follow the edge of the bank for a while in case it's just a hole in the fog. We'll need to keep a sharp lookout for lights and slip back into the fog if we see anything.'

He disappeared down into the cabin and returned a few seconds later. Johann, who had woken up and was making himself a cup of coffee, watched from the companionway as Franz took an instrument from a rough cloth bag and made a few adjustments to it.

'It's a sextant,' Johann said to Ruth, who was looking puzzled. 'Our Franz knows how to take sights from the stars, and the sun, like the ancient mariner he is.'

He laughed.

'He's not that old,' Ruth said, only half amused.

Johann shrugged. 'He's old enough to be your father,' he teased.

'No, he is not,' Ruth said, blushing.

Franz could see a hint of annoyance in her face and frowned at Johann.

'I might not be much older than you,' he said, forcing a smile, 'but I'm a hell of a lot wiser.'

Ruth and Johann watched as he looked up, searching the sky for the star he required.

'I'm going to measure the angle of inclination of the horizon to Polaris, the Pole Star. That's it there.'

He pointed to one of the brightest stars in the sky.

'It's part of the Little Bear constellation,' he said. 'It's always straight up from the North

Pole.'

Once he'd taken the sighting, he wrote down the figures in his notebook.

He looked up into the sky again.

'What are you doing now?' Ruth asked.

'The Pole Star will just tell us our latitude. For longitude as well, we need to do a sighting of another star, or of the sun at noon.'

'We can't do that,' Ruth said. 'We'll be seen.'

'I know. It's why we need to find another star.'

Franz took a second sighting.

'Now for the magic,' Johann said, moving aside to let his brother pass. Franz disappeared into the cabin.

'What is he doing?' Ruth said.

Johann shrugged.

'The devil if I know. He looks through tables in the almanac. He does a few complicated mathematical calculations in his notebook. When that's all done, he tells us where we are.'

'Not quite,' Franz said, returning to the cockpit, 'but close enough.'

'It's all mumbo jumbo,' Johann muttered, before disappearing to make coffee in preparation for coming on watch.

'Do you do this often?' Ruth asked Franz.

'I've only ever done it to keep learning, and to keep my hand in. We've never needed to do it before for real as we've rarely been out of sight of land long enough.'

'So why did you learn to do it?'

Franz sighed.

'I suppose it fascinates me, how seafarers found their way about the world's oceans, so I thought I might as well learn. I didn't know it would come in useful one day.'

She smiled at him.

'Can you teach me?' She giggled. 'It would really shock Manny.'

He looked at her. Her eyes danced with amusement. He would have liked nothing better than to kiss her.

'I love you, Ruth Nussbaum,' he whispered.

'I love you, too, Franz Kästner,' she murmured in his ear. 'Is that a yes?'

'Of course I'll teach you. We'll start now with the sextant itself, then I'll show you how to do all the calculations once we're off watch. It's not as difficult as it looks.'

~~o~~

'It's strange,' Johann said, talking to Franz as he took over the wheel. 'The fog bank doesn't move, but there's a ten-knot wind blowing.'

'I've seen it before. I think it's to do with the temperature of the water. The line of fog marks the junction between a cold-water and a warm-water stream, independent of the wind.'

'Ah. That explains it then.'

CHAPTER 155

[17/04/1941 Thursday]

'Johann,' Manny hissed.

'What?'

Johann had dozed off, sitting in the cockpit, and shook his head to clear the sleep from his brain. Wednesday had drifted into Thursday and there was still a couple of hours to go to sunrise.

'There are lights.'

'Where?' Johann said, looking around frantically.

'Over there,' Manny said, pointing to the north-west, astern of *Der Sturmtaucher* and to starboard.

'I see them,' he said, a hint of relief in his voice. 'They're far enough away.'

'I've been keeping a close lookout. They haven't been there long, and I've not heard an engine, or any sound signals.'

'They're not in the fog, so they wouldn't sound a horn in open water if their navigation lights can be clearly seen.'

'They wouldn't have seen us, would they?'

'No. Not without us showing lights.'

Johann reached down into the locker just inside the companionway and fished out the binoculars.

'It's a sizeable vessel. A freighter, perhaps, trying to sneak across Helgoland Bight under cover of darkness. Heading to Emden or Wilhelmshaven, perhaps.'

'Will it pass close to us?'

'I doubt it,' Johann said, writing in the notebook. 'If we keep checking the ship's bearing from *The Shearwater*, we can see if there's a risk of collision.'

'I remember,' Manny said, pride lighting up his face. 'If the bearing is constant and the range is reducing, the two vessels may collide.'

Johann smiled at him.

'Well done. In the meantime,' he said, 'we'll have to turn back into the fog before sun-up, but I'll speak to Franz first.'

Johann looked at his watch. Just before four. A couple of hours or so until then.

They waited for ten minutes, then Johann took a second bearing to the vessel.

'Five degrees less, and it doesn't look to be closing on us,' he said. 'It's overtaking, and I doubt it'll get nearer than three or four miles.'

They kept a close eye on the ship, always ready to turn *The Shearwater* back into the fog bank if necessary. Ten minutes later, they didn't need to use the hand-bearing compass; it was obvious that the ship was now abeam of the yacht, and still distant enough not to cause concern.

Thirty minutes later, it had disappeared into the dark ahead of them.

~~o~~

Johann spoke briefly with Franz at five, when he and Ruth came on watch, telling him of the encounter.

'I thought it unnecessary to run into the fog,' he said.

'You did right, but we'll need to head back into it before sunrise.'

'Yes. That's what I told Manny. I'll leave you to it. Two-two-five should do it.'

'Two-two-five it is then,' Franz said, turning the wheel five points to port.

Ruth replaced Johann in the cockpit and looked up at the sky, then at the approaching fog bank. She shivered.

'It's a shame we have to go back in so soon,' she said. 'It would have been nice to see the sun.'

'You'll see plenty of sun and blue sky before we get to Britain, and you'll curse it, and pray for fog.'

She smiled.

He was right. He is old and wise.

Franz sat down beside her and put his arm around her, the other on the wheel; no effort was needed in the light wind to keep *The Shearwater* on course but, from time to time, he'd lean forward to check the compass on the binnacle.

Before too long, the first wisps of moisture began drifting over the deck and, within a couple of minutes, they'd been swallowed up again by the fog.

~~o~~

As the blackness of the night faded to a dark, damp grey, then to a dirty, dense white that almost hid the bow of *The Shearwater*, the hatch slid back with a squeak.

Ruth, huddled against Franz, threw off his arm and pulled away from him.

Manny popped his head up without removing the washboards.

'I've just made a pot of coffee. Do you want a mug?'

For a second, neither Ruth nor Franz could meet his gaze.

'Yes, yes, that would be great,' Franz blurted out, the words running together.

Ruth knew that she was blushing and hoped that it wouldn't show in the dull greyness of dawn.

Manny disappeared below and reappeared with two steaming cups, full to the brim.

They thanked him and asked him why he hadn't gone to bed.

'I didn't feel tired. I was reading the sailing directions for the North Sea. We're heading straight for Terschelling in Holland, but we'll have to tack north-westwards long before we get there, won't we, Franz.'

'Yes, Manny. The islands are similar to Langli; low, with marshes and mudflats behind them.'

Manny cringed.

'I don't want to see another mudflat, ever,' he said. He nodded to them and ducked down the companionway, shutting the hatch behind him.

Ruth glanced at Franz, still embarrassed.

'We'll have to be more careful,' she said.

~~o~~

For the rest of the morning *Der Sturmtaucher* sailed inside the fog bank but close to its edges. They developed a technique of sailing for half an hour, then turning a few degrees to starboard for as long as it took for the fog to thin, then turn back to port by five degrees.

In this way, they stayed within the fog's protective cover while maintaining progress westwards, as much as they could.

'How much further south will we need to go?' Ruth asked, her brow furrowed, looking through the companionway hatch to the chart table below.

'I'm hoping that the bank of fog we're sailing in will extend round the coast as we close in on Holland. Then we can strike west while still keeping out of sight.'

'And what if it doesn't?'

'Then we stay in the fog until nightfall and head north-west under cover of dark.'

CHAPTER 156

While *The Shearwater* crept southwards towards the Frisian Islands, back in Kiel, the General fielded sympathetic enquiries from those he came in daily contact with, in the Kriegsmarine, the city council and the army, as well as from his personal staff and his colleagues in the Abwehr.

The news that General Kästner's sons had been missing, and were now presumed drowned on the Swedish coast, had spread throughout Kiel, and further afield.

Maria Kästner and her daughters confined themselves to the house on Drachensee, but the General forced himself to face the well-wishers at Naval Headquarters. It kept him busy, and it allowed him to make certain that all the attention was focussed on the north-east corner of the Skagerrak, where further items from *The Shearwater* had been found at first light.

Captain Bauer had been distraught when he heard the news.

'General Kästner, you shouldn't be in today,' he said. 'No one expects it of you.'

'Nonsense, my boy,' Erich Kästner had said. 'I'd go mad sitting at home, moping. I need to be busy, to occupy my mind.'

'Whatever you say, sir. All the staff have asked me to pass on their condolences; Frau Müller was in tears this morning when she came in.'

'Tell them all I appreciate their support and ask them to try and keep the office running as normal.'

The young man had agreed, but General Kästner could see he had grave reservations and, sure enough, all that morning, a stream of visitors passed through the outer office to sit in front of the General, all professing their intense shock and offering any help they could provide.

In between, the phone rang incessantly, and the General fielded their sympathetic platitudes with embarrassed thanks.

The lies laid heavy on his heart.

At lunchtime, he went home, only to find a distraught Yosef Nussbaum with a summons from the police, and Miriam standing beside him, folding and unfolding a dishcloth.

'We are to be at the police station at Falckstraße 4 by twelve tomorrow, sir,' she said.

'Did they say what it was about?' the General asked, taking the letter from Yosef. He skimmed through it. It simply requested their presence and was signed Kriminalassistent Werner Schmidt.

'He may just be wanting to talk to you about the lack of progress they're making in the search for Ruth and Manny,' the General said, not believing it.

He dismissed the Nussbaums concerns, reassuring them that he would accompany them, deciding that it was only fair to support them despite knowing that it would further incense Maria.

He found his wife sitting in the drawing room, dressed in black, with a black veil on her head, staring out of the window towards the lake.

His heart went out to her.

He went over and laid his hand on her shoulder, and she turned to him, tears in her eyes.

'Oh, Erich,' she said, 'It's awful.'

For the briefest moment, everything was as before, and he wanted to hold her in his arms and tell her the truth about her sons but when he went to take her hand, she pulled it away and stiffened.

'You were at work,' she said, her eyes accusing him.

'Yes. I had to do something, and I thought it would mean that I would hear any further news as soon as they had it,' he said.

'What news do you expect, other than that they've found my sons' bodies?'

'There has been nothing like that, but they did find several more items from *Der Sturmtaucher*; a spar, a life preserver and a wooden box with Franz's initials on it. I think it was the one his sextant was in.'

Maria Kästner let out a cry, then turned away.

'I won't even get to bury them,' she said.

He swallowed. The need to tell her the truth almost broke his resolve, but he stayed silent.

He had been going to mention the Nussbaums' summons to the police station, but he held back. She turned and looked at him.

'My sons are dead, our home is regularly besieged by the police and the Gestapo, I don't know who Antje is anymore, and Eva is heartbroken. This is all down to your obsession with sailing, and your Jewish *family*, and a determination to circumvent the laws laid down by our rightful government. Then, to cap it all, you still go to work and carry on as normal. How can you be so heartless?'

'I've already told you…'

Maria Kästner held up her hand.

'Stop. I'm not listening, Erich. You've made it plain that almost everything is of greater important to you than me. I'm going to my room to grieve for my sons. I'd rather do it alone.'

Erich Kästner's head slumped. When he looked up, she had gone.

~~o~~

Kriminalassistent Heinrich Güllich put the phone down. He smiled grimly at Carl Meyer.

'They've found wreckage. It's *The Shearwater*, without question. They're saying there's no hope the Kästner boys survived.'

'That's it, then, sir.'

The Kriminalassistent stayed silent.

'Sir?'

'I just don't buy it. Two expert yachtsmen, with plenty time to get to shelter, and wreckage conveniently found a week later.'

'You think they staged it?' Carl Meyer's face betrayed his scepticism.

'We have to consider it as a possibility.'

'How would they have done it, sir?'

'Well, you're the expert on sailing, it seems. You tell me if it's feasible.'

Carl Meyer flushed at the Kriminalassistent's unwarranted sarcasm but kept his silence.

'Think about it,' Heinrich Güllich said. 'The Kriegsmarine are looking for them, the boat has been searched once, and they realise that the net is closing. There's the mother of all storms approaching, and they can either run for cover in Norway, where there are German troops and German security service personnel, or they can sail to Sweden, a neutral country, and put themselves ashore, wrecking the boat at the same time, somehow.'

'It's all feasible, sir, apart from the last bit. That would be hard to do.'

'But not impossible?'

'No.'

'So, how would they do it?'

'Well, the easiest way would be to anchor off a beach somewhere, scuttle the yacht and make for shore in the tender.'

'So, what's the problem with that?'

'Sir, by the time they got there, the storm would be raging, and a big sea would be running. Landing on a lee shore like that in a small dinghy would be almost suicide unless…'

'Unless what?'

'They would have needed to find shelter, behind an island, or in a sheltered bay, with deep enough water to sink the boat.'

'Are there any places like that close to where the wreckage was found?'

'The objects they found would have drifted for miles and miles. It's my guess that, if this has been staged, they threw the items overboard not long after they'd been searched, then made for cover.'

'In Sweden?'

'Or Norway, or even back in Denmark, although that's questionable; there's not much shelter there.'

'The Kriegsmarine searched the coast of Norway, and part of the Swedish coast. They found nothing else. Wouldn't the yacht break up and be washed ashore?'

'Not necessarily, sir. It has an iron keel and, if the water was deep enough, the boat would sit on the bottom for years until it rots, well below the waves. They would have cut the rigging, allowing the masts to collapse.'

'Send the Swedish police pictures of the Nussbaums, and the Kästner boys. Tell them that the security services of the Third Reich would appreciate their assistance in apprehending them. Tell them that they are dangerous and…'

He paused.

'Tell them that they are trying to set up a route to smuggle arms and people into Denmark and Germany and to help dangerous resistance fighters escape to Sweden.'

'Yes, sir. Doesn't that request have to go through the foreign office?'

'No. I know an SD officer in the embassy in Stockholm. We will send it directly to him. In the meantime, we can apply a little more pressure to the Nussbaums and the Kästners tomorrow, when we have the Jews in for questioning again. Has that been confirmed?'

'Yes. Werner Schmidt phoned. 'He's expecting them in the station at twelve, midday.'

'Good. And he knows we'll be there?'

'Yes, sir.'

CHAPTER 157

When she finished her watch at eleven that morning, Johann took Ruth's place in the cockpit to speak with Franz, and she found herself sitting alone with Manny for the first time since they'd left Hobo Dyb.

She'd ruffled his hair and he scowled at her, half-boy, half-man brother.

'Are you all right?' she asked him.

'Yes. I'm fine,' he said.

Disappointed that he didn't want to talk to her, she looked away.

It hurts too much for him to speak about them.

For the hundredth time that day, she wondered what her parents were doing.

She saw Manny hesitate for a second, then he spoke again.

'When I came up before, I gave you a start, didn't I?'

She blushed.

'It was so quiet, and I was almost asleep. You caught me unawares.'

He gave her a half-smile, holding his hand out to hers, and taking it.

'I know about you and Franz,' he said.

She stared at him in stunned silence.

'Johann knows too.'

She didn't try to deny it.

'How?' she asked, her face still crimson.

'I'd sort of guessed; it was just the way you acted around each other, then, yesterday, Johann got very embarrassed trying to break it to me gently that you and Franz were together. I think he was relieved when I told him I already knew.'

'I'm sorry, Manny. I didn't mean to hurt you, or Mama or Papa.'

'You haven't,' Manny said, putting his hand over hers. 'I don't know for certain what they would say but I'm sure they'd want you to be happy. There's not a better person around than Franz Kästner; even Johann would say that and, if you are truly fond of him, you should do what you believe is right.'

Tears welled in Ruth's eyes and flowed down her cheeks.

'I thought you'd hate me for it, but I couldn't stop it happening anyway, even if I wanted to. I love Franz as much as I love you, and Mama and Papa. I just didn't want you to think I'd let them down.'

'You haven't. I'm not saying it's right, but I don't know if being right or wrong is as simple as they make out. Not with everything that's happened.'

She bowed her head.

'At school, in Kleiner Kuhberg, they would have disapproved,' he continued, 'but, deep down, I can't, when I see how happy you are. Johann was right.'

'For someone so young, Manny Nussbaum, you are very grown up.'

It was Manny's turn to blush.

Neither of the siblings spoke for a while, then Ruth covered her face with her hands.

'Was it yours or Johann's idea to…' she said, squinting between her fingers at him, unable to meet his gaze.

Manny grinned.

'Have you sleeping in the forepeak?' he said. 'It was Johann's suggestion, but he asked me if I was all right with it. I'm not a child, Ruth.'

Is he right? Why can't he still be my baby brother in some little way, even with what he's been through?

Perhaps, she thought, *a small scrap of the boy did remain.*

But she knew that she thought of him now as a young man now.

Sometimes an old man.

She smiled to herself.

It didn't stop her blushing again.

'I'm not sure I'm entirely comfortable with my little brother discussing something so personal,' she said, 'but I suppose I'm in no position to object.'

'I told Johann that as long as you were both happy, and that Franz cared for you, I could live with it. Whatever you do is between you and him.'

Ruth couldn't hold back her tears.

'Thank you, Manny. And just for the record, Franz loves me. Very much.'

'Johann said that. He told me Franz would never have done anything to hurt you or betray Mama and Papa's trust in him unless that was true. If I'd thought otherwise, I couldn't have looked the other way.'

'That's about how it is,' Ruth said. 'I want you to understand. None of us might survive this trip and, even if we do, we will all be separated, and I might never see Franz again. In normal times, Franz and I would have taken our time to get to know each other properly but these aren't normal times.'

'In normal times you two could never have got together.'

For a brief instant, she wondered where Manny's cynicism had come from, then she thought of all the horrors he'd seen.

'We'll be very discreet,' she said.

'I hope so,' he said, scowling, but the corner of his mouth gave away his smile.

She put her arms around him, and they held each other until Franz shouted that he was coming down, and that Manny should go up.

~~o~~

'Why are we being so strict about just having two on deck, when we're in fog?' Ruth asked, when Franz sat down across from her.

'I don't know if it would make any difference how many people were on board if they found us now but, if someone does spot us, at least there's a chance of talking our way out of it if there are only two of us.'

'But in the fog, they'll never see us.'

'Don't you want to spend all those hours on watch, alone, with me?' Franz teased.

'You know that's not true. Anyway, we don't have to be so secretive now.'

Franz froze.

'Manny,' he said. 'He knows?'

'Johann does too, Manny told me.'

'Scheiße. What did he say?'

'He's all right with it, I think. At least, that's what he said, but I suspect he struggles with the religious implications.'

'Good God, he will do. He seems quite devout, for a teenager.'

'He is, but much of that was a gut reaction to being singled out for being a Jew. It made him want to justify his existence and hold a fist up to those who persecuted him.'

'Does he know… ?'

'I think so. We didn't go into specifics; that would have been horrible, but yes. That's why he and Johann suggested that the off-watch pair should use the forecabin. It was to give us a bit of privacy.'

Franz's face reddened.

'It's bad enough with Johann knowing. I can just imagine the comments I'll get, but Manny. I don't know if I'll be able to look him in the eye.'

She laughed at him, and he laughed along with her.

'We have permission, you know,' she said softly. 'And no one is going to interrupt us…'

He kissed her, holding her head in his hands.

CHAPTER 158

Around lunchtime, *The Shearwater* burst out of the fog bank into bright sunshine, catching Johann by surprise.

Johann, almost blinded by the midday sun, swept his gaze across the horizon and gasped when he saw a vessel five or six miles off their starboard bow.

'A destroyer!' he barked at Manny. 'Helm to port.'

Manny had seen it and was already spinning the wheel. There had been no warning that the fog was thinning out and, when he looked back, the bank of dense white mist looked so unnaturally solid that, for a brief second, it felt that *The Shearwater* was running into a hard wall of ice, to be smashed against it and destroyed.

As the fog swallowed them up again, Johann glanced back and, with a sinking heart, fancied that the warship had changed direction towards them.

'Did they see us?' Manny asked, his face pale and drawn.

'I don't know. We were only out of the fog for twenty seconds at most, but we would have stood out against the whiteness of the fog bank like a polar bear in a coal bunker.'

'Can we not just hide in the fog? They'll never find us.'

'They might have that new radar device. It can see boats at night or in fog.'

'We're done for then,' Manny said.

'It all depends if they have it, or any of their watch officers were looking this way. Rainer Schulze said we don't show up well on radar if we're more than a few miles from them,' Johann said. 'We'll soon hear them if they have.'

'Should we wake Franz?'

Johann thought for a second or two.

'No. There's nothing he can do.'

'We could get into the tender.'

For a brief second, Johann considered it.

'If we hear it coming for us, I'll wake Franz, and I'll mention it. I don't know what use it would be, in the middle of the North Sea.'

'It was just a thought,' Manny said.

'It was a good idea,' Johann said. 'It might still be our only hope.'

'Listen,' Manny said, whispering now, as if those on the destroyer might hear him.

Johann turned his head and heard it, faintly, in the direction he'd seen the ship coming from.

He had his hand on Manny's shoulder, and the boy winced as his grip tightened.

The rhythmic rumble of the ship's propellers, and the swish of its wash was louder now and almost dead in front of them. Johann wondered if the first thing they'd see was the destroyer's bow as it emerged from the mist, cleaving *The Shearwater* in two.

The seconds dragged like minutes as the sounds steadily grew.

'It's an older vessel. That's a reciprocating steam engine, not a diesel or a turbine,' he said, not that it mattered.

'How do you know?'

'It's the absence of engine sound. A turbine has a low soft whine, and an oil-fired engine is loud, and unmistakable.'

He knew he was talking just for the sake of it; anything to distract, in the face of the inevitable.

'It's not getting any louder,' Manny said, his eyes full of hope.

'It may be slowing. They might want to pick us up, not ram us.'

'It's coming from over there now though,' Manny said, pointing further astern.

Johann turned his head a little.

'You're right,' he said, marvelling at the boy's sharpness of hearing.

A few minutes later, the deep rumble of the warship's screws began to recede northwards, and Johann sat down, his head in his hands.

'That was close,' he said.

'They didn't see us after all,' Manny said, grinning.

Johann looked at him and burst out laughing. He thumped Manny on the shoulder, and he didn't flinch this time.

Johann sat for a while, deep in thought. Something niggled at the back of his mind.

'Manny, steer five points to starboard,' he said, getting to his feet and gazing forward.

'But we'll come out of the fog again. The destroyer might still be there.'

'No. It was heading full speed to the north. And anyway, I'm going to go up to the bow. If I see any sunlight, I'll tell you to steer to port, so that we can stay just inside the edge of the fog.'

'Whatever you think,' Manny said, now intrigued.

Johann made his way to the bow and stood, looking out to starboard as *The Shearwater* came round five degrees.

A minute passed, then two, then five.

'Two degrees to port,' Johann shouted, and Manny edged the wheel round, watching the compass needle as it crept one degree, then two.

He looked out to starboard and could see a soft glow in the fog, and the surface of the water on that side now stretched to 100 metres, twice or three times the distance on the port side.

'A point to starboard,' Johann shouted.

'Are you kidding?' Manny said, but he nudged the wheel round and stared at the compass.

'That's a point to starboard,' he said.

Johann smiled at the sceptical tone in his voice.

But the mist around *The Shearwater* slowly cleared and the day brightened until, in a moment so surreal he thought he was dreaming, they were sailing straight along the edge of the fog bank, half-in and half-out of it.

He looked around. Through the occasional wisp of fog, he could see the far horizon, in a long sweep from the bow of the yacht to the stern. It was empty.

Johann clambered back to the cockpit, a grin on his face.

'Look,' he said, pointing

Manny followed his gaze.

The barrier of fog stretched out far ahead in an almost straight line but, perhaps five miles away, the bank veered round to the west, in a long wall of white reaching the far horizon.

'Franz was right,' Johann said. 'That must be the bank of fog off the coast of Holland. We can head west soon.'

We might just make it. Things are going our way, for once.

Manny, cheered by Johann's infectious exhilaration, grinned too.

They hugged.

Johann looked at the compass and made a mental note of the course they'd have to take to follow the edge of the fog.

'Five points to port,' he said.

As the sunlight disappeared, and the cold damp of the fog enveloped them again, he told Manny to steer one-eight-five.

He trailed the log, and the calculation he made confirmed his suspicions. At five knots, it would take them an hour to reach the point where the fog bank curved westwards.

He had sailed enough to know that it was notoriously difficult to gauge distances at sea, but it didn't matter. If they turned too early, they'd just have to turn back in; too late, and they would be a little deeper into the west-going fog bank than they'd intended.

He wanted to tell Franz, but when he slid back the hatch and looked down, the cabin was deserted.

He grinned. Only if the boat were sinking would he risk disturbing them.

'I told Ruth we knew,' Manny said, as if reading Johann's thoughts.

'You did? So, we don't have to tiptoe around them now?'

Manny laughed.

'No, but Franz might want to tell you himself.'

'That's our Franz, but he'll tell me almost nothing, other than that he's in love. He keeps his cards tight to his chest, does my brother.'

'Personally, I'll be happy if they stay there. I don't want to hear any details.'

Johann laughed.

'I suppose you're right. It must be a little strange for you, but I'd be comfortable in the same situation with Eva or Antje, as long as the fellow was a decent sort.'

'You've been with lots of women, haven't you?' Manny said, surprising Johann, who had the grace to look uncomfortable.

'It's probably not something to be proud of,' he said. 'I just love women, and I can't seem to help myself.'

'I'll be fifteen soon. I had a few girlfriends at school, and I kissed a girl once, but I never…'

'There's plenty time for that, Manny,' Johann said, his face serious for once. 'You know, as much as my friends think I'm the cat's whiskers because women come easy to me, a big part of me envies Franz.'

'What do you mean?'

'I fall in love every second week or so, it seems, and it's a blast, but it never lasts. Franz has only ever loved two women; Lise Böhm, who broke his heart, and now, your sister. I hope she might just mend it.'

'So, it's better to be like Franz?'

'My way is more fun, and you might want to try it for a while but, in the end, what Ruth and Franz have is something special.'

'Will you look for a girl like Ruth, one day?'

'I'll look for a girl exactly like Ruth,' he said.

~~o~~

Heinrich Güllich sat at his desk, reading through the Nussbaum file. The whole morning, he'd concentrated on the other cases that demanded his attention and tried to put the General and his Jews out of his mind.

But by lunchtime, when he'd dealt with the most pressing of the outstanding investigations, he opened the folder containing every document pertaining to the missing Nussbaum children and the Kästner family's involvement.

As he read each page, his frustration grew. He knew there were clues in there, but nothing definitive enough to take it to his Kriminaldirektor.

He picked up the telephone transcripts, and reread them, despite knowing them off by heart. Then he stopped, dead, and reread one of them.

'Meyer,' he shouted, 'come in here.'

Carl Meyer jumped whenever his boss required him to, and this time was no exception.

'Read this,' Heinrich Güllich said.

Carl Meyer took the sheet from his boss and read it.

'What am I looking for, sir? There are hundreds of calls like these; Kriegsmarine people wanting to know if there is any news about *Der Sturmtaucher*.'

'Yes, but this one in particular. Captain Hössler's call to the General's office.'

'Yes, sir. He passed on his concerns about the General's sons, sir. But so did half the people in the Kriegsmarine, it appears.'

'What does he say though? What are his exact words?'

Carl Meyer read it again.

'Sorry, sir. I don't see what you're getting at.'

'Dummkopf. "We became very fond of *Der Sturmtaucher*, and your sons".'

The younger man read it again, but a puzzled look remained on his face.

'Why would he say they had become very fond of the Kästner boys?' the Kriminalassistent said, as if to a child, 'unless they had something to do with them, and their yacht.'

'So, they might have been involved in some way?'

496

'Yes. Well done,' Heinrich Güllich said, sarcasm dripping from his words. 'We've ignored what the General's sons were doing in the lead-up to their departure. This Captain Hössler might give us a clue.'

'I see what you mean, sir. I'll chase him up today.'

'No. We'll chase him up now.'

CHAPTER 159

Franz slid back the hatch and looked around.

'How long are your tacks?' he asked.

'About an hour. Four or five miles. Sometimes longer if the fog extends a little further out. We've been heading westward since one o'clock.'

'I thought it was around then. The tacks were very gentle though.'

'Yes. We didn't want to wake you up,' Johann said, a grin at the corner of his mouth.

Franz shook his head. The teasing had started.

He knew Johann would goad the life out of him, but he would put up with it, in as good-natured a manner as he could, because he knew his brother would be overjoyed for him.

'You had a little excitement as well,' Franz said.

Johann reddened.

'We had a close call, but it happened so fast, I didn't want to disturb you.'

He described their encounter with the destroyer and his first sight of the bank of fog in the south, curving round to the west.

Franz nodded.

'I heard the commotion. I'll be up in ten minutes. We're due on watch soon anyway. We'll have a talk.'

'I'll come down,' Manny said.

'No. It will only be for a minute. You can stay. But wait until we are on the starboard tack. We'll be heading back into the fog then.'

~~o~~

Ruth handed up three mugs of coffee.

'Pass up the rum, please,' Franz said.

She rummaged in the locker behind the galley and passed the bottle up, giving him a puzzled look. Franz poured a generous tot into his and Johann's cup and, after a brief hesitation, a smaller measure into Manny's. He gave her the bottle back and she replaced it.

'The reason I want you to stay, Manny, is that I want to explain to you and Johann about Ruth and I.'

Johann sat back in the cockpit, with his hands behind his head. The hint of a smile appeared at the corners of his mouth.

'You don't have to,' Manny said.

Franz held up his hand.

'I do,' he said. 'You both deserve it, for different reasons.'

He took a large gulp of his coffee and screwed up his face.

'Dutch courage,' he said.

He looked straight at Manny.

'In an ideal world,' he continued, 'Ruth and I would have had a long courtship.'

He saw Johann smile to himself and wink at Manny. He ignored it.

'We've all been thrown together over the last few weeks but because of the way the watches were organised, Ruth and I have spent almost all our waking time together, and we've found ourselves liking one another more each day until we realised, by the time we reached Hobo Dyb, that what we felt for each other was far more than just friendship.'

'And you were the one who told me I wasn't to be on watch with Ruth because I might try and seduce her.'

Franz shook his head; he could see the glint of amusement in Johann's eyes.

'I feel bad about that, but I stand by my decision, with your record with women.'

He smiled at his brother.

'Touché,' Johann said, 'but if it was anyone else, I might question your motive.'

Franz frowned at him and turned to Manny.

'Manny, I didn't have any idea that this would happen, believe me. I've always been very fond of you both, and I consider you and your parents to be part of our family, which made it hard for me to reconcile what Ruth and I contemplated with what I promised you all.'

'You promised to get us to safety, and so far, you've delivered on that promise; whatever else happens is between you and Ruth, and while I can't speak for them, I suspect that my parents wouldn't object to you being together.'

~~o~~

Johann turned away to hide his smile. Franz and Manny were almost throwbacks to their grandfathers' days of reserve and deference, but he knew that the Jewish teenager had been forced to grow up fast, and Franz had always had that serious side to his nature that was so alien to Johann.

He turned back and lifted his mug.

'Here's to Franz and Ruth,' he said.

Their coffees finished, Johann and Manny went below, leaving Franz in the cockpit. As Ruth stood at the bottom of the companionway steps, waiting to come up, Johann stepped down and held his arms out. She stepped forward and he held her, somehow managing to whirl her off her feet in the cramped space of the cabin before putting her down.

'I'm so happy for you and the old man,' he said, smiling fondly at her. 'There's only one problem.'

'What's that?' she said, an amused frown on her face.

'You chose the wrong brother,' he said.

She laughed and poked him in the ribs.

As she climbed up the steps to join Franz on watch, still giggling, Johann watched her. He'd been only half-joking.

~~o~~

The marine guardsman held up his hand, and Carl Meyer brought the Gestapo car to a halt in front of the Kriegsmarine victualling yard gates and rolled down his window. A second marine stepped out of the guardhouse and leant down to see the two occupants of the car.

'Do you have passes, sirs?'

'Kriminalassistent Heinrich Güllich and Kriminalassistentanwärter Carl Meyer to see Captain Hössler. We telephoned.'

'Please wait a minute, sir.'

He disappeared into the guardhouse. Carl Meyer could see him through the window, talking on the telephone. When he returned, he told the first marine to open the gates.

'If you just pull over there,' he said, pointing to a low, two-storey building fifty metres inside the gates. 'Captain Hössler will come down and get you.'

With the barest nod of thanks, Carl Meyer drove through the gates, and parked where the man had indicated he should. As they got out, a naval officer emerged from the front door. The two Gestapo men returned his salute.

They followed him up a flight of stairs into his office, where he offered them two rather spartan chairs.

'Sorry about the seating,' he said, taking his place behind his desk. 'What can I do for you. Something about the Kästners' yacht?'

'Yes, as we indicated on the telephone, we are interested in how long the Kästner brothers berthed *Der Sturmtaucher* here before they left for Norway.'

The captain opened a file and scanned the first page.

'They moved her here on the twenty-first of March; that was a Friday. They left again on Wednesday the second of April. Just under a fortnight.'

'Did you see them leave?'

'No. I wasn't here. They left early in the morning. Around seven, I believe. You could ask the harbour master; he'll have all the paperwork.'

The two Gestapo men glanced at each other.

'Ah,' Captain Hössler said. 'I had expected you'd realise, but I suppose it's not common knowledge. Since the beginning of the war, all movements of vessels to and from Kieler Hafen have required clearance papers; indeed, the whole voyage would need clearances, especially as they were travelling to Denmark, then Norway.'

'Where is the harbour master's office?' Heinrich Güllich said.

'It's over at Fischhafen, on Wall. You can't miss it.'

Carl Meyer suppressed a smile. The Kriminalassistent was being made to look like an amateur.

He knew where the fishermen's harbour was and, now that he thought about it, he could picture the building that housed the harbour master's office. He and Heinrich Güllich had called at it a year before, when an SS man had drowned, and the circumstances had been deemed suspicious enough to warrant Gestapo involvement.

'Of course. I remember now,' Heinrich Güllich muttered. 'What is of greater importance is the security at this yard. Were the Kästner brothers permitted to come and go as they pleased?'

'No. Not at all. They were issued with passes and would have been signed in and out every time they entered or left the yard.'

'And no one else visited the boat?'

'Well, yes. The General for one, but he has a pass for most, if not all Kriegsmarine facilities. He would have been signed in, too, though. And, of course, Colonel Schneider, the boat's owner visited on two or three occasions. He was issued with a special pass each time he was here.'

'So, no one else?'

'Not as far as I'm aware of.'

'What about the General's daughter?'

Heinrich Güllich flipped open his notebook and looked down.

'Antje,' he said.

'Ah,' the captain said, blushing a little. 'I think she might have been. The night before they left, to see the boat.'

'And this would all be documented?'

The captain's blush deepened.

'Well, I suppose so. I wasn't here. I'd have to check at the gatehouse.'

'We'll do that on the way out. Is it not a little irregular to let an unaccompanied civilian into a naval base?' Carl Meyer asked, glancing at his boss.

'She wasn't unaccompanied. The General would have been with her.'

'And he is a member of the Kriegsmarine?'

'Not officially, but he is attached to the base in Kiel, and has the highest clearance.'

'Going back to the day before they left, did you see them at all that day?'

'I think I said goodbye to them earlier that day, or perhaps the day before.'

'And you saw nothing suspicious about the boat?'

'Of course not. What do you mean, suspicious?'

Heinrich Güllich ignored the question.

'Are all vehicles searched when they enter and leave the base?' he asked.

'Yes, they are.'

'How thoroughly?'

'Very thoroughly.'

'What about staff vehicles?'

'Yes, mostly. What I mean is, we do spot checks.'

'So, they're not always searched then?'

'Not every time, I suppose.'

'And the General. Would he be considered to be *staff*?'

'No. He would always be treated as a visitor.'

'And his sons?'

'The same.'

'And if one of the admirals came to visit the base?'

The captain blushed again.

'Well?' Heinrich Güllich said, his voice not much more than a whisper.

'The vehicle would probably not be searched. But they would always be in an official Kriegsmarine car.'

'And General Kästner. Are you sure he wouldn't be treated the same? If he was in his official army car?'

Carl Meyer smiled at the captain's discomfort.

'No. I'm sure the men would search every time.'

Carl Meyer thought that the man couldn't have sounded less certain. And he could see beads of sweat on his forehead.

'That will be all, Captain,' he heard Heinrich Güllich say.

Surprised that the Kriminalassistent wasn't pressing on with this, he stood up when his boss did, and shook the naval officer's hand, then saluted.

~~o~~

Carl Meyer waited until they'd swept through the gates before he spoke to Heinrich Güllich.

'Sir, why did you stop your questioning of the captain so abruptly? His nerves were beginning to get the better of him.'

'It suits me better to let him stew a while,' the Kriminalassistent said.

'But neither the Kästner girl nor her cousin were signed in or out. Does that not point to lax security at least, collusion at worst?'

'I'm almost sure the Nussbaum children were smuggled in here. Security, as far as the Kästners went, was woefully slack, but I don't want the captain running to his superiors saying that we were heavy-handed or warn his marines that we're investigating them.'

'I see, sir,' Carl Meyer said. 'But we are going to interview them?'

'Yes. I need you to trace all personnel who were on guard duty over the period *Der Sturmtaucher* was berthed there. Some may have moved on, but I want you to be discreet. And we need to visit the harbour master.'

~~o~~

Franz checked his watch and he and Ruth tacked *The Shearwater*, as if they'd done it together all their lives.

The yacht's bow bit into the water, heading her back to the edge of the fog and, more importantly, westwards and northwards to England.

In the light winds, *The Shearwater* almost sailed herself, only needing the occasional check and minor adjustment to the helm.

They sat together, not minding the dismal light and the constant, dripping damp, nor the need to keep watch. They talked, as always, continuing to condense a year or two of getting to know one another into a few weeks.

And Ruth's English improved a little, day by day.

~~o~~

The harbour master in Kiel was a much more officious individual than his equivalent in Hirtshals, and Heinrich Güllich approved. He and Carl Meyer showed their credentials and were invited into the man's office.

'My clerk will have the records you require in a few minutes,' he said. 'Every single vessel that moves in or out of Kieler Hafen is accounted for.'

'That's excellent. We're trying to find out if there could have been anyone on board *The Shearwater*, in addition to the Kästner brothers.'

'I would doubt it. Their manifest listed only two persons, and no cargo, other than a reasonable quantity of supplies for the length of the journey that was being undertaken.'

'We have suspicions that they may have been trying to smuggle two children out of Germany. Jewish children.'

'Preposterous. Security at the Kriegsmarine dockyard is tight, and the yacht was checked at the marine barrier, against the manifest that was registered here the day before.'

'So, there's no way they could have called at one of the small harbours or jetties after leaving the base?'

'None at all. They would almost certainly have been seen by someone. Anyway, I go back to the fact that the boat was searched again at the marine barrier and, I can tell you, they're very thorough; I receive untold numbers of complaints from the masters of vessels, large and small, every week, and I tell them the same thing.'

'And what is that?' Carl Meyer said. His sarcastic tone earned him a glare from Heinrich

Güllich.

'That if they search every locker, and every corner of the hold, it is only for the safety of the Reich.'

Heinrich Güllich smiled.

'Most commendable,' he said. He pretended to think for a second.

'What about after they'd passed through the marine barrier?' he asked. 'Is there anywhere they could have called in?'

'Well, there's Laboe, on the east shore of Kieler Förde but that's a busy little fishing harbour. Someone would have spotted them.'

'What about the other shore?'

'It's a bit of a detour, but there is Schilksee Hafen, or Strande Hafen. Both are small, and quieter. It should be easy to find out if they called at any of these places, without too much effort.'

'How?' Heinrich Güllich said, glancing at Carl Meyer.

'They must have sailed close to the lightship out at Stollergrund, on their way northwards.'

'What of it? Would they have seen which direction they came from?'

'Perhaps. But even simpler, I know they keep a record of every ship passing. And the time–'

'If they took longer than would be expected, they might have called in somewhere,' Carl Meyer interrupted, rushing his words.

'It could also eliminate the possibility,' the harbour master said, 'if they made good time.'

'Either of these two pieces of information would be useful, Herr Harbour Master,' Heinrich Güllich said.

~~o~~

'Sir, that's three times the boat was checked by the Kriegsmarine, including the search in the Skagerrak. Could we be wrong? I mean, surely they wouldn't all turn a blind eye?'

'Meyer, don't be naïve. There's only one real search they had to get through. The security at the base is lax, especially when it applies to the marvellous Kästner family; the search in the Skagerrak was cursory, I'd imagine. On the surface, it would appear that the personnel at the marine barrier were thorough, but they could be infected with the blindness the rest of the Kriegsmarine are stricken with.'

'I suppose you're right, sir. We'll soon find out; we're almost there.'

The car crossed the Prinz-Heinrich-Brücke that spanned the Nord-Ostsee-Kanal and skirted the airfield. As they rejoined the waterfront, they looked out at the marine barrier stretching across Kieler Förde to the opposite shore, the sentry vessel blocking the gap in its centre.

The marine barrier depot was on the shore front; they'd arranged to be picked up and taken out to the barrier by a Kriegsmarine launch. Heinrich Güllich lit a cigarette, glad it was a benign sort of day. He wasn't sure about his sea legs despite Carl Meyer's assurances to him that the Förde would be flat calm, and that the trip would only take a few minutes.

~~o~~

Kapitänleutnant Meier, the officer who'd inspected *Der Sturmtaucher* on her exit from Kieler Hafen, proved even more officious than the harbour master, but it didn't suit Heinrich Güllich, or his suspicions. He and Carl Meyer came away with the feeling that had the Nussbaums been on *The Shearwater*, they must have been extremely well hidden.

They were fortunate with the lightship keepers who had been on station when the Kästner yacht passed; they were onshore, just off duty, and had taken note of when *Der Sturmtaucher* had passed, heading northwards.

'We sent them a good luck message,' the younger keeper said, laughing.

'What's funny about that?' Carl Meyer said, giving the young man a malevolent stare.

The trainee lighthouse keeper blanched.

'Sorry, sir. It was a little rude. As was their reply. We were all terribly saddened to hear about them.'

'I'm sure you were,' Heinrich Güllich said.

Carl Meyer looked up from the ledger the lighthouse keepers had given him.

'Sir, I don't think they stopped anywhere after leaving the marine barrier. They left it at six minutes past eight and passed the light vessel at nine-thirty. That's just under an hour and a half. It's over seven miles. The winds that day were decent, but they would have been hard pushed to call in at Laboe, far less the harbours on the east shore.'

~~o~~

'We need to find the verdammte boat, if it's still in one piece,' Heinrich Güllich said, on the drive back to the office. 'They must have fashioned a hiding place on it, for these infernal Jews of theirs. You know that Jews are like sewer rats. They can hide in the smallest stinking hole.'

Carl Meyer smiled. He didn't know if the Nussbaums had ever been on the boat, or if the General or his family had anything to do with them vanishing but, in a way, he admired the Kriminalassistent for not letting the facts destroy his belief that he was right.

And a small part of him still harboured the belief that Heinrich Güllich was the only one who saw the truth, and he vowed he would do everything in his power to help him.

CHAPTER 160

Early the next morning, the wind died.

Johann and Manny had come on watch just before midnight, and they'd made steady progress in the small hours of their third Friday on *The Shearwater* but, by four, the wind had turned flukey, backing first to the south, then veering round to the north-west, before dying.

'We're close to the edge of the fog,' Johann said. 'I hope we don't drift out of it, with sunrise coming.'

'Surely if there's no wind we'll just stay in the same place?'

'There's still tide, even if it is weak.'

'Oh,' Manny said. 'I forgot about the tide.'

'We can always row,' Johann said.

Manny laughed.

'No, seriously,' Johann said. 'And we only need one oar.'

Manny frowned. His first thought was that Johann was suffering from a lack of sleep.

'Watch,' Johann said. He climbed onto the side deck and untied the assortment of poles, boat hooks and brushes that were stowed against the coachroof and extracted one of the oars that they used with the tender.

He handed it to Manny, who looked at it in disbelief.

He crossed over to the deck on the port side and unlashed the replacement whisker pole they'd fashioned, used to pole out the jib or fly the balloon foresail, the forerunner of the spinnaker much loved in racing.

Back in the cockpit, he lashed the oar to it, with the blade and part of the shaft extending beyond the end of the pole.

On a cleat on the port stern quarter, he made a loop with a bight of line around the pole and dipped the oar into the water.

'Watch this,' he said, and began rotating the oar in a figure of eight movement, like that used by the gondoliers in Venice.

Manny smirked when nothing happened, then *The Shearwater* stirred, inching forward, leaving gentle ripples in her wake. As Johann worked the makeshift oar, she began to pick up a little speed.

'That's fantastic,' Manny said, shaking his head in disbelief, 'but why don't we just use the engine?'

Johann laughed.

'My brother has a pathological hatred of engines.'

'Why?'

'Ach, he doesn't really hate engines but there are a few reasons we'll not use it unless we have to. The most important one is that while the engine is running, we'll not hear other vessels until they're much closer.'

Manny nodded. 'That makes sense.'

'We also have over 200 miles to go, or perhaps more, and this boat's fuel tanks aren't that big, so Franz wants to keep the fuel in reserve in case we have to make a desperate break for it against the wind, or with no wind at all.'

'There's no wind now.'

'That's true, but we're relatively safe while we're in the fog bank. Later, we may not have that luxury of being hidden from view.'

'So, we just wait for wind?'

'Yes.'

Manny shrugged, but Johann could sense the teenager's nervous frustration.

Johann smiled at him. He lifted the oar from the water and stowed away its constituent parts. He sat down next to Manny again.

'There's another reason why Franz tries to do everything under sail,' he said. 'He likes the idea that men have sailed for millennia without engines and, to be like them, we should only use engines if all else fails. My father has equally strong views on motoring.'

'What about you?'

'I'm with them on this for most of the time, but I get bored, and give in.'

Johann was relieved to see a smile on Manny's face again.

'I like the idea of using sail alone,' Manny said, 'but if it gets us to safety, I'd use the engine.'

'There will be wind, don't worry. And if it comes down to it, Franz will use the engine if we need to. I promise you.'

But for interminable hour after interminable hour, not a breath of wind disturbed *The Shearwater*'s sails. She sat becalmed through the last hour of the watch, and over half of the next one.

~~o~~

Johann woke out of a deep sleep to an intermittent knocking sound. He sat up and looked towards the doorway, expecting Franz or Ruth to open it and tell them it was time for him and Manny to go on watch.

Then he looked at the time; it was only six-thirty and they'd been off watch for less than two hours.

He realised the knocking wasn't coming from the door, but from the hull beside him.

The anchor. It must have come loose.

He hurriedly dressed and slid out of the forepeak, careful not to wake Manny, and made his way across the empty main cabin.

When he opened the hatch and peered out, Franz and Ruth sat huddled together.

'What's wrong?' Franz whispered, and Johann realised that Ruth was dozing, curled up against him.

He crept over to Franz and spoke into his ear.

'I think the anchor's worked loose. It's banging on the side of the hull.'

He looked at Ruth, leaning comfortably against Franz.

'I'll go and sort it,' he said. 'I wouldn't want to spoil your domestic bliss.'

~~o~~

Franz heard Johann laughing quietly and watched him walk up the side deck until he reached the bow, the beam of his torch shining downwards.

He nodded to himself, pleased that Johann had the sense to keep any light shining out from the boat at a minimum.

He saw him freeze in the dim glow of the torch, and stare over the side. The faint sound of laughter died in his throat.

For an age, he didn't move, then he turned slowly to Franz and called to him.

'A mine,' he said quietly, as if shouting would set it off.

Franz felt his heart stop. He gently shook Ruth, and she woke, not knowing quite where she was for a second.

'Stay here,' he said, trying to keep the rising flood of panic from his voice.

He made his way forward, removing the boat hook from its place on the coachroof.

He looked over the bow and, in the light of Johann's torch, saw the mine.

'It's a contact mine,' Johann said, the fear in his voice unmistakable.

Franz handed him the boat hook.

'Be careful,' he said.

Just as Johann reached down to place the boathook on the black, spherical surface to push it away, the mine slowly turned and the Kästner brothers watched with horror as one of the horns touched *The Shearwater*'s hull.

For a second, neither man moved, but nothing happened.

'They must be designed to need a significant force to depress them,' Franz said, 'So that they don't get accidentally set off, by fish, or seals or the like.'

'I wouldn't take a chance on that,' Johann mumbled.

'I'll go and start the engine. When I give the signal, push the mine away, and I'll put us into reverse. And tell Ruth to shout to Manny and get him into the cockpit.'

Johann nodded, although both realised the futility of getting Manny out of the forepeak, where he was within centimetres of the mine, should it go off. They knew that if the mine were to explode, they were all dead, one way or another.

~~o~~

When Franz had gone, Johann looked at both ends of the boathook and frowned. The wooden handle gave him more confidence than the hook, but either of them could slip on the smooth, wet, rounded surface of the mine. He glanced around but could see nothing else he could use.

He took off his oilskin and removed his jumper. He wrapped it around the hook at the end of the pole and tied it with the sleeves, forming a pad that would make it less likely to glance off.

He looked towards the silent cockpit and felt very alone; Franz would be down below, starting the engine, and Ruth would be telling Manny about the mine.

He heard someone moving below deck and hoped it was the Nussbaums leaving the forecabin, then the engine started.

A few seconds later, he heard Franz shout from the cockpit that they were ready.

He leaned over and placed the padded end of the boathook on the surface of the mine, as far away as he could from the terrifying horns sticking out from its casing.

He pushed, but nothing happened for a second, and he wondered if it was still tethered to the bottom. He leaned more heavily on the boathook.

He began to feel the mine give. A gap of a couple of centimetres appeared, and then ten. By the time he was at full stretch, it was almost two metres away. He withdrew the pole, taking care not to touch one of the mine's spikes, and called to Franz.

He felt the boat move backwards and the mine slowly drew away from the bow, its retreat quickening as the boat gathered pace. He followed it with the torch until it disappeared into the fog.

'I'm going to go half a mile north and west of it,' Franz shouted.

'I'll stay up here until we're clear of it, Johann said.

He heard Franz's shouted approval, and Johann stared at the sea ahead while Franz steered *The Shearwater* in a wide circle around the mine's position. Ten minutes later, he heard the engine being killed, and he returned to the cockpit.

Johann began to speak but Franz raised his hand.

'Listen out for a second,' he said.

They all stood silently, straining to hear something but the air around was silent, save for the quiet, gentle creaking of the yacht.

'Good,' Franz said.

'What about using the engine for a while, Franz,' Johann said, glancing at Manny.

'We could,' Franz said, giving Johann a questioning look.

'Even a couple of knots in the right direction would do wonders for morale. We could stop every so often and listen for other boats.'

'If we keep starting and stopping the engine, without running it long enough, we'll flatten the battery.'

'True, but if worst comes to worst, we can hand-start it, and we could keep a lookout up forward. The noise of the engine is less up there, and it would also be useful in case of further mines, like that one.'

Franz knew that what he said made a lot of sense. Any distance they put between themselves and the German Navy was vital, especially as they couldn't guarantee that the fog would stick around forever.

'All right,' Franz said. He looked at his watch.

'We've over half of our watch left. Ruth can helm and I'll go forward first. We'll take turns on lookout. Relieve us at eleven.'

CHAPTER 161

Two hours later, a light breeze filled in from the west. Franz had taken it upon himself to stay as the forward lookout, coming back every ten minutes to cut the engine, check the compass, and listen out for other vessels in the silence, before starting it again and returning to his post at the bow.

Within a few minutes, the wind had increased enough for him to switch the engine off and instruct Ruth to turn southwards until the sails filled.

'It feels better being under sail again,' she said, smiling.

'It's always more satisfying,' Franz said, 'and I feel much safer without the noise of the engine.'

It wasn't entirely soundless; there was still the slap of the small waves against the hull, the gurgle of the wash at the stern and the occasional flap of a luffed sail but these were nothing compared to the rhythmic thump of the motor.

~~o~~

'They'll just have finished breakfast at home,' Ruth said. 'I wonder what is happening.'

Franz looked at her. Her comment had come out of the blue.

'I'm hoping Father has managed to get your parents away by now,' he said, giving her an encouraging smile. 'That's three weeks.'

'It's hard to believe it's been that long. Do you really think they'll be on their way?'

'Father was confident that he could organise it and I know he wanted to have them out of Germany as quickly as possible.'

He could see her fighting back tears.

'Oh, I hope it's true. I know their journey is just as dangerous as ours, but at least they have a chance.'

'I hear you praying for them every night,' he said. 'I'm sure God will listen to you.'

She squeezed his hand and gave him a tearful smile.

~~o~~

Maria Kästner watched in disgust as the General held the door for Miriam and Yosef to get into the car, then climbed in after them. Albert already had the engine running and at a gesture from the General, he pulled out of the drive.

She turned away. The General had told her that morning that he would be back well before twelve to accompany the Nussbaums to the police station.

There had been another blazing row, and she'd stayed upstairs when he'd arrived home, not wanting to have to speak to him, or to the Nussbaums.

She stood back from the window, deep in thought.

Descending the stairs, she then telephoned the countess.

'I was wondering if we could meet up,' she said.

'Of course, my dear Maria. I'm so sorry for your loss. How are you bearing up?'

'I can't tell you the depths of despair I feel, Countess. There are days when I simply can't face anyone.'

'Why don't you come up here? Would tomorrow do?'

'I don't know, although...'

'It would do you good. A change of scenery. You should bring Eva.'

'I believe she and Hugo have plans for tomorrow.'

'Oh, that's so disappointing. They're such a sweet couple.'

Eva's continuing romance with the countess's nephew was the only bright light in the darkness that blighted her life.

'I'll invite a few people over; they're desperate to meet you.'

A surge of disappointment at not having the countess to herself was countered by the possibilities afforded by adding new friends to her repertoire. It would impress the Guild ladies, including the mayor's wife and the foul Beate Böhm.

'That is so kind of you, Countess. What time should I be there?'

'Come for luncheon, my dear, around one. And Maria, please call me Margarethe.'

'I'd be delighted to call you Margarethe. It's such a lovely name.'

'And you and I will get a chance to have a little talk, just the two of us.'

'I'll look forward to that,' Maria Kästner said, immensely pleased with herself, despite her pain.

~~o~~

'Listen. An engine.'

By now, Johann trusted Manny's ears without question.

'Where?'

'North-north-east,' Manny said, without hesitation.

'I'll helm,' Johann said. 'I want you to concentrate on listening to it.'

Within a few minutes, Johann could hear the approaching vessel's engines himself and could tell the sound was coming from somewhere north of them, but as the whine of the ship's turbines grew steadily louder, and the rhythmic beat of her screws vibrated through *Der Sturmtaucher*'s wooden hull, Manny began to look concerned.

'Still north-north-east, Johann.'

'Call Franz and Ruth,' he said, and Manny scurried down the companionway.

A single blast from its horn signalled that the ship was entering the fog bank and Johann hoped that it had slowed down, as it should do in reduced visibility.

Franz, already in his clothes and oilskins, emerged from the companionway.

'The vibration woke me up,' he said. 'What is it?'

'A largish vessel, heading straight for us, I think, at speed. If they have radar, they might see us, but then we're done for, and if they don't, there's a chance they'll cut us in half.'

They could all hear the rush of the ship's wash now as its bow cut through the sea towards them.

'Manny, switch on the engine battery,' Franz called down the companionway, just as Ruth appeared at the head of the steps.

He heard the clunk of the battery switch and pressed the starter. The engine turned four or five times, then rumbled into life. He pushed the throttle forward to engage the propeller and turned to Johann.

'Turn towards it,' Franz said.

'Towards it?' Johann hissed. 'Are you sure?'

'Yes. Just do it.'

~~o~~

Franz knew it went against all the collision regulations but normally, a vessel wasn't trying to remain invisible. In fog, *The Shearwater* should have been making sound signals since leaving Hobo Dyb.

The yacht came round quickly through the wind and the sails filled on the starboard side.

The ship sounded its horn again, dead ahead.

'Manny, Ruth. Lie down, out of sight.'

The two Nussbaums reacted quickly to Franz's urgent command and flattened themselves.

The noise from the ship's bow wave roared like a river now, and the surface of the sea seemed to vibrate with the deep throb of the ship's massive screws.

'Hard to starboard,' Franz shouted, holding his head to one side. He pushed the throttle fully forward and, with the sails and the engine working in tandem, *The Shearwater*'s bow swung round and surged forward.

They watched in horror as, fifty metres away, just off their port side, a whirling vortex appeared in the fog for a second, and a tall blade of grey-painted iron filled their view, crashing towards them.

'Kriegsmarine!' Johann shouted.

The ship's bow towered over *The Shearwater*'s stern as it passed within metres, and the bow wave lifted the yacht as if she were a toy, almost capsizing her.

'Hard to port,' Franz shouted to Johann, feeling *The Shearwater*'s stern being thrown across towards the cold grey of the warship's hull.

Johann turned the wheel and *The Shearwater* surfed down the back of the ship's wash, parallel to the unending grey of the ship's hull.

The sails flapped uselessly, the yacht's wind smothered in the shelter of the warship's lee. Only the drive from the propeller gave them any way at all.

Franz, worried that the engine might be heard by the ship's crew, almost throttled back but decided against it, figuring that it would be drowned out by the noise of the ship itself.

The solid grey wall, towering over *The Shearwater*'s mast, slid past them forever, it seemed, and Franz looked up, expecting to see sailors or marines pointing downwards at them, gesticulating, but the ship appeared bereft of crew, like a modern-day *Marie Celeste*.

The stern cleared them at last, and the deep rumble of its screws turned the surface into a turmoil of tumbling white foam that threatened to suck *The Shearwater* in. As it passed, Franz and Johann craned their necks upwards.

Far above them, at the head of the wide, flattened, overhanging stern with its two cavernous doors, a seaman leaned over the rail, smoking.

Franz and Johann froze. The sailor only had to glance to the side to see them. Franz saw the tip of the man's cigarette glow red as he took a draw, and the column of smoke as he exhaled, quickly dispersed by the breeze.

The seconds seemed to last forever, and Franz couldn't fathom out how the man hadn't seen them. Then, for a second, he appeared to look straight at *Der Sturmtaucher* and straighten, as if he'd noticed them. Then he was gone, leaving nothing but the grey fog surrounding them, and the boiling of the ship's wake.

~~o~~

Johann let out a long breath as the wind caught the sails, and he turned the wheel slowly, as if in a dream.

'It was a minelayer,' Franz said. 'Those two doors at the back are where they drop mines from.'

'*Brummer*,' Manny said, getting up. 'I saw her name as she passed.'

Ruth lifted herself up and sat next to Franz. He put his arm around her, despite her shyness.

'I can't say I've seen her in Kiel,' Franz said, 'but she could be new.'

'Do you think the sailor saw us?' Ruth asked.

Johann realised that Ruth and Manny must have been watching the whole incident with horror, lying on the cockpit floor.

'He might imagine he saw something, but he'll not know what it was. He only caught a glimpse of us as we disappeared into the mist. With any luck, he'll be too unsure of himself to say anything.'

'Either they didn't have radar, or they didn't see us on it,' Johann said.

'I'm not so sure a minelayer would have radar but, if they did, the operator must have dozed off, because they didn't make a move to avoid us.'

'What now?' Johann asked.

'We need to get as far west as we can in this fog by nightfall, then make a dash north-west for the east coast of England.'

'What about just going straight for the Thames estuary. It's the closest point to us.'

'There's more chance of coming across a Kriegsmarine vessel that far south, trying to run the channel or raiding English shipping. We should aim for north of the Wash if we can and, if the wind stays as it is, we can make it without tacking.'

Johann could see the sense of it. A constant broad or beam reach, or even a close reach, would cover a much greater distance towards safety than tacking back and forth. And the two close calls they'd had in the space of a few hours, with the mine and the ship, had shaken him. A thought struck him as Franz and Ruth disappeared down the companionway for the rest of their off-watch spell.

Just how much luck can we expect before it runs out?

~~o~~

Carl Meyer knocked on the Kriminalassistent's office door.

'Come in.'

He opened the door. Heinrich Güllich sat in the smoke-filled room, staring at a file in front of him. Carl Meyer didn't have to ask which one it was.

'Sir, I hope you don't mind, but I've been doing a little research on the yacht.'

The Kriminalassistent turned his head towards the younger Gestapo man, a weary look in his eyes.

'And what brilliant conclusions did you come to?'

'Well, sir. I spoke with one of the Scheindorf brothers from the yard that overhauled the boat during the winter. They say there was no way any hidden compartments could have been built into the yacht and that neither Colonel Schneider, nor indeed Franz Kästner, suggested any alterations which would lead him to believe that they were planning to smuggle anyone on board.'

'You came in here to tell me that?'

'No, sir. The man drew me a rough plan of the yacht. I showed it to my father. He thinks that there are one or two places in the boat where they could have hidden the children.'

'Ah. Your father.'

'Yes, sir. He's been about boats all his life. He said not many places would survive a thorough search.'

'And where were these?'

'The bilges, sir. And the anchor chain locker.'

'The bilges? Where are they?'

'At the bottom of the boat, below the floor of the cabin. Here, sir.'

He pointed them out on the crude diagram.

'And I presume the anchor locker is at the front.'

'Yes, sir. He said that you would have to dispense with much of the chain, but it was just about possible.'

'Did your father say anything else?'

Carl Meyer ignored the deep sarcastic tone in the Kriminalassistent's voice.

'Yes, sir. He said that he'd seen *Der Sturmtaucher* sailing once or twice and, if any boat could survive that storm, she could.'

'None of that helps us, Meyer, does it?'

'Well, sir.' He took a deep breath. 'I took the liberty of contacting everyone who'd been on *Der Sturmtaucher* during her voyage again and questioned them about their time on the yacht. It turns out that neither Kapitänleutnant Meier nor Captain Hössler's team looked in the bilges, nor in the anchor locker. The harbour master at Hirtshals repeated that he'd not done a search of the vessel, but he was there for an hour, at least, and there was no sign of any stowaways. The two officers from the patrol vessel said the same.'

'So, that proves they could still have been hidden. I knew that anyway.'

'We still haven't talked to Rainer Schulze, the officer who conducted the search in the Skagerrak.'

'Ha. Navy pals. They raced yachts together. The elite, looking out for the elite.'

'I don't know, sir. The report on the search sounded as if he'd been extremely thorough.'

'He didn't find the Nussbaums. Obviously, he wasn't thorough enough.'

'I still think it would be worth talking to him. His ship berths in Kiel on Sunday. I believe we should pay him a visit.'

Heinrich Güllich looked at the young detective, and Carl Meyer expected to be given a volley of abuse, but the Kriminalassistent nodded.

'Set it up.'

'I already have, sir.'

Miriam and Yosef looked around and glanced at each other. The police station wasn't quite as intimidating as the Gestapo building, but it filled them both with a sense of dread. It was reassuring having the General in attendance; it gave Miriam hope that they would be returning home later that day rather than be detained in the cells or, worse still, sent to one of the camps.

They'd given their names to the desk sergeant and had taken seats in the waiting area.

Miriam had been a little nervous when the General had taken leave of them, but he'd assured them he'd return once he'd told Albert that he could go back home to see if Maria needed the car.

She'd been happy to see him back, even with an anxious frown on his face.

He leaned in to talk in whispers to them both.

'I don't want you to worry but it's better that you know,' he said. 'I've just seen Heinrich Güllich in the corridor. It may just be coincidence but don't be surprised if he's involved.'

Both the Nussbaums paled. Despite a conditioned sense that the worst could happen, they'd harboured slim hopes that the visit was just a routine update on their missing children and that Werner Schmidt still believed their story.

'I would happily see that one dead,' Miriam said, under her breath.

Yosef glanced around then glared at her.

'No one heard me,' she said, shaking her head at him.

'Miriam Nussbaum. Yosef Nussbaum.'

~~o~~

Werner Schmidt stood in the doorway. The General was the first to rise, and strode over to the policeman, who held out his hand.

'I was sorry to hear about your sons,' the detective said, his face softening, to Erich Kästner's surprise.

'Thank you, Kriminalassistent Schmidt. It has been a hard week. I was wondering if I might be allowed to sit with the Nussbaums during their interview.'

Werner Schmidt smiled to himself. It was exactly as Heinrich Güllich had predicted, and the policeman played the part that he'd been asked to do.

'It's most irregular, Herr General. For myself, I wouldn't mind but there are others involved.'

'The chief?' the General said. 'I'm sure he would have no objections.'

'No, sir. The Gestapo have asked to be observers in this meeting.'

'Then, as it's a meeting, and not an interview, perhaps another "observer" would not be a tall order.'

Werner Schmidt hesitated, as he'd been told to do, then conceded.

'I can't promise that they'll agree, Herr General.'

'Danke.'

~~o~~

Heinrich Güllich was already in the room, sitting with his assistant at the back.

He raised an eyebrow when the General entered and gave Werner Schmidt a quizzical look.

'Herr Güllich,' the KriPo man said, 'General Kästner has asked to be present. I trust you have no objections?'

'It is very irregular, but in the light of his recent loss, it would be churlish to refuse.'

Heinrich Güllich turned to the General.

'We were all very saddened by your sons' deaths,' he said, the lie laid bare by the hint of a smile at the corner of his mouth.

'But one wonders,' he continued, 'at the prudence of attempting such a voyage at this time of year.'

'They were unlucky,' the General said, letting his anger at the Gestapo officer's mocking duplicity show.

He turned to Werner Schmidt.

'Can you tell us the reason for this meeting?'

'Of course,' the policeman said, his eyes turning away from the General's gaze. 'We're here to review the case and to see how we go move it forward'

'That's excellent,' the General said, turning to Yosef and Miriam, 'Isn't it?'

They both nodded numbly, glancing at the two Gestapo men.

'Perhaps not, Herr General,' Werner Schmidt said. 'We haven't been able to make as much progress as we'd expected. It is remarkable that there have been so few sightings of these two young people, despite extensive enquiries.'

'In fact,' interjected Heinrich Güllich, 'apart from the members of the Kästner household, not one further person has seen these *children* for weeks, perhaps months.'

'I find that hard to believe, Herr Güllich,' the General said, his tone soft and restrained. 'I wonder if anyone has interviewed our delivery men, or perhaps the postman? I mean, when one considers that the Nussbaums were under house arrest, it's not surprising that very few people have seen them outside of the confines of their Drachensee *home*.'

The General saw Werner Schmidt and the two Gestapo men flush with anger.

~~o~~

'I-I...' Werner Schmidt stammered. He stared at the Nussbaums.

What did they expect? A full-scale investigation for two Jews?

'It's obvious that they will have been seen around the *Kästner family* property,' Heinrich Güllich said, interrupting the policeman, 'and I'm sure your domestic suppliers will confirm that they have seen the two missing Jews on this or that vague occasion, but that doesn't prove anything.'

'Anyway, we asked along the whole street, and no one saw them wandering off, or being picked up,' Werner Schmidt added, 'and in the absence of any evidence, I'm coming around to Herr Güllich's way of thinking,' he said.

'You surely can't be serious?' the General said, frowning.

Heinrich Güllich smiled. He pulled out a pack of cigarettes and offered one to the KriPo detective. He exhaled a cloud of smoke into the already fetid air.

'My policeman friend has been persuaded by some new evidence that has come to light,' he said.

It wasn't strictly true. Werner Schmidt was just as sceptical, but he wasn't about to argue with a Gestapo officer with the bit between his teeth.

'Evidence? What evidence?' The General laughed.

'Three people were seen on the yacht, near Samsø.'

'Ha. And who witnessed this supposed sighting?'

'A Kriegsmarine midshipman. He and a friend had spent the evening drinking on *The Shearwater* with your boys in Bogense. When they caught them by surprise overtaking them the next day, our man swears that there were three people in the cockpit. He thought one might have been a girl.'

Werner Schmidt gently shook his head. Despite himself, he was impressed with the Gestapo man's embellishment.

'And did anyone else corroborate this, uh, story?' the General asked.

'Unfortunately not. By the time the first officer looked, they'd realised they'd been seen and there was only two on deck.'

'So, when the men were on the yacht, did they see Ruth and Manny?'

'No. But they could have been hiding.'

'And that's what you're basing this ludicrous theory on?' the General said, 'A supposed sighting by a hungover sailor?'

He laughed.

~~o~~

'Herr Güllich,' the General said, still chuckling, 'I don't know if you met my son, Johann, but he seems to have a way with the ladies. In the unlikely event that this drunken midshipman was right, the most plausible explanation is that some Danish girl had been talked into spending a few nights on board the boat, to be dropped off in Hirtshals, or one of the small harbours on the way.'

The General had the satisfaction of seeing a shadow of doubt cross Werner Schmidt's face, and even the junior Gestapo man looked a little uneasy.

Heinrich Güllich's face tensed in anger.

'Let me ask the Nussbaums one question, Herr General.'

He turned to the Nussbaums for the first time.

'If the Kästner men were involved in any attempt to smuggle your children out of Germany, and it can be proved, you do know that the repercussions for the General are unthinkable, don't you?'

He paused and the General saw that the Kriminalassistent's question and his callous smile had driven shards of fear into Miriam and Yosef's chests.

He made to say something, but the Gestapo man held up his hand and told him to stay quiet, on pain of removal.

'However, if you were to tell us what really happened to your offspring, it would help. If the Kästners aren't involved, this would remove any threat of trouble for your beloved General.'

Yosef and Miriam glanced at the General, who gave an almost imperceptible shake of his head. It was fortunate that neither of the Gestapo officers, or Werner Schmidt, saw it.

'Even if the Kästner family were involved, we would be willing to overlook their part in the escape attempt if the children were returned to Kiel; after all, the two Kästner boys are dead and no one wishes to deprive the Third Reich of a highly respected General whom the Kriegsmarine considers almost irreplaceable.'

The cruelty of Heinrich Güllich's proposal enraged the General almost as much as the lie it was founded on; that if the Nussbaums betrayed their children, there would be no repercussions for the General's family.

On the contrary, he and his family would be forever tarnished if Ruth and Manny were detained, and the story of their attempted escape was exposed. And their lives would be in danger. All of them. He hoped that Yosef and Miriam would see the futility of telling the truth, now that the four on board *The Shearwater* were either drowned or had made it to England.

'So, what's it to be?'

The General realised that it was no accident or afterthought that he was present; he was here by design and, once again, he had underestimated the guile of Heinrich Güllich.

'My daughter and son went missing on the fourth of April and we haven't seen them since,' Yosef said.

'That's all we know,' Miriam added. 'We just want them back.'

CHAPTER 163

The General heard the Nussbaums' words, and his heart sang with a cruel mixture of relief and pain. For their sakes, and his, it was the only possible answer and he chastised himself for doubting the couple whose loyalty to him had never wavered.

His eyes rested on Heinrich Güllich; the man's face registered frustration and anger, but most of all, hate.

The General saw Werner Schmidt's shoulders slump.

He doesn't want this case. It's too political. And all the while the children remain unfound, he'll be involved.

'Is there anything else, Herr Schmidt?' the General said.

The policeman flinched and glanced at the Gestapo men.

This time, Heinrich Güllich controlled his anger. He smiled at the General.

Werner Schmidt shook his head.

'No,' he said, glancing at the two Gestapo men. 'I think that is everything.'

The General gathered the Nussbaums and shepherded them towards the door.

'Just a minute, General.'

They all turned at Heinrich Güllich's barked command.

'We have our people in Denmark and Norway looking for your Jews and, in Sweden, the authorities are bending over backwards to help.'

He smiled.

'It's the iron ore, you see. They export over fifty per cent of their production to us.'

The General shook his head sadly.

'You accused the Kriegsmarine of wasting resources, Herr Güllich. I might say the same to you, but I doubt you would listen.'

He turned away and followed the trembling Nussbaums out of the interview room and along the corridor. At the end, Werner Schmidt unlocked the door and stepped aside until the Nussbaums had passed through, back into the waiting room. As the General walked past him, he stopped and looked at the policeman, but Werner Schmidt couldn't meet his gaze.

'Do your job, Kriminalassistent Schmidt,' he said.

~~o~~

17:00 EP: 54°2'62'N, 5°52'00'E. Watch change FK.

Sea slight. Fog. Wind 8-10 knots, westerly. Air pressure 1008mb. Full sail & topsail. 230°M, 4.0 knots. Tide 0.6 knots 090°.

~~o~~

'Sorry, Franz, we had to beat further south than we intended.'

'It can't be helped. The fog bank is following the coast or petering out. We've made good progress westwards, I see.'

Franz, leaning over his brother, pointed to the position Johann, sitting at the chart table, had just plotted.

'If our estimated position is anywhere near correct, yes.'

'It won't be far out. No sign of any other vessels?'

'Nothing, thank God. I don't know if my nerves could have taken much more.'

Franz laughed. Manny was helming, waiting for Franz to come up for his watch, while Ruth kept lookout. It gave them a chance to be on deck together.

'At around midnight, we're going to be crossing the direct route Kriegsmarine ships would take from Rotterdam or Antwerp, or the Channel ports, round the top of Denmark, and we'll be well out of the fog by then.'

'We're showing no lights,' Johann said. 'They shouldn't see us unless they have radar.'

'I'm hoping there won't be a lot of traffic.'

'It only takes one to spot us, or for a ship to steam right through us.' Johann's finger wandered along the line he'd drawn on the chart.

'No point in dwelling on it, I suppose,' he added, 'this will be our last big hurdle. We have to think of that.'

'Don't tell me. It will be on your watch,' Franz said.

Johann laughed, but it had a nervous ring to it.

'I'd better try and get some sleep then,' he said.

'Yes. I'll send Manny and Ruth down when I go up. It's Friday. They'll want to observe Shabbat, as best they can. Don't let him sit up afterwards. I want you two rested.'

~~o~~

In the end, Franz remained awake for most of Johann and Manny's watch as well as his own.

For the four hours it took *The Shearwater* to cross the danger zone, as Friday passed into Saturday, he sat in the companionway, nodding off once in a while, his head barely above the hatch, ready to send Manny below if a searchlight pierced the darkness of night.

They'd taken down the German flag that had flown all the way from Kiel and hoisted a Swedish one; with their blond hair and Franz's smattering of Swedish, there was a slim chance that they would be taken for a neutral boat, and then only if the encounter were fleeting. Most of the personnel in the Kriegsmarine knew about their voyage and, although they were 300 miles away from where they'd gone missing, it wouldn't take a leap of imagination for one of the crew to make the connection, but it was worth a try. Franz hoped they would never have to test its effectiveness.

Two ships crossed their path, both at a safe distance, and neither deviated from their course to investigate them. Only the faraway hum of their engines in the clear night, and their silhouette in the moonlight offered a hint that *The Shearwater* was not alone.

By three, Franz had begun to relax a little. The wind had backed to the south-west shortly after midnight, so they'd been able to make a westerly course for most of Johann and Manny's watch.

At the change of watch, Franz told Ruth to bring the sextant up with her.

'Take a sighting on the Pole Star,' he said to her.

'You can use that?' Manny asked his sister, his mouth hanging open.

'Oh, yes. Franz taught me. It's not as difficult as it seems once you realise it's all geometry.'

She showed him.

'You find the horizon, then the star, then you use this rotating mirror to line them up, and this scale tells you the angle. With the compass, and knowing our course up until now, we can work out our position well enough for our purposes. If not, we can do another star.'

Manny stared at her, and Franz knew that he wouldn't be happy until he'd mastered it too. Not that Ruth would mind; the surprised look on his face when she'd confidently taken her first sighting had been enough reward.

'Best get some sleep now,' she said to her younger brother.

Manny grinned and left, taking the sextant with him.

Ruth and Franz heard Johann's voice floating up from the main cabin, telling Manny to put the verdammte thing down and go to sleep, that he'd explain it to him on their next watch.

They smiled at each other.

CHAPTER 164

[19/04/1941 Saturday]

By nine, Ruth saw the lines of worry return to Franz's face.

He leaned inside and tapped the barometer. It had fallen three millibars in an hour.

'We're in for a bit of a blow again,' he said to her. 'The pressure's dropping fast.'

It was true. The wind had veered. It was now blowing from the west again and had doubled in strength over the space of an hour or two.

And since sunrise, just after six, they'd been in full view of any vessel that passed near to them, for the first time since leaving Hobo Dyb.

With a reef in the main and the mizzen, and a number two jib, the twenty-five knot wind was driving *The Shearwater* ahead at almost six nautical miles every hour, but Ruth, on the helm, was finding it hard to avoid being pushed further north.

The day had changed. From bright sun, with an easy swell on a blue-green sea and an almost warm breeze, it had become cooler, and the waves were now dark and menacing, and beginning to break over the bow of the yacht.

Heavy clouds had replaced the wisps of mare's tails in the clear sky of early morning and Ruth realised that rain wasn't far away.

She felt the first uneasiness in her stomach and went below to find a piece of ginger to chew.

She put on her oilskins and returned to the cockpit.

'What do you think?' she asked.

'We'll be lucky to claw westwards in the teeth of big seas if the wind stays like this, but, on the other hand, it will make us all but invisible, unless a ship passes within a couple of miles of us.'

Ruth looked at the first of the squalls, rapidly approaching.

By the time Johann and Manny came on watch, they were heavily reefed, and once again in the grip of a near gale.

~~o~~

'Erich, my friend.'

Admiral Canaris strode across the General's office and clasped one hand on Erich Kästner's shoulder, shaking his hand with the other.

'Wilhelm. How are you? You shouldn't have come.'

'Nonsense. I'm sorry I wasn't here sooner, but I got away as soon as I could.'

The General had spoken most days with Admiral Canaris by telephone, keeping him up to date with progress on the search for *The Shearwater*, culminating in the call three nights before telling him about the debris from the wreck, and that the boys were officially listed as drowned.

'We need to talk,' the General said. 'But not here. Let's get some fresh air.'

Admiral Canaris raised his eyebrows but said nothing. The General spoke to his secretary on the way out.

'Frau Müller, we'll be back in a while. We're off to let the admiral see a few of the ships we're building.'

They strode down to the water's edge and walked along the Hafenpromenade. They stopped and leaned against the wall and looked across the harbour, the clamour of steel on steel from the shipyards opposite making conversation only possible by both men leaning in close towards the other.

'I suspect Frau Müller listens at every opportunity. I don't know if she's merely an old busybody, or if she is reporting my conversations to someone.'

'You're getting paranoid, like me,' Canaris said. 'I'm glad, my friend. As the war goes on, it may keep you out of trouble.'

'I assume the phones are tapped,' the General said. 'The Gestapo are investigating me for my part in spiriting the Nussbaums' children out of the country.'

'And did you?'

'Yes. Well, I hope so, but there has been a problem. You see, they're on *The Shearwater*…'

~~o~~

'Well, I'll be damned,' Admiral Canaris said, twenty minutes later.

The General had told him the whole of it, from start to finish.

'This must go no further,' he added, gripping the admiral's arm.

'Of course. But you don't know if they survived the storm.'

'*The Shearwater* is a heavy-displacement, long-keeled, gaff-rigged boat. If anything could survive it, she could, but the navy told me that the storm reached force eleven at times, perhaps even twelve. Is it possible that they could ride that out, that could they make way in it?'

'I've seen ships of the line struggle to make headway in seas like that, but I'll say this; if anyone could, it would be Franz and Johann Kästner.'

'If they made it, they should be in England by now. We can only wait for news.'

'It takes up to two months for families of POWs to be informed, my friend. That's if they weren't treated as spies.'

The General stared at him.

'What I mean is, if they didn't surrender as part of a military operation. They may well be under suspicion of trying to land unseen in Great Britain.'

'They'll be sailing in British waters in daylight. They'll be spotted long before they make landfall.'

'I hope you're right,' the admiral said.

'They may not have made it, Wilhelm,' he said. 'At worst, they could have been drowned, at best, they've taken shelter in Norway, Denmark or Sweden.'

'If they get captured, they may wish they'd drowned; for your boys, and for the Nussbaum children.'

'For all of us here, too,' the General added, his head slumped.

'Who all knows?'

'Myself, Antje and the Nussbaums.'

And Dieter. But he doesn't know any details.

'Not Maria?'

'No. I thought it safer.'

The admiral nodded. 'That was sensible.'

'I find it difficult lying to my family and friends, and everyone in the Kriegsmarine, who've been of huge support.'

'Welcome to my world, Erich. My life is in two or three compartments and occasionally, I forget which one I'm in.'

The General smiled, glad that he'd been able to unburden himself to someone he trusted; someone who knew how to keep a secret.

'If there's anything I can do to help…' the admiral added.

'No. It's out of my hands now. If they get caught, no one can help them. Or us.'

The admiral nodded once.

Erich Kästner looked at his friend.

He's relieved. He has my permission to disown us. I owe him that.

The admiral frowned.

'Why are the Gestapo involved? That's something of an overreaction, is it not?'

'I told you that the Gestapo were already sniffing around the Nussbaums over the Weichmann fiasco, and you've already canned me about getting Yosef released from Neuengamme when he was detained as part of the *Kieler Jüdisches Freiheitsnachrichtenblatt* investigation. Because of that, I made a decision to report the Nussbaum children missing three days after *The Shearwater* had left as I felt it was better that the police dealt with it rather than the Gestapo.'

'It backfired?'

'Partly. The Gestapo found out about it, but it bought us a little time. I hadn't counted on how tenacious or clever this Heinrich Güllich fellow would be. He's convinced the Nussbaums were on *The Shearwater*, but he thinks they were bound for Sweden or Norway.'

'There's not much he can do about it if they're on the other side of the Nordsee.'

'No, but he has circulated the Nussbaum children's photographs widely in Norway and Denmark and has enlisted the cooperation of the Swedish authorities to help in their detention.'

'The Swedes have been helpful in handing back Jews who have been caught entering the country illegally but have never been active in seeking them out, so there is a good chance that if they are in Sweden, they'll be safe.'

'Except that the Swedes have their photographs and Heinrich Güllich hinted that his colleagues in Sweden will search for them.'

'They'll not divert resources for something like this,' the admiral said, with a snort.

'I wouldn't be so sure,' the General said, shaking his head. 'He seems to be very persuasive for a mere Kriminalassistent.'

'I'll see what I can find out about him. There may be something we can use.'

'I'd rather you didn't. I wouldn't want him alerted to the fact I'm concerned about him. I've tried to play it that I don't see him as a threat.'

'I'll be very discreet,' the admiral said. 'Leave it with me.'

He turned and grasped Erich Kästner's shoulder.

'They'll make it,' he said. 'Wait and see.'

'Thank you, Canaris,' the General said, smiling. 'It has been good getting that off my chest and not having to lie to you. All I need to do is get Yosef and Miriam out now.'

'How are you going to do that, Kästner?'

'The Haganah, but so far, they haven't got back to us.'

'I can't help you there, I'm afraid. Perhaps you should let the fuss of the children's disappearance die down first.'

'That's why I haven't chased it up, but I have a feeling we can't wait too long.'

'I have to agree. The deportation of Jews has been ramped up from all over Germany and within the occupied zones. If your Jews don't end up in a camp, they'll end up in a ghetto in Poland.'

'I've noticed that it's becoming more challenging to organise transportation for the Kriegsmarine. A significant proportion of the Reichsbahn resources are being diverted to the transports taking Jews east.'

'It's not just that. I shouldn't really tell you this, but I have at last been consulted about the impending invasion of Russia. You were right; they've been working on it since December. Führer directive 21. It's to be called Operation Barbarossa.'

'I'm glad the boys won't be part of it. It will be a disaster.'

'You're right, and I'm doing what I can to stop it. I told the Army High Command that our troops will bleed to death on the icy plains of Russia and, after two years, we won't find a trace of them, but I fear the decision is irrevocable, and the invasion will go ahead. And it's what else I've heard that makes it worse.'

'How can it get worse?'

'I've seen plans for the SS to eliminate every Jew we find in Russia, and it's only a matter of time before that is extended to the Jews held in Poland, and in the camps. Germany will be forever tainted by this horror.'

The General felt his chest constrict and struggled to take a breath.

'No,' he managed to gasp.

'I'm afraid so, my friend. I am in touch with people who feel the same way as us, but we have to be cautious.'

'What can I do?'

'We will need you one day, for the Kriegsmarine. For now, do what you can for your own Jews and keep out of trouble.'

Canaris pointed to the four submarines berthed opposite, waiting to be commissioned.

'I'm sorry now that we spent so much time developing our U-boat strategy. These will keep Britain off our backs and allow us to concentrate on Russia.'

As both men strolled back, they didn't see Carl Meyer turn away and walk briskly in the opposite direction, before turning inland. Crossing Düsternbrooker Weg, it was only a short walk up Reventlouallee to Moltkestraße, and Gestapo Headquarters.

CHAPTER 165

Sat 19th April 1941

14:52. Wind 40 knots, westerly. Sea very rough. Visibility poor. Rain. Air Pressure 995mb. Storm jib & trisail. 010°M, 2.5 knots.

~~o~~

The storm wasn't as ferocious as the one they'd survived the week before; the wind didn't get above gale force nine and the deeper water, around twenty fathoms, didn't kick up the waves as sharply as the five or ten fathom shelf they'd sailed across when the last storm had hit them.

But it was still unpleasant, and as the wind steadily climbed to forty-five knots, threatening a force ten, Ruth hoped it would blow through quicker than the last one.

In the main cabin she clung to Franz as *The Shearwater*'s bow rose and fell, crashing off the top of the waves and burying itself in the next one.

'How can the boat stand this?' she asked, her frightened eyes centimetres from his. He kissed her face, and she buried her head in his shoulder.

'*Der Sturmtaucher* was constructed by men who've been building boats like this since long before you and I were born, and their fathers and grandfathers built countless others before them. She's made for this sort of weather.'

'There's some water coming in.'

She pointed to where the deck above met the hull. In a couple of places, there was a circle of dampness, and a solitary drip ran down the curved planks, petering out before it reached the berth they were lying on.

'All boats, especially wooden boats, leak a little from time to time, especially in rough weather, but this is a dry boat. What you see is nothing when you think of the tonnes of water crashing down on the deck, and against the hull.'

'I suppose so. I just didn't expect it.'

It was the first day they hadn't taken advantage of the privacy of the forecabin to explore one another's bodies. Their hunger, sharpened by the knowledge that their time together was almost over, was undiminished, but the wild pitching and yawing of the forecabin made it uninhabitable.

It was with bittersweet hope that Franz and Ruth longed for, and dreaded, the moment when a British warship would find them and haul them aboard, parting them for the rest of the war.

All through the fog, and until the storm had hit, they'd lain together when they weren't on watch, naked, touching, sleeping, talking, making love, or charting desperate dreams of a future together, when all the madness in Germany, and Europe, was over.

Now, fully clothed, with their oilskins and life preservers hanging ready for immediate use, they lay side by side, Franz reassuring her.

He kissed her and she worked her hand under his sweater and his shirt, caressing the skin of his back, and the hard muscle under it.

'I'm sorry,' she said. 'I must taste awful.'

'I like ginger,' he said, laughing, and kissed her again.

'I don't want to risk not taking it,' she said, knowing that, when the journey was over, she'd never eat anything with ginger in it again.

The sickness hadn't come this time, and she didn't know if the ginger root she constantly chewed played a part in it or not, but she took no chances, and they suffered the taste of it in their kisses with stoic acceptance.

Ruth's eyes grew heavy and, reassured by Franz's faith in *The Shearwater*'s strength, she fell asleep, immune for a while to the crashing waves and the howl of the wind in the rigging.

While the storm raged around them, she dreamt of returning to Germany, of Franz speaking with her father; the wedding, the small cottage overlooking Kieler Förde, perhaps at

Laboe; a boy running around chasing his father while she cradled her newborn daughter in her arms.

Franz's eyes fought sleep for longer, but exhausted from the night before, he drifted off. At the height of the gale, they lost Manny overboard.

CHAPTER 166

Franz awoke with a start. He'd heard a yell, or a cry for help, but couldn't be sure if it was part of a dream.

'Maaaan Overboaaaard.'

This time, he knew he was awake, and it was Johann's voice, and a shaft of cold terror stabbed at his heart.

He scrambled up, shaking Ruth as he tumbled out of the forecabin.

'Manny's in the water,' he gasped at her. 'Get dressed and come up on deck. Put your life preserver on and tie yourself on with your lifeline once you're on deck.'

He stood up at the wet locker to put his feet into his boots and throw on his jacket and oilskins. He almost lost his balance as the boat lurched to one side then straightened, throwing him against the bulkhead.

Good. He's tacked the boat.

It was the first thing to do if a man fell overboard; stop the boat, keeping it as close to the man in the water as possible, and Johann had done that, without thinking, as part of the automatic response that they'd practised countless times over the years.

When Franz reached the cockpit, Johann was looking frantically around, searching the heaving sea surrounding them.

As expected, *The Shearwater* was hove-to. Johann had crash-tacked her almost immediately, and she lay with her storm jib backed, sitting with her shoulder to the sea.

'Did he have his life preserver on?' Franz asked, tying himself onto one of the pad eyes in the cockpit.

'Yes. The sheet was working loose from the storm jib. He'd gone up to sort it. I saw him tie his lifeline to the jackstay but, as he came back after making the bowline sure, a wave came over the bow and he was gone.'

'Did you see him in the water?'

'No, the wave must have washed him behind us.'

'And you tacked right away?'

'Yes, I shouted first, then threw the wheel hard over. She came round at once.'

Franz leaned over and fished a fender out of the stern locker, and a coiled warp, which he tied to the fender.

He threw it overboard.

'That's our marker,' he said. 'It will give us something to base our search on.'

Ruth, pale-faced and tearful, stumbled out into the cockpit.

'Have you found him?' she sobbed.

'Not yet. Tie yourself on.'

She looked at him as if he'd slapped her. He felt terrible, but now wasn't the time for sentiment.

'We're holding into the wind, and he'll be drifting downwind, so we have to assume we're upwind of him. We'll do side to side sweeps, working steadily downwind, keeping the fender in sight. If he's upwind, he'll be drifting towards us.'

Johann nodded, already turning the boat as Franz eased the jib sheet. *The Shearwater* turned across the waves. During the storm off Denmark, the waves had been steeper and shorter, and it would have been almost impossible to find a person in the water. Now, because the troughs were longer, and the waves weren't cresting, Franz thought that there was a glimmer of hope.

'Look out to port,' he told Ruth.

He took out his notebook and wrote down the compass bearing, all the time looking at the fender floating a cable away, until it disappeared over the crest of the next wave.

'Bring her back round through the wind,' he said.

When *The Shearwater* had turned, he could see the fender again, and he told Johann to head towards it, but half a cable downwind.

'Look to starboard,' he told him.

They completed three legs, but still there was no sign of Manny. Franz reckoned the fender, with its coil of rope, would drift at a similar rate to a person, and they were already close to two cables downwind of the fender. He looked at his watch.

Seven minutes.

Ten minutes would feel like an eternity in the cold water of the North Sea. Twenty minutes would be barely survivable. Half an hour would be almost hopeless. And that was only if he hadn't succumbed to the initial shock and had suffered no injuries when he was washed over.

He glanced at Ruth. She was shivering but, in her oilskins and all her layers underneath, it wasn't the cold. He put his hand on her shoulder to comfort her.

As the fender disappeared once more behind them, they turned around again.

Under his grip, he felt Ruth's body freeze.

'What is it?' he said.

'I thought I heard something,' she said, looking back to where they'd turned. 'I'm sure it was a whistle.'

The life preserver had a metal whistle tied onto it with a lanyard, but Franz didn't think Manny should have drifted that far out to the side of the downwind line.

'Turn back,' he told Johann.

Johann swung the boat round again and Franz released the sheet, hauling it in once *The Shearwater* had come through the wind.

They all listened now. Thirty seconds passed, then a minute.

Johann glanced at Franz and shook his head.

'Another minute,' Franz mouthed.

The seconds ticked by. Franz looked at his watch again. Thirty seconds more and he'd tell Johann to turn.

Ahead, and slightly to starboard, a whistle shrilled.

'Manny,' Ruth shouted.

This time there were two blasts of the whistle.

'Twenty degrees to port,' Franz said, desperately searching the sea ahead. 'Keep blowing, Manny,' he shouted.

The whistle sounded again and, a few seconds later they heard another blast, then another.

'I see him,' Ruth called, pointing.

Through the driving rain, and the spray, Franz saw the cream of Manny's life preserver and the boy's pale face, scarcely above it.

'Go a little downwind of him and turn up into the wind.'

Franz cursed himself. It was exactly what Johann would have done anyway, having practised the manoeuvre countless times.

Johann didn't complain.

He judged it well, and *The Shearwater* came to rest with Manny alongside the cockpit on the port side. Franz reached over and grabbed the back of the life vest.

'A rope, quick,' he shouted, but Johann already had it in his hand and passed it under Manny's arms and around the boy's back.

Johann tied a bowline in front of Manny's chest to stop him slipping out through it, then, telling Ruth to help, he began pulling hard on the rope.

Even with all Franz's strength, and Ruth and Johann hauling the rope, they couldn't lift him more than halfway out of the water and Manny himself was too weak to help them.

'Hold him there,' Franz shouted, and crossed to the mast.

He found the jib halyard and unclipped it from the mast. Pulling down on it, he brought the shackle end over to Johann and clipped it onto a bight of the rope supporting Manny.

Returning to the mast, he reached up and took the free end of the halyard and hauled down on it, putting all his weight onto the rope. When nothing happened, he attached the purchase, with its three-to-one increase in traction, and hauled again. This time, Manny's body began to edge upwards with each grunted pull.

A minute later, the boy's dead weight, in his water-sodden clothes, reached the height of the gunwales.

Franz tied off the halyard to the cleat on the mast, and he and Johann pulled Manny inboard, onto the deck, through the guardrails.

'Get him down below,' Franz said, 'and get him undressed. Light the heater and fill a kettle. I'll get the boat squared up and join you.'

He helped lower Manny down the companionway using the rope they'd hauled him out of the water with. The boy's head lolled from side to side and his eyes were closed tight, the skin of his face an almost translucent blue.

After lashing the wheel amidships, he tied the trisail to the boom and shackled the halyard to the gooseneck. Tying himself on, he went forward and dropped the storm jib, lashing it down on deck.

Returning to the cockpit, he pulled out their four longest warps from the stern locker and tied them together in two large bights. Securing each end to cleats on either side of the boat, he threw them overboard to trail behind *The Shearwater*, slowing her drift down and keeping her stern to sea.

He lowered himself down the companionway, slid the washboards into place, and closed the hatch.

'How is he?' he asked, looking over Ruth's shoulder.

'He's alive, but we can't rouse him,' she said.

They'd undressed him and wrapped him in three layers of blankets, and the stove was glowing hot already, warming the cabin in just a few minutes.

'Fill a couple of hot water bottles and wrap them in towels; put them in the blankets, close to his skin.'

Ruth turned to do as he asked, and Franz gave Johann a searching look.

Johann shook his head and lowered his eyes.

Franz began rubbing Manny vigorously and the boy let out an almost inaudible groan. The boat lurched as a wave passed under her. Johann raised an eyebrow.

'We're running under bare poles, trailing warps,' Franz said. 'The boat will be fine, and we have plenty sea room.'

Dealing with Manny was their only concern.

Johann nodded.

Ruth bent down and slid the hot water bottles in their towel cocoons into the blankets.

'Do you think he took any water in?' she asked, her face creased with worry.

'I hope not,' Johann said. 'His breathing sounds fine. I'm sure he's just cold.'

'I thought he was gone,' she said, close to tears.

'It was a miracle we got him back,' Franz said. 'We'll have to be more careful with our lifelines in rough weather.'

'The miracle was you hearing him blowing his whistle,' Johann said, giving Ruth a pained smile.

'I-I-I'm not d-dead, you know.'

They all jumped and stared at Manny.

He was still pale, but a hint of colour had returned to his cheeks and his eyes had opened. Violent shivering caused his voice to tremble uncontrollably.

Ruth flung herself on him, crying.

Franz looked at Johann.

'Shivering is good,' he said. 'It's the body's way of warming itself.'

He poured four coffees from the brewing pot and added four spoonfuls of sugar to Manny's. He waited until Ruth had released her hold on her brother and sat him up, then handed him a mug.

The teenager's fingers shook so much that its contents threatened to spill, but he managed to lift it to his lips and slurp enough of the sweet, hot liquid to keep it from overflowing.

'You gave us a fright, Manny,' Franz said.

'N-Not as much as I d-did myself,' Manny replied, his voice still trembling. 'I thought I'd tied onto the jackstay but I couldn't have done it right. The next thing I knew I was in the water and when I came up, you were half a cable away.'

He gulped another mouthful of warm coffee.

'Take your time,' Johann said.

Manny shook his head.

'By the time I remembered my whistle,' he said, 'you were out of sight. I tried to blow it once every thirty seconds, like you told me, Johann, but it seemed like an age, and I was getting weaker and weaker, and it became such an effort just to get it to make a sound at all.'

'Well, you did, and Ruth heard it, but only just.'

'It's the Shabbat,' Ruth said. 'God was looking out for us.'

'Maybe he was,' Franz said. 'All I know is that I'm glad to have you back on board, and in one piece.'

'Are we hove-to?' Manny asked, realising no one was sailing the boat.

'No, we're running downwind for a bit under bare poles, until we recover ourselves,' Franz said.

'But that's back towards Denmark.'

'Because there are no sails up, we'll be doing a knot at most,' Franz said, the lie coming easily. He saw Johann's mouth twitch in an approving smile.

'I'll be all right by our next watch. We must sail.'

'Don't worry, Manny, we will. Once we've all eaten a hot meal, we'll get going again.'

Manny sat back, propped up against the bulkhead. The shivering had reduced from shudders that shook the whole table to a steady chatter of teeth, and he looked almost like the old Manny.

Franz shook his head.

That's one tough young man.

CHAPTER 167

Heinrich Güllich crumpled up another piece of paper and threw it at the wastebasket in disgust.

When Carl Meyer returned to the office, he'd sent him home; the young man was getting on his nerves and he needed time to think. He'd spent the afternoon writing up his notes, trying to take his mind off the General, and his Jews, but every so often, they would appear without warning at the forefront of his mind.

The knowledge that the smug, arrogant, Jew-loving General thought he'd outsmarted him, and that his sons, and the Nussbaum children were safe, gnawed at his soul.

The arrogant Judenknecht will think he can get the parents out of Germany too.

On a hunch, he'd asked Carl Meyer to watch the Naval Headquarters, having a creeping suspicion that the General would show his hand somehow; that he would make a mistake.

Carl Meyer had spent the whole day watching him and had been told to report back to him if the General went anywhere.

But nothing had come of it. The only time the General had left the building had been to stroll to the waterfront with his boss, Admiral Canaris, and look at the shipyards opposite, like tourists.

The tap on the General's home phone hadn't revealed much beyond his wife having a busier social life than one might expect in the circumstances and that, unlike her husband, she had a healthy regard for the Führer and the Third Reich. And it told him that her daughter was more than likely sexually active with her aristocratic boyfriend.

The tap on the General's office phone would be harder to justify if it ever came to light, and had yielded even less; if anything, it proved that the General was indeed a loyal servant of the Reich who played a significant part in the smooth running of the Kriegsmarine Baltic Command, and that almost everyone else in Kiel, other than Heinrich Güllich and Maria Kästner, thought he was wonderful.

The Kriminalassistent allowed himself a smile. The General's crumbling relationship with his wife was the one thing he could take satisfaction from, and he briefly wondered what it would be like to bed Maria Kästner, and to see the General's face when he found out.

He looked at the blank piece of paper in front of him and wrote the General's name at the top, and the Nussbaums below. He tapped his pen on the paper but nothing else came to him. He'd intended to make a summary of the case, trying to work out what to do next, but his mind kept returning to the smug look on Erich Kästner's face as he ushered his Jewish swine away from the police station.

And what he wanted, more than anything, was to wipe that superior smile from it.

~~o~~

Johann felt a shift and glanced at the compass. It showed east-north-east.

'The wind has backed to the south-west,' he said quietly to Franz.

'You're right. I think we should hoist the trisail and storm jib again. Give me a hand, then Ruth and I can do our watch as usual. By the time you're next on watch I think Manny will be back to himself.'

Johann nodded. 'Let's do it,' he said. 'It will be better than drifting back east.'

By the time they had the storm sails set, Ruth had thrown her assorted layers on and was on deck, standing beside Franz. Johann looked at them and the smallest pang of jealousy niggled him, but he scolded himself. If any two people deserved each other it was his brother and the girl who'd restored his faith in womanhood.

He gave them a smile and made his way down the companionway. Manny was sitting up now, drinking his third cup of warm coffee. He seemed more like himself, but his eyes were unfocussed, gazing blankly at the opposite side of the cabin.

'A penny for them,' Johann said.

Manny shook himself.

'Sorry, I was miles away.'

'What were you thinking of?'

'My parents, Ruth. You and Franz.'

He hesitated.

'When I was in the water at first, I panicked, but after the first shock had passed, I could only think of all the things I wanted to do; girls, a job, money, a sports car like Franz's. I cursed myself for being so stupid but as time went on and I thought maybe you weren't going to find me, it was Mama and Papa and Ruth that filled my mind; how they would feel if I drowned and how I missed them, terribly, and an horrible feeling of guilt took hold of me for not having thought about them more since we left.'

Johann put his hand on Manny's shoulder and gently shook his head.

'It was your way of coping. You'd immersed yourself in the boat, in learning to sail, in pitting yourself against the sea, but I could see times when you were in a dark place, and I could say nothing to help.'

'That's not true. I could speak with Ruth when it got unbearable but the rest of the time, just being able to talk about the boat, and the sea, and listen to your stories about the army, and girls, was enough to keep my mind from dwelling on the past.'

Again, it struck Johann just how grown-up Manny was; at times he thought the fourteen-year-old showed more maturity than himself, but he hoped that, if they reached England, Manny would get a chance to be a boy again.

~~o~~

For the rest of the day, and when the wet, grey sky faded to night, Ruth and Franz fought the gale, edging *The Shearwater* westwards a mile at time.

'We're getting pushed further north than I'd intended,' Franz said, 'but that's not a bad thing. There will be fewer Kriegsmarine vessels in this part of the Nordsee.'

'Will we have to go back south once the storm is passed?'

'No, all we need is a major port. If we're too far north for Hull or Grimsby, we can make Newcastle or Sunderland.'

'Why does it have to be somewhere like that? Can we not use any harbour?'

'No. If we land somewhere small, away from the main ports, we might be arrested as spies. They'd treat us very differently then. Johann and I could even be shot.'

'Oh. I didn't think of that.' She looked back in the darkness to where the flag was flying at the boat's stern. 'I thought we were going to pretend to be Swedish.'

'That's the worst thing we could do. The Swedish flag is just in case the Kriegsmarine see us. As soon as a Royal Navy is close, we'll fly a German flag again. But not a National Socialist one. I hope we'll be picked up long before we get too close to port.'

A wave crashed over the bow and caught them both full in the face.

Ruth gasped with the cold, and she shivered at the thought of being in the water, like Manny.

'How long would he have survived?' she said.

'Not much longer,' Franz said. 'He could barely hold his head up when we lifted him. He would have drowned within minutes.'

Ruth began to cry, and Franz put his arm around her shoulder.

'I nearly lost him,' she sobbed, 'like Mama and Papa.'

'Don't say that. You'll see them both once this is all over.'

She shivered again.

'I don't know if we will,' she said, her voice thin and hard to hear above the wind.

He pulled her in tight to him.

'They're tough, like Manny. They'll do everything to survive.'

'They're so far away now, and in so much danger. I wish we could have brought them.'

'So do I. But it would have been impossible.'

'I know. I only hope they get their chance to get out.'

'My father will see to it; you can be sure of that.'

'You really believe so, don't you?'

'Yes. With all my heart.'

~~o~~

527

The General had got into the habit of talking with Yosef, and sometimes Miriam, after Maria had gone up to bed.

He and Yosef would share a whisky in his study, or all three of them would sit around the Nussbaums' kitchen table, talking about Ruth and Manny, and Franz and Johann.

That evening, the Kästner kitchen was the venue for their daily briefing.

Maria had gone up to her room exceptionally early, even for her, and Miriam was finishing her chores.

The General walked in and sat down at the table. Miriam poured a cup of coffee from the pot sitting on the range and placed it in front of him. She did the same for Yosef when he came in a few moments later.

'How are you two bearing up?' the General asked.

'We get on with it, sir. There's nothing else for it.'

Miriam's voice was flat and tired. The General looked at her. The strain was showing on her face and he thought she looked older. It shouldn't have surprised him; he'd seen himself in the mirror that morning and wondered where the years had gone.

'They should be in Britain by now, but it will be a month or two before we find out.'

'I worry that we'll never know, sir,' Yosef said.

'When the boys are to be made prisoners of war, the British government will be obliged to inform the German government under the Geneva convention.'

'What if they didn't make it to England?' Miriam said.

'I think we would have heard by now if they'd been caught.'

'What if they're still in Denmark or Norway?'

'There's nowhere the boat could be hidden. Too many people know about her. If she had somehow been wrecked, and they'd made it to shore, they would have had to rely on help from local people, and that would have been difficult, I imagine. If they are in Sweden, it might be easier to evade capture. In all three countries, I would expect it would be possible to make some form of contact at some point in the future, to let us know where they were.'

'So, if we don't hear from them soon,' Miriam said, 'they may have drowned?'

'Miriam, don't talk like that,' Yosef said, his face flushing.

'No. She has the right to ask, Yosef. We'll never be able to say for sure, but it is a possibility. There's always that risk when you put to sea, and the navy are still talking about that storm being the worst one in living memory.'

'What is your feeling, General?' Yosef asked, before Miriam could said anything else.

'The storm is my biggest concern, but we can do nothing but wait.'

'And the Gestapo?'

'They're scrambling about in the dark. Heinrich Güllich has five different theories about Ruth and Manny, and not one is correct.'

'But he's getting closer than you expected, sir,' Yosef said.

'That's true, but it will be all be irrelevant if they've made it to Britain. To arrest you, he needs evidence and, if he doesn't get hold of Ruth or Manny, he has nothing substantial, just the word of a solitary sailor who had, by his own admission, been on *The Shearwater* the evening before, without seeing anyone other than Franz or Johann.'

'I have a bad feeling about Herr Güllich, sir. He's not going to let it go.'

'Heinrich Güllich will overstep the mark and he'll get his comeuppance one day, I promise you.'

'I wish I had your faith, sir, but it's of no consequence what happens to us. We'd both be happy if we only knew that Ruth and Manny were safe.'

'You'll know as soon as I do, I promise. Franz and Johann will be permitted to write, but it may take a while for any letters to get here. In the meantime, I think we can assume that Ruth and Manny have made it to safety if we hear that Franz and Johann have arrived in England.'

'We pray for that day, sir.'

'I know. And as for what happens to you, I'll get you out if it kills me to do so.'

'Thank you, sir. I don't suppose the Haganah have made any contact?'

'No. I'm afraid not, but I know they got my message.'

'What will be, will be, sir.'

528

CHAPTER 168

[20/04/1941 Sunday]

By midnight, the wind had eased to a force six. Franz and Johann had stowed the storm sails and hoisted the staysail and a double-reefed main at the change of watch. Manny had made almost a complete recovery, apart from a few bruised ribs from being hauled on board and chafing at the top of his legs where the life preserver belt had rubbed.

The Shearwater, freed from the stopping force of the steeper waves during the gale, threw herself forward, like a terrier released from its leash. They could all see she was eating up miles faster than at any time since leaving Denmark, and on a course which would see them reach landfall.

Sunrise broke to clear skies and a steady twenty knot wind from the south-west. Franz, not long back on watch, projected their track forward and, despite their progress, was a little disappointed to be unable to make anywhere south of the Firth of Forth, in Scotland.

'We could go closer to the wind, couldn't we?' Ruth said. 'We're on a close reach now.'

'Yes, we could beat close to the wind, but we'd lose maybe a knot and a half of speed and we still wouldn't make Newcastle without having to tack so it's to our advantage to keep on the course we're on.'

'I like this better,' she said. 'It feels like we're getting somewhere.'

It was true. They were hitting the waves at a shallower angle and sliding over them, rather than trying to punch through them, and the yacht wasn't as heeled over as she'd been.

For an instant, Franz wished he were at the helm of the army's racing boat, nearly doubling their speed and being able to point much closer to the wind without slowing them down. Then he remembered what *The Shearwater* had brought them through since leaving Hirtshals, and a flush of guilt washed over him.

As the sun climbed above the eastern horizon, he stiffened.

'What's wrong?' Ruth said, staring at him.

'Listen,' he said. 'I can hear an engine.'

They stood still, straining to hear.

'Yes. I hear it,' Ruth said. 'It's from the west, I think. It must be British.'

Franz heard it again. She was right. It was off *The Shearwater*'s port shoulder.

They both scanned the sea.

Visibility was good, so Franz was surprised not to see a ship.

'It must be a smaller vessel, hidden by the waves,' he said, puzzled as to why a boat that size would be out there. He'd been told that the North Sea fisheries had been abandoned for fear of mines and submarines.

'It's a plane, Franz,' Ruth shouted, pointing almost dead ahead.

He saw it now, a black spot just above the horizon.

'We'll be spotted, and they'll have the navy out to us in no time,' Franz said.

'Unless it's one of ours,' Ruth joked.

Franz swallowed. He hadn't considered that it could be a Luftwaffe plane coming out of the west, but he knew there were reconnaissance flights, and supposed it could be one of them on its way back to Germany. In either case, he suspected the plane would spot them, and circle them to verify their identity. It only mattered which nation's colours it flew in.

He glanced behind him. The Swedish flag was still flying at the stern.

Ruth saw him looking.

'Won't you need to change the flag? It might be British.'

He hesitated. She was right.

'No,' he said. 'We can change it once we know it is British. If it's a German plane, we need to convince them that we're neutral.'

Within minutes, the small black spot on the horizon grew larger, its outline recognisable as a plane, with a fuselage and an engine on each wing, its faint hum swelling to a loud drone that filled the sky.

'It's coming straight for us, and it's low,' Franz said, trying to keep any trace of nerves from his voice.

He looked round at Ruth then stepped back and took the wheel from her.

'Go below and hide behind the mast step. Tell Manny and Johann to do the same. Hand me up a white towel first.'

She opened her mouth to argue but saw his look and changed her mind.

She climbed down and grabbed the towel hanging on the grab rails and threw it back to him.

The plane was almost on them now, no more than a few hundred metres in the air.

Franz could see the bubble at the bottom of the nose, and the glazing jutting out at the belly gunner's position.

'It's a bomber,' he shouted, rather pointlessly, then it was on them.

As it passed over, he involuntarily ducked, but had time to see the faces of the pilot and the navigator, and of both the nose and belly gunners, and the black-and-white crosses on the underside of its wings.

'Luftwaffe,' he shouted, wondering if they would hear him down below over the roar of the plane.

He twisted round to look at the plane heading away from them, eastwards, and noticed that only the starboard engine was running, and wisps of smoke streamed out behind the port engine.

Relief flooded over him. It was a returning bomber limping home on one engine and would have no intention of investigating a sailing boat, no matter what flag they'd been flying.

There was only one concern.

If there was a Kriegsmarine vessel in the area, and the commander of the aircraft reported seeing *The Shearwater*, they might just divert the ship to check them out. It was a long shot, and he told himself he was being paranoid, but he couldn't shake the feeling that it had been bad luck to be directly under the homebound route of a lone, stricken, German bomber.

'You're safe now,' he shouted.

~~o~~

Johann was first on deck. Ruth and Manny stuck their heads out of the companionway to catch a glimpse of the receding aircraft.

'So, just a Luftwaffe bomber on its way home on one engine,' Johann said. 'They might report seeing us, but I doubt they'll send a flotilla out here to sink us.'

'No, but I hope they don't put two and two together and realise that it's *The Shearwater*,' Franz said, under his breath. 'That could spell trouble back home.'

Johann paled. He hadn't thought of what it would mean for his father or the Nussbaums.

'Let's hope they don't report it,' he said.

'Or make the connection. There's nothing we can do about it anyway,' Franz said.

He looked up at the sails.

'The wind has dropped again,' he said. 'Let's shake out these reefs and get this boat moving again.'

CHAPTER 169

'Herr Kriminalassistent, the Kriminaldirektor wishes to see you in his office.'

Heinrich Güllich blanched. There was a slight chance that the summons might be about something pleasant, like a promotion, but better to assume that he was going to receive a dressing-down. And if he had to guess what it might be about, his mind didn't have to wander far to think of what that might be.

General Schweinhund Kästner and his litter of Jews.

'Wait here,' he growled at Carl Meyer, wishing he could take the man with him to deflect part of the Kriminaldirektor's wrath.

He climbed the stairs to the next floor and announced himself to the Kriminaldirektor's secretary, wishing he'd had a cigarette to calm his nerves.

'Have a seat, Herr Kriminalassistent,' she said. He sat down and glanced at her when he thought she wasn't looking. She was famed throughout the building as *Dirty Helga*. It was reputed that she spent a lot of time in various hotel rooms with the chief when his wife was out of town.

She certainly had the looks for it and flirted shamelessly with anyone over the rank of Kriminalsekretär. She treated those of lower rank, like Heinrich Güllich, with utter contempt.

He waited five minutes, and during that time he diverted himself with fantasies of what it would be like to rip the brassiere from Helga that was just showing above the cut of her blouse and peel the stockings from her long and shapely legs, unclipping the suspenders that showed so clearly through the fabric of her skirt.

The telephone on her desk rang and she picked it up.

'You can go in now,' she said, as if he was a steaming pile of *Hundescheiße*.

The Kriminaldirektor was a heavy, balding man with a pleasant, open face that he used to great effect to soften his victims, suspects, or errant Gestapo staff, before destroying them.

Heinrich Güllich sat in oppressive silence while the Kriminaldirektor read a file on the desk in front him, without acknowledging the Kriminalassistent's presence.

He tried to keep the image from his mind of a naked Kriminaldirektor on top of Dirty Helga, like a bug under a steamroller.

'Kamerad Kriminalassistent, do you know why you are in here today?'

'No, Herr Kriminaldirektor,' Heinrich Güllich said, back in the real world.

'Indulge me. Let me see if you can guess.'

'I would struggle, sir. Is it one of my cases?'

'Guess.' This time, the sweet tone of the Kriminaldirektor's voice had disappeared.

'Is it the Nussbaum case, sir?' Heinrich Güllich said, trying to soften the blow that he knew was coming by minimising the General's part in it.

'Ah. It's funny that you should come to the right conclusion so soon. Do you know what I did last night?'

Heinrich Güllich hated these guessing games. He presumed this question would be answered by the Kriminaldirektor.

'No, sir.'

'I was at a very stuffy dinner party, with a smorgasbord of Kiel's finest. A smattering of admirals, the fawning little mayor, our wonderful Oberpräsident, Hinrich Lohse and a few others, including the police chief.'

'Yes, sir.'

'My wife is a particular friend of one of the admiral's wives; they attended the same school, I believe. It is why we were invited. Do you know whose name came up in a long and uncomfortable conversation I had with her husband?'

'No, sir.'

'I think you do, Kamerad Kriminalassistent.'

The sweet tone was back, but it had an undercurrent of menace to it.

'Ah. General Kästner, sir.'

'Indeed. Once again you have proved to be a quick learner. If only that could apply on a more general basis if you'll pardon the pun.'

'Sir?'

'You have been given a warning before, I believe,' the Kriminaldirektor said, his voice now hard and chilling.

'Yes, sir.' Heinrich Güllich dropped his head dutifully.

'This man is to be left alone, for now.'

Heinrich Güllich raised his head. There was a glimmer of hope.

'I do not want to have another irritating conversation with my wife about the behaviour of any of my staff. Unless you have a cast-iron reason for being near the General or his staff you will find yourself on guard duty in the far north of Norway where your dick will freeze before you have time to finish taking a piss. Do you understand?'

'Yes, sir.'

'That is all, Herr Kriminalassistent.'

He stood up and saluted. The Kriminaldirektor barely returned it. As he walked down the corridor, he heard the seductively dressed secretary being called in and he wondered if she was being ordered to perform fellatio on the Kriminaldirektor, beneath the rolls of fat of the big man's belly.

He smiled grimly to himself.

CHAPTER 170

The feeling of being exposed grew stronger as the sun climbed high above them towards noon. The horizon stretched monotonously for 360 degrees, and nothing but sky filled their every gaze.

Franz knew that any ship more than twenty miles away wouldn't see them over the horizon, thanks to the curvature of the earth, but it didn't dispel the feeling of vulnerability he harboured, especially after their disconcerting encounter with the German bomber.

Still, every hour drew them six or seven miles nearer to refuge and, with the wind gradually backing to the south, they were able to hold a course much closer to true west again.

He spoke briefly with Johann when the watch changed at eleven.

'Go,' Johann said. 'It shouldn't be much longer.'

Franz nodded, flushing a little, but Johann was right. The next few hours would be the last that he and Ruth would spend together, and there was no knowing how long that separation would last.

They stayed in the forecabin, clinging to one another, trying to save up every sensation they could to see them through the enforced and indefinite parting ahead of them.

'How long do you think it will be?' Ruth asked, tears brimming in her eyes.

'A year, two years perhaps.'

'It's so cruel, being away from my parents, and now you. I feel as if my heart is being ripped out of my chest.'

Franz twisted the piece of fisherman's twine around his neck between his fingers, then lifted it over his head. He untied it and took his one of the rings, his own, from it, then retied it. Lise's ring dangled on the string in the half-light of the forecabin.

'I want you to have this,' he said, reaching out and placing it around her neck. 'I'm sorry it wasn't bought for you, but I have nothing else. I'll buy you a proper ring and we'll get married as soon as this is all over, if you'll have me.'

Tears coursed down her cheeks now.

'Of course I will, and I don't want another ring. I don't care if you bought it for Lise. I know why you wear it, and it means more to me because of that.'

'You fixed my heart, Ruth Nussbaum.'

He fished around in one of the small drawers below the chart table and found an old piece of cotton string. He threaded it through the ring he still held in his palm and tied it and placed it over his head.

They held onto each other as *Der Sturmtaucher* sliced her way through the water, mile after mile closer to the north-east coast of England.

~~o~~

12:00 Noon. Sighting 55°27'30'N, 1°10'01'E.

Sea slight. Clear. Wind 15 knots, sou'westerly. Air pressure 1012mb. Full sail & topsail. 280°M, 6.5 knots. Tide 0.4 knots, 110°T.

~~o~~

Johann's face showed surprise when Ruth and Franz appeared on deck to do a noon sighting, but he had to admit that it was comforting to know exactly where they were. Comparing it with their plotted track, it was with quiet satisfaction that they confirmed their estimated position to be a mere fifteen miles out. And it was in their favour.

'We're around ninety miles from the mouth of the Tyne,' Franz shouted up from the chart table, 'and half of that will be through British minefields.'

Despite their encounter with the stray mine, they had begun to think of the minefields as friends, knowing that no Kriegsmarine ship would dare follow them through.

A Kriegsmarine destroyer could still blow us out of the water from a distance though, Johann thought.

They still glanced behind them from time to time, but the sea had been empty of vessels all day; it was hard to believe that a war was raging around them and that the North Sea was one of its major battlegrounds.

After Ruth and Franz returned below, Johann turned to Manny.

'We'll be picked up later today, or early tomorrow. We'll be separated almost immediately, I'd imagine; Franz and I will be prisoners of war. I hope you two are treated as refugees, but you might be separated; we'll try our best to explain your circumstances.'

Manny's face fell.

'I thought that Ruth and I...' he mumbled. 'I didn't consider...'

His voice trailed off.

'Listen, Manny, my hope is that they allow you and Ruth to stay together, but you'll both have to be prepared for the fact that you may be sent to separate camps, at least for a while; as a child, you might even be cared for by foster parents, I don't know.'

'Papa told me to look after Ruth,' Manny said, his face so pained that Johann could hardly look at him.

'And you have, to the best of your abilities. Just being there for her is all you can do. If she sees that you're struggling, it will make it hard for her so, if you can, try and be as strong as possible. I promise you it won't be forever.'

Johann could almost see Manny's spine stiffen. The boy had immense courage and resilience, perhaps more than anyone he'd ever met, and he fully believed that Manny would get through practically anything the world threw at him, but he knew that he and Franz somehow had to convince the British authorities that the Nussbaums were refugees, and that every effort should be made to keep them together.

'I have to go down below for a minute. Keep an eye out,' he said.

The talk of captivity had reminded him of a task that he and Franz had to do. He found the German flag and laid it on the table, then looked out his kitbag. From the bottom, he pulled out his uniform and laid it out on one of the cabin seats. He found his brother's bag and did the same.

He stared at them.

Mixed with the relief that Manny and Ruth were close to being safe, a smouldering anguish about what he and Franz were about to do lay heavy on his chest.

We're surrendering. Deserting. I'm turning my back on my friends, the Heer, my oath, and my country.

He fought the tears, knowing the truth of it.

I'll never see them again. Maxi. Artur, Fritz. Walther Schneider.

He started to dress.

CHAPTER 171

This time, when the plane flew over, it was British. It came from the south, 2000 feet up but, as it approached, the engine noise changed and it circled them in a wide arc, steadily losing height. Johann ducked down into the cabin and shouted to Franz, telling him to put his uniform on.

Franz looked at Ruth, sitting in the cabin, and Manny, standing on the companionway steps.

'Go up, both of you. We have nothing to hide now.'

Franz changed into his uniform and joined them all in the cockpit.

'I've changed the flag,' Johann said, pointing to the black, white and red stripes of Weimar Germany's ensign now flying at the stern, the black imperial eagle in place of Hitler's swastika.

'Manny, take the helm,' Franz said.

He picked up the white bed sheet he'd brought up with him and handed a corner to Johann.

'Grab an end of this,' he said.

They held it out high between them, hanging onto the backstays to steady themselves.

'What are you doing?' Manny said.

'We're surrendering,' Johann said. 'So that they don't shoot us.'

'Oh. Would they do that?'

'They might. We could be carrying enough explosives to sink a ship, so they won't let us into a harbour, or near a warship without checking us out first.'

'How do we know it's British?'

'The circles on its wings. You'll see them when it's to the east of us, out of the sun.'

The plane was circling lower now, and an Aldis lamp began to flash from the nose of the twin-engine plane that looked surprisingly like the German bomber that had flown over them the previous day.

Franz dropped the sheet and opened his notebook, writing the message down.

'They're telling us to sail north-west, and to await further instructions,' he said. He turned to Manny.

'Steer three-one-five,' he said.

Johann eased the foresail and the staysail sheets as the boat came off the wind, and Franz did the same with the mainsheet and the mizzen.

'They don't want us anywhere near Tyneside,' Johann said, until they check us out.' He looked up. The plane was signalling again.

He pointed, and nudged Franz, who scribbled down the new message.

'We've to continue our present course and we will be intercepted within the next two hours,' he said. 'We'll be safe then.'

He turned and looked up at the plane again. 'Give me a torch,' he said to Ruth, who reached inside the companionway, and fished one out from the locker.

A moment later, he signalled acknowledgement to the circling plane and it banked southwards and was soon a dot on the horizon again, leaving them alone once more.

'It's still our watch,' Johann said, looking at Franz, 'if you two need some time.'

Franz looked at Ruth. She smiled at him.

'No,' he said. 'We've made our goodbyes. We'll stay here with you.'

Johann nodded, understanding. The four of them had been through hell as a crew, and now that they were on the brink of safety, it felt right to share the last few hours together.

'I'll make coffee,' Ruth said. She turned to Manny. 'Give me a hand.'

The boy, with a little reluctance Johann thought, smiling, gave him the wheel.

When they'd disappeared, Johann turned to Franz.

'I only pray they can stay together.'

'I know. They've suffered enough.'

'And you? What about Ruth?'

'It will be terrible, but it's only time. We both know we'll be together, one day. That will make it bearable.'

'I envy you,' Johann said, without a hint of malice.

Franz smiled.

'She's wonderful. There's a girl somewhere for you, like Ruth.'

'I'll need to grow up first, and I don't know if I want to do that yet.'

Franz laughed.

'What are you laughing at?' Ruth asked, handing up the coffees.

'Ah, nothing,' Franz said. 'Just Johann being Johann.'

She smiled and sat down next to him. Johann turned and looked out at the horizon, wiping away the moistness that had uncharacteristically appeared in his eyes.

Another pang of jealousy caught him unawares, but he shook his head.

Every touch for them, no matter how casual, must be painful now.

He looked ahead, waiting for the arrival of the Royal Navy.

'This is almost real sailing,' he said, shifting his sadness by trying to get as much as he could from the yacht.

Touching eight knots now, on a reach, and with just a modest heel, *The Shearwater* seemed to realise she was nearing the end of her journey and responded to Johann's enthusiasm.

While he helmed, Johann watched Ruth and Franz across the cockpit, sitting close together, and wondered how they would suffer being torn apart.

For himself, he knew he would survive whatever happened, despite his despair at losing his friends, and his feelings of guilt. For better or worse, he had always had the ability to be self-reliant, without the agonising close personal bonds that Franz and Ruth had, or Ruth and Manny and their parents possessed; he loved his family, and would miss them, and excepting his friends, perhaps, the separation wouldn't eat away at him as it would with the others.

It struck him that Franz was the one person he wasn't sure he could do without. He had seldom been far from his older brother, following every footstep Franz had taken, ending up at the same military school, training college and Kompanie. And now they were together on this outrageous escape.

He smiled grimly to himself. In all likelihood, they would spend the rest of the war in the same POW camp.

If we're together, that's no bad thing.

Ruth's voice pulled him back to the present.

'Manny and I would like to say something,' she said.

Johann looked at Manny. The teenager's face was even more serious than normal.

'When this was first put to us as a way of getting out of Germany, I had grave reservations,' Ruth said. 'Manny didn't, apart from not wanting to leave Mama and Papa behind. He jumped at the chance for an adventure, and to be away from all of the terrible miseries that we had to suffer in Kiel.'

She paused, taking a breath.

'If I'm honest, I only agreed to come for Manny's sake and, deep down, I didn't believe we were going to make it.'

She smiled at Johann and Franz.

'Well, it appears that we have. Even if we hadn't, I wouldn't have changed this for the world.'

She took Franz's hand in hers.

'When this is all over, Franz and I are going to be married.'

'I should damn well hope so,' said Johann. It prompted laughs all round.

'I'd like to say something too,' Manny said.

He stared westwards.

'I don't know what it's going to be like over there, but I know this has to be better than in Germany, whatever is in front of us. It will be terrible, knowing that Mama and Papa are still in danger but, if they can only find out that we are safe, it will mean the world to them.'

Franz and Johann glanced at each other but didn't interrupt.

'We know that you've given up your family and friends to get us here, and that you will spend the rest of the war, if it ever ends, in prison, and we will never forget that. I also know that parts of this voyage have been terrible for Ruth but for me, I've loved every second.'

'Apart from swimming in the Nordsee,' Johann said, smiling at Manny.

'Yes, apart from that,' Manny said, smiling himself now, 'and the mud.'

'What we're trying to say,' Ruth said, 'is that we can never thank you and Franz enough, or your father and Antje, for all you've risked in getting us here.'

A tear slipped down her cheek, and Franz squeezed her hand.

'There was no other choice,' Johann said, his face serious for once.

~~o~~

Rainer Schulze was desperate to get off the ship; he had a forty-eight-hour furlough and had booked a hotel in the city; his wife of less than six months would be there already, waiting for him.

'Can I not meet with them when I come back, sir? It's surely not that urgent.'

'They were most insistent. Anyway, it shouldn't take long. They're here, waiting.'

One of the midshipmen stuck his head in the door.

'Kriminalassistent Güllich is here to see you, sir. There are two of them. I put them in the wardroom.'

Rainer Schulze followed the midshipman down the corridor. The younger man held the door open for him and he walked in. Two men in black leather coats stood looking at the board with the command structure displayed.

'Heil Hitler,' the older of the two said, turning and saluting.

'Heil Hitler,' the Kriegsmarine man responded. 'I'm Rainer Schulze. You asked to speak to me?'

'Yes. I'm Kriminalassistent Heinrich Güllich, this is Kriminalassistentanwärter Carl Meyer. You're second in command, Herr Kapitänleutnant?'

'Yes, I have that honour. What can I do for you?'

'You were the officer who boarded *Der Sturmtaucher* when torpedo boat *T4* stopped the vessel in the Skagerrak, weren't you?'

'I was.'

'Was it not strange for such a senior officer to be on the boarding party?'

Rainer Schulze smiled.

'Yes, I suppose it was, but I knew the Kästner brothers. I raced against them for a number of years, when they sailed for the army, and I sailed for the navy.'

'So, you were good friends with them?'

'I would say amicable rivals, more than friends. I had a lot of time for them.'

'So, you searched *Der Sturmtaucher*, and found nothing?'

'There was nothing to find. We looked everywhere.'

'A friend's boat? You pulled it apart? Like a policeman would?'

'No. Of course not. But we looked in every locker, under every cushion.'

'Did you look in the bilges?'

Rainer Schulze frowned.

'I did, but why do you ask?' he said, watching the Gestapo men. Both their shoulders slumped.

'It's for us to ask the questions. What about the anchor locker?'

Rainer Schulze laughed.

'What's so funny?' Heinrich Güllich said, his voice cold.

'Sorry, it's just the thought. You would struggle to hide a dog in their anchor locker when the chain is all stowed.'

'It's that small?'

'In that boat, yes. In a larger boat, maybe you could hide a person, but it would be a terrible place to hide.'

'Did you look in the stern locker?'

'Yes. It was full of supplies, fuel and water.'

'And the forepeak locker?'

'Sails.'

'Why did you look surprised when we mentioned the bilge?' Carl Meyer said, risking the wrath of his boss.

Rainer Schulze hesitated.

'It's just that...'

He stopped and shook his head.

'You were going to say?' Heinrich Güllich said, leaning close to Rainer Schulze.

The Kriegsmarine man shrugged. 'They seemed to get terribly nervous when I was in the main cabin. Then, when I noticed a corner of a cotton sheet protruding from the planks covering the bilges, they gave each other a strange look.'

'But you did examine the bilges?'

'Yes. I told you I did. There were a couple of blankets in it, and a bit of sail cloth. They said they stored cans of food there, an overflow from the lockers when the boat was fully stocked. The blankets were to stop them rattling about.'

The two Gestapo men looked at each other.

'And you're sure there couldn't have been anyone else on the boat?'

'I'm ashamed to say, I was suspicious that they were hiding something. I felt terrible, but we searched the boat from top to bottom. No matter what you say, there wasn't another soul on her.'

Heinrich Güllich stood up. 'Thank you for your time, Kapitänleutnant. Your testimony has been most useful. We may contact you again if any further information comes to light.'

~~o~~

'They hid them in the bilges leaving Kiel, and in Bogense and Hirtshals,' Heinrich Güllich said, thumping his fist on the dashboard of the car. 'They must have dropped them off somewhere, or they managed to pull the wool over Kapitän Schulze's eyes. All we need to do is to find out how they smuggled them into the naval base.'

'I've managed to locate most of the marines who were on guard during the period *Der Sturmtaucher* was berthed at the victualling yard,' Carl Meyer said, 'but a few of them have moved on to other posts. Two of them have been seconded to special action forces, The Brandenburgers, and the Wehrmacht is not keen to give out their whereabouts.'

'Good work, Meyer,' the Kriminalassistent said. 'Keep trying, even if we don't get them all.'

'When do you want to start questioning them, sir?'

'When we have the bulk of them. We'll interview them as close together as possible. It will prevent collusion.'

'I hope to have them all by next week, barring the two special action men. Do you really think they jumped ship in Denmark, sir?'

'I very much hope so. Because, if they have, we'll find them. And crucify those who were complicit in their escape.'

For a while, the Kästners and the Nussbaums sat in the cockpit, in comfortable silence, each in their own thoughts.

Then, in the east, Ruth saw a smudge of smoke on the horizon.

'There's a ship behind us,' she said.

They all turned to look. All thoughts of safety evaporated.

Franz cursed. They were almost in the minefields. Surely a German ship wouldn't dare come so close? And not to investigate a yacht, even if they did suspect it was *The Shearwater*.

But it was getting closer and coming straight for them.

'The bomber must have reported back by radio.'

'What do you suggest?' Johann said.

'The Royal Navy should be here soon. Perhaps we could buy some time. Change the flags over again. I can speak enough Swedish to convince them that we're a neutral boat.'

'They might still sink us, just for fun. I mean, who would ever know?'

'We could drop sail, and all hide below,' Manny said. 'They might think *The Shearwater* is an abandoned boat.'

'That won't stop them sinking her,' Johann said.

The ship was approaching fast. They could now clearly make out her tall, thin hull and superstructure.

'It's a destroyer,' Franz said. 'They'll be on us in minutes.'

For the first time, he felt powerless.

'They're signalling,' Ruth shouted.

Franz stared. Ruth was right. An Aldis lamp flashed on its flying bridge.

He screwed his eyes and concentrated. He couldn't make sense of the words for a few seconds, then he froze.

'It's in English,' he yelled, relief flooding over his face. 'It's the Royal Navy.'

At once, they were all laughing and hugging each other. Ruth was crying. Even Johann, caught up in the moment, forgot his guilt about his friends and his country.

He grabbed the bed sheet and waved it in the air. Manny took hold of the other end to hold it up.

'They want us to stop,' Franz said. He turned to Johann. 'Head into the wind,' he said.

Johann let go of the sheet and turned the wheel, and *The Shearwater* came around, heading into the sun, and into the wind, the grey canvas flapping, its job done.

Franz made his way to the mast and dropped the main first, then the foresail.

Hove-to on the mizzen and staysail, *The Shearwater* lay rolling gently on the swell. Franz imagined her letting out a disappointed sigh, that her journey was over. They all watched as the destroyer slowed and circled them, it's large ensign fluttering out behind it, before stopping dead in the water two cables ahead of them.

From a loudspeaker high on its superstructure, a metallic voice rang out.

'Take down your sails and make sure your crew are all standing on deck. Your engine must be stopped.'

The command was repeated in heavily accented German.

Franz waved an acknowledgement. He and Johann dropped the mizzen and the staysail.

'Do you speak English?' the disembodied voice said.

Franz waved again to show he understood.

'Do you have any weapons on board?'

Franz reached down into the chart table and fished out their two service pistols that they'd brought. He held them up in the air by their barrels.

'Lay them down on the foredeck and return to the cockpit. Keep your hands in the air and we will send a boat over.'

They watched as a launch was lowered down the destroyer's port side. There were eight men aboard it. One had an officer's cap, a couple looked like able seamen. And there were five marines.

The ropes were released, and the launch moved away from the side of the ship, towards them.

It came to within fifty metres of *The Shearwater*. The officer had a megaphone in his hand.

'We are going to board you. Keep your hands in the air at all times. We do not need any assistance. Are there only four of you on board?'

'Yes,' shouted Franz.

Franz could see that two of the marines had their guns trained on them as the launch came expertly alongside, and the seamen tied up to the bow and stern cleats. While the two marines covered the crew of *The Shearwater*, the others clambered over and stood on the yacht's side decks, their sub-machine guns in front of them at the ready.

The sub lieutenant stepped on board. He saluted Franz and Johann.

They returned his with a German Army salute.

'I am Sub Lieutenant Archibald of His Majesty's Royal Navy ship *Intrepid*. What are your intentions?'

'Major Franz Kästner, Third Battalion, 69th Infantry Division, Wehrmacht. This is Captain Johann Kästner, of the same Kompanie. We wish to surrender ourselves and our vessel to the Royal Navy.'

'And your other two crew?'

'These are Ruth and Manny Nussbaum, Jewish refugees from Germany. They are brother and sister.'

The sub-officer's eyebrows rose.

'Your English is excellent, Major.'

'Thank you, Sub Lieutenant.'

'What port did you depart from?'

'Kiel. In Germany.'

The officer stiffened.

'Are you sure?' he said, frowning.

'Yes. It's the truth.'

'That's in the Baltic Sea. When did you leave?'

'The beginning of April. The second.'

'And you've been at sea since then?'

Franz couldn't blame the man for the incredulous tone in his voice. It did sound implausible when he said it.

'We took refuge for a week in western Denmark. Near Esbjerg.'

'I find it hard to believe that you weren't caught.'

'It was a very isolated spot. I have our boat's log down below,' Franz said. 'I can get it for you if you like.'

'No. Stay there.' The voice was cold and hard.

Franz froze.

The officer turned to one of the marines, a sergeant.

'Take one of your men and search down below. Be careful. If you see anything suspicious, let me know.'

Franz stayed silent. The man was doing exactly what he would have done had the positions been reversed.

As the two marines climbed carefully down the companionway, one covering the other, the midshipman told a third marine to collect the weapons from the foredeck.

Franz could hear the men below shouting *clear* as they searched the main cabin, then moved forward to the heads, and the forecabin.

The sergeant stuck his head out from the companionway.

'All clear, sir,' he said. 'There's nothing questionable.'

The sub lieutenant turned to Franz.

'Where is the log?'

'It's on the chart table. Our route is marked up on three or four charts. You might find them useful too.'

The officer nodded.

'It's written in German,' Franz added.

'Ich spreche ein bisschen Deutsch,' the sub lieutenant said. *I speak a little German.*

'That's why they sent me over,' he continued, in English. He turned to the marines.

'Have a look for them, Sergeant.'

'Yes, sir. Will I bring them up?'

The sub lieutenant opened his mouth to agree, then changed his mind.

'I'll come down.'

~~o~~

In truth, Sub Lieutenant Archibald was intrigued by the two German soldiers, their strange yacht, and their supposed Jewish crew, and he was curious to see the rest of the boat.

He climbed down the steps and looked around. It looked very well organised and relatively clean and tidy; perhaps over so for the length of voyage that they were claiming to have made.

He sniffed. There was a slight smell of dampness but that would be more than understandable given a passage of any duration, especially with the gales they'd had in the last few days.

There were sleeping bags in both pilot berths and two in the forepeak but only two kitbags were stowed away.

He sat at the chart table and opened the boat's log, flicking through the pages. It had been meticulously kept by at least two different people, judging by the handwriting. He stopped at the page with entries for the ninth of April and stared.

Wind 45 knots, westerly. Massive seas. Barometer still dropping. 988mb

He read it again and shook his head. He remembered the storm of a fortnight ago and found it hard to believe that this vessel could have survived it.

He looked at the charts and followed their track backwards from their current position, southwards and eastwards to their departure from Denmark, then the first part of their journey all the way back to Kiel. He took a few minutes to read the last log entry before they entered Hobo Dyb.

He shook his head.

He rolled up the charts, lifted the boat's log and took them out on deck.

'One at a time, you can go down to the cabin and take any personal items or clothing you need. You can have one bag each, but I notice that there are only two kitbags.'

'Manny and Ruth were smuggled onto the boat in Kiel. They couldn't take much with them. The few belongings they brought were taken to the boat hidden in the stores we took on board, so they have no bags of their own. There are a couple of smaller sail bags they can use, for all that they have. During the voyage, they largely used spare clothes belonging to Johann and I.'

'I see. Well, snap to it, we haven't got all day.'

'Sir, are we not going to sail *The Shearwater* into port?'

The sub lieutenant laughed, then stopped when he saw their faces.

'I'm sorry. I shouldn't have laughed. We cannot afford to hang about nursing a sailing yacht back to Rosyth. It's over 140 miles. It would put our ship and our crew at risk from any passing submarine or aircraft.'

'What will happen to her?' the younger of the brothers said, in a horrified whisper.

'I should imagine we'll scuttle her,' the officer said.

He looked at them. The two German officers had a look of utter devastation on their faces. The younger two looked confused, and turned to their companions, questioning them rapidly in German.

On hearing the reply, the girl began crying, and an angry scowl appeared on the boy's face.

'Can I suggest something, sir?' the one called Franz said.

'I doubt if it will make any difference but go on.'

'We fully understand that you do not wish to put your ship at risk, and we know that leaving *The Shearwater* out here would be a navigational hazard, but we could set her to forereach towards the coast. Perhaps someone could salvage her if she beached. She has a strong hull.'

Before the sub lieutenant could reply, the Franz fellow went on.

'*The Shearwater* means a lot to us, sir. It would break our hearts to see her sunk. She has taken us through conditions that you couldn't imagine and has, without doubt, saved Ruth and Manny from the horrors facing Jews in Germany.'

Sub Lieutenant Graham Archibald wasn't a hard man; in fact, he sometimes felt that he was too soft to be a military officer. And although these people were the enemy, he had a degree of sympathy with what he took to be genuine distress.

Against that, he'd have his commander to answer to.

~~o~~

'Set her up to sail,' the sub lieutenant said to Franz, 'but I can't promise that my captain won't sink her.'

'That's fair.'

Manny and Ruth took turns to go below and return with a small bag each, containing their clothes and personal effects, followed by Johann, then Franz.

Franz packed his sextant, the bottle of whisky, and a few clothes, his spare boots, and a jacket, and put them in the bag with a few of his other personal items.

'We need to hoist the main and the staysail,' he said to the sub lieutenant, coming back on deck.

'Carry on, but we'll be watching you,' he said, still not entirely free of suspicion.

Franz and Johann hoisted the main, with two reefs in it, and the staysail, which they centred in front of the mast.

Johann hauled the mainsheet in tight while Franz lashed the wheel amidships.

'That's her,' he said to the sub lieutenant, as *The Shearwater*'s sails filled, and she began to creep forward.

The Kästner brothers and the Nussbaums climbed into the launch first, followed by the officer, then the marines, who cast off. Ruth looked tearfully back at *The Shearwater* as she picked up speed westwards, then the launch swept them away in a wide curve back to the destroyer.

~~o~~

Guarded by two of the marines, the four young Germans stood in the wardroom, waiting for the captain to see them.

Franz looked at the others numbly.

'We're safe,' he said, bowing his head in relief. 'We're safe.'

Ruth took hold of his head and lifted it up until he was looking at her.

'You did it, Franz. You did what you promised my father. No matter what happens now, we'll never forget that.'

He began to shake. His body, released of all responsibility, gave way to all the terrors and fears that he'd fought to quell for the last eighteen days.

Ruth held his hand tightly, glancing at the marines, then Johann put his arm around his brother's shoulder and held him steady.

'We made it,' he said. 'No one in Germany can touch us now, and Ruth and Manny are safe.'

'I know,' Franz said, pulling himself up straight. 'It will just take a while to sink in.'

CHAPTER 173

[25/08/2001 Saturday]

Maldon, England.

'Nowadays,' Ruth said, leaning towards me with a conspiratorial smile, 'they would call it post-traumatic stress or some such thing. It only lasted for a few minutes, then Franz pulled himself together and began looking after us again.'

She paused for a second, then continued.

'The thing was,' she said, 'when I looked at them both, standing there, I realised that it was Johann who would take it harder.'

'What do you mean?' I asked.

'That was Johann's moment of surrender, she said 'He was a deserter, leaving his country and his friends to fight on their own, without him.'

'But he'd saved you and Manny. And probably himself.'

Ruth sighed.

'For Franz, it was black and white. What he'd been fighting for was evil. His only heartbreak was for me, and Manny, being separated from us, and for those he'd left behind.'

She closed her eyes.

'That was bad enough, but for Johann it was different. It was the guilt. I saw it on his face too often during the journey, and more so as he stood there, waiting to be led away, quietly, like a sheep.'

'I don't think that feeling ever left him.'

CHAPTER 174

North Sea, HMS *Intrepid.*

'I'm not impressed,' the captain said, not hiding his exasperation with his sub lieutenant. 'You should have scuttled it there and then. I've a good mind to send you back over there to do it, were it not for us having to stay here even longer.'

'I'm sorry, sir,' he said and, knowing that he was straying into territory that could get him demoted, he rolled out one of the charts on the chart table in the captain's day cabin.

'Please just have a quick look at these, sir. From what I can see, what they have done is quite remarkable, and they feel that they owe this boat their lives.'

Captain Andrew Stanworth had come up through the ranks of the RNVR in the years leading up to the war, and during the first eighteen months of hostilities, largely due to his quick grasp of navigation and seamanship and an easy way with the men under him, he'd found himself in command of a corvette, then a destroyer. Many of his skills had been honed from an early age, sailing with his father and uncle on their yacht in the Solent.

Putting aside his irritation with his junior officer, a flicker of curiosity prevented him from immediately ordering his most rusty gunnery team to acquire much needed target practice on the abandoned yacht.

'This better be good, Sub,' he said, looking at the chart the officer had smoothed out. 'You have five minutes.'

'Yes, sir,' the midshipman said, pointing to the various places on the chart *The Shearwater* had called at. 'This is the course they took as far as Hirtshals, through the Little Belt, the Kattegat and the eastern Skagerrak. I've had a quick look at their boat's log, and I'd imagine that, apart from the threat of capture, the voyage would have been somewhat routine. It's after leaving Hirtshals that it gets interesting.'

He laid out the second chart, Texel to Bergen, including most of the Skagerrak, and the whole of the west coast of Denmark.

'Sir, the cyclone that caught us late on the seventh of April hit them the next day. They attempted to use the cover of the storm to head westwards to Britain but, according to the yacht's log, they were caught out in the worst conditions the North Sea has seen for decades, without the option to turn back or take refuge close by.'

'Go on.'

'They were out in the teeth of that storm for three days and nights until they found refuge in an isolated anchorage halfway down the coast of Denmark. Sir, you remember what that storm was like.'

HMS *Intrepid*, under Captain Stanworth's command, had been patrolling a hundred miles off the east coast of England when the storm struck. The ship had been only half-full of fuel at the time and without the extra ballast of full tanks, it had taken all the skill of the captain and crew to prevent her foundering in the shallow, vicious waters of the North Sea. She'd crept into the shelter of the Firth of Forth on the second day of the storm.

'If this account is true, it's a remarkable feat of survival, and of seamanship.'

'Think of it, sir. If we alert someone at Coastal Patrol Command, they could organise a tow into the nearest dockyard. I'd imagine someone would find a use for her, sir. It would be a waste of such a brave vessel, sir, if we were to sink her.'

The captain looked at the chart again and read the log entries from *The Shearwater* just before their entrance into Hobo Dyb.

He stared at it for a while.

'Work out the speed and direction of the ruddy vessel and do a half-hour plot of her EPs,' he said, his gruff tone hiding a catch in the back of his throat. He turned to his radio officer.

'Have a signal sent within the hour to Coastal Command North East telling them when she is likely to hit the beach and have them pick her up and take her in before she does. Tell them to let us know where they take her. I'd like to have a look at this *Shearwater*.'

'They translated the name for us, sir, from the German. The boat's name is *Der Sturmtaucher.*'

~~o~~

Franz had recovered his composure.

'The captain will see you now,' Sub Lieutenant Archibald said. 'Come this way.'

The four Germans followed him from the wardroom out onto the deck, and up the steps to the back of the destroyer's bridge, the two marines in close attendance. At the top of the steps, the sub lieutenant stopped and looked out to the south-west. In the distance, now a mile away, Franz saw *The Shearwater* making way slowly under sail, a real-life ghost ship.

'Look, Ruth,' he said, taking her arm and pointing.

They stood, the four of them, watching *The Shearwater* recede towards the horizon, not a dry eye between them, until the sub lieutenant coughed.

'The captain is waiting,' he said.

'Thank you, Sub Lieutenant,' Franz said, saluting the young officer. 'We'll never forget your kindness.'

'She deserved it, from what I've read. Now, hurry, before Captain Stanworth changes his mind.'

~~o~~

They still carried their bags. Before they entered the captain's day cabin, a small compartment behind the bridge, they were asked to leave them with one of the able seamen who were posted at the entrance to the bridge.

Franz asked the marine sergeant if he would be permitted to retrieve something from his kitbag.

The marine and the sailor closely supervised Franz as he withdrew the bottle of whisky and his sextant and showed the items to them.

The captain's day cabin was a place where the vessel's commander could retreat to catch up on sleep in the neat bunk along one wall, or work in relative peace and quiet at his desk, or at the chart table opposite the bunk, and still be available at short notice should he be required.

Franz entered the cabin behind the other three and, on being presented to him, handed the ship's commander the whisky bottle, then saluted him.

'I'd like you to have these, sir, as a token of our appreciation.'

'Ah. Your taste is as impeccable as your English,' he said, eyeing the bottle.

Franz handed him the sextant.

'You keep it, Major,' the captain said.

'No, sir. They'll take it away from me. Give it to one of your junior officers. Perhaps the sub lieutenant.'

The captain took the sextant, turning it over in his hands. 'We'll see,' he said. He placed it on his desk.

'Please take a seat,' he said. 'Some of you may use my bunk.'

He waited until they'd all found somewhere to sit.

'Now, my sub here has persuaded me to let your vessel live. I want to hear from your own lips exactly, and in the greatest detail, if I've made the right decision.'

'Sir, it may take a while.'

'It'll take us five hours to get to port. The sub lieutenant will take notes, so there's no need to rush.'

Franz took a deep breath.

'Well, sir, on the morning of the second of April, we left Kieler Hafen, with a brief to deliver our commanding officer's yacht to Bergen, where we were based...'

CHAPTER 175

Franz and Johann Kästner left the ship in darkness, escorted by the marines, and handed over to troops from the King's Own Scottish Borderers.

The captain had listened to their story for nearly two hours, then left the four prisoners to themselves, guarded by two marines, until the ship docked at Rosyth, in the early hours of Monday, the twenty-first of April, 1941.

Ruth had nodded off in Franz's arms, and Johann and Manny had also fallen asleep, stretched out on the floor as if they didn't have a care in the world.

Franz would have loved to have done the same, but his head buzzed with the enormity of what they'd done, with what they'd left behind, and with the uncertain future ahead of them.

Shortly before they docked, the sub lieutenant had stuck his head in the door and warned them that they'd soon be disembarking.

Manny, fighting back tears, shook both the Kästner brothers' hands before turning away, hiding his face. Ruth hugged Johann first.

'I'll look after him,' she said, seeing the pain in Johann's eyes.

The younger Kästner brother followed Manny out of the cabin.

Ruth turned to Franz.

'I'm not going to cry,' she said. 'I want to remember being happy with you.'

He held her for a minute, until the marine tapped him on the shoulder.

'I'm sorry, sir,' he said. 'It's time to go.'

They took Manny and Ruth first. Franz and Johann stood at the top of the gangway as they were led across the dock to a black car. Two men stood beside it and talked to the two young Jews.

Franz watched numbly.

They look terrified.

Before they got into the car, the two Nussbaums turned round, glanced up at Franz and Johann and gave a last wave. As the car drove along the quay Franz saw Ruth's pale face look back once.

The marines marched the two German officers, in full uniform, down the gangway and onto British soil.

All four saluted the two British soldiers.

'Your prisoners,' barked the marine sergeant.

CHAPTER 176

Maldon, England

'The captain of the destroyer was so kind to us; he could have sunk *Der Sturmtaucher, and he was well within his rights to put us in the cells when they took us aboard the ship, but he did neither. Did you know they had prison cells on a warship?'
'No,' I said, 'but I suppose it makes sense; drunken sailors, and all that.'
Ruth smiled indulgently at my feeble effort at humour, then the smile faded, and that familiar, unfathomable sadness replaced it.
'I didn't know if I'd ever see Franz again, or Johann. I wasn't even sure if Manny and I would be allowed to stay together. And my English was elementary at best.'
She put her hand to her neck.
'Just about the only possession I had to remember Franz by was the ring. Lise's ring.'
She showed it to me. I thought it would be one of the many she wore on her fingers; she loved her jewellery, but no. She reached inside her blouse and, from around her neck, pulled out an old, frayed loop of hemp string.
'I could never bring myself to wear it on my finger,' she said, turning the small, plain gold ring between her fingers, before handing it to me, on its crude necklace. 'It had too much meaning for me, and I wanted to wear it the way he had worn it, to remind me of him, and what we'd been through together.'
Her eyes had that faraway look again. A tear trickled down her deeply wrinkled cheek; her face was still beautiful, suiting the age it carried with immense dignity, and a pride that she had survived. I waited for her to finish speaking.
She shivered.
'It was dark, wet and miserable and we could have been anywhere. The British didn't know what to do with us; two German Jews, both teenagers, and with a smattering of English between us despite my lessons in Saarbrückenstraße and Franz's encouragement on the boat.'
Ruth smiled.
'I couldn't understand their Scottish dialect,' she said, shaking her head, 'and they couldn't understand me any better. It took them a day to find an interpreter.
'The first night, they locked us in a cell in a police station, somewhere in Edinburgh; I never found out where. When the interpreter turned up with officials from the Ministry of Defence, she was horrified. She insisted that we were refugees, and that they immediately find accommodation more fitting for two teenagers.
'After a week, they told us that we would be taken to a camp on an island where they kept German Jews who had reached British shores without visas and often, like us, without passports. All we had was our Kennkarte, our German identity cards.'
'The Isle of Wight?' I asked, the first island that sprang to mind.
'No, we were interned on the Isle of Man.'
Ruth closed her eyes.
'I don't blame them. Even when they admitted that their enquiries had confirmed our story, taking account of the destroyer captain's testimony, Franz's charts, and the logbook from our voyage from Kiel to Scotland, they couldn't let two German citizens go free, no matter what our age.'
'You knew no one in Britain?' I asked her.
'No. Not a soul. If we'd had family or friends here, they might have let them take us in, but we had no one who could vouch for us. Four days later, we were taken to Liverpool and put on a ship with another thirty or forty Jews, under armed guard. We disembarked in Douglas, and we were marched up the street to the camp, with people standing at their doorways watching us. It felt like being back in Germany.'

CHAPTER 177

[25/04/1941 Friday]

North of England

'We'll just have to sit it out and hope that Britain stands firm if Maxi Grabner tries to invade us.'

Franz barely smiled. Johann put his hand on his brother's shoulder.

'She'll be fine,' he said. 'Manny will look out for her.'

They sat in the back of a British Army covered four-tonner. Two soldiers from the King's Own Scottish Borderers sat opposite, watching them with interest. Franz and Johann spoke in German, and neither the corporal nor the private appeared to have any understanding of what they were saying.

'Sprechen Sie Deutsch?' Franz said to the corporal, an older man, wanting to make sure.

'I don't speak your lingo, Kraut,' the man said. Franz recognised his accent as Scottish but found it difficult to understand. 'You speak English, though, we were told.'

'Yes. I speak a little English,' Franz said, 'I find your accent a little difficult, though.'

'Ah. That's because I'm no English. I'm Scottish, born and bred.'

'I thought your accent was Scottish. I met someone who was from Scotland once. From Inverness.'

'A teuchter. That's what we call folk fae up north.'

The private, with a broader accent, spoke.

'Is it true, like, that ye sailed all the way fae Germany, wi two Jews, in an auld yacht?'

Franz smiled.

'Yes. They were friends of ours. We had to get them out of Germany. Jews are being imprisoned and killed in their thousands there.'

'That cannae be right, man. Why would they do that?'

'Adolf Hitler and the National Socialists have stirred up enough hate against the Jews for it to become acceptable. It happened when we captured Poland too.'

'He's a bastard, your Adolf, but killing Jews?' the corporal said. 'In their thousands? I find it hard to believe.'

'It's true. All of it,' Johann said, despite struggling to make out the soldiers' mangled English. He could understand most of Franz's side of the conversation, but he was quite sure that his own limited command of the language was more comprehensible than the strange dialect the two men spoke.

'So, you're deserters then?' the private said, scowling at them.

'No. Well yes, I suppose we are. But if you'd seen what the Wehrmacht, and the SS especially are doing, you'd understand.'

'You're still a deserter, son,' the corporal said, not unkindly. 'And where you're going, I'd keep quiet about it, if I were you. Some of yer pals might no take very weel to it.'

'What do you mean?'

The corporal glanced at the private.

'Well, most of the prisoners we take down to the racecourse are airmen. Luffwaffe, they call themselves, isn't it? Or sailors, mainly from submarines we've sunk, or captured. We've only had a few soldiers before, from Norway, when we were still fighting there. They're all fanatics, doing thon Nazi salute thing to each other every time one of them goes for a pish and singing Nazi songs.'

'How do you know they're Nazi songs?' Franz said, the shortened version of *Nationalsozialisten* rolling off his tongue with an ease that surprised him.

'They told us. The Horst Vessel Song.'

'Horst Wessel,' Franz corrected.

'Aye, that's whit ah said. Awfy proud they were too. We had to tell them tae cut it out after a while. It was getting them all riled up, excited, like. Anyhow, you might want to think about acting a bit like them, if you know what I mean, or you'll stick oot like a sair thumb.'

'Ah,' Franz said. 'We'll keep that in mind. Everyone in Germany seems to be fanatical these days.'

A puzzled look came over Franz's face.

'You said racecourse,' he asked. 'Did I catch you right?'

'Yes. Doncaster Racecourse. It's being used as a transit camp. They call them cages. They're dotted all over Britain. You'll not be there long before you're assigned elsewhere.'

They fell silent for a while, then Johann nudged him.

'Was sagen sie?' he said. *What were they saying?*

'Just that most of the prisoners they transport are all staunch Hitler men. That we should watch what we're saying.'

'I don't see…'

'He's right. Unless we're sure we're alone, never talk about the Nussbaums, and never deviate from our story.'

'I know, I know.' Johann sighed. 'We got caught in the storm, we were terrified that we would be blown onto a lee shore, so we beat out westwards towards the mouth of the Skagerrak. We were foundering when a passing ship picked us up. Trouble is, the ship was a British destroyer. *The Shearwater* was sinking when we left it. Blah-blah-blah.'

'Good. What was the ship's name?'

'HMS *Intrepid.*'

'The captain's name?'

'Captain Stanworth. And the sub lieutenant was called Graham Archibald.'

'Excellent. But don't be tempted to elaborate further. We were put in the cells, then handed over to these soldiers. We know nothing more.'

'All right. Do you think I'm an idiot?'

Franz looked at his brother and smiled.

The truck fell silent apart from the rumble of the engine and the thrum of the tyres on the road. The corporal fell asleep, and although the private did his best to keep his eyes open, by the time the truck had travelled a third of the way to Doncaster, Franz was the only one awake. He smiled. If he'd wanted to escape, he could have jumped out the back when the truck slowed for a junction.

His thoughts drifted to Ruth, and how she was doing, and Manny, and those left in Kiel. It wasn't long before he nodded off too.

He awoke when the truck juddered to a halt at the camp gates.

The corporal jerked out of his sleep at the same time and, just for a second, looked around in the dimness of the back of the lorry in panic. He saw the private, still sleeping, and then the two prisoners and he let out a sigh.

'It's all right. We haven't run away,' Franz said.

The corporal scowled at him, then his face softened.

'Not likely you two would escape, with you wanting to be here in the first place.'

'We wouldn't have done if it hadn't been for our Jewish friends. We're not cowards.'

'No. I suppose. Still, remember what I said. Keep it to yourselves.'

'We will,' Franz said, 'and thank you.'

~~o~~

Franz looked around as he climbed down from the lorry. Barbed wire enclosures covered the whole of the central part of the racecourse, but the white rails were still in place. He wondered if they still held races here, then smiled.

Don't be stupid.

Within the enclosures, there were a mixture of large tents and wooden huts. They were taken through the main gate to the largest hut. A second lorry discharged a larger group of prisoners behind them. The camp guard gestured for Franz and Johann to enter the building, and to wait outside a door marked *Registration.*

After a few minutes, it opened, and Franz was told to go in.

'Do-you-understand-English?' a stocky sergeant, sitting behind a desk, asked him, in slow, enunciated, disinterested speech.

'Yes. I have reasonable English.'

The soldier's bushy eyebrows shot half an inch up his forehead.

'Right,' he said, 'you are required to give your name, rank and regimental number, but I see you've already done that.' The man looked down at his clipboard. 'You're Major Franz Erich Kästner?'

'Yes,' Franz said, confirming the small lie he'd told the sub lieutenant on the ship. His middle name was Eduard, after his maternal grandfather. Erich was Johann's.

'I gave my details to the captain of the destroyer that picked us up,' he added.

'And your unit?'

'With the 69th Infantry Division, Wehrmacht, based in Norway.' There was no point in withholding this. He'd already told Captain Stanworth that they'd been taking the yacht to Norway.

'Yes.'

'But you were captured by a British destroyer, at sea?'

'Yes. We were taking our commanding officer's yacht from Germany to Norway, but we were caught in a storm. One of your destroyers rescued us.'

'I can't imagine your commanding officer will be impressed,' the sergeant said, shaking his head. 'It's a good job you're out of his reach.'

'I suppose you're right. We feel terrible about it.'

'Well, you're here for the duration. He'll have time to calm down.'

'Can I ask a question?'

'Yes, Major. I can't guarantee to answer it though.'

'Are we permitted to write home?'

'Yes. You will be given paper and pen in due course. You can write as many letters as you want but they will only be delivered once per month. I would advise you to keep that in mind if you want to keep the privilege.'

In truth, Franz knew what rights they had. His father had shown him the relevant parts of the most recent version of the Geneva Convention on the Treatment of Prisoners of War, signed by most of the European countries and the United States in Geneva, in 1929.

He could remember it almost word for word.

Countries are required to notify each other of all captures of prisoners as soon as possible through Prisoner Information Bureaux set up at the commencement of hostilities.

As soon as possible, every prisoner shall be enabled to correspond personally with his family. Not later than one week after his arrival in camp, and similarly in case of sickness, each prisoner shall be enabled to send a postcard to his family informing them of his capture and the state of his health.

Each country shall fix periodically the number of letters and postcards which prisoners of war of different categories shall be permitted to send per month. These letters and cards shall be sent by post by the shortest route. They may not be delayed or withheld for disciplinary motives.

As regards prisoners captured at sea, the provisions of the present article shall be observed as soon as possible after arrival in port.

'The British will stick to the agreement,' his father had said. 'They are sticklers for honour.'

Franz looked at the sergeant.

'I would like to let my family know that I and my brother are safe and well, as soon as possible.'

'As part of your registration, you will be asked to fill in a postcard, which will be sent to your relatives, be it your wife or family, back in Germany.'

'Thank you,' Franz said. Despite the General's faith in the British and their sense of fair play, it was a relief to have it confirmed.

'Now, you will be given a medical, and treated for any conditions which would render you a danger to the rest of the camp's population, and any other condition affecting your personal health. Do you understand?'

'Yes.'

'And you will be interviewed with regards to your capture and any additional information you might be willing to give. I must inform you that you are not required to give any of this information to us, and it will not affect the conditions of your incarceration if you refuse to give this information.'

'I understand.'

'However, consider this. The length of time you are incarcerated will depend on how long your country continues its aggression, so it would be in your own interest to furnish us with any information you can give which might shorten the war.'

'I would not be prepared to give any information which would cause harm to my friends and colleagues still fighting for Germany.'

The sergeant gave him a look of resigned disgust but told him to wait by the door of the doctor's office, further along the corridor. Behind him, the sergeant was already talking to Johann.

'Do-you-understand-English?'

'Yes.'

'And you are Captain Johann Eduard Kästner?'

'Yes.' He heard his brother mouth the lie, as the door opened, and the doctor motioned for Franz to enter.

Franz hoped that the swapping of their middle names would not be corrected by the authorities in Germany when they received notification of their capture.

'We'll have to find a way to let you know that Ruth and Manny made it to England,' Franz had said to his father, sitting in his study on their last evening in Drachensee.

'We will have to come up with a few methods in case one fails.'

'Johann and I can transpose our names, but we'll need something else,' Franz had said, sipping the glass of malt his father had poured him. He'd looked at the bottle and smiled. *Glenfiddich.*

CHAPTER 178

```
The War Office,
Whitehall,
London.

To:

Lt. Colonel Anthony James Plenderleith, DSO,
80 London Rd,
Lexden,
Colchester.

20th April 1941,

Dear Sir,

Further to our communications in August of last year, and your
attendance at both the retraining course at Pirbright in
November and the specialist programme in London in February,
you have been appointed as deputy commander of Prisoner of War
camp No. 2, Glen Mill, Oldham, Lancashire.

Accommodation will be provided for you and your family in the
nearby village of Pitses. The property is fully furnished,
although taking a few small pieces of your own would be
acceptable. The address is:

82 Manor Rd
Pitses,
Nr. Oldham
Lancashire

Your new appointment will start on Monday 5th May. The house
will be available from Friday the 2nd May. The keys can be
collected from the Glen Mill camp, Wellyhole Street, Oldham
after 09:00 on the date of entry.

Yours,

Lt. Col. Erskine Cunningham, Adjutant.

PP General David Carruthers.
```

~~o~~

'It's right in the north,' Marjorie Plenderleith said.

'Well, not quite, my dear,' her husband replied. 'Newcastle and Carlisle are further up, and there's the whole of Scotland north of those.'

'I'd hoped you might get something in the Home Counties, or even in the south-west. That would have been lovely.'

'I'm sure it will be fine in Lancashire, and it won't be for long, so don't fret.'

'I suppose you're right. That's why they didn't think it a good idea for us to take our furniture. It would hardly be worth the effort.'

'That's the spirit, my dear, and don't forget, we can come back here when I get a spot of leave.'

They both loved their cottage in Lexden. The small village, a mile west of Colchester, boasted a village shop, an old coaching inn called The Crown that did a lovely Sunday lunch, and a splendid church, St Leonard's.

Lieutenant Colonel Plenderleith chuckled: St Leonard just happened to be the patron saint of prisoners.

~~o~~

'You're an unusual animal in here, Captain…'

'Kästner. Captain Johann Kästner.'

'Pleased to meet you. I'm Kapitän Axel Langefeld, Luftwaffe. This is Kapitänleutnant Gerhard Schlesinger, Kriegsmarine.'

Johann was careful to do the full Hitler salute, mindful of Franz's warning.

'That's my brother, Major Franz Kästner, talking to the guard.'

Franz and Johann, carrying their meagre possessions and two blankets they'd been given, had been shown through a wire-mesh gate into one of the barbed-wire-protected enclosures. Groups of German prisoners milled around, talking or smoking. Others looked at the new arrivals with curiosity. Five or six men, in their vests and rolled-up trousers, were playing a game of football at the far end of the compound.

Johann glanced at the German sailor, but the Kästner name didn't appear to strike a chord with him. Johann presumed that he must have been captured, or had at least left port, before *Der Sturmtaucher* was the talk of the Kriegsmarine. Or perhaps he'd sailed out of Wilhelmshaven.

'Why do you say "unusual", Captain?'

The man laughed.

'There aren't many soldiers in this camp. You may be the only two. By and large, it's downed bomber crew we have in here, or sailors like Kapitänleutnant Schlesinger, from submarines that have been captured or sunk. Apart from a few at the start of the invasion of Norway, the British have captured few of our ground forces.'

Johann had missed the U-boat badge on the Kriegsmarine man's tunic until the Luftwaffe man had mentioned it.

'I suppose so,' he said.

'How were you captured?' the airman said.

'It will sound stupid,' Johann said. He told them their well-rehearsed story.

'We were exhausted when they picked us up,' he finished. 'It took me a few minutes to realise it wasn't one of our ships.'

'It does seem a waste, men like you and your brother, rotting in here…'

Johann looked around at the barbed wire, the tents, the huts, and the watchtowers.

'If it hadn't been for the storm…' Johann said.

The Kriegsmarine sailor clapped Johann on the back. 'What's done is done. You must have seen action in Norway, eh?'

'Yes. And in the Sudetenland, Poland, and France. My brother has an Iron Cross.'

Both the prisoners whistled.

'You've seen plenty action then. More than most in here, I'd say,' the Luftwaffe captain said, a sheepish grin on his face.

'I was shot down on my first flight,' he added, 'and it was only Gerhard's fourth patrol, when the British sank their U-boat.'

'I was lucky,' the Kriegsmarine man said. 'Only ten of us made it out before she sank.'

'What about you, Captain Langefeld? Did you bail out?'

'Ach, call me Axel. We crash-landed in a field. The pilot was a hero, getting us down.'

'Is he in here too?' Johann asked.

Both men laughed.

'He's talking about himself,' the submariner said. 'He often does that.'

Johann joined in the laughter just as Franz walked over.

'This is my brother, Franz,' he said. He turned to his two new companions.

'And this is Captain Axel Langefeld, and Kapitänleutnant Gerhard Schlesinger,' he said to Franz.

'Ah. We have the Luftwaffe and the Kriegsmarine as a welcoming party. And submarines, Herr Kapitänleutnant. I never envied you your posting, no matter how much I loved the sea.'

The U-boat officer laughed and fingered his submariner's badge with pride. It was awarded to submariners who completed their third three patrol; he'd only just received it before embarking for his fourth, and last.

'You say that,' he said, 'but the storm, the one you got caught in. We would just have submerged under it and let it rage over our heads.'

'That hadn't crossed my mind,' Franz said. 'We could certainly have made use of such a capability.'

'Yes, your brother was telling us about your unfortunate capture.'

'In all truth, perhaps, we were lucky. I doubt we would have survived otherwise.'

The airman laughed.

'We're all the same. I'd rather be in here than burning in a wrecked airframe, and I'm sure Gerhard feels the same, God rest his dead comrades.'

'We will be released to fight again, when the Third Reich occupies this sorry country,' the Kapitänleutnant said.

'Heil Hitler,' the Luftwaffe man said, saluting again.

Franz and Johann returned the salute.

'Now, let us introduce you to the others,' the airman said. 'There's Hans and Fritz, another Johann and two Erichs.'

The submariner stopped and looked at Franz and Johann, tilting his head and frowning.

'Kästner,' he said. 'Where are you from?'

'Kiel,' Johann said, knowing what was coming.

'General Kästner. Are you related to him?'

'Yes. He's our father.'

'Ah. I thought I recognised you. I met him a couple of times, and I saw you with him once, at Naval Headquarters, a few years ago.'

He turned to Captain Langefeld.

'General Kästner is based in Kiel. He's part of the army, but he's seconded to the navy. Everyone in the Kriegsmarine speaks highly of him.'

'It sounds strange, a general working for the army. Do they have an air marshal too?'

'My father is a liaison officer between the army, the navy and the Abwehr,' Johann said. 'We're bored of hearing how wonderful the Kriegsmarine think he is.' He laughed.

He saw Franz frowning, but he couldn't see the harm in telling their two companions. Everyone in Kiel knew what their father did.

'And I believe you have an Iron Cross,' Kapitänleutnant Schlesinger said, looking at Franz with admiration.

For a second, Franz's frown deepened, then faded, to be replaced by a resigned and embarrassed look.

'My brother talks too much,' he said, giving Johann a playful cuff on his ear.

'Nonsense,' the Luftwaffe captain said, 'we must hear how you won it over our evening meal, with a glass of wine or two.'

For a second, Johann stared at him, then burst into laughter.

'Wine. Indeed,' he said, still chuckling. 'It's the least the British could do, especially as it is Franz's birthday today.'

Both men clapped Franz on the back.

'Happy birthday, old boy. Come and meet the others,' he said. 'They're always anxious to hear from home, and about our glorious victories. You two will be just the tonic they need. And they'll want to see that Iron Cross of yours.'

CHAPTER 179

Erich Kästner walked into the drawing room. Maria was standing in the centre, staring out of the window at the lake. He saw her shoulders shaking and could hear quiet sobbing. He walked over and put his hand on her shoulder. She looked round at him, and anger replaced the sadness on her face.

'I'm sorry,' he said.

'It's his birthday today, my Franz, but he's gone. And Johann. They were so young. It was so unnecessary.'

He knew that nothing he could say would help, so he kept his silence.

She shrugged his hand from her shoulder and walked towards the window.

'They're still looking,' he said.

'For their bodies. It's cold comfort.'

He longed to tell her, but he couldn't now. It would serve no purpose, other than to drive her into a rage and endanger the whole family. If luck were with them and they had made it to Britain, they'd know in time, and at least that would give her peace from the nightmare he'd inflicted on her.

~~o~~

'How long have you been here?' Franz asked, sitting on the ground outside the hut they'd been assigned to. Axel Langefeld, the airman who'd first spoken to them, sat beside him.

'I've been here two weeks. Gerhard and Kriegsmarine Erich were from different U-boats, but they've been here a month. My pilot friend Erich has been stuck here for over two months and Fritzie spent Christmas here, he says, but most get moved on before that. There doesn't appear to be any rationale to it.'

'Where will they take us after this?'

'They don't tell us, but there are rumours. Wales, Scotland, a place called Devon, wherever that is. Hans there told the officer who interviewed him that he'd be back in Germany in five months, that they couldn't keep him in here. The bastard just laughed and said he'd do well to swim home from Canada.'

'Are they sending prisoners there?' Franz said, the colour draining from his face, the irrational fear of being separated from Ruth by thousands of kilometres catching him by surprise.

His head told him that it didn't matter; it wasn't as if she would be allowed to visit him, even if she were given her own freedom and, anyway, her aim would be to get across the Atlantic with Manny if she could.

His heart told him different. *It did matter.*

'You're right to be worried, my friend,' he heard Captain Langefeld say. 'We all are. Gerhard says our U-boats are sinking every second British ship that tries to cross the Atlantic. Can you imagine being sunk by our own torpedoes? I heard there was nearly a riot at Liverpool docks when they tried to make 500 of our men board an empty cargo ship heading back to Nova Scotia.'

Franz breathed out slowly, relieved that the captain hadn't taken his reaction for anything other than fear. He resolved to be more careful.

'What's with the black patch?' he asked.

Franz and Johann had been given black patches when they'd been processed and told to sit and sew them onto their uniforms. There was a large letter 'C' in the centre, with a minus sign next to it.

'It grades you,' the airman said, spitting on the ground, 'into how much of a *Nazi* you are.'

Franz feigned a puzzled expression.

'It's short for Nationalsozialistische,' the Luftwaffe man said, taking out a pack of cigarettes and offering one to Franz. 'They can't pronounce it.'

'Oh. I see,' said Franz, shaking his head, continuing to pretend ignorance. It wasn't in common usage in Germany, outside of the Jewish community.

Axel Langefeld lit his cigarette and blew a column of smoke into the air.

'We're all graded black in this compound. C-minus,' he said. 'I hear they're keeping C-plus for members of the Waffen-SS.'

'What does it mean?'

'Prisoners with a white badge, graded 'A', are seen as being low-grade Nazis. Those are the ones who tell them that they never wanted to fight, that they don't follow the Führer. Traitors, all of them.'

He spat again.

'Those with grey badges are category 'B' prisoners. They're mostly conscripted men who are just glad to have survived. They give them a questionnaire and, if they state that they only give a salute and a *Heil Hitler when* they're told to, they get a grey badge.'

He shrugged.

'Most officers and good enlisted soldiers who love the Führer are given black patches. I'm surprised you weren't categorised as C-plus when you told them you had an Iron Cross.'

'They ask if you have any medals. I thought I'd better tell the truth. Are black-graded prisoners treated differently?'

'They group us together. I presume we will be sent somewhere with higher security.'

Franz looked over at the other sections; Axel Langefeld was right. In each compound, the men all had matching patches.

'How was your interrogation?' the sailor asked.

'Ach, they didn't press me too hard. I told them only why we'd been in the middle of the Skagerrak, and that we were returning to our Kompanie in Norway.'

'You didn't tell them who your father was?'

'No. They didn't ask.'

Axel Langefeld grinned.

'Good,' he said. 'Give them nothing.'

'They kept calling us Krauts,' Franz said.

'It's short for Sauerkraut. They think they are so amusing, the English. They also call us Fritzies and sometimes Huns, Jerries or, if they are of an age to have fought in the last war, the Boche.'

He spat again.

'And let's not forget, Nazis,' he said. 'They always ask us *are you a Nazi?*'

The young airman laughed.

'As if there are any other kind of real Germans,' he said.

CHAPTER 180

Antje missed the boys more than she thought possible. Although she was accustomed to them being home only on occasional leave, this time was different. On top of that, losing Ruth was as hard to bear as losing her brothers.

No. It's worse.

And, despite trying to tell herself that they were probably safe in England, albeit as prisoners, a worm of doubt ate away at her insides, and she knew she might never find out what had happened to them.

It didn't help having to wear black, like Eva and her mother.

It feels so deceitful.

She found it hard to be in the same room as them, the lie heavy on her heart, but she admitted to herself, in her darkest hours, that it could be true.

They all might be dead.

She would have loved to have visited the Nussbaums when they retired for the night, the common bond of fear and worry drawing her to them and away from her mother and Eva, but something stopped her.

She threw herself into her art, drawing and painting her brothers, and Ruth and Manny, hiding her work lest it give her innermost thoughts away.

And the house, for so long a wonderful place, had a dark, pressing mood. She'd been in the kitchen when the General, with her mother in attendance, had told the Nussbaums that Franz and Johann had been declared drowned.

'I am so sorry, ma'am,' Miriam had said, tears coursing down her cheek, taking Maria's hand in both of hers. 'They were wonderful boys. The best.'

Antje had realised that Miriam and Yosef believed by that time that the yacht *was* lost, with all four of their offspring on it, and that Miriam's sympathy was genuine, made worse by the certain knowledge that her children were dead too, and that the Nussbaums had been the cause of Maria Kästner's grief.

She'd watched her mother squirm at Miriam's deep show of concern, so different to her own recent response to the disappearance of the Jewish couple's two children.

Yosef had come forward to share his sorrow, shaking his mistress's hand and mumbling his regrets, affirming his admiration for her sons. He shook the General's hand, bowing his head in anguish.

Antje had felt tears prick her eyes. This was sadness and pain and guilt and fear on so many complex levels, and it almost overwhelmed her.

'You must feel the same way about Ruth and Manny,' she'd heard her mother say, compelled by politeness, and frowned, hating the hypocrisy, knowing Maria Kästner wished for nothing less than for the Nussbaums to be out of her house, the problem washed away and forgotten.

'Maria is right,' the General had said, rubbing salt into the wounds of the Drachensee house. 'We mustn't forget Ruth and Manny, wherever they are.'

Crieff Herald

Thursday, 1st May 1941

PRISONER OF WAR CAMP – CONSTRUCTION BEGINS.

The first sod has been turned in the construction of a new camp designed to hold up to 4000 Axis prisoners-of-war at Cultybraggan, two miles outside Comrie on the Braco road, on the site of Cultybraggan Farm.

The camp is being built by the 249 (Alien) Company Pioneer Corps, made up of refugees from Nazi Germany.

It is expected that some of the local workforce and Perthshire companies will also assist in the construction and supply of materials for the camp.

Construction is due to be finished by the turn of the year, with German and Italian prisoners arriving in early January.

The army camp, at Cowden, on the southern outskirts of Comrie, will house the soldiers who will guard the prisoners in the main camp. It is expected that civilians connected with both camps will be billeted in homes within the village of Comrie.

~~o~~

[01/05/1941 Thursday]

Ruth looked out of the window. The day was warming up, and the Irish Sea looked less foreboding than on the cold and grey day they'd landed by ferry at Douglas. She busied herself making eggs for Manny and the family that they'd been assigned to live with.

The first night, they'd slept in the single bed in the room they'd been given, huddled together for warmth and comfort but, the next day, Frau Weissberg had taken her aside.

'It's not right for you to have to sleep in the same room as a boy, at your age, even if he is your brother.'

'But Mama and Papa asked me to look after Manny.'

'I know, Ruth, and you are looking after him, but listen to what I have to say.'

Ruth had nodded, unsure, sitting on the edge of the bed.

'I can find an extra bed; you and the girls can have our room; it's the largest, and we'll move Ben's bed into this room, and he and Manny can share. Ben would love that. Aaron and I will have the room the children are in now.'

Ruth thought about it and it made sense. Manny would prefer sharing with young Ben, and the family's daughters, Berta and Frieda, were lovely little girls.

She'd been used to a room of her own, but she knew that her life had changed forever, and freedom from the tyranny of the National Socialists was worth any of the inconveniencies that she and Manny would have to suffer.

'If it's all right with you, that would be fine, Frau Weissberg,' she said, liking the older woman.

'Call me Gella; you're a woman now.'

Ruth blushed, wondering if Frau Weissberg could somehow sense that she'd been with Franz, but she quickly discarded the thought when the older woman continued speaking.

'Anyway,' Frau Weissberg said, 'it will be nice to have a hand with the children and, if we can get you a job of sorts, it will help with the housekeeping.'

'Oh, yes. I'd be happy to do that. But what could I do?'

'Can you sew?'

'Yes. Mama taught me. And I can cook, and bake.'

'We'll find you something. And when we do, you can keep a few shillings back from your wages for you and Manny. We won't leave you without something for yourselves.'

'We have some money with us. Mama and Papa made sure we had a little to get started.'

'Keep it. We'll see about getting you a bank account to put it in. It will be safer.'

'We're allowed a bank account?'

'Oh, yes. The British are very fair, but we might have to wait until we have been released.'

'People on the boat said it was terrible being sent here. That we would be in prison, just like we would be in Germany.'

'It was bad for a while,' the older woman admitted, 'when we were sent here at first.'

'How long have you been here?'

'We arrived in England in December '37. We could see the way things were going in

Germany and, back then, we were welcomed here. We got jobs, most families found homes to rent, or lived with relatives. Others, like us, found warm-hearted British Jews who opened their homes to strangers until we found our feet. Some of the Jews we came over with even got employment again as teachers, or doctors, or nurses, jobs that had been denied to them in Germany for years.'

'What about the language?' Ruth said. 'I went to English lessons in Kiel, but I couldn't make myself understood very well when we arrived.'

'It's the accents, my dear. But stick at it. For the few who spoke good English, it was easier.'

She sighed.

'Then the war came,' she continued. 'There were stories of Jews being traitors and spies in Norway, Holland, and the other countries occupied, assisting the Nazis during the invasion. The British newspapers ran editorial campaigns, demonising German Jews, saying that we were no more trustworthy than the rest of the German people, just because we were Jewish.'

Nazis.

Ruth had heard the term more often since they'd arrived in Britain.

She listened as Gella continued.

'The public were completely ignorant of Hitler's policy of Jewish persecution and, despite a series of tribunals and screenings, where the majority of us were classified as posing no threat, Churchill gave in and ordered us to be interned with the rest of the Germans and Italians.'

She shook her head.

'At first, conditions were terrible. They treated us no better than the Nazis had, kept in prisons, abandoned factories or tents in hastily erected compounds on waste ground. We heard that thousands were deported in ships barely fit for purpose, to Canada and Australia. We were with the first group to be sent here, last May. We walked up the road from the ferry, the locals behind barricades, staring at us as if we were from another planet.'

Ruth looked at Gella Weissberg. She was in her mid-thirties, Ruth supposed, although she could have been younger; her daughters were nine and seven, and Ben, her son, was six.

Like Mama, she has lived with nothing but worry.

'They ringed whole streets of guest houses with barbed wire to keep us in,' Gella continued. 'There were thousands of us around Hutchinson Square, but we were only here a week until they separated the women and children from the men and sent us to a women's camp on the other side of the island, at Rushen. We only got to see our husbands once a month. It was heartbreaking, after having escaped it all in Germany, and elsewhere in Europe, but at least we had work if we wanted it and the good thing was that we were all Jews.'

'Didn't the children miss their fathers?'

'Yes, but they could play on the beach, and in the fields, and the visitors from before the war had left bits and pieces of sports equipment, so they could play games.'

'What about food?'

'We had enough food; the locals helped by supplying fresh fish and dairy produce. The men especially, living in Douglas, got a taste for smoked herrings. The Manx people joked about them, calling them the *Yom Kippers*, and it became the unofficial name for the prisoners of the Hutchinson Square camp.'

Ruth laughed with her new friend, not quite understanding the joke.

'How long was it like that?' Ruth asked.

'Until a month ago. Then they began giving families back apartments in the town. It was heaven, even if each family only had two rooms; any bigger and another family, or parts of families, like you and Manny, would have to share. That's why you are with us.'

'I'm sorry. I know we are an intrusion.'

'You're not. We are lucky to have you. We could have rowdy young men or another couple; a friend of mine can hardly sleep because the husband and wife they have staying with them do nothing but shout at each other. Anyway, you can give me a hand with the children and around the house.'

'I'd be happy to. I'd feel better helping in some way, and I'd be desperate to get a job, but what about my English?'

'There will be someone who speaks the language who will tell you what to do, or you can be like me, and do a little sewing and mending at home, but you'll pick up English in no time at your age, and there are lessons you can go to; the authorities are very keen for us all to learn, though I'm not sure I ever will.'

'And we can go anywhere?'

'Not quite. Our part of the town is barricaded off, but we have greater freedom every week. And they've started releasing people back to the mainland now. There are far less of us here now than there was even a few months ago.'

'So, we may be able to go to England, or Scotland.'

Gella Weissberg glanced at Ruth, a faint smile at the corner of her mouth.

'Scotland?'

Ruth flushed red again.

'It's where we landed. I only saw little bits of it, but I liked it. And the people were nice…'

'Manny told my husband that you'd come from Germany in a sailing boat. I'm guessing you two didn't sail it alone.'

'No… Franz and Johann… well, they're the General's sons, and they…'

Ruth's face crumpled, and large tears began to form in her eyes.

'There, there,' Gella Weissberg said, taking Ruth in her arms.

'I love him,' she said, through the tears, clinging onto a woman she hardly knew. 'And I'll not see him again for the rest of the war; maybe never.'

The older woman held Ruth tight, stroking her hair.

After a minute she pulled away and took Ruth's face in her hands.

'Listen,' she said. 'It will feel like the end of your world, but you are alive and safe; so is Manny, and so are these two boys. This war won't last forever, and you will be together again. Never lose sight of that.'

'I suppose so.' Ruth sniffed, almost managing a grateful smile.

'Now, why don't you tell me all about it. I'm desperate to know who it was, who stole your heart; Franz or Johann.'

Ruth smiled this time.

'Well, when I was a little girl, I wanted nothing more than to marry Johann Kästner one day…'

CHAPTER 181

KIELER MORGENPOST

Thursday 1st May 1941

KINDERLANDVERSCHICKUNG

The first evacuation of children from Kiel to the countryside began today when a train carrying 300 children left Kiel Bahnhof for Bansin, near the town of Swinemünde on the Baltic Sea. In a statement, Mayor Hoffmann said that this was merely a precaution, as the city's air defences, including the many bunkers situated around Kiel, were sufficient to prevent losses within the population. It was, he said, only for the short duration expected before Britain would finally bow to the superiority of the Third Reich and the Luftwaffe and capitulate.

~~o~~

Jakob Teubner hobbled down the steps of the house where services were still held on the Sabbath, when circumstances allowed. He limped slowly along Kleiner Kuhberg to the doorway of number 21. Each neighbouring house held Jews seized from small towns and villages throughout Schleswig-Holstein, awaiting deportation to Poland. There was a steady flow of Jewish families through the building every week.

The Germans reserved number 21 for local Jews and Jakob Teubner shook his head at the German authorities' fondness for segregation and organisation.

The door opened to his knock, and he entered, nodding to the young man who held the door for him, then crossed the hallway and climbed the stairs, grunting with the effort. The after-effects of his beating by the two Gestapo men had left him in more than a little discomfort.

At the top of the stairs, he turned right, and walked along the hallway, before knocking on a familiar door. It opened.

'Jakob,' Emil Liewermann said, hugging the old man, mindful of his damaged ribs.

'Emil, how are you?'

'Better than you, my friend, by the look of you. Still sore, eh?'

'Ach, it's nothing time won't cure. I'm more concerned about you. Are you all ready?'

'Yes. We're packed. A suitcase each. I only hope we have furniture when we get there, or I'll regret leaving all this.'

He swept his arm around the sparsely furnished room. Jakob let out a soft laugh, wary of hurting his chest.

He lowered his eyes.

'I still haven't heard anything from the lawyer,' he said.

'You tried your best, Jakob. The odds were always against them letting Rosa out to come with us. You'll keep trying?'

'You can count on it, as long as I have breath in my body.'

'If she gets out, tell her we are being sent to the ghetto in Łódź, in Poland.' A weary smile crossed Emil's face. 'She would probably be the first Jew applying to go there, but at least we'd be together. I should have a job by then.'

Jakob put a hand on Fischel's head. 'You're a young man now. Help your father as much as you can.'

He turned to Rebeka.

'And you've turned out to be a beautiful young lady and a credit to your mama and your

561

papa.'

'We feel bad about leaving Mama behind,' Rebeka said, a tremor in her voice.

'Oy vey, my girl. She'd want you to go, to make a new life. If she can, she'll join you, I'm sure.'

He turned back to Emil.

'Shalom, my good friend, and may the peace of God go with you. We will drink wine together again when the Nazi scum have been wiped off the face of the earth.'

The two men hugged, neither believing it.

~~o~~

Like most of the Jews deported to ghettos and camps in the east, Emil Liewermann was made to pay for his own transport, prior to embarkation, by a direct money deposit to the SS. It was all part of the *resettlement to work in the East* deception that the German authorities had put in place.

Children under twelve years of age paid half price, and those under four travelled for nothing, but Fischel and Rebeka, being older, were charged an adult tariff.

The SS paid the Reichsbahn four Pfennigs per Jew for each track kilometre they were transported, amounting to a million Reichsmarks every week.

When they got to Łódź, they were housed in a small room, with one bed. Emil gave the bed to his two children, choosing to sleep on the floor, on a quilted blanket he'd managed to purchase on their third day in the ghetto.

It isn't so bad.

CHAPTER 182

Snowgoose, her foresail flapping as her way fell off, glided up to the small stone jetty between Mönkeberg and Kitzeberg. Erich Kästner pushed the tiller over as she came to a halt.

Dieter Maas jumped off and dropped the bow rope over a bollard then walked back and took the stern rope from the General and made it fast too. He stepped back on board and collected the cold beers hanging in a small hessian sack from the midships cleat, just under the water. He opened a bottle and handed it to Erich Kästner, then took one himself.

They'd crossed Kieler Förde on a beam reach from *Snowgoose*'s berth to the rarely used jetty on the east shore, staying silent as the breeze and the yacht's gentle progress through the water cleansed their minds.

Bright sunshine heralded the summer to come but, for the General and the newspaperman, it held no warmth.

'Any news?' Dieter asked.

'None,' the General said. 'It's still too early.'

He knew that it sounded as unconvincing as it felt.

'These things take time,' Dieter Maas said, putting a hand on the General's shoulder. 'Don't give up on them.'

'I haven't given up,' the General said, 'although, at times, it's difficult not to think the worst.'

He let out a sigh.

'How about you?' he asked. 'What are you writing about these days?'

'More deportations. Kleiner Kuhberg bursting at the seams with Jews from all over Schleswig-Holstein. Very few local Jews are still in their own homes, and Jewish houses that have been vacated are being bought up at ridiculously low prices by senior party members; Hinrich Lohse and your friend Herr Hoffmann, our honourable mayor, are amassing quite a property empire.'

The General let out a bitter laugh.

'I hear Herr and Frau Kartoffelkopf are moving out to Düsternbrook, to a large house that has recently come onto the market when its occupants relocated to Poland.'

Dieter Maas laughed.

'Calling the esteemed Mayor and his wife by their *potato-head* moniker will get you arrested,' he said. 'Even the children have stopped calling them that, on pain-of-death warnings from their parents.'

'Talking of children,' the General said. 'Did you see the front page of today's Morgenpost? This *Kinderlandverschickung* business. Are our esteemed leaders getting worried that the *beaten* English will continue to rain bombs down on our city?'

Dieter Maas smiled grimly.

'There's more to it than meets the eye,' he said.

The General raised a questioning eyebrow but said nothing, waiting for the KJF's editor to speak.

'Around half the children being evacuated are going to relatives in rural areas in Germany,' Dieter continued. 'The others are being sent to KLV camps.'

'KLV?' the General said, puzzled. He looked at Dieter Maas and saw his smile.

'Ah,' he said. 'Kinderlandverschickung. KLV. I didn't know about the camps.'

'Guess who's running them?'

'The NSDAP?'

'Close. The Hitlerjugend. The children are being sent there for three to six months, until the bombing ceases. During that time, they will attend *special* classes, I've heard.'

The General shook his head. *The Hitler Youth, and young, impressionable children.*

'There's no end to their ingenuity, is there?'

'No. The parents agree, for the children's safety; they're removed from their influence, and it's easy to indoctrinate them with National Socialist dogma. It's like an extended Hitlerjugend camp for early years.'

'They'll destroy the childhood of every boy and girl in Germany.'

'Yes. And it's indefinite, as far as I can see, unless the British are crushed by the bombing of London, Liverpool and Glasgow, and their other large cities.'

'How do you know about this, Dieter? I mean, who are you talking to?'

Dieter Maas shrugged.

'I'm like a priest. If people wish to tell me things, to get it off their chests, I'm happy to listen.'

'And you don't have the sanctity of the confessional to worry about.' The General laughed.

'No, but I am careful what I do with it. Most of the stuff, I pass on to you alone. Rarely does something appear in print, and only when it concerns my readership.'

'That's sensible.'

'They will be gone in six months anyway,' he said, his eyes clouding. 'We won't have to worry about it anymore.'

The General closed his eyes and shook his head.

'All of them?'

'Yes. I'm sorry.'

'No news from the Haganah?'

'No. They will contact you directly, if at all. They are finding it almost impossible.'

A flock of geese took off from the water with a commotion of sound, and the two men stopped to watch them wheel round, heading for the Schwentine.

'What will you do?' the General said, breaking the silence.

'Perhaps I should relocate to Poland. I'd have the largest circulation of any newspaper in the Third Reich.'

Erich Kästner laughed.

Dieter Maas bowed his head and continued.

'It will only be for a while, I fear. I gather that the death rate in the camps is soaring, and that massive expansion of the camp system is planned, with crematoria being a vital part of that expansion.'

'I can confirm that. We get a memo every week about a new camp opening, or a camp increasing its capacity, or adding to its... facilities.'

'I heard a rumour that a series of new camps are being planned in the Generalgouvernement area.'

'New camps are springing up all over the Reich.'

'But it's a little convenient, is it not, that they'll be so close to the Polish ghettos?'

The General's face paled.

'You think...?'

'Ask your friend, Canaris. He may be able to find out.'

CHAPTER 183

KIELER MORGENPOST

Friday 9th May 1941

THE TELEMANNSCHE HAUS IS DESTROYED

In the early hours of May 8th, the historic Telemannsche Haus on Haßstraße was destroyed in a raid by RAF Bombers. The Morgenpost deplores the indiscriminate bombing of non-military targets by the British, a deliberate tactic, in the view of the Reich ministry for war.

The Telemannsche Haus, one of the oldest of its type in Kiel, was an exceptionally richly decorated half-timbered building from the 16th century. It was built in 1576. It was a rich part of the city's history.

~~o~~

In the grand scheme of things, the destruction of a house was nothing; it was people's lives that mattered, but as Erich Kästner stood looking at the charred ruins of the Telemannsche Haus, it saddened him. As a child, he'd always pleaded with his parents to stop when they passed the timber-fronted house on their occasional Sunday walks through the old town, staring with a boy's wonder at the ornate carvings and the intricate buttresses of the house's facade.

He stood for a while amid the acrid smell of smoke, then, clearing the memory from his mind, walked on.

~~o~~

Daily Mirror

Tuesday, 13th May 1941

HESS, HITLER'S DEPUTY, LANDS IN BRITAIN

Rudolf Hess, Hitler's deputy, the man who knows Germany's every secret, has landed in Scotland, having flown from Germany in defiance of Hitler's desperate attempts to stop him.

This announcement was made to the pressmen of the world at the Ministry of Information a few moments before midnight last night.

~~o~~

'You see, my dear, I told you.'

Lieutenant Colonel Anthony Plenderleith pointed to the headline in the *Daily Mirror*.

'The Nazi party is falling apart,' he continued. 'The war will be over soon now that they're fighting amongst themselves.'

Marjorie Plenderleith looked at the newspaper and screwed up her face.

'The *Daily Mirror*,' she said. 'It's not *The Times*, is it?'

'It's a British newspaper. It tells the truth, even if the headlines are sometimes a little irritating. I can't convince the local paper shop up here to deliver *The Times*.'

'You should listen to the radio, Anthony. The BBC always report the news very sensibly.'

'Marjorie, you know I can't stand that infernal wireless contraption. I'll stick to the newspaper, even if it has to be the *Mirror*.'

It wasn't entirely true. She often caught him pretending not to listen when she had the set turned on, all the more so if it was news reports being broadcast, or a speech by the prime minister.

She'd never let on that she'd noticed.

'I'm glad, though,' she said, 'that the war will be shorter. The house is nice, but it's a bit grim up here sometimes, compared to home.'

~~o~~

[14/05/1941 Wednesday]

'Damn them all!'

Heinrich Güllich thumped his fist on his desk. Carl Meyer had been expecting the outburst since they'd got into the car. All the way back from the Kriegsmarine victualling yard the Kriminalassistent had fumed silently in the passenger seat.

They'd tracked down and interviewed the marines who had been on duty guarding the yard while *Der Sturmtaucher* had been berthed there, before her departure, bar one. They'd all stuck to the same story; apart from the General and his two sons, and the owner of the boat, Colonel Schneider, the only other two visitors had been the General's daughter and her young cousin. And the children had been seen going in, and coming back out again, even if they'd done so without passes, and without paperwork.

'Captain Hössler, the officer of the watch, got to them all to save his own skin. I'm sure of it.'

'There's still Feldwebel Bremer, sir. He's serving in the far north of Norway.'

'He'll be no better, you fool. And he might not be back here for months.'

'Our man in Narvik will interview him in the meantime, sir, when his ship docks.'

'He'll get nothing. Even so, we will interview Bremer when he gets back on leave. And I want to talk to Colonel Schneider. He's lost his boat; he might be keen to discover a few unsavoury truths about the General and his sons.'

The Kriminalassistent paced around the room, dragging hard on his cigarette.

'What about the boy, sir?'

'What boy?' Heinrich Güllich snarled.

'The General's nephew. He's close in age to Manny Nussbaum.'

'We can't talk to him, or his parents. The boy's father has connections high up in the party. They would kick up a fuss, and you and I would be freezing our testicles off in some godforsaken corner of Norway.'

'I suppose you're right, sir.'

'I know I'm right, but we need something, Meyer, to put a bit of pressure on them.'

Carl Meyer took a deep breath.

'I have an idea, sir.'

Heinrich Güllich turned and looked at him.

'Go on,' he said, in an ominous tone that told the younger man that his suggestion had better be good.

'I have a couple of informants who would be willing to swear they saw the Nussbaum brats getting on the boat.'

'In the naval yard? How the devil would they have seen them there?'

'It doesn't have to be at the yard, sir; anywhere would do. And if we had *new* evidence, it would allow us to investigate further.'

'It wouldn't stand up to scrutiny.'

'It only has to be for a few hours, until we could get the Jews in for a thorough interrogation.'

Heinrich Güllich sat for a while, thinking.

'Bring me a map,' he said.

'Where for, sir?'

'North of Kiel. Between here and Eckernförde. And get hold of these two informants of yours.'

CHAPTER 184

Berliner Kreiszeitung

Wednesday, 14th May 1941

HESS FLIGHT LANDS IN ENGLAND

- Deputy Führer captured

~~o~~

The General smiled.

For once, a little piece of good news. Perhaps Hess's unscheduled flight to Britain will destroy a little of Hitler's invincibility.

Dieter Maas had handed him a copy of the Berlin newspaper when they'd met at the boat the evening before.

He'd already heard, in a memo from Canaris the day after Hess's Messerschmidt had crashed, stating that Hitler's deputy had bailed out when his fuel ran out. And that it was in Scotland, not England.

Everyone at Naval Headquarters was talking about it, asking each other what it meant.

The official line was that Hess had suffered some form of mental illness, and that the flight to Scotland was the act of an insane person.

The General wasn't convinced, but he was sure Canaris would enlighten him when they next met.

~~o~~

[21/05/1941 Wednesday]

'I'm sorry, Manny. I'm truly sorry, but we can't.'

'Why not? I heard the other boys saying we could.'

'It would cause untold problems for Mama and Papa, not to mention the General and the rest of the Kästner family.'

'But if they knew we were safe, it would mean the world to them.'

Manny had come to Ruth, asking her to write a letter home because he'd heard one of the boys at the makeshift school he attended talking about it. It was something to do with the Red Cross.

'Franz and Johann told us that we shouldn't,' Ruth said. 'That it would be dangerous for everyone at Drachensee. Anyway, as prisoners of war, they will be permitted to write home and they have ways of letting the General know that we are safe. He will pass it on to Mama and Papa.'

'I miss them so,' Manny said, dropping his head into his hands. 'I just thought…'

She put her arm around his shoulder.

'Franz told me that when a soldier is taken prisoner, the nation that captures them has to inform their home country that they are in captivity. Franz and Johann swapped middle names when they spoke to the captain on the ship, so the General will know that we have reached Britain.'

'I didn't even notice,' Manny said.

'Neither did I,' she said, smiling. 'I was all over the place; happy to be safe but sad knowing that we'd not see Franz or Johann again for a long while.'

'You miss him, don't you?'

'Yes. As much as Mama and Papa, if that's possible.'

'I miss Johann too. He was the best of friends to me.'

Ruth smiled. Despite Johann and Manny's age difference, it was the truth.

'I know,' she said. 'We'll see them again when this is all over.'

'You miss Antje, too, don't you? I've seen you look at the drawing. The Sturmtaucher.'
She blushed.

'It reminds me of her. She was my best friend, and she meant the world to me, more like a sister. She will be good to Mama and Papa, until they can leave.'

They sat for a while, silent, looking out over the sea, on the bench they'd found the first week they'd been here. They came to it every day when they could find time.

'We must practise our English now,' she said, and Manny groaned.

'I'd rather speak German,' he said.

'I know, and we can, for a while. But it's important that we become fluent in English, for when we go to the mainland. We can get jobs and find somewhere to live.'

'But after the war, we don't need to live here. I want to go to Palestine and visit Moshe. Mama and Papa will be there. We must keep learning Hebrew.'

'Learn English first,' she said, but seeing the disappointment in his eyes, she relented.

'Learn both,' she said. 'I'm sure there are people here who would be more than willing to teach you. We have a little money if it costs anything.'

'I'll get a job to pay for it,' he said, the excitement lighting up his face.

'As long as you keep practising English,' she said, stern again.

He laughed. 'You look like Mama when you frown like that.'

She smiled.

'What did you do at school today?'

'Maths and science,' Manny said, his eyes widening. 'Herr Toderman is a good teacher.'

'It sounds marvellous,' she said, wishing she could have gone with him. But she was too old, and she needed to work. The only lessons she attended were the English classes in the evening. To her surprise, she found that she was enjoying them immensely.

'There are classes preparing people for university, you know,' Manny said, looking up at her hopefully.

'I don't have time. The bakery is busy, and it helps Frau Weissberg, the extra money. And don't forget, we can save too. We will need it.'

They both had jobs. Manny delivered bundles of chopped sticks for an hour after he finished school, and Ruth baked scones and cakes at a local bakery. The pay wasn't much, but it made them feel that they were contributing to the household.

'Perhaps, after the war, we can both go to college, or university,' she said.

~~o~~

[21/05/1941 Wednesday]

Werner Schmidt took a long draw of his cigarette and looked at the papers in front of him. The evidence was all circumstantial, but Heinrich Güllich had a way of making it sound compelling.

'And these new witnesses; they're reliable?'

'Yes. A hundred per cent. The children were seen getting into a rowing boat at a jetty at Surendorf.'

'That's around the coast from Strande.'

'Yes. Outside Kieler Förde, and after they'd passed the barrier.'

'We asked along the coast if anyone had seen the yacht. No one had.'

'You read the statements. They stayed well offshore and rowed in for them.'

'It would have taken time. An hour or more. Someone would have seen the yacht.'

'They did. Our witnesses.'

'But the people we talked to were there most of that day. They saw nothing.'

'We'll go back and ask them again,' Heinrich Güllich snapped. 'Show them this evidence. Tell them this is now a Gestapo investigation. I'm sure their memory will improve.'

Werner Schmidt shrugged. Without this, he couldn't see any other way the Nussbaums' offspring had managed to get out of Kiel.

'All right. So, they got on the boat. Where are they now?'

'Denmark, if we're lucky, but more likely Sweden, we think.'

'I thought your men were looking?'

'Yes, but it's a large country, and there are few of them on the ground. The Swedes will provide limited cooperation, but I doubt they'll go out of their way.'

'So why not just wait?'

'Because they might never be found. And in the meantime, these Judenschweine are laughing at us all, and the General believes he has won, that he is untouchable.'

'So, what do you want from me?'

'We can't go near them, even with this evidence,' the Gestapo man said, 'but you can.'

'How?'

Heinrich Güllich pulled out a copy of the *Kieler Jüdisches Freiheitsnachrichtenblatt* and laid it on top of the OrPo detective's desk.

'That might work,' Werner Schmidt said, 'but it's risky. We need to get them out while the General is at work, and the wife is away. And I don't have the manpower to keep watch on them.'

'We'll put a man at the General's house. Once the daughters are at college, or wherever they go, and the driver has taken Frau Kästner to one of her social events, we'll call you. But be ready to move at once. And when you arrest them, don't bring them here.'

'Where, then?'

'The courthouse. On Harmsstraße. We'll sort out a room. We have a good relationship with the district judges.'

Werner Schmidt watched the Gestapo man smile and shivered a little.

'And you wish me to interview them?'

'It might help to soften them up for our interrogation.'

'We might not be able to keep them.'

'We will if they talk. And in the unlikely event they don't, we can dump them somewhere. They won't be in our custody, but the General will have to find them.'

Werner Schmidt hoped they talked, then they'd be out of his hair forever.

~~o~~

[23/05/1941 Friday]

'These aliens are hard workers. They dinnae shirk.'

'I suppose they have nothing else tae dae. Nae families, as far as ah ken.'

'It must be lonely for them, up in thon camp oot at Cultybraggan Farm. Ye very rarely see any o' them in Comrie.'

'They don't have much English. And maybe they're no allowed intae toon.'

'Bobby that works at the sawmill says only the foremen speak English.'

'A cannae understand why they'd want to come all the way up here to work.'

'They say they're all Jews. Prisoners. From Germany and Austria.'

'They don't look like prisoners. I suppose they must have their reasons, for there to be so many of them.'

'Whitever. The place is going up fast. They have a wheen of huts built already, and they watchtower things.'

'Aye, it's a bit different from the camp in the village. A lot mair security. We must be getting Nazis. They wouldnae do it for the Italians, from what I've heard.'

'Well, as long as they keep them locked up, I dinnae mind.'

~~o~~

Manny thought for a moment that he was back on the boat. Something had woken him. He opened his eyes and saw the first grey of morning light seeping through a crack in the curtains, just revealing the faded, flowery wallpaper on the bedroom wall. He listened, then sat up in bed and lowered his feet onto the cold wooden floor. He found the cloth slippers Ruth had made for him and slipped them on.

Padding across the floor, he heard it again. It was someone being sick, but whoever it was, they were trying to make as little noise as possible. Ben was still sound asleep in his bed, so he opened the door, careful to be quiet, and listened in the hallway. Across from him, the bathroom door was closed, and he heard another soft retch.

He recognised the sound; he'd heard it often enough on the boat.

Ruth.

He waited at his bedroom door, and heard the sink running. A minute later, the door opened, and she appeared, her face pale. She frowned when she saw him but gave him a wan smile.

'Seasick again?' he whispered.

She shook her head and tried to laugh.

'No. I must have picked up a bug. I'll be all right.'

'Will you be able to go to work?'

'Yes. I'll be fine. Go back to bed for an hour.'

He went to close the door, then turned round.

'Happy birthday,' he said. 'Wait here.'

He disappeared for a second, then returned with a small package, wrapped in brown paper, tied with sisal string. He handed it to her.

'I'm sorry. I kept a little back from my wages,' he said.

She turned away. He didn't see the tear that fell down her cheek. She untied the string and unwrapped the paper, taking care not to rip it.

'Oh, Manny. It's beautiful.' She held up a bone-handled hairbrush to admire it.

'It's not new,' he said, 'but I cleaned it thoroughly as soon as I bought it. Your hair will soon grow in.'

'I love it,' she said, looking at herself in the small bathroom mirror.

Her hair had grown in a little, but it was still short.

'Thank you,' she said, giving him a hug. 'Go back to bed. I'll be fine by breakfast.'

CHAPTER 185

[23/05/1941 Friday]

Werner Schmidt waited forty-eight hours for the phone call. It came from Carl Meyer.

'Frau Kästner and the driver have just left. Both daughters have left. The General is in a meeting at Naval HQ.'

He put down the phone and nodded to the sergeant and three constables he'd assigned to the task.

~~o~~

They gave neither of the Nussbaums a chance to get to the phone. Werner Schmidt looked at his watch, then through the window at Miriam Nussbaum, working in the kitchen. At the precise time the sergeant pressed the doorbell at the front of the house, he opened the back door and stepped into the kitchen.

He saw her look at the row of bells above the door to the hallway, confused, then at him, then she rested both her hands on the table and bowed her head.

Slipping the handcuffs on, he heard Yosef Nussbaum answer the front door, and the rumble of the sergeant's voice. Werner Schmidt led Miriam through to the hallway to join her now similarly handcuffed husband.

On the way out, Werner Schmidt saw Yosef glance at the telephone.

He smiled. *It might as well be a million kilometres away.*

~~o~~

They were taken to the basement of the courthouse on Harmsstraße. One at a time, they were hauled from their small, airless cells and interrogated in the interview room next door.

For the first hour, Werner Schmidt was given the task of trying to break down the Nussbaums' obdurate adherence to their stories, but they were either telling the truth, which he doubted, or had come to believe their own version of events.

He began by showing them the copy of the *Kieler Jüdisches Freiheitsnachrichtenblatt*. 'We found this in your house.'

'No,' Yosef said, shaking his head. 'We have no copies of the KJF in our house. How would we get it? We have no contact with anyone.'

'How do you suppose it got there?'

'Ask your friends in the Gestapo. I'm sure they're around somewhere.'

'You do realise you can both be sent to a camp, or worse, just for having a copy of this?' Yosef bowed his head.

'Yes. But I can only repeat that I have never seen it. Whether or not you choose to believe me is beyond my control.'

The policeman changed tack.

'We have witnesses who place Ruth and Manny at Surendorf, a few hours after the General's sons left Kieler Förde.'

He showed Yosef the statements from the Gestapo's new witnesses. Instead of the dread that he'd been expecting, he saw Yosef Nussbaum's face relax a little.

'No. They're lying,' he said. 'Ruth and Manny went missing days after the boys left. It couldn't have been them.'

'You do realise this evidence convicts you of conspiracy in an illegal act. It also involves your employer facing the same charges.'

'I didn't read of any mention of General Kästner in the statement. Nor of anyone connected with the General, or his family.'

It had been a mistake, Werner Schmidt realised, to show Yosef Nussbaum the statement. Although it could seal the Nussbaums' fate, it also told the Jew that the police, and the Gestapo, were desperately clutching at straws, if there were no substance to it. And the General might just have enough influence to have a judge dismiss it as an obvious fabrication.

And Yosef Nussbaum was right. The statement made no reference to the Kästners.

Heinrich Güllich had been careful not to include any of them in the statement, knowing that his boss would come down hard on him if he so much as mentioned them.

He knew that the Gestapo man would be listening, but he didn't care.

He lit a cigarette and blew a column of smoke into the air.

'Jew,' he said, 'You do know that if you don't tell me where your children are, others will come and interrogate you?'

'Yes. I can only tell them what I've told you. Do you want me to make up a story?'

'And you wish them to interrogate your wife?'

'They will do what they will, whatever I say.'

Werner Schmidt shook his head and nodded to the constable.

'Take him back. Bring the woman.'

Almost word for word, Miriam Nussbaum's interview echoed her husband's.

This time, he kept a close watch when he handed over the witness statements.

She smiled. It wasn't much, but she definitely smiled. The witnesses are lying.

A cold fury took hold of him, and he left the room.

Heinrich Güllich met him in the corridor.

'You can have them. They deserve it.'

The Gestapo man grinned and put his arm on the policeman's shoulder.

'Stay,' he said. 'You may learn a lot.'

~~o~~

For Carl Meyer, it was fascinating, if frustrating to watch.

Heinrich Güllich ran through the same questions the policeman had asked. Both Nussbaums stuck to the same story.

'Tie her legs,' he said, cursing, when Miriam repeated the now familiar answers, yet again.

Carl Meyer picked up a length of rope from a box in the corner and tied Miriam's ankles to the legs of the chair.

'You can do what you like to me,' she said. 'I can only tell you what I know.'

'Oh, I don't expect you to tell me,' Heinrich Güllich said. 'I'll be asking your husband the questions.'

Carl Meyer smiled and fetched Yosef.

~~o~~

For the next hour, they made Yosef watch, asking him questions while Miriam writhed and groaned. Blood ran from her nose and from the corner of her mouth, until she slumped forward, breathing heavily, almost unconscious.

Manny. Ruth. The Kästner boys. Der Sturmtaucher. The General. The General's friends. The KJF and its new editor. The Weichmanns' money. The Haganah. Esther and Itsik. Jakob Teubner.

Tears ran down Yosef's cheeks with every blow, but his answers remained the same.

My children are missing. The General and his sons haven't spirited them away. We know nothing of the KJF or the money. Jakob, Itsik and Eshter are just friends.

Then they started on him.

They hit him harder, for longer. They poured cold water on Miriam's face to rouse her and make her watch. They asked her the same questions again.

But they'd agreed. No matter what, they would stick to their story.

As the afternoon wore on, there was a knock at the door.

Werner Schmidt crossed to the door and went into the corridor. When he came back, his face had drained of colour.

He motioned for Heinrich Güllich to come outside with him.

Through swollen eyelids, Yosef watched him go. He looked across at Miriam, slumped forward again, and mumbled a prayer.

~~o~~

In the corridor, Heinrich Güllich glared at the detective.

573

'What's wrong?'

'General Kästner is at Police Headquarters. Talking to the chief. I've been told to get them out of here now, and to make sure no one sees them.'

He nodded towards the room the Nussbaums were in.

Heinrich Güllich looked at them. Neither had broken yet. He was sure they would, but he needed more time.

How the hell had the General discovered they'd been arrested so quickly?

'We can't take them to headquarters,' he heard Carl Meyer say. 'The Kriminaldirektor will have our necks.'

He hadn't even noticed his underling listening in.

Heinrich Güllich looked at Werner Schmidt.

'One of your police stations. Can we put them in a cell?'

'No,' the policeman said, shaking his head. 'Not looking like that.'

He nodded to the Nussbaums.

The Jewish couple looked a sorry sight, bruised and bloodied. Yosef's breath rasped, his hair was matted with blood, and Miriam looked no better. One eye was barely open and her face was a florid mess. Her left arm hung limply, still held by the handcuffs to the chair. She sat in a pool of blood, which fell to the floor in a steady drip.

'They're not going to talk anyway, without some specialised tools,' Heinrich Güllich said.

Werner Schmidt paled again, and Carl Meyer laughed.

'It's amazing what a few volts of electricity will do, or a little dental work,' he said, grinning.

'We should just kill them,' Heinrich Güllich said. 'Dump their bodies where they'll never be found. That would eat away at their Jew-loving employer.'

He knew he wouldn't kill the Nussbaums. He wanted to see their faces when he caught their children and tortured the Jewish brats in front of them.

'Why don't we put them in the Judenhaus to stew for a while,' Carl Meyer said. 'The threat of deportation might loosen their tongues.'

Heinrich Güllich laughed and slapped his junior on the back.

'I like your thinking, Kamerad,' he said.

The two Gestapo men untied the prisoners and hauled Yosef to his feet.

'Walk, Jew,' Heinrich Güllich said.

~~o~~

Yosef looked around as Werner Schmidt and his KriPo constable lifted Miriam, helping her to stand. She leant over and groaned. Beneath her skirt, he noticed blood trickling down the inside of her leg.

They've damaged her, inside.

The two detectives half-carried, half-dragged her to the door, followed by the two Gestapo men, with Yosef between them, pushing him down the corridor. Instead of turning right up the stairs, they turned left until they came to a locked metal security door.

'I'll get the car,' Carl Meyer said.

'No,' Heinrich Güllich said. He turned to Werner Schmidt.

'Use the police van.'

Yosef saw the detective open his mouth to argue, then think better of it.

'Go and get it,' he said to the young detective constable. 'Drive it round here.'

'What about her?' the young KriPo man said, looking at Miriam.

'Let her go. She can sit on the floor,' Carl Meyer said.

The two policemen lowered the now unresponsive Miriam to the ground. The constable looked around at her from the doorway, once, then he was gone.

Five minutes later, they heard the soft squeal of the van's brakes as it reversed down the steeply sloping lane, and its doors opening.

The two Gestapo men pushed Yosef through the doorway and shoved him into the back of the van. He lay on the floor, half-stunned, watching as the two policemen lifted Miriam, one end each, and carried her out, sliding her limp, blood-soaked body beside Yosef.

The last clear thought Yosef remembered before he passed out was that they'd killed her.

~~o~~

'Drop them at the Judenhaus. 25, Kleiner Kuhberg,' Heinrich Güllich said.

'We know where it is,' Werner Schmidt said, tersely. He got into the passenger seat of the van and told his younger colleague to drive.

In the driver's wing mirror, he watched as the Gestapo men walked behind the van, got into their car, and followed them.

He shook his head.

'Sir, I don't like this.'

'Just shut up and drive,' he said. 'And not a word to anyone, do you hear?'

'Yes, sir.'

He pulled out a cigarette, but dropped it into the footwell, cursing. He found it and struck a match, drawing the sweet tobacco smoke into his lungs. He blew out slowly.

Every once in a while, Werner Schmidt had to rough up a suspect to further an investigation, most often when it involved habitual criminals or gang members. For them, it was an occupational hazard, but it was becoming less frequent, as the National Socialists cleansed German society of organised crime and replaced it with state terror.

But Werner Schmidt knew that when he resorted to violence, he used it as a means to an end, and he took no pleasure from it. Going back over the Nussbaums' interrogation in his mind, he couldn't rid himself of the look on Heinrich Güllich's face as he worked on Miriam Nussbaum.

It's like sex for him. He gets off on it.

~~o~~

They dumped the beaten couple at the door of the Judenhaus in Kleiner Kuhberg and rang the doorbell. As they pulled away, half a dozen of the Nussbaums' fellow Jews lifted them inside, and someone ran to fetch Jakob Teubner.

Outside, 100 metres up the street, Heinrich Güllich turned to Carl Meyer, sitting in the driver's seat of the black Gestapo sedan.

'We follow anyone who comes out of the house. Let's see how quickly the General finds his Jews. Is Kriminalassistentanwärter Seidel in position?'

'Yes. There's a lane that runs along the back of the buildings. He's watching where it comes out onto Alte Reihe.'

'Good. Now we wait. Did you see the old Jew go in?'

'Yes, sir.'

'He doesn't move so well, eh? You may have been a little sore on him, the last time we met.'

Carl Meyer laughed but, at the time, he thought he'd gone too far when the old man had started coughing up blood.

'Yes, sir. He'll think twice about trying to be clever the next time.'

'Like the General's Jewish pets, eh?'

Carl Meyer closed his eyes for a moment and drifted back to the interrogation of Yosef and Miriam Nussbaum.

CHAPTER 186

Jakob Teubner felt Miriam's wrist for a pulse. He knew that Yosef was still alive; he could hear the crackle of his breathing as he inhaled and exhaled slowly.

Beneath his fingers, he felt the thin, reedy throb in Miriam's wrist, and he let out a long, slow breath.

'Fetch me water and some antiseptic and keep an eye on them. I'll be back in a minute.'

He left number 25 and returned to the house where he lived, the one with the synagogue. He let himself in. Without giving it a glance, he'd noticed the Gestapo car further up the street, but he didn't think they would bother him.

Yet.

He grimaced.

It makes it difficult to get word to the General.

By the time he reached the top floor, his chest was heaving.

Locking the door, he lifted the corner of the carpet in one of the attic rooms and found the loose floorboard. He located it and, taking his knife from his pocket, unfolded the blade and slipped it into the small gap between the floorboard and the one next to it. He worked it slowly until the board began to rise. He grabbed the end with his fingers and lifted it up, exposing a small space below. He reached his arm in and felt around until he found the cloth-wrapped package and pulled it out.

He extracted eight vials of morphine and a syringe and returned the bundle to its hiding place. He tucked the vials into his underpants, muttering apologies under his breath, and slid the syringe into his sock, on the inside of his calf.

Replacing the board and the carpet, he made his way back to number 25.

'Get me Mordecai,' he said to the young woman who was holding Miriam's hand. Once she'd gone, he removed the vials from his underwear and drew a dose up into the syringe. He injected the contents into Miriam's good arm and filled the syringe again, repeating the treatment for Yosef.

As he hid the syringe and the vials again, a young man, perhaps seventeen or eighteen, came in, followed by the girl who'd gone to fetch him.

'Mordecai, I am going to ask you something, but you can say no. There's a degree of risk involved.'

There was a glint of defiance in the young man's eyes.

'I'll not refuse, you know that.'

'I had to ask,' Jakob said, flashing him a brief smile of thanks.

'I need you to go and tell General Kästner that the Nussbaums are here and need help,' he said. 'Medical help.'

'I'll go. Is he at Drachensee?'

He looked at his watch.

'Yes, he'll be home by now, but the Gestapo are watching. You'll have to use the roof.'

'I've done it before. It will take me a little time.'

'They will be watching the back too.'

The young man shrugged.

'I'll come down on Exerzierplatz. No one will take a second look.'

Jakob looked doubtful.

'Trust me.'

~~o~~

An hour later, the Jewish youth dropped the last few feet to the ground and tied the rope to the railings. He undid the bucket of soapy water tied to his belt and hung it next to the rope, with the wet cloth he'd been carrying.

If anyone had seen him, it was a commonplace sight for a window cleaner to use a rope to climb and clean hard-to-reach windows on the high buildings of central Kiel.

He grinned and slipped into the shadows of the narrow back lanes of the city. It wasn't the first time he'd been a runner for the old man, but this one was riskier than most. He stopped at the corner and looked out. The street was clear.

Two hours later, Mordecai reached the Kästner house and it was another fifteen minutes before he was certain that the place wasn't being watched by the Gestapo, and that the General was home alone. He watched as the General moved from room to room and when he saw him in the kitchen, he tapped a couple of times on the glass of the window and stood flattened against the wall by the door.

~~o~~

The General had got home around six. He'd had a fruitless afternoon, calling at each of the police stations in Kiel, culminating in a short meeting at Police Headquarters with Uwe Müller, the police chief, who assured him that the Nussbaums were not in the custody of the police and warned him again to drop it.

His visit to the Gestapo Headquarters might have unnerved him in other circumstances, but his anger and worry banished any fear the building might have provoked.

To his surprise, the head of the Gestapo, the Kriminaldirektor he'd met at some Kriegsmarine function or another, came down and spoke to him, assuring him that the Nussbaums weren't in the custody of the Geheime Staatspolizei, and that he'd warned his men not to harass the Nussbaums.

'You're quite at liberty to look around if it would help convince you,' the man had said. He appeared to be sincere.

It had only been by luck that the General had called home for lunch. The house had been deserted but the back door lay open. He knew that Maria had a busy day organised, so he hadn't expected to find his wife at home, but he was surprised that the Nussbaums weren't around.

He'd called at the cottage, but they weren't there, and a cursory look around the garden hadn't helped. He'd returned to the kitchen with a creeping sense of dread in his stomach. He'd looked around and noticed small signs of a hasty departure; a bowl on the table with flour and two cracked eggs in it, their shells lying on the worktop, and Miriam's apron discarded on the floor beside the chair.

It had sparked off his desperate afternoon search, but it had got him nowhere.

Now arriving home again, the house was empty, and the car still wasn't in the drive. He presumed that Maria and Eva were visiting the countess, or Maria had gone to one of her interminable ladies' evenings, and Eva was with her aristocratic beau. He was surprised Antje wasn't at home but supposed she was on one of the college's art expeditions.

Had she mentioned something this morning?

He couldn't recall.

~~o~~

The General, at his wits' end, heard the tapping on the window and lifted the pan of frying bacon, potato and onion from the ring, and placed it on the cool part of the range. He walked over to the back door and opened it, peering out into the backyard.

'Hello,' he said, puzzled, seeing no one.

'General, I have a message from Jakob Teubner,' a voice hissed, and he stuck his head out and looked around in the direction it had come from. He saw a slight youth leaning against the wall by the rhododendron bush, trying to make himself invisible.

'Come in,' he said, opening the door wide and glancing around.

'No. It's too risky. I can only stay a minute. The Nussbaums are at the Judenhaus in Kleiner Kuhberg. They need medical help. The Gestapo are watching the building.'

'I'll come right away,' the General said.

'Go in the back way, through the lane off Alte Reihe, but be careful. There's a car there, watching.'

'All right. I'll sort something out. Do you want a lift back to Kleiner Kuhberg?'

There was a moment's silence, then the youth spoke again.

'No. It would be dangerous for you, and for me. I'm safer on my own.'

'All right. You're the best judge of that. Thank you for coming to tell me. I know how

577

risky it is.'

Then he was gone. The General shook his head at the young man's bravery.

As he closed the door and went into the hallway, he heard the crunch of tyres on gravel. He glanced out, worried that someone had followed the Jewish youth, but he saw that it was Albert returning with Maria. He opened the door and watched at the top of the steps as his wife and elder daughter emerged, smiling. Then Antje appeared, with a bored look on her face which brightened when she saw him.

Maria said a terse hello and accepted a kiss on both cheeks. She and Eva stood in the hallway, hanging up their coats, chatting in low tones about the evening.

'Just follow my lead,' the General whispered to Antje, as she passed him.

He waited until they were all in the drawing room, then he spoke to Antje, as if he'd just remembered something.

'There was a message for you, Antje. From…' – he went out and picked up a piece of paper from the hall table – '… from Angelina. She wondered if you would like to go over for a while. Something about a project you were doing together.'

'Oh, yes, I'll call her,' she said, without a flicker of hesitation.

'She said there was no need; you've just to go if you could. I can drop you on the way. I have to go to the office. Something urgent has come in.'

'All right, Papa. I'll tell Albert not to put the car in the garage.'

The General turned to his wife.

'I may be some time,' he said. 'I'll send the car to bring Antje back if I'm going to be late. There's food on the stove if you need it.'

He turned and left before Maria could say anything. Explanations would have to wait for later.

~~o~~

Once in the car, the General instructed Albert to stop at the first telephone kiosk.

'What's going on, Albert?' Antje said, glancing up and down the street.

'I have no idea, Miss Antje. Your father told me to drive.'

She turned and watched as the General finished his conversation and replaced the handset.

'Naval Headquarters,' he said to Albert when he got in.

As they drove northwards through the city, the General spoke to Antje, in quiet but urgent tones.

'The Nussbaums have been arrested, and badly beaten, by the sound of it.'

Antje gasped.

'Where are they?'

'At one of the Kleiner Kuhberg houses.'

'Are we going to fetch them?'

'Yes. Well, I am. You're the decoy. I need someone to distract the Gestapo. Would you do it? They'll not touch you.'

'I'll do it,' she said, without hesitation.

'Here's what I want you to do.'

By the time he'd finished telling her what her part in the Nussbaums' rescue was, they'd reached Kriegsmarine Headquarters.

The General spoke to Albert.

'You don't have to be involved, Albert,' he said, 'if you don't want to, but the Nussbaums are in trouble. I need to get medical attention for them. All I require you and Antje to do is to stop the Gestapo from following me. There shouldn't be any danger. If they stop you, just tell them you were told to drive Fräulein Antje, that you were just doing your job.'

'I don't mind, sir. They deserve their comeuppance, the way they've treated everybody.'

'Good. Thank you. Now, Antje will explain the rest. She knows what I want you to do.'

~~o~~

At that moment, the General's army car pulled up.

'Wait just a minute,' the General said. He got out of the car.

Captain Bauer had rolled the window down. The General glanced around, then leaned over to speak to him.

'I came as soon as I could, sir,' Heinz Bauer said. 'What's this all about?'

'I need your help. The Nussbaums need medical attention. It's critical that we get them to Doctor Speer, but they are being watched by the Gestapo. They want me to make a move and incriminate myself.'

'So how are we going to do it?' he said.

The General was impressed that the young captain didn't flinch or question his involvement.

'We'll use the Abwehr car,' he said. 'Antje is going to act as a decoy. Pray God that it works.'

The General returned to where Albert and Antje waited. She opened the door.

'Half an hour should be fine,' he said. 'Then go home and stay there.'

He kissed Antje's cheek and watched as the car pulled away from the kerb, then got into the back of the Abwehr car. Neither man spoke.

After five minutes, as darkness was beginning to fall, the General leaned forward and told him to make his way to Exerzierplatz.

'Take your time though,' he said.

CHAPTER 187

Antje saw the Gestapo man sitting in the car as they passed it on Alte Reihe. Albert turned the car into the narrow lane that gave access to the backyards of the Judenhaus, and the other houses in the row. Antje got out and, as Albert turned the car, she ran up to the back door of number 25 and knocked.

It opened, and Jakob Teubner ushered her in.

'Have the Nussbaums ready to go in five minutes,' she said, then walked back out to the car.

'Drive on, Albert,' she said. 'I hope this works.'

They made it easy for the Gestapo man to follow them by turning left onto Alte Reihe, Albert watching the black car pulling out to follow them in his mirror.

'They've taken the bait, Miss Antje,' he said.

As they reached Großer Kuhberg, they turned left and crossed Holstenstraße onto Klinke, then onto Sophienblatt, towards the railway station.

'Do you think the Gestapo cars have radios?' Antje asked.

'I wouldn't know,' Albert said, 'But I would have thought so. I read that they were to be fitted to all police cars.'

He looked again in his rear-view mirror.

'He's still following,' he said.

'Turn left after the station and head for Wellingdorf,' Antje said. 'We need to waste a little time before going back home.'

She had been going to tell him to drive slowly, but she allowed herself the ghost of a smile as the car crept along the deserted streets.

Albert doesn't do fast.

~~o~~

Albert was correct. Most police cars were fitted with two-way radios, but not all Gestapo cars had them; the car Heinrich Güllich sat in did have a radio, but the one following Albert and Antje didn't. Before it pulled away from the kerb, a second man, unseen by Antje and Albert, had jumped out. He'd hurried around the corner into Kleiner Kuhberg and got into the back of the car Heinrich Güllich and Carl Meyer were sitting in, watching the front of the Judenhaus.

'Well?' Heinrich Güllich had said, stubbing out his cigarette in the ashtray.

'The General's car entered the back lane of the Judenhaus five minutes ago, sir,' the young Kriminalassistentanwärter wheezed, out of breath. 'It left a few minutes later.'

'Are you sure it was the General's car?'

'Yes. The number plate matched the one you gave us.'

'Did you see which direction it went?'

'Yes. It was heading eastwards along Alte Reihe, towards the waterfront. Kriminalassistentanwärter Seidel says he will phone into headquarters when they reach wherever they are going. HQ will pass on the message.'

'Good. He knows not to do something stupid, like try and arrest them, doesn't he?'

'Yes. He said he'd just watch them until you arrive.'

'Excellent. I want to see who General Kästner involves in his attempt to help his Jewish rats. I suspect that Speer fellow, the doctor, will be one. If he takes them for any medical assistance, he is breaking the law. They both are.'

'He'll take them back to Drachensee, surely,' Carl Meyer said.

'He might, but I doubt even he is that stupid. I think he'll take them to the doctor's surgery, or even the house of one of his friends, rather than bring the doctor to his own house, and risk his family's involvement.'

'But he's arrogant, sir, he believes he's untouchable.'

'You might yet be proved right, Kamerad,' Heinrich Güllich said. 'We'll wait and see. It shouldn't be long now. Now how does this damn thing work?'

The radio was in the back; the centre portion of the seat had been removed to accommodate it.

'It's switched on, sir,' Carl Meyer said. 'You'll hear the call coming in. To talk back to them, wait until they say *over*, then press the button to speak.'

'We've never needed them much, but I could see that it would be useful if Kriminalassistentanwärter Seidel had one in his car too. I don't see why all Gestapo vehicles aren't equipped with them.'

'It's all about prioritisation, sir. Since the war began, the focus has been on the military. They need them more than we do, I'm told.'

'Ha. The Wehrmacht. If we don't safeguard our leaders, and make the country safe for decent, true Germans, they won't have anything worth fighting for.'

'I suppose you're right, sir.'

Carl Meyer glanced at the dials of the radio and twiddled the knob to make sure it was working. A blast of interference made the three men flinch, and Carl Meyer hurriedly turned down the squelch control again.

'I thought Kamerad Seidel would have telephoned by now,' he said.

Heinrich Güllich looked at his watch and frowned. Both Doctor Speer's surgery and the Drachensee house were no more than ten minutes by car.

'He's maybe trying to throw off Kriminalassistentanwärter Seidel,' Carl Meyer said. 'If he loses him, should we send a car to both places?'

'Yes. Good thinking. Do that now, just in case. And Kriminalassistentanwärter Seidel will have his testicles served to him in a rich gravy, with mustard, if he has lost him.'

The two junior men laughed, but it was a nervous laugh. Heinrich Güllich's mood could turn in an instant.

~~o~~

Captain Bauer doused his lights and waited until the two cars had passed, then pulled away, turning into Alte Reihe, then into the lane that Albert and Antje had not long exited. As his daughter had done a few minutes earlier, the General jumped out while the captain turned the car. The door opened immediately and two figures, wrapped in blankets, were carried out and placed in the back seats. The General sat between them, an arm around each to prevent them falling over.

'Where to, sir? Doctor Speer's surgery?'

'No. He's not there. His wife told me he was called to the naval hospital at Wik three days ago. He hasn't been home since. He covers for them, occasionally, when they're overwhelmed, as well as helping out at the civilian hospital. They're very busy at the moment.'

'Ah. Is it the wounded from the *Friedrich Eckoldt*, sir?'

Destroyer Z16, the *Friedrich Eckoldt*, had docked at Kiel three days before, badly damaged by a torpedo bomber while patrolling the western end of the Skagerrak. The strike had breached one of the oil tanks, leading to an inferno in the lower decks. She had limped back to Kiel for extensive repairs and to discharge her injured crew to the waiting medical teams at the naval hospital.

'Yes. They say there were sixty or seventy severely burned men, and a stack of less serious injuries. They called in a number of civilian doctors to help out.'

Dr. Speer had been one of them, working day and night like the others, snatching brief naps when he could, on a cot in a storeroom.

~~o~~

It was there, after only an hour's sleep, that Hermann Speer was shaken awake by an orderly.

'Doctor, you're needed in the triage ward. Two new patients for you.'

'Can someone else not see them? I'm dead on my feet.'

'A Captain Bauer asked for you specifically.'

'I don't know anything about it, and I certainly don't know this Captain Bau…'

He stopped and sat up.

Heinz Bauer. The young man who sailed with us. He serves under Erich.

He swung his legs out of the bed.

Two patients? What was Erich up to?

He hurried down the corridor, wide awake now.

The Nussbaums. It must be.

He reached the doors at the bottom and turned left, into the area where military ambulances dropped off wounded personnel to be assessed.

He saw the young captain standing by the doorway. One of the marines guarding the military hospital stood next to him.

'Captain Bauer,' he said, striding toward the young Abwehr man.

'Doctor Speer. I'm glad to see you.'

'Where's General Kästner?'

'Outside. In the car. We have two Abwehr informants who have been... um... injured. They are in urgent need of medical attention, but secrecy is of prime importance. The General has already cleared it with base security.'

'I see. I'll have a room prepared for them, and send a few orderlies out with a couple of gurneys, after I've assessed the patients.'

He gave his instructions to one of the nurses, then pushed his way through the doors.

He could see Erich Kästner sitting in the back of the car and gave him a nod. He opened the back door on the nearside and looked in.

'You're taking an enormous risk, bringing them here,' he said, nodding at the Nussbaums.

'It's the last place they'll look,' the General said, 'And I have some authority here, at least for now. They'll do as I ask, within reason.'

Doctor Speer smiled.

'Telling security that they were Abwehr informants was a touch of genius, I'll give you that, but it may be difficult to keep under wraps; we'll need nursing staff who will be discreet, and you'll have to convince the hospital's commanding officer that these two are who you say they are.'

'I've thought about it; both are achievable. They'll only be here for a couple of days. Once they're better, the Gestapo will be powerless to do anything. Their intention was to catch us in the act of getting medical help for the Nussbaums.'

Doctor Speer shook his head and held his finger up to his lips.

'Don't use their real names anywhere in the hospital,' he said, his voice quiet but firm. 'What are the Abwehr calling them?'

'Johann Schmidt and Hanne Schmidt,' the General said. *John and Jane Smith.*

While he spoke, Doctor Speer examined Yosef.

'Please check Miriam first, Doctor,' Yosef croaked. 'Her injuries are worse than mine.'

His rasping voice was difficult to make out, but Hermann Speer recognised the desperate pleading in it. He moved round to the other side of the car and opened the door.

It wasn't just chivalry on Yosef Nussbaum's part. The medic could see that Miriam's condition was far graver than that of her husband.

'They've both had morphine,' the General said. He handed Doctor Speer a bit of paper. 'Here are the doses, and the times that they were given.'

Doctor Speer glanced at it and put it in his white coat pocket.

'It will be better if you're not seen here. Your face is too well known. I'll contact you when I know something. Leave your captain here to complete the paperwork. I presume he has been briefed?'

'Yes. Thank you, Doc.'

'We may be sharing a cell at Gestapo Headquarters before the week is out.'

'No. The navy will close ranks, as long as we can keep them convinced of our cover story. I'll keep the Gestapo at bay until the Nussbaums are well enough to go home.'

'It's not just that. You will have to get them out of Germany. As soon as they're well.'

'I know. It's not easy, but we're leaving no stone unturned.'

'I understand, my friend,' the doctor said, putting his hand on the General's shoulder. 'Now, leave them with me. The captain will contact you later, or even tomorrow. Yes. That would be better.'

The General nodded and climbed into the front seat.

He wound down the window.

'I hope I can drive this thing,' he said.
The doctor smiled and disappeared inside.
The General wouldn't see the Nussbaums again for seven days.

CHAPTER 188

Carl Meyer flinched as Heinrich Güllich stormed around his office, like a bear in a zoo, cursing the Nussbaums, the General, his family, his driver and the Gestapo's own men who had screwed up.

But most of all, he cursed himself.

'Verdammte Dummkopf. She was a decoy. Her and that tame, traitorous driver of theirs. I should have known.'

He kicked the waste bin across the room.

They'd waited half an hour before the crackled message came over the radio that the General's car was at the Kästner's Drachensee home. Relieved, they'd rushed there to find two Gestapo cars and an apprehensive Kriminalassistentanwärter Seidel pacing the pavement outside. Even in the dim glow of a street lamp fifty metres away, Carl Meyer could see that the young man's face was grey, and beads of sweat coalesced on his brow.

'Are they inside?' Heinrich Güllich had hissed.

'No, sir. I followed the car past the shipyards, through Ellerbek and out to Mönkeberg. They made a couple of stops on the way, but no one got in or out. They then retraced their route and headed back across to the other side of Kieler Hafen.'

'It took them that long to come here?' the Kriminalassistent had said, his voice full of menace.

'No, sir. They drove out towards Russee, then cut across to Mielkendorf. They stopped there briefly, outside a house in Dorfstraße, then headed back here past Schulensee.'

'And?'

'The daughter and the driver got out of the car and went into the Kästner house.'

'And no one else was in the car?'

'No. I waited a few minutes to see if someone would come out to help them, then I crept in and had a look. The car was empty.'

'Are you a hundred per cent sure that no one got in or out at any of the stops the car made?'

'I'm sure. I had a good view of the car at all times.'

'Did they see you?'

'No, I don't think so. I didn't use my headlights and I kept far enough back.'

'Get back in the car,' Heinrich Güllich had said. 'We'll go to the doctor's surgery.'

But it had been fruitless. There were no signs of life. They'd shone their torches through the windows, but the place was deserted.

Heinrich Güllich had waited until he was back in his office before exploding. By then, he'd dismissed the still-sweating Seidel and his companions; only Carl Meyer remained.

'We underestimated the Judenknecht,' the Kriminalassistent said when he'd calmed down a little, his head bowed but his eyes still bulging with anger. 'Where could he have taken them?'

'One of those friends of his, sir? Oskar von Friedeburg; he has properties everywhere.' Heinrich Güllich glanced up.

'Good thinking, Meyer. We'll get a list of the man's holdings in the morning and check them out. We'll have to be careful about it though. He has numerous friends in the party, and we don't want the Kriminaldirektor getting wind of it.'

'Will he not wipe the floor with us about the Nussbaums anyway?' Carl Meyer said, resigned to spending the rest of his career in the remotest Gestapo posting in the Reich.

'Not necessarily. We were careful that no one was there when we seized the Nussbaums from the General's house, and we didn't take them to headquarters or to any of the police stations. There will be no record of our using the room at the courthouse; the judge will make sure of that. We'll just deny it and say they must have taken a stroll and been beaten up by justifiably enraged citizens who took exception to Jewish scum walking around as if they owned the place.'

Carl Meyer laughed, despite his concern.

'It might work, sir.'

'In the meantime, we'll check out the rest of the General's friends. That Maas fellow. He's very cosy with him, and I suppose the doctor could have taken them to another clinic. Make sure we check them all out.'

'Yes, sir. Do we keep tabs on the General?'

'Meyer, you surprise me. You're beginning to think like an investigator. Why did you suggest that?'

'He might lead us to where he has hidden them. Then we can get them together, hopefully with the doctor.'

'Well done, Meyer. It's a pity these two Dummköpfe aren't as sharp as you.'

Carl Meyer checked for a sarcastic tone in his boss's voice but was surprised that his praise appeared to be genuine.

'Put them on the General,' the Kriminalassistent said, 'and tell them not to be seen, or to lose him.'

He paused.

'And while you're talking to Seidel,' he added, 'ask him where the car stopped in Wellingdorf and Mönkeberg, and in Mielkendorf. We'll check them out tomorrow in case the idiot missed something.'

~~o~~

When Antje got into the house, she told Albert to stay over. He'd sleep in the small room in the attic that, in the admiral's day, would have housed a maid. It wasn't out of the ordinary; on occasion, Albert would use the room if he had driven any of the Kästners late in the evening, particularly if they needed him early the next day.

In truth, it worried her how the Gestapo might react when they discovered the subterfuge. On his own, they might just think about taking Albert in for questioning.

'Mama,' she said, sailing into the drawing room as if she had just returned from a friend's house, 'I'm back. Albert is staying over as he may be collecting Papa later, and he says you wish him to drive for you in the morning.'

'That's fine. Tell him he can have something to eat if he likes. Miriam had left a pot of food in the kitchen but, to be honest, it wasn't up to her usual standard.'

'I'll tell him. If you want to go to bed, I'll listen out for the phone. I have some reading to do.'

'Yes. I think I will. Eva's already upstairs. We're going to visit the countess tomorrow. Are you sure you don't wish to come?'

'No Mama, I have classes. You know that.' She smiled. 'I'd only be bored anyway.'

'I suppose so. You looked miserable today. I wish you would make more of an effort, Antje. One day you'll have to mix with these people.'

'They're awfully dull, most of them. The only one I found amusing is the one Eva likes; Ingrid, she called herself.'

'Antje! It's Frau Messner. You should respect your elders.'

'She told me to call her Ingrid, and she said that most of your ladies are nice, if a little dull, but that there are a few nasty old witches amongst them who like nothing better than to spread malicious gossip around.'

'Ingrid Messner can be very rude sometimes.'

It was true, Antje thought. She'd seen her Mama cringe when the woman spoke out of place, or in loud tones, but Antje couldn't help but like her.

'Well, for an old biddy, she was fun. I think you should invite her over for lunch sometime. I'm sure she would amuse Papa.'

Her mother's voice turned cold.

'I couldn't trust your father not to say something controversial, even for Ingrid's ears.'

'Give him a chance, Mama. He's trying his best to look after everyone. He can't give up on people.'

'I'll not discuss it with you, Antje. Your father has his own agenda, and I can't forgive his lack of care for all of us. I've lost two sons, yet he still persists in his obsession with the Nussbaums.'

Antje opened her mouth to tell her mother that what she said was unfair, but she stopped herself.

'He can't help it, Mama,' she said, softening her answer. 'He can't stand aside and let them be victims.'

'He has turned you against me too,' Maria said. 'That's the most hurtful bit of all.'

She turned and walked out of the room.

'Mama…' Antje said.

CHAPTER 189

'What time did you get in last night?' Maria Kästner asked her husband, sitting at breakfast, 'and where have Miriam and Yosef got to? They're really becoming dreadfully unreliable.'

He looked at the table, set for breakfast. He'd got up early to do it as Miriam would have, at least to his mind, and had toasted yesterday's bread on the hotplate, setting out a spread of cheese, cold meats, and jams. He'd just finished percolating the coffee when Maria had appeared for breakfast.

'There's a problem,' he said, swallowing the answer that had been on the tip of his tongue. 'The Gestapo snatched Yosef and Miriam yesterday morning and almost beat them to death.'

Maria froze, and a flicker of compassion crossed her face.

'That's terrible,' she gasped. She glanced at the doorway to the hall.

'Where are they?'

She paled, and Erich Kästner knew by the look on her face what she was thinking. He bowed his head.

'You brought them back here?' she hissed. 'And you had Doctor Speer tend to them? Do you know what they will do if they catch you providing medical help for Jews?'

A cold anger gripped him, but he stifled a barbed retort and fought to keep his voice steady.

'No. I didn't bring them here,' he said. 'As much for their safety as ours. I have them somewhere the Gestapo can't find them. They can return when they have recovered unless I can get them out of Germany before then.'

'If I were you, I would make that your top priority, Erich Kästner.'

She stood up and marched out of the room. She met Albert at the doorway.

'I'm ready when you are, ma'am,' he said.

'I'll be leaving shortly,' she said, the sharpness in her voice causing Albert to lower his gaze.

The driver looked at the General.

'Anything?' he asked.

The General shook his head. News of the Nussbaums would have to wait.

'Do you wish me to drop you off at the office before I take the ladies to visit the countess, sir. I'm sure Miss Eva won't be ready before nine.'

'No, Albert. I have my Abwehr car. I drove it home last night.'

'Ah. It slipped my mind, sir. I hope all goes well.'

'So do I, Albert. So do I.'

~~o~~

Almost as soon as he'd hung up his coat, there was a knock on his office door, and Captain Bauer entered.

'I didn't expect you here, Captain. I was going to send the car for you this morning.'

'I thought it better to involve as few people as possible, sir. Anyway, it was good to have a brisk walk to clear my head.'

The General gave him a grateful smile.

'Thank you for last night. It couldn't have been easy for you.'

'How can they do these things?' the captain said, battling to restrain his anger.

'They do worse, my young friend. They still had their nails, their teeth and all their fingers.'

Heinz Bauer shuddered.

'They still gave them a terrible beating.'

'What did the Doc say?'

'Both the Nussbaums have broken ribs, and Miriam has a dislocated shoulder, which has been fixed, but her arm will require a sling for a few weeks. Yosef's other injuries are mainly confined to severe cuts and bruises, but Miriam has a bleed somewhere inside. Doctor Speer doesn't know where, but he's happy that she's stable this morning. She won't be fit to move for at least three or four days.'

'There's no point in moving Yosef now. We'll keep them there, together. Do the nurses know to say nothing to the other staff, and use their false names?'

'Doctor Speer assured me that they'll not say a word. The base commander, Kapitän von Heeringen, visited as well. He assured me the nursing staff are all enlisted men and women who will be very discreet, and that they all live on the base. He was very sympathetic to the Abwehr's needs and passed on his kindest regards. Knowing that security was vital, he put a marine guard on the door, and all staff have to sign in and out.'

'Excellent work, Captain. I'm sorry I had to involve you in this, but I needed someone I could trust.'

The captain reddened.

'Thank you, sir. I was happy to help.'

'Now. There's nothing more we can do for the moment about the Nussbaums. What else is on the agenda for today?'

'Well, sir, we have a meeting with Mayor Hoffmann and Oberpräsident Lohse at eleven.'

The General groaned.

~~o~~

'Those addresses the General's daughter stopped at last night, sir.'

Heinrich Güllich looked up. He hadn't heard Carl Meyer enter his office.

'Yes, Meyer. Anything of interest?'

'Neither of the ones in Wellingdorf or Ellerbek have any significance, sir, but a Doctor Weiss lives close to where they stopped in Mielkendorf.'

'Ah. Could they have had time to offload the Nussbaums?'

'Seidel insists they couldn't have, and that he had a good view of the car at all times.'

'Do this doctor and the General know each other?'

'Not that we can ascertain, sir. We questioned him. I'm sure he knew nothing about it.'

'A mere coincidence then?'

'Or they were trying to waste our time, sir.'

The Kriminalassistent frowned. His junior was beginning to see things he was missing. Perhaps the young man had potential after all.

'If they were the decoy,' he said, rubbing his chin, 'they would have kept away from where the General was taking the Nussbaums.'

Carl Meyer's eyes widened.

'That's clever, sir. But it still leaves a large chunk of Kiel on this side of Kieler Hafen.'

'I know,' Heinrich Güllich snarled. 'If he has them in Kiel at all.'

His assistant's shoulders slumped.

'Check out Doctor Speer again. He may lead us to them.'

Jakob Teubner stood up on a low table, in the largest room in the Judenhaus. All the residents had crammed into the room, and the hallway outside, along with the Jews from the neighbouring house and the few remaining occupants of the house two doors along, where Jakob and the remainder of his self-help committee lived and worked.

As he placed his hand over his eyes to start the service, the congregation quietened.

In a hushed voice, Jakob intoned the Shema, and, in the packed room, his fellow Jews picked up his chant under their breaths to prevent the sound reaching the street.

'She-ma yisrael, adonai eloheinu, adonai echad.'

Hear O' Israel, the Lord is our God, the Lord is One.

Two men standing by the door glanced out into the street, as if at any moment the authorities would come crashing in and arrest them all at their time of worship.

'Baruch shem kavod malchuto l'olam va-ed,' they whispered with the others.

Blessed is the name of His glorious kingdom for ever and ever.

~~o~~

In another makeshift synagogue, in Douglas, on the Isle of Man, an hour behind Kiel, Ruth and Manny stood in their respective groups; he with the men, she with the women.

The door was open, and people arrived late, their faces and shrugs apologetic.

There were smiles everywhere.

After the Shema, the congregation stood for the Amidah, the standing prayer, then sat to listen to the Torah readings.

Ruth looked around; there was joy in the people's faces as they worshipped.

They have no fear.

She smiled, then the weight of her parents' predicament flooded over her, and her eyes clouded again with pain.

But the reading was an uplifting, hopeful verse from the Pentateuch, the five books of Moses, and she tried to be positive, hoping beyond words that her mother and father were on their way to safety, somehow.

After the service, the congregation stood about in the sun, chatting. Curious Manxmen and women watched as the Jews slowly dispersed to their houses, to share food and drink with their friends and neighbours.

Ruth had watched Manny during the service.

'It's wonderful, isn't it?' she said to him as they walked back behind the Weissbergs.

'Yes. I only wish Mama and Papa could see it.'

'Even with the barbed wire, it still feels free.'

'They say they will remove it soon,' Manny said.

She turned to him, surprised.

'Where did you hear that?'

'Oh. The men. It's just talk. I don't think the Manx authorities see us as a risk to them or give any thought of us trying to escape.'

'They have been good to us,' she said, switching to English, pushing him hard to learn it.

She did it without thinking but, despite her concerns, he was speaking the language of their new home more readily, without her prompting. She'd seen him and the other boys make friends with the island youths, playing football on the waste ground close to the school.

The authorities turned a blind eye when they saw the Manx boys crawl under the loops of coiled wire, knowing that the lure of strange new friends was too tempting for them to resist.

And anyway, she thought. *What harm does it do?*

~~o~~

In Kleiner Kuhberg, the service drew to a close, and the room emptied as the congregation slunk back to their crowded rooms. The occupants of the makeshift meeting room unstacked their pallet beds from around the walls, returning its function to that of a dormitory.

Jakob, after shaking hands with the few of the Judenhaus's residents he knew, made his way back to the house where he lived, two doors up Kleiner Kuhberg. He was accompanied by his wife and the men who made up the vestigial and almost powerless committee running the remnants of Jewish cultural life in the city.

'It's a shame,' he said, 'that we hardly use the synagogue,' he said to Nathan Dreilich and Nossen Deller, the younger men he increasingly relied on.

'Yes. Or the school,' Nossen Deller said. 'After all the effort we put into them.'

'It's safer in number 25. The Goyim would notice if we held it here.'

'It's God's will.'

The three men turned.

Siegmund Eliasowitz walked behind them. He'd listened to their conversation, and no one was surprised that he couldn't stay silent.

'The children of Israel have been persecuted for millenia, since the days of Joseph in Egypt,' the sonorous young man continued, 'and we always will be. Our place of worship is where his people are, and we must teach the children wherever we can make a Cheder.'

'You're right, of course, Herr Eliasowitz. But sometimes, it would be nice if God looked after us all just a little bit better,' Nathan Dreilich said, with a faint smile.

The pious young Jew, who oversaw the religious education of the young men of the dwindling Jewish community, looked at Jakob first, then Nossen Deller, for support. It wasn't forthcoming.

'That's sacrilege,' he said, his face flushing hotly.

'You might be right, Brother Eliasowitz,' Jakob said. 'But it does have a ring of truth.'

CHAPTER 191

Doctor Speer's surgery was closed, and there was no one at the house. A notice on the surgery door listed a telephone number for an alternative doctor, for medical emergencies.

'They might be away for the weekend, sir.'

'It is possible, Kamerad Meyer. Or he could be in a house somewhere in Kiel, illegally tending to a couple of Judenschweine for his military friend.'

'We've no way of knowing, sir.'

'I know. Meyer. I know.'

~~o~~

When the General went to bed, he read for a short while, then turned out the light. Nine times out of ten, the moment he lay his head on the pillow, he fell asleep. It was a talent that had always given him great comfort.

But for once, he lay awake. Something niggled at the back of his mind, and he couldn't quite grasp what it was. He was sure it hadn't been bothering him as he climbed the stairs.

He turned the light back on and looked around. There was something different.

He got up and looked around. He crossed to Maria's dressing table. She'd taken all her hairbrushes and make-up through to the spare bedroom when she'd moved out of theirs, but she'd left the odd personal item lying around. Now, there was nothing. He opened a drawer. It was empty.

He walked over to the wardrobe and opened the doors. Bare boards stared back at him.

He stood in the middle of the floor and bowed his head.

How did we get to this?

He climbed back into bed and lay awake, thinking.

~~o~~

[25/05/1941 Sunday]

'Meyer, I've just had a thought. Go back to the doctor's surgery and get me the phone number on the notice stuck to the door. The one for the alternative doctor. Perhaps Doctor Speer will have told him where he was going.'

'Yes, sir.'

Fifteen minutes later he was back. He handed Heinrich Güllich a piece of paper.

The Kriminalassistent picked up the phone and waited until the doctor picked up the receiver.

'Can I help you?' a tired voice said.

'Yes,' Heinrich Güllich said, his tone oily smooth. 'I'm looking for Doctor Speer, and I was given your number.'

'Are you ill? Is it urgent?'

'No. I'm not a patient. I'm with the Gestapo. I need to ask him a few questions.'

There was a noticeable silence at the end of the line.

'Have you tried the hospital? Both of us work there from time to time, and we cover each other's practices when we need to. Or he might be taking a little time at home; he has been complaining of exhaustion, recently, as we all have. They didn't think about the severe shortage of medical expertise when they banned all the Jewish doctors.'

Heinrich Güllich counted to five in his head and made himself breath slowly.

What is it about the people connected with this investigation?

He was used to the Gestapo name striking terror into even the most upright of citizens, yet the General, Jakob Teubner and now this insignificant doctor dared to air views which could get them arrested.

'He's not at home. Did you mean the general hospital?' he said, his voice polite and reasonable.

'Yes. Out at Hasseldieksdammer Weg. Where else?'

'The geriatric hospital, or the psychiatric hospital on Moltkestraße.'

'I suppose you're right, but he's not a psychiatrist, and the geriatric hospital is nothing but a home for the elderly.'

'What department does he work in at the hospital?'

'We generally cover the accident and emergency department, although they sometimes put us in one of the medical wards.'

'Thank you for your time, Doctor,' Heinrich Güllich said, hoping the doctor detected the sarcasm in his voice. 'You have been most helpful.'

He turned to Carl Meyer, smiling.

'Get your coat. We're going to visit a couple of patients in hospital. It may not be good for their health, but it will do mine no harm at all.'

'He surely wouldn't have dared, would he?' the younger man said. 'I mean, a public hospital.'

'I wouldn't put it past our beloved General to hide them in plain view. He's an arrogant Schwein, and people seem to bend to his wishes.'

~~o~~

An hour later they sat in the hospital administrator's office, asking the harassed man about the general practitioner's work at the hospital.

'Yes,' the harassed official said, 'Doctor Speer does help out from time to time, more often than we'd like, but that is the way it is at present.'

'And is he working here at the moment?'

'I can't be sure. I'll have to phone around.'

Heinrich Güllich had had enough. He picked up the man's telephone and slammed it down on his desk in front of him.

'Make the calls,' he said.

The man's voice shook as he asked the various departments and wards if Doctor Speer was working with them or had done in the previous few days. Their answers were identical, by and large. He'd worked there, but not in the last week, although the doctor in the casualty department thought that he might have been there three days before.

'He says every day runs into the next one,' the administrator said with an apologetic shrug after putting the phone down.

'And you don't have any patients under secure conditions, do you?'

'No. Well, on a rare occasion, the police will place a guard if we're treating a convicted criminal, or a witness to a serious crime, but there hasn't been anything like that for ages.'

'Are you sure?' Heinrich Güllich said. 'It would be unfortunate if we were to discover at a later time that you'd had patients being kept under those conditions.'

'I'll phone around the wards again,' the man said, his words tumbling together.

It took him ten minutes. None of the patients in the hospital had a guard of any kind.

The two Gestapo men returned to the car.

Heinrich Güllich slammed the door shut.

'He has them somewhere safe,' he said. 'Outside Kiel, I suspect. Check and see if the General has any property in the countr…'

He stopped.

'Where do the General's parents live?' he said, gripping his assistant's arm.

'Somewhere in the mountains,' Carl Meyer said, flinching.

'Bavaria? The Alps?'

'No. The Harz mountains, I believe. I heard my father mention it once. It used to be their holiday home.'

'How the other half live,' Heinrich Güllich muttered. 'Would they have risked the journey? It's south of Hanover, isn't it?'

'Yes. A couple of hours further on.'

'Find out from your two inept Kriminalassistentanwärteren what the General is doing. We'll take over their task and keep a watch on him, and they can drive down to the admiral's place in the mountains.'

'Is that wise, sir?'

The Kriminalassistent turned and glared at the younger man.

'What do you mean,' he growled.

'Well, they might not have enough finesse, sir. If the admiral sees them, he may complain.'

'Ah,' Heinrich Güllich said, his anger dissolving. 'You have a point, but I'll have a word with them before they go. They'll be able to observe the place from a distance and confirm if the Nussbaums are there or not, without alerting the admiral or his wife. They can go down and back up in the same day if they leave early enough in the morning.'

~~o~~

KIELER MORGENPOST

Sunday 25th May 1941

BRITISH BATTLESHIP HOOD SUNK BY BISMARCK

The so-called invincible battleship, HMS Hood, has been sunk by the Kriegsmarine's top battleship, the Bismarck, in the first naval battle of the war.

Admiral Schiffer, speaking at the Kriegsmarine Headquarters in Kiel, said that the sinking of the largest and fastest battleship in the world was a decisive victory for Germany and demonstrated that the tactical genius and superior fighting abilities of German naval forces outweighed the Royal Navy's greater numbers and firepower.

CHAPTER 192

[27/05/1941 Tuesday]

Captain Bauer showed Wilhelm Canaris in.

'Kästner!'

'Canaris!'

'How are you doing?' the admiral asked, putting his hand on his friend's shoulder.

'Bearing up, as best as I can,' the General said, the sadness in his voice belying the hearty welcome he'd given Wilhelm Canaris.

The captain slipped out of the room and left them to it.

'Any news?' the admiral said, keeping his voice to a murmur.

'Nothing,' the General said. 'Nothing at all.'

'That's good,' the admiral said. 'It's still too soon to have heard from the British authorities, depending on when they reached England.'

'If they made it. The last few weeks have been the longest in my life, and that includes my time in the trenches of the last war.'

'I have a feeling about them, and about *Der Sturmtaucher*,' the admiral said. He gripped his friend's arm.

'If that had been you and I out there,' he added, 'in that storm, what chance would you have given us?'

'Even with enough sea room, in a boat like that,' the General replied, 'less than evens, and that's with a large slice of luck.'

'And Franz and Johann; what about them?'

'A few years ago, I would have said perhaps less, but now? I think Franz is better than me. And Johann isn't far behind.'

'There you go. Have faith.'

The General gave him a weak smile.

'Remember you told me about the Führer's plans for Russia's Jews when we invade?' he said.

'Yes,' Canaris said. 'What about it?'

'You said that it would sooner or later come to Poland's Jews, and to Germany's.'

'Yes.'

'I'm afraid it already has.'

The General repeated Dieter Maas's reasoning about the new camps being planned in the Generalgouvernement, and their proximity to the evermore crowded ghettos.

The admiral stayed silent for a second or two, then looked at Erich Kästner.

'I hear talk amongst them,' he said. 'Himmler, Heydrich, Göring. Martin Bormann. They trip over one another to do the Führer's bidding. Around a month ago, I overheard a conversation between Himmler and Heydrich, about new camps in Poland with a yet to be defined purpose.'

He paused.

'Belzec, the hub of a string of labour camps on the Bug river, close to the border of Soviet-occupied Poland, is to be expanded. Another two new camps are to be sited elsewhere in the Generalgouvernement. There's also the camp at Oświęcim, just outside the zone, but close to Kraków, one of the five larger ghettos. It is being expanded.'

'So, Dieter is right?'

'I'm afraid so. Whether they work them to death, or just let them die, they intend to kill a significant portion of Europe's Jews.'

'And all the difficulty with transport we're having is down to the number of Jews being transported east, to the ghettos.'

'Much of it, yes.'

'What can we do?'

'What we are doing. Working in the background, trying to curb the excesses of this regime. Even the stuff you do for the navy will help; prioritising the Reichsbahn resources you secure for your navy supply trains will, perhaps, slow down the transports. But keep your views to yourself. The SD and Gestapo are actively weeding out any dissenters in the armed forces.'

'I'll keep it in mind. What about you?'

'I can put a few obstacles in their way, put doubts in their mind about the British, and sow seeds about an American intervention. It might help, and in the meantime, I'll continue talking with groups who see things our way. There are more of them than you might suppose.'

'Take care that you're not betrayed, Canaris,' the General said.

'I'm always careful, but I have to keep in touch with these people. If the chance ever arises, we must have a coordinated response. One group is not capable of overthrowing this regime on its own, but it's too early for them to unite; it wouldn't be safe. At least this way, if one is exposed, the others aren't taken down with them.'

'But the chances are still very much in the favour of the National Socialists?'

'Yes. I'm sorry to say. The odds are stacked against us, and they will be for the foreseeable future. It will take a winter in Russia, or maybe two, to weaken Adolf's grip on power.'

'Unless he wins.'

'Yes. Unless he wins. In the meantime, hundreds of thousands are going to die.'

The General sat, deep in thought, for almost a minute.

'What did you make of the Rudolf Hess story?' he heard his friend say.

'I had hoped that you would have an insider's knowledge.'

'They're trying to write it off as the act of a madman. That he cracked.'

'And what's your view on it?' the General said. 'There are reports that he was in Britain at the Führer's request.'

'I can scotch that rumour,' Canaris said. 'I spoke to Speer, who was standing outside in the corridor when Adolf was told about Hess's flight to Britain. He said his screams of rage could be heard half a kilometre away.'

'So, what did Hess think he would achieve?'

'Maybe he was the only realist in the Third Reich. I mean, attacking Russia while we're still at war with the British. There's where madness lies.'

~~o~~

[27/05/1941 Tuesday]

'General, I have your father on the line for you.'

'Thank you, Frau Müller. Put him through.'

Erich Kästner sat back.

'Father,' he said. 'How are you?'

'Fine, as always, Erich. And you? How are you coping?'

'Ach. One must carry on. How is Mother?'

'She's taking it hard. Her two grandsons. How's Maria?'

'She's not doing well. She's throwing herself into her charity work so that she doesn't have to think about it.'

He felt terrible, lying to the people he loved, even if it was in everyone's interest. He prayed news would come soon and release him from his burden.

'There will be thousands more like her if this war continues,' he heard his father say.

'It will be millions. This will not be a short war. The British are too well defended by the Channel and are frantically regrouping.'

There was an awkward silence at the end of the line, then he heard the admiral speak again.

'There was something I wanted to speak to you about. It's rather delicate…'

'I see. I'm in the middle of something but perhaps it would be better if I telephoned you later, when we could have more time to discuss it?'

'Yes, I apologise. That would do. I'll look forward to hearing from you.'

When his father had hung up, Erich Kästner listened for the click that would tell him Frau Müller had been listening in, but it remained silent. He placed the receiver on his desk and walked softly to the door. As he approached it, he could hear the rattle of his secretary's typewriter. He returned and placed the handset back on its cradle.

He lifted his jacket from the coat stand and left the office, telling Frau Müller he would be gone for a while.

He dialled his father's number at the first telephone kiosk he found.

'Father,' he said. 'I'm calling from a public telephone. Is there a problem?'

'I wondered how safe your office line was. I remembered you saying that you had concerns about the line at the house.'

'I may be paranoid, but best to take no chances. What's bothering you?'

'We had a visit from two shady characters.'

'What did they say?'

'Nothing. They thought they were keeping out of sight, but they were easy to spot. They appeared to be keeping an eye on the place. They had all the hallmarks of Gestapo, or SD perhaps. I assumed that I would be of little interest to them, so I took it that it was about you. Is there any reason why they would be interested in the comings and goings up here?'

'Yes. The Nussbaums. It's a long story but, at the nub of it, they were given a terrible beating by the Gestapo; Miriam's injuries were almost life-threatening. I managed to obtain medical attention for them, but the Gestapo are desperate to catch me at it. They must have thought that I'd sent them to you.'

'Ah. I thought perhaps that it might have had something to do with your outspoken views.'

The General sighed.

'No. I try and keep them to myself and work hard for the Reich, but this Güllich chap doesn't like my efforts to protect the Nussbaums, and the clout I have with the authorities to do so.'

'Be careful, son. These people are dangerous. Don't underestimate them.'

'Unfortunately, I can only agree, and I am taking care. Güllich is especially dangerous, and he will not let it go. The sooner I can get the Nussbaums away, the better.'

'And Ruth and Manny. There's no news?'

'Not yet.'

'I wish there were something I could do.'

'There's nothing anyone can do.'

'If you need a little money, to facilitate…'

'I have enough, should I need it. That's not the problem. It's finding the people who can help Yosef and Miriam, then getting them well enough to travel if they give us the go-ahead.'

'Good luck.'

'Thanks, and it was useful to know about your visitors.'

'Take care, Erich.'

'I will.'

CHAPTER 193

On the way back to the office, the General glanced at the billboard at the news stand.

KIELER MORGENPOST

BISMARCK LOST

He'd heard about the battleship's loss; a memo had come through earlier. He bought the paper, a later edition. He sat down on a bench to read it.

The column was a last-minute addition to the front page. Information was scant. Unlike the sinking of HMS *Hood*, less than a week before, there were no descriptions of brilliant tactics or superior technology, just a lament that the *Bismarck* had been vastly outnumbered by the Royal Navy and that the battleship had suffered a hero's fate.

The General's mind was torn between his pain for the fate of the Bismarck and her crew, and the knowledge that Germany must be defeated, for the sake of the Nussbaums, and rest of Europe's Jews.

And for my nation's future place in the world.

She'd been a fine ship; he'd been at her launch in Hamburg in 1936, one of the hundreds of invited guests, and at her passing out, three years later.

He folded the paper and made his way back to the office.

~~o~~

[28/05/1941 Wednesday]

Kriminalassistentanwärter Seidel stood in front of Heinrich Güllich.

'There's no one there but the old admiral and his wife, sir. And a woman who comes in to clean.'

'You're sure?'

'Yes, sir. They sat out in the garden most of the day and pottered in and out of the house. We'd have seen signs if there had been anyone else in there.'

'And they didn't see you?'

'No, sir. We were very discreet. They were oblivious to us watching.'

'Good. Keep an eye on the General this evening. Kriminalassistentanwärter Meyer and I will take over from you in the morning.'

~~o~~

[31/05/1941 Saturday]

The Nussbaums returned to the cottage under cover of darkness. Captain Bauer picked them up from the naval hospital in the General's Abwehr car and drove them straight to Drachensee.

On Holtenauer Straße, they passed the General, with Albert driving, in the opposite direction, his Gestapo followers trailing three cars behind him.

Neither man waved nor looked across at the other. The two Gestapo men yawned, wishing the Kriminalassistent would give up on his fruitless quest to track the General. It was obvious, even to them, that the General wasn't going to lead them to these Jews of his.

'I mean, it's a Saturday.' Kriminalassistentanwärter Seidel sighed, tailing the General back to Drachensee. 'He goes to the office for fifteen minutes, then he goes back home again. And we follow him like poodles.'

His companion laughed.

'It's what we're paid to do.'

'I thought working with the Gestapo would be glamorous. I even harboured hopes that the uniform would attract girls.'

'It does. You should see the Fräulein I'm seeing just now.'

'She's Gestapo too, even if it is only the typing pool. The rest are too frightened of us.'

'You could always ask Dirty Helga for a date.'

Seidel grimaced.

'I'd give anything for a night with that one, but she wouldn't piss on me if I was on fire. She likes senior meat. And anyway, would you like to face the wrath of the Kriminaldirektor?'

His companion shuddered.

~~o~~

The General waited fifteen minutes, then slipped over to the Nussbaums' cottage. Yosef let him in.

They embraced.

'Sir, thank you for what you did.'

'I only did what needed done. You should thank Doctor Speer and Captain Bauer.'

'We did, sir. They couldn't have been kinder to us.'

'How is Miriam?'

'She's in bed now. Tired, and still sore, but getting better every day.'

'Stay in the cottage. Keep out of sight. I'm going to try the Haganah again tomorrow.'

'Yes, sir. It's getting desperate. Can you get a message to my parents?'

'Yes, as soon as I can. What is it?'

'Tell them that we're all right, but there's no chance of us seeing them.'

'I'll do that. I told them to get out the last time I saw them, but they said they were too old to go anywhere else.'

'I know, sir. We spoke with them at Manny's birthday. They told us to leave if we could. We said our goodbyes then.'

The General turned away for a second and looked out the window.

'They may come again for you. Keep the door locked and don't answer it.'

'They may just break it down, sir.'

'I don't think so. They wouldn't risk leaving proof that they'd been here.'

'But the last time…'

'They took advantage of us all being out. I'll make sure that doesn't happen again.'

'How?'

The General bowed his head.

'I'm sorry, but we'll need to find a new housekeeper. At least it means there will always be someone here.'

'But what about…'

'Miriam's not fit to work yet, and when she's well again, we need to get you out of here.'

'I suppose so, sir.'

The General glanced at Yosef. Pain was etched across his face, and the General knew it hurt him not to be able to work.

'We knew this day would come,' he said. 'My only concern is getting you and Miriam to safety.'

'I understand, sir. Have you heard nothing about the boys?'

The General winced.

I should have told him first.

'Nothing yet,' he said, 'but that means they haven't been caught, or found,' he said, deciding they were too far down the road to ignore the reality of their position.

'It would be good to know, sir, before we left.'

'We should hear any day now.'

'You'd better get on, sir. Frau Kästner will be wondering where you are.'

A shadow crossed the General's face.

'I'm sorry, sir,' Yosef said, 'if we've caused problems for you.'

'You haven't, my friend. But sometimes it takes times like these to realise that you didn't know someone as well as you thought.'

'I...'

'Don't worry, Yosef. It will sort itself out. I'll see you tomorrow.'

'Goodnight, sir.'

CHAPTER 194

[01/06/1941 Sunday]

'The first of June,' Franz said. 'I wonder if they know about us yet.'

'They're bound to have heard by now. That's over a month.'

'They might not have the cards yet. And they only let us write our forenames and surnames on them, so they won't know about Ruth and Manny.'

'I didn't realise how much I'd miss them. I mean, we were only home once in a blue moon, but…'

His voice trailed off.

'It was always going to be hard, not knowing how long we'll be stuck here.'

'I feel guilty,' Johann said. 'I miss my friends almost as much as I miss Mother and Father, and the girls.'

'You spent a lot of time with them. They were like family to you. It's only natural.'

'Even young Manny. I was always very fond of him, but on the boat…'

He looked at Franz, who was staring into the distance.

'I'm sorry,' he said. 'You must miss her.'

'I've never felt hurt like it. We only had a short time, but it was wonderful. I don't know if I can explain it to you.'

Johann gave a rueful smile.

'You mean I wouldn't understand?' he said.

'I didn't say that,' Franz said, blushing.

'Yes, but you were thinking it, and it's probably true. I've never fallen in love like you. Don't get me wrong, I adore women, but I couldn't commit to just one, if you know what I mean.'

Franz shook his head, then smiled.

'No. Not really, but then again, we're very different,' he said, then sighed. 'It's not only Ruth; I miss every one of them. Antje, most of all.'

'Antje is like you. She thinks too much, and she preferred to spend her time with Father. Eva was always a mama's girl.'

'Ha. I suppose you're right.'

Johann punched his brother on the arm.

'Listen to us, moping. We did what we set out to do; to get Ruth and Manny to safety. There's no point in us being any more miserable than we have to be.'

Franz smiled. That was the thing about Johann. Even in his own private hell, he would make the best of any situation, which was why he was good to have around.

A few shouts of laughter drifted over from the group of men sitting by the hut.

'They're all right, if you can see past their loyalty to the Führer,' Johann said, noticing Franz's frown.

'Shh. Someone will hear you.'

'We're too far away. Anyway, they're no worse than our friends in the Kompanie, really.'

Franz glanced sideways at his brother.

'You're wrong. They are worse. Especially Kapitäns Langefeld and Schlesinger. Watch those two.'

'Our friends were just the same; it's just that they were careful what they said when you were around, because they knew what you were like. Deep down, they supported the National Socialists.'

'But…'

Johann held up his hand.

'All right, they weren't extreme Nazis, as they call us over here, but they broadly supported everything Hitler stood for, or at least, they tolerated the worst of his excesses because of what he did for the Wehrmacht.'

'I thought they were upset by the massacre you witnessed?'

'Only Maxi and Fritz were there. They didn't like it but, as Fritz said afterwards, things happen in war that we sometimes have to stomach for the general good.'

'How could they not see the wrong in it?'

Johann bowed his head.

'I was like them. We took an oath. We were desperate to succeed where Father's generation failed.'

'They didn't fail. It couldn't go on. It's almost impossible to imagine what it was like.'

'I didn't mean that. They were betrayed.'

Franz shook his head. 'The men who died or were crippled on both sides were betrayed. It should never have happened, and someone should have stopped it. Why do you think Father couldn't stand the Kaiser and his class?'

Johann stared at him.

'I didn't know,' he said, looking away.

'He didn't talk about it much. He just let slip a few remarks, but Uncle Wilhelm told me a few stories. They must have talked about it, over the years.'

'It's all a mess, isn't it?'

'Yes. And if we invade Russia, it could be worse than the last time. And we'll lose again.'

'My friends,' Johann said, dropping his head into his hands.

'With any luck, they'll get to stay in Norway.'

'No,' he said, shaking his head. 'They won't. They'll do what they did in Poland. They'll put older men into places like Norway and France and send the younger ones to fight the Russians.'

Franz stared numbly at him, knowing he was right.

'There's nothing we can do about it.'

'No, but a big part of me still thinks that we should be there, that we'll be responsible if something happens to them.'

'That's nonsense,' Franz said, but, in his heart, he felt a twinge of guilt. They were his friends too.

They sat together in silence. A minute passed, then Franz nodded towards the hut. A few men were sitting outside.

'They believe the Wehrmacht will invade England, and we'll be released to join back up with our units. If it does happen, we'll have to run. We can't afford to be taken back home.'

'I know,' Johann said.

'Whatever you do,' Franz said, 'don't be tempted to talk to any of the others about any of this. They wouldn't understand, and it could be dangerous.'

'I'm not that stupid,' Johann said, scowling.

They stood up and walked back to the hut.

'Johann,' one of the men shouted, 'We're just going to have a game of cards. Do you fancy it?'

'Yes. Count me in.'

He turned to Franz. 'Are you coming?'

'No. I'll sit it out,' Franz said.

Johann touched his brother lightly on the shoulder and followed the man into the hut. Franz took a pencil and a folded piece of paper from his pocket and opened it out. He added to it every day, even though it would never be posted. He read the first words.

IDear Ruth,

I miss you…

~~o~~

[03/06/1941 Tuesday]

'I've taken on some temporary help while the Nussbaums are indisposed,' Erich Kästner said.

'We should be thinking of a more permanent arrangement,' Maria said, 'and concentrating on finding the Nussbaums a way out, or alternative accommodation.'

'I hear there are great opportunities abroad,' the General said, his voice cold. 'Poland, for instance.'

'That was uncalled for,' Maria said, glaring at her husband, 'although I'm sure you are grossly exaggerating the conditions in these places. More to the point, who is this person you have taken on?'

'I…' The General stopped, seeing Antje at the doorway. He and Maria had caused both their daughters enough pain.

'The wife of one of the admirals used her when their own housekeeper was ill,' he said, trying hard to keep any trace of his anger from his voice. 'He said she was very efficient.'

'And when does she start? It has been awfully difficult without staff.'

'She starts tomorrow. I hope we'll survive until then.'

~~o~~

[13/06/1941 Friday]

Ruth counted the days again. She tried to work out exactly how long it had been since she'd arrived in Britain, but her brain wasn't functioning.

Not that it mattered. However long it was, she was late. A couple of weeks after they'd arrived on the island, she'd felt as if her monthly bleeding had arrived but, apart from a little watery discharge, it hadn't amounted to anything. She'd waited, wondering if the trials of the voyage had affected her womb in some way, but now, when it should have been due again, there was nothing.

And the sickness hadn't stopped. She'd managed to hide it from Manny after that first time, and she was sure no one else had noticed, but she didn't know how long she could keep it a secret.

She sat in the toilet of the bakery, tears gathering in her eyes and rolling down her cheeks.

I have his child inside me.

Ruth sniffed. She dried her eyes and cleaned herself up with cold water at the sink.

They'll not let me keep it. They'll take it away.

She put her hand on the lock and forced herself not to cry again.

As she returned to her bench, the woman beside her asked if she was all right.

'Yes,' she said. 'I'm just missing my family.'

It was a more than plausible excuse for her red-rimmed eyes and, with her parents never far from her thoughts, it wasn't too much of a lie.

She concentrated on filling the pastries and smiled at her companion.

'We've all left someone behind,' the woman said, touching her arm. 'It does get easier with time, you know.'

But Ruth knew it wouldn't.

CHAPTER 195

[16/06/1941 Monday]

'How long have they been back at the cottage?' Heinrich Güllich shouted, punching the wall of his office.

He rubbed his knuckles, cursing.

'We don't know, sir. It was only by chance that we saw the woman.'

Kriminalassistentanwärter Seidel rubbed the sweat from his brow and shifted from foot to foot. Carl Meyer stifled a smile.

At least someone else is taking the brunt this time.

'Go on,' Heinrich Güllich hissed. 'Tell us all how you managed to find the Jewish bitch we've all been desperate to find for the last God knows how long?'

'We were just turning the car, sir, to come back here, when we saw the General's daughter cross the yard to the cottage. We pulled over and watched. The door opened and someone let the girl in. I only caught a brief glimpse, but it was definitely the Nussbaum woman.'

'And none of you noticed her before?'

'No, sir. They must have stayed inside.'

'And there have been no cars coming or going?'

'Just the General, his lady wife, and his daughters, sir.'

'Are you sure?'

'Yes, sir. Oh, wait, the housekeeper came out to hang out the washing.'

Heinrich Güllich scowled.

'No deliveries?'

'Well, yes, sir. Just the usual, but they always park in plain sight.'

'So, they got there by boat. Across the lake?'

'Perhaps, sir.'

Carl Meyer flinched. Seidel had missed the sarcasm in his boss's voice.

The Kriminalassistent threw a book at the young Gestapo man.

'I would doubt it. They would have to go through someone's property and then cross a lake in full view of the neighbours. No. They were taken home when the General was elsewhere, when we were following him, so somebody else is involved.'

'That will be almost impossible to prove now, sir,' Carl Meyer said.

Heinrich Güllich turned towards him, glaring.

'You are quite right, Meyer, but I'm not one to give up. I wish to keep up the surveillance on these Judenläuse and their protectors.'

The three Kriminalassistentanwärteren might have groaned, but with the mood Heinrich Güllich was in, they stayed silent.

Carl Meyer only hoped the Kriminaldirektor wouldn't get to hear about the whole affair. He watched as the Kriminalassistent's face cracked into a cruel smile.

'Fetch me the latest deportation lists for Schleswig-Holstein,' Heinrich Güllich said, 'and request the lists from the Hamburg area too.'

~~o~~

[17/06/1941 Tuesday]

'Number 3 you said, sir?' the army driver asked.

'Yes. Just over there.'

The General pointed to the building on the opposite side of Stoschstraße where Yosef Nussbaum's parents lived. There was a removal van outside and he had to dodge two men lifting a wardrobe up the stairs as he entered the building. He climbed the stairs to the first landing and frowned.

A man in a brown coat was coming out of the Nussbaums' apartment, whistling. A feeling of nausea gripped the General's stomach.

'Excuse me,' the General asked, 'Are Herr and Frau Nussbaum still inside?'

'I wouldn't know, sir,' the man replied, taking his hat off. 'The name on the ticket is Gruber, sir.'

'But what happened to the Nussbaums? They live here.'

The man bowed his head in embarrassment.

'Sir, I… I…'

Full realisation came to the General in a flood.

I should have known.

'When did they move out?'

'I'm sorry, sir, I wouldn't know. We were just told to put all the old furniture in the lorry and move the stuff from the van into the flat.'

'Lorry?'

'Yes, sir. A flatbed. It's parked just up the street. We moved it to allow us to get the van to the door.'

The General ran down the stairs and opened the street door. He looked up Stoschstraße and saw the truck. As he walked towards it, he noticed the familiar couch that had belonged to the Nussbaums, and the old couple's grandfather clock. And sticking out of a wooden crate, he saw the neck of a mandolin. He reached in and lifted it out.

'Oi!'

He looked around. Another of the removal men was coming towards him but, when he saw the General's uniform, his bristling manner became less unsure and, by the time he reached the General, he was apologetic.

'Sorry, sir. Can I help you?'

'The Nussbaums were employees of my father. Their son works for me. I was just looking…'

'Ah. Sorry, sir. I thought…'

The General forced himself to smile.

'You don't know where they went, do you?'

'Sorry, sir. There was nobody here when we arrived. We were just given the key and told to empty the flat, then move the new furniture in.'

'I understand. Where is the furniture being taken?'

The man pulled a sheet from the top pocket of his overall. He showed it to the General.

H. Heidenberg & Sons.

A saleroom.

It confirmed his worst fears.

'Thank you,' he said, handing the docket back to the man. He saw the removal foreman look at the mandolin. He went to hand it back to him.

'You can keep it, sir, if you want. There's no inventory.'

'Thank you. His son will appreciate the gesture.'

The General reached in his pocket and drew out a five Reichsmark note.

'It's not necessary, sir,' the man said.

'It's not payment; just a small gratuity for your help.'

The man took it, and walked back to the removal van, lifting a standard lamp and carrying it towards the building.

The General looked up at the open windows of the Nussbaums' flat, then walked over to the waiting car.

~~o~~

'I'm so sorry, Yosef. If I'd gone a day sooner…'

'You weren't to know, sir.'

'I'll try and find out where they've been sent.'

'Thank you, sir. It will make it easier to find them after the war is over.'

The General looked away, fearful of Yosef seeing the truth in his eyes.

'We received a letter from Hamburg today, sir. From a neighbour of Miriam's parents. They've been deported to Poland too.'

The General gasped. He felt the blood rush from his face and put his hand on the back of the chair to steady himself.

'That's terrible. The timing…'

'It must be a coincidence, sir. It's a miracle it hasn't happened to one of them before now.'

The General was about to argue but stopped himself. The alternative was unthinkable, and would destroy Yosef and Miriam, but in his own mind, he was certain.

This is the work of Heinrich Güllich.

'How's Miriam?' he asked, fighting to keep his voice level.

'Taking it hard, sir. She said this morning that if she were sure we'd be going to the same place as our parents, she would gladly go.'

'Don't even consider it, Yosef, or let Miriam think like that,' he said, a little too stridently.

He turned away again.

They mustn't suspect that where their parents have been sent is not the resettlement in the east they've been told about.

'It's all right, sir. We'll do as you suggest and try and get out, although there has been no word from the Haganah.'

Yosef paused.

'Is there any news…?'

The General shook his head.

'Nothing yet,' he said, putting his arm on Yosef's shoulder. 'It all has to go through official channels; it can take time. I'll let you know as soon as I hear from them.'

'Thank you, sir.'

~~o~~

[21/06/1941 Saturday]

'Maria, I'm not asking much. The police won't come unless the Nussbaums are here on their own.'

'It's dreadfully inconvenient, asking me to stay at home while you run off to Berlin.'

Erich Kästner took a deep breath.

'I'm not running off. This is a very high-level meeting. Hitler himself may be present. And I'm not asking you both to stay here all day, just that one of you should be at home when Antje isn't here.'

'But…'

He held up his hand.

'Antje has promised to be here most of the time,' he said, 'but she has an examination tomorrow at ten o'clock. She'll be back by two. Surely that's not too much of an imposition. I would ask the housekeeper, but she is off today, if you remember. She's travelling to Munich for her aunt's funeral tomorrow.'

She shook her head. 'I suppose I have no choice,' she said, 'but if the Gestapo come hammering at the door, I cannot do anything to stop them taking the Nussbaums.'

'I wouldn't expect you to. I just need your presence here. It will be enough. Thank you.'

He watched a puzzled frown cross her face.

'You're meeting the Führer? What is this all about?'

'I can't say, but do you remember that I told you something a while ago in strictest confidence?'

Maria Kästner's eyes widened.

'Russia? Is it happening?'

'I think so.'

'Soon?'

'Probably.'

'We will win, Erich, I can feel it. Communism will be defeated.'

Taken aback, he took a second to answer.

'It's possible, but…'

He stopped. He looked at his wife. Her eyes were shining, and her face had a light in it he hadn't seen for a while. His sadness was that it wasn't for him.

'Anyway,' he said, taking advantage of her mood, 'thank you for filling in while Antje is away at her art exam. She might have to go out for a short while the following day too.'

He could see that she was still thinking of the march to Moscow, not realising the near impossibility of it.

'I was going to take Eva with me tomorrow. She has a day off. We have an invitation to the Guild in Flensburg, but I can leave her behind. Perhaps Hugo will visit.'

The General raised an eyebrow but said nothing. His wife didn't notice. He hoped that Eva was sensible enough to take precautions.

If Maria wants Eva to marry into the aristocracy, an unwanted child will put a dent in her plans.

'What time are you leaving?' she asked.

'In about an hour.'

'Please don't say anything controversial in front of the Führer, Erich.'

He laughed, causing her to frown.

'I won't. I promise,' he said.

He doubted the Führer would be present, although Keitel, the Wehrmacht's chief of staff, and Reichsmarschall Hermann Göring, most certainly would, but it had been enough to impress Maria.

He'd only been told that the meeting was about urgent naval matters. He'd been invited along by both the Kriegsmarine, and by Canaris, but it was the latter who'd told him that the purpose of the gathering was to finalise the delivery of naval support in the Baltic during the invasion of the Soviet Union.

He would much rather have stayed in Kiel.

CHAPTER 196

KIELER MORGENPOST

Monday 23rd June 1941

THE FÜHRER UNLEASHES THE WEHRMACHT AGAINST THE SOVIETS

Battlefront against Bolshevism from the North Cape to the Black Sea

The Third Reich is now at war with the Soviet Union.

At 3:15 yesterday morning, German forces began the invasion of the Soviet Union with bombing raids against key cities in Soviet-occupied Poland, and deep within Russia and the Ukraine. Following an extensive artillery barrage along the entire front lines of the Soviet defences, ground forces of the Wehrmacht were joined by Finnish and Romanian units, and Lithuanian and Ukrainian nationalist forces, crossing the border along its length from the Baltic to the Black Sea, inflicting heavy defeats on the defending Red Army.

Reich Minister Joseph Goebbels announced the invasion in a radio broadcast early on Sunday morning, quoting the Führer:

"At this moment, a march is taking place that, as regards to its extent, compares with the greatest the world hitherto has seen".

"I therefore decided today again to lay the fate and future of the German Reich and our people in the hands of our soldiers. May God help us especially in this fight!"

Dr. Goebbels added that this was the beginning of a "European crusade against Bolshevism".

~~o~~

The barracks at Ulven Leir, thirty kilometres south of Bergen, housed around 400 soldiers of the 69th Infantry Division and two units of the Norges SS, made up of Norwegian SS recruits commanded by German Schutzstaffel officers.

Generalmajor Walther Schneider sat in his office, surrounded by his senior officers. He looked around.

Brigadier.

His promotion had come through and he'd received the congratulations of his men with the humble grace that he considered the occasion deserved, but it wasn't the same without the Kästner brothers, even if their replacements were slowly filling the gaps left by the pair.

He hadn't realised just how much he'd come to rely on Franz Kästner as an aide until *Der Sturmtaucher* had been lost. He found himself with no one to turn to when difficult decisions needed to be made, and command had become much lonelier because of his absence.

Artur Schweitzer, Fritz Aumeier and Heinrich Öhlman were the only senior officers left of Franz and Johann's cohorts, but they had been joined by a new intake of men, most of whom were a little unsure of the new brigadier, despite the easy relationship he had with his three longest-serving officers.

The last man present was First Lieutenant Maximilian Grabner, included in the group only because it would have been unfair to leave him out. He still hadn't progressed much as a soldier, and the newer officers glanced sideways at him, wondering why the hell he was present.

'Gentlemen,' Brigadier Schneider said, standing up. 'As you might have heard through the rumour mill, we have invaded Russia.'

The officers all glanced at each other. The announcement confirmed what they had already heard.

'We have had no specific orders to mobilise, as yet, but we have been asked to be at instant readiness to move out and that our training schedule should be ramped up. I take this to mean that, as soon as less battle-hardened troops are available to relieve us, we will be sent to the Eastern Front.'

A few murmurs broke out among his men, but he let them settle.

'I've received only scant reports so far, but the news has been encouraging. Our troops have broken through the first lines of Soviet defences and have captured large numbers of Red Army soldiers already, breaking the supply lines of those still engaging with our forces.'

Another rash of murmurs broke out, with a hint of excitement this time.

'Don't get carried away,' the Brigadier said, holding up his hand. 'If we are called to fight in Russia, as I fully expect we will, it won't be easy. The Soviet Union is vast, and it has an almost unlimited supply of men who can replace those captured or killed.'

'But, sir, we have the best fighting army in the world, with the best equipment,' Fritz Aumeier said.

Brigadier Schneider nodded.

'We have the most highly-trained troops but, for instance, the Russians are reported to have tanks that can match ours. And they have a formidable air force. This will be our toughest fight, so far.'

Walther Schneider thought the lie was circumspect. Erich Kästner had told him that the Russian tanks were often superior to the German ones, but the men didn't need to know that.

No point in lowering morale.

'When do you think we'll be going, sir?'

'Soon, I hope. I will try and get you a couple of days' leave before we travel east. Make sure you all see your families.'

Their faces reflected the sobering impact his words had on them.

He dismissed them and thought about the Eastern Front. He'd hidden his real fears; that it would be a long, drawn-out war of attrition like the last one. And he cursed being without Franz and Johann Kästner.

~~o~~

'Franz told me about it,' Ruth said. 'I didn't really believe him.'

She'd read about the invasion of Russia in a newspaper one of the locals had handed in.

'How would Franz know we were going to invade?' Manny said.

'The General, silly.' She let out a laugh, but it died in her throat.

Manny blushed.

'All right. I should have realised. Do you think it will help Mama and Papa?'

Ruth's face clouded. Being pregnant had made the separation from her parents even harder. She longed to be able to ask her mother what she should do to be able to keep her baby once it was born.

'It might,' she said, knowing deep down that it wouldn't. The invasion of Denmark, Norway, Holland and France had, if anything, made things worse.

Russia will be no different.

'It may well make us a little safer here,' she said, trying to comfort Manny. 'The Wehrmacht will hardly invade England while they are fighting the Russians.'

She watched as the three Weissberg children played on the grass of the tree-lined square their temporary home looked onto. Their peals of laughter drifted up to the window and, if she ignored the barbed wire, it wasn't an unpleasant place to be on a summer day.

'I wish we knew what was happening to them,' Manny said.

'So do I,' Ruth said, touching her hand to her stomach.

~~o~~

The General replaced the receiver and stepped out of the telephone kiosk in the hotel lobby.

'Is everything quiet at home?' Admiral Canaris asked him.

'Yes. Maria and Eva are out but Antje is in the house. There has been no sign of either the Gestapo or the KriPo hanging around.'

'And nothing from your Zionist friends?'

'Nothing. They are finding it next to impossible to get people out. I'm considering alternative means.'

'As long as the Abwehr isn't involved in any of them, I'll try and help. What are you thinking?'

'I'm contemplating getting them down through France to Spain. Can you fix travel papers for them?'

'No. But I can point you in the direction of someone who can. It's very risky though, and, if you get caught, I can't give you any assistance.'

'That's fair,' the General said.

Admiral Canaris wrote an address in a small pocket diary, then tore out the sheet. He handed it to the General.

'You didn't get it from me.'

'How do you even know about this sort of thing?'

'Oh, from time to time, we need this man's services.'

He chuckled.

The General shook his head. He looked at the address.

'I'll go tomorrow, before I go back home.'

'You'll have to come back to Berlin to pick them back up. It's not the sort of thing you can send through the post.'

The General gave his friend a rueful smile.

'What time will the meeting finish tomorrow?'

'It depends. The biggest thrust of the work is done. Only the details remain.'

'I'm surprised they wanted me here.'

'They think you are a good negotiator.'

The meeting with the Swedish delegation concerning the use of their waters and the blockade of their ports to Russian vessels had gone well. The Führer hadn't been present, but Göring and Keitel had both made an appearance.

As a result of their negotiations, the whole of the Baltic was nigh on impassable for the Russian Navy, and its merchant vessels. There were a few sticking points, but the General doubted whether his presence at the talks was necessary at this stage.

But Canaris and Raeder had insisted that he stay.

'Now,' said Canaris. 'Do you remember that time we were on leave in Berlin, back in '12?'

'Canaris. We were in our twenties. I hope you're not suggesting some late-night club with doubtful provenance?'

'No. I suppose you're right; we're old men now. But it doesn't stop us having a decent meal and maybe a little light entertainment.'

'There are still places like that?'

'In war, when men are fighting, there are always places like that.'

~~o~~

Antje leaned out of the small attic window, looking up and down the street as far as she could see. High up in the house, it gave her an almost uninterrupted view along Hamburger Chaussee, a few hundred yards in both directions.

There were no parked cars; in this area, they would have stood out, because all the houses had driveways.

And there were no loitering men in dark raincoats and brimmed hats. She ran downstairs and, going out by the kitchen door, she crossed the yard to the Nussbaums' cottage and knocked on the door. Yosef let her in. He peered outside before closing the door behind her.

'It's all right,' Antje said. 'I checked before I came. There's no one about.'

'Is there any news?' Miriam said.

Antje looked at her. She was shocked by how much the older woman had aged. She scolded herself. No one suffering the hell the Nussbaums were living through would look any better.

'No,' she said. 'Not yet, I'm afraid.'

She realised the Nussbaums must have seen her coming over and assumed that she had news of Ruth and Manny.

'I'm so sorry,' she said, 'if I got your hopes up. Papa says there is plenty time yet. It could be months.'

'We might not have months,' Miriam said.

'You'll have to forgive us,' Yosef said. 'We're just so anxious. I know that you must be the same.'

'It's horrible, waiting like this,' Antje said, a tear trickling down her cheek. 'I miss them all terribly.'

Miriam's eyes softened.

'I'm sorry,' she said. 'It's not your fault, and I know you're feeling it every bit as much as us.'

'Father is trying his best,' Antje said. 'He's looking at alternatives if the Haganah don't contact you.'

She hesitated, then spoke again.

'Hitler has invaded Russia,' she said.

Both the Nussbaums gasped.

'When?' Yosef said.

'Yesterday. In the early hours. That's what I came to tell you. Our army is making remarkable progress, if you believe what they say on the wireless.'

For a second, a tide of hope flooded over Yosef, but it ebbed again as soon as it had risen.

'A heavy defeat might finish Adolf Hitler,' he said, 'but if the Wehrmacht provides him with a victory, he will be stronger than ever.'

'I'm glad Franz and Johann aren't part of it,' Miriam said, surprising Antje.

'May God be praised,' Yosef said. 'If we could only hear that they're all safe, we would sleep easy, whatever happens.'

'I'll let you know as soon as I hear anything,' Antje said, rising and making for the door. 'In the meantime, if there's anything you need, just ask.'

'Thank you,' Yosef murmured to her, as she slipped out of the door.

CHAPTER 197

'This is nice,' the General said, his tone implying anything but.

'I was told that it was the place to be,' Canaris said, 'but I'm inclined to agree with your sentiments. It is terrible.'

The club was half-full, if that. A lone girl, dressed in what the General thought was supposed to be a seductive outfit, danced with ill-concealed disinterest on the stage. The General turned to his friend.

'So, the invasion,' he said. 'You didn't manage to stop it.'

'No. I tried my best. I told Keitel that the Russians had been building up forces close to the border for almost a year, and that their tanks outnumbered ours and were technologically superior.'

'You lied again?'

'No. That, my friend, was the truth.'

'So, what happened? We're cutting through them in swathes.'

'Infrastructure, as far as we can tell from our initial intelligence. Lack of ammunition for the Soviet armoured vehicles, and fuel. That, and the absence of any functional command. Moscow appears to have been paralysed for at least half a day. By the time they reacted, their troops were surrounded and surrendering in their tens of thousands; maybe hundreds of thousands.'

'Then we'll do to Moscow what we did to Warsaw and Paris?'

'It's not quite the same. The distance and the sheer numbers of soldiers in the Red Army make that unlikely, if they can mobilise them.'

'And if we don't take Moscow?'

'To succeed, we need to reach Moscow, and we must topple Stalin. You must understand the reasons for this invasion.'

'Adolf Hitler hates the communists. Isn't that enough? The rest of them will scrabble to do whatever pleases him.'

'There's more to it than that. It all goes back to Hitler's plan for *living space* for Germany to grow, feed and clothe itself; space for the people of Germany to live life to the full. As far back as '33, Hitler pronounced that the western part of the Soviet Union had the agricultural resources to allow this *Lebensraum*, and that the Caucasus oil fields would fuel our industrial development. In a way, this invasion was inevitable as soon as the National Socialists took power.'

'If we win, Hitler will dominate Europe for a lifetime.'

'Yes. And he will have the resources to attack Britain.'

The General's chest tightened. He tried not to think what would happen to his sons, or to the Nussbaum siblings, if a German invasion of England were successful. Then guilt flooded through him. If the massacres of the Polish campaign were repeated, hundreds of thousands of innocent people would be slaughtered before the Wehrmacht reached Moscow or London.

'It feels terrible to say, but we must fail,' he said.

'That, my friend, is out of our hands. And consider something else. Would living under a triumphant Stalin be any less palatable?'

A scantily clad waitress approached their table.

'Herr Admiral, Herr General, would you like another drink, or perhaps something else? I can bring you the menu.'

'Thank you. We have already eaten,' the General said. 'Do you have any malt whisky?'

He caught a glimpse of Canaris and the girl exchanging a smirk, and he frowned.

'I will ask,' the girl said, still with a smile at the corner of her mouth.

She left, and Canaris turned to his friend, grinning.

'Don't say a word,' the General said, as the penny dropped. 'How was I to know that the menu was for something other than food, and how the devil did this place survive the fall of the Weimar Republic?'

'Look at it,' Canaris said. 'Discreet booths; a very select clientele, situated within a stone's throw of the Reichstag and the Reich ministries. It has rooms upstairs, of course.

When Hitler and Goebbels and Himmler and Göring decided that the common man should be wholesome and want nothing else other than to fight for his country, or to build cars and tanks, they didn't mean themselves. For the elite, these places still exist.'

'Why did you bring me here?'

'To give you a complete picture. When this place is busy, you'll sit cheek by jowl with Reich ministers, senior civil servants, and the cream of the Kriegsmarine, Heer and the Luftwaffe. Then there's the senior clergy, bankers, rich industrialists and, of course, our leaders. Even your friend, the count. I could go on.'

'The count? He comes here?'

'His class were great supporters of Adolf Hitler. They helped him take power.'

'But I thought…'

'He is, shall we say, sympathetic to his downfall now, but he needs to be seen to keep in with the National Socialist elite. It wouldn't do to fall under suspicion.'

'So, he'll…?'

'He's just one of those who might help, when the time comes. He has been talking to us ever since you put him in touch. I thought you should know, seeing as Maria mixes with them.'

'It makes no difference,' the General said, looking around. 'And I don't care what these so-called leaders do in private. It's what they're doing to our nation that keeps me from sleeping at night.'

'Ah. But don't you see? This gives us hope. They're not all zealous monks who only live for their cause, although there are plenty of those. They have weaknesses, like the rest of us and they are rotten to the core. I don't object to places like this, if they are open and honest and available to everyone.'

'You did during the late twenties, when the freedoms of the Weimar Republic were at their peak. I remember you mumbling about the hedonism that would ruin the moral fibre of the nation.'

The admiral laughed. 'If you remember, you agreed with me.'

'Maybe it went too far, but I always felt comfortable with the Weimar government, and I never pined for an imperial Germany again. I mourned the republic's loss when the National Socialists swept it away.'

Canaris laughed again.

'A communist General! It's a wonder you survived.'

'I kept my thoughts to myself. Perhaps I shouldn't have.'

'You were the first person to warn me about Hitler and the National Socialists.'

'It made little difference, speaking out. Now, there's nothing we can do, other than chip away at the bottom of the edifice and hope that it falls down one day.'

'Or that the Soviets will do it for us.'

'Too many soldiers will die before then.'

'I know.'

~~o~~

Maria Kästner listened to the chatter around her, but her mind was on her husband. Up until now, she'd thought of him as a small but significant cog in the country's armed forces, but a realisation was beginning to dawn on her.

Erich knew about the invasion long before anyone else. At this very moment, he's talking with the Führer and Göring and others at the heart of government. He's close to the centre of it all.

A year ago, it would have excited her. She would have dropped hints to her friends, and to people like Frau Hoffmann and Beate Böhm.

Now she was scared.

She shivered, as if a gust of cold air had chilled the warm June day.

She had horrible visions of her husband being too outspoken, that he'd say something controversial and would be shot, like others had, and she and what remained of her family would be ruined.

Please God that he keeps his thoughts to himself.

She knew it couldn't go on like this; it was beginning to affect her nerves but what could she do?

He won't listen to reason. All he cares about is his Jews.

She looked around. For a moment she felt a shaft of envy; every one of these women had husbands who worked for the party, or supported it.

I'll give him an ultimatum. If the Nussbaums don't go, I will. And I'll take the girls with me. Mama would be delighted to have us.

'A penny for your thoughts, my dear.'

She turned, smiling.

'Oh, nothing much. I'm so glad you could manage today, Countess,' she said. 'The ladies were so thrilled, and just look at the turnout.'

'I was delighted. I have enjoyed myself and, as I told you, please call me Margarethe when it's just the two of us.'

CHAPTER 198

In separate wagons, neither family knowing about the other, Yosef's and Miriam's parents, along with Miriam's brother and his wife, had arrived at Radegast freight station, the arrival and departure point for any Jew entering or leaving the Łódź ghetto.

It was the oldest ghetto in Poland, second only in size to the one in Warsaw, 130 kilometres to the east. The Germans had renamed it, and the city surrounding it, as Litzmannstadt, but nearly all the ghetto's occupants spoke of it by its Polish name, Łódź.

Chaim Rumkowski, the head of the Judenrat, the ghetto's Jewish council, had spoken to the new arrivals later that day.

'We are in charge, here in the ghetto. If it runs smoothly, the KriPo and the Gestapo leave us alone. If we work hard and make money for the Germans in their factories and workshops, we will be fed, watered, and provided with accommodation. And we will live, so, if you feel that we are being too harsh with you, or if some of our decisions don't sit well with you, just remember that we are doing it to keep as many of you alive as possible.'

He'd dismissed them, and they'd queued at the Judenrat house at Ul. Rybna 8 to receive details of their new accommodation.

Neither family had spotted the other in the long line of weary deportees, and each had trudged off to their allotted rooms, sharing with strangers, three doors apart on Ul. Franciszkańska, surrounded by Jews from Schleswig-Holstein, and those from Hamburg.

But it didn't take long, in the way that Jewish communities bind together, for Leonie Sachs to hear the name Nussbaum being mentioned and, within a few days of arriving in the cattle wagons, she'd visited Renate Nussbaum and had embraced Yosef's mother, both women in floods of tears. The families had engineered a swap, and the Nussbaums had moved into the room above the Sachs', sleeping, cooking, and eating together with what little food they could scavenge.

And most evenings, the talk would come round to Yosef and Miriam, and the children.

~~o~~

The Łódź ghetto was home to over 160,000 Jews, crammed into an area of four square kilometres, around seven persons to each available room.

At its western end, Ul. Zgierska, one of the city's major thoroughfares, bisected it, cutting off a smaller area of ghetto which was accessed by two footbridges from the main ghetto. This smaller enclave was further split by Bolesława Limanowskiego into two unequal, smaller, ghettos with one footbridge connecting them.

Despite the Nussbaums and the Liewermann family being well acquainted, they didn't come across each other during their stay in Łódź.

Emil Liewermann and his two children had a small room to themselves in number 6, Ul. Ciesielska, in the smallest of the three interconnected ghettos.

'Why don't we ever go to the large ghetto?' Fischel asked.

'We would have to take the footbridge on Limanowskiego, walk through the other small ghetto, then cross one of the footbridges across Ul. Zgierska. And what for? Everything we need is here.'

Fischel sighed.

Emil Liewermann was unusual in Łódź Ghetto. He didn't work in one of the factories.

When he'd arrived, he'd scavenged a few tools, and bits and pieces of wood, and had set up a small workshop in one half of their living space, making small pieces of furniture for sale or barter.

His pieces, of surprising quality, had caught the eye of one of the ghetto policemen and, from then on, almost all the furniture he produced was snapped up by the German officials who ran the ghetto.

'Keep your head down, turn out as many of these as you can, and you and your children might survive,' one of his neighbours had told him.

And they did. They rarely left the room they called home. Both children helped in the production of his furniture; Rebeka sewed any upholstery that was needed, and Fischel sanded and polished the finished pieces, ready to be collected by a string of officials who valued the quality of Emil's workmanship.

And the extra food, and medicines when needed, kept Emil and his family safe and well. And apart.

Neither the Nussbaums nor the Sachs had occasion to visit the smallest ghetto.

CHAPTER 199

[23/06/1941 Monday]

KIELER JÜDISCHES FREIHEITSNACHRICHTENBLATT

Volume 100

28th of Sivan, 5701

RUSSIA INVADED. GERMAN TROOPS ON THE LONG MARCH TO MOSCOW.

Early on Sunday morning, the Molotov-Ribbentrop Pact was ripped up by the invasion of Soviet-occupied Poland and the Soviet Union itself by an estimated three million troops of the Wehrmacht, supported by extensive artillery barrages and bombing of Polish and Russian cities.

The KJF has expected this invasion for some time and believes that it fits in with the Third Reich's greed for natural resources to further its expansionist aims, and for land suitable for homes required by its growing Aryan population.

What does this mean for the Jews of Germany?

It is the KJF's view that nothing will change. The drive to eliminate Jews from Germany will continue. It now has a name.

Judenrein.

This cleansing of its Jewish presence can apply to a village, a town, a city, a country, or as the KJF suspects, Europe itself.

Deportation, or "resettlement" in official language, will continue to gather pace, with the Generalgouvernement area of Poland being the preferred destination for German Jews.

We have also received confirmed reports that Jews from Holland, Belgium, France and Norway are being transported in large numbers to Poland and that new ghettos and concentration camps are being set up on a weekly basis to cope with the influx.

The KJF has also heard worrying reports, as yet unsubstantiated, that the advancing Wehrmacht has orders to treat Soviet Jews in a similar fashion, perhaps with a further expansion of the concentration camp system in Russia and the Baltic States.

This falls in line with the National Socialist's claim that the invasion of Russia is in self-defence to the Jewish-Bolshevik threat from the east. Ironically, the Jews of Russia and its outlying states have suffered pogrom after pogrom over the centuries, and Jews travelling westwards have always found refuge in Germany.

The only glimmer of hope the KJF harbours is that the two despots, Hitler and Stalin, are locked in a battle that will finish only when they destroy each other.

WORD OF THE WEEK

Judenjagden: Jew hunts, a word from the Eastern Front. Waffen-

SS men of the Einsatzgruppen take part in these Jew hunts. The number of Jews killed are referred to as Stücke.

~~o~~

At risk of death, copies of the KJF were distributed to the remaining Jews of Kiel and Schleswig-Holstein, and to those in a few towns and cities further afield. One found its way through the letterbox of the Nussbaums' cottage; another lay on General Kästner's desk, in an anonymous brown envelope.

A few other notable friends of the Jews, working under the radar of the authorities, received a copy.

A Jew caught trying to purchase a bottle of milk to help feed his infant son, whose mother's breasts had dried up through lack of food, had a copy of the *Kieler Jüdisches Freiheitsnachrichtenblatt* in his pocket when he was arrested.

The man was taken to Gestapo Headquarters, searched, interrogated, and when he was found to have no further useful information, shot.

His copy of the KJF landed on Heinrich Güllich's desk.

~~o~~

Yosef finished reading. The isolation from the Jewish community that had been imposed on them was total, and the KJF was a welcome reminder that there were still a few Jews remaining in Kiel.

He hadn't seen or heard it delivered but he said a silent thank you to the brave people who published it, and those who risked their freedom delivering it.

He looked at Miriam. She hadn't quite recovered from the beating the Gestapo had meted out, and he still saw her flinch every now and again when she stretched to lift something.

She sat, mending clothes to keep her hands busy, staring into space. Yosef worried that she'd been doing much more of that in recent days, but he knew where her mind was when her eyes became glassy, and her hands stopped moving.

Are they safe somewhere in England, or are they at the bottom of the cold, dark depths of the Nordsee?

He handed her the KJF, touching her lightly on the arm to get her attention.

'Here,' he said, giving her a gentle smile.

She took it and glanced at the headlines, but she didn't read it.

'We'll hear from them soon,' Yosef said, but her face told him that she didn't believe him.

'What have we done?' she said, in a voice so soft, he almost didn't hear her.

'We gave them a chance,' he said. 'You know what would have happened to them here; the Gestapo nearly killed you.'

'They wouldn't have done that to the children. They only want me because they know I tricked them out of the money, and because the General protects us. I sometimes think that Güllich hates him more than he hates us.'

'The Gestapo loathe him because he sticks by us. I worry that it will end up drawing the General and his family down with us.'

~~o~~

Miriam didn't contradict Yosef. She knew how much Erich Kästner and his sons had done to help them.

And Antje too. Twice she has taken risks that could have seen her go to prison. But it could all be for nothing, if Ruth and Manny are drowned, and we can do nothing but live in constant fear.

She looked at the KJF again and read it without taking much in. She knew she should care about the Russian Jews, and those from the rest of Europe, but she was exhausted with worry and couldn't find it in herself to add more sorrow to the load she already carried.

Stücke. Pieces. *That's all we are to them.*

A soft knock on the kitchen window interrupted her dark thoughts. She saw Yosef jump up and go to the door, but supposed that it was just Antje again.

She saw her husband standing in the doorway, looking around. He turned to her and shrugged.

~~o~~

Yosef was puzzled; he could see no one, but there had been a tap on the window, unless it had been a bird.

He looked around again.

'Sssssst.'

A hiss came from the direction of the open garage. Albert had forgotten to close one of the doors when he'd taken the car out that morning.

Yosef walked across the yard and slipped inside, peering into the gloom. His heart thumped within his chest.

'Yosef Nussbaum?'

'Yes. Who is it?'

'I have a message for you. From our friends in Palestine.'

Yosef's pulse raced and his breathing quickened.

'The Hagan… ?'

'Quiet. You never know when it's safe.'

'You have arranged for us to go?'

'Yes. You have friends in Palestine.'

Itsik and Esther! What wonderful people.

'Yes. Did they pay for us? We have money.'

He froze.

The General. He's away. I can't get our money.

'I'm told most of it came from Germany.'

Tears stung Yosef's eyes.

Somehow, the General had got the money to Itsik.

'When do we go?'

'This evening. In around an hour. Here are your papers. You are Herr and Frau Kühn. You are ethnic Germans living in Prague, and you were visiting family in Schleswig-Holstein. A car will pick you up and take you to the railway station at Melsdorf. You will change at Rendsburg for Hanover, then take the overnight train to Prague via Magdeburg, Leipzig, and Dresden. Your tickets are all there, with your travel passes. Do you understand?'

Yosef nodded. It sounded a roundabout route, but it avoided getting on the train at Kiel Bahnhof and precluded them having to travel through Berlin. He could see the sense of it. The man continued.

'Someone will meet you in Prague and give you a new set of papers. You will travel to Budapest in Hungary, then through Romania. You'll change trains at Bucharest for Varna in Bulgaria; it's on the Black Sea coast. From there, a boat will take you to Turkey. You will be driven to the Syrian border, where one of our people from Palestine will collect you, and take you across the border, through Syria, into Palestine.'

'Thank you.'

The man shrugged.

'It will be dangerous, and your papers will only hold up to superficial scrutiny. If they interrogate you, they will find out you are Jews and torture you.'

'I know. We have already been… questioned.'

'Tell no one you've gone,' the man said. 'Take no more than you'd expect to carry for a week's travel, as if you were returning home from a holiday in Germany. It's the fashionable thing for ethnic Germans to do, now that the Reich encompasses most of Europe.'

'What about money? We have a little.'

The man shrugged again.

'Take what you can. You are good German citizens. Unless it is tens of thousands of Reichsmarks, it will not arouse suspicion.'

The General. He can send our money on.

Yosef knew that he couldn't leave without letting the General know. He would write a

618

note or tell Antje.

He heard the man talking.

'The password is *Einstein*,' the man said, 'when you are asked.'

Yosef smiled, remembering Ruth's story from school.

The greatest German scientist.

They shook hands.

'Be ready,' the man warned, then he was gone.

Yosef hurried back to the cottage.

He told Miriam what the man had said.

'We must hurry,' he said.

'We can't. We don't know if Ruth and Manny are safe.'

'There's nothing we can do about it. If they're safe, and we want to see them again, this is our only chance.'

'But...'

'Get ready,' he said, harshly, gripping her arm. 'We have no time to lose.'

By the time he'd lifted down two small cases from the top of the wardrobe and returned to the kitchen, he saw that she'd stirred herself and was beginning to grab a few items to pack.

'Take nothing personal that could identify us as Jews.'

He turned away to hide his shame at the way he was treating her, but he couldn't afford to be hampered by emotion at a time like this.

He retrieved the little spare money and the few valuables they had from their hiding place and put them in his pocket. Despite what the man had said, he couldn't bring himself to leave the General in the dark.

When Miriam went upstairs, he slipped out of the cottage and crossed to the big house. Frau Kästner and Eva hadn't returned, so he climbed the stairs and knocked on Antje's door.

She appeared in her paint-smeared smock, with a brush in her hand.

'Yosef,' she said, 'what's the matter?'

'We're going. The Haganah are coming to collect us shortly.'

Antje gasped.

'That's wonderful,' she said, a confusion of joy and pain on her face. 'It's terrible that Papa isn't here to see you off, but he'll be so pleased that you're going, at long last.'

'Say goodbye to him for us, and please give him this, Miss Antje.'

She took the brown envelope from him. Tears gathered and spilled down her cheeks.

'Ruth and Manny...' she said, her face pale.

'I know. Miriam is beside herself.'

'Once you get to Palestine you can find out. The British are in charge. You'll be able to send a letter. If not, try the Red Cross.'

Yosef's face lit up.

'I didn't think of that. That will help Miriam. She's so worried.'

'We all are.'

'I'd better go. We need to be ready.'

'I'll come and say goodbye to Miriam,' Antje said.

CHAPTER 200

The farewell was harrowing. Miriam had practically brought Antje up. She thought of her as a second daughter, and she knew that to Antje, she was as much of a mother as Maria was.

'I'll miss you terribly, Miriam,' Antje said through a flood of tears, 'but you can come back once this horror is over.'

'We will,' Miriam said. 'After the war.'

Miriam nodded and hugged her daughter's closest friend, squeezing her tight to hide the lie on her face. She would never return to Germany if they got out. And she would make sure her children didn't come back.

Antje left, and Miriam was relieved, not wanting to prolong the pain, knowing that she needed time to say goodbye to the house that held all her memories.

Half an hour later, the car arrived. They closed the door of the Drachensee cottage for the last time.

The seven-kilometre journey to Melsdorf station took just under fifteen minutes. The Haganah driver explained that, although Hassee and Russee were closer, the train they were to catch didn't stop at those stations. Before they got out of the car, he wished them good luck.

As the train pulled out, she saw the car turn and head back in the direction of Kiel.

~~o~~

The General phoned around eight. Maria and Eva still weren't home, and Antje answered.

'How's everyone?' he asked.

'Oh, well,' Antje said. 'There's no one home but me, but give me your telephone number and I'll get Mama to call you back later, when she gets in.'

She wrote down the hotel's number and his room number, and chatted for a few minutes about her day, and about his time in Berlin. If there was someone listening to the call, she hoped they wouldn't hear the concern in her voice.

After putting the phone down, Antje checked her purse for change, threw on her coat and left the house. She walked the short distance to the telephone kiosk, glancing up and down Hamburger Chaussee for any sign of the Gestapo.

She picked up the handset and gave the operator the number for the hotel. A pleasant lady on the hotel switchboard put her through to her father's room.

~~o~~

'Antje, what's wrong?'

'Nothing. Our friends are on their way. I just thought you'd want to know.'

The General's stomach lurched.

This is it. God speed them.

'That's great news. Did you speak with them?'

'Yes. A car picked them up a couple of hours ago.'

The General was impressed with his daughter's discretion, even on a public telephone line.

Who knows if an overzealous operator is listening in?

'That's good. They have a chance. I only wish they'd had news of the others before they left.'

'They can find out when they get there,' Antje said.

'True. They'll be well looked after when they arrive.'

He smiled at the thought of the welcome Esther and Itsik Weichmann would give the Nussbaums.

'I'm sure they will,' Antje said.

'Have a word with Mama. She'll be wondering why there are no lights on in the cottage.'

'Yes, Papa. I'll think of something.'

'Excellent. We'll speak further when I return to Kiel.'

The General put down the phone, content that Antje would make up a suitable excuse to give to her mother for the Nussbaums' absence.

She is a bright young woman.

CHAPTER 201

Yosef almost panicked at Rendsburg when, leaving the train, they were guided into the queue waiting to have their papers checked by the two OrPo constables, and he watched with envy as the rest of the passengers walked through the ticket gate unmolested.

Two people ahead of them in line were asked to step aside and were taken through a doorway into an office on the side of the concourse. Yosef felt Miriam grip his hand and squeeze it. He took a deep breath and fought down the bile of fear.

'Papers.'

Yosef handed over their tickets and travel passes. The young policeman scrutinised them, then looked at Yosef and Miriam.

'Have a wonderful trip, Herr Kühn, Frau Kühn.'

He handed their papers back and nodded them through.

Yosef gave the policeman a nod of thanks.

So, this is what it's like if you're Aryan. Policemen are pleasant to you.

It took all Yosef's strength of will not to run from the station. Instead, he checked the departure board and found the platform for their train to Hanover.

'There will be another check at the ticket barrier,' Miriam murmured to him, squeezing his hand again. 'Don't worry. The papers are good.'

Yosef gave her a smile, but it was forced.

They approached the barrier. This time, there was only one policeman, and a ticket inspector. They showed their passes and the Reichsbahn official checked their tickets, and they were through.

They chose a compartment that was almost full, and they took the only two vacant seats. They'd been told to do this if they could – provided their fellow passengers were travelling the whole way to Hanover, no soldier, policeman or SS storm trooper home on leave would sit next to them.

They nodded to their fellow passengers, three older ladies and another couple, with a daughter Miriam reckoned to be about Ruth's age.

There were murmured greetings all round, then each group withdrew into their own cloistered circle. Yosef and Miriam hardly spoke, fearful that they would let something slip that would alert their fellow passengers to the fact that they were travelling with *criminals*.

Even the gentle sway of the carriage and the rhythmic clicking of the wheels that lulled their fellow passengers into intermittent slumber couldn't ease Miriam and Yosef's gnawing fear, but they hid it as well as they could, holding one another's hands beneath Miriam's shawl.

The couple with the teenage daughter left the train at Hamburg and the Nussbaums held their breaths as a stream of people passed in the corridor, looking for a seat. A group of soldiers passed, and one of them pointed at the spare seats, but the others shook their heads, wanting a compartment that would seat them all. They passed down the train as it pulled out of the station.

'Try not to stare the next time,' Miriam whispered to Yosef, when they'd gone.

At Uelzen, a young couple took two of the vacant seats and smiled politely at Yosef and Miriam, and at the three older ladies. The Nussbaums watched them with relief, so wrapped up were they in each other that even polite conversation wasn't expected.

One of the older ladies looked at Yosef curiously and for a brief second, he was filled with horror at the possibility that she was one of the ladies Frau Kästner socialised with, and that she'd recognised him.

A bead of sweat formed on his top lip and he dabbed at it with his handkerchief, but the woman turned away with a curt smile and looked out of the window into the darkness.

At Hanover, they had to face the same security checks when they alighted from the train but, approaching eleven o'clock, the station was quiet, and the solitary policeman appeared to be half asleep, cursorily viewing their passes as they made their way through the barrier and descended the steps to the tunnel that led under the tracks to the station hall.

'The train isn't up yet,' Yosef said, his eyes darting up and down the departures board.

'Stop fidgeting and sit down,' Miriam said. 'It's not due for a while.'

He took a seat next to her in the large station hall, trying not to look at the patrolling policemen. Every so often, he glanced at the board, then the clock, as the minutes ticked by with still no mention of the overnight to Prague.

'I hope it's not delayed,' Yosef said. 'Or cancelled.'

'Where would we go?' Miriam said, glancing around.

'We'd have to find a hotel, or a guest house,' Yosef said, biting his fingernail.

Will our papers be good enough?

He looked up at the board for about the twentieth time. A tile was being changed as he watched.

Platform ten. 11:05. Prague.

He looked at his watch. It was five to eleven. He nudged Miriam and they descended the stairs to the walkway under the tracks.

'It's the furthest platform away,' he said. 'Hurry.'

'We have plenty time,' Miriam said. 'We mustn't appear to be rushing.'

Yosef, who had been almost trotting, slowed down, realising she was right.

As they climbed the stairs to the platform, they saw two policemen standing by the ticket inspector. As their heads emerged above the level of the platform, Miriam tensed, and tightened her grip on Yosef's hand.

He looked through the cast-iron railings. Two men, with the unmistakable appearance of Gestapo, stood beside the policemen.

It was too late to turn round. It would have aroused the policemen's suspicions and, if questioned, a story about finding themselves at the wrong platform would not hold water if they were asked to show their tickets.

Yosef, almost numb with panic, handed their tickets and the passes over. The policemen scrutinised their photographs, glancing up at their faces.

Miriam's injuries had mostly healed, and she'd used a little makeup to hide the few remaining blemishes.

I hope it's enough.

He could see out of the corner of his eye that the two Gestapo men were taking an interest.

'Identity cards, please.'

Yosef fished inside his jacket pocket and handed over the cards. They looked real enough but, as the policeman examined them, one of the Gestapo men held out his hand. The policeman passed them over.

Yosef saw a train approaching on the far side of the platform and wondered if he could run fast enough to jump in front of it, dragging Miriam with him; a quick, painless death would be better than the slow, agonising, lingering one that they would suffer at the hands of the Gestapo.

The leather-coated man handed the cards back to the policeman, who gave them back to Yosef.

'Have a good journey, sir,' he said. The Reichsbahn inspector directed them to the train's guard, who checked their reservations.

'Coach 3, sir. You'll find your seats in a compartment halfway along. Numbers 43 and 44. If you'd like coffee, or a little supper, call first at the restaurant car. It's open for an hour, then again from seven in the morning.'

'Thank you. Can you tell me what time we get to Prague?'

'Yes, sir. 8.45. Will that be all, sir?'

They thanked him and walked towards the front of the train, Yosef's legs almost giving way as fear turned to relief. He would have stumbled but for Miriam's grip, and his face flushed with shame at his weakness.

They found their seats and stowed their bags in the rack above, then walked to the dining car two carriages along. It was busy, and they had to wait a few minutes to be seated. To their horror, half of the carriage's occupants were in military clothing; army officers, largely, but four SS men in their distinctive black sat laughing at one of the tables, a bottle of Schnapps in the centre. Judging by their loudness, it wasn't their first bottle of the evening.

A waiter showed them to a table for two, on the opposite side of the carriage from the larger tables the soldiers occupied. Miriam ordered Gulashsuppe and Yosef opted for the Bratkartoffeln. Too nervous to order wine, they asked for a jug of water and asked for hot chocolate to be served after they'd finished their main course.

'And desert, madam?' the waiter said. 'The crêpes are delicious,' he added.

'We'll both have them,' Miriam said, ignoring Yosef's frown.

'We have to behave as if we're a good German couple returning from our first visit to the Fatherland after years of exile,' Miriam whispered to him once the older man had left.

'Shh,' Yosef hissed, closing his eyes in horror.

Miriam put her hand over his.

'Just eat,' she said, not unkindly. 'We've got this far.'

~~o~~

When they returned to their compartment, two people had taken seats opposite them. Not, as they had dreaded, Wehrmacht personnel, but two brothers, perhaps in their sixties, returning to Vienna after visiting Hanover on business.

'We always travel through Nuremberg, but this train suited us better,' the older one said. 'We will travel from Prague to Vienna in the morning.'

Yosef and Miriam took their seats, lifting the neatly folded travelling rugs provided by the Reichsbahn and spreading them over their legs.

'We are returning home after visiting relatives in Rendsburg,' Miriam said. 'Our nephews, Franz and Johann, served in Austria for a while.'

Yosef swallowed, and hoped that the men had never visited Rendsburg.

'It was the proudest day of our lives, when the German Army marched into Austria,' the man said.

'And it wasn't bad for business either.' The younger brother chuckled.

'What is it you do?' Miriam asked, much to Yosef's dismay.

'We make binoculars. Of exceptional quality,' the first brother said.

'The Wehrmacht like them,' his younger brother said. 'We provide 2000 pairs a month. Our output has trebled since the Anschluss.'

'That is wonderful,' Miriam said, turning to Yosef. 'Isn't it?'

'Yes, indeed,' Yosef said, smiling at the two men, surprised that his voice sounded normal.

'You have been in Prague long?'

'A few years now,' Miriam said.

Yosef was happy to play the hen-pecked husband with a talkative wife who rarely let him get a word in edgeways, but he hoped the conversation would lull before Miriam gave something away about them that would raise suspicion.

'And what is it that you do?' the younger of the two brothers asked.

'I have a small garage just outside Prague. My wife runs a café.'

'Ah. It is a lovely country, I'm told, and Prague is famous for its beautiful buildings. We've never been. Perhaps we should, now that it's part of the Reich.'

'Indeed,' Yosef said, relief flooding through him that the men weren't familiar with the city the Kühns were supposed to be inhabitants of. Still, he was thankful for the short crib sheets that the Haganah man had made them read during the car ride to the station, with the skeleton of their fictional lives.

The first brother yawned and excused himself.

'We've had a hectic few days, and we can't afford to take time off tomorrow,' his sibling said. 'I'm afraid we'll have to try and get a few hours' sleep or suffer in the morning.'

'We understand,' Miriam said. 'We've been travelling a while, and sleep would be most welcome.'

The brothers were snoring within minutes. For Yosef and Miriam, fearful and not used to travelling, sleep eluded them.

'How do you keep so calm?' Yosef whispered. 'Chatting away as if we were on holiday?'

'They have no suspicions about us,' she said, so quietly he could hardly make out her words. 'They'll wake up in the morning and go for breakfast. We will pretend to be asleep.'

We will go along when they come back, and we'll make polite conversation for a few minutes until we arrive at Prague. If we'd been untalkative or rude, it may have just planted a seed of doubt, and you know what it is like in the Third Reich. People relish being good citizens and reporting their fellow countrymen.'

'You're right,' Yosef said. 'I just don't know how you can appear so calm.'

She smiled at him.

'I think of something better. Being with Ruth and Manny again. Seeing Esther, and little Miriam Rosa. Our parents. The waiting was worse. Now, we have a chance.'

He looked at her, amazed as ever.

A few hours before, he'd had to shock her into moving. Now she was the strong one.

'I love you, Miriam Nussbaum,' he said, in her ear.

~~o~~

[24/06/1941 Tuesday]

The train drew to a slow halt at the platform in Prague. The two brothers bade them goodbye and, as soon as it stopped, they rushed to catch their connection to Vienna.

The train hadn't stopped at the border crossing; their passports had been checked between Dresden and Prague, around breakfast time.

On the platform, the chatter of German was the only language that could be heard; few of the train's passengers had been Czechs.

It's a German world now.

Throngs of German soldiers bustled around them, a few of them in the arrogant black of the SS. National Socialist flags hung everywhere around the concourse.

'It's as if we haven't left Germany,' Miriam whispered.

'We haven't,' Yosef replied under his breath.

'Where's the café?' Miriam said, her eyes taking in the ornate dome of the magnificent ticket hall, despite the circumstances.

'We go out the main entrance and turn left. At the national museum we turn left again onto Schwerinova. Locals might still call it Fochova; the Germans changed its name last year. The café is about 200 metres down the street. Café Dobrovský is its name.'

There were few policemen; other than directing traffic, the Gestapo had taken over their role. It was a black-coated Gestapo officer who checked the Nussbaums' papers, waving them through with a polite nod. Miriam allowed herself a brief smile.

We must look like ordinary Germans.

~~o~~

They found the café and took the corner booth they'd been told to sit at. Yosef ordered two coffees and looked around. The place was deserted, save for the proprietor and a bored waitress, who brought their drinks. Five minutes later, the bell above the door rang and a large man in a drab coat and a fur hat entered. He looked across at them, waved, and smiled. He asked the café owner to send over another coffee, then took a seat opposite the Nussbaums.

'How are you?' he said, as if they were old acquaintances.

'We're well. And you?'

'Excellent.' The man lowered his voice. 'I was at the library, looking for a book by that scientist fellow. The one with the hair. What's his name?'

'Einstein?' Yosef said, following the man's lead by talking in low tones.

'That's the one. Albert Einstein. Remarkable man.'

'Indeed. Although I'm surprised any of his books are in the library.'

'They weren't. They've all been removed. It's a shame; I used to teach physics at the university, and he is worth reading.'

'You're a teacher?'

'I still teach night classes but during the day I work in a factory. They closed the university after the student uprising in '39.'

'I'm surprised they let you teach at all.'

'I'm adopted. Only my adoptive parents know that I'm a Jew. My parents died when I was a toddler.'

'How did you know it was us?'

'I followed you from the station. I saw you get off the train.'

'Ah.'

'I have your new papers here. You will be travelling as the Breitlings. You are looking to purchase property by the Black Sea. As German citizens, you have some privileges in the outlying corners of the Third Reich.'

Yosef reached into his pocket.

'What do we do with these?' he said, starting to pull the documents from his pocket that had got them to Prague.

'Not here,' the man said, putting his newspaper down on the table. 'Go to the toilet and tuck them in behind the cistern. I'll collect them once you're gone. Your new passes and tickets are in the newspaper. Pick it up as if you are going to read it and take it with you.'

Yosef nodded.

'Why do we need new papers? These have been perfectly good.'

'Your names were taken at the border crossing, remember. They will be checked again. If you crossed further borders with the same papers, and you were supposed to be travelling no further than Prague, it might alert suspicion.'

'I see,' Yosef said. 'I'll have to remember I'm not Herr Kühn now.'

'Make sure you do. Your train leaves in an hour. Arrive at the station no more than ten minutes before departure. It's riddled with Gestapo, so you don't want to be there too early.'

'What should we do until then?'

'Go shopping, or for another coffee. You're Germans. You own the world.'

He laughed.

Yosef excused himself and went to the toilet. He slid their now redundant papers behind the cistern as instructed. He had a sudden need to urinate, so he stood in front of the bowl and sighed as the stream released the press of his bladder. He washed his hands and dried them, then opened the door.

Two leather-coated men were standing by the table Miriam and their Haganah contact were sitting at.

Miriam's hand was on the newspaper as she looked up and saw Yosef emerge from the toilet. The two Gestapo men turned to look at Yosef and he saw her remove their documents from the newspaper and place them on her lap.

'Papers, please,' one of the Gestapo men said. His tone was respectful.

Yosef's hand went into his inside pocket. He fished about for a second, a puzzled look on his face, then turned to Miriam, who had lifted her bag onto her lap while the Gestapo men had been watching him.

'Ah,' he said, his face lighting up. 'I gave them to my wife.' He turned to Miriam.

'Show them to the gentlemen, dear,' he said.

~~o~~

Miriam handed the Gestapo man their travel papers, for all the world as if she'd just taken them out of her bag. She gripped the table to stop her hand trembling.

It's like the Weichmanns' flat all over again.

The man handed the papers back to her and turned to the Haganah man.

'And yours, sir,' he said.

The big man handed over his identity card and the Gestapo man looked at it.

'You know each other?'

'A little,' the Haganah man said. 'We've met in passing a few times. When I came in, I recognised Herr Breitling and we got talking over a coffee.'

He turned to Yosef.

'What time is your train?'

'Just after ten.' Yosef looked at his watch. It was half-past nine. He looked at the Gestapo men.

'On you go,' the taller of the two men said.

Yosef and Miriam smiled at them, and at their large Czech friend.

The large man nodded.

'Auf wiedersehen. Have a good trip. I'll more than likely bump into you when you get back.'

'Yes. Take care,' Yosef said, opening the door for Miriam. They stepped outside, trying to appear unhurried, and closed the door behind them.

~~o~~

'Now, my Czech friend,' the first Gestapo man said, as the Nussbaums walked up the street. 'We're going to have a little chat. Just because you are on nodding terms with these good German citizens, it doesn't mean you haven't got anything to hide.'

'I'm just a hard-working Czech who has one or two German friends. I've never hidden my admiration for your country, and its recent accomplishments.'

'That may well be, but can we really trust any Slav?' the man said, turning to his colleague.

'I'll have you know that my mother is half-German, and my father's grandfather was from Munich.'

The two Gestapo men looked at each other. The instructions they'd been given was to go easy on the Czech population; von Neurath, the Reichsprotektor of Bohemia and Moravia, the rump of the former Czechoslovakia, was convinced that many Czechs could be Aryanised. Hitler himself had indicated that the Czech population, on the whole, should be encouraged to cooperate as much as possible, to maximise the industrial output of the country, crucial to the expansion of the Wehrmacht.

'And where do you work?' the second Gestapo officer asked.

'In the CKD factory. Making tanks for the German Army. You can check.'

This much was true, if they bothered following up on his story, but it hid the fact that a significant number of the tanks they produced had defects, most of which wouldn't show up for months, or even years.

The Gestapo man stared at the large Czech.

'I have your name. I will run a check on it later.'

He turned to his colleague.

'Hans, get me a cup of coffee. I'm going for a piss.'

'It's so wild,' Ruth said, looking out over the sound to the Calf of Man, the small island off the south tip of the Isle of Man.

'Only the lighthouse keepers live there,' Herr Weissberg said.

Ruth, Manny and the Weissberg family had walked the two-and-a-half miles from Port St. Mary. They intended to spend the afternoon in the port, down at the beach, when they returned.

It hadn't just been the children who were excited as the early bus had trundled its way from Douglas. Their parents, and Ruth and Manny, had been looking forward to getting out of the town, and the confines of the Hutchinson Square area, since the island's authorities had announced that day passes for Jewish internees would be granted, allowing them to travel to other parts of the island.

'Look at the tide,' Manny shouted, pointing to Calf Sound, the turbulent stretch of water between them and the island. It was littered with rocks and a couple of smaller islands, and the sea between them was white with breaking crests and peaks, whipped up by the strong current and the brisk westerly breeze.

'Franz and Johann would love this,' he said, running down to the water's edge, showing the children the swirling eddies.

'Can we go swimming?' they pleaded. 'Please.'

Manny turned.

'It's too dangerous,' he said. 'You'd be swept away by the currents. Wait until we're back at Port St. Mary.'

He took the children's hands and gripped them, just in case. The memory of being alone, drowning in the North Sea still haunted him.

He looked at his sister. She'd been out of sorts in recent weeks, but he knew, like him, that she was missing their parents. And she was hurting for Franz most of all.

She was staring out to sea, oblivious to the children's laughter and squeals.

'Are you all right?' he said, but she didn't hear him. The children let go of his hands and ran to their father.

Manny moved towards Ruth, and was startled when she let out a cry, and pointed.

'Sturmtaucher,' she yelled to him.

He flushed with embarrassment for her and looked round to see if Herr or Frau Weissberg had heard her. He knew she was struggling to cope, but if she was seeing visions, it was a worrying development.

Have the turbulent waters of Calf Sound triggered memories of the storm? Of the heaving decks of the yacht?

'Ruth,' he said, taking hold of her arm. 'We're safe now. We made it, remember?'

She turned to him, puzzled.

'What are you talking about?'

She pointed out towards the Calf.

'Sturmtaucher. Look.'

Manny looked and saw what she was pointing at; the small, dark birds, swooping low over the waves and the foam, flashing white when they turned, their pointed wings steering them across the waves.

He sighed with relief and watched her. A tear trickled down her cheek and he put his arm around her shoulder. He was taller than her now and had begun to fill out. She took hold of his hand and took out a handkerchief to blow her nose.

~~o~~

'It's silly, isn't it,' Ruth said. 'A flock of seabirds, and I'm bubbling like a schoolgirl.'

'You're not silly,' he said. 'You look at Antje's drawing every night. She was your best friend. It's natural to feel that way.'

'Thanks. She was the best of friends. To you and to me. She risked herself for us, you know.'

'I know. They all did; well, most of them.'

'Don't be hard on Frau Kästner. She was just looking after her family. And Eva took her mother's part.'

He scowled. She tried not to smile.

He can still be a little boy in ways.

'It's complicated, the Kästners,' she said, as they watched the children run to the water again, drawn to it. 'The General, Franz, Johann and Antje, were the bravest and most decent people I've ever known, but they're the exception. Frau Kästner and Eva were better than many of the people we know. If we only realised, I would wager that there are more good people than you think who didn't like what was happening but were too frightened to speak out.'

'They abandoned us, and some of them revelled in it.'

'I know. And I'll never forget. But there were acts of kindness too. Remember Rosa's neighbour. And the headmaster at my school.'

'I suppose.'

'It will be over, one day, and we can all return.'

'I'll never go back,' he said, shocking her.

'We must, to see our grandparents, and our friends.'

'I might visit, but I'll never live there. I couldn't. Not after what they've done.'

She looked at him. Manny had the faraway gaze in his eyes, and she shuddered.

'We'll see. We still have to get through this first. Come and rescue these children before they do end up in the water.'

'I know what that feels like.' He grinned, breaking the mood.

She took a last look out at the swooping birds and smiled. For Antje.

CHAPTER 203

'I'll be glad to get out of this place,' Miriam said, looking out of the window at a train arriving at the next platform, 'even if it is a beautiful city.'

'That was too close for comfort. We're lucky they didn't come in a few moments earlier.'

They'd had to force themselves to walk at a normal pace when they left Café Dobrovský, for fear that the two Gestapo officers would be watching them. On the way, they'd found a seat in Vrchuckeho Sady, the park across the road from the station, and familiarised themselves with their new identities. They'd made it onto the train without incident.

The carriage jerked as the train began to move. Yosef let out a long breath.

'We're moving,' he said, laying his hand on top of Miriam's. 'We're one step closer.'

'There's still a long way to go,' Miriam cautioned, but Yosef could see the worried lines of her face fade a little.

He sat back and closed his eyes. He began to imagine what life in Palestine would be like, living with the Weichmanns at first, until they could find a place.

And meeting up with Isaac Stern and his family. How good will that feel?

They'd still worry about the children, of course, but they could, as Antje had suggested, find a way to make enquiries about them, through the British consulate, perhaps.

He was jolted from his thoughts by the sound of the compartment door sliding back, and Miriam gripping his hand.

He blinked for a second at the railway inspector and reached inside his jacket pocket for their tickets.

He froze.

Behind the Czech railway employee stood two men in black raincoats and fedoras. Even without their dark attire he would have known they were Gestapo.

They were the men from the café.

~~o~~

After the Nussbaums had left, their Czech contact had sat, finishing his coffee, hoping the Gestapo men would leave. When they didn't, he abandoned his plan to retrieve the Nussbaums' travel papers from the toilet.

I'll come back later.

He rose from his chair and walked over to the serving counter. He handed the proprietor a five koruna note and waited for his change. He nodded to the man, then reached for the door handle.

'Halt.'

He turned slowly. The second Gestapo man had returned from the toilet and was pointing a pistol at his chest. With his other hand, he dropped the Nussbaums' discarded papers on the table in front of his colleague.

The second Gestapo man looked at them and smiled.

'Ah,' he said. 'What have we here?'

'Travel papers for two Germans from Prague who had been visiting relatives,' the man holding the gun said. 'Such a coincidence, eh?'

~~o~~

Protesting that they were who they said they were, the Nussbaums were escorted along the train corridor to the guard's compartment. When the train slowed to an unscheduled stop at Libeň, a small station in the eastern suburbs of Prague, they were bundled into a car for the ride back to Gestapo Headquarters.

The large, dark, foreboding building in Bredovská Street that terrified almost all of Prague's residents was no more than a block away from the main railway station. Ironically, the building had once housed the former Jewish bank, Petschek and Co, but it had lain empty since the Germans had taken Czechoslovakia. Its owners, sensing the tide of change in

Europe, had left before the invasion for the safety of Great Britain, selling the building for a pittance to the Czech government.

They were shown, still with a modicum of deference, into a room on the first floor and told to sit down. They did as they were asked, sitting together at the table, two empty chairs opposite them. A young Gestapo officer stood guard at the doorway.

'They might just be holding us while they check our papers,' Yosef whispered.

'Do you remember all the details?'

Miriam whispered the address to him when he shook his head. He repeated it under his breath for a few moments, like a prayer.

There was a noise in the corridor and they both looked up. Through the half-open door, they saw a man being dragged, his shoulders sagging, by two Gestapo thugs. As they passed, he looked at them. Despite the terrible state his face was in, the Nussbaums knew with cold certainty that they were staring into the bloodied eyes of their contact in Prague.

In the few seconds the group paused at the door, Yosef couldn't tell if the man's look was one of remorse or defiance. It didn't matter.

The man will almost certainly talk. And so will we. There's no General here to stop them, or to come to our rescue.

Yosef looked at Miriam. He didn't know if the tears in her eyes were for the brave soul who'd risked his life to help them, or for their own predicament, but he saw, in those few moments, the last vestige of hope disappear from her face.

'They did that for our benefit,' Miriam said, bitterly.

Yosef nodded. 'I know. The poor man.'

They sat for an hour, fearful and drained. From somewhere below, they heard a scream. Yosef sat with his arm around Miriam, now numb with despair. Another scream penetrated the walls of the room, then another. There was no telling if it was their friend, but it made no difference. The anguished cries were enough to send a cold shaft of fear through Yosef's body, and he looked at the window, imagining he and Miriam throwing themselves out, ending it before the Gestapo got to work on them.

It's too high up, and it will be locked. The guard would stop us.

Another hour passed, then the two Gestapo men from the café re-entered, and closed the door behind them. They sat down opposite the Nussbaums.

'Now,' the first Gestapo man said. 'We know you've come from the Kiel area, travelling illegally as decent German people. If you hadn't changed papers, you might have got away with it.'

He smiled.

'Your large, Czech, Jew friend was very stubborn, but he told us all he knew, I'm sure, before his sad demise. Unfortunately, he hadn't been furnished with all the information we require.'

'We don't know what you're talking about,' Yosef blustered. 'We're good Germans. We demand to be released and allowed to continue our journey.'

The Gestapo man shook his head.

'It would take us a matter of seconds to strip you and confirm that you are a Jew. And we could persuade you and your filthy Jewish bitch to tell us what you know, but we're not going to. It's your lucky day.'

'You're going to let us go?' Yosef said, instantly regretting his words.

Both men roared with laughter. When they'd got their breath back, the second Gestapo man spoke with difficulty.

'You are going on a journey, but not onwards. More of a return journey.'

'We had an interesting conversation with a colleague in Kiel,' the first man said.

He looked down at his notebook, now open in front of him.

'A Kriminalassistent Güllich is very keen to have a few words with you, Herr Nussbaum,' the man said with a sneer.

Yosef's head bowed and Miriam let out a small cry.

'Ah. Reality dawns,' the man said to his partner, who laughed.

'We're most impressed with Kamerad Güllich's attitude and thoroughness. He explained the case in painstaking detail; your children going *missing*, your Jew-loving employer bending over backwards to help his pet Jews, your constant lying. Herr Güllich's dedication makes us proud to be members of the Geheime Staatspolizei and of the Schutzstaffel.'

'Very proud indeed,' his colleague echoed.

'Which is why we found it easy to accede to his request to leave your interrogation to him.'

'We're being sent back to Kiel?' Yosef said, not quite believing it.

The General. If we are in Kiel, he might be able to help us.

'I detect a sliver of hope,' the first Gestapo officer said, smiling.

Yosef and Miriam's eyes dropped, to hide the truth of his words.

'Enjoy your hope while it lasts. It will wither and die. Your General will not be able to help you now. Impersonation of real Germans by Untermensch Jews, travelling with false papers while attempting to leave the Third Reich? He cannot help you now, even when he does find out that you've been caught, like rats.'

The room was silent for a few moments.

'Well, Jews. Have you nothing to say?'

Yosef shook his head.

'It's ironic, you know,' the man said, smiling again at his companion. 'All those Jewish vermin travelling east, and these two snivelling Judenhund are going west.'

They both laughed.

~~o~~

To Miriam's surprise, they were allowed to sit together. Two Kriminalassistentanwärteren accompanied them on the long journey back to Kiel, retracing the route they'd travelled twenty-four hours before.

They weren't permitted to talk, but there was nothing to say anyway; the same thoughts ran through both their minds and, as they gripped one another's hands, each knew what the other was thinking.

They changed trains twice, each time handcuffed to their escorts to thwart any thought of escape. It would have been futile anyway and, as soon as they were seated on the next train, the handcuffs were removed. No other passengers were permitted to enter their compartment and on the occasion that either of them needed the toilet, one of their guards would accompany them, checking the closet before allowing them to enter. They insisted on the door being left open, an indignity suffered by Miriam with detached misery, knowing that much worse was to come.

Only once did they manage to speak, when the two guards briefly left the compartment to talk to two young women, who had peered in at the four occupants with curious stares.

'It's over,' Yosef whispered, his words hurried, while the girls fawned over the two Gestapo men. 'The General can't help us now.'

'I know. I'm not sorry we tried though. My only regret is that we'll never know if Ruth and Manny made it to Britain.'

'They did. I'm sure of it now. They would have been found otherwise.'

Miriam knew it was a lie, but she loved him for trying. She reached up and kissed him.

'One of us may break, or both,' she said. 'If it's me, please don't hate me for it.'

'I couldn't. Ever. I love you, Miriam Nussbaum. I always have, since I first saw you, and I always will.'

She gripped his hand tighter.

'And I you. From the moment we met. Do you remember it?'

He smiled.

'I'll never forget. Across the synagogue. I asked one of the older men who you were and tried to catch your eye.'

It was her turn to smile.

'It took you three months to pluck up the courage to ask me out.'

'It was worth the wait.'

The door slid open.

'Still halten, Juden!' *Keep quiet.*

The two Fräuleins' eyes grew wide as the young Gestapo man struck Yosef across the face.

He stepped outside again, glaring at the two captives. Miriam could see the two young women listening with wide, excited eyes as the young Kriminalassistentanwärter spoke to them.

He's telling them that we're dangerous Jews, and that his job is of utmost importance to the Reich. They'll fall into bed with them, like whores, after the bastards have delivered us into the hands of Güllich and his assistants.

She sat back and closed her eyes. She thought about Ruth, almost alone, in a strange country.

She's strong. She'll make something of herself. And Manny too. Such a bright boy, and both a credit to us. One day they'll have children, our grandchildren.

~~o~~

Yosef saw her smile, and a tear run down her cheek. He knew what she was thinking, what she was dreaming.

But, in another few hours they would be in Kiel.

And the dreaming would stop.

CHAPTER 204

The General arrived home around seven. Maria and Eva were out.

Antje met him at the door. He gave her a big hug. There were tears in her eyes.

'Papa. I'm so glad you're back. I have a pot of coffee on. And food will be ready soon.'

'Well done, Antje. I could eat a bear.'

She laughed, handing him an envelope. His hand shook a little when he took it. It was addressed simply, in Yosef's neat handwriting.

Erich.

'I'll read this in the study.'

'I'll bring the coffee,' she said.

He gave her a grateful smile and sat behind his desk. He opened the envelope with his paper knife.

~~o~~

My dearest friend, Erich,

It is with a heavy heart that I write this. We would have liked to have said goodbye in person, but it is the nature of these things that, when the chance came, we had to take it.

I don't know how you managed it, but I know that you were responsible for this happening. For that, we will be eternally grateful, and hope that we meet again someday, when this horror is over, to thank you face to face.

We are aware of the dangers but feel that it is our only chance to see our children again. Not knowing where they are is the biggest regret we have in leaving, besides having to abandon you and your family, who have been nothing but wonderful to us.

My earliest memories are of you and I playing as boys in the garden at Drachensee down by the lake and, although I have been your employee since my parents retired, you have never treated me as anything other than a friend. And you welcomed Miriam into your house as if she were one of you.

If, for any reason, we don't make it to Palestine, to the Weichmanns, we have no illusions about what our fate will be. If the worst happens, could you please tell our children someday that we tried to get to them, and pass on the little money that we left with you, to give them a start in life.

Please accept our humble thanks for the incredible care you have always shown us, and God bless you all.

Your true friend, Yosef

~~o~~

When Antje came in with the coffee, her father was staring out of the window, the letter in his hand. He turned when she entered, and she could see his eyes brimming with tears.

He handed her the letter.

As she read, she wept with him, the words blurring on the page. When she'd finished, she handed it back to him.

'How…'

'It doesn't matter. I managed to get money to Itsik. He made sure it got into the right hands.'

'You cannot keep this,' she said.

'I know.'

He placed it in the ashtray and took a lighter from the desk. He lit one corner and waited until the flames grew, and the paper was consumed.

She stood by his side, watching the smoke curl to the ceiling.

'Look at them in black, simpering, and milking everybody's sympathy,' Beate Böhm hissed.

'Now, Beate,' the mayor's wife said, frowning. 'Maria Kästner has just lost her sons, and Eva her brothers.'

'It's not as if they died for their country. For all we know, they may not be dead at all. I wouldn't put it past that family.'

Irmgard Hoffmann glanced around, hoping that no one had heard.

'You can't say that, Beate,' he said, under his breath. 'You're accusing them of desertion.'

'It wouldn't surprise me. None of them would die in the Führer's name.'

'Franz has an Iron Cross, as does his father. Johann has fought in three campaigns. They are just mourning the way any of us would. Your bitterness will get you into a great deal of trouble one day, I've warned you before.'

Beate Böhm shook her head and stared over at Maria Kästner.

'Just look at them, in their black dresses and veils, and all the ladies crowded round them, pandering to their lies.'

The mayor's wife rose. She needed to stay friends with Beate Böhm, her husband had told her. Eberhard Böhm was an important colleague, but it was sometimes difficult. The woman's mouth was dangerous.

~~o~~

[25/06/1941 Wednesday]

Franz approached the guard.

'Excuse me,' he said.

'Yes, what do you want, Kraut?'

The guard's words, harsh at face value, were delivered with a bored indifference that posed no threat, nor indicated anger.

'I was hoping that I might have some writing materials,' Franz said, 'to send a letter to my parents.'

'Haven't they given you any?' the man said.

'No. I've asked a few times, but we've received nothing so far.'

'I'll ask my sergeant at the end of my duty. How's that, Kraut?'

'That would be great. Thank you.'

'Your English is good. Where did you learn to speak like that?'

'At school, then military academy. And sailing. We sailed against English boats often. I was in the army sailing team before the war.'

'Oh. The only sail I did was to the Isle of Wight on the ferry.'

Franz laughed.

'You should try it,' he said. 'You can buy a small sailing dinghy for next to nothing, and there are plenty of wonderful places in your country to sail it, I'm told.'

'Dunno. A rowing boat in the local park is more my style.'

'Think about it. It's a great way to see your wonderful coast.'

Franz saw a few of the prisoners staring at him.

'I must go now,' he said.

'I'll ask about your paper, Kraut.'

'Thank you.'

~~o~~

'You seem to be on very friendly terms with the guard, my friend.'

'Not really. I was just asking him for writing paper, and an envelope.'

Gerhard Schlesinger laughed.

'Girlfriend? Good luck with that one. I doubt mine will wait, even if it is only a year.'

'It's not a woman. I want to write to my parents, tell them I'm well.'

'I wrote a few months ago to my girl,' the submariner said, ignoring Franz's reply. 'I got nothing back. I reckon she's found someone else by now.'

'You don't know that.'

'I do. I know her type. It doesn't bother me. Plenty more fish in the sea.'

Franz laughed.

'You sound like Johann.'

'He's a case, your brother, but you're a quiet one.'

Franz shrugged. 'We've always been the same.'

'Well, don't be getting too friendly with the guards. You'll get no preferential treatment. They don't like us much.'

'I suppose you're right. I don't hold out much hope, but no harm in asking.'

The next day, the guard handed Franz a notepad, and a pack of envelopes.

'Share these among you,' he said.

CHAPTER 205

Carl Meyer had never seen his boss take as much pleasure from inflicting pain as he did for that of Yosef Nussbaum's interrogation.

Until he watched the Kriminalassistent question the Jew's wife.

And Carl Meyer understood why.

It's her eyes.

Even at the end, a glint of defiance shone from the swollen slits, peering out from the crimson pulp that was her face, and he could swear that the corner of her bruised and lacerated lips twitched in the faintest of smiles.

They'd extracted the whole story of their attempted escape from the couple, but there were so many cut-outs and false names, he knew that the Nussbaums' information would not lead them to their Haganah contacts in Germany, or further down the line.

The Gestapo officers in Prague had told them that the man who had met the Nussbaums had been given little information about the next stage of the Nussbaums' proposed journey.

And he was sure that the Nussbaums knew little about the pestilential rag, the *Kieler Jüdisches Freiheitsnachrichtenblatt*, that had somehow resurrected itself even after they'd mopped up its previous editor, other than that it appeared on their doorstep.

For almost a day, they had stuck to their story about their children; that they'd disappeared without trace; that the General had not arranged for them to be spirited out of the country, and that the Kästner brothers had not hidden them in the yacht and delivered them to Sweden, or Norway.

But the Kriminalassistent had been right. Almost no one was able to resist the pain and the terror of the basement of Düppelstraße 23, and it was Yosef Nussbaum who'd cracked first.

'We sent them to my cousin's farm,' he blurted, trying to wrench himself from the thin rope binding him to the arms of the chair.

The words were barely audible, and Heinrich Güllich had to put his ear close to Yosef's mouth to hear them when they were repeated.

'Where?' he said.

Yosef Nussbaum shook his head.

'Where?' the Kriminalassistent repeated, breaking another finger with the pliers he held in his hand.

Yosef screamed.

Heinrich Güllich stood back and waited until his cries had faded to quiet sobs.

'Where?'

'Kaltenhof. It's about a few kilometres outside Karstädt.'

The Kriminalassistent nodded to Carl Meyer, who left the room. He returned a few moments later.

'Kriminalassistentanwärter Seidel is checking it, sir.'

~~o~~

Between the spasms of fresh pain coming from his finger, Yosef hoped that Miriam would remember the fallback story they'd thrashed out when Ruth and Manny had left on the yacht, and they'd been deliberating what to tell the police when they'd reported them missing.

The General had rejected his suggestion that they should say they'd been sent to his cousin's farm, but after the General had gone, he and Miriam had discussed it.

'If we ever get caught,' Yosef had said, 'and we have to tell them something, give them that.'

'Why?' Miriam had said. 'What good will it do?'

'They might believe it, and it will keep the Kästners' name out of it.'

'But how would we have got them to Karstädt?' Miriam had said.

After a few seconds' thought, Yosef had told her his idea, and she'd smiled at the simplicity of it.

Now, through the tears, he hoped she'd remembered.

He heard the Gestapo man talking again.

'And just how did your children get to this farm? Did they walk. Or fly?'

'We paid someone to take them there.'

'Who?'

He knew it would cost him another of his fingers, but it had to sound real.

'I can't tell you,' he said, gritting his teeth.

'Perhaps your wife will be more forthcoming,' Heinrich Güllich said, smiling.

'No, please. She doesn't know.'

'We'll see about that.'

Heinrich Güllich turned to Carl Meyer.

'Bring the whore in.'

The Kriminalassistent watched Yosef while his underling fetched Miriam Nussbaum.

The man dragged her in and tied her to a second chair.

Her head slumped forward.

Heinrich Güllich grabbed her hair and pulled her head back.

'Where did you send your children?' he asked her, his face a few centimetres from hers.

'We didn't. They went missing.'

The Kriminalassistent walked over to the table and lifted a knife. He walked back to Miriam and put it to her throat.

'Tell me. Your sorry husband has already told us.'

Her head jerked up and she gave Yosef an accusatory stare. She shook her head.

Heinrich Güllich grabbed the front of Miriam's dress and the knife flashed down, ripping it all the way down to her waist. He walked around behind her and, grabbing the torn material, pulled it around the back of the chair, and pinned her shoulders to the steel frame.

He came round to the front again and hooked his finger into the centre of her brassiere, sliding the tip of the knife between it and the skin. He slashed upwards, nicking the skin and causing a trickle of blood to run down the centre of Miriam's chest, between her now exposed breasts.

He walked to the table and lifted a pair of medical forceps.

'Your children. Where are they?'

The Gestapo man touched her nipple with the cold steel. From across the room, Yosef let out a yell.

'I told them about the f…'

The back of Carl Meyer's hand connected with his cheek. A tooth flew out, and blood filled his mouth. He began to choke.

Heinrich Güllich ignored him.

'Answer me, bitch,' he said, holding up the stainless-steel clamps in front of her face.

He took her right nipple between his gloved finger and rolled it gently, then squeezed it.

'Not bad for a middle-aged Jewish whore,' he said, examining her breasts with interest. 'Do you think she suckled her young, Meyer?'

'Like a sow, Herr Kriminalassistent. With her litter of Jewish piglets.'

Heinrich Güllich laughed and, with a sudden movement, attached the clamp to the nipple he was holding.

Miriam screamed.

He let it drop, and the forceps hung from Miriam's nipple, pulling her breast downwards.

Yosef tried to make eye contact with Miriam, but her head slumped forward, jerking in sobs.

He saw the Kriminalassistent walk over to the table again, and come back with a small blowtorch, and a piece of wadding. He placed the wadding under the handle of the forceps, lifting them from Miriam's belly.

He lit the blowtorch and let the flames lick against the handle of the forceps. A little smoke rose from the wadding.

'No, no, no,' Yosef screamed. 'Tell him.'

The handle of the forceps began to glow red in the blue flame of the blowtorch, and Yosef thought he could just smell the beginnings of burning flesh. Miriam's sobbing grew louder.

'Tell him,' Yosef screamed.

'The farm,' she said in a small voice, tears streaming down her face. 'In Karstädt.'

Heinrich Güllich took a glass of water from the table and dribbled it onto the clamps. A small cloud of steam hissed from the metal.

'And how did they get there?' he asked.

'Someone came and collected them,' Miriam sobbed. 'We paid them.'

'Who did you pay?'

'I don't know. I really don't know.'

The Kriminalassistent shook his head and relit the blowtorch.

'It was the Bernheim brothers,' Yosef screamed as Heinrich Güllich applied the flame to the handles of the forceps again. He turned to face Yosef.

'Ah. We have decided to cooperate. The Bernheim brothers, you say. The worst of Jewish scum, but useful in their way. You have no idea how many of their fellow Jews they have turned in.'

He smiled at Yosef's bleeding and bruised face.

'We have all we need for now. Your story will be checked, of course, and we will return to ask you a few further questions, depending on what we find. I only hope you have both been telling the truth.'

Yosef glanced at Miriam. He gave the slightest of nods. He couldn't tell if she could see out through the narrow slits in her swollen face where her eyes should have been, and there was little hope of seeing any expression of acknowledgement through the bruises, but his heart eased when she returned his nod with the barest movement of her head.

He knew she'd be asking the same question as him.

Was our account credible enough to satisfy the Gestapo?

He heard Heinrich Güllich speak to Carl Meyer.

'Get Seidel in here. Take these two to the cells. We'll speak to them in the morning.'

It will be a long night, Yosef thought.

But at least we're still alive.

CHAPTER 206

'Your children weren't there,' Heinrich Güllich said. 'Their neighbours told us your cousin and his family had taken a long holiday in Poland.'

Carl Meyer laughed. Heinrich Güllich smiled at him and continued.

'Now, either you're telling us lies, or you have been duped in the most foolish manner.'

Yosef and Miriam stared at him.

'I don't understand,' Yosef said. 'Are they in Poland?'

Heinrich Güllich smiled.

'I'm almost inclined to believe you. For a while, I thought you were sly and devious Judenschweine but perhaps you're not. Can I tell you what I think will have happened to your children, if indeed you put your trust in these gutter Jews?'

He waited for an answer. When none came, he shrugged.

'If the Bernheim brothers left your house with your children, there will have been no three-hour journey through the Elbe Valley to Karstädt. Within ten minutes of leaving Drachensee, your precious Jewish brats would have been thrown down a well, or dumped in sacks into Kieler Förde, weighed down with rocks.'

Thrusting his legs, Yosef threw himself and the chair he was tied to at the Kriminalassistent.

Heinrich Güllich stepped back, surprised, then roared with laughter as Yosef pitched forward to the floor, hitting his head on the corner of the table on the way down.

His body slumped to one side, the chair still attached to him, like a snail or a hermit crab, carrying its home on its back.

For a moment, the Kriminalassistent thought that Yosef had fractured his skull, that he was dead, but he saw the gentle rise and fall of his chest as he lay unconscious.

'See, we don't even have to touch them,' he said. 'The Jews beat themselves up.'

He turned to Carl Meyer.

'Throw some water on the Judenlaus.'

Carl Meyer poured the remainder of the water in the glass onto Yosef's head. After a few seconds, he stirred. The young Gestapo man hauled the chair back up and slid it across the room beside the one Miriam sat in.

Heinrich Güllich waited until Yosef had regained consciousness.

'We're finished with you for now. For crimes against the Reich, you are being imprisoned indefinitely. You may face further questioning at a later date.'

He turned as Kriminalassistentanwärter Seidel opened the door and looked in.

'Take them to the cells,' he said, then turned to Carl Meyer. 'You can give him a hand, Kamerad.'

The two men untied the Nussbaums and led them away.

Heinrich Güllich returned to the office and sat down at his desk.

He was torn between shooting the General's Jews and keeping them alive. It was tempting to be done with them for good but, even if their story was true, he was still convinced that the General still had a hand in it. If he were involved, the Bernheim brothers might have been more inclined to do what they were paid to do, fearful that the General could have them arrested by his police friends and put in one of the camps.

Alive, the Nussbaums were still a lever against the General but, in the meantime, he wasn't sure how he should use them. His immediate boss, the Kriminalsekretär, had told him when the Nussbaums had been brought back to Kiel that he had just forty-eight hours, then they would have to disappear, one way or the other.

He made up his mind and picked up the phone.

'Kommandant,' he said. 'Guten Abend.'

~~o~~

When they were pulled from the van, Yosef knew at once where they were.

Neuengamme.

The place had changed little. He looked around. The shuffling prisoners in thin striped clothes, the dried, barren mud, with barely a weed pushing through, in contrast to the lush green of the farmland and trees beyond the wire. It was as if he'd never left.

The only thing missing is the biting wind, the clinging mud, and the driving rain.

A worried frown creased his bruised and battered face.

There are no women here. What will they do with Miriam?

They'd said their goodbyes many times in the last few days, never knowing when it would be the last. He suspected that the one during their journey to the camp would be their final farewell.

He watched as two female guards approached and read out Miriam's name. She could barely stand. She gave a weak nod and was rewarded with a blow across her back.

'Yes,' she said, through swollen and bleeding lips.

They took her by her arms and began dragging her towards a pair of gates on one side of the reception compound. As the gates were opened, Miriam looked over her shoulder and her eyes locked with Yosef's for a slow, lingering second. A thousand unsaid words passed between them in the time before her head was snapped round by one of her guards. The gates closed behind them.

Yosef's head slumped, but he made himself watch as she was bundled into a building beyond the gates. One of the women said something and her companion laughed, then closed the door behind them.

'Nussbaum. Schnell.'

The riding crop hit the back of his neck, almost causing him to black out. He had so many cuts and bruises, that any blow found its mark on flesh that was already flayed.

He stumbled forward, towards the lines of huts that held Neuengamme's male prisoners.

~~o~~

'Why Neuengamme, sir?'

If he were honest, Heinrich Güllich didn't fully know his reasons for keeping the Nussbaums alive. He was convinced that they hadn't told him all they knew but, if that was the case, they were two of the toughest people that had passed through Gestapo Headquarters in Kiel.

Could that be true of two Jewish Untermenschen like them?

'You know why. If we'd kept them here, their tame Jew-lover would have found out they were at Gestapo Headquarters and kicked up a storm, sooner or later. I couldn't trust the Kriminaldirektor not to cave in.'

'Why not just kill them, sir, and dump their bodies in the nearest river?'

'While they're alive, the General might show his hand and make a mistake. And there's always the chance the Jewish brats will be found. If they are, I want to see the look in their parents' eyes when we shoot them.'

Carl Meyer laughed.

'You showed commendable restraint, sir. I have one question about technique.'

'Yes? What is it?' the Kriminalassistent grumbled, a slight frown creasing his brow.

'You held back from having the woman sexually assaulted. I was trying to work out why. Wouldn't even the threat of it have made the husband talk sooner?'

Heinrich Güllich rarely raped any of the women he questioned. But he would allow one of his underlings to do it for him, when the occasion required it. Often, it was one of the thugs they used as part of their regime of terror but, once or twice, when he could see them itching, he had allowed Carl Meyer and his fellow Kriminalassistentanwärteren to forcibly take a particularly difficult female subject.

But not usually Jews. It was against the blood and German honour laws. On a rare occasion, however, it was sometimes necessary, as a tool of interrogation. It was especially effective in extracting information from fathers or husbands.

He'd noticed his assistant's interest when he'd tortured the Nussbaum woman, particularly when he'd slashed her clothes and attached the clamp to her nipple.

'You have to learn restraint,' he said. 'As much as you may have wanted to show the Jewish bitch all she's good for, you have to think of the bigger picture if you are ever going to advance.'

'But, sir, I…'

The Kriminalassistent held up his hand.

'I have my own agenda, and I'll not let your base desires interfere with my plans for these two.'

In truth, he had been as aroused as his underling and would have liked nothing better than to rape the Jew in front of her screaming husband. But he prided himself on his cast-iron willpower and professionalism, enjoying the mental torture of his clients as much as the physical pain and debasement he could inflict.

And it was there in reserve if it were needed.

'You're young. You'll learn to be patient, to step away and be dispassionate when necessary.

'Yes, sir. What do we do now?'

'We sit back and wait, and we let them all stew in their own broth.'

CHAPTER 207

When Miriam's name was called, she'd tried to walk, but she'd struggled to keep pace with the two SS women who escorted her. When she stumbled, one of them had hit her with the stick she carried. They'd passed through another gate into a small compound where there were only two huts.

The two guards had marched Miriam to the door of the first hut and barked an order. The door opened and a woman stood to one side. She'd also held a stick, but she was in grey prison garb.

The SS women had dragged Miriam up the steps and threw her to the floor.

'A new one for you. The Gestapo want her alive for now.'

When they'd left, the woman with the stick turned and shouted at the watching prisoners.

'Schnell. Schnell. Give her a bunk. Clean her up. I don't want the blame of her dying.'

Miriam felt hands grabbing her and helping her to her feet. They led her to the back of the hut and told her to lie down on a bottom bunk. A rough straw mattress covered the pallet of hard wooden slats, barely wide enough to lie on, but she slumped onto it gratefully.

A woman brought a pail of water and another a piece of rag. Miriam protested, but they insisted on cleaning her up. Through the narrow slits between her swollen eyelids, Miriam looked at the women who tended to her.

'Why are you helping…?'

'Ssshhh,' a young woman whispered, shaking her head. 'The Kapo doesn't let us talk in case we make plans to escape, or to kill her.' She smiled.

'But…' This time, the woman, *a young girl*, really, Miriam thought, put her finger to Miriam's lips and gave a more determined shake of her head.

'Later,' she whispered.

Miriam closed her eyes. She wanted to sleep, and not waken up. Every part of her body ached. Her only comfort was that they hadn't raped her; she'd heard it could happen during interrogations by the Gestapo.

She opened her eyes again. Four or five women surrounded her now, their faces pale with horror. She wondered what she must look like to evoke such strong revulsion.

One of the women looked familiar but, in the deepening gloom, it was hard to be sure. She closed her eyes again. This time, she drifted into a fitful sleep.

~~o~~

Yosef stood in front of the deputy Kommandant. The SS-Sturmbannführer looked at the paperwork on the desk in front of him.

'I see that you've been a prisoner here before.'

'Yes, sir. It was a few months ago.'

'You'll know what to expect then, so I'll not repeat myself. The Gestapo wish to keep you alive, for reasons of their own. As a result, I am going to place you with the workers who are building the new brickworks. The work is less strenuous, and the workers are given extra rations. You will be given your uniform shortly and taken to your barrack.'

The Kommandant lit another cigarette and blew the smoke into the air.

'Do not be tempted to abuse your position,' he continued. 'The current requirement to keep you alive does not preclude punishment and, don't forget, once the Gestapo are finished with you, and you are of no further use to them, it will be a small matter to transfer you to one of the sections digging the canal. If, on the other hand, you prove an adept worker, you might remain in the brick factory, staying away from the Arbeitskommandos. Do you understand?'

'Yes, sir. Kommandant. Sir.'

'Off with you then. One of the Kapos is waiting outside. Go with him.'

Yosef turned to go.

'Oh. There's one more thing, Jew.'

'Yes, sir?' Yosef said. The man was smiling, but Yosef shivered.

'Your General will not be coming for you this time.'

CHAPTER 208

[27/06/1941 Friday]

Miriam woke to the wail of a siren outside. The women scrambled to the door. One of them looked back and hissed at Miriam to follow.

Miriam rolled out of bed onto the floor and pulled herself up using the corner post of the bunk. She stumbled towards the door, barely seeing where she was going. The young woman from the night before grabbed the thin cloth of Miriam's sleeve.

'Come on,' she said. 'You must make Appell, or they'll take you away to the hospital, or shoot you. Either way, you're not coming back.'

She followed the woman outside to where the roll-call took place and stood at the end of the row. She heard the rest of the women answer to their names being called, then her mind drifted away.

'Nussbaum!'

The shout and the crack of a blow to her side came at the same time.

She somehow acknowledged her name, and, after they'd all done the same, the women filed back into the block.

As she waited to go through the door, she got a better view of the women in the light of day. In contrast to the walking skeletons she'd seen shuffling around the men's compound the day before, most of her fellow inmates were on the thin side, but not painfully so. And there were only a handful of them.

She followed the last of the women through the door and, taking her cue from the others, made up her bed, folding the thin sheet and stacking the mattress on its side. She shuddered to think what it would be like in winter. The young woman who had looked after her the night before slept in the bunk above her. In the little daylight that filtered through the small windows high up on the wall Miriam saw that she was no more than Ruth's age.

'They bring food to the hut,' the young girl said. 'Once we have eaten, the women chosen to work are taken away. The rest of us can stay here, in the hut, or outside in the compound.'

'Doesn't everyone work?' Miriam mumbled, through swollen lips. 'My husband was in here a few months ago and every prisoner had to work ten or twelve hours a day.'

The girl gave her a strange smile.

'We only work when they want us to,' she said, turning away. 'Today, I'm to go. They'll not make you work for a while; not while you look like that.'

She pointed at the injuries on Miriam's face.

'Listen,' she said. 'I have to go. Just do what the other women tell you. It will keep you out of trouble.'

'Thank you for your help,' Miriam said.

The girl blushed.

'It was nothing. I'm Frieda.' She held out her hand.

'I'm Miriam.'

Then she was gone. Miriam hobbled over to one of the small windows and looked out. The compound they were in was small, as was the one next to it. She saw a group of women sitting on the ground outside and made for the door. The bright sunshine stung her raw eyes and she shaded them with her hand. She looked around to see if any guards were nearby and limped towards the group of women. As she approached them, she frowned. Through the stinging sun, she looked at the woman from last night, unsure. She stopped dead.

Rosa. It can't be. I should have known, but it was dark last night.

She felt the blood drain from her face and the world spun around her, then went black.

~~o~~

When she came round, she looked up at four faces peering at her. She sat up.

'Rosa,' she said, her eyes fixed on her friend's face. A little thinner, and older-looking, perhaps, but it was unmistakably her.

Rosa stared at her, uncomprehending for a second, then her face crumpled.

'Miriam!'

She cradled Miriam's head in her arms and held her to her chest, weeping.

'Rosa,' Miriam repeated, mumbling. 'You're still alive. I can't believe it.'

The other women knelt in silence beside them, giving the two friends time. Rosa turned to them, tears coursing down her face.

'This is my best friend, Miriam Nussbaum.' She turned back to Miriam. 'We'll introduce you to the rest later, but this is Katherine, Lizbet and Edith. The girl you bunk with is Frieda.'

'I know. She told me. She's away to work,' Miriam said. 'It's strange that you don't all have to work every day.'

She looked at them, squinting through her swollen eyelids.

'You look healthy,' she said. 'Are the women treated different from the men?'

The other three women stared at Miriam, then got up. They gave Rosa what looked like a sympathetic glance.

'It's better that you...' one of them said.

Rosa nodded. When her three friends had gone, she turned to Miriam and looked her straight in the eye. Miriam recognised Rosa's defiant look of old.

'They keep us like this for a reason,' she said. 'They use us.'

For a moment Miriam stared, frowning, then bowed her head.

'No,' she said. 'Not you.'

'Yes, me. And you will too. Or you'll die.'

'How can you?' Miriam said, but instantly regretted it.

What kind of friend am I?

'I'm sorry,' she said. 'I shouldn't have...'

'Judged?' Rosa said, but her tone was resigned rather than angry.

'I've gone beyond judging,' she went on. 'At first, I fought against it, then I justified to myself that I was staying alive for my family. Now, I just do it to survive, and to have enough food, unlike those wretches.'

She nodded towards the men's compound.

Miriam took hold of Rosa's hand and squeezed it.

'I'm not going to judge you, Rosa. Do what you need to do, but I can't.'

'Then you'll die, Miriam. And before you do, they'll rape you anyway. They'll give you to the Kapos, and the thugs they use to punish the male prisoners, or they'll take you to the hospital, and use you for god knows what.'

'I know. But...' She took her friend's face in her bruised hands. 'I'm not condemning you, and I don't want to die without seeing my children again, but I don't think I could face them again if I...'

Her voice trailed off.

'I beg you to do it, if only for me. I would never have wished to see you in here, but it is the sweetest thing to be able to talk to you again.'

She paled, and stared at Miriam.

'What?' Miriam said, frowning.

'Emil, the children. Have you any news of them? Have you heard anything?'

'They are well. They were brought back to Kiel. They're living at the Judenhaus in Kleiner Kuhberg.'

The lie came easily. She wasn't going to be the one to crush Rosa's hope.

Rosa started crying again, and hugged Miriam.

'Thank you. Thank you. Thank you.'

'I haven't heard from Esther for a while. There's no mail. Most of Kiel's Jews have either been deported to Poland or have been put in the Judenhaus. Those who haven't stay at home or move around only when they must. Few people are willing to associate with Jews now.'

'What about Yosef?'

Miriam glanced across at the shuffling skeletons through the wire.

'Oh, no,' Rosa said.

Miriam nodded.

'What about Manny, and Ruth?'

Miriam hesitated. She and Yosef had sworn never to tell anyone about their children's escape, but this was Rosa.

'We paid the Bernheim brothers to take them to Yosef's cousin's farm. From there, they were going to try and make for Bavaria, then over the border into Switzerland with his son and daughter. We don't know if they made it.'

She hated lying to Rosa, even if was only one more untruth in the long line of lies she'd told to the people she loved.

'Oh, honey,' Rosa said, hugging Miriam. 'They might have succeeded.'

'The Gestapo say the whole family were deported to Poland. We don't know if Ruth and Manny were with them. They could have been lying to us.'

She justified her own lie by telling herself that it wasn't as far from the truth as all that; they'd entrusted two brothers to try and get Ruth and Manny out of Germany. She didn't know if they'd got there, or even if they were still alive. And now she would never know.

'What about Yosef's parents, and yours?' she heard Rosa say.

'They were deported a couple of weeks ago. I don't know where to.'

'Oh. At least they stayed out of the camps.'

'We all tried so hard to get you out, so that you could be with Emil and the children.'

'I know. They let me meet a lawyer, once.'

'Once? The lawyer told Jakob that he saw you on a regular basis.'

'No. It was only once. He told me there was nothing he could do.'

Miriam turned away, the anger bubbling up inside her.

'Why are you in here?' Rosa asked.

'We tried to get to Palestine, with the Haganah. We only got as far as Prague.'

'I'm surprised they didn't shoot you, honey.'

'There's a Gestapo man in Kiel. He's determined to use us to get to the General because he tried to protect us.'

She didn't tell Rosa about the Weichmanns' money, and how it had paid for her lawyer, who'd cheated them out of it, as it turned out. Or that it was the Gestapo's suspicions that she'd stolen it that had first brought her to the attention of Heinrich Güllich.

'What did we do to make people do this to us?' Rosa said, looking around at the wire, and the towers, and the shuffling prisoners in the next compound. 'I keep asking myself.'

'We did nothing. It's them. And one day, they'll pay for it.'

'You think so? I'm not so sure, here or in the afterlife. God seems to have a strange way of looking after his people.'

'Rosa!'

'It's true. I'm not so sure I even believe anymore. Why would any God allow this to happen?'

Miriam had no answer for Rosa. If she were honest, she'd asked the same question herself.

Neither woman said anything for a while. Then Rosa took Miriam's hand again.

'They'll not want you working while you look like that. If you can stand more pain, you can keep your face looking that way for a while.'

'I'd rather have pain than be…'

Her voice faded away. 'I'm sorry,' she said.

'Don't be,' Rosa said. 'I made a choice. I have to live with it.'

'Why do they have you in here? Is it not illegal for an Aryan man to go with a Jewish woman?'

Rosa laughed softly, but it had a bitter edge to it.

'When it suits them, they forget that we are Jewish.'

'Are the rest…'

'No. I'm the only Jew. I'm here by accident, like you.'

'How do you stand it?'

'I try and imagine I'm somewhere else. With Emil, or my children, or my parents. Or with you and Esther.'

Miriam felt sick at the thought.

'How often…?'

'When you're working, you might see six or eight men in a day. We work four or five days out of each week.'

She gave a bitter laugh.

'They look after us,' she said. 'They give us good food, regular medicals, and treatment if we need it.'

She bowed her head.

'It's not for us, needless to say,' she continued. 'It's for the men. So that we don't give them anything.'

'How did it start?'

'I was sent here by mistake, I think. There weren't many women here; just a few to service the guards and the Kapos. They put me in a cell with little food and water, and no heating. It was January, and the cold was terrible.'

She stared past Miriam.

'They offered me food, and warmth. I knew I couldn't survive otherwise, and I just wanted to live for the chance to see my family again.'

Tears ran down her cheeks, and Miriam wrapped her arms around her, holding her tight.

'You did right. You're still here and you have a chance to live and see them.'

'I tell myself that I'm being raped, every day. That I'm powerless to stop it, but it's not true.'

'Yes, it is. You said yourself; they kill you if you don't do as you're told.'

Rosa gave her a tired smile.

'Then why don't you think about it. I don't want to lose you.'

'I couldn't, Rosa. I just couldn't. I'd rather die.'

The two women sat in silence. They heard a laugh come from Rosa's friends, and they smiled. Then Rosa's face darkened.

'Do you ever ask yourself?'

'What?'

'If we'd only gone to Palestine, with Esther?'

'Every day.'

~~o~~

The female guard looked over and frowned at the two women, sitting talking together.

Scheming, more than likely. Nothing a couple of blows with a stick won't fix.

She made to walk towards them, but she turned at a shout from the gate and saw that her relief had arrived.

'About time,' she said, looking at her watch.

'Sorry. Her Highness wanted a word. She'll likely catch you on the way out. It's about that new one.'

She nodded towards Miriam.

'What about her?'

'She's not to be touched.'

'Beaten, you mean?'

'Yes. Or made to work. For now. But she's not to be told, under any circumstances.'

'Unusual. Anything to do with the Gestapo men from Kiel?'

'The ones that brought them in? I suppose so.'

The outgoing guard breathed a sigh of relief as she walked towards the admin block.

What would I have told the Lagerführer if I'd half-killed the Jewish bitch?

CHAPTER 209

Yosef watched the sorry line of prisoners of the Arbeitskommando trudge into the camp through the gates. Although he was exhausted after a day mixing mortar for the construction of the new brickworks, he was glad not to have been digging all day, without respite, in the mud and clay at the bottom of the huge trench that would, one day, connect the camp with the Dove-Elbe river.

Or working in the clay pits within the camp itself.

He waited in line for food, holding the bowl which was his lifeline; without it, he wouldn't eat, so, like every other prisoner, he kept it by him at all times. The thin, tasteless soup with half-rotten vegetables and an occasional scrap of meat was all that the men of the Arbeitskommandos were given to eat, three times a day, and it showed in the way that their striped jackets and trousers hung from their emaciated frames.

For the skilled men building the brickworks, a slice of coarse bread, with cheese or something resembling cold meat, was provided in the middle of the day and Yosef, despite being a labourer, was included. It kept him alive.

Even so, it was nothing near to what he was used to, and he knew that the work, and the diet would, over the course of time, sap his energy. He needed to get better, and make himself useful, if he were to survive.

And when the winter comes…

His broken fingers, taped together with strips of cloth, sent shafts of pain up his arms every time he threw a shovelful of sand or lime into the mix, and working the paddles proved beyond him.

'Just keep shovelling,' the man in charge of the mortar said. 'I'll mix.'

Yosef did what he was told and, when they stood in line for food, he thanked the man who'd been kind to him.

'Don't thank me. If you held us back, we'd all get punished. You'll make up for it when your body heals, I'll make sure of that.'

'I need to keep this job,' Yosef said. 'I couldn't survive the canal, or the pits.'

'No one does. Not for longer than a few months anyway, at most.'

'How do I stay here?'

'Be useful. What did you do before?'

Yosef told him. The man laughed.

'Driving? Gardening? There's not much call for that in here, but if you're good with your hands, you could learn to make bricks, or help the joiners.'

'What about you?'

'I'm the best mortar mixer in the camp. All the bricklayers want my mortar.'

'Thanks. I'll maybe just learn to mix mortar.'

'Listen, I saw you today. Not many would have worked as hard as you did with hands like that. I'll have a word with the foreman.'

'I couldn't make bricks at the moment, but I'm comfortable working with my hands.'

'Leave it with me. In the meantime, just do as you are doing.'

The man looked at him.

'What is it?' Yosef said.

'They beat you up like that, then they give you a job that keeps you alive?'

Yosef shrugged. Trust no one, Jakob had told him the last time.

'They must want something from you,' the man said, handing him an extra piece of bread.

~~o~~

[28/06/1941 Saturday]

Chief Petty Officer Neuer handed the General a small brown envelope.

'It was handed in at the guardhouse, sir.'

'Thank you, Günter,' the General said. He often used his officer's first names, much to

Frau Müller's disgust.

'It's good to have you back, sir.'

'It's a relief to be back. I can only take so much of Berlin, and the people I have to deal with there.'

The chief petty officer laughed.

'I'll stick to my post here, sir, if you don't mind.' He turned and left.

The General tore open the note.

Meet me at the boat. Oskar.

The General frowned. He walked over to the window and looked across to the dock. A lone figure stood halfway along it, looking out over Kieler Hafen.

He reached for his coat and folded it over his arm.

'I'll be out for a short while, Frau Müller. If anyone calls, I'll get back to them as soon as I return.'

On the way out, he spoke to Günter Neuer.

'I'll be down at the boat. I've been informed she has a little water lying in her.'

'Do you want a hand, sir?'

'No. It will be something minor. Perhaps I left a seacock open. One of them was weeping a little.'

'Very good, sir. I'll come and get you if someone starts a war.'

The General laughed then walked down the corridor towards the entrance hall, trying not to hurry.

When he reached the boat, Oskar von Friedeburg turned to him, his face pale and like stone.

The General glanced around, then stared at his friend.

'What's wrong, Oskar. Are you in trouble...?'

'No, of course not. It's not that.'

'Then what?'

'My Swedish business agent received a message from Palestine. From Itsik Weichmann. He asked me to pass on a message. They know that I have access to you, and that I can be trusted.'

'Yosef? Miriam? They've been killed?'

'They don't know. But the Haganah say they didn't reach Bulgaria, where they were to cross the Black Sea to Turkey. And their man in Prague is missing.'

'You think they're still in Czechoslovakia?'

'They don't know. Possibly Romania. They've suspended all activities in the meantime, until they find out what happened. They can't afford to lose any more people.'

The General looked out across the water. He'd almost begun to believe that they'd made it.

He turned back to Oskar.

'Thank you, my friend. You took a risk. If anyone asks, you were passing, and you noticed *Snowgoose* had a little water in her.'

Oskar smiled. A sad smile.

'She has. You'd better pump her out, while you're here.'

~~o~~

'We need to talk. I'm at the usual number.'

General Kästner put the phone down and looked out the window. No one else was using the telephone booth along the seafront from the Kriegsmarine Headquarters. He knew Canaris would find a public phone near his office and try both the numbers he'd given him the last time he was in Berlin. The second number was for the telephone kiosk at Drachensee.

Five minutes later, he stood at the booth. The telephone rang, and the General answered it.

'Canaris.'

'Kästner. What can I do for you?'

The General hesitated for a second.

'I have a big favour to ask.'

'Go on.' The admiral's voice was guarded.

'Do you have any operatives inside the Gestapo?'

The General heard a groan from the other end of the telephone line.

'The Nussbaums. They've got themselves arrested again?'

'They've gone missing between Prague and Bulgaria. Along with their Haganah contact.'

'How do you know?'

'I knew they'd left. It was around a week ago. The Haganah contacted me to say they were missing.'

'You shouldn't be seen associating with these people. It would only take one sharp-eyed Gestapo or SD officer to put you in a very compromising situation.'

'The approach was through a third party. Two in fact.'

The admiral grunted again. The General took it to indicate reluctant approval.

'I can't promise anything. I'll not compromise a source for personal matters; neither yours nor anyone else's.'

'I understand.'

'Do you know the name of the Haganah operative?'

'No. I'm afraid not.'

'It's a big ask, but I'll try. I don't have a Gestapo contact in Prague, but we have men in the city. Gestapo security is risible; they're too arrogant to care and, anyway, they don't mind a few stories leaking out, true or otherwise. They think it enhances their reputation and keeps the locals in line.'

'Thank you, Canaris. I just need to know.'

'I'll be in touch.'

~~o~~

Lt. Colonel Anthony James Plenderleith held up the letter, frowning.

'I'm sorry, Marjorie. I wouldn't have signed up for this war business if I'd have known.'

'Don't worry, my dear. It's a real feather in your cap that you've been asked.'

'But, in the middle of nowhere, in the Scottish Highlands? What will you do?'

'We'll make the most of it, Anthony. It's not every day that you'll be asked to be the commandant of a prisoner-of-war camp. What's it called?'

'Cultybraggan. It's close to a small village, Comrie, near Crieff, in Perthshire.'

'We've been to Crieff. Don't you remember we had that holiday in Scotland? We travelled through it on our way to the Trossachs. We stayed in a lovely big hotel there.'

'Yes. The Crieff Hydro.' He gave her a sardonic grin. 'We'll not be staying there, I'm afraid. The Ministry of Defence have requisitioned it for the use of the Free Polish Forces.'

'Oh. I didn't know there were such people.'

'Yes. I believe they escaped from Poland when the infernal Nazis took over their country. I'm told that they want to take part in the fight against Hitler, but in the meantime, a few of them may be stationed as camp guards at Cultybraggan.'

'Oh, goodness. Will you have to learn Polish?'

'No, the onus will be on them to speak decent English, but I suppose it will vary from man to man. I suspect that they will have spokesmen who will communicate my commands to the rest.'

'What about a house? And when do we go?'

'We will be billeted in Comrie. We leave tomorrow. The War Office man assures me that our accommodation will be a sizeable cottage with a large garden, and that the village is charming and friendly. The camp is only half finished.'

'Oh well. I guess we'll be made most welcome. Scotland is a beautiful place.'

'Yes. In summer. I'm not so sure about winter.'

CHAPTER 210

[29/06/1941 Sunday]

'Canaris! What are you doing here?'

'I was passing through and I have some news for you. It's not good, I'm afraid, although there is a glimmer of hope.'

'The Nussbaums? They're still alive?'

'Yes, and not more than a kilometre from where we are standing.'

'What? They're in Kiel?'

'They were moved to Gestapo Headquarters three days ago. They were arrested in Prague, on the train to Bucharest.'

'Did someone betray them?'

'It doesn't look like it. My agent thinks it was just bad luck. The Gestapo is openly boasting that they'd arrested a Jewish resistance leader. I presume that was the Haganah man. They said he had accomplices.'

'He was under surveillance?'

'No. It appears as if it was just a routine check. It justifies their high security presence.'

'I'll get right over there. The head of the Gestapo assured me that he would not sanction harassment of my household staff. His wife and Maria are friends.'

'Ah. Preferential treatment for the elite,' Canaris said, then held up his hand in apology.

'Seriously, I would be careful if I were you. This time, the Nussbaums have been caught breaking the law; fraud, obtaining false identities, defying travel bans, attempting to leave the Reich without permission. This is no longer harassment. It is legitimate incarceration. The best you can hope for is that your influence will keep them from being shot after they've been interrogated.'

The General stared at his friend. He realised with a terrible certainty that what Canaris was saying was the truth.

'I must at least try and see that they are being treated well.'

'Don't expect too much. The Gestapo will have questioned them with vigour. I'd be surprised if they hadn't told them about their children. Very few can resist.'

'The Nussbaums would never…'

'Don't rely on it. Few have the courage to resist. In most cases, only death prevents a subject yielding to their methods. You might end up having to deny their claims.'

'Never. That would be the death of them. I'd rather admit it.'

'That would be stupid, my friend. It won't save them, and it will be your downfall.'

'I don't need this job. I'll retire again. What can they do?'

'Without your position and influence, they can do what they like to you and your family. In a way, Maria was right. You have put them all in jeopardy.'

The General slumped.

'I cannot abandon them. You must understand that.'

'You may have to make the choice between the Nussbaums and your wife and children.'

Neither man said anything for a while, then the General got up and began to pace around the room.

'I need to find out. I'll speak to the Gestapo chief. He will at least let me know what is happening to them.'

'I can't stop you but take care. You're dealing with a nest of vipers.'

CHAPTER 211

Doncaster racecourse transit camp, 29th June 1941

Dear Father and Mother,

They have finally allowed us to write. By now, you will know that although The Shearwater did not survive, we did.

We are well. The storm hit us with a ferocity that I have never before experienced, and we realised that to make for shore and an unknown port would have risked certain death, so we decided to try and keep away from land as far as possible, beating our way westwards to give ourselves as much sea room as possible towards the western end of the Skagerrak, hoping to ride out the storm and make for Norway once it had passed.

We lasted nearly a day, but the wind continued to increase, and even our scrap of storm jib was overpowered. The waves began to swamp the boat, then the rudder broke. We jury-rigged a replacement, but it couldn't hold us to wind, so we decided to run downwind with bare poles. We were broached several times, then when we thought it couldn't get any worse, we were knocked down and rolled.

Incredible as it seems, The Shearwater came back up, although the main mast had broken, and the boom was trailing over the side. We cut loose all the rigging and let it go. By this time, we'd taken on a lot of water, and the bilge pump jammed so we had to bail out by hand, but it was a losing battle; The Shearwater was shipping more water with every wave than we could bail.

We'd almost given up hope, resigning ourselves to dying, when a ship appeared. It almost hit us, but they spotted us just in time. This is where our good luck ended; the ship was a destroyer of the British Royal Navy. What it was doing so far east is beyond me, but it saved our lives.

I suppose we should be grateful that we were rescued, and they did treat us well, but we are devastated to be spending the rest of the war in captivity in England.

Johann is fine. His letter should accompany mine as they gave us all paper and envelopes yesterday, but you know Johann. We should be permitted to write every month, or every second month.

I hope this letter finds you all well at Drachensee. Please pass on my love and best wishes to Eva and Antje, and my grandparents.

Have they found Ruth and Manny yet? Pass on our concerns to Yosef and Miriam. All four of them are in our thoughts.

I said earlier that the British had treated us well, father. Johann and I, needless to say, were exhausted and just about at our wits' end when we were rescued. Once they'd allowed us a hot shower, we were taken to see Captain Stanworth, who sat us down and asked us all sorts of questions but didn't insist on interrogating us further when we stuck to our rights and only gave our names, ranks and Wehrmacht numbers.

It turns out that he sailed yachts at home in the Solent. And you will like this, Father. When he poured us a stiff drink each, I expected that it would be navy rum but, you won't believe it; he was a whisky man. It was a Glenfiddich!

No harm to all the great whiskies you've introduced me to over the years, but a glass of malt never tasted better!

I must go now. There is not much more to tell; life is very humdrum here at the racecourse. Perhaps when we are moved to a permanent camp there will be more to do but at present the men all just hang around talking or playing football.

We are both missing you all, although Johann has already made a crowd of new friends, which shouldn't surprise you.

You have my deepest devotion,

Your son,

Franz

~~o~~

Franz placed the letter in the envelope. He didn't seal it: the censors would do that once they had scrutinised it. He looked around for Johann and found his brother standing with the usual crowd of prisoners, laughing and joking.

He marvelled at the ease with which Johann could make himself at home with any group of people, no matter where.

'Johann,' he said, approaching the group.

'Franz. We're just going to have a game of cards. Do you want in?'

'No, thanks. I'm going to hand in my letter. Have you written yours?'

'Not yet. I was going to do it tonight.'

'Your brother tells us you met the Führer,' Axel Langefeld, the Luftwaffe officer said.

'Yes. Twice. Johann was most disappointed that he spoke to me in Paris, not him.'

The flying officer laughed.

'He told me,' he said. 'I think he still harbours a degree of bitterness about it.'

'Yes,' Johann snorted, but with a glint of a smile in his eyes. 'Major Kästner this, Major Kästner that. Always the man in charge of the boat, or at the head of the guard of honour. Who else would the Führer wish to talk to? Not the crew who do all the work, or the captain who makes sure all Major Kästner's men are suitably turned out, and well-trained. No. He only wishes to speak to Major Kästner.'

'Technically, you're Major Kästner now,' Franz said, smiling.

'I know, but you're always one step ahead.'

'Whoa, gentlemen. What's all this about promotions? You didn't say anything.'

'We hadn't actually received our new commissions when we were captured,' Johann said. 'They were to come through on our return to our unit.'

'So, that would make you Oberst, Franz?'

'No, not a full colonel. Lieutenant colonel.'

'You're the most senior officer here then.'

'No. There are a few other majors, and my new rank was never ratified, so I'm still a lowly major.'

The aircraftman lowered his voice.

'A few of us are talking about trying to break out. Get aboard a fishing boat and head across the North Sea. We have experienced Kriegsmarine men among us. You could command it. What do you say?'

Franz shook his head.

'I sail yachts. I have never been in a fishing boat, far less skippered one, and the Kriegsmarine men are all submariners. They have no experience of surface ships, and don't forget, I was almost drowned in the North Sea a short while ago. What makes you think I would want to risk that again?'

'Because you are a soldier of the Wehrmacht, and it is your duty to do everything possible within your power to fight for the Reich.'

'If I must fight, I will. But I am not a professional sailor, and I will not take unnecessary risks with men's lives on a crazy scheme that would fail, for sure.'

Axel Langefeld shrugged.

'What about you, Johann? Would you be man enough to do it?'

He laughed, but Franz detected an edge to it.

Johann shook his head.

'I'm not going to sea without Franz.'

Franz could have hugged his brother, but he realised that being branded as a coward in a POW camp could leave him with a big target on his back.

'If you find me a professional seaman, an officer, and not a submariner, who is willing to take the risk,' Franz said, 'I'll go with him as crew.'

I won't, but I'll cross that bridge when I need to.

Axel Langefeld nodded.

'I suppose that's fair, but it's disappointing. Ach, well, we may just have to steal a plane.'

'If you can find a pilot here that hasn't crashed, I'll go with you,' Johann joked.

This time, the Luftwaffe man's laughter was genuine. Once again, Franz envied his brother's easy way of diffusing a situation without having to think about it.

'That's assuming you could get out of this place,' he said.

CHAPTER 212

'Herr Kriminaldirektor, it was good of you to agree to see me.'

'General, if I can't help such an esteemed colleague, what would that make me?'

'You're very gracious. I do appreciate you taking the time.'

'What can I do for you, Erich? May I call you Erich?'

'By all means, Herr Kriminaldirektor. Our wives appear to be on intimate terms.'

An exaggeration, perhaps, and the General hoped his wife would never find out.

'Excellent,' the corpulent Gestapo chief said. 'And please call me Gerhard.'

'That would be a privilege, Gerhard. The thing is, as you already know, I have a problem.'

'Yes. Your Jewish staff.'

'They have been arrested.'

'Yes. In Prague. With false papers. And associating with an enemy of the state.'

'Gerhard, both you and I know they were trying to get to Palestine. That is their only crime.'

'I know, Erich. I know. But, still, it is a crime, these days. Why did they not leave when it was encouraged?'

'That was an error on their part, and on mine, for not insisting.'

'I'm afraid it will be a costly mistake. Even as the head of the Gestapo in Kiel, my hands are tied, Erich. While Kriminalassistent Güllich's suspicions were unfounded and, to be honest, grounded in what I thought at the time was an obsession, I could keep him in check. Now, I'm afraid, due to the seriousness of the offences your employees have committed, there's not much I can do to help.'

'What do you mean?'

'Kriminalassistent Güllich has already finished his interrogation. The Nussbaums are not here, I'm afraid.'

'They've been executed?' the General asked, barely controlling the anger in his voice.

'No. As a matter of fact, they have been detained indefinitely. The Kriminalassistent seems to think that they may be of future help with other investigations. He was within his rights to have them shot.'

'I see,' the General said, barely hiding his relief. 'Where are they being held?'

'They're at a camp close to Hamburg, I believe.'

The General felt his stomach lurch.

Neuengamme.

He hesitated. His next actions could put him, and his family, in a great deal of danger.

'Perhaps there is a charity, for returning SS veterans, for instance, that would benefit from a donation, in gratitude for the help you have given, and could give.'

'It's a kind offer, Erich. As you know, we are making enormous strides towards Moscow and although the Wehrmacht is suffering remarkably low casualties, there are some unfortunate souls who need help. My only caveat is that any further assistance I could provide would be limited.'

'How limited?'

'They cannot be released. As much as is possible, I can promise you that they will not be executed by anyone under my command, but I cannot guarantee their safety.'

'I think that is fair,' the General said, relieved to have achieved the little he had.

'I must be allowed to see them,' he continued, deciding to push for as much as possible.

'I cannot promise you that, but I will make enquiries.'

'It would be a pointless exercise if I weren't allowed to confirm that they were alive,' the General said.

The Gestapo chief laughed.

'Everything they say about you is true. You drive a hard bargain, and still leave the other party glad to have done business with you.'

The General smiled.

'I apologise if I have been too forward,' he said, 'but I need to make sure I get my money's worth.'

'Touché,' the Gestapo man said, smiling. 'I will try my best to make this possible.'

The General coughed.

'How much of a donation would help the veterans?' he asked.

As the big man laughed, the General noticed the rolls of fat on his neck shaking, like jellied fruit.

'I'll let you decide,' the Gestapo chief said, when his laughter had subsided. 'What are your Jews worth to you?'

~~o~~

[30/06/1941 Monday]

Erich Kästner sat on the gunnels of the dinghy, watching his daughter tack the little boat expertly around the lake without much help from him. They'd got into the habit of taking a sail on Drachensee if he came home from Kriegsmarine Headquarters if time allowed, and there was enough wind.

She'd become quite adept at handling the dinghy in the confined waters of the small lake and as he watched her, he realised that she was as expert as he was at trimming the little craft's sails, and tacking and gybing, to get the best speed out of her.

'You could sail *Snowgoose* yourself now,' he said to her. 'With the navigation you've learned over the last few years from the boys and I…'

His voice trailed off at the thought of his sons.

'Surely we would have heard by now,' Antje said, saying out loud the exact thought that was in his mind.

'No. It's still too early to think like that. These things can take time and there may have been complications with Ruth and Manny.'

'What do you mean?'

'Well…' The General hesitated.

He sighed.

'If a soldier, or an airman, or a sailor is captured, the rules are simple. They are prisoners of war. Even prisoners who surrender without having been involved in combat should be treated the same way, but Franz and Johann have travelled across the sea to an enemy's border in the company of two civilians. There could be suspicions of espionage, and it could take some time to sort out. If they were found to be spies, they could be imprisoned without the rights of POWs, or even shot.'

Antje gasped.

'No. Surely not. They were only trying to help Ruth and Manny.'

'We discussed it before they went. I'm quite sure the British will listen to reason. And don't forget that Franz has excellent English.'

'That could work against them though,' Antje said, as she tacked the dinghy round the small buoy at the far end of the lake.

'That's true, but no. I think they'll be treated well.'

'So, you still think there's hope that they made it?'

'Yes. Definitely.' He looked at his daughter. She'd turned into a delightful young woman; not as sophisticated as Eva, or as likely to turn heads, but that was only because she played down her looks, making little effort with hair, make-up, or clothes, much to her mother's disgust. He didn't even know if there was a boy on the scene.

He took a deep breath.

'I brought you out here for a reason tonight,' he said.

'It's the Nussbaums,' she said, the blood draining from her face, 'isn't it?'

'Yes. I'm sorry. They were captured in Prague and brought back to Kiel.'

'They're back here?' she said, her eyes wide in horror.

'No. They were interrogated by the Gestapo in Kiel, but they've been moved. They must have said nothing about Ruth and Manny, and Franz and Johann, or Güllich would have been at our door, asking all sorts of questions. Anyway, they've been sent to Neuengamme, where Yosef was before.'

'Can't you get them out, like you did the last time?'

'There's little hope, I'm afraid. They were caught with false papers, contravening travel restrictions.'

'What will happen to them?' she said, in a small voice, a tear brimming over and rolling down her cheek.

'They're strong people. If I can provide a little help…'

'How?'

'I have contacts; I can put pressure on the authorities, and a little money might buy preferential treatment, like easier work details and extra food helpings. You just have to find the right person to channel it through.'

'Have you spoken to Yosef and Miriam?'

'No. Mama is friendly with the Gestapo chief's wife. I've spoken to him, and I've made a *donation* to the SS welfare fund. He has promised to try and get me in to see them.'

Tears ran down her face. He handed her his handkerchief. It was one of the reasons he'd taken her out on the lake. By the time they returned to the house, she'd have time to compose herself again.

'You must keep this to yourself. The only other person who knows is Uncle Wilhelm. It was he who found out what had happened to them.'

'What about Mama? And Eva?'

'I don't want to say anything just yet. Keep this between ourselves. You know what Mama is like. She'll try and stop me from helping them.'

'Why would she do that, after all those years?'

Bright red spots appeared high on Antje's cheeks.

'She's frightened for you and Eva, and herself, like everyone else in the country.'

'She's just concerned about what her *ladies* think.'

'You're being harsh, Antje. You have to see it from her point of view.'

'Why are you defending her? She's horrible to you. Don't think I haven't noticed that she's moved everything of hers from your bedroom? That she barely speaks to you?'

'Antje. That's enough. That's between me and your mama.'

'Not when I see what it's doing to our family.'

'It's as much my fault as hers. I'm stubborn.'

'But you're right. She's wrong.'

'It's not that simple,' he said. 'Ask Eva.'

'Eva just doesn't want to lose out on the chance to be married to the aristocratic Hugo or lose her job with the National Socialists.'

'She doesn't work with the NSDAP. She works for the government, like a lot of good people who aren't National Socialists.'

Antje snorted.

'The government is the party. And what she does is very secretive, but she has let a few remarks slip.'

The General stayed silent, digesting the new information.

My own daughter.

'Good jobs are hard to come by these days,' he said, 'especially for girls. She speaks three languages fluently. Where else would she get a job like that?'

Antje bowed her head.

'Nowhere,' she mumbled. 'But it doesn't make it right.'

The General looked at Antje. He frowned.

'You're not involved with anything at college, are you?'

Antje flushed.

'Antje,' the General said, taking a grip of her hand, but she drew it away to gybe the dinghy at the mark near to the dock.

'It's nothing. We just talk. You can't tell me to be careful when you publicly stand up against all of this… this… madness.'

'That's different. I have the protection afforded me by my position in the Wehrmacht. You have nothing.'

'You always said that if ordinary people had stood up to them, we wouldn't have got into this mess.'

He knew she was right, but it filled him with horror to think of the consequences if she were reported for anti-government activities.

His shoulders slumped.

'Just be careful who you trust,' he said.

'I am. Truly. But it's comforting to know that not everyone's like them.'

He smiled at her.

He thought about the others. He knew that he'd as good as lost Eva, and it pained him to the depths of his soul. Johann, the least serious of them all, would survive anywhere, and would adapt to anything life threw at him. He valued his friends as much as his family, perhaps more so.

And Franz. He was the most like him, and they could talk about anything together. They had few differences, and the sorrow he felt at his absence left a deep hole in his being.

But it was Antje who melted his heart, every time he saw her.

He took her hand again.

'Promise me that you won't take risks,' he said.

'If you'll do the same,' she replied.

He stared at her, angry for a second, and he opened his mouth to scold her.

Then he laughed, quietly, but his shoulders shook.

She looked at him for a second or two, puzzled, then she giggled too. She let go of the tiller and the mainsheet and the boat slewed to a halt, rounding up into the wind.

She leaned forward and he wrapped his arms around her.

'I hope they're not watching from the house,' she said.

'I'll tell them you've just broken up with your latest boyfriend, and that I was consoling you, convincing you that you were too good for him, and that there are plenty more fish in the sea.'

She laughed, blushing.

'So, there is someone?' he said.

'No one too serious, just yet, Papa, but I'll let you meet him sometime.'

'Do what makes you happy,' the General said, 'but be careful.'

They looked at each other and laughed.

'Sorry, that sounded like a different kind of advice.'

'I'll be careful in every way, Papa.'

'Bring him home,' he said.

'No. I'll take you to him, if at all. In town.'

'Ah. I see.'

~~o~~

'We have invaded Russia.'

Johann stared at his brother. 'When? How do you know?'

'I overheard two of the guards talking. It appears we have advanced halfway across Russian-occupied Poland already. They said that the Red Army had crumbled.'

'What does it mean for us, for the Nussbaums?'

Franz rubbed his chin.

'There will be no invasion of England now, unless…'

'Unless what?'

'If we take Moscow, we'll have all the resources we'll ever need. It would only be a matter of time before the Führer turns his gaze back across the English Channel.'

'We'd be in the Scheiße then.'

'Yes. And Ruth and Manny too.'

'Will you tell Axel?'

'Yes. He'll find out anyway.'

CHAPTER 213

Chief of the Security Police and the SD

B. No. IV - 1100/41 Top Secret
B. No. g. Rs. 02/07/41

EK 3

Reich Secret Document
a) To the Higher SS and Police Leader
SS Obergruppenführer Jeckeln
b) To the Higher SS and Police Leader
SS Gruppenführer von dem Bach
c) To the Higher SS and Police Leader
SS Gruppenführer Pruetzmann
d) To the Higher SS and Police Leader
SS Oberführer Korsemann

Owing to the fact that the Chief of the Ordnungspolizei invited
the Higher SS and Police Leaders to Berlin and commissioned
them to take part in policing during Operation Barbarossa
without informing me of this in time, I was unfortunately not
in a position to provide them with basic instructions for the
sphere of jurisdiction of the Security Police and SD.

In the following letter I will make known briefly the most
important instructions given by me to the Einsatzgruppen and
Kommandos of the Security Police and the SD, with the request
to take note of them.

Executions

All the following are to be executed:

Officials of the Comintern (together with professional
Communist politicians in general);

Top- and medium-level officials and radical lower-level
officials of the Party, Central Committee and district and sub-
district committees;

People's Commissars;

Jews in Party and State employment, and other radical elements
(saboteurs, propagandists, snipers, assassins, inciters, etc)
insofar as they are, in any particular case, required or no
longer required to supply information on political or economic
matters which are of special importance for the further
operations of the Security Police, or for the economic
reconstruction of the Occupied Territories.

~~o~~

[04/07/1941 Friday]

Erich Kästner placed the transcribed copy of Heydrich's letter on the desk. It had arrived in
the daily internal post from Berlin, addressed to him, from Admiral Wilhelm Canaris, Chef der
Abwehr.

The note accompanying it read *I thought you'd be interested.*

He put it in the inside pocket of his jacket and looked at the clock. He would phone Dieter Maas from a public telephone and arrange to meet him at the boat.

He needs to see this.

CHAPTER 214

[12/07/1941 Saturday]

It was unfortunate that when Ruth Nussbaum fainted, she was standing at the top of the stairs in the house in Hutchinson Square that she and Manny shared with the Weissberg family.

It was Frau Weissberg, making Gefilte fish in the kitchen for the evening meal, who heard the thump and clatter as Ruth fell the twenty steps down to the hallway, and rushed out to see what the commotion was.

'Ruth,' she shouted as she spotted the unmoving body at the foot of the stairs, wiping her hands on her apron before touching the young woman's face, as if laying a hand on her would tell her if she was still alive.

Ruth let out a groan, causing Frau Weissberg to jump.

'Manny!' she screamed, knowing that she'd need help.

'What is it?' he shouted from the top of the stairs.

'Hurry. It's Ruth.'

He took one glance at Ruth's body lying crumpled in the hallway and leapt down the stairs three steps at a time.

'What happened?' he said, kneeling beside his sister.

'I don't know. I just heard the noise and came running. I found her only a few seconds ago. Go and fetch Doctor Ginsberg.'

Jewish immigrant doctors and dentists were permitted to practise, in a limited manner, within the confines of the Jewish prisoner community. Anything more serious would be dealt with by one of the island's general practitioners.

By the time Manny returned, saying that the doctor was on the way, Ruth was beginning to stir, letting out low moans and trying to sit up.

'Lie still, Meydaleh,' Frau Weissberg said. *Little girl.*

~~o~~

Ruth's eyes flickered open and darted around, staring first at the older woman who had become her friend, then at Manny, a dazed look in her eyes.

'You fell, Ruth. Don't try and move. We're waiting for the doctor.'

'I'll be all right. Help me to sit up. I'm just winded. I don't know what happened. Everything just went black.'

She tried to lift herself to a sitting position, but her head swam, and she lay back down again.

She winced as a spasm of pain in her lower abdomen overrode the ache elsewhere in her body; her ribs, her left arm and both her legs throbbed, and the beginning of a sharp headache made it difficult for her to see clearly.

She must have passed out again because when she opened her eyes next, a grey-haired, well-dressed small man with round glasses was crouching over her, a stethoscope in his ears. He was listening to her chest.

'I'm sorry, my dear,' he said, seeing Ruth's agitated stare. 'I had to...'

He continued to listen to her chest, then took the chestpiece of the stethoscope from under Ruth's blouse.

'You have no fractured ribs, and your lungs are fine. Your heart is strong, but it's racing a little faster than I would like. Probably the shock.'

He examined all her limbs in turn, talking her through his findings.

'No fractures. You will be badly bruised, and it would be better if you lay still for a few days or maybe longer.'

He pressed on her abdomen and frowned.

'You are sore, here?' he said.

'A little.'

He turned to Frau Weissberg.

'She will need to drink warm broth, and plenty fluids. Now, could you both help me to lift her to her bed?'

Manny rushed to help, but Frau Weissberg insisted on fetching the man next door. The doctor instructed the three of them how he wanted Ruth lifted. Between them, they managed to get her upstairs and into bed, and to make her comfortable.

'I will need you to run to the chemist shop for tablets for your sister, for the pain,' the doctor said to Manny, while Frau Weissberg showed the neighbour out and explained the circumstances to her.

The doctor scribbled a quick note. 'Show them this, and the guards will let you through to fetch the medicine,' he said.

When Manny had left, the doctor turned to Ruth.

'You must let me know if you have any bleeding, in your stools or in your urine. It is vitally important.'

Ruth blushed, but appreciated the doctor's discretion.

'And you might lose your baby,' he said, lowering his voice. 'There's just a chance, I'm afraid.'

'How did you know?' Ruth gasped.

The doctor gave her a sad smile.

'I've seen enough young women in your condition to spot the symptoms and hazard a guess, but it was the way you touched your stomach, and looked down at yourself for signs of bleeding that gave it away.'

Ruth began to cry.

'There,' the doctor said. 'Nothing can be done about it now. It's in God's hands, but if you lie very still and don't leave this bed, there is a chance that your baby will survive.'

'I'll need to go to the toilet.'

'I'll instruct a nurse to call in three times a day to help you. A few of our fellow prisoners were very proficient nurses, until the National Socialists took that away from them, and I'm sure Frau Weissberg will help too. I'll suggest to her that I'm worried about your back for now, but you'll need to tell her sometime.'

'Thank you,' Ruth said, drying her tears. 'It happened on the boat, coming here. We didn't know if we were going to live or die. I loved him.'

She knew she wasn't making much sense, but it felt important to her that he understood that she wanted the baby, and that it hadn't been conceived in a careless encounter.

'It is not for me to judge, especially in these times. Even if the baby survives, you have a hard hill to climb.'

He looked at her and put his hand on hers.

'I will call back every day to check on you. In the meantime, get as much rest as you can. If anything untoward happens, tell Frau Weissberg and she will fetch me at once.'

'Thank you, Doctor,' Ruth said, her dark eyes gaunt in her pale face.

~~o~~

He let himself out. At the foot of the stairs, he gave Frau Weissberg instructions for the patient's care, and left. The older woman climbed the stairs and knocked on the bedroom door before entering.

'How are you feeling now?' she asked.

'Sore. And very silly. I don't want to be a nuisance.'

'Don't fret. The doctor thinks you fainted, and that you may have hurt your back. You've not to get out of bed.'

Ruth turned away, flushing.

'Don't worry there, my love. It will be easier than you imagine; just a little awkward. I nursed my mama when she was ill, and we had to do everything for her. At least you'll be up in a few days. The girls can sleep in our bedroom for now.'

'Oh, no. Don't put them out, for me.'

'Not at all. We can't have you being nursed with those two scallywags getting in the way. If there's anything you need, or you just want to talk, let me know.'

'No. I'll be fine,' Ruth said, with a slight hesitation. 'I'll be fine.'

'I'll go and make a pot of broth. The doctor says you need plenty fluids.'

She went to the door and looked back at Ruth.

'I'll send Manny up for little while.'

She saw a tear trickle down Ruth's cheek as she closed the door. She wondered when Ruth would tell her that she was pregnant.

Is it better that she loses the baby? It's in God's hands now.

She sent Manny up the stairs with the strict admonishment that he should stay no more than a few minutes with Ruth. She busied herself chopping vegetables for the soup.

She'd suspected that Ruth was pregnant weeks before but had waited for the girl to come to her, rather than try and drag it from her.

Neither brother nor sister had hidden the fact that Ruth had fallen in love with the General's oldest son, and that it wasn't just because he and his brother had saved their lives and secured their freedom.

Gella Weissberg remembered her own first flames of love and smiled. If she and her husband had been given the opportunities to be alone like Ruth and Franz, it would have been difficult to deny each other what they had both ached for.

Now, he looks at me like I'm a heiferlump.

She laughed. It wasn't quite that bad, but three children, and now two lodgers, made it difficult.

The doctor had looked worried, and not because of the girl's back.

She shrugged. She would do her best to help Ruth, whatever the outcome.

~~o~~

[13/07/1941 Sunday]

KIELER JÜDISCHES FREIHEITSNACHRICHTENBLATT

Volume 101

18th of Tamuz, 5701

SOVIET INVASION: CONTINUED SUCCESS

The German advance into Russia, the Ukraine and Russian-occupied Poland continues apace.

In the north, the Wehrmacht is within striking distance of Leningrad.

From the centre, the 2nd, 3rd, 4th and 9th Armies have taken most of Poland and have now encircled Smolensk, in Russia, 360 kilometres west of Moscow. It is expected that the city will fall within a few days.

In the south, German troops are fighting a few kilometres short of Kiev, in Ukraine.

The KJF has no reason to doubt these claims by the ministry of propaganda and has been able to verify that most of the reports are credible.

The KJF has also received information from a reliable source that there has been a policy change and that large numbers of political opponents and Jews are being eliminated behind the advancing German Army.

The KJF believes that the only thing that will halt or slow down the advance of the forces of the German invasion is the weather. If history is anything to go by, the leaders of the Third Reich should look to Napoleon Bonaparte's fate at the hands of the Russian winter and Imperial Russia's vast reserves of soldiers. In the meantime, the situation for Jews in Germany and in the occupied territories remains perilous.

WORD OF THE WEEK

Einsatzkommandos: Special, mobilised sub-units of
Einsatzgruppen, tasked with eliminating Jews and other
'Untermenschen' on the Eastern Front.

CHAPTER 215

[14/07/1941 Monday]

The bleeding started two days after Ruth fell. Gella Weissberg heard the soft but terrible cries coming from the bedroom and knew at once. One look at Ruth's face when she entered the room told her she was right.

The nurse was due in an hour, but she sent her oldest daughter, Berta, to fetch Doctor Ginsberg.

'Tell him to hurry,' she told her, but she knew that no amount of haste could help Ruth's baby now.

She sat on the bed and cradled Ruth, her racking sobs breaking the older woman's heart.

'The doctor's coming, my dear,' she said. 'He'll be here soon.'

'It'll do no good,' she said, as she doubled up with another cramp. 'It's finished.'

She was right, and Gella Weissberg knew it. But she couldn't bring herself to say that to Ruth.

'You never know. Women have bled before now, and they've gone on to have their babies.'

Ruth stared at her through the tears.

'You knew?'

'I guessed as much. The sickness, the tiredness. The constant worry. And you hadn't washed your menstrual rags since you came here. Women notice these things.'

'Why didn't you say?'

Gella Weissberg shrugged and gave Ruth a tired smile.

'Ach. You'd have come to me in your own time if this hadn't happened.'

Ruth began to cry again, and the older woman held her. Another spasm ripped through her abdomen, and she clutched Gella Weissberg's hand.

'I know it would have been difficult,' she said, when the pain had passed, 'but I wanted to keep the baby. It's all I have of Franz. We might never see each other again.'

Gella Weissman took hold of Ruth's shoulders.

'Listen,' she said. 'Those two boys will be well looked after. The British are sticklers for the rules. You needn't worry on that score.'

'But what if Hitler invades Britain?'

'Then we'll have more to worry about than your young man. We'd have to get out first, and we're fast running out of places that will take us.'

For a moment, she saw real fear in Ruth's eyes. Then another barb of pain tightened its grip on the girl's womb and turned her mind back to the present.

~~o~~

[28/07/1941 Monday]

At the end of the evening meal, after the housekeeper had cleared away the dishes, the General told his wife and daughters that he had some bad news.

'Franz and Johann,' Eva gasped. Her face, like her mother's, was pale and drawn.

'No, don't be silly. There has been nothing. I would have told you right away. This is about the Nussbaums.'

Neither Eva nor Maria Kästner could hide the relief that flooded over their faces. It was Antje, who'd been warned to act surprised, who reacted.

'What about them, Papa?' she said, playing her part.

The General marvelled again at his youngest daughter's acting abilities. Even to him, she sounded convincing.

'They've been captured trying to get to Palestine.'

In fairness, the shock returned to Maria Kästner's face.

'No,' she said. 'The poor souls. When did this happen?'

'A little while ago. I waited until I was completely sure before I told you.'

'You knew?'

'I'd heard rumours, but you know how difficult it is to confirm anything these days. They're in Neuengamme. They were questioned by the Gestapo.'

'How long have you known?' There was a cold shiver of accusation in Maria Kästner's voice.

'That doesn't matter. All I know is that I had to be sure.'

'I sometimes think you don't trust us.'

'That's not fair. If I'd told you, and it had turned out to be wrong, it would have upset you for no good reason. Anyway, had you even noticed that they'd gone?'

Maria Kästner's face flushed with anger.

'That's cruel and unwarranted,' she said. 'You did promise to find them a way to leave Germany. I'd hoped they might be on their way.'

She turned her head, evading his stare.

'What happened, Papa?' Antje said.

'They were caught in Prague,' the General said, glad that his daughter had intervened.

He got up and stood at the window, looking down at the evening shadows lengthening on the lawn, and the lake beyond.

'They were making for Romania, then Bulgaria,' he continued. 'The plan was to cross over to Turkey, then down through Syria to Palestine.'

'Erich, please don't make a fuss this time. I can't be having the Gestapo visiting the house. As much as it pains me that the Nussbaums are in one of these camps, it would be foolhardy for you to try and get them out.'

'There doesn't seem to be much chance of having them released,' the General said. His voice hid the cold fury stirred by her only care being for herself.

'But I am trying to arrange to see them,' he added, 'to let them know we haven't completely abandoned them.'

The relief on his wife's face froze.

'What good will it do,' she said, her face taut, 'even if you do manage to get in? It will only give them false hope.'

'But Mama, Papa might be able to shield them a little from the hardships of the camp. He has contacts.'

Antje turned to her father.

'Isn't that right?' she pleaded.

'I'll try, Antje,' he said. 'I've spoken to the Gestapo chief.'

He turned to Maria. 'I believe you know his wife,' he said.

'Indeed I do not,' she said, bristling.

'She's friendly with Admiral Schiffer's wife. We met them at the dinner we were at a few months ago. Frau Keppler.'

'Nonsense. Her husband is an Obersturmführer in the SS.'

'That is true. He is also the chief of the Geheime Staatspolizei in Kiel. All Gestapo personnel are part of the SS and have an equivalent SS rank. I suppose at these dinner parties, it is almost as distasteful to be a member of the Gestapo as it is to be a Jew.'

'Erich. That was uncalled for.'

'I'm sorry. You're right. A Jew would be at a quite different dinner party. With a few thousand fellow guests, being served a thin potato gruel.'

Maria Kästner's face paled for a second, then reddened. The anger on Eva's face mirrored her mother's.

'You've gone too far this time, Erich Kästner,' Maria said, her eyes blazing. 'I will not be spoken to like that.'

'Yes, Father. Mama is right,' Eva said, as angry as her mother.

'Mama, Papa, please stop this,' Antje said.

The General's shoulders slumped.

'I'm sorry, Antje,' he said. 'You're right. We'll discuss this again when we've all had time to think about it.'

'There's nothing to discuss,' Maria Kästner said. 'Come with me, Eva. We don't have to listen to one of your father's hateful rants.'

'Wait, Mama,' Antje said.

'No, Antje. It's about time that you realised that you may have to make a choice between your father's shameful rhetoric and my moderation. Between his reckless behaviour and our family's safety.'

'No, Mama. I won't. I love you both, but I also loved the Nussbaums.'

'You've made your choice, I see. Come, Eva. There's no point in staying.'

She turned to the General.

'We'll be in the drawing room. You are both quite welcome to join us if you think you can manage to take part in a civilised conversation.'

The General gave a sad shake of his head.

'Do what you must,' he said.

When his wife and elder daughter had left the room, he turned to Antje.

'I'm sorry,' he said. 'Her attitude towards the Nussbaums sickens me.'

'I know, Papa, but you must try hard not to bait her, even if it is sometimes warranted. It does no good, in the long term.'

'It makes me feel better at the time, but you're right. I shouldn't.'

He gave her a cheerless smile.

'I'll speak to her,' she said, 'when she's calmed down a little.'

'Thank you. What would I do without you?'

'Have you heard anything?' she asked.

'No. Nothing. I'd hoped that I would have been allowed in to see them by now. I contacted Herr Keppler today at Gestapo Headquarters, to find out if there has been any progress. He told me that I had no patience.'

Despite the sadness in the house, Antje gave a soft laugh at her father's mournful expression.

'I can't imagine that went down well.'

He returned her smile.

'You're right. It did dent my pride. But he's wrong about something. I can be very patient when I need to be.'

CHAPTER 216

[29/07/1941 Tuesday]

It suited Miriam that her injuries healed much slower the second time. She supposed that her body was tired of fighting to mend itself, only to be broken again.

And, according to Rosa, it bought her a little time before her body would be required for a different use, as a receptacle for men's lustful needs and, Rosa thought, their hatred of women.

'Why else would they want to take a woman without any desire on her part?' Rosa said, on one of the days she wasn't working in the next-door compound.

'I'd never really thought about it,' Miriam said. 'I mean, all these stories you hear, about soldiers raping civilians. I always thought it was exaggerated, but now…'

'Don't all soldiers have it in them?' Rosa asked.

'No.'

'How can you be so sure?'

'Because Yosef was a soldier. The General is a soldier, and his sons are soldiers. Emil was once one too, Rosa.'

'And you know for certain that none of them took women in the chaos of combat?'

'Yes. I'm sure. I know them.'

'There are thousands, maybe millions of women saying the same thing about their husbands. Even the men who use me; most of them will go home to their wives and children, and they'll be none the wiser.'

She stared at the barbed wire fence.

'They must know something,' Miriam said. 'They just won't admit it, even to themselves.'

~~o~~

From:

Hermann Göring
Der Reichsmarschall des Reiches
Beauftragter für den Vierjahresplan.

To:

Chef der Sicherheitspolizei und des SD
SS-Gruppenführer Heydrich.
Berlin, 31.07.1941

In addition to the task you received with the order of January 24, 1939 to solve the Jewish question of emigration or evacuation in a manner feasible according to the current circumstances, I hereby command you to make all necessary organisational, functional, and material preparations for a complete solution of the Jewish question in the German sphere of influence in Europe.

In cases where this affects the responsibilities of other central organisations, these shall participate as required.

I further instruct you to submit to me, in the near future, an overall concept of the organisational, factual and material measures to carry out the desired final solution of the Jewish question.

Göring

~~~o~~~

[01/08/1941 Friday]

Canaris read the memo again. It was a photograph of the original, taken at great personal risk by one of the Abwehr chief's agents. In places it was indistinct and difficult to read, but its message was stark. He placed it in a small brown envelope and stood up. He glanced at the safe built into the wall of his office but passed it by and walked to the corner of the room.

Opening the door of his personal toilet, he entered, and locked it behind him. He knelt on the floor in front of the toilet; anyone watching might have thought he was going to be sick and, after reading the memo, Canaris could see why he might feel nauseous, but there was no bile rising in his throat.

He lifted the corner of the linoleum behind the toilet and pulled it back. He listened for a second, then slid one of the floorboards along a few millimetres, then removed it, exposing a small steel safe with a combination dial on it; he'd had a trusted operative, who did all sorts of jobs for the Abwehr, install it when he'd first been given the position as Chef der Abwehr, and it contained only a few selected documents but each, to his mind, was highly significant. It also contained a personal record which he kept on a weekly basis.

Only he, and the man who put it there, knew about it, and that was a risk he had been prepared to take. If he survived the war, its contents would help ensure that there could be no denial on the part of the members of the regime, the armed forces, and the security services of the Third Reich about their part in taking his beloved nation down the path they did. If he died, it would likely die with him.

He slipped the envelope in beside the others and closed the safe, spinning the dial to lock it. He replaced the board and the linoleum and flushed the toilet.

Sitting back at his desk, he lifted his telephone and waited for his adjutant to answer.

'I'm going to Schleswig-Holstein tomorrow. Arrange for my driver to be available and reschedule my three o'clock meeting with General Albertz for the next day. I'll leave about seven.'

'Yes, Admiral. Will you be returning the same day, or the next morning?'

'I'll be back tomorrow night.'

He put the phone down. He would think about what to do on the drive to Plön.

~~~o~~~

'Canaris.'

'Kästner.'

'I'm sorry I was late. You didn't give me much warning.'

'It was a last-minute thing. I needed to speak to you.'

The General had known it was something of great import. Canaris's adjutant had left a terse message for him, telling him to make his way to the Stadtheide barracks, forthwith.

They waited until Corporal Lubinus had taken the General's coat and had left the room.

'What's so critical that you couldn't speak on the telephone?'

'I received a copy of a memo from Göring to Heydrich.'

'You did? Let me see it then.'

'I didn't bring it. It would be too dangerous to be caught with a copy.'

'You destroyed it?'

Admiral Canaris hesitated. The General noticed but said nothing.

'No. It's in a safe place. But I can tell you its contents.'

His eyes hooded, he quoted Göring's memo word for word. The General listened, the blood draining from his face.

'They don't just want Germany free of Jews,' he said, when Canaris had finished speaking.

'No. They intend to rid Europe of Jews. Perhaps the world.'

'They'll never succeed.'

'The world, no. I don't believe that they can ever beat the Americans, or the Chinese, should it get that far, even if they succeed in defeating the Soviet Union.'

'But Europe? You think they can kill every Jew?'

'They've shown they have the will. And they are slaughtering Jews by their thousands in Russia, and in the camps. They don't appear to take any notice of foreign opinion.'

'Does the world know what is going on?'

'I have been feeding information to the British. So were the Poles. I would expect they would share it with the Americans.'

'So why is there not an outcry?'

'Only the few at the very top, at the very centre of things, know its full extent. I believe it is not in their interest to make it public.'

'But why?'

'We are winning the battle of the Atlantic. Our *Unterseeboot* wolf packs are sinking British merchantmen in the hundreds of thousands of tonnes each week. We are 300 kilometres from taking Moscow. The British will clutch at anything that diverts resources to either of those two fronts. If that means sacrificing a few Jews, they might be willing to accept that.'

'I can't believe the British would do that.'

'Think about it from their point of view. They believed a year ago that an invasion of their country was imminent. They know that if Russia falls, it will be Britain next. They're rearming, but it's a slow process. The Royal Navy is defending the Atlantic convoys with obsolete destroyers sold to them by the Americans in exchange for handing over military bases elsewhere in the world.'

The General stayed silent as Canaris's words hit home.

'I will continue to pass information to the British. And to the Americans. We're working on better contacts over there. Here, there are people working behind the scenes, waiting for their chance, but the Führer is too well protected.'

'Then we can do nothing?'

'In our own small way, we can make a difference, but against this, we can only hope for a miracle.'

He gripped the General's arm.

'You warned me. I didn't listen. It's my biggest regret.'

'I didn't see anything like this coming,' the General said, shaking his head. 'How could I have?'

'You saw more than most. Far more than anyone else I can think of.'

'Other than hundreds of thousands of communists, and other dissenters, who are now dead, or in camps, for standing up to them.'

'Their differences were political, and an extension of their fight against capitalism. Your opposition was on the grounds that the National Socialists were morally corrupt, that they were evil, even if you were a nationalist, like the rest of us.'

'I've not been a nationalist since the end of the last war. Just a man who was proud to be German.'

There was a long silence.

'I need to ask you something,' Canaris said, bowing his head.

'Go on.'

'It means putting aside your attempts to help your people.'

'The Nussbaums, you mean?'

'Yes.'

'You know I can't.'

'Not even for the greater good?'

The General said nothing.

'If you persist in your very public efforts to save the Nussbaums, it will have no effect if the contents of Göring's memo are true, and they implement their plan. On the other hand, if you toe the party line, and work quietly in the background, we can attempt to undermine everything they do.'

'Canaris, you know me better than any living soul, apart from my wife, perhaps. You know that I can't desert them, no matter how bleak their future is.'

Admiral Canaris closed his eyes and shook his head.

'Listen,' the General said. 'By now, the Nussbaums will have been interrogated in the most terrifying of ways; it's part of the reason, I think, that they've delayed me seeing them for so long. But consider this. If, at any point, they'd broken and told the Gestapo about Franz and Johann's involvement in Ruth and Manny's escape attempt, the Gestapo would have arrested me, or at least questioned me and my family. Do you know what that means?'

'Yes. They are incredibly brave people. But like you, they are foolish. They would be better off killing themselves. That's the harsh reality, Erich.'

The General stared at his friend. It was impossible to argue with his reasoning, but it was a difficult truth to hear.

'I'm sorry. I must try.'

'I thought that's what you would say, but I had to ask.'

'Why?'

'It's nothing, my friend. Forget I asked.'

The General knew he had failed a test. It saddened him to have let Canaris down, but his conscience wouldn't let him drop his efforts to save the Nussbaums.

'What do you want me to do?' he asked.

'The same as ever. Do as you are doing and hope that, one day, it will bear fruit.'

The two men embraced, and the General saw Canaris out to his car. They shook hands.

'I'll be in touch.'

~~o~~

As the car sped off, Canaris smiled, despite his disappointment. He couldn't risk telling the General of his secret depository or his other clandestine enterprises but, in a way, he was relieved. He wasn't sure how he would have felt if his oldest friend had agreed to abandon the Nussbaums.

The only problem is, there is no one else I can trust like Erich Kästner.

~~o~~

[03/08/1941 Sunday]

'At last. One of the clergy has found a conscience, and a pair of balls.'

'Erich!' Maria Kästner scolded her husband. 'You're not on the barrack square now. Please keep your language under control.'

'I'm sorry,' the General said, looking anything but. 'It's just a surprise that one of these so-called men of God has had the courage to call out the National Socialists on their crimes.'

'What are you talking about?'

Erich Kästner held up the newspaper.

'It's in the Morgenpost. That alone is a miracle. They've maybe grown a pair too.'

He ignored his wife's cold stare.

'Bishop Clemens August Graf von Galen of Muenster denounces the euthanasia programme,' he read out. 'He does this in a public sermon.'

'That's ridiculous. There's no such thing.'

'Oh, but there is. It is administered by the Reich Committee for the Scientific Registration of Hereditary and Congenital Illnesses, from its headquarters in Tiergartenstraße 4 in Berlin. I've seen the documents. Canaris sent them to me. Those deemed to be Lebensunwertes Leben are being marked for euthanasia.'

'I don't believe it. Life unworthy of life? It's another piece of communist propaganda.'

'No, it's not. We have documentation. The crippled, the mentally ill, chronic alcoholics, even; they're all being killed. Merciful death, they call it.'

'You believe whatever you want to believe, and I'm sure you'll try and talk me round but, as far as I'm concerned, the National Socialists have resurrected German pride and nationhood, and if you can't be pleased about that, I don't know that you can call yourself German.'

'I suppose it helps that the Nussbaums are out of the way?'

'That's unfair. You can't blame me for their problems. I told you to get rid… get them out earlier, but both you and they were too pig-headed to do as I suggested.'

'They were just an inconvenience for you. Does it not bother you that your precious National Socialist government has put them in a camp with a fifty or sixty per cent mortality rate?'

672

Maria's face paled, then reddened in anger.

'They tried to get out of Germany using false papers. You encouraged them. What did you expect?'

'I hoped they would make it. If they got caught, I expected they would die, one way or another. It's a miracle they're still alive.'

'And you'll have us all in one of these camps with them, trying to have them released.'

'No. That will be impossible, but I am going to see them, to do my best to make sure they're being looked after, if that's possible.'

'You should think of your own family. Haven't you noticed that your own daughter is avoiding you?'

'I had, but I thought that part of it was her desire to see more of her young man. A lot more.'

'Erich! How can you say that?'

'I knew you were blind to the Nussbaums' plight, but I thought you might have been a little better informed about what Eva was up to.'

'Eva wouldn't. I assure you.'

'Ask her,' he said, regretting it instantly. He'd lashed out, but if Maria repeated his words to his oldest daughter, it would alienate her still further from him.

For a minute, a cold silence filled the room.

'I will. Now. What have you done about permanent replacements for the Nussbaums?'

Erich Kästner shook his head, sadness like a lead weight on his chest.

'They're irreplaceable,' he said. 'I don't have the stomach for it. You will have to find a suitable couple yourself.'

'And how am I to do that?' she said, her tone indignant.

'I'm sure there are plenty non-Jewish domestic staff who will jump at the chance. Ask your precious countess. A recommendation from her will work wonders. Or perhaps I could ask Heydrich, or Himmler, or Göring for suggestions for staff who are racially pure and up to speed on National Socialist dogma.'

'Don't be sarcastic with me, Erich Kästner. The temporary woman is fine, but you do know she's moving on. It will be a different story when your meals aren't on the table for you.'

She had a point, he thought; the temporary cook and housekeeper had already indicated that she had another position lined up.

Somewhere less contentious, in all likelihood.

'I'll ask around,' he said, letting out a sigh, 'and pass the names on to you. I'll be satisfied with whoever you engage.'

He stood up and left the room before she could reply.

CHAPTER 217

[06/08/1941 Wednesday]

Before the Nussbaums left, it would have been Yosef who collected the post from the box at the top of the Kästners' drive to lay it on the breakfast table, or give to the General in the kitchen, if he were breakfasting on his own.

Since they'd left, the General made it his first job in the morning to walk to the entrance gates, unlock the small iron box, and remove the day's mail.

Still saddened by the state of his relationship with his wife, he lifted the post and flicked through it. As he got to the end, he froze, his heart racing.

There were two postcards addressed to him and Maria.

He read the words on the first card almost in a daze:

Army Perm W3054
PRISONERS OF WAR POST CARD

Kriegsgefangenensendung.

NUR FÜR DIE ADRESSE

An:
Herr and Frau Kästner,
246 Hamburger Chaussee
Kiel
Schleswig-Holstein
Deutschland.

Zur Beachtung, Nichts hinzufügen. Widrigenfalls wird

Die Karte vernichtet.

Erich Kästner smiled at the dire warning on the card: *Please note, add nothing, otherwise the card will be destroyed.*

A British Army stamp reinforced the officiousness of the card. He turned it over and read the words in stilted German, probably written by an English officer with a smattering of the language.

Ich bin in Englische gefangenschaft geraten

Bin Leicht verwunder. Feste Adresse folgt.

Absender: *Major Franz Kästner*
Regiment: *69th Infantry Division*
Datum: *25th April 1941*

~~o~~

The second card had Johann's name on it; it was also spelled correctly, and only forenames and surnames were given. The General cursed. One of the prearranged signals he and the boys had agreed to let the Nussbaums know that Manny and Ruth had made it to England was for Franz, Johann, or both to misspell their names when they first surrendered. Another was that they would transpose part of their names.

Either the Nussbaums hadn't made it, or the British had checked the names against their tags. And they hadn't been allowed to write their middle names.

There was still another couple of ways the boys could confirm that the Nussbaums had made it.

A letter. I need a letter from Franz. Or Johann.

He took a deep breath and strode down the driveway and threw open the front door. Now, there would be a little less lying.

'Maria,' he shouted. 'It's the boys. They're alive.'

~~o~~

Afterwards, he wasn't convinced she believed him.

'No, no, no,' she'd whispered when he showed her the cards. 'It can't be true.'

'It is, Maria. Why would the British send cards to us? And the handwriting is Franz's and Johann's.'

'I know, but how?'

'I don't know. A British ship, maybe a submarine, in the Skagerrak. I can't say, but it doesn't matter, does it. They're alive.'

Tears ran down her face and the General felt a terrible guilt for all the suffering he'd caused her. Truth be told, he'd almost convinced himself that his sons had indeed both perished, along with the Nussbaum children, but that didn't alter the fact that he'd deceived the woman he loved, and his oldest daughter.

'Eva and Antje will be beside themselves with joy,' Maria said, fingering the black cloth of her dress, 'and your father and mother. You must phone them immediately.'

'I will, but I wanted to tell you first.'

His wife's eyes glowed with happiness and part of his guilt evaporated; she now knew that they were safe, and she didn't have the burden of knowledge that he and Antje had about the boys' defection.

And in time, if the war on the Eastern Front went as badly as Canaris expected, and the youth of Germany returned home in coffins in their thousands, she might come to welcome their imprisonment in Britain.

After the war, if his marriage survived, he would tell them everything. Maria and Eva, and his parents, friends, and colleagues. Not all of them would forgive him, but he was sure the ones who were important to him would.

His wife's voice brought him back to the present with a jolt.

'Sorry,' he said. 'What did you say?'

'I said that you don't appear terribly surprised at the news.'

He'd heard her, but the age-old trick of buying time came easily to him.

'I was as shocked as you when I first saw the cards, out at the postbox. I've had a few minutes for it to sink in.'

'Oh, I see. I suppose that's true.'

'My mind is still reeling with the thought that somewhere in Britain, they're sitting in a POW camp somewhere, thinking of home; perhaps they're even writing letters as we speak.'

Her eyes widened.

'They're allowed to write home? Can we write to them?'

'Yes. It's in the Geneva Convention. The Red Cross organise it. We can even send them food parcels and clothing.'

'How do you know all this?'

'It's a commander's duty to know what happens to his men when they are captured. Our training is updated at regular intervals.'

'How will they be treated?' she asked, a worried look crossing her face.

'The British will look after them well, I'm sure. They are meticulous when it comes to fighting with honour; at least, they were in the last war.'

'And what does it involve?'

'Basic barrack accommodation, nourishing food, if not always tasty, medical attention if needed and, depending on the officers running the camp, all sorts of activities in education, entertainment and perhaps even sport.'

'It sounds just like a normal army camp. They should be used to those conditions.'

'Don't get me wrong, it is still a prison, but it's in no one's interest to have a camp full of bored and resentful young men.'

'I suppose that makes sense.'

'And if you think about it, it will spare them for what fate awaits the Wehrmacht in

Russia.'

She glared at him.

'You say that, but they will have missed out on the chances that you had in the last war,' she said. 'You surely can't imagine that they'll promote POWs when they come home after it's all over, do you?'

'I'd rather they were alive. And anyway, I doubt there will be a German Army after this war is over. It might be a thousand years before the world ever trusts us again.'

'You always have to be so negative, don't you? I'm surprised that the army haven't dismissed you.'

'I'm not employed by the army. And someone has to try and keep a check on the madness of our leaders.'

'And why does that have to be you?'

The General shrugged.

~~o~~

Antje sat with Eva on the tram home; it would have looked strange if they hadn't, but it was largely completed in silence.

Antje was convinced that Eva had completely thrown her hat in with the National Socialists, to the point where she wouldn't dare tell Eva her friends' names and wasn't interested in what her sister had to say about her day, or her friends.

And she knew that Eva considered her to be reactionary and far too much in sympathy with their father's views, and that she worried that her choice of companions would impact on the family one day.

The result was that the only conversation they had was about the weather, and what might be for dinner.

They alighted from the tram together and walked to the gates of the Drachensee house. Eva seemed in a hurry to Antje.

She's probably keen to get home and get ready to go out with Hugo.

Antje's only wish was to go to her room after dinner and paint. It was her way of dealing with the pain of imagining what the Nussbaums were going through, and the worry about her brothers, and about Ruth and Manny.

They were only halfway down the drive when Maria opened the door to them, crying and laughing at the same time, unable to speak. It was the General who told them the news.

'The boys are alive,' he said, catching Antje's eyes in a gentle warning. 'They must have been rescued by a British ship.'

'They're prisoners?' Eva said, disbelief etched on her face.

'Yes,' Maria said. 'but they're alive.' She hugged her older daughter.

Antje stood frozen in the doorway. The General touched her arm.

Her face crumpled. All the worry and pain, and the secrecy and the lies caught up with her. She covered her face with her hands and sobbed, the relief giving her release, but it was tempered with unanswered questions.

As Eva and Maria turned and walked down the hall, Antje looked at her father. She silently mouthed to him, 'Any news of Ruth and Manny?'

He gave her the barest shake of his head, and her eyes clouded.

'They must have made it too,' he whispered to her as she passed by him. 'I'll speak to you later.'

They reached the drawing room where Maria handed the General a bottle of champagne to open and, for a brief moment, they were a family again.

They laughed at the printed wording on the card, especially on the reverse.

I've been captured by the English. I'm a little surprised. My fixed address will follow.

'We'll not see them for years,' Eva said.

'Nonsense,' Maria said. 'Once we defeat the Russians, the British will surrender, rather than be destroyed. The boys can come back and rejoin their units.'

Antje glanced at her father.

She saw his frown and said nothing.

'The main thing is that they're alive,' the General said. 'Let's all drink to that.'

CHAPTER 218

[07/08/1941 Thursday]

'Rudolf!'

Rudolf clicked his heels sharply and returned Arnulf Eicke's Hitler salute.

'Obersturmbannführer. How are you?'

'Never been better. How are you finding command, Hauptsturmführer?'

Rudolf Mey gripped his former commanding officer's hand and shook it vigorously.

'Excellent, sir. And it's all thanks to you. It was most kind of you to recommend me for promotion.'

'Nonsense. Both of us know you deserved it. You're an outstanding young SS officer.'

'Thank you, sir. How is your lovely wife?'

'Ah. Delightful and supportive as usual. Yours?'

Rudolf's face darkened for a second, then he smiled.

'Never better, sir.'

'I bumped into her and her mother, in Kiel, the last time I was there. Didn't she tell you?'

'No, sir. It must have slipped her mind.'

'Fine-looking women, mother and daughter, eh?'

Arnulf Eicke nudged Rudolf and winked.

'Yes, sir. I never really took any notice of Lise's mother, sir.'

'Oh, come now. Has it never crossed your mind what it would be like to do the mother?'

Rudolf's face reddened.

'No, sir. Never. She's my mother-in-law.'

'You were always a stickler for the proprieties, Kamerad. Such a waste. These older women are often the keenest to please, my young friend. Their husbands ignore them or take them for granted, and when a dashing young SS officer shows a little interest, well…'

Rudolf blushed again and fidgeted with his sleeve.

The Obersturmbannführer laughed and Rudolf forced himself to join in.

'What are you doing in this neck of the woods, sir?'

'Did your commanding officer not tell you? I'm here to do a little scouting for Kamerad Heydrich. See the lie of the land and how the Einsatzgruppen are doing, and to give you and your men a little guidance, shall we say.'

'You're in SS central command now, sir?'

'It's only temporary. I'm to be second in command of Einsatzgruppe 'E' after I've reported back to the Oberst-Gruppenführer in Berlin. We're following the army through Ukraine.'

'Congratulations, sir. You might be the first into Moscow.'

'I hope so. Now, how are things at the front?'

'Very good, sir. We have orders to work behind advancing Wehrmacht units and apprehend and execute all high- and mid-ranking communist officials. We've had great success.'

'Yes, your commanding officer told me, but I wanted to hear first-hand from the soldiers on the front line, who are doing this important work.'

'Well, sir. The biggest problem is clarity. What about the Jews? Do we shoot them, don't we shoot them? What about Gypsies, or homosexuals?'

'What are you doing at present?'

'Killing them, naturally, where there is any resistance, but the army sometimes insists on taking them prisoner, and sending them back west.' The young SS man sneered.

The Obersturmbannführer held up his hand.

'Part of my duties is to find out what is happening on the ground; my other responsibility is to pass on some key strategic information.'

'The regular Heer units interfere more than they should,' Rudolf said, frowning. 'It would be better if they'd concentrate on sending Russian soldiers back to the camps in

Germany and leave the rest of it to us. That's our job.'

'Don't worry, Kamerad. Herr Heydrich is in negotiations to demarcate the Heer's responsibilities. You will receive clearer instructions in due course. In the meantime, feel free to shoot them all. Communists, Jews, deviants. I can promise you there will be no repercussions.'

'Pah. That doesn't worry me, sir. We just need to keep these spineless army people out of the way.'

'Are you seeing much resistance from the local population?'

'On the contrary, sir,' Rudolf Mey said. 'When we were in Kovno, we and the SD encouraged the local Lithuanian population to help relocate their Jewish neighbours. Unfortunately, things got a little out of hand. By the time we stepped in, they'd clubbed most of the prisoners to death.'

He finished with a laugh, and the senior SS man thumped him on the back and joined in.

'Ah. Delegation,' he said between breaths. 'Marvellous.'

He put his arm around Rudolf's shoulders.

'So, all is well, ja?' he said, when his mirth had subsided.

'Yes, sir. For the glory of the Fatherland.'

'Mark my words, Kamerad Mey. It's back to good old times, like the Polish campaign.'

'Yes, sir, those were the days. Do you remember Mayer, sir?'

'Yes. A big brute of a soldier. Not much between the ears.'

'That's him, sir. He has a new thing, sir.'

'Oh, what's that?'

'When there's a piece of nice, fresh Jewish meat, he takes them and, just when he's about to finish, he shoots them in the head.'

'Really. That's most interesting.'

'He says the death spasm makes him come like a stallion!'

They both laughed.

'Have you tried it, Mey?'

Rudolf coloured.

'No, sir.'

'But you want to, don't you?'

'I suppose you could say I'm curious.'

'As am I, Kamerad. Perhaps I might give it a go. One can never discount something until one has tried it.'

'You're right, sir. We should have open minds.'

The Obersturmbannführer stood up.

'Well, Mey, it's been a pleasure to catch up. I'm travelling through Kiel. Would you like me to call in with a message for your wife?'

The grin froze on Rudolf Mey's face but, after a second's hesitation, he nodded, and gave his senior officer a forced smile.

'That would be great, sir. Tell her that I'm missing her, and that I'm doing the Führer's vital work.'

'I'll do that. She must be missing you terribly, and you her. She's a most remarkable woman. You should try and get leave soon.'

'Yes, sir,' he said, a sudden chill making him shudder. He didn't know why, but there was something about the idea of the Obersturmbannführer visiting Lise that bothered him.

~~o~~

[09/08/1941 Saturday]

'Herr General.'

Erich Kästner stood at the front door. Heinrich Güllich was the last person he wanted to see but he knew that his request to see the Nussbaums had made the man's visit inevitable.

But on a Saturday? At home? It must be deliberate.

'Herr Kriminalassistent, what can I do for you?'

'It's more of what I can do for you, but perhaps we can do each other a favour.'

'Come in. I'll have the maid bring coffee if you like.'

'Ah. You have replaced your former staff.'

'We have a temporary woman until the Nussbaums are released.'

Heinrich Güllich laughed as the General led the Gestapo investigator to his study.

'Both you and I know that that is not going to happen,' the Kriminalassistent said as he sat down opposite the General.

'I never discount anything, Herr Güllich. Now, you said you could help me?'

'My boss, the Kriminaldirektor, has asked me to inform you that it might be possible for you to visit the Nussbaums at their place of incarceration.'

'Yes. Neuengamme. I spoke to him about it a few weeks ago.'

'The camp authorities are dragging their heels a little; they don't like the routine of the camp disrupted in any way by outside influences.'

'I am in the process of contacting the Kommandant, Obersturmbannführer Weiß to discuss the Nussbaums' situation. I served with his father during the last war.'

He had the satisfaction of watching the blood drain from the Gestapo man's face.

It was true. However, the older man was dead, and there was no reason to suppose the son would give his father's old colleague any special treatment.

'I also had a long chat about the situation with Reichsmarschall Göring during his recent visit to Kiel.' This wasn't true but the Kriminalassistent had no way of checking.

Heinrich Güllich flinched and, for a moment, a tic appeared above his right eye and the General thought he might explode but, after a few moments' hesitation, he smiled at the General.

'Your Jews are guilty of serious crimes,' he said. 'You'll be lucky if they're alive in three months unless you cooperate. I'm interested to know why they would have tried to escape when they had such an impressive level of immunity?'

'Perhaps it was the serious assault carried out by you and your colleagues that made them fear for their lives. I can't blame them for trying to escape a country where people like you are above the law.'

'We are the law,' Heinrich Güllich said, his voice rising.

'It would seem so, but one day, you will be made to answer for your actions,' the General said. Although he didn't raise his voice, his words had a cold steel that made the Gestapo man flinch again.

'I hope you're not talking about the afterlife, Herr General,' he said with a brittle laugh.

'There is that, too, but I suspect you don't believe in any authority higher than the Führer. No, I'm talking about more temporal judges, or do you still believe in the thousand-year Reich?'

'The Reich will be here long after you are dead and gone, Herr General. One day, you will put a foot wrong, and I will be there to see you fall.'

They stared at each other, both despising everything they could see in the man sitting opposite them.

The housekeeper knocked the door and entered and laid the tray on the desk.

'Coffee?' the General asked.

'No, thanks,' the Gestapo man said, in a parody of politeness. 'I must be going.'

The General got up and saw him to the door.

'You'll be hearing from me, Herr General.'

'I look forward to it, Herr Güllich.'

~~o~~

As the door closed, Heinrich Güllich walked up the driveway, cursing himself for letting General Kästner get under his skin. He'd wasted the chance to ask a series of questions of the Abwehr officer by being riled by the man. In a fit of anger, he wondered if the General had made a point of goading him.

Then he smiled. He looked at his watch. Colonel Schneider would be in Lübeck in a few hours, home on leave before his battalion was shipped out to fight the Soviets, and he'd arranged to meet him the following day. There was still something not right about the Nussbaums' version of events and he was determined to pursue every avenue open to him.

Even if nothing came of it, sowing the seeds of doubt in the minds of the General's military colleagues would give satisfaction enough, and he mulled over the possibility of trying to get an interview with Admiral Canaris, the General's superior officer.

Being cashiered would wipe the smug grin from the General's face.

As he reached the car, he dropped the last of his cigarette and ground it out with his foot. A sudden thought struck him, and he turned back and made for the neighbouring house.

Herr and Frau Böhm. Perhaps it isn't just the General's colleagues who should be alerted to the man's deceit.

~~o~~

Ruth took to English far better than she'd ever expected and, in contrast to the progress she'd made in the classes in Kiel, something clicked, and she made huge strides almost every day. In part, it was the only activity she'd found that exercised her brain, and kept her mind, at least for a little while, from her loss.

It also reminded her of Franz, and their long watches on *Der Sturmtaucher*, growing closer each day while he sat with great patience, teaching her the words and phrases that had proved so useful to her in the first few difficult months in Britain.

Even her teacher was amazed.

'It's a difficult language, English,' he'd said. 'It has no logic, yet so many rules.'

'Why do countless words sound the same,' Ruth asked with a sigh, 'but have different spellings, while others are spelled the same, but sound so dissimilar?'

The man had shrugged. 'The reason is that the English language is a motley collection of words from Celtic, Norse, Saxon, Norman, Latin and Greek and German, with more recent additions from India, and Britain's other colonies.'

'They use the same word for three or four entirely different purposes,' she said, shaking her head. 'How do you know which is which?'

'It's all about context. Take *stem*, for instance. You can *stem* the tide, something can *stem* from a mistake, and a flower has a thorny *stem*. The word's meaning is obvious from the words around it.'

'I suppose so. But it's so hard to learn.'

'It's also the reason why so many of the world's great literary works are written in English. Its chaotic nature makes for interesting prose.'

'I'll never master it.'

'Ruth Nussbaum. You're the brightest pupil I've ever taught. Just keep at it, and you'll be fluent before you know it. We'll have you reading *Pride and Prejudice* and *Jane Eyre* by Hanukkah.'

Ruth blushed, bringing a little colour to her pale cheeks.

~~o~~

Ruth's teacher looked at her. He was fond of her, and it hadn't been empty flattery. She was by far the quickest learner he'd taught but, for two or three weeks, she hadn't looked quite herself, and had missed a week's lessons.

I hope, whatever it was, that she's getting over it.

CHAPTER 219

When Beate Böhm opened the front door, Heinrich Güllich noted the familiar wariness that his appearance often provoked in the average citizen but, with the Kästners' neighbour, it was fleeting at most.

'Yes,' she said. 'Can I be of help?'

'Ah, Frau Böhm, I hope you can. I'm doing a little background research on the Nussbaums, who were the General's household staff, and wondered if I could have a few moments of your time.'

'Of course, Herr…'

'I do apologise. He reached into his pocket and pulled out one of the new cards he'd had printed. He'd seen his immediate boss, one of the three Kriminalsekretäre in Kiel, handing a similar card to a high-ranking party member during an internal investigation, and had been taken with the idea.

She looked at the card. Her frown evaporated.

'Herr Güllich. I remember now,' she said. 'You spoke to my husband and I when the Nussbaums' brats went missing.'

'Indeed. Now that their parents have been arrested, they…'

He stopped, seeing the woman's shocked expression, followed a second or two later by a smile that lit up her face. He realised that she was a rather attractive woman, for her age.

Why did the rich men of places like Drachensee end up with the most beautiful of wives?

He knew the answer to his own question.

Money. Power. Or both.

He thought of Dirty Helga and the grossly overweight Kriminaldirektor. His conclusion was reinforced when Herr Böhm, also fat and balding, appeared at the door beside his wife, asking what was wrong.

Heinrich Güllich had married too young, and too plain, when his prospects hadn't looked so promising, but he saw little of his mousy wife. His job kept him busy, and he was seldom home, except to eat and sleep, and get a change of clothing. Sex was something he took from her when he felt the urge, but it had no passion or real interest to him, or to her, he thought. He wondered what it would be like to fuck a woman like Beate Böhm.

After I've screwed Maria Kästner, of course.

'So, the Nussbaums…'

Beate Böhm interruption forced his mind back to the present.

'When were they arrested?' she asked.

'About six weeks ago.'

'She never said a word. Maria high-and-mighty Kästner kept quiet about that.'

'Beate!' Eberhard Böhm admonished, under his breath.

'Oh, no. Don't tell me to be quiet. She's always so superior. Wait till the ladies hear of this. She won't be quite so in demand then.'

Heinrich Güllich watched the woman's reaction with interest and realised the potential to cause the General and his pestilential family a ream of trouble.

'Frau Böhm, I remember that you had a few reservations about the General's over-tolerant attitude to his Jewish staff…'

'Jew-loving, more like. And his son. He almost ruined my daughter.'

Heinrich Güllich racked his brain.

Yes. The daughter was engaged to Franz Kästner but had broken it off for some reason.

'How so?' The Kriminalassistent looked past the Böhms, into the house.

'I'm sorry, Herr Kriminalassistent,' Beate said. 'It was rude of us not to invite you in.'

She stood aside to let the Gestapo man pass and instructed her husband to find the maid and have coffee sent to the lounge.

For the next half hour, Heinrich Güllich listened as Beate Böhm gave chapter and verse on her neighbour's social climbing ways, her husband's love of Jews, and not just his own employees, but Jews in general. Then, in great detail, she catalogued the catastrophic engagement of her daughter to his Jew-loving and Führer-hating son, Franz.

When she left the room to chase up the maid, he spoke to Herr Böhm.

'You were once close, the two families?'

'Ach, the whole affair was a mess. I was a close friend of Erich's; I was vice president of the Rotary club while he was president, and he was always decent enough to me.'

'But he had anti-government tendencies?' the Kriminalassistent asked.

'He wasn't the Führer's greatest fan,' Eberhard Böhm admitted, frowning, 'or a great supporter of the National Socialist ideals, but that was his only fault, I'd say.'

'And the son?'

'Very like his father but, from what I hear, a good soldier. Even my son-in-law, Lise's husband, doesn't have a bad word to say against him. And he's an SS Hauptsturmführer.'

'So, you have nothing to do with the Kästners now?'

'Of course we don't,' Beate Böhm said, coming back into the room, the maid in tow with the coffee.

'You'll have a cup, Herr Güllich?'

'I wouldn't mind,' the Gestapo man said.

Beate Böhm watched while the maid poured three cups.

'May I ask what the Nussbaums were arrested for?'

'I don't see why not. It's no secret. They tried to escape to Palestine with the Haganah, using false papers. They were arrested in Prague by vigilant Gestapo officers.'

'The ungrateful Judenläuse,' Beate Böhm said, ignoring her husband's frown.

'Indeed,' the Gestapo man said, warming to the Böhm woman.

'You've been extremely helpful,' he said. 'I may need to have a word with your daughter. What is her address?'

'She has just moved to a new flat. It's in Holtenauer Straße.' She scribbled the details on a piece of notepaper.

'Thank you,' Heinrich Güllich said. 'If anything comes to mind, just telephone the number on the card and leave your name. I'll get back to you.'

~~o~~

Gella Weisberg looked over at Ruth. She was helping young Benjamin with his homework.

She has so much patience, and tenderness. She'll make a great mama, one day.

Manny was out. She knew he and a few of his friends hung around the men, watching them smoke, listening to all their wild war-talk, but Aaron said that they were a good bunch, and that neither she nor Ruth should worry.

'Can I go out and play?' Benjamin asked, finishing his exercise.

'Yes, but stay in the square, where I can see you.'

Ruth still sat at the table, staring out of the window. A tear slid down her cheek.

Gella sat down and put her arm around her. Ruth leaned into the older woman.

'I'm sorry,' she said. 'I just can't seem to snap out of it.'

'It's not something you can recover from, just like that,' Gella said, snapping her fingers, 'and you've nothing to be sorry for. You shouldn't even be back at work.'

'I couldn't stand doing nothing. Work takes my mind off things.'

'And your English lessons. My word, I don't know how you pick it up so quickly. It's incomprehensible to me.'

'You can speak Yiddish and German. English is just one more language.'

'I think in Yiddish and German. I don't have to scramble about for the right word.'

'My teacher says it will be like that with English, too, if I stick with it.'

'It will, for you. And maybe for me, one day. Perhaps it's too easy just to speak German here. Once we're back in Finchley…'

Both women sat in silence for a while, Gella stroking Ruth's hair, which was beginning to grow back in again.

'The doctor said I should still be able to have children,' Ruth said.

'That's good,' Gella said. 'Wait and see, you'll not be five minutes back together with Franz and it will happen again.'

Ruth blushed.

'Do you think we were wrong,' she asked, 'to do what we did?'

Gella Weissberg sighed.

'If it were my own daughters, I'd tell them to wait until they're married, but the situation you found yourself in, I couldn't find fault with what you did.'

'It didn't feel wrong,' Ruth said, 'but I do worry about telling Mama and Papa.'

'They don't need to know. Let's keep that our secret.'

She paused. 'Anyway,' she said, 'I'm sure they won't condemn you for it. You love Franz. They'll understand.'

~~o~~

[09/08/1941 Saturday]

Carl Meyer had never seen Heinrich Güllich so angry. He could barely speak.

'I'll kill them!' he screamed.

It had been the young Kriminalassistentanwärter's unfortunate privilege to inform his boss, on his return from Drachensee, that the Kästner brothers had survived the storm and that they were being held in a British prisoner-of-war camp.

He looked out the open door of the Kriminalassistent's office. It was fortunate that the rest of the building was almost empty. Another of the Gestapo's showpiece interrogations was in progress in the basement, this time of a leading Kiel businessman who had been passing information via his connections in Switzerland to the British.

His wife was a beautiful former actress of minor fame, twenty years younger than him, and it was her hotly anticipated questioning that was attracting most of the Gestapo investigators to the interrogation rooms.

'One day, sir, when we defeat the British, we will deal with them.'

'Not them, you fool, although I will travel in person to England to shoot them once our glorious Wehrmacht forces have crushed the British, and we fly the flag of the Third Reich above their famous Houses of Parliament.'

'Who then, sir?'

'The Jews. The ones we have in custody. I'll make them suffer. No holding back this time.'

'Is that wise, sir? Remember what the Kriminaldirektor said. The Nussbaums are not to be touched.'

'He'll change his mind when I tell him about this. You know what it means, don't you?'

'Yes, sir. I think so.'

'If these Jew-loving insults to the German Army survived, so did the young Judenschweine they took with them.'

'But, sir, if they weren't on the boat when it was searched in the Skagerrak, how...'

Heinrich Güllich slammed his fist down on the desk.

'Fool. They were on the boat. That Schulze fellow was either covering up for them, or he was inept.'

'Sir, I've gone through his report, and I ran it past my father. There's nowhere else the Jews could have been hiding unless they were in the water.'

'Then they were in the water.'

'But, sir, the search took at least twenty minutes. A man would struggle to survive that long, far less two children.'

Carl Meyer regretted his words almost as soon as he'd spoken them. Heinrich Güllich's face turned puce, and the veins on his neck stood out.

'The girl was not a child, and the boy was barely one. And Jews, like most vermin, are hard to kill.'

'You think they are in Britain, sir?'

'I'm sure of it, now. And I'll grind it out of the parents if it's the last thing I do.'

'What will be the last thing you do?'

Both men started at the voice and turned, shocked to see the bulk of the Kriminaldirektor almost blocking the doorway.

'Sir, we didn't see you there,' a grovelling Carl Meyer said.

To Heinrich Güllich's credit, he gave his assistant a disgusted stare, and faced the Gestapo chief.

'You've heard, sir, that General Kästner's sons have turned up in a POW camp somewhere in Britain?'

'Yes, Kriminalassistent Güllich, the whole of Kiel is talking about it. A miracle indeed.'

'But, sir, surely you can see what this means?'

'I know what you *think* this means, and I can sympathise with your view, but it proves nothing.'

'But, sir, I can make the Nussbaums talk.'

'I can't afford that. For the moment, at least.'

The Kriminaldirektor moved forward until his eyes were no more than a hand's width from Heinrich Güllich's face.

'You will not lay a finger on the General's Jewish rats. Do-you-understand?'

Heinrich Güllich returned his chief's stare for a full two seconds. Carl Meyer flinched, sweating as he waited for the Kriminaldirektor to wipe the floor with the Kriminalassistent.

'Yes,' Heinrich Güllich said, in a voice close to a whisper. 'I understand.'

'Now,' the Kriminaldirektor said with a broad smile. 'That doesn't mean you can't make further enquiries.'

Carl Meyer breathed out, scarcely able to believe that he and his boss were not heading somewhere close to the Eastern Front, rooting out Jews and communists in small villages in the middle of the nowhere.

'But why can't we interview the Nussbaums again?' he heard Heinrich Güllich say. He willed his superior officer to keep his mouth shut and accept the breadcrumbs that the Kriminaldirektor had thrown them.

'Because I say so. Not at present. They are still recovering from your last attempts to extract the truth from them. Did you ever get anything from the Bernheim brothers?'

'No, sir. They deny any knowledge of the whole thing. They're lying Jewish scum but, in this instance, I'm inclined to believe them, in light of the news about the Kästner brothers.'

'Güllich,' the Kriminaldirektor said. 'I want you to treat this investigation like a box of eggs. Break one, and you will be freezing your testicles off in the coming Soviet winter. Have you got that?'

'Yes, sir.' He hesitated for a second then, to Carl Meyer's horror, he spoke again.

'Sir, do you still intend to let General Kästner see the Nussbaums?'

'Yes. I do. For my own reasons.'

'When is this likely to happen?'

'I'm going to let him stew a little while longer. He has already made further enquiries about the delay. It won't hurt for him to wait. Why do you ask?'

'Would it be possible for me to listen in, or better still, be present when the meeting takes place?'

The Kriminaldirektor looked at his Kriminalassistent. To Carl Meyer's surprise, it was a look of grudging respect.

'Go on,' he said.

'Well, sir. They might give something away. Something we could use to prove that the General was a party to the whole affair.'

'Even if we could show he was involved, it would be a brave man who tries to take the General down, particularly when he has been so effective in saving the Kriegsmarine millions of Reichsmarks and solving its many supply-chain problems. And he has powerful allies in the party.'

'But, sir, he's a criminal, sir, flouting every law possible in the reprehensible shielding of his pet Jews.'

'I will consider it, but any action taken must go through me first. And I will not have the Gestapo accused of acting in a way that would be detrimental to the furtherment of the war effort. I don't wish to join you in your outpost in Siberia.'

The Kriminaldirektor smiled and put his arm around Heinrich Güllich's shoulders. His grip was gentle, but it was enough to let the Kriminalassistent feel the raw physical power of the man.

'Tread warily and keep me informed. Heil Hitler,' he said.

'Heil Hitler,' the two younger men chorused, returning the chief's salute.

The large man turned and left them, heading for the top floor.

'I thought we were finished, sir,' Carl Meyer said.

'You need balls in this job, Meyer. Never forget that. And you need to believe that you're right.'

He lit a cigarette and opened the folder that sat on his desk.

'Now,' he said. 'We have work to do.'

CHAPTER 220

Lise Böhm heard the news about Franz and Johann at almost the same time as Carl Meyer told Heinrich Güllich. It was the first thing her mother said to her when she arrived at Drachensee Villa, the Böhm family home.

'It's not a shock,' Lise said. 'Those traitors deserve to be prisoners. It's only a shame that they're not in one of our camps. It wouldn't surprise me if they engineered their capture, so that they didn't need to fight again.'

'Lise!' Eberhard Böhm scolded, 'You can't say that. Franz has an Iron Cross.'

She gave him a withering look.

'Lise is right,' Beate Böhm said. 'And their Jew-loving father should be in prison too; we all know he's a communist. It would be better if you were less of an apologist for that family, Eberhard.'

'I'm not. I was just saying that Iron Crosses are not handed out without reason. He saved German soldiers' lives, pulling them out of a burning tank, for God's sake.'

'A fabricated story, no doubt,' Beate Böhm sneered. 'I mean, Maria Kästner has always been one to be sparing with the truth. If it hadn't been for the nice Gestapo man, we would never have known about the Nussbaums.'

Eberhard Böhm shook his head and left his wife and daughter to it. He sometimes felt like an outsider in his own home when the two women got together. And it was becoming more frequent, even though Rudolf and Lise had a lovely new flat in Holtenauer.

It's such a shame that Rudolf doesn't get much leave. They don't get much time together.

~~o~~

In the living room, a similar thought passed through Beate Böhm's mind.

'No news from Rudolf?' she said.

'He'll be home on leave soon, but he'll be so stressed out, Mama, I'm not sure he'll manage over to see you this time.'

'I understand, dear. You two will need the time together.'

'I don't know why Rudolf hasn't got an Iron Cross. He's in the front line on the Russian campaign and, from what the Obersturmbannführer said, Rudolf is a courageous commander, never shirking from leading his men into battle.'

'You spoke to Obersturmbannführer Eicke?' Beate Böhm said lightly. 'He was in town?'

'Yes. He was passing through. He called in to see me with a message from Rudolf. They'd met in Lithuania or Byelorussia, while he was travelling around visiting the various Einsatzgruppen, including Rudolf's.'

'That was nice of him. Doesn't he command his own unit now?'

'He was on secondment to staff command, working for Reinhard Heydrich. He's taking charge of his own Einsatzgruppe after he has been home on leave.'

Lise's beautiful forehead creased a little. For a moment, she'd seen a flash of irritation cross her mother's face, but it was so fleeting, she wondered if she'd imagined it.

It's this thing about the Kästners. It's so galling.

'How long was he in Kiel for?' she heard her mother ask. There was still a strange tone in her voice; almost petulant.

'Oh, just one night, I believe,' she said. 'He was staying at the Europäischer Hof. I only saw him briefly.'

Lise looked out of the window to hide her smile, remembering the Obersturmbannführer's touch, his controlled strength, and her complete surrender to the waves of pleasure that he always brought to her bed.

The casual way he'd left her afterwards hadn't been so pleasing. It left her feeling like a discarded toy, sitting in the flat, vowing to snub him the next time he phoned at his whim.

But she knew she never would again. The last time she'd tried, he'd ignored her until she crawled back to him.

She turned away from the window. Her mother was speaking.

'Maria Kästner is trying to make out that her boys tried to fight off being captured.'

'Ha. More likely they stood like snivelling cowards, pleading to surrender. I hear that the 69th Infantry Division is now being transferred to the Eastern Front. Quite a coincidence, don't you think, that Franz and Johann should be safe in a British POW camp just when their Kompanie is deployed to Russia?'

'You're right, Lise, and I'm sure that their father knew about that in advance. That's what I've been telling the ladies. That stuck-up bitch next door will soon be the laughing stock of Kiel. The countess will drop her in no time once she hears she has two deserters for sons.'

~~o~~

Brigadier Schneider's division was indeed in transit from Norway, preparing to join the rest of the 4th Army as part of Operation Barbarossa. The Brigadier stood, looking out of his window.

The conquest of Russia. What will be the cost?

He was spending a few well-deserved days in Lübeck with his family, and it irritated him that he had to give up part of that precious time to meet with a trumped-up Gestapo officer with a bee in his bonnet about the legitimacy of the Kästner brothers' fateful trip to Norway.

At least I don't have their deaths on my conscience now.

He'd been informed of Franz and Johann's capture on disembarking from the company's transport to Kiel and had rushed to Kriegsmarine Headquarters to speak with the General and pass on the delight and relief that the news had given him.

The General had been grateful for his visit, but Walther Schneider could see that the boys' supposed deaths had taken its toll on the man. He'd looked his age for the first time, the colonel thought.

The doorbell rang and his maid informed him that Kriminalassistent Güllich was in the front room.

He straightened up his uniform and strode through to meet him.

No non-combatant SS upstart is going to intimidate me.

'Ah, Herr Güllich,' he said, snapping his heels together with an outstretched arm. 'Heil Hitler.'

'Heil Hitler.'

Heinrich Güllich's salute was just as crisp.

'I'm glad you could spare me the time, Colonel Schneider. I know you only have a short spell at home, and I'll try not to take up too much of it.'

'Thank you. It's Brigadier Schneider now, by the way, Herr Güllich.'

'Congratulations, sir. You must be delighted.'

'My only desire is to do my duty for my country.'

'That's very admirable, sir. I'll try not to hold you back.'

'I'm not sure it will be worth your while. I can't see what I can tell you.'

'Let me be the judge of that, shall we? First, we have no interest in your reasons for allowing the voyage to take place. It is the Kästners' part in it that interests us.'

A minor sense of relief passed over the Brigadier. He'd had a reprimand from staff command for allowing two of his senior officers to go missing, presumed drowned, but his promotion hadn't been rescinded and, as far as he could tell, the Heer were content to leave it at that. But he'd wondered if the report on the incident would reach the desk of someone higher up in the Wehrmacht and trigger further action.

And it bridled him that this snake of a man should question his decisions.

'I should think not,' he said. 'It was a quite acceptable voyage for them to make, given their experience. The only reason I didn't join them was because I couldn't get away. The storm was just sheer bad luck, a once in a decade event.'

'As I said, I'm not here to debate the possible rights and wrongs of the enterprise. If I might be allowed, can I start with who first suggested the trip?'

The Brigadier, still irked at the implied criticism of his decision to allow the voyage to go ahead, answered curtly.

'I did, of course. It was my boat.'

'And neither of the boys hinted that it might be a good idea.'

'No. They jumped at the chance to do it when I asked them but, after all, they were in the army sailing team, and had cruised with their father to Norway before. They were highly experienced sailors, among the best in Germany.'

'I see. So, you wanted your boat in Norway, while you were stationed there?'

'Yes. You must understand, I use the boat as part of my officer training syllabus. Having a crew away for a few days tells me a lot about how my officers will handle combat; it takes them out of their comfort zone and brings out the best in some and highlights deficiencies in others.'

'And Franz and Johann Kästner were in the former category, I presume?'

'Very much so, especially Franz. I'm glad they survived. I believe if he hadn't been captured, he would have been a full colonel by the time we've conquered Europe, and Great Britain. Both Kästner brothers had been approved for promotion.'

'He was that good?'

'The best I've ever seen. It wouldn't surprise me if he were better than his father one day.'

'Ah. The General. Do you know him well?'

'I served under him. He was the making of me, you could say. An extraordinary military man. I hear he does wonders with the Kriegsmarine in Kiel. I'm sure they would make him an admiral if they could get away with it.'

Walther Schneider laughed.

~~o~~

It was Heinrich Güllich's turn to fume. He was sick and tired of hearing about General Kästner's near legendary abilities.

'So, the idea to take the boat to Norway was yours. Did the Kästners ever try and dissuade you from going on the trip?'

'No. On the contrary, they urged me to go.'

Heinrich Güllich saw a brief shadow cross Walther Schneider's face.

'There is a problem?' he asked.

'No. It was nothing. It was just something the General said, long before then, when we were discussing sailing the boat to Norway. He asked me if I'd ever thought of having it shipped out.'

'That would have been feasible?'

'Oh, yes. It could have been craned onto a cradle on the deck of a supply ship and lashed down.'

'He suggested it, did he?'

'It wasn't so much of a suggestion, more of a throwaway remark.'

'But he didn't hint that you should sail the boat to Norway.'

'No. He just said that the sailing in Norway was as good as anywhere.'

Heinrich Güllich paused while he scribbled a few lines in his notebook.

'Did you try to have the boat shipped to Norway?'

'I made enquiries. It was considered a frivolous use of resources.'

'And yet, sending two of your best officers to collect it wasn't?'

'No. And I'm not sure I like what you're implying.'

'I apologise. I'll rephrase that. Did you let the army know your intentions to have the boat sailed over by two of your men?'

'Yes. They were quite happy. And General Kästner was delighted that his sons were being given the chance to do it.'

'Oh, you asked the General?'

'Well, I ran it past him. To see if he was comfortable with Franz and Johann sailing *Der Sturmtaucher* to Norway. He was. I'm sure he even toyed with the idea of making the trip with them.'

'He did, did he? That's interesting. Did he take any part in the preparation?'

'Yes. He was most helpful. I was in Norway, and he kept an eye on the boat during its refit.'

Heinrich Güllich made a few more notes.

'He also helped provision the boat and, without me dropping his name in the conversation, I doubt we would have had the use of the Kriegsmarine's victualling yard to prepare for the passage.'

'It sounds as if he had a large part in the whole affair.'

'Oh, I wouldn't say that. Franz and Johann did most of it, but the General's contacts in the Kriegsmarine were extremely useful. We had charts showing the minefields, planned ship movements and, as you would expect, weather reports.'

'Ah. The weather. It has been said that, despite the adverse reports, the Kästner brothers took a risk when they left Hirtshals for Grimstad.'

Walther Schneider's eyes narrowed.

'You seem to know a lot about the trip.'

'I've studied it in quite a bit of depth.'

'Are you a sailor yourself?'

'God forbid. My assistant's father crewed on the Krupp boat for his whole working life. He has been a useful source of information. The weather, as I was saying?'

'Forecasting is an inexact science, but there were reports of a storm brewing. I spoke to Franz by telephone the night before he left, and he was happy that they would make landfall before the storm. In hindsight, we were all wrong.'

'Yes. The storm came in sooner than was expected, and was ferocious, I'm told.'

'I spoke to several commanders who were out in the early part of it. They said that in a small boat, it was not survivable.'

'Yet, they survived.'

'Yes. By a miracle. But the yacht didn't. Although they're in enemy hands, I'm relieved that a British ship rescued them. It takes a weight off my conscience.'

'Did you visit the yacht before it left Kiel?'

Heinrich Güllich knew the answer. He had a copy of the victualling yard gate logs for the whole period *Der Sturmtaucher* was berthed there.

'I went twice, as I recall. The last time was the night before they left.'

'And everything was as you expected?'

'What do you mean?'

'There was nothing new on the boat, no modifications?'

'No. Why would they? I'd directed the boatyard to make necessary repairs and replace worn or damaged rigging, blocks and planks.'

'And the Kästners didn't ask the boatyard to make any changes?'

'No. They would have spoken to me first.'

Then he smiled.

'There was one little modification they made,' he said. 'I thought it was quite clever of them. They'd drilled a small hole in one of the boards that covered the bilges, to let the water drain away quicker if they were pooped.'

'Could you explain that? For a non-sailor, like me.'

'If the boat is overwhelmed by a wave, and the cockpit fills with water, it can be extremely dangerous. That's why we have large cockpit drains fitted. If the washboards are open, water can also flood down into the cabin. Normally, it drains into the bilges and is pumped out. Franz and Johann drilled a drainage hole in one of the boards so that the water could drain quicker. I told them to make a matching hole in the board on the port side.'

'And did they?'

'I don't know. I presume so.'

~~o~~

Heinrich Güllich nodded and looked at his notebook again.

'Were the provisions they took adequate for a journey of that length?' he said, adding a few words to his notebook with each answer.

Walther Schneider looked at the Gestapo man, puzzled.

'Yes, I'd say so. They had to top up with fresh food like milk and cheese each time they were in harbour, but they had plenty of tinned food, potatoes, and flour to make bread. They had enough supplies for a week at a push if they had to use anchor all the way up the coast of

Norway.'

'So, they weren't over provisioned?'

'No,' the army man snapped. 'This has gone on long enough. What are these questions about? The journey was well planned and well executed. They were just unlucky and it's unfair to try and blacken their names when they can't answer to you.'

Heinrich Güllich put down his pen and closed his notebook.

'What if I told you we have evidence that your boat was used by the Kästners to spirit two Jewish children out of the country?'

Walther Schneider laughed.

'I'd say you were mad. They were searched twice. Thoroughly. They would never have been able to smuggle them onto the boat at the yard. What evidence do you have for this ludicrous theory?'

'A sighting, for one thing, of at least three people on the boat; the Nussbaum children went missing around the time that the Kästner brothers left Kiel, and they've never been found. Then the Kästners turn up in England. A miracle.'

'That's tenuous, to say the least.'

For the next half hour, Heinrich Güllich laid out every scrap of evidence in front of the Brigadier. It was mostly circumstantial, he admitted; the lax security at the naval yard, the whole Kriegsmarine being so besotted with the Kästners that they failed to do proper searches, Antje and the cousin being at the boat the night before they left.

'And now you tell me they made a small hole in the bilge boards. A perfect air hole if someone was hiding there, no?'

'It's all the product of a vivid imagination, I'm afraid. Even if it were true, how would they have arranged for a Royal Navy boat to pick them up in German-controlled water, risking one of their ships in the middle of the worst storm in living memory?'

'What if they sailed your boat to England, themselves?'

'Impossible. They could not have survived that storm.'

'You said yourself that they were among the best sailors in Germany. I presume your boat was a solid one. I'm told it was.'

'Yes, but no vessel that size would have made it through that storm. It was close to being a hurricane. Even the largest of Kriegsmarine ships ran for port.'

He paused, considering the possibility, then he shook his head.

'No,' he said. 'They foundered, and they were picked up by a British ship. It's the only explanation.'

'Then this mythical British ship must have been there to rendezvous with them.'

'For what? Two German junior officers and two Jewish servants' children?'

'They may have had information to trade.'

'Franz and Johann, good officers as they were, had nothing of enough importance to prompt the British to make a naval vessel available like that, with all the risks it would entail.'

'No, but their father might have. Perhaps he furnished them with information.'

'Not the General. Never. He may have his flaws; his determination to keep his Jewish staff is one of them, but he is no traitor. Ask around the Kriegsmarine. The man has done more for the German war effort than anyone else in Kiel.'

'So everyone says.'

'Because it's true. If you were much of an investigator, you should make sure to consider all the facts before you make those sorts of accusations.'

Both men were rattled.

Walther Schneider could see that he'd stung Heinrich Güllich with his barb about his investigative skills but, despite his stout defence of the Kästners, a niggle of doubt had crept into the Brigadier's mind and he resolved to do a little delving around of his own, after he'd got rid of the obnoxious and arrogant Gestapo officer.

He'd resolved to have a word with the man's superiors but reasoned that it could wait until he was clear in his own mind that the man was out of order.

He saw Heinrich Güllich force a smile.

'If anything comes to mind that might shed light on the case, please give me a call,' the Gestapo man said, oozing an oily charm.

Walther Schneider grunted his agreement, and they parted with a Hitler salute.

For a long while after the Gestapo man left, Brigadier Schneider stared out of the window.

CHAPTER 221

With the bit between his teeth, Heinrich Güllich was delighted when Carl Meyer told him that the last of the naval yard marines, Feldwebel Weber, was in Kiel on leave.

'I'll ask him to come in for an interview, sir,' the younger man said.

'No. Tell him we'll meet him somewhere. It will be less intimidating. One of the cafés along the promenade will do.'

When the two Gestapo men arrived, the sergeant was already sitting at the table. Even from a distance, Heinrich Güllich saw that the man wasn't happy.

'Feldwebel Weber,' he said, shaking the marine's hand. 'Don't get up. You'll have a coffee?'

'I've ordered. Here it comes now.'

The waiter placed the coffee on the table and took the Gestapo men's orders. They sat down opposite Feldwebel Weber.

'Now, do you know why we want to talk to you?'

'Not really. Something to do with the base.'

'Yes. First, you're not in any sort of trouble. This has nothing to do with you, or your colleagues. We just need to clear something up.'

'I didn't think it was anything I'd done,' he said, but Carl Meyer thought a weight had lifted from the marine's shoulders. Still, he remembered his boss's adage that everyone was guilty of something, and he wondered if it could be exploited.

It turned out that there was no need. As soon as Heinrich Güllich asked the sergeant about the Kästners, he talked freely.

'It's been niggling at the back of my mind for ages, but there was never enough to talk to anyone about it. Did Private Hemming tell you?'

'No, no one said anything.' Carl Meyer made a note of Hemming's name.

'What is it that bothers you?'

'Well, the night before they left, the Kästner brothers arrived at the gatehouse in the little sports car of the major's, with his sister and a young boy in tow, their young cousin. The Kästners had been back and forward numerous times to the yard and, because of their father's standing with the Kriegsmarine, we just made a note of the names and let them through. The General turned up half an hour later and I spoke with him; by then, I knew him quite well. He was a great man for making time for everyone. He made you feel that you were important. If I'm honest, it doesn't feel quite right talking about this.'

'Don't be fooled. The General has a talent for lowering people's guard and ensuring their loyalty to him. Carry on.'

'Well, when the General left, he gave us a chart with his sons' proposed passage marked on it, and he came into the guardhouse to show us. When he got back into the car, he said something, as if there was someone in the back. I got a quick glimpse of a bundle on the seat as he drove out but thought nothing of it.'

He paused and looked at the two Gestapo men, his face colouring.

'A short while later, Colonel Schneider arrived. We searched his car, as was normal protocol, and we talked about the boat, and the journey while we were doing it. We also searched it again when the colonel left a short while later.'

'Then what happened?'

'The Kästner brothers drove up to the gatehouse a while later, but the boy wasn't with them.'

'The sister, Antje, was though?'

'Yes. We couldn't help but notice. She is very pretty, sir.'

'Quite. That sort of thing sticks in a sailor's mind, doesn't it?'

The marine laughed.

'Yes. I suppose it does.'

'Did you ask where the boy was?'

'Yes. Major Kästner looked surprised and said that he thought his father would have told us; the boy had been tired, and a little nauseous, and had gone home with the General.'

'Ah. They were alluding to this so-called person in the back seat of the General's car?'

'Yes, sir. And it could have been, easily. But something bothered me. I don't even know what it was. When they'd all gone, I went down to the boat with Hemming and checked it over. It was locked, and I'm sure no one was on it, but I rocked the boat from side to side, just to make sure. If a child had been inside, he would have cried out.'

'Anything else?'

'No. I finished my watch at midnight. By the time I came back on duty the next day, the boat had gone. We followed their progress, like many in the Kriegsmarine, until we got news that they were missing, presumed drowned.'

'And what did you think when you heard that they were in a British POW camp?'

'It was a shock, sir, but I was glad they'd survived.'

'And you didn't consider coming forward with your information?'

The marine sergeant's eyes narrowed, and his face became guarded.

'No, sir. As I told you, I wasn't convinced I'd seen anything.'

'And you told us because you thought Hemming might have said something?'

'No, sir. Well, perhaps a little, but it has been bothering me, sir, and I'm glad to get it off my chest. Will there be any trouble over it?'

'Not for you. Captain Vossler may find himself in a posting somewhere cold and miserable because of the lax security, but that's for the Kriegsmarine to decide. You've been most helpful, Feldwebel Weber. I would caution you against saying anything about this to anyone else, especially private Hemming.'

The marine sergeant's eyes dropped for a second and Heinrich Güllich knew he was right to have warned him. He smiled and shook the man's hand.

Once he'd gone, he turned to Carl Meyer.

'A switch,' he said. 'That's how they got them in. Now, we need a little background on the brothers. Did you contact the men in the Kästners' unit?'

'Yes, sir. These are the four that were their closest friends.'

He handed the Kriminalassistent a list.

'How did you find out?' Heinrich Güllich said.

'I asked the adjutant when I telephoned to arrange your interview with Brigadier Schneider. They're all coming back to Kiel today, to report for duty again. I've arranged for us to interview them at five o'clock, at the barracks in Plön.'

'Good.'

'I'll also contact all the Danish, Swedish and Norwegian ports for a final time about sightings of a yacht, or wreckage washed up on shore. There might be something else.'

'I doubt it, Meyer, but well done.'

Carl Meyer beamed.

'There's one more thing,' the Kriminalassistent said. 'We must go back and talk to the Kriegsmarine. I want to know if it would have been feasible for a British Navy vessel to get in and out of the Skagerrak that day, unseen.'

'Yes, sir.' Carl Meyer said, looking at his watch. 'We should really be going, sir, if we're to be there for five.'

~~o~~

They'd got to Plön ten minutes late. The four men had been standing in a line, waiting.

On the way back to Kiel, Carl Meyer turned to Heinrich Güllich, who sat fuming.

'It was to be expected, sir. They were always going to be loyal to their friends.'

Heinrich Güllich exploded.

'They are servants of the Third Reich,' he shouted. 'That should always come before any feelings of personal allegiance to their friends.'

Artur Schweitzer, Fritz Aumeier, Heinrich Öhlman and Maximilian Grabner hadn't deviated from the line that Franz and Johann Kästner were true German patriots and fine soldiers.

Artur Schweitzer had told them that Franz Kästner was the best young officer in the

Kompanie, and the others had all echoed his sentiments. They'd made no secret of the fact that Franz, like his father, did not approve of the way that the government was treating its Jewish citizens, but they all insisted that it did not affect his duties as a soldier.

'But what did he do when asked to take action against Jewish resistance fighters, for instance?' Heinrich Güllich had asked.

'He treated them like any other armed resistance; if they didn't surrender, the fight would be to the death,' the soldier had replied, with a scathing look reserved for those non-combatants who condemned active soldiers from the safety of a position hundreds of kilometres away from the fighting.

'And if he'd been ordered to shoot Jewish prisoners?'

'Brigadier Schneider wouldn't have put him in that position,' the major had said, looking the Gestapo officer straight in the eye. 'Nor did he ever ask any of us to kill prisoners. We left that to the SS.'

Carl Meyer knew that, if he had been outside, in the open air, the man would have spat on the ground. He'd seen his boss's neck tense and redden.

'Did either of the Kästners ever do anything to prevent such an action?'

'Not as far as I'm aware of. But I suspect Franz would have, had the situation arisen.'

'That would have been disobeying orders, would it not?'

'In battle, German officers are given a fair bit of leeway as to their actions. It is one of the reasons the Wehrmacht has been so successful. We can react more readily than the forces who face us.'

The answers the remaining three men gave had been so similar, Carl Meyer was convinced that they'd rehearsed beforehand. And all of them, without being asked, had attempted to tell them of Franz's actions when he'd won his Iron Cross. Each time, the Kriminalassistent had cut them off, saying that it had no relevance.

As the four men stood in line after their interviews, Heinrich Güllich had dismissed them in disgust.

'You may judge it to be clever to close ranks and protect your fellow officers,' he'd told them, 'but be warned that if charges of treason are brought against your former colleagues, your part in their duplicity will be under question. Think about that.'

To everyone's surprise, it was Maximilian Grabner who had responded, his words to be repeated in the canteen and the barracks, and in the battalion's trucks on their way to Russia.

'Herr Kriminalassistent,' he'd said, with no fear. 'In two days, we are being sent east to engage with Soviet forces who will fight to the last man to defend their homeland. Many of us will not return. Do you think we will lose any sleep over the words of an SS policeman who has never seen action?'

Carl Meyer had seen, in the grim pride on the faces of his friends, that Maximilian Grabner, the least impressive soldier of the four, would return to his Kompanie as a legend. It had not left Heinrich Güllich in a cheerful frame of mind.

~~o~~

The young Gestapo man drove, keeping his eyes on the road in front. He waited for the Kriminalassistent to continue his tirade.

When Heinrich Güllich stayed silent, Carl Meyer waited for a minute, then steeled himself.

'We've been looking for a British Navy ship, or a submarine, sir,' he said, not knowing if it was wise, 'I know it's a long shot, but perhaps it wasn't a warship that picked them up.'

'What do you mean?' Heinrich Güllich said.

'Well, I was talking to my father. He served with the Reichsmarine in the last war, and he said that both sides used trawlers for various duties, including clandestine missions. Could the Kästners and the Nussbaums have been picked up by a trawler?'

The Kriminalassistent pursed his lips. He stared at the younger man, who had beads of sweat gathering on his forehead.

'A trawler wouldn't have coped much better than the yacht with the storm,' Heinrich Güllich said, but Carl Meyer could see that he was giving the idea serious consideration.

'No, but it could have hidden among the other fishing boats in any of the Danish

694

harbours,' he said.

'They would have been spotted.'

'Not by our people and, although the Danes didn't put up much of a fight, they're not inclined to cooperate either.'

'Someone would have informed on them. There's always someone who doesn't fit in with the rest, or is resentful of his fellow countrymen, or thinks there could be money in it.'

'Not necessarily. These fishing communities are very tight. Remember Hirtshals.'

Heinrich Güllich appeared to think about it for a second then his face darkened.

'If what you're saying is true, it's possible the Kästners and their Judenhunde were still in Hirtshals when we were there. We might have been this close to finding them.'

He held his finger and thumb up to Carl Meyer's face, millimetres apart.

'It's possible,' the younger man said.

'When we get back, contact the Kriegsmarine and ask for reports of vessels fishing in the area just after the storm. While you're onto them, ask them to circulate a memo to all their ships asking that any sighting of civilian vessels, no matter how inconsequential they might appear, should be reported and passed to us.'

Carl Meyer was relieved. The Kriminalassistent's foul temper had passed, and the younger man pressed home his advantage.

'I'll also put in a request to the Luftwaffe command to send us any reported sightings from the air, for the week after the yacht went missing.'

'That's good thinking, Kamerad Meyer,' the Kriminalassistent said.

~~o~~

The General was surprised when his wife met him at the front door.

She waited while he took his coat off.

'I've hired a new cook,' she told him, walking behind him as he made for the drawing room. She followed him in.

'Excellent,' he said.

'I've hired a gardener as well. He's the cook's husband. We'll still need a handyman from time to time.'

'That's fine. There will be someone local. What about the housekeeper?'

'I've kept her on. The cook was not prepared to take on a cleaning role, and the housekeeper's new position has fallen through.'

'As long as you're happy with their work, I don't see a problem with that.'

Maria Kästner hesitated.

'Both the cook and the housekeeper enquired if accommodation would be available.'

The General sighed.

'I suppose so, but do we have to have people living upstairs? I don't mind Albert staying over the odd time but a cook and a maid? It will feel like we're back in my father and mother's time.'

'There's always the cottage…'

The General froze. In his mind, he slowly counted.

Eins. Zwei. Drei. Vier…

'It's a little early to consider using Yosef and Miriam's home for other staff,' he said, his voice even. 'The more I think about it, perhaps they should stay where they are, for now.'

Maria Kästner opened her mouth to retort but she bit her lip and said nothing.

She crossed to the door, then turned.

'I'll need to give them extra travelling money,' she said.

'Do what it takes,' he said, staring out of the window, towards the lake.

CHAPTER 222

'Sir, the Luftwaffe were almost completely grounded for most of the period the storm was raging, from the eighth to the twelfth of April, and high-altitude reconnaissance took place only during the very beginning of that period, and when the storm passed.'

'That was a waste of effort then, Meyer,' Heinrich Güllich said with a sneer, 'Let's concentrate on the job in hand.'

Carl Meyer shook his head, despite his boss's scowl.

'Sir, they sent me the whole month's reports, not just the returns for that week. I searched through all of them. There might just be something, but the timing is way out.'

'What are you talking about, Meyer? We have work to do. This better be worthwhile.'

'Sir, please hear me out. I don't know how it could tie in, but the co-pilot of a bomber crew returning from a mission on the south coast of England on the twentieth of April noted that they'd seen a sailing vessel around 150 kilometres off the east coast of England.'

'That's two weeks after the last sighting of the Kästners, Meyer. What relevance does that have to our investigation?'

'Well, the bomber had sustained significant damage, and was limping home on one engine. The pilot was concentrating on keeping the plane in the air, and the belly gunner had lost consciousness at that point; he didn't make it. But the co-pilot got a better view of it, as did the nose gunner. They both said it had two masts and was sailing towards the coast. The nose gunner swears that it was flying a Swedish flag.'

'It's just coincidence, Meyer, although why a Swedish yacht should be in the North Sea during a war beats me. Are these sailing people off their heads?'

'It is possible, sir. Sweden is a neutral country and I suppose there's nothing to stop a Swedish yachtsman from deciding to sail around the world, despite the war, but it would be madness.'

He paused and looked at his feet.

'There's another possibility,' he said, raising his head.

'What? You think that *Der Sturmtaucher* fought the storm for days and days, battering its way slowly to England in a storm that everyone says was unsurvivable, even your father. They wouldn't have carried enough food or water for a start.'

'And I'm sure that's right, sir. But what if they took shelter somewhere, then struck out again for Britain once the storm had passed?'

'They would have been spotted. You can't hide a boat like that, then sail it across the North Sea without being seen.'

'I spoke with my father this morning, just before I came in. There's just a slight possibility that it could have happened, exactly like that.'

Carl Meyer unrolled a chart of the North Sea.

'It's my father's,' he said.

Heinrich Güllich glanced at it, then gave a scornful laugh.

'You're saying they sheltered in one of the Norwegian fjords for a week, then made a dash for it across to Britain?' the Kriminalassistent said, pointing at the coast of southern Norway on the chart.

'No, sir, although there are abundant places in southern Norway where they could have hidden, but this boat was spotted much too far south for that. No, if it was them, they must have somehow made shelter in Denmark, to ride out the worst of the storm. And that makes more sense, sir, because it would have given them a chance to get across to England unseen, at least for part of the way.'

'What do you mean?'

'Fog, sir. The southern part of the North Sea is very prone to severe fog. I've checked with the Kriegsmarine. For the week after the storm abated, the whole area was covered by extensive fog banks. They could have crept across, running south towards Helgoland, then west along the coasts of northern Germany and Holland, making a dash north-west towards

England when they ran out of cover.'

'They'd have been seen by one of our ships, or planes.'

'I believe they were, sir. This bomber.'

'It's preposterous. Someone would have spotted them in Denmark.'

'There are a multitude of places it is possible to hide a boat, all the way down the coast of Denmark or even behind some of the less populated Frisian Islands of northern Germany or Holland.'

'But they would have had to get there during the worst of this storm everyone keeps talking about.'

'My father says that, in the right hands, the yacht was as capable as any boat that size of surviving a storm like that as long as they weren't trying to make way against it.'

'What does that mean? Tell me in plain German.'

'The wind was in the west for most of the storm. If they'd tried to head into the storm, the waves and the wind would have stopped them dead, my father says, but if they made their way southwards, it's just possible that they could have reached shelter.'

Heinrich Güllich pulled out his cigarettes and lit one, rubbing his chin.

'And they would have had the whole sea to themselves, I suppose?'

'Yes. Every other vessel was tied up in harbour during that storm. My father says that, if they did it, it was an incredible feat of seamanship; maybe the best he's ever heard of.'

'Yes, yes, yes,' Heinrich Güllich said, 'we've heard enough about how *wunderbar* these Kästner men are. More to the point, did anyone else see them? Let's ask our friends in Denmark to put out a few feelers.'

'I've already done that, sir, and I've asked the Kriegsmarine to circulate a memo asking all ships if there were any unusual sightings of vessels at sea during the entire period between *Der Sturmtaucher* going missing and this report by the bomber, sir.'

'Very good, Meyer. I'm impressed. This must have taken you a while.'

'I was up all night, sir.'

The Kriminalassistent thumped him on the arm.

'That's what I meant when I told you that you need dedication. We'll make a Gestapo man out of you yet.'

He paused for a second.

'Arrange to speak with the bomber crew. They may have more information than they realise.'

~~o~~

Carl Meyer stared at the young sailor who sat in front of them. The rating's hands moving in a constant nervous dance.

'I'd just checked the racks, and I… I thought I'd have cigarette, s… sir.'

'Don't be anxious, sailor,' Heinrich Güllich said, smiling. 'This isn't anything to be worried about. We're just delighted that you came forward.'

It seemed to disarm the young rating, who had contacted the Gestapo office in Kiel after seeing a notice in the galley on board his ship.

'Sorry, sir. I'm a little nervous.'

'Take your time. Now, what are these racks that you're talking about?'

'Ah, those, sir. They're the mine racks, sir, where we store the mines, ready for deployment. It's essential that we check them frequently when we are underway in case they come loose. That would be a disaster, sir.'

Carl Meyer smiled. It was clever, asking the young sailor about something he knew a great deal about.

'Yes. I can imagine,' Heinrich Güllich said. 'So, what did you see?'

'Well, I'd just lit up, and I'd taken a draw when I looked down at our wake, sir. It's quite a sight if I'm honest.'

'Yes. Our warships are very impressive. Go on.'

'Well, I was sure that I saw a wooden sailing ship, sir, but only for the briefest of seconds, and then it was gone. I thought it was my imagination.'

'I suppose that's what you would think. I mean, why would a sailing ship be out there?'

'That's exactly what I thought, sir.'

'So, you didn't tell anyone?'

The young man's face reddened. He dropped his head.

'I… I didn't want to look stupid. They would have ribbed me rotten, my mates, and the older men. They'd have said I w… was seeing things, sir.'

'You should have told one of your officers,' Heinrich Güllich said.

Carl Meyer was sure he was going to tear the rating a new arsehole; if the young sailor had acted like he should have done, and said something, *Der Sturmtaucher* would surely have been detained.

But the Kriminalassistent didn't.

'Do you know where your ship was when you saw it?'

'We weren't far out of Emden, perhaps two or three hours away, so it was around fifty miles north of there, and a little bit to the west. It was the eighteenth of April. I know because we got home leave for five days while they repaired the radar.'

'Ah. The *Brummer* was fitted with radar then?'

'Yes, but it began malfunctioning while we were laying mines off the coast of Norway. They made us return home to have it repaired.'

'You weren't using radar on the day in question?'

'We were, sir, but they had it running on low power. It would only pick up large vessels.'

'Not a sailing ship?'

'Not one that size, sir.'

'What about fishing boats?'

The man shrugged. 'They shouldn't have been there, sir. They can only be fishing in permitted waters, away from the routes Kriegsmarine ships use.'

The Kriminalassistent looked thoughtful for a second.

'Why Emden? I would have thought Wilhelmshaven would have been a more likely destination.'

'They're building and repairing Kriegsmarine ships in every shipyard in Germany now. Emden was the only place that could fit us in, the sub lieutenant told us.'

Heinrich Güllich assured the sailor that he'd been right to come to them with the information; that it had been helpful. Then he dismissed him.

When he'd left, Carl Meyer took out the North Sea chart his father had given him. He marked the approximate position the sailor had provided, and the time and date. He drew a line on the chart from there to the point he'd plotted earlier, where the bomber had sighted the sailing boat. He took out a set of dividers and measured the distance the way his father had shown him.

'That's 150 miles, sir. In two days. They're more than capable of that.'

'Why would it have taken them so long, Meyer? Even I know they can go faster than that.'

'I believe another low-pressure system crossed the North Sea during that time. It was nothing like the storm they'd been through the week before, but it would have slowed them up.'

'You're convinced that it's them, aren't you?'

'Yes, sir. For the first time, really. But there's nothing concrete that would convince the Kriminaldirektor yet. May I show my father this?'

Heinrich Güllich's eyes narrowed, then he smiled.

'Why not? He has been useful so far. Ask him if he thinks it is feasible but tell him that it's highly confidential.'

'That goes without saying, sir. He'll understand.'

CHAPTER 223

[13/08/1941 Wednesday]

'General Kästner is not a committee member anymore; he hasn't been for some time. In fact, he's not even a member of the club.'

'I see. Did he leave, or was he asked to go?'

Heinrich Güllich didn't show it, but Carl Meyer knew that his boss would be disappointed. The Kriminalassistent aimed to undermine the General's social standing by disseminating rumours of disloyalty, and even treason, among his sailing colleagues.

The Clubkapitän sat across the enormous committee table from the two Gestapo men. Carl Meyer looked around at the glass cases with the club's trophies and the mementos of its royal heritage; a large portrait of the Kaiser as commodore of the club still hung on the wall behind the Clubkapitän.

This place reeks of money, power, and influence. The Führer will smash all of this, one day.

'The General left of his own accord,' the Clubkapitän said, but he'd hesitated for a second, and Carl Meyer wondered why.

'Can you tell me his reasons,' the Kriminalassistent asked.

The Clubkapitän swallowed and stared at the two Gestapo men.

'A difference of opinion on how the club should be run,' he said.

~~o~~

The Clubkapitän was tempted to lie, to tell them something plausible that would send them away with a juicy morsel about disparaging comments about the Führer, but with the General's parting words still surprisingly fresh in his mind, he decided to stick to the facts.

The self-righteous bastard wouldn't think twice about carrying through his threats to ruin my reputation.

'A Jewish couple who were guests of one of our members were asked to leave,' he said. 'The General took exception to this.'

'And he left the club because of that?' Carl Meyer interjected.

'Yes. Erich Kästner couldn't move with the times and see the benefits that the government's policy on Jewish matters would bring.'

'Yes. It's part of the reason for this investigation,' Heinrich Güllich said.

The Clubkapitän raised an eyebrow.

'The General is being investigated?'

'We are looking at several aspects of his life, shall we say. We have his Jewish servants in custody. They were trying to get to Palestine with false papers. We are trying to find out how much involvement the General had in the attempt.'

'Ah. That does not surprise me. I had to have a word with the General about allowing his servant's daughter to accompany his own girl to sailing club events.'

'When was this?'

'The most embarrassing one wasn't a club event, but a regatta for the armed forces. The army and the navy used our facilities. I believe it was the first year it was held; 1934, I think. He had the temerity to introduce the girl to the Führer.'

The Gestapo men both leaned forward.

'He did what?'

'He introduced the Jewish girl to the Führer. He had only just been made chancellor at that point, but even so…'

'What did the Führer say?'

'Nothing. As far as I remember he didn't find out she was Jewish, fortunately. But one of the guests made a bit of a scene afterwards, rightly, and the General had her blackballed for comments she made about the girl.'

'The poor woman,' Carl Meyer said.

'Oh, I wouldn't worry. As soon as the General left the club, she and her husband joined.

He's now on the committee, in fact.'

'Could you give me their names,' Heinrich Güllich said, taking out his notebook, 'We would like to talk to them.'

'I'd be happy to, but there's no need. They're here in the club. I can ask them to speak with you now if you like.'

'That would be excellent. You have been very accommodating.'

The man hesitated again.

'I hate to say it, but it's about time someone put Erich Kästner in his place.'

He left the two Gestapo men sitting and returned a few minutes later.

~~o~~

Carl Meyer frowned when the Clubkapitän took a seat at the end of the table and introduced the couple.

He glanced at his boss, but Heinrich Güllich seemed unperturbed by the man's continued presence.

'I'm Kriminalassistent Güllich,' he said to the new arrivals. 'Thank you for speaking with us.'

'It's the least we can do,' the woman said. 'It was intolerable the way that man treated us. We're very well-respected people, you know.'

Carl Meyer thought she was the worst kind of woman. Brash, self-important and a social parasite. He almost felt sorry for her husband.

'Your Clubkapitän mentioned that you had an unfortunate run-in with General Kästner, a few years ago.'

'Yes,' the woman said, 'the way he treated me that day was nothing short of disgraceful.'

Carl Meyer realised that the woman had waited all these years to get it off her substantial chest.

'Not to mention his disdain for the Führer's sensitivities,' Heinrich Güllich said.

'It was shocking. I told him so at the time.'

'And he had you blackballed?'

'That's right. It was humiliating, but I knew that I'd done the right thing, that it was that disgusting man who was in the wrong. I mean, introducing a filthy Jew to the Führer.'

The woman's eyes blazed with righteous anger. 'It's not the only time he showed that he was a Jew-lover,' she added. 'Fellow members have told me of countless times when he flouted the rules and brought his Jews here, or sounded off about the rights of Jews within the club.'

'Your outrage is commendable,' Heinrich Güllich said. 'We may require you to appear as a witness at some point. We'll be in touch.'

Carl Meyer saw the triumph in the woman's eyes.

The Kriminalassistent got up to leave, then turned to the three yacht club people.

'Just one last question,' he said. 'Did you all know the General's sons well?'

'I knew them very well,' the Clubkapitän said. 'They'd been part of the yacht club since they joined as young cadets; all their lives, really.'

'Did they leave the club at the same time as the General?'

'By that time, the boys were away in the army, but they were still occasionally here after that, I'm sure. Certainly, Johann was, I'm not sure about Franz. I'd have to check their membership records.'

'Can you do that, please?'

'By all means. Excuse me for a moment.'

He disappeared through a door in the corner and, after an awkward few minutes' silence, he strode back to the table, holding two record cards.

He looked up at the two Gestapo men.

'Franz's membership lapsed in 1937, the year his father resigned.'

'But he didn't resign?'

'No. He just didn't pay the renewal fee. It is surprising, in retrospect, although the fact that he no longer lived in Kiel might explain it.'

'What do you mean, surprising?'

'Well, it's such a prestigious club. Most people would continue their membership even if they left Kiel. It is key to getting into the right places all over Germany.'

Carl Meyer sensed the Kriminalassistent stiffening, but he hid his loathing of the man, and the couple, very well.

'And Johann?' the senior Gestapo man said.

'From what I can see, he is still a member. He last paid his dues in January of this year.'

'What did you all think about their trip to Norway?'

The three sailing club members glanced at each other.

'It was the talk of Kiel,' the Clubkapitän said, 'especially within the Kriegsmarine and the sailing community. They saw it as quite an adventure. For us, it was something a good few of our members do each year; a decent trip, but not anything out of the ordinary.'

'So, it wasn't foolhardy?'

'No, although there was always a risk, that early in the season, that they would encounter bad weather.'

'And on the day they left Hirtshals with a heavy storm forecast? That wasn't reckless?'

'Perhaps. It would depend on how much time they reckoned on having before the storm hit. I'm sure they put a lot of thought into it.'

'What did you think when you heard that they'd survived, and were prisoners in England?'

'Relieved, more than anything. Despite having a father like that, they were decent boys, and always respectful.'

~~o~~

'Go home, have a square meal, a sleep, and show your father what we've found. He's been a great help.'

Carl Meyer glanced at Heinrich Güllich, but he could see no guile. And it had been a long few days, with only snatches of sleep. If he looked as tired as he felt, it was no wonder his boss was sending him home, even if it was uncharacteristic of the Kriminalassistent.

They'd returned to the office in Düppelstraße from the yacht club, and Carl Meyer had expected to be given a hundred tasks to do, a daunting thought in his exhausted state.

He'd been at his father's home before reporting for duty early that morning and the one before, grilling him about the Kästner route to make sure that Heinrich Güllich couldn't find fault. The Kriminalassistent's praise was the first time he'd said anything pleasant about Carl Meyer's father, and the young Gestapo officer beamed with gratitude.

He gratefully accepted his boss's offer, before he changed his mind.

~~o~~

After he'd sent Carl Meyer away, Heinrich Güllich extracted his notebook from his pocket and skimmed through the last few pages.

He knew that, if the General's case came up in front of a court with a sympathetic National Socialist judge, the likes of the socialites at the sailing club would help paint a picture of a man determined to help Jews, whoever they were, and at any cost. When he'd heard the woman's testimony about the General introducing the Jewish child to the Führer, he knew for certain that it had been a deliberate act of provocation on his part, and that it would come across well if the case ever reached trial.

But he needed more. He needed to show that the General's sons were in league with him, that they were rotten like their father. Frau Böhm was the only one of his witnesses who hated Franz as much as she hated the General. It didn't matter if the younger son couldn't be tarnished as a Jew-lover; it would do to have him painted as being duped, of just blindly following his brother, but it would give him intense pleasure to put Major Franz Kästner in the same box as his father.

He looked at his notebook again.

Lise Böhm. If she was as bitter as her mother, she might well have something to add.

He lifted his coat from the stand and made for the door. It was only a few minutes' walk to the girl's flat. Checking the address, he closed his notebook and slipped it inside his pocket. He could easily fit the visit in between his other duties.

CHAPTER 224

Lise Mey took a while to answer the doorbell and tell him to come up. He climbed the stairs and knocked on the door of her flat. When she opened it for him, she was in a bathrobe.

'I'm sorry, Fräulein Böhm. Would it be more convenient for me to come back another time?'

'No, no. Come on in. I was taking a bath. It has been a long day.'

She motioned for him to pass her into the hallway and closed the door behind him.

'It's Frau Mey,' she said. 'I'm married.'

'My apologies,' Heinrich Güllich said. 'Your parents did say. You'll have to excuse my oversight.'

'It's of no consequence,' Lise said. 'Please, go on in. The living room is straight ahead. I've been expecting you to call. My mother said you were investigating the Kästners.'

She said the name with a venom that surprised him.

Heinrich Güllich noticed the wine bottle and glass on the table. The glass was almost empty, but the bottle was still three-quarters full.

'Would you like a glass, Herr…'

'I'm sorry. It's Kriminalassistent Güllich,' he said, handing her a card.

'Of course. Güllich. My mother mentioned it. Would you like a glass, or are you like policemen; you can't drink on duty?'

'Yes. I mean, no thank you. I don't drink while I'm working.'

In truth, Heinrich Güllich wasn't a big drinker, unlike many of the Gestapo men. A glass of wine with a meal, a few beers on the odd occasion he went to a bar for a colleague's birthday, or the birth of a child. He detested the false bonhomie it engendered in him, and the loss of his sense of control.

'You don't mind if I…'

She pointed to the bottle.

'No. By all means, go ahead.'

He watched her as she poured. She was an incredible woman. Every movement she made was lithe and, even in a bathrobe, he could see that she had the figure to match the beauty and compelling nature of her face.

He gave himself an imperceptible shake and willed himself to concentrate on the job in hand.

Looking like that, she would be dynamite on the witness stand.

'So, you wish to ask me about the Kästners,' she said, sitting down opposite him with her legs tucked under her.

'Yes. Franz Kästner, to be specific. I believe you were engaged to him?'

She stiffened, and her face hardened.

'It was the worst mistake of my life, getting engaged to that traitor.'

Heinrich Güllich's eyes narrowed, and he leaned forward. 'How long were you engaged for?' he asked.

'Only a few days, until I found out what he was really like. I should have known though.'

'Did he do something, or say something, that would have made you suspicious, before you became engaged?'

'To be honest, I thought nothing of it. Perhaps I was making excuses for him because I thought I was in love with him, but it was the way he was so familiar with the servants, as if they were part of the family. They'd always been like that, ever since we were all children.'

'The Nussbaums?'

'Yes. It was sickening to watch, once I realised what was going on.'

'But at the time, you thought it was normal?'

'Yes. We'd been brought up, living next door. As children, we spent all our time together, both of our families, and the Nussbaum brats. Even my parents thought nothing of it, until the Führer taught us what the Jews had done to us, and to Germany.'

'And when was the first time you noticed that Franz had tendencies, shall we say.'

'It was during the Olympics. We'd just got engaged and they were all besotted with that negro, who won all the races.'

'Owens? He shouldn't have been allowed to compete.'

'I agree. I told Franz that. He wanted him to win, even if it was an afront to the Führer.'

'Too many of our citizens fell under Owens' spell, just like they did with the Jews.'

'That's exactly how I felt. I told Franz that. He took exception to me saying that and tried to tell me that it was somehow normal to want a non-German to win, and black to boot. It was a travesty that he won all these races.'

'Perhaps it's because they're closer to being animals, these negroes,' Heinrich Güllich said.

'I'm sure he must have been cheating, however he managed it.'

Heinrich Güllich was warming to Lise Mey. She was a true Aryan in all senses of the word, and a credit to German womanhood. He breathed in. She smelled wonderful too.

'Is that when you broke off your engagement?' he asked.

'He got annoyed. He tried to force himself on me. I was only seventeen.'

Despite his hatred of the Kästners, Heinrich Güllich found it hard to believe that Franz Kästner was a rapist. And looking at Lise Böhm, he doubted that, at seventeen, she was as innocent as she was implying, but he wasn't going to say anything to contradict her version of events.

'What did you do, Frau Mey?' He engineered as much shock as he could into his voice. A tear ran down Lise's face.

'I managed to fight him off. I threw his ring at him and told him he was a traitor, and a disgrace to the uniform, then I left. I haven't spoken to him since.'

'That's terrible. I didn't realise. Your mother didn't say.'

'Was my father there? She wouldn't say in front of him. He would have killed Franz Kästner if he'd known.'

Heinrich Güllich couldn't imagine Eberhard Böhm killing anything bigger than a fly.

'Would you be willing to testify if it ever came to trial?'

'It would be humiliating, and degrading, but I would do it, to see the Kästners get what they deserve.'

She reached for a handkerchief and dabbed at her eyes.

'I'm sorry,' she said.

'Don't be. At least things turned out well for you. Your father told me that you are married to an SS officer now.'

'Yes. Rudolf. He's a Hauptsturmführer. With an Einsatzgruppe.'

'You must be immensely proud of him.'

'I am,' she said, but her voice faltered, and another tear ran down her cheek.

'Frau Mey, what's the matter?'

'Nothing. It's nothing.'

'It must be difficult, with your husband being away fighting. But it's for the Fatherland and for the Führer, no?'

He touched her on the shoulder, genuinely sorry for the hardships suffered by such a model German couple.

'Sometimes, things aren't as they seem on the surface,' she said quietly.

'What do you mean, Fräulein... I mean Frau Mey?'

'It's not his fault. The fighting, the horrors they see; their Kameraden killed by cowardly Bolsheviks and Jews, and it's only when he gets drunk. It's not surprising.'

'What is?' His eyes widened. 'Can he not... ?'

'No,' she said quickly, frowning. 'It's not that. I shouldn't really say.'

Heinrich Güllich could see a way that would make this young woman indebted to him but, for the sake of her credibility as a witness, there had to be no hint of scandal in her marriage, the more so when it was to one of the Reich's shining examples, a front-line SS-Hauptsturmführer.

'Please. I might be able to help.'

'No one can help. My parents don't even know. I'm too afraid to tell them.'

'Tell them what? Does he hit you?'

In Heinrich Güllich's opinion, the odd slap didn't do a woman any harm. On the contrary, it kept them in check. Some even enjoyed it, he'd been led to believe.

'He almost killed me the last time. It took me a month to recover.'

'What did you tell your parents?'

'That I fell down the stairs. It's one of the reasons Papa found me this flat. The ones at our old place were steep and twisting.'

'And they believed you?'

'I told them I'd had too much to drink. I don't think my mother believed me, but she said nothing.'

'Why don't you leave him?'

'That's what F...' She stopped.

'My friend, Francesca. She's the only one I've told.'

She said nothing for a minute.

'How can you leave an SS officer, when he's laying his life on the line for the Führer?'

'But what if he does it again?'

'He doesn't have a key for the flat. He doesn't even know where it is.'

'Let me know the next time he's home. I can arrange protection for you.'

She stared at him.

'You'd do that for me?'

'I have to look after my star witness,' he said, then regretted it as her face clouded. *Surely, she didn't think...*

He felt a stirring in his groin.

'Oh. I see. I suppose you're right. Whatever the reason, it will be a comfort.'

'And we will have to keep your relationship problems with your husband under wraps,' he said.

Her face clouded again.

'I don't wish it to be public knowledge anyway. With Rudolf away all the time, no one need know.'

An awkward silence descended on the room.

After a minute, Heinrich Güllich made to get up.

'Don't go. Please. It has been a relief to talk to someone about it.'

Heinrich Güllich looked at his watch.

'It's getting late.'

'Your wife? She is expecting you?'

'No. I work all sorts of hours. She knows not to wait for me.'

'You have to be somewhere?'

'No. I was mindful of your reputation. A Gestapo officer comes to your house in the early evening. That will cause tongues to wag. The longer I stay, the more they will gossip.'

'I don't care what people think, and they'll not dare say anything to an SS wife. Anyhow, I'll explain that you are an old friend of Rudolf, from SS school, or whatever you call it.'

A few strands had fallen from her piled-up hair and lay against her neck.

God. What must it be like? Perhaps he should stay a little while. See that she's all right.

'Would you like a coffee?'

He eyed the bottle of wine.

'Perhaps I might make an exception and have just one glass of wine.'

She got up and went to fetch him a glass. He watched her walk across the room. She moved with the grace of a cat. He loosened his collar a little, the sudden warmth uncomfortable.

She returned with a glass and handed it to him. As she leaned forward, the top of her dressing gown opened out a little and he saw her neck where it ran into the swell of her breasts. A few drops of moisture appeared on his brow.

'Are you warm, Herr Güllich?' she asked him, with an innocence in her voice that made him doubt himself.

'It is a little hot.'

'You should remove your jacket. You will be more comfortable.'

She moved around behind him and, as he leant forward, she took hold of his jacket. With an awkward struggle, he removed his arms and she lifted it from him.

'There,' she said. 'That's better, I'm sure.' She sat back down on the couch and looked at him. Her gaze, just like the slight touch of her fingers on his neck when she'd taken his jacket, sent shivers of electricity through his body.

He told himself he was a Kriminalassistent with the Geheime Staatspolizei and not an awkward youth of seventeen on the verge of his first sexual encounter.

'Do you have any children, Herr Güllich?'

'No,' he said, blushing at her directness.

'It never happened,' he added.

'It's why he beats me,' she said. 'I won't carry his child.'

He was sweating again.

'It is the duty of an SS officer's wife to provide children for the Reich.'

'And your wife? She has failed.'

'Not through any fault of her own.'

'You know this for sure?'

'Yes. I do. Yes.'

'I loved Rudolf. I would have had his children, some day. But I chose not to for a while, because I loved being with him, in and out of the bedroom, and I haven't seen a marriage yet that hasn't gone stale once children arrived.'

'Did he know?'

'No. But the ungrateful fool should have thanked God that he had a wife like me, not tried to punish me for keeping myself for him alone; for his pleasure.'

'His loyalty to the Führer, and to the Reich, would have been greater than his personal pleasure,' Heinrich Güllich said.

'I think it's difficult for you to judge, having not been in the Hauptsturmführer's position.'

'I know my love for the Führer comes before anything.'

'Perhaps we should put that to the test,' she said, leaning forward and putting her hand on his knee.

CHAPTER 225

She was right. The man is a fool.

Heinrich Güllich walked briskly to the corner of Holtenauer and Düppelstraße as if he'd just finished a routine call, questioning a witness, or intimidating an errant citizen.

But inside, his mind was reeling. He hadn't known women like that existed.

He stopped to light a cigarette and glanced around, expecting the world to look different.

He thought of his wife, mousy and subservient, like her mother; for her, sex was a duty, to be furnished when her husband required it, and as a way of trying to conceive the child she so desperately wanted.

An impregnation.

He felt no guilt. It had been something of another world, with no connection or similarity to what went on in his marital bed. And it wasn't the first time he'd taken a woman outside of his marriage. He'd used whores as and when he felt the urge, and working women often found it necessary, for business reasons, to give some of their time for free to members of the Gestapo, if they wished to continue their trade.

And more than once, in the early days, he'd given in to his impulses and taken one of his women suspects forcibly, as part of an interrogation or as punishment when they failed to provide the desired information.

But he hadn't indulged since he'd been promoted, feeling that, as a Kriminalassistent, he should be above it.

And now I've slept with a key witness.

He knew there would be no repercussions; the sex had been consensual and largely led by her, but no one could ever know about it. She was too useful a witness, should the General ever face trial.

How do I do that, if every cell in my body wants to go back there tomorrow?

He would find a way, because she'd let him know that that would be available to him again, at her discretion.

He made the wrong choice, her husband.

He had to admit that it was easier for him, with no strings attached. Screwing Lise Böhm, or Lise Mey, would not affect his ability or his desire to do his job, and he was under no obligation to put her in child. But he knew, if he had been Rudolf Mey, it would have been enough.

Let someone else provide the Reich with new Aryans. At least for a while.

~~o~~

'They're missing?' Heinrich Güllich said, the vein in his temple throbbing. 'You can't be serious.'

'Sorry, sir. They didn't return from their last mission.'

Carl Meyer had tracked down the crew of the bomber who had reported the sighting of the yacht in the western part of the North Sea. He'd arranged for them to be available to talk to Heinrich Güllich and him, at their base in Achmer, near Osnabrück, close to the border with Holland.

They'd driven the 300 kilometres that morning, only stopping for a coffee in Nienburg. Heinrich Güllich had stayed in the car while Carl Meyer had gone into the guardhouse at the gate, to return with the shattering news.

'Damn Luftwaffe. They could have telephoned us and saved us the trip.'

'To be fair, sir, they were due back in the early hours of this morning, and Air Command have been contacting other airfields nearer the coast to see if they'd landed at one of them. It's not uncommon, I'm told, if they have engine problems.'

'We've come this far. We can go to one of these infernal airfields.'

'There's no word, sir. They would have landed by now. They've either been shot down over England and they're in enemy hands, or they've ditched in the sea.'

'Or they're dead.'

'Or they're dead, sir.' Carl Meyer nodded.

'What's the chance of them being picked up by one of our vessels if they ditched?'

'I asked. The airman on guard says there's little chance. They'll telephone us if they turn up.'

'Could they not have lasted one more mission?' Heinrich Güllich muttered.

'I know, sir,' Carl Meyer said as he turned the car. 'What next, sir?'

'I want to interview Rainer Schulze again, the Kapitän who searched the yacht when it was intercepted on its way to Norway. You're convinced he conducted a proper search. Let's see if he did.'

'Yes, sir. I'll find out when he's next home on leave. Anything else, sir?'

'Yes. I interviewed the Böhms, the Kästners next-door neighbours. They were most helpful. They hate the General with a passion, and Franz too, after the way he treated their daughter.'

'I've heard she's quite a stunner, sir.'

'Yes, I suppose she is.'

'She was there when you interviewed the Böhms, sir?'

'No, no. I visited Lise Böhm at her flat. Anyway, She's Lise Mey now. Married to an SS-Hauptsturmführer. He's serving with an Einsatzgruppe in Russia.'

Carl Meyer raised his eyebrows.

'She says Franz was close to being a communist,' Heinrich Güllich continued. 'And that he hated the Führer and National Socialism. She also echoed her mother's testimony, that he loved Jews and was a big fan of Jesse Owens. He seemed to think that negroes were real people.'

'A radical, sir? Is the General one too?'

The Kriminalassistent winced as the car went round a sharp bend, then smiled. The occasional bit of discomfort from the scratches she'd given him were a small price to pay for an evening with Lise Böhm, provided he remembered not to let his wife see his back, until they had healed.

'Sir. Do you believe that Franz Kästner and his father are radicals?'

He looked up. Carl Meyer was glancing at him, a frown on his face.

'Sorry. I heard you the first time. I was thinking.'

Scheiße. I can't afford to slip up. Meyer is clever enough to notice.

'Perhaps she's exaggerating a little,' he continued. 'It's very personal with her, but I do think they all have a fundamental disdain for the Führer's vision for the Reich, and the whole Jewish question; it's not just about their own Jews.'

'Did they say anything else? Were there any strange comings and goings at the Kästner house?'

'No. They didn't say. That's good thinking, Meyer. I'll go back and ask them.'

'We could call in on the way back, sir, if you like.'

'Yes, why not. I had a feeling there might be more they can tell us. After all, they've lived next door to them for years.'

'Do you want to call on the daughter too?'

'No. Leave that to me. She's a little nervous, almost frightened. I don't know about what, but we don't want to go in mob-handed.'

'Yes, sir. If you think so, sir.'

Heinrich Güllich glanced at his underling, but Carl Meyer's eyes were on the road, unblinking.

'These people are important if we can bring the General to trial for sedition, or treason,' he explained. 'They'll help paint a picture of the General as someone who isn't just trying to keep his Jewish servants with him for selfless reasons, like he tries to portray, but of a man who does not believe in the ideals of the National Socialist party, and who is willing to act on his beliefs.'

'You're right, I suppose, sir, but why does it need to come to trial, sir? If we find enough evidence, would it not be simpler just to throw him in one of the camps?'

'No, Meyer. He has too much influence. In this case, we will have to go through the whole criminal justice system; everything has to be seen to be done by the book.'

'Generals have been shot before for treason. Why not him?'

'Ah. There's a difference, but it's a valid point, Meyer. Those people were exposed by others with the same rank, or higher. They have the power to act in exceptional circumstances, for the good of the nation. We, on the other hand, must build a case that will stand up in court, so that the people can see the type of man who has betrayed the future of the Reich.'

'I understand, sir.'

'I'm glad. And once we invade England, and *liberate* our brave prisoners of war, his sons will stand trial with him.'

CHAPTER 226

'I had an interesting conversation a few days ago with Herr Küblböck, the administrator of the psychiatric hospital.'

The General looked at the Doc.

'That's the one in Düsternbrook, on Moltkestraße?' he said.

'Yes, out by the park.'

'What was he saying? Are they still killing the mentally disturbed?'

'Yes, to a certain extent, if they are included in their *unfit to live* category, but that's not what he spoke to me about.'

'What then?'

The four friends still met up from time to time, always in the bar at the Europäischer Hof. It didn't happen every week, but they tried to make it at least once or twice a month.

Dieter and Oskar still hadn't arrived, but they'd sent a message. A rush print job had come up, and they'd be along later.

'He says they are getting an increasing number of young patients,' the Doc continued.

'I thought the psychiatric hospital was full of young patients. Do they not put the older ones in the geriatric hospital?'

'They do, but these are even younger than usual. Around thirty per cent of psychiatric admissions are now soldiers who've served in Russia.'

'I'm not surprised. From what I hear, the fighting is fierce in parts, and these young men will have seen sights that would make you and I lose sleep, even if we've seen it all before.'

Doc Speer shook his head.

'These aren't front-line soldiers. They're SS troopers, mostly from the Einsatzgruppen. He says there was a trickle during the Polish campaign, but now it's a regular flow. He described them having something akin to shell shock.'

'The Einsatzgruppen don't see any action, as such, from what I hear. How the hell do they get shell shock?'

'It's not quite the same. He says that he spoke with one of the SS commanders who visited the men. Many of them are alcoholics, or they're addicted to drugs of various description, morphine and the like. It's apparently all down to the traumatic effects of their role.'

The General snorted.

'You do know what Einsatzgruppen do, don't you?'

The Doc sighed. 'Yes. You told me. And that's the problem.'

Erich Kästner's brow furrowed, and he stared at Hermann Speer.

'What do you mean?'

'Their problems arise from them having to kill all these people, face to face.'

'From what I hear, it's often with a shot to the back of the head.'

'You know what I mean. It's personal. One to one.'

'You're telling me these poor souls, these young fragile men who kill innocent people in their thousands, are to be pitied?'

'No. I suspect that they're chosen for their... let's say... suitability, but it doesn't mean that they don't suffer psychologically.'

'I have more empathy with their victims, I'm afraid.'

'It was something else that the commander mentioned that worried me more,' the Doc said. 'He told me that Heinrich Himmler had visited his unit at their headquarters in Minsk, to discuss the problem of recruitment, and retaining personnel.'

'Ah, now we come to the nub of the problem.'

'He said that our beloved Reichsführer had assured him that they were working on a solution to the problem, that his men would not be expected to have to kill in such numbers for very much longer.'

'I doubt very much if they will stop the killings.'

Again, Hermann Speer shook his head.

'The man was grinning when he told me this,' he said. 'I forced myself not to react, in the hope that he'd say more, but he didn't.'

'They must be testing new ways of killing people. Injections, possibly.'

'I doubt it. That is just as personal, and it's time-consuming.'

'Canaris told me once that he'd seen a group of men locked into a synagogue and burned to death.'

'That would cause similar problems for these SS men.'

'I'll talk to Canaris about it. Thanks for telling me. Now, where are these two? I can understand Dieter working late, but it's not like Oskar getting his hands dirty.'

~~o~~

[22/08/1941 Friday]

'We are convinced the Jews were on board. All the evidence points to it.'

Rainer Schulze returned Heinrich Güllich's stare.

'I've told you before. We searched that boat from top to bottom. There was no one else on it, other than Franz and Johann.'

'Then the Jews were in the water, clinging to the side, while you were searching.'

The torpedo boat captain laughed.

'What's so funny?' Heinrich Güllich said, stiffening.

Carl Meyer could see the congested blood vessels clearly in the whites of his boss's eyes.

'The temperature in that water is barely above freezing; there was still a little ice in parts of the Ostsee, and the Nordsee isn't much warmer. We were on that boat for half an hour, and we had it under close observation for five or ten minutes before that. They couldn't have survived immersion in water at that temperature for that length of time.'

'What if they wore some sort of diver's suit?'

Rainer Schulze laughed.

'Really? You believe that? For a start, it would have taken immense foresight and planning to have them to hand and, anyway, where do you think you could source something like that? It's very specialised equipment.'

'The General has contacts.'

Rainer Schulze gave Heinrich Güllich such a look of contempt that, for a second, Carl Meyer thought that his boss might pull his pistol and shoot the man.

Instead, he turned away, but the young Gestapo man could see a vein pulse in his boss's neck.

'When you searched the boat, was there nowhere that you could possibly have missed?' Carl Meyer said, to give his boss time to calm down.

'No. We searched every cabin, every locker, and under every bunk.'

'And there couldn't have been a false bottom in any of them, or in the bilges?'

'No. We went through all this before. There just wasn't room. I know yachts. I've sailed them for years.'

'And did you empty every locker? Could they have hidden underneath something; piles of ropes, fenders, or something?'

'Yes. We emptied everything. We even checked under the tender. I...'

He stopped.

'What?' Carl Meyer said.

'The locker in the forecabin. I didn't take the sail bags out, but I checked around them. There was no one hiding underneath them.'

Heinrich Güllich had turned back to face Rainer Schulze.

'How big were these sail bags?' he said, in a low voice, full of menace.

'Quite large. On a boat like that, the sails are very bulky.'

'Were the bags spacious enough for a person?'

'No. Well, yes, I suppose, but I would have felt a body through the material. They definitely had sails in them.'

'And if a *small* person were to hide between the folds of the sail. Could you have missed them?'

Rainer Schulze flushed crimson, and it was Heinrich Güllich's turn to give the naval officer a look of contempt.

'Yes,' he said in a whisper, lowering his head into his hands. 'It's possible.'

'Danke,' Heinrich Güllich said.

CHAPTER 227

KIELER MORGENPOST

Monday 1st September 1941

REICH JEWS MUST WEAR STAR OF DAVID

Reich Minister of the Interior, Wilhelm Frick, has decreed that, from today, Jews living in the Greater German Reich of six years of age and over are required to wear a yellow Star of David on their outer clothing in public at all times.

The penalties for non-compliance with this law will be severe.

The minister has also introduced strict regulations obliging Jews to live in designated areas of German cities, in Judenhäuser specifically allocated to them. Any Jew found living in a house not thus designated will be liable for arrest and imprisonment.

~~o~~

KIELER JÜDISCHES FREIHEITSNACHRICHTENBLATT

Volume 102

9th of Elul, 5701

RESPONSE BY GERMAN CITIZENS TO YELLOW STAR BADGES.

In an unusual show of empathy, there have been widespread reports of ordinary German citizens of Kiel, and wider Germany, approaching Jews wearing the new yellow Star of David badges and passing on their feelings of sympathy and disapproval.

The new regulations came into force earlier this week and Jews have been threatened with severe penalties if they refuse to wear badges identifying them as Jews. This move was, in the view of the KJF, inevitable; a similar scheme was introduced in the Generalgouvernement region of occupied Poland in 1939 by Governor General Hans Frank, where all Jews over the age of ten were made to wear a white armband affixed with a blue six-sided "Jewish" star, worn over the right upper sleeve of their outer garments.

The KJF has heard that in some quarters of the Jewish community there is scepticism about the response of the Aryan community. One prominent Jewish teacher said that it was "too little, too late; where were these people when they took away our rights, our jobs, and our children's futures?".

The KJF would prefer to take the sympathetic gestures at face value and hopes that such gestures will signal the start of a backlash against the National Socialist's treatment of the Jewish population in Germany, and in the occupied territories.

STOP PRESS

Just before publication, the KJF has been handed a pamphlet issued by the Department of Propaganda and Enlightenment to all non-Jewish households.

In it, citizens are given guidance as to how they should respond when encountering former neighbours wearing the new badge. It includes such advice as "do not engage in unnecessary conversation with the wearer of the badge, nor make any kind of sign that would indicate sympathy for the Jew". It also exhorted decent German citizens to inform the authorities if they believe a person of Jewish nature is seen to be without a badge.

WORD OF THE WEEK

We are blessed with a glut of new words this week. In official German documents and publications,

the terms "Evakuierung", "Umsiedlung nach dem Osten", and "Absiedlung" are the latest euphemisms for deportations of Jews to the ghettos in Poland.

~~o~~

Erich Kästner stared at his copy of the KJF.

Evacuation. Relocation to the East. Resettlement. The National Socialists have invented a completely new language to cover their crimes.

He slipped the printed sheet into the folder he kept in a locked drawer in the desk in his study; he would add it to the file of documents he thought were important to preserve, for generations only just being born.

CHAPTER 228

'I should have seen him by now. I watch every day.'

Rosa looked at her friend.

It was true; Miriam spent much of her time looking through the wire at the men's compound hoping for a glimpse of Yosef.

'He must be dead,' she said.

'Don't think like that, honey. There are thousands of men; you just haven't spotted him yet, or he could have been moved to another camp; there's talk of us being shifted.'

'What do you mean? How do you know?'

'Men say things when they're...'

'Oh.'

'This isn't really a camp for women. The only reason the few of us are here is to service the guards, and the Kapos. There are other camps which have women in them, working just like the men. Ask Edith. She was at Sachsenhausen before they brought her here.'

Rosa glanced at Miriam.

She almost looks like herself again.

Miriam's face had all but healed; even the scars were less angry now, but she still limped, and she didn't have full use of her left arm.

'But I'll be away from Yosef if they move us,' she said. Her head dropped.

'I know, honey,' Rosa said, 'but it's not as if he's...'

Rosa's voice trailed off.

'I know I can't see him but if he's here, he's close, and I know if he's alive, he'll be thinking of me.'

'He'll be thinking of you wherever he is.'

'I'd just like to see him again. Am I being selfish? You haven't seen Emil since... how long?'

'It was January. January 1940. A year and a half.'

'I'm sorry, Rosa.'

'I think about them every day. Rebeka. Fischel. Emil. I wonder what they are doing and whether they still remember me.'

'Of course they do. Emil was beside himself, trying to get you out.'

'I'll never see them again.'

'Don't say that. You will, I promise.'

'Tell me again about the last time you saw them...'

The only time Yosef Nussbaum was in the main compound was when he stood with the others in the Appellplatz for roll-call, morning and night, and to sleep, two to a bunk in the middle level of three.

Someone was looking out for him, he knew, because he'd been given a job in the brickworks, making bricks to build the new, larger, more modern facility that was being constructed closer to the clay pits.

It was hard work, but nowhere near as back-breaking as the work on the canal or in the pits. And it was skilled, so the extra rations that made the difference between life and death continued.

'As long as you keep producing bricks, they'll keep you alive,' the foreman said.

Yosef nodded. 'I'll do my best,' he said.

His first few batches had been poor, but he'd very quickly learned, and, by the end of the week, he was turning out bricks without having to think about it. He knew that, if he'd been in one of the Arbeitskommandos, he would be dead by now.

The General has done this. I pray that he has done the same for Miriam.

He thought of her often, and of Ruth, and Manny. His hut wasn't near the compound where she'd been taken, so he never got the chance to look for her. He worked seven days a week and, in the shortening days, it was barely light when he left in the morning and when he returned in the evening.

I know she's still here, and she's alive. And my children are too.

He chose to believe it, even though he knew it to be a lie.

They might all be dead.

CHAPTER 229

Memo: Geh.KdoS. ABW 27/09/41 CAC1461.1

For Attention Only: All senior executive officers, Abwehr.

From: Admiral Wilhelm Canaris, Chef der Abwehr.

Reinhard Heydrich has been appointed Deputy Reich Protector of the Protectorate of Bohemia and Moravia. He will be assisting the Reich Protector, Konstantin von Neurath in the control of the territory of the former Czechoslovakia annexed to the Reich on 15 March 1939.

This follows his promotion three days ago to SS-Obergruppenführer and General der Polizei of the Greater Reich. It is expected that he will continue to serve in both posts. [END]

~~o~~

'Canaris.'

'Kästner.'

'I'm getting sick and tired of finding new telephone kiosks every time you wish to converse.'

'Stop complaining. It gets you off your fat backside and gives you a bit of exercise.'

Erich Kästner burst out laughing.

'Canaris, you make me smile, my friend.'

'It's not easy to find a smile these days. Did you read my memo about Heydrich?'

'Yes. Is he out of our hair now? Who will we get in his place?'

'No one. It's as I said in the memo. He'll continue in both roles, although he may have to delegate somewhat to his minions who, I can assure you, are ready and willing to do his bidding.'

'Why the move?'

'There's unrest in Prague, and other cities in the parts of Czechoslovakia that we control, and there's a growing anti-German sentiment, with widespread strikes and sabotage. The Führer is concerned about the region's industrial output; we rely on it heavily for military and commercial vehicles, as well as cars, motorbikes, and trams. It also supplies a significant part of our military resources, including arms and ammunition.'

'So, von Neurath has lost control?'

'Yes. Adolf thinks he is too soft on the Czechs. He remains the territory's titular head, but he has been given indefinite extended leave, *for family reasons*, so Heydrich will be in charge. The Czechs have a shock coming.'

'He'll not tolerate any resistance,' the General said.

'No. Did you hear what he said when he got there?'

'No, but I guess it wasn't something placatory.'

'He told his aides that he will Germanise the Czech vermin, and that those he couldn't Germanise, he would crush. They'd do well to believe him.'

'Anything else?' the General asked.

'Yes. Our worst fears about the Einsatzgruppen have been confirmed. I received an urgent report from one of our operatives in the Ukraine. Over two days, they shot over 30,000 Jews just outside Kiev, at a place called Babi Yar.'

There was silence on the phone.

'Did you say 30,000?'

'Yes. It could have been more, my man said. There were notices posted all over Kiev two days before, in Ukrainian, Russian, and German. I'll read one out to you.'

The General heard the rustle of paper, then Canaris's voice.

'All Yids of the city of Kiev and its environs are ordered to gather on Monday, September 29, 1941, by eight o'clock in the morning at the junction of streets Melnyk and Dokterivskaya (near to the cemetery). You must bring documents, money, linen, etc. Yids who do not obey this order will be shot.'

There was another silence.

'They walked to their own deaths,' Canaris continued, his voice quiet. 'And it wasn't just the Einsatzgruppen who carried it out. They were aided by units of the Wehrmacht's 6th Army and the Ukrainian Auxiliary Police.'

He paused. When he spoke again, the General heard a mixture of raw anger and despair in his voice.

'They've even developed a technique for making maximum use of the space in mass graves,' Canaris said. 'It's called the Jeckeln System.'

'What does it involve?' the General asked. He dreaded what he was about to hear, but he sensed that he needed to know.

'The Einsatzgruppen shooting teams were finding that when people were shot at the edge of a pit,' Canaris continued, in a matter-of-fact voice that Erich Kästner found chilling, 'they would fall in on top of those who had been shot a few moments earlier, and their bodies would crumple every which way. This resulted in unused and wasted space between the bodies. It meant digging more pits than would be needed than if the bodies had fallen into neat rows. Friedrich Jeckeln, an SS general, solved this problem. He called his solution *Sardinenpackung.*'

'They shoot them, and then get the other prisoners to stack them? That's horrific.'

'It's worse than that. They make the Jews lie in rows on top of the layer of people who have just been killed, then they shoot them in the back of the neck.'

'And the poor souls just do as they're told?'

'Yes, knowing what is going to happen to them.'

'What can be done?' the General said, knowing the answer.

'Nothing, but one day, the world will remember Babi Yar and Germany will be forever tainted by it. Perhaps the Ukraine will be too.'

'There must be something that we can do.'

'I've had the information about this, and other Einsatzgruppen massacres, passed on to the British, and to the Vatican.'

'At least the world will know then. How can they not act?'

He gave a brittle laugh. 'I'm one to talk,' he said.

'What do you mean? You're doing what you can.'

'It's not that. It might be only a small thing in the light of what is going on in the Soviet Union and Poland, but you'll have seen the Star of David badges that Jews are being forced to wear?'

'Yes. What about them?'

'That was down to me, a long time ago, before...' His voice trailed off for a second.

'You know what I mean,' he said.

'I still don't get it. The Star of David badges. That was your idea?'

'More or less. It was during the formation of the Generalgouvernement region in Poland. Hitler, Himmler, Göring and I were discussing ways of identifying the Jews in Warsaw. Every method involved constant checking by the police, or by the army. I suggested that we should put a large cross on their backs, or even better, make them wear one of their beloved six-pointed stars that they were so proud of.'

'And they went for it.'

'Yes. They jumped on it. Slapped me on the back. Adolf shook my hand, and they were all laughing, congratulating me for being a genius. Of course, there was an hour-long discussion on how it should be implemented but they finally decided on an armband. Blue on white.'

'Yes. I've seen photographs. I wonder why they've gone for a badge this time, and why they chose yellow.'

Canaris gave another dry laugh.

'The armband was too easy for the Jews to slip on and off when they wanted, to sneak out of the ghetto. With a badge sewn onto their clothes, it wasn't so easy.'

'Ah. I see. And yellow stands out.'

The General paused.

'It's not your fault, Canaris. We all make mistakes. I can't forgive myself for not getting the Nussbaums out when I could.'

'We weren't to know how bad it would get. None of us, even you, my friend.'

'No. But it's sometimes hard to live with,' the General said.

He was just about to hang up when he remembered his conversation with the Doc.

'Canaris?' he said.

'Yes?'

'I was talking to my friend, Hermann Speer. I think you've met him.'

'Yes. The doctor fellow. A nice chap.'

'That's him. He was saying that the SS are having terrible problems with the mental health of the men in the Einsatzgruppen. The psychiatric hospitals are filling up with them, and they're finding it hard to maintain squad numbers.'

'I heard that too. Himmler and Heydrich are extremely concerned. They're working on a solution.'

'Yes. The Doc said that. Have you any idea what it could be?'

There was a silence on the end of the telephone for a few seconds.

'Canaris?'

'I've heard stories. They've been doing experiments for years. I think the first ones were in '39. They're gassing prisoners.'

'Gas, like they used in the trenches?'

'No. The Einsatzgruppen are using vans now. They lock the prisoners in, then they divert the exhaust gases into the back of the van.'

'That's horrific.'

'Yes, but the SS troopers don't have to watch them die.'

'It must be time-consuming though.'

'They're working on more efficient ways to do it, and with different gasses.'

'How long have you known this?'

'I've suspected it for a long while. What your Doc says just confirms that the SS are having problems. I should know more soon.'

'Keep me posted.'

'I will.'

CHAPTER 230

[29/09/1941 Monday]

Maria Kästner tore open the envelope. As she read the letter, tears spilled down her cheeks, dripping onto the page. She hurried to wipe them off, terrified that the ink might run.

██████████████ *transit camp, 29th June 1941*

Dear Father and Mother,

They have finally allowed us to write. By now, you will know that although The Shearwater did not survive, we did.

We are well. The storm hit us with such ferocity as I have never seen before, and we realised that to make for shore and an unknown port would have risked certain death, so we decided to try and keep away from land as far as possible, beating our way westwards to give ourselves as much sea room as possible towards the western end of the ███████, hoping to ride out the storm and make for ████ once it had passed.

We lasted nearly a day, but the wind continued to increase, and even our scrap of storm jib was overpowered. The waves began to swamp the boat, then the rudder broke. We jury-rigged a replacement, but it couldn't hold us to wind, so we decided to run downwind with bare poles. We were broached several times, then when we thought it couldn't get any worse, we were knocked down and rolled.

Incredible as it seems, The Shearwater came back up, although the main mast had broken, and the boom was trailing over the side. We cut loose all the rigging and let it go. By this time, we'd taken on a lot of water, and the bilge pump jammed so we had to bail out by hand, but it was a losing battle; The Shearwater was shipping more water with every wave than we could bail.

We'd almost given up hope, resigning ourselves to dying, when a ship appeared. It almost hit us, but they spotted us just in time. This is where our good luck ended; the ship was ██████████ of the British Royal Navy. ██████████ ██████████████ it saved our lives.

I suppose we should be grateful that we were rescued, and they did treat us well, but we are devastated to be spending the rest of the war in captivity in England.

Johann is fine. His letter should accompany mine as they gave us all paper and envelopes yesterday, but you know Johann. We should be permitted to write every month, or every second month.

I hope this letter finds you all well at Drachensee. Please pass on my love and best wishes to Eva and Antje, and my grandparents.

Have they found Ruth and Manny yet? Pass on our concerns to Yosef and Miriam. All four of them are in our thoughts.

I said earlier that the British had treated us well, father. Johann and I, needless to say, were exhausted and just about at our wits' end when we were rescued. Once they'd allowed us a hot shower, we were taken to see ██████████████, who sat us down and asked us all sorts of questions but didn't insist on interrogating us further when we stuck to our rights and only gave our names, ranks and Wehrmacht numbers.

It turns out that he sailed yachts ██████████████. And you will like this, Father. When he poured us a stiff drink each, I expected that it would be navy rum but, you won't believe it, he was a whisky man. It was a Glenfiddich!

No harm to all the great whiskies you've introduced me to over the years, but a glass of malt never tasted better!

I must go now. There is not much more to tell; life is very humdrum here █████

███████ *. Perhaps when we are moved to a permanent camp there will be more to do but at present the men all just hang around talking or playing football.*

We are both missing you all, although Johann has already made a crowd of new friends, which shouldn't surprise you.

You have my deepest devotion,

Your son,

Franz

~~o~~

Despite herself, Maria Kästner telephoned her husband at work.

'Erich,' she said, when Frau Müller had connected the call, 'It's a letter from Franz.'

'What does it say?'

'They're well. They were picked up by a British ship when they were sinking. They're in a camp, and they're being looked after.'

'Anything else? No. Wait. I'll come home. I'll be there shortly.'

When he arrived, it took all his willpower not to snatch the letter from her. He hugged her first, seeing her tears.

Then he read. When he'd finished, he found he also had tears in his eyes.

'It's wonderful,' she said, 'isn't it. Even though they're in a POW camp.'

'Yes. It's wonderful,' he said, meaning it. 'Where are Eva and Antje?'

'Oh. Eva's at work. She'll be thrilled to hear from Franz. Antje will be home soon. She said she would be back for lunch.'

She took the letter from him and looked at it again.

'He hasn't given us an address to write to, Erich.'

'It's done through the Red Cross. I'll find out today. All we need is their Heer registration number, I think.'

'I'm going to make up a parcel each. Bratwurst and pickles and ham and cheese. And a few warm clothes for winter.'

He smiled.

'Wait and see what we are permitted to send. Perishable goods might not be suitable.'

'Oh. That didn't occur to me.'

'I'll make enquiries this afternoon. You can send it tomorrow.'

Unthinking, she kissed him on the cheek, then turned away, embarrassed.

'Thank you,' she said.

An awkward silence filled the hallway then, the front door burst open.

'Antje,' they both said at once.

She smiled, surprised at seeing her parents happy together.

'There's a letter from Franz,' Maria said, handing it to her.

Antje, without the General's reserve, grabbed it and read it, then read it again.

'They've blanked out half of it,' she said. Her huffed look made the General smile.

'That will be the British,' he said, although he was sure the German authorities would have had a good look at it too. 'They cross out anything that could be deemed as compromising to their security.'

'They don't know that Ruth and Manny are still missing, or that Yosef and Miriam are in a Konzentrationslager,' she said, her eyes full of tears.

The General marvelled at his daughter's acting ability.

She should have studied drama instead of art.

Something made him look at his wife. The smile had turned to a frown. He realised why.

Antje mentioned the Nussbaums. Even now, Maria didn't want them involved.

'We can write and tell them if you want,' he said. 'They would want to know.'

He was sure that the Gestapo would monitor the mail to Franz and Johann, and it was important for them to keep up a pretence.

'Are you going back to work, Papa?' Antje said.

'Yes. But I'll have lunch first. Why don't we have it by the lake, or at the summer house.'

'That would be nice,' Maria said, smiling again. 'The summer house would be lovely. I'll go and ask Frau Helder to prepare something. Why don't you two put out the table and chairs and I'll fetch a tablecloth.'

'All right, Mama,' Antje said.

As they walked to the summer house, the General looked back to see that Maria hadn't followed and spoke quietly to Antje.

'Ruth and Manny made it. They're safe in England.'

'How do you know? They boys only said they were safe.'

'It's the whisky. If he mentioned a fine malt, they were safe. If they weren't, it was to be *Loch Scavaig*.'

He explained that the bottle her mother had bought him, although it looked good, had been the worst whisky he'd ever tasted.

She laughed.

'It was an immense relief,' he said. 'We only had one more sign he could have used. The name switches and misspellings didn't work.'

'What else did you have?'

'He would have called the boat *The Sandpiper* if something had happened to Ruth and Manny.'

'You have to get in to see Yosef and Miriam now. They need to know, whatever happens to them.'

'I know. I'll contact the Gestapo tomorrow.'

CHAPTER 231

'It's Yom Kippur, today. I can't eat.'

'You must eat, Miriam, holy day or not. You'll need all the strength you can get.'

'For what? I will not give myself to any man.'

'If you don't, they'll take you by force, then kill you.'

'That is their choice and, if they don't pay for it on earth, God will see that they pay in Gehinnom.'

Rosa, although not a scholar when it came to religion, knew the difference between *Gehinnom*, a place after death where a soul could be punished for evil deeds on earth and *Sheol*, a sort of holding pen for the dead until they could enter *Gan Eden*, the Garden of Eden, the closest idea of heaven that she could imagine as a Jew.

Only the truly righteous went straight to Gan Eden.

'If there is a God, I pray that he will punish these bastards with all the power he can muster. If he's looking for an assistant, I'll happily volunteer.'

'Rosa, you can't talk about him like that, and on the day of atonement. It would serve you better to say your prayers.'

'I am. I'm praying that God will make them suffer, as we have. Every last one of them.'

~~o~~

Miriam shook her head. She was getting stronger by the day, and her bones and flesh had almost healed, but the pain of being separated from her husband, and her children, had only deepened.

She closed her eyes and prayed under her breath. It didn't do to let the guards hear, but she required to pray five times on Yom Kippur, two more than on any other day.

'They'll make you go over there soon,' Rosa said, nodding towards the other compound. 'I'm surprised that they haven't done it already.'

Miriam had watched the girls take their turns to pass through the gates and disappear inside the hut, and she'd seen the constant stream of men who entered by a second gate, always accompanied by a female guard, or one of the Kapos, trusted inmates who did the guards' dirty work for the price of a meal and somewhere better to sleep. And to stay alive.

'You know,' Miriam said, 'I didn't realise how bad it was for all the other Jews, until later.'

Rosa smiled.

'I knew,' she said.

'Why didn't you say?'

'We did our share of moaning but hearing it second-hand from us is never quite the same.'

'It was the General, Rosa. We were shielded from a lot of it. The shortages, the humiliation of having storekeepers ignore you, being spat at. But you and Esther, my parents and Yosef's parents, you all had it from the beginning.'

'It was hard. That's why Esther went to Palestine, even though she knew she would hate it, and it's why we spent our savings trying to get to America.'

'We should all have left when we could. Like the rabbi told us.'

~~o~~

Rosa said nothing. There was nothing to say. She inspected Miriam's injuries. The bruising had almost disappeared and the scabs on her wounds were dry and fresh-looking, helped by the saltwater bathing that Rosa and the other women had given them. She glanced through the wire to the hut next door.

'I'll not go,' Miriam said.

'They'll drag you.'

'I'll not open my legs for them.'

'They'll hold you down and, if you're lucky, they'll take it in turns to rape you. They may use a rifle or a baton instead, just to show you they're in charge. Then they'll send you back here until you heal, then do it again. When they get fed up, they will put a bullet in your head.'

'I'll die then.'

'You'll never see your children again,' Rosa hissed, tears welling up in her eyes.

Miriam looked at Rosa in silence for a second or two, then held out her arms.

Rosa couldn't find it in herself to be angry with Miriam for long, and she hugged her.

'The God I know will not punish you, Rosa Liewermann, for what you're doing, and I would never condemn you, but you do understand why I can't do the same.'

'Yes. I do. I wish I could have been as strong. Emil won't have me back, even if we do survive.'

'Yes, he will, because you won't tell him. What you're forced to do in here is finished when you walk out of this place, do you hear me?'

'Then why can't you do that?'

'Because I'm a stubborn fool.'

CHAPTER 232

Admiral Wilhelm Canaris looked out of the window of the General's office. In the still warm October sunshine, the citizens of Kiel, mingling with soldiers and sailors, some with girlfriends on their arms, strolled along the promenade, pointing at the shipyards opposite. An ice-cream stall did a roaring trade, even if the wartime ersatz cones were a poor imitation of the ones its customers remembered.

'I wonder if they know what is being done in their name,' he said, his back to the General.

'I doubt they know the details, but they've seen enough on their own doorsteps to have a broad understanding.'

'You think so?'

'Yes, unless they are burying their collective heads in the sand, or up their arses.'

'You're wrong. They don't know, and they don't want to know. All they care for is that the forces of the Third Reich are victorious.'

'And if they knew? Would it make a difference to them?'

'I'm not sure.'

'You're very morose today, Canaris. It must be bad for you to be like this.'

The admiral turned to his friend. He reached inside his pocket and pulled out a folded sheet of paper.

'Read this.'

The General sat down at his desk and, putting on his glasses, began to read.

From: OKW

Directive IA 1601/41

06/09/1941 11:00

To: Army Group North.

From the commencement of the encircling of the City of Leningrad, there can be no intention of the City and its inhabitants being captured. Any requests for negotiations re: surrender are to be rejected, as the feeding and housing of the population cannot be made the responsibility of the Wehrmacht. [END]

~~o~~

'You came here to show me this?'

'No, I was in the area, but I did want you to see it.'

'They mean to eradicate a whole city? How many people?'

'Three million souls.'

'How do they intend to do it?'

'A siege like no other. A combination of a systematic bombing of the city and starvation. I'm told that the commanders encircling the city are to have access to unlimited supplies of ammunition.'

'How long do they reckon it will take?'

'They expect a significant percentage of the population will escape into the countryside and make for other cities but, for those that remain, our scientists predict four to eight weeks. It depends on how effectively we can cut off the water supply.'

'It's murder, on an unprecedented scale.'

'It seems to be the only policy our leaders understand.'

The General stared at Admiral Canaris, numb with horror.

'And after that?' he said. 'Moscow?'

The admiral nodded.

'Even as we speak, our forces are advancing eastwards through Belarus. They hope to take the capital before winter sets in.'

'Can we do it?'

'I'm hearing reports that the autumn rains have turned the roads to mud, and that progress has slowed, but once the winter freeze sets in, we should be able to move faster.'

'What about Leningrad? Will it fall as soon as they say?'

'The collective minds of the High Command appear to believe it will. I heard a rumour yesterday that Adolf Hitler was so confident of capturing Leningrad that he had invitations printed to the victory celebrations to be held in the city's Hotel Astoria. I think in the light of the directive, that's unlikely. There won't be a building left standing.'

'God rest their souls,' the General said.

CHAPTER 233

Memo: Geh.KdoS. ABW 03/10/41 CAC1494.1

For Attention Only: General Erich Kästner, Abwehr, Kiel office.

From: Admiral Wilhelm Canaris, Chef der Abwehr.

The Abwehr has received reports that the policy of deportation of Jews from Germany to exclusive Jewish residential areas has been rescinded in favour of direct deportation to work camps. It is not expected that additional transport resources will be required in the short term. [END]

~~o~~

[04/10/1941 Saturday]

For Hauptsturmführer Rudolf Mey, his return home was both humiliating and heartbreaking. For months before, he had spent all his free hours refining his speech of contrition that would allow Lise and him to start afresh.

His letters requesting that she should meet him had been returned unanswered, and he almost decided to cancel his leave, or go to Berlin instead, but he'd fought his inner demons and travelled to Kiel on an overnight troop train from Smolensk.

He'd been billeted in the Russian city while his Einsatzgruppen cleared the countryside between the Smolensk and the front line, eighty kilometres to the east, of communists, deviants, Gypsies, and, of course, Jews.

Arriving at their flat, hoping to see Lise and explain to her that he'd changed, he'd heard a man's footsteps on the stairs below and, hiding in a doorway, he'd been horrified to see a young Kriegsmarine officer let himself into the flat with a key.

She has a lover. One with his own key, so it must have been going on for months.

The thudding of blood in his ears drowned out any rational thought. He crossed to the door as the man pushed it shut behind him and stuck his foot in the opening to prevent it closing.

'Hey,' the man yelled, and gave the door another sharp push.

But Rudolf had seen too much close-quarter action to give way, and he was in the flat with his hands around the throat of the midshipman before the sailor could shout out again.

'How long?' Rudolf hissed as the young man writhed and kicked, his face turning red then puce.

Rudolf realised the man could not answer and loosened his grip on his throat.

'How long?' he repeated.

'I don't know what you...'

His words ended in a strangled scream as Rudolf tightened his grip again.

'What the hell are you doing?'

Rudolf looked up to see a stranger, a young woman, staring at him in abject horror. Something made him release the pressure on the young man's throat.

'Who are you?' he demanded of the woman.

'I live here!' she screamed at him. 'Leave my husband alone or I'll call the police.'

'Your husband? Why are you in my house?'

'It's our apartment. We moved in two months ago.'

Rudolf took his hands from the naval officer's throat and looked down at him, then up at her.

A rattling wheeze came from the young man's throat and his wife fell to her knees, leaning over him to undo his collar, letting him breathe.

'What have you done?' she said. 'Why did you attack him?'

'I'm sorry. It's a mistake. I thought...'

'You're the SS man, the husband. The neighbours spoke about you. Your wife left you,

you fool.'

Rudolf, who had been full of genuine regret at his mistake, stared at the woman and the pulsing beat in his brain grew again. He stood up.

'I have been fighting on the front line for the last year. I have killed countless people with these alone.'

He held up his gloved hands.

'I'd consider your next words with care if I were you,' he added, moving towards the woman.

'Let it be,' croaked the man, pulling himself up to sit against the wall, with deep, rasping breaths.

His wife looked at him, then at the menacing figure of Rudolf Mey.

'Go,' she said. 'Just get out before I change my mind and telephone the police.'

Rudolf turned to go, then stopped.

'Her forwarding address,' he said. 'You have it.'

'No,' she said. 'We rented the flat from the landlord. We pass any mail to him.'

Rudolf remembered the man. He lived on the ground floor.

'Once again, I do apologise.' He withdrew his wallet and threw a fifty-mark note on the floor.

'Go out for a meal or buy something nice.'

Rudolf turned and left.

~~o~~

The woman picked up the note and looked at it for a minute.

'Give this away. I don't want it. I might still report him.'

'We can't. I've heard stories about him, and if the Gestapo get involved, they will take his side; they're all SS, after all.'

'Why should we be terrorised by people like that?' she said.

'Let it go,' he said, stumbling down the hall, leaning on her shoulder. 'We'll never see him again.'

~~o~~

The landlord was out of town. A note on his door said he would be absent for a week but didn't give the date he'd left.

Dummkopf.

Rudolf left the building and walked towards Drachensee, black thoughts of confronting Lise's parents pounding in his head but, by the time he'd reached their house, his rage had calmed to cold anger. He found a spot in the wood opposite the Kästners' house, and he made himself comfortable, wedged in the fork of a tree, ten feet up from the ground.

~~o~~

[05/10/1941 Sunday]

By morning, no one had entered or left the Böhm house, and Rudolf was cold and sore, but it was no worse than some of the billets they'd suffered in Poland, Lithuania, or Belarus. He looked around, but his cover was adequate. He had a good view of the front door of Drachensee Villa, the Böhm's stylish house, and he was hidden from sight by the branches of the surrounding trees, and the bushes below them.

He watched Herr and Frau Böhm leave for church around ten and was rewarded two hours later when they returned, Lise with them.

His heart melted when he saw her. If anything, she looked more beautiful than he remembered. The light summer dress and tailored jacket complemented her startling face and exquisite figure without flaunting the sensuality that he knew lay just under the surface.

But he felt it, even from a distance.

He climbed down from his hiding place and, picking up his kitbag from under a bush, he crossed the road and made his way through the dense woodland beyond the Kästner house to the water's edge.

Removing his clean shirt from the bag, he laid it to one side and stripped off to the waist.

He washed and shaved, towelling himself with the shirt he'd worn overnight, before stuffing it back in his pack with his toilet bag. He applied a splash of cologne and slapped his face a couple of times to bring a little colour back into his cheeks, and brushed a few small fragments of leaf from his uniform.

When he had finished dressing, he made his way back to Hamburger Chaussee and walked down past the Kästner house. He briefly thought of the Kästner brothers, returned from the dead by some miracle, only to rot in a British POW camp.

I'd rather be dead.

When he reached the entrance to Lise's parents' house, he pushed open the gate.

She won't make a scene here.

He smoothed down his jacket and gave himself a final check.

I can't. What if she's told them what I've done?

Indecision gripped him. He stood for a minute, then turned and left. He walked towards town and found a café, where he ordered coffee and thin slices of toast, with ham, cheese and jam. From time to time, he glanced through the café window but there were few passers-by.

He idled the time away by going over in his mind what he was going to say to her, ordering another cup of coffee every time the café owner looked at him with restless eyes.

Around three, he saw her walking down the opposite side of the road towards town and, unhurried, he settled his bill, standing at the counter while she passed.

Leaving the café, he saw her a hundred metres ahead. He crouched and retied his shoelace and waited until she was twice that distance away, then followed her.

Twice he came close to losing her, but she chose to walk along the front as far as Bootshafen, then cut up through Kleiner Kiel between the two small lakes, on to Holtenauer Straße, where he caught up with her again. She walked along the bustling street and, just before it joined with Knooper Weg, close to the Schauspielhaus theatre, she let herself into one of the apartment blocks, through a doorway between a haberdashery shop and a bakery.

He watched for a while and was pleased to see Lise come to one of the windows on the second floor. He saw her take off her jacket and look down the street. He turned his face away for a second, but he was confident she'd not see him in the shop doorway, where he'd taken cover.

He found another café on the opposite side of the street to the flat, half a block down towards Waitzstraße, and ordered a glass of wine. He wasn't quite ready to confront her, just yet.

One glass. Just to steady the nerves.

CHAPTER 234

Since calling on her parents with Carl Meyer, Heinrich Güllich had visited Lise twice. He'd also called in at Drachensee Villa but, to his disappointment, neither Lise or her parents could remember any strange visitors, or night-time movements of people or vehicles to or from the Kästner house.

But each visit to the flat on Holtenauer had been better than the last. She'd been eager for him to stay on both occasions, despite him offering her an excuse that he should leave.

Despite her treatment at her husband's hands, she seemed to like the Gestapo uniform and took great pleasure in getting him out of it; quickly, the first time he returned and with a teasing slowness on his second visit.

Now, walking down Holtenauer, he wondered when she would get bored of him and tell him it was over.

He had no illusions that he was her only lover. He was sure he'd seen her once having coffee with a senior SS officer in the Europäischer Hotel in the weeks before he'd first interviewed her.

And he knew that she'd get tired of him, in time. She was far too much of a woman for him to leave his wife for because he understood, even if she were still interested in him, he could never trust other men to leave her alone.

It hadn't stopped him telling his wife he had something to do at the office after a dreary Sunday lunch with her parents and walking the short distance to Lise's apartment.

He glanced around as he pressed the bell on the street door. Holtenauer Straße was unusually quiet and there were few souls around. He heard the click of the lock opening and he entered, closing the door behind him.

~~o~~

In the café opposite, Rudolf Mey frowned. There was no mistaking that the man who had just entered the building was Gestapo. He waited with interest to see if someone was going to be hauled out, protesting. It was doubtful; the man was on his own and didn't appear to have a vehicle nearby.

Someone getting shaken down, more than likely.

A few minutes later, Rudolf stared at Lise's window, his heart pounding. The Gestapo man had appeared, looked up and down the street, then stepped back out of view. It was so brief that Rudolf questioned for a second if he'd seen him.

It was Lise's window. What has she been up to? Surely to God, it couldn't be anything that the Gestapo were interested in?

He readied himself to move, if need be, but stayed in his seat, waiting for a car to draw up, or another Gestapo officer to arrive, but neither happened. He ordered another glass of wine while he waited.

An hour later, the Gestapo man left the building, looked around and closed the door behind him. He crossed the road towards the café that Rudolf was sitting in. Rudolf lifted a menu and studied it, hiding his face from the stranger, and watched as the man walked past.

He was smiling. And there was something else about him that Rudolf couldn't quite put his finger on.

Then it hit him. It was the smug, languid, self-satisfied look of a man who had just had sex. With Lise.

He knew the feeling.

It's as if you'd just been granted a special favour from God.

And his blood boiled.

He sat for a minute, then got up, paid his bill, and looked up at the window of Lise's flat, checking that she wasn't looking out. He left the café and crossed over.

He looked down the line of bell pushes. There was no Mey, or even Böhm, but there was one without a name next to it. He pressed it and waited. The lock clicked open and he took the stairs, two at a time, to the second floor. There were two flats on the landing, but one of the doors was unlatched. He heard Lise's voice from inside.

'It's open.'

He pushed it and stepped inside. He could smell Lise's perfume but there was another smell.

He followed the sound of her voice. She was sitting in the living room with her back to him.

'What have you forgo…'

She turned and stared.

'Rudolf!'

Her eyes darted to the window, then the bedroom door, then back to her husband. He saw a glimpse of fear in them, then she recovered.

'I didn't know you were home. You didn't write.'

'You moved. You left no forwarding address. The new people say they give any mail to the landlord.'

'Did you speak to him?'

It struck him as a strange question to ask. A tic pulsed in his left eye, and he hoped it wasn't noticeable.

'No,' he said, 'but I know what he would have told me.'

'And just what would he say?'

He watched as small spots of anger burned on her cheeks. She stared at him, defiant.

'That you didn't leave an address for him to forward any mail in case I came looking for you.'

She looked away, only for the briefest of seconds.

'You nearly killed me. I needed to be safe.'

All the fight appeared to leave her, and his heart melted. Then, like a wreath of smoke from a doused fire, the smell pierced his consciousness again.

It was the smell of sex.

'You've betrayed me, Lise,' he said, all the conciliatory words he'd meant to say wiped from his mind by the knowledge of what she'd done, less than an hour ago, with the man in the leather coat.

'No. It's not true. What are you talking about?'

'The Gestapo officer. I'm not stupid.'

'He was here to question me about Franz, Rudolf. Go and ask him. He's investigating General Kästner and his sons.'

She gave him a look of dismissive anger and, for a few seconds, Rudolf hesitated. He stared at her. He couldn't see anything but truth on her face.

Then the smell reached his nostrils again.

Before he knew what he was doing, his hand was in her hair, dragging her to the bedroom.

'Did he question you in here?' he said, staring at the crumpled, tangled and sweat-soaked sheets.

'I don't sleep well. I have nightmares. I've had them since the last time you were here.'

This time, the lie flickered in her eyes.

'I came home to plead to you to take me back, that I loved you more than life itself,' he said, a dreadful coldness in his voice.

'Don't hurt me, Rudolf. We can talk about it. We can make a fresh start.'

He smiled at the pleading desperation in her voice.

'It's too late,' he said.

CHAPTER 235

KIELER MORGENPOST

Tuesday 7th October 1941

THE ADVANCE ON MOSCOW CONTINUES

The unstoppable advance of our victorious troops on the Soviet
capital continues. In a statement from the War Ministry
yesterday, a spokesman said that the towns of Bryansk and Oryol
had been taken with few casualties.

"We expect to have made significant progress to Moscow over the
next week or so", the spokesman added.

From somewhere, Maria Kästner had procured a map of Europe, including western Russia, and she'd taken to reading the Morgenpost each day and marking in towns and cities that had been captured by the advancing Wehrmacht.

The General suspected that she did it in response to his pessimistic predictions about the success of *Operation Barbarossa.*

'You've never shown an interest in the affairs of the army before, even when I was fighting in the last war,' he said, smiling.

Or followed the progress of your sons' advances across Europe.

'I find it fascinating,' she said with a smile that lit up her face. 'Group Army South has taken Bryansk and Oryol.'

She took out a red pencil and circled the two Russian towns on the map.

There had been an entente between them since Franz's letter had arrived, helped since he'd explained to her how she could send food parcels and letters to her sons.

He didn't know what Maria, Eva and Antje had written in their letters but, in his note to Franz, he'd passed on the sad news that Ruth and Manny had never been found, despite extensive searches by the police, and that Yosef and Miriam had been arrested.

He had no faith that the German censors would let any of it pass, but he'd done all he could. And he was sure that the Gestapo would want to scrutinise them first. He hadn't mentioned Neuengamme, but he hoped his reference to the younger Nussbaums would be noted, and muddy the waters.

His wife's voice broke into his thoughts.

'Our troops will be in Moscow by the end of November. The Russians will be forced to surrender and without many casualties. Isn't it wonderful?'

'Don't believe everything you read, Maria. There's more resistance than they're letting on.'

'Can't you be positive about something for once,' she said, shaking our head. 'The sooner this is over the better for us, and for our soldiers. Think of your friend, the colonel, and his men; Franz and Johann's friends.'

'I never stop thinking about them, and all the others. I just don't want you getting your hopes up that Moscow will be taken without bloodshed, and that its capture will be the end of it.'

'Look at the map. It doesn't lie. See how far they've come, and Moscow is only another 300 kilometres away.'

'The closer they get to Moscow, the harder it will get. It will be the most gruelling 300 kilometres of the campaign and, anyway, there are still major battles raging behind the line of advance. And despite what they tell you, the casualties are beginning to mount.'

'Nonsense. They've taken these towns...' she said, checking the Morgenpost, '...

Bryansk and Oryol, with few casualties. That's what it says. Why would they lie?'

He laughed.

'Because that's how the politicians have convinced the people of Germany that we're undefeatable. For instance, they did capture both these towns, but the Soviet Army is holding positions outside of Bryansk, south and north of it. We've surrounded them but they're still fighting, tying up thousands of our troops and armour, until we can force them to surrender, or annihilate them. Either way, it will slow up our advance for weeks. And men lost or injured during those battles are not reported, as Bryansk and Oryol have already been taken.'

'Whatever I say, you always have an answer, Erich Kästner. How do you know you can trust your information any more than I can trust mine?'

'Because we have men on the ground, reporting back to us. The Morgenpost prints what the Ministry of Propaganda tells them to; what it thinks the public wants to hear.'

'Rubbish, Erich. Last week they said they'd met stiff resistance at Leningrad, and they haven't advanced as fast as they would have liked.'

'No. They had to admit that but, even then, they only told a small part of the story.'

'What do you mean?'

'They're going to starve the people of Leningrad to death, even if they do try to surrender.'

'You're talking nonsense again. How can they starve a whole city?'

'Simple. You surround it. You don't let anything in or out. They starve. All three million of the city's inhabitants; men, women and children.'

She shook her head, her face flushing crimson. 'You're exaggerating,' she fumed. 'They couldn't kill that number of civilians.'

'Our scientists reckon it will take six to eight weeks, but it could be longer. After all, if they can kill 30,000 Jews in two days, imagine how many Russians they can kill in two months.'

'You're blinded by your hatred of the Führer. You can't see anything other than what you want to see. This madness will destroy your career and what's left of your family. I *will* not allow you to do that.'

He'd never seen her quite so angry.

'It's God's honest truth,' he said.

'Don't bring God into it. You don't even go to church these days.'

'Because the churches, and this whole country, are Godless.'

She let out a scream of frustration, turned, and marched out of the room, muttering to herself.

Erich Kästner sighed. He picked up the paper and read the article. In a way, he couldn't argue with it. What it said was true, as far as it went, but it was what was left out that he took issue with.

CHAPTER 236

'It will stop your wounds healing,' Rosa said. 'They will not make you work if you have open sores.'

'But what if they turn septic and cause blood poisoning?' Miriam asked, frowning.

'They won't. Not if you use your own hair and urine.'

Rosa Liewermann was sure she'd heard that somewhere.

'So, I just pull a few hairs from my head and urinate on them?' Miriam asked, unsure.

'You can take hairs from wherever you want. Pluck them from down there if you don't want the bother of urinating on them.'

She pointed to her own pubic area.

Despite the horror surrounding them, they laughed. They did it quietly, into themselves, so as not to give the guards an excuse to beat them.

'Perhaps I should just laugh out loud,' Miriam said. 'If they beat me hard enough, they couldn't make me work.'

'A beating could be fatal, if one of the guards is in the wrong mood. This way is safer, and less painful.'

Miriam pulled a couple of strands of hair from her scalp.

'I'll be back in a minute,' she said.

'Just do it here. No one will notice.'

'No. I'll go to the latrine.'

A few minutes later, she returned.

'I couldn't,' she said. 'It just wouldn't come.'

'You are hopeless, Miriam Nussbaum. Go and try again.'

This time, when she returned, she held out three wet hairs between her fingers. She wrinkled her nose in disgust.

'Give me your arm,' Rosa said.

Miriam did as she was asked. Rosa looked around and began to pick at the edge of the biggest scab. Once it started to peel, she told Miriam to place the urine-soaked hairs underneath it.

'I'm not going to do it for you,' she said, turning up her nose.

Miriam laughed.

'You'll pick my scab, but you won't touch my hair, just because I've urinated on it.'

'Yes. That would be disgusting.'

'You all washed me the first day I was in here.'

'That's different. Now keep quiet and hold the scab shut until the blood coagulates.'

For five minutes, they sat, saying nothing.

'You know,' Rosa said, breaking the silence. 'I shouldn't say it, but it's been nice having you here.'

'I know what you mean. I don't know what I'd have done here without you.'

'You'd have got on with it. Like I do. But I'm glad Esther isn't in here with us.'

Miriam looked at Rosa. They both understood. Esther would not have coped in a place like Neuengamme.

'So am I,' Miriam said.

~~o~~

Beate Böhm seethed. How could the countess not see through the Kästner lies?

She'd stayed close to the elegant old aristocrat from the start of the fundraiser, wanting to see in person the destruction of Maria Kästner's social standing.

Instead, the countess had embraced the woman like a long-lost friend.

'My dearest Maria,' she'd gushed, 'It's so wonderful. I'm so relieved for you. It must have been a terrible ordeal.'

Beate Böhm watched a simpering Maria Kästner allow herself to be congratulated by all the ladies on her sons' miraculous return from the dead.

'Don't you worry that they've been captured by the British,' the countess continued. 'I have a few close relatives in England, and they're a stickler for doing the right thing; they'll be well looked after.'

'It's so disappointing. Franz had just been told he was being promoted to Oberstleutnant, and Johann was to be a major. Now they're...'

Beate Böhm felt sick as her neighbour sniffed into her handkerchief, comforted by the countess.

The mayor's wife, Irmgard Hoffmann, weighed in.

'They will be liberated when the Wehrmacht take Russia,' she simpered, 'then England.'

'Irmgard is right,' another of the Guild's ladies said.

Beate Böhm turned away, not wanting the anger showing on her face to be seen by the others, but she caught Ingrid Messner, Eva's sometime mentor, staring at her.

She glared back and made her way to the ladies'. She looked at herself in the mirror.

One day. They'll all see through her deceit, and her falseness.

She forced herself to smile. She knew it had been careless, letting the old crone see her anger.

When Maria Kästner is disgraced, I'll be there to see it.

~~o~~

[08/10/1941 Wednesday]

Miriam looked at her wound. It was red at the edges, and a sticky pus oozed from beneath the scab. It throbbed almost constantly and when the pain eased, it itched.

It's nothing. Compared to what I've suffered already.

She could have asked the guard to be taken to the hospital, but Rosa advised against it.

'Let it fester a few more days, then ask. They will give you dressing for it, and wound powder. Use it as sparingly as you can. We can pass the surplus to the men.'

Miriam stared at Rosa.

'You can communicate with the men?'

'Only through the Kapo. She will pass things on if you give her money, or cigarettes, or some of the wound powder.'

'But I thought it was to help the men?'

'It is. But she'll keep a little for herself. To sell.'

'Can she get a message across?'

'That's more dangerous. If you get caught...'

'I don't care. Tell me how to do it.'

~~o~~

[11/10/1941 Saturday]

Yosef Nussbaum held out his plate for the ladleful of stew he was entitled to, if you could call it that. He counted one small piece of meat among the potato and rotten cabbage, but he knew that he shouldn't complain. It was more than the inmates on the work parties received.

The prisoner dishing out the food handed him a hard, blackened, almost inedible roll. As he passed it over, he gripped Yosef's hand.

'Inside,' he whispered, through unmoving lips. 'Look inside.'

The roll looked like it always did, but when Yosef risked a closer glance, he noticed a small hole at one end.

Yosef took it and shuffled back to his bench, where the mould lay for the next batch of bricks. He dipped the cloth they were provided with into the bucket of cold water and wiped the surface of the mould. It was ready for the next load of clay, but it also doubled as a table, for him to eat his meal.

He looked around him, then broke open the roll.

Making sure not to be seen, he palmed the tiny piece of paper he found inside and hid it at the bottom of the pocket of his striped uniform, under his bricklayer's apron.

After he'd eaten his stew, which had two lumps of meat, much to his satisfaction, and chewed the roll until his mouth hurt, the guard blew his whistle and the next bucketload of clay landed with a thump in his mould.

He carefully tamped it down and smoothed it off then, using the wires the way the foreman had shown him, cut the clay into eight evenly-sized bricks. He drew his trowel back along the top of the bricks, leaving a small valley, almost identical in each brick. That was the skilled part, and he'd taken to it quickly, impressing both the foreman and the Blockführer in charge of the factory.

For the next five hours, Yosef made brick after brick after brick. He'd always enjoyed working with his hands, and he was good at it, so time passed. But every so often, he would think of Miriam, and Ruth and Manny, and a dark shadow would cross his face.

When he saw a similar look on his fellow prisoners' faces, from time to time, he knew they were doing the same.

At six, Yosef shuffled to the Appellplatz, with the rest of his squad. Then they were counted, like sheep, and fed again with the thin, pallid soup that tasted of nothing.

They were housed in a separate hut from the other prisoners, and he watched with pity every night as the men of the Arbeitskommando dragged themselves into the camp, barely able to stand in line for their meagre rations, and he blessed his benefactor, or whatever slice of good fortune that had kept him away from their suffering.

He always looked to see if any of his former friends from Kleiner Kuhberg were among them, but if they were, they were too emaciated to be recognisable.

Most likely they're dead.

In the quiet of the hut, with just enough light to see, Yosef looked around to make sure he was alone, and extracted the piece of paper he'd hidden in the fold at the bottom of his pocket.

I am well. I love you. Shalom. M.

He felt the dampness on his face as a tear rolled down his cheek. He wiped it away. It didn't do to show any sign of weakness in Neuengamme, even among the elite workers.

From under his bunk, tucked away in a gap between the planks, he extracted a tiny piece of wood, sharpened at one end, the tip burnt black against the stove.

He turned the paper over and wrote on the back.

I'm also well. Shalom Aleichem. I love you too. Y.

~~o~~

[12/10/1941 Sunday]

The next day, when his food was dished out, he dropped the small piece of paper in the container that held the rolls. It was acknowledged with the barest of nods.

~~o~~

That night, Rosa comforted Miriam when she cried at Yosef's reply. She put her hand on her friend's arm when Miriam tore off another piece of the paper wrapping that the wound powder had come in, and started to write.

'Miriam, honey, you'll just tie yourself in knots, writing back and forth. And you'll get caught, and you'll both be beaten, or even killed. Leave it for a while; a month or so.'

Miriam stared at Rosa, then replaced the paper in its hiding place underneath one of the slats of her bunk.

'You're right,' Miriam said, but while Rosa was in the compound next door the following day, servicing the SS guards, she knew that Miriam Nussbaum would stand at the perimeter fence of the compound, staring through the wire towards the main camp in the hope of catching the smallest glimpse of her husband.

CHAPTER 237

[16/10/1941 Thursday]

Lise looked in the mirror. It had been eleven days since her husband had visited. She began to apply the make-up which would cover what remained of the bruising on her face.

Most of the swelling had subsided and she was relieved to see that there was no scarring, but she was staggered by the healing powers of her own body. Her hand was coming along well; the splints on her broken fingers had done their job.

After Rudolf had gone, she'd lain for a day on the floor, unable to move, slipping in and out of consciousness. The next morning, she'd dragged herself to the telephone in the hallway, and had phoned for a doctor first, then she'd spoken to her mother.

'Mama, I'll be away for a week,' she'd said in what she hoped sounded like breathless excitement. 'Rudolf is being stationed in Berlin for a week; special training, he told me, but he's in a hotel, and he's free in the evenings, so I'm going to go to him.'

'I'll come and see you before you go,' Beate had said.

'No, I'm leaving shortly. The taxi is waiting. I'll see you when I get back.'

In truth, the catch in her breath came from the broken ribs that Rudolf's boots had inflicted, and it had taken her all her efforts to speak clearly, with her swollen and lacerated tongue. She hoped she'd been convincing.

It must have worked, because her mother didn't return the call, or visit the flat. But Kriminalassistent Güllich had, the day after the doctor had called.

She'd sat quietly while he rang the doorbell repeatedly, waiting until he'd gone. Picking up the telephone, she'd dialled the number on the card he'd given her the first day he visited and left a message with a young Kriminalassistentanwärter to pass on to Kriminalassistent Güllich that Frau Mey would be out of town for a week, at least, and that she would contact him on her return, if she had any further information for him.

She'd had enough food that would have lasted the week; it wasn't the most appetising and she hadn't starved but, by the fourth day, she managed to don a lace shawl and shuffle downstairs like an old woman to the grocer's, two doors down, for milk, and to the bakery next door, for bread. Neither of the two shopkeepers had made any comment about her health, and her face was well hidden by the fine black material.

The doctor had told her that she was lucky to be alive. Three or four broken ribs. Another broken cheekbone, and fortunate not to lose an eye. There was also a hairline fracture of her skull, in addition to the broken bones of her hand when he'd crushed her fingers in a drawer.

And she'd known she'd take little pleasure from sex for a long while, if ever. The rape had been bad enough, and the three back teeth smashed by the muzzle of his pistol, rammed into her mouth while he violated her, were a reminder of the assault every time she ran her tongue over the place where they'd been.

But he'd not stopped there. She'd passed out by then, but the pain that burned in her groin when she'd woken, and the empty, bloodied wine bottle discarded next to her, told her what he'd done to her.

When the doctor told her she might never conceive, she wondered if that had been Rudolf's purpose. She knew she'd made the attack worse by telling him she'd screwed the Hauptsturmführer, his mentor, but it was almost worth the pain to see the look of blind rage on her husband's face every time she closed her eyes and thought of him.

It was all Franz Kästner's fault. If he hadn't been such a Jew-lover, and a traitor, she would be happily married to an Oberstleutnant, the wife of the holder of an Iron Cross, with expectations of being the mistress of the Kästner family home, a door away from her parents.

Just give me the chance to testify. I'll see them all in prison.

~~o~~

[18/10/1941 Saturday]

Lise telephoned Gestapo Headquarters two days later, almost a fortnight after Rudolf's visit, and said she had further information for Kriminalassistent Güllich.

Leaving the flat, she took a tram out to Drachensee and visited her parents. She'd made a good job of her make-up, and her mother made no comment, but Lise could see that she knew. *I'll tell her about it in my own time.*

When she got back to the flat, Heinrich Güllich was standing on the pavement waiting for her, the smoke from the cigarette he held curling upwards in the crisp autumn air.

A man walking by glanced at Lise, and Heinrich Güllich gave him an angry glare. She told herself that he'd have to get used to other men staring if he was around her for long.

Lise let herself into the apartment block, and he followed, checking the street, closing the door behind him.

~~o~~

As Heinrich Güllich and the girl disappeared inside, Dieter Mass turned into Waitzstraße. It was only a hundred metres to his home, but he walked past the door to his flat, then stopped and pretended to tie his shoelace, taking the opportunity to look behind him. He let out a long slow breath when he saw that he hadn't been followed.

His stomach had lurched when the Gestapo man looked straight at him. At any other time, he would never have made eye contact with a member of the Geheime Staatspolizei, but it was unfortunate that the woman the man had been with was Lise Mey.

Dieter Maas had only ever seen her a few times before, but she had such a striking face that he'd instantly recognised her. He was surprised to see her with a Gestapo officer, and he'd looked away too late to prevent the man from seeing him staring at her. What's more, he'd recognised the Gestapo man.

He trawled his brain for the man's name.

Güllich. That's it. Kriminalassistent Güllich. The man who's causing Erich so much trouble.

He let himself into the house and threw his jacket onto the coat stand. He went into the kitchen and he poured himself a stiff Schnapps.

Looking out the window, he checked the street, but it was empty.

He downed his drink in one go.

~~o~~

Heinrich Güllich lay back, spent.

When they'd entered her flat, he'd reached for Lise, desperate to have her naked, and wanting him. It had been a long two weeks since he'd been with her, and he knew that she was an addiction that needed purged.

But Lise had held out her hand and, while not pushing him away, she'd stopped him from touching her.

A flash of anger crossed his face, but he saw a tear fall down her cheek and his rage evaporated.

'What's wrong?' he asked, surprising himself that he cared.

'Sit down,' she said. He did as he was told.

She stood in front of him and undid the top button of her blouse, then the next. His excitement, which had died, began to grow again until they were all undone and she slipped her arm, wincing, from her sleeve, exposing the skin of her chest and arm. She showed him her still swollen fingers, and he gasped at the fading yellow bruises and healing skin of her ribcage and abdomen. He'd handed out enough beatings to know how sustained and thorough the assault had been, and how long ago it had happened.

'He was home. He did this to you.'

'Yes. Almost two weeks ago. That's why I couldn't see anybody.'

'Did you get a doctor?'

'Yes.'

'I can arrest him if you want. He shouldn't be able to get away with this.'

'You know that the SS will hush it all up. They don't want the nation's heroes tarnished.'

'There's still a rule of law,' Heinrich Güllich said, but his face echoed her scepticism.

'At the very least, I'll have a word with him, to warn him off.'

'You'd do that for me?'

'Of course. I believe we must protect the good women of the German Reich, or we won't have built a decent society. That's what we're all striving for, isn't it?'

'That's very sweet of you. I'm glad I have someone like you I can rely on. I know you would never hurt me.'

He watched with a sinking heart as she covered herself, cursing his luck.

'I can't be with you,' she said. 'It would hurt too much.'

She told him what Rudolf had done to her with the bottle.

Heinrich Güllich was incensed. He knew the damage that could be inflicted, having used the same method to extract information from a *filthy Jew bitch* about where she'd hidden her brood to avoid them being deported.

Damn the bloody man. I hope he catches a bullet.

Her voice broke into an image in his mind of the top of Rudolf Mey's head being blown off.

'Sorry, what did you say?'

She smiled at him in that way she had.

'It doesn't mean that you should miss out.'

He felt the heat spread through his body from his groin.

Kneeling in front of him, she unbuttoned his shirt and kissed his chest, working her way down. Her good hand worked with his belt, then his buttons, then she slipped it inside his underpants. With her fingers and her lips, she teased and tormented him until finally, he gave in to the waves of pleasure her touch provoked.

'What did the doctor say?' he asked when he could breathe again.

'That I may never have children, but I should heal. I don't believe it's as bad as he thought.'

She looked at him, with those eyes that almost extinguished any other thought. It struck him with new appreciation why intelligence operators used women as traps for diplomats, or military officers. He knew that he could never betray his oath to the SS, but it would be close to unbearable to have to choose between her and his Führer.

He cursed letting himself be drawn into such a position of weakness, then he smiled grimly to himself.

I'll not have to make that choice. It will be her decision to discard me.

He heard her speak again.

'I wanted you now,' she said, 'but I couldn't dare risk it. No intercourse for at least six weeks, the doctor said.'

Heinrich Güllich couldn't help himself doing the quick calculation in his head.

Four more weeks.

He watched the hint of a smile appear at the corner of her mouth. He blushed.

She can read what I'm thinking.

'It will pass quickly,' she said, putting her hand between his legs again. 'It will be worth it; wait and see.'

In a distant part of his brain, he knew it would feel like a long month, but he was finding it difficult to process any rational thought. He looked at her face as she closed her hand on him tightly, causing him to flinch and draw a sharp breath.

Her eyes, through narrow slits, looked distant.

When she slipped her injured hand down and gently stroked him, still maintaining her biting grip with the other, the pain seemed to intensify the overpowering sensation that flooded his core.

He gave into it and lay back, almost blacking out.

When he'd finished, he looked at her through eyes that could barely focus. Her breathing was as fast as his, her face as flushed.

She finished too. On her own. Just by doing that to me.

He wondered if she'd pushed herself against him, or the chair; he couldn't recall.

'Do you mind if I come back before you can...?' he said, trying to keep any hint of pleading from his voice.

'Don't come,' she said. 'I find it difficult to stop. Leave it until then. I promise it will be worth the wait.'

He believed her, but he wasn't sure he could live that long without her.

'Of course,' he said. 'As you wish.'

'Don't huff,' she said, making him blush again.

'It's just…'

'I know. It's the same for me.'

He wasn't entirely sure that it was.

~~o~~

From a phone box, Dieter Maas dialled the General's office, and was put through after a short wait.

'Dieter, what a pleasure. What can I do for you?'

'I just wondered if you were needing a hand with the boat, at some point.'

'Yes. I was going to call you. She's out of the water. I was hoping to get her scraped down and varnished next week.'

'I'll be glad to help. Just let me know when.'

'I will do. It will be good to catch up, Dieter.'

~~o~~

An hour later, both men sat in the cockpit of Erich Kästner's yacht, talking.

When they'd finished, Dieter Maas rose and began descending the ladder to the yard below. He stopped, with his head still above the coaming.

'By the way,' he said, 'I thought you might like to know. I bumped into Lise Mey earlier. She must have a flat in Holtenauer Straße.'

'Oh. I thought she lived in Lange Reihe.'

'No, it was Holtenauer. The strange thing was, she was with a friend of yours.'

'A friend of mine?'

'Yes. An SS officer, but not her husband. Gestapo.'

The General's pulse quickened.

'Did you recognise him?'

'Yes. You pointed him out to me once. Güllich. The one who'd caused you so much trouble.'

'Interesting,' the General said. 'Strange bedfellows, eh?'

'Indeed. Well. I must go. It was good to talk.'

Dieter's head disappeared and a moment later the General saw him stroll along the promenade in the direction of town.

He turned and looked out across Kieler Hafen.

Lise Böhm and Heinrich Güllich. If it's just a coincidence, why is there a creeping tingle at the back of my neck?

CHAPTER 238

Heinrich Güllich, all thoughts of Lise Böhm expunged from his mind, at least for a short while, was filled with the righteous indignation that only those who know they are being cheated by life can truly feel. He faced General Kästner with ill-concealed disgust.

'You will be informed shortly when access to your Jewish criminals has been arranged. The Kriminaldirektor told me to tell you that he is satisfied that everything is in place, and that he saw to it in person that your request had been granted.'

'When is it likely to be?' the General asked, his matter-of-fact tone further infuriating the Kriminalassistent.

'When I say it will be,' Heinrich Güllich snapped.

~~o~~

'I'd like to know how much the Jew-lover paid the Kriminaldirektor, and perhaps even the camp Kommandant, for the privilege of getting in to see his Judenhunde,' the Kriminalassistent said, as he and Carl Meyer entered Gestapo Headquarters on their return from their visit to the General.

'It wouldn't be so bad, sir, if some of the money filtered down. I mean, if it weren't for the likes of us, these people wouldn't be in prison.'

'That's not the point, Meyer. We should all be above this sort of thing. The General should never have been allowed access to his Dreckjuden. They should have rotted away, instead of being kept in luxury at the state's expense. And all just to allow the Kriminaldirektor to lavish a bit of cash on Dirty Helga.'

Filthy Jews. Carl Meyer smiled at that, then looked around nervously. The Kriminalassistent was on dangerous ground.

If the Kriminaldirektor heard comments like these...

He also knew that it was hypocritical of his boss to talk of bribes, and ethics. Carl Meyer had seen Güllich pocket the small brown envelopes, had watched him shake down suspects, and accept gifts from anxious businessmen. And none of the money ever trickled his way.

But he agreed with the Kriminalassistent that it was sickening that someone like the General, with his money and power, could buy preferential treatment for his Judenhunde.

Carl Meyer comforted himself with one thought.

Herr Güllich is right. He'll make a mistake one day, and fall. And we will be there, ready.

~~o~~

'They're fools.'

Brigadier Schneider knew his words could earn him a rap on the knuckles at the very least, but he was angry.

'How so, sir?'

The battalion, in support of the 2nd Army, were entrenched around the rump of the Red Army forces holding out in an enclave north of Bryansk. The Brigadier sat talking to Artur Schweitzer, newly promoted to Oberstleutnant, the rank Franz Kästner should have held.

Not for the first time, Walther Schneider missed the elder Kästner brother, despite the seed of doubt that the verdammte Gestapo investigator had somehow managed to plant in the back of his mind.

He walked over to the map laid out on his makeshift desk and pointed.

'We're stuck here in a war of attrition against a collection of poorly armed but determined Soviet troops who could hold out for weeks. In the meantime, advance units of the 2nd have taken Oryol, a hundred or so kilometres to the east, with little resistance, but they've stopped there, waiting for us to come and support them.'

'Is that not wise, sir?'

Again, Walther Schneider wished that it were Franz standing beside him.

He would have understood straight away.

'Have a look at the road from Oryol, Oberstleutnant.'

'The road to Moscow, sir?'

'Yes. What's the next large town?'

Artur Schweitzer traced the road north-east, then stopped.

'Tula, sir?'

'Yes. Do you notice anything about it?'

The Oberstleutnant scrutinised the map, his brow furrowed. Past conversations with his commanding officer taught him to take his time and study things thoroughly.

'Roads, sir, and railways,' he said, with considerable relief.

'Correct. Tula is the hub of the transport network between Moscow and the south. Capture it and we control the approach to the capital, and the country. We have intelligence that shows it is lightly defended, for now. We should be advancing hell for leather and taking it. Instead, we're stuck here, doing nothing.'

'Is there not a danger that the encircled troops would break out if we did that, and attack our rear?'

'We could leave half a division to hold them, instead of tying up an entire battle group with the intention of crushing them. Once they'd learned that we'd taken Tula, and there was no hope of rescue or resupply, they'd have been forced to surrender. In the meantime, we'd have southern Russia in our hands.'

'Perhaps we can still do that, sir?'

'You can bet on your life, Oberstleutnant Schweitzer, that the Soviets will be moving heaven and earth to bolster the small garrison at Tula as we speak. Because we've prevaricated, they'll be there before us. It could take months to get past it.'

'The men have been talking, sir. They think we'll be in Moscow before the snows arrive.'

'We might have been, but not now, unless our Group North colleagues are more decisive.'

Artur Schweitzer left, worried. He'd never seen the Brigadier so despondent.

Walther Schneider stared at the map. Despite the astonishing progress they'd made, casualties were beginning to mount and, although the Russians were losing ten soldiers for every one of his, he knew the Soviet Army could sustain these losses, and still have reserves to fight if the conditions turned against the Wehrmacht.

And at the back of his mind, a festering wound itched him.

Did Franz and Johann Kästner betray me? And their Fatherland?

CHAPTER 239

[05/11/1941 Wednesday]

'It's shocking the way these Jews are prepared to live.'

Canaris watched as the three fawning civil servants soaked up the words of the Reichsminister for Public Enlightenment and Propaganda, Joseph Goebbels.

'I know, Herr Reichsminister,' one of the hangers-on said, the others nodding.

'I returned yesterday from a visit to the ghetto in Wilna. I was appalled.'

'Wilna, sir. In Lithuania?'

'No, you fool. It's in occupied Poland,' the Reichsminister said, frowning in irritation at the junior bureaucrat.

'It used to be in Lithuania,' Canaris interjected. 'There was some dispute about who owned it, and the Poles took hold of it after the Great War.'

The Reichsminister scowled at the head of the Abwehr.

'An irrelevance, Admiral. You can imagine my disgust at the squalor that I found the Jewish inhabitants were prepared to live in. And they wonder why we don't want them in Germany.'

'Perhaps that is because they have no choice, Herr Reichsminister. We put them there, in grossly overcrowded conditions.'

'Die Juden sind die Läuse der zivilisierten Menschheit,' the Reichsminister said.

Canaris stared at him.

The Jews are the lice of civilised humanity. What does that make us?

He became aware that the three civil servants were staring at him and cursed himself for getting drawn into a debate with Goebbels.

He stifled his intended response and nodded.

'I suppose they are,' he said, in as bland a voice as he could muster. He watched as the faces of the four men relaxed into smiles.

He wondered what Erich Kästner would have said.

KIELER MORGENPOST

Wednesday 5th November 1941

BAN ON ASSOCIATION WITH JEWS

From today, it is illegal for Reich citizens to have any association with Jews or any person with Jewish blood. Severe penalties have been introduced for any German found to be flouting the ban.

The sole exception to this rule is for members of the police and security services, applicable only in the performance of their duties.

~~o~~

Memo: Geh.KdoS. ABW 07/11/41 CAC1512.1

For Attention Only: General Erich Kästner, Abwehr, Kiel office.

From: Admiral Wilhelm Canaris, Chef der Abwehr.

The Abwehr has received information that units of Einsatzgruppe B, commanded by Arthur Nebe, rounded up 13,000 Jews from the

Minsk ghetto and executed them in the nearby village of Tuchinka. [END]

~~o~~

[07/11/1941 Friday]

It had started as an ordinary, humdrum day. The General breakfasted alone in the dining room because the new housekeeper had chased him the first day he had eaten in the kitchen, and he hadn't repeated his error.

He read the paper with his usual mixture of disgust and incredulity, then left for work, saying good morning to a barely awake Antje on the way out. He offered Eva a lift into town but, as always, she declined. He couldn't make up his mind if it was because of her loyalty to her mother, or if she had a genuine concern about being seen with him.

He shook his head sadly, the full weight of his family's troubles on his shoulders.

Arriving at the office, he read Canaris's memo, he pulled out the black leather-bound ledger from his desk drawer. He'd started keeping it the year before and he wrote the date of the Tuchinka massacre in his neat handwriting, with brief details, adding the name of the commander of the SS death squad to it.

Around nine-thirty, Captain Bauer knocked and entered without waiting, his face pale and taut.

'What's up?' the General said, getting to his feet.

'It's Herr Güllich, sir. He says you must go with him.'

'Did he say why?' the General said.

'No, sir. Do you wish me to ask Chief Petty Officer Neuer to accompany you, sir?'

The General smiled.

'No, I don't think that will be necessary. Show Kriminalassistent Güllich in, Captain.'

'Yes, sir.'

The young captain shook his head in disbelief.

'How can you be so calm, sir?'

'It takes practice, Heinz,' the General said. 'You'll find out when you get your first command.'

When the captain left, the General sat back down and slid the ledger back into the bottom drawer of his desk and locked it. Inside, his heart was racing, and he took a couple of deep breaths to steady himself.

If only the young man knew.

The door opened again, and Captain Bauer ushered the Gestapo man in, accompanied by his sidekick.

'Ah. Herr Güllich, Herr Meyer. It is good to see you.'

'Herr General,' Heinrich Güllich said, saluting. 'Heil Hitler.'

'Heil Hitler,' the General said, giving a perfunctory Hitler greeting. He watched with satisfaction as the two Gestapo men frowned. 'How can I be of help?'

'It is I who can be of help, Herr General. You can see your Jews now. I have been told to accompany you to Neuengamme by my Kriminaldirektor.'

Heinrich Güllich smiled as the General fought to remain impassive, but the shock drained his face of colour, despite his best efforts.

A terrible sense of foreboding threatened to crush him.

'They're still alive?' he blurted.

Heinrich Güllich laughed.

'Of course. The Kriminaldirektor gave you his word.'

In truth, the General would not have been surprised had they been dead, and he had paid for the privilege of seeing their bodies.

'I'll get my driver to…'

'We have a car,' Heinrich Güllich interrupted. 'The camp Kommandant insisted that you were to be accompanied at all times, and that only an official SS vehicle was acceptable.'

Ignoring Captain Bauer's worried look, the General nodded and smiled.

CHAPTER 240

Erich Kästner tried to keep the shock from his face when the guards brought them into the room, Yosef first, then Miriam.

Their appearance helped. They were thin but, compared to the poor souls he'd seen on the other side of the fence while he waited to be admitted to the camp, they looked a picture of health.

But they'd aged ten years in five months.

And, within seconds, the General realised it was the first time the Nussbaums had seen one another since their incarceration.

It was only a fleeting glance, but the General read their desperate need to hold each other in their eyes. He couldn't understand why they didn't rush into an embrace, then he looked at the sneering guards, male and female.

They're institutionalised. To let the guards see even a hint of emotion would be to show weakness.

'You can leave us alone,' he said to the guards. 'They're not going to kill me.'

'Sir, we were ordered to stay,' the male guard said.

'Ask your superior. Tell him that the Kriminaldirektor promised me a private meeting.'

The guard looked doubtful but went to the door and tapped on it. When it opened, he went out and closed it behind him. A short while later, he returned and beckoned for the female guard to leave.

'You have ten minutes,' he said. 'If there is any contact, the visit will be terminated. Do you understand?'

'Yes,' the General said. The guard left and closed the door behind him.

The General had no illusions about the privacy of the meeting. They were in what looked to be a prison cell, with a large steel door sporting two peepholes. In the ceiling, the General counted three ventilation grilles, any of which could have microphones hidden behind them.

He was certain that Heinrich Güllich and Carl Meyer were watching and listening, and that their conversation was being recorded; it was even possible they were being filmed.

Three wooden chairs had been provided. The General indicated that the Nussbaums should sit down in the two that were close together.

'It is good to see you both,' he said. 'We've all been desperately worried.'

'We're all right, sir,' Yosef said, glancing again at Miriam. 'It's not too bad in here, this time.'

The General saw changes in them both which hinted at the horror of the torture and the beatings they'd suffered. Both moved with the stiff gait of bodies not yet fully healed. The scars had faded but would never disappear; Miriam's cheek and Yosef's forehead were the most obvious but, when he looked closer, the General could see others, and one of Yosef's fingers did not align itself with the rest, like a tine on a bent fork.

But it was in their bearing that he noticed the biggest shift. The fight had been knocked out of them, and he wondered if they'd given up.

'It's been tolerable here, sir,' Miriam said in a voice so drab and listless the General wondered if she was drugged. 'We have enough food, and we get medicine, if we need it. If we do as we are told, we are left alone.'

She looked at the floor as she spoke, only raising her eyes for a second.

Have they been broken?

'How's everyone at Drachensee, sir?' Miriam asked.

'They're all well. And I have news for you. Johann and Franz are alive.'

It must have taken all their strength of will but, apart from a barely perceptible stiffening, neither of the Nussbaums reacted, other than with the understandable relief that might have been expected.

'That's great news, sir,' Yosef said, not quite overcoming the weariness in his manner. 'Are they home?'

The General let his face fall, hoping that the Gestapo were watching.

'No. I'm afraid not. Their yacht sank, and only by sheer luck were they picked up by a

British warship. They're in a prisoner-of-war camp in England.'

'I'm sorry, sir, but at least they're alive.'

'Yes. It lifted a heavy load from Maria and the girls too. They pass on their best wishes, by the way.'

'Thank you, sir,' Miriam said. For a moment, her eyes met his.

'Sir, have the police managed to find our children yet?' Yosef asked, his voice breaking.

The General bowed his head and shook it slowly from side to side.

'No, I'm afraid we've heard nothing. They don't appear to be getting anywhere. They've tried all they can, but there's not a sign of them. It's as if they've disappeared from the face of the earth.'

Both Miriam and Yosef seemed to slump. The General hoped it looked like disappointment, and that only he knew it was relief. They'd played their part far better than he could have hoped for.

When they looked up at him again, he saw a light in both their eyes that hadn't been there before.

'If we don't make it, sir,' Yosef said, 'thank you for trying to help us. I know what you have done to make our time here bearable.'

'I'll do what I can, but you must look after yourselves.'

'We will, sir. Tell Maria and the girls that we were happy to hear about Franz and Johann.'

'Danken got zey zenen zikher,' the General said.

Thank God they are safe.

Neither Yosef nor Miriam blinked at his use of Yiddish.

'Gat zal eykh bentshn,' they said together. *God bless you.*

The General noticed that the Jewish couple's hands had come together by the sides of their chairs, and their fingers were entwined. He saw Yosef squeeze Miriam's hand and was surprised that the guards hadn't come in to terminate the meeting.

Perhaps a few thousand marks buys the odd extra privilege.

He couldn't put a price on what that short, sweet touch would mean to the Nussbaums.

'I'll try and come again, but it might be difficult.'

'We understand, sir,' Miriam said. 'You've done enough already.'

She nodded, and the General felt the strain ease a little.

They've understood. They know their children are safe.

'We don't have much longer,' the General said. 'Just remember what I told you. Do you have jobs?'

'I make bricks, sir. It's hard work, but I don't mind it, in all honesty. It keeps me busy. The other inmates are all decent sorts, although we're seeing a lot of Russian soldiers coming through the gates. They sometimes cause a bit of trouble in the first few weeks they are here, but they soon settle down.'

The General could imagine how easily the fight would be knocked out of them by the hell of the work details.

'What about you, Miriam?' he said.

'There's nothing for me, sir. I wish they would put me to work in the kitchen. The days pass slowly, and there's too much time to think, but I'm not complaining.'

The door rattled and opened.

'Your time is up,' the male guard said, gripping Yosef's arm roughly.

'Wait,' the General said.

He took Yosef's hand in both of his and shook it, looking straight at his friend.

'Be strong,' he said.

The guard shook his head in disgust but allowed the General to do the same with Miriam before the Nussbaums were led away. A third guard entered and indicated that he would escort the General to reception.

As he walked along the corridor a few minutes later, he looked out of the window. Yosef was being led away to the large compound, shuffling behind the guard. To his right, the female guard led Miriam to the smaller compound where two or three groups of women milled around. When they saw Miriam at the gate, a woman moved towards her and, with a start, the General recognised her.

Rosa Liewermann. She's still alive. What a godsend that will be for Miriam.
He didn't know why, but it made leaving them there more bearable.

CHAPTER 241

'The arrogant bastard can wait all day, as far as I'm concerned.'

Heinrich Güllich had waited until his Kriminaldirektor had left with the camp Kommandant before he exploded. The Gestapo chief's parting words to him were that he'd better not leave the General lingering for long.

The Kriminalassistent had thought it was a step in the right direction when his boss turned up to view the meeting between the General and his Jewish filth; Erich Kästner had been right when he'd suspected that the Gestapo would film the entire encounter. The camera was mounted behind the door, using one of its peepholes; they'd scrutinise it once it had been developed.

Heinrich Güllich was convinced that the General had somehow used the meeting to let the Nussbaums know their children were in Britain.

A guard had been sent to fetch one of the Jewish Kapos when the General had spoken in Yiddish, but the innocuous translation he'd provided from the tape recording had left Heinrich Güllich frustrated, and his boss unimpressed.

'I'm sorry, Kriminalassistent Güllich,' the Kriminaldirektor had said. 'I heard nothing during that meeting that would indicate to me whether or not the Kästner brothers smuggled the Jewish brats to England, or if the General was involved. He did not communicate any information to his Jews about their children, other than to say that the police hadn't found them, and that he hadn't either.'

'He's lying, sir. I know it.'

'No, Güllich. You choose to believe it. There's a difference. Unfortunately, when you're dealing with a man in General Kästner's position, you'll need hard proof before we could even think of making that sort of accusation.'

'But sir. You've read my report. There's overwhelming evidence that I'm right. And don't forget, these Jews are the worst type of criminals; they were suspects in two other criminal investigations before we caught them in the end, using false papers.'

'You failed to provide any evidence that the Nussbaums were any more involved in distribution of the KJF bile than any other Jew in Kiel. And the money thing. You had your chance, and you squandered it. Let it go. That's an order.'

'Yes, sir,' Heinrich Güllich said, seething inside.

'You can question them again, once more,' the Kriminaldirektor said, throwing his most tenacious investigator a scrap of meat, 'but I want them alive. And intact.'

'Yes, sir. Thank you, sir.'

'I've arranged for you to come back tomorrow. Now, don't keep the General waiting. He's a busy man.'

~~o~~

The next day, while Heinrich Güllich drove to Neuengamme, wondering how to inflict as much pain as he could to the Nussbaums without causing too much obvious damage, the General sat in his study, thinking.

He knew that continued donations to the Kriminaldirektor, some of which would find its way into the camp Kommandant's pockets, would ensure that the Nussbaums would receive preferential treatment, but Neuengamme was still a dangerous place for a Jew, and the protection his money could buy was not guaranteed.

But there was no possibility of them being released.

For their sakes, and for the lives of every other Jew still living under the shadow of the Third Reich, Canaris is right. I need to consider the big picture.

And he started to plan.

~~o~~

The reason Miriam Nussbaum died was because she chose to. In a few whispered words, in the only moments they had the chance to talk before she was killed, she told her husband why she had decided to do what she did.

'They will rape me first, then they will make me work as a prostitute for those Goyim camp guards,' she whispered, putting her finger to his lips to prevent him arguing while the two Gestapo men talked to one of the camp guards. 'I cannot do that.'

'What about Ruth and Manny?' he said in an agonised mumble.

'They're safe. You heard the General. I can die happy.'

She stared at him, willing him to accept her decision, and say goodbye.

He looked away, tears running down his cheeks.

'No,' he said. 'Please, No.'

'I must. I cannot be their *whore*.'

They looked at each other for a final time, a flood of unspoken words passing between them.

~~o~~

Afterwards, when Heinrich Güllich thought about it, he realised that she'd tricked them, that she'd planned the whole thing.

At first, he had been collected and methodical, applying pain when necessary, attempting to use the Nussbaums' pathetic devotion to each other as leverage.

And he'd discovered her weak spot. And her husband's. *Her virtue.*

He didn't want to admit it, but Carl Meyer had been right. He should have done it sooner.

He'd been stymied in how far he could go inflicting pain on the Jewish bitch, but the Kriminaldirektor had said nothing about sexually assaulting her. His first thought had been to allow his assistant to violate the woman but the echoes of the Kriminaldirektor's taunting dismissal of his investigation had smouldered deep within his soul.

The thought of the Jewish slut looking back at the Weichmanns' flat and waving at Carl Meyer, and of the smug look he imagined she had every time her Jew-loving General arranged for them to be released from his custody stirred a profound anger in him and, with it, the desire to force himself on her.

Simmering under it all, his anger at Lise's treatment by her SS husband hadn't improved his temper.

'Keep an eye on him,' he said, nodding to Yosef. He grabbed Miriam's hair and dragged her across the cell to the door, still tied to the chair, and undid one of the handcuffs, slipping it through the long, vertical door handle, and snapped it shut around her wrist again.

He cut the ties holding her legs and threw the chair to the side. Taking a hold of the top of her prison uniform, he ripped it downwards, exposing her bare chest.

She tried to cross her legs to stop him ripping the striped trousers from her, but he punched her in the stomach, and she doubled over, as far as her arms would let her without them being pulled from their sockets.

It was easy for him to tear her trousers and, once he'd discarded them, he turned to Carl Meyer.

'You can have her after me,' he said, 'and I'll get every guard in the camp in here after you're finished with her until she talks.'

'No,' Yosef shouted. 'Leave her alone. She won't talk.'

'No, but you might,' Heinrich Güllich said, laughing while he undid his belt and hung it over the chair.

He unbuttoned his trousers and let them drop to the floor. He slipped his underpants down and moved towards her.

'Take a look,' he said, grabbing her hair and shoving her head down, making her look at him. He kicked her ankle, moving it outward, and when she tried to move it back, he stamped down hard, hearing the snap of the small bones in her foot.

~~o~~

Carl Meyer opened his mouth to remind the Kriminalassistent of their chief's words, then thought better of it. He watched with growing excitement as Heinrich Güllich put his hand between the Jewish whore's legs and forced his fingers upwards, making her scream. He felt the husband tense under his grip and screwed his arm further up his back to dispel any thought the man might have of protecting his wife's honour.

He saw the Kriminalassistent move between the woman's legs and waited for the thrust and the squeal of the Jewish sow but Heinrich Güllich stopped. Then Carl Meyer noticed the woman's lips moving.

'We are about to find out the truth,' Heinrich Güllich said, leaning close to try and hear what Miriam Nussbaum was mumbling.

Carl Meyer scowled, disappointed, as the Kriminalassistent listened to the woman, then saw Heinrich Güllich freeze. Just as his neck reddened, he watched Miriam Nussbaum bring her knee up hard between his legs, causing him to almost double over, and the breath rush out of him.

~~o~~

Yosef also watched, with a mixture of morbid fascination and despair, as the Kriminalassistent staggered to his feet and grabbed the chair, swinging it round at Miriam's face in a wide, deceptively slow arc.

The chair connected with her nose, caving in the front of her face.

Yosef screamed her name and got to his feet, struggling to loosen himself from the chair. The last thing he saw before Carl Meyer dragged him and the chair to the ground was Miriam's head collapsing onto her chest, and her body falling forward until her shoulders, supporting the dead weight of her, snapped out of their sockets with a sickening crack.

~~o~~

As Heinrich Güllich swung the chair again, Carl Meyer dived across the room to catch his arm, but only succeeded in slowing down the blow, which connected with the top of Miriam's skull.

He stared at the woman hanging from her own arms, a pool of blood spreading on the floor below her.

'You've killed her, sir. What did she say to you?'

Carl Meyer didn't know why it was important; the damage had been done, but he needed an answer.

'She told me that her children were free in England,' Heinrich Güllich said, 'and that they took the money from the Weichmanns with them, and that...'

Carl Meyer grabbed his boss's arm as he tried to swing what was left of the broken chair at Miriam Nussbaum's head.

'What, sir?'

'She said that the General was laughing at me, that he'd won, that two Jewish children and a few decent Germans had beaten me.'

And Carl Meyer knew that she was right. She'd won. If Heinrich Güllich wasn't shot for killing her, he was bound to lose his rank, spending the rest of the war as a private in a front-line SS Kompanie in Russia, just as winter was at its deepest. And he also knew that there was every chance he, Carl Meyer, would accompany him.

EPILOGUE

[16/09/2001 Sunday]

Maldon, England

'I thought I would know, in my heart, if something had happened to Mama. It turns out that I didn't. I had no inkling, just the dread that stayed with me all through the dark years of the war.'
    I said nothing. I waited for her to continue.
    'The not knowing, that was the worst. It ate away at me, and thoughts of Mama and Papa were never far away.'
    Ruth stared out the window across the River Chelmer to the Saltings, a tear rolling down her time-weathered cheek.
    She let out a sigh. When she spoke, there was terrible sadness in her voice.
    'But,' she said, 'as Gella Weissberg once told me, life must go on.'

The end.

The Turn of the Tide, the third and final book in the *Sturmtaucher trilogy*, continues the story of the Nussbaums and the Kästners as Adolf Hitler and his National Socialists tighten their hold on Europe, and its Jews.

For further information, visit www.alanjonesbooks.co.uk/sturmtaucher_trilogy.html

ACKNOWLEDGEMENTS

The list of people to thank for help and support during the writing of Flight of the Shearwater is much the same as it was for The Gathering Storm, with a few addtitions.

Leif Sigvaldsen for the image of a Colin Archer rescue ketch for the front cover, and for Jeppe jul Nielsen for finding it for me

Catrin Jeans and Fraser McDonald, for their advice and input regarding the covers

The National Library of Scotland and The British Library, for their wonderful collection of maps and sea charts, and the British Newspaper Archive for such a vast collection of newspaper from every corner of Britain.

Gav Don, for recommending that I read Victor Klemperer's Diaries

Tom Cunliffe, for being easily approachable for advice, and for his book Hand, Reef and Steer, my bible for gaff-rigged sailing.

Jacob Madsen and Jens Kirketerp Jensen: Information on Hirtshals Hafn.

Dr. Julian Freche, Kieler Stadt- und Schifffahrtsmuseum, Kiel, for taking the time to speak with me during my visit to Germany.
www.kiel.de/de/kultur_freizeit/museum/schifffahrtsmuseum_fischhalle

Anne Cater, Random Things Tours for the blog tour on the Trilogy's launch
www.randomthingsthroughmyletterbox.blogspot.com

All the blog tour participants: Bookchatter @cookiebiscuit, Reflections Of A Reader @LeahJMoyse, The Magic of Wor(l)ds @MagicOfWorldsBE, Steph's Book Blog @sjroth21, By The Letter Book Reviews @sarahhardy681, The Book Magnet @thebookmagnet, Beyond The Books @ShazzieRimmel, Wild Writing Life @wildwritinglife, Cal Turner Reviews @calturner, Hair Past A Freckle @karlou, Cheryl M-M's Book Blog @mm_cheryl, Berty Boy 123 @arabat

And the other bloggers who supported the launch: Yvonnne - Me and My Books @yvonnembee, jerasjamboree @shazgoodwin @ElenaSharp1, Books from dusk til dawn @susanhampson57, The Book Review Café @ReviewCafe, Mark Fearn @BookMark on Facebook, Patricias Books @PatriciasBooks, Crimebookjunkie @nholten40, Fiction Books @Fiction_Books, ChapterInMyLife @Sbairden.

Book bloggers have given me and my books incredible support over the years, doing an amazing amount of hard work and asking nothing in return but a story.

All my remarkably loyal readers, especially Val Spencer and Susan Hunter, who have been unremitting in their enthusiasm for my writing, and Melanie Preston Lewis, Dee Groocock, and Audrey Gibson for their amazing support since The Gathering Storm was published.

Sharon Bairden and Noelle Holten, 'The Twinnies', for having my back, and for advice and support ad nauseum.

Sarah Hardy, for much advice and support, for being the first blogger to read 'The Gathering

Storm and Flight of the Shearwater', and for being so enthusiastic about it.
https://bytheletterbookreviews.com

The Book Club on Facebook, and its Reviewers Group, for once again finding me so many beta readers and ARC readers, and for the enthusiasm and support of its members, Tracy Fenton, and her team.

The Historical Fiction Novel Society, who's members enthusiastically responded to my request for beta readers and the Second World War Club for the amazing response of its members.

My wonderful beta readers for their time, patience, encouragement and critical feedback. As a self-published author, I couldn't do it without them. They are, in no particular order:

Gill Lynch, Stuart Clachan, Teresa Murphy, Susan McDonald, Rob Lee, Gordon Smith, Gabi Gerganova, Marc Kelly, Mary Jeans, Simon Caldecut, Marion Simmons, Kenny Stirling, Katrina Taylor, David Petherick, Fraser McDonald, Sapna Chamaria, Lauren Cohen, Fiona McCormick, Sally Stackhouse, Theresa Webber, Amanda Williams, Susan Hunter, Sydney Clark, Amanda Nellist, and Breffni Martin.

During the publication of The Gathering Storm, one of my beta readers, a wonderful friend and fellow lifeboatman, Ian Mclymont, sadly passed away. I'll never forget him, or his contribution.

In addition, there were a handful of beta readers who also turned out to be my technical support section:

Mark Jardine, for gaff-rigged sailing expertise. https://www.boattripsiona.com

Pauline Mullender, for German proofreading, a former resident of Kiel.

Olaf Meys, for advice on the Wehrmacht, and National Socialist document translation.

Charlotte Bidstrup, for Danish proofreading.

Nigel and Lia Court, for their input on Jewish religion, language and culture, and for proofreading the Yiddish content, and for their humbling enthusiasm for the books.

Madeleine Black, whose father was a Holocaust survivor. https://madeleineblack.co.uk

Ian Skewis, for proof-reading with great patience. www.ianskewis.com/

My wife Mary, for support and forbearance, and watching me disappear for five years into my 'writing hole'.

My children, and my grandchildren, and to all my extended family and friends. In the words of Erich Kästner, if it weren't for them, none of it would matter.

REFERENCES & ATTRIBUTIONS

02/07/1941 Heydrich's letter to Einsatzgruppen. With permission of Yad Vashem
https://www.yadvashem.org/docs/heydrich-guidelines-for-leaders-in-occupied-soviet-union.html

31/07/1941 Goring's letter to Heydrich Re: final solution.   Original, transcript and translation
Public domain: https://commons.wikimedia.org/wiki/File:Carta_G%C3%B6ring.JPG

23/06/1941 Hitler's announement of Operation Babarossa Public Domain:
http://www.ibiblio.org/pha/policy/1941/410622a.html

02/07/1941 Heydrich's Guidelines for the Soviet Union. Documents on the Holocaust:
Selected Sources on the Destruction of the Jews of Germany and Austria, Poland, and the
Soviet Union by Yisrael Gutman (Editor), Yitzhak Arad (Editor), Abraham Margaliot
(Editor), & 2 more (Yad Vashem)

29/09/1941 Babi Yar notice to Jews. Google Translation by author, checked by Olaf Meyes:
https://commons.wikimedia.org/wiki/File:Bigbabijar14.jpg

BIBLIOGRAPHY

LITERATURE

Although this is not an exhaustive list, these are the books I referred to most often during the writing of the Sturmtaucher Trilogy.

IBM and the Holocaust *Black, Edwin*

I Shall Bear Witness: The Diaries Of Victor Klemperer 1933-41 *Klemperer, Victor*

To The Bitter End: The Diaries of Victor Klemperer 1942-45 *Klemperer, Victor*

Language of the Third Reich *Klemperer, Victor*

Ordinary Men: Reserve Police Battalion 101 and the Final Solution in Poland *Browning, Christopher R.*

The Holocaust: The Jewish Tragedy *Martin, Gilbert*

Reeds Nautical Almanac 1944 *Watts, Oswald M., Ed., Adlard Coles*

Hand, Reef and Steer *Cunliffe, Tom*

Heavy Weather Sailing *Bruce, Peter*

The Windfall Yachts - a legacy of goodwill' by *Cudmore, Michael*

Documents on the Holocaust *Arak, Yitshak; Gutman, Israel; Margaliot, Abraham*

Sexual Violence Against Jewish Women During The Holocaust *Hedgepeth, Sonia M. and Saidel, Rochelle G.*

Battleships of the Scharnhorst Class: Warships of the Kriegsmarine *Koop, Gerard, and Schmolke, Klaus-Peter*

Jane's fighting ships of World War II *Preston, Antony*

Minenschiffe 1939-1945 *Kutzbelen, Karl. V. ; Schroeder, William; Brennecke, Jochen*

German Battleships 1939–45 Williamson, Gordon

Camp 21 Cultybraggan History *Cultybraggan Local History Group for Comrie Development Trust*

Camp 21 Comrie *Campbell, Valerie*

"German Railroads and the Holocaust: Uncovering the Tracks" *Ben-Horin, Lisa*

Jewish women's sexual behaviour and sexualized abuse during the Nazi era *Beverley Chalmers* www.utpjournals.press/doi/pdf/10.3138/cjhs.242-A10

Conti Atlas für Kraftfahrer. Deutschland 1 : 500 000 mit den Reichskraftfahrbahnen.. *Conti. - Ed.*

Baltic Pilot *Stan Townsend \ Adlard Coles*

Heil Hitler, Das Schwien ist Tot *Herzog, Rudolf*

Admiralty Tidal Stream Atlas North Sea Eastern Part *Admiralty UK Hydrographic Dept.*

Yiddish-English English-Yiddish *Michael James*

Road Atlas of Great Britain *John Bartholemew*

WEBSITES

As well as the books I used in my research, I trawled through thousands of websites over a five-year period, too numerous to mention individually, but I found myself going back to a few sites again and again. Here is a short list.

HebCal - Hebrew date convertor www.hebcal.com/converter

Historical US Dollars to German Marks currency conversion
https://marcuse.faculty.history.ucsb.edu/projects/currency.htm

Measuring Worth - Purchasing Power of the Pound.
www.measuringworth.com/calculators/ukcompare

Wikipedia en.wikipedia.org/wiki/

Jewish Virtual Library www.jewishvirtuallibrary.org

Railways of Germany Forum (English) www.tapatalk.com/groups/germanrailfr/index.php

United States Holocaust Memorial Museum Holocaust Encyclopedia
encyclopedia.ushmm.org/

US library of Congress www.loc.gov/collections/

Yad Vashem www.yadvashem.org/

Kiel municipal website www.kiel.de/

Kiel WW2 Bunker list www.bunker-kiel.com/

Air strikes Kiel kiel-wiki.de/Luftangriffe_auf_Kiel

Konzentrationslager-Gedenkstaette-Neuengamme www.kz-gedenkstaette-neuengamme.de/en

British Library - Maps and Charts
explore.bl.uk/primo_library/libweb/action/search.do?vid=BLVU1

Danish overlaid historical Maps - The Danish Agency for Data Supply and Efficiency
sdfekort.dk/spatialmap

Mapster (Poland) German Historical Maps 1:25 000
igrek.amzp.pl/mapindex.php?cat=M841W~

The University of Texas Libraries - Maps legacy.lib.utexas.edu/maps/

Kiel Municipal photograph Archive fotoarchiv-stadtarchiv.kiel.de/

Traces of War (Information World War Two Foundation) www.tracesofwar.com/default.asp

World Time Date - Sun and moon calculators www.world-timedate.com/astronomy/index.php

Heinrich Böll Foundation -Sexual Violence in the Holocaust: Perspectives from Ghettos and Camps in Ukraine www.boell.de/en/2020/05/18/sexual-violence-holocaust-perspectives-ghettos-and-camps-ukraine

Comrie Development Trust - Cultybraggan POW camp comriedevelopmenttrust.org.uk/

RAILSCOT | Crieff Junction Railway www.railscot.co.uk/Crieff_Junction_Railway/index.php

AKENS (Arbeitskreis zur Erforschung des Nationalsozialismus in Schleswig-Holstein) www.akens.org/

ABOUT

Alan Jones is a Scottish author with three gritty crime stories to his name, the first two set in Glasgow, the third one based in London. He has now switched genres, and his WW2 trilogy will be published from August to December 2021. It is a Holocaust story set in Northern Germany.

He is married with four grown up children and four wonderful grandchildren.

He has recently retired as a mixed-practice vet in a small Scottish coastal town in Ayrshire and is one of the coxswains on the local RNLI lifeboat. He makes furniture in his spare time, and maintains and sails a 45-year-old yacht, cruising in the Irish Sea and on the beautiful west coast of Scotland. He loves reading, watching films and cooking. He still plays football despite being just the wrong side of sixty.

His crime novels are not for the faint-hearted, with some strong language, violence, and various degrees of sexual content. The first two books also contain a fair smattering of Glasgow slang.

He is one of the few self-published authors to be given a panel at the Bloody Scotland crime fiction festival in Stirling and has done two pop-up book launches at previous festivals.

He has spent the last five years researching and writing the Sturmtaucher Trilogy.

To find out more, please visit www.alanjonesbooks.co.uk

GLOSSARY

A freylekhn geburtstag....Yiddish, Happy birthday. Literally 'a good birthday'
Abaft....Behind. 'Abaft the beam'
Abeam....To the side. 'A boat-length abeam'
Absender....Sender
Abwehr....German Army intelligence
Admiral....Kriegsmarine, Admiral
Aft....In front. 'Aft of the mast'
Ahnenpaß \ ahnenpass....Certification of being Aryan
Akvavit....Scandinavian spiced alcoholic drink. 'Water of life'
Aleichem Shalom....Reply to Shalom, 'Peace'
Alter furz....Old fart
Alter\alte....Old
amidships....Towards the centre of a ship or boat
Anschluss....Political union of Austria with Germany
Appell....Roll-call in POW or Concentration camp
Appellplatz....Roll-call Square
Aquarelle....Watercolors
Arbeiter....Worker(s)
Arbeitskommando....Work detail
Arbeitsscheue....Work shy, targetting the unemployed
Arsch....Arse, profanity
Arschleckern....Arse-licker
Arschloch....Asshole
Aryan....Germans of Nordic type, untainted
Aryanised....Process where non-Germans deemed suitable to be classified as Aryans
Auf....On
Auffangslager....Reception camp, transit camp
Aufstehen....Get to your feet, stand up
Aus....Out
Auschwitz....A Nazi concentration camp near Oświęcim in southern Poland
Ausschaltung....Elimination, often a euphemism for murder by the state
Auswanderung....Emigration, often a euphemism for deportation to Ghettos and camps
Backstay....Part of the rigging, from the top of the mast to the stern of the boat.
Bahnhof....Railway station
Bar-mitzvah....The initiation ceremony of a boy into adulthood at the age of 13
Bataillonen....Battalion, typically commanded by a lieutenant colonel, divided into companies
Bat-mitzvah....The initiation ceremony of a girl into adulthood at the age of 13
Bauernhof....Farm
BDM....Bund Deutscher Mädel, girls' wing of the Nazi Party youth movement, the Hitler Youth
Be'ezrát hashém....God willing, with the help of God
Beam....To the side. 'on the beam'
Beauftragter....Representative
Beer hall putsch....Attempted coup by Adolf Hitler and his party in 1923
BEF....British Expeditionary Force
Belzec....a Nazi German extermination camp southeast of Lublin
BerlinerTageblatt....German liberal newspaper, shut down by the National Socialists in 1939
Besetzten....Occupied
Beyz....Evil
Bier....Beer
Bight....A bay or recess in a coastline, also a loop of rope
Bimah....A raised platform in a synagogue where the Torah is read from
binnacle....A vertical wooden stand that holds the boat's wheel

Bitte....Please\You're welcome

Blitzkrieg....A military tactic utilising speed, surprise, excellent communications and air support.

Blockführer....SS concentration camp guard in charge of a prisoner barrack

Blut....Blood

Blut und boden....Blood and Soil. Used as slogan for NSDAP campaign for German citizens to grow food for the nation

Blutschande....Blood shame', the adulteration of German racial purity by intermarriage with other non-Germanic races

Boche....British derogatory name for the German Army or German soldiers.

Bohemia....Western region of Czechoslovakia, part of Austrian empire before WW1

Bolshevik....Radical left wing party associated with the Soviet Union

Boom....The spar that supports the bottom of the mainsail

Bootshafen....Boat Harbour

Bootshaus....Boathouse

Bow....Front end of a boat

Bratkartoffeln....Fried potato dish

Bratwurst....German sausage

Brigadeführer-SS....SS-Brigade Leader, Brigadier General

Broaching....A sudden change of a yacht's direction due to loss of control in strong winds or following waves

Brownshirts....Sturmabteilung, SA, so called because of their brown uniform

Brücke....Bridge, gangway, pier

Bubbe....Yiddish, grandmother

Bubbeleh....Yiddish term of endearment for a child

Buchenwald....A Nazi concentration camp near Weimar in central Germany

Bund Deutscher Mädel....BDM, Girls' wing of the Nazi Party youth movement, the Hitler Youth

Buoy....A floating marker for navigational or racing purposes

C\O....Commanding officer

Caserne....Barracks

CB....Confined to barracks

Challah bread....Braided loaf, with part of the dough, or Challah, set aside as an offering

Chametz....Leavening foods, forbidden on the Jewish holiday of Passover

Chamudah....Yiddish term of endearment, 'cutie-pie'

Chanukkah....Jewish festival commemorating Jerusalem's recapture and the rededication of the Second Temple

Cheder....A traditional school teaching children the basics of Judaism and the Hebrew language

Chef der....Chief of (Police, Abwehr, etc.)

cleat....A necked deck or spar fitting for attaching lines or warps to

Clubkapitän....Club captain

coamings....The raised protective barrier around a yacht's cockpit

cockpit....The recessed area for the crew in a yacht, and the steering position.

Comintern....The international wing of the Soviet Communist Party

cresting....Waves that are breaking. They are very dangerous to vessels

Crosstrees....The spar crossing the mast which holds the shrouds away from the mast

Cutter....Sailing vessel with two foresails

Dachau....A Nazi concentration camp near Munich in southern Germany

Dankgottesdienste....Thanksgiving service

davits....Arms used to hold and lower a lifeboat or launch on a ship

Deck-stepped....A mast whose base sits on the keel deck, supported by bulkheads below deck

depowering....Letting a sail flap loose to lose its drive. Also luffing or stalling

Der Stürmer....Nazi newspaper famous for its rabid antisemitism

Derasha\derashah....Sermon

Deutsche\en\er\es....German

Deutschland....Germany

Deutschnationale Volkspartei....DNVP, a German Nationalist political party in coalition with the National Socialist Party in 1933

Deutsch-ostafrika....German East Africa

Deutsch-westafrika....German West Africa

Diaspora....A scattered population whose origin lies in a separate geographic locale. Historically, it has often referred to the dispersion of Jews

Dinghy....A small sailing vessel or rowing boat

DNVP...Deutschnationale Volkspartei, a German Nationalist political party in coalition with the National Socialist Party in 1933

Dornier....German aeroplane manufacturer

Downwind....Sailing with the wind directly behind the boat, or close to it

Drogue....A small canvas open ended cone used to slow a boat, to prevent broaching by following waves

DSO....Distinguished Service Order (DSO) is a British military decoration

Dummkopf\dummköpfe....Idiot

Dumplingwurst....German term of endearment. Literally 'Dumpling sausage'

Ebb, ebbing....The outgoing tide

Ehre....Honour

Ehrenzeichen....Badge of honour

Ein....a

Eins. Zwei. Drei. Vier....A count to four in German

Einsatz....commitment

Einsatzgruppen....SS death squads in Nazi Germany responsible for mass killings during WW2

EP....Estimated position, using course, speed, time and tide

Erbhöfe....Hereditary farm

Ersatzkaffe ....Substitute coffee, used when real coffee became unavailable

Esterwegen....Nazi concentration camp in the northwest of Germany

F1-12....Beaufort scale, Force 0 (windless) to Force 12 (hurricaine)

Fachschule....Technical school

Fähnrich....Sub-company Sergeant Major

Feh....A Yiddish expression of disgust or disappointment

Feldpolizei....The secret military police of the German Wehrmacht

Feldwebel....Kriegsmarine, Petty Officer

Feldwebel....Wehrmacht, Company Sergeant Major

Fischhafen....Fishing Harbour

Förde....Fjord, narrow inlet of water

Fore....Towards the front of the boat

Fore-and-aft....Front and back of the boat. 'Fore-and-aft rigged'

Forecabin....The accomodation at the bow of the boat

Foredeck....The part of the deck in front of the main mast

Foremast....Furthest forward mast in multiple-masted boat

Forepeak....A small locker at the bow of a boat

Fore-reaching....Setting sails amidships and lashing the rudder over for unhanded sailing

Foresail....The sail, or sails, set in front of the mast, usually on the forestay

Forestay....Rigging wire or rope that holds the mast vertically from the bow

Forward....Towards the front of the boat. 'forward of the mast'

Frau....Mrs,salutation

Fräulein....Miss, salutation, or a young woman

Fregattenkapitän....Kriegsmarine, Frigate captain, Commander

Frei....Free

Freiheit....Freedom

Freiheitsnachrichtenblatt....Freedom news sheet. 'Kieler Jüdisches Freiheitsnachrichtenblatt'

Friedhof....Cemetery

Fritzies....British derogatory name for the Germans

Froy....Yiddish, woman

Führer....Leader

Funkmessgerät....Radar
Für....For
Furz\fürze....Farts
Furzmaschinen....Fart machines
Gaff....Spar supporting the top of a sail, usually at around 30° from mast
Gaff-rigged....Sailing set up incorporating at least one gaff sail
Gärtnerei....Nursery
Gauleiter....Regional governor under Nazi rule
Gebiete....Areas
Gebietsführer....Area leader
Geburtstag....Birthday
gefangenschaft....captured
Gefilte....Jewish poached fish patties
Gefreiter....Lance Corporal
Gegen....Against
Geh.kdos....Abbreviation for Secret Command, For senior officers only
Geheime staatspolizei ....Gestapo, German secret police
Gehinnom....A place to go after death to atone for one's sins. A jewish version of purgatory
General der Infanterie, Artillerie etc.....Lieutenant General, commands Corps
Generaladmiral....Kriegsmarine, Admiral
General-Feldmarschall....Field Marshall, commands Armies
Generalgouvernement....Part of Poland not incorporated into the Third Reich. Governed by Hans Frank, destination for the bulk of Europe's Jews during WW2
Generalissimo....Leader of the armed forces, specifically General Franco, Fascist leader of Spain
Generalleutnant....Major General, commands Division
Generalmajor....Brigadier, commands Brigade
Generaloberst....General, commands Army, Armies
Gentile....Hebrew term for a non-Jew
gesellschaft....Company, industrial
Gesetze....Laws
Gespräch....Conversation, chat
Gestapo....Geheime staatspolizei, German secret police
Giftpilz....Toadstool, 'The poisonous mushroom'
Gimballed....Instrument or appliance suspended on arms allowing it to stay level despite the heel, or tilt, of a yacht
Glockengeläut....Church bell ringing
gooseneck....The connecting joint between the mast and the boom
Goose-winging....Sailing directly downwind with mainsail and foresail set out on opposite sides of the yacht
Goyim....Yiddish, non-Jews, not complimentary
Großadmiral....Kriegsmarine, Admiral of the Fleet
Großer....Greater
Ground....To Ground a boat is to touch the bottom, to run aground
Grundschule....Infant School
Gruppenführer-SS....SS-Group Leader, Major General
guardrail....Usually wire, they stop crew falling overboard
Gunwale....the upper edge or planking of the side of a boat or ship
Guten Abend....Good evening
Guten morgen....Good morning
Gybe....Turning a yacht with the wind crossing behind the stern. Can be a dangerous manoeuvre if uncontrolled
Haavara agreement....A German scheme to encourage Jewish emigration to Palestine from 1933 -1933
Hafen....Harbour
Haganah....Jewish paramilitary organization in the Palestine Mandate 1920 - 1948
Haggadah ....The Jewish text that sets forth the order of the Passover Seder

Halakha....The collective body of Jewish religious laws derived from the written and Oral Torah
Half-tracks....Military vehicle with front wheels and tracks behind
Halyards....Lines on a yacht that are used to hoist sails and spars
Hank....to attach the jib to the forestay by it's hanks, allowing it to be hoisted by the jib halyard
Hannukah....See Chanukkah
Hashém\hashem....Jewish name for God
Hauptamt....Main office
Hauptbahnhof....Main railway station
Hauptmann....Captain, 2nd-I-C to Major (Company)
Hauptscharführer....SS-Head Company Leader
Hauptscharführer-SS....SS-Head Company Leader, Master Sergeant
Hauptsturmführer....SS-Head Storm Leader
Hauptsturmführer....Head storm leader
Hauptsturmführer-SS....SS-Head Storm Leader, Captain
Havn....Harbour in Danish
hawsepipe....A right angled pipe set through the deck to take the anchor chain to its locker
Heer....German Army after 1935
Heeresleitung....Army command
Heil....Hail
Heinkel....German aeroplane manufacturer
Herr....Mr, Salutation
Himbeerschnitt....Raspberry shortbread
Hitlerjugend, HJ....Hitler Youth, National Socialist organisation for boys
Hoch....High
Höchste geheimhaltung....Maximum confidentiality (Top Secret)
Hof....Court, often used in hotel names
Höhere....Higher
Hora....Hebrew group dance, usually done by men
HQ....Headquarters
HSSPF....Regional Security Representative directly accountable to Heinrich Himmler
hydrophones....Listening device on a submarine for ships engines
Im yirtzeh hashem....God willing
Innenhafen....Inner Harbour
Jachtclub....Yacht Club
Juda....Jewish peoples
Jude, Juden....Jew, Jews
Judenfrei....Free of Jews
Judenhaus\ Judenhäuser....House(s) set aside to accommodate Jews made homeless by Nazi laws
Judenhund, Judenhunde....
Judenjagden....Jew hunts, carried out by Einzatzgruppen
Judenknecht....servant of the Jews
Judenlaus\ Judenläuse....Jew-louse\Lice
Judenliebhaber....Jew lover
Judenrat....Jewish council, appointed by Nazi authorities to control Jewish populations
Judenrein....Cleansed of its Jewish presence
Judensau....Jew-sow
Judenscheiße....Jew-shit
Judenschwein\Judenschweine....Jew-pig(s)
Jüdische \ Jüdisches....Jewish
Jungvolk....Young people
Kaddish....Jewish spoken hymn, often refers to mourner's Kaddish, a prayer for the dead
Kaffee....Coffee
Kaffeeklatsch....Coffee gossip
Kaiser....German emperor
Kamerad\Kameraden....Friend(s), comrade(s)

Kamft....Fight, battle
Kampf....Struggle
Kapitän zur see, captain....Captain
Kapitän zur See, Captain....Kriegsmarine, Captain
Kapitänleutnant....Lieutenant
Kapitänleutnant....Kriegsmarine, Lieutenant
Karte....Card
Kartoffelkopf....Potato-head
Kauf....Purchase
kedge anchor....A second anchor, usually at the stern, to hold a vessel aligned to the sea or the wind
Keel....Lowest part of a boat
Keelboats....Yacht with an inbuilt Keel
keel-stepped....A mast whose base sits on the keel and penetrates the deck
Kennkarte....German Identification card
Keriah....A strip of cloth ripped during a funeral, symbolic of rending of clothing
Ketch....Two masted sailing vessel with the mizzen mast in front of the rudder
Kibbutz....A collective community in Israel traditionally based on agriculture.
Kinderlandverschickung (KLV)....The evacuation of children in Germany during the World War II
Kindertransport....Trains used to transport thousands of Jewish children from Germany to Britain just prior to WW2
Kippah....Brimless hat worn by Jewish men as a head covering
Kirche....Church
Kirchenfest....Church festival
Knödel....Savoury dumplings
Kommodore....Kriegsmarine, Commodore
Kompanie....Company, a unit of soldiers, around 100 - 150 men, usually commanded by a Major
Konteradmiral....Kriegsmarine, Rear-Admiral, Counter Admiral
Korvette....Corvette, a small naval fighting vessel
Korvettenkapitän....Kriegsmarine, Lieutenant-Commander
Kosher....Food that complies with the strict dietary standards of traditional Jewish law
KPD....Communist party of Germany during the Weimar Republic
Kriegsakademie....Naval academy
Kriegsmarine....German Navy after 1935
Kriegsschule....Navy college
Kriminalassistent....Criminal Assistant, Gestapo, rank 2
Kriminalassistentanwärter....Criminal Assistant Guard, Gestapo rank 1
Kriminaldirektor....Criminal Director, Gestapo rank 6
Kriminalinspektor....Criminal Inspector, Gestapo rank 4
Kriminalkommissar....Criminal Commissioner, Gestapo rank 5
Kriminalpolizei, KriPo....Criminal Investigation Department CPD
Kriminalsekretär....Criminal Secretary, Gestapo rank 3
Kristallnacht....The night of broken glass', a pogrom against Jews in response to the assasination of a German diplomat in Paris
Kübelwagen....German equivalent of a jeep or landrover
Kuchen....Cake
Kunsthalle....Art Gallery
Künstlerspaint....Artist's paints
Lagerführer....Camp leader
Länderbahnen....Regional railways
Landesbischof....Archbishop
Landespolizei....National Police
lashed....Tied down

Lebensborn....Nazi breeding program for unmarried mothers. The resulting babies were to be raised by the Reich

Lebensraum....Living space', the concept of German territorial expansion to provide homes and resources for German citizens

Lebensunwertes Leben ....Unfit for life', disabled, the old and the mentally ill, euthanased by the Nazi authorities

Leberknödel....Small liver dumplings

Lederhosen....Traditional leather breeches

leech....The front edge of a sail, attached vertically to the mast or to a stay

leeway....The amount of sideways drift of a vessel due to wind

Leutnant....2nd Lieutenant

Lieblingsmädchen....Term of endearment, 'favourite girl'

Lines....Ropes

Lt....Shortened form of light, or lighthouse, used in navigation

luff....The rear edge of a sail

luffed....An unfilled, or stalled sail

Luftwaffe....German air force

Mädchen, Mädel....Girl

Maginot line....A series of defensive fortresses that guarded the French border with Germany

mainsail....The primary sail flying from the main mast, with a swinging boom at its foot

mainsheet....The rope that controls the boom, and hence the mainsail

Major....Major, commands Company: 100-150 men

Mamzer....A person who is born as the result of certain forbidden relationships or incest

Marineunteroffizierschule....Naval NCO school

Mark....Short for Reichsmark, currency from 1924 to 1948

Markt....Market

Marktplatz....Market place, market square

Marzahn....A Nazi concentration camp in Berlin that housed mainly Gypsies

Matjes....pickled herrings

Matratzen....Mattresses

Matrose....Kriegsmarine, Ordinary rating/seaman

Matrosengefreiter....Kriegsmarine, Able rating/seaman

Matrosenhaupgefreiter....Kriegsmarine, Leading Hand

Matrosenstabsgefreiter....Kriegsmarine, Petty Officer

Matzah....Unleavened bread, eaten during Passover

Matzah ball....Jewish soup dumplings

Maultaschen....Pasta dish

Mauthausen....A Nazi concentration camp near Munich in upper Austria

Menorah....A nine-lamp candelabrum used on the Jewish holiday of Hanukka

Mentsh....Yiddish, a good person

Meshugener....Yiddish, a crazy person

Mettwurst....A strongly flavored German sausage made from raw minced pork preserved by curing and smoking, often with garlic

Meydaleh....Little girl

Mischling, Mischlinge(pl)....A person of mixed Jewish blood

mizzen....Primary sail on the mizzenmast

mizzenmast....Second, smaller mast aft of the main mast on ketch or a yawl

Morgen....Morning

Nase....Nose

National socialist party, NSDAP....Fascist party of Adolf Hitler, shortened to Nazi by Western Allies

Nationalsozialistische....Nationalsozialistische Deutsche Arbeiterpartei, National Socialist Party

Near-gale....Force 7 on Beaufort scale, wind 28-33 knots

Neuengamme....Concentration camp close to Hamburg

Nisht gefloygn....Yiddish, unbelievable

NM....Nautical mile, equal to 1.15 statute miles, 1 minute of latitude

Non-aryan....Not conforming to racial stereotype required in Nazi Germany

Nord-Ostsee-Kanal....The canal that runs from the Elbe estuary in the north sea to Kiel on the Baltic

Nordsee....North Sea

Nsdap....Nationalsozialistische Deutsche Arbeiterpartei, National Socialist Party

Nuremberg....City in Bavaria, in south of Germany, home of some of the largest Nazi rallies and birthplace of the Nuremberg race laws

Oberbannführer....Hitler Youth, Senior Banner Leader

Oberbürgermeister....Lord Mayor

Oberfähnrich....Division Sergeant Major

Oberfähnrich zur See....Kriegsmarine, Midshipman

Oberfeldwebel....Kriegsmarine, Chief Petty Officer

Oberfeldwebel....Battalion Sergeant Major

Oberführer-SS....SS-Senior Leader, Colonel

Obergefreiter....Corporal

Obergruppenführer-SS....SS-Senior Group Leader, Lieutenant General

Oberkommando der Wehrmacht....OKW, High Command of the Wehrmach

Oberleutnant....Lieutenant, commands Platoon \ Trup\ Unit :30 men

Oberleutnant zur See....Kriegsmarine, Sub-Lieutenant

Oberpräsident....High President, usually of one or more of the Reichs's regions

Oberscharführer-SS....SS-Senior Company Leader, Sergeant 1st Class

Oberschütze....Private 1st Class

Oberschütze-SS....SS-Head Private

Oberst....Colonel,Brigade\ division, command or 2nd-I-C

Oberstgruppenführer-SS....SS-Supreme Group Leader, General

Oberstleutnant....Lieutenant Colonel, commands Sub units of up to 650 men

Obersturmbannführer-SS....SS-Senior Storm Command Leader, Lieutenant Colonel

Obersturmführer-SS....SS-Senior Storm Leader, 1st Lieutenant

OKW....Oberkommando der Wehrmacht, High Command of the Wehrmach

Oog....Island

Orcas....Killer whales

OrPo....Ordnungspolizei, 'Order Police'. Uniformed police force

Österrreich....Austria

Ostjuden....Eastern Jews, usually emigrated to Germany from Russia due to pogroms in late 1800s, early 1900s

Ostsee....Baltic Sea

Oświęcim....Village in Southern Poland, close to Auschwitz-Birkinau death camp

outhaul....A line that tensions the mainsail out along the boom

Pah....German expression of disbelief or frustration

Paradeplatz....Parade square

passage-making....Sailing a yacht from one destination to another

Pentateuch....The first five books of the Torah, and the Christian bible

Pfennig....Penny, German currency

PHM....Port hand mark, a buoy marking the left side of the channel

Platz....Place, Square

Poch....A German card game

Pogrom....Organised violence aimed at the massacre or expulsion of an ethnic or religious group

Polacks....Derogatory term for Polish people

Polnischen....Polish

Pooped....Yacht's cockpit filled with water, usually from a wave crashing over the stern

Port....The left side of a vessel, looking forward

Purchase....Two wooden blocks, or pulleys, with a reduction gear of 3 or 4 to one, to exert greater pull on a rope.

Purim....Jewish holy day, 'The deliverence of the Jews'

Putsch....Coup

R\T....Radiotelephonic communications

Rassenschande....Racial disgrace
Rathaus....Town hall
Raus....Out
Ravensbrück....Concentration camp 90 Km north of Berlin
Reaching....Sailing with the wind across the deck, often the fastest point of sail
Realschule....Secondary school, equivalent to comprehensive school
Regatta....Sailing race festival
Reich....Realm, empire. Used by National Socialists for Germany and all territories occupied during WW2
Reichsadler....The eagle insignia of the Third Reich
Reichsbahn....German railways
Reichsbank....National bank of Germany
Reichschancellery....The office of the Chancellor of Germany
Reichsführer-SS....SS-Command. Heinrich Himmler
Reichsheer....German Army prior to 1935
Reichskanzler....Chancellor
Reichsmarine....German Navy prior to 1935
Reichsmarks, RM....German currency from 1924 to 1948
Reichsminister....Minister of the German government
Reichspost....German national post office
Reichstag....German parliament
Reichsvereinigung....Reich Association
Reichswehr....German Armed forces prior to 1935
Rheinland....Rhineland, a region of Germany ceded to France after WW1 in the Versailles Treaty
Rigging....The wires or ropes that hold up the mast or masts on a yacht
Rinderrouladen....Rolls of stuffed beef
RNVR....Royal Naval Volunteer Reserve (RNVR), to utilise amateur sailors during wartime
Rosh Hashanah....Jewish new year
Rottenführer-SS....SS-Band Leader, Corporal
RSHA....Reichssicherheitshauptamt, Reich Security Main Office
Rugelach....A filled pastry product originating in the Jewish communities of Poland
Rührer....Stirrer
Running Backstay....Paired backstays on both sides of mainsail, used alternately. Changed over when gybing
Running fix ....A way of fixing a boat's position on the chart with only one point of reference
SA....Sturmabteilung
Saar, Saarland....A region of Germany administered by France after WW1 in the Versailles Treaty
Sachsenhausen....Concentration camp 35 km north of Berlin
Samson post....A strong metal bollard at the bow or stern of a vessel to tie lines to
Sandtorte....German cake, very popular in Schleswig Holstein
Sardinenpackung....Sardine packing', the method of shooting Jews to stack more into a mass grave
Sauerbraten....A beef dish marinated for days, then slow-cooked for twelve hours
Sauerkraut....Pickled Cabbage
scandalising....Lifting the boom of a sail to depower it quickly
Schadenfreude....The deriving of pleasure, or relief, from someone else's misfortune
Scharführer-SS....SS-Company Leader, Staff Sergeant
Schatzi....Sweetheart
Scheiße....Shit, shite, faeces
Scheißkerl....Shit guy, literal - general insult
Scheißköpfe....Shitheads
Schlagball....Similar to the British game of rounders
Schleswig-holstein....Most northern of the German states, borders with Denmark, with whom the territory was historically disputed
Schloss....Castle or palace

Schmeckel....Yiddish insult. Penis
Schmutziger....Dirty
Schnapps....An alcoholic beverage that may take several forms, including distilled fruit brandies and flavored liqueurs
Schneebälle....Snowball', a shortcrust pastry treat
Schneegans....Snowgoose
Schnell....Fast, quick
Schule....School
Schütze....Private
Schütze-SS....SS-Private
Schutzstaffel ....SS, National Socialist political armed wing
Schwachkopf....Bonehead, imbecile, halfwit
Schwein\Schweine....Pig(s)
Schweinhund....Pig-dog
SD....Sicherheitsdienst des reichsführers-ss, German Security Service, part of SS
Seacock....A through-hull valve for the expulsion or intake of water
See....German for a body of water, lake or sea
Shabbat....Jewish Sabbath, from just before sunset on Friday to nightfall on Saturday
Shalom....Jewish greeting, 'peace'
Shalom aleichem ....peace be upon you
Shanah Tovah....greeting on Rosh Hashanah, 'have a good year'
Shanah Tovah Umetukah....Happy Jewish New Year
Sheets....Lines that control sails on a yacht
Shema....A prayer that serves as a centerpiece of the morning and evening Jewish prayer services
Shiksa....Yiddish, Gentile woman
Shkoyekh....Yiddish, thankyou
Shlaym....Yiddish, scum
Shleger ....Yiddish, Bully
SHM....Starboard hand mark, a buoy marking the right side of the channel
shoal....An area of shallow seabed
Shrouds....Rigging wires or ropes that hold the mast vertically at each side. Often in pairs
Sicherheitsdienst des reichsführers-ss....SD, German Security Service, part of SS
Sicherheitspolizei(SiPo)....Nazi state political and criminal investigation security agencies
Sieg....Victory
sounding....Taking a depth reading, usually with a lead line in the 1930s and 40s
Sparkasse....Savings bank
Spars....A wooden pole used in the rigging of a yacht to support its sail. Includes yards, booms, and masts
Spindrift....Spray blown from cresting waves during a gale
spinnaker....A large sail for downwind sailing that flies from the front of the yacht
SS....Schutzstaffel, National Socialist political armed wing
Staatsgeheimnisse declaration ....Similar to signing the Official Secrets Act
Staatspolizei....State Police
Stabsfeldwebel....Kriegsmarine, Chief Petty Officer
Stabsfeldwebel....Regimental Sergeant Major
Stabskapitänleutnant....Kriegsmarine, Lieutenant
Stabsoberfeldwebel....Kriegsmarine, Warrant Officer
Städtische....City, urban
Standartenführer-SS....SS-Standard Leader, Colonel
Starboard....The right side of a vessel, looking forward
staysail....A second foresail set aft of the Genoa or Jib, in parallel or alone in high winds
Stillgestanden....Stand still. Stand to attention
Stormtrooper....SS soldier
Strafing....Aerial attack of ground targets using mounted automatic weapons
Strandkörbe....Beach chairs
Straße....Street

Streuselkuchen....Crumb cake
Stücke....Literally 'pieces', The number of Jews killed on an Einsatzgruppen aktion
Stuka....Junkers Ju 88s. German dive bomber
Stukas....Junkers Ju 87, a Luftwaffe dive-bomber
Sturmabteilung....SA, Paramilitary wing of National Socialists. Eventually superceded by SS
Sturmbannführer-SS....SS-Storm Command Leader, Major
Stürmerkasten....Street-corner billboards for the public to read Der Stürmer
Sturmmann-SS....SS-Storm Man, Lance Corporal
Sturmscharführer-SS....SS-Storm Company Leader, Sergeant Major
Sturmtaucher....Shearwater
Sudetendeutsche....Ethnic Germans from the Sudeten area of Czechoslovakia
Sudetenland....The Sudeten area of Czechoslovakia, ceded to the Czechs after WW1
tacking....The process of sailing upwind by making a series of legs at 45° angle to the wind
Talmud....The central book of Rabbinic Judaism, the source of much Jewish religious law
Tell-tails....A piece of yarn or fabric attached to a sail, a stay, or any rigging to indicate wind flow
The hard....Concrete or stone slip for launching small boats, usually at a yacht club
topmast....A small spar at the top of the main mast to carry the topsail
topping lift....A halyard that holds the boom up when not supported by the mainsail
topsail....A small sail that fits between the mainsail's gaff and the topmast
Topsides....Part of the hull between the waterline and the deck
Torah....The Hebrew Bible, often refers to the five books of Moses, but can include up to 24
Totenkopfverbände....SS Death's head units
Tsuris....Yiddish, worries
Tyrol....Historical region in the alps, split between Austria and Italy
Über....Over
U-boat....Submarine
Ul.....Abbreviation for Ulica, street in Polish
Unterfeldwebel....Platoon Sergeant Major
Untermensch\Untermenschen....Sub-human(s) Term used for Jews in Nazi Germany
Unteroffizier....Sergeant
Unterscharführer-SS....SS-Under Company Leader, Sergeant
Unterseeboot....U-boat, submarine
Untersturmführer-SS....SS-Under Storm Leader, 2nd Lieutenant
Veer....Usally refers to the wind, swinging round to clockwise on the compass
Verboten....Forbidden
Verdammt....Curse. Damned
Vermögens....Riches, property, fortune
Verordnung....Decree, regulation
Versailles....Town in France where the Treaty of Versailles at the end of WW1
Vierjahresplan....The Four Year Plan was a series of economic measures overseen by Hermann Göring
Vizeadmiral....Kriegsmarine, Vice-Admiral
Völkischer beobachter....The newspaper of the Nazi Party (NSDAP) from 25 December 1920
Warps....Ropes used to secure a vessel to the shore
Warps....Ropes securing a vessel to a harbour wall or jetty
Washboards....The removable boards closing off the companionway on a Yacht
Watches....The splitting up of the day into 4-6 hour periods to rotate crew on deck
Watchkeeping....To be on watch, to navigate the yacht and keep a lookout
Way....When a vessel is moving under control it has way on
Wehrmacht....German armed services after 1935
Wiener schnitzel....Thin, breaded, fried veal cutlet
Winch....A drum shaped mechanical device used to control halyards and sheets
Windlass....A winch on a ship, often for hauling an Anchor on a yacht
Withy sticks....Tall willow sticks used to mark the sides of small little-used channels
Wunderbar....Wonderful
Yirtzeh Hashem.....God willing

Yom Kippers....Affectionate name given to interned Jews by Isle of Man residents for their love of smoked fish

Yom Kippur.......Day of Atonement, the holiest day of the year in Judaism

Printed in Great Britain
by Amazon

25457984R00435

edition suhrkamp

Redaktion: Günther Busch

Karin Struck wurde 1947 in Schlagtow/Mecklenburg geboren.

Den Inhalt des Romans *Klassenliebe* referieren hieße, die Erfahrungen, die Hoffnungen und Leiden einer ganzen Klasse nacherzählen, hieße Arbeitsverhältnisse und Lebensläufe beschreiben, soziale Sprachnot und unterdrückte Sinnlichkeit hervorheben; es hieße aber auch, reden von der Sehnsucht nach Gesundheit, nach einer natürlichen Natur und nach einer menschlicheren Gesellschaft. Karin Strucks erstes Buch ist der ungewöhnliche literarische Ausdruck ihres Klassenhasses und der Liebe zu ihrer Klasse.

In einer Art Tagebuch vom 16. Mai bis zum 25. August 1972 erzählt sie die Geschichte ihrer Herkunft, die Jugend im westfälischen Schloß Holte, die Arbeit in der Fabrik, die erdrückenden sozialen Verhältnisse, den Bekannten- und Freundeskreis, die Mühe mit der Dissertation, ihre Ehe etc. Auslösendes Moment dieses ebenso rücksichtslosen wie befreienden Selbstbekenntnisses ist die Bekanntschaft mit Z., an dem sie »sehen und sprechen« lernt – eine Begegnung mit einem anderen Menschen aus einer fernen Zeit und einer fremden Klasse, für die das »happy end« ein ganz und gar unmöglicher Abschluß wäre.

Indem Karin Struck von sich selbst spricht – über die Selbstentfremdung, ihre Todesängste und die Vorbereitungen für ein ungezwungeneres Leben –, spricht sie von allen, mit denen sie zusammenhängt, beschreibt sie die Recherchen ihrer Familie und ihrer Klasse. Durch Zitate aus Büchern, Briefen und Gesprächen entsteht ein kollektives Erzählen von unverwechselbarer Subjektivität und konkreter Sinnlichkeit, das durch seine leidenschaftliche Sprache, durch seine Sensibilität für Verhaltensweisen und durch sein kritisches Wahrnehmungsvermögen fasziniert und betroffen macht.